THE TIME TRAVELER'S ALMANAC

THE TIME TRAVELER'S ALMANAC

Edited by Ann and Jeff VanderMeer

Editorial Assistants
Tessa Kum and Dominik Parisien

TOR®

A Tom Doherty Associates Book
New York

THE TIME TRAVELER'S ALMANAC

Copyright © 2013 by Ann and Jeff VanderMeer

Introduction copyright © 2013 by Rian Johnson; Preface copyright © by Ann and Jeff VanderMeer; "Top Ten Tips for Time Travellers" copyright © by Charles Yu; "Time Travel in Theory and Practice" copyright © 2013 by Stan Love; "Trousseau: Fashion for Time Travellers" copyright © 2013 by Genevieve Valentine; "Music for Time Travellers" copyright © 2013 by Jason Heller

Originally published in Great Britain by Head of Zeus Ltd.

All rights reserved.

A Tor Book
Published by Tom Doherty Associates, LLC
175 Fifth Avenue
New York, NY 10010

www.tor-forge.com

Tor® is a registered trademark of Tom Doherty Associates, LLC.

ISBN 978-0-7653-7421-9 (hardcover)
ISBN 978-0-7653-7424-0 (trade paperback)
ISBN 978-1-4668-4145-1 (e-book)

The Library of Congress Cataloging-in-Publication Data is available upon request.

Tor books may be purchased for educational, business, or promotional use. For information on bulk purchases, please contact Macmillan Corporate and Premium Sales Department at 1-800-221-7945, extension 5442, or write specialmarkets@macmillan.com.

First U.S. Edition: March 2014

Printed in the United States of America

0 9 8 7 6 5 4 3 2 1

CONTENTS

PREFACE

"I gave a party for time-travelers, but I didn't send out the invitations until after the party. I sat there a long time, but no one came."

Stephen Hawking (from an interview with *Ars Technica*)

Time travelers, as you will soon discover, are often too busy to attend parties – and the parties they attend are only those they know in advance are going to be good ones. Just because you travel through time does not mean that you can take time out from saving the universe, preserving history, finding your true love, or hunting dinosaurs just to confirm a famous physicist's theories. Indeed, the shadowy Preservationists Guild,[1] founded in 2150, would argue that the worst thing for time travelers would be to show up at such a party.

Thus, most of us are left with the stories, the speculations – some of them based on facts and personal experiences – offered up by a variety of fiction writers. Which is not such a bad place to be. Because one thing we chrononauts know for sure: for more than a century, readers have been enthralled by time travel stories with classics from writers like H.G. Wells, Ray Bradbury, Richard Matheson, and Isaac Asimov becoming fixtures of modern fiction. Whether thrilling, cautionary, or adventurous, these imaginative *what-if* tales transport us to other worlds, most often right here on our own planet.

Today, time travel is as familiar a concept to readers as space travel. Such stories are more popular than ever, including such recent bestsellers as Stephen King's *11/22/63*, Charles Yu's *How to Live Safely in a Science Fictional Universe*, and Audrey Niffenegger's *The Time Traveler's Wife*. The resurgence of iconic TV series like *Doctor Who* has fed into this trend. In addition, time travel often incorporates elements of such hot subgenres like steampunk and historical fiction, further extending its appeal. Time travel has also been popular with teens ever since the publication of such classics as Madeleine L'Engle's *A Wrinkle in Time*, extending to the present-day and such popular youth novels as *When You Reach Me* by Newberry winner Rebecca Stead. Meanwhile, movies like *The Terminator*, *Back to the Future*, *Time Bandits*, *Donnie Darko*, and *Safety Not Guaranteed* have shown the cinematic range of such tales.

Oddly, however, never before has there been an anthology that demonstrated the full depth and breadth of the time travel story. Perhaps this has something

---

1   For those of our readers from 2150 and beyond: any and all comments about the Preservationist Guild herein are not actionable by twenty-first-century law; therefore, the editors cannot be extradited to the future under any current and future time-travel statutes.

to do with the Preservationist Guild's Fifth Dictum: "Diffuse, disguise, confuse, obfuscate, deny." Most prior attempts have zeroed in on excellent yet decidedly science-fictional tales in which the focus has been on the dreaded "time paradox" – otherwise known as either "And Then I Found Out I Was My Own Father" or "Will I Be Kissing My Grandmother By Mistake?" That may be the bedrock of time travel fiction, but there is so much more: tales of fantasy and horror that involve travel through time like Kim Newman's "Is There Anybody There?," E.F. Benson's "In the Tube," and Rick Bowes's "The Mask of the Rex," – in addition to such truly strange science fiction as "Traveller's Rest," by David Masson, "Loob" by Bob Leman, and "Hwang's Billion Brilliant Daughters" by Alice Sola Kim.

Not all effective stories of time travel focus on epic consequences or seismic shifts in the course of history, either. What would you do if you could go backwards or forwards in time? Perhaps you might do what Christine does in Karen Haber's "3 RMS, Good View" – use that ability to find a better apartment. Maybe you'd use it to escape a war-torn country, as in Greg Egan's "The Lost Continent." Perhaps you'd even try to use it to get better grades in school ("The Most Important Thing in the World," Steve Bein), win an election ("The Final Days," David Langford), or, for that most delicate and yet powerful of reasons, for love ("If Ever I Should Leave You," Pamela Sargent).

You don't even need a time machine, believe it or not. Time machines are expensive to build and notoriously unpredictable – jury-rigged and perhaps even tampered with by the Preservationist Guild. That dial you spin to pick an era is always either stuck or spinning too fast or subject to variation from the slightest encounter with a paradox pebble while in the space-time corridor. You might wind up exiled forever making fungi spaghetti for yourself and a squirrel-like distant ancestor in a lonely shale cave at the butt-end of the Cretaceous Period if you're not careful.

So, no time machine? That's okay. You can time travel via the Devil's Intent, like Enoch Soames in Max Beerbohm's accurate historical account of the same name or by eating a special plant like Dr. Phipps' patient in Norman Spinrad's "The Weed of Time." You might even travel by means of magic, as in Tamsyn Muir's "The House That Made Sixteen Loops of Time." That might not seem very scientific, but you should see what the propaganda wing of the Preservationist Guild calls "magic" as opposed to "science." But the ways are myriad, and the Guild's members finite – they cannot be everywhere, suppress everything. Black holes, the telephone, mutation – any of these might suffice to move you from the twenty-first century to, say, Leonardo Da Vinci's bedroom as he secretly dressed up and painted himself in the mirror for *Mona Lisa*.

Obviously, the sheer variety of time travel stories has created some organizational challenges. Therefore, we have divided *The Time Traveler's Almanac* into four distinct sections, each corresponding to some major strand of time travel endeavor. (Each section is also bookended with nonfiction: educational palate-cleansers for your enjoyment.)

- **Experiments** – Stories in which individuals or organizations are experimenting with time travel or are subjects of experimentation.

- **Reactionaries and Revolutionaries** – Stories in which people are trying to protect the past from change or because they are curious tourists or academicians and want to accurately document different times.

- **Mazes and Traps** – Stories in which the paradox of time travel is front-and-center, and characters become trapped in those paradoxes.

- **Communiqués** – Stories about people trying to get a message to either someone in the past or in the future – out of their own time.

These categories may seem stable and grounded in time-honored tradition. But we must, as a public service, point out that time travel stories are devious narratives. While we have managed to lock each tale into a particular category, we cannot guarantee that some anomaly or future temporal attacks by rival anthology editors will not mean that the copy you hold in your hands fails to match up exactly. There may even be wormholes and rifts that warp the very nature of the pages. (We cannot recommend the eel-skin 2040 edition, for example, nor the "cheese cloth" edition of 2079.)

For this reason, we hope you will dive deep in these sections, but do so while attached to a rope or bungee cord. Because some of these stories will pull you into other times and other places so immersively that you may find it hard to get back to your era after reading them.

Because the truth is, fiction is one of the most effective time travel machines in the universe and always has been.

Ann & Jeff VanderMeer
Tallahassee, Florida, 2013 and 2150

INTRODUCTION

Rian Johnson

L et's time travel. Right now. Are you ready?

After this paragraph I'm going to type a symbol that is a sort of hidden Easter egg on the Mac keyboard, and after you see it, once your brain absorbs its contours and angles, a metaphysical displacement will occur and in the space between two beats of your heart we will both be transported through time. Alright. Let's do this. Here we go.

°¥˄

We have now hopped into the near future, and you have already read a good chunk of this book.

How am I certain of this? Oh, subtle changes in the room. An almost imperceivable ghosting of dust on the desk. A different charge to the ions in the air. A shift in the quality of the light. But most of all, I am certain that you have already read a big chunk of this book because nobody in their right mind would pick up this volume filled with some of the best science fiction writing from the last one hundred and fifty years from the greatest writers the genre has known on the most beguiling and thematically rich topic sci-fi has produced, *nobody* would pick this up and read the "Introduction by Rian Johnson" first. Hell, just looking over the table of contents, I want to flip ahead myself. (Go ahead and flip at any time, by the way. I encourage it. It seems fitting.)

The stories in this collection span across the past century and a half, from the nascent beginnings of genre itself in Edward Page Mitchell's pre-Wells "The Clock That Went Backward" (1881) through those gilded golden years of the 1950s with (my own personal favorite) Bradbury, into the cultural cross-currents that sci-fi charted for our generation in the late twentieth century, and finally forging into some of the best and brightest voices in the genre today.

As a broad survey it's invaluable, and in one way this book can be seen as a cultural almanac. Charting how we've used this infinitely malleable tool of time travel to engage with the changing landscape around us is a tempting method for mapping our recent history. A back-to-back reading of Wells's "The Time Machine" with Bradbury's "A Sound of Thunder" makes your stomach drop, as within a few quick pages we plunge from the scientific advancements of the late 1800s that were opening the world up for mankind to those of the 1950s that were threatening to bring the sky down onto his puny head. Flip a few more pages into Reagan's 1980s in Gibson's "The Gernsback Continuum," in which the enemy (and focal point of the story) is no longer technology at all but a vision of a utopian society rising from the mythologies of the past to crush what makes modern man human.

Sci-fi attracts armchair tinkerers. I know that I'm one myself. It makes sense that the take-it-apart-and-see-why-it-works (or if-it-works) instinct is drawn to this impossibly broad realm of fiction whose one unifying element is some degree of world-building. The one thing you know when you pick up a science fiction story is that there will be some sort of geared mechanism at its core that you can take apart and analyze, whether it's a PKDish thought puzzle or an Asmovian interplanetary society. If you're denying your healthy (and encouraged!) flipping instinct and are still reading this introduction in a few paragraphs I'll passionately argue that this is not the essential appeal of great sci-fi, but it's a biggie. When it comes to time travel stories this tinkering instinct kicks up into a higher gear, but is also (to badly mix bad metaphors) a double-edged sword.

On the one hand, the pleasure of time travel dissection is a beautiful and necessary thing. If someone hands you a kinked-up slinky, what do they expect you to do with it? Turn it over in your hands and appreciate the beauty of the tangle? Nuts to that. "Let's see if we can untangle and make sense of this thing" is part of its purpose, and a good time travel story will have an interior logic that encourages and stands up to untangling, and smoothly slinks down the stairs when you're finished. However, with time travel stories there's also a unique danger to this untangling. There is, I believe, a right and a wrong way to do it, and the wrong way can very easily lead to becoming "that guy." You know the guy I'm talking about. He's the guy who can talk to you for an hour at a party (in a tone pitched between the Comic Book Guy from *The Simpsons* and a Whit Stillman character) about why this or that slinky is well tangled or isn't, but doesn't seem to actually enjoy playing with them.

When we're talking about whether or not a story's "time travel logic" makes sense, it is important to remember that every story builds its own framework for its own logic. In that sense, time travel is more of a fantasy-based story element than a science-based one. Time travel does not exist in the real world, and any broadly accepted rules for how it can and can't work were derived from a bunch of "that guys" talking about time travel *fiction*. There is no "makes sense" in the universal sense – that is to say, criticizing a time travel story because its rules do not line up with rules in the real world is akin to dismissing the Harry Potter books because the conductive properties of wood could never sustain the energy required for spell casting.

Approaching a time travel story with a dogmatic measuring stick in hand also denies the unique pleasure that the genre affords tinkerers. A good story's internal logic is flawless, and everything in between its first and last word makes sense on its own terms. In that way, it presents the tinkerer with the literary equivalent of an Escher drawing. Internally, step by step, the logic of Escher's staircase makes (or makes you believe it makes) nefariously perfect sense, and its dissonance with what we know to be possible is not something you have to "just accept and get over to enjoy it," but is the very source of what's enjoyable about it.

For all its pleasures, though, the untangling-game cannot sustain a story, let alone a sub-genre that has thrived for so many years. Something about the concept of time travel snaps into our selves like a jigsaw-puzzle piece, just like invisibility or the power of flight. It is wish fulfillment on a primeval level of the psyche. When I fly in my dreams I'm not doing any of the "wouldn't it be cool to . . ." things that our conscious minds wish for, like saving time getting across town or arriving at parties through the window or having lunch on top of the Empire State Building. In my dreams I'm just flying, and just that feeling of soaring through the air feels like it scratches some deeply rooted itch.

Meeting Abraham Lincoln, hunting dinosaurs, making a fortune on the stock market, giving your younger self one piece of advice, all these "wouldn't it be cool" reasons we'd like to time travel do not get to the root of why we really *want* to time travel. I think partly it has to do with the cruel cold clockwork of this defined span of years each of us is assigned, the linear piece of chain we're all rolling across like a gear from beginning to inevitable end. Few wishes in life go deeper than the desire to give that chain the finger.

There's also something deeply familiar about time travel. It feels like something that is not at all foreign to our brains; it makes sense in an odd way. How much of our lives do we live in the past or future, looking forward or looking back, whether regretting or pining or fearing? Speaking for myself, the answer is a sheepish "lots." Time travel stories give us the dual pleasure of the carrot and the stick, on one hand letting us imagine going physically to where our minds can only take us, to re-experience that perfect day or change that awful thing, and on the other hand warning us that actually doing this would not turn out well, and that our place is in the present.

Ultimately, though, there is only one base ingredient that everything in this book absolutely has in common: they are all damn good stories by damn good storytellers.

But I don't have to tell you this. You've already read them. And I feel bad about that. Wouldn't it be nice to be able to go back and experience all these incredible stories for the first time again?

Rian Johnson

TOP TEN TIPS FOR TIME TRAVELERS

Charles Yu

1. Here's the thing: you're doing something that you don't understand. That's not a knock on you. It's just a fact. Humans can't wrap their heads around time travel, and it's not a software thing. It's hardware. Our brains just don't get it. Not yet. Maybe someday. But that will take, for lack of a better word, time. We could evolve, as a species, but that would require a selection pressure, some environmental advantage for minds unburdened by the illusion of temporal sequence, of the notion of cause and effect. But that's not what we have. What we have is the opposite. What we have are minds that are very good at being trapped in time. We are geniuses, each and every one of us. We are unbelievable machines, capable of incredible feats of psychological athleticism. We are full-grown, half-starved Bengal tigers, pacing in our cages, and we know every inch of the space in front of us, and behind, and to either side. We have evolved to survive as prisoners, and so, when one of us manages to get free, we look for walls, for a ceiling. We want to get back indoors, back inside time. We look for our cages. We look for rules.

2. So, the most important thing is, forget any rules. If you're really going to do this, you're going to have to open your mind. If you go into it with preconceived notions about what time is, what causality is, well, then, you're only going to see it through those conceptual lenses. You'll understand it, of course, because that's what we do. We understand things. But sometimes understanding gets in the way. Especially when something can't be understood.

3. But, but, but, you say. What do you mean? What could it even mean to understand something that can't be understood? Well, that's easy. When things can't be understood, and you understand them, well, then, what you're doing is just making stuff up. A circle looks at a sphere, and it understands it as a circle. A cross-section, it understands it exactly to the extent that it already makes sense to it.

4. So if you can't understand it, then what are you supposed to do? Well, not supposed to do, that's not right. You can't suppose anything, that's the point. You are free. As free as any human who has ever lived. You broke out. Of the ultimate constraint. There have been a few others – go look in your library books. Maybe in your religious texts – they've got stories of people who have done the same. Although you might not think of them as time travelers, that's what they were. We tend to worship them, tell stories about them. People might tell stories about you, too, depending on how you handle this.

     So get rid of the concept of supposed to do. Suppose anything. You can, you know. Suppose that you are a time traveler. Sounds like some kind of philosophical experiment, doesn't it? And that's the thing. You're traveling in time, my friend. That's pretty philosophical. And the ultimate experiment.

5. Which is not to say you are imagining this. This is as real as anything.

6. What kinds of tips are these? You thought you were going to get some advice about avoiding paradoxes. About ripple effects and avoiding stable time loops and all of that. Don't kill grandma, do kill Hitler, don't step on that twig. No kissing family members. All good ideas, to be sure. Don't need to repeat them here.

     Or maybe you wanted a brochure. A guide from the tourism office. Some good times to visit, catch the show. Back-row seats at some key moments in the history of the world. Crucial moments in the history of the world.

     But that's not what you're getting.

     What you're getting is this instead. Ask yourself, who am I? Am I important?

7. You are. You're very important. By definition. You're a time traveler, and with that comes some level of responsibility. Think about it. Your whole life, you've imagined time travel. You have the power to affect the flow of events, the lives of other people, the course of the universe, in a way that is unique and ineffably strange. How did you get to be one of these select, chosen few? What makes you so special?

8. Here is what makes you so special: you remember. You always had a gift, a knack, a predisposition to this. You look ahead. You knew there was more to it. That there had to be, if not a way out, a way up, and around, and back in. That there was something fishy about the whole infrastructure. Why build roads if no one can go anywhere? Why do we have all of this temporal equipment inside of us, if we can never use it? You were right. You

didn't know how right you were. Everyone thought it was poetic. A grand metaphor. A way of thinking about our psychology. You knew it was more, waited for the moment, waited for this moment. You were right, and you had no idea how right you were.

9. Here is what you need to ask yourself: how did you come to be a time traveler? Did you choose this, or did it choose you? Are you on some kind of mission? Do you feel like you might be stuck in a stable time loop? Is there anyone in your life who you need to go see in the past? Have you ever had dreams about the future that might not be dreams but premonitions? Are you lost and adrift outside of time and if so do you want to get back in? Who is asking you these rhetorical questions? Why are you looking for tips, and especially from someone or something that you don't know anything about? How do you know you're not asking yourself these questions, that this isn't your own diary you are reading, from the past or the future or the present and that you haven't read this eleven million seven hundred ninety three thousand four hundred sixty one times? And will read it an infinite number of times more? That these tips are all that you have, all that there ever will be, or ever was, which is the same thing, because nothing has ever existed that has not always existed, that you live in an eternal block universe, timeless and frozen, and that time, as you knew it when you started this, that time is in the past, but it's still there, and you can go back, and then you can come back here, and you have, and you will.

    You wanted some tips. You have some tips. Probably not quite what you were expecting. But what were you expecting? Time travel is a lonely activity. Time travel means you can never go home again. But maybe it also means always being able to see home from here. Don't you remember? These tips are what got you into trouble in the first place.

10. Now that you know this information, go back to tip number 2 above. Go back to the time when you first read that, and read it again. There are no rules. Okay? None. Now: what a concept. Now. Now: you've got your whole life, what came before and what will come after, gathered up here in this little area here, the whole thing. What are you going to do with your life? What was it, what is it, what will it be?

EXPERIMENTS

DEATH SHIP

Richard Matheson

Richard Matheson was an American author and screenwriter most known for his work in fantasy, horror, and science fiction. Some of his best-known works are *The Shrinking Man*, *Hell House*, and *I Am Legend* (the latter having been made into full-length films three times). In addition to the many feature films adapted from his work, he also wrote several episodes of *The Twilight Zone* original series in the 1960s. "Death Ship" was first published in *Fantastic Story Magazine* in 1953 and then later adapted for television as Episode 6, Season 4, of *The Twilight Zone* in 1963.

Mason saw it first.

He was sitting in front of the lateral viewer taking notes as the ship cruised over the new planet. His pen moved quickly over the graph-spaced chart he held before him. In a little while they'd land and take specimens. Mineral, vegetable, animal – if there were any. Put them in the storage lockers and take them back to Earth. There the technicians would evaluate, appraise, judge. And, if everything was acceptable, stamp the big, black inhabitable on their brief and open another planet for colonization from overcrowded Earth.

Mason was jotting down items about general topography when the glitter caught his eye.

"I saw something," he said.

He flicked the viewer to reverse lensing position.

"Saw what?" Ross asked from the control board.

"Didn't you see a flash?"

Ross looked into his own screen.

"We went over a lake, you know," he said.

"No, it wasn't that," Mason said. "This was in that clearing beside the lake."

"I'll look," said Ross, "but it probably was the lake."

His fingers typed out a command on the board and the big ship wheeled around in a smooth arc and headed back.

"Keep your eyes open now," Ross said. "Make sure. We haven't got any time to waste."

"Yes, sir."

Mason kept his unblinking gaze on the viewer, watching the earth below move past like a slowly rolled tapestry of woods and fields and rivers. He was thinking, in spite of himself, that maybe the moment had arrived at last. The moment in which Earthmen would come upon life beyond Earth, a race evolved from other cells and other muds. It was an exciting thought. 1997 might be the year. And he and Ross and Carter might now be riding a new *Santa Maria* of discovery, a silvery, bulleted galleon of space.

"There!" he said. "There it is!"

He looked over at Ross. The captain was gazing into his viewer plate. His face bore the expression Mason knew well. A look of smug analysis, of impending decision.

"What do you think it is?" Mason asked, playing the strings of vanity in his captain.

"Might be a ship, might not be," pronounced Ross.

Well, for God's sake, let's go down and see, Mason wanted to say, but knew he couldn't. It would have to be Ross's decision. Otherwise they might not even stop.

"I guess it's nothing," he prodded.

He watched Ross impatiently, watched the stubby fingers flick buttons for the viewer. "We might stop," Ross said. "We have to take samples anyway. Only thing I'm afraid of is . . ."

He shook his head. Land, man! The words bubbled up in Mason's throat. For God's sake, let's go down!

Ross evaluated. His thickish lips pressed together appraisingly. Mason held his breath.

Then Ross's head bobbed once in that curt movement which indicated consummated decision. Mason breathed again. He watched the captain spin, push and twist dials. Felt the ship begin its tilt to upright position. Felt the cabin shuddering slightly as the gyroscope kept it on an even keel. The sky did a ninety-degree turn, clouds appeared through the thick ports. Then the ship was pointed at the planet's sun and Ross switched off the cruising engines. The ship hesitated, suspended a split second, then began dropping toward the earth.

"Hey, we settin' down already?"

Mickey Carter looked at them questioningly from the port door that led to the storage lockers. He was rubbing greasy hands over his green jumper legs.

"We saw something down there," Mason said.

"No kiddin'," Mickey said, coming over to Mason's viewer. "Let's see."

Mason flicked on the rear lens. The two of them watched the planet billowing up at them.

"I don't know whether you can . . . oh, yes, there it is," Mason said. He looked over at Ross.

"Two degrees east," he said.

Ross twisted a dial and the ship then changed its downward movement slightly.

"What do you think it is?" Mickey asked. "Hey!"

Mickey looked into the viewer with even greater interest. His wide eyes examined the shiny speck enlarging on the screen. "Could be a ship," he said. "Could be."

Then he stood there silently, behind Mason, watching the earth rushing up.

"Reactors," said Mason.

Ross jabbed efficiently at the button and the ship's engines spouted out their flaming gases. Speed decreased. The rocket eased down on its roaring fire jets. Ross guided.

"What do you think it is?" Mickey asked Mason.

"I don't know," Mason answered. "But if it's a ship," he added, half wishfully thinking, "I don't see how it could possibly be from Earth. We've got this run all to ourselves."

"Maybe they got off course," Mickey dampened without knowing.

Mason shrugged. "I doubt it," he said.

"What if it is a ship?" Mickey said. "And it's not ours?"

Mason looked at him and Carter licked his lips.

"Man," he said, "that'd be somethin'."

"Air spring," Ross ordered.

Mason threw the switch that set the air spring into operation. The unit which made possible a landing without then having to stretch out on thick-cushioned couches. They could stand on deck and hardly feel the impact. It was an innovation on the newer government ships.

The ship hit on its rear braces.

There was a sensation of jarring, a sense of slight bouncing. Then the ship was still, its pointed nose straight up, glittering brilliantly in the bright sunlight.

"I want us to stay together," Ross was saying. "No one takes any risks. That's an order."

He got up from his seat and pointed at the wall switch that let atmosphere into the small chamber in the corner of the cabin.

"Three to one we need our helmets," Mickey said to Mason.

"You're on," Mason said, setting into play their standing bet about the air or lack of it in every new planet they found. Mickey always bet on the need for apparatus. Mason for unaided lung use. So far, they'd come out about even.

Mason threw the switch and there was a muffled sound of hissing in the chamber. Mickey got the helmet from his locker and dropped it over his head. Then he went through the double doors. Mason listened to him clamping the doors behind him. He kept wanting to switch on the side viewers and see if he could locate what they'd spotted. But he didn't. He let himself enjoy the delicate nibbling of suspense.

Through the intercom they heard Mickey's voice.

"Removing helmet," he said.

Silence. They waited. Finally, a sound of disgust.

"I lose again," Mickey said.

The others followed him out.

"God, did they hit!"

Mickey's face had an expression of dismayed shock on it. The three of them stood there on the greenish-blue grass and looked.

It *was* a ship. Or what was left of a ship for, apparently, it had struck the earth at terrible velocity, nose first. The main structure had driven itself about fifteen feet into the hard ground. Jagged pieces of superstructure had been ripped off by the crash and were lying strewn over the field. The heavy engines had been torn loose and nearly crushed the cabin. Everything was deathly silent, and the wreckage was so complete they could hardly make out what type of ship it was. It was as if some enormous child had lost fancy with the toy model and had dashed it to earth, stamped on it, banged on it insanely with a rock.

Mason shuddered. It had been a long time since he'd seen a rocket crash. He'd almost forgotten the everpresent menace of lost control, of whistling fall through space, of violent impact. Most talk had been about being lost in an orbit. This reminded him of the other threat in his calling. His throat moved unconsciously as he watched.

Ross was scuffing at a chunk of metal at his feet.

"Can't tell much," he said. "But I'd say it was our own." Mason was about to speak, then changed his mind. "From what I can see of that engine up there, I'd say it was ours," Mickey said.

"Rocket structure might be standard," Mason heard himself say, "everywhere."

"Not a chance," Ross said. "Things don't work out like that. It's ours all right. Some poor devils from Earth. Well, at least their death was quick."

"Was it?" Mason asked the air, visualizing the crew in their cabin, rooted with fear as their ship spun toward earth, maybe straight down like a fired cannon shell, maybe end-over-end like a crazy, fluttering top, the gyroscope trying in vain to keep the cabin always level.

The screaming, the shouted commands, the exhortations to a heaven they had never seen before, to a God who might be in another universe. And then the planet rushing up and blasting its hard face against their ship, crushing them, ripping the breath from their lungs. He shuddered again, thinking of it. "Let's take a look," Mickey said.

"Not sure we'd better," Ross said. "We say it's ours. It might not be."

"Jeez, you don't think anything is still alive in there, do you?" Mickey asked the captain.

"Can't say," Ross said.

But they all knew he could see that mangled hulk before him as well as they. Nothing could have survived that.

The look. The pursed lips. As they circled the ship. The head movement, unseen by them.

"Let's try that opening there," Ross ordered. "And stay together. We still have work to do. Only doing this so we can let the base know which ship this is." He had already decided it was an Earth ship.

They walked up to a spot in the ship's side where the skin had been laid open along the welded seam. A long, thick plate was bent over as easily as a man might bend paper.

"Don't like this," Ross said. "But I suppose . . ."

He gestured with his head and Mickey pulled himself up to the opening. He tested each handhold gingerly, then slid on his work gloves as he found some sharp edge. He told the other two and they reached into their jumper pockets. Then Mickey took a long step into the dark maw of the ship.

"Hold on, now!" Ross called up. "Wait until I get there."

He pulled himself up, his heavy boot toes scraping up the rocket skin. He went into the hole, too. Mason followed.

It was dark inside the ship. Mason closed his eyes for a moment to adjust to the change. When he opened them, he saw two bright beams searching up through the twisted tangle of beams and plates. He pulled out his own flash and flicked it on.

"God, is this thing wrecked," Mickey said, awed by the sight of metal and machinery in violent death. His voice echoed slightly through the shell. Then, when the sound ended, an utter stillness descended on them. They stood in the murky light and Mason could smell the acrid fumes of broken engines.

"Watch the smell, now," Ross said to Mickey who was reaching up for support. "We don't want to get ourselves gassed."

"I will," Mickey said. He was climbing up, using one hand to pull his thick, powerful body up along the twisted ladder. He played the beam straight up.

"Cabin is all out of shape," he said, shaking his head.

Ross followed him up. Mason was last, his flash moving around endlessly over the snapped joints, the wild jigsaw of destruction that had once been a powerful new ship. He kept hissing in disbelief to himself as his beam came across one violent distortion of metal after another.

"Door's sealed," Mickey said, standing on a pretzel-twisted catwalk, bracing himself against the inside rocket wall. He grabbed the handle again and tried to pull it open.

"Give me your light," Ross said. He directed both beams at the door and Mickey tried to drag it open. His face grew red as he struggled. He puffed.

"No," he said, shaking his head. "It's stuck."

Mason came up beside them. "Maybe the cabin is still pressurized," he said softly. He didn't like the echoing of his own voice.

"Doubt it," Ross said, trying to think. "More than likely the jamb is twisted." He gestured with his head again. "Help Carter."

Mason grabbed one handle and Mickey the other. Then they braced their feet against the wall and pulled with all their strength. The door held fast. They shifted their grip, pulled harder.

"Hey, it slipped!" Mickey said. "I think we got it."

They resumed footing on the tangled catwalk and pulled the door open. The frame was twisted, the door held in one corner. They could only open it enough to wedge themselves in sideways.

The cabin was dark as Mason edged in first. He played his light beam toward the pilot's seat. It was empty. He heard Mickey squeeze in as he moved the light to the navigator's seat.

There was no navigator's seat. The bulkhead had been stove in there, the viewer, the table and the chair all crushed beneath the bent plates. There was a clicking in Mason's throat as he thought of himself sitting at a table like that, in a chair like that, before a bulkhead like that.

Ross was in now. The three beams of light searched. They all had to stand, legs spraddled, because the deck slanted.

And the way it slanted made Mason think of something. Of shifting weights, of *things* sliding down . . .

Into the corner where he suddenly played his shaking beam.

And felt his heart jolt, felt the skin on him crawling, felt his unblinking eyes staring at the sight. Then felt his boots thud him down the incline as if he were driven.

"Here," he said, his voice hoarse with shock.

He stood before the bodies. His foot had bumped into one of them as he held himself from going down any further, as he shifted his weight on the incline.

Now he heard Mickey's footsteps, his voice. A whisper. A bated, horrified whisper.

"*Mother of God.*"

Nothing from Ross. Nothing from any of them then but stares and shuddering breaths.

Because the twisted bodies on the floor were theirs, all three of them. And all three . . . dead.

*

Mason didn't know how long they stood there, wordlessly, looking down at the still, crumpled figures on the deck.

How does a man react when he is standing over his own corpse? The question plied unconsciously at his mind. What does a man say? What are his first words to be? A poser, he seemed to sense, a loaded question.

But it was happening. Here he stood – and there he lay dead at his own feet. He felt his hands grow numb and he rocked unsteadily on the tilted deck.

"*God!*"

Mickey again. He had his flash pointed down at his own face. His mouth twitched as he looked. All three of them had their flash beams directed at their own faces, and the bright ribbons of light connected their dual bodies.

Finally Ross took a shaking breath of the stale cabin air.

"Carter," he said, "find the auxiliary light switch, see if it works." His voice was husky and tightly restrained.

"The light switch – the light switch!" Ross snapped.

Mason and the captain stood there, motionless, as Mickey shuffled up the deck. They heard his boots kick metallic debris over the deck surface. Mason closed his eyes, but was unable to take his foot away from where it pressed against the body that was his. He felt bound.

"I don't understand," he said to himself.

"Hang on," Ross said.

Mason couldn't tell whether it was said to encourage him or the captain himself.

Then they heard the emergency generator begin its initial whining spin. The light flickered, went out. The generator coughed and began humming and the lights flashed on brightly.

They looked down now. Mickey slipped down the slight deck hill and stood beside them. He stared down at his own body. Its head was crushed in. Mickey drew back, his mouth a box of unbelieving terror.

"I don't get it," he said. "I don't get it. What is this?"

"Carter," Ross said.

"That's *me!*" Mickey said. "God, it's *me!*"

"Hold on!" Ross ordered.

"The three of us," Mason said quietly, "and we're all dead."

There seemed nothing to be said. It was a speechless nightmare. The tilted cabin all bashed in and tangled. The three corpses all doubled over and tumbled into one corner, arms and legs flopped over each other. All they could do was stare.

Then Ross said, "Go get a tarp. Both of you."

Mason turned. Quickly. Glad to fill his mind with simple command. Glad to crowd out tense horror with activity. He took long steps up the deck. Mickey backed up, unable to take his unblinking gaze off the heavy-set corpse with the green jumper and the caved-in, bloody head.

Mason dragged a heavy, folded tarp from the storage locker and carried it back into the cabin, legs and arms moving in robotlike sequence. He tried to numb his brain, not think at all until the first shock had dwindled.

Mickey and he opened up the heavy canvas sheet with wooden motions. They tossed it out and the thick, shiny material fluttered down over the bodies. It settled, outlining the heads, the torsos, the one arm that stood up stiffly like a spear, bent over wrist and hand like a grisly pennant.

Mason turned away with a shudder. He stumbled up to the pilot's seat and slumped down. He stared at his outstretched legs, the heavy boots. He reached out and grabbed his leg and pinched it, feeling almost relief at the flaring pain.

"Come away," he heard Ross saying to Mickey. "I said, *come away*!"

He looked down and saw Ross half dragging Mickey up from a crouching position over the bodies. He held Mickey's arm and led him up the incline.

"We're dead," Mickey said hollowly. "That's us on the deck. We're *dead*!"

Ross pushed Mickey up to the cracked port and made him look out.

"There," he said. "There's our ship over there. Just as we left it. This ship isn't ours. And those bodies. They . . . can't be ours."

He finished weakly. To a man of his sturdy opinionation, the words sounded flimsy and extravagant. His throat moved, his lower lip pushed out in defiance of this enigma. Ross didn't like enigmas. He stood for decision and action. He wanted action now.

"You saw yourself down there," Mason said to him. "Are you going to say it isn't you?"

"That's exactly what I'm saying," Ross bristled. "This may seem crazy, but there's an explanation for it. There's an explanation for everything."

His face twitched as he punched his bulky arm.

"This is me," he claimed. "I'm solid." He glared at them as if daring opposition. "I'm alive," he said.

They stared blankly at him.

"I don't get it," Mickey said weakly. He shook his head and his lips drew back over his teeth.

Mason sat limply in the pilot's seat. He almost hoped that Ross's dogmatism would pull them through this. That his staunch bias against the inexplicable would save the day. He wanted for it to save the day. He tried to think for himself, but it was so much easier to let the captain decide.

"We're all dead," Mickey said.

"Don't be a fool!" Ross exclaimed. "Feel yourself!"

Mason wondered how long it would go on. Actually, he began to expect a sudden awakening, him jolting to a sitting position on his bunk to see the two of them at their tasks as usual, the crazy dream over and done with.

But the dream went on. He leaned back in the seat and it was a solid seat. From where he sat he could run his fingers over solid dials and buttons and switches. All real. It was no dream. Pinching wasn't even necessary.

"Maybe it's a vision," he tried, vainly attempting thought, as an animal mired tries hesitant steps to solid earth.

"That's enough," Ross said.

Then his eyes narrowed. He looked at them sharply. His face mirrored decision. Mason almost felt anticipation. He tried to figure out what Ross was working on. Vision? No, it couldn't be that. Ross would hold no truck with visions. He noticed Mickey staring open-mouthed at Ross. Mickey wanted the consoling of simple explanation too.

"Time warp," said Ross.

They still stared at him.

"What?" Mason asked.

"Listen," Ross punched out his theory. More than his theory, for Ross never bothered with that link in the chain of calculation. His certainty.

"Space bends," Ross said. "Time and space form a continuum. Right?"

No answer. He didn't need one.

"Remember they told us once in training of the possibility of circumnavigating time. They told us we could leave Earth at a certain time. And when we came back we'd be back a year earlier than we'd calculated. Or a year later.

"Those were just theories to the teachers. Well, I say it's happened to us. It's logical, it could happen. We could have passed right through a time warp. We're in another galaxy, maybe different space lines, maybe different time lines."

He paused for effect.

"I say we're in the future," he said.

Mason looked at him.

"How does that help us?" he asked. "If you're right."

"We're not dead!" Ross seemed surprised that they didn't get it.

"If it's in the future," Mason said quietly, "then we're going to die."

Ross gaped at him. He hadn't thought of that. Hadn't thought that his idea made things even worse. Because there was only one thing worse than dying. And that was knowing you were going to die. And where. And how.

Mickey shook his head. His hands fumbled at his sides. He raised it to his lips and chewed nervously on a blackened nail.

"No," he said weakly, "I don't get it."

Ross stood looking at Mason with jaded eyes. He bit his lips, feeling nervous with the unknown crowding him in, holding off the comfort of solid, rational thinking. He pushed, he shoved it away. He persevered.

"Listen," he said, "we're agreed that those bodies aren't ours."

No answer.

"Use your heads!" Ross commanded. "Feel yourself!"

Mason ran numbed fingers over his jumper, his helmet, the pen in his pocket. He clasped solid hands of flesh and bone. He looked at the veins in his arms. He pressed an anxious finger to his pulse. It's true, he thought. And the thought drove lines of strength back into him. Despite all, despite Ross's desperate advocacy, he was alive. Flesh and blood were his evidence.

His mind swung open then. His brow furrowed in thought as he lightened up. He saw a look almost of relief on the face of a weakening Ross.

"All right then," he said, "we're in the future."

Mickey stood tensely by the port. "Where does that leave us?" he asked.

The words threw Mason back. It was true, where did it leave them?

"How do we know how distant a future?" he said, adding weight to the depression of Mickey's words. "How do we know it isn't in the next twenty minutes?"

Ross tightened. He punched his palm with a resounding smack.

"How do we know?" he said strongly. "We don't go up, we can't crash. That's how we know."

Mason looked at him.

"Maybe if we went up," he said, "we might bypass our death altogether and leave it in this space-time system. We could get back to the space-time system of our own galaxy and . . ."

His words trailed off. His brain became absorbed with twisting thought.

Ross frowned. He stirred restlessly, licked his lips. What had been simple was now something else again. He resented the uninvited intrusion of complexity.

"We're alive now," he said, getting it set in his mind, consolidating assurance with reasonable words, "and there's only one way we can stay alive."

He looked at them, decision reached. "We have to stay here," he said.

They just looked at him. He wished that one of them, at least, would agree with him, show some sign of definition in their minds.

"But. . . what about our orders?" Mason said vaguely.

"Our orders don't tell us to kill ourselves!" Ross said. "No, it's the only answer. If we never go up again, we never crash. We . . . we avoid it, we prevent it!"

His head jarred once in a curt nod. To Ross, the thing was settled.

Mason shook his head.

"I don't know," he said. "I don't . . ."

"I do," Ross stated. "Now let's get out of here. This ship is getting on our nerves."

Mason stood up as the captain gestured toward the door. Mickey started to move, then hesitated. He looked down at the bodies.

"Shouldn't we . . . ?" he started to inquire.

"What, what?" Ross asked, impatient to leave.

Mickey stared at the bodies. He felt caught up in a great, bewildering insanity.

"Shouldn't we . . . bury ourselves?" he said.

Ross swallowed. He would hear no more. He herded them out of the cabin. Then, as they started down through the wreckage, he looked in at the door. He looked at the tarpaulin with the jumbled mound of bodies beneath it. He pressed his lips together until they were white.

"I'm alive," he muttered angrily.

Then he turned out the cabin light with tight, vengeful fingers and left.

*

They all sat in the cabin of their own ship. Ross had ordered food brought out from the lockers, but he was the only one eating. He ate with a belligerent rotation of his jaw as though he would grind away all mystery with his teeth.

Mickey stared at the food.

"How long do we have to stay?" he asked, as if he didn't clearly realize that they were to remain permanently.

Mason took it up. He leaned forward in his seat and looked at Ross.

"How long will our food last?" he said.

"There's edible food outside, I've no doubt,' Ross said, chewing.

"How will we know which is edible and which is poisonous?"

"We'll watch the animals," Ross persisted.

"They're a different type of life," Mason said. "What they can eat might be poisonous to us. Besides, we don't even know if there are any animals here."

The words made his lips raise in a brief, bitter smile. And he'd actually been hoping to contact another people. It was practically humorous.

Ross bristled. "We'll . . . cross each river as we come to it," he blurted out as if he hoped to smother all complaint with this ancient homily.

Mason shook his head. "I don't know," he said.

Ross stood up.

"Listen," he said. "It's easy to ask questions. We've all made a decision to stay here. Now let's do some concrete thinking about it. Don't tell me what we can't do. I know that as well as you. Tell me what we can do."

Then he turned on his heel and stalked over to the control board. He stood there glaring at blank-faced gauges and dials. He sat down and began scribbling rapidly in his log as if something of great note had just occurred to him. Later Mason looked at what Ross had written and saw that it was a long paragraph which explained in faulty but unyielding logic why they were all alive.

Mickey got up and sat down on his bunk. He pressed his large hands against his temples. He looked very much like a little boy who had eaten too many green apples against his mother's injunction and who feared retribution on both counts. Mason knew what Mickey was thinking. Of that still body with the skull forced in. The image of himself brutally killed in collision. He, Mason, was thinking of the same thing. And, behavior to the contrary, Ross probably was too.

Mason stood by the port looking out at the silent hulk across the meadow. Darkness was falling. The last rays of the planet's sun glinted off the skin of the crashed rocket ship. Mason turned away. He looked at the outside temperature gauge. Already it was seven degrees and it was still light. Mason moved the thermostat needle with his right forefinger.

Heat being used up, he thought. The energy of our grounded ship being used up faster and faster. The ship drinking its own blood with no possibility of transfusion. Only operation would recharge the ship's energy system. And they were without motion, trapped and stationary.

"How long can we last?" he asked Ross again, refusing to keep silence in the face of the question. "We can't live in this ship indefinitely. The food will run out in a couple of months. And a long time before that the charging system will go. The heat will stop. We'll freeze to death."

"How do we know the outside temperature will freeze us?" Ross asked, falsely patient.

"It's only sundown," Mason said, "and already it's. . . minus thirteen degrees."

Ross looked at him sullenly. Then he pushed up from his chair and began pacing.

"If we go up," he said, "we risk . . . *duplicating* that ship over there."

"But would we?" Mason wondered. "We can only die once. It seems we already have. In this galaxy. Maybe a person can die once in every galaxy. Maybe that's afterlife. Maybe . . ."

"Are you through?" asked Ross coldly.

Mickey looked up.

"Let's go," he said. "I don't want to hang around here."

He looked at Ross.

Ross said, "Let's not stick out our necks before we know what we're doing. Let's think this out."

"I have a wife!" Mickey said angrily. "Just because you're not married—"

"Shut up!" Ross thundered.

Mickey threw himself on the bunk and turned to face the cold bulkhead. Breath shuddered through his heavy frame. He didn't say anything. His fingers opened and closed on the blanket, twisting it, pulling it out from under his body.

Ross paced the deck, abstractedly punching at his palm with a hard fist. His teeth clicked together, his head shook as one argument after another fell before his bullheaded determination. He stopped, looked at Mason, then started pacing again. Once he turned on the outside spotlight and looked to make sure it was not imagination.

The light illumined the broken ship. It glowed strangely, like a huge, broken tombstone. Ross snapped off the spotlight with a soundless snarl. He turned to face them. His broad chest rose and fell heavily as he breathed.

"All right," he said. "It's *your* lives too. I can't decide for all of us. We'll hand vote on it. That thing out there may be something entirely different from what we think. If you two think it's worth the risk of our lives to go up, we'll . . . go up."

He shrugged. "Vote," he said. "I say we stay here."

"I say we go," Mason said.

They looked at Mickey.

"Carter," said Ross, "what's your vote?"

Mickey looked over his shoulder with bleak eyes.

"Vote," Ross said.

"Up," Mickey said. "Take us up. I'd rather die than stay here."

Ross's throat moved. Then he took a deep breath and squared his shoulders.

"All right," he said quietly. "We'll go up."

"God have mercy on us," Mickey muttered as Ross went quickly to the control board.

The captain hesitated a moment. Then he threw switches. The great ship began shuddering as gases ignited and began to pour like channeled lightning from the rear vents. The sound was almost soothing to Mason. He didn't care any more; he was willing, like Mickey, to take a chance. It had only been a few hours. It had seemed like a year. Minutes had dragged, each one weighted with oppressive recollections. Of the bodies they'd seen, of the shattered rocket – even more of the Earth they would never see, of parents and wives and sweethearts and children. Lost to their sight forever. No, it was far better to try to get back. Sitting and waiting was always the hardest thing for a man to do. He was no longer conditioned for it.

Mason sat down at his board. He waited tensely. He heard Mickey jump up and move over to the engine control board.

"I'm going to take us up easy," Ross said to them. "There's no reason why we should . . . have any trouble."

He paused. They snapped their heads over and looked at him with muscle-tight impatience.

"Are you both ready?" Ross asked.

"*Take us up!*" Mickey said.

Ross jammed his lips together and shoved over the switch that read: *Vertical Rise.*

They felt the ship tremble, hesitate. Then it moved off the ground, headed up with increasing velocity. Mason flicked on the rear viewer. He watched the dark earth recede, tried not to look at the white patch in the corner of the screen, the patch that shone metallically under the moonlight.

"Five hundred," he read. "Seven-fifty . . . one thousand . . . fifteen hundred . . ."

He kept waiting. For explosion. For an engine to give out. For their rise to stop.

They kept moving up.

"Three thousand," Mason said, his voice beginning to betray the rising sense of elation he felt. The planet was getting farther and farther away. The other ship was only a memory now. He looked across at Mickey. Mickey was staring, open-mouthed, as if he were about ready to shout out *"Hurry!"* but was afraid to tempt the fates.

"Six thousand . . . *seven thousand!*" Mason's voice was jubilant. "We're *out* of it!"

Mickey's face broke into a great, relieved grin. He ran a hand over his brow and flicked great drops of sweat on the deck.

"God," he said, gasping, "my God."

Mason moved over to Ross's seat. He clapped the captain on the shoulder.

"We made it," he said. "Nice flying."

Ross looked irritated.

"We shouldn't have left," he said. "It was nothing all the time. Now we have to start looking for another planet." He shook his head. "It wasn't a good idea to leave," he said.

Mason stared at him. He turned away, shaking his head, thinking . . . you can't win.

"If I ever see another glitter," he thought aloud, "I'll keep my big mouth shut. To hell with alien races anyway."

Silence. He went back to his seat and picked up his graph chart. He let out a long shaking breath. Let Ross complain, he thought, I can take anything now. Things are normal again. He began to figure casually what might have occurred down there on that planet. Then he happened to glance at Ross.

Ross was thinking. His lips pressed together. He said something to himself. Mason found the captain looking at him. "Mason," he said.

"What?"

"Alien race, you said."

Mason felt a chill flood through his body. He saw the big head nod once in decision. Unknown decision. His hands started to shake. A crazy idea came. No, Ross wouldn't do that, not just to assuage vanity. Would he?

"I don't . . ." he started. Out of the corner of his eye he saw Mickey watching the captain too.

"*Listen*," Ross said. "I'll tell you what happened down there. I'll *show* you what happened!"

They stared at him in paralyzing horror as he threw the ship around and headed back.

"What are you doing!" Mickey cried.

"Listen," Ross said. "Didn't you understand me? Don't you see how we've been tricked?"

They looked at him without comprehension. Mickey took a step toward him.

"Alien race," Ross said. "That's the short of it. That time-space idea is all wet. But I'll tell you what idea isn't all wet. So we leave the place. That's our first instinct as far as reporting it? Saying it's uninhabitable? We'd do more than that. We wouldn't report it at all."

"Ross, you're not taking us back!" Mason said, standing up suddenly as the full terror of returning struck him.

"You bet I am!" Ross said, fiercely elated.

"You're crazy!" Mickey shouted at him, his body twitching, his hands clenched at his sides menacingly.

"Listen to me!" Ross roared at them. "Who would be benefited by us not reporting the existence of that planet?"

They didn't answer. Mickey moved closer.

"Fools!" he said. "Isn't it obvious? There *is* life down there. But life that isn't strong enough to kill us or chase us away with force. So what can they do? They don't want us there. So what can they do?"

He asked them like a teacher who cannot get the right answers from the dolts in his class.

Mickey looked suspicious. But he was curious now, too, and a little timorous as he had always been with his captain, except in moments of greatest physical danger. Ross had always led them, and it was hard to rebel against it even when it seemed he was trying to kill them all. His eyes moved to the viewer screen where the planet began to loom beneath them like a huge dark ball.

"We're alive," Ross said, "and I say there never was a ship down there. We saw it, sure. We *touched* it. But you can see anything if you believe it's there! All your senses can tell you there's something when there's nothing. All you have to do is *believe* it!"

"What are you getting at?" Mason asked hurriedly, too frightened to realize. His eyes fled to the altitude gauge. Seventeen thousand . . . sixteen thousand . . . fifteen . . .

"Telepathy," Ross said, triumphantly decisive. "I say those men, or whatever they are, saw us coming. And they didn't want us there. So they read our minds and saw the death fear, and they decided that the best way to scare us away was to show us our ship crashed and ourselves dead in it. And it worked . . . until now."

"So it worked!" Mason exploded. "Are you going to take a chance on killing us just to prove your damn theory?"

"It's *more* than a theory!" Ross stormed, as the ship fell, then Ross added with the distorted argument of injured vanity, "My orders say to pick up specimens from every planet. I've always followed orders before and, by God, I still will!"

"You saw how cold it was!" Mason said. "No one can live there anyway! Use your head, Ross!"

"Damn it, *I'm* captain of this ship!" Ross yelled. "And I give the orders!"

"Not when our lives are in your hands!" Mickey started for the captain.

"Get back!" Ross ordered.

That was when one of the ship's engines stopped and the ship yawed wildly.

"You fool!" Mickey exploded, thrown off balance. "You *did* it, you *did* it!"

Outside the black night hurtled past.

The ship wobbled violently. *Prediction true* was the only phrase Mason could think of. His own vision of the screaming, the numbing horror, the exhortations to a deaf heaven – all coming true. That hulk would be this ship in a matter of minutes. Those three bodies would be . . .

"Oh . . . *damn!*" He screamed it at the top of his lungs, furious at the enraging stubbornness of Ross in taking them back, of causing the future to be as they saw – all because of insane pride.

"No, they're not going to fool us!" Ross shouted, still holding fast to his last idea like a dying bulldog holding its enemy fast in its teeth.

He threw switches and tried to turn the ship. But it wouldn't turn. It kept plunging down like a fluttering leaf. The gyroscope couldn't keep up with the abrupt variations in cabin equilibrium and the three of them found themselves being thrown off balance on the tilting deck.

"Auxiliary engines!" Ross yelled.

"It's no use!" Mickey cried.

"*Damn it!*" Ross clawed his way up the angled deck, then crashed heavily against the engine board as the cabin inclined the other way. He threw switches over with shaking fingers.

Suddenly Mason saw an even spout of flame through the rear viewer again. The ship stopped shuddering and headed straight down. The cabin righted itself.

Ross threw himself into his chair and shot out furious hands to turn the ship about. From the floor Mickey looked at him with a blank, white face. Mason looked at him, too, afraid to speak.

"Now shut up!" Ross said disgustedly, not even looking at them, talking like a disgruntled father to his sons. "When we get down there you're going to see that it's true. That ship'll be gone. And we're going to go looking for those bastards who put the idea in our minds!"

They both stared at their captain humbly as the ship headed down backwards. They watched Ross's hands move efficiently over the controls. Mason felt a sense of confidence in his captain. He stood on the deck quietly, waiting for the landing without fear. Mickey got up from the floor and stood beside him, waiting.

The ship hit the ground. It stopped. They had landed again. They were still the same. And . . .

"Turn on the spotlight," Ross told them.

Mason threw the switch. They all crowded to the port. Mason wondered for a second how Ross could possibly have landed in the same spot. He hadn't even appeared to be following the calculations made on the last landing.

They looked out.

Mickey stopped breathing. And Ross's mouth fell open.

The wreckage was still there.

They had landed in the same place and they had found the wrecked ship still there. Mason turned away from the port and stumbled over the deck. He felt lost, a victim of some terrible universal prank, a man accursed.

"You said . . ." Mickey said to the captain.

Ross just looked out of the port with unbelieving eyes.

"Now we'll go up again," Mickey said, grinding his teeth. "And we'll *really* crash this time. And we'll be killed. Just like those . . . those . . ."

Ross didn't speak. He stared out of the port at the refutation of his last clinging hope. He felt hollow, void of all faith in belief in sensible things.

Then Mason spoke.

"We're not going to crash –" he said somberly –"ever."

"What?"

Mickey was looking at him. Ross turned and looked too.

"Why don't we stop kidding ourselves?" Mason said. "We all know what it is, don't we?"

He was thinking of what Ross had said just a moment before. About the senses giving evidence of what was believed. Even if there was nothing there at all . . .

Then, in a split second, with the knowledge, he saw Ross and he saw Carter. As they *were*. And he took a short shuddering breath, a last breath until illusion would bring breath and flesh again.

"Progress," he said bitterly, and his voice was an aching whisper in the phantom ship. "The Flying Dutchman takes to the universe."

RIPPLES IN THE DIRAC SEA

Geoffrey A. Landis

Geoffrey A. Landis, who appears later in this anthology with "At Dorado," is a NASA scientist whose first novel, *Mars Crossing*, was published by Tor Books in 2000, winning a Locus Award. He has also won the Analog Analytical Laboratory Award for the novelette *The Man in the Mirror* (2009). A short-story collection, *Impact Parameter and Other Quantum Realities*, was published by Golden Gryphon Press in 2001. His 2010 novella *The Sultan of the Clouds* won the Sturgeon award for best short science fiction story. "Ripples in the Dirac Sea" was first published in *Asimov's Science Fiction Magazine* in 1988 and won the 1989 Nebula Award for best short story.

My death looms over me like a tidal wave, rushing toward me with an inexorable slow-motion majesty. And yet I flee, pointless though it may be.

I depart, and my ripples diverge to infinity, like waves smoothing out the footprints of forgotten travellers.

We were so careful to avoid any paradox, the day we first tested my machine. We pasted a duct-tape cross onto the concrete floor of a windowless lab, placed an alarm clock on the mark, and locked the door. An hour later we came back, removed the clock and put the experimental machine in the room, with a super-eight camera set between the coils. I aimed the camera at the X, and one of my grad students programmed the machine to send the camera back half an hour, stay in the past five minutes, then return. It left and returned without even a flicker. When we developed the film, the time on the clock was half an hour before we loaded the camera. We'd succeeded in opening the door into the past. We celebrated with coffee and champagne.

Now that I know a lot more about time, I understand our mistake, that we had not thought to put a movie camera in the room with the clock to photograph the machine as it arrived from the future. But what is obvious to me now was not obvious then.

I arrive, and the ripples converge to the instant *now* from the vastness of the infinite sea.

To San Francisco, June 8, 1965. A warm breeze riffles across dandelion-speckled

grass, while puffy white clouds form strange and wondrous shapes for our entertainment. Yet so very few people pause to enjoy it. They scurry about, diligently
preoccupied, believing that if they act busy enough, they must be important.
"They hurry so," I say. "Why can't they slow down, sit back, enjoy the day?"

"They're trapped in the illusion of time," says Dancer. He lies on his back
and blows a soap bubble, his hair flopping back long and brown in a time when
"long" hair meant anything below the ear. A puff of breeze takes the bubble
down the hill and into the stream of pedestrians. They uniformly ignore it.
"They're caught in the belief that what they do is important to some future
goal." The bubble pops against a briefcase, and Dancer blows another. "You
and I, we know how false an illusion that is. There is no past, no future, only
the now, eternal."

He was right, more right than he could have imagined. Once I, too, was
preoccupied and self-important. Once I was brilliant and ambitious. I was
twenty-eight years old, and I made the greatest discovery in the world.

From my hiding place I watched him come up the service elevator. He was thin
almost to the point of starvation, a nervous man with stringy blonde hair and
an armless white T-shirt. He looked up and down the hall, but failed to see me
hidden in the janitor's closet. Under each arm was a two-gallon can of gasoline,
in each hand another. He put down three of the cans and turned the last one
upside down, then walked down the hall, spreading a pungent trail of gasoline.
His face was blank. When he started on the second can, I figured it was about
enough. As he passed my hiding spot, I walloped him over the head with a
wrench, and called hotel security. Then I went back to the closet and let the
ripples of time converge.

I arrived in a burning room, flames licking forth at me, the heat almost too
much to bear. I gasped for breath – a mistake – and punched at the keypad.

NOTES ON THE THEORY AND PRACTICE OF TIME TRAVEL:
1) Travel is possible only into the past.
2) The object transported will return to exactly the time and place of departure.
3) It is not possible to bring objects from the past to the present.
4) Actions in the past cannot change the present.

One time I tried jumping back a hundred million years, to the Cretaceous, to
see dinosaurs. All the picture books show the landscape as being covered with
dinosaurs. I spent three days wandering around a swamp – in my new tweed
suit – before even catching a glimpse of any dinosaur larger than a basset hound.
That one – a theropod of some sort, I don't know which – skittered away as soon
as it caught a whiff of me. Quite a disappointment.

My professor in transfinite math used to tell stories about a hotel that had
an infinite number of rooms. One day all the rooms are full, and another guest
arrives. "No problem," says the desk clerk. He moves the person in room one
into room two, the person in room two into room three, and so on. Presto! A
vacant room.

A little later, an infinite number of guests arrive. "No problem," says the dauntless desk clerk. He moves the person in room one into room two, the person in room two into room four, the person in room three into room six, and so on. Presto! An infinite number of rooms vacant.

My time machine works on just that principle.

Again I return to 1965, the fixed point, the strange attractor to my chaotic trajectory. In years of wandering I've met countless people, but Daniel Ranien – Dancer – was the only one who truly had his head together. He had a soft, easy smile, a battered secondhand guitar, and as much wisdom as it has taken me a hundred lifetimes to learn. I've known him in good times and bad, in summer days with blue skies that we swore would last a thousand years, in days of winter blizzards with drifted snow piled high over our heads. In happier times we have laid roses into the barrels of rifles, we laid our bodies across the city streets in the midst of riots, and not been hurt. And I have been with him when he died, once, twice, a hundred times over.

He died on February 8, 1969, a month into the reign of King Richard the Trickster and his court fool Spiro, a year before Kent State and Altamont and the secret war in Cambodia slowly strangled the summer of dreams. He died, and there was – is – nothing I can do. The last time he died I dragged him to a hospital where I screamed and ranted until finally I convinced them to admit him for observation, though nothing seemed wrong with him. With X-rays and arteriograms and radioactive tracers, they found the incipient bubble in his brain; they drugged him, shaved his beautiful long brown hair, and operated on him, cutting out the offending capillary and tying it off neatly. When the anesthetic wore off, I sat in the hospital room and held his hand. There were big purple blotches under his eyes; he gripped my hand and stared, silent, into space. Visiting hours or no, I didn't let them throw me out of the room. He just stared. In the grey hours just before dawn he sighed softly and died. There was nothing at all that I could do.

Time travel is subject to two constraints: conservation of energy, and causality. The energy to appear in the past is only borrowed from the Dirac sea, and since ripples in the Dirac sea propagate in the negative direction, transport is only into the past. Energy is conserved in the present as long as the object transported returns with zero time delay, and the principle of causality assures that actions in the past cannot change the present. For example, what if you went in the past and killed your father?

Who, then, would invent the time machine?

Once I tried to commit suicide by murdering my father, before he met my mother, twenty-three years before I was born. It changed nothing, of course, and even when I did it I knew it would change nothing. But you have to try these things. How else could I know for sure?

Next we tried sending a rat back. It made the trip through the Dirac sea and back undamaged. Then we tried a trained rat, one we borrowed from the psychology lab across the green without telling them what we wanted it for. Before its little trip it had been taught to run through a maze to get a piece of bacon. Afterwards, it ran the maze as fast as ever.

We still had to try it on a human. I volunteered myself and didn't allow anyone to talk me out of it. By trying it on myself, I dodged the university regulations about experimenting on humans.

The dive into the negative energy sea felt like nothing at all. One moment I stood in the center of the loop of Renselz coils, watched by my two grad students and a technician; the next I was alone, and the clock had jumped back exactly one hour. Alone in a locked room with nothing but a camera and a clock, that moment was the high point of my life.

The moment when I first met Dancer was the low point. I was in Berkeley, a bar called "Trishia's," slowly getting trashed. I'd been doing that a lot, caught between omnipotence and despair. It was 1967. 'Frisco then – it was the middle of the hippy era – seemed somehow appropriate.

There was a girl, sitting at a table with a group from the university. I walked over to her table and invited myself to sit down. I told her she didn't exist, that her whole world didn't exist, it was all created by the fact that I was watching, and would disappear back into the sea of unreality as soon as I stopped looking. Her name was Lisa, and she argued back. Her friends, bored, wandered off, and in a while Lisa realized just how drunk I was. She dropped a bill on the table and walked out into the foggy night.

I followed her out. When she saw me following, she clutched her purse and bolted.

He was suddenly there under the streetlight. For a second I thought he was a girl. He had bright blue eyes and straight brown hair down to his shoulders. He wore an embroidered Indian shirt with a silver and turquoise medallion around his neck and a guitar slung across his back. He was lean, almost stringy, and moved like a dancer or a karate master. But it didn't occur to me to be afraid of him.

He looked me over. "That won't solve your problem, you know," he said.

And instantly I was ashamed. I was no longer sure exactly what I'd had in mind or why I'd followed her. It had been years since I'd first fled my death, and I had come to think of others as unreal, since nothing I could do would permanently affect them. My head was spinning. I slid down the wall and sat down, hard, on the sidewalk. What had I come to?

He helped me back into the bar, fed me orange juice and pretzels, and got me to talk. I told him everything. Why not, since I could unsay anything I said, undo anything I did? But I had no urge to. He listened to it all, saying nothing. No one else had ever listened to the whole story before. I can't explain the effect it had on me. For uncountable years I'd been alone, and then, if only for a moment. . . . It hit me with the intensity of a tab of acid. If only for a moment, I was not alone.

We left arm in arm. Half a block away, Dancer stopped, in front of the alley. It was dark.

"Something not quite right here." His voice had a puzzled tone.

I pulled him back. "Hold on. You don't want to go down there—" He pulled free and walked in. After a slight hesitation, I followed.

The alley smelled of old beer, mixed with garbage, urine, and stale vomit. In a moment, my eyes became adjusted to the dark.

Lisa was cringing in a corner behind some trash cans. Her clothes had been cut away with a knife, and lay scattered around. Blood showed dark on her thighs and one arm. She didn't seem to see us. Dancer squatted down next to her and said something soft. She didn't respond. He pulled off his shirt and wrapped it around her, then cradled her in his arms and picked her up. "Help me get her to my apartment."

"Apartment, hell. We'd better call the police," I said.

"Call the pigs? Are you crazy? You want them to rape her, too?"

I'd forgotten; this was the sixties. Between the two of us, we got her to Dancer's VW bug and took her to his apartment in The Hashbury. He explained it to me quietly as we drove, a dark side of the summer of love that I'd not seen before. It was greasers, he said. They come down to Berkeley because they heard that hippy chicks gave it away free, and get nasty when they meet one who thought otherwise.

Her wounds were mostly superficial. Dancer cleaned her, put her in bed, and stayed up all night beside her, talking and crooning and making little reassuring noises. I slept on one of the mattresses in the hall. When I woke up in the morning, they were both in his bed. She was sleeping quietly. Dancer was awake, holding her. I was aware enough to realize that that was all he was doing, holding her, but still I felt a sharp pang of jealousy, and didn't know which one of them it was that I was jealous of.

NOTES FOR A LECTURE ON TIME TRAVEL

The beginning of the twentieth century was a time of intellectual giants, whose likes will perhaps never again be equalled. Einstein had just invented relativity, Heisenberg and Schrödinger quantum mechanics, but nobody yet knew how to make the two theories consistent with each other. In 1930, a new person tackled the problem. His name was Paul Dirac. He was twenty-eight years old. He succeeded where the others had failed.

His theory was an unprecedented success, except for one small detail. According to Dirac's theory, a particle could have either positive or negative energy. What did this mean, a particle of negative energy? How could something have negative energy? And why don't ordinary – positive energy – particles fall down into these negative energy states, releasing a lot of free energy in the process?

You or I might have merely stipulated that it was impossible for an ordinary positive energy particle to make a transition to negative energy. But Dirac was not an ordinary man. He was a genius, the greatest physicist of all, and he had an answer. If every possible negative energy state was already occupied, a particle couldn't drop into a negative energy state. Ah ha! So Dirac postulated that the entire universe is entirely filled with negative energy particles. They surround us, permeate us, in the vacuum of outer space and in the center of the earth, every possible place a particle could be. An infinitely dense "sea" of negative energy particles. The Dirac sea.

His argument had holes in it, but that comes later.

Once I went to visit the crucifixion. I took a jet from Santa Cruz to Tel Aviv, and a bus from Tel Aviv to Jerusalem. On a hill outside the city, I dove through the Dirac sea.

I arrived in my three-piece suit. No way to help that, unless I wanted to travel naked. The land was surprisingly green and fertile, more so than I'd expected. The hill was now a farm, covered with grape arbors and olive trees. I hid the coils behind some rocks and walked down to the road. I didn't get far. Five minutes on the road, I ran into a group of people. They had dark hair, dark skin, and wore clean white tunics. Romans? Jews? Egyptians? How could I tell? They spoke to me, but I couldn't understand a word. After a while two of them held me, while a third searched me. Were they robbers, searching for money? Romans, searching for some kind of identity papers? I realized how naïve I'd been to think I could just find appropriate dress and somehow blend in with the crowds. Finding nothing, the one who'd done the search carefully and methodically beat me up. At last he pushed me face down in the dirt. While the other two held me down, he pulled out a dagger and slashed through the tendons on the back of each leg. They were merciful, I guess. They left me with my life. Laughing and talking incomprehensibly among themselves, they walked away.

My legs were useless. One of my arms was broken. It took me four hours to crawl back up the hill, dragging myself with my good arm. Occasionally people would pass by on the road, studiously ignoring me. Once I reached the hiding place, pulling out the Renselz coils and wrapping them around me was pure agony. By the time I entered return on the keypad I was wavering in and out of consciousness. I finally managed to get it entered. From the Dirac sea the ripples converged and I was in my hotel room in Santa Cruz. The ceiling had started to fall in where the girders had burned through. Fire alarms shrieked and wailed, but there was no place to run. The room was filled with a dense, acrid smoke. Trying not to breathe, I punched out a code on the keypad, somewhen, anywhen other than that one instant and I was in the hotel room, five days before. I gasped for breath. The woman in the hotel bed shrieked and tried to pull the covers up. The man screwing her was too busy to pay any mind. They weren't real anyway. I ignored them and paid a little more attention to where to go next. Back to '65, I figured. I punched in the combo and was standing in an empty room on the thirtieth floor of a hotel just under construction. A full moon gleamed on the silhouettes of silent construction cranes. I flexed my legs experimentally. Already the memory of the pain was beginning to fade. That was reasonable, because it had never happened. Time travel. It's not immortality, but it's got to be the next best thing.

You can't change the past, no matter how you try.

In the morning I explored Dancer's pad. It was crazy, a small third-floor apartment a block off Haight Ashbury that had been converted into something from another planet. The floor of the apartment had been completely covered with old mattresses, on top of which was a jumbled confusion of quilts, pillows, Indian blankets, stuffed animals. You took off your shoes before coming in – Dancer always wore sandals, leather ones from Mexico with soles cut from old tires. The radiators, which didn't work anyway, were spray-painted in dayglo colors. The walls were plastered with posters: Peter Max prints, brightly colored Eschers, poems by Allen Ginsberg, record album covers, peace rally posters, a "Haight is Love" sign, FBI ten most-wanted posters torn down from a post office with photos of famous antiwar activists circled in blue magic-marker, a huge peace symbol in passion-pink. Some of the posters were illuminated with black light and luminesced in impossible colors. The air was musty with incense and the banana-sweet smell of dope. In one corner a record player played *Sergeant Pepper's Lonely Hearts Club Band* on infinite repeat. Whenever one copy of the album got too scratchy, inevitably one of Dancer's friends would bring in another. He never locked the door. "Somebody wants to rip me off, well, hey, they probably need it more than I do anyway, okay? It's cool." People dropped by any time of day or night.

I let my hair grow long. Dancer and Lisa and I spent that summer together, laughing, playing guitar, making love, writing silly poems and sillier songs, experimenting with drugs. That was when LSD was blooming onto the scene like sunflowers, when people were still unafraid of the strange and beautiful world on the other side of reality. That was a time to live. I knew that it was Dancer that Lisa truly loved, not me, but in those days free love was in the air like the scent of poppies, and it didn't matter. Not much, anyway.

NOTES FOR A LECTURE ON TIME TRAVEL (continued)
Having postulated that all of space was filled with an infinitely dense sea of negative energy particles, Dirac went on further and asked if we, in the positive-energy universe, could interact with this negative energy sea. What would happen, say, if you added enough energy to an electron to take it out of the negative energy sea? Two things: first, you would create an electron, seemingly out of nowhere. Second, you would leave behind a "hole" in the sea. The hole, Dirac realized, would act as if it were a particle itself, a particle exactly like an electron except for one thing: it would have the opposite charge. But if the hole ever encountered an electron, the electron would fall back into the Dirac sea, annihilating both electron and hole in a bright burst of energy. Eventually they gave the hole in the Dirac sea a name of its own: "positron." When Anderson discovered the positron two years later to vindicate Dirac's theory, it was almost an anticlimax.

And over the next fifty years, the reality of the Dirac sea was almost ignored by physicists. Antimatter, the holes in the sea, was the important feature of the theory; the rest was merely a mathematical artifact.

Seventy years later, I remembered the story my transfinite math teacher told and put it together with Dirac's theory. Like putting an extra guest into a hotel with an infinite number of rooms, I figured out how to borrow energy from the Dirac sea. Or, to put it another way: I learned how to make waves.

And waves on the Dirac sea travel backward in time.

Next we had to try something more ambitious. We had to send a human back farther into history, and obtain proof of the trip. Still we were afraid to make alterations in the past, even though the mathematics stated that the present could not be changed.

We pulled out our movie camera and chose our destinations carefully.

In September of 1853 a traveller named William Hapland and his family crossed the Sierra Nevadas to reach the California coast. His daughter Sarah kept a journal, and in it she recorded how, as they reached the crest of Parker's ridge, she caught her first glimpse of the distant Pacific ocean exactly as the sun touched the horizon, "in a blays of cryms'n glorie," as she wrote. The journal still exists. It was easy enough for us to conceal ourselves and a movie camera in a cleft of rocks above the pass, to photograph the weary travellers in their ox-drawn wagon as they crossed.

The second target was the great San Francisco earthquake of 1906. From a deserted warehouse that would survive the quake – but not the following fire – we watched and took movies as buildings tumbled down around us and embattled firemen in horse-drawn firetrucks strove in vain to quench a hundred blazes. Moments before the fire reached our building, we fled into the present.

The films were spectacular.

We were ready to tell the world.

There was a meeting of the AAAS in Santa Cruz in a month. I called the program chairman and wangled a spot as an invited speaker without revealing just what we'd accomplished to date. I planned to show those films at the talk. They were to make us instantly famous.

The day that Dancer died we had a going-away party, just Lisa and Dancer and I. He knew he was going to die; I'd told him and somehow he believed me. He always believed me. We stayed up all night, playing Dancer's second-hand mandolin, painting psychedelic designs on each other's bodies with grease-paint, competing against each other in a marathon game of cut-throat Monopoly, doing a hundred silly, ordinary things that took meaning only from the fact that it was the last time. About four in the morning, as the glimmer of false-dawn began to show in the sky, we went down to the bay and, huddling together for warmth, went tripping. The last thing he said, he told us not to let our dreams die; to stay together.

We buried Dancer, at city expense, in a welfare grave. We split up three days later.

I kept in touch with Lisa, vaguely. In the late seventies she went back to school, first for an MBA, then law school. I think she was married for a while. We wrote each other cards at Christmas for a while, then I lost track of her. Years later I got a letter from her. She said that she was finally able to forgive me for causing Dan's death.

It was a cold and foggy February day, but I knew I could find warmth in 1965. The ripples converged.

ANTICIPATED QUESTIONS FROM THE AUDIENCE:

Q (old, stodgy professor): It seems to me this proposed temporal jump of yours violates the law of conservation of mass/energy. For example, when a transported object is transported into the past, a quantity of mass will appear to vanish from the present, in clear violation of the conservation law.

A (me): Since the return is to the exact time of departure, the mass present is constant.

Q: Very well, but what about the arrival in the past? Doesn't this violate the conservation law?
A: No. The energy needed is taken from the Dirac sea, by the mechanism I explain in detail in the Phys Rev paper. When the object returns to the "future," the energy is restored to the sea.

Q (intense young physicist): Then doesn't Heisenberg uncertainty limit the amount of time that can be spent in the past?
A: A good question. The answer is yes, but because we borrow an infinitesimal amount of energy from an infinite number of particles, the amount of time spent in the past can be arbitrarily large. The only limitation is that you must leave the past an instant before you depart from the present.

In half an hour I was scheduled to present the paper that would rank my name with Newton's and Galileo's – and Dirac's. I was twenty-eight years old, the same age that Dirac was when he announced his theory. I was a firebrand, preparing to set the world aflame. I was nervous, rehearsing the speech in my hotel room. I took a swig out of an old Coke that one of my grad students had left sitting on top of the television. The evening news team was babbling on, but I wasn't listening.

I never delivered that talk. The hotel had already started to burn; my death was already foreordained. Tie neat, I inspected myself in the mirror, then walked to the door. The doorknob was warm. I opened it onto a sheet of fire. Flame burst through the opened door like a ravening dragon. I stumbled backward, staring at the flames in amazed fascination.

Somewhere in the hotel I heard a scream, and all at once I broke free of my spell. I was on the thirtieth story; there was no way out. My thought was for my machine. I rushed across the room and threw open the case holding the time machine. With swift, sure fingers I pulled out the Renselz coils and wrapped them around my body. The carpet had caught on fire, a sheet of flame between me and any possible escape. Holding my breath to avoid suffocation, I punched an entry into the keyboard and dove into time.

I return to that moment again and again. When I hit the final key, the air was already nearly unbreathable with smoke. I had about thirty seconds left to live, then. Over the years I've nibbled away my time down to ten seconds or less.

I live on borrowed time. So do we all, perhaps. But I know when and where my debt will fall due.

Dancer died on February 9, 1969. It was a dim, foggy day. In the morning, he said he had a headache. That was unusual, for Dancer never had headaches. We decided to go for a walk through the fog. It was beautiful, as if we were alone in a strange, formless world. I'd forgotten about his headache altogether, until, looking out across the sea of fog from the park over the bay, he fell over. He was dead before the ambulance came. He died with a secret smile on his face. I've never understood that smile. Maybe he was smiling because the pain was gone.

Lisa committed suicide two days later.

You ordinary people, you have the chance to change the future. You can father children, write novels, sign petitions, invent new machines, go to cocktail parties, run for president. You affect the future with everything you do. No matter what I do, I cannot. It is too late for that, for me. My actions are written in flowing water. And having no effect, I have no responsibilities. It makes no difference what I do, not at all.

When I first fled the fire into the past, I tried everything I could to change it. I stopped the arsonist, I argued with mayors, I even went to my own house and told myself not to go to the conference.

But that's not how time works. No matter what I do, talk to a governor or dynamite the hotel, when I reach that critical moment – the present, my destiny, the moment I left – I vanish from whenever I was, and return to the hotel room, the fire approaching ever closer. I have about ten seconds left. Every time I dive through the Dirac sea, everything I changed in the past vanishes. Sometimes I pretend that the changes I make in the past create new futures, though I know this is not the case. When I return to the present, all the changes are wiped out by the ripples of the converging wave, like erasing a blackboard after a class.

Someday I will return and meet my destiny. But for now, I live in the past. It's a good life, I suppose. You get used to the fact that nothing you do will ever have any effect on the world. It gives you a feeling of freedom. I've been places no one has ever been, seen things no one alive has ever seen. I've given up physics, of course. Nothing I discover could endure past that fatal night in Santa Cruz. Maybe some people would continue for the sheer joy of knowledge. For me, the point is missing.

But there are compensations. Whenever I return to the hotel room, nothing is changed but my memories. I am again twenty-eight, again wearing the same three-piece suit, again have the fuzzy taste of stale Cola in my mouth. Every time I return, I use up a little bit of time. One day I will have no time left.

Dancer, too, will never die. I won't let him. Every time I get to that final February morning, the day he died, I return to 1965, to that perfect day in June. He doesn't know me, he never knows me. But we meet on that hill, the only two willing to enjoy the day doing nothing. He lies on his back, idly fingering chords on his guitar, blowing bubbles and staring into the clouded blue sky. Later I will introduce him to Lisa. She won't know us either, but that's okay. We've got plenty of time.

"Time," I say to Dancer, lying in the park on the hill. "There's so much time."

"All the time there is," he says.

NEEDLE IN A TIMESTACK

Robert Silverberg

Robert Silverberg is an American writer widely known for his science fiction and fantasy stories. He is a many-time winner of the Hugo and Nebula awards, was named to the Science Fiction Hall of Fame in 1999, and in 2004 was designated a Grand Master by the Science Fiction Writers of America. His books and stories have been translated into forty languages. Among his best-known titles are *Nightwings*, *Dying Inside*, *The Book of Skulls*, and the three volumes of the Majipoor Cycle: *Lord Valentine's Castle*, *Majipoor Chronicles*, and *Valentine Pontifex*. His collected short stories, covering nearly sixty years of work, have been published in nine volumes by Subterranean Press. His attraction to the time travel theme is most notable in his novel-length work in books such as *Hawksbill Station*, *House of Bones*, and *Up the Line*. This story was originally published in *Playboy* in June of 1983.

B etween one moment and the next the taste of cotton came into his mouth, and Mikkelsen knew that Tommy Hambleton had been tinkering with his past again. The cotton-in-the-mouth sensation was the standard tip-off for Mikkelsen. For other people it might be a ringing in the ears, a tremor of the little finger, a tightness in the shoulders. Whatever the symptom, it always meant the same thing: your time-track has been meddled with, your life has been retroactively transformed. It happened all the time. One of the little annoyances of modern life, everyone always said. Generally, the changes didn't amount to much.

But Tommy Hambleton was out to destroy Mikkelsen's marriage, or, more accurately, he was determined to unhappen it altogether, and that went beyond Mikkelsen's limits of tolerance. In something close to panic he phoned home to find out if he still had Janine.

Her lovely features blossomed on the screen – glossy dark hair, elegant cheekbones, cool sardonic eyes. She looked tense and strained, and Mikkelsen knew she had felt the backlash of this latest attempt too.

"Nick?" she said. "Is it a phasing?"

"I think so. Tommy's taken another whack at us, and Christ only knows how much chaos he's caused this time."

"Let's run through everything."

"All right," Mikkelsen said. "What's your name?"

"Janine."

"And mine?"

"Nick. Nicholas Perry Mikkelsen. You see? Nothing important has changed."

"Are you married?"

"Yes, of course, darling. To you."

"Keep going. What's our address?"

"11 Lantana Crescent."

"Do we have children?"

"Dana and Elise. Dana's five, Elise is three. Our cat's name is Minibelle, and—"

"Okay," Mikkelsen said, relieved. "That much checks out. But I tasted the cotton, Janine. Where has he done it to us this time? What's been changed?"

"It can't be anything major, love. We'll find it if we keep checking. Just stay calm."

"Calm. Yes." He closed his eyes. He took a deep breath. The little annoyances of modern life, he thought. In the old days, when time was just a linear flow from *then* to *now*, did anyone get bored with all that stability? For better or for worse it was different now. You go to bed a Dartmouth man and wake up Columbia, never the wiser. You board a plane that blows up over Cyprus, but then your insurance agent goes back and gets you to miss the flight. In the new fluid way of life there was always a second chance, a third, a fourth, now that the past was open to anyone with the price of a ticket. But what good is any of that, Mikkelsen wondered, if Tommy Hambleton can use it to disappear me and marry Janine again himself?

They punched for readouts and checked all their vital data against what they remembered. When your past is altered through time-phasing, all records of your life are automatically altered too, of course, but there's a period of two or three hours when memories of your previous existence still linger in your brain, like the phantom twitches of an amputated limb. They checked the date of Mikkelsen's birth, parents' names, his nine genetic coordinates, his educational record. Everything seemed right. But when they got to their wedding date the readout said 8 Feb 2017, and Mikkelsen heard warning chimes in his mind. "I remember a summer wedding," he said. "Outdoors in Dan Levy's garden, the hills all dry and brown, the 24th of August."

"So do I, Nick. The hills wouldn't have been brown in February. But I can see it – that hot dusty day—"

"Then five months of our marriage are gone, Janine. He couldn't unmarry us altogether, but he managed to hold us up from summer to winter." Rage made his head spin, and he had to ask his desk for a quick buzz of tranks. Etiquette called for one to be cool about a phasing. But he couldn't be cool when the phasing was a deliberate and malevolent blow at the center of his life. He wanted to shout, to break things, to kick Tommy Hambleton's ass. He wanted his marriage left alone. He said, "You know what I'm going to do one of these days? I'm going to go back about fifty years and eradicate Tommy completely. Just arrange things so his parents never get to meet, and—"

"No, Nick. You mustn't."

"I know. But I'd love to." He knew he couldn't, and not just because it would be murder. It was essential that Tommy Hambleton be born and grow up and meet Janine and marry her, so that when the marriage came apart she would meet and marry Mikkelsen. If he changed Hambleton's past, he would change hers too, and if he changed hers, he would change his own, and anything might happen. Anything. But all the same he was furious. "Five months of our past, Janine—"

"We don't need them, love. Keeping the present and the future safe is the main priority. By tomorrow we'll always think we were married in February of 2017, and it won't matter. Promise me you won't try to phase him."

"I hate the idea that he can simply—"

"So do I. But I want you to promise you'll leave things as they are."

"Well—"

"Promise."

"All right," he said. "I promise."

Little phasings happened all the time. Someone in Illinois makes a trip to eleventh-century Arizona and sets up tiny ripple currents in time that have a tangential and peripheral effect on a lot of lives, and someone in California finds himself driving a silver BMW instead of a gray Toyota. No one minded trifling changes like that. But this was the third time in the last twelve months, so far as Mikkelsen was able to tell, that Tommy Hambleton had committed a deliberate phasing intended to break the chain of events that had brought about Mikkelsen's marriage to Janine.

The first phasing happened on a splendid spring day – coming home from work, sudden taste of cotton in mouth, sense of mysterious disorientation. Mikkelsen walked down the steps looking for his old ginger tomcat, Gus, who always ran out to greet him as though he thought he was a dog. No Gus. Instead a calico female, very pregnant, sitting placidly in the front hall.

"Where's Gus?" Mikkelsen asked Janine.

"Gus? Gus who?"

"Our cat."

"You mean Max?"

"Gus," he said. "Sort of orange, crooked tail—"

"That's right. But Max is his name. I'm sure it's Max. He must be around somewhere. Look, here's Minibelle." Janine knelt and stroked the fat calico. "Minibelle, where's Max?"

"Gus," Mikkelsen said. "Not Max. And who's this Minibelle?"

"She's our cat, Nick," Janine said, sounding surprised. They stared at each other.

"Something's happened, Nick."

"I think we've been time-phased," he said.

Sensation as of dropping through trapdoor – shock, confusion, terror. Followed by hasty and scary inventory of basic life-data to see what had changed. Everything appeared in order except for the switch of cats. He didn't remember having a female calico. Neither did Janine, although she had accepted the presence of the cat without surprise. As for Gus – Max – he was getting foggier about his name, and Janine couldn't even remember what he looked like. But she did recall that he had been a wedding gift from some close friend, and Mikkelsen remembered that the friend was Gus Stark, for whom they had named him, and

Janine was then able to dredge up the dimming fact that Gus was a close friend of Mikkelsen's and also of Hambleton and Janine in the days when they were married, and that Gus had introduced Janine to Mikkelsen ten years ago when they were all on holiday in Hawaii.

Mikkelsen accessed the household callmaster and found no Gus Stark listed. So the phasing had erased him from their roster of friends. The general phone directory turned up a Gus Stark in Costa Mesa. Mikkelsen called him and got a freckle-faced man with fading red hair, who looked more or less familiar. But he didn't know Mikkelsen at all, and only after some puzzling around in his memory did he decide that they had been distantly acquainted way back when, but had had some kind of trifling quarrel and had lost touch with each other years ago.

"That's not how I think I remember it," Mikkelsen said. "I remember us as friends for years, really close. You and Donna and Janine and I were out to dinner only last week, is what I remember, over in Newport Beach."

"Donna?"

"Your wife."

"My wife's name is Karen. Jesus, this has been one hell of a phasing, hasn't it?" He didn't sound upset.

"I'll say. Blew away your marriage, our friendship, and who knows what-all else."

"Well, these things happen. Listen, if I can help you any way, fella, just call. But right now Karen and I were on our way out, and—"

"Yeah. Sure. Sorry to have bothered you," Mikkelsen told him.

He blanked the screen.

Donna. Karen. Gus. Max. He looked at Janine.

"Tommy did it," she said.

She had it all figured out. Tommy, she said, had never forgiven Mikkelsen for marrying her. He wanted her back. He still sent her birthday cards, coy little gifts, postcards from exotic ports.

"You never mentioned them," Mikkelsen said.

She shrugged. "I thought you'd only get annoyed. You've always disliked Tommy."

"No," Mikkelsen said, "I think he's interesting in his oddball way, flamboyant, unusual. What I dislike is his unwillingness to accept the notion that you stopped being his wife a dozen years ago."

"You'd dislike him more if you knew how hard he's been trying to get me back."

"Oh?"

"When we broke up," she said, "he phased me four times. This was before I met you. He kept jaunting back to our final quarrel, trying to patch it up so that the separation wouldn't have happened. I began feeling the phasings and I knew what must be going on, and I told him to quit it or I'd report him and get his jaunt-license revoked. That scared him, I guess, because he's been pretty well behaved ever since, except for all the little hints and innuendoes and invitations to leave you and marry him again."

"Christ," Mikkelsen said. "How long were you and he married? Six months?"

"Seven. But he's an obsessive personality. He never lets go."

"And now he's started phasing again?"

"That's my guess. He's probably decided that you're the obstacle, that I really do still love you, that I want to spend the rest of my life with you. So he needs to make us unmeet. He's taken his first shot by somehow engineering a breach between you and your friend Gus a dozen years back, a breach so severe that you never really became friends and Gus never fixed you up with me. Only it didn't work out the way Tommy hoped. We went to that party at Dave Cushman's place and I got pushed into the pool on top of you and you introduced yourself and one thing led to another and here we still are."

"Not all of us are," Mikkelsen said. "My friend Gus is married to somebody else now."

"That didn't seem to trouble him much."

"Maybe not. But he isn't my friend any more, either, and that troubles *me*. My whole past is at Tommy Hambleton's mercy, Janine! And Gus the cat is gone too. Gus was a damned good cat. I miss him."

"Five minutes ago you weren't sure whether his name was Gus or Max. Two hours from now you won't know you ever had any such cat, and it won't matter at all."

"But suppose the same thing had happened to you and me as happened to Gus and Donna?"

"It didn't, though."

"It might the next time," Mikkelsen said.

But it didn't. The next time, which was about six months later, they came out of it still married to each other. What they lost was their collection of twentieth-century artifacts – the black-and-white television set and the funny old dial telephone and the transistor radio and the little computer with the typewriter keyboard. All those treasures vanished between one instant and the next, leaving Mikkelsen with the telltale cottony taste in his mouth, Janine with a short-lived tic below her left eye, and both of them with the nagging awareness that a phasing had occurred.

At once they did what they could to see where the alteration had been made. For the moment they both remembered the artifacts they once had owned, and how eagerly they had collected them in '21 and '22, when the craze for such things was just beginning. But there were no sales receipts in their files and already their memories of what they had bought were becoming blurry and contradictory. There was a grouping of glittery sonic sculptures in the corner, now, where the artifacts had been. What change had been effected in the pattern of their past to put those things in the place of the others?

They never really were sure – there was no certain way of knowing – but Mikkelsen had a theory. The big expense he remembered for 2021 was the time jaunt that he and Janine had taken to Aztec Mexico, just before she got pregnant with Dana. Things had been a little wobbly between the Mikkelsens back then, and the time jaunt was supposed to be a second honeymoon. But their guide on the jaunt had been a hot little item named Elena Schmidt, who had made a very determined play for Mikkelsen and who had had him considering, for at least half an hour of lively fantasy, leaving Janine for her.

"Suppose," he said, "that on our original time-track we never went back to the Aztecs at all, but put the money into the artifact collection. But then Tommy went back and maneuvered things to get us interested in time jaunting, and at the same time persuaded that Schmidt cookie to show an interest in me. We couldn't afford both the antiques and the trip; we opted for the trip, Elena did her little number on me, it didn't cause the split that Tommy was hoping for, and now we have some gaudy memories of Moctezuma's empire and no collection of early electronic devices. What do you think?"

"Makes sense," Janine said.

"Will you report him, or should I?"

"But we have no proof, Nick!"

He frowned. Proving a charge of time-crime, he knew, was almost impossible, and risky besides. The very act of investigating the alleged crime could cause an even worse phase-shift and scramble their pasts beyond repair. To enter the past is like poking a baseball bat into a spiderweb: it can't be done subtly or delicately.

"Do we just sit and wait for Tommy to figure out a way to get rid of me that really works?" Mikkelsen asked.

"We can't just confront him with suspicions, Nick."

"You did it once."

"Long ago. The risks are greater now. We have more past to lose. What if he's not responsible? What if he gets scared of being blamed for something that's just coincidence, and *really* sets out to phase us? He's so damned volatile, so unstable – if he feels threatened, he's likely to do anything. He could wreck our lives entirely."

"If *he* feels threatened? What about—"

"Please, Nick. I've got a hunch Tommy won't try it again. He's had two shots and they've both failed. He'll quit it now. I'm sure he will."

Grudgingly Mikkelsen yielded, and after a time he stopped worrying about a third phasing. Over the next few weeks, other effects of the second phasing kept turning up, the way losses gradually make themselves known after a burglary. The same thing had happened after the first one. A serious attempt at altering the past could never have just one consequence; there was always a host of trivial – or not so trivial – secondary shifts, a ramifying web of transformations reaching out into any number of other lives. New chains of associations were formed in the Mikkelsens' lives as a result of the erasure of their plan to collect electronic artifacts and the substitution of a trip to pre-Columbian Mexico. People they had met on that trip now were good friends, with whom they exchanged gifts, spent other holidays, shared the burdens and joys of parenthood. A certain hollowness at first marked all those newly ingrafted old friendships, making them seem curiously insubstantial and marked by odd inconsistencies. But after a time everything felt real again, everything appeared to fit.

Then the third phasing happened, the one that pushed the beginning of their marriage from August to the following February, and did six or seven other troublesome little things, as they shortly discovered, to the contours of their existence.

"I'm going to talk to him," Mikkelsen said.

"Nick, don't do anything foolish."

"I don't intend to. But he's got to be made to see that this can't go on."

"Remember that he can be dangerous if he's forced into a corner," Janine said. "Don't threaten him. Don't push him."

"I'll tickle him," Mikkelsen said.

He met Hambleton for drinks at the Top of the Marina, Hambleton's favorite pub, swiveling at the end of a jointed stalk a thousand feet long rising from the harbor at Balboa Lagoon. Hambleton was there when Mikkelsen came in – a small sleek man, six inches shorter than Mikkelsen, with a slick confident manner. He was the richest man Mikkelsen knew, gliding through life on one of the big microprocessor fortunes of two generations back, and that in itself made him faintly menacing, as though he might try simply to buy back, one of these days, the wife he had loved and lost a dozen years ago when all of them had been so very young.

Hambleton's overriding passion, Mikkelsen knew, was time-travel. He was an inveterate jaunter – a compulsive jaunter, in fact, with that faintly hyperthyroid goggle-eyed look that frequent travelers get. He was always either just back from a jaunt or getting his affairs in order for his next one. It was as though the only use he had for the humdrum real-time event horizon was to serve as his springboard into the past. That was odd. What was odder still was where he jaunted. Mikkelsen could understand people who went zooming off to watch the battle of Waterloo, or shot a bundle on a first-hand view of the sack of Rome. If he had anything like Hambleton's money, that was what he would do. But according to Janine, Hambleton was forever going back seven weeks in time, or maybe to last Christmas, or occasionally to his eleventh birthday party. Time-travel as tourism held no interest for him. Let others roam the ferny glades of the Mesozoic: he spent fortunes doubling back along his own time-track, and never went anywher other. The purpose of Tommy Hambleton's time-travel, it seemed, was to edit his past to make his life more perfect. He went back to eliminate every little contretemps and faux pas, to recover fumbles, to take advantage of the new opportunities that hindsight provides – to retouch, to correct, to emend. To Mikkelsen that was crazy, but also somehow charming. Hambleton was nothing if not charming. And Mikkelsen admired anyone who could invent his own new species of obsessive behavior, instead of going in for the standard hand-washing routines, or stamp-collecting or sitting with your back to the wall in restaurants.

The moment Mikkelsen arrived, Hambleton punched the autobar for cocktails and said, "Splendid to see you, Mikkelsen. How's the elegant Janine?"

"Elegant."

"What a lucky man you are. The one great mistake of my life was letting that woman slip through my grasp."

"For which I remain forever grateful, Tommy. I've been working hard lately to hang on to her, too."

Hambleton's eyes widened. "Yes? Are you two having problems?"

"Not with each other. Time-track troubles. You know, we were caught in a couple of phasings last year. Pretty serious ones. Now there's been another one. We lost five months of our marriage."

"Ah, the little annoyances of—"

"– modern life," Mikkelsen said. "Yes. A very familiar phrase. But these are what I'd call frightening annoyances. I don't need to tell you, of all people, what a splendid woman Janine is, how terrifying it is to me to think of losing her in some random twitch of the time-track."

"Of course. I quite understand."

"I wish I understood these phasings. They're driving us crazy. And that's what I wanted to talk to you about."

He studied Hambleton closely, searching for some trace of guilt or at least uneasiness. But Hambleton remained serene.

"How can I be of help?"

Mikkelsen said, "I thought that perhaps you, with all your vast experience in the theory and practice of time-jaunting, could give me some clue to what's causing them, so that I can head the next one off."

Hambleton shrugged elaborately. "My dear Nick, it could be anything! There's no reliable way of tracing phasing effects back to their cause. All our lives are interconnected in ways we never suspect. You say this last phasing delayed your marriage by a few months? Well, then, suppose that as a result of the phasing you decided to take a last bachelor fling and went off for a weekend in Banff, say, and met some lovely person with whom you spent three absolutely casual and nonsignificant but delightful days, thereby preventing her from meeting someone else that weekend with whom in the original time-track she had fallen in love and married. You then went home and married Janine, a little later than originally scheduled, and lived happily ever after; but the Banff woman's life was totally switched around, all as a consequence of the phasing that delayed your wedding. Do you see? There's never any telling how a shift in one chain of events can cause interlocking upheavals in the lives of utter strangers."

"So I realize. But why should we be hit with three phasings in a year, each one jeopardizing the whole structure of our marriage?"

"I'm sure I don't know," said Hambleton. "I suppose it's just bad luck, and bad luck always changes, don't you think? Probably you've been at the edge of some nexus of negative phases that has just about run its course." He smiled dazzlingly. "Let's hope so, anyway. Would you care for another filtered rum?"

He was smooth, Mikkelsen thought. And impervious. There was no way to slip past his defenses, and even a direct attack – an outright accusation that he was the one causing the phasings – would most likely bring into play a whole new line of defense. Mikkelsen did not intend to risk that. A man who used time-jaunting so ruthlessly to tidy up his past was too slippery to confront. Pressed, Hambleton would simply deny everything and hasten backward to clear away any traces of his crime that might remain. In any case, making an accusation of time-crime stick was exceedingly difficult, because the crime by definition had to have taken place on a track that no longer existed. Mikkelsen chose to retreat. He accepted another drink from Hambleton; they talked in a desultory way for a while about phasing theory, the weather, the stock market, the excellences of the woman they both had married, and the good old days of 2014 or so when they all used to hang out down in dear old La Jolla, living golden lives of wondrous irresponsibility. Then he extricated himself from the conversation and headed for home in a dark and brooding mood. He had no doubt that Hambleton would strike again, perhaps quite soon. How could he be held at bay? Some sort of pre-emptive strike, Mikkelsen wondered? Some bold leap into the past that would neutralize the menace of Tommy Hambleton forever? Chancy, Mikkelsen thought. You could lose as much as you gained, sometimes, in that sort of maneuver. But perhaps it was the only hope.

He spent the next few days trying to work out a strategy. Something that would get rid of Hambleton without disrupting the frail chain of circumstance that bound his own life to that of Janine – was it possible? Mikkelsen sketched out ideas, rejected them, tried again. He began to think he saw a way.

Then came a new phasing on a warm and brilliantly sunny morning that struck him like a thunderbolt and left him dazed and numbed. When he finally shook away the grogginess, he found himself in a bachelor flat ninety stories above Mission Bay, a thick taste of cotton in his mouth, and bewildering memories already growing thin of a lovely wife and two kids and a cat and a sweet home in mellow old Corona del Mar.

Janine? Dana? Elise? Minibelle?

Gone. All gone. He knew that he had been living in this condo since '22, after the breakup with Yvonne, and that Melanie was supposed to be dropping in about six. That much was reality. And yet another reality still lingered in his mind, fading vanishing.

So it had happened. Hambleton had really done it, this time.

There was no time for panic or even for pain. He spent the first half hour desperately scribbling down notes, every detail of his lost life that he still remembered, phone numbers, addresses, names, descriptions. He set down whatever he could recall of his life with Janine and of the series of phasings that had led up to this one. Just as he was running dry the telephone rang. Janine, he prayed.

But it was Gus Stark. "Listen," he began, "Donna and I got to cancel for tonight, on account of she's got a bad headache, but I hope you and Melanie aren't too disappointed, and—" He paused. "Hey, guy, are you okay?"

"There's been a bad phasing," Mikkelsen said.

"Uh-oh."

"I've got to find Janine."

"Janine?"

"Janine – Carter," Mikkelsen said. "Slender, high cheekbones, dark hair – you know."

"Janine," said Stark. "Do I know a Janine? Hey, you and Melanie on the outs? I thought—"

"This had nothing to do with Melanie," said Mikkelsen.

"Janine Carter." Gus grinned. "You mean Tommy Hambleton's girl? The little rich guy who was part of the La Jolla crowd ten-twelve years back when—"

"That's the one. Where do you think I'd find her now?"

"Married Hambleton, I think. Moved to the Riviera, unless I'm mistaken. Look, about tonight, Nick—"

"Screw tonight," Mikkelsen said. "Get off the phone. I'll talk to you later."

He broke the circuit and put the phone into search mode, all directories worldwide, Thomas and Janine Hambleton. While he waited, the shock and anguish of loss began at last to get to him, and he started to sweat, his hands shook, his heart raced in double time. I won't find her, he thought. He's got her hidden behind seven layers of privacy networks and it's crazy to think the phone number is listed, for Christ's sake, and—

The telephone. He hit the button. Janine calling, this time.

She looked stunned and disoriented, as though she were working hard to keep her eyes in focus. "Nick?" she said faintly. "Oh, God, Nick, it's you, isn't it?"

"Where are you?"

"A villa outside Nice. In Cap d'Antibes, actually. Oh, Nick – the kids – they're gone, aren't they? Dana. Elise. They never were born, isn't that so?"

"I'm afraid it is. He really nailed us, this time."

"I can still remember just as though they were real – as though we spent ten years together – oh, Nick—"

"Tell me how to find you. I'll be on the next plane out of San Diego."

She was silent a moment.

"No. No, Nick. What's the use? We aren't the same people we were when we were married. An hour or two more and we'll forget we ever were together."

"Janine—"

"We've got no past left, Nick. And no future."

"Let me come to you!"

"I'm Tommy's wife. My past's with him. Oh, Nick, I'm so sorry, so awfully sorry – I can still remember, a little, how it was with us, the fun, the running along the beach, the kids, the little fat calico cat – but it's all gone, isn't it? I've got my life here, you've got yours. I just wanted to tell you—"

"We can try to put it back together. You don't love Tommy. You and I belong with each other. We—"

"He's a lot different, Nick. He's not the man you remember from the La Jolla days. Kinder, more considerate, more of a human being, you know? It's been ten years, after all."

Mikkelsen closed his eyes and gripped the edge of the couch to keep from falling. "It's been two hours," he said. "Tommy phased us. He just tore up our life, and we can't ever have that part of it back, but still we can salvage something, Janine, we can rebuild, if you'll just get the hell out of that villa and—"

"I'm sorry, Nick." Her voice was tender, throaty, distant, almost unfamiliar. "Oh, God, Nick, it's such a mess. I loved you so. I'm sorry, Nick. I'm so sorry."

The screen went blank.

Mikkelsen had not time-jaunted in years, not since the Aztec trip, and he was amazed at what it cost now. But he was carrying the usual credit cards and evidently his credit lines were okay, because they approved his application in five minutes. He told them where he wanted to go and how he wanted to look, and for another few hundred the makeup man worked him over, taking that dusting of early gray out of his hair and smoothing the lines from his face and spraying him with the good old Southern California tan that you tend to lose when you're in your late thirties and spending more time in your office than on the beach. He looked at least eight years younger, close enough to pass. As long as he took care to keep from running into his own younger self while he was back there, there should be no problems.

He stepped into the cubicle and sweet-scented fog enshrouded him, and when he stepped out again it was a mild December day in the year 2012, with a faint hint of rain in the northern sky. Only fourteen years back, and yet the world looked prehistoric to him, the clothing and the haircuts and the cars all wrong, the buildings heavy and clumsy, the advertisements floating overhead offering archaic and absurd products in blaring gaudy colors. Odd that the world of 2012 had not looked so crude to him the first time he had lived through it; but then the present never looks crude, he thought, except through the eyes of the future. He enjoyed the strangeness of it: it told him that he had really gone backward in time. It was like walking into an old movie. He felt very calm. All the pain was behind him now; he remembered nothing of the life that he had lost, only that it was important for him to take certain countermeasures against the man who had stolen something precious from him. He rented a car and drove quickly up to La Jolla. As he expected, everybody was at the beach club except for young Nick Mikkelsen, who was back in Palm Beach with his parents. Mikkelsen had put this jaunt together quickly but not without careful planning.

They were all amazed to see him – Gus, Dan, Leo, Christie, Sal, the whole crowd. How young they looked! Kids, just kids, barely into their twenties, all that hair, all that baby fat. He had never before realized how young you were when you were *young*. "Hey," Gus said, "I thought you were in Florida!" Someone handed him a popper. Someone slipped a capsule to his ear and raucous overload music began to pound against his cheekbone. He made the rounds, grinning, hugging, explaining that Palm Beach had been a bore, that he had come back early to be with the gang. "Where's Yvonne?" he asked.

"She'll be here in a little while," Christie said.

Tommy Hambleton walked in five minutes after Mikkelsen. For one jarring instant Mikkelsen thought that the man he saw was the Hambleton of his own time, thirty-five years old, but no: there were little signs, and a certain lack of tension in this man's face, a certain callowness about the lips, that marked him as younger. The truth, Mikkelsen realized, is that Hambleton had *never* looked really young, that he was ageless, timeless, sleek and plump and unchanging. It would have been very satisfying to Mikkelsen to plunge a knife into that impeccably shaven throat, but murder was not his style, nor was it an ideal solution to his problem. Instead, he called Hambleton aside, bought him a drink and said quietly, "I just thought you'd like to know that Yvonne and I are breaking up."

"Really, Nick? Oh, that's so sad! I thought you two were the most solid couple here!"

"We were. We were. But it's all over, man. I'll be with someone else New Year's Eve. Don't know who, but it won't be Yvonne."

Hambleton looked solemn. "That's so sad, Nick."

"No. Not for me and not for you." Mikkelsen smiled and nudged Hambleton amiably. "Look, Tommy, it's no secret to me that you've had your eye on Yvonne for months. She knows it too. I just wanted to let you know that I'm stepping out of the picture, I'm very gracefully withdrawing, no hard feelings at all. And if she asks my advice, I'll tell her that you're absolutely the best man she could find. I mean it, Tommy."

"That's very decent of you, old fellow. That's extraordinary!"

"I want her to be happy," Mikkelsen said.

Yvonne showed up just as night was falling. Mikkelsen had not seen her for years, and he was startled at how uninteresting she seemed, how bland, how unformed, almost adolescent. Of course, she was very pretty, close-cropped blonde hair, merry greenish-blue eyes, pert little nose, but she seemed girlish and alien to him, and he wondered how he could ever have become so involved with her. But of course all that was before Janine. Mikkelsen's unscheduled return from Palm Beach surprised her, but not very much, and when he took her down to the beach to tell her that he had come to realize that she was really in love with Hambleton and he was not going to make a fuss about it, she blinked and said sweetly, "In love with Tommy? Well, I suppose I *could* be – though I never actually saw it like that. But I could give it a try, couldn't I? That is, if you truly are tired of me, Nick." She didn't seem offended. She didn't seem heartbroken. She didn't seem to care much at all.

He left the club soon afterward and got an express-fax message off to his younger self in Palm Beach: *Yvonne has fallen for Tommy Hambleton. However upset you are, for God's sake get over it fast, and if you happen to meet a young woman named Janine Carter, give her a close look. You won't regret it, believe me. I'm in a position to know.*

He signed it *A Friend,* but added a little squiggle in the corner that had always been his own special signature-glyph. He didn't dare go further than that. He hoped young Nick would be smart enough to figure out the score.

Not a bad hour's work, he decided. He drove back to the jaunt-shop in downtown San Diego and hopped back to his proper point in time.

There was the taste of cotton in his mouth when he emerged. So it feels that way even when you phase *yourself*, he thought. He wondered what changes he had brought about by his jaunt. As he remembered it, he had made the hop in order to phase himself back into a marriage with a woman named Janine, who apparently he had loved quite considerably until she had been snatched away from him in a phasing. Evidently the unphasing had not happened, because he knew he was still unmarried, with three or four regular companions – Cindy, Melanie, Elena and someone else – and none of them was named Janine. Paula, yes, that was the other one. Yet he was carrying a note, already starting to fade, that said: *You won't remember any of this, but you were married in 2016 or 17 to the former Janine Carter, Tommy Hambleton's ex-wife, and however much you may like your present life, you were a lot better off when you were with her.* Maybe so, Mikkelsen thought. God knows he was getting weary of the bachelor life, and now that Gus and Donna were making it legal, he was the only singleton left in the whole crowd. That was a little awkward. But he hadn't ever met anyone he genuinely wanted to spend the rest of his life with, or even as much as a year with. So he had been married, had he, before the phasing? Janine? How strange, how unlike him.

He was home before dark. Showered, shaved, dressed, headed over to the

Top of the Marina. Tommy Hambleton and Yvonne were in town, and he had agreed to meet them for drinks. Hadn't seen them for years, not since Tommy had taken over his brother's villa on the Riviera. Good old Tommy, Mikkelsen thought. Great to see him again. And Yvonne. He recalled her clearly, little snub-nosed blonde, good game of tennis, trim compact body. He'd been pretty hot for her himself, eleven or twelve years ago, back before Adrienne, before Charlene, before Georgiana, before Nedra, before Cindy, Melanie, Elena, Paula. Good to see them both again. He stepped into the skylift and went shooting blithely up the long swivel-stalk to the gilded little cupola high above the lagoon. Hambleton and Yvonne were already there.

Tommy hadn't changed much – same old smooth slickly dressed little guy – but Mikkelsen was astonished at how time and money had altered Yvonne. She was poised, chic, sinuous, all that baby-fat burned away, and when she spoke there was the smallest hint of a French accent in her voice. Mikkelsen embraced them both and let himself be swept off to the bar.

"So glad I was able to find you," Hambleton said. "It's been years! Years, Nick!"

"Practically forever."

"Still going great with the women, are you?"

"More or less," Mikkelsen said. "And you? Still running back in time to wipe your nose three days ago, Tommy?"

Hambleton chuckled. "Oh, I don't do much of that any more. Yvonne and I went to the Fall of Troy last winter, but the short-hop stuff doesn't interest me these days. I – oh. How amazing?"

"What is it?" Mikkelsen asked, seeing Hambleton's gaze go past him into the darker corners of the room.

"An old friend," Hambleton said. "I'm sure it's she! Someone I once knew – briefly, glancingly—" He looked toward Yvonne and said, "I met her a few months after you and I began seeing each other, love. Of course, there was nothing to it, but there could have been – there could have been—" A distant wistful look swiftly crossed Hambleton's features and was gone. His smile returned. He said, "You should meet her, Nick. If it's really she, I know she'll be just your type. How amazing! After all these years! Come with me, man!"

He seized Mikkelsen by the wrist and drew him, astounded, across the room. "Janine?" Hambleton cried. "Janine Carter?"

She was a dark-haired woman, elegant, perhaps a year or two younger than Mikkelsen, with cool perceptive eyes. She looked up, surprised. "Tommy? Is that you?"

"Of course, of course. That's my wife, Yvonne, over there. And this – this is one of my oldest and dearest friends, Nick Mikkelsen. Nick – Janine—"

She stared up at him. "This sounds absurd," she said, "but don't I know you from somewhere?"

Mikkelsen felt a warm flood of mysterious energy surging through him as their eyes met. "It's a long story," he said. "Let's have a drink and I'll tell you all about it."

ANOTHER STORY *or* A FISHERMAN OF THE INLAND SEA

Ursula K. Le Guin

Ursula K. Le Guin is an American writer born in 1929 in Berkeley, California, who now lives in Portland, Oregon. An iconic figure in fantasy, science fiction, and general fiction, she has published twenty-one novels, eleven volumes of short stories, four collections of essays, twelve books for children, six volumes of poetry, and four books in translation. Le Guin has received many honors and awards including the Hugo, Nebula, National Book Award, and PEN-Malamud. Her most recent publications are *Finding My Elegy: New and Selected Poems, 1960–2010* and *The Unreal and the Real: Selected Stories.* "Another Story" was first published in *Tomorrow* in 1994.

To the Stabiles of the Ekumen on Hain, and to Gvonesh,
Director of the Churten Field Laboratories at Ve Port:
from Tiokunan'n Hideo, Farmholder of the Second
Sedoretu of Udan, Derdan'nad, Oket, on O.

I shall make my report as if I told a story, this having been the tradition for some time now. You may, however, wonder why a farmer on the planet O is reporting to you as if he were a Mobile of the Ekumen. My story will explain that. But it does not explain itself. Story is our only boat for sailing on the river of time, but in the great rapids and the winding shallows, no boat is safe.

So: once upon a time when I was twenty-one years old I left my home and came on the NAFAL ship *Terraces of Darranda* to study at the Ekumenical Schools on Hain.

The distance between Hain and my home world is just over four light-years, and there has been traffic between O and the Hainish system for twenty centuries. Even before the Nearly As Fast As Light drive, when ships spent a hundred years of planetary time instead of four to make the crossing, there were people who would give up their old life to come to a new world. Sometimes they returned; not often. There were tales of such sad returns to a world that had forgotten the voyager. I knew also from my mother a very old story called "The Fisherman of the Inland Sea," which came from her home world, Terra. The life of a ki'O child is full of stories, but of all I heard told by her and my othermother and my fathers and grandparents and uncles and aunts and teachers, that one was my favorite. Perhaps I liked it so well because my mother told it with deep feeling, though very plainly, and always in the same words (and I would not let her change the words if she ever tried to).

The story tells of a poor fisherman, Urashima, who went out daily in his boat alone on the quiet sea that lay between his home island and the mainland. He was a beautiful young man with long, black hair, and the daughter of the king of the sea saw him as he leaned over the side of the boat and she gazed up to see the floating shadow cross the wide circle of the sky.

Rising from the waves, she begged him to come to her palace under the sea with her. At first he refused, saying, "My children wait for me at home." But how could he resist the sea king's daughter? "One night," he said. She drew him down with her under the water, and they spent a night of love in her green palace, served by strange undersea beings. Urashima came to love her dearly, and maybe he stayed more than one night only. But at last he said, "My dear, I must go. My children wait for me at home."

"If you go, you go forever," she said.

"I will come back," he promised.

She shook her head. She grieved, but did not plead with him. "Take this with you,' she said, giving him a little box, wonderfully carved, and sealed shut. "Do not open it, Urashima."

So he went up onto the land, and ran up the shore to his village, to his house: but the garden was a wilderness, the windows were blank, the roof had fallen in. People came and went among the familiar houses of the village, but he did not know a single face. "Where are my children?" he cried. An old woman stopped and spoke to him: "What is your trouble, young stranger?"

"I am Urashima, of this village, but I see no one here I know!"

"Urashima!" the woman said – and my mother would look far away, and her voice as she said the name made me shiver, tears starting to my eyes "Urashima! My grandfather told me a fisherman named Urashima was lost at sea, in the time of his grandfather's grandfather. There has been no one of that family alive for a hundred years."

So Urashima went back down to the shore; and there he opened the box, the gift of the sea king's daughter. A little white smoke came out of it and drifted away on the sea wind. In that moment Urashima's black hair turned white, and he grew old, old, old; and he lay down on the sand and died.

Once, I remember, a traveling teacher asked my mother about the fable, as he called it. She smiled and said, "In the Annals of the Emperors of my nation of Terra it is recorded that a young man named Urashima, of the Yosa district, went away in the year 477, and came back to his village in the year 825, but soon departed again. And I have heard that the box was kept in a shrine for many centuries." Then they talked about something else.

My mother, Isako, would not tell the story as often as I demanded it. "That one is so sad," she would say, and tell instead about Grandmother and the rice dumpling that rolled away, or the painted cat who came alive and killed the demon rats, or the peach boy who floated down the river. My sister and my germanes, and older people, too, listened to her tales as closely as I did. They were new stories on O, and a new story is always a treasure. The painted cat story was the general favorite, especially when my mother would take out her brush and the block of strange, black, dry ink from Terra, and sketch the animals – cat, rat – that none of us had ever seen: the wonderful cat with arched back and brave round eyes, the fanged and skulking rats, "pointed at both ends" as my sister said. But I waited always, through all other stories, for her to catch my eye, look away, smile a little and sigh, and begin, "Long, long ago, on the shore of the Inland Sea there lived a fisherman . . ."

Did I know then what that story meant to her? that it was her story? that if she were to return to her village, her world, all the people she had known would have been dead for centuries?

Certainly I knew that she "came from another world", but what that meant to me as a five-, or seven-, or ten-year-old, is hard for me now to imagine, impossible to remember. I knew that she was a Terran and had lived on Hain; that was something to be proud of. I knew that she had come to O as a Mobile of the Ekumen (more pride, vague and grandiose) and that "your father and I fell in love at the Festival of Plays in Sudiran." I knew also that arranging the marriage had been a tricky business. Getting permission to resign her duties had not been difficult – the Ekumen is used to Mobiles going native. But as a foreigner, Isako did not belong to a ki'O moiety, and that was only the first problem. I heard all about it from my othermother, Tubdu, an endless source of family history, anecdote, and scandal. "You know," Tubdu told me when I was eleven or twelve, her eyes shining and her irrepressible, slightly wheezing, almost silent laugh beginning to shake her from the inside out – "you know, she didn't even know women got married? Where she came from, she said, women don't marry."

I could and did correct Tubdu: "Only in her part of it. She told me there's lots of parts of it where they do." I felt obscurely defensive of my mother, though Tubdu spoke without a shadow of malice or contempt; she adored Isako. She had fallen in love with her "the moment I saw her – that black hair! that mouth!" – and simply found it endearingly funny that such a woman could have expected to marry only a man.

"I understand," Tubdu hastened to assure me. "I know – on Terra it's different, their fertility was damaged, they have to think about marrying for children. And they marry in twos, too. Oh, poor Isako! How strange it must have seemed to her! I remember how she looked at me—" And off she went again into what we children called The Great Giggle, her joyous, silent, seismic laughter.

To those unfamiliar with our customs I should explain that on O, a world with a low, stable human population and an ancient climax technology, certain social arrangements are almost universal. The dispersed village, an association of farms, rather than the city or state, is the basic social unit. The population consists of two halves or moieties. A child is born into its mother's moiety, so that all ki'O (except the mountain folk of Ennik) belong either to the Morning People, whose time is from midnight to noon, or the Evening People, whose time is from noon to midnight. The sacred origins and functions of the moieties are recalled in the Discussions and the Plays and in the services at every farm shrine. The original social function of the moiety was probably to structure exogamy into marriage and so discourage inbreeding in isolated farmholds, since one can have sex with or marry only a person of the other moiety. The rule is severely reinforced. Transgressions, which of course occur, are met with shame, contempt, and ostracism. One's identity as a Morning or an Evening Person is as deeply and intimately part of oneself as one's gender, and has quite as much to do with one's sexual life.

A ki'O marriage, called a sedoretu, consists of a Morning woman and man and an Evening woman and man; the heterosexual pairs are called Morning and Evening according to the woman's moiety; the homosexual pairs are called Day – the two women, and Night – the two men.

So rigidly structured a marriage, where each of four people must be sexually compatible with two of the others while never having sex with the fourth – clearly this takes some arranging. Making sedoretu is a major occupation of my people. Experimenting is encouraged; foursomes form and dissolve, couples "try on" other couples, mixing and matching. Brokers, traditionally elderly widowers, go about among the farmholds of the dispersed villages, arranging meetings, setting up field dances, serving as universal confidants. Many marriages begin as a love match of one couple, either homosexual or heterosexual, to which another pair or two separate people become attached. Many marriages are brokered or arranged by the village elders from beginning to end. To listen to the old people under the village great tree making a sedoretu is like watching a master game of chess or tidhe. "If that Evening boy at Erdup were to meet young Tobo during the flour-processing at Gad'd . . ." "Isn't Hodin'n of the Oto Morning a programmer? They could use a programmer at Erdup. . . ." The dowry a prospective bride or groom can offer is their skill, or their home farm. Otherwise undesired people may be chosen and honored for the knowledge or the property they bring to a marriage. The farmhold, in turn, wants its new members to be agreeable and useful. There is no end to the making of marriages on O. I should say that all in all they give as much satisfaction as any other arrangement to the participants, and a good deal more to the marriage-makers.

Of course many people never marry. Scholars, wandering Discussers, itinerant artists and experts, and specialists in the Centers seldom want to fit themselves into the massive permanence of a farmhold sedoretu. Many people attach themselves to a brother's or sister's marriage as aunt or uncle, a position with limited, clearly defined responsibilities; they can have sex with either or both spouses of the other moiety, thus sometimes increasing the sedoretu from four to seven or eight. Children of that relationship are called cousins. The children of one mother are brothers or sisters to one another; the children of the Morning and the children of the Evening are germanes. Brothers, sisters, and first cousins may not marry, but germanes may. In some less conservative parts of O germane marriages are looked at askance, but they are common and respected in my region.

My father was a Morning man of Udan Farmhold of Derdan'nad Village in the hill region of the Northwest Watershed of the Saduun River, on Oket, the smallest of the six continents of O. The village comprises seventy-seven farmholds, in a deeply rolling, stream-cut region of fields and forests on the watershed of the Oro, a tributary of the wide Saduun. It is fertile, pleasant country, with views west to the Coast Range and south to the great floodplains of the Saduun and the gleam of the sea beyond. The Oro is a wide, lively, noisy river full of fish and children. I spent my childhood in or on or by the Oro, which runs through Udan so near the house that you can hear its voice all night, the rush and hiss of the water and the deep drumbeats of rocks rolled in its current. It is shallow and quite dangerous. We all learned to swim very young in a quiet bay dug out as a swimming pool, and later to handle rowboats and kayaks in the swift current full of rocks and rapids. Fishing was one of the children's responsibilities. I liked to spear the fat, beady-eyed, blue ochid; I would stand heroic on a slippery boulder in midstream, the long spear poised to strike. I was good at it. But my germane Isidri, while I was prancing about with my spear, would slip into the water and catch six or seven ochid with her bare hands. She could catch eels and even the darting ei. I never could do it. "You just sort of move with the water and get transparent," she said. She could stay underwater longer than any of us, so long you were sure she had drowned. "She's too bad to drown," her mother, Tubdu, proclaimed. "You can't drown really bad people. They always bob up again."

Tubdu, the Morning wife, had two children with her husband Kap: Isidri, a year older than me, and Suudi, three years younger. Children of the Morning, they were my germanes, as was Cousin Had'd, Tubdu's son with Kap's brother Uncle Tobo. On the Evening side there were two children, myself and my younger sister. She was named Koneko, an old name in Oket, which has also a meaning in my mother's Terran language: "kitten," the young of the wonderful animal "cat" with the round back and the round eyes. Koneko, four years younger than me, was indeed round and silky like a baby animal, but her eyes were like my mother's, long, with lids that went up towards the temple, like the soft sheaths of flowers before they open. She staggered around after me, calling, "Deo! Deo! Wait!" – while I ran after fleet, fearless, ever-vanishing Isidri, calling, "Sidi! Sidi! Wait!"

When we were older, Isidri and I were inseparable companions, while Suudi, Koneko, and Cousin Had'd made a trinity, usually coated with mud, splotched with scabs, and in some kind of trouble – gates left open so the yamas got into the crops, hay spoiled by being jumped on, fruit stolen, battles with the children from Drehe Farmhold. "Bad, bad," Tubdu would say. "None of 'em will ever drown!" And she would shake with her silent laughter.

My father Dohedri was a hardworking man, handsome, silent, and aloof. I think his insistence on bringing a foreigner into the tight-woven fabric of village and farm life, conservative and suspicious and full of old knots and tangles of passions and jealousies, had added anxiety to a temperament already serious. Other ki'O had married foreigners, of course, but almost always in a "foreign marriage," a pairing; and such couples usually lived in one of the Centers, where all kinds of untraditional arrangements were common, even (so the village gossips hissed under the great tree) incestuous couplings between two Morning people! two Evening people! Or such pairs would leave O to live on Hain, or would cut all ties to all homes and become Mobiles on the NAFAL ships, only touching different worlds at different moments and then off again into an endless future with no past.

None of this would do for my father, a man rooted to the knees in the dirt of Udan Farmhold. He brought his beloved to his home, and persuaded the Evening People of Derdan'nad to take her into their moiety, in a ceremony so rare and ancient that a Caretaker had to come by ship and train from Noratan to perform it. Then he had persuaded Tubdu to join the sedoretu. As regards her Day marriage, this was no trouble at all, as soon as Tubdu met my mother; but it presented some difficulty as regards her Morning marriage. Kap and my father had been lovers for years; Kap was the obvious and willing candidate to complete the sedoretu; but Tubdu did not like him. Kap's long love for my father led him to woo Tubdu earnestly and well, and she was far too good-natured to hold out against the interlocking wishes of three people, plus her own lively desire for Isako. She always found Kap a boring husband, I think; but his younger brother, Uncle Tobo, was a bonus. And Tubdu's relation to my mother was infinitely tender, full of honor, of delicacy, of restraint. Once my mother spoke of it. "She knew how strange it all was to me," she said. "She knows how strange it all is."

"This world? Our ways?" I asked.

My mother shook her head very slightly. "Not so much that," she said in her quiet voice with the faint foreign accent. "But men and women, women and women, together – love – It is always very strange. Nothing you know ever prepares you. Ever."

The saying is, "a marriage is made by Day," that is, the relationship of the two women makes or breaks it. Though my mother and father loved each other deeply, it was a love always on the edge of pain, never easy. I have no doubt that the radiant childhood we had in that household was founded on the unshakable joy and strength Isako and Tubdu found in each other.

So, then: twelve-year-old Isidri went off on the suntrain to school at Herhot, our district educational Center, and I wept aloud, standing in the morning sunlight in the dust of Derdan'nad Station. My friend, my playmate, my life was gone. I was bereft, deserted, alone forever. Seeing her mighty eleven-year-old elder brother weeping, Koneko set up a howl too, tears rolling down her cheeks in dusty balls like raindrops on a dirt road. She threw her arms about me, roaring, "Hideo! She'll come back! She'll come back!"

I have never forgotten that. I can hear her hoarse little voice, and feel her arms round me and the hot morning sunlight on my neck.

By afternoon we were all swimming in the Oro, Koneko and I and Suudi and Had'd. As their elder, I resolved on a course of duty and stern virtue, and led the troop off to help Second-Cousin Topi at the irrigation control station, until she drove us away like a swarm of flies, saying, "Go help somebody else and let me get some work done!" We went and built a mud palace.

So, then: a year later, twelve-year-old Hideo and thirteen-year-old Isidri went off on the suntrain to school, leaving Koneko on the dusty siding, not in tears, but silent, the way our mother was silent when she grieved.

I loved school. I know that the first days I was achingly homesick, but I cannot recall that misery, buried under my memories of the full, rich years at Herhot, and later at Ran'n, the Advanced Education Center, where I studied temporal physics and engineering.

Isidri finished the First Courses at Herhot, took a year of Second in literature, hydrology, and oenology, and went home to Udan Farmhold of Derdan'nad Village in the hill region of the Northwest Watershed of the Saduun.

The three younger ones all came to school, took a year or two of Second, and carried their learning home to Udan. When she was fifteen or sixteen, Koneko talked of following me to Ran'n; but she was wanted at home because of her excellence in the discipline we call "thick planning" – farm management is the usual translation, but the words have no hint of the complexity of factors involved in thick planning, ecology politics profit tradition aesthetics honor and spirit all functioning in an intensely practical and practically invisible balance of preservation and renewal, like the homeostasis of a vigorous organism.

Our "kitten" had the knack for it, and the Planners of Udan and Derdan'nad took her into their councils before she was twenty. But by then, I was gone.

Every winter of my school years I came back to the farm for the long holidays. The moment I was home I dropped school like a book bag and became pure farm boy overnight – working, swimming, fishing, hiking, putting on Plays and farces in the barn, going to field dances and house dances all over the village, falling in and out of love with lovely boys and girls of the Morning from Derdan'nad and other villages.

In my last couple of years at Ran'n, my visits home changed mood. Instead of hiking off all over the country by day and going to a different dance every night, I often stayed home. Careful not to fall in love, I pulled away from my old, dear relationship with Sota of Drehe Farmhold, gradually letting it lapse, trying not to hurt him. I sat whole hours by the Oro, a fishing line in my hand, memorizing the run of the water in a certain place just outside the entrance to our old swimming bay. There, as the water rises in clear strands racing towards two mossy, almost-submerged boulders, it surges and whirls in spirals, and while some of these spin away, grow faint, and disappear, one knots itself on a deep center, becoming a little whirlpool, which spins slowly downstream until, reaching the quick, bright race between the boulders, it loosens and unties itself, released into the body of the river, as another spiral is forming and knotting itself round a deep center upstream where the water rises in clear strands above the boulders. . . . Sometimes that winter the river rose right over the rocks and poured smooth, swollen with rain; but always it would drop, and the whirlpools would appear again.

In the winter evenings I talked with my sister and Suudi, serious, long talks by the fire. I watched my mother's beautiful hands work on the embroidery of new curtains for the wide windows of the dining room, which my father had sewn on the four-hundred-year-old sewing machine of Udan. I worked with him on reprogramming the fertilizer systems for the east fields and the yama rotations, according to our thick-planning council's directives. Now and then he and I talked a little, never very much. In the evenings we had music; Cousin Had'd was a drummer, much in demand for dances, who could always gather a group. Or I would play Word-Thief with Tubdu, a game she adored and always lost at because she was so intent to steal my words that she forgot to protect her own. "Got you, got you!" she would cry, and melt into The Great Giggle, seizing my letterblocks with her fat, tapering, brown fingers; and next move I would take all my letters back along with most of hers. "How did you see that?" she would ask, amazed, studying the scattered words. Sometimes my otherfather Kap played with us, methodical, a bit mechanical, with a small smile for both triumph and defeat.

Then I would go up to my room under the eaves, my room of dark wood walls and dark red curtains, the smell of rain coming in the window, the sound of rain on the tiles of the roof. I would lie there in the mild darkness and luxuriate in sorrow, in great, aching, sweet, youthful sorrow for this ancient home that I was going to leave, to lose forever, to sail away from on the dark river of time. For I knew, from my eighteenth birthday on, that I would leave Udan, leave O, and go out to the other worlds. It was my ambition. It was my destiny.

I have not said anything about Isidri, as I described those winter holidays. She was there. She played in the Plays, worked on the farm, went to the dances, sang the choruses, joined the hiking parties, swam in the river in the warm rain with the rest of us. My first winter home from Ran'n, as I swung off the train at Derdan'nad Station, she greeted me with a cry of delight and a great embrace, then broke away with a strange, startled laugh and stood back, a tall, dark, thin girl with an intent, watchful face. She was quite awkward with me that evening. I felt that it was because she had always seen me as a little boy, a child, and now, eighteen and a student at Ran'n, I was a man. I was complacent with Isidri, putting her at her ease, patronizing her. In the days that followed, she remained awkward, laughing inappropriately, never opening her heart to me in the kind of long talks we used to have, and even, I thought, avoiding me. My whole last tenday at home that year, Isidri spent visiting her father's relatives in Sabtodiu Village. I was offended that she had not put off her visit till I was gone.

The next year she was not awkward, but not intimate. She had become interested in religion, attending the shrine daily, studying the Discussions with the elders. She was kind, friendly, busy. I do not remember that she and I ever touched that winter until she kissed me good-bye. Among my people a kiss is not with the mouth; we lay our cheeks together for a moment, or for longer. Her kiss was as light as the touch of a leaf, lingering yet barely perceptible.

My third and last winter home, I told them I was leaving: going to Hain, and that from Hain I wanted to go on farther and forever.

How cruel we are to our parents! All I needed to say was that I was going to Hain. After her half-anguished, half-exultant cry of "I knew it!" my mother said in her usual soft voice, suggesting not stating, "After that, you might come back, for a while." I could have said, "Yes." That was all she asked. Yes, I might come back, for a while. With the impenetrable self-centeredness of youth, which mistakes itself for honesty, I refused to give her what she asked. I took from her the modest hope of seeing me after ten years, and gave her the desolation of believing that when I left she would never see me again. "If I qualify, I want to be a Mobile," I said. I had steeled myself to speak without palliations. I prided myself on my truthfulness. And all the time, though I didn't know it, nor did they, it was not the truth at all. The truth is rarely so simple, though not many truths are as complicated as mine turned out to be.

She took my brutality without the least complaint. She had left her own people, after all. She said that evening, "We can talk by ansible, sometimes, as long as you're on Hain." She said it as if reassuring me, not herself. I think she was remembering how she had said good-bye to her people and boarded the ship on Terra, and when she landed a few seeming hours later on Hain, her mother had been dead for fifty years. She could have talked to Terra on the ansible; but who was there for her to talk to? I did not know that pain, but she did. She took comfort in knowing I would be spared it, for a while.

Everything now was "for a while." Oh, the bitter sweetness of those days! How I enjoyed myself – standing, again, poised on the slick boulder amidst the roaring water, spear raised, the hero! How ready, how willing I was to crush all that long, slow, deep, rich life of Udan in my hand and toss it away!

Only for one moment was I told what I was doing, and then so briefly that I could deny it.

I was down in the boathouse workshop, on the rainy, warm afternoon of a day late in the last month of winter. The constant, hissing thunder of the swollen river was the matrix of my thoughts as I set a new thwart in the little red row-boat we used to fish from, taking pleasure in the task, indulging my anticipatory nostalgia to the full by imagining myself on another planet a hundred years away remembering this hour in the boathouse, the smell of wood and water, the river's incessant roar. A knock at the workshop door. Isidri looked in. The thin, dark, watchful face, the long braid of dark hair, not as black as mine, the intent, clear eyes. "Hideo," she said, "I want to talk to you for a minute."

"Come on in!" I said, pretending ease and gladness, though half-aware that in fact I shrank from talking with Isidri, that I was afraid of her – why?

She perched on the vise bench and watched me work in silence for a little while. I began to say something commonplace, but she spoke: "Do you know why I've been staying away from you?"

Liar, self-protective liar, I said, "Staying away from me?"

At that she sighed. She had hoped I would say I understood, and spare her the rest. But I couldn't. I was lying only in pretending that I hadn't noticed that she had kept away from me. I truly had never, never until she told me, imagined why.

"I found out I was in love with you, winter before last," she said. "I wasn't going to say anything about it because – well, you know. If you'd felt anything like that for me, you'd have known I did. But it wasn't both of us. So there was no good in it. But then, when you told us you're leaving ... At first I thought, all the more reason to say nothing. But then I thought, that wouldn't be fair. To me, partly. Love has a right to be spoken. And you have a right to know that somebody loves you. That somebody has loved you, could love you. We all need to know that. Maybe it's what we need most. So I wanted to tell you. And because I was afraid you thought I'd kept away from you because I didn't love you, or care about you, you know. It might have looked like that. But it wasn't that." She had slipped down off the table and was at the door.

"Sidi!" I said, her name breaking from me in a strange, hoarse cry, the name only, no words – I had no words. I had no feelings, no compassion, no more nostalgia, no more luxurious suffering. Shocked out of emotion, bewildered, blank, I stood there. Our eyes met. For four or five breaths we stood staring into each other's soul. Then Isidri looked away with a wincing, desolate smile, and slipped out.

I did not follow her. I had nothing to say to her: literally. I felt that it would take me a month, a year, years, to find the words I needed to say to her. I had been so rich, so comfortably complete in myself and my ambition and my destiny, five minutes ago; and now I stood empty, silent, poor, looking at the world I had thrown away.

That ability to look at the truth lasted an hour or so. All my life since I have thought of it as "the hour in the boathouse." I sat on the high bench where Isidri had sat. The rain fell and the river roared and the early night came on. When at last I moved, I turned on a light, and began to try to defend my purpose, my planned future, from the terrible plain reality. I began to build up a screen of emotions and evasions and versions; to look away from what Isidri had shown me; to look away from Isidri's eyes.

By the time I went up to the house for dinner I was in control of myself. By the time I went to bed I was master of my destiny again, sure of my decision, almost able to indulge myself in feeling sorry for Isidri – but not quite. Never did I dishonor her with that. I will say that much for myself. I had had the pity that is self-pity knocked out of me in the hour in the boathouse. When I parted from my family at the muddy little station in the village, a few days after, I wept, not luxuriously for them, but for myself, in honest, hopeless pain. It was too much for me to bear. I had had so little practice in pain! I said to my mother, "I will come back. When I finish the course – six years, maybe seven – I'll come back, I'll stay a while."

"If your way brings you," she whispered. She held me close to her, and then released me.

So, then: I have come to the time I chose to begin my story, when I was twenty-one and left my home on the ship *Terraces of Darranda* to study at the Schools on Hain.

Of the journey itself I have no memory whatever. I think I remember entering the ship, yet no details come to mind, visual or kinetic; I cannot recollect being on the ship. My memory of leaving it is only of an overwhelming physical sensation, dizziness. I staggered and felt sick, and was so unsteady on my feet I had to be supported until I had taken several steps on the soil of Hain.

Troubled by this lapse of consciousness, I asked about it at the Ekumenical School. I was told that it is one of the many different ways in which travel at near-lightspeed affects the mind. To most people it seems merely that a few hours pass in a kind of perceptual limbo; others have curious perceptions of space and time and event, which can be seriously disturbing; a few simply feel they have been asleep when they "wake up" on arrival. I did not even have that experience. I had no experience at all. I felt cheated. I wanted to have felt the voyage, to have known, in some way, the great interval of space: but as far as I was concerned, there was no interval. I was at the spaceport on O, and then I was at Ve Port, dizzy, bewildered, and at last, when I was able to believe that I was there, excited.

My studies and work during those years are of no interest now. I will mention only one event, which may or may not be on record in the ansible reception file at Fourth Beck Tower, EY 21-11-93/1645. (The last time I checked, it was on record in the ansible transmission file at Ran'n, ET date 30-11-93/1645. Urashima's coming and going was on record, too, in the Annals of the Emperors.) 1645 was my first year on Hain. Early in the term I was asked to come to the ansible center, where they explained that they had received a garbled screen transmission, apparently from O, and hoped I could help them reconstitute it. After a date nine days later than the date of reception, it read:

les oku n hide problem netru emit it hurt di it may not be salv devir

The words were gapped and fragmented. Some were standard Hain-ish, but *oku* and *netru* mean "north" and "symmetrical" in Sio, my native language. The ansible centers on O had reported no record of the transmission, but the Receivers thought the message might be from O because of these two words and because the Hainish phrase "it may not be salvageable" occurred in a transmission received almost simultaneously from one of the Stabiles on O, concerning a wave-damaged de-salinization plant. "We call this a creased message," the Receiver told me, when I confessed I could make nothing of it and asked how often ansible messages came through so garbled. "Not often, fortunately. We can't be certain where or when they originated, or will originate. They may be effects of a double field – interference phenomena, perhaps. One of my colleagues here calls them ghost messages."

Instantaneous transmission had always fascinated me, and though I was then only a beginner in ansible principle, I developed this fortuitous acquaintance with the Receivers into a friendship with several of them. And I took all the courses in ansible theory that were offered.

When I was in my final year in the school of temporal physics, and considering going on to the Cetian Worlds for further study – after my promised visit home, which seemed sometimes a remote, irrelevant daydream and sometimes a yearning and yet fearful need – the first reports came over the ansible from Anarres of the new theory of transilience. Not only information, but matter, bodies, people might be transported from place to place without lapse of time. "Churten technology" was suddenly a reality, although a very strange reality, an implausible fact.

I was crazy to work on it. I was about to go promise my soul and body to the School if they would let me work on churten theory when they came and asked me if I'd consider postponing my training as a Mobile for a year or so to work on churten theory, judiciously and graciously, I consented. I celebrated all over town that night. I remember showing all my friends how to dance the fen'n, and I remember setting off fireworks in the Great Plaza of the Schools, and I think I remember singing under the Director's windows, a little before dawn. I remember what I felt like next day, too; but it didn't keep me from dragging myself over to the Ti-Phy building to see where they were installing the Churten Field Laboratory.

Ansible transmission is, of course, enormously expensive, and I had only been able to talk to my family twice during my years on Hain; but my friends in the ansible center would occasionally "ride" a screen message for me on a transmission to O. I sent a message thus to Ran'n to be posted on to the First Sedoretu of Udan Farmhold of Derdan'nad Village of the hill district of the Northwest Watershed of the Saduun, Oket, on O, telling them that "although this research will delay my visit home, it may save me four years' travel." The flippant message revealed my guilty feeling; but we did really think then that we would have the technology within a few months.

The Field Laboratories were soon moved out to Ve Port, and I went with them. The joint work of the Cetian and Hainish churten research teams in those first three years was a succession of triumphs, postponements, promises, defeats, breakthroughs, setbacks, all happening so fast that anybody who took a week off was out-of date. "Clarity hiding mystery," Gvonesh called it. Every time it all came clear it all grew more mysterious. The theory was beautiful and maddening. The experiments were exciting and inscrutable. The technology worked best when it was most preposterous. Four years went by in that laboratory like no time at all, as they say.

I had now spent ten years on Hain and Ve, and was thirty-one. On O, four years had passed while my NAFAL ship passed a few minutes of dilated time going to Hain, and four more would pass while I returned: so when I returned I would have been gone eighteen of their years. My parents were all still alive. It was high time for my promised visit home.

But though churten research had hit a frustrating setback in the Spring Snow Paradox, a problem the Cetians thought might be insoluble, I couldn't stand the thought of being eight years out-of-date when I got back to Hain. What if they broke the paradox? It was bad enough knowing I must lose four years going to O. Tentatively, not too hopefully, I proposed to the Director that I carry some experimental materials with me to O and set up a fixed double-held auxiliary to the ansible link between Ve Port and Ran'n. Thus I could stay in touch with Ve, as Ve stayed in touch with Urras and Anarres; and the fixed ansible link might be preparatory to a churten link. I remember I said, "If you break the paradox, we might eventually send some mice."

To my surprise my idea caught on; the temporal engineers wanted a receiving field. Even our Director, who could be as brilliantly inscrutable as churten theory itself, said it was a good idea. "Mouses, bugs, gholes, who knows what we send you?" she said.

So, then: when I was thirty-one years old I left Ve Port on the NAFAL transport *Lady of Sorra* and returned to O. This time I experienced the near-lightspeed flight the way most people do, as an unnerving interlude in which one cannot think consecutively, read a clockface, or follow a story. Speech and movement become difficult or impossible. Other people appear as unreal half presences, inexplicably there or not there. I did not hallucinate, but everything seemed hallucination. It is like a high fever – confusing, miserably boring, seeming endless, yet very difficult to recall once it is over, as if it were an episode outside one's life, encapsulated. I wonder now if its resemblance to the "churten experience" has yet been seriously investigated.

I went straight to Ran'n, where I was given rooms in the New Quadrangle, fancier than my old student room in the Shrine Quadrangle, and some nice lab space in Tower Hall to set up an experimental transilience field station. I got in touch with my family right away and talked to all my parents; my mother had been ill, but was fine now, she said. I told them I would be home as soon as I had got things going at Ran'n. Every tenday I called again and talked to them and said I'd be along very soon now. I was genuinely very busy, having to catch up the lost four years and to learn Gvonesh's solution to the Spring Snow Paradox. It was, fortunately, the only major advance in theory. Technology had advanced a good deal. I had to retrain myself, and to train my assistants almost from scratch. I had had an idea about an aspect of double-field theory that I wanted to work out before I left. Five months went by before I called them up and said at last, "I'll be there tomorrow." And when I did so, I realized that all along I had been afraid.

I don't know if I was afraid of seeing them after eighteen years, of the changes, the strangeness, or if it was myself I feared.

Eighteen years had made no difference at all to the hills beside the wide Saduun, the farmlands, the dusty little station in Derdan'nad, the old, old houses on the quiet streets. The village great tree was gone, its replacement had a pretty wide spread of shade already. The aviary at Udan had been enlarged. The yama stared haughtily, timidly at me across the fence. A road gate that I had hung on my last visit home was decrepit, needing its post reset and new hinges, but the weeds that grew beside it were the same dusty, sweet-smelling summer weeds. The tiny dams of the irrigation runnels made their multiple, soft click and thump as they closed and opened. Everything was the same, itself. Timeless, Udan in its dream of work stood over the river that ran timeless in its dream of movement.

But the faces and bodies of the people waiting for me at the station in the hot sunlight were not the same. My mother, forty-seven when I left, was sixty-five, a beautiful and fragile elderly woman. Tubdu had lost weight; she looked shrunken and wistful. My father was still handsome and bore himself proudly, but his movements were slow and he scarcely spoke at all. My otherfather Kap, seventy now, was a precise, fidgety, little old man. They were still the First Sedoretu of Udan, but the vigor of the farmhold now lay in the Second and Third Sedoretu.

I knew of all the changes, of course, but being there among them was a different matter from hearing about them in letters and transmissions. The old house was much fuller than it had been when I lived there. The south wing had been reopened, and children ran in and out of its doors and across courtyards that in my childhood had been silent and ivied and mysterious.

My sister Koneko was now four years older than I instead of four years younger. She looked very like my early memory of my mother. As the train drew in to Derdan'nad Station, she had been the first of them I recognized, holding up a child of three or four and saying, "Look, look, our Uncle Hideo!"

The Second Sedoretu had been married for eleven years: Koneko and Isidri, sister-germanes, were the partners of the Day. Koneko's husband was my old friend Sota, a Morning man of Drehe Farmhold. Sota and I had loved each other dearly when we were adolescents, and I had been grieved to grieve him when I left. When I heard that he and Koneko were in love I had been very surprised, so self-centered am I, but at least I am not jealous: it pleased me very deeply. Isidri's husband, a man nearly twenty years older than herself, named Hedran, had been a traveling scholar of the Discussions. Udan had given him hospitality, his visits had led to the marriage. He and Isidri had no children. Sola and Koneko had two Evening children, a boy of ten called Murmi, and Lasako, Little Isako, who was four.

The Third Sedoretu had been brought to Udan by Suudi, my brother-ger-mane, who had married a woman from Aster Village; their Morning pair also came from farmholds of Aster. There were six children in that sedoretu. A cousin whose sedoretu at Ekke had broken had also come to live at Udan with her two children; so the coming and going and dressing and undressing and washing and slamming and running and shouting and weeping and laughing and eating was prodigious. Tubdu would sit at work in the sunny kitchen courtyard and watch a wave of children pass. "Bad!" she would cry. "They'll never drown, not a one of 'em!" And she would shake with silent laughter that became a wheezing cough.

My mother, who had after all been a Mobile of the Ekumen, and had trav-eled from Terra to Hain and from Hain to O, was impatient to hear about my research. "What is it, this churtening? How does it work, what does it do? Is it an ansible for matter?"

"That's the idea," I said. "Transilience: instantaneous transference of being from one s-tc point to another."

"No interval?"

"No interval."

Isako frowned. "It sounds wrong," she said. "Explain."

I had forgotten how direct my soft-spoken mother could be; I had forgotten that she was an intellectual. I did my best to explain the incomprehensible.

"So," she said at last, "you don't really understand how it works."

"No. Nor even what it does. Except that – as a rule – when the field is in oper-ation, the mice in Building One are instantaneously in Building Two, perfectly cheerful and unharmed. Inside their cage, if we remembered to keep their cage inside the initiating churten field. We used to forget. Loose mice everywhere."

"What's *mice?*" said a little Morning boy of the Third Sedoretu, who had stopped to listen to what sounded like a story.

"Ah," I said in a laugh, surprised. I had forgotten that at Udan mice were unknown, and rats were fanged, demon enemies of the painted cat. "Tiny, pretty, furry animals," I said, "that come from Grandmother Isako's world. They are friends of scientists. They have traveled all over the Known Worlds."

"In tiny little spaceships?" the child said hopefully.

"In large ones, mostly," I said. He was satisfied, and went away.

"Hideo," said my mother, in the terrifying way women have of passing with-out interval from one subject to another because they have them all present in their mind at once, "you haven't found any kind of relationship?"

I shook my head, smiling.

"None at all?"

"A man from Alterra and I lived together for a couple of years," I said. "It was a good friendship; but he's a Mobile now. And . . . oh, you know . . . people here and there. Just recently, at Ran'n, I've been with a very nice woman from East Oket."

"I hoped, if you intend to be a Mobile, that you might make a couple-marriage with another Mobile. It's easier, I think," she said. Easier than what? I thought, and knew the answer before I asked.

"Mother, I doubt now that I'll travel farther than Hain. This churten business is too interesting; I want to be in on it. And if we do learn to control the technology, you know, then travel will be nothing. There'll be no need for the kind of sacrifice you made. Things will be different. Unimaginably different! You could go to Terra for an hour and come back here: and only an hour would have passed."

She thought about that. "If you do it, then," she said, speaking slowly, almost shaking with the intensity of comprehension, "you will . . . you will shrink the galaxy – the universe? – to . . ." and she held up her left hand, thumb and fingers all drawn together to a point.

I nodded. "A mile or a light-year will be the same. There will be no distance."

"It can't be right," she said after a while. "To have event without interval . . . Where is the dancing? Where is the way? I don't think you'll be able to control it, Hideo." She smiled. "But of course you must try."

And after that we talked about who was coming to the field dance at Drehe tomorrow.

I did not tell my mother that I had invited Tasi, the nice woman from East Oket, to come to Udan with me and that she had refused, had, in fact, gently informed me that she thought this was a good time for us to part. Tasi was tall, with a braid of dark hair, not coarse bright black like mine but soft, fine, dark, like the shadows in a forest. A typical ki'O woman, I thought. She had deflated my protestations of love skillfully and without shaming me. "I think you're in love with somebody, though," she said. "Somebody on Hain, maybe. Maybe the man from Alterra you told me about?" No, I said. No, I'd never been in love. I wasn't capable of an intense relationship, that was clear by now. I'd dreamed too long of traveling the galaxy with no attachments anywhere, and then worked too long in the churten lab, married to a damned theory that couldn't find its technology. No room for love, no time.

But why had I wanted to bring Tasi home with me?

Tall but no longer thin, a woman of forty, not a girl, not typical, not comparable, not like anyone anywhere, Isidri had greeted me quietly at the door of the house. Some farm emergency had kept her from coming to the village station to meet me. She was wearing an old smock and leggings like any field worker, and her hair, dark beginning to grey, was in a rough braid. As she stood in that wide doorway of polished wood she was Udan itself, the body and soul of that thirty-century-old farmhold, its continuity, its life. All my childhood was in her hands, and she held them out to me.

"Welcome home, Hideo," she said, with a smile as radiant as the summer light on the river. As she brought me in, she said, "I cleared the kids out of your old room. I thought you'd like to be there – would you?" Again she smiled, and I felt her warmth, the solar generosity of a woman in the prime of life, married, settled, rich in her work and being. I had not needed Tasi as a defense. I had nothing to fear from Isidri. She felt no rancor, no embarrassment. She had loved me when she was young, another person. It would be altogether inappropriate for me to feel embarrassment, or shame, or anything but the old affectionate loyalty of the years when we played and worked and fished and dreamed together, children of Udan.

So, then: I settled down in my old room under the tiles. There were new curtains, rust and brown. I found a stray toy under the chair, in the closet, as if I as a child had left my playthings there and found them now. At fourteen, after my entry ceremony in the shrine, I had carved my name on the deep window jamb among the tangled patterns of names and symbols that had been cut into it for centuries. I looked for it now. There had been some additions. Beside my careful, clear *Hideo,* surrounded by my ideogram, the cloudflower, a younger child had hacked a straggling *Dohedri,* and nearby was carved a delicate three-roofs ideogram. The sense of being a bubble in Udan's river, a moment in the permanence of life in this house on this land on this quiet world, was almost crushing, denying my identity, and profoundly reassuring, confirming my identity. Those nights of my visit home I slept as I had not slept for years, lost, drowned in the waters of sleep and darkness, and woke to the summer mornings as if reborn, very hungry.

The children were still all under twelve, going to school at home. Isidri, who taught them literature and religion and was the school planner, invited me to tell them about Hain, about NAFAL travel, about temporal physics, whatever I pleased. Visitors to ki'O farmholds are always put to use. Evening-Uncle Hideo became rather a favorite among the children, always good for hitching up the yama-cart or taking them fishing in the big boat, which they couldn't yet handle, or telling a story about his magic mice who could be in two places at the same time. I asked them if Evening-Grandmother Isako had told them about the painted cat who came alive and killed the demon rats – "And his mouf *was* all BLUGGY in the morning!" shouted Lasako, her eyes shining. But they didn't know the tale of Urashima.

"Why haven't you told them 'The Fisherman of the Inland Sea?'" I asked my mother.

She smiled and said, "Oh, that was your story. You always wanted it."

I saw Isidri's eyes on us, clear and tranquil, yet watchful still.

I knew my mother had had repair and healing to her heart a year before, and I asked Isidri later, as we supervised some work the older children were doing, "Has Isako recovered, do you think?"

"She seems wonderfully well since you came. I don't know. It's damage from her childhood, from the poisons in the Terran biosphere; they say her immune system is easily depressed. She was very patient about being ill. Almost too patient."

"And Tubdu – does she need new lungs?"

"Probably. All four of them are getting older, and stubborner . . . But you look at Isako for me. See if you see what I mean."

I tried to observe my mother. After a few days I reported back that she seemed energetic and decisive, even imperative, and that I hadn't seen much of the patient endurance that worried Isidri. She laughed.

"Isako told me once," she said, "that a mother is connected to her child by a very fine, thin cord, like the umbilical cord, that can stretch light-years without any difficulty. I asked her if it was painful, and she said, 'Oh, no, it's just there, you know, it stretches and stretches and never breaks.' It seems to me it must be painful. But I don't know. I have no child, and I've never been more than two days' travel from my mothers." She smiled and said in her soft, deep voice, "I think I love Isako more than anyone, more even than my mother, more even than Koneko . . ."

Then she had to show one of Suudi's children how to reprogram the timer on the irrigation control. She was the hydrologist for the village and the oenologist for the farm. Her life was thick-planned, very rich in necessary work and wide relationships, a serene and steady succession of days, seasons, years. She swam in life as she had swum in the river, like a fish, at home. She had borne no child, but all the children of the farmhold were hers. She and Koneko were as deeply attached as their mothers had been. Her relation with her rather fragile, scholarly husband seemed peaceful and respectful. I thought his Night marriage with my old friend Sota might be the stronger sexual link, but Isidri clearly admired and depended on his intellectual and spiritual guidance. I thought his teaching a bit dry and disputatious; but what did I know about religion? I had not given worship for years, and felt strange, out of place, even in the home shrine. I felt strange, out of place, in my home. I did not acknowledge it to myself.

I was conscious of the month as pleasant, uneventful, even a little boring. My emotions were mild and dull. The wild nostalgia, the romantic sense of standing on the brink of my destiny, all that was gone with the Hideo of twenty-one. Though now the youngest of my generation, I was a grown man, knowing his way, content with his work, past emotional self-indulgence. I wrote a little poem for the house album about the peacefulness of following a chosen course. When I had to go, I embraced and kissed everyone, dozens of soft or harsh cheek-touches. I told them that if I stayed on O, as it seemed I might be asked to do for a year or so, I would come back next winter for another visit. On the train going back through the hills to Ran'n, I thought with a complacent gravity how I might return to the farm next winter, finding them all just the same; and how, if I came back after another eighteen years or even longer, some of them would be gone and some would be new to me and yet it would be always my home, Udan with its wide dark roofs riding time like a dark-sailed ship. I always grow poetic when I am lying to myself.

I got back to Ran'n, checked in with my people at the lab in Tower Hall, and had dinner with colleagues, good food and drink – I brought them a bottle of wine from Udan, for Isidri was making splendid wines, and had given me a case of the fifteen-year-old Kedun. We talked about the latest breakthrough in churten technology, "continuous-field sending," reported from Anarres just yesterday on the ansible. I went to my rooms in the New Quadrangle through the summer night, my head full of physics, read a little, and went to bed. I turned out the light and darkness filled me as it filled the room. Where was I? Alone in a room among strangers. As I had been for ten years and would always be. On one planet or another, what did it matter? Alone, part of nothing, part of no one. Udan was not my home. I had no home, no people. I had no future, no destiny, any more than a bubble of foam or a whirlpool in a current has a destiny. It is and it isn't. Nothing more.

I turned the light on because I could not bear the darkness, but the light was worse. I sat huddled up in the bed and began to cry. I could not stop crying. I became frightened at how the sobs racked and shook me till I was sick and weak and still could not stop sobbing. After a long time I calmed myself gradually by clinging to an imagination, a childish idea: in the morning I would call Isidri and talk to her, telling her that I needed instruction in religion, that I wanted to give worship at the shrines again, but it had been so long, and I had never listened to the Discussions, but now I needed to, and I would ask her, Isidri, to help me. So, holding fast to that, I could at last stop the terrible sobbing and lie spent, exhausted, until the day came.

I did not call Isidri. In daylight the thought which had saved me from the dark seemed foolish; and I thought if I called her she would ask advice of her husband, the religious scholar. But I knew I needed help. I went to the shrine in the Old School and gave worship. I asked for a copy of the First Discussions, and read it. I joined a Discussion group, and we read and talked together. My religion is godless, argumentative, and mystical. The name of our world is the first word of its first prayer. For human beings its vehicle is the human voice and mind. As I began to rediscover it, I found it quite as strange as churten theory and in some respects complementary to it. I knew, but had never understood, that Cetian physics and religion are aspects of one knowledge. I wondered if all physics and religion are aspects of one knowledge.

At night I never slept well and often could not sleep at all. After the bountiful tables of Udan, college food seemed poor stuff; I had no appetite. But our work, my work went well – wonderfully well.

"No more mouses," said Gvonesh on the voice ansible from Hain. "Peoples."

"What people?" I demanded.

"Me," said Gvonesh.

So our Director of Research churtened from one corner of Laboratory One to another, and then from Building One to Building Two – vanishing in one laboratory and appearing in the other, smiling, in the same instant, in no time.

"What did it feel like?" they asked, of course, and Gvonesh answered, of course, "Like nothing."

Many experiments followed; mice and gholes churtened halfway around Ve and back; robot crews churtened from Anarres to Urras, from Hain to Ve, and then from Anarres to Ve, twenty-two light-years. So, then, eventually the *Shoby* and her crew of ten human beings churtened into orbit around a miserable planet seventeen light-years from Ve and returned (but words that imply coming and going, that imply distance traveled, are not appropriate) thanks only to their intelligent use of entrainment, rescuing themselves from a kind of chaos of dissolution, a death by unreality, that horrified us all. Experiments with high-intelligence lifeforms came to a halt.

"The rhythm is wrong," Gvonesh said on the ansible (she said it "rithkhom"). For a moment I thought of my mother saying, "It can't be right to have event without interval." What else had Isako said? Something about dancing. But I did not want to think about Udan. I did not think about Udan. When I did I felt, far down deeper inside me than my bones, the knowledge of being no one, no where, and a shaking like a frightened animal.

My religion reassured me that I was part of the Way, and my physics absorbed my despair in work. Experiments, cautiously resumed, succeeded beyond hope. The Terran Dalzul and his psychophysics took everyone at the research station on Ve by storm; I am sorry I never met him. As he predicted, using the continuity field he churtened without a hint of trouble, alone, first locally, then from Ve to Hain, then the great jump to Tadkla and back. From the second journey to Tadkla, his three companions returned without him. He died on that far world. It did not seem to us in the laboratories that his death was in any way caused by the churten field or by what had come to be known as "the churten experience," though his three companions were not so sure.

"Maybe Dalzul was right. One people at a time," said Gvonesh; and she made herself again the subject, the "ritual animal," as the Hainish say, of the next experiment. Using continuity technology she churtened right around Ve in four skips, which took thirty-two seconds because of the time needed to set up the coordinates. We had taken to calling the ion-interval in time/real interval in space a "skip." It sounded light, trivial. Scientists like to trivialize.

I wanted to try the improvement to double-field stability that I had been working on ever since I came to Ran'n. It was time to give it a test; my patience was short, life was too short to fiddle with figures forever. Talking to Gvonesh on the ansible I said, "I'll skip over to Ve Port. And then back here to Ran'n. I promised a visit to my home farm this winter." Scientists like to trivialize.

"You still got that wrinkle in your field?" Gvonesh asked. "Some kind, you know, like a fold?"

"It's ironed out, ammar," I assured her.

"Good, fine," said Gvonesh, who never questioned what one said. "Come."

So, then: we set up the fields in a constant stable churten link with ansible connection; and I was standing inside a chalked circle in the Churten Field Laboratory of Ran'n Center on a late autumn afternoon and standing inside a chalked circle in the Churten Research Station Field Laboratory in Ve Port on a late summer day at a distance of 4.2 light-years and no interval of time.

"Feel nothing?" Gvonesh inquired, shaking my hand heartily. "Good fellow, good fellow, welcome, ammar, Hideo. Good to see. No wrinkle, hah?"

I laughed with the shock and queerness of it, and gave Gvonesh the bottle of Udan Kedun '49 that I had picked up a moment ago from the laboratory table on O.

I had expected, if I arrived at all, to churten promptly back again, but Gvonesh and others wanted me on Ve for a while for discussions and tests of the field. I think now that the Director's extraordinary intuition is at work; the "wrinkle," the "fold" in the Tiokunan'n Field still bothered her. "Is unaesthetical," she said.

"But it works," I said.

"It worked," said Gvonesh.

Except to retest my field, to prove its reliability, I had no desire to return to O. I was sleeping somewhat better here on Ve, although food was still unpalatable to me, and when I was not working I felt shaky and drained, a disagreeable reminder of my exhaustion after the night which I tried not to remember when for some reason or other I had cried so much. But the work went very well.

"You got no sex, Hideo?" Gvonesh asked me when we were alone in the Lab one day, I playing with a new set of calculations and she finishing her box lunch.

The question took me utterly aback. I knew it was not as impertinent as Gvonesh's peculiar usage of the language made it sound. But Gvonesh never asked questions like that. Her own sex life was as much a mystery as the rest of her existence. No one had ever heard her mention the word, let alone suggest the act.

When I sat with my mouth open, stumped, she said, "You used to, hah," as she chewed on a cold varvet.

I stammered something. I knew she was not proposing that she and I have sex, but inquiring after my well-being. But I did not know what to say.

"You got some kind of wrinkle in your life, hah," Gvonesh said. "Sorry. Not my business."

Wanting to assure her I had taken no offense I said, as we say on O, "I honor your intent."

She looked directly at me, something she rarely did. Her eyes were clear as water in her long, bony face softened by a fine, thick, colorless down. "Maybe is time you go back to O?" she asked.

"I don't know. The facilities here—"

She nodded. She always accepted what one said. "You read Harraven's report?" she asked, changing one subject for another as quickly and definitively as my mother.

All right, I thought, the challenge was issued. She was ready for me to test my field again. Why not? After all, I could churten to Ran'n and churten right back again to Ve within a minute, if I chose, and if the Lab could afford it. Like ansible transmission, churtening draws essentially on inertial mass, but setting up the field, disinfecting it, and holding it stable in size uses a good deal of local energy. But it was Gvonesh's suggestion, which meant we had the money. I said, "How about a skip over and back?"

Fine, Gvonesh said. "Tomorrow."

So the next day, on a morning of late autumn, I stood inside a chalked circle in the Field Laboratory on Ve and stood—

A shimmer, a shivering of everything – a missed beat – skipped—

in darkness. A darkness. A dark room. The lab? A lab – I found the light panel. In the darkness I was sure it was the laboratory on Ve. In the light I saw it was not. I didn't know where it was. I didn't know where I was. It seemed familiar yet I could not place it. What was it? A biology lab? There were specimens, an old subparticle microscope, the maker's ideogram on the battered brass casing, the lyre ideogram. . . . I was on O. In some laboratory in some building of the Center at Ran'n? It smelled like the old buildings of Ran'n, it smelled like a rainy night on O. But how could I have not arrived in the receiving field, the circle carefully chalked on the wood floor of the lab in Tower Hall? The field itself must have moved. An appalling, an impossible thought.

I was alarmed and felt rather dizzy, as if my body had skipped that beat, but I was not yet frightened. I was all right, all here, all the pieces in the right places, and the mind working. A slight spatial displacement? said the mind.

I went out into the corridor. Perhaps I had myself been disoriented and left the Churten Field Laboratory and come to full consciousness somewhere else. But my crew would have been there; where were they? And that would have been hours ago; it should have been just past noon on O when I arrived. A slight temporal displacement? said the mind, working away. I went down the corridor looking for my lab, and that is when it became like one of those dreams in which you cannot find the room which you must find. It was that dream. The building was perfectly familiar: it was Tower Hall, the second floor of Tower, but there was no Churten Lab. All the labs were biology and biophysics, and all were deserted. It was evidently late at night. Nobody around. At last I saw a light under a door and knocked and opened it on a student reading at a library terminal.

"I'm sorry," I said. "I'm looking for the Churten Field Lab—"

"The what lab?"

She had never heard of it, and apologized. "I'm not in Ti Phy, just Bi Phy," she said humbly.

I apologized too. Something was making me shakier, increasing my sense of dizziness and disorientation. Was this the "chaos effect" the crew of the *Shoby* and perhaps the crew of the *Galba* had experienced? Would I begin to see the stars through the walls, or turn around and see Gvonesh here on O?

I asked her what time it was. "I should have got here at noon," I said, though that of course meant nothing to her.

"It's about one," she said, glancing at the clock on the terminal. I looked at it too. It gave the time, the ten-day, the month, the year.

"That's wrong," I said.

She looked worried.

"That's not right," I said. "The date. It's not right." But I knew from the steady glow of the numbers on the clock, from the girl's round, worried face, from the beat of my heart, from the smell of the rain, that it was right, that it was an hour after midnight eighteen years ago, that I was here, now, on the day after the day I called "once upon a time" when I began to tell this story.

A major temporal displacement, said the mind, working, laboring.

"I don't belong here," I said, and turned to hurry back to what seemed a refuge, Biology Lab 6, which would be the Churten Field Lab eighteen years from now, as if I could re-enter the field, which had existed or would exist for .004 second.

The girl saw that something was wrong, made me sit down, and gave me a cup of hot tea from her insulated bottle.

"Where are you from?" I asked her, the kind, serious student.

"Herdud Farmhold of Deada Village on the South Watershed of the Saduun," she said.

"I'm from downriver," I said. "Udan of Derdan'nad." I suddenly broke into tears. I managed to control myself, apologized again, drank my tea, and set the cup down. She was not overly troubled by my fit of weeping. Students are intense people, they laugh and cry, they break down and rebuild. She asked if I had a place to spend the night: a perceptive question. I said I did, thanked her, and left.

I did not go back to the biology laboratory, but went downstairs and started to cut through the gardens to my rooms in the New Quadrangle. As I walked the mind kept working; it worked out that somebody else had been/would be in those rooms then/now.

I turned back towards the Shrine Quadrangle, where I had lived my last two years as a student before I left for Hain. If this was in fact, as the clock had indicated, the night after I had left, my room might still be empty and unlocked.

It proved to be so, to be as I had left it, the mattress bare, the cyclebasket unemptied.

That was the most frightening moment. I stared at that cyclebasket for a long time before I took a crumpled bit of outprint from it and carefully smoothed it on the desk. It was a set of temporal equations scribbled on my old pocketscreen in my own handwriting, notes from Sedharad's class in Interval, from my last term at Ran'n, day before yesterday, eighteen years ago.

I was now very shaky indeed. You are caught in a chaos field, said the mind, and I believed it. Fear and stress, and nothing to do about it, not till the long night was past. I lay down on the bare bunk-mattress, ready for the stars to burn through the walls and my eyelids if I shut them. I meant to try and plan what I should do in the morning, if there was a morning. I fell asleep instantly and slept like a stone till broad daylight, when I woke up on the bare bed in the familiar room, alert, hungry, and without a moment of doubt as to who or where or when I was.

I went down into the village for breakfast. I didn't want to meet any colleagues – no, fellow students – who might know me and say, "Hideo! What are you doing here? You left on the *Terraces of Darranda* yesterday!"

I had little hope they would not recognize me. I was thirty-one now, not twenty-one, much thinner and not as fit as I had been; but my half-Terran features were unmistakable. I did not want to be recognized, to have to try to explain. I wanted to get out of Ran'n. I wanted to go home.

O is a good world to time-travel in. Things don't change. Our trains have run on the same schedule to the same places for centuries. We sign for payment and pay in contracted barter or cash monthly, so I did not have to produce mysterious coins from the future. I signed at the station and took the morning train to Saduun Delta.

The little suntrain glided through the plains and hills of the South Watershed and then the Northwest Watershed, following the ever-widening river, stopping at each village. I got off in the late afternoon at the station in Derdan'nad. Since it was very early spring, the station was muddy, not dusty.

I walked out the road to Udan. I opened the road gate that I had re-hung a few days/eighteen years ago; it moved easily on its new hinges. That gave me a little gleam of pleasure. The she-yamas were all in the nursery pasture. Birthing would start any day; their woolly sides stuck out, and they moved like sailboats in a slow breeze, turning their elegant, scornful heads to look distrustfully at me as I passed. Rain clouds hung over the hills. I crossed the Oro on the hump-backed wooden bridge. Four or five great blue ochid hung in a backwater by the bridgefoot; I stopped to watch them; if I'd had a spear... The clouds drifted overhead trailing a fine, faint drizzle. I strode on. My face felt hot and stiff as the cool rain touched it. I followed the river road and saw the house come to view, the dark, wide roofs low on the tree-crowned hill. I came past the aviary and the collectors, past the irrigation center, under the avenue of tall bare trees, up the steps of the deep porch, to the door, the wide door of Udan. I went in.

Tubdu was crossing the hall – not the woman I had last seen, in her sixties, grey-haired and tired and fragile, but Tubdu of The Great Giggle, Tubdu at forty-five, fat and rosy-brown and brisk, crossing the hall with short, quick steps, stopping, looking at me at first with mere recognition, there's Hideo, then with puzzlement, is that Hideo? and then with shock – that can't be Hideo!

"Ombu," I said, the baby word for othermother, "Ombu, it's me, Hideo, don't worry, it's all right, I came back." I embraced her, pressed my cheek to hers.

"But, but—" She held me off, looked up at my face. "But what has happened to you, darling boy?" she cried, and then, turning, called out in a high voice, "Isako! Isako!"

When my mother saw me she thought, of course, that I had not left on the ship to Hain, that my courage or my intent had failed me; and in her first embrace there was an involuntary reserve, a withholding. Had I thrown away the destiny for which I had been so ready to throw away everything else? I knew what was in her mind. I laid my cheek to hers and whispered, "I did go, mother, and I came back. I'm thirty-one years old. I came back—"

She held me away a little just as Tubdu had done, and saw my face. "Oh, Hideo!" she said, and held me to her with all her strength. "My dear, my dear!"

We held each other in silence, till I said at last, "I need to see Isidri."

My mother looked up at me intently but asked no questions. "She's in the shrine, I think."

"I'll be right back."

I left her and Tubdu side by side and hurried through the halls to the central room, in the oldest part of the house, rebuilt seven centuries ago on the foundations that go back three thousand years. The walls are stone and clay, the roof is thick glass, curved. It is always cool and still there. Books line the walls, the Discussions, the discussions of the Discussions, poetry, texts and versions of the Plays; there are drums and whispersticks for meditation and ceremony; the small, round pool which is the shrine itself wells up from clay pipes and brims its blue-green basin, reflecting the rainy sky above the skylight. Isidri was there. She had brought in fresh boughs for the vase beside the shrine, and was kneeling to arrange them.

I went straight to her and said, "Isidri, I came back. Listen—"

Her face was utterly open, startled, scared, defenseless, the soft, thin face of a woman of twenty-two, the dark eyes gazing into me.

"Listen, Isidri: I went to Hain, I studied there, I worked on a new kind of temporal physics, a new theory – transilience – I spent ten years. Then we began experiments, I was in Ran'n and crossed over to the Hainish system in no time, using that technology, in no time, you understand me, literally, like the ansible – not at lightspeed, not faster light, but in no time. In one place and in another place instantaneously, you understand? And it went fine, it worked, but coming back there was . . . there was a fold, a crease, in my field. I was in the same place in a different time. I came back eighteen of your years, ten of mine. I came back to the day I left, but I didn't leave, I came back, I came back to you."

I was holding her hands, kneeling to face her as she knelt by the silent pool. She searched my face with her watchful eyes, silent. On her cheekbone there was a fresh scratch and a little bruise; a branch had lashed her as she gathered the evergreen boughs.

"Let me come back to you," I said in a whisper.

She touched my face with her hand. "You look so tired," she said. "Hideo . . .

Are you all right?"

"Yes," I said. "Oh, yes. I'm all right."

And there my story, so far as it has any interest to the Ekumen or to research in transilience, comes to an end. I have lived now for eighteen years as a farm-holder of Udan Farm of Derdan'nad Village of the hill region of the Northwest Watershed of the Saduun on Oket, on O. I am fifty years old. I am the Morning husband of the Second Sedoretu of Udan; my wife is Isidri; my Night marriage is to Sota of Drehe, whose Evening wife is my sister Koneko. My children of the Morning with Isidri are Latubdu and Tadri; the Evening children are Murmi and Lasako. But none of this is of much interest to the Stabiles of the Ekumen.

My mother, who had had some training in temporal engineering, asked for my story, listened to it carefully, and accepted it without question; so did Isidri. Most of the people of my farmhold chose a simpler and far more plausible story, which explained everything fairly well, my severe loss of weight and ten-year age gain overnight. At the very last moment, just before the space ship left, they said, Hideo decided not to go to the Ekumenical School on Hain after all. He came back to Udan, because he was in love with Isidri. But it had made him quite ill, because it was a very hard decision and he was very much in love.

Maybe that is indeed the true story. But Isidri and Isako chose a stranger truth.

Later, when we were forming our sedoretu, Sota asked me for that truth. "You aren't the same man, Hideo, though you are the man I always loved," he said. I told him why, as best I could. He was sure that Koneko would understand it better than he could, and indeed she listened gravely, and asked several keen questions which I could not answer.

I did attempt to send a message to the temporal physics department of the Ekumenical Schools on Hain. I had not been home long before my mother, with her strong sense of duty and her obligation to the Ekumen, became insistent that I do so.

"Mother," I said, "what can I tell them? They haven't invented churten theory yet!"

"Apologize for not coming to study, as you said you would. And explain it to the Director, the Anarresti woman. Maybe she would understand."

"Even Gvonesh doesn't know about churten yet. They'll begin telling her about it on the ansible from Urras and Anarres about three years from now. Anyhow, Gvonesh didn't know me the first couple of years I was there." The past tense was inevitable but ridiculous; it would have been more accurate to say, "She won't know me the first couple of years I won't be there."

Or *was* I there on Hain, now? That paradoxical idea of two simultaneous existences on two different worlds disturbed me exceedingly. It was one of the points Koneko had asked about. No matter how I discounted it as impossible under every law of temporality, I could not keep from imagining that it was possible, that another I was living on Hain, and would come to Udan in eighteen years and meet myself. After all, my present existence was also and equally impossible.

When such notions haunted and troubled me I learned to replace them with a different image: the little whorls of water that slid down between the two big rocks, where the current ran strong, just above the swimming bay in the Oro. I would imagine, those whirlpools forming and dissolving, or I would go down to the river and sit and watch them. And they seemed to hold a solution to my question, to dissolve it as they endlessly dissolved and formed.

But my mother's sense of duty and obligation was unmoved by such trifles as a life impossibly lived twice. "You should try to tell them,' she said.

She was right. If my double transilience field had established itself permanently, it was a matter of real importance to temporal science, not only to myself. So I tried. I borrowed a staggering sum in cash from the farm reserves, went up to Ran'n, bought a five-thousand-word ansible screen transmission, and sent a message to my director of studies at Ekumenical School, trying to explain why, after being accepted at the School, I had not arrived – if in fact I had not arrived.

I take it that this was the "creased message" or "ghost" they asked me to try to interpret, my first year there. Some of it is gibberish, and some words probably came from the other, nearly simultaneous transmission; parts of my name are in it, and other words may be fragments or reversals from my long message – problem, churten, return, arrived, time.

It is interesting, I think, that at the ansible center the Receivers used the word "creased" for a temporally disturbed transilient, as Gvonesh would use it for the anomaly, the "wrinkle" in my churten field. In fact, the ansible field was meeting a resonance resistance, caused by the ten-year anomaly in the churten field, which did fold the message back into itself, crumple it up, inverting and erasing. At that point, within the implication of the Tiokunan'n Double Field, my existence on O as I sent the message was simultaneous with my existence on Hain when the message was received. There was an I who sent and an I who received, so long as the encapsulated field anomaly existed, the simultaneity literally a point, an instant, a crossing without further implication in either the ansible or the churten field.

An image for the churten field in this case might be a river winding in its floodplain, winding in deep, redoubling curves, folding back upon itself so closely that at last the current breaks through the double banks of the S and runs straight, leaving a whole reach of the water aside as a curving lake, cut off from the current, unconnected. In this analogy, my ansible message would have been the one link, other than my memory, between the current and the lake.

But I think a truer image is the whirlpools of the current itself, occurring and recurring; the same? Or not the same?

I worked at the mathematics of an explanation in the early years of my marriage, while my physics was still in good working order. See the "Notes toward a Theory of Resonance Interference in Doubled Ansible and Churten Fields," appended to this document. I realize that the explanation is probably irrelevant, since, on this stretch of the river, there is no Tiokunan'n Field. But independent research from an odd direction can be useful. And I am attached to it, since it is the last temporal physics I did. I have followed churten research with intense interest, but my life's work has been concerned with vineyards, drainage, the care of yamas, the care and education of children, the Discussions, and trying to learn how to catch fish with my bare hands.

Working on that paper, I satisfied myself in terms of mathematics and physics that the existence in which I went to Hain and became a temporal physicist specializing in transilience was in fact encapsulated (enfolded, erased) by the churten effect. But no amount of theory or proof could quite allay my anxiety, my fear – which increased after my marriage and with the birth of each of my children – that there was a crossing point yet to come. For all my images of rivers and whirlpools, I could not prove that the encapsulation might not reverse at the instant of transilience. It was possible that on the day I churtened from Ve to Ran'n I might undo, lose, erase my marriage, our children, all my life at Udan, crumple it up like a bit of paper tossed into a basket. I could not endure that thought.

I spoke of it at last to Isidri, from whom I have only ever kept one secret.

"No," she said, after thinking a long time, "I don't think that can be. There was a reason, wasn't there, that you came back – here."

"You," I said.

She smiled wonderfully. "Yes," she said. She added after a while, "And Sota, and Koneko, and the farmhold . . . But there'd be no reason for you to go back there, would there?"

She was holding our sleeping baby as she spoke; she laid her cheek against the small silky head.

"Except maybe your work there," she said. She looked at me with a little yearning in her eyes. Her honesty required equal honesty of me.

"I miss it sometimes," I said. "I know that. I didn't know that I was missing you. But I was dying of it. I would have died and never known why, Isidri. And anyhow, it was all wrong – my work was wrong."

"How could it have been wrong, if it brought you back?" she said, and to that I had no answer at all.

When information on churten theory began to be published I subscribed to whatever the Center Library of O received, particularly the work done at the Ekumenical Schools and on Ve. The general progress of research was just as I remembered, racing along for three years, then hitting the hard places. But there was no reference to a Tiokunan'n Hideo doing research in the field. Nobody worked on a theory of a stabilized double field. No churten field research station was set up at Ran'n.

At last it was the winter of my visit home, and then the very day; and I will admit that, all reason to the contrary, it was a bad day. I felt waves of guilt, of nausea. I grew very shaky, thinking of the Udan of that visit, when Isidri had been married to Hedran, and I a mere visitor.

Hedran, a respected traveling scholar of the Discussions, had in fact come to teach several times in the village. Isidri had suggested inviting him to stay at Udan. I had vetoed the suggestion, saying that though he was a brilliant teacher there was something I disliked about him. I got a sidelong flash from Sidi's clear dark eyes: *Is he jealous?* She suppressed a smile. When I told her and my mother about my "other life," the one thing I had left out, the one secret I kept, was my visit to Udan. I did not want to tell my mother that in that "other life" she had been very ill. I did not want to tell Isidri that in that "other life" Hedran had been her Evening husband and she had had no children of her body. Perhaps I was wrong, but it seemed to me that I had no right to tell these things, that they were not mine to tell.

So Isidri could not know that what I felt was less jealousy than guilt, I had kept knowledge from her. And I had deprived Hedran of a life with Isidri, the dear joy, the center, the life of my own life.

Or had I shared it with him? I didn't know. I don't know.

That day passed like any other, except that one of Suudi's children broke her elbow falling out of a tree. "At least we know she won't drown," said Tubdu, wheezing.

Next came the date of the night in my rooms in the New Quadrangle, when I had wept and not known why I wept. And a while after that, the day of my return, transilient, to Ve, carrying a bottle of Isidri's wine for Gvonesh. And finally, yesterday, I entered the churten field on Ve, and left it eighteen years ago on O. I spent the night, as I sometimes do, in the shrine. The hours went by quietly; I wrote, gave worship, meditated, and slept. And I woke beside the pool of silent water.

So, now: I hope the Stabiles will accept this report from a farmer they never heard of, and that the engineers of transilience may see it as at least a footnote to their experiments. Certainly it is difficult to verify, the only evidence for it being my word, and my otherwise almost inexplicable knowledge of churten theory. To Gvonesh, who does not know me, I send my respect, my gratitude, and my hope that she will honor my intent.

HWANG'S BILLION BRILLIANT DAUGHTERS

Alice Sola Kim

Alice Sola Kim is an American writer. Her short stories can be found in *Asimov's Science Fiction Magazine*, *Lady Churchill's Rosebud Wristlet*, and *Strange Horizons*. "Hwang's Billion Brilliant Daughters" was first published in *Lightspeed* in November 2010.

When Hwang finds a time that he likes, he tries to stay awake. The longest he has ever stayed awake is three days. The longest someone has ever stayed awake is eleven days. If Hwang sleeps enough times, he will eventually reach a time in which people do not have to sleep. Unfortunately, this can only come about through expensive gene therapy that has to be done long before one is born. Thus, it is the rich who do not have to sleep. They stay awake all night and bound across their useless beds, shedding crumbs and drops of sauce as they eat everyone else's food.

Whenever Hwang goes to sleep, he jumps forward in time. This is a problem. This is not a problem that is going to solve itself.

Sometimes Hwang wakes to find that he's only jumped forward a few days. The most Hwang has ever jumped is one hundred seventy years.

After a while, his daughters stop looking exactly Asian. His genes – previously distilled from a population in a small section of East Asia for thousands of years – have mixed with genes from other populations and continued to do so while Hwang slept. In fact, it all started with Hwang and his ex-wife. Hwang's daughters are a crowd of beautiful, muddled, vigorous hybrids, with the occasional recessive trait exploding like fireworks – squash-colored hair, gray eyes, albinism.

Backward, fool, backward! You were supposed to take me backward! He wishes he could find Grishkov and scream at him, but Grishkov is dead, of course. He died sometime that night, the first night Hwang slept and jumped through days, years, decades.

Later, Hwang awakes in a world with no men. Reproduction occurs through parthenogenesis. Scientists discovered that the genes of the father are the ones that shorten human lifespan; scientists decided to do something about it.

There are people walking around who look like men, but they aren't men. But if they look like men, walk like men, talk like men, maybe they are men?

There are new categories of gender that Hwang is unable to comprehend. Men are men. He finds a daughter who is a man, so she must actually be a son, but in Hwang's mind – his mind that he cannot change – he is his daughter and always will be.

If you could flip through Hwang's life like a book – which I am able to do – you would see that Hwang and women have been a calamitous combination. It is not Hwang's fault or the women's fault but it is unfortunate nevertheless. I wish there was someone to blame.

Once, Hwang awakes to find no one. He walks around the city for hours before seeing a woman in a coverall. She is pulling vines off the side of a building and stuffing them into a trash bag. *I am paid millions a year for this work*, she says.

Even for the future, that is a lot of money.

It turns out that everyone has been uploaded into virtual space, but a few people still have to stick around to make sure that buildings stay up and the tanks are clean and operational.

Later, everyone comes back, because it turns out that no one really likes uploaded life.

Hwang's wife was a research scientist. When they divorced, Hwang was granted temporary full custody and his wife went to Antarctica. Sometimes she sent their three children humorous emails about falling asleep on the toilet because it was so cold.

When their daughters were kidnapped walking home from school, Hwang's wife and Hwang both blamed Hwang. Their son turned fifteen, became a goth, and moved in with his mother when she returned from Antarctica.

Hwang, alone, rested his head on pillowcases permanently smudged with black. And slept for days.

Hwang says, *When people are able to live forever, that is when I will get my life back. I can marry again. We can have a family. When I awake, they will still be there, old as cedars. My cedar family, planted in the living room.*

I will live forever, but marriage between Hwang and I is out of the question.

Sometimes one of Hwang's daughters will buy him new clothes, but he always wakes up wearing his old clothes. He has been frumpy, archaic, obscene, unworthy of notice, and perfectly in style – all those things, in that order.

There is a future in which skanky summer is quite popular. People walk around in bathing suits, waterproof briefs, shorts, breast-baring monokinis, sarongs – all with personal climate control units attached to the base of their necks.

Hwang emerges from his room, shivering in a wrinkled button-down sweater, and corduroy pants. That day, the rain drifts down as gently as snow, and it gets you wet so gradually that you are startled to realize it, like a boiled frog in a pot of water.

Hwang never sees his son again. Upon waking for the first time, Hwang goes out into the world and finds that his son is a computer mogul who lives in a cheesy yet terrifying house surrounded by a moat. This house has no right angles, and a viscous red substance continually flows down the sides and into the moat.

A security guard grabs the back of Hwang's jacket as he backs up to get a running start so he can jump the moat. *You'll never make it*, she says, and he realizes that the security guard is his daughter. She sighs, looking him up and down. *There's a shelter a few miles away. You can get a decent meal. I'll drive you.*

His daughter does not look how he'd expect, but her eyes, when she glances at him in the rear-view mirror, are familiar and bright. *But I'm his father*, says Hwang. She laughs.

The computer mogul, famously, has no father (and says so often). Of course. Hwang sits in the back seat like a lump. He realizes that he can no longer enumerate to himself the ways in which he has failed, that his failure has turned into an exponential number residing within him, sleek and unutterably dense and deadly.

There is a time during which Hwang's visits are foreseen. His daughters tell him that his story has been passed down from their mothers. That their great-great-great. . .will come into their lives, recognizable by his blue sweater and brown corduroy pants (*You dress like a fucking teddy bear*, his son used to say – it felt like affection).

And then what? It is disputed. Is Hwang a force of good? Is he evil? How does he choose which daughters he appears to? Is he a matrilineal family curse? He tries to explain but it is not satisfying to his daughters.

The next time he jumps, it is a hundred years later and his story has been forgotten.

Hwang's daughter listens to his story. When he is done, she pulls a pill case from her bag. *Sounds like you need to change your point of view*, she says. *Try a Chip or a Barbara.*

Hwang chooses a pill from the compartment labeled "Chip." Chip and Barbara are personality construct drugs, named for the people from whom they originated.

In an hour, he feels loose. He is young, and has plenty of time to decide what he wants to be when he grows up. He doesn't know if he wants to have kids yet. Come on, man, that's ages away. Let's have some fun before fun ends.

Hwang is still Chip when he goes to sleep, but it wears off in the night. He goes to find it again, to feel simultaneously free yet locked into the right time with no sense of slippage, but discovers that Chip and Barbara have been taken off the market.

In bare feet, Hwang was half an inch shorter than his wife, which seemed within the bounds of acceptability. But the world conspired to tip this delicate balance, with slanted sidewalks, with Italian heels, with poor posture. Hwang and his ex-wife each thought that the other cared more about their height discrepancy.

Your wife is white? said a sophisticated older aunt. *Then your daughters will be beautiful.* They were, because all daughters were beautiful; that is what Hwang believed. But Hwang was never one to be proud of their beauty. He was proud because they were brilliant, or they were about to be; they were at the age at which youthful precocity grew distinct and immutable. That is where they stayed.

Hwang always wakes up in the lab. The lab is always the same.

The time machine is a gnarled, charred mess on the floor, and the curtains are skeletons. Grishkov's body is curled like a cat in the corner; his face is untouched like a peaceful waxwork, and for that, Hwang is grateful. Hwang sleeps on the couch, which has blackened and split like a bratwurst. As unkind and sooty as the lab is, Hwang lingers there to hold off timeshock and cultureshock.

When he needs to use the bathroom, he has to leave.

In time, Hwang begins to suspect that he is not only being pulled forward in time as he sleeps; he is also being pulled sideways in space, to parallel universes.

He thinks he has confirmation of this fact when he arrives at a time when everyone is green. (Don't worry – there is still racism!)

Hwang sits with his daughter at a diner and tries to question her about what has happened. She explains, but language has changed, and he has trouble understanding her. *Lincoln*, he says. *Kennedy. Were they assassinated in this timeline?* She opens her mouth and taps at her translator earbud.

Doowah? she says.

Soon there are no more bananas. The iconic Cavendish banana, tall and bright and constant, has gone extinct. It is true that no one's favorite fruit is the banana. But now that bananas as he knew them are gone, Hwang feels like he's been trapped in a house without windows.

There is no backwards from this forwards. No more bananas for anyone ever again.

Hwang has learned a valuable life lesson: never allow someone to test a time machine on you.

No matter how certain they are it will work.

No matter how certain you are that it will enable you to fix your life and the lives of your loved ones.

But Hwang must have done some good for his later daughters; he has to have done some good; he has to.

Would it all be worth it, then?

Once, he wakes up, opens the door to the lab, and steps into water. He doesn't know how to swim. He is a giant lead teddy bear sinking to the bottom of the ocean, and as he flails in the water, his thoughts are not about how it's all over thank god, they are about expelling water from his lungs and if he could just take another breath please that would be perfect thank you thank you thank you let me live.

Someone grabs him and pulls him up. It's a woman wearing a cheap waiter's tuxedo. All around them, houses and restaurants and offices bob impossibly.

Do you have a reservation? the woman, his daughter, asks. He is exhausted. *Fine*, his daughter says. *Wait here. I'll bring something. Don't touch anything. You need to be disinfected.* His daughters are always so exasperated with him.

The time after that, everything is dry again. Hwang asks his daughter where the ocean is. His daughter shrugs. *We put it somewhere else. It was in the way.*

Hwang needs to understand that someday he will wake up and no one will be around, for good.

Once, when Hwang was thirteen, he came home to find his father strangling his mother. They rearranged themselves right as Hwang walked into the house; they must have heard his key. Stranglings can be quiet. He stood and saw his father flexing his hands and smiling, his mother wiping water out of her eyes and turning a sob into a smile, the way she turned seemingly random organic matter into food, work into money, disorder into order. If she was anti-entropic then his father was the opposite. Money for booze; so much grain goes into alcohol; carbohydrates are then wasted in the fermentation process; it is not sensible. Hwang had been sent to the library. When he came home early, it was awkward; Hwang did not know before then that the terrible could also be awkward.

His father did not murder his mother that day.

There comes a stable time, a time during which Hwang does not jump forward too crazily. He only goes a few days each time he sleeps. He sees his daughter often. He follows her around and pleads with her not to take the photon train to school; it is too fast. It is unnatural. She laughs. She goes to school in another state and her commute only takes half an hour.

Judgmental Hwang is aghast that people in the future react so placidly to risk, but he remembers things like bisphenol A and airborne toxic events and revealing your crush to a homophobe who will get so embarrassed that he will murder you, and then Hwang must admit that there were so many things in his time that he hadn't thought to worry about.

Soon enough, his daughter becomes less amused by this great-great-great . . .popping up in her world every few days. *Just go away*, she says. *Stop interloping. Get your own life.* She shakes his arm off and kicks the wall. He watches as the wall slowly bulges out and undents itself.

That night he goes to sleep, vowing to find some way to protect his daughter, and he wakes up one hundred seventy years later.

Hwang wonders: when he dies, will his cells disperse and mass elsewhere to such an extent that there will be achronological patches in the air? Space dust that travels through time?

What is sleep for a single cell?

Once, I built Hwang a new life, made to look and feel like the early years of the second millennium, but he would not accept it. He stepped out of the lab and the lab was where it is supposed to be. There, on the street, a man in basketball shorts was peeling and eating a banana, which was, well, which was a little on the nose, but I wished for him to know that bananas were back and he could be happy again. (Right?) As were vehicles powered by fossil fuels, as was orthodontia, as was AIDS, as was lithium. For a moment, his face was the face of someone who has woken up from a dream and feels enormous relief that it is not real, what just happened.

But it didn't last. He shook his head until his cheeks wobbled. He stamped his foot. The sidewalk began to sink and whirl beneath him.

Knew it, he shouted. *No backwards from this forwards.*

Up to his knees in the sidewalk, he sloshed ahead with effort and tried to touch whatever he could. The man eating the banana melted. The car melted. The German shepherd melted. Finally, the world rose above Hwang's eyes and, after a brief burbling, he went silent.

Well. I did try.

Hwang tries to look at it this way: time jumps forward when you sleep no matter who you are.

The first time Hwang jumps forward in time, he comes out of his room into fifty years later. The time machine had caught fire, and Grishkov had had to pull him out before the sequence completed countdown. The fire spread and trapped them; they knew already that the dusty red fire extinguisher had been emptied three years ago during a prank and never refilled. Grishkov succumbed to the smoke first, bad-heart Grishkov still clutching Hwang by the forearms as he swanned to the floor. Then Hwang fainted, too.

When Hwang awakes, many people are dead and many new people are alive and everything seems somehow worse, despite all the new machines and pills and fashions.

As Hwang is drawn to his daughters, his daughters are drawn to him.

Hwang does not want to die, but there would not be a very good reason to stay alive if life was only jumping through time rapidly. (*Wait.*) He is now part of the time machine, and although he is broken he remains magnetized to his descendants, his daughters. Down a street, in a tree, in a bar, driving a hovercar— they always find one another. His daughters feed him, imagining that they are experiencing a random surge of kindness toward a dusty, gentle homeless man.

Hwang is guilty about this; he feels that he is enslaving his daughters and the best thing to do would be to release all of them from this obligation. That is when he does want to die.

But he decides to wait it out. He will reach the end of time. He will reach the end of daughters. Then he can end, too.

When Hwang is now, nobody knows. He is sleeping. He has been sleeping all night, his eyelids fluttering and his mouth twitching from the struggle to stay asleep. He wants time to keep moving; he doesn't want to stop anywhere, even though the light is seeping in around the curtains and the hours turn to day. I say to him, *Dad, I won't forget. I'll be the one who remembers the story.*

Still he sleeps. I watch him still. In his mind, I am already blurring.

HOW THE FUTURE GOT BETTER

Eric Schaller

Eric Schaller's fiction has appeared in such magazines as *Sci Fiction*, *Postscripts*, *Shadows & Tall Trees*, and *Lady Churchill's Rosebud Wristlet*, and been reprinted in *The Year's Best Fantasy and Horror*, *Best of the Rest*, and *Fantasy: The Best of the Year*. His illustrations can be found in Jeff VanderMeer's *City of Saints and Madmen* and Hal Duncan's *An A to Z of the Fantastic City*, among others. He is coeditor of *The Revelator*. This story was first published in *Sybil's Garage #7* in 2010.

The FoTax process. "Your taxes fo' nothing," is how Uncle Walt defined it. He stole that joke from a late-night talk show. But even though he didn't bother to read the brochure, he had caught at least one TV special and knew that Fo stood for photon and Tax for tachyon. "Now pass me another roll," he said, "a warm one from the bottom of the bucket."

Mom always insisted that everyone sit down as a family for dinner, but had consented to eating a half-hour earlier than usual so we could watch when FoTax went live. Five-thirty in the pee-em, would you believe it? "Might as well be eating lunch twice," is how Uncle Walt phrased it, but he said it soft so that Mom couldn't hear, and out of the corner of his mouth just in case she could lip read. "Hey! What about that roll? A man could die from hunger at his own table." Little sister Susie, Suz to the family, passed him the bucket and let him dig for his own roll. He probably fingered every one, muttering the whole time: "Cold and hard as a goddamn rock. Probably break a tooth and wouldn't that be just my luck. There's a sucker born every minute and, by God, this time that sucker is me." Took him so long to find his roll and butter it that, by the time he got around to taking a bite, we were already talking about ice cream. "Hold your cotton-picking horses," Uncle Walt said. "What's the future got that we ain't got now?" But he powered through his chicken, coleslaw, and dessert and long-legged it to the living room before anyone grabbed his favorite lounger.

Mom played with the settings on the new Sony receiver by the TV set, squinting at a pamphlet in her hand labeled READ THIS FIRST. "Set it five minutes ahead," big sister Elizabeth called from her seat on the couch between Dad and Gramps. Elizabeth insisted upon being called by all four syllables of her given name but, to her credit, had memorized the instruction manual as soon as it was out of its plastic wrapper. Probably memorized the Spanish edition too, just in case. "Setting the time closer to now reduces the chance of gray spaces and ghost-ing," she said. "Don't forget to tune to channel one-hundred-and-thirty-one."

She might have said more but was interrupted by a frantic knocking at our apartment door. It was the Willard family, Pa Willard in the lead, Ma at his elbow, and all the little Willards, indistinguishable from each other with their chocolate-smeared mouths and cherubic curls, peering through the bars of their parents' legs. "Can we join you?" Pa Willard asked. "Our receiver didn't arrive." Ma Willard shot him a dirty look. "You forgot to sign up," she said. Before the argument could escalate, and the Willards were always arguing, Mom said, "Come on in. Everyone's in the living room. Suz, would you grab some more chairs for the Willards?"

Which is why, when FoTax went live, there were fourteen of us crammed together in one small room. Our TV was seven feet on the diagonal, and the Willards might have come over even if Pa Willard had remembered to order their receiver. Last anyone knew they still had their old 42-inch model. As you might guess with both families together, and even granting that Grammy started to nod off as soon as she settled into her chair, it was kind of noisy. But everyone went quiet and stared at the TV screen when the little green numbers on the receiver flickered to six o'clock.

But nothing happened.

Nothing changed.

All you could see was the blue of an empty channel.

"What a gyp," said Uncle Walt. "You made me rush dessert for this?"

"Maybe it's not set to the right channel," said Elizabeth. "One-hundred-and-thirty-one is what the manual said."

Mom reacted like she had just been called stupid, but got up and checked the setting again anyway. "One-three-one," she said. "See, it says one-three-one."

Then without preamble or warning, while Mom tapped her finger on the illuminated part of the screen that, to her credit, did display the proper channel designation, an image abruptly replaced the blue background.

An image of us.

Or most of us anyway. The vantage point looked to be above and a little behind from where we were sitting. But you could see Uncle Walt's balding head protruding above his lounger, the shoulders and hair of Dad and Elizabeth and Gramps on the couch, and, beside them, Mom sitting rigidly in one of the wooden chairs brought in from the dining table. Two of the golden-haired Willard kids shared another wooden chair beside her. In the image, they, or rather we were all watching the TV. You could see just about one-third of the TV screen, and on that image of the TV there were tinier versions of us clustered around a still tinier version of the TV. And on that miniature TV . . . well, you get the picture.

Suz, surprisingly, was the first to notice the difference between the image on TV and the positioning of those of us clustered around it. "Hey, Mom," she said, "you're sitting down in the TV picture. On a chair." Which of course was true. But just as true was the fact that here, in the real world, Mom was still standing beside the TV where she had been checking the channel.

"That's because it's the future. And in the future Mom's already sat down again." Elizabeth said this using her most infuriating know-it-all voice, as if she had also seen the same thing but hadn't bothered to say a word because it was all so self-evident.

"What if I chose not to sit down?" said Mom, suddenly inspired as she looked at the seated image of herself on the screen. "What if I continued to stand here by the TV?" Even as she said this, before she had finished speaking, her image on the TV started to turn gray and fade away like smoke.

"Hey, you're ghosting," said Elizabeth, genuinely excited. "I read about that. Maybe you'll disappear altogether."

"Oh, I don't like that," said Mom. She sat down in the nearest empty chair, and the image of her on TV came back clear and sharp.

"I want to ghost too," said one of the Willard kids, already making a move like he was going to jump out of his chair and dance around the room.

"No you don't," said Ma Willard, and shot him a look that could freeze, and did.

Uncle Walt was the next one to make a discovery. "You know what?"

"What?" Mom said. She didn't look at him but kept her eyes fixed on her seated TV image.

"I was wrong."

"You wrong? Now that I find hard to believe." Uncle Walt was Mom's younger brother and, according to her, had been so spoiled while growing up it was a wonder he didn't stink all the way to China. "Not that I find it hard to believe you were wrong, mind you," Mom said. "But that you would admit it. That I find hard to believe. Please tell, and I hope to God someone is recording this."

"I was wrong about the future. It does look better."

"Better than what?"

"Better than now."

"How's that?"

"In the future, I got a beer." Uncle Walt gave a little nod like he had just scored a major debating point, but was too polite to rub it in. He was right. The TV version of Uncle Walt was reclined in his lounger, an extra pillow behind his head, just like the real version here in the living room. But on the TV, in the cup holder of his lounger, was a silver can of Coors Light.

Uncle Walt got up, went to the kitchen, and returned brandishing his Coors Light like it was the Holy Grail. He triumphantly popped its top and settled back into his lounger. Now there was absolutely no difference between the version of Uncle Walt on TV and the one in our living room.

We watched then in silence, waiting to see if we could pick out anything else, waiting to see what we would do next, even trying to make out what was being shown on those screens within screens within screens that should, by rights, show us the future in five-minute increments. In some ways it was like a What's Wrong With This Picture game where you study two seemingly identical pictures and try to discover the differences. Only here they didn't tell you how many differences there were.

And that wasn't really fair.

Pretty soon Mom started talking about the obits with Ma Willard. Dad told Pa Willard about the funny noise our refrigerator made, sometimes squealing like there was a mouse trapped inside it, and Pa Willard responded with the obvious,

"Well, maybe there is a mouse trapped inside it." Elizabeth told the Willard kids a ghost story, with Suz adding atmospheric wailings at the appropriate moments. Gramps asked Gramma if she wanted a bedtime martini, then laughed when all he got in response was a colossal snore.

Uncle Walt wasn't the sort to say he was getting bored with a program, at least when he was one of the stars. But after about fifteen minutes, he leaned over to me and asked, "Isn't there a new episode of 'Nut Jobs' on?"

I tried to remember what day of the week 'Nut Jobs' ran, and if they were maybe already into repeats. I was just about to check the listings when I saw it. I spotted a difference. Me. Not Suz. Not Uncle Walt. And certainly not all four syllables of Elizabeth.

"No," I told him. "'Nut Jobs' isn't on. But there's something just as good."

"How do you know?"

I pointed at the TV.

Five minutes into the future we were already watching it.

PALE ROSES

Michael Moorcock

Michael Moorcock is an English writer currently living in the United States. Although primarily known for his science fiction and fantasy works, he has also published literary novels. He was the editor of the British magazine *New Worlds* from 1964–1971 and 1976–1996, and is credited with developing the New Wave literary style in science fiction. Although his Nebula Award–winning novella "Behold the Man" is often thought to be his most famous time travel story, Moorcock does not consider the tale to include any time travel. "Pale Rose," included herein, is one of Moorcock's favorites of his own stories and is both ribald and complex. It was first published in *New Worlds Quarterly* in 1976.

> *Short summer-time and then, my heart's desire,*
> *The winter and the darkness: one by one*
> *The roses fall, the pale roses expire*
> *Beneath the slow decadence of the sun.*
> Ernest Dowson, "Transition"

I. IN WHICH WERTHER IS INCONSOLABLE

"**Y**ou can still amuse people, Werther, and that's the main thing," said Mistress Christia, lifting her skirts to reveal her surprise.

It was rare enough for Werther de Goethe to put on an entertainment (though this one was typical – it was called "Rain") and rare, too, for the Everlasting Concubine to think in individual terms to please her lover of the day.

"Do you like it?" she asked as he peered into her thighs.

Werther's voice in reply was faintly, unusually animated. "Yes." His pale fingers traced the tattoos, which were primarily on the theme of Death and the Maiden, but corpses also coupled, skeletons entwined in a variety of extravagant carnal embraces – and at the centre, in bone-white, her pubic hair had been fashioned in the outline of an elegant and somehow quintessentially feminine skull. "You alone know me, Mistress Christia."

She had heard the phrase so often, from so many, and it always delighted her. "Cadaverous Werther!"

He bent to kiss the skull's somewhat elongated lips.

His rain rushed through dark air, each drop a different gloomy shade of green, purple or red. And it was actually wet so that when it fell upon the small audience (the Duke of Queens, Bishop Castle, My Lady Charlotina, and one or two recently arrived, absolutely bemused, time travellers from the remote past) it soaked their clothes and made them shiver as they stood on the shelf of glassy rock overlooking Werther's Romantic Precipice (below, a waterfall foamed through fierce, black rock).

"Nature," exclaimed Werther. "The only verity!"

The Duke of Queens sneezed. He looked about him with a delighted smile, but nobody else had noticed. He coughed to draw their attention, tried to sneeze again, but failed. He looked up into the ghastly sky; fresh waves of black cloud boiled in: there was lightning now, and thunder. The rain became hail. My Lady Charlotina, in a globular dress of pink veined in soft blue, giggled as the little stones fell upon her gilded features with an almost inaudible ringing sound.

But Bishop Castle, in his nodding, crenellated tete (from which he derived the latter half of his name and which was twice his own height), turned away, saturnine and bored, plainly noting a comparison between all this and his own entertainment of the previous year, which had also involved rain, but with each drop turning into a perfect mannikin as it touched the ground. There was nothing in his temperament to respond to Werther's rather innocent re-creation of a Nature long since departed from a planet which could be wholly re-modelled at the whim of any one of its inhabitants.

Mistress Christia, ever quick to notice such responses, eager for her present lover not to lose prestige, cried: "But there is more, is there not, Werther? A finale?"

"I had thought to leave it a little longer . . ."

"No! No! Give us your finale now, my dear!"

"Well, Mistress Christia, if it is for you." He turned one of his power rings, disseminating the sky, the lightning, the thunder, replacing them with pearly clouds, radiated with golden light through which silvery rain still fell.

"And now," he murmured, "I give you Tranquillity, and in Tranquillity – Hope . . ."

A further twist of the ring and a rainbow appeared, bridging the chasm, touching the clouds.

Bishop Castle was impressed by what was an example of elegance rather than spectacle, but he could not resist a minor criticism. "Is black exactly the shade, do you think? I should have supposed it expressed your Idea, well, perhaps not perfectly . . ."

"It is perfect for me," answered Werther a little gracelessly.

"Of course," said Bishop Castle, regretting his impulse. He drew his bushy red brows together and made a great show of studying the rainbow. "It stands out so well against the background."

Emphatically (causing a brief, ironic glint in the eye of the Duke of Queens) Mistress Christia clapped her hands. "It is a beautiful rainbow, Werther. I am sure it is much more as they used to look."

"It takes a particularly original kind of imagination to invent such – simplicity." The Duke of Queens, well known for a penchant in the direction of vulgarity, fell in with her mood.

"I hope it does more than merely represent." Satisfied both with his creation and with their responses, Werther could not resist indulging his nature, allowing a tinge of hurt resentment in his tone.

All were tolerant. All responded, even Bishop Castle. There came a chorus of consolation. Mistress Christia reached out and took his thin, white hand, inadvertently touching a power ring.

The rainbow began to topple. It leaned in the sky for a few seconds while Werther watched, his disbelief gradually turning to miserable reconciliation; then, slowly, it fell, shattering against the top of the cliff, showering them with shards of jet.

Mistress Christia's tiny hand fled to the rosebud of her mouth; her round, blue eyes expressed horror already becoming laughter (checked when she noted the look in Werther's dark and tragic orbs). She still gripped his hand; but he slowly withdrew it, kicking moodily at the fragments of the rainbow. The sky was suddenly a clear, soft grey, actually lit, one might have guessed, by the tired rays of the fading star about which the planet continued to circle, and the only clouds were those on Werther's noble brow. He pulled at the peak of his bottle-green cap, he stroked at his long, auburn hair, as if to comfort himself. He sulked.

"Perfect!" praised My Lady Charlotina, refusing to see error.

"You have the knack of making the most of a single symbol, Werther." The Duke of Queens waved a brocaded arm in the general direction of the now disseminated scene. "I envy you your talent, my friend."

"It takes the product of panting lust, of pulsing sperm and eager ovaries, to offer us such brutal originality!" said Bishop Castle, in reference to Werther's birth (he was the product of sexual union, born of a womb, knowing childhood – a rarity, indeed). "Bravo!"

"Ah," sighed Werther, "how cheerfully you refer to my doom: to be such a creature, when all others came into this world as mature, uncomplicated adults!"

"There was also Jherek Carnelian," said My Lady Charlotina. Her globular dress bounced as she turned to leave.

"At least he was not born malformed," said Werther.

"It was the work of a moment to re-form you properly, Werther," the Duke of Queens reminded him. "The six arms (was it?) removed, two perfectly fine ones replacing them. After all, it was an unusual exercise on the part of your mother. She did very well, considering it was her first attempt."

"And her last," said My Lady Charlotina, managing to have her back to Werther by the time the grin escaped. She snapped her fingers for her air car. It floated towards her, a great, yellow rocking horse. Its shadow fell across them all.

"It left a scar," said Werther, "nonetheless."

"It would," said Mistress Christia, kissing him upon his black velvet shoulder. "A terrible scar."

"Indeed!" said the Duke of Queens in vague affirmation, his attention wandering. "Well, thank you for a lovely afternoon, Werther. Come along, you two!" He signed to the time travellers, who claimed to be from the eighty-third millennium and were dressed in primitive transparent "exoskin", which was not altogether stable and was inclined to writhe and make it seem that they were covered in hundreds of thin, excited worms. The Duke of Queens had acquired them for his menagerie. Unaware of the difficulties of returning to their own time (temporal travel had, apparently, only just been re-invented in their age), they were inclined to treat the Duke as an eccentric who could be tolerated until it suited them to do otherwise. They smiled condescendingly, winked at each other, and followed him to an air car in the shape of a cube whose sides were golden mirrors decorated with white and purple flowers. It was for the pleasure of enjoying the pleasure they enjoyed, seemingly at his expense, that the Duke of Queens had brought them with him today. Mistress Christia waved at his car as it disappeared rapidly into the sky.

At last they were all gone, save herself and Werther de Goethe. He had seated himself upon a mossy rock, his shoulders hunched, his features downcast, unable to speak to her when she tried to cheer him.

"Oh, Werther," she cried at last, "what would make you happy?"

"Happy?" His voice was a hollow echo of her own. "Happy?" An awkward, dismissive gesture. "There is no such thing as happiness for such as I!"

"There must be some sort of equivalent, surely?"

"Death, Mistress Christia, is my only consolation!"

"Well, die, my dear! I'll resurrect you in a day or two, and then . . ."

"Though you love me, Mistress Christia – though you know me best – you do not understand. I seek the inevitable, the irreconcilable, the unalterable, the inescapable! Our ancestors knew it. They knew Death without Resurrection; they knew what it was to be Slave to the Elements. Incapable of choosing their own destinies, they had no responsibility for their own actions. They were tossed by tides. They were scattered by storms. They were wiped out by wars, decimated by disease, ravaged by radiation, made homeless by holocausts, lashed by lightnings . . ."

"You could have lashed yourself a little today, surely?"

"But it would have been my decision. We have lost what is Random, we have banished the Arbitrary, Mistress Christia. With our power rings and our gene banks we can, if we desire, change the courses of the planets, populate them with any kind of creature we wish, make our old sun burst with fresh energy or fade completely from the firmament. We control All. Nothing controls us!"

"There are our whims, our fancies. There are our characters, my moody love."

"Even those can be altered at will."

"Except that it is a rare nature which would wish to change itself. Would you change yours? I, for one, would be disconsolate if, say, you decided to be more like the Duke of Queens or the Iron Orchid."

"Nonetheless, it is possible. It would merely be a matter of decision. Nothing is impossible, Mistress Christia. Now do you realize why I should feel unfulfilled?"

. "Not really, dear Werther. You can be anything you wish, after all. I am not, as you know, intelligent – it is not my choice to be – but I wonder if a love of Nature could be, in essence, a grandiose love of oneself – with Nature identified, as it were, with one's ego?" She offered this without criticism.

For a moment he showed surprise and seemed to be considering her observation. "I suppose it could be. Still, that has little to do with what we were discussing. It's true that I can be anything – or, indeed, anyone – I wish. That is why I feel unfulfilled!"

"Aha," she said.

"Oh, how I pine for the pain of the past! Life has no meaning without misery!"

"A common view then, I gather. But what sort of suffering would suit you best, dear Werther? Enslavement by Esquimaux?" She hesitated, her knowledge of the past being patchier than most people's. "The beatings with thorns? The barbed-wire trews? The pits of fire?"

"No, no – that is primitive. Psychic, it would have to be. Involving – um – morality."

"Isn't that some sort of wall-painting?"

A large tear welled and fell. "The world is too tolerant. The world is too kind. They all – you most of all – approve of me! There is nothing I can do which would not amuse you – even if it offended your taste – because there is no danger, nothing at stake. There are no crimes, inflamer of my lust. Oh, if I could only sin!"

Her perfect forehead wrinkled in the prettiest of frowns. She repeated his words to herself. Then she shrugged, embracing him.

"Tell me what sin is," she said.

II. IN WHICH YOUR AUDITOR INTERPOSES

Our time travellers, once they have visited the future, are only permitted (owing to the properties of Time itself) at best brief returns to their present. They can remain for any amount of time in their future, where presumably they can do no real damage to the course of previous events, but to come back at all is difficult for even the most experienced; to make a prolonged stay has been proved impossible. Half-an-hour with a relative or a loved one, a short account to an auditor, such as myself, of life, say, in the 75th century, a glimpse at an artefact allowed to some interested scientist – these are the best the time traveller can hope for, once he has made his decision to leap into the mysterious future.

As a consequence our knowledge of the future is sketchy, to say the least: we have no idea of how civilizations will grow up or how they will decline; we do not know why the number of planets in the Solar System seems to vary drastically between, say, half-a-dozen to almost a hundred; we cannot explain the popularity in a given age of certain fashions striking us as singularly bizarre or perverse. Are beliefs which we consider fallacious or superstitious based on an understanding of reality beyond our comprehension?

The stories we hear are often partial, hastily recounted, poorly observed, perhaps misunderstood by the traveller. We cannot question him closely, for he is soon whisked away from us (Time insists upon a certain neatness, to protect her own nature, which is essentially of the practical, ordering sort, and should that nature ever be successfully altered, then we might, in turn, successfully alter the terms of the human condition), and it is almost inevitable that we shall never have another chance of meeting him.

Resultantly, the stories brought to us of the Earth's future assume the character of legends rather than history and tend, therefore, to capture the imagination of artists, for serious scientists need permanent, verifiable evidence with which to work, and precious little of that is permitted them (some refuse to believe in the future, save as an abstraction; some believe firmly that returning time travellers' accounts are accounts of dreams and hallucinations and that they have not actually travelled in Time at all!). It is left to the Romancers, childish fellows like myself, to make something of these tales. While I should be delighted to assure you that everything I have set down in this story is based closely on the truth, I am bound to admit that while the outline comes from an account given me by one of our greatest and most famous temporal adventuresses, Miss Una Persson, the conversations and many of the descriptions are of my own invention, intended hopefully to add a little colour to what would otherwise be a somewhat spare, a rather dry recounting of an incident in the life of Werther de Goethe.

That Werther will exist, only a few entrenched sceptics can doubt. We have heard of him from many sources, usually quite as reliable as the admirable Miss Persson, as we have heard of other prominent figures of that Age we choose to call "the End of Time". If it is this age which fascinates us more than any other, it is probably because it seems to offer a clue to our race's ultimate destiny.

Moralists make much of this period and show us that on the one hand it describes the politeness of human existence or, on the other, the whole point. Romancers are attracted to it for less worthy reasons; they find it colourful, they find its inhabitants glamorous, attractive; their imaginations sparked by the paradoxes, the very ambiguities which exasperate our scientists, by the idea of a people possessing limitless power and using it for nothing but their own amusement, like gods at play. It is pleasure enough for the Romancer to describe a story; to colour it a little, to fill in a few details where they are missing, in the hope that by entertaining himself he entertains others.

Of course, the inhabitants at the End of Time are not the creatures of our past legends, not mere representations of our ancestors' hopes and fears, not mere metaphors, like Siegfried or Zeus or Krishna, and this could be why they fascinate us so much. Those of us who have studied this Age (as best as it can be studied) feel on friendly terms with the Iron Orchid, with the Duke of Queens, with Lord Jagged of Canaria and the rest, and even believe that we can guess something of their inner lives.

Werther de Goethe, suffering from the *knowledge* of his, by the standards of his own time, unusual entrance into the world, doubtless felt himself apart from his fellows, though there was no objective reason why he should feel it. (I trust the reader will forgive my abandoning any attempt at a clumsy future tense.) In a society where eccentricity is encouraged, where it is celebrated no matter how extreme its realization, Werther felt, we must assume, uncomfortable: wishing for peers who would demand some sort of conformity from him. He could not retreat into a repressive past age; it was well known that it was impossible to remain in the past (the phenomenon had a name at the End of Time: it was called the Morphail Effect), and he had an ordinary awareness of the futility of re-creating such an environment for himself – for he would have created it; the responsibility would still ultimately be his own. We can only sympathize with the irreconcilable difficulties of leading the life of a gloomy fatalist when one's fate is wholly, decisively, in one's own hands!

Like Jherek Carnelian, whose adventures I have recounted elsewhere, he was particularly liked by his fellows for his vast and often naive enthusiasm in whatever he did. Like Jherek, it was possible for Werther to fall completely in love – with Nature, with an idea, with Woman (or Man, for that matter).

It seemed to the Duke of Queens (from whom we have it on the excellent authority of Miss Persson herself) that those with such a capacity must love themselves enormously and such love is enviable. The Duke, needless to say, spoke without disapproval when he made this observation: "To shower such largesse upon the Ego! He kneels before his soul in awe – it is a moody king, in constant need of gifts which must always seem rare!" And what is Sensation, our Moralists might argue, but Seeming Rarity? Last year's gifts re-gilded.

It might be true that young Werther (in years no more than half-a-millennium) loved himself too much and that his tragedy was his inability to differentiate between the self-gratifying sensation of the moment and what we would call a lasting and deeply felt emotion. We have a fragment of poetry, written, we are assured, by Werther for Mistress Christia:

> At these times, I love you most when you are sleeping;
>   Your dreams internal, unrealized to the world at large:
> And do I hear you weeping?

Most certainly a reflection of Werther's views, scarcely a description, from all that we know of her, of Mistress Christia's essential being.

Have we any reason to doubt her own view of herself? Rather, we should doubt Werther's view of everyone, including himself. Possibly this lack of insight was what made him so thoroughly attractive in his own time – *le Grand Naif!*

And, since we have quoted one, it is fair to quote the other, for happily we have another fragment, from the same source, of Mistress Christia's verse:

> To have my body moved by other hands;
>   Not only those of Man,
> But Woman, too!
>   My Liberty in pawn to those who understand:
> That Love, alone, is True.

Surely this displays an irony entirely lacking in Werther's fragment. Affectation is also here, of course, but affectation of Mistress Christia's sort so often hides an equivalently sustained degree of self-knowledge. It is sometimes the case in our own age that the greater the extravagant outer show the greater has been the plunge by the showman into the depths of his private conscience. Consequently, the greater the effort to hide the fact, to give the world not what one is, but what it wants. Mistress Christia chose to reflect with consummate artistry the desires of her lover of the day; to fulfil her ambition as subtly as she did reveals a person of exceptional perspicacity.

I intrude upon the flow of my tale with these various bits of explanation and speculation only, I hope, to offer credibility for what is to follow – to give a hint at a natural reason for Mistress Christia's peculiar actions and poor Werther's extravagant response. Some time has passed since we left our lovers. For the moment they have separated. We return to Werther . . .

III. IN WHICH WERTHER FINDS A SOUL MATE

Werther de Goethe's pile stood on the pinnacle of a black and mile-high crag about which, in the permanent twilight, black vultures swooped and croaked. The rare visitor to Werther's crag could hear the vultures' voices as he approached. "Nevermore!" and "Beware the Ides of March!" and "Picking a Chicken with You" were three of the least cryptic warnings they had been created to caw.

At the top of the tallest of his thin, dark towers, Werther de Goethe sat in his favourite chair of unpolished quartz, in his favourite posture of miserable introspection, wondering why Mistress Christia had decided to pay a call on My Lady Charlotina at Lake Billy the Kid.

"Why should she wish to stay here, after all?" He cast a suffering eye upon the sighing sea below. "She is a creature of light – she seeks colour, laughter, warmth, no doubt to try to forget some secret sorrow – she needs all the things I cannot give her. Oh, I am a monster of selfishness!" He allowed himself a small sob. But neither the sob nor the preceding outburst produced the usual satisfaction; self-pity eluded him. He felt adrift, lost, like an explorer without chart or compass in an unfamiliar land. Manfully, he tried again:

"Mistress Christia! Mistress Christia! Why do you desert me? Without you I am desolate! My pulsatile nerves will sing at your touch only! And yet it must be my doom forever to be destroyed by the very things to which I give my fullest loyalty. Ah, it is hard! It is hard!"

He felt a little better and rose from his chair of unpolished quartz, turning his power ring a fraction so that the wind blew harder through the unglazed windows of the tower and whipped at his hair, blew his cloak about, stung his pale, long face. He raised one jackbooted foot to place it on the low sill and stared through the rain and the wind at the sky like a dreadful, spreading bruise overhead, at the turbulent, howling sea below.

He pursed his lips, turning his power ring to darken the scene a little more, to bring up the wind's wail and the ocean's roar. He was turning back to his previous preoccupation when he perceived that something alien tossed upon the distant waves; an artefact not of his own design, it intruded upon his careful conception. He peered hard at the object, but it was too far away for him to identify it. Another might have shrugged it aside, but he was painstaking, even prissy, in his need for artistic perfection. Was this some vulgar addition to his scene made, perhaps, by the Duke of Queens in a misguided effort to please him?

He took his parachute (chosen as the only means by which he could leave his tower) from the wall and strapped it on, stepping through the window and tugging at the rip cord as he fell into space. Down he plummeted and the scarlet balloon soon filled with gas, the nacelle opening up beneath him, so that by the time he was hovering some feet above the sombre waves, he was lying comfortably on his chest, staring over the rim of his parachute at the trespassing image he had seen from his tower. What he saw was something resembling a great shell, a shallow boat of mother-of-pearl, floating on that dark and heaving sea.

In astonishment he now realized that the boat was occupied by a slight figure, clad in filmy white, whose face was pale and terrified. It could only be one of his friends, altering his appearance for some whimsical adventure. But which? Then he caught, through the rain, a better glimpse and he heard himself saying:

"A child? A child? Are you a child?"

She could not hear him; perhaps she could not even see him, having eyes only for the watery walls which threatened to engulf her little boat and carry her down to the land of Davy Jones. How could it be a child? He rubbed his eyes. He must be projecting his hopes – but there, that movement, that whimper! It was a child! Without doubt!

He watched, open-mouthed, as she was flung this way and that by the elements – his elements. She was powerless: actually powerless! He relished her terror; he envied her her fear. Where had she come from? Save for himself and Jherek Carnelian there had not been a child on the planet for thousands upon thousands of years.

He leaned further out, studying her smooth skin, her lovely rounded limbs. Her eyes were tight shut now as the waves crashed upon her fragile craft; her delicate fingers, unstrong, courageous, clung hard to the side; her white dress was wet, outlining her new-formed breasts; water poured from her long, auburn hair. She panted in delicious impotence.

"It is a child!" Werther exclaimed. "A sweet, frightened child!"

And in his excitement he toppled from his parachute with an astonished yell, and landed with a crash, which winded him, in the sea-shell boat beside the girl. She opened her eyes as he turned his head to apologize. Plainly she had not been aware of his presence overhead. For a moment he could not speak, though his lips moved. But she screamed.

"My dear . . ." The words were thin and high and they faded into the wind. He struggled to raise himself on his elbows. "I apologize . . ."

She screamed again. She crept as far away from him as possible. Still she clung to her flimsy boat's side as the waves played with it: a thoughtless giant with too delicate a toy; inevitably, it must shatter. He waved his hand to indicate his parachute, but it had already been borne away. His cloak was caught by the wind and wrapped itself around his arm; he struggled to free himself and became further entangled; he heard a new scream and then some demoralized whimpering.

"I will save you!" he shouted, by way of reassurance, but his voice was muffled even in his own ears. It was answered by a further pathetic shriek. As the cloak was saturated it became increasingly difficult for him to escape its folds. He lost his temper and was deeper enmeshed. He tore at the thing. He freed his head.

"I am not your enemy, tender one, but your saviour," he said. It was obvious that she could not hear him. With an impatient gesture he flung off his cloak at last and twisted a power ring. The volume of noise was immediately reduced. Another twist and the waves became calmer. She stared at him in wonder.

"Did you do that?" she asked.

"Of course. It is my scene, you see. But how you came to enter it, I do not know!"

"You are a wizard, then?" she said.

"Not at all. I have no interest in sport." He clapped his hands and his parachute re-appeared, perhaps a trifle reluctantly as if it had enjoyed its brief independence, and drifted down until it was level with the boat. Werther lightened the sky. He could not bring himself, however, to dismiss the rain, but he let a little sun shine through it.

"There," he said. "The storm has passed, eh? Did you like your experience?"

"It was horrifying! I was so afraid. I thought I would drown."

"Yes? And did you like it?"

She was puzzled, unable to answer as he helped her aboard the nacelle and ordered the parachute home.

"You are a wizard!" she said. She did not seem disappointed. He did not quiz her as to her meaning. For the moment, if not for always, he was prepared to let her identify him however she wished.

"You are actually a child?" he asked hesitantly. "I do not mean to be insulting. A time traveller, perhaps? Or from another planet?"

"Oh, no. I am an orphan. My father and mother are now dead. I was born on Earth some fourteen years ago." She looked in faint dismay over the side of the craft as they were whisked swiftly upward. "*They* were time travellers. We made our home in a forgotten menagerie – underground, but it was pleasant. My parents feared recapture, you see. Food still grew in the menagerie. There were books, too, and they taught me to read – and there were other records through which they were able to present me with a reasonable education. I am not illiterate. I know the world. I was taught to fear wizards."

"Ah," he crooned, "the world! But you are not a part of it, just as I am not a part."

The parachute reached the window and, at his indication, she stepped gingerly from it to the tower. The parachute folded itself and placed itself upon the wall. Werther said: "You will want food, then? I will create whatever you wish!"

"Fairy food will not fill mortal stomachs, sir," she told him.

"You are beautiful," he said. "Regard me as your mentor, as your new father. I will teach you what this world is really like. Will you oblige me, at least, by trying the food?"

"I will." She looked about her with a mixture of curiosity and suspicion. "You lead a Spartan life." She noticed a cabinet. "Books? You read, then?"

"In transcription," he admitted. "I listen. My enthusiasm is for Ivan Turgiditi, who created the Novel of Discomfort and remained its greatest practitioner. In, I believe, the 900th (though they could be spurious, invented, I have heard) . . ."

"Oh, no, no! I have read Turgiditi." She blushed. "In the original. *Wet Socks* – four hours of discomfort, every second brought to life and in less than a thousand pages!"

"My favourite," he told her, his expression softening still more into besotted wonderment. "I can scarcely believe – in this Age – one such as you! Innocent of device. Uncorrupted! Pure!"

She frowned. "My parents taught me well, sir. I am not . . ."

"You cannot know! And dead, you say? Dead! If only I could have witnessed – but no, I am insensitive. Forgive me. I mentioned food."

"I am not really hungry."

"Later, then. That I should have so recently mourned such things as lacking in this world. I was blind. I did not look. Tell me everything. Whose was the menagerie?"

"It belonged to one of the lords of this planet. My mother was from a period she called the October Century, but recently recovered from a series of interplanetary wars and fresh and optimistic in its rediscoveries of ancestral technologies. She was chosen to be the first into the future. She was captured upon her arrival and imprisoned by a wizard like yourself."

"The word means little. But continue."

"She said that she used the word because it had meaning for her and she had no other short description. My father came from a time known as the Preliminary Structure, where human kind was rare and machines proliferated. He never mentioned the nature of the transgression he made from the social code of his day, but as a result of it he was banished to this world. He, too, was captured for the same menagerie and there he met my mother. They lived originally, of course, in separate cages, where their normal environments were re-created for them. But the owner of the menagerie became bored, I think, and abandoned interest in his collection . . ."

"I have often remarked that people who cannot look after their collections have no business keeping them," said Werther. "Please continue, my dear child." He reached out and patted her hand.

"One day he went away and they never saw him again. It took them some time to realize that he was not returning. Slowly the more delicate creatures, whose environments required special attention, died."

"No one came to resurrect them?"

"No one. Eventually my mother and father were the only ones left. They made what they could of their existence, too wary to enter the outer world in case they should be recaptured, and, to their astonishment, conceived me. They had heard that people from different historical periods could not produce children."

"I have heard the same."

"Well, then, I was a fluke. They were determined to give me as good an upbringing as they could and to prepare me for the dangers of your world."

"Oh, they were right! For one so innocent, there are many dangers. I will protect you, never fear."

"You are kind." She hesitated. "I was not told by my parents that such as you existed."

"I am the only one."

"I see. My parents died in the course of this past year, first my father, then my mother (of a broken heart, I believe). I buried my mother and at first made an attempt to live the life we had always led, but I felt the lack of company and decided to explore the world, for it seemed to me I, too, could grow old and die before I had experienced anything!"

"Grow old," mouthed Werther rhapsodically, "and die!"

"I set out a month or so ago and was disappointed to discover the absence of ogres, of malevolent creatures of any sort – and the wonders I witnessed, while a trifle bewildering, did not compare with those I had imagined I would find. I had fully expected to be snatched up for a menagerie by now, but nobody has shown interest, even when they have seen me."

"Few follow the menagerie fad at present." He nodded. "They would not have known you for what you were. Only I could recognize you. Oh, how lucky I am. And how lucky you are, my dear, to have met me when you did. You see, I, too, am a child of the womb. I, too, made my own hard way through the uterine gloom to breathe the air, to find the light of this faded, this senile globe. Of all those you could have met, you have met the only one who understands you, who is likely to share your passion, to relish your education. We are soul mates, child!"

He stood up and put a tender arm about her young shoulders.

"You have a new mother, a new father now! His name is Werther!"

IV. IN WHICH WERTHER FINDS SIN AT LAST

Her name was Catherine Lilly Marguerite Natasha Dolores Beatrice Machine-shop-Seven Flambeau Gratitude (the last two names but one being her father's and her mother's respectively).

Werther de Goethe continued to talk to her for some hours. Indeed, he became quite carried away as he described all the exciting things they would do, how they would live lives of the purest poetry and simplicity from now on, the quiet and tranquil places they would visit, the manner in which her education would be supplemented, and he was glad to note, he thought, her wariness dissipating, her attitude warming to him.

"I will devote myself entirely to your happiness," he informed her, and then, noticing that she was fast asleep, he smiled tenderly: "Poor child. I am a worm of thoughtlessness. She is exhausted."

He rose from his chair of unpolished quartz and strode to where she lay curled upon the iguana-skin rug; stooping, he placed his hands under her warm-smelling, her yielding body, and somewhat awkwardly lifted her. In her sleep she uttered a tiny moan, her cherry lips parted and her newly budded breasts rose and fell rapidly against his chest once or twice until she sank back into a deeper slumber.

He staggered, panting with the effort, to another part of the tower, and then he lowered her with a sigh to the floor. He realized that he had not prepared a proper bedroom for her.

Fingering his chin, he inspected the dank stones, the cold obsidian which had suited his mood so well for so long and now seemed singularly offensive. Then he smiled.

"She must have beauty," he said, "and it must be subtle. It must be calm."

An inspiration, a movement of a power ring, and the walls were covered with thick carpets embroidered with scenes from his own old book of fairy tales. He remembered how he had listened to the book over and over again – his only consolation in the lonely days of his extreme youth.

Here, Man Shelley, a famous harmonican, ventured into Odeon (a version of Hell) in order to be re-united with his favourite three-headed dog, Omnibus. The picture showed him with his harmonica (or "harp") playing "Blues for a Nightingale" – a famous lost piece. There, Casablanca Bogard, with his single eye in the middle of his forehead, wielded his magic spade, Sam, in his epic fight with that ferocious bird, the Malted Falcon, to save his love, the Acrilan Queen, from the power of Big Sleepy (a dwarf who had turned himself into a giant) and Mutinous Caine, who had been cast out of Hollywood (or paradise) for the killing of his sister, the Blue Angel.

Such scenes were surely the very stuff to stir the romantic, delicate imagination of this lovely child, just as his had been stirred when – he felt the *frisson* – he had been her age. He glowed. His substance was suffused with delicious compassion for them both as he recalled, also, the torments of his own adolescence.

That she should be suffering as he had suffered filled him with the pleasure all must feel when a fellow spirit is recognized, and at the same time he was touched by her plight, determined that she should not know the anguish of his earliest years. Once, long ago, Werther had courted Jherek Carnelian, admiring him for his fortitude, knowing that locked in Jherek's head were the memories of bewilderment, misery and despair which would echo his own. But Jherek, pampered progeny of that most artificial of all creatures, the Iron Orchid, had been unable to recount any suitable experiences at all, had, whilst cheerfully eager to please Werther, recalled nothing but pleasurable times, had reluctantly admitted, at last, to the possession of the happiest of childhoods. That was when Werther had concluded that Jherek Carnelian had no soul worth speaking of, and he had never altered his opinion (now he secretly doubted Jherek's origins and sometimes believed that Jherek merely pretended to have been a child – merely one more of his boring and superficial affectations).

Next, a bed – a soft, downy bed, spread with sheets of silver silk, with posts of ivory and hangings of precious Perspex, antique and yellowed, and on the floor the finely tanned skins of albino hamsters and marmalade cats.

Werther added gorgeous lavs of intricately patterned red and blue ceramic, their bowls filled with living flowers: with whispering toadflax, dragonsnaps, goldilocks and shanghai lilies, with blooming scarlet margravines (his adopted daughter's name-flower, as he knew to his pride), with soda-purple poppies and tea-green roses, with iodine and cerise and crimson hanging johnny, with golden cynthia and sky-blue truelips, calomine and creeping larrikin, until the room was saturated with their intoxicating scents.

Placing a few bunches of hitler's balls in the corners near the ceiling, a toy fish-tank (capable of firing real fish), which he remembered owning as a boy, under the window, a trunk (it could be opened by pressing the navel) filled with clothes near the bed, a full set of bricks and two bats against the wall close to the doorway, he was able, at last, to view the room with some satisfaction.

Obviously, he told himself, she would make certain changes according to her own tastes. That was why he had shown such restraint. He imagined her naive delight when she wakened in the morning. And he must be sure to produce days and nights of regular duration, because at her age routine was the main thing a child needed. There was nothing like the certainty of a consistently glorious sunrise! This reminded him to make an alteration to a power ring on his left hand, to spread upon the black cushion of the sky crescent moons and stars and starlets in profusion. Bending carefully, he picked up the vibrant youth of her body and lowered her to the bed, drawing the silver sheets up to her vestal chin. Chastely he touched lips to her forehead and crept from the room, fashioning a leafy door behind him, hesitating for a moment, unable to define the mood in which he found himself. A rare smile illumined features set so long in lines of gloom. Returning to his own quarters, he murmured:

"I believe it is Contentment!"

A month swooned by. Werther lavished every moment of his time upon his new charge. He thought of nothing but her youthful satisfactions. He encouraged her in joy, in idealism, in a love of Nature. Gone were his blizzards, his rocky spires, his bleak wastes and his moody forests, to be replaced with gentle landscapes of green hills and merry, tinkling rivers, sunny glades in copses of poplars, rhododendrons, redwoods, laburnum, banyans and good old amiable oaks. When they went on a picnic, large-eyed cows and playful gorillas would come and nibble scraps of food from Catherine Gratitude's palm. And when it was day, the sun always shone and the sky was always blue, and if there were clouds, they were high, hesitant puffs of whiteness and soon gone.

He found her books so that she might read. There was Turgiditi and Uto, Pett Ridge and Zakka, Pyat Sink – all the ancients. Sometimes he asked her to read to him, for the luxury of dispensing with his usual translators. She had been fascinated by a picture of a typewriter she had seen in a record, so he fashioned an air car in the likeness of one, and they travelled the world in it, looking at scenes created by Werther's peers.

"Oh, Werther," she said one day, "you are so good to me. Now that I realize the misery which might have been mine (as well as the life I was missing underground), I love you more and more."

"And I love you more and more," he replied, his head a-swim. And for a moment he felt a pang of guilt at having forgotten Mistress Christia so easily. He had not seen her since Catherine had come to him, and he guessed that she was sulking somewhere. He prayed that she would not decide to take vengeance on him.

They went to see Jherek Carnelian's famous "London, 1896", and Werther manfully hid his displeasure at her admiration for his rival's buildings of white marble, gold and sparkling quartz. He showed her his own abandoned tomb, which he privately considered in better taste, but it was plain that it did not give her the same satisfaction.

They saw the Duke of Queens' latest, "Ladies and Swans", but not for long, for Werther considered it unsuitable. Later they paid a visit to Lord Jagged of Canaria's somewhat abstract "War and Peace in Two Dimensions", and Werther thought it too stark to please the girl, judging the experiment "successful". But Catherine laughed with glee as she touched the living figures, and found that somehow it was true. Lord Jagged had given them length and breadth but not a scrap of width – when they turned aside, they disappeared.

It was on one of these expeditions, to Bishop Castle's "A Million Angry Wrens" (an attempt in the recently revised art of Aesthetic Loudness), that they encountered Lord Mongrove, a particular confidant of Werther's until they had quarrelled over the method of suicide adopted by the natives of Uranus during the period of the Great Sodium Breather. By now, if Werther had not found a new obsession, they would have patched up their differences, and Werther felt a pang of guilt for having forgotten the one person on this planet with whom he had, after all, shared something in common.

In his familiar dark green robes, with his leonine head hunched between his massive shoulders, the giant, apparently disdaining an air carriage, was riding home upon the back of a monstrous snail.

The first thing they saw, from above, was its shining trail over the azure rocks of some abandoned, half-created scene of Argonheart Po's (who believed that nothing was worth making unless it tasted delicious and could be eaten and digested). It was Catherine who saw the snail itself first and exclaimed at the size of the man who occupied the swaying howdah on its back.

"He must be ten feet tall, Werther!"

And Werther, knowing whom she meant, made their typewriter descend, crying:

"Mongrove! My old friend!"

Mongrove, however, was sulking. He had chosen not to forget whatever insult it had been which Werther had levelled at him when they had last met. "What? Is it Werther? Bringing freshly sharpened dirks for the flesh between my shoulder blades? It is that Cold Betrayer himself, whom I befriended when a bare boy, pretending carelessness, feigning insouciance, as if he cannot remember, with relish, the exact degree of bitterness of the poisoned wine he fed me when we parted. Faster, steed! Bear me away from Treachery! Let me fly from further Insult! No more shall I suffer at the hands of Calumny!" And, with his long, jewelled stick he beat upon the shell of his molluscoid mount. The beast's horns waved agitatedly for a moment, but it did not really seem capable of any greater speed. In good-humoured puzzlement, it turned its slimy head towards its master.

"Forgive me, Mongrove! I take back all I said," announced Werther, unable to recall a single sour syllable of the exchange. "Tell me why you are abroad. It is rare for you to leave your doomy dome."

"I am making my way to the Ball," said Lord Mongrove, "which is shortly to be held by My Lady Charlotina. Doubtless I have been invited to act as a butt for their malice and their gossip, but I go in good faith."

"A Ball? I know nothing of it."

Mongrove's countenance brightened a trifle. "You have not been invited? Ah!"

"I wonder . . . But, no – My Lady Charlotina shows unsuspected sensitivity. She knows that I now have responsibilities – to my little Ward here. To Catherine – to my Kate."

"The child?"

"Yes, to my child. I am privileged to be her protector. Fate favours me as her new father. This is she. Is she not lovely? Is she not innocent?"

Lord Mongrove raised his great head and looked at the slender girl beside Werther. He shook his huge head as if in pity for her.

"Be careful, my dear," he said. "To be befriended by de Goethe is to be embraced by a viper!"

She did not understand Mongrove; questioningly she looked up at Werther. "What does he mean?"

Werther was shocked. He clapped his hands to her pretty ears.

"Listen no more! I regret the overture. The movement, Lord Mongrove, shall remain unresolved. Farewell, spurner of good-intent. I had never guessed before the level of your cynicism. Such an accusation! Goodbye, for ever, most malevolent of mortals, despiser of altruism, hater of love! You shall know me no longer!"

"You have known yourself not at all," snapped Mongrove spitefully, but it was unlikely that Werther, already speeding skyward, heard the remark.

And thus it was with particular and unusual graciousness that Werther greeted My Lady Charlotina when, a little later, they came upon her.

She was wearing the russet ears and eyes of a fox, riding her yellow rocking horse through the patch of orange sky left over from her own turbulent "Death of Neptune". She waved to them. "Cock-a-doodle-do!"

"My dear Lady Charlotina. What a pleasure it is to see you. Your beauty continues to rival Nature's mightiest miracles."

It is with such unwonted effusion that we will greet a person, who has not hitherto aroused our feelings, when we are in a position to compare him against another, closer, acquaintance who has momentarily earned our contempt or anger.

She seemed taken aback, but received the compliment equably enough.

"Dear Werther! And is this that rarity, the girl-child I have heard so much about and whom, in your goodness, you have taken under your wing? I could not believe it! A child! And how lucky she is to find a father in yourself – of all our number the one best suited to look after her."

It might almost be said that Werther preened himself beneath the golden shower of her benediction, and if he detected no irony in her tone, perhaps it was because he still smarted from Mongrove's dash of vitriol.

"I have been chosen, it seems," he said modestly, "to lead this waif through the traps and illusions of our weary world. The burden I shoulder is not light . . ."

"Valiant Werther!"

". . . but it is shouldered willingly. I am devoting my life to her upbringing, to her peace of mind." He placed a bloodless hand upon her auburn locks, and, winsomely, she took his other one.

"You are tranquil, my dear?" asked My Lady Charlotina kindly, arranging her blue skirts over the saddle of her rocking horse. "You have no doubts?"

"At first I had," admitted the sweet child, "but gradually I learned to trust my new father. Now I would trust him in anything!"

"Ah," sighed My Lady Charlotina, "trust!"

"Trust," said Werther. "It grows in me, too. You encourage me, charming Charlotina, for a short time ago I believed myself doubted by all."

"Is it possible? When you are evidently so reconciled – so – happy!"

"And I am happy, also, now that I have Werther," carolled the commendable Catherine.

"Exquisite!" breathed My Lady Charlotina. "And you will, of course, both come to my Ball."

"I am not sure . . ." began Werther, "perhaps Catherine is too young . . ."

But she raised her tawny hands. "It is your duty to come. To show us all that simple hearts are the happiest."

"Possibly . . ."

"You must. The world must have examples, Werther, if it is to follow your Way."

Werther lowered his eyes shyly. "I am honoured," he said. "We accept."

"Splendid! Then come soon. Come now, if you like. A few arrangements, and the Ball begins."

"Thank you," said Werther, "but I think it best if we return to my castle for a little while." He caressed his ward's fine, long tresses. "For it will be Catherine's first Ball, and she must choose her gown."

And he beamed down upon his radiant protegee as she clapped her hands in joy.

My Lady Charlotina's Ball must have been at least a mile in circumference, set against the soft tones of a summer twilight, red-gold and transparent so that, as one approached, the guests who had already arrived could be seen standing upon the inner wall, clad in creations extravagant even at the End of Time.

The Ball itself was inclined to roll a little, but those inside it were undisturbed; their footing was firm, thanks to My Lady Charlotina's artistry. The Ball was entered by means of a number of sphincterish openings, placed more or less at random in its outer wall. At the very centre of the Ball, on a floating platform, sat an orchestra comprised of the choicest musicians, out of a myriad of ages and planets, from My Lady's great menagerie (she specialized, currently, in artists).

When Werther de Goethe, a green-gowned Catherine Gratitude upon his blue velvet arm, arrived, the orchestra was playing some primitive figure of My Lady Charlotina's own composition. It was called, she claimed as she welcomed them, "On the Theme of Childhood", but doubtless she thought to please them, for Werther believed he had heard it before under a different title.

Many of the guests had already arrived and were standing in small groups chatting to each other. Werther greeted an old friend, Li Pao, of the 27th century, and such a kill-joy that he had never been wanted for a menagerie. While he was forever criticizing their behaviour, he never missed a party. Next to him stood the Iron Orchid, mother of Jherek Carnelian, who was not present. In contrast to Li Pao's faded blue overalls, she wore rags of red, yellow and mauve, thousands of sparkling bracelets, anklets and necklaces, a headdress of woven peacocks' wings, slippers which were moles and whose beady eyes looked up from the floor.

"What do you mean – waste?" she was saying to Li Pao. "What else could we do with the energy of the universe? If our sun burns out, we create another. Doesn't that make us conservatives? Or is it preservatives?"

"Good evening, Werther," said Li Pao in some relief. He bowed politely to the girl. "Good evening, miss."

"Miss?" said the Iron Orchid. "What?"

"Gratitude."

"For whom?"

"This is Catherine Gratitude, my Ward," said Werther, and the Iron Orchid let forth a peal of luscious laughter.

"The girl-bride, eh?"

"Not at all," said Werther. "How is Jherek?"

"Lost, I fear, in Time. We have seen nothing of him recently. He still pursues his paramour. Some say you copy him, Werther."

He knew her bantering tone of old and took the remark in good part. "His is a mere affectation," he said. "Mine is Reality."

"You were always one to make that distinction, Werther," she said. "And I will never understand the difference!"

"I find your concern for Miss Gratitude's upbringing most worthy," said Li Pao somewhat unctuously. "If there is any way I can help. My knowledge of twenties' politics, for instance, is considered unmatched – particularly, of course, where the 26th and 27th centuries are concerned . . ."

"You are kind," said Werther, unsure how to take an offer which seemed to him overeager and not entirely selfless.

Gaf the Horse in Tears, whose clothes were real flame, flickered towards them, the light from his burning, unstable face almost blinding Werther. Catherine Gratitude shrank from him as he reached out a hand to touch her, but her expression changed as she realized that he was not at all hot – rather, there was something almost chilly about the sensation on her shoulder. Werther did his best to smile. "Good evening, Gaf."

"She is a dream!" said Gaf. "I know it, because only I have such a wonderful imagination. Did I create her, Werther?"

"You jest."

"Ho, ho! Serious old Werther." Gaf kissed him, bowed to the child, and moved away, his body erupting in all directions as he laughed the more. "Literal, literal Werther!"

"He is a boor," Werther told his charge. "Ignore him."

"I thought him sweet," she said.

"You have much to learn, my dear."

The music filled the Ball and some of the guests left the floor to dance, hanging in the air around the orchestra, darting streamers of coloured energy in order to weave complex patterns as they moved.

"They are very beautiful," said Catherine Gratitude. "May we dance soon, Werther?"

"If you wish. I am not much given to such pastimes as a rule."

"But tonight?"

He smiled. "I can refuse you nothing, child."

She hugged his arm and her girlish laughter filled his heart with warmth.

"Perhaps you should have made yourself a child before, Werther?" suggested the Duke of Queens, drifting away from the dance and leaving a trail of green fire behind him. He was clad all in soft metal which reflected the colours in the Ball and created other colours in turn. "You are a perfect father. Your metier."

"It would not have been the same, Duke of Queens."

"As you say." His darkly handsome face bore its usual expression of benign amusement. "I am the Duke of Queens, child. It is an honour." He bowed, his metal booming.

"Your friends are wonderful," said Catherine Gratitude. "Not at all what I expected."

"Be wary of them," murmured Werther. "They have no conscience."

"Conscience? What is that?"

Werther touched a ring and led her up into the air of the Ball. "I am your conscience, for the moment, Catherine. You shall learn in time."

Lord Jagged of Canaria, his face almost hidden by one of his high, quilted collars, floated in their direction.

"Werther, my boy! This must be your daughter. Oh! Sweeter than honey! Softer than petals! I have heard so much – but the praise was not enough! You must have poetry written about you. Music composed for you. Tales must be spun with you as the heroine." And Lord Jagged made a deep, an elaborate bow, his long sleeves sweeping the air below his feet. Next, he addressed Werther:

"Tell me, Werther, have you seen Mistress Christia? Everyone else is here, but not she."

"I have looked for the Everlasting Concubine without success," Werther told him.

"She should arrive soon. In a moment My Lady Charlotina announces the beginning of the masquerade – and Mistress Christia loves the masquerade."

"I suspect she pines," said Werther.

"Why so?"

"She loved me, you know."

"Aha! Perhaps you are right. But I interrupt your dance. Forgive me."

And Lord Jagged of Canaria floated, stately and beautiful, towards the floor.

"Mistress Christia?" said Catherine. "Is she your Lost Love?"

"A wonderful woman," said Werther. "But my first duty is to you. Regretfully I could not pursue her, as I think she wanted me to do."

"Have I come between you?"

"Of course not. Of course not. That was infatuation – this is sacred duty."

And Werther showed her how to dance – how to notice a gap in a pattern which might be filled by the movements from her body. Because it was a special occasion he had given her her very own power ring – only a small one, but she was proud of it, and she gasped so prettily at the colours her train made that Werther's anxieties (that his gift might corrupt her precious innocence) melted entirely away. It was then that he realized with a shock how deeply he had fallen in love with her.

At the realization, he made an excuse, leaving her to dance with, first, Sweet Orb Mace, feminine tonight, with a latticed face, and then with O'Kala Incarnadine who, with his usual preference for the bodies of beasts, was currently a bear. Although he felt a pang as he watched her stroke O'Kala's ruddy fur, he could not bring himself just then to interfere. His immediate desire was to leave the Ball, but to do that would be to disappoint his ward, to raise questions he would not wish to answer. After a while he began to feel a certain satisfaction from his suffering and remained, miserably, on the floor while Catherine danced on and on.

And then My Lady Charlotina had stopped the orchestra and stood on the platform calling for their attention.

"It is time for the masquerade. You all know the theme, I hope." She paused, smiling. "All, save Werther and Catherine. When the music begins again, please reveal your creations of the evening."

Werther frowned, wondering her reasons for not revealing the theme of the masquerade to him. She was still smiling at him as she drifted towards him and settled beside him on the floor.

"You seem sad, Werther. Why so? I thought you at one with yourself at last. Wait. My surprise will flatter you, I'm sure!"

The music began again. The Ball was filled with laughter – and there was the theme of the masquerade!

Werther cried out in anguish. He dashed upward through the gleeful throng, seeing each face as a mockery, trying to reach the side of his girl-child before she should realize the dreadful truth.

"Catherine! Catherine!"

He flew to her. She was bewildered as he folded her in his arms.

"Oh, they are monsters of insincerity! Oh, they are grotesque in their apings of all that is simple, all that is pure!" he cried.

He glared about him at the other guests. My Lady Charlotina had chosen "Childhood" as her general theme. Sweet Orb Mace had changed himself into a gigantic single sperm, his own face still visible at the glistening tail; the Iron Orchid had become a monstrous newborn baby with a red and bawling face which still owed more to paint than to Nature; the Duke of Queens, true to character, was three-year-old Siamese twins (both the faces were his own, softened); even Lord Mongrove had deigned to become an egg.

"What ith it, Werther?" lisped My Lady Charlotina at his feet, her brown curls bobbing as she waved her lollipop in the general direction of the other guests. "Doeth it not pleathe you?"

"Ugh! This is agony! A parody of everything I hold most perfect!"

"But, Werther . . ."

"What is wrong, dear Werther?" begged Catherine. "It is only a masquerade."

"Can you not see? It is you – what you and I mean – that they mock. No – it is best that you do not see. Come, Catherine. They are insane; they revile all that is sacred!" And he bore her bodily towards the wall, rushing through the nearest doorway and out into the darkened sky.

He left his typewriter behind, so great was his haste to be gone from that terrible scene. He fled with her willy-nilly through the air, through daylight, through pitchy night. He fled until he came to his own tower, flanked now by green lawns and rolling turf, surrounded by songbirds, swamped in sunshine. And he hated it: landscape, larks and light – all were hateful.

He flew through the window and found his room full of comforts – of cushions and carpets and heady perfume – and with a gesture he removed them. Their particles hung gleaming in the sun's beams for a moment. But the sun, too, was hateful. He blacked it out and night swam into that bare chamber. And all the while, in amazement, Catherine Gratitude looked on, her lips forming the question, but never uttering it. At length, tentatively, she touched his arm.

"Werther?"

His hands flew to his head. He roared in his mindless pain.

"Oh, Werther!"

"Ah! They destroy me! They destroy my ideals!"

He was weeping when he turned to bury his face in her hair.

"Werther!" She kissed his cold cheek. She stroked his shaking back. And she led him from the ruins of his room and down the passage to her own apartment.

"Why should I strive to set up standards," he sobbed, "when all about me they seek to pull them down. It would be better to be a villain!"

But he was quiescent; he allowed himself to be seated upon her bed; he felt suddenly drained. He sighed. "They hate innocence. They would see it gone forever from this globe."

She gripped his hand. She stroked it. "No, Werther. They meant no harm. I saw no harm."

"They would corrupt you. I must keep you safe."

Her lips touched his and his body came alive again. Her fingers touched his skin. He gasped.

"I must keep you safe."

In a dream, he took her in his arms. Her lips parted, their tongues met. Her young breasts pressed against him – and for perhaps the first time in his life Werther understood the meaning of physical joy. His blood began to dance to the rhythm of a sprightlier heart. And why should he not take what they would take in his position? He placed a hand upon a pulsing thigh. If cynicism called the tune, then he would show them he could pace as pretty a measure as any. His kisses became passionate, and passionately were they returned.

"Catherine!"

A motion of a power ring and their clothes were gone, the bed hangings drawn.

And your auditor, not being of that modern school which salaciously seeks to share the secrets of others' passions (secrets familiar, one might add, to the great majority of us), retires from this scene.

But when he woke the next morning and turned on the sun, Werther looked down at the lovely child beside him, her auburn hair spread across the pillows, her little breasts rising and falling in tranquil sleep, and he realized that he had used his reaction to the masquerade to betray his trust. A madness had filled him; he had raised an evil wind and his responsibility had been borne off by it, taking Innocence and Purity, never to return. His lust had lost him everything.

Tears reared in his tormented eyes and ran cold upon his heated cheeks. "Mongrove was perceptive indeed," he murmured. "To be befriended by Werther is to be embraced by a viper. She can never trust me – anyone – again. I have lost my right to offer her protection. I have stolen her childhood."

And he got up from the bed, from the scene of that most profound of crimes, and he ran from the room and went to sit in his old chair of unpolished quartz, staring listlessly through the window at the paradise he had created outside. It accused him; it reminded him of his high ideals. He was astonished by the consequences of his actions: he had turned his paradise to hell.

A great groan reverberated in his chest. "Oh, now I know what sin is!" he said. "And what terrible tribute it exacts from the one who tastes it!"

And he sank almost luxuriously into the deepest gloom he had ever known.

V. IN WHICH WERTHER FINDS REDEMPTION OF SORTS

He avoided Catherine Gratitude all that day, even when he heard her calling his name, for if the landscape could fill him with such agony, what would he feel under the startled inquisition of her gaze? He erected himself a heavy dungeon door so that she could not get in, and, as he sat contemplating his poisoned paradise, he saw her once, walking on a hill he had made for her. She seemed unchanged, of course, but he knew in his heart how she must be shivering with the chill of lost innocence. That it should have been himself, of all men, who had introduced her so young to the tainted joys of carnal love! Another deep sigh and he buried his fists savagely in his eyes.

"Catherine! Catherine! I am a thief, an assassin, a despoiler of souls. The name of Werther de Goethe becomes a synonym for Treachery!"

It was not until the next morning that he thought himself able to admit her to his room, to submit himself to a judgement which he knew would be worse for not being spoken. Even when she did enter, his shifty eye would not focus on her for long. He looked for some outward sign of her experience, somewhat surprised that he could detect none.

He glared at the floor, knowing his words to be inadequate. "I am sorry," he said.

"For leaving the Ball, darling Werther! The epilogue was infinitely sweeter."

"Don't!" He put his hands to his ears. "I cannot undo what I have done, my child, but I can try to make amends. Evidently you must not stay here with me. You need suffer nothing further on that score. For myself, I must contemplate an eternity of loneliness. It is the least of the prices I must pay. But Mongrove would be kind to you, I am sure." He looked at her. It seemed that she had grown older. Her bloom was fading now that it had been touched by the icy fingers of that most sinister, most insinuating of libertines, called Death. "Oh," he sobbed, "how haughty was I in my pride! How I congratulated myself on my high-mindedness. Now I am proved the lowliest of all my kind!"

"I really cannot follow you, Werther dear," she said. "Your behaviour is rather odd today, you know. Your words mean very little to me."

"Of course they mean little," he said. "You are unworldly, child. How can you anticipate . . . ah, ah . . ." and he hid his face in his hands.

"Werther, please cheer up. I have heard of *le petit mal*, but this seems to be going on for a somewhat longer time. I am still puzzled . . ."

"I cannot, as yet," he said, speaking with some difficulty through his palms, "bring myself to describe in cold words the enormity of the crime I have committed against your spirit – against your childhood. I had known that you would – eventually – wish to experience the joys of true love – but I had hoped to prepare your soul for what was to come – so that when it happened it would be beautiful."

"But it *was* beautiful, Werther."

He found himself experiencing a highly inappropriate impatience with her failure to understand her doom.

"It was not the right *kind* of beauty," he explained.

"There are certain correct kinds for certain times?" she asked. "You are sad because we have offended some social code?"

"There is no such thing in this world, Catherine – but you, child, could have known a code. Something I never had when I was your age – something I wanted for you. One day you will realize what I mean." He leaned forward, his voice thrilling, his eye hot and hard. "And if you do not hate me now, Catherine, oh, you will hate me then. Yes! You will hate me then."

Her answering laughter was unaffected, unstrained. "This is silly, Werther. I have rarely had a nicer experience."

He turned aside, raising his hands as if to ward off blows. "Your words are darts – each one draws blood in my conscience." He sank back into his chair.

Still laughing, she began to stroke his limp hand. He drew it away from her.

"Ah, see! I have made you lascivious. I have introduced you to the drug called lust!"

"Well, perhaps to an aspect of it!"

Some change in her tone began to impinge on Werther, though he was still stuck deep in the glue of his guilt. He raised his head, his expression bemused, refusing to believe the import of her words.

"A wonderful aspect," she said. And she licked his ear.

He shuddered. He frowned. He tried to frame words to ask her a certain question, but he failed.

She licked his cheek and she twined her fingers in his lacklustre hair. "And one I should love to experience again, most passionate of anachronisms. It was as it must have been in those ancient days – when poets ranged the world, stealing what they needed, taking any fair maiden who pleased them, setting fire to the towns of their publishers, laying waste the books of their rivals: ambushing their readers. I am sure you were just as delighted, Werther. Say that you were!"

"Leave me!" he gasped. "I can bear no more."

"If it is what you want."

"It is."

With a wave of her little hand, she tripped from the room.

And Werther brooded upon her shocking words, deciding that he could only have misheard her. In her innocence she had seemed to admit an understanding of certain inconceivable things. What he had half-interpreted as a familiarity with the carnal world was doubtless merely a child's romantic conceit. How could she have had previous experience of a night such as that which they had shared?

She had been a virgin. Certainly she had been that.

He wished that he did not then feel an ignoble pang of pique at the possibility of another having also known her. Consequently this was immediately followed by a further wave of guilt for entertaining such thoughts and subsequent emotions. A score of conflicting glooms warred in his mind, sent tremors through his body.

"Why," he cried to the sky, "was I born! I am unworthy of the gift of life. I accused My Lady Charlotina, Lord Jagged and the Duke of Queens of base emotions, cynical motives, yet none are baser or more cynical than mine! Would I turn my anger against my victim, blame her for my misery, attack a little child because she tempted me? That is what my diseased mind would do. Thus do I seek to excuse myself my crimes. Ah, I am vile! I am vile!"

He considered going to visit Mongrove, for he dearly wished to abase himself before his old friend, to tell Mongrove that the giant's contempt had been only too well founded; but he had lost the will to move; a terrible lassitude had fallen upon him. Hating himself, he knew that all must hate him, and while he knew that he had earned every scrap of their hatred, he could not bear to go abroad and run the risk of suffering it.

What would one of his heroes of Romance have done? How would Casablanca Bogard or Eric of Marylebone have exonerated themselves, even supposing they could have committed such an unbelievable deed in the first place?

He knew the answer.

It drummed louder and louder in his ears. It was implacable and grim. But still he hesitated to follow it. Perhaps some other, more original act of retribution would occur to him? He racked his writhing brain. Nothing presented itself as an alternative.

At length he rose from his chair of unpolished quartz. Slowly, his pace measured, he walked towards the window, stripping off his power rings so that they clattered to the flagstones.

He stepped upon the ledge and stood looking down at the rocks a mile below at the base of the tower. Some jolting of a power ring as it fell had caused a wind to spring up and to blow coldly against his naked body. "The Wind of Justice," he thought.

He ignored his parachute. With one final cry of "Catherine! Forgive me!" and an unvoiced hope that he would be found long after it proved impossible to resurrect him, he flung himself, unsupported, into space.

Down he fell and death leapt to meet him. The breath fled from his lungs, his head began to pound, his sight grew dim, but the spikes of black rock grew larger until he knew that he had struck them, for his body was a-flame, broken in a hundred places, and his sad, muddled, doom-clouded brain was chaff upon the wailing breeze. Its last coherent thought was: *Let none say Werther did not pay the price in full*. And thus did he end his life with a proud negative.

VI. IN WHICH WERTHER DISCOVERS CONSOLATION

"Oh, Werther, what an adventure!"

It was Catherine Gratitude looking down on him as he opened his eyes. She clapped her hands. Her blue eyes were full of joy.

Lord Jagged stood back with a smile. "Re-born, magnificent Werther, to sorrow afresh!" he said.

He lay upon a bench of marble in his own tower. Surrounding the bench were My Lady Charlotina, the Duke of Queens, Gaf the Horse in Tears, the Iron Orchid, Li Pao, O'Kala Incarnadine and many others. They all applauded.

"A splendid drama!" said the Duke of Queens.

"Amongst the best I have witnessed," agreed the Iron Orchid (a fine compliment from her).

Werther found himself warming to them as they poured their praise upon him; but then he remembered Catherine Gratitude and what he had meant himself to be to her, what he had actually become, and although he felt much better for having paid his price, he stretched out his hand to her, saying again, "Forgive me."

"Silly Werther! Forgive such a perfect role? No, no! If anyone needs forgiving, then it is I." And Catherine Gratitude touched one of the many power rings now festooning her fingers and returned herself to her original appearance.

"It is you!" He could make no other response as he looked upon the Everlasting Concubine. "Mistress Christia?"

"Surely you suspected towards the end?" she said. "Was it not everything you told me you wanted? Was it not a fine 'sin', Werther?"

"I suffered . . ." he began.

"Oh, yes! *How* you suffered! It was unparalleled. It was equal, I am sure, to anything in History. And, Werther, did you not find the 'guilt' particularly exquisite?"

"You did it for me?" He was overwhelmed. "Because it was what I said I wanted most of all?"

"He is still a little dull," explained Mistress Christia, turning to their friends. "I believe that is often the case after a resurrection."

"Often," intoned Lord Jagged, darting a sympathetic glance at Werther. "But it will pass, I hope."

"The ending, though it could be anticipated," said the Iron Orchid, "was absolutely right."

Mistress Christia put her arms around him and kissed him. "They are saying that your performance rivals Jherek Carnelian's," she whispered. He squeezed her hand. What a wonderful woman she was, to be sure, to have added to his experience and to have increased his prestige at the same time.

He sat up. He smiled a trifle bashfully. Again they applauded.

"I can see that this was where 'Rain' was leading," said Bishop Castle. "It gives the whole thing point, I think."

"The exaggerations were just enough to bring out the essential mood without being too prolonged," said O'Kala Incarnadine, waving an elegant hoof (he had come as a goat).

"Well, I had not . . ." began Werther, but Mistress Christia put a hand to his lips.

"You will need a little time to recover," she said.

Tactfully, one by one, still expressing their most fulsome congratulations, they departed, until only Werther de Goethe and the Everlasting Concubine were left.

"I hope you did not mind the deception, Werther," she said. "I had to make amends for ruining your rainbow and I had been wondering for ages how to please you. My Lady Charlotina helped a little, of course, and Lord Jagged – though neither knew too much of what was going on."

"The real performance was yours," he said. "I was merely your foil."

"Nonsense. I gave you the rough material with which to work. And none could have anticipated the wonderful, consummate use to which you put it!"

Gently, he took her hand. "It was everything I have ever dreamed of," he said. "It is true, Mistress Christia, that you alone know me."

"You are kind. And now I must leave."

"Of course." He looked out through his window. The comforting storm raged again. Familiar lightnings flickered; friendly thunder threatened; from below there came the sound of his old consoler the furious sea flinging itself, as always, at the rock's black fangs. His sigh was contented. He knew that their liaison was ended; neither had the bad taste to prolong it and thus produce what would be, inevitably, an anti-climax, and yet he felt regret, as evidently did she.

"If death were only permanent," he said wistfully, "but it cannot be. I thank you again, granter of my deepest desires."

"If death," she said, pausing at the window, "were permanent, how would we judge our successes and our failures? Sometimes, Werther, I think you ask too much of the world." She smiled. "But you are satisfied for the moment, my love?"

"Of course."

It would have been boorish, he thought, to have claimed anything else.

THE GERNSBACK CONTINUUM

William Gibson

William Gibson is an American-Canadian novelist most closely associated with the science fiction subgenre cyberpunk. He has won many awards for his fiction, including the Hugo Award, the Nebula Award, the Philip K. Dick Award, and the Arthur C. Clarke Award in addition to numerous nominations and other recognition in the field. Many of his works have been made into feature films, such as *Johnny Mnemonic*. "The Gernsback Continuum" was first published in *Universe 11* in 1981.

Mercifully, the whole thing is starting to fade, to become an episode. When I do still catch the odd glimpse, it's peripheral; mere fragments of mad-doctor chrome, confining themselves to the corner of the eye. There was that flying-wing liner over San Francisco last week, but it was almost translucent. And the shark-fin roadsters have gotten scarcer, and freeways discreetly avoid unfolding themselves into the gleaming eighty-lane monsters I was forced to drive last month in my rented Toyota. And I know that none of it will follow me to New York; my vision is narrowing to a single wavelength of probability. I've worked hard for that. Television helped a lot.

I suppose it started in London, in that bogus Greek taverna in Battersea Park Road, with lunch on Cohen's corporate tab. Dead steam-table food and it took them thirty minutes to find an ice bucket for the retsina. Cohen works for Barris-Watford, who publish big, trendy "trade" paperbacks: illustrated histories of the neon sign, the pinball machine, the windup toys of Occupied Japan. I'd gone over to shoot a series of shoe ads; California girls with tanned legs and frisky Day-Glo jogging shoes had capered for me down the escalators of St. John's Wood and across the platforms of Tooting Bec. A lean and hungry young agency had decided that the mystery of London Transport would sell waffle-tread nylon runners. They decide; I shoot. And Cohen, whom I knew vaguely from the old days in New York, had invited me to lunch the day before I was due out of Heathrow. He brought along a very fashionably dressed young woman named Dialta Downes, who was virtually chinless and evidently a noted pop-art historian. In retrospect, I see her walking in beside Cohen under a floating neon sign that flashes THIS WAY LIES MADNESS in huge sans-serif capitals.

Cohen introduced us and explained that Dialta was the prime mover behind the latest Barris-Watford project, an illustrated history of what she called

"American Streamlined Moderne." Cohen called it "raygun Gothic." Their working title was *The Airstream Futuropolis: The Tomorrow That Never Was.*

There's a British obsession with the more baroque elements of American pop culture, something like the weird cowboys-and-Indians fetish of the West Germans or the aberrant French hunger for old Jerry Lewis films. In Dialta Downes this manifested itself in a mania for a uniquely American form of architecture that most Americans are scarcely aware of. At first I wasn't sure what she was talking about, but gradually it began to dawn on me. I found myself remembering Sunday morning television in the Fifties.

Sometimes they'd run old eroded newsreels as filler on the local station. You'd sit there with a peanut butter sandwich and a glass of milk, and a static-ridden Hollywood baritone would tell you that there was A Flying Car in Your Future. And three Detroit engineers would putter around with this big old Nash with wings, and you'd see it rumbling furiously down some deserted Michigan runway. You never actually saw it take off, but it flew away to Dialta Downes's never-never land, true home of a generation of completely uninhibited technophiles. She was talking about those odds and ends of "futuristic" Thirties and Forties architecture you pass daily in American cities without noticing: the movie marquees ribbed to radiate some mysterious energy, the dime stores faced with fluted aluminum, the chrome-tube chairs gathering dust in the lobbies of transient hotels. She saw these things as segments of a dream-world, abandoned in the uncaring present; she wanted me to photograph them for her.

The Thirties had seen the first generation of American industrial designers; until the Thirties, all pencil sharpeners had looked like pencil sharpeners – your basic Victorian mechanism, perhaps with a curlicue of decorative trim. After the advent of the designers, some pencil sharpeners looked as though they'd been put together in wind tunnels. For the most part, the change was only skin-deep; under the streamlined chrome shell, you'd find the same Victorian mechanism. Which made a certain kind of sense, because the most successful American designers had been recruited from the ranks of Broadway theater designers. It was all a stage set, a series of elaborate props for playing at living in the future.

Over coffee, Cohen produced a fat manila envelope full of glossies. I saw the winged statues that guard the Hoover Dam, forty-foot concrete hood ornaments leaning steadfastly into an imaginary hurricane. I saw a dozen shots of Frank Lloyd Wright's Johnson Wax Building, juxtaposed with the covers of old *Amazing Stories* pulps, by an artist named Frank R. Paul; the employees of Johnson Wax must have felt as though they were walking into one of Paul's spray-paint pulp Utopias. Wright's building looked as though it had been designed for people who wore white togas and Lucite sandals. I hesitated over one sketch of a particularly grandiose prop-driven airliner, all wing, like a fat, symmetrical boomerang with windows in unlikely places. Labeled arrows indicated the locations of the grand ballroom and two squash courts. It was dated 1936.

"This thing couldn't have flown . . . ?" I looked at Dialta Downes.

"Oh, no, quite impossible, even with those twelve giant props; but they loved the look, don't you see? New York to London in less than two days, first-class dining rooms, private cabins, sun decks, dancing to jazz in the evening . . . The designers were populists, you see; they were trying to give the public what it wanted. What the public wanted was the future."

I'd been in Burbank for three days, trying to suffuse a really dull-looking rocker with charisma, when I got the package from Cohen. It is possible to photograph what isn't there; it's damned hard to do, and consequently a very marketable talent. While I'm not bad at it, I'm not exactly the best, either, and this poor guy strained my Nikon's credibility. I got out depressed because I do like to do a good job, but not totally depressed, because I did make sure I'd gotten the check for the job, and I decided to restore myself with the sublime artiness of the Barris-Watford assignment. Cohen had sent me some books on Thirties design, more photos of streamlined buildings, and a list of Dialta Downes's fifty favorite examples of the style in California.

Architectural photography can involve a lot of waiting; the building becomes a kind of sundial, while you wait for a shadow to crawl away from a detail you want, or for the mass and balance of the structure to reveal itself in a certain way. While I was waiting, I thought of myself in Dialta Downes's America. When I isolated a few of the factory buildings on the ground glass of the Hasselblad, they came across with a kind of sinister totalitarian dignity, like the stadiums Albert Speer built for Hitler. But the rest of it was relentlessly tacky; ephemeral stuff extruded by the collective American subconscious of the Thirties, tending mostly to survive along depressing strips lined with dusty motels, mattress wholesalers, and small used-car lots. I went for the gas stations in a big way.

During the high point of the Downes Age, they put Ming the Merciless in charge of designing California gas stations. Favoring the architecture of his native Mongo, he cruised up and down the coast erecting raygun emplacements in white stucco. Lots of them featured superfluous central towers ringed with those strange radiator flanges that were a signature motif of the style and which made them look as though they might generate potent bursts of raw technological enthusiasm if you could only find the switch that turned them on. I shot one in San Jose an hour before the bulldozers arrived and drove right through the structural truth of plaster and lathing and cheap concrete.

"Think of it," Dialta Downes had said, "as a kind of alternate America: a 1980 that never happened. An architecture of broken dreams."

And that was my frame of mind as I made the stations of her convoluted socioarchitectural cross in my red Toyota – as I gradually tuned in to her image of a shadowy America-that-wasn't, of Coca-Cola plants like beached submarines, and fifth-run movie houses like the temples of some lost sect that had worshiped blue mirrors and geometry. And as I moved among these secret ruins, I found myself wondering what the inhabitants of that lost future would think of the world I lived in. The Thirties dreamed white marble and slipstream chrome, immortal crystal and burnished bronze, but the rockets on the covers of the Gernsback pulps had fallen on London in the dead of night, screaming. After the war, everyone had a car – no wings for it – and the promised superhighway to drive it down, so that the sky itself darkened, and the fumes ate the marble and pitted the miracle crystal . . .

And one day, on the outskirts of Bolinas, when I was setting up to shoot a particularly lavish example of Ming's martial architecture, I penetrated a fine membrane, a membrane of probability . . .

Ever so gently, I went over the Edge—

And looked up to see a twelve-engined thing like a bloated boomerang, all wing, thrumming its way east with an elephantine grace, so low that I could count the rivets in its dull silver skin, and hear – maybe – the echo of jazz.

I took it to Kihn. Merv Kihn, freelance journalist with an extensive line in Texas pterodactyls, redneck UFO contactees, bush-league Loch Ness monsters, and the Top Ten conspiracy theories in the loonier reaches of the American mass mind.

"It's good," said Kihn, polishing his yellow Polaroid shooting glasses on the hem of his Hawaiian shirt, "but it's not *mental*; lacks the true quill."

"But I saw it, Mervyn." We were seated poolside in brilliant Arizona sunlight. He was in Tucson waiting for a group of retired Las Vegas civil servants whose leader received messages from Them on her microwave oven. I'd driven all night and was feeling it.

"Of course you did. Of course you saw it. You've read my stuff; haven't you grasped my blanket solution to the UFO problem? It's simple, plain and country simple: people" – he settled the glasses carefully on his long hawk nose and fixed me with his best basilisk glare – "*see* . . . things. People see these things. Nothing's there, but people *see* them anyway. Because they need to, probably. You've read Jung, you should know the score . . . In your case, it's so obvious: You admit you were thinking about this crackpot architecture, having fantasies . . . Look, I'm sure you've taken your share of drugs, right? How many people survived the Sixties in California without having the odd hallucination? All those nights when you discovered that whole armies of Disney technicians had been employed to weave animated holograms of Egyptian hieroglyphs into the fabric of your jeans, say, or the times when—"

"But it wasn't like that."

"Of course not. It wasn't like that at all; it was 'in a setting of clear reality,' right? Everything normal, and then there's the monster, the mandala, the neon cigar. In your case, a giant Tom Swift airplane. It happens *all the time*. You aren't even crazy. You know that, don't you?" He fished a beer out of the battered foam cooler beside his deck chair.

"Last week I was in Virginia. Grayson County. I interviewed a sixteen-year-old girl who'd been assaulted by a *bar hade*."

"A what?"

"A bear head. The severed head of a bear. This *bar hade*, see, was floating around on its own little flying saucer, looked kind of like the hubcaps on cousin Wayne's vintage Caddy. Had red, glowing eyes like two cigar stubs and telescoping chrome antennas poking up behind its ears." He burped.

"It assaulted her? How?"

"You don't want to know; you're obviously impressionable. 'It was cold'" – he lapsed into his bad Southern accent – "'and metallic.' It made electronic noises. Now that is the real thing, the straight goods from the mass unconscious, friend; that little girl is a witch. There's no place for her to function in this society. She'd have seen the devil if she hadn't been brought up on 'The Bionic Woman' and all those 'Star Trek' reruns. She is clued into the main vein. And she knows that it happened to her. I got out ten minutes before the heavy UFO boys showed up with the polygraph."

I must have looked pained, because he set his beer down carefully beside the cooler and sat up.

"If you want a classier explanation, I'd say you saw a semiotic ghost. All these contactée stories, for instance, are framed in a kind of sci-fi imagery that permeates our culture. I could buy aliens, but not aliens that look like Fifties' comic art. They're semiotic phantoms, bits of deep cultural imagery that have split off and taken on a life of their own, like the Jules Verne airships that those old Kansas farmers were always seeing. But you saw a different kind of ghost, that's all. That plane was part of the mass unconscious, once. You picked up on that, somehow. The important thing is not to worry about it."

I did worry about it, though.

Kihn combed his thinning blond hair and went off to hear what They had had to say over the radar range lately, and I drew the curtains in my room and lay down in air-conditioned darkness to worry about it. I was still worrying about it when I woke up. Kihn had left a note on my door; he was flying up north in a chartered plane to check out a cattle-mutilation rumor ("muties," he called them; another of his journalistic specialties).

I had a meal, showered, took a crumbling diet pill that had been kicking around in the bottom of my shaving kit for three years, and headed back to Los Angeles.

The speed limited my vision to the tunnel of the Toyota's headlights. The body could drive, I told myself, while the mind maintained. Maintained and stayed away from the weird peripheral window dressing of amphetamine and exhaustion, the spectral, luminous vegetation that grows out of the corners of the mind's eye along late-night highways. But the mind had its own ideas, and Kihn's opinion of what I was already thinking of as my "sighting" rattled endlessly through my head in a tight, lopsided orbit. Semiotic ghosts. Fragments of the Mass Dream, whirling past in the wind of my passage. Somehow this feedback-loop aggravated the diet pill, and the speed-vegetation along the road began to assume the colors of infrared satellite images, glowing shreds blown apart in the Toyota's slipstream.

I pulled over, then, and a half-dozen aluminum beer cans winked goodnight as I killed the headlights. I wondered what time it was in London, and tried to imagine Dialta Downes having breakfast in her Hampstead flat, surrounded by streamlined chrome figurines and books on American culture.

Desert nights in that country are enormous; the moon is closer. I watched the moon for a long time and decided that Kihn was right. The main thing was not to worry. All across the continent, daily, people who were more normal than I'd ever aspired to be saw giant birds, Bigfeet, flying oil refineries; they kept Kihn busy and solvent. Why should I be upset by a glimpse of the 1930s pop imagination loose over Bolinas? I decided to go to sleep, with nothing worse to worry about than rattlesnakes and cannibal hippies, safe amid the friendly roadside garbage of my own familiar continuum. In the morning I'd drive down to Nogales and photograph the old brothels, something I'd intended to do for years. The diet pill had given up.

The light woke me, and then the voices. The light came from somewhere behind me and threw shifting shadows inside the car. The voices were calm, indistinct, male and female, engaged in conversation.

My neck was stiff and my eyeballs felt gritty in their sockets. My leg had gone to sleep, pressed against the steering wheel. I fumbled for my glasses in the pocket of my work shirt and finally got them on.

Then I looked behind me and saw the city.

The books on Thirties design were in the trunk; one of them contained sketches of an idealized city that drew on *Metropolis* and *Things to Come*, but squared everything, soaring up through an architect's perfect clouds to zeppelin docks and mad neon spires. That city was a scale model of the one that rose behind me. Spire stood on spire in gleaming ziggurat steps that climbed to a central golden temple tower ringed with the crazy radiator flanges of the Mongo gas stations. You could hide the Empire State Building in the smallest of those towers. Roads of crystal soared between the spires, crossed and recrossed by smooth silver shapes like beads of running mercury. The air was thick with ships: giant wing-liners, little darting silver things (sometimes one of the quicksilver shapes from the sky bridges rose gracefully into the air and flew up to join the dance), mile-long blimps, hovering dragonfly things that were gyrocopters . . .

I closed my eyes tight and swung around in the seat. When I opened them, I willed myself to see the mileage meter, the pale road dust on the black plastic dashboard, the overflowing ashtray.

"Amphetamine psychosis," I said. I opened my eyes. The dash was still there, the dust, the crushed filter tips. Very carefully, without moving my head, I turned the headlights on.

And saw them.

They were blond. They were standing beside their car, an aluminum avocado with a central shark-fin rudder jutting up from its spine and smooth black tires like a child's toy. He had his arm around her waist and was gesturing toward the city. They were both in white: loose clothing, bare legs, spotless white sun shoes. Neither of them seemed aware of the beams of my headlights. He was saying something wise and strong, and she was nodding, and suddenly I was frightened, frightened in an entirely different way. Sanity had ceased to be an issue; I knew, somehow, that the city behind me was Tucson – a dream Tucson thrown up out of the collective yearning of an era. That it was real, entirely real. But the couple in front of me lived in it, and they frightened me.

They were the children of Dialta Downes's '80-that-wasn't; they were Heirs to the Dream. They were white, blond, and they probably had blue eyes. They were American. Dialta had said that the Future had come to America first, but had finally passed it by. But not here, in the heart of the Dream. Here, we'd gone on and on, in a dream logic that knew nothing of pollution, the finite bounds of fossil fuel, or foreign wars it was possible to lose. They were smug, happy, and utterly content with themselves and their world. And in the Dream, it was *their* world.

Behind me, the illuminated city: Searchlights swept the sky for the sheer joy of it. I imagined them thronging the plazas of white marble, orderly and alert, their bright eyes shining with enthusiasm for their floodlit avenues and silver cars.

It had all the sinister fruitiness of Hitler Youth propaganda.

I put the car in gear and drove forward slowly, until the bumper was within three feet of them. They still hadn't seen me. I rolled the window down and listened to what the man was saying. His words were bright and hollow as the pitch in some chamber of commerce brochure, and I knew that he believed in them absolutely.

"John," I heard the woman say, "we've forgotten to take our food pills." She clicked two bright wafers from a thing on her belt and passed one to him. I backed onto the highway and headed for Los Angeles, wincing and shaking my head.

I phoned Kihn from a gas station. A new one, in bad Spanish Modern. He was back from his expedition and didn't seem to mind the call.

"Yeah, that is a weird one. Did you try to get any pictures? Not that they ever come out, but it adds an interesting *frisson* to your story, not having the pictures turn out . . ."

But what should I do?

"Watch lots of television, particularly game shows and soaps. Go to porn movies. Ever see *Nazi Love Motel*? They've got it on cable, here. Really awful. Just what you need."

What was he talking about?

"Quit yelling and listen to me. I'm letting you in on a trade secret: really bad media can exorcise your semiotic ghosts. If it keeps the saucer people off my back, it can keep these Art Deco futuroids off yours. Try it. What have you got to lose?"

Then he begged off, pleading an early-morning date with the Elect.

"The who?"

"These oldsters from Vegas; the ones with the microwaves."

I considered putting a collect call through to London, getting Cohen at Barris-Watford and telling him his photographer was checked out for a protracted season in the Twilight Zone. In the end, I let a machine mix me a really impossible cup of black coffee and climbed back into the Toyota for the haul to Los Angeles.

Los Angeles was a bad idea, and I spent two weeks there. It was prime Downes country; too much of the Dream there, and too many fragments of the Dream waiting to snare me. I nearly wrecked the car on a stretch of overpass near Disneyland when the road fanned out like an origami trick and left me swerving through a dozen minilanes of whizzing chrome teardrops with shark fins. Even worse, Hollywood was full of people who looked too much like the couple I'd seen in Arizona. I hired an Italian director who was making ends meet doing darkroom work and installing patio decks around swimming pools until his ship came in; he made prints of all the negatives I'd accumulated on the Downes job. I didn't want to look at the stuff myself. It didn't seem to bother Leonardo, though, and when he was finished I checked the prints, riffling through them like a deck of cards, sealed them up, and sent them air freight to London. Then I took a taxi to a theater that was showing *Nazi Love Motel* and kept my eyes shut all the way.

Cohen's congratulatory wire was forwarded to me in San Francisco a week later. Dialta had loved the pictures. He admired the way I'd "really gotten into it," and looked forward to working with me again. That afternoon I spotted a flying wing over Castro Street, but there was something tenuous about it, as if it were only half there. I rushed to the nearest newsstand and gathered up as much as I could find on the petroleum crisis and the nuclear energy hazard. I'd just decided to buy a plane ticket for New York.

"Hell of a world we live in, huh?" The proprietor was a thin black man with bad teeth and an obvious wig. I nodded, fishing in my jeans for change, anxious to find a park bench where I could submerge myself in hard evidence of the human near-dystopia we live in. "But it could be worse, huh?"

"That's right," I said, "or even worse, it could be perfect."

He watched me as I headed down the street with my little bundle of condensed catastrophe.

THE THREADS OF TIME

C.J. Cherryh

C.J. Cherryh is an American science fiction and fantasy writer. She used her initials early in her writing career in order to disguise the fact that she was a female science fiction writer. She is the recipient of the Hugo Award and the Locus Award, among others, and has had an asteroid named after her. This story was first published in 1978 in the *Darkover Grand Council Program Book IV* and later in *The Collected Short Fiction of C. J. Cherryh*.

I t was possible that the Gates were killing the qhal. They were everywhere, on every world, had been a fact of life for five thousand years, and linked the whole net of qhalur civilization into one present-tense coherency.

They had not, to be sure, invented the Gates. Chance gave them that gift . . . on a dead world of their own sun. One Gate stood – made by unknown hands.

And the qhal made others, imitating what they found. The Gates were instantaneous transfer, not alone from place to place, but, because of the motion of worlds and suns and the traveling galaxies – involving time.

There was an end of time. Ah, qhal *could* venture anything. If one supposed, if one believed, if one were very *sure,* one could step through a Gate to a Gate that would/might exist on some other distant world.

And if one were wrong?

If it did not exist?

If it never had?

Time warped in the Gate-passage. One could step across light-years, unaged; so it was possible to outrace light and time.

Did one not want to die, bound to a single lifespan? Go forward. See the future. Visit the world/worlds to come.

But never go back. Never tamper. Never alter the past.

There was an End of Time.

It was the place where qhal gathered, who had been farthest and lost their courage for traveling on. It was the point beyond which no one had courage, where descendants shared the world with living ancestors in greater and greater numbers, the jaded, the restless, who reached this age and felt their will erode away.

It was the place where hope ended. Oh, a few went farther, and the age saw them – no more. They were gone. They did not return.

They went beyond, whispered those who had lost their courage. They went out a Gate and found nothing there.

They died.

Or was it death – to travel without end? And what was death? And was the universe finite at all?

Some went, and vanished, and the age knew nothing more of them.

Those who were left were in agony – of desire to go; of fear to go farther.

Of changes.

This age – did change. It rippled with possibilities. Memories deceived. One remembered, or remembered that one had remembered, and the fact grew strange and dim, contradicting what obviously *was*. People remembered things that never had been true.

And one must never go back to see. Backtiming – had direst possibilities. It made paradox.

But some tried, seeking a time as close to their original exit point as possible. Some came too close, and involved themselves in time-loops, a particularly distressing kind of accident and unfortunate equally for those involved as bystanders.

Among qhal, between the finding of the first Gate and the End of Time, a new kind of specialist evolved: time-menders, who in most extreme cases of disturbance policed the Gates and carefully researched afflicted areas. They alone were licensed to violate the back-time barrier, passing back and forth under strict non-involvement regulations, exchanging intelligence only with each other, to minutely adjust reality.

Evolved.

Agents recruited other agents at need – but at whose instance? There might be some who knew. It might have come from the far end of time – in that last (or was it last?) age beyond which nothing seemed certain, when the years since the First Gate were more than five thousand, and the Now in which all Gates existed was – very distant. Or it might have come from those who had found the Gate, overseeing their invention. Someone knew, somewhen, somewhere along the course of the stars toward the end of time.

But no one said.

It was hazardous business, this time-mending, in all senses. Precisely *what* was done was something virtually unknowable after it was done, for alterations in the past produced (one believed) changes in future reality.

Whole time-fields, whose events could be wiped and redone, with effects which widened the farther down the timeline they proceeded. Detection of time-tampering was almost impossible.

A stranger wanted something to eat, a long time ago. He shot himself his dinner.
A small creature was not where it had been, when it had been.
A predator missed a meal and took another . . . likewise small.
A child lost a pet.
And found another.
And a friend she would not have had. She was happier for it.
She met many people she had never/would never meet.
A man in a different age had breakfast in a house on a hill.

Agent Harrh had acquired a sense about disruptions, a kind of extrasensory queasiness about a just-completed timewarp. He was not alone in this. But the time-menders (Harrh knew three others of his own age) never reported such experiences outside their own special group. Such reports would have been meaningless to his own time, involving a past which (as a result of the warp) was neither real nor valid nor perceptible to those in Time Present. Some time-menders would reach the verge of insanity because of this. This was future fact. Harrh knew this.

He had been there.

And he refused to go again to Now, that Now to which time had advanced since the discovery of the Gate – let alone to the End of Time, which was the farthest that anyone imagined. He was one of a few, a very few, licensed to do so, but he refused.

He lived scattered lives in ages to come, and remembered the future with increasing melancholy.

He had visited the End of Time, and left it in the most profound despair. He had seen what was there, and when he had contemplated going beyond, that most natural step out the Gate which stood and beckoned—

He fled. He had never run from anything but that. It remained, a recollection of shame at his fear.

A sense of a limit which he had never had before.

And this in itself was terrible, to a man who had thought time infinite and himself immortal.

In his own present of 1003 since the First Gate, Harrh had breakfast, a quiet meal. The children were off to the beach. His wife shared tea with him and thought it would be a fine morning.

"Yes," he said. "Shall we take the boat out? We can fish a little, take the sun."

"Marvelous," she said. Her gray eyes shone. He loved her – for herself, for her patience. He caught her hand on the crystal table, held slender fingers, not speaking his thoughts, which were far too somber for the morning.

They spent their mornings and their days together. He came back to her, time after shifting time. He might be gone a month; and home a week; and gone two months next time. He never dared cut it too close. They lost a great deal of each other's lives, and so much – so much he could not share with her.

"The island," he said. "Mhreihrrinn, I'd like to see it again."

"I'll pack," she said.

And went away.

He came back to her never aged; and she bore their two sons; and reared them; and managed the accounts: and explained his absences to relatives and the world. *He travels,* she would say, with that right amount of secrecy that protected secrets.

And even to her he could never confide what he knew.

"I trust you," she would say – knowing what he was, but never what he did.

He let her go. She went off to the hall and out the door – He imagined happy faces, holiday, the boys making haste to run the boat out and put on the bright colored sail. She would keep them busy carrying this and that, fetching food and clothes – things happened in shortest order when Mhreihrrinn set her hand to them.

He wanted that, wanted the familiar, the orderly, the homely. He was, if he let his mind dwell on things – afraid. He had the notion never to leave again.

He had been to the Now most recently – 5045, and his flesh crawled at the memory. There was recklessness there. There was disquiet. The Now had traveled two decades and more since he had first begun, and he felt it more and more. The whole decade of the 5040's had a queasiness about it, ripples of instability as if the whole fabric of the Now were shifting like a kaleidoscope.

And it headed for the End of Time. It had become more and more like that age, confirming it by its very collapse.

People had illusions in the Now. They perceived what had not been true.

And yet it *was* when he came home.

It had grown to be so – while he was gone.

A university stood in Morurir, which he did not remember.

A hedge of trees grew where a building had been in Morurir.

A man was in the Council who had died.

He would not go back to Now. He had resolved that this morning. He had children, begotten before his first time-traveling. He had so very much to keep him – this place, this home, this stability – He was very well to do. He had invested well – his own small tampering. He had no lack, no need. He was mad to go on and on. He was done.

But a light distracted him, an opal shimmering beyond his breakfast nook, arrival in that receptor which his fine home afforded, linked to the master gate at Pyvrrhn.

A young man materialized there, opal and light and then solidity, a distraught young man.

"Harrh," the youth said, disregarding the decencies of meeting, and strode forward unasked. "Harrh, is everything all right here?"

Harrh arose from the crystal table even before the shimmer died, beset by that old queasiness of things out of joint. This was Alhir from 390 Since the Gate, an experienced man in the force: he had used a Master Key to come here – had such access, being what he was.

"Alhir," Harrh said, perplexed. "What's wrong?"

"You don't know." Alhir came as far as the door.

"A cup of tea?" Harrh said. Alhir had been here before. They were friends. There were oases along the course of suns, friendly years, places where houses served as rest-stops. In this too Mhreihrrinn was patient. "I've got to tell you— No, don't tell me. I don't want to know. I'm through. I've made up my mind. You can carry that where you're going. – But if you want the breakfast—"

"There's been an accident."

"I don't want to hear."

"He got past us."

"I don't want to know." He walked over to the cupboard, took another cup. "Mhreihrrinn's with the boys down at the beach. You just caught us." He set the cup down and poured the tea, where Mhreihrrinn had sat. "Won't you? You're always welcome here. Mhreihrrinn has no idea what you are. My young friend, she calls you. She doesn't know. Or she suspects. She'd never say. – Sit *down.*"

Alhir had strayed aside, where a display case sat along the wall, a lighted case of mementoes, of treasures, of crystal. "Harrh, there was a potsherd here."

"No," Harrh said, less and less comfortable. "Just the glasses. I'm quite sure."

"Harrh, it was very old."

"No," he said. "I promised Mhreihrrinn and the boys – I mean it. I'm through. I don't want to know."

"It came from Silen. From the digs at the First Gate, Harrh. It was a very valuable piece. You valued it very highly. – You don't remember."

"No," Harrh said, feeling fear thick about him, like a change in atmosphere. "I don't know of such a piece. I never had such a thing. Check your memory, Alhir."

"It was from the ruins by the *First Gate,* don't you understand?"

And then Alhir did not exist.

Harrh blinked, remembered pouring a cup of tea. But he was sitting in the chair, his breakfast before him.

He poured the tea and drank.

He was sitting on rock, amid the grasses blowing gently in the wind, on a clifftop by the sea.

He was standing there. "Mhreihrrinn," he said, in the first chill touch of fear.

But that memory faded. He had never had a wife, nor children. He forgot the house as well.

Trees grew and faded.

Rocks moved at random.

The time-menders were in most instances the only ones who survived even a little while.

Wrenched loose from time and with lives rooted in many parts of it, they felt it first and lived it longest, and not a few were trapped in back-time and did not die, but survived the horror of it and begot children who further confounded the time-line.

Time, stretched thin in possibilities, adjusted itself.

He was Harrh.

But he was many possibilities and many names.

In time none of them mattered.

He was many names; he lived. He had many bodies; and the souls stained his own.

In the end he remembered nothing at all, except the drive to live.

And the dreams.

And none of the dreams were true.

TRICERATOPS SUMMER

Michael Swanwick

Michael Swanwick is an American writer of novels and stories who has received the Hugo, Nebula, Theodore Sturgeon, and World Fantasy awards for his work. His stories have appeared in *Omni*, *Penthouse*, *Amazing*, *Asimov's Science Fiction Magazine*, *High Times*, *New Dimensions*, *Starlight*, *Universe*, *Full Spectrum*, *TriQuarterly*, and elsewhere. Many have been reprinted in year's best anthologies, and translated into several foreign languages. His books include *In the Drift*, an Ace Special; *Vacuum Flowers*; *Griffin's Egg*; *Stations of the Tide*; *The Iron Dragon's Daughter*, a *New York Times* Notable Book; and *Jack Faust*. This story was first published by *Amazon Shorts* in 2005.

The dinosaurs looked all wobbly in the summer heat shimmering up from the pavement. There were about thirty of them, a small herd of what appeared to be *Triceratops*. They were crossing the road – don't ask me why – so I downshifted and brought the truck to a halt, and waited.

Waited and watched.

They were interesting creatures, and surprisingly graceful for all their bulk. They picked their way delicately across the road, looking neither to the right nor the left. I was pretty sure I'd correctly identified them by now – they had those three horns on their faces. I used to be a kid. I'd owned the plastic models.

My next-door neighbor, Gretta, who was sitting in the cab next to me with her eyes closed, said, "Why aren't we moving?"

"Dinosaurs in the road," I said.

She opened her eyes.

"Son of a bitch," she said.

Then, before I could stop her, she leaned over and honked the horn, three times. Loud.

As one, every *Triceratops* in the herd froze in its tracks, and swung its head around to face the truck.

I practically fell over laughing.

"What's so goddamn funny?" Gretta wanted to know. But I could only point and shake my head helplessly, tears of laughter rolling down my cheeks.

It was the frills. They were beyond garish. They were as bright as any circus poster, with red whorls and yellow slashes and electric orange diamonds – too many shapes and colors to catalog, and each one different. They looked like Chinese kites! Like butterflies with six-foot wingspans! Like Las Vegas on acid! And then, under those carnival-bright displays, the most stupid faces imaginable, blinking and gaping like brain-damaged cows. Oh, they were funny, all right, but if you couldn't see that at a glance, you never were going to.

Gretta was getting fairly steamed. She climbed down out of the cab and slammed the door behind her. At the sound, a couple of the *Triceratops* pissed themselves with excitement, and the lot shied away a step or two. Then they began huddling a little closer, to see what would happen next.

Gretta hastily climbed back into the cab. "What are those bastards up to now?" she demanded irritably. She seemed to blame me for their behavior. Not that she could say so, considering she was in my truck and her BMW was still in the garage in South Burlington.

"They're curious," I said. "Just stand still. Don't move or make any noise, and after a bit they'll lose interest and wander off."

"How do you know? You ever see anything like them before?"

"No," I admitted. "But I worked on a dairy farm when I was a young fella, thirty, forty years ago, and the behavior seems similar."

In fact, the *Triceratops* were already getting bored and starting to wander off again when a battered old Hyundai pulled wildly up beside us, and a skinny young man with the worst-combed hair I'd seen in a long time jumped out. They decided to stay and watch.

The young man came running over to us, arms waving. I leaned out the window. "What's the problem, son?"

He was pretty bad upset. "There's been an accident – an *incident*, I mean. At the Institute." He was talking about the Institute for Advanced Physics, which was not all that far from here. It was government-funded and affiliated in some way I'd never been able to get straight with the University of Vermont. "The verge stabilizers failed and the meson-field inverted and vectorized. The congruence factors went to infinity and . . ." He seized control of himself. "You're not supposed to see *any* of this."

"These things are yours, then?" I said. "So you'd know. They're *Triceratops*, right?"

"*Triceratops horridus*," he said distractedly. I felt unreasonably pleased with myself. "For the most part. There might be a couple other species of *Triceratops* mixed in there as well. They're like ducks in that regard. They're not fussy about what company they keep."

Gretta shot out her wrist and glanced meaningfully at her watch. Like everything else she owned, it was expensive. She worked for a firm in Essex Junction that did systems analysis for companies that were considering downsizing. Her job was to find out exactly what everybody did and then tell the CEO who could be safely cut. "I'm losing money," she grumbled.

I ignored her.

"Listen," the kid said. "You've got to keep quiet about this. We can't afford to have it get out. It has to be kept a secret."

"A secret?" On the far side of the herd, three cars had drawn up and stopped. Their passengers were standing in the road, gawking. A Ford Taurus pulled up behind us, and its driver rolled down his window for a better look. "You're planning to keep a herd of dinosaurs secret? There must be dozens of these things."

"Hundreds," he said despairingly. "They were migrating. The herd broke up after it came through. This is only a fragment of it."

"Then I don't see how you're going to keep this a secret. I mean, just look at them. They're practically the size of tanks. People are bound to notice."

"My God, my God."

Somebody on the other side had a camera out and was taking pictures. I didn't point this out to the young man.

Gretta had been getting more and more impatient as the conversation proceeded. Now she climbed down out of the truck and said, "I can't afford to waste any more time here. I've got work to do."

"Well, so do I, Gretta."

She snorted derisively. "Ripping out toilets, and nailing up sheet rock! Already, I've lost more money than you earn in a week."

She stuck out her hand at the young man. "Give me your car keys."

Dazed, the kid obeyed. Gretta climbed down, got in the Hyundai, and wheeled it around. "I'll have somebody return this to the Institute later today."

Then she was gone, off to find another route around the herd.

She should have waited, because a minute later the beasts decided to leave, and in no time at all were nowhere to be seen. They'd be easy enough to find, though. They pretty much trampled everything flat in their wake.

The kid shook himself, as if coming out of a trance. "Hey," he said. "She took my *car*."

"Climb into the cab," I said. "There's a bar a ways up the road. I think you need a drink."

He said his name was Everett McCoughlan, and he clutched his glass like he would fall off the face of the Earth if he were to let go. It took a couple of whiskeys to get the full story out of him. Then I sat silent for a long time. I don't mind admitting that what he'd said made me feel a little funny. "How long?" I asked at last.

"Ten weeks, maybe three months, tops. No more."

I took a long swig of my soda water. (I've never been much of a drinker. Also, it was pretty early in the morning.) Then I told Everett that I'd be right back.

I went out to the truck, and dug the cell phone out of the glove compartment.

First I called home. Delia had already left for the bridal shop, and they didn't like her getting personal calls at work, so I left a message saying that I loved her. Then I called Green Mountain Books. It wasn't open yet, but Randy likes to come in early and he picked up the phone when he heard my voice on the machine. I asked him if he had anything on *Triceratops*. He said to hold on a minute, and then said yes, he had one copy of *The Horned Dinosaurs* by Peter Dodson. I told him I'd pick it up next time I was in town.

Then I went back in the bar. Everett had just ordered a third whiskey, but I pried it out of his hand. "You've had enough of that," I said. "Go home, take a nap. Maybe putter around in the garden."

"I don't have my car," he pointed out.

"Where do you live? I'll take you home."

"Anyway, I'm supposed to be at work. I didn't log out. And technically I'm still on probation."

"What difference does that make," I asked, "now?"

Everett had an apartment in Winooski at the Woolen Mill, so I guess the Institute paid him good money. Either that or he wasn't very smart how he spent it. After I dropped him off, I called a couple contractors I knew and arranged for them to take over what jobs I was already committed to. Then I called the *Free Press* to cancel my regular ad, and all my customers to explain I was having scheduling problems and had to subcontract their jobs. Only old Mrs. Bremmer gave me any trouble over that, and even she came around after I said that in any case I wouldn't be able to get around to her Jacuzzi until sometime late July.

Finally, I went to the bank and arranged for a second mortgage on my house. It took me a while to convince Art Letourneau I was serious. I'd been doing business with him for a long while, and he knew how I felt about debt. Also, I was pretty evasive about what I wanted the money for. He was half-suspicious I was having some kind of late onset mid-life crisis. But the deed was in my name and property values were booming locally, so in the end the deal went through.

On the way home, I stopped at a jewelry store and at the florist's.

Delia's eyes widened when she saw the flowers, and then narrowed at the size of the stone on the ring. She didn't look at all the way I'd thought she would. "This better be good," she said.

So I sat down at the kitchen table and told her the whole story. When I was done, Delia was silent for a long while, just as I'd been. Then she said, "How much time do we have?"

"Three months if we're lucky. Ten weeks in any case," Everett said.

"You believe him?"

"He seemed pretty sure of himself."

If there's one thing I am, it's a good judge of character, and Delia knew it. When Gretta moved into the rehabbed barn next door, I'd said right from the start she was going to be a difficult neighbor. And that was before she'd smothered the grass on her property under three different colors of mulch, and then complained about me keeping my pickup parked in the driveway, out in plain sight.

Delia thought seriously for a few minutes, frowning in that way she has when she's concentrating, and then she smiled. It was a wan little thing, but a smile nonetheless. "Well, I've always wished we could afford a real first-class vacation."

I was glad to hear her say so, because that was exactly the direction my own thought had been trending in. And happier than that when she flung out her arms and whooped, "I'm going to *Disney*world!"

"Hell," I said. "We've got enough money to go to Disneyworld, Disneyland, *and* Eurodisney, one after the other. I think there's one in Japan too."

We were both laughing at this point, and then she dragged me up out of the chair, and the two of us were dancing around and round the kitchen, still a little spooked under it all, but mostly being as giddy and happy as kids.

We were going to sleep in the next morning, but old habits die hard and anyway, Delia felt she owed it to the bridal shop to give them a week's notice. So, after she'd left, I went out to see if I could find where the *Triceratops* had gone.

Only to discover Everett standing by the side of the road with his thumb out.

I pulled over. "Couldn't get somebody at the Institute to drive your car home?" I asked when we were underway again.

"It never got there," he said gloomily. "That woman who was with you the other day drove it into a ditch. Stripped the clutch and bent the frame out of shape. She said she wouldn't have had the accident if my dinosaurs hadn't gotten her upset. Then she hung up on me. I just started at this job. I don't have the savings to buy a new car."

"Lease one instead," I said. "Put it on your credit card and pay the minimum for the next two or three months."

"I hadn't thought of that."

We drove on for a while and then I asked, "How'd she manage to get in touch with you?" She'd driven off before he mentioned his name.

"She called the Institute and asked for the guy with the bad hair. They gave her my home phone number."

The parking lot for the Institute for Advanced Physics had a card system, so I let Everett off by the side of the road. "Thanks for not telling anybody," he said as he climbed out. "About . . . you know."

"It seemed wisest not to."

He started away and then turned back suddenly and asked, "Is my hair really that bad?"

"Nothing that a barber couldn't fix," I said.

I'd driven to the Institute by the main highway. Returning, I went by back ways, through farmland. When I came to where I'd seen the *Triceratops*, I thought for an instant there'd been an accident, there were so many vehicles by the side of the road. But it turned out they were mostly gawkers and television crews. So apparently the herd hadn't gone far. There were cameras up and down the road and lots of good-looking young women standing in front of them with wireless microphones.

I pulled over to take a look. One *Triceratops* had come right up to the fence and was browsing on some tall weeds there. It didn't seem to have any fear of human beings, possibly because in its day mammals never got much bigger than badgers. I walked up and stroked its back, which was hard and pebbly and warm. It was the warmth that got to me. It made the experience real.

A newswoman came over with her cameraman in tow. "You certainly look happy," she said.

"Well, I always wanted to meet a real live dinosaur." I turned to face her, but I kept one hand on the critter's frill. "They're something to see, I'll tell you. Dumb as mud but lots more fun to look at."

She asked me a few questions, and I answered them as best I could. Then, after she did her wrap, she got out a notebook and took down my name and asked me what I did. I told her I was a contractor but that I used to work on a dairy farm. She seemed to like that.

I watched for a while more, and then drove over to Burlington to pick up my book. The store wasn't open yet, but Randy let me in when I knocked. "You bastard," he said after he'd locked the door behind me. "Do you have any idea how much I could have sold this for? I had a foreigner," by which I understood him to mean somebody from New York State or possibly New Hampshire, "offer me two hundred dollars for it. And I could have got more if I'd had something to dicker with!"

"I'm obliged," I said, and paid him in paper bills. He waved off the tax but kept the nickel. "Have you gone out to see 'em yet?"

"Are you nuts? There's thousands of people coming into the state to look at those things. It's going to be a madhouse out there."

"I thought the roads seemed crowded. But it wasn't as bad as all of that."

"It's early still. You just wait."

Randy was right. By evening the roads were so congested that Delia was an hour late getting home. I had a casserole in the oven and the book open on the kitchen table when she staggered in. "The males have longer, more elevated horns, where the females have shorter, more forward-directed horns," I told her. "Also, the males are bigger than the females, but the females outnumber the males by a ratio of two to one."

I leaned back in my chair with a smile. "Two to one. Imagine that."

Delia hit me. "Let me see that thing."

I handed her the book. It kind of reminded me of when we were new-married, and used to go out bird-watching. Before things got so busy. Then Delia's friend Martha called and said to turn on Channel 3 quick. We did, and there I was saying, "dumb as mud."

"So you're a cattle farmer now?" Delia said, when the spot was over.

"That's not what I told her. She got it mixed up. Hey, look what I got." I'd been to three separate travel agents that afternoon. Now I spread out the brochures: Paris, Dubai, Rome, Australia, Rio de Janeiro, Marrakech. Even Disneyworld. I'd grabbed everything that looked interesting. "Take your pick, we can be there tomorrow."

Delia looked embarrassed.

"What?" I said.

"You know that June is our busy season. All those young brides. Francesca begged me to stay on through the end of the month."

"But—"

"It's not that long," she said.

For a couple of days it was like Woodstock, the Super Bowl, and the World Series all rolled into one – the Interstates came to a standstill, and it was worth your life to actually have to go somewhere. Then the governor called in the National Guard, and they cordoned off Chittenden County so you had to show your ID to get in or out. The *Triceratops* had scattered into little groups by then. Then a dozen or two were captured and shipped out of state to zoos where they could be more easily seen. So things returned to normal, almost.

I was painting the trim on the house that next Saturday when Everett drove up in a beat-up old clunker. "I like your new haircut," I said. "Looks good. You here to see the trikes?"

"Trikes?"

"That's what they're calling your dinos. *Triceratops* is too long for common use. We got a colony of eight or nine hanging around the neighborhood." There were woods out back of the house and beyond them a little marsh. They liked to browse the margins of the wood and wallow in the mud.

"No, uh . . . I came to find out the name of that woman you were with. The one who took my car."

"Gretta Houck, you mean?"

"I guess. I've been thinking it over, and I think she really ought to pay for the repairs. I mean, right's right."

"I noticed you decided against leasing."

"It felt dishonest. This car's cheap. But it's not very good. One door is wired shut with a coat hanger."

Delia came out of the house with the picnic basket then and I introduced them. "Ev's looking for Gretta," I said.

"Well, your timing couldn't be better," Delia said. "We were just about to go out trike-watching with her. You can join us."

"Oh, I can't—"

"Don't give it a second thought. There's plenty of food." Then, to me, "I'll go fetch Gretta while you clean up."

So that's how we found ourselves following the little trail through the woods and out to the meadow on the bluff above the Tylers' farm. The trikes slept in the field there. They'd torn up the crops pretty bad. But the state was covering damages, so the Tylers didn't seem to mind. It made me wonder if the governor knew what we knew. If he'd been talking with the folks at the Institute.

I spread out the blanket, and Delia got out cold cuts, deviled eggs, lemonade, all the usual stuff. I'd brought along two pairs of binoculars, which I handed out to our guests. Gretta had been pretty surly so far, which made me wonder how Delia'd browbeat her into coming along. But now she said, "Oh, look! They've got babies!"

There were three little ones, only a few feet long. Two of them were mock-fighting, head-butting and tumbling over and over each other. The third just sat in the sun, blinking. They were all as cute as the dickens, with their tiny little nubs of horns and their great big eyes.

The other trikes were wandering around, pulling up bushes and such and eating them. Except for one that stood near the babies, looking big and grumpy and protective. "Is that the mother?" Gretta asked.

"That one's male," Everett said. "You can tell by the horns." He launched into an explanation, which I didn't listen to, having read the book.

On the way back to the house, Gretta grumbled, "I suppose you want the number for my insurance company."

"I guess," Everett said.

They disappeared into her house for maybe twenty minutes and then Everett got into his clunker and drove away. Afterwards, I said to Delia, "I thought the whole point of the picnic was you and I were going to finally work out where we were going on vacation." She hadn't even brought along the travel books I'd bought her.

"I think they like each other."

"Is that what this was about? You know, you've done some damn fool things in your time—"

"Like what?" Delia said indignantly. "When have I ever done anything that was less than wisdom incarnate?"

"Well . . . you married me."

"Oh, that." She put her arms around me. "That was just the exception that proves the rule."

So, what with one thing and the other, the summer drifted by. Delia took to luring the *Triceratops* closer and closer to the house with cabbages and bunches of celery and such. Cabbages were their favorite. It got so that we were feeding the trikes off the back porch in the evenings. They'd come clomping up around sunset, hoping for cabbages but willing to settle for pretty much anything.

It ruined the yard, but so what? Delia was a little upset when they got into her garden, but I spent a day putting up a good strong fence around it, and she replanted. She made manure tea by mixing their dung with water, and its effect on the plants was bracing. The roses blossomed like never before, and in August the tomatoes came up spectacular.

I mentioned this to Dave Jenkins down at the home-and-garden and he looked thoughtful. "I believe there's a market for that," he said. "I'll buy as much of their manure as you can haul over here."

"Sorry," I told him, "I'm on vacation."

Still, I couldn't get Delia to commit to a destination. Not that I quit trying. I was telling her about the Atlantis Hotel on Paradise Island one evening when suddenly she said, "Well, look at this."

I stopped reading about swimming with dolphins and the fake undersea ruined city, and joined her at the door. There was Everett's car – the new one that Gretta's insurance had paid for – parked out front of her house. There was only one light on, in the kitchen. Then that one went out too.

We figured those two had worked through their differences.

An hour later, though, we heard doors slamming, and the screech of Everett's car pulling out too fast. Then somebody was banging on our screen door. It was Gretta. When Delia let her in, she burst out into tears. Which surprised me. I wouldn't have pegged Everett as that kind of guy.

I made some coffee while Delia guided her into a kitchen chair, and got her some tissues, and soothed her down enough that she could tell us why she'd thrown Everett out of her house. It wasn't anything he'd done apparently, but something he'd said.

"Do you know what he *told* me?" she sobbed.

"I think I do," Delia said.

"About timelike—"

"—loops. Yes, dear."

Gretta looked stricken. "You too? Why didn't you tell me? Why didn't you tell everybody?"

"I considered it," I said. "Only then I thought, what would folks do if they knew their actions no longer mattered? Most would behave decently enough. But a few would do some pretty bad things, I'd think. I didn't want to be responsible for that."

She was silent for a while.

"Explain to me again about timelike loops," she said at last. "Ev tried, but by then I was too upset to listen."

"Well, I'm not so sure myself. But the way he explained it to me, they're going to fix the problem by going back to the moment before the rupture occurred and preventing it from ever happening in the first place. When that happens, everything from the moment of rupture to the moment when they go back to apply the patch separates from the trunk timeline. It just sort of drifts away, and dissolves into nothingness – never was, never will be."

"And what becomes of us?"

"We just go back to whatever we were doing when the accident happened. None the worse for wear."

"But without memories."

"How can you remember something that never happened?"

"So Ev and I—"

"No, dear," Delia said gently.

"How much time do we have?"

"With a little luck, we have the rest of the summer," Delia said. "The question is, how do you want to spend it?"

"What does it matter," Gretta said bitterly, "if it's all going to end?"

"Everything ends eventually. But after all is said and done, it's what we do in the meantime that matters, isn't it?"

The conversation went on for a while more. But that was the gist of it.

Eventually, Gretta got out her cell and called Everett. She had him on speed dial, I noticed. In her most corporate voice, she said, "Get your ass over here," and snapped the phone shut without waiting for a response.

She didn't say another word until Everett's car pulled up in front of her place. Then she went out and confronted him. He put his hands on his hips. She grabbed him and kissed him. Then she took him by the hand and led him back into the house.

They didn't bother to turn on the lights.

I stared at the silent house for a little bit. Then I realized that Delia wasn't with me anymore, so I went looking for her.

She was out on the back porch. "Look," she whispered.

There was a full moon and by its light we could see the *Triceratops* settling down to sleep in our backyard. Delia had managed to lure them all the way in at last. Their skin was all silvery in the moonlight; you couldn't make out the patterns on their frills. The big trikes formed a kind of circle around the little ones. One by one, they closed their eyes and fell asleep.

Believe it or not, the big bull male snored.

It came to me then that we didn't have much time left. One morning soon we'd wake up and it would be the end of spring and everything would be exactly as it was before the dinosaurs came. "We never did get to Paris or London or Rome or Marrakech," I said sadly. "Or even Disneyworld."

Without taking her eyes off the sleeping trikes, Delia put an arm around my waist. "Why are you so fixated on going places?" she asked. "We had a nice time here, didn't we?"

"I just wanted to make you happy."

"Oh, you idiot. You did that decades ago."

So there we stood, in the late summer of our lives. Out of nowhere, we'd been given a vacation from our ordinary lives, and now it was almost over. A pessimist would have said that we were just waiting for oblivion. But Delia and I didn't see it that way. Life is strange. Sometimes it's hard, and other times it's painful enough to break your heart. But sometimes it's grotesque and beautiful. Sometimes it fills you with wonder, like a *Triceratops* sleeping in the moonlight.

THE MOST IMPORTANT THING IN THE WORLD

Steve Bein

Steve Bein is a philosopher, photographer, professor, translator, traveler, and award-winning author of genre-bending fiction. His short fiction has appeared in *Asimov's Science Fiction Magazine*, *Interzone*, *Writers of the Future*, and in international translation. His Fated Blades novels have met with critical acclaim. Bein divides his time between Rochester, Minnesota, and Rochester, New York. This story was first published in *Asimov's Science Fiction Magazine* in 2011.

Ernie Sisco knows what the most important thing in the world is. It took him a long time to figure it out, but he knows what it is now. He knows because somebody forgot it in the back of his cab.

Ernie's been driving cabs thirty-two years now, and in that time he's seen people leave all kinds of things behind. Crazy things, things he'd never have believed somebody could forget in a taxi. Wallets and purses are commonplace. So are asthma inhalers, epi-pens, medications the fare's literally going to die without. Once a fare actually left her baby in the back seat, a ten-month-old in one of those tan Graco baby carriers.

The kid was sleeping right behind Ernie's seat, right where he couldn't see her, and he'd gone on a good half a mile before he had to pull over to take a leak. Good thing for the fare, too.

When he drove back she was crying her eyes out on the street corner, too scared to tell anyone what she'd done.

Sometimes people will say their kids are the most important thing in the world, but Ernie doesn't think that's right. In any case the ten-month-old wasn't what helped him figure it out.

What sent him in the right direction was folded up in a silver Samsonite carry-on.

Ernie picks up the fare at Logan, a skinny white kid, the type that doesn't surprise a guy when they tell him to drive to Harvard. The kid's got two bags, matching hard cases the color that car companies call Lunar Mist or Ingot Silver Metallic.

Ernie puts the big one in the trunk. The kid insists on keeping the carry-on with him in the back seat. "Plenty of room," Ernie says, but the kid says whatever's in the case is too important to risk getting rear-ended. It's obvious the kid doesn't think much of Ernie's driving but Ernie shrugs it off and starts the meter running.

They get to the Yard and figure out where the kid's conference is going to meet. It's on theoretical physics or temporal physics or something like that. Ernie took physics in high school, but that was a million years ago and he was never any good at it anyway. He was never the math-science type; Ernie's more of a reader. Look under the driver's seat and you'll find yellowed copies of *For Whom the Bell Tolls* and *Zen and the Art of Motorcycle Maintenance*. Ernie doesn't know anything about motorcycles, Zen, or the Spanish Civil War; he's just got a thing for fiction that leans toward autobiography and lately he's been boning up on American authors.

A lot of Harvard types don't tend to think much of Ernie. They see a chunky bald guy behind the wheel of a cab and they make certain assumptions. But Ernie's no dope. He's got a cushy job where he can sit and read all day if he wants to.

Park it on the corner of Brattle and James and he can spend all afternoon reading without getting a call. Some might call it lazy – in fact, there's one in particular who calls it lazy every chance she gets – but Ernie can read the same great books as all the other Harvard types and he can do it without dropping any thirty or forty grand a year.

Ernie drops the kid off on Kirkland and sure enough the kid forgets the little Samsonite in the back. The campus has that effect on first-timers. It's beautiful, especially on a bright summer day: all green leaves and red brick and bright whitewashed windows. And there's the whole reputation thing too. Thinking about how they're going to impress all the muckety-mucks has a way of leaving people a little scatterbrained. Sometimes they ignore guys like Ernie completely, and then they go walking off toward the nearest red-brick building without leaving a tip and without remembering to check the back seat.

Ernie forgets all about it too, and doesn't hear the case clunking around back there until he's in the line at Fenway in the top of the ninth. There's big business at Fenway, a lot of fares, and they usually tip pretty well when the Sox win.

They're up six-nothing when Ernie pulls up, so he stows the kid's carry-on in the trunk and figures he'll drop it off the next time a fare takes him out that way.

One of the buckles comes undone when he drops the case in the trunk and curiosity gets the better of Ernie. He takes a peek.

Inside there's this funny-looking suit, a bit like a wetsuit but with copper wires running all over the outside. The neoprene smells strongly of neoprene. It's the same shade of blue the Royals wear, and with the hood and goggles it looks like something you'd wear if you wanted to get in a fistfight with Spiderman. On the chest there's a steel box with a little readout screen and what looks like a phone keypad.

That's as good a look as Ernie gets before the roar goes up in Fenway. It sounds like a third out pop fly. Ernie's back on. By the time he's done running Fenway fares he's hungry, and by the time he finishes a brat and a soft pretzel he's sick of working and so he heads home. It's not until he's a beer down and watching Sox highlights on ESPN that he remembers the funny-looking suit.

His first thought when he gets it laid out on his sofa is that he's going to have a hell of a hard time fitting into it. Thirty-some years sitting behind the wheel of a cab hasn't done much for his physique. But he's just got to try it on. Whatever it is, the kid said it was too important to risk damaging. He's careful with it, but he's got to know what it is.

The boots are too big and the arms are too long, and it's all Ernie can do to suck in his gut enough to get the front zipped. The stink of neoprene overpowers even the legions of cigarettes Ernie and Janine have smoked in this room. The stainless steel box hangs around his neck the way tourists hang their big black cameras, fixed to a sling of webbing, and on top of the box is that little readout screen. It's about impossible to read the numbers on it unless he's wearing the goggles, and as soon as he puts the goggles on he learns the big plastic rings around them house a bunch of ultra-bright LEDs. The goggles shift everything he sees toward the yellow-orange part of the spectrum, kind of like ski goggles, and the LEDs spotlight everything he looks at.

The readout screen on the chest unit is actually two screens. On the left you can set the date and time and the right side seems to work like a kitchen timer. The date and time are way off: six o'clock in the morning on March 13th, the year after next. Ernie sets it right, which for him means five minutes fast. Janine used to yell at him all the time for being late, and though he'll be the first to admit she didn't fix everything she says is wrong with him, at least he's never late anymore.

Next he looks at the kitchen timer. By now he's sweating his balls off even in the air conditioning, but he's damned if he's taking off this ridiculous suit before he figures out what it does. He sets the timer for two minutes and hits Start.

The world stops. The ESPN guy, in the midst of saying something about the Cubs, freezes on the "ah" of "Chicago" and just keeps saying "aaaaaah." There's a steady drone coming from the air conditioner, not the usual back and forth rattle but a constant monotone. The thin ribbon of smoke snaking up from Ernie's ashtray stops dead and just hangs there.

"Weird," Ernie's about to say, but saying this is weird is like saying Ted Williams could hit a little bit, so Ernie doesn't bother. Apart from him, the only things moving in the whole house are the numbers counting down on the kitchen timer.

Even the air feels like it's stuck in place. Ernie's got to suck it in like a milkshake through a straw. Standing up is hard and walking is like pushing through chest-deep water.

There's a compression left in the couch cushion where he was sitting a second ago, still squished down though there's no big cabbie ass to squish it. He wades over to the ashtray and touches the cigarette smoke with a gloved finger. It doesn't move under a light touch, but a little nudge frees it up somehow and the part he touched starts its slow crawl toward the ceiling. The rest just hangs there like a question mark made of white cotton candy.

He fiddles with other stuff for a minute or two.

Everything he tries to pick up feels like it's glued down, but he can budge it if he muscles it. The TV remote doesn't do anything, though; it's still just whatshisname saying "aaaaah" with a not-so-bright look on his face.

The kitchen holds the best surprises. That brat he picked up for dinner wasn't doing the trick, so before he turned on the TV and cracked open that beer he put a pot on for spaghetti.

When he gets to the kitchen, the flames under the pot look like they've been airbrushed there. They don't move a bit. The water looks like it's boiling and frozen at the same time, the bubbles stock-still, a big one half-popped on the surface and looking like a crater.

Then bam, the world starts moving again. Bubbles bubble. Flames flicker. The couch cushion springs up from the ass print he left on it. The ESPN guy finally finishes whatever he was going to say about the Cubs. Ernie looks down at the box on his chest and he sees the timer's at zero.

Ernie dumps some angel hair in the pot, then sits in front of the air conditioner and sweats, trying to figure out what the hell just happened. In the four and a half minutes it takes the angel hair to cook, he comes up with nothing. He goes back to the kitchen, grabs a black pasta spoon, and hooks a noodle to taste it. They're perfect. Then the world gets funny again.

One second he's holding the cheap plastic spoon over the pot. The next he's holding a hot drooping handle and there's spatters of black plastic all over the stovetop. The business end of the spoon is bumping around in the pot, half an inch of melted handle curling down from one side like a tail.

To beat that, his angel hair's gone from al dente to mush.

He finds that out after he drains it and fishes out what's left of his spoon. Right about then is when he sees the red light blinking on the answering machine. Ernie's old school. He has an answering machine, a big brown-and-black one, and despite the fact that there were no messages on it when he got home, now there is one and he never heard the phone ring.

He plays the message. It's Janine. She says she's coming over in a few minutes. According to the time stamp she left the message while he was standing five feet from the phone, watching his angel hair and his pasta spoon turn to garbage in something like a millionth of a second.

Then it hits him. She's coming over in a few minutes. He's dressed to go scuba diving with Buck Rogers.

He struggles out of the suit, which is no easier getting out of than in. He's in his boxers, shirtless and sweating like a dockworker, when he hears her key slide into the lock. He stuffs the blue suit behind the couch and gets turned back around just in time not to look suspicious. And desperate. He hopes.

She takes one look at him and says, "Jesus, Ernie."

Janine's the type of woman you can tell was beautiful once.

The tanning she did when they were in their twenties isn't so easy to wear anymore, but hot damn was she a looker back then.

Gravity hasn't been so kind to what used to draw long looks from every guy on the street, but back then every last one of them was wishing he was Ernie. She's not what she used to be, but to Ernie she's still Rita Hayworth.

He's not even sure he realized that himself, not even just the night before, when the yelling got bad and she slammed the door on her way out. Now, after the day he's been having, it feels damn good to have her in the house again.

"You're letting yourself go," she says.

"Just getting changed," he says. "Long day at work."

"If it was a long day at work," she says, "you'd still be out working. You knock off after the game again today?"

"Again with the game," he says, wishing he could take it back the second it leaves his mouth. "Look, they tip good over there," he says. "I don't have to work a full eight hours on game days."

"I'll worry about eight after you put in six," she says. "I just came for some clothes."

Ernie follows her to the bedroom and sweeps yesterday's jeans off the end of the unmade bed. "You want to stay for dinner?" he says.

She doesn't answer. She doesn't need to.

She rolls an armful of bras and underwear in a T-shirt and drapes another shirt and a pair of jeans on top. Ernie asks her if she's staying at her sister's again tonight. She says yes.

On her way back to the door, she says, "Christ, Ernie, did you steal something from a fare?"

"No," he says – maybe a second too soon. It's been a point of pride for him. You wouldn't believe how many cabbies figure a fare leaves something in the cab, that means they must not want it that bad. It's been a point of pride for Janine, too.

She always said he was better than those other guys.

She gives him a cold look and says, "Where's that suitcase from, then?"

The silver Samsonite's sitting right there on the couch.

He only has to look at it for a second before he answers. "It's for you," he says. "I figured maybe you'd need it to get your stuff."

Her eyes get colder. "Bull," she says. "You're telling me you're making it easier for me to get out of here?"

"No," he says. "I'm making it easier for you to come back."

It softens her for a second. She puts her stuff in the suitcase. He invites her again to stay for dinner. "You put in a full day's work and maybe I'll stay," she says. Then she walks out.

He stays up late thinking about things – about Janine, about the suit and the timer on it – and before he knows it it's nine in the morning and the snooze on his alarm clock's been yelling at him for over an hour. Some cabbies have to drive when the company tells them to, but Ernie owns his own car so he drives when he wants. That's part of the problem with Janine.

By the time he fell asleep, he'd managed to convince himself things weren't so bad. He didn't steal the suit from that kid. Right from the beginning he meant to give it back.

He just forgot. And things with Janine weren't as bad as they could've been. She was pissed, sure, but she still had her ring on. She never did get pissed off the way Ernie does. She stores everything up, lets it build, and it takes just as long for her to bleed the pressure off. Ernie, he's more the firecracker type. Short fuse, short burst, then back to peace and quiet.

But he figures she meant it when she said she'd stay for dinner. Too bad that's not going to happen anymore. It's too late to get a full day's worth of fares and be home by dinnertime. He missed the morning rush and the Sox are on the road. But before he nodded off he got himself an idea about the suit. He told himself he wasn't going to go through with it, but that was before he slept through the morning rush. Now the more he thinks about it, the more he figures there isn't another way. Before he tries it, though, he's got to try an experiment.

He sets up the suit exactly the same way he did the night before – two minutes on the timer, the clock set five minutes fast – only this time he doesn't put the suit on. He holds the suit up over his head and gives it a little upward toss the second he hits Start on the timer.

The suit's on the ground without falling there. He's looking at it overhead and then it's on his feet. He never sees it fall. He'd have said this is pretty weird, but the weirdest part is this is exactly what he thought would happen.

He's got five minutes to wait before the next part of the experiment, and during that time he learns five minutes is way too long to think about whether being near this suit is going to give him cancer or something. For all he knows, the suit's radioactive. For all he knows, he ought to be wearing a lead jock strap.

At the end of the five minutes, he pokes and prods at the suit with a big stubby toe. He can't move it. He kicks it.

Can't even ruffle the neoprene. A harder kick and all he does is hurt his foot.

Just for grins he pours a glass of water on the suit. The water looks like it slides off the suit without ever touching it. Not like rain on a waxed car, where it beads up on the wax; it's as if the suit's not wet because the water can't touch it at all. There's a dark spot in Ernie's orange shag carpeting and not a drop on the neoprene. For two minutes nothing he can do affects the suit.

By this time he figures he's got a pretty good idea of what this suit is and what it does. He can't even begin to imagine how it's possible, but at this point he can't afford to care.

This little jewel is the end of all his worries. Never mind a full day's pay; what he needs is for Janine to take him back, and with this thing he can get her back for good.

He stuffs the suit in an old duffel bag and heads downtown.

He doesn't turn his lights on, doesn't roll by the hospital or the Huntington Avenue hotels to see if there's a fare, doesn't even bother calling in to dispatch. Whatever he'd make from fares isn't squat compared to what the suit can do for him.

Ernie parks at the first Seven-Eleven he sees, grabs the duffel bag, and asks the old guy behind the counter if he can use the john. In the bathroom he changes into the suit, sets the clock one hour fast, and sets the timer for ten minutes.

Then he punches Start.

It's hard to breathe again and opening the door feels like he's pulling it through water. He finally manages to get it open, though, and outside the whole store's frozen. The second hand on the clock isn't moving. The little hot dog rollers don't roll. The hot dogs don't even blister under the heat lamps.

It feels like wading as he makes his way to the cash register. There's a little portable radio on behind the counter; he can't tell what it's playing because there's just the one note coming from it, like someone leaning on a car horn.

The old guy is staring at the chest of a busty eighteen-year-old buying *Cosmo* and cigarettes. Her eyes are fixed in mid-blink, her teeth at half-chew on her gum. Their hands are stone still above the counter, her change in mid-slide from his hand to hers. The till is open.

It's hard to pull up the black plastic drawer, and not just because it's stuck there like glue: Ernie doesn't know if bumping into the old guy will be like nudging the smoke, freeing him, so he's got to be careful not to touch him. It takes him about a minute to lift the drawer. One minute to make a solid day's worth of fares. It wouldn't be too hard to pick up the hundred dollar bills if he could use his fingernails, but they're gloved under an eighth of an inch of blue neoprene and so he needs to use the edge of a quarter to pry them up. He takes all three, and the fifty too, and leaves the checks.

He leaves the rest of the cash too. No point in bankrupting the place. Nor does he go after the white Coach purse hanging from the girl's shoulder. He's got nothing against her. Nothing against the old guy or Seven-Eleven either. It's just that he's got to get his wife back and this is the only way he can see to do it.

He heads to the bathroom, drags the door open, and grabs his duffel bag. The timer on his chest says he's got four more minutes. It takes him a little over a minute to open one of the cooler doors and pry a can of Dr. Pepper off the shelf. Another minute to wade over to the front door of the store. Half a second to realize that leaving now would mean that apart from the teenage girl and the old cashier, the only person the security camera's going to show is a chubby balding white guy who walked into the men's room and never came out. He wades back to the john, he locks himself in, and he waits.

When the timer hits zero, he unzips the suit and crams it back in the duffel. By the time he gets out of the bathroom, the girl's gone and the old man still doesn't have the slightest clue what happened. And why would he? He hasn't opened the drawer again yet.

The clock on the dash said it was eleven o'clock on the dot when he parked the cab in front of the store. When he starts her up again, it says eleven-oh-four. Still plenty of time.

On the way home he stops by a J.C. Penney and buys a small silver Samsonite just like the one he gave Janine the night before. He tucks the receipt in his wallet, and when he gets home he stows the carry-on with all the rest of the crap he's got piled up under the basement stairs. Then he waits.

Just before noon, he makes sure to be sitting right in front of his alarm clock. He waits for it to hit. He's sitting on the edge of the bed looking at the big red digits telling him it's 11:59. He blinks.

When his eyes open it's 12:10.

He didn't fall asleep. He knows he didn't. The time just passed, like a movie he didn't buy a ticket to. He hits the streets again with the suit in his duffel.

It turns out he got lucky at the Seven-Eleven. The next men's room he uses is at a gas station, and when he gets to the cash register the drawer's closed and nothing he can do can make it open. He figures he'll make the best of it so he goes outside and tries to fill up on gas. He can pull the nozzle loose and force it into the mouth of his gas tank, but squeezing the handle doesn't do a thing. It isn't like the Dr. Pepper, where prying loose the can pries loose everything inside it. The gas is separate from the nozzle, and it's all still frozen in that big reservoir under the pavement.

It's a senseless waste of ten free minutes. He tries again at a Dunkin Donuts with the same results. The next time he wises up and hits a really busy gas station. He figures the way to boost his odds is to find a place where the drawer's going to be open a lot.

The till's got five hundred and thirty bucks in it, counting just the big bills, twenties and up. He leaves the rest of the cash; these people have to eat too, and Ernie really isn't a bad guy. Taking out what he paid for the luggage, he's close to seven hundred for the day. Not bad. Not bad at all.

This time when he gets out of the john, the cashier's losing it. She knows the cash is gone but she doesn't know how.

Ernie practically has a heart attack when she threatens to lock the whole store and call the cops. Breathing is so hard while he's wearing the suit that he's already feeling like he ran the Boston Marathon. Having her freak out isn't any help. But Ernie's luck is still holding: there's a pair of young black men by the magazine rack in Charlestown High football jackets. Society is what it is, and that means nobody in this town is going to suspect a middle-aged, out-of-shape white guy of robbing a gas station when they've got two black guys right there in Bloods colors.

Ernie gets the hell out of there ASAP. Those boys aren't going to see jail time for this. There's no evidence against them. That's what Ernie tells himself, anyway, and he's almost certainly right. And, he tells himself, there's not much point in taking fares today, so he goes home and cracks open some James Ellroy and waits for the call from Janine.

She's not happy.

She doesn't even bother calling. She just comes over.

"Where you been?" she says. Not even a hello.

"I been working," says Ernie, and he shows her a fat wad of bills. "I had a great day."

He tells her a story about a couple of French businessmen he picked up at Logan, how they didn't really get the whole tipping thing and how even though he tried to talk them out of it they left him a hundred bucks each. "Bullshit," she says.

"Your dispatcher called me," she says, "trying to get a hold of you. They say some kid's been calling every ten minutes wondering if anyone's turned in a bag he left in his cab. Silver carry-on. Sound familiar?"

"Hey, yeah," says Ernie. "Kind of like the bag I bought you, huh?"

"Just like it," she says. "Don't you dare try to talk your way out of this."

He doesn't. He shows her the receipt from his wallet, with most of the date eaten up by a convenient Dr. Pepper stain.

"You're up to something," she says. "Your dispatcher said you hadn't logged in all day. Now you got two days' worth of tips. What's going on?"

"Nothing," he says. He's been making the airport run all day, he says, so what's the point of calling dispatch? Janine doesn't buy it. He tries to talk her into dinner. She's not buying that either.

"Come on," he says. "You said if I had the money, you'd stay."

"It's not about the money," she says. "It's about reliability. It's about me not having to pick up extra shifts at the last minute to make sure the bills get paid. Good night, Ernie."

"G'night." There's nothing else to say.

It takes him an hour to realize he's got nothing else going that night, and with all the stuff with Janine he knows he isn't getting to sleep any time soon. He heads out to the cab and calls in to take a couple of fares. Roberta at dispatch asks him where he's been all day. Ernie says thanks a lot and tells her to go screw herself.

One of his fares takes him within half a mile of Harvard Yard. He can't help thinking about that kid. He rolls down Mass Ave but the Yard's dark and empty, the way it usually is when school's out. Then he sees a dozen people walking past Memorial Church. Most of them look Indian or Chinese, but there's one tall skinny white guy straggling at the back. It's the kid who forgot the suit.

He slides into a parking space half a block down and leaves her running, his eye fixed on the rear view. Soon enough he catches sight of the Indians and Chinese and the skinny kid again. They turn down Dunster and Ernie figures he knows where they're headed. He turns off the car, feeds the meter and makes for the Brew House.

John Harvard's Brew House is just the sort of place you go if you're a tourist who just got done with a conference at Harvard. It's close, it's popular, and it's got that ambience the tourists go for. It is not, therefore, a good place to sit by yourself and drown your sorrows. By the time Ernie gets inside, the Indians and Chinese are talking loudly in the corner, boisterous and drinking like tourists. The skinny kid's by himself at the bar, hunched over a beer like he's whispering secrets to it.

He's the kind of skinny Ernie only ever sees in pictures of foreigners, East African refugees or the Jews in Auschwitz.

He's the kind of skinny that makes you stare. Ernie tries not to.

The kid finishes his beer and orders another. Ernie sits down two stools away and orders a Summer Blonde. They sit there a few minutes, quiet. The kid looks up at Ernie and his eyes are red around the edges. They have a kind of light to them.

Cruel, Ernie wants to call it. Cold. But as soon as he thinks he sees it, it's gone, and everything in the kid's face tells Ernie he doesn't recognize him at all. That's good.

Ernie asks him how he's doing. Fine, he says. "You don't look it," Ernie says. "Hope you don't mind me saying so, but you look more stressed out than I ever been in my life, and I been held up twice. Once at gunpoint, once at knifepoint. Even then I wasn't as stressed as you."

"Yeah," the kid says, "well, the last couple of days have been pretty rough." He knocks back the last half of his drink in one gulp.

Ernie orders him another. "Whatsa matter?" he says. "Lose your job or something?"

"You could say that," he says. "My job, my fellowship, my future. Maybe my wife. I don't know."

"Come on," says Ernie. "It can't be that bad. You're young and full of beans. You got your whole life ahead of you."

He gives Ernie a disdainful look. "Platitudes and beer?" he says. "That's what I need to solve all my problems? Maybe we'll do a cliché chaser after this."

"Hey, sorry," Ernie says. "Just trying to help. The point I was gonna make is, whatever's wrong, you got plenty of time to fix it. You're smart, you're young... how old are you anyway?"

"That depends on how you look at it," says the kid. Ernie gives him a funny look and the kid changes his answer right away. "Twenty-nine," he says.

"There you go," Ernie tells him. "Plenty of time."

"Mister," says the kid, "no offense, but I know a lot more about time than you ever will."

That's the hook Ernie needs. Years ago, it used to be that people talked to their cabbies. These days they're in the back on their iPods or cell phones or whatever, but for a good twenty years a big part of Ernie's job was making chitchat. He's still good enough at it that he can prod the kid in the right direction. Now that he's got him talking about time, he keeps him there.

At first Ernie's only pretending to be interested, but actually the kid's got some pretty neat stuff to say. Once Ernie gets him talking about his research at school, it's hard to shut the kid up long enough to order another round. The truth is, Ernie can't follow half of what the kid's telling him.

He's been meaning to put Hawking and Greene and Tyson on his reading list for years; now he's wishing he'd gotten around to it. His favorite used book store is right across the square and Ernie's half-wishing they were still open so he could run over there and do some digging.

But they're not, so he can't, and at any rate he needs to concentrate a hundred percent on what the kid's telling him. It turns out the kid is some kind of physics genius. Ernie never went to college – to him it always seemed like too much work for too little reward – but he knows enough to know you have to be some kind of genius to be finishing a double doctorate by twenty-nine.

Even if most of what the kid says is over his head, Ernie comes to understand they didn't start with a suit. The first experiments worked with lumps of some kind of radioactive material Ernie thinks he remembers hearing of once. Cesium, it's called. Ernie's pretty sure cesium's in the periodic table but he's not positive. The kid explained how you can use whatever these lumps give off to measure the passage of time – something about half-lifes and atomic clocks and a bunch of other stuff Ernie hasn't thought about since high school.

But Ernie understands the long and short of it well enough.

The bottom line is, the kid and his professor at school found a way to make these lumps spend some of their own future in the present.

"No way," Ernie tells him. "That's impossible."

"It's not," says the kid, and he buries Ernie under a lot more stuff there's no way he'd have been able to follow if he hadn't seen the suit do its thing. It all had to do with "four dimensional space-time" and thinking of time as cause and effect, and what is cause and effect except the transfer of energy? By the time Ernie's ass leaves the bar stool he'll have forgotten almost all of this, but he'll remember that question because the kid poses it to him about a hundred times.

Over the next hour Ernie wraps his lightly liquored brain around the idea that we've been storing energy and converting it and moving it around for a long time, and that if causality is a kind of energy then if you understand it right you can basically move cause and effect. Ernie tries to sum it up like this: "So what you're saying is, you're majoring in time travel."

"It's not time travel," says the kid. "It's more like borrowing time. Think of it as taking a link from a chain and inserting it earlier in the chain."

He finishes his beer and Ernie signals the girl behind the bar for another round. The kid's a lightweight drinking-wise, but Ernie has to admit he's pretty damn smart even this many beers down. Ernie's a couple behind him and he's only an inch away from just plain lost.

The kid says, "Never mind the chain," and he goes back to the radioactive lumps. Eventually he gets Ernie to see the big picture. You take two of these lumps, the exact same size, and you pop one of them in a machine that does what the suit does.

You set the machine to borrow an hour from one o'clock that afternoon. You turn the machine on and bam, lump one – the one in the machine – is smaller than lump two. Then, at one o'clock, all of a sudden lump one isn't radioactive anymore. It stays that way for an hour, not radioactive and not shrinking.

Then, by two o'clock, both lumps are radioactive again and both of 'em are back to the exact same size.

It's weird stuff. And Ted Williams could hit a little bit.

Ernie would have said the kid was full of crap if he hadn't been doing that very experiment all afternoon. "So what's the point?" he says. "Give a hammer and chisel and I figure I could make your lump smaller for you. I wouldn't need two hours and a college degree, neither."

"What's the point?" asks the kid, and he squints at Ernie like Ernie just asked him which one's worth more, a nickel or a hundred dollar bill. "We didn't limit the experiments to lumps of cesium," he says. "We built a bodysuit," he says, and he tells Ernie all about it.

Ernie gets it. He gets it just fine. The suit is free money. It's the ultimate blank check. According to the kid the college types invented it to see if something that borrowed time from its own future could pull other things into its timestream, but Ernie's got bigger fish to fry. And he's got bigger questions too, but he can't ask them flat out without tipping the kid off that he has the suit. So he sits. And he listens.

And he waits.

When the kid's done, Ernie says, "Sounds like you're living the dream, sport. You and your prof went and invented the ring of Gyges."

"What do you mean?" says the kid.

Ernie rolls his eyes, wondering what they're teaching kids in college these days. He says, "In the suit you can do whatever you want, right? And nobody can do anything about it, right? 'Cause you're the only time traveler? My friend, what you got is action without consequences. You got the ultimate get out of jail free card."

"It's not free," the kid says. "And the consequences are far too high."

Ernie's finally got him where he wants him. "What're the consequences?" he says. "What's the downside to this time traveling of yours?"

"It isn't time travel," says the kid. "And it isn't free. This is borrowing time. Take it from me: if you do it enough, you'll destroy your life."

Ernie's balls shrink up into his gut. He knew it. He just knew it. There had to be a downside. Cancer. Something. But he can't let any of that show on his face.

Instead he says, "What do you mean? You don't look dead to me."

"Not yet," the kid says, "but I'm living on borrowed time."

He laughs at himself and drains his beer. They've had four together so far. Ernie orders another round.

"My life isn't my own anymore," the kid tells him. "My daughter was born the day after I defended my second proposal. Seeta. My wife's family's Indian. Beautiful, beautiful girl."

He stops to take another drink. "I had a brand new baby," he says, "two dissertations to write, and only a year before my grant money ran out. Do you know what kind of pressure that is? No. Of course you don't. A year wasn't enough. I needed more time."

That look comes back in his eyes. "I put on the device," he says. "Every night, as soon as Lakshmi and Seeta were asleep, I set it for eight hours. At first I was planning to use the time to write, but my computer wouldn't work. I could dislodge the keys into my time-stream but not the electrons in the wires. So I wrote during the day and used my extra eight hours a night to read. I finished my thesis on Poincaré's special relativity in ten months flat. I'm halfway through the second one now."

"Let me get this straight," says Ernie. "You been doing this every night?"

"I've been living thirty-two hour days for over a year," the kid tells him.

"Jesus," says Ernie. "No wonder you look tired. How much you borrowed so far?"

"Eight hours a night for a year is just short of a hundred and twenty-two days," says the kid. He chuckles into his mug.

"I'd be in the hundred and fifty range by now if it weren't for the interest."

Ernie doesn't get it, and says so.

"It was a recent discovery," the kid says. "Six weeks ago we tried stopwatches instead of cesium samples, to make the results of the experiments more easily understandable to lay people. For funding, you see. It never even occurred to us that radioactivity would have anything to do with the time lending process."

Ernie gulps. Cancer. The suit's radioactive after all.

Then he figures out the kid's talking about the cesium. Even with that realization he still wants to grab his nuts to make sure they're still there.

"Borrow a minute from a stopwatch's future," the kid says, "and you get it back just over a minute fast. We haven't yet figured out why. My advisor thinks it has something to do with the mass – the cesium was always lighter when it paid back its time – but I think it's more to do with the radioactivity itself. At any rate, the discrepancy magnifies exponentially as you increase the time borrowed. Borrow an hour and it comes back almost sixty-six minutes fast."

"How about borrowing eight hours?" asks Ernie.

"Nine hundred and fifty-odd minutes," the kid says. "When it comes time, I'll pay back nearly sixteen hours for every eight I've borrowed." He finishes his drink and Ernie keeps 'em coming. "My driver's license says I'm twenty-nine," he says. "Chronologically, my body is approaching its thirty-first birthday."

Ernie's thinking, Cry me a river. Here he is, fifty-three and staring down the barrel of a divorce, and this kid's bitching about thirty-one.

But Ernie doesn't say any of that. He asks him where he's getting the time from.

"Next summer," says the kid, and just saying it makes him come damn close to puking.

"What's gonna happen to you?" says Ernie.

"I had it all planned," the kid says, and the words start tumbling out like they're tripping over each other to get out of his mouth. "It was going to happen in the summer," he says. "I was going to slip out of time. Secure a post-doc, find a little cabin in the woods, and just slip out. Now," he says, "now...," and all the rest is gibberish.

"Come on," Ernie tells him, "hold it together. What's gonna happen to you?"

"I'm going to slip out of time," says the kid. His eyes are rimmed with red; he's halfway ready to cry. Ernie can't stand seeing a grown man cry. "When it hits," the kid says, "when I get to the point I've been borrowing from, I'm just going to freeze. However I'm sitting right then, I'll just sit that way. From May 15th next year until the following March."

"What," Ernie says, "like being in a coma?"

The kid shakes his head. Getting him back to talking about the science seems to sober him up a bit. "I won't feel any time pass," he says. "For everyone else, I'll be like a statue. My heart won't beat. I won't breathe. If they try to resuscitate me, they'll fail. If my eyes are open, no one will understand why they don't dry out."

"Jesus," says Ernie. "You could wake up in a coffin."

The kid nods and says, "I've thought of that. I'll have to make it clear I want to be cremated."

Ernie coughs up a mouthful of beer. "What are you, nuts?" he says. "You want to wake up burnt to a crisp?"

"You forget," says the kid, "burning is a kind of change. Change can only take place over time, and I'll have spent that time by then. When you're borrowing time, dislodging something from its own time-stream into yours is difficult but it's possible. Once you've borrowed the time, though, you've spent it; if you were to experience change then, that would be real time travel."

"So nothing bad can happen to you," says Ernie.

The kid gives him that sullen, cold-eyed stare again.

"Suppose the first one to find me is my daughter," he says. "She'll be almost two years old. Her father will be worse than comatose. He'll be a zombie. A vampire."

"Nah," says Ernie. "You'll explain it to her. Your wife'll explain it. You got a year yet, right?"

"Then suppose I'm not at home," he says. "What if when it happens I'm someplace where nobody knows me? Or what if I'm driving? If I'm in traffic when it hits me, I could kill someone."

"Nah," Ernie says again. "You're a smart kid. You won't let that happen. I bet you already got a backup plan."

"You want to hear my plan?" says the kid. He makes a face like he's gonna puke again. He says, "The big plan was to lock up a post-doc my advisor says I'm in the running for. He says our experiments make me a shoo-in. I secure the fellowship for next year's fall semester. I take a summer vacation 'to write'" – he gives Ernie the air quotes – "and find myself a cabin in the woods somewhere. I slip out of time for the summer, come back mid-October, and throw something together to satisfy the post-doc people in between mailing out résumés and applying for jobs."

Ernie shrugs. It sounds like a good plan.

"Don't you get it?" says the kid. "That was when I thought I'd be out for five months. With the discrepancy, do you know how much time I've got to pay back?"

"I'm guessing it's not five months," says Ernie.

The kid's voice gets sharp and cold. "If I stop borrowing today," he says, "I'm looking at three hundred and one days, fourteen hours, fifty-two minutes." The numbers roll off his tongue as easily as his Social Security number. Ernie wonders how long he's spent dwelling on this. "By the time I come back," the kid says, "the best jobs will be gone. My fellowship deadline will be blown and I'll have nothing to give them. Nothing. I'll miss Christmas with Seeta. At her age she's not even going to remember who I am. Her dad's going to disappear on her for almost a year with nothing to show for it. Christ, what am I going to do?"

He's practically crying now and it makes Ernie squirm in his seat. "Kid," he tells him, "believe me when I tell you this: if that's the worst this suit can do to you, you're no different from the rest of us. Here I been thinking you're gonna tell me the suit'll give you a heart attack. Seriously, kid, nothing bad can happen to you while you're slipped out of time? No cancer or nothing?"

"I'll answer that," he says, "just as soon as you give back the device."

Ernie chokes on his beer and sputters. Then he puts on the most innocent face he can and asks him what he's talking about.

All the kid's emotion has drained out onto the floor.

"Face it," he says, "cab drivers don't usually go out to bars to discuss temporal physics."

Wicked smart, this kid. Ernie's looking at his shirt, his jacket, his hands, wondering what the kid saw that gave him away. He can't figure it out so he asks, "How'd you know I was a cabbie?"

"You drove me from the airport," says the kid.

Ernie says he thought the kid didn't recognize him. "I know," says the kid. "That's what you were supposed to think. Now, do you have the device with you, or are we going back to your place?"

As the kid gets in the back seat, Ernie says, "So seriously, there's got to be risks. Doesn't there? To using the suit?"

"As if living on borrowed time isn't bad enough," says the kid. "As if lying to my wife every night for the last year isn't bad enough."

They pull out into light after-bar traffic. Ernie's feeling a touch of fuzziness on the backs of his eyes. He's in no shape to drive and he knows it, but the kid threatened to call the cops if Ernie didn't take him straight to the suit.

"Come on," he says. "Look at you. They invited you to bring your suit all the way to Harvard. That's why you're here, isn't it? If it weren't for that suit, you and I never would've met because you wouldn't have your conference to go to."

A guffaw from the kid cuts Ernie off. "Are you kidding?" he says. "I'm just here because my advisor's here. He said he'd introduce me to – no, no, 'the suit' – hell, I was never even supposed to take it out of the lab. Do you have any idea how completely fucked I am if I don't get it back?"

"Hey, take it easy," Ernie says. The booze is taking over now, jumbling the kid's words, getting him all excitable, and Ernie doesn't want to wait and find out if he's a violent drunk.

"My point is, you're getting away with it, aren't you? You caught me, kid. I'm taking you back to the suit. How can you say this thing destroyed your life?"

"You ought to know," he says. "You've been wearing it."

Ernie thinks about lying but he can't see the point.

"Yeah," he says. "It's harder to move. Harder to breathe. Money feels like it's glued down. I got to tell you, though, if that's all there is, it isn't much of a downside."

"Isn't it?" The kid's giving him that dead-eyed stare in the rearview. "In my book selling out all your values isn't such a small price to pay. Or is it your own glued-down money you've been stealing? You have been stealing, haven't you?"

Ernie feels his cheeks flush. Better than those other guys. That's what Janine always said. I guess she was wrong, Ernie thinks. I guess we were both wrong.

That doesn't sit well with Ernie, so he does what he always does when it comes to stuff like this: he talks himself out of it. "So what?" he says. "You said it yourself: I took myself out of the loop of cause and effect. Even if it's only for ten minutes, for ten minutes there's no consequences."

"What else have you done?" says the kid. "Do you find yourself lying more often? Breaking the rules in general? Even when you're not wearing the device?"

"Hey," Ernie says, "don't get all high and mighty on me. You're just a kid. What do you know?"

"I know I never meant to lie to my wife," he says. "I know the human body needs a little something extra to make it through thirty-two hour days. I know...."

Ernie can hear it in his voice: the kid wants to stop himself, but the booze went and loosened his tongue and now he can't stop talking. He says, "I know the first time I fell asleep wearing the device I told myself I'd never make such a waste of it again. I've been taking ephedrine every night ever since, and to be honest I'm not sure I can stop. I'm on sleeping pills to counteract the epinephrine and I'm not sure I can quit on those either."

The kid starts crying. "And what's the point?" he says.

Ernie really cannot stand seeing a grown man cry. Maybe it's a generational thing. Maybe it's old-fashioned machismo.

Whatever it is, there's not enough beer in the world to make Ernie cry in front of a man he hardly knows. His eyes dodge the rearview like they might see his sister in it naked.

"All that to finish in a year," the kid says. "I've become a drug addict so I can look better on paper. So I can land a job where I'll always have to wonder if the reason I got hired was because I had an unfair advantage. You had it all wrong," he says, sobbing. "You never escape cause and effect. You just draw your cards from the deck in the wrong order."

Habit makes Ernie glance up at the mirror. Big mistake.

"Jesus H.," he says. "Why're you telling me all this, kid?"

"So you'll give it back to me," the kid says, his voice quivering. His whole face is red and wet; his eyes are bloodshot. "So I won't have to call the cops," he says. "So I can get the device back without having to admit I lost it. So I can go back to screwing up my life, I guess."

He starts crying again.

"Jesus," says Ernie.

They get to Ernie's place. "That'll be fifty-eight fifty," he says. The kid looks up at Ernie and laughs. At least he can take a joke.

Ernie asks him what his name is. "Ernest," the kid says.

"You gotta be kidding," Ernie says with a laugh. "That's my name! My folks named me after Hemingway."

"Mine too," says Ernest. His voice is real quiet. "They wanted me to go into literature."

"Hell," says Ernie, "I don't know what they wanted for me, but it sure as hell wasn't driving cabs. Wait here."

He goes inside, gets the Samsonite carry-on from the basement and crams the suit in it. It's not a hard decision.

It might have been if they'd started their conversation on Ernie's front porch, but they were driving all the way from Cambridge and Ernie had plenty of time to think. Plenty of places to turn off, places he could've dropped the kid and kept driving. This time of night, the wrong neighborhood, maybe skinny little Ernest never comes back.

Maybe. Or maybe Ernie just drives him someplace secluded, lets him out, breaks both his knees with the front bumper. Pick a dark place and turn the lights off and no one could get a good look at his plates. He could've made skinny little Ernest a speed bump, even backed over him to make sure, and the only description the cops would've had is "a taxi cab."

Ernie could have done it but he didn't. He can't exactly explain why, either. Maybe it's because he wasn't sure he could have gotten away with it. Maybe it's because he got away with everything so far and he didn't want to push his luck. Or maybe getting away with it isn't as easy as it sounds. Ernie's not sure. He just knows this one wasn't the hard decision.

Ernie gets behind the wheel, passes the case back to Ernest, and pulls a U-turn to take the kid back to the Yard.

"This isn't my suitcase," says Ernest.

"Yeah, well, the suit's in it," says Ernie. "Don't get picky on me."

"No," the kid says. "You don't understand." Ernie can hear him futzing with zippers. "There was a journal," he says. "It had a log of the time I've borrowed. I need it back or I won't know where to start borrowing from again."

Maybe you ought to lay off the borrowing, Ernie wants to say. Maybe it'll help you quit the pills. But Ernie figures it's not for him to get all high and mighty on this kid. "My wife's got it," he says.

"I need it back," says Ernest.

Ernie looks at him through the mirror. "Kid," he says, "you don't know what you're asking."

All the kid says is, "I need it back."

Ernie pulls up in front of Janine's sister's place and the living-room drapes are thin enough that he can see they've still got the kitchen lights on. He sighs and says, "Give me the damn suitcase."

He rings the doorbell and her sister peeks out between the drapes. Janine comes down after a minute. Ernie takes a deep breath. "I need to tell you something," he says, "and I'm gonna tell it to you straight."

It's a month later when Ernie gets a call. It's seven PM and Ernie's been driving since seven that morning. That's become a regular thing for him. He knocks off for half an hour once or twice to grab a bite and read, but otherwise he's running Logan and Brigham and Massachusetts General like clockwork. He does it for Janine, he says, but when he takes the time to think about it he knows it's more than just that.

He's got another regular thing going these days: he tends to take lunch at a particular Seven-Eleven. The old guy behind the counter there probably thinks Ernie's a scatterbrain, what with him always forgetting his change on the counter when he leaves. Ernie would do the same at a particular gas station too, only the girl they used to have got fired. It wasn't even over Ernie robbing the place. The poor kid was too honest to keep the change he kept leaving on the counter, and her boss canned her for being over whenever she closed out her register.

Ernie talked Roberta at dispatch into getting her a job but the kid hasn't taken to it. Ernie'll tell you it just goes to show how hard it is to do right by somebody after you did them wrong.

He's at home on the sofa reading Sherman Alexie when the phone rings. It's Ernest; he recognizes the voice right away.

He doesn't know how the kid got his number, but then the kid is wicked smart. "I just wanted to thank you," he says.

"For what?" says Ernie.

"Returning the device," says Ernest. "And the suitcase and the journal."

Ernie laughs. He ended up driving that kid all the way back to the Yard for free that night, but does he get thanks for that? "You don't have to thank a guy for returning what he stole from you," he says.

"Yeah, well, thanks anyway."

"How you doing with those pills?" says Ernie.

"How are you doing with that wife?" says Ernest.

Ernie laughs again, but for once he's pretty happy on that front. Janine spent the night. They both had a few drinks in them the night before and in the morning Janine said it was probably a mistake, but Ernie liked the sound of the word probably. She let him give her a kiss on his way out the door, and that's not bad.

The night he came to get the kid's carry-on he told her the whole shebang. She didn't believe him. Called him a lying sack of shit, actually, but he was surprised to learn he really didn't care whether she believed him or not. The big thing was that he told her the truth. It was the hardest decision he'd made in a long time. He still can't say it felt good, but it felt right.

That's not much comfort, by the way, and he'll be the first to say so. He'll say, You know that satisfaction people talk about? The one you get from doing the right thing? Well, that and a buck'll get you a cup of coffee.

On the phone he says, "Let me tell you this, kid: it's not easy to make things right with someone when she don't believe you. It's even harder when the true story is the most cockamamie thing you ever heard of. So thanks for inventing that suit, huh? And for leaving it in my cab. You damn Harvard types."

Now the kid laughs. He says, "You're the one who put it on. I suppose you're going to blame me for that too?"

A memory comes back to Ernie: the image of a skinny drunk in his back seat on the drive back to the Yard, folding that suit over and over in his hands. He looked like he was thinking pretty hard about it. Ernie doesn't know the kid well or anything, but for some reason he's got hope for him.

"Hey, you're not going to believe what happened to me today," Ernie says. "I'm dropping off a couple of Frenchmen at their hotel and they don't understand tipping. Fifty bucks they left me. I tell you what, me and Janine are eating steak tonight."

"That's great, Ernie."

The kid's tone is flat and Ernie knows their conversation is over. "Listen," he says, "you take care of your girls, kid. Keep 'em close."

"You too, Ernie," says the kid, his tone still flat, and Ernie's not sure he'll ever hear from him again.

But if it's the last thing the kid ever told him, at least it was good advice. Ernie's going to keep Janine as close as he can. He's already decided he's taking her to Davio's tonight if she's up for it. If not, the next night, maybe. He figures it'll all work itself out. They've got time.

HIMSELF IN ANACHRON

Cordwainer Smith

Cordwainer Smith was the pseudonym of American writer Paul M.A.
Linebarger. As a child, he traveled and lived overseas in Europe and
also the Far East with his family and was fluent in several languages.
His first professional science fiction story, "Scanners Live in Vain,"
was published in *Fantasy Book* in 1950; however, it wasn't until the
mid-1950s that he was encouraged to write more. Most of his science
fiction was written between 1955 and 1966. In addition to his many
short stories, he also wrote one science fiction novel, *Norstrilia*, and
three mainstream novels, *Ria*, *Corola*, and *Atomsk*. This story was
published posthumously in his definitive collection, *The Rediscovery
of Man*, in 2003.

And Time there is
And Time there was
And Time goes on, before –
But what is the Knot
That binds the time
That holds it here, and more –
Oh, the Knot in Time
Is a secret place
They sought in times of yore –
Somewhere in Space
They seek it still
But Tasco hunts no more . . .
HE FOUND IT
　　from "Mad Dita's Song"

First they threw out every bit of machinery which was not vital to their
lives or the function of the ship. Then went Dita's treasured honeymoon
items (foolishly and typically she had valued these over the instruments).
Next they ejected every bit of nutrient except the minimum for survival for two
persons. Tasco knew then. It was not enough. The ship still had to be lightened.

*He remembered that the Subchief had said, bitterly enough: "So you got leave
to time-travel together! You fool! I don't know whether it was your idea or
hers to have a 'honeymoon in time,' but with everyone watching your marriage
you've got the sentimental mob behind you. 'Honeymoon in time,' indeed. Why?
Is it that your woman is jealous of your time trips? Don't be an idiot, Tasco.*

You know that ship's not built for two. You don't even have to go at all; we can send Vomact. He's single." Tasco remembered, too, the quick warmth of his jealousy at the mention of Vomact. *If anything had been needed to steel his determination, that name had done it. How could he possibly have backed out after the publicity over his proposed flight to find the Knot. The Subchief must have realized from the expression on his face something of his feelings; he had said with a knowledgeable grin: "Well, if anybody can find the Knot, it'll be you. But listen, leave her here. Take her later if you like but go first alone."* But Tasco could remember, too, Dita's kitten-soft body as she nestled up to him holding his eyes with her own and murmuring, *"But, darling, you promised . . ."*

Yes, he had been warned, but that didn't make the tragedy any easier. Yes, he could have left her behind, but what kind of marriage would they have had with the blot of her bitterness on the first days of their married life? And how could he have lived with himself if he had let Vomact go in his place? How, even, would Dita have regarded him? He could not deceive himself; he knew that Dita loved him, loved him dearly, but he had been a hero ever since she had known him and how much would she have loved him without the hero image? He loved her enough not to want to find out.

And now, one of them must go, be lost in space and time forever. Tasco looked at her, his beloved. He thought, *I have loved you forever, but in our case forever was only three earth days. Shall I love you there in space and timelessness?* To postpone, if only for minutes, the eternal parting, he pretended to find some other instrument which could be disposed of, and sent through the hatch one person's share of the remaining nutrient. Now the decision was made. Dita came over to stand beside him.

"Does that do it, Tasco? Is the ship light enough now for us to get out of the Knot? Instead of answering he held her tightly against him. *I've done what I had to,* he thought . . . *Dita, Dita, not to hold you ever again . . .*

Softly, not to disturb the moon-pale curve of her hair, he passed his hand over her head. Then he released her.

"Get ready to take over, Dita. I could not murder you, oh my darling, and unless the ship is lightened by the weight of one of us we will both die here in the Knot. You must take it back, you have to take back the ship and all the instrument-gathered data. It's not you or me or us now. We're the servants of the Instrumentality. You must understand . . ."

Still within his arms, she backed away enough to look at his face. She was dewy-eyed, loving, frightened, her lips trembling with affection. She was adorable, and Cranch! how incompetent. But she'd make it; she had to. She said nothing at first, trying to hold her lips steady, and then she said the thing that would annoy him most. "Don't, darling, don't. I couldn't stand it . . . Please don't leave me."

His reaction was completely spontaneous: His open hand caught her across the cheek, hard. A reciprocal anger flashed across her eyes and mouth, but she gained control of herself. She returned to pleading.

"Tasco, Tasco, don't be bad to me. If we have to die together, I can face it. Don't leave me, please don't leave me. I don't blame you . . ." *I don't blame you!* he thought. *By the Forgotten One, that's really rather good!*

He said, as quietly as he could, "I've told you. Somebody has got to take this ship back to our own time and place. We've found the Knot. This is the Knot in Time. Look."

He pointed. The Merochron swung slightly back and forth, from +1,000,000:1 to –500,000:1. "Look hard – twenty-years-a-minute-plus to ten-years-a-minute-minus. The ship has a chance of getting out if the load is lightened. We've thrown everything else we could out. Now I'm going. I love you; you love me. It will be as hard for me to leave you as for you to see me go. A lifetime with you would not have been enough. But, Dita, you owe me this . . . to take the ship back safely. Don't make it harder for me. If you can hold it on Left Subformal Probability, do it. If not, keep on trying to slow down in backtime."

"But, darling . . ."

He wanted to be tender. Words caught in his throat. But *their* time had run out. Their honeymoon had been a gamble, their own gamble, and now it and their life together were over. Three earth days! The Instrumentality remained; the Chiefs and Lords waited; a million lives would be a cheap price for a fix on the Knot in Time. Dita could do it. Even she could do it if the ship were lighter by a man.

His farewell kiss was not one she would remember. He was in a hurry now to finish it; the sooner he left, the better her chances were of getting back. And still she looked at him as if she expected him to stay and talk. Something in her eyes made him suspicious that she would try to hinder him. He cut in his helmet speaker and said:

"Goodbye. I love you. I have to go now, quickly. Please do as I ask and don't get in my way."

She was weeping now. "Tasco, you're going to die . . ."

"Maybe," he said.

She reached for him, tried to hold him. "Darling, don't. Don't go. Don't hurry so."

Roughly he pushed her back into the control seat. He tried to hold his anger that she would not let him do even this right, to die for her. She would make it a scene. "Sweetheart," he said, "don't make me say it all over again. Anyhow, I may not die. I'll aim for a planet full of nymphs and I'll live a thousand years."

He had half expected to stir her to jealousy or anger . . . at least some other emotion, but she disregarded his poor joke and went on quietly weeping. A wisp of smoke rising in the hot moving air of the cabin made them look to the control panel. The Probability Selector was glowing. Tasco kept his face immobile, glad that she did not realize the significance of the reading. *Now no one will ever find me, even if I live,* he thought. *But go, go, go!*

He smiled at her through his shimmering suit. He touched her arm with his metal claw. Then, before she could stop him he backed into the escape hatch, slammed the door on himself, fumbled for the ejector gun, pressed the button. Pressed it hard.

Thunder, and a wash like water. There went his world, his wife, his time, himself . . . He floated free in anachron. Others had gone astray between the Probabilities; none had come back. They had borne it, he supposed. If they could, he could too. And then it caught him. The others, had they left wives and sweethearts? Was it for them too a personal tragedy? *Himself and Dita, they had not had to come. Vanity, pride, jealousy, stubbornness. They had come. And now: himself in anachron.*

He felt himself leaping from Probability to Probability like a pebble bouncing down a corrugated plastic roof. He couldn't even tell whether he was going toward Formal or Resolved. Perhaps he was still somewhere in Left Subformal.

The clatter ceased. He waited for more blows.

One more came. Only one, and sharp.

He felt tension go out of him. He felt the Probabilities firming around him, listened to the selector working in his helmet as it coded him into a time-space combination fit for human life. The thing had a murmur in it which he had never heard in a practice jump, but then, this wasn't practice. He had never before gotten out between the Probabilities, never floated free in anachron.

A feeling of weight and direction made him realize that he was coming back to common space. His feet were touching ground. He stood still, attempting to relax while a world took shape around him. There was something very strange about the whole business. The grey color of the space around him resembled the grey of fast backtiming, the blind blur which he had so often seen from the cabin window when, having chosen a Probability, he had coursed it down until the Selectors had given him an opening he could land in. *But how could he be backtiming with no ship, no power?*

Unless—

Unless the Knot in Time in flinging him out had imparted to him a time-momentum in his own body. But even if that were so he should decelerate. Was he coming down in ratio? This still felt like hightiming, 10,000:1 or higher.

He tried briefly to think of Dita but his personal situation outweighed everything else. A new worry hit him. What was his own personal consumption of time? With time so high outside his unit was it also rising inside? How long would his nutrients last? He tried to be aware of his own body, to feel hunger, to catch a glimpse of himself. Was the automatic nutrition keeping up with the changing time? On inspiration, he rubbed his face against the mask to see if his whiskers had grown since he left the ship.

He had a beard. Plenty.

Before he could figure that one out, there was one last *Snap!* and he fainted.

When he recovered, he was still erect. Some kind of frame supported him. Who had put it there, and how? By the continued greyness he could tell that his physiological time and external time had not yet met. He felt a violent impatience. There should be some way to slow down. His helmet felt heavy. Disregarding the risks, he clawed at the mask until it came off.

The air was sweet but thick, thick. He had to fight to breathe it in. It was hardly worth the struggle.

He was still hightiming, more so than he had thought anybody could with an exposed body. He looked down and saw his beard tremble as it grew. He felt the stab of fingernails growing against his palms; there should have been an automatic cut-off but time was going too fast. Clenching his hand, he broke off the nails roughly. His boots had apparently broken off his toenails, and although his feet were uncomfortable the pressure was bearable. Anyway there was nothing he could do about it.

His immense tiredness warned him that the automatic nutrient system was not keeping up with his bodily time. With effort he fitted his claw to his belt and twisted until the supplementary food vial was released. He felt the needle pierce the skin of his belly; he twisted again until the hot surge of nourishment told him that the food-injector had reached a vein. Almost immediately his strength began to rise.

He watched the blur of buildings flashing into instantaneous shape around him, standing a moment, and then melting slowly away. Now he could see a little more of his surroundings. He seemed to be standing in the mouth of a cave or in a great doorway. It was curious, that, about the buildings. All the other buildings he had seen in time had worked the other way. First the slow upthrust as they were built, then the greying evenness of age, then the flash of removal. But, he reminded himself tiredly, he was backtiming and he thought it probable that no other human being had ever backtimed so hard and fast or for so long a time.

He seemed now to be rapidly decelerating. A building appeared around him, then he was outside of it, then back in again. Suddenly a great light shone in front of him.

Now he was inside a large palace. He seemed to be placed on a pedestal, high up at the center of things. Shimmering masses began to take form around him at rhythmic intervals: people? There was something wrong about the way they moved; why did they move with that strange awkwardness?

As the light persisted and this building seemed solid, he made an effort to squint to try to see more. His eyeballs were the only part of his anatomy that seemed to move freely. His breaking growing breaking fingernails and toenails and the growing beard reminded him to break off another food needle in his vein. His skin itched intolerably. As he realized the increasing immobility of his arms he felt panic and while there was still time pushed the continuous-flow button on the supplementary nutrients. Despite the food, enough to keep him alive in the cold of space, he could no longer move his hands and fingers. And still, it seemed only minutes since he had left the ship. (*Dita, Dita, are you out of the Knot? Did you manage it in time? If only I calculated the weight load right . . .*)

The building continued stable around him. He rolled his eyes to try to see where he was, when he was.

I'm still alive, he thought. *Nobody else ever got out of anachron. That's something. Nobody else ever stepped out of time to be seen again.*

Deceleration continued. The bright light before him remained even and he found he could see better. In front of him was a sort of picture, high and large. What was it? Panels, a series of panels, paintings from some remote past.

He peered harder and recognized that the panel at the top left was himself, Tasco Magnon. There he was: shimmering space suit, marble armrests, pedestal below him. But they had given him wings like the wings of angels of the Old Strong Religion. Great white wings. And they had put a halo around his head. The next panel showed him as he felt: suit shimmering but his face old and tired.

The panels on the lower level were equally curious. The first showed a bed of grass or moss with luminescence glowing above it. The second showed a skeleton standing in a frame.

His tired mind sought to make sense of the panels.

People became plainer in the blur around him. Sometimes he could almost see individuals. The colors of the paintings brightened, brightened, until they flashed gay and bold, then disappeared.

Disappeared completely, flatly.

His brain, so old and tired now, struggled with immense effort to reach the truth. Physiological time was utterly deranged. Each minute seemed years. His thoughts became old memories while he thought them. But the truth came through to him:

He was still backtiming.

He had passed the time of his arrival and resurrection in this world. The resurrection was wisely prophesied by the beings who built the palace, painted the wings and halo around him.

He would die soon, in the remote past of this civilization.

Long afterwards, centuries before his own death, his alien remains would fade into the system of this time-space locus; and in fading, they would seem to glow and to assemble. They must have been untouchable and beyond manipulation. The people who had built the palace and their forefathers had watched dust turn to skeleton, skeleton heave upright, skeleton become mummy, mummy become corpse, corpse become old man, old man become young – himself as he had left the spaceship. He had landed in his own tomb, his own temple.

He had yet to fulfil the things which these people had seen him do, and had recorded in the panels of his temple.

Across his fatigue he felt a thrill of weary remote pride: he knew that he was sure to fulfil the godhood which these people had so faithfully recorded. He knew he would become young and glorious, only to disappear. He'd done it, a few minutes or millennia ago.

The clash of time within his body tore at him with peculiar pain. The food needle seemed to have no further effect. His vitals felt dry.

The building glowed as it seemed to come nearer.

The ages thrust against him. He thought, "I am Tasco Magnon and have been a god. I will become one again."

But his last conscious thought was nothing grandiose. A glimpse of moon-pale hair, a half-turned cheek. In the aching lost silence of his own mind he called,

Dita! Dita!

The twisted timeship took form at the Dateport of the Instrumentality. Officials and engineers rushed up, opened the door. The young woman who sat at the controls staring blindly was white-faced beyond all weeping. They tried to rouse her from her trance-like state but she clung desperately to the controls, repeating like a chant:

"He jumped out. Tasco jumped out. He jumped out. Alone, alone in anachron . . ."

Gravely and gently, the officials lifted her from the controls so that they could remove the now-priceless instruments.

THE TIME MACHINE

H.G. Wells

H.G. Wells was an English writer best known for his science fiction books. "The Chronic Argonauts" is considered the short story that served as the initial inspiration for Wells's classic novella *The Time Machine*, which is excerpted here. Although it is popularly believed that "The Chronic Argonauts" was the first fiction published with a time-travel theme, another story, also in this anthology, predates it by almost a decade: Edward Page Mitchell's "The Clock That Went Backward." In addition to *The Time Machine*, Wells's other famous and popular books include *The War of the Worlds*, *The Invisible Man,* and *The Island of Doctor Moreau*. *The Time Machine* was first published in 1895.

'I told some of you last Thursday of the principles of the Time Machine, and showed you the actual thing itself, incomplete in the workshop. There it is now, a little travel-worn, truly; and one of the ivory bars is cracked, and a brass rail bent; but the rest of it's sound enough. I expected to finish it on Friday, but on Friday, when the putting together was nearly done, I found that one of the nickel bars was exactly one inch too short, and this I had to get remade; so that the thing was not complete until this morning. It was at ten o'clock to-day that the first of all Time Machines began its career. I gave it a last tap, tried all the screws again, put one more drop of oil on the quartz rod, and sat myself in the saddle. I suppose a suicide who holds a pistol to his skull feels much the same wonder at what will come next as I felt then. I took the starting lever in one hand and the stopping one in the other, pressed the first, and almost immediately the second. I seemed to reel; I felt a nightmare sensation of falling; and, looking round, I saw the laboratory exactly as before. Had anything happened? For a moment I suspected that my intellect had tricked me. Then I noted the clock. A moment before, as it seemed, it had stood at a minute or so past ten; now it was nearly half-past three!

'I drew a breath, set my teeth, gripped the starting lever with both hands, and went off with a thud. The laboratory got hazy and went dark. Mrs. Watchett came in and walked, apparently without seeing me, towards the garden door. I suppose it took her a minute or so to traverse the place, but to me she seemed to shoot across the room like a rocket. I pressed the lever over to its extreme position. The night came like the turning out of a lamp, and in another moment came to-morrow. The laboratory grew faint and hazy, then fainter and ever fainter. To-morrow night came black, then day again, night again, day again, faster and faster still. An eddying murmur filled my ears, and a strange, dumb confusedness descended on my mind.

'I am afraid I cannot convey the peculiar sensations of time travelling. They are excessively unpleasant. There is a feeling exactly like that one has upon a switchback – of a helpless headlong motion! I felt the same horrible anticipation, too, of an imminent smash. As I put on pace, night followed day like the flapping of a black wing. The dim suggestion of the laboratory seemed presently to fall away from me, and I saw the sun hopping swiftly across the sky, leaping it every minute, and every minute marking a day. I supposed the laboratory had been destroyed and I had come into the open air. I had a dim impression of scaffolding, but I was already going too fast to be conscious of any moving things. The slowest snail that ever crawled dashed by too fast for me. The twinkling succession of darkness and light was excessively painful to the eye. Then, in the intermittent darknesses, I saw the moon spinning swiftly through her quarters from new to full, and had a faint glimpse of the circling stars. Presently, as I went on, still gaining velocity, the palpitation of night and day merged into one continuous greyness; the sky took on a wonderful deepness of blue, a splendid luminous color like that of early twilight; the jerking sun became a streak of fire, a brilliant arch, in space; the moon a fainter fluctuating band; and I could see nothing of the stars, save now and then a brighter circle flickering in the blue.

'The landscape was misty and vague. I was still on the hill-side upon which this house now stands, and the shoulder rose above me grey and dim. I saw trees growing and changing like puffs of vapour, now brown, now green; they grew, spread, shivered, and passed away. I saw huge buildings rise up faint and fair, and pass like dreams. The whole surface of the earth seemed changed–melting and flowing under my eyes. The little hands upon the dials that registered my speed raced round faster and faster. Presently I noted that the sun belt swayed up and down, from solstice to solstice, in a minute or less, and that consequently my pace was over a year a minute; and minute by minute the white snow flashed across the world, and vanished, and was followed by the bright, brief green of spring.

'The unpleasant sensations of the start were less poignant now. They merged at last into a kind of hysterical exhilaration. I remarked indeed a clumsy swaying of the machine, for which I was unable to account. But my mind was too confused to attend to it, so with a kind of madness growing upon me, I flung myself into futurity. At first I scarce thought of stopping, scarce thought of anything but these new sensations. But presently a fresh series of impressions grew up in my mind – a certain curiosity and therewith a certain dread – until at last they took complete possession of me. What strange developments of humanity, what wonderful advances upon our rudimentary civilization, I thought, might not appear when I came to look nearly into the dim elusive world that raced and fluctuated before my eyes! I saw great and splendid architecture rising about me, more massive than any buildings of our own time, and yet, as it seemed, built of glimmer and mist. I saw a richer green flow up the hill-side, and remain there, without any wintry intermission. Even through the veil of my confusion the earth seemed very fair. And so my mind came round to the business of stopping.

'The peculiar risk lay in the possibility of my finding some substance in the space which I, or the machine, occupied. So long as I travelled at a high velocity through time, this scarcely mattered; I was, so to speak, attenuated – was slipping like a vapour through the interstices of intervening substances! But to come to a stop involved the jamming of myself, molecule by molecule, into whatever lay in my way; meant bringing my atoms into such intimate contact with those of the obstacle that a profound chemical reaction – possibly a far-reaching explosion – would result, and blow myself and my apparatus out of all possible dimensions – into the Unknown. This possibility had occurred to me again and again while I was making the machine; but then I had cheerfully accepted it as an unavoidable risk – one of the risks a man has got to take! Now the risk was inevitable, I no longer saw it in the same cheerful light. The fact is that, insensibly, the absolute strangeness of everything, the sickly jarring and swaying of the machine, above all, the feeling of prolonged falling, had absolutely upset my nerve. I told myself that I could never stop, and with a gust of petulance I resolved to stop forthwith. Like an impatient fool, I lugged over the lever, and incontinently the thing went reeling over, and I was flung headlong through the air.

'There was the sound of a clap of thunder in my ears. I may have been stunned for a moment. A pitiless hail was hissing round me, and I was sitting on soft turf in front of the overset machine. Everything still seemed grey, but presently I remarked that the confusion in my ears was gone. I looked round me. I was on what seemed to be a little lawn in a garden, surrounded by rhododendron bushes, and I noticed that their mauve and purple blossoms were dropping in a shower under the beating of the hail-stones. The rebounding, dancing hail hung in a cloud over the machine, and drove along the ground like smoke. In a moment I was wet to the skin. "Fine hospitality," said I, "to a man who has travelled innumerable years to see you."

'Presently I thought what a fool I was to get wet. I stood up and looked round me. A colossal figure, carved apparently in some white stone, loomed indistinctly beyond the rhododendrons through the hazy downpour. But all else of the world was invisible.

'My sensations would be hard to describe. As the columns of hail grew thinner, I saw the white figure more distinctly. It was very large, for a silver birch-tree touched its shoulder. It was of white marble, in shape something like a winged sphinx, but the wings, instead of being carried vertically at the sides, were spread so that it seemed to hover. The pedestal, it appeared to me, was of bronze, and was thick with verdigris. It chanced that the face was towards me; the sightless eyes seemed to watch me; there was the faint shadow of a smile on the lips. It was greatly weather-worn, and that imparted an unpleasant suggestion of disease. I stood looking at it for a little space – half a minute, perhaps, or half an hour. It seemed to advance and to recede as the hail drove before it denser or thinner. At last I tore my eyes from it for a moment and saw that the hail curtain had worn threadbare, and that the sky was lightening with the promise of the sun.

'I looked up again at the crouching white shape, and the full temerity of my voyage came suddenly upon me. What might appear when that hazy curtain was altogether withdrawn? What might not have happened to men? What if cruelty had grown into a common passion? What if in this interval the race had lost its manliness and had developed into something inhuman, unsympathetic, and overwhelmingly powerful? I might seem some old-world savage animal, only the more dreadful and disgusting for our common likeness – a foul creature to be incontinently slain.

'Already I saw other vast shapes – huge buildings with intricate parapets and tall columns, with a wooded hill-side dimly creeping in upon me through the lessening storm. I was seized with a panic fear. I turned frantically to the Time Machine, and strove hard to readjust it. As I did so the shafts of the sun smote through the thunderstorm. The grey downpour was swept aside and vanished like the trailing garments of a ghost. Above me, in the intense blue of the summer sky, some faint brown shreds of cloud whirled into nothingness. The great buildings about me stood out clear and distinct, shining with the wet of the thunderstorm, and picked out in white by the unmelted hailstones piled along their courses. I felt naked in a strange world. I felt as perhaps a bird may feel in the clear air, knowing the hawk wings above and will swoop. My fear grew to frenzy. I took a breathing space, set my teeth, and again grappled fiercely, wrist and knee, with the machine. It gave under my desperate onset and turned over. It struck my chin violently. One hand on the saddle, the other on the lever, I stood panting heavily in attitude to mount again.

'But with this recovery of a prompt retreat my courage recovered. I looked more curiously and less fearfully at this world of the remote future. In a circular opening, high up in the wall of the nearer house, I saw a group of figures clad in rich soft robes. They had seen me, and their faces were directed towards me.

'Then I heard voices approaching me. Coming through the bushes by the White Sphinx were the heads and shoulders of men running. One of these emerged in a pathway leading straight to the little lawn upon which I stood with my machine. He was a slight creature – perhaps four feet high – clad in a purple tunic, girdled at the waist with a leather belt. Sandals or buskins – I could not clearly distinguish which – were on his feet; his legs were bare to the knees, and his head was bare. Noticing that, I noticed for the first time how warm the air was.

'He struck me as being a very beautiful and graceful creature, but indescribably frail. His flushed face reminded me of the more beautiful kind of consumptive – that hectic beauty of which we used to hear so much. At the sight of him I suddenly regained confidence. I took my hands from the machine.

YOUNG ZAPHOD PLAYS IT SAFE

Douglas Adams

Douglas Adams was an English writer responsible for the phenomenon known as *The Hitchhiker's Guide to the Galaxy*. This humorous series began as a popular BBC radio show that first aired in 1978. Adams was the youngest writer to win Britain's Golden Pan Award, one of many awards acquired by this multi-talented writer. This story is a prequel to the events in the books, where we meet a young Zaphod Beeblebrox before he became president of the galaxy. It was originally published in 1986 in an anthology coedited by Adams entitled *The Utterly Utterly Merry Comic Relief Christmas Book*, which raised money for Comic Relief.

A large flying craft moved swiftly across the surface of an astoundingly beautiful sea. From midmorning onward it plied back and forth in great, widening arcs, and at last attracted the attention of the local islanders, a peaceful, seafood-loving people who gathered on the beach and squinted up into the blinding sun, trying to see what was there.

Any sophisticated, knowledgable person who had knocked about, seen a few things, would probably have remarked on how much the craft looked like a filing cabinet – a large and recently burgled filing cabinet lying on its back with its drawers in the air and flying. The islanders, whose experience was of a different kind, were instead struck by how little it looked like a lobster.

They chattered excitedly about its total lack of claws, its stiff, unbendy back, and the fact that it seemed to experience the greatest difficulty staying on the ground. This last feature seemed particularly funny to them. They jumped up and down on the spot a lot to demonstrate to the stupid thing that they themselves found staying on the ground the easiest thing in the world. But soon this entertainment began to pall for them. After all, since it was perfectly clear to them that the thing was not a lobster, and since their world was blessed with an abundance of things that were lobsters (a good half a dozen of which were now marching succulently up the beach towards them), they saw no reason to waste any more time on the thing, but decided instead to adjourn immediately for a late lobster lunch.

At that exact moment the craft stopped suddenly in midair, then upended itself and plunged headlong into the ocean with a great crash of spray that sent the islanders shouting into the trees. When they re-emerged, nervously, a few minutes later, all they were able to see was a smoothly scarred circle of water and a few gulping bubbles.

That's odd, they said to each other between mouthfuls of the best lobster to be had anywhere in the Western Galaxy, that's the second time that's happened in a year.

The craft that wasn't a lobster dived directly to a depth of two hundred feet, and hung there in the heavy blueness, while vast masses of water swayed about it. High above, where the water was magically clear, a brilliant formation of fish flashed away. Below, where the light had difficulty reaching, the colour of the water sank to a dark and savage blue.

Here, at two hundred feet, the sun streamed feebly. A large, silk-skinned sea mammal rolled idly by, inspecting the craft with a kind of half-interest, as if it had half expected to find something of this kind round about here, and then it slid on up and away towards the rippling light.

The craft waited here for a minute or two, taking readings, and then descended another hundred feet. At this depth it was becoming seriously dark. After a moment or two the internal lights of the craft shut down, and in the second or so that passed before the main external beams suddenly stabbed out, the only visible light came from a small, hazily illuminated pink sign that read, THE BEEBLEBROX SALVAGE AND REALLY WILD STUFF CORPORATION.

The huge beams switched downwards, catching a vast shoal of silver fish, which swivelled away in silent panic.

In the dim control room that extended in a broad bow from the craft's blunt prow, four heads were gathered round a computer display that was analysing the very, very faint and intermittent signals that were emanating from deep on the seabed.

"That's it," said the owner of one of the heads finally.

"Can we be quite sure?" said the owner of another of the heads.

"One hundred per cent positive," replied the owner of the first head.

"You're one hundred per cent positive that the ship which is crashed on the bottom of this ocean is the ship which you said you were one hundred per cent positive could one hundred per cent positively never crash?" said the owner of the two remaining heads. "Hey" – he put up two of his hands – "I'm only asking."

The two officials from the Safety and Civil Reassurance Administration responded to this with a very cold stare, but the man with the odd, or rather the even number of heads, missed it. He flung himself back on the pilot couch, opened a couple of beers – one for himself and the other also for himself – stuck his feet on the console, and said "Hey, baby," through the ultra-glass at a passing fish.

"Mr. Beeblebrox . . ." began the shorter and less reassuring of the two officials in a low voice.

"Yup?" said Zaphod, rapping a suddenly empty can down on some of the more sensitive instruments. "You ready to dive? Let's go."

"Mr. Beeblebrox, let us make one thing perfectly clear . . ."

"Yeah, let's," said Zaphod. "How about this for a start. Why don't you just tell me what's really on this ship."

"We have told you," said the official. "By-products."

Zaphod exchanged weary glances with himself.

"By-products," he said. "By-products of what?"

"Processes," said the official.

"What processes?"

"Processes that are perfectly safe."

"Santa Zarquana Voostra!" exclaimed both of Zaphod's heads in chorus. "So safe that you have to build a zarking fortress ship to take the by-products to the nearest black hole and tip them in! Only it doesn't get there because the pilot does a detour – is this right? – to pick up some lobster? Okay, so the guy is cool, but . . . I mean own up, this is barking time, this is major lunch, this is stool approaching critical mass, this is . . . this is . . . total vocabulary failure!"

"Shut up!" his right head yelled at his left. "We're flanging!"

He got a good calming grip on the remaining beer can.

"Listen, guys," he resumed after a moment's peace and contemplation. The two officials had said nothing. Conversation at this level was not something to which they felt they could aspire. "I just want to know," insisted Zaphod, "what you're getting me into here."

He stabbed a finger at the intermittent readings trickling over the computer screen. They meant nothing to him, but he didn't like the look of them at all. They were all squiggly, with lots of long numbers and things.

"It's breaking up, is that it?" he shouted. "It's got a hold full of epsilonic radiating aorist rods or something that'll fry this whole space sector for zillions of years back, and it's breaking up. Is that the story? Is that what we're going down to find? Am I going to come out of that wreck with even more heads?"

"It cannot possibly be a wreck, Mr. Beeblebrox," insisted the official. "The ship is guaranteed to be perfectly safe. It cannot possibly break up."

"Then why are you so keen to go and look at it?"

"We like to look at things that are perfectly safe."

"Freeeooow!"

"Mr. Beeblebrox," said the official patiently, "may I remind you that you have a job to do?"

"Yeah, well maybe I don't feel so keen on doing it all of a sudden. What do you think I am, completely without any moral whatsits, what are they called, those moral things?"

"Scruples?"

"Scruples, thank you, whatsoever? Well?"

The two officials waited calmly. They coughed slightly to help pass the time. Zaphod sighed a what-is-the-world-coming-to sort of sigh to absolve himself from all blame, and swung himself round in his seat.

"Ship?" he called.

"Yup?" said the ship.

"Do what I do."

The ship thought about this for a few milliseconds and then, after double-checking all the seals on its heavy-duty bulkheads, it began slowly, in-exorably, in the hazy blaze of its lights, to sink to the lowest depths.

*

Five hundred feet.

A thousand.

Two thousand.

Here, at a pressure of nearly seventy atmospheres, in the chilling depths where no light reaches, nature keeps its most heated imaginings. Two-foot-long nightmares loomed wildly into the bleaching light, yawned, and vanished back into the blackness.

Two and a half thousand feet.

At the dim edges of the ship's lights, guilty secrets flitted by with their eyes on stalks.

Gradually the topography of the distantly approaching ocean bed resolved with greater and greater clarity on the computer displays until at last a shape could be made out that was separate and distinct from its surroundings. It was like a huge, lopsided, cylindrical fortress that widened sharply halfway along its length to accommodate the heavy ultra-plating with which the crucial storage holds were clad, and which were supposed by its builders to have made this the most secure and impregnable spaceship ever built. Before launch, the material structure of this section had been battered, rammed, blasted, and subjected to every assault its builders knew it could withstand, in order to demonstrate that it could withstand them.

The tense silence in the cockpit tightened perceptibly as it became clear that it was this section that had broken rather neatly in two.

"In fact it's perfectly safe," said one of the officials. "It's built so that even if the ship does break up, the storage holds cannot possibly be breached."

Three thousand eight hundred twenty-five feet.

Four Hi-Presh-A SmartSuits moved slowly out of the open hatchway of the salvage craft and waded through the barrage of its lights towards the monstrous shape that loomed darkly out of the sea night. They moved with a sort of clumsy grace, near weightless though weighed on by a world of water.

With his right-hand head, Zaphod peered up into the black immensities above him, and for a moment his mind sang with a silent roar of horror. He glanced to his left and was relieved to see that his other head was busy watching the Brockian Ultra-Cricket broadcasts on the helmet vid without concern. Slightly behind him to his left walked the two officials from the Safety and Civil Reassurance Administration, and slightly in front of him to his right walked the empty suit, carrying their implements and testing the way for them.

They passed the huge rift in the broken-backed starship *Billion Year Bunker*, and played their flashlights up into it. Mangled machinery loomed between torn and twisted bulkheads two feet thick. A family of large transparent eels lived in there now and seemed to like it. The empty suit preceded them along the length of the ship's gigantic, murky hull, trying the airlocks. The third one it tested ground open uneasily. They crowded inside it and waited for several long minutes while the pump mechanisms dealt with the hideous pressure that the ocean exerted, and slowly replaced it with an equally hideous pressure of air and inert gases. At last the inner door slid open and they were admitted to a dark outer holding area of the starship *Billion Year Bunker*.

Several more high-security Titan-O-Hold doors had to be passed through, each of which the officials opened with a selection of quark keys. Soon they were so deep within the heavy security fields that the Ultra-Cricket broadcasts were beginning to fade, and Zaphod had to switch to one of the rock video stations, since there was nowhere that they were not able to reach.

A final doorway slid open, and they emerged into a large, sepulchral space. Zaphod played his flashlight against the opposite wall and it fell full on a wild-eyed, screaming face.

Zaphod screamed a diminished fifth himself, dropped his light, and sat heavily on the floor, or rather on a body that had been lying there undisturbed for around six months, and that reacted to being sat on by exploding with great violence. Zaphod wondered what to do about all this and, after a brief but hectic internal debate, decided that passing out would be the very thing.

He came to a few minutes later, and pretended not to know who he was, where he was, or how he had got there, but was not able to convince anybody. He then pretended that his memory suddenly returned with a rush and that the shock caused him to pass out again, but he was helped unwillingly to his feet by the empty suit – which he was beginning to take a serious dislike to – and forced to come to terms with his surroundings.

They were dimly and fitfully lit and unpleasant in a number of respects, the most obvious of which was the colourful arrangement of parts of the ship's late lamented navigation officer over the floor, walls, and ceiling, and especially over the lower half of his, Zaphod's, suit. The effect of this was so astoundingly nasty that we shall not be referring to it again at any point in this narrative – other than to record briefly the fact that it caused Zaphod to throw up inside his suit, which he therefore removed and swapped, after suitable headgear modifications, with the empty one. Unfortunately the stench of the fetid air in the ship, followed by the sight of his own suit walking around casually draped in rotting intestines, was enough to make him throw up in the other suit as well, which was a problem that he and the suit would simply have to live with.

There. All done. No more nastiness.

At least, no more of that particular nastiness.

The owner of the screaming face had calmed down very slightly now and was bubbling away incoherently in a large tank of yellow liquid – an emergency suspension tank.

"It was crazy," he babbled, "crazy! I told him we could always try the lobster on the way back, but he was crazy. Obsessed! Do you ever get like that about lobster? Because I don't. Seems to me it's all rubbery and fiddly to eat, and not that much taste, well, I mean is there? I infinitely prefer scallops, and said so. Oh Zarquon, I said so!"

Zaphod stared at this extraordinary apparition, flailing in its tank. The man was attached to all kinds of life-support tubes, and his voice was bubbling out of speakers that echoed insanely round the ship, returning as haunting echoes from deep and distant corridors.

"That was where I went wrong," the madman yelled. "I actually said that I preferred scallops and he said it was because I hadn't had real lobster like they did where his ancestors came from, which was here, and he'd prove it. He said it was no problem, he said the lobster here was worth a whole journey, let alone the small diversion it would take to get here, and he swore he could handle the ship in the atmosphere, but it was madness, madness!" he screamed, and paused with his eyes rolling, as if the word had rung some kind of bell in his mind. "The ship went right out of control! I couldn't believe what we were doing and just to prove a point about lobster which is really so overrated as a food, I'm sorry to go on about lobsters so much, I'll try and stop in a minute, but they've been on my mind so much for the months I've been in this tank, can you imagine what it's like to be stuck in a ship with the same guys for months eating junk food when all one guy will talk about is lobster and then spend six months floating by yourself in a tank thinking about it. I promise I will try and shut up about the lobsters, I really will. Lobsters, lobsters, lobsters – enough! I think I'm the only survivor. I'm the only one who managed to get to an emergency tank before we went down. I sent out the mayday and then we hit. It's a disaster, isn't it? A total disaster, and all because the guy liked lobsters. How much sense am I making? It's really hard for me to tell."

He gazed at them beseechingly, and his mind seemed to sway slowly back down to earth like a falling leaf. He blinked and looked at them oddly, like a monkey peering at a strange fish.

He scrabbled curiously with his wrinkled-up fingers at the glass side of the tank. Tiny, thick yellow bubbles loosed themselves from his mouth and nose, caught briefly in his swab of hair, and strayed on upwards.

"Oh Zarquon, oh heavens," he mumbled pathetically to himself, "I've been found. I've been rescued . . ."

"Well," said one of the officials, briskly, "you've been found at least." He strode over to the main computer bank in the middle of the chamber and started checking quickly through the ship's main monitor circuits for damage reports.

"The aorist rod chambers are intact," he said.

"Holy dingo's dos," snarled Zaphod, "there are aorist rods on board!"

Aorist rods were devices used in a now happily abandoned form of energy production. When the hunt for new sources of energy had at one point got particularly frantic, one bright young chap suddenly spotted that one place which had never used up all its available energy was – the past. And with the sudden rush of blood to the head that such insights tend to induce, he invented a way of mining it that very same night, and within a year huge tracts of the past were being drained of all their energy and simply wasting away. Those who claimed that the past should be left unspoilt were accused of indulging in an extremely expensive form of sentimentality. The past provided a very cheap, plentiful, and clean source of energy, there could always be a few Natural Past Reserves set up if anyone wanted to pay for their upkeep, and as for the claim that draining the past impoverished the present, well, maybe it did, slightly, but the effects were immeasurable and you really had to keep a sense of proportion.

It was only when it was realised that the present really was being impoverished, and that the reason for it was that those selfish plundering wastrel bastards up in the future were doing exactly the same thing, that everyone realised that every single aorist rod, and the terrible secret of how they were made, would have to be utterly and forever destroyed. They claimed it was for the sake of their grandparents and grandchildren, but it was of course for the sake of their grandparents' grandchildren, and their grandchildren's grandparents.

The official from the Safety and Civil Reassurance Administration gave a dismissive shrug. "They're perfectly safe," he said. He glanced up at Zaphod and suddenly said with uncharacteristic frankness, "There's worse than that on board. At least," he added, tapping at one of the computer screens, "I hope it's on board."

The other official rounded on him sharply.

"What the hell do you think you're saying?" he snapped.

The first shrugged again. He said, "It doesn't matter. He can say what he likes. No one would believe him. It's why we chose to use him rather than do anything official, isn't it? The more wild the story he tells, the more it'll sound like he's some hippy adventurer making it up. He can even say that we said this and it'll make him sound like a paranoid." He smiled pleasantly at Zaphod, who was seething in a suit full of sick. "You may accompany us," he told him, "if you wish."

*

"You see?" said the official, examining the ultra-titanium outer seals of the aorist rod hold. "Perfectly secure, perfectly safe."

He said the same thing as they passed holds containing chemical weapons so powerful that a teaspoonful could fatally infect an entire planet.

He said the same thing as they passed holds containing zeta-active compounds so powerful that a teaspoonful could blow up a whole planet.

He said the same thing as they passed holds containing theta-active compounds so powerful that a teaspoonful could irradiate a whole planet.

"I'm glad I'm not a planet," muttered Zaphod.

"You'd have nothing to fear," assured the official from the Safety and Civil Reassurance Administration. "Planets are very safe. Provided," he added – and paused. They were approaching the hold nearest to the point where the back of the starship *Billion Year Bunker* was broken. The corridor here was twisted and deformed, and the floor was damp and sticky in patches.

"Ho-hum," he said, "ho very much hum."

"What's in this hold?" demanded Zaphod.

"By-products," said the official, clamming up again.

"By-products . . ." insisted Zaphod, quietly, "of what?"

Neither official answered. Instead they examined the hold door very carefully and saw that its seals were twisted apart by the forces that had deformed the whole corridor. One of them touched the door lightly. It swung open to his touch. There was darkness inside, with just a couple of dim yellow lights deep within it.

"Of what?" hissed Zaphod.

The leading official turned to the other.

"There's an escape capsule," he said, "that the crew were to use to abandon ship before jettisoning it into the black hole," he said. "I think it would be good to know that it's still there." The other official nodded and left without a word.

The first official quietly beckoned Zaphod in. The large dim yellow lights glowed about twenty feet from them.

"The reason," he said quietly, "why everything else in this ship is, I maintain, safe, is that no one is really crazy enough to use them. No one. At least no one that crazy would ever get near them. Anyone that mad or dangerous rings very deep alarm bells. People may be stupid, but they're not that stupid."

"By-products," hissed Zaphod again – he had to hiss in order that his voice shouldn't be heard to tremble – "of what?"

"Er, Designer People."

"What?"

"The Sirius Cybernetics Corporation were awarded a huge research grant to design and produce synthetic personalities to order. The results were uniformly disastrous. All the 'people' and 'personalities' turned out to be amalgams of characteristics which simply could not coexist in naturally occurring life-forms. Most of them were just poor pathetic misfits, but some were deeply, deeply dangerous. Dangerous because they didn't ring alarm bells in other people. They could walk through situations the way that ghosts walk through walls, because no one spotted the danger.

"The most dangerous of all were three identical ones – they were put in this hold, to be blasted, with this ship, right out of this universe. They are not evil, in fact they are rather simple and charming. But they are the most dangerous creatures that ever lived because there is nothing they will not do if allowed, and nothing they will not be allowed to do . . ."

Zaphod looked at the dim yellow lights, the two dim yellow lights. As his eyes became accustomed to the light, he saw that the two lights framed a third space where something was broken. Wet, sticky patches gleamed dully on the floor.

Zaphod and the official walked cautiously toward the lights. At that moment, four words came crashing into the helmet headsets from the other official.

"The capsule has gone," he said tersely.

"Trace it," snapped Zaphod's companion. "Find exactly where it has gone. We must know where it has gone!"

Zaphod approached the two remaining tanks. A quick glance showed him that each contained an identical floating body. He examined one more carefully. The body, that of an elderly man, was floating in a thick yellow liquid. The man was kindly looking, with lots of pleasant laugh lines round his face. His hair seemed unnaturally thick and dark for someone of his age, and his right hand seemed continually to be weaving forward and back, up and down, as if shaking hands with an endless succession of unseen ghosts. He smiled genially, babbled and burbled like a half-sleeping baby, and occasionally seemed to rock very slightly with little tremors of laughter, as if he had just told himself a joke he hadn't heard before, or didn't remember properly. Waving, smiling, chortling, with little yellow bubbles beading on his lips, he seemed to inhabit a distant world of simple dreams.

Another terse message suddenly came through his helmet headset. The planet toward which the escape capsule had headed had already been identified. It was in Galactic Sector ZZ9 Plural Z Alpha.

Zaphod found a small speaker by the tank, and turned it on. The man in the yellow liquid was babbling gently about a shining city on a hill.

He also heard the Official from the Safety and Civil Reassurance Administration issue instructions to the effect that the missing escape capsule contained a "Reagan" and that the planet in ZZ9 Plural Z Alpha must be made "Perfectly safe."

TIME TRAVEL IN THEORY AND PRACTICE

Stan Love

We are all time travelers.

But time travel as it's commonly practiced is not as much fun as it ought to be. We're doing it all the time, so it gets monotonous. We can't control our routing very well, so there are surprises and disappointments. We can't change our speed, a stately 3600 seconds per hour, except at the infinitesimal end of a long string of decimal places. Not exactly adventure travel. We are all stuck on the same train, and for practical purposes it never speeds up, slows down, or goes backward.

Those are the uninteresting facts as we know them today. But science fiction stirs some fun into the facts by asking, "what if?" What if we could visit the future and see what will become of ourselves and the things we know? Better yet, what if we could travel into the past, view history with our own eyes, and maybe even use the gift of hindsight to adjust events to our advantage?

Those questions have provided fertile ground for writers of short stories, books, and movies, going back at least as far as Mark Twain. An incomplete list of written works on time travel might feature H.G. Wells's *The Time Machine*, Robert A. Heinlein's *The Door into Summer*, Ray Bradbury's *A Sound of Thunder*, Fritz Leiber's *The Big Time*, Lester Del Rey's *Tunnel Through Time*, Kurt Vonnegut's *Slaughterhouse-Five*, Clifford D. Simak's *Mastodonia*, Anne McCaffrey's *Dragonflight*, Frederik Pohl's *Gateway*, Julian May's Pliocene Exile series, and the literally unsurpassable *The Restaurant at the End of the Universe* by Douglas Adams. Time travel movies and TV shows include *Time Bandits*, *The Terminator*, *Back to the Future*, *Groundhog Day*, *12 Monkeys*, *Meet the Robinsons*, *The Girl Who Leapt Through Time*, a double handful of *Star Trek* episodes and movies, and decades of *Doctor Who*.

Plenty of exciting, inspiring, and even funny reading and viewing. But is it all just fantasy? Is our steady journey together into the future really all there is? Might science somehow, someday imitate art and make time travel – real time travel, with the ability to make big changes in speed and direction – possible?

Let's take a look.

Fast Forward

Traveling forward in time is allowed by physics. And simulating it is downright easy. You can get all the main effects without the need for any special equipment. Just go on a long trip. You'll return to find a lot of undone work and an over-flowing mailbox. Stay away long enough (maybe for an overseas deployment or a prison sentence) and when you return you'll be disoriented about current events. Technology will have advanced. Everyone you know will have changed, and they may not recognize you.

But time travel the old-fashioned way is too slow to satisfy the purist. Part of the allure of traveling to the future is being able to see it before our friends do, and to get there without ageing. What we want is a shortcut. Fortunately, Albert Einstein showed us not just one but two shortcuts. According to Dr. Einstein, there is a Special way to move quickly into the future, and a General way.

> *Special Relativity*
> *The classroom clock crawls*
> *As we speed through our studies.*
> *Relativity.*

Einstein's Theory of Special Relativity predicts that things moving at almost the speed of light experience an array of strange effects. Lengths contract. Masses increase. Things that happen simultaneously as seen by one observer happen at different times as seen by another. And, crucially, time slows down.

The Twin Paradox is a famous "thought experiment" that has been used since the early 1900s to illustrate the time-distorting effects of travel at relativistic speeds. In the experiment, which has to be done in thought because we can't do it for real yet, one twin travels out into space and then back to Earth on a ship moving at relativistic speed. Because of the immense speed she's traveling at, time runs slow for her. If her brother (they don't have to be identical twins) watches her through a powerful telescope, he will see her moving in slow motion, the hands of her wall clock turning at a reduced rate, and the light from her reading lamp shifted to longer, redder wavelengths. When she comes back to Earth after her voyage, she will have experienced a fraction of the time that her brother has. She will have aged less than he. She will have effectively traveled into the future.

If you are wondering why that story represents a paradox, bravo for you. It doesn't. The paradox arises when you consider what the sister sees through *her* telescope when she looks back at her brother. To her, *he* is the one who is moving at high speed and whose clock should be running slow. Formally resolving the paradox takes a lot of math: seven pages in my college relativity textbook, the one with the rhinoceroses on the cover. Leaving the calculations as an exercise for the abnormally interested reader, the paradox really does resolve, and the far-traveling twin really does age less than her brother. Robert A. Heinlein's classic *Time for the Stars* explores the Twin Paradox in detail, using plenty of actual twins. The story may be getting a little creaky in the joints, but Mr. Heinlein did his physics homework correctly.

The great thing about special relativity is that it is totally fair and square. The theory has been verified by experiment over and over again. Even lettered physicists who love deflating the balloons of science-fiction lovers can't declare that moving quickly into the future is impossible.

So it's not impossible . . . but it is very hard. To dramatically slow down your clock, you must dramatically speed up your self. The speed of light is about 300,000 kilometers per second. To get a meaningful slowing of the clock, you need to go almost as fast as that: say, 240,000 km/s for a time-dilation factor of 60%. The fastest speed any human being has ever achieved is about 11 km/s, experienced by the *Apollo* astronauts whose capsules fell all the way from the Moon. Gaining even that pokey velocity was so difficult and expensive that humanity managed it only a handful of times, back when NASA was enjoying a ten-times-larger share of Federal discretionary spending than it gets today. The fastest we've ever made an unpiloted spacecraft go is about 70 km/s, for the *Helios* solar mission and the *Galileo* Jupiter entry probe. Neither value is close to 300,000 km/s. In another branch of science, we are able to accelerate things up to within a time-dilated gnat's eyelash of light speed, but none of those things are bigger than a single atom, and it takes a particle accelerator with the length and power consumption of a small town to do it. If we want to use special relativity for time travel, we've got a long way to go in the propulsion department. When we get there, though, we'll get the stars as a side benefit.

General Relativity

> *The Theory of General Relativity*
> *Attributes to mass this proclivity:*
> *Sufficient self-gravity*
> *Creates a dark cavity*
> *That holds even light in captivity.*

General relativity offers another way to move into the future. Get close to an object with an escape velocity near or equal to the speed of light, and your clock will run slow as seen by an observer out in free space. Again, totally kosher, and confirmed by every experiment that has investigated it, including the recent and exquisitely sensitive Gravity Probe B space mission. Even the gravitational time dilation effect of the Earth, whose 11.2 km/s escape velocity is nowhere near the speed of light, is measurable and known. The GPS unit in your phone has to compensate for general relativity or it wouldn't work.

But the Earth doesn't slow time very much. Neither does the Sun, which has a surface escape velocity of about 600 km/s; close flybys yield way more scorched paint than temporal displacement. For a meaningful effect on the flow of time, you need a neutron star or a black hole. These are very unneighborly objects. They raise tides strong enough to rip apart any known material, including specifically your soft pink body. They may feature intense high-energy radiation and magnetic fields strong enough to short-circuit your nervous system. You must approach a black hole or neutron star very closely indeed to make time slow down, and somehow hang out there for a while to let the days add up. Landing is not a survivable option, but perhaps you could enter a low orbit, whipping around the monster hundreds of times a second. You will somehow have to endure the tides and radiation. Then, to enjoy your trip to the future, you must get away again, which takes a vehicle that can overcome that near-light-speed escape velocity! Compared to special relativity, this approach is messy and risky – but both earn a solid endorsement from physics.

Rewind

Moving forward in time would be great, but moving backward would be even better. Making piles of money on the stock market is just one of the attractive possibilities.

Astronomers know that it is possible, indeed unavoidable, to at least *see* things as they were in the past. Whenever we aim a telescope at a distant object, we're looking back into history. Even at its dazzling speed of travel, the light that falls on earthly mirrors and detectors takes time to get here. We see the Moon as it was 1.3 seconds ago, the Sun as it was eight minutes ago, the Andromeda Galaxy as it was two and a half million years ago. Out at the limit of observable space, we can see the afterglow of the Big Bang: the infant universe as it was almost fourteen billion years ago.

But at those distances it's hard to see any details interesting at a human scale, and we are naturally more interested in our own history than that of a distant galaxy. And many of us won't be satisfied by just looking. We would much prefer to go in person.

So could we do it for real?

The scientific answer is a definite Maybe.

Fair warning: after this point, things are going to get weird, even according to standards that find relativistic time dilation perfectly normal. Moving forward in time is fully authorized by a mature theory that is backed up by experiment to great accuracy. Backward, not so much. Einstein recognized nothing in his work that supported the possibility of going back in time.

But Einstein was not the only, nor the last, smart person on Earth.

Among the smartest people currently on Earth is a Caltech professor named Kip Thorne. You may not have heard of him, but you have probably heard of the brilliant wheelchair-bound physicist Stephen Hawking. Kip Thorne makes bets about relativity with Stephen Hawking. Sometimes he wins. Dr. Thorne is the world's authority on practical time machines. He has written a readable book called *Black Holes and Time Warps: Einstein's Outrageous Legacy*. Most of what I know on this topic comes from Dr. Thorne's lectures and book.

It turns out that there are several theoretical possibilities for making a real time machine. None are supported by experiment, and even the theories are contentious. And let us be clear: the engineering would be incredibly difficult. Even if the theory holds up, we will not be ready to build the first working time machine until a far-off future when our technology is almost unimaginably advanced. We'll be commuting to work at the relativistic speeds we talked about earlier. Our kids will be terraforming planets for Science Fair projects. But let's say we've gotten that far.

One theoretical possibility is to build a massive cylinder of infinite length (not merely as long as the universe is wide, but infinitely long). We set it rotating about its long axis at nearly the speed of light, and then play tag with it in very capable vehicles. Certain flight paths around the beast return to the same point in space, but at an earlier time. Voilá, a time machine.

But infinite cylinders require infinite budgets, and that's not the way science funding seems to be headed. We might not have to build one, though. Cosmologists have postulated that similar things might have been produced naturally in the early universe: linear black holes called "cosmic string," which Earthly astronomers might be able to detect because circles drawn around them have fewer than 360 degrees. (I told you it was going to get weird.) I'm not going to say any more about infinite cylinders here because a different method is cooler and has an interesting connection to science fiction.

Another writer who famously did his homework was Carl Sagan. For his novel *Contact*, he wanted a physically plausible way for his heroine to travel to the star Vega and back quickly. He came up with a method that an incredibly advanced alien culture might develop, and mailed a description to Kip Thorne to ask his opinion. Dr. Thorne had a better idea. He shared it with Dr. Sagan, who incorporated it into the book.

Dr. Thorne's suggestion is known to the initiated as an Einstein-Rosen bridge and to producers and consumers of science fiction as a wormhole. (Check out the Wikipedia article on wormholes for details and pictures, including a formally ray-traced image of a wormhole connecting two places on Earth.) Simply connect the throat of a black hole near Vega with that of another near the Earth, and bingo! We've built a shortcut to the stars, and the universe is ours.

But wait, it sounds like we're talking about faster-than-light travel. What does this have to do with time travel?

Everything. Remember, the central tenet of Einstein's relativity is that space and time are different aspects of the same fundamental thing. Bend one, and you twist the other.

Dr. Thorne and other theorists have suggested that it might be possible to turn a wormhole into a time machine. Leave one mouth of the tunnel at home, and take the other on a Twin Paradox sortie out into space. The traveling mouth experiences less time than the homebound one. When it returns, you can enter the latter and come out the former in the past. It's a bona fide time machine. (Physicists use the term "closed timelike curves" when discussing them in print, in an attempt to head off media headlines screaming about scientists inventing time machines.)

The wormhole time machine is limited. It's hard to adjust the time interval between the two mouths. You can do it only by taking one mouth or the other on a high-speed jaunt. And you can never go back to a time before you built the wormhole, a disappointment to people interested in altering the outcomes of still-earlier elections, sporting events, or armed conflicts. But you could still use it to make a fortune on Wall Street, or assassinate an ancestor and finally put to rest all philosophical posturing about the Grandfather Paradox.

General relativity may allow for the possibility of wormholes, but that doesn't mean they're a done deal. There are some construction challenges we don't yet know how to overcome. First, every normal black hole contains an evil singularity in the center. Anything that crosses the hole's horizon must fall into that singularity, be disrupted by it, and become one with it. Ouch. Next, there is not an obvious way to coax two black holes to connect with one another. Finally, theorists predict that if two holes are somehow spliced together, the resulting tunnel will pinch itself off before anything could pass through. Considerable intellectual energy has been invested in these topics, though, and there could be a way to solve them.

It might be possible to make two connected and singularity-free black holes out of something besides ordinary mass, which could then counteract the natural tendency of the tunnel to collapse. Theory suggests that this requirement would be met by a substance with negative mass and negative pressure. That's right: to build a traversable wormhole, we'll need to use something that weighs less than nothing and is emptier than a perfect vacuum. (Did you not believe me when I said it was going to get weird?) Engineers joke about "unobtainium" for applications that demand materials with unrealistic physical properties, but this stuff takes the cake.

Yet off in the fringes of physics there do seem to be things that exert negative pressure. The mysterious "dark energy" that is accelerating the expansion of our universe against the pull of its own gravity might be one. Another is the Casimir effect. It may be possible to build a traversable wormhole using the Casimir effect, so it's worth covering here.

Physicists believe that at the tiniest-size scales and the briefest flickers of time, our universe is a seething froth of instability, constantly creating pairs of subatomic particles that recombine and vanish before they can be detected. These are called "virtual particles." Among the virtual particles are photons, the wiggles of electricity and magnetism that make up light, radio, X-rays, and so on. Photons both real and virtual cannot travel very well through electrical conductors such as metals. So if we take two very smooth flat metal surfaces, and place them very close together, they'll suppress the creation of virtual photons with a wavelength longer than the separation between them. But outside the plates are virtual photons of all wavelengths, which exert a tiny bit more radiation pressure on the back sides of the plates than does the restricted range of wavelengths available between them. If all of this weirdness is really true, then there should be a very tiny force – effectively a negative pressure – pushing the plates toward one another.

This force exists and has been measured in experiments.

There are some difficulties with building wormholes using the Casimir effect. It operates only over very short distances. Also it's rather weak. It's not as heavy a hammer for knocking holes in spacetime as, say, the collapsing core of a massive star. But if our kids are terraforming planets and we don't want to be outdone, we should go for it. We start by building a spherical metal shell with the diameter of the orbit of Pluto, a supersized Dyson sphere. We then build another one surrounding the first, carefully maintaining the gap between them at one Ångstrom unit, roughly the size of an atom. If we accomplish these things, says Dr. Thorne, the Casimir effect will warp space so that we will no longer be able to tell which sphere is the inner one and which is the outer. We will have built a wormhole that allows us to travel the massive distance of one ten-billionth of a meter. Not a practical transportation device, unfortunately. But it's a real wormhole, and by sending one end on a high-speed trip we might possibly be able to turn it into a real time machine.

Back to the Present

Unfortunately, our own less-than-incredibly-advanced culture won't be building Matryoshka-doll Dyson spheres and accelerating them to relativistic speeds any time soon. But that doesn't diminish the appeal of time travel. It remains a fruitful topic for both science fiction and theoretical physics. As in the case of *Contact*, sometimes the interplay between the two helps make both stronger. And as our train moves inexorably forward at 3600 seconds per hour, the day when we can engineer time machines must be moving just as inexorably closer. Maybe, somewhere up the track, they're sending people even further along, to still more distant futures where they can send people back.

REACTIONARIES AND REVOLUTIONARIES

A SOUND OF THUNDER

Ray Bradbury

Ray Bradbury was one of the most celebrated twentieth-century American writers. He wrote science fiction, horror, and mystery fiction. Many of Bradbury's works have been adapted into comic books, television shows, and films. This story was first published in *Collier's* magazine in 1952. The term "the Butterfly Effect" was coined because of this famous story – which may be the most reprinted science fiction tale in history.

The sign on the wall seemed to quaver under a film of sliding warm water. Eckels felt his eyelids blink over his stare, and the sign burned in this momentary darkness:

> TIME SAFARI, INC.
> SAFARIS TO ANY YEAR IN THE PAST.
> YOU NAME THE ANIMAL.
> WE TAKE YOU THERE.
> YOU SHOOT IT.

Warm phlegm gathered in Eckels' throat; he swallowed and pushed it down. The muscles around his mouth formed a smile as he put his hand slowly out upon the air, and in that hand waved a check for ten thousand dollars to the man behind the desk.

"Does this safari guarantee I come back alive?"

"We guarantee nothing," said the official, "except the dinosaurs." He turned. "This is Mr. Travis, your Safari Guide in the Past. He'll tell you what and where to shoot. If he says no shooting, no shooting. If you disobey instructions, there's a stiff penalty of another ten thousand dollars, plus possible government action, on your return."

Eckels glanced across the vast office at a mass and tangle, a snaking and humming of wires and steel boxes, at an aurora that flickered now orange, now silver, now blue. There was a sound like a gigantic bonfire burning all of Time, all the years and all the parchment calendars, all the hours piled high and set aflame.

A touch of the hand and this burning would, on the instant, beautifully reverse itself. Eckels remembered the wording in the advertisements to the letter. Out of chars and ashes, out of dust and coals, like golden salamanders, the old years, the green years, might leap; roses sweeten the air, white hair turn Irish-black, wrinkles vanish; all, everything fly back to seed, flee death, rush down to their beginnings, suns rise in western skies and set in glorious easts, moons eat themselves opposite to the custom, all and everything cupping one in another like Chinese boxes, rabbits into hats, all and everything returning to the fresh death, the seed death, the green death, to the time before the beginning. A touch of a hand might do it, the merest touch of a hand.

"Unbelievable," Eckels breathed, the light of the Machine on his thin face. "A real Time Machine." He shook his head. "Makes you think. If the election had gone badly yesterday, I might be here now running away from the results. Thank God Keith won. He'll make a fine President of the United States."

"Yes," said the man behind the desk. "We're lucky. If Deutscher had gotten in, we'd have the worst kind of dictatorship. There's an anti-everything man for you, a militarist, anti-Christ, anti-human, anti-intellectual. People called us up, you know, joking but not joking. Said if Deutscher became President they wanted to go live in 1492. Of course it's not our business to conduct Escapes, but to form Safaris. Anyway, Keith's President now. All you got to worry about is—"

"Shooting my dinosaur," Eckels finished it for him.

"A *Tyrannosaurus Rex*. The Tyrant Lizard, the most incredible monster in history. Sign this release. Anything happens to you, we're not responsible. Those dinosaurs are hungry."

Eckels flushed angrily. "Trying to scare me!"

"Frankly, yes. We don't want anyone going who'll panic at the first shot. Six Safari leaders were killed last year, and a dozen hunters. We're here to give you the severest thrill a real hunter ever asked for. Traveling you back sixty million years to bag the biggest game in all of Time. Your personal check's still there. Tear it up."

Mr. Eckels looked at the check. His fingers twitched.

"Good luck," said the man behind the desk. "Mr. Travis, he's all yours."

They moved silently across the room, taking their guns with them, toward the Machine, toward the silver metal and the roaring light.

First a day and then a night and then a day and then a night, then it was day-night-day-night. A week, a month, a year, a decade! A.D. 2055. A.D. 2019. 1999! 1957! Gone! The Machine roared.

They put on their oxygen helmets and tested the intercoms.

Eckels swayed on the padded seat, his face pale, his jaw stiff. He felt the trembling in his arms and he looked down and found his hands tight on the new rifle. There were four other men in the Machine. Travis, the Safari Leader, his assistant, Lesperance, and two other hunters, Billings and Kramer. They sat looking at each other, and the years blazed around them.

"Can these guns get a dinosaur cold?" Eckels felt his mouth saying.

"If you hit them right," said Travis on the helmet radio. "Some dinosaurs have two brains, one in the head, another far down the spinal column. We stay away from those. That's stretching luck. Put your first two shots into the eyes, if you can, blind them, and go back into the brain."

The Machine howled. Time was a film run backward. Suns fled and ten million moons fled after them. "Think," said Eckels. "Every hunter that ever lived would envy us today. This makes Africa seem like Illinois."

The Machine slowed; its scream fell to a murmur. The Machine stopped.

The sun stopped in the sky.

The fog that had enveloped the Machine blew away and they were in an old time, a very old time indeed, three hunters and two Safari Heads with their blue metal guns across their knees.

"Christ isn't born yet," said Travis. "Moses has not gone to the mountains to talk with God. The Pyramids are still in the earth, waiting to be cut out and put up. Remember that. Alexander, Caesar, Napoleon, Hitler – none of them exists."

The man nodded.

"That" – Mr. Travis pointed – "is the jungle of sixty million two thousand and fifty-five years before President Keith."

He indicated a metal path that struck off into green wilderness, over streaming swamp, among giant ferns and palms.

"And that," he said, "is the Path, laid by Time Safari for your use. It floats six inches above the earth. Doesn't touch so much as one grass blade, flower, or tree. It's an anti-gravity metal. Its purpose is to keep you from touching this world of the past in any way. Stay on the Path. Don't go off it. I repeat. *Don't go off*. For *any* reason! If you fall off, there's a penalty. And don't shoot any animal we don't okay."

"Why?" asked Eckels.

They sat in the ancient wilderness. Far birds' cries blew on a wind, and the smell of tar and an old salt sea, moist grasses, and flowers the color of blood.

"We don't want to change the Future. We don't belong here in the Past. The government doesn't *like* us here. We have to pay big graft to keep our franchise. A Time Machine is finicky business. Not knowing it, we might kill an important animal, a small bird, a roach, a flower even, thus destroying an important link in a growing species."

"That's not clear," said Eckels.

"All right," Travis continued, "say we accidentally kill one mouse here. That means all the future families of this one particular mouse are destroyed, right?"

"Right."

"And all the families of the families of the families of that one mouse! With a stamp of your foot, you annihilate first one, then a dozen, then a thousand, a million, a billion possible mice!"

"So they're dead," said Eckels. "So what?"

"So what?" Travis snorted quietly. "Well, what about the foxes that'll need those mice to survive? For want of ten mice, a fox dies. For want of ten foxes a lion starves. For want of a lion, all manner of insects, vultures, infinite billions of life forms are thrown into chaos and destruction. Eventually it all boils down to this: fifty-nine million years later, a caveman, one of a dozen on the entire world, goes hunting wild boar or saber-toothed tiger for food. But you, friend, have stepped on all the tigers in that region. By stepping on one single mouse. So the caveman starves. And the caveman, please note, is not just any expendable man, no! He is an entire future nation. From his loins would have sprung ten sons. From their loins one hundred sons, and thus onward to a civilization. Destroy this one man, and you destroy a race, a people, an entire history of life. It is comparable to slaying some of Adam's grandchildren. The stomp of your foot, on one mouse, could start an earthquake, the effects of which could shake our earth and destinies down through Time, to their very foundations. With the death of that one caveman, a billion others yet unborn are throttled in the womb. Perhaps Rome never rises on its seven hills. Perhaps Europe is forever a dark forest, and only Asia waxes healthy and teeming. Step on a mouse and you crush the Pyramids. Step on a mouse and you leave your print, like a Grand Canyon, across Eternity. Queen Elizabeth might never be born, Washington might not cross the Delaware, there might never be a United States at all. So be careful. Stay on the Path. *Never* step off!"

"I see," said Eckels. "Then it wouldn't pay for us even to touch the grass?"

"Correct. Crushing certain plants could add up infinitesimally. A little error here would multiply in sixty million years, all out of proportion. Of course maybe our theory is wrong. Maybe Time can't be changed by us. Or maybe it can be changed only in little subtle ways. A dead mouse here makes an insect imbalance there, a population disproportion later, a bad harvest further on, a depression, mass starvation, and finally, a change in social temperament in far-flung countries. Something much more subtle, like that. Perhaps only a soft breath, a whisper, a hair, pollen on the air, such a slight, slight change that unless you looked close you wouldn't see it. Who knows? Who really can say he knows? We don't know. We're guessing. But until we do know for certain whether our messing around in Time can make a big roar or a little rustle in history, we're being careful. This Machine, this Path, your clothing and bodies, were sterilized, as you know, before the journey. We wear these oxygen helmets so we can't introduce our bacteria into an ancient atmosphere."

"How do we know which animals to shoot?"

"They're marked with red paint," said Travis. "Today, before our journey, we sent Lesperance here back with the Machine. He came to this particular era and followed certain animals."

"Studying them?"

"Right," said Lesperance. "I track them through their entire existence, noting which of them lives longest. Very few. How many times they mate. Not often. Life's short. When I find one that's going to die when a tree falls on him, or one that drowns in a tar pit, I note the exact hour, minute, and second. I shoot a paint bomb. It leaves a red patch on his side. We can't miss it. Then I correlate our arrival in the Past so that we meet the Monster not more than two minutes before he would have died anyway. This way, we kill only animals with no future, that are never going to mate again. You see how *careful* we are?"

"But if you came back this morning in Time," said Eckels eagerly, "you must've bumped into us, our Safari! How did it turn out? Was it successful? Did all of us get through – alive?"

Travis and Lesperance gave each other a look.

"That'd be a paradox," said the latter. "Time doesn't permit that sort of mess – a man meeting himself. When such occasions threaten, Time steps aside. Like an airplane hitting an air pocket. You felt the Machine jump just before we stopped? That was us passing ourselves on the way back to the Future. We saw nothing. There's no way of telling if this expedition was a success, if we got our monster, or whether all of us – meaning you, Mr. Eckels – got out alive."

Eckels smiled palely.

"Cut that," said Travis sharply. "Everyone on his feet!"

They were ready to leave the Machine.

The jungle was high and the jungle was broad and the jungle was the entire world forever and forever. Sounds like music and sounds like flying tents filled the sky, and those were pterodactyls soaring with cavernous gray wings, gigantic bats of delirium and night fever. Eckels, balanced on the narrow Path, aimed his rifle playfully.

"Stop that!" said Travis. "Don't even aim for fun, blast you! If your guns should go off—"

Eckels flushed. "Where's our *Tyrannosaurus?*"

Lesperance checked his wristwatch. "Up ahead. We'll bisect his trail in sixty seconds. Look for the red paint! Don't shoot till we give the word. Stay on the Path. *Stay on the Path!*"

They moved forward in the wind of morning.

"Strange," murmured Eckels. "Up ahead, sixty million years, Election Day over. Keith made President. Everyone celebrating. And here we are, a million years lost, and they don't exist. The things we worried about for months, a lifetime, not even born or thought of yet."

"Safety catches off, everyone!" ordered Travis. "You, first shot, Eckels. Second, Billings, Third, Kramer."

"I've hunted tiger, wild boar, buffalo, elephant, but now, this is it," said Eckels. "I'm shaking like a kid."

"Ah," said Travis.

Everyone stopped.

Travis raised his hand. "Ahead," he whispered. "In the mist. There he is. There's His Royal Majesty now."

The jungle was wide and full of twitterings, rustlings, murmurs, and sighs.

Suddenly it all ceased, as if someone had shut a door.

Silence.

A sound of thunder.

Out of the mist, one hundred yards away, came *Tyrannosaurus Rex.*

"It," whispered Eckels. "It . . ."

"Sh!"

It came on great oiled, resilient, striding legs. It towered thirty feet above half of the trees, a great evil god, folding its delicate watchmaker's claws close to its oily reptilian chest. Each lower leg was a piston, a thousand pounds of white bone, sunk in thick ropes of muscle, sheathed over in a gleam of pebbled skin like the mail of a terrible warrior. Each thigh was a ton of meat, ivory, and steel mesh. And from the great breathing cage of the upper body those two delicate arms dangled out front, arms with hands which might pick up and examine men like toys, while the snake neck coiled. And the head itself, a ton of sculptured stone, lifted easily upon the sky. Its mouth gaped, exposing a fence of teeth like daggers. Its eyes rolled, ostrich eggs, empty of all expression save hunger. It closed its mouth in a death grin. It ran, its pelvic bones crushing aside trees and bushes, its taloned feet clawing damp earth, leaving prints six inches deep wherever it settled its weight. It ran with a gliding ballet step, far too poised and balanced for its ten tons. It moved into a sunlit area warily, its beautifully reptilian hands feeling the air.

"Why, why," Eckels twitched his mouth. "It could reach up and grab the moon."

"Sh!" Travis jerked angrily. "He hasn't seen us yet."

"It can't be killed." Eckels pronounced this verdict quietly, as if there could be no argument. He had weighed the evidence and this was his considered opinion. The rifle in his hands seemed a cap gun. "We were fools to come. This is impossible."

"Shut up!" hissed Travis.

"Nightmare."

"Turn around," commanded Travis. "Walk quietly to the Machine. We'll remit half your fee."

"I didn't realize it would be this *big*," said Eckels. "I miscalculated, that's all. And now I want out."

"It *sees* us!"

"There's the red paint on its chest!"

The Tyrant Lizard raised itself. Its armored flesh glittered like a thousand green coins. The coins, crusted with slime, steamed. In the slime, tiny insects wriggled, so that the entire body seemed to twitch and undulate, even while the monster itself did not move. It exhaled. The stink of raw flesh blew down the wilderness.

"Get me out of here," said Eckels. "It was never like this before. I was always sure I'd come through alive. I had good guides, good safaris, and safety. This time, I figured wrong. I've met my match and admit it. This is too much for me to get hold of."

"Don't run," said Lesperance. "Turn around. Hide in the Machine."

"Yes." Eckels seemed to be numb. He looked at his feet as if trying to make them move. He gave a grunt of helplessness.

"Eckels!"

He took a few steps, blinking, shuffling.

"Not *that* way!"

The Monster, at the first motion, lunged forward with a terrible scream. It covered one hundred yards in six seconds. The rifles jerked up and blazed fire. A windstorm from the beast's mouth engulfed them in the stench of slime and old blood. The Monster roared, teeth glittering with sun.

The rifles cracked again. Their sound was lost in shriek and lizard thunder. The great level of the reptile's tail swung up, lashed sideways. Trees exploded in clouds of leaf and branch. The Monster twitched its jeweler's hands down to fondle at the men, to twist them in half, to crush them like berries, to cram them into its teeth and its screaming throat. Its boulderstone eyes leveled with the men. They saw themselves mirrored. They fired at the metallic eyelids and the blazing black iris.

Like a stone idol, like a mountain avalanche, *Tyrannosaurus* fell. Thundering, it clutched trees, pulled them with it. It wrenched and tore the metal Path. The men flung themselves back and away. The body hit, ten tons of cold flesh and stone. The guns fired. The Monster lashed its armored tail, twitched its snake jaws, and lay still. A fount of blood spurted from its throat. Somewhere inside, a sac of fluids burst. Sickening gushes drenched the hunters. They stood, red and glistening.

The thunder faded.

The jungle was silent. After the avalanche, a green peace. After the nightmare, morning.

Billings and Kramer sat on the pathway and threw up. Travis and Lesperance stood with smoking rifles, cursing steadily. In the Time Machine, on his face, Eckels lay shivering. He had found his way back to the Path, climbed into the Machine.

Travis came walking, glanced at Eckels, took cotton gauze from a metal box, and returned to the others, who were sitting on the Path.

"Clean up."

They wiped the blood from their helmets. They began to curse too. The Monster lay, a hill of solid flesh. Within, you could hear the sighs and murmurs as the furthest chambers of it died, the organs malfunctioning, liquids running a final instant from pocket to sac to spleen, everything shutting off, closing up forever. It was like standing by a wrecked locomotive or a steam shovel at quitting time, all valves being released or levered tight. Bones cracked; the tonnage of its own flesh, off balance, dead weight, snapped the delicate forearms, caught underneath. The meat settled, quivering.

Another cracking sound. Overhead, a gigantic tree branch broke from its heavy mooring, fell. It crashed upon the dead beast with finality.

"There." Lesperance checked his watch. "Right on time. That's the giant tree that was scheduled to fall and kill this animal originally." He glanced at the two hunters. "You want the trophy picture?"

"What?"

"We can't take a trophy back to the Future. The body has to stay right here where it would have died originally, so the insects, birds, and bacteria can get at it, as they were intended to. Everything in balance. The body stays. But we can take a picture of you standing near it."

The two men tried to think, but gave up, shaking their heads.

They let themselves be led along the metal Path. They sank wearily into the Machine cushions. They gazed back at the ruined Monster, the stagnating mound, where already strange reptilian birds and golden insects were busy at the steaming armor. A sound on the floor of the Time Machine stiffened them. Eckels sat there, shivering.

"I'm sorry," he said at last.

"Get up!" cried Travis.

Eckels got up.

"Go out on that Path alone," said Travis. He had his rifle pointed. "You're not coming back in the Machine. We're leaving you here!"

Lesperance seized Travis's arm. "Wait—"

"Stay out of this!" Travis shook his hand away. "This fool nearly killed us. But it isn't *that* so much, no. It's his shoes! Look at them! He ran off the Path. That *ruins* us! We'll forfeit! Thousands of dollars of insurance! We guarantee no one leaves the Path. He left it. Oh, the fool! I'll have to report to the government.

They might revoke our license to travel. Who knows *what* he's done to Time, to History!"

"Take it easy, all he did was kick up some dirt."

"How do we *know*?" cried Travis. "We don't know anything! It's all a mystery! Get out of here, Eckels!"

Eckels fumbled his shirt. "I'll pay anything. A hundred thousand dollars!"

Travis glared at Eckels' checkbook and spat. "Go out there. The Monster's next to the Path. Stick your arms up to your elbows in his mouth. Then you can come back with us."

"That's unreasonable!"

"The Monster's dead, you idiot. The bullets! The bullets can't be left behind. They don't belong in the Past; they might change anything. Here's my knife. Dig them out!"

The jungle was alive again, full of the old tremorings and bird cries. Eckels turned slowly to regard the primeval garbage dump, that hill of nightmares and terror. After a long time, like a sleepwalker he shuffled out along the Path.

He returned, shuddering, five minutes later, his arms soaked and red to the elbows. He held out his hands. Each held a number of steel bullets. Then he fell. He lay where he fell, not moving.

"You didn't have to make him do that," said Lesperance.

"Didn't I? It's too early to tell." Travis nudged the still body. "He'll live. Next time he won't go hunting game like this. Okay." He jerked his thumb wearily at Lesperance. "Switch on. Let's go home."

*

1492. 1776. 1812.

They cleaned their hands and faces. They changed their caking shirts and pants. Eckels was up and around again, not speaking. Travis glared at him for a full ten minutes.

"Don't look at me," cried Eckels. "I haven't done anything."

"Who can tell?"

"Just ran off the Path, that's all, a little mud on my shoes – what do you want me to do – get down and pray?"

"We might need it. I'm warning you, Eckels, I might kill you yet. I've got my gun ready."

"I'm innocent. I've done nothing!"

1999. 2000. 2055.

The Machine stopped.

"Get out," said Travis.

The room was there as they had left it. But not the same as they had left it. The same man sat behind the same desk. But the same man did not quite sit behind the same desk. Travis looked around swiftly. "Everything okay here?" he snapped.

"Fine. Welcome home!"

Travis did not relax. He seemed to be looking through the one high window.

"Okay, Eckels, get out. Don't ever come back."

Eckels could not move.

"You heard me," said Travis. "What're you *staring* at?"

Eckels stood smelling the air, and there was a thing to the air, a chemical taint so subtle, so slight, that only a faint cry of his subliminal senses warned him it was there. The colors, white, gray, blue, orange, in the wall, in the furniture, in the sky beyond the window, were . . . were . . . And there was a feel. His flesh twitched. His hands twitched. He stood drinking the oddness with the pores of his body. Somewhere, someone must have been screaming one of those whistles that only a dog can hear. His body screamed silence in return. Beyond this room, beyond this wall, beyond this man who was not quite the same man seated at this desk that was not quite the same desk . . . lay an entire world of streets and people. What sort of world it was now, there was no telling. He could feel them moving there, beyond the walls, almost, like so many chess pieces blown in a dry wind . . .

But the immediate thing was the sign painted on the office wall, the same sign he had read earlier today on first entering. Somehow, the sign had changed:

> TYME SEFARI INC.
> SEFARIS TU ANY YEER EN THE PAST.
> YU NAIM THE ANIMALL.
> WEE TAEK YU THAIR.
> YU SHOOT ITT.

Eckels felt himself fall into a chair. He fumbled crazily at the thick slime on his boots. He held up a clod of dirt, trembling. "No, it can't be. Not a little thing like that. No!"

Embedded in the mud, glistening green and gold and black, was a butterfly, very beautiful and very dead.

"Not a little thing like *that*! Not a butterfly!" cried Eckels.

It fell to the floor, an exquisite thing, a small thing that could upset balances and knock down a line of small dominoes and then big dominoes and then gigantic dominoes, all down the years across Time. Eckels' mind whirled. It *couldn't* change things. Killing one butterfly couldn't be that important! Could it?

His face was cold. His mouth trembled, asking: "Who – who won the presidential election yesterday?"

The man behind the desk laughed. "You joking? You know very well. Deutscher, of course! Who else? Not that fool weakling Keith. We got an iron man now, a man with guts!" The official stopped. "What's wrong?"

Eckels moaned. He dropped to his knees. He scrabbled at the golden butterfly with shaking fingers. "Can't we," he pleaded to the world, to himself, to the officials, to the Machine, "can't we take it back, can't we make it alive again? Can't we start over? Can't we—"

He did not move. Eyes shut, he waited, shivering. He heard Travis breathe loud in the room; he heard Travis shift his rifle, click the safety catch, and raise the weapon.

There was a sound of thunder.

VINTAGE SEASON

Henry Kuttner & C.L. Moore

Henry Kuttner was an American science fiction and fantasy writer. He collaborated on many stories with his wife, C.L. Moore, who he met through "Lovecraft's Circle." He was considered one of the most important writers in genre in the 1940s. Although he wrote many novels, he is best known for his short fiction. Catherine L. Moore was an American science fiction and fantasy writer, most often known as C.L. Moore. She was one of the first women to write in either genre, and paved the way for many other female speculative fiction writers. Her earliest stories appeared in *Weird Tales*. Many of her stories were collaborations with her husband, Henry Kuttner, although this particular story is often credited to her alone. It was first published in *Astounding Science Fiction* in 1946 under the pseudonym Lawrence O'Donnell. "Vintage Season" inspired Robert Silverberg's time travel story "In Another Country," taking place at the same time yet told from a different point of view. In later years she wrote for television, most notably for *Maverick* and *77 Sunset Strip*.

Three people came up the walk to the old mansion just at dawn on a perfect May morning. Oliver Wilson in his pajamas watched them from an upper window through a haze of conflicting emotions, resentment predominant. He didn't want them there.

They were foreigners. He knew only that much about them. They had the curious name of Sancisco, and their first names, scrawled in loops on the lease, appeared to be Omerie, Kleph and Klia, though it was impossible as he looked down upon them now to sort them out by signature. He hadn't even been sure whether they would be men or women, and he had expected something a little less cosmopolitan.

Oliver's heart sank a little as he watched them follow the taxi driver up the walk. He had hoped for less self-assurance in his unwelcome tenants, because he meant to force them out of the house if he could. It didn't look very promising from here.

The man went first. He was tall and dark, and he wore his clothes and carried his body with that peculiar arrogant assurance that comes from perfect confidence in every phase of one's being. The two women were laughing as they followed him. Their voices were light and sweet, and their faces were beautiful, each in its own exotic way, but the first thing Oliver thought of when he looked at them was, Expensive!

It was not only that patina of perfection that seemed to dwell in every line of their incredibly flawless garments. There are degrees of wealth beyond which wealth itself ceases to have significance. Oliver had seen before, on rare occasions, something like this assurance that the earth turning beneath their well-shod feet turned only to their whim.

It puzzled him a little in this case, because he had the feeling as the three came up the walk that the beautiful clothing they wore so confidently was not clothing they were accustomed to. There was a curious air of condescension in the way they moved. Like women in costume. They minced a little on their delicate high heels, held out an arm to stare at the cut of a sleeve, twisted now and then inside their garments as if the clothing sat strangely on them, as if they were accustomed to something entirely different.

And there was an elegance about the way the garments fitted them which even to Oliver looked strikingly unusual. Only an actress on the screen, who can stop time and the film to adjust every disarrayed fold so that she looks perpetually perfect, might appear thus elegantly clad. But let these women move as they liked, and each fold of their clothing followed perfectly with the movement and fell perfectly into place again. One might almost suspect the garments were not cut of ordinary cloth, or that they were cut according to some unknown, subtle scheme, with many artful hidden seams placed by a tailor incredibly skilled at his trade.

They seemed excited. They talked in high, clear, very sweet voices, looking up at the perfect blue and transparent sky in which dawn was still frankly pink. They looked at the trees on the lawn, the leaves translucently green with an under color of golden newness, the edges crimped from constriction in the recent bud.

Happily and with excitement in their voices they called to the man, and when he answered his own voice blended so perfectly in cadence with theirs that it sounded like three people singing together. Their voices, like their clothing, seemed to have an elegance far beyond the ordinary, to be under a control such as Oliver Wilson had never dreamed of before this morning.

The taxi driver brought up the luggage, which was of a beautiful pale stuff that did not look quite like leather, and had curves in it so subtle it seemed square until you saw how two or three pieces of it fitted together when carried, into a perfectly balanced block. It was scuffed, as if from much use. And though there was a great deal of it, the taxi man did not seem to find his burden heavy. Oliver saw him look down at it now and then and heft the weight incredulously.

One of the women had very black hair and skin like cream, and smoke-blue eyes heavy-lidded with the weight of her lashes. It was the other woman Oliver's gaze followed as she came up the walk. Her hair was a clear, pale red, and her face had a softness that he thought would be like velvet to touch. She was tanned to a warm amber darker than her hair.

Just as they reached the porch steps the fair woman lifted her head and looked up. She gazed straight into Oliver's eyes and he saw that hers were very blue, and just a little amused, as if she had known he was there all along. Also they were frankly admiring.

Feeling a bit dizzy, Oliver hurried back to his room to dress.

*

"We are here on a vacation," the dark man said, accepting the keys. "We will not wish to be disturbed, as I made clear in our correspondence. You have engaged a cook and housemaid for us, I understand? We will expect you to move your own belongings out of the house, then, and—"

"Wait," Oliver said uncomfortably. "Something's come up. I—" He hesitated, not sure just how to present it. These were such increasingly odd people. Even their speech was odd. They spoke so distinctly, not slurring any of the words into contractions. English seemed as familiar to them as a native tongue, but they all spoke as trained singers sing, with perfect breath control and voice placement.

And there was a coldness in the man's voice, as if some gulf lay between him and Oliver, so deep no feeling of human contact could bridge it.

"I wonder," Oliver said, "if I could find you better living quarters somewhere else in town. There's a place across the street that—"

The dark woman said, "Oh, no!" in a lightly horrified voice, and all three of them laughed. It was cool, distant laughter that did not include Oliver.

The dark man said, "We chose this house carefully, Mr. Wilson. We would not be interested in living anywhere else."

Oliver said desperately, "I don't see why. It isn't even a modern house. I have two others in much better condition. Even across the street you'd have a fine view of the city. Here there isn't anything. The other houses cut off the view, and—"

"We engaged rooms here, Mr. Wilson," the man said with finality. "We expect to use them. Now will you make arrangements to leave as soon as possible?"

Oliver said, "No," and looked stubborn. "That isn't in the lease. You can live here until next month, since you paid for it, but you can't put me out. I'm staying."

The man opened his mouth to say something. He looked coldly at Oliver and closed it again. The feeling of aloofness was chill between them. There was a moment's silence. Then the man said, "Very well. Be kind enough to stay out of our way."

It was a little odd that he didn't inquire into Oliver's motives. Oliver was not yet sure enough of the man to explain. He couldn't very well say, "Since the lease was signed, I've been offered three times what the house is worth if I'll sell it before the end of May." He couldn't say, "I want the money, and I'm going to use my own nuisance-value to annoy you until you're willing to move out." After all, there seemed no reason why they shouldn't. After seeing them, there seemed doubly no reason, for it was clear they must be accustomed to surroundings infinitely better than this timeworn old house.

It was very strange, the value this house had so suddenly acquired. There was no reason at all why two groups of semi-anonymous people should be so eager to possess it for the month of May.

In silence Oliver showed his tenants upstairs to the three big bedrooms across the front of the house. He was intensely conscious of the red-haired woman and the way she watched him with a sort of obviously covert interest, quite warmly, and with a curious undertone to her interest that he could not quite place. It was familiar, but elusive. He thought how pleasant it would be to talk to her alone, if only to try to capture that elusive attitude and put a name to it.

Afterward he went down to the telephone and called his fiancée.

Sue's voice squeaked a little with excitement over the wire.

"Oliver, so early? Why, it's hardly six yet. Did you tell them what I said? Are they going to go?"

"Can't tell yet. I doubt it. After all, Sue, I did take their money, you know."

"Oliver, they've got to go! You've got to do something!"

"I'm trying, Sue. But I don't like it."

"Well, there isn't any reason why they shouldn't stay somewhere else. And we're going to need that money. You'll just have to think of something, Oliver."

Oliver met his own worried eyes in the mirror above the telephone and scowled at himself. His straw-colored hair was tangled and there was a shining stubble on his pleasant, tanned face. He was sorry the red-haired woman had first seen him in his untidy condition. Then his conscience smote him at the sound of Sue's determined voice and he said: "I'll try, darling. I'll try. But I did take their money."

They had, in fact, paid a great deal of money, considerably more than the rooms were worth even in that year of high prices and high wages. The country was just moving into one of those fabulous eras which are later referred to as the Gay Forties or the Golden Sixties – a pleasant period of national euphoria. It was a stimulating time to be alive – while it lasted.

"All right," Oliver said resignedly. "I'll do my best."

*

But he was conscious, as the next few days went by, that he was not doing his best. There were several reasons for that. From the beginning the idea of making himself a nuisance to his tenants had been Sue's, not Oliver's. And if Oliver had been a little less determined the whole project would never have got under way. Reason was on Sue's side, but—

For one thing, the tenants were so fascinating. All they said and did had a queer sort of inversion to it, as if a mirror had been held up to ordinary living and in the reflection showed strange variations from the norm. Their minds worked on a different basic premise, Oliver thought, from his own. They seemed to derive covert amusement from the most unamusing things; they patronized, they were aloof with a quality of cold detachment which did not prevent them from laughing inexplicably far too often for Oliver's comfort.

He saw them occasionally, on their way to and from their rooms. They were polite and distant, not, he suspected, from anger at his presence but from sheer indifference.

Most of the day they spent out of the house. The perfect May weather held unbroken and they seemed to give themselves up wholeheartedly to admiration of it, entirely confident that the warm, pale-gold sunshine and the scented air would not be interrupted by rain or cold. They were so sure of it that Oliver felt uneasy.

They took only one meal a day in the house, a late dinner. And their reactions to the meal were unpredictable. Laughter greeted some of the dishes, and a sort of delicate disgust others. No one would touch the salad, for instance. And the fish seemed to cause a wave of queer embarrassment around the table.

They dressed elaborately for each dinner. The man – his name was Omerie – looked extremely handsome in his dinner clothes, but he seemed a little sulky and Oliver twice heard the women laughing because he had to wear black. Oliver entertained a sudden vision, for no reason, of the man in garments as bright and as subtly cut as the women's, and it seemed somehow very right for him. He wore even the dark clothing with a certain flamboyance, as if cloth-of-gold would be more normal for him.

When they were in the house at other mealtimes, they ate in their rooms. They must have brought a great deal of food with them, from whatever mysterious place they had come. Oliver wondered with increasing curiosity where it might be. Delicious odors drifted into the hall sometimes, at odd hours, from their closed doors. Oliver could not identify them, but almost always they smelled irresistible. A few times the food smell was rather shockingly unpleasant, almost nauseating. It takes a connoisseur, Oliver reflected, to appreciate the decadent. And these people, most certainly, were connoisseurs.

Why they lived so contentedly in this huge ramshackle old house was a question that disturbed his dreams at night. Or why they refused to move. He caught some fascinating glimpses into their rooms, which appeared to have been changed almost completely by additions he could not have defined very clearly from the brief sights he had of them. The feeling of luxury which his first glance at them had evoked was confirmed by the richness of the hangings they had apparently brought with them, the half-glimpsed ornaments, the pictures on the walls, even the whiffs of exotic perfume that floated from half-open doors.

He saw the women go by him in the halls, moving softly through the brown dimness in their gowns so uncannily perfect in fit, so lushly rich, so glowingly colored they seemed unreal. That poise born of confidence in the subservience of the world gave them an imperious aloofness, but more than once Oliver, meeting the blue gaze of the woman with the red hair and the soft, tanned skin, thought he saw quickened interest there. She smiled at him in the dimness and went by in a haze of fragrance and a halo of incredible richness, and the warmth of the smile lingered after she had gone.

He knew she did not mean this aloofness to last between them. From the very first he was sure of that. When the time came she would make the opportunity to be alone with him. The thought was confusing and tremendously exciting. There was nothing he could do but wait, knowing she would see him when it suited her.

On the third day he lunched with Sue in a little downtown restaurant overlooking the great sweep of the metropolis across the river far below. Sue had shining brown curls and brown eyes, and her chin was a bit more prominent than is strictly accordant with beauty. From childhood Sue had known what she wanted and how to get it, and it seemed to Oliver just now that she had never wanted anything quite so much as the sale of this house.

"It's such a marvelous offer for the old mausoleum," she said, breaking into a roll with a gesture of violence. "We'll never have a chance like that again, and prices are so high we'll need the money to start housekeeping. Surely you can do *something*, Oliver!"

"I'm trying," Oliver assured her uncomfortably.

"Have you heard anything more from that madwoman who wants to buy it?"

Oliver shook his head. "Her attorney phoned again yesterday. Nothing new. I wonder who she is."

"I don't think even the attorney knows. All this mystery – I don't like it, Oliver. Even those Sancisco people— What did they do today?"

Oliver laughed. "They spent about an hour this morning telephoning movie theaters in the city, checking up on a lot of third-rate films they want to see parts of."

"Parts of? But why?"

"I don't know. I think . . . oh, nothing. More coffee?"

The trouble was, he thought he did know. It was too unlikely a guess to tell Sue about, and without familiarity with the Sancisco oddities she would only think Oliver was losing his mind. But he had from their talk, a definite impression that there was an actor in bit parts in all these films whose performances they mentioned with something very near to awe. They referred to him as Golconda, which didn't appear to be his name, so that Oliver had no way of guessing which obscure bit-player it was they admired so deeply. Golconda might have been the name of a character he had once played – and with superlative skill, judging by the comments of the Sanciscos – but to Oliver he meant nothing at all.

"They do funny things," he said, stirring his coffee reflectively. "Yesterday Omerie – that's the man – came in with a book of poems published about five years ago, and all of them handled it like a first edition of Shakespeare. I never even heard of the author, but he seems to be a tin god in their country, wherever that is."

"You still don't know? Haven't they even dropped any hints?"

"We don't do much talking," Oliver reminded her with some irony.

"I know, but— Oh, well, I guess it doesn't matter. Go on, what else do they do?"

"Well, this morning they were going to spend studying 'Golconda' and his great art, and this afternoon I think they're taking a trip up the river to some sort of shrine I never heard of. It isn't very far, wherever it is, because I know they're coming back for dinner. Some great man's birthplace, I think – they promised to take home souvenirs of the place if they could get any. They're typical tourists, all right – if I could only figure out what's behind the whole thing. It doesn't make sense."

"Nothing about that house makes sense any more. I do wish—"

She went on in a petulant voice, but Oliver ceased suddenly to hear her, because just outside the door, walking with imperial elegance on her high heels, a familiar figure passed. He did not see her face, but he thought he would know that poise, that richness of line and motion, anywhere on earth.

"Excuse me a minute," he muttered to Sue, and was out of his chair before she could speak. He made the door in half a dozen long strides, and the beautifully elegant passerby was only a few steps away when he got there. Then, with the words he had meant to speak already half-uttered, he fell silent and stood there staring.

It was not the red-haired woman. It was not her dark companion. It was a stranger. He watched, speechless, while the lovely, imperious creature moved on through the crowd and vanished, moving with familiar poise and assurance and an equally familiar strangeness as if the beautiful and exquisitely fitted garments she wore were an exotic costume to her, as they had always seemed to the Sancisco women. Every other woman on the street looked untidy and ill at ease beside her. Walking like a queen, she melted into the crowd and was gone.

She came from *their* country, Oliver told himself dizzily. So someone else nearby had mysterious tenants in this month of perfect May weather. Someone else was puzzling in vain today over the strangeness of the people from the nameless land.

In silence he went back to Sue.

The door stood invitingly ajar in the brown dimness of the upper hall. Oliver's steps slowed as he drew near it, and his heart began to quicken correspondingly. It was the red-haired woman's room, and he thought the door was not open by accident. Her name, he knew now, was Kleph.

The door creaked a little on its hinges and from within a very sweet voice said lazily, "Won't you come in?"

The room looked very different indeed. The big bed had been pushed back against the wall and a cover thrown over it that brushed the floor all around looked like soft-haired fur except that it was a pale blue-green and sparkled as if every hair were tipped with invisible crystals. Three books lay open on the fur, and a very curious-looking magazine with faintly luminous printing and a page of pictures that at first glance appeared three-dimensional. Also a tiny porcelain pipe encrusted with porcelain flowers, and a thin wisp of smoke floating from the bowl.

Above the bed a broad picture hung, framing a square of blue water so real Oliver had to look twice to be sure it was not rippling gently from left to right. From the ceiling swung a crystal globe on a glass cord. It turned gently, the light from the windows making curved rectangles in its sides.

Under the center window a sort of chaise-longue stood which Oliver had not seen before. He could only assume it was at least partly pneumatic and had been brought in the luggage. There was a very rich-looking quilted cloth covering and hiding it, embossed all over in shining metallic patterns.

Kleph moved slowly from the door and sank upon the chaise-longue with a little sigh of content. The couch accommodated itself to her body with what looked like delightful comfort. Kleph wriggled a little and then smiled up at Oliver.

"Do come on in. Sit over there, where you can see out the window. I love your beautiful spring weather. You know, there never was a May like it in civilized times." She said that quite seriously, her blue eyes on Oliver's, and there was a hint of patronage in her voice, as if the weather had been arranged especially for her.

Oliver started across the room and then paused and looked down in amazement at the floor, which felt unstable. He had not noticed before that the carpet was pure white, unspotted, and sank about an inch under the pressure of the feet. He saw then that Kleph's feet were bare, or almost bare. She wore something like gossamer buskins of filmy net, fitting her feet exactly. The bare soles were pink as if they had been rouged, and the nails had a liquid gleam like tiny mirrors. He moved closer, and was not as surprised as he should have been to see that they really were tiny mirrors, painted with some lacquer that gave them reflecting surfaces.

"Do sit down," Kleph said again, waving a white-sleeved arm toward a chair by the window. She wore a garment that looked like short, soft down, loosely cut but following perfectly every motion she made. And there was something curiously different about her very shape today. When Oliver saw her in street clothes, she had the square-shouldered, slim-flanked figure that all women strove for, but here in her lounging robe she looked – well, different. There was an almost swanlike slope to her shoulders today, a roundness and softness to her body that looked unfamiliar and very appealing.

"Will you have some tea?" Kleph asked, and smiled charmingly.

A low table beside her held a tray and several small covered cups, lovely things with an inner glow like rose quartz, the color shining deeply as if from within layer upon layer of translucence. She took up one of the cups – there were no saucers – and offered it to Oliver.

It felt fragile and thin as paper in his hand. He could not see the contents because of the cup's cover, which seemed to be one with the cup itself and left only a thin open crescent at the rim. Steam rose from the opening.

Kleph took up a cup of her own and tilted it to her lips, smiling at Oliver over the rim. She was very beautiful. The pale red hair lay in shining loops against her head and the corona of curls like a halo above her forehead might have been pressed down like a wreath. Every hair kept order as perfectly as if it had been painted on, though the breeze from the window stirred now and then among the softly shining strands.

Oliver tried the tea. Its flavor was exquisite, very hot, and the taste that lingered upon his tongue was like the scent of flowers. It was an extremely feminine drink. He sipped again, surprised to find how much he liked it.

The scent of flowers seemed to increase as he drank, swirling through his head like smoke. After the third sip there was a faint buzzing in his ears. The bees among the flowers, perhaps, he thought incoherently – and sipped again.

Kleph watched him, smiling.

"The others will be out all afternoon," she told Oliver comfortably. "I thought it would give us a pleasant time to be acquainted."

Oliver was rather horrified to hear himself saying, "What makes you talk like that?" He had had no idea of asking the question; something seemed to have loosened his control over his own tongue.

Kleph's smile deepened. She tipped the cup to her lips and there was indulgence in her voice when she said, "What do you mean 'like that?'"

He waved his hand vaguely, noting with some surprise that at a glance it seemed to have six or seven fingers as it moved past his face.

"I don't know – precision, I guess. Why don't you say 'don't,' for instance?"

"In our country we are trained to speak with precision," Kleph explained. "Just as we are trained to move and dress and think with precision. Any slovenliness is trained out of us in childhood. With you, of course—" She was polite. "With you, this does not happen to be a national fetish. With us, we have time for the amenities. We like them."

Her voice had grown sweeter and sweeter as she spoke, until by now it was almost indistinguishable from the sweetness of the flower-scent in Oliver's head, and the delicate flavor of the tea.

"What country do you come from?" he asked, and tilted the cup again to drink, mildly surprised to notice that it seemed inexhaustible.

Kleph's smile was definitely patronizing this time. It didn't irritate him. Nothing could irritate him just now. The whole room swam in a beautiful rosy glow as fragrant as the flowers.

"We must not speak of that, Mr. Wilson."

"But—" Oliver paused. After all, it was, of course, none of his business. "This is a vacation?" he asked vaguely.

"Call it a pilgrimage, perhaps."

"Pilgrimage?" Oliver was so interested that for an instant his mind came back into sharp focus. "To – what?"

"I should not have said that, Mr. Wilson. Please forget it. Do you like the tea?"

"Very much."

"You will have guessed by now that it is not only tea, but an euphoriac."

Oliver stared. "Euphoriac?"

Kleph made a descriptive circle in the air with one graceful hand, and laughed. "You do not feel the effects yet? Surely you do?"

"I feel," Oliver said, "the way I'd feel after four whiskeys."

Kleph shuddered delicately. "We get our euphoria less painfully. And without the aftereffects your barbarous alcohols used to have." She bit her lip. "Sorry. I must be euphoric myself to speak so freely. Please forgive me. Shall we have some music?"

Kleph leaned backward on the chaise-longue and reached toward the wall beside her. The sleeve, falling away from her round tanned arm, left bare the inside of the wrist, and Oliver was startled to see there a long, rosy streak of fading scar. His inhibitions had dissolved in the fumes of the fragrant tea; he caught his breath and leaned forward to stare.

Kleph shook the sleeve back over the scar with a quick gesture. Color came into her face beneath the softly tinted tan and she would not meet Oliver's eyes. A queer shame seemed to have fallen upon her.

Oliver said tactlessly, "What is it? What's the matter?"

Still she would not look at him. Much later he understood that shame and knew she had reason for it. Now he listened blankly as she said:

"Nothing . . . nothing at all. A . . . an inoculation. All of us . . . oh, never mind. Listen to the music."

This time she reached out with the other arm. She touched nothing, but when she had held her hand near the wall a sound breathed through the room. It was the sound of water, the sighing of waves receding upon long, sloped beaches. Oliver followed Kleph's gaze toward the picture of the blue water above the bed.

The waves there were moving. More than that, the point of vision moved. Slowly the seascape drifted past, moving with the waves, following them toward shore. Oliver watched, half-hypnotized by a motion that seemed at the time quite acceptable and not in the least surprising.

The waves lifted and broke in creaming foam and ran seething up a sandy beach. Then through the sound of the water music began to breathe, and through the water itself a man's face dawned in the frame, smiling intimately into the room. He held an oddly archaic musical instrument, lute-shaped, its body striped light and dark like a melon and its long neck bent back over his shoulder. He was singing, and Oliver felt mildly astonished at the song. It was very familiar and very odd indeed. He groped through the unfamiliar rhythms and found at last a thread to catch the tune by – it was "Make-Believe," from *Showboat*, but certainly a showboat that had never steamed up the Mississippi.

"What's he doing to it?" he demanded after a few moments of outraged listening. "I never heard anything like it!"

Kleph laughed and stretched out her arm again. Enigmatically she said, "We call it kyling. Never mind. How do you like this?"

It was a comedian, a man in semi-clown make-up, his eyes exaggerated so that they seemed to cover half his face. He stood by a broad glass pillar before a dark curtain and sang a gay, staccato song interspersed with patter that sounded impromptu, and all the while his left hand did an intricate, musical tattoo of the nailtips on the glass of the column. He strolled around and around it as he sang. The rhythms of his fingernails blended with the song and swung widely away into patterns of their own, and blended again without a break.

It was confusing to follow. The song made even less sense than the monologue, which had something to do with a lost slipper and was full of allusions which made Kleph smile, but were utterly unintelligible to Oliver. The man had a dry, brittle style that was not very amusing, though Kleph seemed fascinated. Oliver was interested to see in him an extension and a variation of that extreme smooth confidence which marked all three of the Sanciscos. Clearly a racial trait, he thought.

Other performances followed, some of them fragmentary as if lifted out of a completer version. One he knew. The obvious, stirring melody struck his recognition before the figures – marching men against a haze, a great banner rolling backward above them in the smoke, foreground figures striding gigantically and shouting in rhythm, "Forward, forward the lily banners go!"

The music was tinny, the images blurred and poorly colored, but there was a gusto about the performance that caught at Oliver's imagination. He stared, remembering the old film from long ago. Dennis King and a ragged chorus, singing "The Song of the Vagabonds" from – was it *Vagabond King*?

"A very old one," Kleph said apologetically. "But I like it."

The steam of the intoxicating tea swirled between Oliver and the picture. Music swelled and sank through the room and the fragrant fumes and his own euphoric brain. Nothing seemed strange. He had discovered how to drink the tea. Like nitrous oxide, the effect was not cumulative. When you reached a peak of euphoria, you could not increase the peak. It was best to wait for a slight dip in the effect of the stimulant before taking more.

Otherwise it had most of the effects of alcohol – everything after awhile dissolved into a delightful fog through which all he saw was uniformly enchanting and partook of the qualities of a dream. He questioned nothing. Afterward he was not certain how much of it he really had dreamed.

There was the dancing doll, for instance. He remembered it quite clearly, in sharp focus – a tiny, slender woman with a long-nosed, dark-eyed face and a pointed chin. She moved delicately across the white rug – knee-high, exquisite. Her features were as mobile as her body, and she danced lightly, with resounding strokes of her toes, each echoing like a bell. It was a formalized sort of dance, and she sang breathlessly in accompaniment, making amusing little grimaces. Certainly it was a portrait-doll, animated to mimic the original perfectly in voice and motion. Afterward, Oliver knew he must have dreamed it.

What else happened he was quite unable to remember later. He knew Kleph had said some curious things, but they all made sense at the time, and afterward he couldn't remember a word. He knew he had been offered little glittering candies in a transparent dish, and that some of them had been delicious and one or two so bitter his tongue still curled the next day when he recalled them, and one – Kleph sucked luxuriantly on the same kind – of a taste that was actively nauseating.

As for Kleph herself – he was frantically uncertain the next day what had really happened. He thought he could remember the softness of her white-downed arms clasped at the back of his neck, while she laughed up at him and exhaled into his face the flowery fragrance of the tea. But beyond that he was totally unable to recall anything, for a while.

There was a brief interlude later, before the oblivion of sleep. He was almost sure he remembered a moment when the other two Sanciscos stood looking down at him, the man scowling, the smoky-eyed woman smiling a derisive smile.

The man said, from a vast distance, "Kleph, you know this is against every rule—" His voice began in a thin hum and soared in fantastic flight beyond the range of hearing. Oliver thought he remembered the dark woman's laughter, thin and distant too, and the hum of her voice like bees in flight.

"Kleph, Kleph, you silly little fool, can we never trust you out of sight?"

Kleph's voice then said something that seemed to make no sense. "What does it matter, *here*?"

The man answered in that buzzing, faraway hum. "The matter of giving your bond before you leave, not to interfere. You know you signed the rules—"

Kleph's voice, nearer and more intelligible: "But here the difference is . . . it does not matter *here*! You both know that. How could it matter?"

Oliver felt the downy brush of her sleeve against his cheek, but he saw nothing except the slow, smokelike ebb and flow of darkness past his eyes. He heard the voices wrangle musically from far away, and he heard them cease.

When he woke the next morning, alone in his own room, he woke with the memory of Kleph's eyes upon him very sorrowfully, her lovely tanned face looking down on him with the red hair falling fragrantly on each side of it and sadness and compassion in her eyes. He thought he had probably dreamed that. There was no reason why anyone should look at him with such sadness.

Sue telephoned that day.

"Oliver, the people who want to buy the house are here. That madwoman and her husband. Shall I bring them over?"

Oliver's mind all day had been hazy with the vague, bewildering memories of yesterday. Kleph's face kept floating before him, blotting out the room. He said, "What? I . . . oh, well, bring them if you want to. I don't see what good it'll do."

"Oliver, what's wrong with you? We agreed we needed the money, didn't we? I don't see how you can think of passing up such a wonderful bargain without even a struggle. We could get married and buy our own house right away, and you know we'll never get such an offer again for that old trashheap. Wake up, Oliver!"

Oliver made an effort. "I know, Sue – I know. But—"

"Oliver, you've got to think of something!" Her voice was imperious.

He knew she was right. Kleph or no Kleph, the bargain shouldn't be ignored if there was any way at all of getting the tenants out. He wondered again what made the place so suddenly priceless to so many people. And what the last week in May had to do with the value of the house.

A sudden sharp curiosity pierced even the vagueness of his mind today. May's last week was so important that the whole sale of the house stood or fell upon occupancy by then. Why? *Why?*

"What's going to happen next week?" he asked rhetorically of the telephone. "Why can't they wait till these people leave? I'd knock a couple of thousand off the price if they'd . . ."

"You would not, Oliver Wilson! I can buy all our refrigeration units with that extra money. You'll just have to work out some way to give possession by next week, and that's that. You hear me?"

"Keep your shirt on," Oliver said practically. "I'm only human, but I'll try."

"I'm bringing the people over right away," Sue told him. "While the Sanciscos are still out. Now you put your mind to work and think of something, Oliver." She paused, and her voice was reflective when she spoke again. "They're . . . awfully odd people, darling."

"Odd?"

"You'll see."

It was an elderly woman and a very young man who trailed Sue up the walk. Oliver knew immediately what had struck Sue about them. He was somehow not at all surprised to see that both wore their clothing with the familiar air of elegant self-consciousness he had come to know so well. They, too, looked around them at the beautiful, sunny afternoon with conscious enjoyment and an air of faint condescension. He knew before he heard them speak how musical their voices would be and how meticulously they would pronounce each word.

There was no doubt about it. The people of Kleph's mysterious country were arriving here in force – for something. For the last week of May? He shrugged mentally; there was no way of guessing – yet. One thing only was sure: all of them must come from that nameless land where people controlled their voices like singers and their garments like actors who could stop the reel of time itself to adjust every disordered fold.

The elderly woman took full charge of the conversation from the start. They stood together on the rickety, unpainted porch, and Sue had no chance even for introductions.

"Young man, I am Madame Hollia. This is my husband." Her voice had an underrunning current of harshness, which was perhaps age. And her face looked almost corseted, the loose flesh coerced into something like firmness by some invisible method Oliver could not guess at. The make-up was so skillful he could not be certain it was make-up at all, but he had a definite feeling that she was much older than she looked. It would have taken a lifetime of command to put so much authority into the harsh, deep, musically controlled voice.

The young man said nothing. He was very handsome. His type, apparently, was one that does not change much no matter in what culture or country it may occur. He wore beautifully tailored garments and carried in one gloved hand a box of red leather, about the size and shape of a book.

Madame Hollia went on. "I understand your problem about the house. You wish to sell to me, but are legally bound by your lease with Omerie and his friends. Is that right?"

Oliver nodded. "But—"

"Let me finish. If Omerie can be forced to vacate before next week, you will accept our offer. Right? Very well. Hara!" She nodded to the young man beside her. He jumped to instant attention, bowed slightly, said, "Yes, Hollia," and slipped a gloved hand into his coat.

Madame Hollia took the little object offered on his palm, her gesture as she reached for it almost imperial, as if royal robes swept from her outstretched arm.

"Here," she said, "is something that may help us. My dear –" she held it out to Sue – "if you can hide this somewhere about the house, I believe your unwelcome tenants will not trouble you much longer."

Sue took the thing curiously. It looked like a tiny silver box, no more than an inch square, indented at the top and with no line to show it could be opened.

"Wait a minute," Oliver broke in uneasily. "What is it?"

"Nothing that will harm anyone, I assure you."

"Then what—"

Madame Hollia's imperious gesture at one sweep silenced him and commanded Sue forward. "Go on, my dear. Hurry, before Omerie comes back. I can assure you there is no danger to anyone."

Oliver broke in determinedly. "Madame Hollia, I'll have to know what your plans are. I—"

"Oh, Oliver, please!" Sue's fingers closed over the silver cube. "Don't worry about it. I'm sure Madame Hollia knows best. Don't you want to get those people out?"

"Of course I do. But I don't want the house blown up or—"

Madame Hollia's deep laughter was indulgent. "Nothing so crude, I promise you, Mr. Wilson. Remember, we want the house! Hurry, my dear."

Sue nodded and slipped hastily past Oliver into the hall. Outnumbered, he subsided uneasily. The young man, Hara, tapped a negligent foot and admired the sunlight as they waited. It was an afternoon as perfect as all of May had been, translucent gold, balmy with an edge of chill lingering in the air to point up a perfect contrast with the summer to come. Hara looked around him confidently, like a man paying just tribute to a stageset provided wholly for himself. He even glanced up at a drone from above and followed the course of a big transcontinental plane half dissolved in golden haze high in the sun. "Quaint," he murmured in a gratified voice.

Sue came back and slipped her hand through Oliver's arm, squeezing excitedly. "There," she said. "How long will it take, Madame Hollia?"

"That will depend, my dear. Not very long. Now, Mr. Wilson, one word with you. You live here also, I understand? For your own comfort, take my advice and . . ."

Somewhere within the house a door slammed and a clear high voice rang wordlessly up a rippling scale. Then there was the sound of feet on the stairs, and a single line of song. *Come hider, love, to me—*

Hara started, almost dropping the red leather box he held.

"Kleph!" he said in a whisper. "Or Klia. I know they both just came on from Canterbury. But I thought . . ."

"Hush." Madame Hollia's features composed themselves into an imperious blank. She breathed triumphantly through her nose, drew back upon herself and turned an imposing facade to the door.

Kleph wore the same softly downy robe Oliver had seen before, except that today it was not white, but a pale, clear blue that gave her tan an apricot flush. She was smiling.

"Why, Hollia!" Her tone was at its most musical. "I thought I recognized voices from home. How nice to see you. No one knew you were coming to the—" She broke off and glanced at Oliver and then away again. "Hara, too," she said. "What a pleasant surprise."

Sue said flatly, "When did you get back?"

Kleph smiled at her. "You must be the little Miss Johnson. Why, I did not go out at all. I was tired of sightseeing. I have been napping in my room."

Sue drew in her breath in something that just escaped being a disbelieving sniff. A look flashed between the two women, and for an instant held – and that instant was timeless. It was an extraordinary pause in which a great deal of wordless interplay took place in the space of a second.

Oliver saw the quality of Kleph's smile at Sue, that same look of quiet confidence he had noticed so often about all of these strange people. He saw Sue's quick inventory of the other woman, and he saw how Sue squared her shoulders and stood up straight, smoothing down her summer frock over her flat hips so that for an instant she stood posed consciously, looking down on Kleph. It was deliberate. Bewildered, he glanced again at Kleph.

Kleph's shoulders sloped softly, her robe was belted to a tiny waist and hung in deep folds over frankly rounded hips. Sue's was the fashionable figure – but Sue was the first to surrender.

Kleph's smile did not falter. But in the silence there was an abrupt reversal of values, based on no more than the measureless quality of Kleph's confidence in herself, the quiet, assured smile. It was suddenly made very clear that fashion is not a constant. Kleph's curious, out-of-mode curves without warning became the norm, and Sue was a queer, angular, half-masculine creature beside her.

Oliver had no idea how it was done. Somehow the authority passed in a breath from one woman to the other. Beauty is almost wholly a matter of fashion; what is beautiful today would have been grotesque a couple of generations ago and will be grotesque a hundred years ahead. It will be worse than grotesque; it will be outmoded and therefore faintly ridiculous.

Sue was that. Kleph had only to exert her authority to make it clear to everyone on the porch. Kleph was a beauty, suddenly and very convincingly, beautiful in the accepted mode, and Sue was amusingly old-fashioned, an anachronism in her lithe, square-shouldered slimness. She did not belong. She was grotesque among these strangely immaculate people.

Sue's collapse was complete. But pride sustained her, and bewilderment. Probably she never did grasp entirely what was wrong. She gave Kleph one glance of burning resentment and when her eyes came back to Oliver there was suspicion in them, and mistrust.

Looking backward later, Oliver thought that in that moment, for the first time clearly, he began to suspect the truth. But he had no time to ponder it, for after the brief instant of enmity the three people from – elsewhere – began to speak all at once, as if in a belated attempt to cover something they did not want noticed.

Kleph said, "This beautiful weather—" and Madame Hollia said, "So fortunate to have this house—" and Hara, holding up the red leather box, said loudest of all, "Cenbe sent you this, Kleph. His latest."

Kleph put out both hands for it eagerly, the eiderdown sleeves falling back from her rounded arms. Oliver had a quick glimpse of that mysterious scar before the sleeve fell back, and it seemed to him that there was the faintest trace of a similar scar vanishing into Hara's cuff as he let his own arm drop.

"Cenbe!" Kleph cried, her voice high and sweet and delighted. "How wonderful! What period?"

"From November 1664," Hara said. "London, of course, though I think there may be some counterpoint from the 1347 November. He hasn't finished – of course." He glanced almost nervously at Oliver and Sue. "A wonderful example," he said quickly. "Marvelous. If you have the taste for it, of course."

Madame Hollia shuddered with ponderous delicacy. "That man!" she said. "Fascinating, of course – a great man. But – so *advanced*!"

"It takes a connoisseur to appreciate Cenbe's work fully," Kleph said in a slightly tart voice. "We all admit that."

"Oh yes, we all bow to Cenbe," Hollia conceded. "I confess the man terrifies me a little, my dear. Do we expect him to join us?"

"I suppose so," Kleph said. "If his – work – is not yet finished, then of course. You know Cenbe's tastes."

Hollia and Hara laughed together. "I know when to look for him, then," Hollia said. She glanced at the staring Oliver and the subdued but angry Sue, and with a commanding effort brought the subject back into line.

"So fortunate, my dear Kleph, to have this house," she declared heavily. "I saw a tridimensional of it – afterward – and it was still quite perfect. Such a fortunate coincidence. Would you consider parting with your lease, for a consideration? Say, a coronation seat at . . ."

"Nothing could buy us, Hollia," Kleph told her gaily, clasping the red box to her bosom.

Hollia gave her a cool stare. "You may change your mind, my dear Kleph," she said pontifically. "There is still time. You can always reach us through Mr. Wilson here. We have rooms up the street in the Montgomery House – nothing like yours, of course, but they will do. For us, they will do."

Oliver blinked. The Montgomery House was the most expensive hotel in town. Compared to this collapsing old ruin, it was a palace. There was no understanding these people. Their values seemed to have suffered a complete reversal.

Madame Hollia moved majestically toward the steps.

"Very pleasant to see you, my dear," she said over one well-padded shoulder. "Enjoy your stay. My regards to Omerie and Klia. Mr. Wilson—" she nodded toward the walk. "A word with you."

Oliver followed her down toward the street. Madame Hollia paused halfway there and touched his arm.

"One word of advice," she said huskily. "You say you sleep here? Move out, young man. Move out before tonight."

Oliver was searching in a half-desultory fashion for the hiding place Sue had found for the mysterious silver cube, when the first sounds from above began to drift down the stairwell toward him. Kleph had closed her door, but the house was old, and strange qualities in the noise overhead seemed to seep through the woodwork like an almost visible stain.

It was music, in a way. But much more than music. And it was a terrible sound, the sounds of calamity and of all human reaction to calamity, everything from hysteria to heartbreak, from irrational joy to rationalized acceptance.

The calamity was – single. The music did not attempt to correlate all human sorrows; it focused sharply upon one and followed the ramifications out and out. Oliver recognized these basics to the sounds in a very brief moment. They were essentials, and they seemed to beat into his brain with the first strains of the music which was so much more than music.

But when he lifted his head to listen he lost all grasp upon the meaning of the noise and it was sheer medley and confusion. To think of it was to blur it hopelessly in the mind, and he could not recapture that first instant of unreasoning acceptance.

He went upstairs almost in a daze, hardly knowing what he was doing. He pushed Kleph's door open. He looked inside . . . What he saw there he could not afterward remember except in a blurring as vague as the blurred ideas the music roused in his brain. Half the room had vanished behind a mist, and the mist was a three-dimensional screen upon which were projected – he had no words for them. He was not even sure if the projections were visual. The mist was spinning with motion and sound, but essentially it was neither sound nor motion that Oliver saw.

This was a work of art. Oliver knew no name for it. It transcended all art-forms he knew, blended them, and out of the blend produced subtleties his mind could not begin to grasp. Basically, this was the attempt of a master composer to correlate every essential aspect of a vast human experience into something that could be conveyed in a few moments to every sense at once.

The shifting visions on the screen were not pictures in themselves, but hints of pictures, subtly selected outlines that plucked at the mind and with one deft touch set whole chords ringing through the memory. Perhaps each beholder reacted differently, since it was in the eye and the mind of the beholder that the truth of the picture lay. No two would be aware of the same symphonic panorama, but each would see essentially the same terrible story unfold.

Every sense was touched by that deft and merciless genius. Color and shape and motion flickered in the screen, hinting much, evoking unbearable memories deep in the mind; odors floated from the screen and touched the heart of the beholder more poignantly than anything visual could do. The skin crawled sometimes as if to a tangible cold hand laid upon it. The tongue curled with remembered bitterness and remembered sweet.

It was outrageous. It violated the innermost privacies of a man's mind, called up secret things long ago walled off behind mental scar tissue, forced its terrible message upon the beholder relentlessly though the mind might threaten to crack beneath the stress of it.

And yet, in spite of all this vivid awareness, Oliver did not know what calamity the screen portrayed. That it was real, vast, overwhelmingly dreadful he could not doubt. That it had once happened was unmistakable. He caught flashing glimpses of human faces distorted with grief and disease and death – real faces, faces that had once lived and were seen now in the instant of dying. He saw men and women in rich clothing superimposed in panorama upon reeling thousands of ragged folk, great throngs of them swept past the sight in an instant, and he saw that death made no distinction among them.

He saw lovely women laugh and shake their curls, and the laughter shriek into hysteria and the hysteria into music. He saw one man's face, over and over – a long, dark, saturnine face, deeply lined, sorrowful, the face of a powerful man wise in worldliness, urbane – and helpless. That face was for a while a recurring motif, always more tortured, more helpless than before.

The music broke off in the midst of a rising glide. The mist vanished and the room reappeared before him. The anguished dark face for an instant seemed to Oliver printed everywhere he looked, like after-vision on the eyelids. He knew that face. He had seen it before, not often, but he should know its name—

"Oliver, Oliver—" Kleph's sweet voice came out of a fog at him. He was leaning dizzily against the doorpost looking down into her eyes. She, too, had that dazed blankness he must show on his own face. The power of the dreadful symphony still held them both. But even in this confused moment Oliver saw that Kleph had been enjoying the experience.

He felt sickened to the depths of his mind, dizzy with sickness and revulsion because of the superimposing of human miseries he had just beheld. But Kleph – only appreciation showed upon her face. To her it had been magnificence, and magnificence only.

Irrelevantly Oliver remembered the nauseating candies she had enjoyed, the nauseating odors of strange food that drifted sometimes through the hall from her room.

What was it she had said downstairs a little while ago? Connoisseur, that was it. Only a connoisseur could appreciate work as – as *advanced* – as the work of someone called Cenbe.

A whiff of intoxicating sweetness curled past Oliver's face. Something cool and smooth was pressed into his hand.

"Oh, Oliver, I am so sorry," Kleph's voice murmured contritely. "Here, drink the euphoriac and you will feel better. Please drink!"

The familiar fragrance of the hot sweet tea was on his tongue before he knew he had complied. Its relaxing fumes floated up through his brain and in a moment or two the world felt stable around him again. The room was as it had always been. And Kleph—

Her eyes were very bright. Sympathy showed in them for him, but for herself she was still brimmed with the high elation of what she had just been experiencing.

"Come and sit down," she said gently, tugging at his arm. "I am so sorry – I should not have played that over, where you could hear it. I have no excuse, really. It was only that I forgot what the effect might be on one who had never heard Cenbe's symphonies before. I was so impatient to see what he had done with . . . with his new subject. I am so very sorry, Oliver!"

"What was it?" His voice sounded steadier than he had expected. The tea was responsible for that. He sipped again, glad of the consoling euphoria its fragrance brought.

"A . . . a composite interpretation of . . . oh, Oliver, you know I must not answer questions!"

"But—"

"No – drink your tea and forget what it was you saw. Think of other things. Here, we will have music – another kind of music, something gay . . ."

She reached for the wall beside the window, and as before, Oliver saw the broad framed picture of blue water above the bed ripple and grow pale. Through it another scene began to dawn like shapes rising beneath the surface of the sea.

He had a glimpse of a dark-curtained stage upon which a man in a tight dark tunic and hose moved with a restless, sidelong pace, his hands and face startlingly pale against the black about him. He limped; he had a crooked back and he spoke familiar lines. Oliver had seen John Barryrnore once as the crook-backed Richard, and it seemed vaguely outrageous to him that any other actor should essay that difficult part. This one he had never seen before, but the man had a fascinatingly smooth manner and his interpretation of the Plantagenet king was quite new and something Shakespeare probably never dreamed of.

"No," Kleph said, "not this. Nothing gloomy." And she put out her hand again. The nameless new Richard faded and there was a swirl of changing pictures and changing voices, all blurred together, before the scene steadied upon a stageful of dancers in pastel ballet skirts, drifting effortlessly through some complicated pattern of motion. The music that went with it was light and effortless too. The room filled up with the clear, floating melody.

Oliver set down his cup. He felt much surer of himself now, and he thought the euphoriac had done all it could for him. He didn't want to blur again mentally. There were things he meant to learn about. Now. He considered how to begin.

Kleph was watching him. "That Hollia," she said suddenly. "She wants to buy the house?"

Oliver nodded. "She's offering a lot of money. Sue's going to be awfully disappointed if . . ." He hesitated. Perhaps, after all, Sue would not be disappointed. He remembered the little silver cube with the enigmatic function and he wondered if he should mention it to Kleph. But the euphoriac had not reached that level of his brain, and he remembered his duty to Sue and was silent.

Kleph shook her head, her eyes upon his warm with – was it sympathy?

"Believe me," she said, "you will not find that – important – after all. I promise you, Oliver."

He stared at her. "I wish you'd explain."

Kleph laughed on a note more sorrowful than amused. But it occurred to Oliver suddenly that there was no longer condescension in her voice. Imperceptibly that air of delicate amusement had vanished from her manner toward him. The cool detachment that still marked Omerie's attitude, and Klia's, was not in Kleph's any more. It was a subtlety he did not think she could assume. It had to come spontaneously or not at all. And for no reason he was willing to examine, it became suddenly very important to Oliver that Kleph should not condescend to him, that she should feel toward him as he felt toward her. He would not think of it.

He looked down at his cup, rose-quartz, exhaling a thin plume of steam from its crescent-slit opening. This time, he thought, maybe he could make the tea work for him. For he remembered how it loosened the tongue, and there was a great deal he needed to know. The idea that had come to him on the porch in the instant of silent rivalry between Kleph and Sue seemed now too fantastic to entertain. But some answer there must be.

Kleph herself gave him the opening.

"I must not take too much euphoriac this afternoon," she said, smiling at him over her pink cup. "It will make me drowsy, and we are going out this evening with friends."

"More friends?" Oliver asked. "From your country?"

Kleph nodded. "Very dear friends we have expected all this week."

"I wish you'd tell me," Oliver said bluntly, "where it is you come from. It isn't from here. Your culture is too different from ours – even your names . . ." He broke off as Kleph shook her head.

"I wish I could tell you. But that is against all the rules. It is even against the rules for me to be here talking to you now."

"What rules?"

She made a helpless gesture. "You must not ask me, Oliver." She leaned back on the chaise-longue, which adjusted itself luxuriously to the motion, and smiled very sweetly at him. "We must not talk about things like that. Forget it, listen to the music, enjoy yourself if you can—" She closed her eyes and laid her head back against the cushions. Oliver saw the round tanned throat swell as she began to hum a tune. Eyes still closed, she sang again the words she had sung upon the stairs. "*Come hider, love, to me . . .*"

A memory clicked over suddenly in Oliver's mind. He had never heard the queer, lagging tune before, but he thought he knew the words. He remembered what Hollia's husband had said when he heard that line of song, and he leaned forward. She would not answer a direct question, but perhaps—

"Was the weather this warm in Canterbury?" he asked, and held his breath. Kleph hummed another line of the song and shook her head, eyes still closed.

"It was autumn there," she said. "But bright, wonderfully bright. Even their clothing, you know . . . everyone was singing that new song, and I can't get it out of my head." She sang another line, and the words were almost unintelligible – English, yet not an English Oliver could understand.

He stood up. "Wait," he said. "I want to find something. Back in a minute."

She opened her eyes and smiled mistily at him, still humming. He went downstairs as fast as he could – the stairway swayed a little, though his head was nearly clear now – and into the library. The book he wanted was old and battered, interlined with the penciled notes of his college days. He did not remember very clearly where the passage he wanted was, but he thumbed fast through the columns and by sheer luck found it within a few minutes. Then he went back upstairs, feeling a strange emptiness in his stomach because of what he almost believed now.

"Kleph," he said firmly, "I know that song. I know the year it was new."

Her lids rose slowly; she looked at him through a mist of euphoriac. He was not sure she had understood. For a long moment she held him with her gaze. Then she put out one downy-sleeved arm and spread her tanned fingers toward him. She laughed deep in her throat.

"*Come hider, love, to me,*" she said.

He crossed the room slowly, took her hand. The fingers closed warmly about his. She pulled him down so that he had to kneel beside her. Her other arm lifted. Again she laughed, very softly, and closed her eyes, lifting her face to his.

The kiss was warm and long. He caught something of her own euphoria from the fragrance of the tea breathed into his face. And he was startled at the end of the kiss, when the clasp of her arms loosened about his neck, to feel the sudden rush of her breath against his cheek. There were tears on her face, and the sound she made was a sob.

He held her off and looked down in amazement. She sobbed once more, caught a deep breath, and said, "Oh, Oliver, Oliver—" Then she shook her head and pulled free, turning away to hide her face. "I . . . I am sorry," she said unevenly. "Please forgive me. It does not matter . . . I *know* it does not matter . . . but—"

"What's wrong? What doesn't matter?"

"Nothing. Nothing . . . please forget it. Nothing at all." She got a handkerchief from the table and blew her nose, smiling at him with an effect of radiance through the tears.

Suddenly he was very angry. He had heard enough evasions and mystifying half-truths. He said roughly, "Do you think I'm crazy? I know enough now to—"

"Oliver, please!" She held up her own cup, steaming fragrantly. "Please, no more questions. Here, euphoria is what you need, Oliver. Euphoria, not answers."

"What year was it when you heard that song in Canterbury?" he demanded, pushing the cup aside.

She blinked at him, tears bright on her lashes. "Why . . . what year do you think?"

"I know," Oliver told her grimly. "I know the year that song was popular. I know you just came from Canterbury – Hollia's husband said so. It's May now, but it was autumn in Canterbury, and you just came from there, so lately the song you heard is still running through your head. Chaucer's Pardoner sang that song some time around the end of the fourteenth century. Did you see Chaucer, Kleph? What was it like in England that long ago?"

Kleph's eyes fixed his for a silent moment. Then her shoulders drooped and her whole body went limp with resignation beneath the soft blue robe. "I am a fool," she said gently. "It must have been easy to trap me. You really believe what you say?"

Oliver nodded.

She said in a low voice, "Few people do believe it. That is one of our maxims, when we travel. We are safe from much suspicion because people before The Travel began will not believe."

The emptiness in Oliver's stomach suddenly doubled in volume. For an instant the bottom dropped out of time itself and the universe was unsteady about him. He felt sick. He felt naked and helpless. There was a buzzing in his ears and the room dimmed before him.

He had not really believed – not until this instant. He had expected some rational explanation from her that would tidy all his wild half-thoughts and suspicions into something a man could accept as believable. Not this.

Kleph dabbed at her eyes with the pale-blue handkerchief and smiled tremulously.

"I know," she said. "It must be a terrible thing to accept. To have all your concepts turned upside down. We know it from childhood, of course, but for you . . . here, Oliver. The euphoriac will make it easier."

He took the cup, the faint stain of her lip rouge still on the crescent opening. He drank, feeling the dizzy sweetness spiral through his head, and his brain turned a little in his skull as the volatile fragrance took effect. With that turning, focus shifted and all his values with it.

He began to feel better. The flesh settled on his bones again, and the warm clothing of temporal assurance settled upon his flesh, and he was no longer naked and in the vortex of unstable time.

"The story is very simple, really," Kleph said. "We – travel. Our own time is not terribly far ahead of yours. No. I must not say how far. But we still remember your songs and poets and some of your great actors. We are a people of much leisure, and we cultivate the art of enjoying ourselves.

"This is a tour we are making – a tour of a year's seasons. Vintage seasons. That autumn in Canterbury was the most magnificent autumn our researchers could discover anywhere. We rode in a pilgrimage to the shrine – it was a wonderful experience, though the clothing was a little hard to manage.

"Now this month of May is almost over – the loveliest May in recorded times. A perfect May in a wonderful period. You have no way of knowing what a good, gay period you live in, Oliver. The very feeling in the air of the cities – that wonderful national confidence and happiness – everything going as smoothly as a dream. There were other Mays with fine weather, but each of them had a war or a famine, or something else wrong." She hesitated, grimaced and went on rapidly. "In a few days we are to meet at a coronation in Rome," she said. "I think the year will be 800 – Christmastime. We—"

"But why," Oliver interrupted, "did you insist on this house? Why do the others want to get it away from you?"

Kleph stared at him. He saw the tears rising again in small bright crescents that gathered above her lower lids. He saw the look of obstinacy that came upon her soft, tanned face. She shook her head.

"You must not ask me that." She held out the steaming cup. "Here, drink and forget what I have said. I can tell you no more. No more at all."

When he woke, for a little while he had no idea where he was. He did not remember leaving Kleph or coming to his own room. He didn't care, just then. For he woke to a sense of overwhelming terror.

The dark was full of it. His brain rocked on waves of fear and pain. He lay motionless, too frightened to stir, some atavistic memory warning him to lie quiet until he knew from which direction the danger threatened. Reasonless panic broke over him in a tidal flow; his head ached with its violence and the dark throbbed to the same rhythms.

A knock sounded at the door. Omerie's deep voice said, "Wilson! Wilson, are you awake?"

Oliver tried twice before he had breath to answer. "Y-yes – what is it?"

The knob rattled. Omerie's dim figure groped for the light switch and the room sprang into visibility. Omerie's face was drawn with strain, and he held one hand to his head as if it ached in rhythm with Oliver's.

It was in that moment, before Omerie spoke again, that Oliver remembered Hollia's warning. "Move out, young man – move out before tonight." Wildly he wondered what threatened them all in this dark house that throbbed with the rhythms of pure terror.

Omerie in an angry voice answered the unspoken question.

"Someone has planted a subsonic in the house, Wilson. Kleph thinks you may know where it is."

"S-subsonic?"

"Call it a gadget," Omerie interpreted impatiently. "Probably a small metal box that—"

Oliver said, "Oh," in a tone that must have told Omerie everything.

"Where is it?" he demanded. "Quick. Let's get this over."

"I don't know." With an effort Oliver controlled the chattering of his teeth. "Y-you mean all this – all this is just from the little box?"

"Of course. Now tell me how to find it before we all go crazy."

Oliver got shakily out of bed, groping for his robe with nerveless hands. "I s-suppose she hid it somewhere downstairs," he said. "S-she wasn't gone long."

Omerie got the story out of him in a few brief questions. He clicked his teeth in exasperation when Oliver had finished it.

"That stupid Hollia—"

"Omerie!" Kleph's plaintive voice wailed from the hall. "Please hurry, Omerie! This is too much to stand! Oh, Omerie, please!"

Oliver stood up abruptly. Then a redoubled wave of the inexplicable pain seemed to explode in his skull at the motion, and he clutched the bedpost and reeled.

"Go find the thing yourself," he heard himself saying dizzily. "I can't even walk—"

Omerie's own temper was drawn wire-tight by the pressure in the room. He seized Oliver's shoulder and shook him, saying in a tight voice, "You let it in – now help us get it out, or—"

"It's a gadget out of your world, not mine!" Oliver said furiously.

And then it seemed to him there was a sudden coldness and silence in the room. Even the pain and the senseless terror paused for a moment. Omerie's pale, cold eyes fixed upon Oliver a stare so chill he could almost feel the ice in it.

"What do you know about our – world?" Omerie demanded.

Oliver did not speak a word. He did not need to; his face must have betrayed what he knew. He was beyond concealment in the stress of this night-time terror he still could not understand.

Omerie bared his white teeth and said three perfectly unintelligible words. Then he stepped to the door and snapped, "Kleph!"

Oliver could see the two women huddled together in the hall, shaking violently with involuntary waves of that strange, synthetic terror. Klia, in a luminous green gown, was rigid with control, but Kleph made no effort whatever at repression. Her downy robe had turned soft gold tonight; she shivered in it and the tears ran down her face unchecked.

"Kleph," Omerie said in a dangerous voice, "you were euphoric again yesterday?"

Kleph darted a scared glance at Oliver and nodded guiltily.

"You talked too much." It was a complete indictment in one sentence. "You know the rules, Kleph. You will not be allowed to travel again if anyone reports this to the authorities."

Kleph's lovely creamy face creased suddenly into impenitent dimples.

"I know it was wrong. I am very sorry – but you will not stop me if Cenbe says no."

Klia flung out her arms in a gesture of helpless anger. Omerie shrugged. "In this case, as it happens, no great harm is done," he said, giving Oliver an unfathomable glance. "But it might have been serious. Next time perhaps it will be. I must have a talk with Cenbe."

"We must find the subsonic first of all," Klia reminded them, shivering. "If Kleph is afraid to help, she can go out for a while. I confess I am very sick of Kleph's company just now."

"We could give up the house!" Kleph cried wildly. "Let Hollia have it! How can you stand this long enough to hunt—"

"Give up the house?" Klia echoed. "You must be mad! With all our invitations out?"

"There will be no need for that," Omerie said. "We can find it if we all hunt. You feel able to help?" He looked at Oliver.

With an effort Oliver controlled his own senseless panic as the waves of it swept through the room. "Yes," he said. "But what about me? What are you going to do?"

"That should be obvious," Omerie said, his pale eyes in the dark face regarding Oliver impassively. "Keep you in the house until we go. We can certainly do no less. You understand that. And there is no reason for us to do more, as it happens. Silence is all we promised when we signed our travel papers."

"But—" Oliver groped for the fallacy in that reasoning. It was no use. He could not think clearly. Panic surged insanely through his mind from the very air around him. "All right," he said. "Let's hunt."

It was dawn before they found the box, tucked inside the ripped seam of a sofa cushion. Omerie took it upstairs without a word. Five minutes later the pressure in the air abruptly dropped and peace fell blissfully upon the house.

"They will try again," Omerie said to Oliver at the door of the back bedroom. "We must watch for that. As for you, I must see that you remain in the house until Friday. For your own comfort, I advise you to let me know if Hollia offers any further tricks. I confess I am not quite sure how to enforce your staying indoors. I could use methods that would make you very uncomfortable. I would prefer to accept your word on it."

Oliver hesitated. The relaxing of pressure upon his brain had left him exhausted and stupid, and he was not at all sure what to say.

Omerie went on after a moment. "It was partly our fault for not insuring that we had the house to ourselves," he said. "Living here with us, you could scarcely help suspecting. Shall we say that in return for your promise, I reimburse you in part for losing the sale price on this house?"

Oliver thought that over. It would pacify Sue a little. And it meant only two days indoors. Besides, what good would escaping do? What could he say to outsiders that would not lead him straight to a padded cell?

"All right," he said wearily. "I promise."

By Friday morning there was still no sign from Hollia. Sue telephoned at noon. Oliver knew the crackle of her voice over the wire when Kleph took the call. Even the crackle sounded hysterical; Sue saw her bargain slipping hopelessly through her grasping little fingers.

Kleph's voice was soothing. "I am sorry," she said many times, in the intervals when the voice paused. "I am truly sorry. Believe me, you will find it does not matter. I know . . . I am sorry—"

She turned from the phone at last. "The girl says Hollia has given up," she told the others.

"Not Hollia," Klia said firmly.

Omerie shrugged. "We have very little time left. If she intends anything more, it will be tonight. We must watch for it."

"Oh, not tonight!" Kleph's voice was horrified. "Not even Hollia would do that!"

"Hollia, my dear, in her own way is quite as unscrupulous as you are," Omerie told her with a smile.

"But – would she spoil things for us just because she can't be here?"

"What do you think?" Klia demanded.

Oliver ceased to listen. There was no making sense out of their talk, but he knew that by tonight whatever the secret was must surely come into the open at last. He was willing to wait and see.

For two days excitement had been building up in the house and the three who shared it with him. Even the servants felt it and were nervous and unsure of themselves. Oliver had given up asking questions – it only embarrassed his tenants – and watched.

All the chairs in the house were collected in the three front bedrooms. The furniture was rearranged to make room for them, and dozens of covered cups had been set out on trays. Oliver recognized Kleph's rose-quartz set among the rest. No steam rose from the thin crescent-openings, but the cups were full. Oliver lifted one and felt a heavy liquid move within it, like something half-solid, sluggishly.

Guests were obviously expected, but the regular dinner hour of nine came and went, and no one had yet arrived. Dinner was finished; the servants went home. The Sanciscos went to their rooms to dress, amid a feeling of mounting tension.

Oliver stepped out on the porch after dinner, trying in vain to guess what it was that had wrought such a pitch of expectancy in the house. There was a quarter moon swimming in haze on the horizon, but the stars which had made every night of May thus far a dazzling translucency, were very dim tonight. Clouds had begun to gather at sundown, and the undimmed weather of the whole month seemed ready to break at last.

Behind Oliver the door opened a little, and closed. He caught Kleph's fragrance before he turned, and a faint whiff of the fragrance of the euphoriac she was much too fond of drinking. She came to his side and slipped a hand into his, looking up into his face in the darkness.

"Oliver," she said very softly. "Promise me one thing. Promise me not to leave the house tonight."

"I've already promised that," he said a little irritably.

"I know. But tonight – I have a very particular reason for wanting you indoors tonight." She leaned her head against his shoulder for a moment, and despite himself his irritation softened. He had not seen Kleph alone since that last night of her revelations; he supposed he never would be alone with her again for more than a few minutes at a time. But he knew he would not forget those two bewildering evenings. He knew too, now, that she was very weak and foolish – but she was still Kleph and he had held her in his arms, and was not likely ever to forget it.

"You might be – hurt – if you went out tonight," she was saying in a muffled voice. "I know it will not matter, in the end, but – remember you promised, Oliver."

She was gone again, and the door had closed behind her, before he could voice the futile questions in his mind.

The guests began to arrive just before midnight. From the head of the stairs Oliver saw them coming in by twos and threes, and was astonished at how many of these people from the future must have gathered here in the past weeks. He could see quite clearly now how they differed from the norm of his own period. Their physical elegance was what one noticed first – perfect grooming, meticulous manners, meticulously controlled voices. But because they were all idle, all, in a way, sensation-hunters, there was a certain shrillness underlying their voices, especially when heard all together. Petulance and self-indulgence showed beneath the good manners. And tonight, an all-pervasive excitement.

By one o'clock everyone had gathered in the front rooms. The teacups had begun to steam, apparently of themselves, around midnight, and the house was full of the faint, thin fragrance that induced a sort of euphoria all through the rooms, breathed in with the perfume of the tea.

It made Oliver feel light and drowsy. He was determined to sit up as long as the others did, but he must have dozed off in his own room, by the window, an unopened book in his lap.

For when it happened he was not sure for a few minutes whether or not it was a dream. The vast, incredible crash was louder than sound. He felt the whole house shake under him, felt rather than heard the timbers grind upon one another like broken bones, while he was still in the borderland of sleep. When he woke fully he was on the floor among the shattered fragments of the window.

How long or short a time he had lain there he did not know. The world was still stunned with that tremendous noise, or his ears still deaf from it, for there was no sound anywhere.

He was halfway down the hall toward the front rooms when sound began to return from outside. It was a low, indescribable rumble at first, prickled with countless tiny distant screams. Oliver's eardrums ached from the terrible impact of the vast unheard noise, but the numbness was wearing off and he heard before he saw it the first voices of the stricken city.

The door to Kleph's room resisted him for a moment. The house had settled a little from the violence of the – the explosion? – and the frame was out of line. When he got the door open he could only stand blinking stupidly into the darkness within. All the lights were out, but there was a breathless sort of whispering going on in many voices.

The chairs were drawn around the broad front windows so that everyone could see out; the air swam with the fragrance of euphoria. There was light enough here from outside for Oliver to see that a few onlookers still had their hands to their ears, but all were craning eagerly forward to see.

Through a dreamlike haze Oliver saw the city spread out with impossible distinctness below the window. He knew quite well that a row of houses across the street blocked the view – yet he was looking over the city now, and he could see it in a limitless panorama from here to the horizon. The houses between had vanished.

On the far skyline fire was already a solid mass, painting the low clouds crimson. That sulphurous light reflecting back from the sky upon the city made clear the rows upon rows of flattened houses with flame beginning to lick up among them, and farther out the formless rubble of what had been houses a few minutes ago and was now nothing at all.

The city had begun to be vocal. The noise of the flames rose loudest, but you could hear a rumble of human voices like the beat of surf a long way off, and staccato noises of screaming made a sort of pattern that came and went continuously through the web of sound. Threading it in undulating waves the shrieks of sirens knit the web together into a terrible symphony that had, in its way, a strange, inhuman beauty.

Briefly through Oliver's stunned incredulity went the memory of that other symphony Kleph had played there one day, another catastrophe retold in terms of music and moving shapes.

He said hoarsely, "Kleph—"

The tableau by the window broke. Every head turned, and Oliver saw the faces of strangers staring at him, some few in embarrassment avoiding his eyes, but most seeking them out with that avid, inhuman curiosity which is common to a type in all crowds at accident scenes. But these people were here by design, audience at a vast disaster timed almost for their coming.

Kleph got up unsteadily, her velvet dinner gown tripping her as she rose. She set down a cup and swayed a little as she came toward the door, saying, "Oliver . . . Oliver—" in a sweet, uncertain voice. She was drunk, he saw, and wrought up by the catastrophe to a pitch of stimulation in which she was not very sure what she was doing.

Oliver heard himself saying in a thin voice not his own, "W-what was it, Kleph? What happened? What—" But "happened" seemed so inadequate a word for the incredible panorama below that he had to choke back hysterical laughter upon the struggling questions, and broke off entirely, trying to control the shaking that had seized his body.

Kleph made an unsteady stoop and seized a steaming cup. She came to him, swaying, holding it out – her panacea for all ills.

"Here, drink it, Oliver – we are all quite safe here, quite safe." She thrust the cup to his lips and he gulped automatically, grateful for the fumes that began their slow, coiling surcease in his brain with the first swallow.

"It was a meteor," Kleph was saying. "Quite a small meteor, really. We are perfectly safe here. This house was never touched."

Out of some cell of the unconscious Oliver heard himself saying incoherently, "Sue? Is Sue—" He could not finish.

Kleph thrust the cup at him again. "I think she may be safe – for a while. Please, Oliver – forget about all that and drink."

"But you knew!" Realization of that came belatedly to his stunned brain. "You could have given warning, or—"

"How could we change the past?" Kleph asked. "We knew – but could we stop the meteor? Or warn the city? Before we come we must give our word never to interfere—"

Their voices had risen imperceptibly to be audible above the rising volume of sound from below. The city was roaring now, with flames and cries and the crash of falling buildings. Light in the room turned lurid and pulsed upon the walls and ceiling in red light and redder dark.

Downstairs a door slammed. Someone laughed. It was high, hoarse, angry laughter. Then from the crowd in the room someone gasped and there was a chorus of dismayed cries. Oliver tried to focus upon the window and the terrible panorama beyond, and found he could not.

It took several seconds of determined blinking to prove that more than his own vision was at fault. Kleph whimpered softly and moved against him. His arms closed about her automatically, and he was grateful for the warm, solid flesh against him. This much at least he could touch and be sure of, though everything else that was happening might be a dream. Her perfume and the heady perfume of the tea rose together in his head, and for an instant, holding her in this embrace that must certainly be the last time he ever held her, he did not care that something had gone terribly wrong with the very air of the room.

It was blindness – not continuous, but a series of swift, widening ripples between which he could catch glimpses of the other faces in the room, strained and astonished in the flickering light from the city.

The ripples came faster. There was only a blink of sight between them now, and the blinks grew briefer and briefer, the intervals of darkness more broad.

From downstairs the laughter rose again up the stairwell. Oliver thought he knew the voice. He opened his mouth to speak, but a door nearby slammed open before he could find his tongue, and Omerie shouted down the stairs.

"Hollia?" he roared above the roaring of the city. "Hollia, is that you?"

She laughed again, triumphantly. "I warned you!" her hoarse, harsh voice called. "Now come out in the street with the rest of us if you want to see any more!"

"Hollia!" Omerie shouted desperately. "Stop this or—"

The laughter was derisive. "What will you do, Omerie? This time I hid it too well – come down in the street if you want to watch the rest."

There was angry silence in the house. Oliver could feel Kleph's quick, excited breathing light upon his cheek, feel the soft motions of her body in his arms. He tried consciously to make the moment last, stretch it out to infinity. Everything had happened too swiftly to impress very clearly on his mind anything except what he could touch and hold. He held her in an embrace made consciously light, though he wanted to clasp her in a tight, despairing grip, because he was sure this was the last embrace they would ever share.

The eye-straining blinks of light and blindness went on. From far away below the roar of the burning city rolled on, threaded together by the long, looped cadences of the sirens that linked all sounds into one.

Then in the bewildering dark another voice sounded from the hall downstairs. A man's voice, very deep, very melodious, saying:

"What is this? What are you doing here? Hollia – is that you?"

Oliver felt Kleph stiffen in his arms. She caught her breath, but she said nothing in the instant while heavy feet began to mount the stairs, coming up with a solid, confident tread that shook the old house to each step. Then Kleph thrust herself hard out of Oliver's arms. He heard her high, sweet, excited voice crying, "Cenbe! Cenbe!" and she ran to meet the newcomer through the waves of dark and light that swept the shaken house.

Oliver staggered a little and felt a chair seat catching the back of his legs. He sank into it and lifted to his lips the cup he still held. Its steam was warm and moist in his face, though he could scarcely make out the shape of the rim.

He lifted it with both hands and drank.

When he opened his eyes it was quite dark in the room. Also it was silent except for a thin, melodious humming almost below the threshold of sound. Oliver struggled with the memory of a monstrous nightmare. He put it resolutely out of his mind and sat up, feeling an unfamiliar bed creak and sway under him.

This was Kleph's room. But no – Kleph's no longer. Her shining hangings were gone from the walls, her white resilient rug, her pictures. The room looked as it had looked before she came, except for one thing.

In the far corner was a table – a block of translucent stuff – out of which light poured softly. A man sat on a low stool before it, leaning forward, his heavy shoulders outlined against the glow. He wore earphones and he was making quick, erratic notes upon a pad on his knee, swaying a little as if to the tune of unheard music.

The curtains were drawn, but from beyond them came a distant, muffled roaring that Oliver remembered from his nightmare. He put a hand to his face, aware of a feverish warmth and a dipping of the room before his eyes. His head ached, and there was a deep malaise in every limb and nerve.

As the bed creaked, the man in the corner turned, sliding the earphones down like a collar. He had a strong, sensitive face above a dark beard, trimmed short. Oliver had never seen him before, but he had that air Oliver knew so well by now, of remoteness which was the knowledge of time itself lying like a gulf between them.

When he spoke his deep voice was impersonally kind.

"You had too much euphoriac, Wilson," he said, aloofly sympathetic. "You slept a long while."

"How long?" Oliver's throat felt sticky when he spoke.

The man did not answer. Oliver shook his head experimentally. He said, "I thought Kleph said you don't get hangovers from—" Then another thought interrupted the first, and he said quickly, "Where is Kleph?" He looked confusedly toward the door.

"They should be in Rome by now. Watching Charlemagne's coronation at St. Peter's on Christmas Day a thousand years from here."

That was not a thought Oliver could grasp clearly. His aching brain sheered away from it; he found thinking at all was strangely difficult. Staring at the man, he traced an idea painfully to its conclusion.

"So they've gone on – but you stayed behind? Why? You . . .you're Cenbe? I heard your – symphonia, Kleph called it."

"You heard part of it. I have not finished yet. I needed – this." Cenbe inclined his head toward the curtains beyond which the subdued roaring still went on.

"You needed – the meteor?" The knowledge worked painfully through his dulled brain until it seemed to strike some area still untouched by the aching, an area still alive to implication. "The *meteor*? But—"

There was a power implicit in Cenbe's raised hand that seemed to push Oliver down upon the bed again. Cenbe said patiently, "The worst of it is past now, for a while. Forget if you can. That was days ago. I said you were asleep for some time. I let you rest. I knew this house would be safe – from the fire at least."

"Then – something more's to come?" Oliver only mumbled his question. He was not sure he wanted an answer. He had been curious so long, and now that knowledge lay almost within reach, something about his brain seemed to refuse to listen. Perhaps this weariness, this feverish, dizzy feeling would pass as the effect of the euphoriac wore off.

Cenbe's voice ran on smoothly, soothingly, almost as if Cenbe too did not want him to think. It was easiest to lie here and listen.

"I am a composer," Cenbe was saying. "I happen to be interested in interpreting certain forms of disaster into my own terms. That is why I stayed on. The others were dilettantes. They came for the May weather and the spectacle. The aftermath – well, why should they wait for that? As for myself – I suppose I am a connoisseur. I find the aftermath rather fascinating. And I need it. I need to study it at first hand, for my own purposes."

His eyes dwelt upon Oliver for an instant very keenly, like a physician's eyes, impersonal and observing. Absently he reached for his stylus and the note pad. And as he moved, Oliver saw a familiar mark on the underside of the thick, tanned wrist.

"Kleph had that scar, too," he heard himself whisper. "And the others."

Cenbe nodded. "Inoculation. It was necessary, under the circumstances. We did not want disease to spread in our own time-world."

"Disease?"

Cenbe shrugged. "You would not recognize the name."

"But, if you can inoculate against disease—" Oliver thrust himself up on an aching arm. He had a half-grasp upon a thought now which he did not want to let go. Effort seemed to make the ideas come more clearly through his mounting confusion. With enormous effort he went on.

"I'm getting it now," he said. "Wait. I've been trying to work this out. You can change history? You can! I know you can. Kleph said she had to promise not to interfere. You all had to promise. Does that mean you really could change your own past – our time?"

Cenbe laid down his pad again. He looked at Oliver thoughtfully, a dark, intent look under heavy brows. "Yes," he said. "Yes, the past can be changed, but not easily. And it changes the future, too, necessarily. The lines of probability are switched into new patterns – but it is extremely difficult, and it has never been allowed. The physiotemporal course tends to slide back to its norm, always. That is why it is so hard to force any alteration." He shrugged. "A theoretical science. We do not change history, Wilson. If we changed our past, our present would be altered, too. And our time-world is entirely to our liking. There may be a few malcontents there, but they are not allowed the privilege of temporal travel."

Oliver spoke louder against the roaring from beyond the windows. "But you've got the power! You could alter history, if you wanted to – wipe out all the pain and suffering and tragedy—"

"All of that passed away long ago," Cenbe said.

"Not – now! Not – this!"

Cenbe looked at him enigmatically for a while. Then— "This, too," he said.

*

And suddenly Oliver realized from across what distances Cenbe was watching him. A vast distance, as time is measured. Cenbe was a composer and a genius, and necessarily strongly empathic, but his psychic locus was very far away in time. The dying city outside, the whole world of now was not quite real to Cenbe, falling short of reality because of that basic variance in time. It was merely one of the building blocks that had gone to support the edifice on which Cenbe's culture stood in a misty, unknown, terrible future.

It seemed terrible to Oliver now. Even Kleph – all of them had been touched with a pettiness, the faculty that had enabled Hollia to concentrate on her malicious, small schemes to acquire a ringside seat while the meteor thundered in toward Earth's atmosphere. They were all dilettantes, Kleph and Omerie and the other. They toured time, but only as onlookers. Were they bored – sated – with their normal existence?

Not sated enough to wish change, basically. Their own time-world was a fulfilled womb, a perfection made manifest for their needs. They dared not change the past – they could not risk flawing their own present.

Revulsion shook him. Remembering the touch of Kleph's lips, he felt a sour sickness on his tongue. Alluring she had been; he knew that too well. But the aftermath—

There was something about this race from the future. He had felt it dimly at first, before Kleph's nearness had drowned caution and buffered his sensibilities. Time traveling purely as an escape mechanism seemed almost blasphemous. A race with such power—

Kleph – leaving him for the barbaric, splendid coronation at Rome a thousand years ago – how had she seen him? Not as a living, breathing man. He knew that, very certainly Kleph's race were spectators.

But he read more than casual interest in Cenbe's eyes now. There was an avidity there, a bright, fascinated probing. The man had replaced his earphones – he was different from the others. He was a connoisseur. After the vintage season came the aftermath – and Cenbe.

Cenbe watched and waited, light flickering softly in the translucent block before him, his fingers poised over the note pad. The ultimate connoisseur waited to savor the rarities that no non-gourmet could appreciate.

Those thin, distant rhythms of sound that was almost music began to be audible again above the noises of the distant fire. Listening, remembering, Oliver could very nearly catch the pattern of the symphonia as he had heard it, all intermingled with the flash of changing faces and the rank upon rank of the dying—

He lay back on the bed, letting the room swirl away into the darkness behind his closed and aching lids. The ache was implicit in every cell of his body, almost a second ego taking possession and driving him out of himself, a strong, sure ego taking over as he himself let go.

Why, he wondered dully, should Kleph have lied? She had said there was no aftermath to the drink she had given him. No aftermath – and yet this painful possession was strong enough to edge him out of his own body.

Kleph had not lied. It was no aftermath to drink. He knew that – but the knowledge no longer touched his brain or his body. He lay still, giving them up to the power of the illness which was aftermath to something far stronger than the strongest drink. The illness that had no name – yet.

Cenbe's new symphonia was a crowning triumph. It had its premiere from Antares Hall, and the applause was an ovation. History itself, of course, was the artist – opening with the meteor that forecast the great plagues of the fourteenth century and closing with the climax Cenbe had caught on the threshold of modern times. But only Cenbe could have interpreted it with such subtle power.

Critics spoke of the masterly way in which he had chosen the face of the Stuart king as a recurrent motif against the montage of emotion and sound and movement. But there were other faces, fading through the great sweep of the composition, which helped to build up to the tremendous climax. One face in particular, one moment that the audience absorbed greedily. A moment in which one man's face loomed huge in the screen, every feature clear. Cenbe had never caught an emotional crisis so effectively, the critics agreed. You could almost read the man's eyes.

After Cenbe had left, he lay motionless for a long while. He was thinking feverishly—

I've got to find some way to tell people. If I'd known in advance, maybe something could have been done. We'd have forced them to tell us how to change the probabilities. We could have evacuated the city.

If I could leave a message—

Maybe not for today's people. But later. They visit all through time. If they could be recognized and caught somewhere, sometime, and made to change destiny—

It wasn't easy to stand up. The room kept tilting. But he managed it. He found pencil and paper and through the swaying of the shadows he wrote down what he could. Enough. Enough to warn, enough to save.

He put the sheets on the table, in plain sight, and weighted them down before he stumbled back to bed through closing darkness.

The house was dynamited six days later, part of the futile attempt to halt the relentless spread of the Blue Death.

THIRTY SECONDS FROM NOW

John Chu

John Chu designs microprocessors by day and writes by night. His fiction has been published in *Asimov's Science Fiction Magazine*, and *Tor.com*, among others. This is his first published story, which appeared in the *Boston Review* in 2011.

One second from now, the bean bag will thunk into Scott's left palm. From reflex, his fingers will wrap around it before he'll toss it back up again. The trick of juggling lies not in the catch but in the toss. The bean bag will arc up from his right hand, but Scott sees his left hand blur now. Phantom left hands at the few places his left hand may be one second from now overlap with each other, and with his real left hand about a foot above the cold tile floor he's sitting on. The same holds for the phantom bean bags. They overlap each other and the result looks nearly as cubic, red, and solid in the air, stark against the dorm room's blank walls, as the bean bag does right now resting in Scott's right hand.

He's making a good toss. This catch will be easy. His three bean bag cascade looks to him the way he imagines it must look to anyone else, well, if they were near-sighted and missing their glasses.

When he makes a bad toss, translucent Scotts scatter across the room. They reach for the beds on either side of him, lunge for his or his roommate's desk, and dive over his bed for the closet. They all stretch for the myriad translucent bean bags raining from the stucco ceiling. The bean bags threaten to knock over the desk lamps, bury themselves in the acting textbooks that line his closet shelf and smack against the window blinds. A desperate enough toss and a phantom bean bag may fly through the doorway into the hall.

He does not need his time-skewed senses to know he will eventually make a bad toss. As hard as he tries to keep his sight solid, to make his life predictable, he will drop a bean bag. That's why he's sitting on the floor. It's easier to pick up dropped bean bags that way.

Five seconds from now, someone will walk past the open door of his dorm room. Scott doesn't recognize him. He's just arrived at the university and can barely recognize his roommate, a long-haired rail of a man who left him to eat breakfast in the basement cafeteria. The man who will walk past the door is about the same height as the bulletin board across from Scott's room. His thick body will block what he's posting from view. His dark hair will lie on his head like a mane. Looking at the man's back, Scott sees a rounded teddy bear quality to him. What attracts Scott, though, is the man's clarity.

Scott can read the man's T-shirt. It lists films the Department of Media Studies screened at a festival this past summer. Five distinct fingers will splay to hold his flyer in place as the other hand pushes pins into the cork. His actions show none of the uncertainty, the blurriness that everyone else's shows. It's been years since anyone has looked so clear to him.

The future is messy. Scott's senses feed him all possible futures at once. He's learned to wander only a few seconds ahead. That's close, but it's still not normal. This man, though, is a relief to his senses. He makes everything clean. Scott wonders for how long he can ogle the man and if he'll ever walk by the room again. He untethers his senses, and the future rushes in.

Thirty seconds from now, the man, when he turns to leave, will see Scott juggling. He will rip the flyer he posted off of the bulletin board. The dorm room door will bounce against the closet wall when he knocks on it. A boom will punctuate the bounce. The man will stare at the door chagrined. Scott finds him even more like a teddy bear from the front.

"Hey, I'm Tony." He'll shrug as if to say that he didn't know his own strength. "How long have you been juggling?"

No alternate phrasings or completely different sentences overlap Tony's words. Scott hears what Tony will say as clearly as if Tony were speaking to him now.

"Five years." Juggling taught him control, to work in the now. "Why?"

"My senior project—" Tony's hands will play with his crumpled flyer. "Can I come in?"

Tony's smile will be warm and Scott's a sucker for a warm smile. Scott will nod.

"Here's the deal." Tony will toss his flyer into the wastebasket. "I want to be the next Fellini. I need a juggler for my senior project. And I want you." He will dig a finger into Scott's shoulder. Phantom bean bags will fall around Scott. "Interested?"

"Don't know enough about your senior project." The bean bag may fall two inches to the left of Scott's left hand. His juggling is blurry, but his words to Tony sound as clear as Tony's words to him. "Also, the Department of Theater and Dance has a mixer tonight in the atrium of the Center for the Arts. I should find out about everyone else's projects too. Stop by tomorrow, maybe."

"Sure." Tony will look disappointed as he backs out of the room. "Tomorrow."

About nine hours from now, the roommate will be downstairs partying with friends. He will have mentioned something to Scott about either jello shots or kamakazes and Scott will have said no. The dorm room will be dark and empty when its door unlocks. A hand will fumble for the light switch. It'll be Tony's. His other arm will be around Scott, trying to slow his breathing.

"What happened to you, anyway?" Tony will set Scott's keys on the closest desk. When Scott pulls away, Tony'll let go of him. "One moment, you're standing by yourself in a corner of the atrium. The next moment, you can't breathe."

Scott will have already plucked his bean bags, sitting next to his keys, from his desk. Seated on the floor between the beds, he'll juggle.

"I didn't expect so many people at the mixer," Scott will say.

He doesn't do well with crowds. A bad trait for an actor. The multiple alternate selves fill a room and their cacophony sounds like the chaos of all future conversations heard at once. That noise is not the certainty of rehearsed lines and preset blocking on stage. It's what he's worked so hard to avoid and what he doesn't hear when he's talking to Tony.

Tony will sit on Scott's bed. His gaze will follow the bean bags up and down.

"Better now?" Tony will lean forward, his hands on his thighs. "I can stay for a while if you want. To make sure you're OK."

"You don't need to do that." To Scott, the bean bags look nearly as sharply defined as Tony. "I'll be fine."

"Of course, I don't need to do that." He'll open his palms to Scott. "I don't need to do anything."

"You don't even know my name."

"Which is . . .?" Tony's face will hang, expectant.

"Scott." Right now, he's staring at Tony, but about nine hours from now, he will be studying the bean bags as they arc through the air. "For now, I just need to be alone and juggle, OK?"

"Fine, Scott. But you haven't seen the last of me yet." Tony will point his finger repeatedly at him. "I will get you into my movie."

Tony will back out of the room again.

Four days from now, Scott will have his jacket on, his juggling gear in his backpack, when the dorm room door will rattle with polite knocking. It'll be Tony. His right hand will clutch a paper bag. The smell of roasted chicken and cornbread will waft through the doorway.

"Hey, Scott." Tony will smile and the rest of the world will dim a little. "Doing anything tonight?"

This will be the third day in a row Tony has stood at Scott's door trying to have dinner with him. Right now, parsing the future, Scott wonders why Tony's so insistent. Maybe they will have also talked elsewhere. He can't hear those conversations unless he also goes there to listen. Or maybe Tony will need a juggler really badly.

"Getting a quick bite down in the basement, then I'm going to Juggling Club."

Tony will look disapprovingly at Scott, but he will only be able to keep it up for a second before he'll smile. The power of Tony's smile worries Scott.

"You don't want to do that." Tony will hold up the paper bag. "Real food. They're serving yellow stuff and brown stuff in the basement. I checked. Besides, I have to tell you about my senior project."

Scott will look back at the room and sigh. His roommate will have used the floor as his closet. In four days, he will know exactly what his roommate has scattered on the floor. Right now, to Scott's time-shifted gaze, clothing of some sort lies smeared over the tile like a gray carpet. Tony is unusual in that Scott can envision him distinctly even four days ahead. The yellow and black checkerboard of Tony's button-down shirt is hideous, but on him, it almost looks good.

"Scott, you know that you don't come close to blocking the door, right?" Tony will pretend to jump to see over Scott. "I can see past you just fine. Just tell me none of that underwear is yours."

Scott will step aside and they will sit opposite each other on the tangle of sheets and blanket covering his bed to eat chicken, cornbread, and greens. The juices will dribble down his chin. The sweet, salty, tender chicken is everything he already misses about real food.

"The movie is about a charismatic, womanizing director." Tony will gesticulate with his fork and a piece of cornbread. "The conceit is that the world is a circus. We'll shoot in black and white . . ."

Scott will listen intently, facing Tony at first. As the conversation wears on, they'll talk about Hemingway, Fitzgerald, and the Jazz Age. Tony's gaze will invite Scott and he won't refuse. He'll find himself resting against Tony's chest, within the embrace of Tony's arms. The Juggling Club will meet then break for the night without him.

About two weeks from now, Tony will swap rooms with Scott's roommate. Tony will have suggested that this will be more convenient for everyone. No games with ties on doorknobs to show who is where.

Movie posters will cover the walls. Scott does not recognize most of them yet. Maybe he will in two weeks. Right now, studying the walls that will be, he recognizes only *Roma*, *La Dolce Vita*, and *8½*.

Tony's stuff will dominate their room. All Scott has brought with him to school are his clothes, a laptop, and his juggling gear. He sees Tony's stuff as clearly as he sees Tony. Cases of lights, cameras, and lenses will sit against their own wall. A refrigerator will hum between their desks. Reference texts will fill Tony's closet, along with hangers of perfectly pressed clothes. To make space for everything, they will have bunked their beds, not that they expect both beds to get much use.

The shirts they'll wear will become sticky with sweat as they move Tony in, and the smell assaults Scott. After they'll have finished unpacking, Tony will take off his shirt as he struts to the refrigerator. He'll hand Scott a beer. Scott will stare back at him puzzled.

"You've never had a beer before?" His face will contort into an incredulous scowl. "This is the perfect drink after moving lots of heavy boxes. Trust me. You'll love it."

Scott will be so parched that he barely notices any bitterness. Astringency rides on bubbles that explode in his mouth and flow down his throat. His second sip will be a chug.

"Hey, don't drink it all at once." Tony will hold his own bottle out to him. "To my, among other things, best buddy."

Scott will nearly choke on the beer. Tony will pound Scott's back. When Scott's finished coughing, he'll find Tony's left arm around his shoulders.

"What's the matter?" Tony will squeeze Scott's shoulders. "Didn't you ever have a best buddy before?"

Scott didn't. High school was an acting exercise. Camouflage. Pretending he never heard all the things people might say. Pretending he never saw all the things they might do. Pretending he was what everyone else expected.

About four weeks from now, Scott will be on the floor in his pajamas, juggling, waiting up for Tony. The door will rattle against the jamb several times before Scott hears a key inserted into the lock. Scott likes to keep the door locked. Tony always assumes the door will be unlocked. Scott, through his time-shifted sight, has seen Tony forget the door will be locked several times already in the two weeks since they started living together.

"Where have you been?" Scott will stifle a yawn. He will catch his bean bags then rub his bleary eyes. "I need to tell you something."

"I'm starting production of my movie." Tony will drop his backpack on his desk. "Are you OK?"

Tony will wrap himself around Scott on the floor. His lips will touch Scott's neck. Well beyond the point when Tony ought to have been a scattered, transparent ghost, the hair on his arms will be crisp, sharp, and distinct. Scott will share with Tony the secret he's never shared with anyone else.

"Something I want you to know about me." Scott's words will be slow as much from fear as from tiredness. "I sense future sights, sounds, whatever while I sense the present."

"You know the future?" Tony will laugh. "Tell me that one of these days, I'll get all the locations for my movie sorted out."

"I don't know the future," Scott will say. "It's like my body is jet-lagged compared to my senses, and all possible futures stack on top of each other." Scott will lean back into Tony. "Wherever I am, I experience all the things that may happen there. The more likely it is, the clearer and stronger it is. When I'm near you, the future clears. I never see alternative yous."

"I never see alternative yous either." Tony's whisper will brush Scott's ear and undercut its gently mocking tone. As Tony stands, he will squeeze Scott's shoulder. "You're tired. Get to sleep."

Some 50 days from now, Scott will wake to the door crashing back and forth against the jamb. This will not be the first time Tony will return without his key. Nights when Tony needs the juggler on set, this will not be a problem, but the juggler is not a large part.

Scott will stumble to open the door. Tony will march in, forcing Scott back until he is crushed against the bunk beds.

"What the fuck is the matter with you?" Tony will launch his backpack towards his desk. When it lands, a sheaf of paper will scatter and a few pens will crash to the floor. "How many times do I need to tell you? When I'm not in, the door stays open."

"I don't want anyone to sneak in while I'm asleep." Scott's voice will be small. They will have been building to this conversation for weeks. "We're not supposed to leave the door open."

"If you can actually see the future," Tony will say, folding his arms across his chest, "shouldn't you know if someone is going to sneak in while you're sleeping?"

Scott will roll his eyes. He will have lost count of how often he has explained this.

"I don't want my senses any further ahead than they have to be. And I never see what will be. I see everything that may be. Well, you I always see clearly, but you're special."

"You stupid motherfucker. You've got it all worked out, don't you? You get to be a special snowflake but never have to prove it."

For an instant, Tony will blur and scatter. Scott, now sensing almost two months ahead, has never seen Tony do this before. Tony, like everyone else, has multiple potential futures. Until now, however, Scott has never seen them.

As translucent Tonys scatter around the room, so do translucent Scotts. One Tony slams a Scott against a wall, punching his stomach. Another hits Scott where they stand. Some step back toward the closets, the desk, and Tony's film gear, turning away from Scott. Others stare at Scott stunned. Only one lays his arms around Scott, gently stroking his back.

Scott and his future self both feel all these alternatives at once. His mind reels from the shock of pain breaking against his nose. A salty, metallic taste slides down his throat, even though he may not bleed that night. Tony's potential punches to his torso stun, and even if they never happen, they will still knock the wind out of Scott about 50 days from now. Simultaneous with the pain, Tony's phantom gentle arms caress him. Phantom whispers, like the rustle of leaves, soothe him.

An instant later, Tony will snap back into focus. As the phantom Tonys collapse back into the real one, the phantom Scotts collapse too.

Tony will stare at Scott, his jaw slack. His gaze will sweep over Scott, taking in the grimaces, tears, and the body twisted with pain from the futures that Tony will not have chosen.

"I'm sorry I didn't believe you." Tony will caress Scott, his arm moving smoothly across Scott's back. "I'll never even think about hurting you again. I promise. The actors who I picked have been real assholes, but I shouldn't take it out on you. I'm sorry."

Tony will be unusually attentive that night. He won't press, though, when Scott refuses the attention.

Three and a half months from now, both closets will be empty. Tony's gear will be stacked in black boxes almost exactly where Scott is sitting right now. The future Scott will be sitting on the bottom bunk, cross-legged, folding his shirts. His pants will already be packed in the suitcase sitting on his desk. The refrigerator will be empty and unplugged, its door ajar.

The dorm room door will swing open and clang against the wall. Tony, wrapped in his winter coat, will look like the snowman a five-year-old might make. As far as Scott's time-shifted sight has shown him, Tony will have been true to his word. He will not have hurt Scott.

Tony will reach for a box of lenses, then stop. "Are you ashamed of me?"

Scott will look at up him. "What?" He will drop his cast T-shirt from the Theater and Dance Department's fall musical onto his lap. "Why would you think that?"

"You never bring any of your friends here." His gaze will sweep past him like a final exam. "You do have other friends, right?"

Scott will look at his bean bags on the desk, his acting texts sitting on the closet shelf, and climbing gear lying on the closet floor. "Sure. But this is the room where I don't have to work to untangle my senses. Bringing my friends here would make it like the rest of the world for me."

Tony's face will twist into a frown. He'll pull his chair from his desk and sit in it backwards facing Scott. Tony's arms will rest on top of the chair back.

"It's ironic that I have to talk to you about the future." He'll take a deep breath. "You know this will end, right? It's winter break." He'll shrug. "After the spring semester, I'll be gone, but you'll still be here."

"You've met someone else?"

Tony will laugh. "No, I only direct like Fellini. Six months from now, I'm going to graduate. You should keep your options open."

Scott's brow will furrow. He'll look at the boxes of gear, stacked ready to go. "You're moving out?" He'll pick up his T-shirt and twist it in his hands.

"No, of course not, Scott. And you're not moving out either." Tony will sit next to Scott, his hand on Scott's thigh. "If you want to keep fucking, I'm completely willing. As much and as often as you want. But us, it's going to end in six months. You have lots of possible futures and they probably don't involve me. Just saying . . ."

Scott's eyes itch. His T-shirt will be a pretzel in his hands.

"Can you leave me alone for a moment?"

Tony will nod. He'll stand, avoiding the top bunk, his face apologetic. His hands will slap onto his topmost box of gear. With a grunt, he will heft it out of the room.

Right now, the bean bag thunks into Scott's left palm. His eyes still itch and he feels the grief he'll feel again at the end of the semester. A ghost Scott moves to shut the dorm room door. If he closes the door, he and Tony will never meet. Tony will never learn how to hurt Scott in a way that only he can be hurt. Tony will never hurt him in a way that anyone can be hurt.

Scott sighs. All he's done for years is hide. He's already lived that kind of hurt. He throws a bean bag into the air and waits for the man with the flyer to arrive. He's seen the movie of his life. Now, he'll live the whole thing.

FORTY, COUNTING DOWN

Harry Turtledove

Harry Turtledove is an American writer sometimes known as the Master of Alternate History. In addition to writing fiction, he has also edited anthologies, including one on the theme of time travel. This story was first published in *Asimov's Science Fiction Magazine* in 1999 and is a companion piece to his other story in this anthology, "Twenty-one, Counting Up." Both stories feature the same main character, Justin Kloster.

"Hey, Justin!" Sean Peters' voice floated over the top of the Superstrings, Ltd., cubicle wall. "It's twenty after six – quitting time and then some. Want a drink or two with me and Garth?"

"Hang on," Justin Kloster answered. "Let me save what I'm working on first." He told his computer to save his work as it stood, generate a backup, and shut itself off. Having grown up in the days when voice-recognition software was imperfectly reliable, he waited to make sure the machine followed orders. It did, of course. Making that software idiotproof had put Superstrings on the map a few years after the turn of the century.

Justin got up, stretched, and looked around. Not much to see: the grayish-tan fuzzy walls of the cubicle and an astringently neat desktop that held the computer, a wedding photo of Megan and him, and a phone/fax. His lips narrowed. The marriage had lasted four years – four and a half, actually. He hadn't come close to finding anybody else since.

Footsteps announced Peters' arrival. He looked like a high-school linebacker who'd let most of his muscle go to flab since. Garth O'Connell was right behind him. He was from the same mold, except getting thin on top instead of going gray. "How's the Iron Curtain sound?" Peters asked.

"Sure," Justin said. "It's close, and you can hear yourself think – most of the time, anyhow."

They went out into the parking lot together, bitching when they stepped from air conditioning to San Fernando Valley August heat. Justin's eyes started watering, too; L.A. smog wasn't so bad as it had been when he was young, but it hadn't disappeared.

An Oasis song was playing when the three software engineers walked into the Iron Curtain, and into air conditioning chillier than the office's. The music took Justin back to the days when he'd been getting together with Megan, though he'd liked Blur better. "Look out," Sean Peters said. "They've got a new fellow behind the bar." He and Garth chuckled. They knew what was going to happen. Justin sighed. So did he.

Peters ordered a gin and tonic, O'Connell a scotch on the rocks. Justin asked for a Bud. Sure as hell, the bartender said, "I'll be right with you two gents" – he nodded to Justin's co-workers – "but for you, sir, I'll need some ID."

With another sigh, Justin produced his driver's license. "Here."

The bartender looked at him, looked at his picture on the license, and looked at his birthdate. He scowled. "You were born in 1978? No way."

"His real name's Dorian Gray," Garth said helpfully.

"Oh, shut up," Justin muttered, and then, louder, to the bartender, "Yeah, I really turned forty this past spring." He was slightly pudgy, but he'd been slightly pudgy since he was a toddler. And he'd been very blond since the day he was born. If he had any silver mixed with the gold, it didn't show. He also stayed out of the sun as much as he could, because he burned to a crisp when he didn't. That left him with a lot fewer lines and wrinkles than his buddies, who were both a couple of years younger than he.

Shaking his head, the bartender slid Justin a beer. "You coulda fooled me," he said. "You go around picking up high-school girls?" His hands shaped an hourglass in the air.

"No." Justin stared down at the reflections of the ceiling lights on the polished bar.

"Middle school," Garth suggested. He'd already made his scotch disappear. Justin gave him a dirty look. It was such a dirty look, it got through to Sean Peters. He tapped Garth on the arm. For a wonder, Garth eased off.

Justin finished the Bud, threw a twenty on the bar, and got up to leave. "Not going to have another one?" Peters asked, surprised.

"Nope." Justin shook his head. "Got some things to do. See you in the morning." Out he went, walking fast so his friends couldn't stop him.

As soon as the microchip inside Justin's deadbolt lock shook hands with the one in his key, his apartment came to life. Lamps came on. The stereo started playing the Pulp CD he'd left in there this morning. The broiler heated up to do the steak the computer knew was in the refrigerator. From the bedroom, the computer called, "Now or later?"

"Later," Justin said, so the screen stayed dark.

He went into the kitchen and tossed a couple of pieces of spam snailmail into the blue wastebasket for recycling. The steak went under the broiler; frozen mixed vegetables went into the microwave. Eight minutes later, dinner.

After he finished, he rinsed the dishes and silverware and put them in the dishwasher. When he closed the door, the light in it came on; the machine judged it was full enough to run a cycle in the middle of the night.

Like the kitchen, his front room was almost as antiseptically tidy as his cubicle at Superstrings. But for a picture of Megan and him on their honeymoon, the coffee table was bare. All his books and DVDs and audio CDs were arranged alphabetically by author, title, or group. None stood even an eighth of an inch out of place. It was as if none of them dared move without his permission.

He went into the bedroom. "Now," he said, and the computer monitor came to life.

A picture of Megan and him stood on the dresser, another on the nightstand. Her high-school graduation picture smiled at him whenever he sat down at the desk. Even after all these years, he smiled back most of the time. He couldn't help it. He'd always been happy around Megan.

But she hadn't been happy around him, not at the end. Not for a while before the end, either. He'd been a long, long time realizing that. "Stupid," he said. He wasn't smiling now, even with Megan's young, glowing face looking right at him out of the picture frame. "I was stupid. I didn't know enough. I didn't know how to take care of her."

No wonder he hadn't clicked with any other woman. He didn't want any other woman. He wanted Megan – and couldn't have her any more.

"E-mail," he told the computer, and gave his password. He went through it, answering what needed answering and deleting the rest. Then he said, "Banking." The computer had paid the monthly Weblink bill, and the cable bill, too. "All good," he told it.

The CD in the stereo fell silent. "Repeat?" the computer asked.

"No." Justin went out to the front room. He took the Pulp CD out of the player, put it in its jewel box, and put the jewel box exactly where it belonged on the shelf. Then he stood there in a rare moment of indecision, wondering what to pull out next. When he chose a new CD, he chuckled. He doubted Sean or Garth would have heard of the Trash Can Sinatras, let alone heard any of their music. His work buddies had listened to grunge rock back before the turn of the century, not British pop.

As soon as *Cake* started, he went back into the bedroom and sat down at the computer again. This time, he did smile at Megan's picture. She'd been crazy for the Trash Can Sinatras, too.

The music made him especially eager to get back to work. "Superstrings," he said, and gave a password, and "Virtual reality" and another password, and "Not so virtual" and one more. Then he had to wait. He would have killed for a Mac a quarter this powerful back in 1999, but it wasn't a patch on the one he used at the office. The company could afford the very best. He couldn't, not quite.

He went to the keyboard for this work: for numbers, it was more precise than dictating. And he had to wait again and again, while the computer did the crunching. One wait was long enough for him to go take a shower. When he got back, hair still damp, the machine hadn't finished muttering to itself. Justin sighed. But the faster Macs at the office couldn't leap these numbers at a single bound. What he was asking of his home computer was right on the edge of what it could do.

Or maybe it would turn out to be over the edge. In that case, he'd spend even more lunch hours in his cubicle in the days ahead than he had for the past six months. He was caught up on everything the people above him wanted. They thought he worked his long hours to stay that way.

"What they don't know won't hurt them," Justin murmured. "And it may do me some good."

He didn't think anyone else had combined superstring physics, chaos theory, and virtual reality this way. If anyone had, he was keeping quiet about it – nothing in the journals, not a whisper on the Web. Justin would have known; he had virbots out prowling all the time. They'd never found anything close. He had this all to himself . . . if he hadn't been wasting his time.

Up came the field parameters, at long, long last. Justin studied them. As the computer had, he took his time. He didn't want to let enthusiasm run away with him before he was sure. He'd done that half a lifetime ago, and what had it got him? A divorce that blighted his life ever since. He wouldn't jump too soon. Not again. Not ever again. But things looked good.

"Yes!" he said softly. He'd been saying it that particular way since he was a teenager. He couldn't have named the disgraced sportscaster from whom he'd borrowed it if he'd gone on the rack.

He saved the parameters, quit his application, and had the computer back up everything he'd done. The backup disk went into his briefcase. And then, yawning, he hit the sack.

Three days later, Garth O'Connell was the first to gape when Justin came into the office. "Buzz cut!" he exclaimed, and ran a hand over his own thinning hair. Then he laughed and started talking as if the past twenty years hadn't happened: "Yo, dude. Where's the combat boots?"

In my closet, Justin thought. He didn't say that. What he did say was, "I felt like doing something different, that's all."

"Like what?" Garth asked. "Globalsearching for high-school quail, like the barkeep said? The competition doesn't wear short hair any more, you know."

"Will you melt it down?" Justin snapped.

"Okay. Okay." Garth spread his hands. "But you better get used to it, 'cause everybody else is gonna say the same kind of stuff."

Odds were he was right, Justin realized gloomily. He grabbed a cup of coffee at the office machine, then ducked into his cubicle and got to work. That slowed the stream of comments, but didn't stop them. People would go by the cubicle, see the side view, do a double take, and start exclaiming.

Inside half an hour, Justin's division head came by to view the prodigy. She rubbed her chin. "Well, I don't *suppose* it looks unbusinesslike," she said dubiously.

"Thanks, Ms. Chen," Justin said. "I just wanted to—"

"Start your midlife crisis early." As it had a few evenings before, Sean Peters' voice drifted over the walls of the cubicle.

"And thank *you*, Sean." Justin put on his biggest grin. Ms. Chen smiled, which meant he'd passed the test. She gave his hair another look, nodded more happily than she'd spoken, and went off to do whatever managers did when they weren't worrying about haircuts.

Sean kept his mouth shut till lunchtime, when he stuck his head into Justin's cubicle and said, "Feel like going over to Omino's? I've got a yen for Japanese food." He laughed. Justin groaned. That made Peters laugh harder than ever.

Justin shook his head. Pointing toward his monitor, he said, "I'm brownbagging it today. Got a ton of stuff that needs doing."

"Okay." Peters shrugged. "Anybody'd think you worked here or something. I'll see you later, then."

Between noon and half past one, Superstrings was nearly deserted. Munching on a salami sandwich and an orange, Justin worked on his own project, his private project. The office machine was better than his home computer for deciding whether possible meant practical.

"Yes!" he said again, a few minutes later, and then, "Time to go shopping."

Being the sort of fellow he was, he shopped with a list. Vintage clothes came from Aaardvark's Odd Ark, undoubtedly the funkiest secondhand store in town, if not in the world. As with his haircut, he did his best to match the way he'd looked just before the turn of the century.

Old money was easier; he had to pay only a small premium for old-fashioned smallhead bills at the several coin-and-stamp shops he visited. "Why do you want 'em, if you don't care about condition?" one dealer asked.

"Maybe I think the new bills are ugly," he answered. The dealer shrugged, tagging him for a nut but a harmless one. When he got to $150,000, he checked *money* off the list.

He got to the office very early the next morning. The security guard chuckled as he unlocked the door. "Old clothes and everything. Looks like you're moving in, pal."

"Seems like that sometimes, too, Bill." Justin set down his suitcases for a moment. "But I'm going out of town this afternoon. I'd rather have this stuff indoors than sitting in the trunk of my car."

"Oh, yeah." Bill nodded. He had to be seventy, but his hair wasn't any lighter than iron gray. "I know that song." He knew lots of songs, many dating back to before Justin was born. He'd fought in Vietnam, and been a cop, and now he was doing this because his pension hadn't come close to keeping up with skyrocketing prices. Justin wondered if his own would, come the day.

But he had different worries now. "Thanks," he said when the guard held the door for him.

He staggered up the stairs; thanks to the stash of cash (a new compact car here, nothing more, even with the premium he'd had to pay, but a young fortune before the turn of the century), some period clothes scrounged – like the Dilbert T-shirt and baggy jeans he had on – from secondhand stores, and the boots, those suitcases weren't light, and he'd never been in better shape than he could help. The backpack in which he carried his PowerBook and VR mask did nothing to make him more graceful, either.

Once he got up to the second floor, he paused and listened hard. "Yes!" he said when he heard nothing. Except for Bill down below, he was the only person here.

He went into the men's room, piled one suitcase on the other, and sat down on them. Then he took the laptop out of its case. He plugged the VR mask into its jack, then turned on the computer. As soon as it came up, he put on the mask. The world went black, then neutral gray, then neutral . . . neutral: no color at all, just virtual reality waiting to be made real.

It all took too long. He wished he could do this back at his desk, with an industrial-strength machine. But he didn't dare take the chance. This building had been here nineteen years ago. This men's room had been here nineteen years ago. He'd done his homework as well as he could. But his homework hadn't been able to tell him where the goddamn cubicle partitions were back before the turn of the century.

And so . . . the john. He took a deep breath. "Run program super-strings-slash-virtual reality-slash-not so virtual," he said.

The PowerBook quivered, ever so slightly, on his lap. His heart thudded. Talk about your moments of truth. Either he was as smart as he thought he was, or Garth or Sean or somebody would breeze in and ask, "Justin, what the *hell* are you doing?"

A string in space-time connected this place now to its earlier self, itself in 1999. As far as Justin knew, nobody but him had thought of accessing that string, of sliding along it, with VR technology. When the simulation was good enough, it became the reality – for a while, anyhow. That was what the math said. He thought he'd done a good enough job here.

And if he had . . . oh, if he had! He knew a hell of a lot more now, at forty, than he had when he was twenty-one. If he-now could be back with Megan for a while instead of his younger self, he could make things right. He could make things last. He knew it. He had to, if he ever wanted to be happy again.

I'll fix it, he thought. *I'll fix everything. And when I slide back to here-and-now, I won't have his emptiness in my past. Everything will be the way it could have been, the way it should have been.*

An image began to emerge from the VR blankness. It was the same image he'd seen before slipping on the mask: blue tile walls with white grouting, acoustic ceiling, sinks with a mirror above them, urinals off to the left, toilet stalls behind him.

"Dammit," he muttered under his breath. Sure as hell, the men's room hadn't changed at all.

"Program superstrings-slash-virtual reality-slash-not so virtual reality is done," the PowerBook told him.

He took off the mask. Here he sat, on his suitcases, in the men's room of his office building. 2018? 1999? He couldn't tell, not staying in here. If everything had worked out the way he'd calculated, it would be before business hours back when he'd arrived, too. All he had to do was walk out that front door and hope the security guard wasn't right there.

No. What he really had to hope was that the security guard wasn't Bill.

He put the computer in his backpack again. He picked up the suitcases and walked to the men's-room door. He set down a case so he could open the door. His heart pounded harder than ever. Yes? Or no?

Justin took two steps down the hall toward the stairs before he whispered, "Yes!" Instead of the gray-green carpet he'd walked in on, this stuff was an ugly mustard yellow. He had no proof he was in 1999, not yet. But he wasn't in Kansas any more.

The place had the quiet-before-the-storm feeling offices get waiting for people to show up for work. That fit Justin's calculations. The air conditioner was noisier, wheezier, than the system that had been – would be – in his time. But it kept the corridor noticeably cooler than it had been when he lugged his stuff into the men's room. The '90s had ridden an oil glut. They burned lavishly to beat summer heat. His time couldn't.

There was the doorway that led to the stairs. Down he went. The walls were different: industrial yellow, not battleship gray. When he got to the little lobby, he didn't recognize the furniture. What was there seemed no better or worse than what he was used to, but it was different.

If there was a guard, he was off making his rounds. Justin didn't wait for him. He opened the door. He wondered if that would touch off the alarm, but it didn't. He stepped out into the cool, fresh early-morning air of . . . when?

He walked through the empty lot to the sidewalk, then looked around. Across the street, a woman out power-walking glanced his way, but didn't stop. She wore a cap, a T-shirt, and baggy shorts, which proved nothing. But then he looked at the parked cars, and began to grin a crazy grin. Most of them had smooth jelly-bean lines, which, to his eyes, was two style changes out of date. If this wasn't 1999, it was damn close.

With a clanking rumble of iron, a MetroLink train pulled into the little station behind his office. A couple of people got off; a handful got on. In his day, with gas ever scarcer, ever costlier, that commuter train would have far more passengers.

Standing on the sidewalk, unnoticed by the world around him, he pumped a fist in the air. "I did it!" he said. "I really did it!"

Having done it, he couldn't do anything else, not for a little while. Not much was open at half past five. But there was a Denny's up the street. Suitcases in hand, he trudged toward it. The young, bored-looking Hispanic waitress who seated him gave him a fishy stare. "You coulda left your stuff in the car," she said pointedly.

His answer was automatic: "I don't have a car." Her eyebrows flew upward. If you didn't have a car in L.A., you were nobody. If you didn't have a car and did have suitcases, you were liable to be a dangerously weird nobody. He had to say something. Inspiration struck: "I just got off the train. Somebody should've picked me up, but he blew it. Toast and coffee, please?"

She relaxed. "Okay – coming up. White, rye, or whole wheat?"

"Wheat." Justin looked around. He was the only customer in the place. "Can you keep an eye on the cases for a second? I want to buy a *Times*." He'd seen the machine out front, but hadn't wanted to stop till he got inside. When the waitress nodded, he got a paper. It was only a quarter. That boggled him; he paid two bucks weekdays, five Sundays.

But the date boggled him more. *June 22, 1999*. Right on the money. He went back inside. The coffee waited for him, steaming gently. The toast came up a moment later. As he spread grape jam over it, he glanced at the *Times* and wondered what his younger self was doing now.

Sleeping, you dummy. He'd liked to sleep late when he was twenty-one, and finals at Cal State Northridge would have just ended. He'd have the CompUSA job to go to, but the place didn't open till ten.

Megan would be sleeping, too. He thought of her lying in a T-shirt and sweats at her parents' house, wiggling around the way she did in bed. Maybe she was dreaming of him and smiling. She would be smiling now. A few years from now . . . Well, he'd come to fix that.

He killed forty-five minutes. By then, the restaurant was filling up. The waitress started to look ticked. Justin ordered bacon and eggs and hash browns. They bought him the table for another hour. He tried not to think about what the food was doing to his coronary arteries. His younger self wouldn't have cared. His younger self loved Denny's. *My younger self was a fool*, he thought.

He paid, again marveling at how little things cost. Of course, people didn't make much, either; you could live well on $100,000 a year. He tried to imagine living on $100,000 in 2018, and shook his head. You couldn't do it, not if you felt like eating, too.

When he went out to the parking lot, he stood there for forty minutes, looking back toward the train station. By then, it was getting close to eight o'clock. Up a side street from the Denny's was a block of apartment buildings with names like the Tivoli, the Gardens, and the Yachtsman. Up the block he trudged. The Yachtsman had a vacancy sign.

The manager looked grumpy at getting buzzed so early, but the sight of greenbacks cheered him up in a hurry. He rented Justin a one-bedroom furnished apartment at a ridiculously low rate. "I'm here on business," Justin said, which was true . . . in a way. "I'll pay three months in advance if you fix me up with a TV and a stereo. They don't have to be great. They just have to work."

"I'd have to root around," the manager said. "It'd be kind of a pain." He waited. Justin passed him two fifties. He nodded. So did Justin. This was business, too. The manager eyed his suitcases. "You'll want to move in right away, won't you?"

Justin nodded again. "And I'll want to use your phone to set up my phone service."

"Okay," the manager said with a sigh. "Come into my place here. I'll get things set up." His fish-faced wife watched Justin with wide, pale, unblinking eyes while he called the phone company and made arrangements. The manager headed off with a vacuum cleaner. In due course, he came back. "You're ready. TV and stereo are in there."

"Thanks." Justin went upstairs to the apartment. It was small and bare, with furniture that had seen better decades. The TV wasn't new. The stereo was so old, it didn't play CDs, only records and cassettes. Well, his computer could manage CDs. He accepted a key to the apartment and another for the security gates, then unpacked. He couldn't do everything he wanted till he got a phone, but he was here.

He used a pay phone to call a cab, and rode over to a used-car lot. He couldn't do everything he wanted without wheels, either. He had no trouble proving he was himself; he'd done some computer forgery before he left to make his driver's license expire in 2003, as it really did. His number hadn't changed. Security holograms that would have given a home machine trouble here-and-now were a piece of cake to graphics programs from 2018. His younger self didn't know he'd just bought a new old car: a gray early-'90s Toyota much like the one he was already driving.

"Insurance is mandatory," the salesman said. "I can sell you a policy . . ." Justin let him do it, to his barely concealed delight. It was, no doubt, highway robbery, especially since Justin was nominally only twenty-one. He'd dressed for the age he affected, in T-shirt and jeans. To him, though, no 1999 prices seemed expensive. He paid cash and took the car.

Getting a bank account wasn't hard, either. He chose a bank his younger self didn't use. Research paid off: he deposited only $9,000. Ten grand or more in cash and the bank would have reported the transaction to the government. He didn't want that kind of notice. He wanted no notice at all. The assistant manager handed him a book of temporary checks. "Good to have your business, Mr. Kloster. The personalized ones will be ready in about a week."

"Okay." Justin went off to buy groceries. He wasn't a great cook, but he was a lot better than his younger self. He'd had to learn, and had.

Once the groceries were stowed in the pantry and the refrigerator, he left again, this time to a bookstore. He went to the computer section first, to remind himself of the state of the art. After a couple of minutes, he was smiling and shaking his head. Had he done serious work with this junk? He supposed he had, but he was damned if he saw how. Before he was born, people had used slide rules because there weren't any computers yet, or even calculators. He was damned if he saw how they'd done any work, either.

But the books didn't have exactly what he wanted. He went to the magazine rack. There was a *MacAddict* in a clear plastic envelope. The CD-ROM that came with the magazine would let him start an account on a couple of online services. Once he had one, he could e-mail his younger self, and then he'd be in business.

If I – or I-then – don't flip out altogether, he thought. Things might get pretty crazy. Now that he was here and on the point of getting started, he felt in his belly how crazy they might get. And he knew both sides of things. His younger self didn't.

Would Justin-then even listen to him? He had to hope so. Looking back, he'd been pretty stupid when he was twenty-one. No matter how stupid he'd been, though, he'd have to pay attention when he got his nose rubbed in the facts. Wouldn't he?

Justin bought the *MacAddict* and took it back to his apartment. As soon as he got online, he'd be ready to roll.

He chose AOL, not Earthlink. His younger self was on Earthlink, and looked down his nose at AOL. And AOL let him pay by debiting his checking account. He didn't have any credit cards that worked in 1999. He supposed he could get one, but it would take time. He'd taken too much time already. He thought he had about three months before the space-time string he'd manipulated would snap him back to 2018. With luck, with skill, with what he knew then that he hadn't known now, he'd be happier there. But he had no time to waste.

His computer, throttled down to 56K access to the outside world, might have thought the same. But AOL's local access lines wouldn't support anything faster. "Welcome," the electronic voice said as he logged on. He ignored it, and went straight to e-mail. He was pretty sure he remembered his old e-mail address. *If*

I don't, he thought, chuckling a little as he typed, *whoever is using this address right now will get awfully confused.*

He'd pondered what he would say to get his younger self's attention, and settled on the most provocative message he could think of. He wrote, *Who but you would know that the first time you jacked off, you were looking at Miss March 1993, a little before your fifteenth birthday? Nobody, right? Gorgeous blonde, wasn't she? The only way I know that is that I am you, more or less. Let me hear from you.* He signed it, *Justin Kloster, age 40,* and sent it.

Then he had to pause. His younger self would be working now, but he'd check his e-mail as soon as he got home. Justin remembered religiously doing that every day. He didn't remember getting e-mail like the message he'd just sent, of course, but that was the point of this exercise.

Waiting till half past five wasn't easy. He wished he could use his time-travel algorithm to fast-forward to late afternoon, but he didn't dare. Too many super-strings might tangle, and even the office machine up in 2018 hadn't been able to work out the ramifications of that. In another ten years, it would probably be child's play for a computer, but he wouldn't be able to pretend he was twenty-one when he was fifty. Even a baby face and pale gold hair wouldn't stretch that far. He hoped they'd stretch far enough now.

At 5:31, he logged onto AOL again. "Welcome!" the voice told him, and then, "You've got mail!"

"You've got spam," he muttered under his breath. And one of the messages in his mailbox *was* spam. He deleted it without a qualm. The other one, though, was from his younger self @earthlink.net.

Heart pounding, he opened the e-mail. *What kind of stupid joke is this?* his younger self wrote. *Whatever it is, it's not funny.*

Justin sighed. He supposed he shouldn't have expected himself-at-twenty-one to be convinced right away. This business was hard to believe, even for him. But he had more shots in his gun than one. *No joke,* he wrote back. *Who else but you would know you lost your first baby tooth in a pear at school when you were in the first grade? Who would know your dad fed you Rollos when he took you to work with him that day you were eight or nine? Who would know you spent most of the time while you were losing your cherry staring at the mole on the side of Lindsey Fletcher's neck? Me, that's who: you at 40.* He typed his name and sent the message.

His stomach growled, but he didn't go off and make supper. He sat by the computer, waiting. His younger self would still be online. He'd have to answer . . . wouldn't he? Justin hadn't figured out what he'd do if himself-at-twenty-one wanted nothing to do with him. The prospect had never crossed his mind. Maybe it should have.

"Don't be stupid, kid," he said softly. "Don't complicate things for me. Don't complicate things for yourself, either."

He sat. He waited. He worried. After what seemed forever but was less than ten minutes, the AOL program announced, "You've got mail!"

He read it. *I don't watch* X-Files *much,* his younger self wrote, *but maybe I ought to. How could you know all that about me? I never told* anybody *about Lindsey Fletcher's neck.*

So far as Justin could recall, he hadn't told anyone about her neck by 2018, either. That didn't mean he'd forgotten. He wouldn't forget till they shoveled dirt over him.

How do I know? he wrote. *I've told you twice now – I know because I am you, you in 2018. It's not* X-Files *stuff – it's good programming.* The show still ran in endless syndication, but he hadn't watched it for years. He went on, *Believe me, I'm back here for a good reason,* and sent the e-mail.

Again, he waited. Again, the reply came back fast. He imagined his younger self eyeing the screen of his computer, eyeing it and scratching his head. His younger self must have been scratching hard, for what came back was, *But that's impossible.*

Okay, he typed. *It's impossible. But if it is impossible, how do I know all this stuff about you?*

More waiting. *The hell with it,* he thought. He'd intended to broil lamb chops, but he would have had to pay attention to keep from cremating them. He took a dinner out of the freezer and threw it into the tiny microwave built in above the stove. He could punch a button and get it more or less right. Back to the computer.

"You've got mail!" it said once more, and he did. *I don't know,* his younger self had written. *How do you know all this stuff about me?*

Because it's stuff about me, too, he answered. *You don't seem to be taking that seriously yet.*

The microwave beeped. Justin started to go off to eat, but the PowerBook told him he had more mail. He called it up. *If you're supposed to be me,* himself-at-twenty-one wrote, *then you'll look like me, right?*

Justin laughed. His younger self wouldn't believe that. He'd probably think it would make this pretender shut up and go away. But Justin wasn't a pretender, and didn't need to shut up – he could put up instead. *Right,* he replied. *Meet me in front of the B. Dalton's in the Northridge mall tomorrow night at 6:30 and I'll buy you dinner. You'll see for yourself.* He sent the message, then did walk away from the computer.

Eating frozen food reminded him why he'd learned to cook. He chucked the tray in the trash, then returned to the bedroom to see what his younger self had answered. Three words: *See you there.*

The mall surprised Justin. In his time, it had seen better years. In 1999, just a little after being rebuilt because of the '94 earthquake, it still seemed shiny and sparkly and new. Justin got there early. With his hair short, with the Cow Pi T-Shirt and jeans and big black boots he was wearing, he fit in with the kids who shopped and strutted and just hung out.

He found out how well he fit when he eyed an attractive brunette of thirty or so who was wearing business clothes. She caught him doing it, looked horrified for a second, and then stared through him as if he didn't exist. At first, he thought her reaction was over the top. Then he realized it wasn't. *You may think she's cute, but she doesn't think you are. She thinks you're wet behind the ears.*

Instead of leaving him insulted, the woman's reaction cheered him. *Maybe I can bring this off.*

He leaned against the brushed-aluminum railing in front of the second-level B. Dalton's as if he had nothing better to do. A gray-haired man in maroon polyester pants muttered something about punk kids as he walked by. Justin grinned, which made the old fart mutter more.

But then the grin slipped from Justin's face. What replaced it was probably astonishment. Here came his younger self, heading up from the Sears end of the mall.

He could tell the moment when his younger self saw him. Himself-at-twenty-one stopped, gaped, and turned pale. He looked as if he wanted to turn around and run away. Instead, after gulping, he kept on.

Justin's heart pounded. He hadn't realized just how strange seeing himself would feel. And he'd been expecting this. For his younger self, it was a bolt from the blue. That meant he had to be the one in control. He stuck out his hand. "Hi," he said. "Thanks for coming."

His younger self shook hands with him. They both looked down. The two right hands fit perfectly. *Well, they would, wouldn't they?* Justin thought. His younger self, still staring, said, "Maybe I'm not crazy. Maybe you're not crazy, either. You look just like me."

"Funny how that works," Justin said. Seeing his younger self wasn't like looking in a mirror. It wasn't because himself-at-twenty-one looked that much younger – he didn't. It wasn't even because his younger self wasn't doing the same things he did. After a moment, he figured out what it was: his younger self's image wasn't reversed, the way it would have been in a mirror. That made him look different.

His younger self put hands on hips. "Prove you're from the future," he said.

Justin had expected that. He took a little plastic coin purse, the kind that can hook onto a key chain, out of his pocket and squeezed it open. "Here," he said. "This is for you." He handed himself-at-twenty-one a quarter.

It looked like any quarter – till you noticed the date. "It's from 2012," his younger self whispered. His eyes got big and round again. "Jesus. You weren't kidding."

"I told you I wasn't," Justin said patiently. "Come on. What's the name of that Korean barbecue place on . . . Reseda?" He thought that was right. It had closed a few years after the turn of the century.

His younger self didn't notice the hesitation. "The Pine Tree?"

"Yeah." Justin knew the name when he heard it. "Let's go over there. I'll buy you dinner, like I said in e-mail, and we can talk about things."

"Like what you're doing here," his younger self said.

He nodded. "Yeah. Like what I'm doing here."

None of the waitresses at the Pine Tree spoke much English. That was one reason Justin had chosen the place: he didn't want anybody eavesdropping. But he liked garlic, he liked the odd vegetables, and he enjoyed grilling beef or pork or chicken or fish on the gas barbecue set into the tabletop.

He ordered for both of them. The waitress scribbled on her pad in the odd characters of *hangul*, then looked from one of them to the other. "Twins," she said, pulling out a word she did know.

"Yeah," Justin said. *Sort of,* he thought. The waitress went away.

His younger self pointed at him. "Tell me one thing," he said.

"What?" Justin asked. He expected anything from *What are you doing here?* to *What is the meaning of life?*

But his younger self surprised him: "That the Rolling Stones aren't still touring by the time you're – I'm – forty."

"Well, no," Justin said. That was a pretty scary thought, when you got down to it. He and his younger self both laughed. They sounded just alike. *We would,* he thought.

The waitress came back with a couple of tall bottles of OB beer. She hadn't asked either one of them for an ID, for which Justin was duly grateful. His younger self kept quiet while she was around. After she'd gone away, himself-at-twenty-one said, "Okay, I believe you. I didn't think I would, but I do. You know too much – and you couldn't have pulled that quarter out of your ear from nowhere." He sipped at the Korean beer. He looked as if he would sooner have gone out and got drunk.

"That's right," Justin agreed. *Stay in control. The more you sound like you know what you're doing, the more he'll think you know what you're doing. And he has to think that, or this won't fly.*

His younger self drank beer faster than he did, and waved for a second tall one as soon as the first was empty. Justin frowned. He remembered drinking more in his twenties than he did at forty, but didn't care to have his nose rubbed in it. He wouldn't have wanted to drive after two big OBs, but his younger self didn't worry about it.

With his younger self's new beer, the waitress brought the meat to be grilled and the plates of vegetables. She used aluminum tongs to put some pork and some marinated beef over the fire. Looking at the strips of meat curling and shrinking, himself-at-twenty-one exclaimed, "Oh my God! They killed Kenny!"

"Huh?" Justin said, and then, "Oh." He managed a feeble chuckle. He hadn't thought about *South Park* in a long time.

His younger self eyed him. "If you'd said that to me, I'd have laughed a lot harder. But the show's not hot for you any more, is it?" He answered his own question before Justin could: "No, it wouldn't be. 2018? Jesus." He took another big sip of beer.

Justin grabbed some beef with the tongs. He used chopsticks to eat, ignoring the fork. So did his younger self. He was better at it than himself-at-twenty-one; he'd had more practice. The food was good. He remembered it had been.

After a while, his younger self said, "Well, *will* you tell me what this is all about?"

"What's the most important thing in your life right now?" Justin asked in return.

"You mean, besides trying to figure out why I'd travel back in time to see me?" his younger self returned. He nodded, carefully not smiling. He'd been looser, sillier, at twenty-one than he was now. Of course, he'd had fewer things go wrong then, too. And his younger self went on, "What could it be but Megan?"

"Okay, we're on the same page," Justin said. "That's why I'm here, to set things right with Megan."

"Things with Megan don't need setting right." Himself-at-twenty-one sounded disgustingly complacent. "Things with Megan are great. I mean, I'm taking my time and all, but they're great. And they'll stay great, too. How many kids do we have now?"

"None." Justin's voice went flat and harsh. A muscle at the corner of his jaw jumped. He touched it to try to calm it down.

"None?" His younger self wasn't quick on the uptake. He needed his nose rubbed in things. He looked at Justin's left hand. "You're not wearing a wedding ring," he said. He'd just noticed. Justin's answering nod was grim. His younger self asked, "Does that mean we don't get married?"

Say it ain't so. Justin did: "We get married, all right. And then we get divorced."

His younger self went as pale as he had when he first saw Justin. Even at twenty-one, he knew too much about divorce. Here-and-now, his father was living with a woman not much older than he was. His mother was living with a woman not much older than he was, too. That was why he had his own apartment: paying his rent was easier for his mom and dad than paying him any real attention.

But, however much himself-at-twenty-one knew about divorce, he didn't know enough. He'd just been a fairly innocent bystander. He hadn't gone through one from the inside. He didn't understand the pain and the emptiness and the endless might-have-beens that kept going through your mind afterwards.

Justin had had those might-have-beens inside his head since he and Megan fell apart. But he was in a unique position, sitting here in the Pine Tree eating *kimchi*. He could do something about them.

He could. If his younger self let him. Said younger self blurted, "That can't happen."

"It can. It did. It will," Justin said. The muscle started twitching again.

"But – how?" Himself-at-twenty-one sounded somewhere between bewildered and shocked. "We aren't like Mom and Dad – we don't fight all the time, and we don't look for something on the side wherever we can find it." Even at twenty-one, he spoke of his parents with casual contempt. Justin thought no better of them in 2018.

He said, "You can fight about sex, you can fight about money, you can fight about in-laws. We ended up doing all three, and so . . ." He set down his chopsticks and spread his hands wide. "We broke up – will break up – if we don't change things. That's why I figured out how to come back: to change things, I mean."

His younger self finished the second OB. "You must have wanted to do that a lot," he remarked.

"You might say so." Justin's voice came harsh and ragged. "Yeah, you just might say so. Since we fell apart, I've never come close to finding anybody who makes me feel the way Megan did. If it's not her, it's nobody. That's how it looks from here, anyhow. I want to make things right for the two of us."

"Things *were* going to be right." But his younger self lacked conviction. Justin sat and waited. He was better at that than he had been half a lifetime earlier. Finally, himself-at-twenty-one asked, "What will you do?"

He didn't ask, *What do you want to do?* He spoke as if Justin were a force of nature. Maybe that was his youth showing. Maybe it was just the beer. Whatever it was, Justin encouraged it by telling his younger self what he *would* do, not what he'd like to do: "I'm going to take over your life for a couple of months. I'm going to be you. I'm going to take Megan out, I'm going to make sure things are solid – and then the superstring I've ridden to get me here will break down. You'll live happily ever after: I'll brief you to make sure you don't screw up what I've built. And when I get back to 2018, I *will have lived* happily ever after. How does that sound?"

"I don't know," his younger self said. "You'll be taking Megan out?"

Justin nodded. "That's right."

"You'll be . . . taking Megan back to the apartment?"

"Yeah," Justin said. "But she'll think it's you, remember, and pretty soon it'll be you, and it'll keep right on being you till you turn into me, if you know what I mean."

"I know what you mean," his younger self said. "Still . . ." He grimaced. "I don't know. I don't like it."

"You have a better idea?" Justin folded his arms across his chest and waited, doing his best to be the picture of inevitability. Inside, his stomach tied itself in knots. He'd always been better at the tech side of things than at sales.

"It's not fair," himself-at-twenty-one said. "You *know* all this shit, and I've gotta guess."

Justin shrugged. "If you think I did all this to come back and tell you lies, go ahead. That's fine." It was anything but fine. But he couldn't let his younger self see that. "You'll see what happens, and we'll both be sorry."

"I don't know." His younger self shook his head, again and again. His eyes had a trapped-animal look. "I just don't know. Everything sounds like it hangs together, but you could be bullshitting, too, just as easy."

"Yeah, right." Justin couldn't remember the last time he'd said that, but it fit here.

Then his younger self got up. "I won't say yes and I won't say no, not now I won't. I've got your e-mail address. I'll use it." Out he went, not quite steady on his feet.

Justin stared after him. He paid for both dinners – it seemed like peanuts to him – and went home himself. His younger self needed time to think things through. He saw that. Seeing it and liking it were two different things. And every minute himself-at-twenty-one dithered was a minute he couldn't get back. He stewed. He fumed. He waited. What other choice did he have?

You could whack him and take over for him. But he rejected the thought with a shudder. He was no murderer. All he wanted was some happiness. Was that too much to ask? He didn't think so, not after all he'd missed since Megan made him move out. He checked e-mail every hour on the hour.

Two and a half mortal days. Justin thought he'd go nuts. He'd never dreamt his younger self would make him wait so long. At last, the computer told him, "You've got mail!"

All right, dammit, himself-at-twenty-one wrote. *I still don't know about this, but I don't think I have any choice. If me and Megan are going to break up, that can't happen. You better make sure it doesn't.*

"Oh, thank God," Justin breathed. He wrote back, *You won't be sorry.*

Whatever, his younger self replied. *Half of me is sorry already. More than half.*

Don't be, Justin told him. *Everything will be fine.*

It had better be, his younger self wrote darkly. *How do you want to make the switch?*

Meet me in front of the B. Dalton's again, Justin answered. *Park by the Sears. I will, too. Bring whatever you want in your car. You can move it to the one I'm driving. I'll do the same here. See you in two hours?*

Whatever, his younger self repeated. Justin remembered saying that a lot. He hoped it meant *yes* here. The only things he didn't want his younger self getting his hands on here were his laptop (though it would distract himself-at-twenty-one from worrying about Megan if anything would) and some of his cash. He left behind the TV and the stereo and the period clothes – and, below the underwear and socks, the cash he wasn't taking along. His younger self could eat and have some fun, too, provided he did it at places where Megan wouldn't run into him.

This time, his younger self got to the mall before him. Thoroughly grim, himself-at-twenty-one said, "Let's get this over with."

"Come on. It's not a root canal," Justin said. Now his younger self looked blank – he didn't know about root canals. Justin wished *he* didn't; that was a bit of the future less pleasant to contemplate than life with Megan. He went on, "Let's go do it. We'll need to swap keys, you know."

"Yeah." Himself-at-twenty-one nodded. "I had spares made. How about you?"

"Me, too." Justin's grin twisted up one corner of his mouth. "We think alike. Amazing, huh?"

"Amazing. Right." His younger self started back toward Sears. "This better work."

"It will," Justin said. *It has to, goddammit.*

They'd parked only a couple of rows apart. His younger self had a couple of good-sized bundles. He put them in Justin's car while Justin moved his stuff to the machine himself-at-twenty-one had been driving. "You know where I live," his younger self said after they'd swapped keys. "What's my new address?"

"Oh." Justin told him. "The car's insured, and you'll find plenty of money in the underwear drawer." He put a hand on his younger self's shoulder. "It'll be fine. Honest. You're on vacation for a couple of months, that's all."

"On vacation from my *life*." Himself-at-twenty-one looked grim again. At twenty-one, everything was urgent. "Don't fuck up, that's all."

"It's my life, too, remember." Justin got into the car his younger self had driven to the mall. He fumbled a little, finding the right key. When he fired up the engine, the radio started playing KROQ. He laughed. Green Day was the bomb now, even if not quite to his taste. It wasn't music for people approaching middle age and regretting it. He cranked the radio and drove back to his younger self's apartment.

The Acapulco. He nodded as he drove up to it. It looked familiar. That made him laugh again. It hadn't changed. He had.

After he drove through the security gate, he found his old parking space more by letting his hands and eyes guide his brain than the other way round. He couldn't remember his apartment number at all, and had to go the the lobby to see which box had KLOSTER Dymo-taped onto it. He walked around the pool and past the rec room hardly anybody used, and there it was – his old place. But it wasn't old now. This was where his younger self had lived and would live, and where he was living now.

As soon as he opened the door, he winced. He hadn't remembered the bile-colored carpet, either, but it came back in a hurry. He looked around. Here it was – all his old stuff, a lot of it things he hadn't seen in half a lifetime. Paperbacks, CDs, that tiny statuette of a buglike humanoid standing on its hind legs and giving a speech . . . During which move had that disappeared? He shrugged. He'd been through a lot of them. He fondly touched an antenna as he went past the bookcase, along a narrow hall, and into the bedroom.

"My old iMac!" he exclaimed. But it wasn't old; the model had been out for less than a year. Bondi blue and ice case – to a taste formed in 2018, it looked not just outmoded but tacky as hell, but he'd thought it was great when it came out.

His younger self had left a note by the keyboard. *In case you don't remember, here's Megan's phone number and e-mail. Don't screw it up, that's all I've got to tell you.*

He had remembered her e-mail address, but not her phone number. "Thanks, kid," he said to himself-at-twenty-one. There by the phone on the nightstand lay his younger self's address book, but having things out in the open made it easier.

Instead of calling her, he walked into the bathroom. His hand shook as he flipped on the light. He stared at the mirror. *Can I do this?* He ran a palm over his cheek. *Yeah, I look young. Do I look that young? What will Megan think when I come to the door? What will her folks think? I'm only a couple of years younger than they are, for Christ's sake.*

If I come to the door wearing his – my – clothes, though, and talking like me, and knowing things only I could know, who else would I be but Justin Kloster? She'll think I'm me, because I can't possibly be anybody else. And I'm not anybody else – except I am.

He was still frowning and looking for incipient wrinkles when the telephone rang. As he hurried back to the bedroom, he hoped it would be a telemarketer. *I'm not ready, I'm not ready, I'm not . . .* "Hello?"

"Hiya? How the hell are you?" It was Megan, all right. He hadn't heard her in more than ten years, but he knew her voice. He hadn't heard her sound bouncy and bubbly and glad to be talking to *him* in a lot more than ten years. Before he could get a word in, she went on, "You mad at me? You haven't called in two days."

By the way she said it, it might have been two years. "I'm not mad," Justin answered automatically. "Just – busy."

"Too busy for *me*?" Now she sounded as if she couldn't imagine such a thing. Justin's younger self must have been too caught up in everything else to have time for her. At least he hadn't blabbed about Justin's return to 1999. "What were you doing? Who were you doing it with – or to?"

She giggled. Justin remembered her asking him questions like that later on, in an altogether different tone of voice. Not now. She didn't know she would do that. If he changed things here, she wouldn't. "Nothing," he said. "Nobody. Things have been hairy at work, that's all."

"A likely story." But Megan was still laughing. He remembered her doing things like that. He remembered her stopping, too. She said, "Well, you're not working now, right? Suppose I come over?"

"Okay," he said, thinking about baptism by total immersion. Either this would work, or it would blow up in his face. *What do I do if it blows up? Run back to 2018 with my tail between my legs, that's what.*

But Megan didn't even give him time to panic. "Okay?" she said, mock-fierce. "Okay? I'll okay you, mister, you see if I don't. Ten minutes." She hung up.

Justin ran around like a madman, to remind himself where things were and to clean up a little. He hadn't remembered his younger self as such a slob. He checked the refrigerator. Frozen dinners, beer, cokes – about what he'd expected.

He waited for the buzz that would mean Megan was at the security door. But he'd forgotten he'd given her a key. The first thing he knew she was there was the knock on the door. He opened it. "Hi," he said, his voice breaking as if he really were twenty-one, or maybe sixteen.

"Hiya." Megan clicked her tongue between her teeth. "You do look tired. Poor baby."

He was looking at her, too, looking and trying not to tremble. She looked just like all the photos he'd kept: a swarthy brunette with flashing dark eyes, a little skinny maybe, but with some meat on her bones even so. She always smiled as if she knew a secret. He'd remembered. Remembering and seeing it in the flesh when it was fresh and new and a long way from curdling were very different things. He hadn't imagined how different.

"How tired *are* you?" she said. "Not *too* tired, I hope." She stepped forward, put her arms around him, and tilted her face up.

Automatically, his arms went around her. Automatically, he brought his mouth down to hers. She made a tiny noise, deep in her throat, as their lips met.

Justin's heart pounded so hard, he was amazed Megan couldn't hear it. He wanted to burst into tears. Here he was, holding the only woman he'd ever truly loved, the woman who'd so emphatically stopped loving him – only now she did again. If that wasn't a miracle, he didn't know what was.

She felt soft and smooth and warm and firm. Very firm, he noticed – a lot firmer than the women he'd been seeing, no matter how obsessively they went to the gym. And that brought the second realization, almost as blinding as realizing he, Justin, was alone with her, Megan: he, a forty-year-old guy, was alone with her, a twenty-year-old girl.

What had the bartender asked? *You go around picking up high-school girls?* But it wasn't like that, dammit. Megan didn't know he was forty. She thought he was his going-into-senior-year self. He had to think that way, too.

Except he couldn't, or not very well. He'd lived half a lifetime too long. He tried not to remember, but he couldn't help it. "Wow!" he gasped when the kiss finally ended.

"Yeah." Megan took such heat for granted. She was twenty. Doubt never entered her mind. "Not bad for starters." Without waiting for an answer, she headed for the bedroom.

Heart pounding harder than ever, Justin followed. Here-and-now, they hadn't been lovers very long, and neither had had a whole lot of experience beforehand. That was part of what had gone wrong; Justin was sure of it. They'd gone stale, without knowing how to fix things. Justin knew a lot more now than he had at twenty-one. And here he was, getting a chance to use it when it mattered.

He almost forgot everything the next instant, because Megan was getting out of her clothes and lying down on the bed and laughing at him for being so slow. He didn't stay slow very long. As he lay down beside her, he thanked God and Superstrings, Ltd., not necessarily in that order.

His hands roamed her. She sighed and leaned toward him for another kiss. *Don't hurry*, he thought. *Don't rush*. In a way, that was easy. He wanted to touch her, caress her, taste her, forever. In another way . . . He wanted to do more, too.

He made himself go slow. It was worth it. "Oh, Justin," Megan said. Some time later, she said, "Ohhh, Justin." He didn't think he'd ever heard her sound like that the first time around. What she said a few minutes after that had no words, but was a long way from disappointed.

Then it was his turn. He kept having the nagging thought that he was taking advantage of a girl half his age who didn't know exactly who he was. But then, as she clasped him with arms and legs, all the nagging thoughts went away. And it was just as good as he'd hoped it would be, which said a great deal.

Afterwards, they lay side by side, sweaty and smiling foolishly. Justin kept stroking her. She purred. She stroked him, too, expectantly. When what she was expecting didn't happen, she gave him a sympathetic look. "You *must* be tired," she said.

Did she think he'd be ready again right then? They'd just finished! But memory, now that he accessed it, told him she did. He clicked his tongue between his teeth. He might look about the same at forty as he had at twenty-one, but he couldn't perform the same. Who could?

Had he thought of this beforehand, he would have brought some Viagra back with him. In his time, it was over-the-counter. He wasn't even sure it existed in 1999. He hadn't had to worry about keeping it up, not at twenty-one.

But Megan had given him an excuse, at least this time. "Yeah, day from hell," he said. "Doesn't mean I can't keep you happy." He proceeded to do just that, and took his time about it, teasing her along as much as he could.

Once the teasing stopped, she stared at him, eyes enormous. "Oh, sweetie, why didn't you ever do anything like that before?" she asked. All by itself, the question made him sure he'd done the right thing, coming back. It also made him sure he needed to give his younger self a good talking-to before he slid up the superstring to 2018. But Megan found another question: "Where did you *learn* that?"

Did she think he had another girlfriend? Did she wonder if that was why he could only do it once with her? Or was she joking? He hoped she was. How would his younger self have answered? With pride. "I," he declared, "have a naturally dirty mind."

Megan giggled. "Good."

And it was good. A little later, in the lazy man's position, he managed a second round. That was very good. Megan thought so, too. He couldn't stop yawning afterwards, but he'd already said he was tired. "See?" he told her. "You wear me out." He wasn't kidding. Megan didn't know how much he wasn't kidding.

She proved that, saying, "I was thinking we'd go to a club tonight, but I'd better put you to bed. We can go tomorrow." She went into the bathroom, then came back and started getting dressed. "We can do all sorts of things tomorrow." The smile she gave him wasn't just eager; it was downright lecherous.

Christ, he thought, *she'll expect me to be just as horny as I was tonight.* His younger self would have been. To him, the prospect seemed more nearly exhausting than exciting. *Sleep. I need sleep.*

Megan bent down and kissed him on the end of the nose. "Pick me up about seven? We'll go to the Probe, and then who knows what?"

"Okay," he said around another yawn. "Whatever." Megan laughed and left. Justin thought he heard her close the door, but he wasn't sure.

He couldn't even sleep late. He had to go do his younger self's job at CompUSA, and himself-at-twenty-one didn't keep coffee in the apartment. He drank cokes instead, but they didn't pack the jolt of French roast.

Work was hell. All the computers were obsolete junk to him. Over half a lifetime, he'd forgotten their specs. Why remember when they were obsolete? And his boss, from the height of his late twenties, treated Justin like a kid. He wished he'd told his younger self to keep coming in. But Megan stopped by every so often, and so did other people he knew. He wanted himself-at-twenty-one out of sight, out of mind.

His younger self probably *was* going out of his mind right now. He wondered what the kid was doing, what he was thinking. Worrying, he supposed, and dismissed himself-at-twenty-one as casually as his boss had dismissed him believing him to be his younger self.

His shift ended at five-fifteen. He drove home, nuked some supper, showered, and dressed in his younger self's club-hopping clothes: black pants and boots, black jacket, white shirt. The outfit struck him as stark. You needed to be skinny to look good in it, and he'd never been skinny. He shrugged. It was what you wore to go clubbing.

Knocking on the door to Megan's parents' house meant more strangeness. He made himself forget all the things they'd say after he and Megan went belly-up. And, when Megan's mother opened the door, he got another jolt: she looked pretty damn good. He'd always thought of her as old. "H-hello, Mrs. Tricoupis," he managed at last.

"Hello, Justin." She stepped aside. No, nothing old about her – somewhere close to his own age, sure enough. "Megan says you've been working hard."

"That's right." Justin nodded briskly.

"I believe it," Mrs. Tricoupis said. "You look tired." Megan had said the same thing. It was as close as they could come to, *You look forty.* But her mother eyed him curiously. He needed a minute to figure out why: he'd spoken to her as an equal, not as his girlfriend's mother. *Gotta watch that*, he thought. It wouldn't be easy; he saw as much. Even if nobody else did, he knew how old he was.

Before he could say anything else to raise eyebrows, Megan came out. She fluttered her fingers at Mrs. Tricoupis. "See you later, Mom."

"All right," her mother said. "Drive safely, Justin."

"Yeah," he said. Nobody'd told him that in a long time. He grinned at Megan. "The Probe."

He'd had to look up how to get there in the Thomas Brothers himself-at-twenty-one kept in the car; he'd long since forgotten. It was off Melrose, the center of youth and style in the '90s – and as outmoded in 2018 as the corner of Haight and Ashbury in 1999.

On the way down, Megan said, "I hear there's going to be another rave at that place we went to a couple weeks ago. Want to see?"

"Suppose." Justin hoped he sounded interested, not alarmed. After-hours illicit bashes didn't hold the attraction for him they once had. And he had no idea where they'd gone then. His younger self would know. He didn't.

He had as much trouble not grinning at the fashion statements the kids going into the club were making as Boomers did with tie-dye and suede jackets with fringe. Tattoos, pierced body parts . . . Those fads had faded. Except for a stud in his left ear, he'd never had more holes than he'd been born with.

Somebody waved to Megan and him as they went in. He waved back. His younger self would have known who it was. He'd long since forgotten. He got away with it. And he got carded when he bought a beer. That made him laugh. Then he came back and bought another one for Megan, who wasn't legal yet.

She pointed toward the little booth with the spotlight on it. "Look. Helen's deejaying tonight. She's good!"

"Yeah." Justin grinned. Megan sounded so excited. Had he cared so passionately about who was spinning the music? He probably had. He wondered why. The mix hadn't been that much different from one deejay to another.

When the music started, he thought the top of his head would blow off. Coming home with ears ringing had been a sign of a good time – and a sign of nerve damage, but who cared at twenty-one? He cared now.

"What's the matter?" Megan asked. "Don't you want to dance?" He thought that was what she said, anyhow; he read her lips, because he couldn't hear a word.

"Uh, sure." He hadn't been a great dancer at twenty-one, and hadn't been on the floor in a lot of years since. But Megan didn't criticize. She'd always liked getting out there and letting the music take over. The Probe didn't have a mosh pit, for which Justin was duly grateful. Looking back, pogoing in a pit reminded him more of line play at the Super Bowl than of dancing.

He hadn't been in great shape when he was twenty-one, either. Half a lifetime riding a desk hadn't improved things. By the time the first break came, he was blowing like a whale. Megan's face was sweaty, too, but she loved every minute of it. She wasn't even breathing hard. "This is *so* cool!" she said.

She was right. Justin had long since stopped worrying about whether he was cool. You could stay at the edge till you were thirty – thirty-five if you really pushed it. After that, you were either a fogy or a grotesque. He'd taken fogydom for granted for years. Now he had to ride the crest of the wave again. He wondered if it was worth it.

Helen started spinning more singles. Justin danced till one. At least he had the next day off. Even so, he wished he were home in bed – not with Megan but alone, blissfully unconscious. No such luck. Somebody with enough rings in his ears to set off airport metal detectors passed out xeroxed directions to the rave. That told Justin where it was. He didn't want to go, but Megan did. "You wearing out on me?" she asked. They went.

He wondered who owned the warehouse – a big Lego block of a building – and if whoever it was had any idea what was going on inside. He doubted it. It was a dreadful place for a big party – concrete floor, wires and metal scaffolding overhead, acoustics worse than lousy. But Megan's eyes glowed. The thrill of the not quite legal. The cops might show up and throw everybody out.

He knew they wouldn't, not tonight, because they hadn't. And, at forty, the thrill of the not quite legal had worn off for him. Some smiling soul came by with little plastic bottles full of greenish liquid. "Instant Love!" he said. "Five bucks a pop."

Megan grabbed two. Justin knew he had to grab his wallet. "What's in it?" he asked warily.

"Try it. You'll like it," the guy said. "A hundred percent natural."

Megan had already gulped hers down. She waited expectantly for Justin. He remembered taking a lot of strange things at raves, but that had been a long time ago – except it wasn't. Nothing had killed him, so he didn't suppose this would.

And it didn't, but not from lack of trying. The taste was nasty plus sugar. The effect . . . when the shit kicked in, Justin stopped wishing for coffee. He felt as if he'd just had seventeen cups of the strongest joe ever perked. His heart pounded four hundred beats a minute. His hands shook. He could feel the veins on his eyeballs sticking out every time he blinked.

"Isn't it *great*?" Megan's eyes were bugging out of her head.

"Whatever." When Justin was twenty-one, he'd thought this kind of rush was great, too. Now he wondered if he'd have a coronary on the spot. He did dance a lot more energetically.

And, when he took Megan back to his place, he managed something else, too. With his heart thudding the way it was, remembering anything related to fore-play wasn't easy, but he did. Had he been twenty-one, it surely would have been wham-bam-thank-you-ma'am. Megan seemed suitably appreciative; maybe that Instant Love handle wasn't altogether hype.

But his real age told. Despite the drug, whatever it was, and despite the company, he couldn't have gone a second round if he'd had a crane to get it up. If that bothered Megan, she didn't let on.

Despite his failure, he didn't roll over and go to sleep, the way he had the first night. He wondered if he'd sleep for the next week. It was past four in the morning. "Shall I take you home?" he asked. "Your folks gonna be worried?"

Megan sat up naked on the bed and shook her head. Everything moved when she did that; it was marvelous to watch. "No problem," she said. "They aren't on me twenty-four-seven like some parents. You don't want to throw me out, I'd just as soon stay a while." She opened her eyes very wide to show she wasn't sleepy, either.

"Okay. Better than okay." Justin reached out and brushed the tip of her left breast with the backs of his fingers. "I like having you around, you know?" She had no idea how much he wanted to have her around. With luck, she'd never find out.

"I like being around." She cocked her head to one side. "You've been kind of funny the last couple days, you know?"

To cover his unease – hell, his fear – Justin made a stupid face. "Is that funny enough for you?" he asked.

"Not funny like that," Megan said. He made a different, even more stupid, face. It got a giggle from her, but she persisted: "Not funny like that, I told you. Funny a different sort of way."

"Like how?" he asked, though he knew.

Megan didn't, but groped toward it: "Lots of little things. The way you touch me, for instance. You didn't used to touch me like that." She looked down at the wet spot on the sheets. "I like what you're doing, believe me I do, but it's not what you were doing last week. How did you . . . find this out, just all of a sudden? It's great, like I say, but . . ." She shrugged. "I shouldn't complain. I'm *not* complaining. But . . ." Her voice trailed off again.

If I'd known then what I know now – everybody sang that song. But he didn't just sing it. He'd done something about it. This was the thanks he got? At least she hadn't come right out and asked him if he had another girlfriend.

He tried to make light of it: "Here I spent all night laying awake, trying to think of things you'd like, and—"

"I do," Megan said quickly. She wasn't lying, not unless she was the best actress in the world. But she went on, "You looked bored in the Probe tonight. You never looked bored in a club before."

Damn. He hadn't known it showed. What was hot at twenty-one wasn't at forty. *Been there, done that.* That was what people said in the '90s. One more thing he couldn't admit. "Tired," he said again.

Megan nailed him for it. "You never said that, either, not till yesterday – day before yesterday now." Remorselessly precise.

"Sorry," Justin answered. "I'm just me. Who else would I be?" Again, he was conscious of knowing what she didn't and keeping it from her. It felt unkosher, as if he were the only one in class who took a test with the book open. But what else could he do?

Megan started getting into her clothes. "Maybe you'd better take me home." But then, as if she thought that too harsh, she added some teasing: "I don't want to eat what you'd fix for breakfast."

He could have made her a damn fine breakfast. He started to say so. But his younger self couldn't have, not to save his life. He shut up and got dressed, too. Showing her more differences was the last thing he wanted.

Dawn was turning the eastern sky gray and pink when he pulled up in front of her parents' house. Before she could take off her seat belt, he put his arm around her and said, "I love you, you know?"

His younger self wouldn't say those words for another year. *Taking my time*, the socially backwards dummy called it. For Justin at forty, the words weren't just a truth, but a truth that defined his life – for better and, later on, for worse. He had no trouble bringing them out.

Megan stared at him. Maybe she hadn't expected him to say that for quite a while yet. After a heartbeat, she nodded. She leaned over and kissed him, half on the cheek, half on the mouth. Then she got out and walked to her folks' front door. She turned and waved. Justin waved back. He drove off while she was working the deadbolt.

He finally fell asleep about noon. The Instant Love kept him up and bouncing till then. At two-thirty, the phone rang. By the way he jerked and thrashed, a bomb might have gone off by his head. He grabbed the handset, feeling like death. "Hello?" he croaked.

"Hi. How are things?"

Not Megan. A man's voice. For a second, all that meant was that it didn't matter, that he could hang up on it. Then he recognized it: the voice on his own answering machine. But it wasn't a recording. It was live, which seemed more than he could say right now. His younger self.

He had to talk, dammit. "Things are fine," he said. "Or they were till you called. I was asleep."

"*Now?*" The way himself-at-twenty-one sounded, it might have been some horrible perversion. "I called now 'cause I figured you wouldn't be."

"Never mind," Justin said. The cobwebs receded. He knew they'd be back pretty soon. "Yeah, things are okay. We went to the Probe last night, and—"

"*Did* you?" His younger self sounded – no, *suspicious* wasn't right. *Jealous.* That was it. "What else did you do?"

"That after-hours place. Some guy came through with fliers, so I knew how to get there."

"Lucky you. And what *else* did you do?" Yeah. Jealous. A-number-one jealous. Justin wondered how big a problem that would be. "About what you'd expect," he answered tightly. "I'm you, remember. What would you have done?"

The sigh on the other end of the line said his younger self knew exactly what he would have done, and wished he'd been doing it. *But I did it better, you little geek.*

Before his younger self could do anything but sigh, Justin added, "And when I took her home, I told her I loved her."

"Jesus!" himself-at-twenty-one exclaimed. "What did you go and do that for?"

"It's true, isn't it?"

"That doesn't mean you've got to *say* it, for Christ's sake," his younger self told him. "What am I supposed to do when you go away?"

"Marry her, doofus," Justin said. "Live happily ever after, so I get to live happily ever after, too. Why the hell do you think I came back here?"

"For your good time, man, not mine. I'm sure not having a good time, I'll tell you."

Was I really that stupid? Justin wondered. But it wasn't quite the right question. *Was my event horizon that short?* Holding on to patience with both hands, he said, "Look, chill for a while, okay? I'm doing fine."

"Sure you are." His younger self sounded hot. "You're doing fucking great. What about me?"

Nope, no event horizon at all. Justin said, "You're fine. Chill. You're on vacation. Go ahead. Relax. Spend my money. That's what it's there for."

That distracted his younger self. "Where'd you get so much? What did you do, rob a bank?"

"It's worth a lot more now than it will be then," Justin answered. "Inflation. Have some fun. Just be discreet, okay?"

"You mean, keep out of your hair." His younger self didn't stay distracted long.

"In a word, yes."

"While you're in Megan's hair." Himself-at-twenty-one let out a long, angry breath. "I don't know, dude."

"It's for you." Justin realized he was pleading. "It's for her and you."

Another angry exhalation. "Yeah." His younger self hung up.

Everything went fine till he took Megan to the much ballyhooed summer block-buster two weekends later. She'd been caught up in the hype. And she thought the leading man was cute, though he looked like a boy to Justin. On the other hand, Justin looked like a boy himself, or he couldn't have got away with this.

But that wasn't the worst problem. Unlike her, he'd seen the movie before. He remembered liking it, though he'd thought the plot a little thin. Seen through forty-year-old eyes, it had no plot at all. He had a lot less tolerance for loud soundtracks and things blowing up every eight and a half minutes than his younger self would have. And even the most special special effects seemed routine to somebody who'd been through another twenty years of computer-generated miracles.

As the credits finally rolled, he thought, *No wonder I don't go to the movies much any more.*

When Megan turned to him, though, her eyes were shining. "Wasn't that great?" she said as they headed for the exit.

"Yeah," he said. "Great."

A different tone would have saved him. He realized that as soon as the words were out of his mouth. Too late. The one he'd used couldn't have been anything but sarcastic. And Megan noticed. She was good at catching things like that – better than he'd ever been, certainly. "What's the matter?" she demanded. "Why didn't you like it?"

The challenge in her voice reminded Justin of how she'd sounded during the quarrels before their breakup. She couldn't know that. His younger self wouldn't have known, either – he hadn't been through it. But Justin had, and reacted with a challenge of his own: "Why? Because it was really dumb."

It was a nice summer night, clear, cooling down from the hot day, a few stars in the sky – with the lights of the San Fernando Valley, you never saw more than a few. None of that mattered to Megan. She stopped halfway to the car. "How can you say that?"

Justin saw the special-effects stardust in her eyes, and the effect of a great many closeups of the boyishly handsome – pretty, to his newly jaundiced eye – leading man. He should have shut up. But he reacted viscerally to that edge in her voice. Instead of letting things blow over, he told her exactly why the movie was dumb.

He finished just as they got to the Toyota. He hadn't let her get in word one. When he ran down, she stared at him. "Why are you so mean? You never sounded so mean before."

"You asked. I told you," he said, still seething. But when he saw her fighting back tears as she fastened her seat belt, he realized he'd hit back too hard. It wasn't quit like kicking a puppy, but it was close, too close. He had a grown man's armor and weapons to pierce a grown woman's – all the nastier products of experience – and he'd used them on a kid. Too late, he felt like an asshole. "I'm sorry," he mumbled.

"Whatever." Megan looked out the window toward the theater complex, not at him. "Maybe you'd better take me home."

Alarm tore through him. "Honey, I said I was sorry. I meant it."

"I heard you." Megan still wouldn't look at him. "You'd better take me home anyhow."

Sometimes, the more you argued, the bigger the mess you made. This looked like one of those times. Justin recognized that now. A couple of minutes sooner would have been better. "Okay," he said, and started the car.

The ride back to her folks' house was almost entirely silent. When he pulled up, Megan opened the door before the car stopped rolling. "Goodnight," she said. She started for the front door at something nearly a run.

"Wait!" he called. If that wasn't raw panic in his voice, it would do. She heard it, too, and stopped, looking back warily, like a frightened animal that *would* bolt at any wrong move. He said, "I won't do that again. Promise." To show how much he meant it, he crossed his heart. He hadn't done that since about the third grade.

Megan's nod was jerky. "All right," she said. "But don't call me for a while anyway. We'll both chill a little. How does that sound?"

Terrible. Justin hated the idea of losing any precious time here. But he saw he couldn't argue. He wished he'd seen that sooner. He made himself nod, made himself smile, made himself say, "Okay."

The porch light showed relief on Megan's face. Relief she wouldn't be talking to him for a while. He had to live with that all the way home.

He wished he could have walked away from his younger self's job at CompUSA, but it would have looked bad. He'd needed a few days to have the details of late-1990s machines come back to him. Once they did, he rapidly got a reputation as a maven. His manager bumped him a buck an hour – and piled more hours on him. He resisted as best he could, but he couldn't always.

Three days after the fight with Megan, his phone rang as he got into his – well, his younger self's – apartment. He got to it just before the answering machine could. "Hello?" He was panting. If it was himself-at-twenty-one, he was ready to contemplate murder – or would it be suicide?

But it was Megan. "Hiya," she said. "Didn't I ask you not to call for a little bit? I know I did."

"Yeah, you did. And I—" Justin broke off. *He* hadn't called her. What about his younger self? *Maybe I ought to rub him out, if he's going to mess things up.* But that thought vanished. He couldn't deny a conversation she'd surely had. "I just like talking to you, that's all."

Megan's laughter was rainbows to his ears. "You were *so* funny," she said. "It was like we hadn't fought at all. I couldn't stay pissed. Believe me, I tried."

"I'm glad you didn't," Justin said. *And I do* need *to have a talk with my younger self.* "You want to got out this weekend?"

"Sure," Megan answered. "But let's stay away from the movies. What do you think?"

"Whatever," he said. "Okay with me."

"Good." More relief. "Plenty of other things we can do. Maybe I should just come straight to your place."

His younger self would have slavered at that. He liked the idea pretty well himself. But, being forty and not twenty-one, he heard what Megan didn't say, too. What she meant, or some of what she meant, was, *You're fine in bed. Whenever we're not in bed, whenever we go somewhere, you get weird.*

"Sure," he said, and then, to prove he wasn't only interested in her body, he went on, "Let's to Sierra's and stuff ourselves full of tacos and enchiladas. How's that?"

"Fine," Megan said.

Justin thought it sounded fine, too. Sierra's was a Valley institution. It had been there since twenty years before he was born, and would still be going strong in 2018. He didn't go there often then; he had too many memories of coming there with Megan. Now those memories would turn from painful to happy. That was why he was here. Smiling, he said, "See you Saturday, then."

"Yeah," Megan said. Justin's smile got bigger.

Ring. Ring. Ring. "Hello?" his younger self said.

"Oh, good," Justin said coldly. "You're home."

"Oh. It's you." Himself-at-twenty-one didn't sound delighted to hear from him, either. "No, *you're* home. I'm stuck here."

"Didn't I tell you to lay low till I was done here?" Justin demanded. "God damn it, you'd better listen to me. I just had to pretend I knew what Megan was talking about when she said I'd been on the phone with her."

"She's my girl, too," his younger self said. "She was my girl first, you know. I've got a *right* to talk with her."

"Not if you want her to keep being your girl, you don't," Justin said. "You're the one who's going to screw it up, remember?"

"That's what you keep telling me," his younger self answered. "But you know what? I'm not so sure I believe you any more. When I called her, Megan sounded like she was really torqued at me – at you, I mean. So it doesn't sound like you've got all the answers, either."

"*Nobody* has *all* the answers," Justin said with such patience as he could muster. He didn't think he'd believed that at twenty-one; at forty, he was convinced it was true. He was convinced something else was true, too: "If you think you've got more of them than I do, you're full of shit."

"You want to be careful how you talk to me," himself-at-twenty-one said. "Half the time, I still think your whole setup is bogus. If I decide to, I can wreck it. You know damn well I can."

Justin knew only too well. It scared the crap out of him. But he didn't dare show his younger self he was afraid. As sarcastically as he could, he said, "Yeah, go ahead. Screw up your life for good. Keep going like this and you will."

"You sound pretty screwed up now," his younger self said. "What have I got to lose?"

"I had something good, and I let it slip through my fingers," Justin said. "That's enough to mess anybody up. You wreck what I'm doing now, you'll go through life without knowing what a good thing was. You want that? Just keep sticking your nose in where it doesn't belong. You want to end up with Megan or not?"

Where nothing else had, that hit home. "All right," his younger self said sullenly. "I'll back off – for now." He hung up. Justin stared at the phone, cursed, and put it back in its cradle.

Megan stared at her empty plate as if she couldn't imagine how it had got that way. Then she looked at Justin. "Did I really eat all that?" she said. "Tell me I didn't really eat all that."

"Can't do it," he said solemnly.

"Oh, my God!" Megan said: not Valley-girl nasal but sincerely astonished. "All those refried beans! They'll go straight to my thighs."

"No, they won't." Justin spoke with great certainty. For as long as he'd known – would know – Megan, her weight hadn't varied by more than five pounds. He'd never heard that she'd turned into a blimp after they broke up, either. He lowered his voice. "I like your thighs."

She raised a dark eyebrow, as if to say, *You're a guy. If I let you get between them, of course you like them.* But the eyebrow came down. "You talk nice like that, maybe you'll get a chance to prove it. Maybe."

"Okay." Justin's plate was as empty as hers. Loading up on heavy Mexican food hadn't slowed him down when he was twenty-one. Now it felt like a bowling ball in his stomach. But he figured he'd manage. Figuring that, he left a bigger tip than he would have otherwise.

The waiter scooped it up. "*Gracias, señor.*" He sounded unusually sincere.

Driving north up Canoga Avenue toward his place, Justin used a sentence that had the phrase "after we're married" in it.

Megan had been looking at the used-car lot across the street. Her head whipped around. "After we're what?" she said. "Not so fast, there."

For the very first time, Justin thought to wonder whether his younger self knew what he was doing when he took another year to get around to telling Megan he loved her. He-now had the advantage of hindsight; he knew he and Megan would walk down the aisle. But Megan didn't know it. Right this minute, she didn't sound delighted with the idea.

Worse, Justin couldn't explain that he knew, or how he knew. "I just thought—" he began.

Megan shook her head. Her dark hair flipped back and forth. She said, "No. You didn't think. You're starting your senior year this fall. I'm starting my junior year. We aren't ready to think about getting married yet, even if . . ." She shook her head again. "We aren't ready. What would we live on?"

"We'd manage." Justin didn't want to think about that *even if*. It had to be the start of something like, *even if I decide I want to marry you.* But Megan hadn't said all of it. Justin clung to that. He had nothing else to cling to.

"We'd manage?" Megan said. "Yeah, right. We'd go into debt so deep, we'd never get out. I don't want to do that, not when I'm just starting. I didn't think you did, either."

He kept driving for a little while. Clichés had women eager for commitment and men fleeing from it as if from a skunk at a picnic. He'd gone and offered to commit, and Megan reacted as if he ought to be committed. What did that say about clichés? Probably not to pay much attention to them.

"Hey." Megan touched his arm. "I'm not mad, not for that. But I'm not ready, either. Don't push me, okay?"

"Okay." But Justin had to push. He knew it too damn well. He couldn't stay in 1999 very long. Things between Megan and him had to be solid before he left the scene and his younger self took over again. His younger self, he was convinced, could fuck up a wet dream, and damn well had fucked up what should have been a perfect, lifelong relationship.

He opened the window and clicked the security key into the lock. The heavy iron gate slid open. He drove in and parked the car. They both got out. Neither said much as they walked to his apartment.

Not too much later, in the dark quiet of the bedroom, Megan clutched the back of his head with both hands and cried out, "Ohhh, Justin!" loud enough to make him embarrassed to show his face to the neighbors – or make him a minor hero among them, depending. She lay back on the bed and said, "You drive me crazy when you do that."

"We aim to please." Did he sound smug? If he did, hadn't he earned the right? Megan laughed. "Bull's-eye!" Her voice still sounded shaky.

He slid up to lie beside her, running his hands along her body as he did. *Strike while the iron is hot*, he thought. He felt pretty hot himself. He said, "And you don't want to talk about getting married yet?"

"I don't want to talk about anything right now," Megan said. "What I want to do is . . ." She did it. If Justin hadn't been a consenting adult, it would have amounted to criminal assault. As things were, he couldn't think of any stretch of time he'd enjoyed more.

"Jesus, I love you," he said when he was capable of coherent speech.

Megan kept straddling him – not that he wanted to escape. Her face was only a couple of inches above his. Now she leaned down and kissed him on the end of the nose. "I love this," she said, which wasn't the same thing at all.

He ran a hand along the smooth, sweat-slick curves of her back. "Well, then," he said, as if the two things were the same.

She laughed and shook her head. Her hair brushed back and forth across his face, full of the scent of her. Even though she kissed him again, she said, "But we can't do this all the time." At that precise moment, he softened and flopped out of her. She nodded, as if he'd proved her point. "See what I mean?"

Justin wished for his younger self's body. Had himself-at-twenty-one been there, he would have been hard at it again instead of wilting at the worst possible time. But he had to play the hand he'd been dealt. He said, "I know it's not the only reason to get married, but isn't it a nice one?" To show how nice it was, he slid his hand between her legs.

Megan let it stay there for a couple of seconds, but then twisted away. "I asked you not to push me about that, Justin," she said, all the good humor gone from her voice.

"Well, yeah, but—" he began.

"You didn't listen," she said. "People who get married have to, like, listen to each other, too, you know? You can't just screw all the time. You really can't. Look at my parents, for crying out loud."

"*My* parents are screwing all the time," Justin said.

"Yeah, but not with each other." Megan hesitated, then said, "I'm sorry."

"Why? It's true." Justin's younger self had been horrified at his parents' antics. If anything, that horror had got worse since. Up in 2018, he hadn't seen or even spoken to either one of them for years, and he didn't miss them, either.

Then he thought, *So Dad chases bimbos and Mom decided she wasn't straight after all. What you're doing here is a lot weirder than any of that.* But was it? All he wanted was a happy marriage, one like Megan's folks had, one that probably looked boring from the outside but not when you were in it.

Was that too much to ask? The way things were going, it was liable to be.

Megan said, "Don't get me wrong, Justin. I like you a lot. I wouldn't go to bed with you if I didn't. Maybe I even love you, if you want me to say that. But I don't know if I want to try and spend my whole life with you. And if you keep riding me twenty-four-seven about it, I'll decide I don't. Does that make any sense to you?"

Justin shook his head. All he heard was a clock ticking on his hopes. "If we've got a good thing going, we ought to take it as far as we can," he said. "Where will we find anything better?" He'd spent the rest of his life looking not for something better but for something close to as good. He hadn't found it.

"Goddammit, it's not a good thing if you won't listen to me. You don't want to notice that." Megan got up and went into the bathroom. When she came back, she started dressing. "Take me home, please."

"Shouldn't we talk some more?" Justin heard the panic in his own voice.

"No. Take me home." Megan sounded very sure. "Every time we talk lately, you dig the hole deeper for yourself. Like I said, Justin, I like you, but I don't think we'd better talk for a while. It's like you don't even hear me, like you don't even have to hear me. Like you're the grownup and I'm just a kid to you, and I don't like that a bit."

How seriously did a forty-year-old need to take a twenty-year-old? Unconsciously, Justin must have decided, *not very.* That looked to be wrong. "Honey, please wait," he said.

"It'll just get worse if I do," she answered. "Will you drive me, or shall I call my dad?"

He was in Dutch with her. He didn't want to get in Dutch with her folks, too. "I'll drive you," he said dully.

Even more than the drive back from the movie theater had, this one passed in tense silence. At last, as Justin turned onto her street, Megan broke it: "We've got our whole lives ahead of us, you know? The way you've been going lately, it's like you want everything nailed down tomorrow. That's not gonna happen. It can't happen. Neither one of us is ready for it."

"I am," Justin said.

"Well, I'm not," Megan told him as he stopped the car in front of her house. "And if you keep picking at it and picking at it, I'm never going to be. In fact . . ."

"In fact, what?"

"Never mind," she said. "Whatever." Before he could ask her again, she got out and hurried up the walk toward the house. He waved to her. He blew her a kiss. She didn't look back to see the wave or the kiss. She just opened the door and went inside. Justin sat for a couple of minutes, staring at the house. Then, biting his lip, he drove home.

Over the next three days, he called Megan a dozen times. Every time, he got the answering machine or one of her parents. They kept telling him she wasn't home. At last, fed up, he burst out, "She doesn't want to talk to me!"

Her father would have failed as White House press secretary. All he said was, "Well, if she doesn't, you can't make her, you know" – hardly a ringing denial.

But that's what I came back for! Justin wanted to scream it. That wouldn't have done any good. He knew as much. He still wanted to scream it. He'd come back to make things better, and what had he done? Made them worse.

On the fourth evening, the telephone rang as he walked in the door from his shift at CompUSA. His heart sank as he hurried into the bedroom. His younger self would be flipping out if he'd tried to call Megan and discovered she wouldn't talk to him. He'd told his younger self not to do that, but how reliable was himself-at-twenty-one? Not very. "Hello?"

"Hello, Justin." It wasn't his younger self. It was Megan.

"Hi!" He didn't know whether to be exalted or terrified. Not knowing, he ended up both at once. "How are you?"

"I'm okay." She paused. Terror swamped exaltation. When she went on, she said, "I've been talking with my folks the last few days."

That didn't sound good. Trying to pretend he didn't know how bad it sounded, he asked, "And?" The word hung in the air.

Megan paused again. At last, she said, "We – I've – decided I'd better not see you any more. I'm sorry, Justin, but that's how things are."

"They're making you say that!" If Justin blamed Megan's parents, he wouldn't have to blame anyone else: himself, for instance.

But she said, "No, they aren't. My mom, especially, thought I ought to give you another chance. But I've given you a couple chances already, and you don't know what to do with them. Things got way too intense way too fast, and I'm not ready for that. I don't want to deal with it, and I don't have to deal with it, and I'm not going to deal with it, and that's that. Like I said, I'm sorry and everything, but I can't."

"I don't believe this," he muttered. Refusing to believe it remained easier than blaming himself. "What about the sex?"

"It was great," Megan said at once. "I won't tell you any lies. If you make other girls feel the way you make – *made* – me feel, you won't have any trouble finding somebody else. I hope you do."

Christ, Justin thought. *She's letting me down easy. She's trying to, anyhow, but she's only twenty and she's not very good at it.* He didn't want to be let down easy, or at all. He said, "What about you?"

"I'll keep looking. If you can do it for me, probably other fellows can, too," Megan answered with devastating pragmatism. Half to herself, she added, "Maybe I need to date older guys, or something, if I can find some who aren't too bossy."

That would have been funny, if only it were funny. Justin whispered, "But I love you. I've always loved you." He'd loved her for about as long as she'd been alive here in 1999. What did he have to show for it? Getting shot down in flames not once but twice.

"Don't make this harder than it has to be. Please?" Megan said. "And don't call here any more, okay? You're not going to change my mind. If I decide I was wrong, I'll call your place, all right? Goodbye, Justin." She hung up without giving him a chance to answer.

Don't call us. We'll call you. Everybody knew what that meant. It meant what she'd been telling him anyhow: so long. He didn't want to hang up. Finally, after more than a minute of dial tone, he did.

"What do I do now?" he asked himself, or possibly God. God might have known. Justin had no clue.

He thought about calling his younger self and letting him know things had gone wrong: he thought about it for maybe three seconds, then dropped the idea like a live grenade. Himself-at-twenty-one would want to slaughter him. He metaphorically felt like dying, but not for real.

Why not? he wondered. *What will it be like when you head back to your own time? You wanted to change the past. Well, you've done that. You've screwed it up big-time. What kind of memories will you have when you come back to that men's room in 2018? Not memories of being married to Megan for a while and then having things go sour, that's for sure. You don't even get those. It'll be nineteen years of nothing – a long, lonely, empty stretch.*

He lay down on the bed and wept. He hadn't done that since Megan told him she was leaving him. *Since the last time Megan told me she was leaving me,* he thought. Hardly noticing he'd done it, he fell asleep.

When the phone rang a couple of hours later, Justin had trouble remembering when he was and how old he was supposed to be. The old-fashioned computer on the desk told him everything he needed to know. Grimacing, he picked up the telephone. "Hello?"

"You son of a bitch." His younger self didn't bellow the words. Instead, they were deadly cold. "You goddamn stupid, stinking, know-it-all son of a bitch."

Since Justin was calling himself the same things, he had trouble getting angry when his younger self cursed him. "I'm sorry," he said. "I tried to—"

He might as well have kept quiet. His younger self rode over him, saying, "I just tried calling Megan. She said she didn't want to talk to me. She said she never wanted to talk to me again. She said she'd told me she never wanted to talk to me again, so what was I doing on the phone right after she told me that? Then she hung up on me."

"I'm sorry," Justin repeated. "I—"

"Sorry?" This time, his younger self did bellow. "You think you're sorry now? You don't know what sorry is, but you will. I'm gonna beat the living shit out of you, dude. Fuck up my life, will you? You think you can get away with that, you're full of—" He slammed down the phone.

Justin had never been much for fisticuffs, not at twenty-one and not at forty, either. But his younger self was so furious now, who could guess what he'd do? What with rage and what had to be a severe case of testosterone poisoning, he was liable to mean what he'd said. Justin knew to the day how many years he was giving away.

He also knew his younger self had keys to this apartment. If himself-at-twenty-one showed up here in fifteen minutes, did he want to meet him?

That led to a different question: did he want to be here in 1999 at all any more? All he'd done was the opposite of what he'd wanted. Why hang around, then? Instead of waiting to slide back along the superstring into 2018 in a few more weeks, wasn't it better to cut the string and go back to his own time, to try to pick up the pieces of whatever life would be left to him after he'd botched things here?

Justin booted up the PowerBook from his own time. The suitcases he'd brought to 1999 were at the other apartment. So was a lot of the cash. His mouth twisted. He didn't think he could ask his younger self to return it.

As he slipped the VR mask onto his head, he hoped he'd done his homework right, and that he would return to the men's room from which he'd left 2018. That was what his calculations showed, but how good were they? Only real experience would tell. If this building still stood then and he materialized in somebody's bedroom, he'd have more explaining to do than he really wanted.

He also wondered what memories he'd have when he got back to his former point on the timeline. The old ones, as if he hadn't made the trip? The old ones, plus his memories of seeing 1999 while forty? New ones, stemming from the changes he'd made back here? Some of each? He'd find out.

From its initial perfect blankness, the VR mask view shifted to show the room in which he now sat, PowerBook on his lap. "Run program super-strings-slash-virtual reality-slash-not so virtual-slash-reverse," he said. The view began to shift. Part of that was good old-fashioned morphing software, so what he saw in the helmet looked less and less like this bedroom and more and more like the restroom that was his destination. And part was the superstring program, pulling him from one point on the string to the other. He hoped part of it was the superstring software, anyhow. If the program didn't run backwards, he'd have to deal with his angry younger self, and he wasn't up to that physically or mentally.

On the VR screen, the men's room at the Superstrings building had completely replaced the bedroom of his younger self's apartment. "Program super-strings-slash-virtual reality-slash-not so virtual reality-slash-reverse is done," the PowerBook said. Justin kept waiting. If he took off the helmet and found himself still in that bedroom . . .

When he nerved himself to shed the mask, he let out a long, loud sigh of relief: what he saw without it matched what he'd seen with it. His next worry – his mind coughed them up in carload lots – was that he'd gone to the right building, but in 1999, not 2018.

His first step out of the men's room reassured him. The carpeting was its old familiar color, not the jarring one from 1999. He looked at the VR mask and PowerBook he was carrying. He wouldn't need them any more today, and he didn't feel like explaining to Sean and Garth and everybody else why he'd brought them. He headed downstairs again, to stow them in the trunk of his car.

As he walked through the lobby toward the front door, the security guard opened it for him. "Forget something, sir?" the aging Boomer asked.

"Just want to put this stuff back, Bill." Justin held up the laptop and mask. Nodding, the guard stepped aside.

Justin was halfway across the lot before he realized the car toward which he'd aimed himself wasn't the one he'd parked there before going back to 1999. It was in the same space, but it wasn't the same car. He'd driven here in an aging Ford, not a top-of-the-line Volvo.

He looked around the lot. No Ford. No cars but the Volvo and Bill's ancient, wheezing Hyundai. If he hadn't got here in the Volvo, how had he come? Of itself, his hand slipped into his trouser pocket and came out with a key ring. The old iron ring and the worn leather fob on it were familiar; he'd had that key ring a long time. The keys . . .

One was a Volvo key. He tried it in the trunk. It turned in the lock. Smoothly, almost silently, the lid opened. Justin put the computer and the VR mask in the trunk, closed it, and slid the keys back into his pants pocket.

They weren't the pants he'd worn when he left his apartment that morning: instead of 1990s-style baggy jeans, they were slacks, a lightweight wool blend. His shoes had changed, too, and he was wearing a nice polo shirt, not a Dilbert T-shirt.

He ran his left hand over the top of his head. His hair was longer, the buzz cut gone. He started to wonder if he was really himself. His memories of what he'd been before he went back and changed his own past warred with the ones that had sprung from the change. He shook his head; his brain felt overcrowded.

He started back toward the Superstrings building, but wasn't ready to go in there again quite yet. He needed to sit down somewhere quiet for a while and straighten things out inside his own mind.

When he looked down the street, he grinned. There was the Denny's where he'd had breakfast right after going back to 1999. It hadn't changed much in the years since. He sauntered over. He was still on his own time.

"Toast and coffee," he told the middle-aged, bored-looking Hispanic waitress.

"White, rye, or whole wheat?"

"Wheat," he answered.

"Yes, sir," she said. She brought them back with amazing speed. He smeared the toast with grape jelly, let her refill his cup two or three times, and then, still bemused but caffeinated, headed back to Superstrings, Ltd.

More cars in the lot now, and still more pulling in as he walked up. There was Garth O'Connell's garish green Chevy. Justin waved. "Morning, Garth. How you doing?"

O'Connell smiled. "Not too bad. How are you, Mr. Kloster?"

"Could be worse," Justin allowed. Part of him remembered Garth being on a first-name basis with him. The other part, the increasingly dominant part, insisted that had never happened.

They went inside and upstairs together, talking business. Garth headed off into the maze of cubicles that made up most of the second floor. Justin started to follow him, but his feet didn't want to go that way. He let them take him where they would. They had a better idea of where exactly he worked than his conscious mind did right now.

His secretary was already busy at the computer in the anteroom in front of his office. She nodded. "Good morning, Mr. Kloster."

"Good morning, Brittany," he said. Had he ever seen her in all his life? If he hadn't, how did he know her name? How did he know she'd worked for him the past three years?

He went into the office – *his* office – and closed the door. Again, he had that momentary disorientation, as if he'd never been here before. But of course he had. If the founder and president of Superstrings, Ltd., didn't deserve the fanciest office in the building, who did?

The part of him that had traveled back through time still felt confused. Not the rest, the part that had been influenced by his trip back to 1999. Knowing such things were possible – and having the seed money his time-traveling self left behind – wouldn't he naturally have started getting involved in this area as soon as he could? Sure he would have – he damn well had. On the wall of the office, framed, hung, not the first dollar he'd ever made, but a quarter dated 2012. He'd had it for nineteen years.

He sat down at his desk. The view out the window wasn't much, but it beat the fuzzy, grayish-tan wall of a cubicle. On the desk stood a framed picture of a smiling blond woman and two boys he'd never seen before – his sons, Saul and Lije. When he stopped and thought, it all came back to him, just as if he'd really lived it. As a matter of fact, he had. *He'd* never got over Megan. His younger self, who'd never married her, was a different story – from the way things looked, a better story.

Why, he even knew how the image had been ever so slightly edited. She could be vain about the silliest things. His phone buzzed. He picked it up. "Yes, Brittany?"

"Your wife's on the line, Mr. Kloster," his secretary said. "Something she wants you to get on the way home."

"Sure, put her through." Justin was still chuckling when his wife came on the line. "Okay, what do you need at the store, Lindsey?"

THE FINAL DAYS

David Langford

David Langford is a British writer, editor, and critic, mostly known for his work in the science fiction field. He publishes the science fiction fanzine and newsletter *Ansible*. In addition to several novels, he has written many short stories, including parodies and other works of dark humor. He has won the Hugo Award more than twenty-five times and has also received much recognition as an editor, writer, and speaker. This story was first published in 1981 in the anthology *A Spadeful of Spacetime*, edited by Fred Saberhagen.

It was under the hot lights that Harman always felt most powerful. The air throbbed and sang with dazzlement and heat, wherein opponents – Ferris merely the most recent – might shrivel and wilt; but Harman sucked confidence from cameras, glad to expose something of himself to a nation of watchers, and more than a nation. Just now the slick, machine-stamped interviewer was turned away, towards Ferris; still Harman knew better than to peer surreptitiously at his own solid, blond and faintly smiling image in the monitor. Control was important, and Harman's image was imperturbable: his hands lay still and relaxed, the left on the chair-arm, the right on his thigh, their stillness one of the many small negative mannerisms which contributed to the outward Harman's tough dependability.

Gradually the focus was slipping away from Ferris, whose mere intelligence and sincerity should not be crippling his handling of the simplest, the most hypothetical questions.

"What would be *your* first act as President, Mr. Ferris?"

"Well, er . . . it would depend on . . ."

And the monitor would ruthlessly cut back to Harman in relaxed close-up, faintly smiling. One of the tricks was to be always the same. Ferris, alternately tense and limp, seemed scarcely camera-trained. Why? Ferris did not speak naturally toward the interviewer, nor oratorically into the camera which now pushed close, its red action-light ablink; his gaze wavered as he assembled libertarian platitudes, and his attention was drawn unwillingly beyond the arena's heat and light, to something that troubled him. Harman glanced easily about the studio, and followed Ferris's sick fascination to his own talisman, the magic box which traced the threads of destiny. (Always to be ready with a magniloquent phrase; that was another of the tricks.)

He could have laughed. Ferris, supposedly a seasoned performer and a dangerous opponent, could not adapt to this novelty. Four days to go, and his skill was crumbling under the onslaught of a gigantically magnified stage-fright. Posterity was too much for him.

Looking up from the box, the technician intercepted Harman's tightly relaxed gaze and held up five fingers; and five more; and four. Harman's self-confidence and self-belief could hardly burn brighter. Fourteen watchers. Favoured above all others, he had never before scored higher than ten. The wheel still turned his way, then. *Ecce homo*; man of the hour; man of destiny; he half-smiled at the clichés, but no more than half.

The interviewer swivelled his chair to Harman, leaving Ferris in a pool of sweat. His final questions had been gentle, pityingly gentle; and Ferris with flickering eyes had fumbled nearly all.

"Mr. Ferris has explained his position, Mr. Harman, and I'm sure that you'd like to state yours before I ask you a few questions."

Harman let his practised voice reply at once, while his thoughts sang *fourteen . . . fourteen.*

"I stand, as I have said before, for straight talking and honest action. I stand for a rejection of the gutless compromises which have crippled our economy. I want a fair deal for everyone, and I'm ready to fight to see they get it."

The words were superfluous. Harman's followers had a Sign.

"I'll tell you a true story about something that happened to me a while ago. I was walking home at night, in a street where vandals had smashed up half the lights, and a mugger came up to me. One of those scum who will be swept from the streets when our program of police reform goes through."

(He detected a twitch of resentment from Ferris; but Ferris was off-camera now.)

"He showed me a knife and asked for my wallet, the usual line of talk. Now I'm not a specially brave man, but this was what I'd been talking about when I laid it on the line about political principles. You just don't give in to threats like that. So I said damn you, come and try it, and you know, he just crumpled up. There's a moral in that story for this country, a moral you'll see when you think who's threatening us right now—"

It was a true story. As it happened, the security man on Harman's tail had shot the mugger as he wavered.

"A few questions, then," said the interviewer. "I think we're all waiting to hear more about the strangest gimmick ever included in a Presidential campaign. A lot of people are pretty sceptical about these scientists' claims, you know. Perhaps you could just briefly tell the viewers what you yourself think about these eyes, these watchers—?"

When you're hot, you're hot. Harman became still chattier.

"It's not a gimmick and it's not really part of my campaign. Some guys at the Gravity Research Foundation discovered that we – or some of us – are being watched. By, well, posterity. As you'll know from the newspapers, they were messing about with a new way of picking up gravity waves, which is something a plain man like me knows nothing about; and instead their gadget spotted these (what did they call them?) little knots of curdled space. The nodes, they called them later, or the peepholes. The gadget tells you when they're looking and how many are looking. It turns out that ordinary folk" – he suppressed the reflexive *like you and me* – "aren't watched at all; important people might get one or two or half-a-dozen eyes on them . . ."

At a sign from the interviewer, a previously dormant camera zoomed in on the technician and the unremarkable-looking Box. "Can you tell us how many – eyes – are present in this studio, sir?"

The technician paused to make some minor adjustment, doubtless eager for his own tiny share of limelight. He looked up after a few seconds, and said:

"Fifteen."

Ferris shuddered very slightly.

"Of course," said Harman smoothly, "some of these will be for Mr. Ferris." Ferris, he knew, had two watchers; intermittently; and it seemed that he hated it. The interviewer, giant of this tiny studio world, was never watched for his own sake when alone. He was marking time now, telling the tale of Sabinnen, that artist whom they tagged important in earlier tests of the detectors. Sabinnen was utterly obscure at that time; that ceased when they tracked the concentration of eight eyes, and his cupboardful of paintings came to light, and did it not all hang together, this notion of the Future watching the famous before their fame?

Harman revelled in the silent eyes which so constantly attended him. It recalled the curious pleasure of first finding his home and office bugged; such subtle flattery might dismay others, but Harman had nothing to hide.

"But I must emphasize that this is only a pointer," he said, cutting in at the crucial moment. "The people have this hint of the winning side, as they might from newspaper predictions or opinion polls – but the choice remains theirs, a decision which we politicians must humbly accept. Of course I'm glad it's not just today's voters who have faith in me—" He was full of power; the words came smoothly, compellingly, through the final minutes – while Ferris stared first morosely at his shoe and then bitterly at Harman, while the interviewer (momentarily forgetful of the right to equal time, doubtless reluctant to coax the numbered Ferris through further hoops) listened with an attentive silence which clearly said *In four days you will be President.*

Then it was over, and Harman moved through a triumphal procession of eager reporters, scattering bonhomie and predictions of victory, saluted again and again by electronic flashes which for long minutes burnt green and purple on his retinas; and so to the big, quiet car with motorcycles before and behind, off into the anonymous night. He wondered idly whether any reporter had been kind enough to beg an opinion or two from Ferris.

*

He refused to draw the car's shades, of course, preferring to remain visible to the public behind his bullet-proof glass. There was a risk of assassination, but though increasing it was still small. (How the eyes must have hovered over JFK, like a cloud of eager flies. But no one could wish to assassinate Harman . . . surely.) He settled in the rear seat, one hand still relaxed upon the leather, the other resting calmly on his own right thigh. The outline of the chauffeur's head showed dimly through more impervious glass . . . In four days he would rate six motor-cyclists before and behind; with two only to supplement the eye-detector's van and this purring car, he felt almost alone. Better to recall the seventeen watchers (the number had been rising still, the Argus eyes of destiny marking him out); or the eye of the camera, which held within it a hundred million watchers here and now. The show had gone well. He felt he might have succeeded without the silent eyes, the nodes of interference born of the uncertainty principle which marked where information was siphoned into the years ahead. How far ahead? No one knew; and it did not matter. Harman believed in himself and knew his belief to be sincere, even without this sign from heaven to mark him as blessed of all men.

And *that* was strangely true, he knew. The princes and powers of the world had been scanned for the stigmata of lasting fame (not the Soviets, of course, nor China); politicians – Harman smiled – often scored high, yet none higher than eight or nine. *Seventeen* showed almost embarrassing enthusiasm on the part of the historians, the excellent, discriminating historians yet to be.

I shall deserve it, Harman told himself as his own home came into view, search-lights splashing its pale walls and throwing it into due prominence. In a brief huddle of guards he passed within to the theoretical privacy of his personal rooms, sincere and knowing again that he was sincere. He would fulfil his promises to the letter, honest and uncompromising, ready to risk even his reputation for the good of Democracy. He paced the mildly austere bedroom (black and white, grey and chrome); he fingered the chess set and *go*-board which magazines had shown to the nation. The recorders whirred companionably. His clothes were heavy with sweat, inevitable under the hot lights; the trick was not to look troubled by heat, not ever to subside and mop oneself like Ferris, poor Ferris.

This room had no windows, for sufficient reasons; but Harman knew of six optical bugs at the least. Naked in the adjoining shower, he soaped himself and smiled. Seventeen watchers – or perhaps nineteen or twenty, for the power was still rising within him – the bugs and the watchers troubled him not at all. That, he was certain, was his true strength. He had nothing to hide from the future, nor from the present; in all his life, he believed there was no episode which could bring shame to his biography. Let the eyes peer! The seedy Ferris might weaken himself with drink, with women, but Harman's energies flowed cool and strong in a single channel, which for convenience he called The Good Of The Nation.

He tumbled into pyjamas, his erection causing some small discomfort. Four days. Only four days and then: no compromise. The hard line. Straight talk, nation unto nation. He would give them good reason to watch him, Harman, the ultimate politician. He felt, as though beneath his fingers, the Presidential inheritance of red telephones and red buttons.

The eyes of time were upon him. He knew he would not fail them.

FIRE WATCH

Connie Willis

Connie Willis is an American writer who has won eleven Hugo Awards and eight Nebula Awards – more than any other writer. She was inducted into the Science Fiction Hall of Fame in 2009 and the Science Fiction Writers of America named her its twenty-eighth Grand Master in 2011. This story, first published in *Asimov's Science Fiction Magazine* in 1982, won both the Hugo Award and the Nebula Award.

History hath triumphed over time, which besides it nothing but eternity hath triumphed over.
Sir Walter Raleigh, *The History of the World*

September 20 – Of course the first thing I looked for was the fire watch stone. And of course it wasn't there yet. It wasn't dedicated until 1951, accompanying a speech by the Very Reverend Dean Walter Matthews, and this is only 1940. I knew that. I went to see the fire watch stone only yesterday, with some kind of misplaced notion that seeing the scene of the crime would somehow help. It didn't.

The only things that would have helped were a crash course in London during the Blitz and a little more time. I had not gotten either.

"Traveling in time is not like taking the tube, Mr Bartholomew," the esteemed Dunworthy had said, blinking at me through those antique spectacles of his. "Either you report on the twentieth or you don't go at all."

"But I'm not ready," I'd said. "Look, it took me four years to get ready to travel with St Paul. *St Paul*. Not St Paul's. You can't expect me to get ready for London in the Blitz in two days."

"Yes," Dunworthy had said. "We can." End of conversation.

"Two days!" I had shouted at my roommate Kivrin. "All because some computer adds an 's'. And the esteemed Dunworthy doesn't even bat an eye when I tell him. 'Time travel is not like taking the tube, young man,' he says. 'I'd suggest you get ready. You're leaving the day after tomorrow.' The man's a total incompetent."

"No," she said. "He isn't. He's the best there is. He wrote the book on St Paul's. Maybe you should listen to what he says."

I had expected Kivrin to be at least a little sympathetic. She had been practically hysterical when she got her practicum changed from fifteenth- to fourteenth-century England, and how did either century qualify as a practicum? Even counting infectious diseases they couldn't have been more than a five. The Blitz is an eight, and St Paul's itself is, with my luck, a ten.

"You think I should go see Dunworthy again?" I said.

"Yes."

"And then what? I've got two days. I don't know the money, the language, the history. Nothing."

"He's a good man," Kivrin said. "I think you'd better listen to him while you can." Good old Kivrin. Always the sympathetic ear.

The good man was responsible for my standing just inside the propped-open west doors, gawking like the country boy I was supposed to be, looking for a stone that wasn't there. Thanks to the good man, I was about as unprepared for my practicum as it was possible for him to make me.

I couldn't see more than a few feet into the church. I could see a candle gleaming feebly a long way off and a closer blur of white moving towards me. A verger, or possibly the Very Reverend Dean himself. I pulled out the letter from my clergyman uncle in Wales that was supposed to gain me access to the dean, and patted my back pocket to make sure I hadn't lost the microfiche *Oxford English Dictionary, Revised, with Historical Supplements* I'd smuggled out of the Bodleian. I couldn't pull it out in the middle of the conversation, but with luck I could muddle through the first encounter by context and look up the words I didn't know later.

"Are you from the ayarpee?" he said. He was no older than I am, a head shorter and much thinner. Almost ascetic-looking. He reminded me of Kivrin. He was not wearing white, but clutching it to his chest. In other circumstances I would have thought it was a pillow. In other circumstances I wouldn't know what was being said to me, but there had been no time to unlearn sub-Mediterranean Latin and Jewish law and learn Cockney and air raid procedures. Two days, and the esteemed Dunworthy, who wanted to talk about the sacred burdens of the historian instead of telling me what the ayarpee was.

"Are you?" he demanded again.

I considered whipping out the OED after all on the grounds that Wales was a foreign country, but I didn't think they had microfilm in 1940. Ayarpee. It could be anything, including a nickname for the fire watch, in which case the impulse to say no was not safe at all. "No," I said.

He lunged suddenly toward and past me and peered out the open doors. "Damn," he said, coming back to me. "Where are they then? Bunch of lazy bourgeois tarts!" And so much for getting by on context.

He looked at me closely, suspiciously, as if he thought I was only pretending not to be with the ayarpee. "The church is closed," he said finally.

I held up the envelope and said, "My name's Bartholomew. Is Dean Matthews in?"

He looked out the door a moment longer as if he expected the lazy bourgeois tarts at any moment and intended to attack them with the white bundle; then he turned and said, as if he were guiding a tour, "This way, please," and took off into the gloom.

He led me to the right and down the south aisle of the nave. Thank God I had memorized the floor plan or at that moment, heading into total darkness, led by a raving verger, the whole bizarre metaphor of my situation would have been enough to send me out the west doors and back to St John's Wood. It helped a little to know where I was. We should have been passing number twenty-six: Hunt's painting of *The Light of the World* – Jesus with his lantern – but it was too dark to see it. We could have used the lantern ourselves.

He stopped abruptly ahead of me, still raving. "We weren't asking for the bloody Savoy, just a few cots. Nelson's better off than we are – at least he's got a pillow provided." He brandished the white bundle like a torch in the darkness. It was a pillow after all. "We asked for them over a fortnight ago, and here we still are, sleeping on the bleeding generals from Trafalgar because those bitches want to play tea and crumpets with the Tommies at Victoria and the hell with us!"

He didn't seem to expect me to answer his outburst, which was good, because I had understood perhaps one key word in three. He stomped on ahead, moving out of sight of the one pathetic altar candle and stopping again at a black hole. Number twenty-five: stairs to the Whispering Gallery, the Dome, the library (not open to the public). Up the stairs, down a hall, stop again at a medieval door and knock. "I've got to go wait for them," he said. "If I'm not there they'll likely take them over to the Abbey. Tell the Dean to ring them up again, will you?" And he took off down the stone steps, still holding his pillow like a shield against him.

He had knocked, but the door was at least a foot of solid oak, and it was obvious the Very Reverend Dean had not heard. I was going to have to knock again. Yes, well, and the man holding the pinpoint had to let go of it, too, but even knowing it will all be over in a moment and you won't feel a thing doesn't make it any easier to say, "Now!" So I stood in front of the door, cursing the history department and the esteemed Dunworthy and the computer that had made the mistake and brought me here to this dark door with only a letter from a fictitious uncle that I trusted no more than I trusted the rest of them.

Even the old reliable Bodleian had let me down. The batch of research stuff I cross-ordered through Balliol and the main terminal is probably sitting in my room right now, a century out of reach. And Kivrin, who had already done her practicum and should have been bursting with advice, walked around as silent as a saint until I begged her to help me.

"Did you go to see Dunworthy?" she said.

"Yes. You want to know what priceless bit of information he had for me? 'Silence and humility are the sacred burdens of the historian.' He also told me I would love St Paul's. Golden gems from the Master. Unfortunately, what I need to know are the times and places of the bombs so one doesn't fall on me." I flopped down on the bed. "Any suggestions?"

"How good are you at memory retrieval?" she said.

I sat up. "I'm pretty good. You think I should assimilate?"

"There isn't time for that," she said. "I think you should put everything you can directly into long-term."

"You mean endorphins?" I said.

The biggest problem with using memory-assistance drugs to put information into your long-term memory is that it never sits, even for a microsecond, in your short-term memory, and that makes retrieval complicated, not to mention unnerving. It gives you the most unsettling sense of déjà vu to suddenly know something you're positive you've never seen or heard before.

The main problem, though, is not eerie sensations but retrieval. Nobody knows exactly how the brain gets what it wants out of storage, but short-term is definitely involved. That brief, sometimes microscopic, time information spends in short-term is apparently used for something besides tip-of-the-tongue availability. The whole complex sort-and-file process of retrieval is apparently centered in the short-term, and without it, and without the help of the drugs that put it there or artificial substitutes, information can be impossible to retrieve. I'd used endorphins for examinations and never had any difficulty with retrieval, and it looked like it was the only way to store all the information I needed in anything approaching the time I had left, but it also meant that I would *never* have known any of the things I needed to know, even for long enough to have forgotten them. If and when I could retrieve the information, I would know it. Till then I was as ignorant of it as if it were not stored in some cobwebbed corner of my mind at all.

"You can retrieve without artificials, can't you?" Kivrin said, looking skeptical.

"I guess I'll have to."

"Under stress? Without sleep? Low body endorphin levels?" What exactly had her practicum been? She had never said a word about it, and undergraduates are not supposed to ask. Stress factors in the Middle Ages? I thought everybody slept through them.

"I hope so," I said. "Anyway, I'm willing to try this idea if you think it will help."

She looked at me with that martyred expression and said, "Nothing will help." Thank you, St Kivrin of Balliol.

But I tried it anyway. It was better than sitting in Dunworthy's rooms having him blink at me through his historically accurate eyeglasses and tell me I was going to love St Paul's. When my Bodleian requests didn't come, I overloaded my credit and bought out Blackwell's. Tapes on World War II, Celtic literature, history of mass transit, tourist guidebooks, everything I could think of. Then I rented a high-speed recorder and shot up. When I came out of it, I was so panicked by the feeling of not knowing any more than I had when I started that I took the tube to London and raced up Ludgate Hill to see if the fire watch stone would trigger any memories. It didn't.

"Your endorphin levels aren't back to normal yet," I told myself and tried to relax, but that was impossible with the prospect of the practicum looming up before me. And those are real bullets, kid. Just because you're a history major doing his practicum doesn't mean you can't get killed. I read history books all the way home on the tube and right up until Dunworthy's flunkies came to take me to St John's Wood this morning.

Then I jammed the microfiche OED in my back pocket and went off feeling as if I would have to survive by my native wit and hoping I could get hold of artificials in 1940. Surely I could get through the first day without mishap, I thought, and now here I was, stopped cold by almost the first word that was spoken to me.

Well, not quite. In spite of Kivrin's advice that I not put anything in short-term, I'd memorized the British money, a map of the tube system, a map of my own Oxford. It had gotten me this far. Surely I would be able to deal with the Dean.

Just as I had almost gotten up the courage to knock, he opened the door, and as with the pinpoint, it really was over quickly and without pain. I handed him my letter and he shook my hand and said something understandable like, "Glad to have another man, Bartholomew." He looked strained and tired and as if he might collapse if I told him the Blitz had just started. I know, I know: Keep your mouth shut. The sacred silence, etc.

He said, "We'll get Langby to show you round, shall we?" I assumed that was my Verger of the Pillow, and I was right. He met us at the foot of the stairs, puffing a little but jubilant.

"The cots came," he said to Dean Matthews. "You'd have thought they were doing us a favor. All high heels and hoity-toity. 'You made us miss our tea, luv,' one of them said to me. 'Yes, well, and a good thing, too,' I said. 'You look as if you could stand to lose a stone or two.'"

Even Dean Matthews looked as though he did not completely understand him. He said, "Did you set them up in the crypt?" and then introduced us. "Mr Bartholomew's just got in from Wales," he said. "He's come to join our volunteers." Volunteers, not fire watch.

Langby showed me round, pointing out various dimnesses in the general gloom, and then dragged me down to see the ten folding canvas cots set up among the tombs in the crypt, also in passing, Lord Nelson's black marble sarcophagus. He told me I don't have to stand a watch the first night and suggested I go to bed, since sleep is the most precious commodity in the raids. I could well believe it. He was clutching that silly pillow to his breast like his beloved.

"Do you hear the sirens down here?" I asked, wondering if he buried his head in it.

He looked round at the low stone ceilings. "Some do, some don't. Brinton has to have his Horlick's. Bence-Jones would sleep if the roof fell in on him. I have to have a pillow. The important thing is to get your eight in no matter what. If you don't, you turn into one of the walking dead. And then you get killed."

On that cheering note he went off to post the watches for tonight, leaving his pillow on one of the cots with orders for me to let nobody touch it. So here I sit, waiting for my first air raid siren and trying to get all this down before I turn into one of the walking or non-walking dead.

I've used the stolen OED to decipher a little Langby. Middling success. A tart is either a pastry or a prostitute (I assume the latter, although I was wrong about the pillow). Bourgeois is a catchall term for all the faults of the middle class. A Tommy's a soldier. Ayarpee I could not find under any spelling and I had nearly given up when something in long-term about the use of acronyms and abbreviations in wartime popped forward (bless you, St Kivrin) and I realized it must be an abbreviation. ARP. Air Raid Precautions. Of course. Where else would you get the bleeding cots from?

September 21 – Now that I'm past the first shock of being here, I realize that the history department neglected to tell me what I'm supposed to do in the three-odd months of this practicum. They handed me this journal, the letter from my uncle, and ten pounds of pre-war money and sent me packing into the past. The ten pounds (already depleted by train and tube fares) is supposed to last me until the end of December and get me back to St John's Wood for pickup when the second letter calling me back to Wales to sick uncle's bedside comes. Till then I live here in the crypt with Nelson, who, Langby tells me, is pickled in alcohol inside his coffin. If we take a direct hit, will he burn like a torch or simply trickle out in a decaying stream onto the crypt floor, I wonder. Board is provided by a gas-ring, over which are cooked wretched tea and indescribable kippers. To pay for all this luxury I am to stand on the roofs of St Paul's and put out incendiaries.

I must also accomplish the purpose of this practicum, whatever it may be. Right now the only purpose I care about is staying alive until the second letter from uncle arrives and I can go home.

I am doing make-work until Langby has time to "show me the ropes". I've cleaned the skillet they cook the foul little fishes in, stacked wooden folding chairs at the altar end of the crypt (flat instead of standing because they tend to collapse like bombs in the middle of the night), and tried to sleep.

I am apparently not one of the lucky ones who can sleep through the raids. I spend most of the night wondering what St Paul's risk rating is. Practica have to be at least a six. Last night I was convinced this was a ten, with the crypt as ground zero, and that I might as well have applied for Denver.

The most interesting thing that's happened so far is that I've seen a cat. I am fascinated, but trying not to appear so, since they seem commonplace here.

September 22 – Still in the crypt. Langby comes dashing through periodically cursing various government agencies (all abbreviated) and promising to take me up on the roofs. In the meantime I've run out of make-work and taught myself to work a stirrup pump. Kivrin was overly concerned about my memory retrieval abilities. I have not had any trouble so far. Quite the opposite. I called up fire-fighting information and got the whole manual with pictures, including instructions on the use of the stirrup pump. If the kippers set Lord Nelson on fire, I shall be a hero.

Excitement last night. The sirens went early and some of the chars who clean offices in the City sheltered in the crypt with us. One of them woke me out of a sound sleep, going like an air raid siren. Seems she'd seen a mouse. We had to go whacking at tombs and under the cots with a rubber boot to persuade her it was gone. Obviously what the history department had in mind: murdering mice.

September 24 – Langby took me on rounds. Into the choir, where I had to learn the stirrup pump all over again, assigned rubber boots and a tine helmet. Langby says Commander Allen is getting us asbestos firemen's coats, but hasn't yet, so it's my own wool coat and muffler and very cold on the roofs even in September. It feels like November and looks it, too, bleak and cheerless with no sun. Up to the dome and onto the roofs, which should be flat but in fact are littered with towers, pinnacles, gutters, statues, all designed expressly to catch and hold incendiaries out of reach. Shown how to smother an incendiary with sand before it burns through the roof and sets the church on fire. Shown the ropes (literally) lying in a heap at the base of the dome in case somebody has to go up one of the west towers or over the top of the dome. Back inside and down to the Whispering Gallery.

Langby kept up a running commentary through the whole tour, part practical instruction, part church history. Before we went up into the Gallery he dragged me over to the south door to tell me how Christopher Wren stood in the smoking rubble of Old St Paul's and asked a workman to bring him a stone from the graveyard to mark the cornerstone. On the stone was written in Latin, "I shall rise again," and Wren was so impressed by the irony that he had the word inscribed above the door. Langby looked as smug as if he had not told me a story every first-year history student knows, but I suppose without the impact of the fire watch stone, the other is just a nice story.

Langby raced me up the steps and onto the narrow balcony circling the Whispering Gallery. He was already halfway round to the other side, shouting dimensions and acoustics at me. He stopped facing the wall opposite and said softly, "You can hear me whispering because of the shape of the dome. The sound waves are reinforced around the perimeter of the dome. It sounds like the very crack of doom up here during a raid. The dome is one hundred and seven feet across. It is eighty feet above the nave."

I looked down. The railing went out from under me and the black-and-white marble floor came up with dizzying speed. I hung onto something in front of me and dropped to my knees, staggered and sick at heart. The sun had come out, and all of St Paul's seemed drenched in gold. Even the carved wood of the choir, the white stone pillars, the leaden pipes of the organ, all of it golden, golden.

Langby was beside me, trying to pull me free. "Bartholomew," he shouted, "what's wrong? For God's sake, man."

I knew I must tell him that if I let go, St Paul's and all the past would fall in on me, and that I must not let that happen because I was an historian. I said something, but it was not what I intended because Langby merely tightened his grip. He hauled me violently free of the railing and back onto the stairway, then let me collapse limply on the steps and stood back from me, not speaking.

"I don't know what happened in there," I said. "I've never been afraid of heights before."

"You're shaking," he said sharply. "You'd better lie down." He led me back to the crypt.

September 25 – Memory retrieval: ARP manual. Symptoms of bombing victims. Stage one – shock; stupefaction; unawareness of injuries; words may not make sense except to victim. Stage two – shivering; nightmares; nausea; injuries, losses felt; return to reality. Stage three – talkativeness that cannot be controlled; desire to explain shock behavior to rescuers.

Langby must surely recognize the symptoms, but how does he account for the fact there was no bomb? I can hardly explain my shock behavior to him, and it isn't just the sacred silence of the historian that stops me.

He has not said anything, in fact assigned me my first watches for tomorrow night as if nothing had happened and he seems no more preoccupied than anyone else. Everyone I've met so far is jittery (one thing I had in short-term was how calm everyone was during the raids) and the raids have not come near us since I got here. They've been mostly over the East End and the docks.

There was reference tonight to a UXB, and I have been thinking about the Dean's manner and the church being closed when I'm almost sure I remember reading it was open through the entire Blitz. As soon as I get a chance, I'll try to retrieve the events of September. As to retrieving anything else, I don't see how I can hope to remember the right information until I know what it is I am supposed to do here, if anything.

There are no guidelines for historians, and no restrictions either. I could tell everyone I'm from the future if I thought they would believe me. I could murder Hitler if I could get to Germany. Or could I? Time paradox talk abounds in the history department, and the graduate students back from their practica don't say a word one way or the other. Is there a tough, immutable past? Or is there a new past every day and do we, the historians, make it? And what are the consequences of what we do, if there are consequences? And how do we dare do anything without knowing them? Must we interfere boldly, hoping we do not bring about all our downfalls? Or must we do nothing at all, not interfere, stand by and watch St Paul's burn to the ground if need be so that we don't change the future?

All those are fine questions for a late-night study session. They do not matter here. I could no more let St Paul's burn down than I could kill Hitler. No, that is not true. I found that out yesterday in the Whispering Gallery. I could kill Hitler if I caught him setting fire to St Paul's.

September 26 – I met a young woman today. Dean Matthews has opened the church, so the watch have been doing duties as chars and people have started coming in again. The young woman reminded me of Kivrin, though Kivrin is a good deal taller and would never frizz her hair like that. She looked as if she had been crying. Kivrin looked like that since she got back from her practicum. The Middle Ages were too much for her. I wonder how she would have coped with this. By pouring out her fears to the local priest, no doubt, as I sincerely hoped her look-alike was not going to do.

"May I help you?" I said, not wanting in the least to help. "I'm a volunteer."

She looked distressed. "You're not paid?" she said, and wiped at her reddened nose with a handkerchief. "I read about St Paul's and the fire watch and all, and I thought perhaps there's a position there for me. In the canteen, like, or something. A paying position." There were tears in her red-rimmed eyes.

"I'm afraid we don't have a canteen," I said as kindly as I could, considering how impatient Kivrin always makes me, "and it's not actually a real shelter. Some of the watch sleep in the crypt. I'm afraid we're all volunteers, though."

"That won't do, then," she said. She dabbed at her eyes with the handkerchief. "I love St Paul's, but I can't take on volunteer work, not with my little brother Tom back from the country." I was not reading this situation properly. For all the outward signs of distress she sounded quite cheerful and no closer to tears than when she had come in. "I've got to get us a proper place to stay. With Tom back, we can't go on sleeping in the tubes."

A sudden feeling of dread, the kind of sharp pain you get sometimes from involuntary retrieval, went over me. "The tubes?" I said, trying to get at the memory.

"Marble Arch, usually," she went on. "My brother Tom saves us a place early and I go . . ." She stopped, held the handkerchief close to her nose, and exploded into it. "I'm sorry," she said, "this awful cold!"

Red nose, watering eyes, sneezing. Respiratory infection. It was a wonder I hadn't told her not to cry. It's only by luck that I haven't made some unforgivable mistake so far, and this is not because I can't get at the long-term memory. I don't have half the information I need even stored: cats and colds and the way St Paul's looks in full sun. It's only a matter of time before I am stopped cold by something I do not know. Nevertheless, I am going to try for retrieval tonight after I come off watch. At least I can find out whether and when something is going to fall on me.

I have seen the cat once or twice. He is coal-black with a white patch on his throat that looks as if it were painted on for the blackout.

September 27 – I have just come down from the roofs. I am still shaking. Early in the raid the bombing was mostly over the East End. The view was incredible. Searchlights everywhere, the sky pink from the fires and reflecting in the Thames, the exploding shells sparkling like fireworks. There was a constant, deafening thunder broken by the occasional droning of the planes high overhead, then the repeating stutter of the ack-ack guns.

About midnight the bombs began falling quite near with a horrible sound like a train running over me. It took every bit of will I had to keep from flinging myself flat on the roof, but Langby was watching. I didn't want to give him the satisfaction of watching a repeat performance of my behavior in the dome. I kept my head up and my sand bucket firmly in hand and felt quite proud of myself.

The bombs stopped roaring past about three, and there was a lull of about half an hour, and then a clatter like hail on the roofs. Everybody except Langby dived for shovels and stirrup pumps. He was watching me. And I was watching the incendiary.

It had fallen only a few meters from me, behind the clock tower. It was much smaller than I had imagined, only about thirty centimeters long. It was sputtering violently, throwing greenish-white fire almost to where I was standing. In a minute it would simmer down into a molten mass and begin to burn through the roof. Flames and the frantic shouts of firemen, and then the white rubble stretching for miles, and nothing, nothing left, not even the fire watch stone.

It was the Whispering Gallery all over again. I felt that I had said something, and when I looked at Langby's face he was smiling crookedly.

"St Paul's will burn down," I said. "There won't be anything left."

"Yes," Langby said. "That's the idea, isn't it? Burn St Paul's to the ground? Isn't that the plan?"

"Whose plan?" I said stupidly.

"Hitler's, of course," Langby said. "Who did you think I meant?" and, almost casually, picked up his stirrup pump.

The page of the ARP manual flashed suddenly before me. I poured the bucket of sand around the still sputting bomb, snatched up another bucket and dumped that on top of it. Black smoke billowed up in such a cloud that I could hardly find my shovel. I felt for the smothered bomb with the tip of it and scooped it into the empty bucket, then shoveled the sand in on top of it. Tears were streaming down my face from the acrid smoke. I turned to wipe them on my sleeve and saw Langby.

He had not made a move to help me. He smiled. "It's not a bad plan, actually. But of course we won't let it happen. That's what the fire watch is here for. To see that it doesn't happen. Right, Bartholomew?"

I know now what the purpose of my practicum is. I must stop Langby from burning down St Paul's.

September 28 – I try to tell myself I was mistaken about Langby last night, that I misunderstood what he said. Why would he want to burn down St Paul's unless he is a Nazi spy? How can a Nazi spy have gotten on the fire watch? I think about my faked letter of introduction and shudder.

How can I find out? If I set him some test, some fatal thing that only a loyal Englishman in 1940 would know, I fear I am the one who would be caught out. I *must* get my retrieval working properly.

Until then, I shall watch Langby. For the time being at least that should be easy. Langby has just posted the watches for the next two weeks. We stand everyone together.

September 30 – I know what happened in September. Langby told me.

Last night in the choir, putting on our coats and boots, he said, "They've already tried once, you know."

I had no idea what he meant. I felt as helpless as that first day when he asked me if I was from the ayarpee.

"The plan to destroy St Paul's. They've already tried once. The tenth of September. A high explosive bomb. But of course you didn't know about that. You were in Wales."

I was not even listening. The minute he had said "high explosive bomb", I had remembered it all. It had burrowed in under the road and lodged on the foundations. The bomb squad had tried to defuse it, but there was a leaking gas main. They decided to evacuate St Paul's, but Dean Matthews refused to leave, and they got it out after all and exploded it in Barking Marshes. Instant and complete retrieval.

"The bomb squad saved her that time," Langby was saying. "It seems there's always somebody about."

"Yes," I said, "there is," and walked away from him.

October 1 – I thought last night's retrieval of the events of September tenth meant some sort of breakthrough, but I have been lying here on my cot most of the night trying for Nazi spies in St Paul's and getting nothing. Do I have to know exactly what I'm looking for before I can remember it? What good does that do me?

Maybe Langby is not a Nazi spy. Then what is he? An arsonist? A madman? The crypt is hardly conducive to thought, being not at all as silent as a tomb. The chars talk most of the night and the sound of the bombs is muffled, which somehow makes it worse. I find myself straining to hear them. When I did get to sleep this morning, I dreamed about one of the tube shelters being hit, broken mains, drowning people.

*

October 4 – I tried to catch the cat today. I had some idea of persuading it to dispatch the mouse that has been terrifying the chars. I also wanted to see one up close. I took the water bucket I had used with the stirrup pump last night to put out some burning shrapnel from one of the antiaircraft guns. It still had a bit of water in it, but not enough to drown the cat, and my plan was to clamp the bucket over him, reach under, and pick him up, then carry him down to the crypt and point him at the mouse. I did not even come close to him.

I swung the bucket, and as I did so, perhaps an inch of water splashed out. I thought I remembered that the cat was a domesticated animal, but I must have been wrong about that. The cat's wide complacent face pulled back into a skull-like mask that was absolutely terrifying, vicious claws extended from what I had thought were harmless paws, and the cat let out a sound to top the chars.

In my surprise I dropped the bucket and it rolled against one of the pillars. The cat disappeared. Behind me, Langby said, "That's no way to catch a cat."

"Obviously," I said, and bent to retrieve the bucket.

"Cats hate water," he said, still in that expressionless voice.

"Oh," I said, and started in front of him to take the bucket back to the choir. "I didn't know that."

"Everybody knows it. Even the stupid Welsh."

October 8 – We have been standing double watches for a week – bomber's moon. Langby didn't show up on the roofs, so I went looking for him in the church. I found him standing by the west doors talking to an old man. The man had a newspaper tucked under his arm and he handed it to Langby, but Langby gave it back to him. When the man saw me, he ducked out. Langby said, "Tourist. Wanted to know where the Windmill Theatre is. Read in the paper the girls are starkers."

I know I looked as if I didn't believe him because he said, "You look rotten, old man. Not getting enough sleep, are you? I'll get somebody to take the first watch for you tonight."

"No," I said coldly. "I'll stand my own watch. I like being on the roofs," and added silently, where I can watch you.

He shrugged and said, "I suppose it's better than being down in the crypt. At least on the roofs you can hear the one that gets you."

October 10 – I thought the double watches might be good for me, take my mind off my inability to retrieve. The watched-pot idea. Actually, it sometimes works. A few hours of thinking about something else, or a good night's sleep, and the fact pops forward without any prompting, without any artificials.

The good night's sleep is out of the question. Not only do the chars talk constantly, but the cat has moved into the crypt and sidles up to everyone, making siren noises and begging for kippers. I am moving my cot out of the transept and over by Nelson before I go on watch. He may be pickled, but he keeps his mouth shut.

*

October 11 – I dreamed Trafalgar, ships' guns and smoke and falling plaster and Langby shouting my name. My first waking thought was that the folding chairs had gone off. I could not see for all the smoke.

"I'm coming," I said, limping toward Langby and pulling on my boots. There was a heap of plaster and tangled folding chairs in the transept. Langby was digging in it. "Bartholomew!" he shouted, flinging a chunk of plaster aside. "Bartholomew!"

I still had the idea it was smoke. I ran back for the stirrup pump and then knelt beside him and began pulling on a splintered chair back. It resisted, and it came to me suddenly: there is a body under here. I will reach for a piece of the ceiling and find it is a hand. I leaned back on my heels, determined not to be sick, then went at the pile again.

Langby was going far too fast, jabbing with a chair leg. I grabbed his hand to stop him, and he struggled against me as if I were a piece of rubble to be thrown aside. He picked up a large flat square of plaster, and under it was the floor. I turned and looked behind me. Both chars huddled in the recess by the altar. "Who are you looking for?" I said, keeping hold of Langby's arm.

"Bartholomew," he said, and swept the rubble aside, his hands bleeding through the coating of smoky dust.

"I'm here," I said. "I'm all right." I choked on the white dust. "I moved my cot out of the transept."

He turned sharply to the chars and then said quite calmly, "What's under here?"

"Only the gas ring," one of them said timidly from the shadowed recess, "and Mrs Galbraith's pocketbook." He dug through the mess until he had found them both. The gas ring was leaking at a merry rate, though the flame had gone out.

"You've saved St Paul's and me after all," I said, standing there in my underwear and boots and holding the useless stirrup pump. "We might all have been asphyxiated."

He stood up. "I shouldn't have saved you," he said.

Stage one: shock, stupefaction, unawareness of injuries, words may not make sense except to victim. He would not know his hand was bleeding yet. He would not remember what he had said. He had said he shouldn't have saved my life.

"I shouldn't have saved you," he repeated. "I have my duty to think of."

"You're bleeding," I said sharply. "You'd better lie down." I sounded just like Langby in the Gallery.

October 13 – It was a high explosive bomb. It blew a hole in the choir, and some of the marble statuary is broken, but the ceiling of the crypt did not collapse, which is what I thought at first. It only jarred some plaster loose.

I do not think Langby has any idea what he said. That should give me some sort of advantage, now that I am sure where the danger lies, now that I am sure it will not come crashing down from some other direction. But what good is all this knowing, when I do not know what he will do? Or when?

Surely I have the facts of yesterday's bomb in long-term, but even falling plaster did not jar them loose this time. I am not even trying for retrieval, now. I lie in the darkness waiting for the roof to fall in on me. And remembering how Langby saved my life.

October 15 – The girl came in again today. She still has the cold, but she has gotten her paying position. It was a joy to see her. She was wearing a smart uniform and open-toed shoes, and her hair was in an elaborate frizz around her face. We are still cleaning up the mess from the bomb, and Langby was out with Allen getting wood to board up the choir, so I let the girl chatter at me while I swept. The dust made her sneeze, but at least this time I knew what she was doing.

She told me her name is Enola and that she's working for the WVS, running one of the mobile canteens that are sent to the fires. She came, of all things, to thank me for the job. She said that after she told the WVS that there was no proper shelter with a canteen for St Paul's they gave her a run in the City. "So I'll just pop in when I'm close and let you know how I'm making out, won't I just?"

She and her brother Tom are still sleeping in the tubes. I asked her if that was safe and she said probably not, but at least down there you couldn't hear the one that got you and that was a blessing.

October 18 – I am so tired I can hardly write this. Nine incendiaries tonight and a land mine that looked as though it was going to catch on the dome till the wind drifted its parachute away from the church. I put out two of the incendiaries. I have done that at least twenty times since I got here and helped with dozens of others, and still it is not enough. One incendiary, one moment of not watching Langby, could undo it all.

I know that is partly why I feel so tired. I wear myself out every night trying to do my job and watch Langby, making sure none of the incendiaries falls without my seeing it. Then I go back to the crypt and wear myself out trying to retrieve something, anything, about spies, fires, St Paul's in the fall of 1940, anything. It haunts me that I am not doing enough, but I don't now know what else to do. Without the retrieval, I am as helpless as these poor people here, with no idea what will happen tomorrow.

If I have to, I will go on doing this till I am called home. He cannot burn down St Paul's so long as I am here to put out the incendiaries. "I have my duty," Langby said in the crypt.

And I have mine.

October 21 – It's been nearly two weeks since the blast and I just now realized we haven't seen the cat since. He wasn't in the mess in the crypt. Even after Langby and I were sure there was no one in there, we sifted through the stuff twice more. He could have been in the choir, though.

Old Bence-Jones says not to worry. "He's all right," he said. "The jerries could bomb London right down to the ground and the cats would waltz out to greet them. You know why? They don't love anybody. That's what gets half of us killed. Old lady out in Stepney got killed the other night trying to save her cat. Bloody cat was in the Anderson."

"Then where is he?"

"Someplace safe, you can bet on that. If he's not around St Paul's, it means we're for it. That old saw about the rats deserting a sinking ship, that's a mistake, that is. It's cats, not rats."

October 25 – Langby's tourist showed up again. He cannot still be looking for the Windmill Theatre. He had a newspaper under his arm again today, and he asked for Langby, but Langby was across town with Allen, trying to get the asbestos firemen's coats. I saw the name of the paper. It was *The Worker*. A Nazi newspaper?

November 2 – I've been up on the roofs for a week straight, helping some incompetent workmen patch the hole the bomb made. They're doing a terrible job. There's still a great gap on one side a man could fall into, but they insist it'll be all right because, after all, you wouldn't fall clear through but only as far as the ceiling, and "the fall can't kill you". They don't seem to understand it's a perfect hiding place for an incendiary.

And that is all Langby needs. He does not even have to set a fire to destroy St Paul's. All he needs to do is let one burn uncaught until it is too late.

I could not get anywhere with the workmen. I went down into the church to complain to Matthews, and saw Langby and his tourist behind a pillar, close to one of the windows. Langby was holding a newspaper and talking to the man. When I came down from the library an hour later, they were still there. So is the gap. Matthews says we'll put planks across it and hope for the best.

November 5 – I have given up trying to retrieve. I am so far behind on my sleep I can't even retrieve information on a newspaper whose name I already know. Double watches the permanent thing now. Our chars have abandoned us altogether (like the cat), so the crypt is quiet, but I cannot sleep.

If I do manage to doze off, I dream. Yesterday I dreamed Kivrin was on the roofs, dressed like a saint. "What was the secret of your practicum?" I said. "What were you supposed to find out?"

She wiped her nose with a handkerchief and said, "Two things. One, that silence and humility are the sacred burdens of the historian. Two" – she stopped and sneezed into the handkerchief – "don't sleep in the tubes."

My only hope is to get hold of an artificial and induce a trance. That's a problem. I'm positive it's too early for chemical endorphins and probably hallucinogens. Alcohol is definitely available, but I need something more concentrated than ale, the only alcohol I know by name. I do not dare ask the watch. Langby is suspicious enough of me already. It's back to the OED, to look up a word I don't know.

November 11 – The cat's back. Langby was out with Allen again, still trying for the asbestos coats, so I thought it was safe to leave St Paul's. I went to the grocer's for supplies, and hopefully an artificial. It was late, and the sirens sounded before I had even gotten to Cheapside, but the raids do not usually start until after dark. It took a while to get all the groceries and to get up my courage to ask whether he had any alcohol – he told me to go to a pub – and when I came out of the shop, it was as if I had pitched suddenly into a hole.

I had no idea where St Paul's lay, or the street, or the shop I had just come from. I stood on what was no longer the sidewalk, clutching my brown-paper parcel of kippers and bread with a hand I could not have seen if I held it up before my face. I reached up to wrap my muffler closer about my neck and prayed for my eyes to adjust, but there was no reduced light to adjust to. I would have been glad of the moon, for all St Paul's watch cursed it and called it a fifth columnist. Or a bus, with its shuttered headlights giving just enough light to orient myself by. Or a searchlight. Or the kickback flare of an ack-ack gun. Anything.

Just then I did see a bus, two narrow yellow slits a long way off. I started toward it and nearly pitched off the curb. Which meant the bus was sideways in the street, which meant it was not a bus. A cat meowed, quite near, and rubbed against my leg. I looked down into the yellow lights I had thought belonged to the bus. His eyes were picking up light from somewhere, though I would have sworn there was not a light for miles, and reflecting it flatly up at me.

"A warden'll get you for those lights, old tom," I said, and then as a plane droned overhead, "Or a jerry."

The world exploded suddenly into light, the searchlights and a glow along the Thames seeming to happen almost simultaneously, lighting my way home.

"Come to fetch me, did you, old tom?" I said gaily. "Where've you been? Knew we were out of kippers, didn't you? I call that loyalty." I talked to him all the way home and gave him half a tin of the kippers for saving my life. Bence-Jones said he smelled the milk at the grocer's.

November 13 – I dreamed I was lost in the blackout. I could not see my hands in front of my face, and Dunworthy came and shone a pocket torch at me, but I could only see where I had come from and not where I was going.

"What good is that to them?" I said. "They need a light to show them where they're going."

"Even the light from the Thames? Even the light from the fires and the ack-ack guns?" Dunworthy said.

"Yes. Anything is better than this awful darkness." So he came closer to give me the pocket torch. It was not a pocket torch, after all, but Christ's lantern from the Hunt picture in the south nave. I shone it on the curb before me so I could find my way home, but it shone instead on the fire watch stone and I hastily put the light out.

November 20 – I tried to talk to Langby today. "I've seen you talking to that old gentleman," I said. It sounded like an accusation. I meant it to. I wanted him to think it was and stop whatever he was planning.

"Reading," he said. "Not talking." He was putting things in order in the choir, piling up sandbags.

"I've seen you reading then," I said belligerently, and he dropped a sandbag and straightened.

"What of it?" he said. "It's a free country. I can read to an old man if I want, same as you can talk to that little WVS tart."

"What do you read?" I said.

"Whatever he wants. He's an old man. He used to come home from his job, have a bit of brandy and listen to his wife read the papers to him. She got killed in one of the raids. Now I read to him. I don't see what business it is of yours."

It sounded true. It didn't have the careful casualness of a lie, and I almost believed him, except that I had heard the tone of truth from him before. In the crypt. After the bomb.

"I thought he was a tourist looking for the Windmill," I said.

He looked blank only a second, and then he said, "Oh, yes, that. He came in with the paper and asked me to tell him where it was. I looked it up to find the address. Clever, that. I didn't guess he couldn't read it for himself." But it was enough. I knew that he was lying.

He heaved a sandbag almost at my feet. "Of course you wouldn't understand a thing like that, would you? A simple act of human kindness."

"No," I said coldly. "I wouldn't."

None of this proves anything. He gave away nothing, except perhaps the name of an artificial, and I can hardly go to Dean Matthews and accuse Langby of reading aloud.

I waited till he had finished in the choir and gone down to the crypt. Then I lugged one of the sandbags up to the roof and over to the chasm. The planking has held so far, but everyone walks gingerly around it, as if it were a grave. I cut the sandbag open and spilled the loose sand into the bottom. If it had occurred to Langby that this is the perfect spot for an incendiary, perhaps the sand will smother it.

November 21 – I gave Enola some of "uncle's" money today and asked her to get me the brandy. She was more reluctant than I thought she'd be, so there must be societal complications I am not aware of, but she agreed.

I don't know what she came for. She started to tell me about her brother and some prank he'd pulled in the tubes that got him in trouble with the guard, but after I asked her about the brandy, she left without finishing the story.

November 25 – Enola came today, but without bringing the brandy. She is going to Bath for the holidays to see her aunt. At least she will be away from the raids for a while. I will not have to worry about her. She finished the story of her brother and told me she hopes to persuade this aunt to take Tom for the duration of the Blitz but is not at all sure the aunt will be willing.

Young Tom is apparently not so much an engaging scapegrace as a near criminal. He has been caught twice picking pockets in the Bank tube shelter, and they have had to go back to Marble Arch. I comforted her as best I could, told her all boys were bad at one time or another. What I really wanted to say was that she needn't worry at all, that young Tom strikes me as a true survivor type, like my own tom, like Langby, totally unconcerned with anybody but himself, well-equipped to survive the Blitz and rise to prominence in the future.

Then I asked her whether she had gotten the brandy.

She looked down at her open-toed shoes and muttered unhappily, "I thought you'd forgotten all about that."

I made up some story about the watch taking turns buying a bottle, and she seemed less unhappy, but I am not convinced she will not use this trip to Bath as an excuse to do nothing. I will have to leave and buy it myself, and I don't dare leave Langby alone in the church. I made her promise to bring the brandy today before she leaves. But she is still not back, and the sirens have already gone.

November 26 – No Enola, and she said their train left at noon. I suppose I should be grateful that at least she is safely out of London. Maybe in Bath she will be able to get over her cold.

Tonight one of the ARP girls breezed in to borrow half our cots and tell us about a mess over in the East End where a surface shelter was hit. Four dead, twelve wounded. "At least it wasn't one of the tube shelters!" she said. "Then you'd see a real mess, wouldn't you?"

November 30 – I dreamed I took the cat to St John's Wood.

"Is this a rescue mission?" Dunworthy said.

"No, sir," I said proudly. "I know what I was supposed to find in my practicum. The perfect survivor. Tough and resourceful and selfish. This is the only one I could find. I had to kill Langby, you know, to keep him from burning down St Paul's. Enola's brother has gone to Bath, and the others will never make it. Enola wears open-toed shoes in the winter and sleeps in the tubes and puts her hair up on metal pins so it will curl. She cannot possibly survive the Blitz."

Dunworthy said, "Perhaps you should have rescued her instead. What did you say her name was?"

"Kivrin," I said, and woke up cold and shivering.

December 5 – I dreamed Langby had the pinpoint bomb. He carried it under his arm like a brown paper parcel, coming out of St Paul's Station and around Ludgate Hill to the west doors.

"This is not fair," I said, barring his way with my arm. "There is no fire watch on duty."

He clutched the bomb to his chest like a pillow. "That is your fault," he said, and before I could get to my stirrup pump and bucket, he tossed it in the door.

The pinpoint was not even invented until the end of the twentieth century, and it was another ten years before the dispossessed communists got hold of it and turned it into something that could be carried under your arm. A parcel that could blow a quarter mile of the City into oblivion. Thank God that is one dream that cannot come true.

It was a sunlit morning in the dream, and this morning when I came off watch the sun was shining for the first time in weeks. I went down to the crypt and then came up again, making the rounds of the roofs twice more, then the steps and the grounds and all the treacherous alleyways between where an incendiary could be missed. I felt better after that, but when I got to sleep I dreamed again, this time of fire and Langby watching it, smiling.

December 15 – I found the cat this morning. Heavy raids last night, but most of them over toward Canning Town and nothing on the roofs to speak of. Nevertheless the cat was quite dead. I found him lying on the steps this morning when I made my own, private rounds. Concussion. There was not a mark on him anywhere except the white blackout patch on his throat, but when I picked him up, he was all jelly under the skin.

I could not think what to do with him. I thought for one mad moment of asking Matthews if I could bury him in the crypt. Honorable death in war or something. Trafalgar, Waterloo, London, died in battle. I ended by wrapping him in my muffler and taking him down Ludgate Hill to a building that had been bombed out and burying him in the rubble. It will do no good. The rubble will be no protection from dogs or rats, and I shall never get another muffler. I have gone through nearly all of uncle's money.

I should not be sitting here. I haven't checked the alleyways or the rest of the steps, and there might be a dud or a delayed incendiary or something that I missed.

When I came here, I thought of myself as the noble rescuer, the savior of the past. I am not doing very well at the job. At least Enola is out of it. I wish there were some way I could send St Paul's to Bath for safekeeping. There were hardly any raids last night. Bence-Jones said cats can survive anything. What if he was coming to get me, to show me the way home? All the bombs were over Canning Town.

December 16 – Enola has been back a week. Seeing her, standing on the west steps where I found the cat, sleeping in Marble Arch and not safe at all, was more than I could absorb. "I thought you were in Bath," I said stupidly.

"My aunt said she'd take Tom but not me as well. She's got a houseful of evacuation children, and what a noisy lot. Where is your muffler?" she said. "It's dreadful cold up here on the hill."

"I . . ." I said, unable to answer. "I lost it."

"You'll never get another one," she said. "They're going to start rationing clothes. And wool, too. You'll never get another one like that."

"I know," I said, blinking at her.

"Good things just thrown away," she said. "It's absolutely criminal, that's what it is."

I don't think I said anything to that, just turned and walked away with my head down, looking for bombs and dead animals.

December 20 – Langby isn't a Nazi. He's a communist. I can hardly write this. A communist.

One of the chars found *The Worker* wedged behind a pillar and brought it down to the crypt as we were coming off the first watch.

"Bloody communists," Bence-Jones said. "Helping Hitler, they are. Talking against the king, stirring up trouble in the shelters. Traitors, that's what they are."

"They love England same as you," the char said.

"They don't love nobody but themselves, bloody selfish lot. I wouldn't be surprised to hear they were ringing Hitler up on the telephone," Bence-Jones said. "'Ello, Adolf, here's where to drop the bombs."

The kettle on the gas ring whistled. The char stood up and poured the hot water into a chipped teapot, then sat back down. "Just because they speak their minds don't mean they'd burn down old St Paul's, does it now?"

"Of course not," Langby said, coming down the stairs. He sat down and pulled off his boots, stretching his feet in their wool socks. "Who wouldn't burn down St Paul's?"

"The communists," Bence-Jones said, looking straight at him, and I wondered if he suspected Langby too.

Langby never batted an eye. "I wouldn't worry about them if I were you," he said. "It's the jerries that are doing their bloody best to burn her down tonight. Six incendiaries so far, and one almost went into that great hole over the choir." He held out his cup to the char, and she poured him a cup of tea.

I wanted to kill him, smashing him to dust and rubble on the floor of the crypt while Bence-Jones and the char looked on in helpless surprise, shouting warnings to them and the rest of the watch. "Do you know what the communists did?" I wanted to shout. "Do you? We have to stop him." I even stood up and started toward him as he sat with his feet stretched out before him and his asbestos coat still over his shoulders.

And then the thought of the Gallery drenched in gold, the communist coming out of the tube station with the package so casually under his arm, made me sick with the same staggering vertigo of guilt and helplessness, and I sat back down on the edge of my cot and tried to think what to do.

They do not realize the danger. Even Bence-Jones, for all his talk of traitors, thinks they are capable only of talking against the king. They do not know, cannot know, what the communists will become. Stalin is an ally. Communists mean Russia. They have never heard of Karinsky or the New Russia or any of the things that will make "communist" into a synonym for "monster". They will never know it. By the time the communists become what they became, there will be no fire watch. Only I know what it means to hear the name "communist" uttered here, so carelessly, in St Paul's.

A communist. I should have known. I should have known.

December 22 – Double watches again. I have not had any sleep and I am getting very unsteady on my feet. I nearly pitched into the chasm this morning, only saved myself by dropping to my knees. My endorphin levels are fluctuating wildly, and I know I must get some sleep soon or I will become one of Langby's walking dead, but I am afraid to leave him alone on the roofs, alone in the church with his communist party leader, alone anywhere. I have taken to watching him when he sleeps.

If I could just get hold of an artificial, I think I could induce a trance, in spite of my poor condition. But I cannot even go out to a pub. Langby is on the roofs constantly, waiting for his chance. When Enola comes again I must convince her to get the brandy for me. There are only a few days left.

December 28 – Enola came this morning while I was on the west porch, picking up the Christmas tree. It has been knocked over three nights running by concussion. I righted the tree and was bending down to pick up the scattered tinsel when Enola appeared suddenly out of the fog like some cheerful saint. She stooped quickly and kissed me on the cheek. Then she straightened up, her nose red from her perennial cold, and handed me a box wrapped in colored paper.

"Merry Christmas," she said. "Go on then, open it. It's a gift."

My reflexes are almost totally gone. I knew the box was far too shallow for a bottle of brandy. Nevertheless I believed she had remembered, had brought me my salvation. "You darling," I said, and tore it open.

It was a muffler. Gray wool. I stared at it for fully half a minute without realizing what it was. "Where's the brandy?" I said.

She looked shocked. Her nose got redder and her eyes started to blur. "You need this more. You haven't any clothing coupons and you have to be outside all the time. It's been so dreadful cold."

"I *needed* the brandy," I said angrily.

"I was only trying to be kind," she started, and I cut her off.

"Kind?" I said. "I asked you for brandy. I don't recall ever saying I needed a muffler." I shoved it back at her and began untangling a string of colored lights that had shattered when the tree fell.

She got that same holy martyr look Kivrin is so wonderful at. "I worry about you all the time up here," she said in a rush. "They're *trying* for St Paul's, you know. And it's so close to the river. I didn't think you should be drinking. I – it's a crime when they're trying so hard to kill us all that you won't take care of yourself. It's like you're in it with them. I worry some day I'll come up to St Paul's and you won't be here."

"Well, and what exactly am I supposed to do with a muffler? Hold it over my head when they drop the bombs?"

She turned and ran, disappearing into the gray fog before she had gone down two steps. I started after her, still holding the string of broken lights, tripped over it, and fell almost all the way to the bottom of the steps.

Langby picked me up. "You're off watches," he said grimly.

"You can't do that," I said.

"Oh, yes, I can. I don't want any walking dead on the roofs with me."

I let him lead me down here to the crypt, make me a cup of tea, put me to bed, all very solicitous. No indication that this is what he has been waiting for. I will lie here till the sirens go. Once I am on the roofs he will not be able to send me back without seeming suspicious. Do you know what he said before he left, asbestos coat and rubber boots, the dedicated fire watcher? "I want you to get some sleep." As if I could sleep with Langby on the roofs. I would be burned alive.

December 30 – The sirens woke me, and old Bence-Jones said, "That should have done you some good. You've slept the clock round."

"What day is it?" I said, going for my boots.

"The twenty-ninth," he said, and as I dived for the door, "No need to hurry. They're late tonight. Maybe they won't come at all. That'd be a blessing, that would. The tide's out."

I stopped by the door to the stairs, holding on to the cool stone. "Is St Paul's all right?"

"She's still standing," he said. "Have a bad dream?"

"Yes," I said, remembering the bad dreams of all the past weeks – the dead cat in my arms in St John's Wood, Langby with his parcel and his *Worker* under his arm, the fire watch stone garishly lit by Christ's lantern. Then I remembered I had not dreamed at all. I had slept the kind of sleep I had prayed for, the kind of sleep that would help me remember.

Then I remembered. Not St Paul's, burned to the ground by the communists. A headline from the dailies. "Marble Arch hit. Eighteen killed by blast." The date was not clear except for the year. 1940. There were exactly two more days left in 1940. I grabbed my coat and muffler and ran up the stairs and across the marble floor.

"Where the hell do you think you're going?" Langby shouted to me. I couldn't see him.

"I have to save Enola," I said, and my voice echoed in the dark sanctuary. "They're going to bomb Marble Arch."

"You can't leave now," he shouted after me, standing where the fire watch stone would be. "The tide's out. You dirty—"

I didn't hear the rest of it. I had already flung myself down the steps and into a taxi. It took almost all the money I had, the money I had so carefully hoarded for the trip back to St John's Wood. Shelling started while we were still in Oxford Street, and the driver refused to go any farther. He let me out into pitch blackness, and I saw I would never make it in time.

Blast. Enola crumpled on the stairway down to the tube, her open-toed shoes still on her feet, not a mark on her. And when I try to lift her, jelly under the skin. I would have to wrap her in the muffler she gave me, because I was too late. I had gone back a hundred years to be too late to save her.

I ran the last blocks, guided by the gun emplacement that had to be in Hyde Park, and skidded down the steps into Marble Arch. The woman in the ticket booth took my last shilling for a ticket to St Paul's Station. I stuck it in my pocket and raced toward the stairs.

"No running," she said placidly. "To your left, please." The door to the right was blocked off by wooden barricades, the metal gates beyond pulled to and chained. The board with names on it for the stations was x-ed with tape, and a new sign that read ALL TRAINS was nailed to the barricade, pointing left.

Enola was not on the stopped escalators or sitting against the wall in the hallway. I came to the first stairway and could not get through. A family had set out, just where I wanted to step, a communal tea of bread and butter, a little pot of jam sealed with waxed paper, and a kettle on a ring like the one Langby and I had rescued out of the rubble, all of it spread on a cloth embroidered at the corners with flowers. I stood staring down at the layered tea, spread like a waterfall down the steps.

"I – Marble Arch—" I said. Another twenty killed by flying tiles. "You shouldn't be here."

"We've as much right as anyone," the man said belligerently. "And who are you to tell us to move on?"

A woman lifting saucers out of a cardboard box looked up at me, frightened. The kettle began to whistle.

"It's you that should move on," the man said. "Go on then." He stood off to one side so I could pass. I edged past the embroidered cloth apologetically.

"I'm sorry," I said. "I'm looking for someone. On the platform."

"You'll never find her in there, mate," the man said, thumbing in that direction. I hurried past him, nearly stepping on the tea cloth, and rounded the corner into hell.

It was not hell. Shopgirls folded coats and leaned back against them, cheerful or sullen or disagreeable, but certainly not damned. Two boys scuffled for a shilling and lost it on the tracks. They bent over the edge, debating whether to go after it, and the station guard yelled to them to back away. A train rumbled through, full of people. A mosquito landed on the guard's hand and he reached out to slap it and missed. The boys laughed. And behind and before them, stretching in all directions down the deadly tile curves of the tunnel like casualties, backed into the entranceways and onto the stairs, were people. Hundreds and hundreds of people.

I stumbled back onto the stairs, knocking over a teacup. It spilled like a flood across the cloth.

"I told you, mate," the man said cheerfully. "It's hell in there, ain't it? And worse below."

"Hell," I said. "Yes." I would never find her. I would never save her. I looked at the woman mopping up the tea, and it came to me that I could not save her either. Enola or the cat or any of them, lost here in the endless stairways and cul-de-sacs of time. They were already dead a hundred years, past saving. The past is beyond saving. Surely that was the lesson the history department sent me all this way to learn. Well, fine, I've learned it. Can I go home now?

Of course not, dear boy. You have foolishly spent all your money on taxicabs and brandy, and tonight is the night the Germans burn the City. (Now it is too late, I remember it all. Twenty-eight incendiaries on the roofs.) Langby must have his chance, and you must learn the hardest lesson of all and the one you should have known from the beginning. You cannot save St Paul's.

I went back out onto the platform and stood behind the yellow line until a train pulled up. I took my ticket out and held it in my hand all the way to St Paul's Station. When I got there, smoke billowed toward me like an easy spray of water. I could not see St Paul's.

"The tide's out," a woman said in a voice devoid of hope, and I went down in a snake pit of limp cloth hoses. My hands came up covered with rank-smelling mud, and I understood finally (and too late) the significance of the tide. There was no water to fight the fires.

A policeman barred my way and I stood helplessly before him with no idea what to say. "No civilians allowed here," he said. "St Paul's is for it." The smoke billowed like a thundercloud, alive with sparks, and the dome rose golden above it.

"I'm fire watch," I said, and his arm fell away, and then I was on the roofs.

My endorphin levels must have been going up and down like an air raid siren. I do not have any short-term from then on, just moments that do not fit together: the people in the church when we brought Langby down, huddled in a corner playing cards, the whirlwind of burning scraps of wood in the dome, the ambulance driver who wore open-toed shoes like Enola and smeared salve on my burned hands. And in the center, the one clear moment when I went after Langby on a rope and saved his life.

I stood by the dome, blinking against the smoke. The City was on fire and it seemed as if St Paul's would ignite from the heat, would crumble from the noise alone. Bence-Jones was by the northwest tower, hitting at an incendiary with a spade. Langby was too close to the patched place where the bomb had gone through, looking toward me. An incendiary clattered behind him. I turned to grab a shovel, and when I turned back, he was gone.

"Langby!" I shouted, and could not hear my own voice. He had fallen into the chasm and nobody saw him or the incendiary. Except me. I do not remember how I got across the roof. I think I called for a rope. I got a rope. I tied it around my waist, gave the ends of it into the hands of the fire watch, and went over the side. The fires lit the walls of the hole almost all the way to the bottom. Below me I could see a pile of whitish rubble. He's under there, I thought, and jumped free of the wall. The space was so narrow there was nowhere to throw the rubble. I was afraid I would inadvertently stone him, and I tried to toss the pieces of planking and plaster over my shoulder, but there was barely room to turn. For one awful moment I thought he might not be there at all, that the pieces of splintered wood would brush away to reveal empty pavement, as they had in the crypt.

I was numbed by the indignity of crawling over him. If he was dead I did not think I could bear the shame of stepping on his helpless body. Then his hand came up like a ghost's and grabbed my ankle, and within seconds I had whirled and had his head free.

He was the ghastly white that no longer frightens me. "I put the bomb out," he said. I stared at him, so overwhelmed with relief I could not speak. For one hysterical moment I thought I would even laugh, I was so glad to see him. I finally realized what it was I was supposed to say.

"Are you all right?" I said.

"Yes," he said, and tried to raise himself on one elbow. "So much the worse for you."

He could not get up. He grunted with pain when he tried to shift his weight to his right side and lay back, the uneven rubble crunching sickeningly under him. I tried to lift him gently so I could see where he was hurt. He must have fallen on something.

"It's no use," he said, breathing hard. "I put it out."

I spared him a startled glance, afraid that he was delirious and went back to rolling him onto his side.

"I know you were counting on this one," he went on, not resisting me at all. "It was bound to happen sooner or later with all these roofs. Only I went after it. What'll you tell your friends?"

His asbestos coat was torn down the back in a long gash. Under it his back was charred and smoking. He had fallen on the incendiary. "Oh, my God," I said, trying frantically to see how badly he was burned without touching him. I had no way of knowing how deep the burns went, but they seemed to extend only in the narrow space where the coat had torn. I tried to pull the bomb out from under him, but the casing was as hot as a stove. It was not melting, though. My sand and Langby's body had smothered it. I had no idea if it would start up again when it was exposed to the air. I looked around, a little wildly, for the bucket and stirrup pump Langby must have dropped when he fell.

"Looking for a weapon?" Langby said, so clearly it was hard to believe he was hurt at all. "Why not just leave me here? A bit of overexposure and I'd be done for by morning. Or would you rather do your dirty work in private?"

I stood up and yelled to the men on the roof above us. One of them shone a pocket torch down at us, but its light didn't reach.

"Is he dead?" somebody shouted down to me.

"Send for an ambulance," I said. "He's been burned."

I helped Langby up, trying to support his back without touching the burn. He staggered a little and then leaned against the wall, watching me as I tried to bury the incendiary, using a piece of the planking as a scoop. The rope came down and I tied Langby to it. He had not spoken since I helped him up. He let me tie the rope around his waist, still looking steadily at me. "I should have let you smother in the crypt," he said.

He stood leaning easily, almost relaxed against the wooden supports, his hands holding him up. I put his hands on the slack rope and wrapped it once around them for the grip I knew he didn't have. "I've been onto you since that day in the Gallery. I knew you weren't afraid of heights. You came down here without any fear of heights when you thought I'd ruined your precious plans. What was it? An attack of conscience? Kneeling there like a baby, whining, "What have we done? What have we done?" You made me sick. But you know what gave you away first? The cat. Everybody knows cats hate water. Everybody but a dirty Nazi spy."

There was a tug on the rope. "Come ahead," I said, and the rope tautened.

"That WVS tart? Was she a spy, too? Supposed to meet you in Marble Arch? Telling me it was going to be bombed. You're a rotten spy, Bartholomew. Your friends already blew it up in September. It's open again."

The rope jerked suddenly and began to lift Langby. He twisted his hands to get a better grip. His right shoulder scraped the wall. I put my hands and pushed him gently so that his left side was to the wall. "You're making a big mistake, you know," he said. "You should have killed me. I'll tell."

I stood in the darkness, waiting for the rope. Langby was unconscious when he reached the roof. I walked past the fire watch to the dome and down to the crypt.

This morning the letter from my uncle came and with it a five-pound note.

December 31 – Two of Dunworthy's flunkies met me in St John's Wood to tell me I was late for my exams. I did not even protest. I shuffled obediently after them without even considering how unfair it was to give an exam to one of the walking dead. I had not slept in – how long? Since yesterday when I went to find Enola. I had not slept in a hundred years.

Dunworthy was in the Examination Buildings, blinking at me. One of the flunkies handed me a test paper and the other one called time. I turned the paper over and left an oily smudge from the ointment on my burns. I stared uncomprehendingly at them. I had grabbed at the incendiary when I turned Langby over, but these burns were on the backs of my hands. The answer came to me suddenly in Langby's unyielding voice. "They're rope burns, you fool. Don't they teach you Nazi spies the proper way to come up a rope?"

I looked down at the test. It read, "Number of incendiaries that fell on St Paul's_____ Number of land mines_____ Number of high explosive bombs_____ Method most commonly used for extinguishing incendiaries_____ land mines_____ high explosive bombs_____ Number of volunteers on first watch_____ second watch_____ Casualties_____ Fatalities_____." The questions made no sense. There was only a short space, long enough for the writing of a number, after any of the questions. Method most commonly used for extinguishing incendiaries. How would I ever fit what I knew into that narrow space? Where were the questions about Enola and Langby and the cat?

I went up to Dunworthy's desk. "St Paul's almost burned down last night," I said. "What kind of questions are these?"

"You should be answering questions, Mr Bartholomew, not asking them."

"There aren't any questions about the people," I said. The outer casing of my anger began to melt.

"Of course there are," Dunworthy said, flipping to the second page of the test. "Number of casualties, 1940. Blast, shrapnel, other."

"Other?" I said. At any moment the roof would collapse on me in a shower of plaster dust and fury. "Other? Langby put out a fire with his own body. Enola has a cold that keeps getting worse. The cat . . . ." I snatched the paper back from him and scrawled "one cat" in the narrow space next to "blast". "Don't you care about them at all?"

"They're important from a statistical point of view," he said, "but as individuals they are hardly relevant to the course of history."

My reflexes were shot. It was amazing to me that Dunworthy's were almost as slow. I grazed the side of his jaw and knocked his glasses off. "Of course they're relevant!" I shouted. "They *are* the history, not all these bloody numbers!"

The reflexes of the flunkies were very fast. They did not let me start another swing at him before they had me by both arms and were hauling me out of the room.

"They're back there in the past with nobody to save them. They can't see their hands in front of their faces and there are bombs falling down on them and you tell me they aren't important? You call that being an historian?"

The flunkies dragged me out the door and down the hall. "Langby saved St Paul's. How much more important can a person get? You're no historian! You're nothing but a—" I wanted to call him a terrible name, but the only curses I could summon up were Langby's. "You're nothing but a dirty Nazi spy!" I bellowed. "You're nothing but a lazy bourgeois tart!"

They dumped me on my hands and knees outside the door and slammed it in my face. "I wouldn't be an historian if you paid me!" I shouted, and went to see the fire watch stone.

December 31 – I am having to write this in bits and pieces. My hands are in pretty bad shape, and Dunworthy's boys didn't help matters much. Kivrin comes in periodically, wearing her St Joan look, and smears so much salve on my hands that I can't hold a pencil.

St Paul's Station is not there, of course, so I got out at Holborn and walked, thinking about my last meeting with Dean Matthews on the morning after the burning of the city. This morning.

"I understand you saved Langby's life," he said. "I also understand that between you, you saved St Paul's last night."

I showed him the letter from my uncle and he stared at it as if he could not think what it was. "Nothing stays saved forever," he said, and for a terrible moment I thought he was going to tell me Langby had died. "We shall have to keep on saving St Paul's until Hitler decides to bomb something else."

The raids on London are almost over, I wanted to tell him. He'll start bombing the countryside in a matter of weeks. Canterbury, Bath, aiming always at the cathedrals. You and St Paul's will both outlast the war and live to dedicate the fire watch stone.

"I am hopeful, though," he said. "I think the worst is over."

"Yes, sir." I thought of the stone, its letters still readable after all this time. No sir, the worst is not over.

I managed to keep my bearings almost to the top of Ludgate Hill. Then I lost my way completely, wandering about like a man in a graveyard. I had not remembered that the rubble looked so much like the white plaster dust Langby had tried to dig me out of. I could not find the stone anywhere. In the end I nearly fell over it, jumping back as if I had stepped on a body.

It is all that's left. Hiroshima is supposed to have had a handful of untouched trees at ground zero. Denver the capitol steps. Neither of them says, "Remember men and women of St Paul's Watch who by the grace of God saved this cathedral." The grace of God.

Part of the stone is sheared off. Historians argue there was another line that said, "for all time," but I do not believe that, not if Dean Matthews had anything to do with it. And none of the watch it was dedicated to would have believed it for a minute. We saved St Paul's every time we put out an incendiary, and only until the next one fell. Keeping watch on the danger spots, putting out the little fires with sand and stirrup pumps, the big ones with our bodies, in order to keep the whole vast complex structure from burning down. Which sounds to me like a course description for History Practicum 401. What a fine time to discover what historians are for when I have tossed my chance for being one out the windows as easily as they tossed the pinpoint bomb in! No, sir, the worst is not over.

There are flash burns on the stone, where legend says the Dean of St Paul's was kneeling when the bomb went off. Totally apocryphal, of course, since the front door is hardly an appropriate place for prayers. It is more likely the shadow of a tourist who wandered in to ask the whereabouts of the Windmill Theatre, or the imprint of a girl bringing a volunteer his muffler. Or a cat.

Nothing is saved forever, Dean Matthews, and I knew that when I walked in the west doors that first day, blinking in the gloom, but it is pretty bad nevertheless. Standing here knee-deep in rubble out of which I will not be able to dig any folding chairs or friends, knowing that Langby died thinking I was a Nazi spy, knowing that Enola came one day and I wasn't there. It's pretty bad.

But it is not as bad as it could be. They are both dead, and Dean Matthews too, but they died without knowing what I knew all along, what sent me to my knees in the Whispering Gallery, sick with grief and guilt: that in the end none of us saved St Paul's. And Langby cannot turn to me, stunned and sick at heart, and say, "Who did this? Your friends the Nazis?" And I would have to say, "No, the communists." That would be the worst.

I have come back to the room and let Kivrin smear more salve on my hands. She wants me to get some sleep. I know I should pack and get gone. It will be humiliating to have them come and throw me out, but I do not have the strength to fight her. She looks so much like Enola.

January 1 – I have apparently slept not only through the night, but through the morning mail drop as well. When I woke just now, I found Kivrin sitting on the end of the bed holding an envelope. "Your grades came," she said.

I put my arm over my eyes. "They can be marvelously efficient when they want to, can't they?"

"Yes," Kivrin said.

"Well, let's see it," I said, sitting up. "How long do I have before they come and throw me out?"

She handed the flimsy computer envelope to me. I tore it along the perforation. "Wait," she said. "Before you open it, I want to say something." She put her hand gently on my burns. "You're wrong about the history department. They're very good."

It was not exactly what I expected her to say. "Good is not the word I'd use to describe Dunworthy," I said and yanked the inside slip free.

Kivrin's look did not change, not even when I sat there with the printout on my knees where she could surely see it.

"Well," I said.

The slip was hand-signed by the esteemed Dunworthy. I have taken a first. With honors.

January 2 – Two things came in the mail today. One was Kivrin's assignment. The history department thinks of everything – even to keeping her here long enough to nursemaid me, even to coming up with a prefabricated trial by fire to send their history majors through.

I think I wanted to believe that was what they had done, Enola and Langby only hired actors, the cat a clever android with its clockwork innards taken out for the final effect, not so much because I wanted to believe Dunworthy was not good at all, but because then I would not have this nagging pain at not knowing what had happened to them.

"You said your practicum was England in 1400?" I said, watching her as suspiciously as I had watched Langby.

"1349," she said, and her face went slack with memory. "The plague year."

"My God," I said. "How could they do that? The plague's a ten."

"I have a natural immunity," she said, and looked at her hands.

Because I could not think of anything to say, I opened the other piece of mail. It was a report on Enola. Computer-printed, facts and dates and statistics, all the numbers the history department so dearly loves, but it told me what I thought I would have to go without knowing: that she had gotten over her cold and survived the Blitz. Young Tom had been killed in the Baedaker raids on Bath, but Enola had lived until 2006, the year before they blew up St Paul's.

I don't know whether I believe the report or not, but it does not matter. It is, like Langby's reading aloud to the old man, a simple act of human kindness. They think of everything.

Not quite. They did not tell me what happened to Langby. But I find as I write this that I already know: I saved his life. It does not seem to matter that he might have died in hospital next day, and I find, in spite of all the hard lessons the history department has tried to teach me, I do not quite believe this one: that nothing is saved forever. It seems to me that perhaps Langby is.

January 3 – I went to see Dunworthy today. I don't know what I intended to say – some pompous drivel about my willingness to serve in the fire watch of history, standing guard against the falling incendiaries of the human heart, silent and saintly.

But he blinked at me nearsightedly across his desk, and it seemed to me that he was blinking at that last bright image of St Paul's in sunlight before it was gone forever and that he knew better than anyone that the past cannot be saved, and I said instead, "I'm sorry I broke your glasses, sir."

"How did you like St Paul's?" he said, and like my first meeting with Enola, I felt I must be somehow reading the signals all wrong, that he was not feeling loss, but something quite different.

"I loved it, sir," I said.

"Yes," he said. "So do I."

Dean Matthews is wrong. I have fought with memory my whole practicum only to find that it is not the enemy at all, and being an historian is not some saintly burden after all. Because Dunworthy is not blinking against the fatal sunlight of the last morning, but into the bloom of that first afternoon, looking at the great west doors of St Paul's at what is, like Langby, like all of it, every moment, in us, saved forever.

NOBLE MOLD

Kage Baker

Kage Baker was an award-winning American writer of novels and stories. Her novels have been translated into Spanish, French, Italian, Hebrew, and German. Before she became a professional writer, Baker spent quite a bit of time in the theatre. Her beloved and popular Company series tells the story of time traveling agents who work for the mysterious Company. "Noble Mold" was the first short story written in that series. It is also the first story of hers that she read to her mother.

This was the first Company story ever to appear in print, while In the Garden of Iden *was still in search of a publisher. It is also the only story of mine my mother ever heard.*

She was a person of epic personality and style, rather like the late great Jennifer Patterson of Two Fat Ladies *fame, outrageous, artistic, and endlessly nurturing. Naturally enough, I spent most of my life refusing to be anything she wanted me to be. I never let her read anything I wrote, although she loved science fiction.*

Then she was, abruptly, diagnosed with something awful and lasted only a month. Every day after work I would visit her in her hospital room, where of course the truth hit me like a grand piano dropped out a window: I desperately wanted *her to read my stuff. And now she couldn't hold a book or even focus her eyes. And the train was pulling out of the station so fast, and I was standing there like an idiot on the platform, with almost no time to say I was sorry.*

But, pacing by her bed, I explained the whole Company idea, and made up a short story to illustrate the way it worked, about Mendoza and Joseph trying to steal a rare plant. I acted it out, did all the voices, everything I could think of to hold her attention and get the idea across. She liked it, thank God. I wrote it down after she died.

Mea culpa, mea culpa, mea maxima culpa.

This introduction first appeared in *Black Projects, White Knights,* by Golden Gryphon Press, 2002, introducing "Noble Mold," the first story to be published of The Company Dossiers and, indeed, of Kage Baker's.

For a while I lived in this little town by the sea. Boy, it was a soft job. Santa Barbara had become civilized by then: no more Indian rebellions, no more pirates storming up the beach, nearly all the grizzly bears gone. Once in a while some bureaucrat from Mexico City would raise hell with us, but by and large the days of the old Missions were declining into forlorn shades, waiting for the Yankees to come.

The Company operated a receiving, storage, and shipping terminal out of what looked like an oaken chest in my cell. I had a mortal identity as an alert little padre with an administrative career ahead of him, so the Church kept me pretty busy pushing a quill. My Company duties, though, were minor: I logged in consignments from agents in the field and forwarded communiqués.

It was sort of a forty-year vacation. There were fiestas and fandangos down in the pueblo. There were horse races along the shore of the lagoon. My social standing with the De La Guerra family was high, so I got invited out to supper a lot. And at night, when the bishop had gone to bed and our few pathetic Indians were tucked in for the night, I would sneak a little glass of Communion wine and then relax out on the front steps of the church. There I'd sit, listening to the night sounds, looking down the long slope to the night sea. Sometimes I'd sit there until the sky pinked up in the east and the bells rang for Matins. We Old Ones don't need much sleep.

One August night I was sitting like that, watching the moon drop down toward the Pacific, when I picked up the signal of another immortal somewhere out there in the night. I tracked it coming along the shoreline, past the point at Goleta; then it crossed the Camino Real and came straight uphill at me. Company business. I sighed and broadcast, *Quo Vadis?*

Hola, came the reply. I scanned, but I knew who it was anyway. *Hi, Mendoza,* I signaled back, and leaned up on my elbows to await her arrival. Pretty soon I picked her up on visual, too, climbing up out of the mists that flowed along the little stream; first the wide-brimmed hat, then the shoulders bent forward under the weight of the pack, the long walking skirt, the determined lope of the field operative without transportation.

Mendoza is a botanist, and has been out in the field too long. At this point she'd been tramping around Alta California for the better part of twelve decades. God only knew what the Company had found for her to do out in the back of beyond; I'd have known, if I'd been nosy enough to read the Company directives I relayed to her from time to time. I wasn't her case officer anymore, though, so I didn't.

She raised burning eyes to me and my heart sank. She was on a Mission, and I don't mean the kind with stuccoed arches and tile roofs. Mendoza takes her work way too seriously. "How's it going, kid?" I greeted her in a loud whisper when she was close enough.

"Okay." She slung down her pack on the step beside me, picked up my wine and drank it, handed me back the empty glass and sat down.

"I thought you were back up in Monterey these days," I ventured.

"No. The Ventana," she replied. There was a silence while the sky got a little brighter. Far off, a rooster started to crow and then thought better of it.

"Well, well. To what do I owe the pleasure, et cetera?" I prompted.

She gave me a sharp look. "Company Directive 080444-C," she said, as though it were really obvious.

I'd developed this terrible habit of storing incoming Green Directives in my tertiary consciousness without scanning them first. The soft life, I guess. I accessed hastily. "They're sending you after grapes?" I cried a second later.

"Not just grapes." She leaned forward and stared into my eyes. "*Mission* grapes. All the cultivars around here that will be replaced by the varieties the Yankees introduce. I'm to collect genetic material from every remaining vine within a twenty-five-mile radius of this building." She looked around disdainfully. "Not that I expect to find all that many. This place is a wreck. The Church has really let its agricultural program go to hell, hasn't it?"

"Hard to get slave labor nowadays." I shrugged. "Can't keep 'em down on the farm without leg irons. We get a little help from the ones who really bought into the religion, but that's about it."

"And the Holy Office can't touch them." Mendoza shook her head. "Never thought I'd see the day."

"Hey, things change." I stretched out and crossed my sandaled feet one over the other. "Anyway. The Mexicans hate my poor little bishop and are doing their level best to drive him crazy. In all the confusion with the Missions being closed down, a lot of stuff has been looted. Plants get dug up and moved to people's gardens in the dark of night. There are still a few Indian families back in some of the canyons, too, and a lot of them have tiny little farms. Probably a lot of specimens out there, but you'll really have to hunt around for them."

She nodded, all brisk. "I'll need a processing credenza. Bed and board, too, and a cover identity. That's your job. Can you arrange them by 0600 hours?"

"Gosh, this is just like old times," I said without enthusiasm. She gave me that look again.

"I have work to do," she explained with exaggerated patience. "It is very important work. I'm a good little machine and I love my work. Nothing is more important than *My Work*. You taught me that, remember?"

Which I had, so I just smiled my most sincere smile as I clapped her on the shoulder. "And a damned good machine you are, too, I know you'll do a great job, Mendoza. And I feel that your efficiency will be increased if you don't rush this job. Take the time to do it right, you know? Mix a little rest and rec into your schedule. After all, you really deserve a holiday, a hard-working operative like you. This is a great place for fun. You could come to one of our local cascaron balls. Dance the night away. You used to like to dance."

Boy, was that the wrong thing to say. She stood up slowly, like a cobra rearing back.

"I haven't owned a ballgown since 1703. I haven't attended a mortal party since 1555. If you've chosen to forget that miserable Christmas, I can assure you I haven't. *You* play with the damned monkeys, if you're so fond of them." She drew a deep breath. "I, myself, have better things to do." She stalked away up the steps, but I called after her:

"You're still sore about the Englishman, huh?"

She didn't deign to respond but shoved her way between the church doors, presumably to get some sleep behind the altar screen where she wouldn't be disturbed.

She was still sore about the Englishman.

I may have a more relaxed attitude toward my job than some people I could mention, but I'm still the best at it. By the time Mendoza wandered squinting into morning light I had her station set up, complete with hardware, in one of the Mission's guest cells. For the benefit of my fellow friars she was my cousin from Guadalajara, visiting me while she awaited the arrival of her husband from Mexico City. As befitted the daughter of an old Christian family, the señora was of a sober and studious nature, and derived much innocent pleasure from painting flowers and other subjects of natural history.

She didn't waste any time. Mendoza went straight out to what remained of the Mission vineyard and set to work, clipping specimens, taking soil samples, doing all those things you'd have to be an obsessed specialist to enjoy. By the first evening she was hard at work at her credenza, processing it all.

When it came time to loot the private gardens of the *Gentes de Razon* her social introductions went okay, too, once I got her into some decent visiting clothes. I did most of the talking to the Ortegas and Carrillos and the rest, and the fact that she was a little stiff and silent while taking grape brandy with them could easily be explained away by her white skin and blue veins. If you had any Spanish blood you were sort of expected to sneer about it in that place, in those days.

Anyway it was a relief for everybody when she'd finished in the pueblo and went roving up and down the canyons, pouncing on unclaimed vines. There were a few Indians settled back in the hills, ex-neophytes scratching out a living between two worlds, on land nobody else had wanted. What they made of this woman, white as their worst nightmares, who spoke to them in imperious and perfectly accented Barbareno Chumash, I can only imagine. However she persuaded them, though, she got samples of their vines too. I figured she'd soon be on her way back to the hinterlands, and had an extra glass of Communion wine to celebrate. Was *that* ever premature!

I was hearing confessions when her scream of excitement cut through the subvocal ether, followed by delighted profanity in sixteenth-century Galician. My parishioner went on:

" . . . which you should also know, Father, was that I have coveted Juana's new pans. These are not common iron pans but enamelware, white with a blue stripe, very pretty, and they came from the Yankee trading ship. It disturbs me that such things should imperil my soul."

Joseph! Joseph! Joseph!

"It is good to be concerned on that account, my child." I shut out Mendoza's transmission so I could concentrate on the elderly mortal woman on the other side of the screen. "To covet worldly things is very sinful indeed, especially for the poor. The Devil himself sent the Yankees with those pans, you may be certain." But Mendoza had left her credenza and was coming down the arcade in search of me, ten meters, twenty meters, twenty-five . . . "For this, and for your sinful dreams, you must say thirty Paternosters and sixty Ave Marias . . ." Mendoza was coming up the church steps two at a time . . . "Now, recite with me the Act of Contrition—"

"Hey!" Mendoza pulled back the door of the confessional. Her eyes were glowing with happiness. I gave her a stern look and continued the Act of Contrition with my somewhat disconcerted penitent, so Mendoza went out to stride up and down in front of the church in her impatience.

"Don't you know better than to interrupt me when I'm administering a sacrament?" I snapped when I was finally able to come out to her. "Some Spaniard you are!"

"So report me to the Holy Office. Joseph, this is important. One of my specimens read out with an F-M Class One rating."

"And?" I put my hands in my sleeves and frowned at her, refusing to come out of the role of offended friar.

"Favorable Mutation, Joseph, don't you know what that means? It's a Mission grape with a difference. It's got Saccharomyces with style and Botrytis in rare bloom. Do you know what happens when a field operative discovers an F-M Class One, Joseph?"

"You get a prize," I guessed.

"Si, Señor!" She did a little dance down the steps and stared up at me in blazing jubilation. I hadn't seen her this happy since 1554. "I get a Discovery Bonus! Six months of access to a lab for my own personal research projects, with the very finest equipment available! Oh joy, oh rapture. So I need you to help me."

"What do you need?"

"The Company wants the parent plant I took the specimen from, the whole thing, root and branch. It's a big vine, must have been planted years ago, so I need you to get me some Indians to dig it up and bring it back here in a carreta. Six months at a Sciences Base, can you imagine?"

"Where did you get the specimen?" I inquired.

She barely thought about it. "Two kilometers south-southeast. Just some Indian family back in the hills, Joseph, with a hut in a clearing and a garden. Kasmali, that was what they called themselves. You know the family? I suppose we'll have to pay them something for it. You'll have to arrange that for me, okay?"

I sighed. Once again the kindly padre was going to explain to the Indian why it was necessary to give up yet another of his belongings. Not my favorite role, all things considered.

But there we were that afternoon, the jolly friar and his haughty cousin, paying a call on the Kasmali family.

They were good parishioners of mine, the old abuela at Mass every day of the week, rain or shine, the rest of the family lined up there every Sunday. That was a lot to expect of our Indians in this day and age. They were prosperous, too, as Indians went: they had three walls of a real adobe house and had patched in the rest with woven brush. They had terraced their tiny hillside garden and were growing all kinds of vegetables on land not fit for grazing. There were a few chickens, there were a few little brown children chasing them, there were a few cotton garments drying on the bushes. And, on the crest of the hill, a little way from the house, there was the vineyard: four old vines, big as trees, with branches spreading out to shade most of an acre of land.

The children saw us coming and vanished into the house without a sound. By the time we reached the top of the winding stony path, they had all come out and were staring at us: the toothless old woman from daily Mass, a toothless old man I did not know, the old son, the two grown grandsons, their wives, and children of assorted ages. The elder of the grandsons came forward to greet us.

"Good evening, little Father." He looked uneasily at Mendoza. "Good evening, lady."

"Good evening, Emidio." I paused and pretended to be catching my breath after the climb, scanning him. He was small, solidly built, with broad and very dark features; he had a stiff black moustache. His wide eyes flickered once more to Mendoza, then back to me. "You have already been introduced to my cousin, I see."

"Yes, little Father." He made a slight bow in her direction. "The lady came yesterday and cut some branches off our grapevines. We did not mind, of course."

"It is very kind of you to permit her to collect these things." I eyed Mendoza, hoping she'd been tactful with them.

"Not at all. The lady speaks our language very well."

"That is only courtesy, my son. Now, I must tell you that one of your vines has taken her fancy, for its extraordinary fruit and certain virtues in the leaves. We have come back here today, therefore, to ask you what you will accept for that near vine at the bottom of the terrace."

The rest of the family stood like statues, even the children. Emidio moved his hands in a helpless gesture and said, "The lady must of course accept our gift."

"No, no," said Mendoza. "We'll pay you. How much do you want for it?" I winced.

"She must accept the gift, please, Father." Emidio's smile was wretched.

"Of course she shall," I agreed. "And, Emidio, I have a gift I have been meaning to give you since the feast of San Juan. Two little pigs, a boar and a sow, so they may increase. When you bring down the vine for us you may collect them."

The wives lifted up their heads at that. This was a good deal. Emidio spread out his hands again. "Of course, little Father. Tomorrow."

"Well, that was easy," Mendoza remarked as we picked our way down the hill through the chaparral. "You're so good with mortals, Joseph. You just have to treat Indians like children, I guess, huh?"

"No, you don't," I sighed. "But it's what they expect you to do, so they play along." There was more to it than that, of course, but something else was bothering me. I had picked up something more than the usual stifled resentment when I had voiced my request: someone in the family had been badly frightened for a second. Why? "You didn't do anything to, like, scare those people when you were there before, did you, Mendoza? Didn't threaten them or anything, did you?"

"Heavens, no." She stopped to examine a weed. "I was quite polite. They weren't comfortable around me, actually, but then mortals never are. Look at this! I've never seen this blooming so late in the year, have you?"

"Nice." I glanced at it. I don't know from plants. I know a lot about mortals, though.

So I was surprised as hell next day when Emidio and his brother appeared at the Mission, trundling a cart full of swaying leaves into the open space by the fountain. I went out to greet them and Mendoza was behind me like a shadow. She must have been prowling her room, listening for the squeak of wheels.

"This is very good, my sons, I am proud of you—" I was saying heartily, when Mendoza transmitted a blast of subvocal fury.

Damn it, Joseph, this is wrong! These are just clippings, they haven't brought the whole vine!

"– but I perceive there has been a misunderstanding," I continued. "My cousin requested the vine itself, with its roots, that she may replant it. You have brought only cut branches, apparently." The Indians exchanged glances.

"Please forgive us, little Father. We did not understand." They set down the traces and Emidio reached into the back. "We did bring all the grapes that were ripe. Maybe it was these the lady wanted?" And he proffered a big woven dish of grapes. I looked close and noticed they did have a funny look to them, a bloom on the skin so heavy it was almost . . . furry?

"No," said Mendoza, in clearest Chumash. "Not just the grapes. I want the vine. The whole plant. You need to dig it up, roots and all, and bring it here. Do you understand now?"

"Oh," said Emidio. "We're very sorry. We didn't understand."

"But you understand now?" she demanded.

"I am certain they do," I said smoothly. "What remarkable grapes these are, my sons, and what a beautiful basket! Come in and rest in the shade, my sons, and have a cool drink. Then we will go catch one of the little pigs I promised you."

By the time we got back, Mendoza had vanished; the grapes and the vine cuttings were gone too. The brothers trudged away up the hill with their cart and one squealing shoat, his legs bound with twine. Pig Number Two remained in the Mission pen, to be paid on delivery of the vine. I figured if the wives got that message they'd see to it the job got done.

Mendoza came out when they were gone. She looked paler than usual. She handed me a sheet of paper from her credenza. "This is a Priority Order," she told me. "I sent them the codes on the grapes and clippings anyway, but it's not enough."

I read the memo. She wasn't kidding; it was a first-class trans-departmental Priority Gold telling me I was to do everything in my power to facilitate, expedite and et cetera. "What have we got here, anyway, cancer cures from grapes?" I speculated.

"You don't need to know and neither do I," said Mendoza flatly. "But the Company means business now, Joseph. We must get that vine."

"We'll get it tomorrow," I told her. "Trust me."

Next day, same hour, the brothers came with hopeful smiles and a big muddy mess of a vine trailing out of their cart. Such relief! Such heartfelt praise and thanks the kindly friar showered on his obedient sons in Christ! Mendoza heard their arrival and came tearing out into the courtyard, only to pull up short with an expression of baffled rage.

THAT'S NOT THE VINE! she transmitted, with such intensity I thought for a second we were having an earthquake.

" . . . And yet, my sons, I am afraid we have not understood each other once again," I went on wearily. "It appears that, although you have brought us *a* whole vine, you have not brought *the* particular vine that was specifically asked for by my cousin."

"We are so sorry," replied Emidio, averting his eyes from Mendoza. "How stupid we were! But, Father, this is a very good vine. It's in much better condition than the other one and bears much prettier grapes. Also, it was very difficult to dig it all up and we have brought it a long way. Maybe the lady will be satisfied with this vine instead?"

Mendoza was shaking her head, not trusting herself to speak, although the air around her was wavering like a mirage. Hastily I said:

"My dearest sons, I am sure it is an excellent vine, and we would not take it from your family. You must understand that it is the *other* vine we want, the very one you brought cuttings from yesterday. That vine and no other, and all of that vine. Now, you have clearly worked very hard and in good faith, so I will certainly send you home with your other pig, but you must come back tomorrow with the right vine."

The brothers looked at each other and I picked up a flash of despair from them, and some weird kind of fear too. "Yes, little Father," they replied.

But on the next day they didn't come at all.

Mendoza paced the arcade until nine in the evening, alarming the other friars. Finally I went out to her and braced myself for the blast.

"You know, you lost yourself two perfectly good pigs," she informed me through gritted teeth. "Damned lying Indians."

I shook my head. "Something's wrong here, Mendoza."

"You bet something's wrong! You've got a three-day delay on a Priority Gold."

"But there's some reason we're not getting. Something is missing from this picture . . ."

"We never should have tried to bargain with them, you know that? They offered it as a gift in the first place. We should have just taken it. Now they know it's really worth something! I'll go up there with a spade and dig the damned vine up myself, if I have to."

"No! You can't do that, not now. They'll know who took it, don't you see?"

"One more crime against the helpless Indians laid at the door of Spain. As if it mattered any more!" Mendoza turned on her heel to stare at me. Down at the other end of the arcade one of my brother friars put his head out in discreet inquiry.

It does matter! I dropped to a subvocal hiss. *It matters to them and it matters to me! I call them my beloved sons, but they know I've got the power to go up there and confiscate anything they have on any excuse at all because that's how it's always been done! Only I don't. They know Father Rubio won't do that to them. I've built up a cover identity as a kindly, honorable guy because I've got to live with these people for the next thirty years! You'll get your damn specimen and go away again into the sagebrush, but I've got a character to maintain!*

My God, she sneered, *He wants his little Indians to love him.*

Company policy, baby. It's easier to deal with mortals when they trust you. Something you used to understand. So just you try screwing with my cover identity! Just you try it and see what happens.

She widened her eyes at that, too furious for words, and I saw her knuckles go white; little chips of whitewash began falling from the walls. We both looked up at them and cooled down in a hurry.

Sorry. But I mean what I say, Mendoza. We handle this my way.

She threw her hands up in the air. *What are you going to do, then, smart guy? You have to do something.*

Day four of the Priority Gold, and Company Directive 081244-A anxiously inquired why no progress on previous trans-departmental request for facilitation?

Situation Report follows, I responded. *Please stand by.* Then I put on my walking sandals and set off up the canyon alone.

Before I had toiled more than halfway, though, I met Emidio coming in my direction. He didn't try to avoid me, but as he approached he looked down the canyon past me in the direction of the Mission. "Good morning, little Father," he called.

"Good morning, my son."

"Is your cousin lady with you?" He dropped his voice as he drew close.

"No, my son. We are alone."

"I need to speak with you, little Father, about the grapevine." He cleared his throat. "I know the lady must be very angry, and I am sorry. I don't mean to make you angry too, little Father, because I know she is your cousin—"

"I understand, my son, believe me. And I am not angry."

"Well then." He drew a deep breath. "This is the matter. The grapevines do not belong to me, nor to my father. They belong to our grandfather Diego. And he will not let us dig up the vine the lady wants."

"Why will he not?"

"He won't tell us. He just refuses. Don't be stupid, we told him. Father Rubio has been good to us, he has treated us fairly. Look at the fine pigs he has given us, we said. He just sits in the sun and rocks himself, and refuses us. And our grandmother came and touched his feet and cried, though she didn't say anything, but he wouldn't even look at her."

"I see."

"We have said everything we could say to him, but he will not let us dig up that vine. We tried to fool the lady twice by pretending to make mistakes (and that was a sin, little Father, and I'm sorry), but it didn't work. Somehow she knew. Then our grandfather—" he paused in obvious embarrassment. "I don't know how to say this, little Father – you know the old people are superstitious and still believe foolish things – I think he somehow has the idea that your cousin lady is a *nunasis*. Please don't take this the wrong way—"

"No, no, go on—"

"We have an old story about a spirit who walks on the mountains and wears a hat like hers, you see, throwing a shadow cold as death. I know it's stupid. Even so, Grandfather won't let us dig up that vine. Now, you might say, our grandfather is only an old man and a little bit crazy now, and we're strong, so he can be put aside as though he were a little baby; but if we did that, we would be breaking the commandment about honoring the old people. It seems to us that would be a worse sin than the white lady not getting what she wanted. What do you think, little Father?"

Boy, oh, boy. "This is very hard, my son," I said, and I meant it. "But you are right."

Emidio studied me in silence for a long moment, his eyes narrowed. "Thank you," he said at last. After another pause he added, "Is there anything we can do that will make the lady happy? She'll be angry with you, now."

I found myself laughing. "She will make my life a Purgatory, I can tell you," I said. "But I will offer it up for my sins. Go home, Emidio, and don't worry. Perhaps God will send a miracle."

1 wasn't laughing when I got back to the Mission, though, and when Mendoza came looking for me she saw my failure right away.

"No dice, huh?" She squinted evilly. "Well. This is no longer a matter of me and my poor little bonus now, Joseph. *The Company wants that vine.* I suggest you think of something fast or there are liable to be some dead Indians around here soon, pardon my indelicate phrasing."

"I'm working on it," I told her.

And I was. I went to the big leatherbound books that held the Mission records. I sat down in a corner of the scriptorium and went over them in minute detail.

1789 – here was the baptism of Diego Kasmali, age given as thirty years. 1790, marriage to Maria Conception, age not given. 1791 through 1810, a whole string of baptisms of little Kasmalis: Agustin, Xavier, Pablo, Juan Bautista, Maria, Dolores, Guadalupe, Dieguito, Marta, Tomas, Luisa, Bartolomeo. First Communion for Xavier Kasmali, 1796. One after the other, a string of little funerals: Agustin age two days, Pablo age three months six days, Juan Bautista age six days, Maria age two years . . . too sad to go on down the list, but not unusual. Confirmation for Xavier Kasmali, 1802. Xavier Kasmali married to Juana Catalina of the Dos Pueblos rancheria, age 18 years, 1812. Baptism of Emidio Kasmali, 1813. Baptism of Salvador Kasmali, 1814. Funeral of Juana Catalina, 1814. First Communions, Confirmations, Marriages, Baptisms, Extreme Unctions . . . not a sacrament missed. Really good Catholics.

Why the old, old woman was at Mass every single day of the year, rain or shine, though she was propped like a bundle of sticks in the shadows at the back of the church. Maria Conception, wife of Diego Kasmali. But Diego never, ever at Mass. Why not? On a desperate hunch I went to my transmitter and typed in a request for something unusual.

The reply came back: *Query: first please resolution Priority Gold status?*

Request relates Priority, I replied. *Resolving now. Requisition Sim ParaN Phenom re: Priority resolution?*

That gave them pause. They verified and counterverified my authority, they re-scanned the original orders and mulled over their implications. At least, I guessed they were doing that, as the blue screen flickered. Feeling I had them on the run, I pushed for a little extra, just for my own satisfaction: *Helpful Priority specify mutation. What? Why?*

Pause while they verified me again, then the bright letters crawled onscreen in a slow response:

Patent Black Elysium.

I fell back laughing, though it wasn't exactly funny. The rest of the message followed in a rapid burst: *S-P Requisition approved. Specify Tech support?*

I told them what I needed.

Estimate resolution time Priority Gold?

I told them how long it would take.

Expecting full specimen consign & report then, was the reply, and they signed off.

"Why don't they ever put convenient handles on these things?" grumbled Mendoza. She had one end of the transport trunk and a shovel; I had the other end of the trunk and the other shovel. It was long after midnight and we were struggling up the rocky defile that led to the Kasmali residence.

'Too much T-field drag," I explained.

"Well, you would think that an all-powerful cabal of scientists and business-men, with advance knowledge of every event in recorded history *and* infinite time in which to take every possible advantage of said events, *and* every possible technological resource at their command, *and* unlimited wealth—" Mendoza shifted the trunk again and we went on "– you'd think they could devise some-thing as simple as a recessed handle."

"They tried it. The recess cuts down on the available transport space inside," I told her.

"You're kidding me."

"No. I was part of a test shipment. Damn thing got me right in the third cervical vertebra."

"I might have known there'd be a reason."

"The Company has a reason for everything, Mendoza."

We came within earshot of the house, so conversation ended. There were three big dogs in the yard before the door. One slept undisturbed, but two raised their heads and began to growl. We set down the trunk. I opened it and from the close-packed contents managed to prize out the hush unit. The bigger of the dogs got to his feet, preparing to bark.

I switched on the unit. Good dog, what a sleepy doggie; he fell over with a woof and did not move again. The other dog dropped his head on his paws. Dog Number Three would not wake at all now, nor would any of the occupants of the house, not while the hush field was being generated.

I carried the unit up to the house and left it by the dogs, Mendoza dragging the trunk after me. We removed the box of golden altar vessels and set off up the hill with it.

The amazing mutated vine was pretty sorry-looking now, with most of its branches clipped off in the attempt to appease Mendoza. I hoped to God their well-meaning efforts hadn't killed it. Mendoza must have been thinking the same thing, but she just shrugged grimly. We began to dig.

We made a neat hole, small but very deep, just behind the trunk and singled slightly under it. There was no way to hide our disturbance of the earth, but fortunately the ground had already been so spaded up and trampled over that our work shouldn't be that obvious.

"How deep does this have to be?" I panted when we had gone about six feet and I was in the bottom passing spadefuls up to Mendoza.

"Not much deeper; I'd like it buried well below the root ball." She leaned in and peered.

"Well, how deep is that?" Before she could reply my spade hit something with a metallic clank. We halted.

Mendoza giggled nervously. "Jesus, don't tell me there's *already* buried treasure down there!"

I scraped a little with the spade. "There's something like a hook," I said. "And something else." I got the spade under it and launched it up out of the hole with one good heave. The whole mass fell on the other side of the dirt heap, out of my view. "It looked kind of round," I remarked.

"It looks kind of like a hat—" Mendoza told me cautiously, bending down and turning it over. Abruptly she yelled and danced back from it. I scrambled up out of the hole to see what was going on.

It was a hat, all right, or what was left of it; one of the hard-cured leather kind Spain had issued to her soldiers in the latter half of the last century. I remembered seeing them on the presidio personnel. Beside the hat, where my spade-toss had dislodged it, was the head that had been wearing it. Only a brown skull now, the eyes blind with black earth. Close to it was the hilt of a sword, the metallic thing I'd hit.

"Oh, *gross!*" Mendoza wrung her hands.

"Alas, poor Yorick," was all I could think of to say.

"Oh, God, how disgusting. Is the rest of him down there?"

I peered down into the hole. I could see a jawbone and pieces of what might have been cavalry boots. "Looks like it, I'm afraid."

"What do you suppose he's doing down there?" Mendoza fretted, from behind the handkerchief she had clapped over her mouth and nose.

"Not a damn thing nowadays," I guessed, doing a quick scan of the bones. "Take it easy: no pathogens left. This guy's been dead a long time."

"Sixty years, by any chance?" Mendoza's voice sharpened.

"They must have planted him with the grapevine," I agreed. In the thoughtful silence that followed I began to snicker. I couldn't help myself. I leaned back and had myself a nice sprawling guffaw.

"I fail to see what's so amusing," said Mendoza.

"Sorry. Sorry. I was just wondering: do you suppose you could cause a favorable mutation in something by planting a dead Spaniard under it?"

"Of course not, you idiot, not unless his sword was radioactive or something."

"No, of course not. What about those little wild yeast spores in the bloom on the grapes, though? You think they might be influenced somehow by the close proximity of a gentleman of Old Castile?"

"What are you talking about?" Mendoza took a step closer.

"This isn't a cancer cure, you know." I waved my hand at the vine-stock, black against the stars. "I found out why the Company is so eager to get hold of your Favorable Mutation, kid. This is the grape that makes Black Elysium."

"The dessert wine?" Mendoza cried.

"The very expensive dessert wine. The hallucinogenic-controlled-substance dessert wine. The absinthe of the twenty-fourth century. The one the Company holds the patent on. That stuff. Yeah."

Stunned silence from my fellow immortal creature. I went on:

"I was just thinking, you know, about all those decadent technocrats sitting around in the future getting bombed on an elixir produced from . . ."

"So it gets discovered here, in 1844," said Mendoza at last. "It isn't genetically engineered cultivar at all. And the wild spores somehow came from. . . ?"

"But nobody else will ever know the truth, because we're removing every trace of this vine from the knowledge of mortal men, see?" I explained. "Root and branch and all."

"I'd sure better get that bonus," Mendoza reflected.

"Don't push your luck. You aren't supposed to know." I took my shovel and clambered back into the hole. "Come on, let's get the rest of him out of here. The show must go on."

Two hours later there was a tidy heap of brown bones and rusted sled moldering away in a new hiding place, and a tidy sum in gold plate occupying the former burial site. We filled in the hole, set up the rest of the equipment we'd brought, tested it, camouflaged it, turned it on and hurried away back down the canyon to the Mission, taking the hush unit with us. I made it in time for Matins.

News travels fast in a small town. By nine there were Indians, and some of the *Gentes de Razon* too, running in from all directions to tell us that the Blessed Virgin had appeared in the Kasmalis' garden. Even if I hadn't known already, I would have been tipped off by the fact that old Maria Conception did not show up for morning Mass.

By the time we got up there, the bishop and I and all my fellow friars and Mendoza, a cloud of dust hung above the dirt track from all the traffic. The Kasmalis' tomatoes and corn had been trampled by the milling crowd. People ran everywhere, waving pieces of grapevine; the oilier plants had been stripped as bare as the special one. The rancheros watched from horseback, or urged their mounts closer across the careful beds of peppers and beans.

Around the one vine, the family had formed a tight circle. Some of them watched Emidio and Salvador, who were digging frantically, already about five feet down in the hole; others stared unblinking at the floating image of the Virgin of Guadalupe who smiled upon them from midair above the vine. She was complete in every detail, nicely three-dimensional and accompanied by heavenly music. Actually it was a long tape loop of Ralph Vaughan Williams's *Fantasia on a Theme by Thomas Tallis,* which nobody would recognize because it hadn't been composed yet.

"Little Father!" One of the wives caught me by my robe. "It's the Mother of God! She told us to dig up the vine, she said there was treasure buried underneath!"

"Has she told you anything else?" I inquired, making the sign of the cross. My brother friars were falling to their knees in raptures, beginning to sing the Ave Maria; the bishop was sobbing.

"No, not since this morning," the wife told me. "Only the beautiful music has gone on and on."

Emidio looked up and noticed me for the first time. He stopped shoveling for a moment, staring at me, and a look of dark speculation crossed his face. Then his shovel was moving again, clearing away the earth, and more earth, and more earth.

At my side, Mendoza turned away her face in disgust. But I was watching the old couple, who stood a little way back from the rest of the family. They clung to each other in mute terror and had no eyes for the smiling Virgin. It was the bottom of the ever-deepening hole they watched, as birds watch a snake.

And I watched them. Old Diego was bent and toothless now, but sixty years ago he'd had teeth, all right; sixty years ago his race hadn't yet learned never to fight back against its conquerors. Maria Conception, what had she been sixty years ago when those vines were planted? Not a dried-up shuffling old thing back then. She might have been a beauty, and maybe a careless beauty.

The old bones and the rusting steel could have told you, sixty years ago. Had he been a handsome young captain with smooth ways, or just a soldier who took what he wanted? Whatever he'd been, or done, he'd wound up buried under that vine, and only Diego and Maria knew he was there. All those years, through the children and grandchildren and great-grandchildren, he'd been there. Diego never coming to Mass because of a sin he couldn't confess. Maria never missing Mass, praying for someone.

Maybe that was the way it had happened. Nobody would ever tell the story, I was fairly sure. But it was clear that Diego and Maria, alone of all those watching, did not expect to see treasure come out of that hole in the ground.

So when the first glint of gold appeared, and then the chalice and altar plate were brought up, their old faces were a study in confusion.

"The treasure!" cried Salvador. "Look!"

And the rancheros spurred their horses through the crowd to get a better look, lashing the Indians out of the way; but I touched the remote hidden in my sleeve and the Blessed Virgin spoke, in a voice as sweet and immortal as a synthesizer:

"This, my beloved children, is the altar plate that was lost from the Church at San Carlos Borromeo, long ago in the time of the pirates. My beloved Son has caused it to be found here as a sign to you all that ALL SINS ARE FORGIVEN!"

I touched the remote again and the Holy Apparition winked out like a soap bubble, and the beautiful music fell silent.

Old Diego pushed his way forward to the hole and looked in. There was nothing else there in the hole now, nothing at all. Maria came timidly to his side and she looked in too. They remained there staring a long time, unnoticed by the mass of the crowd, who were watching the dispute that had already erupted over the gold.

The bishop had pounced on it like a duck on a June bug, as they say, asserting the right of Holy Mother Church to her lost property. Emidio and Salvador had let it be snatched from them with hard patient smiles. One of the *Gentes de Razon* actually got off his horse to tell the bishop that the true provenance of the items had to be decided by the authorities in Mexico City, and until they could be contacted the treasure had better be kept under lock and key at the alcalde's house. Blessed Virgin? Yes, there had seemed to be an apparition of some kind; but then again, perhaps it had been a trick of the light.

The argument moved away down the hill – the bishop had a good grip on the gold and kept walking with it, so almost everyone had to follow him. I went to stand beside Diego and Maria, in the ruins of their garden.

"She forgave us," whispered Diego.

"A great weight of sin has been lifted from you today, my children," I told them. "Rejoice, for Christ loves you both. Come to the church with me now and I will celebrate a special Mass in your honor."

I led them away with me, one on either arm. Unseen behind us, Mendoza advanced on the uprooted and forgotten vine with a face like a lioness kept from her prey.

Well, the old couple made out all right, anyway. I saw to it that they got new grapevines and food from the Mission supplies to tide the family over until their garden recovered. Within a couple of years they passed away, one after the other, and were buried reasonably near one another in the consecrated ground of the Mission cemetery, in which respect they were luckier than the unknown captain from Castile, or wherever he'd come from.

They never got the golden treasure, but being Indians there had never been any question that they would. Their descendants lived on and multiplied in the area, doing particularly well after the coming of the Yankees, who (to the mortification of the *Gentes de Razon)* couldn't tell an Indian from a Spanish Mexican and lumped them all together under the common designation of Greaser, treating one no worse than the other.

Actually I never kept track of what happened to the gold. The title dispute dragged on for years, I think, with the friars swearing there had been a miracle and the rancheros swearing there hadn't been. The gold may have been returned to Carmel, or it may have gone to Mexico City, or it may have gone into a trunk underneath the alcalde's bed, I didn't care; it was all faked Company-issue reproductions anyway. The bishop died and the Yankees came and were the new conquerors, and maybe nothing ever did get resolved either way.

But Mendoza got her damned vine and her bonus, so she was as happy as she ever is. The Company got its patent on Black Elysium secured. I lived on at the Mission for years and years before (apparently) dying of venerable old age and (apparently) being buried in the same cemetery as Diego and Maria. God forgave us all, I guess, and I moved on to less pleasant work.

Sometimes, when I'm in that part of the world, I stop in as a tourist and check out my grave. It's the nicest of the many I've had, except maybe for that crypt in Hollywood. Well, well; life goes on.

Mine does anyway.

UNDER SIEGE

George R.R. Martin

George R.R. Martin is an American writer of fantasy and science fiction best known for his *A Song of Ice and Fire* epic fantasy series, now the HBO original series *Game of Thrones*. According to myth, he began his career selling monster stories to other neighborhood children for pennies. Subsequent work has won many awards, including the Hugo and World Fantasy awards. In this story, first published in *Omni* magazine in 1985, a wise-cracking mutant travels from the future to save the world from cataclysmic war.

On the high ramparts of Vargön, Colonel Bengt Anttonen stood alone and watched phantasms race across the ice.

The world was snow and wind and bitter, burning cold. The winter sea had frozen hard around Helsinki, and in its icy grip it held the six island citadels of the great fortress called Sveaborg. The wind was a knife drawn from a sheath of ice. It cut through Anttonen's uniform, chafed at his cheeks, brought tears to his eyes and froze them as they trickled down his face. The wind howled around the towering gray granite walls, forced its way through doors and cracks and gun emplacements, insinuated itself everywhere. Out upon the frozen sea, it snapped and shrieked at the Russian artillery, and sent puffs of snow from the drifts running and swirling over the ice like strange white beasts, ghostly animals all asparkle, wearing first one shape and then another, changing constantly as they ran.

They were creatures as malleable as Anttonen's thoughts. He wondered what form they would take next and where they were running to so swiftly, these misty children of snow and wind. Perhaps they could be taught to attack the Russians. He smiled, savoring the fancy of the snow beasts unleashed upon the enemy. It was a strange, wild thought. Colonel Bengt Anttonen had never been an imaginative man before, but of late his mind had often been taken by such whimsies.

Anttonen turned his face into the wind again, welcoming the chill, the numbing cold. He wanted it to cool his fury, to cut into the heart of him and freeze the passions that seethed there. He wanted to be numb. The cold had turned even the turbulent sea into still and silent ice; now let it conquer the turbulence within Bengt Anttonen. He opened his mouth, exhaled a long plume of breath that rose from his reddened cheeks like steam, inhaled a draught of frigid air that went down like liquid oxygen.

But panic came in the wake of that thought. Again, it was happening again.

What was liquid oxygen? Cold, he knew somehow; colder than the ice, colder than this wind. Liquid oxygen was bitter and white, and it steamed and flowed. He knew it, knew it as certainly as he knew his own name. But *how*?

Anttonen turned from the ramparts. He walked with long swift strides, his hand touching the hilt of his sword as if it could provide some protection against the demons that had invaded his mind. The other officers were right; he was going mad, surely. He had proved it this afternoon at the staff meeting.

The meeting had gone very badly, as they all had of late. As always, Anttonen had raised his voice against the others, hopelessly, stupidly. He was right, he *knew* that. Yet he knew also that he could not convince them, and that each word further undermined his status, further damaged his career.

Jägerhorn had brought it on once again. Colonel F. A. Jägerhorn was everything that Anttonen was not; dark and handsome, polished and politic, an aristocrat with an aristocrat's control. Jägerhorn had important connections, had influential relatives, had a charmed career. And, most importantly, Jägerhorn had the confidence of Vice-Admiral Carl Olof Cronstedt, commandant of Sveaborg.

At the meeting, Jägerhorn had had a sheaf of reports.

"The reports are wrong," Anttonen had insisted. "The Russians do not outnumber us. And they have barely forty guns, sir. Sveaborg mounts ten times that number."

Cronstedt seemed shocked by Anttonen's tone, his certainty, his insistence. Jägerhorn simply smiled. "Might I ask how you come by this intelligence, Colonel Anttonen?" he asked.

That was the question Bengt Anttonen could never answer. "I know," he said stubbornly.

Jägerhorn rattled the papers in his hand. "My own intelligence comes from Lieutenant Klick, who is in Helsinki and has direct access to reliable reports of enemy plans, movements, and numbers." He looked to Vice-Admiral Cronstedt. "I submit, sir, that this information is a good deal more reliable than Colonel Anttonen's mysterious certainties. According to Klick, the Russians outnumber us already, and General Suchtelen will soon be receiving sufficient reinforcements to enable him to launch a major assault. Furthermore, they have a formidable amount of artillery on hand. Certainly more than the forty pieces that Colonel Anttonen would have us believe the extent of their armament."

Cronstedt was nodding, agreeing. Even then Anttonen could not be silent. "Sir," he insisted, "Klick's reports must be discounted. The man cannot be trusted. Either he is in the pay of the enemy or they are deluding him."

Cronstedt frowned. "That is a grave charge, Colonel."

"Klick is a fool and a damned Anjala traitor!"

Jägerhorn bristled at that, and Cronstedt and a number of junior officers looked plainly aghast. "Colonel," the commandant said, "it is well known that Colonel Jägerhorn has relatives in the Anjala League. Your comments are offensive. Our situation here is perilous enough without my officers fighting among themselves over petty political differences. You will offer an apology at once."

Given no choice, Anttonen had tendered an awkward apology. Jägerhorn accepted with a patronizing nod.

Cronstedt went back to the papers. "Very persuasive," he said, "and very alarming. It is as I have feared. We have come to a hard place." Plainly his mind was made up. It was futile to argue further. It was at times like this that Bengt Anttonen most wondered what madness had possessed him. He would go to staff meetings determined to be circumspect and politic, and no sooner would he be seated than a strange arrogance would seize him. He argued long past the point of wisdom; he denied obvious facts, confirmed in written reports from reliable sources; he spoke out of turn and made enemies on every side.

"No, sir," he said, "I beg of you, disregard Klick's intelligence. Sveaborg is vital to the spring counteroffensive. We have nothing to fear if we can hold out until the ice melts. Once the sea lanes are open, Sweden will send help."

Vice-Admiral Cronstedt's face was drawn and weary, an old man's face. "How many times must we go over this? I grow tired of your argumentative attitude, and I am quite aware of Sveaborg's importance to the spring offensive. The facts are plain. Our defenses are flawed, and the ice makes our walls accessible from all sides. Sweden's armies are being routed—"

"We know that only from the newspapers the Russians allow us, sir," Anttonen blurted. "French and Russian papers. Such news is unreliable."

Cronstedt's patience was exhausted. "Quiet!" he said, slapping the table with an open palm. "I have had enough of your intransigence, Colonel Anttonen. I respect your patriotic fervor, but not your judgment. In the future, when I require your opinion, I shall ask for it. Is that clear?"

"Yes, sir," Anttonen had said.

Jägerhorn smiled. "If I may proceed?"

The rebuke had been as smarting as the cold winter wind. It was no wonder Anttonen had felt driven to the cold solitude of the battlements afterwards.

By the time he returned to his quarters, Bengt Anttonen's mood was bleak and confused. Darkness was falling, he knew. Over the frozen sea, over Sveaborg, over Sweden and Finland. And over America, he thought. Yet the afterthought left him sick and dizzy. He sat heavily on his cot, cradling his head in his hands. America, America, what madness was that, what possible difference could the struggle between Sweden and Russia make to that infant nation so far away?

Rising, he lit a lamp, as if light would drive the troubling thoughts away, and splashed some stale water on his face from the basin atop the modest dresser. Behind the basin was the mirror he used for shaving; slightly warped and dulled by corrosion, but serviceable. As he dried his big, bony hands, he found himself staring at his own face, the features at once so familiar and so oddly, frighteningly strange. He had unruly graying hair, dark gray eyes, a narrow straight nose, slightly sunken cheeks, a square chin. He was too thin, almost gaunt. It was a stubborn, common, plain face. The face he had worn all his life. Long ago, Bengt Anttonen had grown resigned to the way he looked. Until recently, he scarcely gave his appearance any thought. Yet now he stared at himself, unblinking, and felt a disturbing fascination welling up inside him, a sense of satisfaction, a pleasure in the cast of his image that was alien and troubling.

Such vanity was sick, unmanly, another sign of madness. Anttonen wrenched his gaze from the mirror. He lay himself down with a will.

For long moments he could not sleep. Fancies and visions danced against his closed eyelids, sights as fantastic as the phantom animals fashioned by the wind:

flags he did not recognize, walls of polished metal, great storms of fire, men and women as hideous as demons asleep in beds of burning liquid. And then, suddenly, the thoughts were gone, peeled off like a layer of burned skin. Bengt Anttonen sighed uneasily, and turned in his sleep . . .

*

. . . before the awareness is always the pain, and the pain comes first, the only reality in a still quiet empty world beyond sensation. For a second, an hour I do not know where I am and I am afraid. And then the knowledge comes to me; returning, I am returning, in the return is always pain, I do not want to return, but I must. I want the sweet clean purity of ice and snow, the bracing touch of the winter wind, the healthy lines of Bengt's face. But it fades, fades though I scream and clutch for it, crying, wailing. It fades, fades, and then is gone.

I sense motion, a stirring all around me as the immersion fluid ebbs away. My face is exposed first. I suck in air through my wide nostrils, spit the tubes out of my bleeding mouth. When the fluid falls below my ears, I hear a gurgling, a greedy sucking sound. The vampire machines feed on the juices of my womb, the black blood of my second life. The cold touch of air on my skin pains me. I try not to scream, manage to hold the noise down to a whimper.

Above, the top of my tank is coated by a thin ebony film that has clung to the polished metal. I can see my reflection. I'm a stirring sight, nostril hairs aquiver on my noseless face, my right cheek bulging with a swollen greenish tumor. Such a handsome devil. I smile, showing a triple row of rotten teeth, fresh new incisors pushing up among them like sharpened stakes in a field of yellow toadstools. I wait for release. The tank is too damned small, a coffin. I am buried alive, and the fear is a palpable weight upon me. They do not like me. What if they just leave me in here to suffocate and die? "Out!" I whisper, but no one hears.

Finally the lid lifts and the orderlies are there. Rafael and Slim. Big strapping fellows, blurred white colossi with flags sewn above the pockets of their uniforms. I cannot focus on their faces. My eyes are not so good at the best of times, and especially bad just after a return. I know the dark one is Rafe, though, and it is he who reaches down and unhooks the IV tubes and the telemetry, while Slim gives me my injection. Ahhh. Good. The hurt fades. I force my hands to grasp the sides of the tank. The metal feels strange; the motion is clumsy, deliberate, my body slow to respond. "What took you so long?" I ask.

"Emergency," says Slim. "Rollins." He is a testy, laconic sort, and he doesn't like me. To learn more, I would have to ask question after question. I don't have the strength. I concentrate instead on pulling myself to a sitting position. The room is awash with a bright blue-white fluorescent light. My eyes water after so long in darkness. Maybe the orderlies think I'm crying with joy to be back. They're big but not too bright. The air has an astringent, sanitized smell and the hard coolness of air conditioning. Rafe lifts me up from the coffin, the fifth silvery casket in a row of six, each hooked up to the computer banks that loom around us. The other coffins are all empty now. I am the last vampire to rise this night, I think. Then I remember. Four of them are gone, have been gone for a long time. There is only Rollins and myself, and something has happened to Rollins.

They set me in my chair and Slim moves behind me, rolls me past the empty caskets and up the ramps to debriefing. "Rollins," I ask him.

"We lost him."

I didn't like Rollins. He was even uglier than me, a wizened little homunculus with a swollen, oversized cranium and a distorted torso without arms or legs. He had real big eyes, lidless, so he could never close them.

Even asleep, he looked like he was staring at you. And he had no sense of humor. No goddamned sense of humor at all. When you're a geek, you got to have a sense of humor. But whatever his faults, Rollins was the only one left, besides me. Gone now. I feel no grief, only a numbness.

The debriefing room is cluttered but somehow impersonal. They wait for me on the other side of the table. The orderlies roll me up opposite them and depart. The table is a long Formica barrier between me and my superiors, maybe a *cordon sanitaire*. They cannot let me get too close, after all, I might be contagious. They are normals. I am . . . what am I? When they conscripted me, I was classified as a HM_3. Human Mutation, third category. Or a hum-three, in the vernacular. The hum-ones are the nonviables, stillborns and infant deaths and living veggies. We got millions of 'em. The hum-twos are viable but useless, all the guys with extra toes and webbed hands and funny eyes. Got thousands of them. But us hum-threes are a fucking *elite*, so they tell us. That's when they draft us. Down here, inside the Graham Project bunker, we get new names. Old Charlie Graham himself used to call us his "timeriders" before he croaked, but that's too romantic for Major Salazar. Salazar prefers the official government term: G. C., for Graham Chrononaut. The orderlies and grunts turned G. C. into "geek' of course, and we turned it right back on 'em, me and Nan and Creeper, when they were still with us. *They* had a terrific sense of humor, now. The killer geeks, we called ourselves. Six little killer geeks riding the timestream biting the heads off vast chickens of probability. Heigh-ho.

And then there was one.

Salazar is pushing papers around on the table. He looks sick. Under his dark complexion I can see an unhealthy greenish tinge, and the blood vessels in his nose have burst beneath the skin. None of us are in good shape down here, but Salazar looks worse than most. He's been gaining weight, and it looks bad on him. His uniforms are all too tight now, and there won't be any fresh ones. They've closed down the commissaries and the mills, and in a few years we'll all be wearing rags. I've told Salazar he ought to diet, but no one will listen to a geek, except when the subject is chickens. "Well," Salazar says to me, his voice snapping. A hell of a way to start a debriefing. Three years ago, when it began, he was full of starch and vinegar, very correct and military, but even the Maje has no time left for decorum now.

"What happened to Rollins?" I ask.

Doctor Veronica Jacobi is seated next to Salazar. She used to be chief head-shrinker down here, but since Graham Crackers went and expired she's been heading up the whole scientific side of the show. "Death trauma," she says, professionally. "Most likely, his host was killed in action."

I nod. Old story. Sometimes the chickens bite back. "He accomplish anything?"

"Not that we've noticed," Salazar says glumly.

The answer I expected. Rollins had gotten rapport with some ignorant grunt of a footsoldier in the army of Charles XII. I had this droll mental picture of him marching the guy up to his loon of a teenaged king and trying to tell the boy to stay away from Poltava. Charles probably hanged him on the spot though, come to think of it, it had to be something quicker, or else Rollins would have had time to disengage.

"Your report" prompts Salazar.

"Right, Maje," I say lazily. He hates to be called Maje, though not so much as he hated Sally, which was what Creeper used to call him. Us killer geeks are an insolent lot. "It's no good," I tell them. "Cronstedt is going to meet with General Suchtelen and negotiate for surrender. Nothing Bengt says sways him one damned bit. I been pushing too hard. Bengt thinks he's going crazy. I'm afraid he may crack."

"All timeriders take that risk," Jacobi says. "The longer you stay in rapport, the stronger your influence grows on the host, and the more likely it becomes that your presence will be felt. Few hosts can deal with that perception." Ronnie has a nice voice, and she's always polite to me. Well-scrubbed and tall and calm and even friendly, and above all ineffably polite. I wonder if she'd be as polite if she knew that she'd figured prominently in my masturbation fantasies ever since we'd been down here? They only put five women into the Cracker Box, with thirty-two men and six geeks, and she's by far the most pleasant to contemplate.

Creeper liked to contemplate her, too. He even bugged her bedroom, to watch her in action. She never knew. Creeper had a talent for that stuff, and he'd rig up these tiny little audio-video units on his workbench and plant them everywhere. He said that if he couldn't live life, at least he was going to watch it. One night he invited me into his room, when Ronnie was entertaining big, red-haired Captain Halliburton, the head of the base security, and her fella in those early days. I watched, yeah; got to confess that I watched. But afterward I got angry. Told Creeper he had no right to spy on Ronnie, or on any of them. "They make us spy on our hosts," he said, "right inside their fucking *heads*, you geek. Turnabout is fair play." I told him it was different, but I got so mad I couldn't explain why.

It was the only fight Creeper and me ever had. In the long run, it didn't mean much. He went on watching, without me. They never caught the little sneak, but it didn't matter, one day he went timeriding and didn't come back. Big strong Captain Halliburton died too, caught too many rads on those security sweeps, I guess. As far as I know, Creeper's hookup is still in place; from time to time I've thought about going in and taking a peek, to see if Ronnie has herself a new lover. But I haven't. I really don't want to know. Leave me with my fantasies and my wet dreams; they're a lot better anyway.

Salazar's fat fingers drum upon the table. "Give us a full report on your activities," he says curtly.

I sigh and give them what they want, everything in boring detail. When I'm done, I say, "Jägerhorn is the key to the problem. He's got Cronstedt's ear. Anttonen don't."

Salazar is frowning. "If only you could establish rapport with Jägerhorn," he grumbles. What a futile whiner. He knows that's impossible.

"You takes what you gets," I tell him. "If you're going to wish impossible wishes, why stop at Jägerhorn? Why not Cronstedt? Hell, why not the god-damned *Czar?*"

"He's right, Major," Veronica says. "We ought to be grateful that we've got a link with Anttonen. At least he's a colonel. That's better than we did in any of the other target periods."

Salazar is still unhappy. He's a military historian by trade. He thought this would be easy when they transferred him out from West Point, or what was left of it. "Anttonen is peripheral," he declares. "We must reach the key figures. Your chrononauts are giving me footnotes, bystanders, the wrong men in the wrong place at the wrong time. It is impossible."

"You knew the job was dangerous when you took it," I say. A killer geek quoting Superchicken; I'd get thrown out of the union if they knew. "We don't get to pick and choose."

The Maje scowls at me. I yawn. "I'm tired of this," I say. "I want something to eat. Some ice cream. I want some rocky road ice cream. Seems funny, don't it? All that goddamned ice, and I come back wanting ice cream." There is no ice cream, of course. There hasn't been any ice cream for half a generation, anywhere in the godforsaken mess they call a world. But Nan used to tell me about it. Nan was the oldest geek, the only one born before the big crash, and she had lots of stories about the way things used to be. I liked it best when she talked about ice cream. It was smooth and cold and sweet, she said. It melted on your tongue, and filled your mouth with liquid, delicious cold. Sometimes she would recite the flavors for us, as solemnly as Chaplain Todd reading his Bible: vanilla and strawberry and chocolate, fudge swirl and praline, rum raisin and heavenly hash, banana and orange sherbet and mint chocolate chip, pistachio and butterscotch and coffee and cinnamon and butter pecan. Creeper used to make up flavors to poke fun at her, but there was no getting to Nan. She just added his inventions to her list, and spoke fondly thereafter of anchovy almond and liver chip and radiation ripple, until I couldn't tell the real flavors from the made-up ones any more, and didn't really care.

Nan was the first we lost. Did they have ice cream in St Petersburg back in 1917? I hope they did. I hope she got a bowl or two before she died.

Major Salazar is still talking, I realize. He has been talking for some time, ". . . our last chance now," he is saying. He begins to babble about Sveaborg, about the importance of what we are doing here, about the urgent need to *change* something somehow, to prevent the Soviet Union from ever coming into existence, and thus forestall the war that has laid the world to waste. I've heard it all before, I know it all by heart. The Maje has terminal verbal diarrhea, and I'm not so dumb as I look.

It was all Graham Cracker's idea, the last chance to win the war or maybe just save ourselves from the plagues and bombs and the poisoned winds. But the Maje was the historian, so he got to pick all the targets, when the computers had done their probability analysis. He had six geeks and he got six tries. "Nexus points," he called 'em. Critical points in history. Of course, some were better than others. Rollins got the Great Northern War, Nan got the Revolution, Creeper got to go all the way back to Ivan the Terrible, and I got Sveaborg. Impregnable, invincible Sveaborg. Gibraltar of the North.

"There is no reason for Sveaborg to surrender," the Maje is saying. It is his own ice-cream litany. History and tactics give him the sort of comfort that butter brickle gave to Nan. "The garrison is seven thousand strong, vastly outnumbering the besieging Russians. The artillery inside the Fortress is much superior. There is plenty of ammunition, plenty of food. If Sveaborg only holds out until the sea lanes are open, Sweden will launch its counteroffensive and the siege will be broken easily. The entire course of the war may change! You must make Cronstedt listen to reason."

"If I could just lug back a history text and let him read what they say about him, I'm sure he'd jump through flaming hoops," I say. I've had enough of this. "I'm tired," I announce. "I want some food." Suddenly, for no apparent reason, I feel like crying. "I want something to eat, damn it, I don't want to talk anymore, you hear, I want *something to eat.*"

Salazar glares, but Veronica hears the stress in my voice, and she is up and moving around the table. "Easy enough to arrange," she says to me, and to the Maje, "We've accomplished all we can for now. Let me get him some food." Salazar grunts, but he dares not object. Veronica wheels me away, toward the commissary.

Over stale coffee and a plate of mystery meat and overcooked vegetables, she consoles me. She's not half bad at it; a pro, after all. Maybe, in the old days, she wouldn't have been considered especially striking – I've seen the old magazines, after all, even down here we have our old *Playboys,* our old video tapes, our old novels, our old record albums, our old funny books, nothing *new* of course, nothing recent, but lots and lots of the old junk. I ought to know, I practically mainline the stuff; when I'm not flailing around inside Bengt's cranium, I'm planted in front of my tube, running some old TV show or a movie, maybe reading a paperback at the same time, trying to imagine what it would be like to live back then, before they screwed up everything. So I know all about the old standards, and maybe it's true that Ronnie ain't up to, say, Bo or Marilyn or Brigitte or Garbo.

Still, she's nicer to look at than anybody else down in this damned septic tank. And the rest of us don't quite measure up either. Creeper wasn't no Groucho, no matter how hard he tried; me, I look just like Jimmy Cagney, but the big green tumor and all the extra yellow teeth and the want of a nose spoil the effect, just a little.

I push my fork away with the meal half-eaten. "It has no taste. Back then, food had *taste.*"

Veronica laughs. "You're lucky. You get to taste it. For the rest of us, this is all there is."

"Lucky? Ha-ha. I know the difference, Ronnie. You don't. Can you miss something you never had?" I'm sick of talking about it, though; I'm sick of it all. "You want to play chess?"

She smiles and gets up in search of our set. An hour later, she's won the first game and we're starting the second. There are about a dozen chess players down here in the Cracker Box; now that Graham and Creeper are gone, I can beat all of them except Ronnie. The funny thing is, back in 1808 I could probably be world champion. Chess has come a long way in the last two hundred years, and I've memorized openings that those old guys never even dreamed of.

"There's more to the game than book openings," Veronica says, and I realize I've been talking aloud.

"I'd still win," I insist. "Hell, those guys have been dead for centuries, how much fight can they put up?"

She smiles, and moves a knight. "Check," she says.

I realize that I've lost again. "Some day I've got to learn to play this game," I say. "Some world champion."

Veronica begins to put the pieces back in the box. "This Sveaborg business is a kind of chess game too," she says conversationally, "a chess game across time, us and the Swedes against the Russians and the Finnish nationalists. What move do you think we should make against Cronstedt?"

"Why did I know that the conversation was going to come back to that?" I say. "Damned if I know. I suppose the Maje has an idea."

She nods. Her face is serious now. Pale soft face, framed by dark hair. "A desperate idea. These are desperate times."

What would it be like if I did succeed, I wonder? If I changed something? What would happen to Veronica and the Maje and Rafe and Slim and all the rest of them? What would happen to *me*, lying there in my coffin full of darkness? There are theories, of course, but no one really knows. "I'm a desperate man, ma'am," I say to her, "ready for any desperate measures. Being subtle sure hasn't done diddly-squat. Let's hear it. What do I gotta get Bengt to do now? Invent the machine gun? Defect to the Russkis? Expose his privates on the battlements? What?"

She tells me.

I'm dubious. "Maybe it'll work," I say. "More likely, it'll get Bengt slung into the deepest goddamned dungeon that place has. They'll really think he's nuts. Jägerhorn might just shoot him outright."

"No, she says. "In his own way, Jägerhorn is an idealist. A man of principle. I agree, it is a chancy move. But you don't win chess games without taking chances. Will you do it?"

She has such a nice smile; I think she likes me. I shrug. "Might as well," I say. "Can't dance."

*

". . . shall be allowed to dispatch two couriers to the King, the one by the northern, the other by the southern road. They shall be furnished with passports and safeguards, and every possible facility shall be given them for accomplishing their journey. Done at the island of Lonan, 6 April, 1808."

The droning voice of the officer reading the agreement stopped suddenly, and the staff meeting was deathly quiet. A few of the Swedish officers stirred uneasily in their seats, but no one spoke.

Vice-Admiral Cronstedt rose slowly. "This is the agreement," he said. "In view of our perilous position, it is better than we could have hoped for. We have used a third of our powder already, our defenses are exposed to attack from all sides because of the ice, we are outnumbered and forced to support a large number of fugitives who rapidly consume our provisions. General Suchtelen might have demanded our immediate surrender. By the grace of God, he did not. Instead we have been allowed to retain three of Sveaborg's six islands, and will regain two of the others, should five Swedish ships-of-the-line arrive to aid us before the third of May. If Sweden fails us, we must surrender. Yet the fleet shall be restored to Sweden at the conclusion of the war, and this immediate truce will prevent any further loss of life."

Cronstedt sat down. At his side, Colonel Jägerhorn came crisply to his feet. "In the event the Swedish ships do not arrive on time, we must make plans for an orderly surrender of the garrison." He launched into a discussion of the details.

Bengt Anttonen sat quietly. He had expected the news, had somehow known it was coming, but it was no less dismaying for all that. Cronstedt and Jägerhorn had negotiated a disaster. It was foolish. It was craven. It was hopelessly doomed. Immediate surrender of Wester-Svartö, Langorn, and Oster-Lilla-Svartö, the rest of the garrison to come later, capitulation deferred for a meaningless month. History would revile them. School children would curse their names. And he was helpless.

When the meeting at last ended, the others rose to depart. Anttonen rose with them, determined to be silent, to leave the room quietly for once, let them sell Sveaborg for thirty pieces of silver if they would. But as he led to turn, the compulsion seized him, and he went instead to where Cronstedt and Jägerhorn lingered. They both watched him approach. In their eyes, Anttonen thought he could see a weary resignation.

"You must not do this," he said heavily.

"It is done," Cronstedt replied. "The subject is not open for further discussion, Colonel. You have been warned. Go about your duties." He climbed to his feet, turned to go.

"The Russians are cheating you," Anttonen blurted.

Cronstedt stopped and looked at him.

"Admiral, please, you must listen to me. This provision, this agreement that we will retain the fortress if five ships-of-the-line reach us by the third of May, it is a fraud. The ice will not have melted by the third of May. No ship will be able to reach us. The armistice agreement provides that the ships must have entered Sveaborg's harbor by noon on the third of May. General Suchtelen will use the time afforded by the truce to move his guns and gain control of the sea approaches. Any ship attempting to reach Sveaborg will come under heavy attack. And there is more. The messengers you are sending to the King, sir, they –" Cronstedt's face was ice and granite. He held up a hand. "I have heard enough. Colonel Jägerhorn, arrest this madman." He gathered up his papers, refusing to look Anttonen in the face, and strode angrily from the room.

"Colonel Anttonen, you are under arrest," Jägerhorn said, with surprising gentleness in his voice. "Don't resist, I warn you, that will only make it worse."

Anttonen turned to face the other colonel. His heart was sick. "You will not listen. None of you will listen. Do you know what you are doing?"

"I think I do," Jägerhorn said.

Anttonen reached out and grabbed him by the front of his uniform. "You do *not*. You think I don't know what you are, Jägerhorn? You're a nationalist, damn you. This is the great age of nationalism. You and your Anjala League, your damned Finnlander noblemen, you're all Finnish nationalists. You resent Sweden's domination. The Czar has promised you that Finland will be an autonomous state under his protection, so you have thrown off your loyalty to the Swedish crown."

Colonel F. A. Jägerhorn blinked. A strange expression flickered across his face before he regained his composure. "You cannot know that," he said. "No one knows the terms – I—"

Anttonen shook him bodily. "History is going to laugh at you, Jägerhorn. Sweden will lose this war, because of you, because of Sveaborg's surrender, and you'll get your wish, Finland will become an autonomous state under the Czar. But it will be no freer than it is now, under Sweden. You'll swap your King like a secondhand chair at a flea market, for the butchers of the Great Wrath, and gain nothing by the transaction."

"Like a . . . a market for fleas? What is that?"

Anttonen scowled. "A flea market, a flea . . . I don't know," he said. He released Jägerhorn, turned away. "Dear God, I do know. It is a place where . . . where things are sold and traded. A fair. It has nothing to do with fleas, but it is full of strange machines, strange smells." He ran his fingers through his hair, fighting not to scream. "Jägerhorn, my head is full of demons. Dear God, I must confess. Voices, I hear voices day and night, even as the French girl, Joan, the warrior maid. I know things that will come to pass." He looked into Jägerhorn's eyes, saw the fear there, and held his hands up, entreating now. "It is no choice of mine, you must believe that. I pray for silence, for release, but the whispering continues, and these strange fits seize me. They are not of my doing, yet they must be sent for a reason, they must be true, or why would God torture me so? Have mercy, Jägerhorn. Have mercy on me, and listen!"

Colonel Jägerhorn looked past Anttonen, his eyes searching for help, but the two of them were quite alone. "Yes," he said. "Voices, like the French girl. I did not understand."

Anttonen shook his head. "You hear, but you will not believe. You are a patriot, you dream you will be a hero. You will be no hero. The common folk of Finland do not share your dreams. They remember the Great Wrath. They know the Russians only as ancient enemies, and they hate. They will hate you as well. And Cronstedt, ah, poor Admiral Cronstedt. He will be reviled by every Finn, every Swede, for generations to come. He will live out his life in this new Grand Duchy of Finland, on a Russian stipend, and he will die a broken man on April 7, 1820, twelve years and one day after he met with Suchtelen on Lonan and gave Sveaborg to Russia. Later, years later, a man named Runeberg will write a series of poems about this war. Do you know what he will say of Cronstedt?"

"No," Jagerhorn said. He smiled uneasily. "Have your voices told you?"

"They have taught me the words by heart," said Bengt Anttonen.

He recited:

> *"Call him the arm we trusted in,*
> *that shrank in time of stress,*
> *call him Affliction, Scorn, and Sin,*
> *and Death and Bitterness,*
> *but mention not his former name,*
> *lest they should blush who bear the same.*

"That is the glory you and Cronstedt are winning here, Jägerhorn," Anttonen said bitterly. "That is your place in history. Do you like it?"

Colonel Jägerhorn had been carefully edging around Anttonen; there was a clear path between him and the door. But now he hesitated. "You are speaking madness," he said. "And yet – and yet – how could you have known of the Czar's promises? You would almost have me believe you. Voices? Like the French girl? The voice of God, you say?"

Anttonen sighed. "God? I do not know. Voices, Jägerhorn, that is all I hear. Perhaps I am mad."

Jägerhorn grimaced. "They will revile us, you say? They will call us traitors and denounce us in poems?"

Anttonen said nothing. The madness had ebbed; he was filled with a help-less despair.

"No," Jägerhorn insisted. "It is too late. The agreement is signed. We have staked our honor on it. And Vice-Admiral Cronstedt, he is so uncertain. His family is here, and he fears for them. Suchtelen has played him masterfully and we have done our part. It cannot be undone. I do not believe this madness of yours, yet even if I believed, there is no hope for it, nothing to be done. The ships will not come in time. Sveaborg must yield, and the war must end with Sweden's defeat. How could it be otherwise? The Czar is allied with Bonaparte himself, he cannot be resisted!"

"The alliance will not last," Anttonen said, with a rueful smile. "The French will march on Moscow and it will destroy them as it destroyed Charles XII. The winter will be their Poltava. All of this will come too late for Finland, too late for Sveaborg."

"It is too late even now," Jägerhorn said. "Nothing can be changed."

For the first time, Bengt Anttonen felt the tiniest glimmer of hope. "It is not too late."

"What course do you urge upon us, then? Cronstedt has made his decision. Should we mutiny?"

"There will be a mutiny in Sveaborg, whether we take part or not. It will fail."

"What then?"

Bengt Anttonen lifted his head, stared Jägerhorn in the eyes. "The agreement stipulates that we may send two couriers to the King, to inform him of the terms, so the Swedish ships may be dispatched on time."

"Yes. Cronstedt will choose our couriers tonight, and they will leave tomor-row, with papers and safe passage furnished by Suchtelen."

"You have Cronstedt's ear. See that I am chosen as one of the couriers."

"You?" Jägerhorn looked doubtful. "What good will that serve?" He frowned. "Perhaps this voice you hear is the voice of your own fear. Perhaps you have been under siege too long, and it has broken you, and now you hope to run free."

"I can prove my voices speak true," Anttonen said.

"How?" snapped Jägerhorn.

"I will meet you tomorrow at dawn at Ehrensvärd's tomb, and I will tell you the names of the couriers that Cronstedt has chosen. If I am right, you will convince him to send me in the place of one of those chosen. He will agree, gladly. He is anxious to be rid of me."

Colonel Jägerhorn rubbed his jaw, considering. "No one could know the choices but Cronstedt. It is a fair test." He put out his hand. "Done."

They shook. Jägerhorn turned to go. But at the doorway he turned back. "Colonel Anttonen," he said, "I have forgotten my duty. You are in my custody. Go to your own quarters and remain there, until the dawn."

"Gladly," said Anttonen. "At dawn, you will see that I am right."

"Perhaps," said Jägerhorn, "but for all our sakes, I shall hope very much that you are wrong."

*

. . . and the machines suck away the liquid night that enfolds me, and I'm screaming, screaming so loudly that Slim draws back, a wary look on his face. I give him a broad geekish smile, rows on rows of yellow rotten teeth. "Get me out of here, turkey," I shout. The pain is a web around me, but this time it doesn't seem as bad, this time I can almost stand it, this time the pain is *for* something.

They give me my shot, and lift me into my chair, but this time I'm eager for the debriefing. I grab the wheels and give myself a push, breaking free of Rafe, rolling down the corridors like I used to do in the old days, when Creeper was around to race me. There's a bit of a problem with one ramp, and they catch me there, the strong silent guys in their ice-cream suits (that's what Nan called 'em, anyhow), but I scream at them to leave me alone. They do. Surprises the hell out of me.

The Maje is a little startled when I come rolling into the room all by my lonesome. He starts to get up. "Are you . . ."

"Sit down, Sally," I say. "It's good news. Bengt psyched out Jägerhorn good. I thought the kid was gonna wet his pants, believe me. I think we got it socked. I'm meeting Jägerhorn tomorrow at dawn to clinch the sale." I'm grinning, listening to myself. Tomorrow, hey, I'm talking about 1808, but tomorrow is how it feels. "Now here's the sixty-four thousand dollar question. I need to know the names of the two guys that Cronstedt is going to try and send to the Swedish king. Proof, y'know?

"Jägerhorn says he'll get me sent if I can convince him. So you look up those names for me, Maje, and once I say the magic words, the duck will come down and give us Sveaborg."

"This is very obscure information," Salazar complains. "The couriers were detained for weeks, and did not even arrive in Stockholm until the day of the surrender. Their names may be lost to history." What a whiner, I'm thinking; the man is never satisfied.

Ronnie speaks up for me, though. "Major Salazar, those names had better not be lost to history, or to us. You were our military historian. It was your job to research each of the target periods *thoroughly.*" The way she's talking to him, you'd never guess he was the boss. "The Graham Project has every priority. You have our computer files, our dossiers on the personnel of Sveaborg, and you have access to the war college at New West Point. Maybe you can even get through to someone in what remains of Sweden. I don't care how you do it, but it must be done. The entire project could rest on this piece of information. The entire world. Our past and our future. I shouldn't need to tell you that." She turns to me. I applaud. She smiles. "You've done well," she says. "Would you give us the details?"

"Sure," I say. "It was a piece of cake. With ice cream on top. What'd they used to call that?"

"A la mode."

"Sveaborg a la mode," I say, and I serve it up to them. I talk and talk. When I finally finish, even the Maje looks grudgingly pleased.

Pretty damn good for a geek, I think. "OK," I say when I'm done with the report. "What's next? Bengt gets the courier job, right? And I get the message through somehow. Avoid Suchtelen, don't get detained, the Swedes send in the cavalry."

"Cavalry?" Sally looks confused.

"It's a figure of speech," I say, with unusual patience. The Maje nods. "No," he says. "The couriers – it's true that General Suchtelen lied, and held them up as an extra form of insurance. The ice might have melted, after all. The ships might have come through in time. But it was an unnecessary precaution. That year, the ice around Helsinki did not melt until well after the deadline date." He gives me a solemn stare. He has never looked sicker, and the greenish tinge of his skin undermines the effect he's trying to achieve. "We must make a bold stroke. You will be sent out as a courier, under the terms of the truce. You and the other courier will be brought before General Suchtelen to receive your safe conducts through Russian lines. That is the point at which you will strike. The affair is settled, and war in those days was an honorable affair. No one will expect treachery."

"Treachery?" I say. I don't like the sound of what I'm hearing.

For a second, the Maje's smile looks almost genuine; he's finally lit on something that pleases him. "Kill Suchtelen," he says.

"Kill Suchtelen?" I repeat.

"Use Anttonen. Fill him with rage. Have him draw his weapon. Kill Suchtelen." I see. A new move in our crosstime chess game. The geek gambit.

"They'll kill Bengt," I say.

"You can disengage," Salazar says.

"Maybe they'll kill him fast," I point out. "Right there, on the spot, y'know."

"You take that risk. Other men have given their lives for our nation. This is war." The Maje frowns. "Your success may doom us all. When you change the past, the present as it now exists may simply cease to exist, and us with it. But our nation will live, and millions we have lost will be restored to us. Healthier, happier versions of ourselves will enjoy the rich lives that were denied us. You yourself will be born whole, without sickness or deformity."

"Or talent," I say. "In which case I won't be able to go back to do this, in which case the past stays unchanged."

"The paradox does not apply. You have been briefed on this. The past and the present and future are not co-temporaneous. And it will be Anttonen who affects the change, not yourself. He is of that time." The Maje is impatient. His thick, dark fingers drum on the tabletop. "Are you a coward?"

"Fuck you and the horse you rode in on," I tell him. "You don't get it. I couldn't give a shit about me. I'm better off dead. But they'll kill *Bengt*."

He frowns. "What of it?"

Veronica has been listening intently. Now she leans across the table and touches my hand, gently. "I understand. You identify with him, don't you?"

"He's a good man," I say. Do I sound defensive? Very well, then; I *am* defensive. "I feel bad enough that I'm driving him around the bend, I don't want to get him killed. I'm a freak, a geek, I've lived my whole life under siege and I'm going to die here, but Bengt has people who love him, a life ahead of him. Once he gets out of Sveaborg, there's a whole world out there."

"He has been dead for almost two centuries," Salazar says.

"I was inside his head this afternoon," I snap.

"He will be a casualty of war," the Maje says. "In war, soldiers die. It is a fact of life, then as now."

Something else is bothering me. "Yeah, maybe, he's a soldier, I'll buy that. He knew the job was dangerous when he took it. But he cares about *honor*, Sally. A little thing we've forgotten. To die in battle sure, but you want me to make him goddamned assassin, have him violate a flag of truce. He's an honorable man. They'll revile him."

"The ends justify the means," says Salazar bluntly. "Kill Suchtelen, kill him under the flag of truce, yes. It will kill the truce as well. Suchtelen's second-in-command is far less wily, more prone to outbursts of temper, more eager for a spectacular victory. You will tell him that Cronstedt *ordered* you to cut down Suchtelen. He will shatter the truce, will launch a furious attack against the fortress, an attack that Sveaborg, impregnable as it is, will easily repulse. Russian casualties will be heavy, and Swedish determination will be fired by what they will see as Russian treachery. Jägerhorn, with proof before him that the Russian promises are meaningless, will change sides. Cronstedt, the hero of Ruotsinsalmi, will become the hero of Sveaborg as well. The fortress will hold. With the spring the Swedish fleet will land an army at Sveaborg, behind Russian lines, while a second Swedish army sweeps down from the north. The entire course of the war will change. When Napoleon marches on Moscow, a Swedish army will already hold St Petersburg. The Czar will be caught in Moscow, deposed, executed. Napoleon will install a puppet government, and when his retreat comes, it will be north, to link up with his Swedish allies at St Petersburg. The new Russian regime will not survive Bonaparte's fall, but the Czarist restoration will be as short-lived as the French restoration, and Russia will evolve toward a liberal parliamentary democracy. The Soviet Union will never come into being to war against the United States." He emphasizes his final words by pounding his fist on the conference table.

"Sez you," I say mildly.

Salazar gets red in the face. "That is the computer projection," he insists. He looks away from me, though. Just a quick little averting of the eyes, but I catch it. Funny. He can't look me in the eyes.

Veronica squeezes my hand. "The projection may be off," she admits. "A little or a lot. But it is all we have. And this is our last chance. I understand your concern for Anttonen, really I do. It's only natural. You've been part of him for months now, living his life, sharing his thoughts and feelings. Your reservations do you credit. But now millions of lives are in the balance, against the life of this one man. This one, dead man. It's your decision. The most important decision in all of human history, perhaps, and it rests with you alone." She smiles. "Think about it carefully, at least." When she puts it like that, and holds my little hand all the while, I'm powerless to resist. Ah, Bengt. I look away from them, sigh.

"Break out the booze tonight," I say wearily to Salazar, "the last of that old prewar stuff you've been saving."

The Maje looks startled, discomfited; the jerk thought his little cache of prewar Glenlivet and Irish Mist and Remy Martin was a well-kept secret.

And so it was until Creeper planted one of his little bugs, heigh-ho. "I do not think drunken revelry is in order," Sally says. Defending his treasure. He's homely and mean-spirited, but nobody ever said he wasn't selfish. "Shut up and come across," I say. Tonight I ain't gonna be denied. I'm giving up Bengt, the Maje can give up some booze. "I want to get shit-faced," I tell them. "It's time to drink to the goddamned dead and toast the living, past and present. It's in the rules, damn you. The geek always gets a bottle before he goes out to meet the chickens."

*

Within the central courtyard of the Vargön citadel, Bengt Anttonen waited in the predawn chill. Behind him stood Ehrensvard's tomb, the final resting place of the man who had built Sveaborg, and now slept securely within the bosom of his creation, his bones safe behind her guns and her thick granite walls, guarded by all her daunting might. He had built her impregnable, and impregnable she stood, so none would come to disturb his rest. But now they wanted to give her away.

The wind was blowing. It came howling down out of a black empty sky, stirred the barren branches of the trees that stood in the empty courtyard, and cut through Anttonen's warmest coat. Or perhaps it was another sort of chill that lay upon him; the chill of fear. Dawn was almost at hand. Above, the stars were fading. And his head was empty, echoing, mocking. Light would soon break over the horizon, and with the light would come Colonel Jägerhorn, hard-faced, imperious, demanding, and Anttonen would have nothing to say to him.

He heard footsteps. Jägerhorn's boots rang on the stones. Anttonen turned to face him, watching him climb the few small steps up to Ehrensvard's memorial. They stood a foot apart, conspirators huddled against the cold and darkness. Jägerhorn gave him a curt, short nod. "I have met with Cronstedt."

Anttonen opened his mouth. His breath steamed in the frigid air. And just as he was about to succumb to the emptiness, about to admit that his voices had failed him, something whispered deep inside him. He spoke two names.

There was such a long silence that Anttonen once again began to fear. Was it madness after all, and not the voice of God? Had he been wrong? But then Jägerhorn looked down, frowning, and clapped his gloved hands together in a gesture that spoke of finality. "God help us all," he said, "but I believe you."

"I will be the courier?"

"I have already broached the subject with Vice-Admiral Cronstedt." Jägerhorn said. "I have reminded him of your years of service, your excellent record. You are a good soldier and a man of honor, damaged only by your own patriotism and the pressure of the siege. You are that sort of warrior who cannot bear inaction, who must always be doing something. You deserve more than arrest and disgrace, I have argued. As a courier, you will redeem yourself, I have told him I have no doubt of it. And by removing you from Sveaborg, we will remove also a source of tension and dissent around which mutiny might grow. The

Vice-Admiral is well aware that a good many of the men are most unwilling to honor our pact with Suchtelen. He is convinced." Jägerhorn smiled wanly. "I am nothing if not convincing, Anttonen. I can marshal an argument as Bonaparte marshals his armies. So this victory is ours. You are named courier."

"Good," said Anttonen. Why did he feel so sick at heart? He should have been full of jubilation.

"What will you do?" Jägerhorn asked. "For what purpose do we conspire?"

"I will not burden you with that knowledge," Anttonen replied. It was knowledge he lacked himself. He must be the courier, he had known that since yesterday, but the why of it still eluded him, and the future was cold as the stone of Ehrensvärd's tomb, as misty as Jägerhorn's breath. He was full of a strange foreboding, a sense of approaching doom.

"Very well," said Jägerhorn. "I pray that I have acted wisely in this." He moved his glove, offered his hand. "I will count on you, on your wisdom and your honor."

"My honor," Bengt repeated. Slowly, too slowly, he took off his own glove to shake the hand of the dead man standing there before him. Dead man? He was no dead man; he was live, warm flesh. But it was frigid there under those bare trees, and when Anttonen clasped Jägerhorn's hand, the other's skin felt cold to the touch.

"We have had our differences," said Jägerhorn, "but we are both Finns, after all, and patriots, and men of honor, and now too we are friends."

"Friends," Anttonen repeated. And in his head, louder than it had ever been before, so clear and strong it seemed almost as if someone had spoken behind him, came a whisper, sad somehow, and bitter. *C'mon, Chicken Little,* it said, *shake hands with your pal the geek.*

*

Gather ye Four Roses while ye may, for time is still aflying, and this same geek what smiles today tomorrow may be dying. Heigh-ho, drunk again, second night inna row, chugging all the Maje's good booze, but what does it matter, he won't be needing it. After this next little timeride, he won't even exist, or that's what they tell me. In fact, he'll never have existed, which is a real weird thought. Old Major Sally Salazar, his big thick fingers, his greenish tinge, the endearing way he had of whining and bitching, he sure seemed real this afternoon at that last debriefing, but now it turns out there never was any such person. Never was a Creeper, never a Rate or a Slim, Nan never ever told us about ice cream and reeled off the names of all those flavors, butter pecan and rum raisin are one with Nineveh and Tyre, heigh-ho. Never happened, nope, and I slug down another shot, drinking alone, in my room, in my cubicle, the savior at this last liquid supper, where the hell are all my fucking apostles? Ah, drinking, drinking, but not with me.

They ain't s'posed to know, nobody's s'posed to know but me and the Maje and Ronnie, but the word's out, yes it is, and out there in the corridors it's turned into a big wild party, boozing and singing and lighting, a little bit of screwing for those lucky enough to have a partner, of which number I am not one, alas. I want to go out and join in, hoist a few with the boys, but no, the Maje says no, too dangerous, one of the motley horde might decide that even this kind of has-been life is better than a never-was nonlife, and therefore off the geek, ruining everybody's plans for a good time. So here I sit on geek row, in my little room boozing alone, surrounded by five other little rooms, and down at the end of the corridor is a most surly guard, pissed off that he isn't out there getting a last taste, who's got to keep me in and the rest of them out.

I was sort of hoping Ronnie might come by, you know, to share a final drink and beat me in one last game of chess and maybe even play a little kissy-face, which is a ridiculous fantasy on the face of it, but somehow I don't wanna die a virgin, even though I'm not really going to die, since once the trick is done, I won't ever have lived at all. It's goddamned noble of me if you ask me and you got to 'cause there ain't nobody else around to ask. Another drink now but the bottle's almost empty, I'll have to ring the Maje and ask for another. Why won't Ronnie come by? I'll never be seeing her again, after tomorrow, tomorrow-tomorrow and two-hundred-years-ago-tomorrow. I could refuse to go, stay here and keep the happy lil' family alive, but I don't think she'd like that. She's a lot more sure than me. I asked her this afternoon if Sally's projections could tell us about the side effects. I mean, we're changing this war, and we're keeping Sveaborg and (we hope) losing the Czar and (we hope) losing the Soviet Union and (we sure as hell hope) maybe losing the big war and all, the bombs and the rads and the plagues and all that good stuff, even radiation ripple ice cream which was the Creeper's favorite flavor, but what if we lose other stuff? I mean, with Russia so changed and all, are we going to lose Alaska? Are we gonna lose vodka? Are we going to lose George Orwell? Are we going to lose Karl Marx? We tried to lose Karl Marx, actually, one of the other geeks, Blind Jeffey, he went back to take care of Karlie, but it didn't work out. Maybe vision was too damn much for him. So we got to keep Karl, although come to think of it, who cares about Karl Marx, are we gonna lose Groucho? No Groucho, no Groucho ever, I don't like that concept, last night I shot a geek in my pajamas and how he got in my pajamas I'll never know, but maybe, who the hell knows how us geeks get anyplace, all these damn dominoes falling every which way, knocking over other dominoes, dominoes was never my game, I'm a chess player, world chess champion in temporal exile, that's me, dominoes is a dumb damn game. What if it don't work, I asked Ronnie, what if we take out Russia, and, well, Hitler wins World War II so we wind up swapping missiles and germs and biotoxins with Nazi Germany? Or England? Or fucking Austria-Hungary, maybe, who can say? The superpower Austria-Hungary, what a thought, last night I shot a Hapsburg in my pajamas, the geeks put him there, heigh-ho.

Ronnie didn't make me no promises, kiddies. Best she could do was shrug and tell me this story about a horse. This guy was going to get his head cut off by some old-timey king, y'see, so he pipes up and tells the king that if he's given a year, he'll teach the king's horse to talk. The king likes this idea, for some reason, maybe he's a Mister Ed fan, I dunno, but he gives the guy a year. And afterwards, the guy's friends say, hey, what is this, you can't get no horse to talk. So the guy says, well, I got a year now, that's a long time, all kinds of things could happen. Maybe the king will die. Maybe I'll die. Maybe the horse will die. Or maybe the horse will talk.

I'm too damn drunk, I am I am, and my head's full of geeks and talking horses and falling dominoes and unrequited love, and all of a sudden I got to see her. I set down the bottle, oh so carefully, even though it's empty, don't want no broken glass on geek row, and I wheel myself out into the corridor, going slow, I'm not too coordinated right now. The guard is at the end of the hall, looking wistful. I know him a little bit. Security guy, big black fellow, name of Dex. "Hey, Dex," I say as I come wheeling up, "screw this shit, let's us go party, I want to see lil' Ronnie." He just looks at me, shakes his head. "C'mon," I say. I bat my baby-blues at him. Does he let me by? Does the Pope shit in the woods? Hell no, old Dex says, "I got my orders, you stay right here." All of a sudden I'm mad as hell, this ain't fair, I want to see Ronnie. I gather up all my strength and try to wheel right by him. No cigar; Dex turns, blocks my way, grabs the wheelchair and pushes. I go backwards fast, spin around when a wheel jams, flip over and out of the chair. It hurts. Goddamn it hurts. If I had a nose, I woulda bloodied it, I bet. "You stay where you are, you fucking freak," Dex tells me. I start to cry, damn him anyhow, and he watches me as I get my chair upright and pull myself into it. I sit there staring at him. He stands there staring at me. "Please," I say finally. He shakes his head. "Go get her then," I say. "Tell her I want to see her." Dex grins. "She's busy," he tells me. "Her and Major Salazar. She don't want to see you."

I stare at him some more. A real withering, intimidating stare. He doesn't wither or look intimidated. It can't be, can it? Her and the Maje? Her and old Sally Greenface? No way, he's not her type, she's got better taste than that, I know she has. Say it ain't so, Joe. I turn around, start back to my cubicle. Dex looks away. Heigh-ho, fooled him.

Creeper's room is the one beyond mine, the last one at the end of the hall. Everything's just like he left it. I turn on the set, play with the damn switches, trying to figure out how it works. My mind isn't at its sharpest right at this particular minute, it takes me a while, but finally I get it, and I jump from scene to scene down in the Cracker Box, savoring all these little vignettes of life in these United States as served up by Creeper's clever ghost. Each scene has its own individual charm. There's a gang bang going on in the commissary, right on top of one of the tables where Ronnie and I used to play chess. Two huge security men are fighting up in the airlock area; they've been at it a long time, their faces are so bloody I can't tell who the hell they are, but they keep at it, staggering at each other blindly, swinging huge awkward fists, grunting, while a few others stand around and egg them on. Slim and Rafe are sharing a joint, leaning up against my coffin. Slim thinks they ought to rip out all the wires, fuck up everything so I can't go timeriding. Rafe thinks it'd be easier to just bash my head in. Somehow I don't think he loves me no more. Maybe I'll cross him off my Christmas list. Fortunately for the geek, both of them are too stoned and screwed up to do anything at all. I watch a half-dozen other scenes, and finally, a little reluctantly, I go to Ronnie's room, where I watch her screwing Major Salazar.

Heigh-ho, as Creeper would say, what'd you expect, really?

I could not love thee, dear, so much, loved I not honor more. She walks in beauty like the night. But she's not so pretty, not really, back in 1808 there were lovelier women, and Bengt's just the man to land 'em too, although Jägerhorn probably does even better. My Veronica's just the queen bee of a corrupt poisoned hive, that's all. They're done now. They're talking. Or rather the Maje is talking, bless his soul, he's into his ice-cream litany, he's just been making love to Ronnie and now he's lying there in bed talking about Sveaborg, damn him. " . . . only a thirty percent chance that the massacre will take place," he's saying, "the fortress is very strong, formidably strong, but the Russians have the numbers, and if they do bring up sufficient reinforcements, Cronstedt's fears may prove to be substantial. But even that will work out. The assassination, well, the rules will be suspended, they'll slaughter everyone inside, but Sveaborg will become a sort of Swedish Alamo, and the branching paths ought to come together again. Good probability. The end results will be the same." Ronnie isn't listening to him, though; there's a look on her face I've never seen, drunken, hungry, scared, and now she's moving lower on him and doing something I've only seen in my fantasies, and now I don't want to watch anymore, no, oh no, no, oh no.

*

General Suchtelen had established his command post on the outskirts of Helsinki, another clever ploy. When Sveaborg turned its cannon on him, every third shot told upon the city the fortress was supposed to protect, until Cronstedt finally ordered the firing stopped. Suchtelen took advantage of that concession as he had all the rest. His apartments were large and comfortable; from his windows, across the white expanse of ice and snow, the gray form of Sveaborg loomed large. Colonel Bengt Anttonen stared at it morosely as he waited in the anteroom with Cronstedt's other courier and the Russians who had escorted them to Suchtelen. Finally the inner doors opened and the dark Russian captain emerged. "The general will see you now," he said.

General Suchtelen sat behind a wide wooden desk. An aide stood by his right arm. A guard was posted at the door, and the captain entered with the Swedish couriers. On the broad, bare expanse of the desk was an inkwell, a blotter, and two signed safe conducts, the passes that would take them through the Russian lines to Stockholm and the Swedish king, one by the southern and the other by the northern route. Suchtelen said something, in Russian; the aide provided a translation. Horses had been provided, and fresh mounts would be available for them along the way, orders had been given. Anttonen listened to the discussion with a curiously empty feeling and a vague sense of disorientation. Suchtelen was going to let them go. Why did that surprise him? Those were the terms of the agreement, after all, those were the conditions of the truce. As the translator droned on, Anttonen felt increasingly lost and listless. He had conspired to get himself here, the voices had told him to, and now here he was, and he did not know why, nor did he know what he was to do.

They handed him one of the safe conducts, placed it in his outstretched hand. Perhaps it was the touch of the paper; perhaps it was something else. A sudden red rage filled him, an anger so fierce and blind and all-consuming that for an instant the world seemed to flicker and vanish and he was somewhere else, seeing naked bodies twining in a room whose walls were made of pale green blocks. And then he was back, the rage still hot within him, but cooling now, cooling quickly. They were staring at him, all of them. With a sudden start, Anttonen realized that he had let the safe conduct fall to the floor, that his hand had gone to the hilt of his sword instead, and the blade was now half-drawn, the metal shining dully in the sunlight that streamed through Suchtelen's window. Had they acted more quickly, they might have stopped him, but he had caught them all by surprise. Suchtelen began to rise from his chair, moving as if in slow motion. Slow motion, Bengt wondered briefly, what was that? But he knew, he knew. The sword was all the way out now. He heard the captain shout something behind him, the aide began to go for his pistol, but Quick Draw McGraw he wasn't, Bengt had the drop on them all, heigh-ho. He grinned, spun the sword in his hand, and offered it, hilt first, to General Suchtelen.

"My sword, sir, and Colonel Jägerhorn's compliments," Bengt Anttonen heard himself say with something approaching awe. "The fortress is in your grasp. Colonel Jägerhorn suggests that you hold up our passage for a month. I concur. Detain us here, and you are certain of victory. Let us go, and who knows what chance misfortune might occur to bring the Swedish fleet? It is a long time until the third of May. In such a time, the king might die, or the horse might die, or you or I might die. Or the horse might talk."

The translator put away his pistol and began to translate; the other courier began to protest, ineffectually. Bengt Anttonen found himself possessed of an eloquence that even his good friend might envy. He spoke on and on. He had one moment of strange weakness, when his stomach churned and his head swam, but somehow he knew it was nothing to be alarmed at, it was just the pills taking effect, it was just a monster dying far away in a metal coffin full of night, and then there were none, heigh-ho, one siege was ending and another would go on and on, and what did it matter to Bengt, the world was a big, crisp, cold, jeweled oyster. He thought this was the beginning of a beautiful friendship, and what the hell, maybe he'd save their asses after all, if he happened to feel like it, but he'd do it his way.

After a time, General Suchtelen, nodding, reached out and accepted the proffered sword.

*

Colonel Bengt Anttonen reached Stockholm on the third of May, in the Year of Our Lord Eighteen-Hundred-and-Eight, with a message for Gustavus IV Adolphus, King of Sweden. On the same date, Sveaborg, impregnable Sveaborg, Gibraltar of the North, surrendered to the inferior Russian forces.

At the conclusion of hostilities, Colonel Anttonen resigned his commission in the Swedish army and became an émigré, first to England, and later to America. He took up residence in New York City, where he married, fathered nine children, and became a well-known and influential journalist, widely respected for his canny ability to sense coming trends. When events proved him wrong, as happened infrequently, Anttonen was always surprised. He was a founder of the Republican Party, and his writings were instrumental in the election of John Charles Fremont to the Presidency in 1856.

In 1857, a year before his death, Anttonen played Paul Morphy in a New York chess tournament, and lost a celebrated game. Afterward, his only comment was, "I could have beat him at dominoes," a phrase that Morphy's biographers are fond of quoting.

WHERE OR WHEN

Steven Utley

Steven Utley was an American writer who helped found the famous
Turkey City Writer's Workshop in Texas that also included Bruce
Sterling, Howard Waldrop, and many other prominent writers. Utley
authored five story collections, including *Ghost Seas*, *The Beasts of
Love*, and *Where or When*. His series of Silurian Tales appeared in
Asimov's Science Fiction Magazine, *The Magazine of Fantasy & Science
Fiction*, *Analog Science Fiction and Fact*, *SciFiction*, and many other
venues. He coedited the anthologies *Lone Star Universe* (with George
W. Proctor, 1976) and *Passing for Human* (with Michael Bishop, 2009)
and also wrote poems, humorous essays, and other nonfiction over
the course of his career. He died in early 2013 and is much missed.
This story was first published in *Asimov's Science Fiction Magazine* in
1991.

Suddenly, we were *going*. Just as suddenly, but completely unexpectedly, I
came tumbling through dense, tangled underbrush, crashed heavily into
an arrester net of creepers, and half-lay, half-hung there, panting, aching,
astonished. Above me were draperies of vines and the interlaced branches of
scrub pines; patches of blue sky were visible through the interstices. All about
me were gloom and silence. Then, from afar, came a long, rippling burst of noise,
pow pop-pop-pop pow.

Before the sounds could fade completely, there was a second burst, more
ragged than the first but also more sustained, pop-pop-pow, and a pause, and
then pop-pop-pop, pause, pow-pow-pop. It must have gone on like that for half
a minute or more, during which time an unpleasant suspicion began to form in
my mind. As the racket subsided, I cupped my hands around my mouth and sang
out hopefully, "John!"

There was no answer, only another long series of rippling pops.

After some minutes' thrashing about, I managed to find footing and get up
and out of the creepers. I found myself on a slope, surrounded by stunted pines
and up to my waist in underbrush. My stick and beaver hat were gone, and my
Dundreary whiskers were full of twigs, burrs, and bits of leaves. My clothes were
torn and dirty. The day was very warm, and I was already slimy with sweat;
my hand came away streaked with a film of mud when I wiped my forehead.
Self-pity welled up in me. I would never be allowed into the exposition in my
present disheveled state.

I called out John's name again. This time someone called back, "Help!" and before I could decide from which direction the cry had come, there were other sounds, of flailing limbs, cracking rotten wood, shredding fabric, and eloquent profanity, and a woman burst headfirst halfway through a mass of foliage some yards from where I stood. I didn't recognize her immediately, though I had been introduced to her not an hour before, subjective time. She, too, had been in John's party and should have been in it still. Now she had lost her cap and her parasol, and her coiffure, which had been so carefully done up for this jaunt, had been undone by branches, thorns, and simple gravity. She had a long, bloody scratch along the curve of one fine cheekbone and looked mad enough to bite into a live badger.

"Don't just *stand* there!" she snapped. "I'm *caught*! I'm upside-down in this goddamn *stupid* bush!"

I made for her, but it was hard going. The legs of my trousers ended in loops that passed under the shanks of my black Wellington boots; a loop would catch on one stick of wood or another every time I took a step. Finally, I had to stop, sit, and get out my pen-knife. It was a replica of an exquisite nineteenth-century instrument and razor-sharp. I cut the loops off and disgustedly flung them away into the underbrush.

The woman grabbed me as soon as I had come within grabbing distance. I let her cling to me for a few seconds while I got my breath back. Then I tried to pull her out of the bush. It was no use.

I said, "Can't you just sort of back out of there?"

"Not with these clothes on. I can't *move*. This is the height of mid-nineteenth-century fashion I've got on, and it's like wearing a circus tent. I can't breathe, either. They made me wear some goddamn piece of armor-plated underwear."

"They always have been sticklers for accuracy of period detail."

"Who in eighteen fifty-one's gonna get to see what I wear under my dress?"

"Well, you just never know, do you?" and I gave her a wryly apologetic grin that absolutely failed to endear me to her, took out my trusty pen-knife again, and got around behind her. Viewed from that side, she rather resembled an enormous blossom. Her legs, sheathed in long, lace-trimmed drawers, were the stamens, and her numerous and varied petticoats, the petals.

I said, "Good God, how many petticoats are you wearing?"

"Eighty or ninety."

"There's enough silk here for a parachute battalion."

"It's not silk, it's muslin."

"Whatever."

"Just cut, cut! Jesus Christ!"

I began to saw at the material. She began to curse, first somebody named George, whose idea it evidently had been, and then John, whose fault it all was. She stopped in mid-slander as the rippling pops were repeated.

"What's that noise?" she said.

"Well, I don't want to alarm you, but—"

"Alarm me?" She glared around at me as best she could. "Gosh, you mean to say something's *wrong* with this picture? You mean to tell me this *isn't* the goddamn Crystal Palace? Jesus! *I* never would've guessed!"

She was within her rights to be upset, upended in a small tree as she was, and probably lost in time and space as well. Still, her sarcasm stung. I tried not to let her irritation infect me and kept ripping at her layers of petticoats. "I think we've landed near a battle or something," I told her. "I think that sound like popcorn popping is guns being fired. A lot of guns."

"Oh, that's great, that's just great. Look, while you're trying to cop a feel back there, reach up and cut through this corset."

"You're going to have to undo some buttons or something at your end first, so I can get up under your jacket and blouse."

We fumbled and fussed for several minutes more. At last she was able to slither forward out of both bush and most of her clothes. She did still have on her jacket and blouse, her long drawers, stockings, and boots, and I had made a point of leaving some fabric below the waist, so that she now wore a droopy, uneven, knee-length skirt adorned with a few bedraggled ribbons and bows. I watched as she reached into what remained of her clothing and began to tug at something. She caught me watching and paused to look me straight in the eye.

"A *gentleman* averts his gaze when a lady removes her corset."

"A thousand pardons."

I averted my gaze, and she fell to grunting and gasping. After a time, during which I heard two more or less distinct volleys of pops from not so far off as before, there came a final, triumphant exhalation from behind me. A moment later, trailing imprecations and strings or straps or possibly poison-barbed tendrils, an odd rectangular object sailed semi-rigidly over my head and lodged itself in the branches of a scrub pine.

"Okay to look now," she said crisply, so I looked. Stood right-side-up and free of the undergarment from Hell, she was a rather attractive brunette in her early or middle thirties. I found that I had to admire the way she raked some errant strands of hair out of her face, brushed dirt and leaves from one sleeve of her jacket, adjusted a soiled glove just so, with the air of one who need do no more to restore herself to presentability. She stepped toward me and offered her hand. Not everyone can look terribly, terribly formal in not much more than clothing remnants and a hairdo that has exploded, so I was duly impressed.

"We were introduced before," she said, "but I'm no good at remembering people's names. I'm Elizabeth Hazel."

"Lewis Alisdair. Charmed." I took her hand and made a little bow over it. I was stuck in character. Amusement flickered at the corners of her mouth, and she made a slight curtsying motion. We had signed on with John to go play-act, and, by God, with or without John, here we were, play-acting.

"Okay," she said, dropping my hand and her own show of formality as though both suddenly just bored the daylights out of her, "now let's go find John so I can kill him for dumping me into a damn bush. No, wait, first I'll sue him for every penny he's got. The Institute, too. *Then* I'll kill him."

"I don't think you can sue him, or the Institute, either. That waiver you signed—"

"Oh hell, that's right. Well, I'll just have to settle for killing him, then."

"These things have been known to happen. It may not have been John's fault."

"Who else's fault might it be? He is our guide. He *is* supposed to know what he's doing. He was supposed to deliver us safe and sound to London in eighteen fifty-one." Fists on hips, she glared around unhappily at the woods. "I don't know where the hell we are, but I sure don't expect to run into Queen Vicky and Albert around here. We've obviously missed the exposition by God knows how many years or miles – or both, most likely. So kindly stop defending that asshole, okay?" Now she was glaring unhappily at me. "What are you, anyway, the Institute's liability-law boy, public relations, what?"

"I'm a sightseer, too. Bought a ticket, same as you," and I gave her what was meant to be a rueful, we're-in-this-together kind of look, to which she responded with all the warmth of a frozen dinner. Falteringly, I slogged on. "It's not that I'm – I'm not defending John, but I have known him a long time, and I've traveled with him before, and I'm just saying—"

"He is an asshole, you know. He revels in it."

"The point is—"

"He was coming on to the women in the group before we left." She feigned a shudder. "Made my skin crawl, he's such a creep. I think being a creep must go with the job or something. Like whatever it is that makes someone able to time-travel also makes him a creep. Like there aren't already enough goddamn asshole creeps who *can't* travel through time."

I waited before speaking to make sure that she had exhausted the subject of creeps for the time being. "The point *is*," I said, "John will find us. Wherever we go in time or space, outside our proper matrix, we're anomalies. We leave a trail John can't miss in a hundred years."

That was time-travel humor, but old time-travel humor. She didn't even bother to smile politely. "I *know* we're not marooned here forever or anything. At least we better not be. But what do we do until that jerk gets here?"

"We're supposed to stay put when something like this happens, but that may not be such a good idea under the circumstances. The battle sounds like it's coming our way."

After a moment, she said, "Any idea where we are or who's making all the fuss?"

"Judging from the trees, somewhere in the northern temperate latitudes."

"That narrows it down."

"Judging from the gunfire—" I shrugged helplessly. "My specialty is nineteenth-century English literature."

She looked at me in frank dismay. "How fascinatingly interesting," she said, in the voice women usually reserve for dealing with lecherous bores. "I don't suppose you also happen to know any woodcraft, do you? As in how to figure out which way we should go? Or how to start a fire and find food and water, just in case we do get stuck here? No? Great. I need Tarzan, Daniel Boone. I get a prissy English lit specialist."

Heat was creeping up my neck and face, and in the back of my mind was a bubbling sound like vinegar and baking soda stirred together. Sometimes, the natural product of chemistry between a man and a woman is a stink bomb. I said, "I cannot imagine how you expected to pass yourself off as a well-bred Englishwoman of the nineteenth or any other century."

"Now what's that supposed to mean?"

"How in the world did you ever get past screening? Good God, your accent's bad enough – what *is* that, Dallas? Texarkana? But. Worse by far. Proper nineteenth-century ladies do not use the s-word in conversation, or the f-word, or any other a-to-z word, for that matter. Proper nineteenth-century ladies probably don't even *think* those words."

I might as well have insulted her pet cat. She gave me the most belligerent look I had seen on a human face since my first marriage. "You got a problem with the way I talk?"

"I've got a problem with you, period. And another thing I've got is a strong aversion to getting mobbed. When we do get where we're going, don't speak to anyone until I'm clear of you. You'll probably start a riot by saying fuck in front of the queen."

"Don't think I can play the part, huh?" She sat up straight all of a sudden, folded her hands in her lap, drew a breath, fixed me with cold old Pleistocene ice in her eye. She said, perfectly calmly, perfectly veddy-English-thenk-yew-snootily, "I can do anything to which I put my mind, Mister Alisdair, up to and beyond impersonating a well-bred Englishwoman." By comparison, her earlier show of formality amounted to a hug and a howdy-do from a loose and crazy woman.

"I have degrees in history and linguistics," she went on, "and I have professional-acting experience. I speak four languages and numerous dialects." She paused, cleared her throat softly, and another amazing change came over her. Her new voice dripped Canarsie. "On my second excursion, I met Anne of Austria." Enn ahv *Aw*streeuh. "She was Louis the Thirteenth of France's girl friend." Ghil frin. "I hid my recording equipment in my wig." She had come around again to East Texas for that. "Get the picture, *asshole*?"

"Well, shut my mouth," and I did.

Probably we could have sat there, not speaking, not looking at each other, until John found us or Hell froze over, whichever occurred first, but another volley of gunfire made us peer nervously into the surrounding woods. It was impossible to see more than twenty yards in any direction, but it seemed to me that the popping noises were coming from directly up the slope. I could hear people yelling now, too, and had a horrible thought. What if they were Apache Indians or Nazis or other barbarians who were notorious for cruelty?

Elizabeth was looking around wonderingly. "Who'd be dumb enough," she said, "to bring an army into this place?" Obviously, no one as smart as she. "There're probably snakes in these woods. There're probably *ticks*," and I saw her shudder again. This time, the shudder seemed genuine. "Yuck. Ticks."

"Let's get out of here." I pointed downhill. "I think we should go that way."

"I think so, too. And fast."

We turned and lumbered down the slope. The growth fought us every step of the way. As though the underbrush were not bad enough, the land here was as choppy as the surface of a gale-swept sea: we had traveled very little distance at all before we found ourselves slogging uphill; then the ground dipped again, more sharply this time. And as though thicket and broken terrain were not a bad enough combination, neither of us was outfitted for a trek through the wild woods. We hadn't gone ten yards before her stockings were only a memory. Her fashionable boots looked as though they were already beginning to disintegrate.

Mine were just starting to pinch my feet.

Yet we pushed on, until we came to a sluggish creek that had cut a shallow, steep-sided ravine through the tangle. There we practically collapsed. We were dripping perspiration and covered with burrs and approximately three hundred fresh scratches apiece.

We had managed to put some distance between the fighting and ourselves, but not much, and certainly not enough. The shooting still sounded close. I couldn't be sure, because I now discovered that my watch had been torn from its chain, but my guess was that it had taken us the better part of an hour to cover, at most, a quarter of a mile of ground.

Elizabeth knelt in the mud beside the creek, dipped in her handkerchief, *oohed* gratefully as she dabbed it against her face. "I'm so thirsty," she said.

"Me, too, but not enough to drink this stuff." I did scoop up some water in my hand and splash it on my face. "Inoculations or no."

"Where's your spirit of adventure?"

"Left it on the expressway in rush-hour traffic this morning. I almost missed getting to the jump-off on time."

"I bet now you wish you had." She re-wetted her handkerchief and swabbed her face some more. "I wish I had. This is the worst blind date I've ever had."

We were actually grinning at each other. Exhaustion had taken a little of the starch out of both of us.

The shooting sounded very close now.

I said, "We'd better keep moving," she muttered something heartfelt, and we picked ourselves up and trudged on.

The ravine widened and deepened as we moved downstream, and as the banks drew away from us on both sides, scrub pines and saplings closed in densely. Soon, neither bank was visible. The creek itself broadened and deepened and meandered. The ground became swampy underfoot. We were soon exhausted again and had to take another rest. Maddeningly, the sounds of gunfire seemed no farther behind us than ever.

"John'll never find us in this place," Elizabeth said.

"He certainly does have his work cut out." I reached over and started to give her a reassuring pat on the arm, but she recoiled.

"Look," she said, "just don't mess with me, okay?"

Mercurial bitch, I thought.

Not looking at each other, we listened to another volley or two.

I heard her sigh. "Guess we'd better go."

Still not looking at her, I started to get to my feet and gripped the bole of a dead pine to steady myself. Just about eight inches above the spot where I had placed my hand, a patch of bark as big around as a saucer suddenly exploded with a zing, spraying me with splinters and grit. My hand dropped to my side, very quickly, seemingly of its own volition, for it took me another couple of seconds to decide to drop to the ground. I looked around frantically but could see only trees and creepers and, hanging among the pines, a small puff of bluish smoke. Elizabeth was still on her feet. She looked down at me exasperatedly, as though I were a total stranger who had embarrassed her by willfully falling at her feet in public and having a fit.

"Elizabeth," I said.

"What's the matter with—"

I grabbed her and pulled her down and rolled halfway on top of her, and there was a moment as short as a heartbeat during which she was too surprised to react and the woods were silent except for a subdued, almost featureless sort of background bee swarm murmur, and then, abruptly, the murmur resolved itself into the sounds of men and masses of men thrashing and crashing about in the underbrush, and yells of excitement, and an eruption of reports, quite close this time, and quite emphatic, and now much less like the sound of popcorn popping than like that of pebbles or dried peas being shaken in a large gourd, and there were more zinging explosions among the trees. Some of the yelling turned anguished. The sounds were all around us now; we weren't near a battle, we were in it. I risked a look but there was nothing to see except a thick haze of gunsmoke drifting among the trees. I pulled my head back in and lay on my belly beside Elizabeth in the mud.

The woods grew gloomier as gunsmoke collected under the branches. There was a bitter smoky stench in the air that stung our eyes and burned our throats, and now, between blasts of gunfire, we could hear men crying out in pain and terror. From just downstream, off to our left, came a blurry bawled command, the rustle and crash of heavy movement through underbrush, then splashing noises. I glimpsed shadowy forms pushing through knee-deep water at the nearest bend of the creek. From upstream came another thunderous rattle of gunfire. Orange flames flickered among the trees, and there were more cries, more sounds of movement.

There were other sounds, too, a rising roar of wind among the treetops, a crackling, a hissing. I couldn't imagine what they signified. Then came a different sort of smoke smell, and at almost the same moment Elizabeth put her mouth close to my ear and yelled, "The woods are on fire! We've got to get out of here!"

As though on cue, flame curled through a tripod of dead pines not twenty feet from where we lay. Elizabeth made to get up. I grabbed her arm roughly.

"You want to get yourself shot?"

She jerked away. "I sure as hell don't want to burn to death or suffocate!"

"Keep down, or you won't have to worry!"

"Come on, if you're coming!" and she slid herself into the water.

Better shot than cooked, I decided, and followed. I found myself wading in knee-deep water, with soft, ankle-deep mud sucking at my boots. Behind us, the fire suddenly roared along the bank, seeming to leap from treetop to treetop, consuming everything immediately combustible, scorching everything else. The air filled with sparks, and the heat was so intense, the smoke so thick, that we were momentarily driven onto the other bank. A cloud of airborne burning bits engulfed us like a swarm of hellish insects, stinging as they alighted on our faces and hands. Breathing was like swallowing heated needles. Our hair and clothing began to smolder, and Elizabeth screamed and started beating at herself. I looped an arm around her waist, forced her back into the water, dunked us both. She pulled free and surfaced several feet away, sputtering and clawing hair out of her eyes.

"Go!" I yelled at her. "Go! Go!"

And we went, blistered, half-blinded, and choking, through Hell.

Everywhere there was fire and smoke and noise and horror.

Once, we heard someone in one of the thickets along the bank cry out that he was burning and beg to be shot. His pleas abruptly broke off in a wail of agony that must have persisted for a full minute. Elizabeth unexpectedly grabbed my hand, and I felt her fingernails bite into my palm; under the mud and the soot, her face was bone white.

Farther downstream, as we skirted a fire that burned all the way down the bank to the water, a flame-swathed figure lurched blindly out of the inferno. It was pawing at itself and moaning hideously, and as it broke through the thicket, burning vines dragged and snatched at it as though to pull it back into the heart of the blaze. It slipped in the mud on the bank opposite us and seemed to dissolve in a boiling cloud of steam.

I covered my eyes with my hands as we plunged past.

In some places there was no fire, only shadows and that infernal, constant pow-pow-pop, now close by, now remote. Once again, we were caught in a cross-fire and lay clutching each other in terror against a reedy bank while bullets clipped small branches and pieces of bark overhead. The shooting quickly rose to a furious crescendo, then died away as abruptly and unexpectedly as it had begun.

When we had heard only distant battle sounds for a long time, Elizabeth leaned close to me and said, "This is it for me. I'm worn out, and I've lost a shoe in the mud. This is as far as I go."

"We aren't safe here."

"We aren't safe anywhere in this goddamn swamp. May as well die here as anywhere else."

"We're not going to die. John—"

"Oh, screw John, and screw you, too," and with that she crawled up the soggy bank and flung herself down on relatively dry ground. There was nothing for me to do but follow her into the thicket. For no reason I could imagine save that I was stuck in character again, I pulled off my ruined jacket and offered it to her. She looked at it and at me with consummate distaste and declined to accept. The whole exchange was leaden pantomime. We were too tired for actual argument any more, though not too tired to disagree. She wadded up her own jacket for a pillow and apparently fell asleep as soon as her head touched it. I was dead tired, too, and hungry and thirsty as well, but I was too worried to fall asleep. Where was John?

And night fell, but the shooting never died away completely, and neither did the brush-fires. I could hear the intermittent crash of gunfire all about, often punctuated by shouts. The smell of burning was everywhere, and its crimson glow was reflected among the trees and against the sky. One blaze flared up not twenty yards from us. I went forward to keep an eye on its progress, and by its light saw dead men lying among a jackstraw pile of pine trunks. The fire had already gone over them, charring them and their garments beyond recognition and leaving a sickening seared-meat smell hanging about the area. As I turned to leave, I was startled by some firecracker-like explosions among the smouldering corpses – lingering flames were setting off the unused cartridges in the dead men's pouches.

I returned to Elizabeth, sat down beneath a tree, leaned against it. Though it seemed that I closed my eyes for only a moment, when I opened them, the woods were suffused with a sickly gray light, and somewhere a bird was cawing.

Before me stood a stranger.

He was dressed in rather dusty and shabby dark clothes and carried an antiquated but effective-looking short rifle. The muzzle, which was pointed at my midriff, looked wide enough to accommodate a banana. By his right hip hung an equally antiquated revolver in a holster, by his left, a wooden canteen on a strap. His black slouch hat had seen better days. The shadow of its brim smudged the details of his face above his whiskery chin and solemn mouth.

I raised my hands and showed him my palms.

He gestured with the rifle in the general direction of the burned area and asked, in a low, soft drawl, "You looked at all that?"

I found my voice, but it was barely more than a hoarse whisper. "Y-yes."

"What do you think?"

"It – it's horrible."

The stranger tilted his head back slightly, and something like a smile distorted the solemn mouth. "Oh, I don't know. Those're the first Yankees I've seen in a while that are cooked just the way I like 'em."

I had the distinct sensation of icy fingers stroking my shoulder blades.

"Not much like the videos at all," he said, "now, is it?"

"You're from up the way!"

"You folks ain't from around here, either." The "ain't" sounded like an affectation. "I could tell that even without seeing your trails. You're anachronistic at worst," and he shot a look at Elizabeth, "and inappropriate at best."

Elizabeth was still asleep, with her knees drawn up and her arms wrapped protectively around her head. I knelt beside her and shook her gently. She gave a grunt and a heave, and that was all.

I shook her again and got a petulant moan out of her this time. She rolled onto her back, ran her parched tongue over her cracked, blackened lips, peered out from under the arch of her elbow.

"Company," I said, nodding in the stranger's direction.

She blinked, not understanding. I helped her into a sitting position, and then she noticed him. They studied each other for several seconds.

"Another time-traveler," I told her. Elizabeth looked relieved. I didn't know how to set her straight.

"Judging from your clothes," he said, "or what's left of 'em, I'd say you're just a couple of lost sightseers." There was offhanded contempt in his voice as he spoke the word "sightseers."

"I think she's some kind of reporter—"

"Documentary film-maker!"

"– and I'm from the University of—"

He cut us short with an impatient wave of his rifle. "Where you folks suppose' to be?"

"The Crystal Palace exposition in London, England," I said. "Eighteen fifty-one."

"That so? Then you only missed it by about a dozen years and a couple thousand miles. This is Virginia—"

"Virginia!" Elizabeth and I exclaimed in unison.

"– and it's the first week of May, eighteen sixty-four."

He let us gnaw on that all we could stand. After a while, Elizabeth struck her knee with her fist and bawled, "Where the hell is *John*?"

The stranger made a shushing sound at her with his mouth, a shushing motion with his hand. "My guess is your guide's trying to sort your trail out from everybody else's. There's been a lot of fighting right around here over the last few years, and there'll be some more for a while to come. There was a big battle over by Chancellorsville just last year. Big or little, past or future, each one of these fights has got its own crowd of spectators. You can just see 'em out of the corner of your eye. Well, I guess you can't see any of 'em, since you're just passengers. But when I look, this whole area's all criss-crossed with – it's like seeing one of those time-exposed photos of a highway at night. All streaks of light, except that this ain't just a time-exposed picture. It's double- and triple-exposed a hundred times over."

"May we please have some water?"

Elizabeth had cut in just as he obviously was getting going on a subject dear to him. He stopped and glared and seemed to have to shift mental gears.

"We're very thirsty," she continued. "We haven't had anything to drink since yesterday. We're incredibly hungry, too."

He stared at her for a moment more, then shifted his rifle to draw the canteen strap up over his head. He handed the canteen to me. I uncorked it and handed it to Elizabeth. "You're so gallant," she said as she took it.

"Now don't gulp," the stranger warned her.

She took a gulp and began to cough.

"Serves you right," said the stranger. "Sip."

She gulped again and coughed again.

Since she patently wasn't listening to him, he spoke to me. "Can't give you food. Only got some hardtack and a little salt meat, and it's got to last me a bit. Just make you thirsty again anyway. But you won't starve before your guide finds you and takes you home."

"I'll be sure to mention your solicitude to the folks back home," Elizabeth said, dangerously close to sarcasm. I could have strangled her.

"I'll be obliged if you don't mention my solicitude or anything else to the folks back home."

Elizabeth handed the canteen over to me. I raised it to my lips and took a careful sip. The water was warm and strange-tasting. The idea crossed my mind that tadpoles had probably swum in it, perhaps swam in it even now, but I didn't care, and I swallowed gratefully. Then the idea crossed my mind that burning men may have been extinguished in it as well, and I quickly re-corked the canteen and handed it to its owner. He slipped the canteen's strap back over his head.

"You'd best lay low here till your guide comes. Last thing anybody wants is dead passengers around here, so you keep your heads down. This is a dangerous place for you. Actually" – there was that smile again – "this is a dangerous place for just about anybody. There're Yankee soldiers and Confederates scattered every which way in these woods. You're just off the end of the whole battle line."

Without further ado, he turned to go.

"Wait!" Elizabeth said. "Can't we stay with your passengers until our guide gets here?"

"Don't carry passengers." He was already walking away.

She called after him plaintively, "Can't you *please* take us home?"

He paused, half-turned, touched his hat brim. "Ma'am," he said, "this is home," and with that he strode off and was quickly lost to view and to hearing as well.

I suddenly realized that I had been holding my breath for some time. I let the air rush out of me and sagged deflated against a tree.

"Now there," Elizabeth murmured, "is a truly weird person."

"You don't know the half of it."

She looked at me curiously, but I just turned away. My hands and knees were shaking. I didn't know much about the American Civil War, but I recalled reading or hearing that northern Virginia was some of the most fought-over real estate in North America. Anyone who wanted to be a spectator to the Civil War could do worse than to visit Virginia. Anyone who wanted to *live* the Civil War, and had the power to reach it, and didn't burden himself with passengers, could come to this place at this time and stay indefinitely and never run out of opportunities to participate – if not, perhaps, in the crazy hope of changing the outcome, then only, perhaps, with the crazy joy of contributing to the carnage.

I felt those cold fingers brush along my spine again.

"What do you think he meant," Elizabeth said, "when he said this was home?"

"I think," I began, and paused to ask myself if I really wanted to go on and tell her I believed he meant that this was a mighty fine place to kill people. The answer was no, so I shrugged and lied. "I haven't the faintest idea."

And we fell silent then, and sat almost together in our thicket, fearful and attentive, she listening to the distant incessant clatter of firearms, and I for any sound that might be the stranger returning. I took no comfort from his assurance that he preferred not to have our corpses discovered in his slaughter-house. Sociopaths changed their minds, too. When, at length, we did hear the unmistakable crack of wood snapping underfoot, both of us uttered hoarse little cries of fright and spun around – just as John stepped out from behind a tree. He beamed at us and said, in his infuriatingly cheerful way, "Not too much the worse for wear, I trust."

He was dressed as I had last seen him, in a striped cloth suit and a beaver hat. His hair was immaculately waved and curled, and there didn't seem to be a speck of dirt anywhere on his person.

Elizabeth squawled at him in the voice cats use when their tails get caught in doors: "*Where the hell have you been?*"

He looked at her amusedly. "Oh, around. Before that, at the exposition, of course. I think everybody in England must've been there." He fingered his silk cravat, stroked his moustache, looked past her to give me a man-to-man kind of smirk. "Don't ever let anybody tell you that nineteenth-century gals weren't lookers, or that they didn't know how to have a good time."

"John," said Elizabeth, "I am riven with nausea at the mere thought."

He laughed. "I just didn't know you two'd gotten lost. Not at first, anyway.

When we arrived in London," and he looked very pointedly at me, "you weren't around," and he looked as pointedly at Elizabeth, "and she wasn't around, and I just sort of figured both of you'd run off into the crowd or, ah, somewhere."

Beside me, Elizabeth groaned in disgust. "Give me a break!"

I took my cue from that and said to him, "We didn't even know each other before we wound up here. We don't seem to like each other now that we have gotten acquainted."

"Pity. She's really not bad-looking underneath all that dirt, you know."

Elizabeth went straight at him, spewing curses. Though he would have made two and a half of her, he retreated, stepping surprisingly daintily through the plant debris as she reached for his lapels with her two very dirty hands. She was half-unshod, however, and there were thorns in the mat of plant stuff underfoot, and it was no time at all before her lavish description of his mating habits was cut short by a yelp of pain. She grabbed her foot and hopped backward a couple of steps to sit on a fallen bole.

I asked myself, bitterly and not for the first time in all the long while I had known John, why he had to be the one with the special affinity for my favorite place and period of history. I stepped over to Elizabeth and knelt before her. "Let me see your foot."

"Oh God, what *is* this? Sight of blood turn you on or – ow! Damn it!"

I showed her the thorn, then tossed it aside. "John," I said, "give me your handkerchief."

I noted with a certain sense of satisfaction that he looked distressed as he drew the handkerchief from his pocket. "This is real silk, Lew. *Silk*."

"So it is, John, so it is."

"Ah, jeeze."

"God," Elizabeth murmured as I bound her foot, "for a guy who can't find his own ass in the woods, you're such a damn Boy Scout."

She said it almost tenderly. Very surprised, I looked up at her face. She smiled fleetingly. After a moment's hesitation, I smiled back. Removing a thorn from someone's foot is vastly underrated as a bonding experience. I felt like Androcles.

Then her attention swung from me and her foot back to John, and she immediately took on the aspect of Mount Pelée about to blow.

"Hey," he told her, "give *me* a break, okay? I did have other people to look after on this little excursion. I *am* sorry about losing you. But you know how it is. These little slippages happen."

Mount Pelée exploded. "*This* little slippage nearly got us killed!"

"But it didn't actually get you killed. And I *did* come looking for you as soon as I realized that you really *weren't* around. And now I have found you, haven't I? Well? Haven't I?"

Elizabeth sullenly yeah-yeahed. I didn't respond. I was dead tired. All I wanted to do was go home, and he grated on the little I had left that could be grated on. There is no one more smug than somebody who has your signed waiver stashed someplace safe.

A resounding crash of gunfire from downstream made us look around. John's expression was mildly reproachful. "Boy," he said, "everybody seems to have got up on the wrong side of bed this morning. But, as I was saying. Sorry it took so long to locate you. You've really got no idea how many time-travelers are wandering around this area right now, right at this very minute. Their trails are everywhere. I mean, *everywhere*. New trails and old ones, too. Who'd think so many people'd want to come watch two armed mobs chase each other around the countryside? Give me the good times, thank you."

"Let's get out of here," I said wearily. "The battle's starting up again."

He nodded, but he also said, "Where's your spirit of adventure, Lew?"

"Same place as my sense of humor. Gone."

"Boy, I guess so. Well, come on, the twenty-first-century express is now boarding." He stepped closer, gave his spotless gloves a sorrowful look, held out his hands to us. I took one. Elizabeth started to take the other, then held back.

"My hands are dirty," she told him. "Mustn't mess up your nice clean gloves."

She reached out and deliberately wiped her black fingers against the front of his coat.

"Much better," she declared, and entwined her still-nasty fingers with his.

He sighed. "Lady, you are no lady."

"Cut the crap," she said, "and just take us home."

There was a moment's lightheadedness, a sensation of blacking out, and then the three of us were floating together through the treetops, unmindful of gravity and spiky branches alike. Now, as we emerged into the open sky, I saw the vast extent of the forest and caught a glimpse of a road below and ahead, and a long swarm of men.

It was only a glimpse, though. Among the trees were many opaque puffs of grayish-white smoke. Rising here and there were columns of darker stuff, some of it shot with red and orange flames. As far as the eye could see, the world lay obscured by a translucent, pungent haze.

Beside me, John said, "I even ran into some visitors from our own future. First time for me. It was some historian with a pack of grad students in tow. Fun bunch *they* were, too, let me tell you. They got all sniffy when I asked 'em about things up the way. Said it was against the rules. Rules? I said, and the old guy just grinned at me and cackled, There'll be *laws* one day, and cops, too. Can you imagine? Cops!"

I remembered the stranger's smile as he talked of Yankees cooked just right, and I nodded, more to myself than to John. I could imagine cops.

Then, suddenly, we were *going*.

TIME GYPSY

Ellen Klages

Ellen Klages is an American writer who has published two acclaimed young-adult novels. *The Green Glass Sea*, which won the Scott O'Dell Award, the New Mexico Book Award, and the Judy Lopez Memorial Award, and *White Sands, Red Menace*, which won the California and New Mexico Book awards. Her short stories have been nominated for the Nebula Award, the Hugo Award, World Fantasy Award, and Campbell Award. Her story, "Basement Magic," won a Nebula in 2005. She lives in San Francisco, in a small house full of strange and wondrous things. "Time Gypsy" was first published in 1998, in *Bending the Landscape: Science Fiction*, edited by Nicola Griffith and Stephen Pagel.

Friday, February 10, 1995. 5:00 p.m.

As soon as I walk in the door, my officemate Ted starts in on me. Again. "What do you know about radiation equilibrium?" he asks.

"Nothing. Why?"

"That figures." He holds up a faded green volume. "I just found this insanely great article by Chandrasekhar in the '45 *Astrophysical Journal*. And get this – when I go to check it out, the librarian tells me I'm the first person to take it off the shelf since 1955. Can you believe that? Nobody reads anymore." He opens the book again. "Oh, by the way, Chambers was here looking for you."

I drop my armload of books on my desk with a thud. Dr. Raymond Chambers is the chairman of the Physics department, and a Nobel Prize winner, which even at Berkeley is a very, very big deal. Rumor has it he's working on some top secret government project that's a shoe-in for a second trip to Sweden.

"Yeah, he wants to see you in his office, pronto. He said something about Sara Baxter Clarke. She's that crackpot from the 50s, right? The one who died mysteriously?"

I wince. "That's her. I did my dissertation on her and her work." I wish I'd brought another sweater. This one has holes in both elbows. I'd planned a day in the library, not a visit with the head of the department.

Ted looks at me with his mouth open. "Not many chick scientists to choose from, huh? And you got a post-doc here doing that? Crazy world." He puts his book down and stretches. "Gotta run. I'm a week behind in my lab work. Real science, you know?"

I don't even react. It's only a month into the term, and he's been on my case about one thing or another – being a woman, being a dyke, being close to 30

– from day one. He's a jerk, but I've got other things to worry about. Like Dr. Chambers, and whether I'm about to lose my job because he found out I'm an expert on a crackpot.

Sara Baxter Clarke has been my hero since I was a kid. My pop was an army technician. He worked on radar systems, and we traveled a lot – six months in Reykjavik, then the next six in Fort Lee, New Jersey. Mom always told us we were gypsies, and tried to make it seem like an adventure. But when I was eight, mom and my brother Jeff were killed in a bus accident on Guam. After that it didn't seem like an adventure any more.

Pop was a lot better with radar than he was with little girls. He couldn't quite figure me out. I think I had too many variables for him. When I was ten, he bought me dresses and dolls, and couldn't understand why I wanted a stack of old physics magazines the base library was throwing out. I liked science. It was about the only thing that stayed the same wherever we moved. I told Pop I wanted to be a scientist when I grew up, but he said scientists were men, and I'd just get married.

I believed him, until I discovered Sara Baxter Clarke in one of those old magazines. She was British, went to MIT, had her doctorate in theoretical physics at 22. At Berkeley, she published three brilliant articles in very, very obscure journals. In 1956, she was scheduled to deliver a controversial fourth paper at an international physics conference at Stanford. She was the only woman on the program, and she was just 28.

No one knows what was in her last paper. The night before she was supposed to speak, her car went out of control and plunged over a cliff at Devil's Slide – a remote stretch of coast south of San Francisco. Her body was washed out to sea. The accident rated two inches on the inside of the paper the next day – right under a headline about some vice raid – but made a small uproar in the physics world. None of her papers or notes were ever found; her lab had been ransacked. The mystery was never solved.

I was fascinated by the mystery of her the way other kids were intrigued by Amelia Earhart. Except nobody'd ever heard of my hero. In my imagination, Sara Baxter Clarke and I were very much alike. I spent a lot of days pretending I was a scientist just like her, and even more lonely nights talking to her until I fell asleep.

So after a master's in Physics, I got a Ph.D. in the History of Science – studying her. Maybe if my obsession had been a little more practical, I wouldn't be sitting on a couch outside Dr. Chambers's office, picking imaginary lint off my sweater, trying to pretend I'm not panicking. I taught science in a junior high for a year. If I lose this fellowship, I suppose I could do that again. It's a depressing thought.

The great man's secretary finally buzzes me into his office. Dr. Chambers is a balding, pouchy man in an immaculate, perfect suit. His office smells like lemon furniture polish and pipe tobacco. It's wood-paneled, plushly carpeted, with about an acre of mahogany desk. A copy of my dissertation sits on one corner.

"Dr. McCullough." He waves me to a chair. "You seem to be quite an expert on Sara Baxter Clarke."

"She was a brilliant woman," I say nervously, and hope that's the right direction for the conversation.

"Indeed. What do you make of her last paper, the one she never presented?" He picks up my work and turns to a page marked with a pale green Post-it. "'An Argument for a Practical Tempokinetics?'" He lights his pipe .and looks at me through the smoke.

"I'd certainly love to read it," I say, taking a gamble. I'd give anything for a copy of that paper. I wait for the inevitable lecture about wasting my academic career studying a long-dead crackpot.

"You would? Do you actually believe Clarke had discovered a method for time travel?" he asks. "Time travel, Dr. McCullough?"

I take a bigger gamble. "Yes, I do."

Then Dr. Chambers surprises me. "So do I. I'm certain of it. I was working with her assistant, Jim Kennedy. He retired a few months after the accident. It's taken me 40 years to rediscover what was tragically lost back then."

I stare at him in disbelief. "You've perfected time travel?"

He shakes his head. "Not perfected. But I assure you, tempokinetics is a reality."

Suddenly my knees won't quite hold me. I sit down in the padded leather chair next to his desk and stare at him. "You've actually done it?"

He nods. "There's been a great deal of research on tempokinetics in the last 40 years. Very hush-hush, of course. A lot of government money. But recently, several key discoveries in high-intensity gravitational field theory have made it possible for us to finally construct a working tempokinetic chamber."

I'm having a hard time taking this all in. "Why did you want to see me?" I ask.

He leans against the corner of his desk. "We need someone to talk to Dr. Clarke."

"You mean she's alive?" My heart skips several beats.

He shakes his head. "No."

"Then—?"

"Dr. McCullough, I approved your application to this university because you know more about Sara Clarke and her work than anyone else we've found. I'm offering you a once in a lifetime opportunity." He clears his throat. "I'm offering to send you back in time to attend the 1956 International Conference for Experimental Physics. I need a copy of Clarke's last paper."

I just stare at him. This feels like some sort of test, but I have no idea what the right response is. "Why?" I ask finally.

"Because our apparatus works, but it's not practical," Dr. Chambers says, tamping his pipe. "The energy requirements for the gravitational field are enormous. The only material that's even remotely feasible is an isotope they've developed up at the Lawrence lab, and there's only enough of it for one round trip. I believe Clarke's missing paper contains the solution to our energy problem."

After all these years, it's confusing to hear someone taking Dr. Clarke's work seriously. I'm so used to being on the defensive about her, I don't know how to react. I slip automatically into scientist mode – detached and rational. "Assuming your tempokinetic chamber is operational, how do you propose that I locate Dr. Clarke?"

He picks up a piece of stiff ivory paper and hands it to me. "This is my invitation to the opening reception of the conference Friday night, at the St.

Francis Hotel. Unfortunately I couldn't attend. I was back east that week. Family matters."

I look at the engraved paper in my hand. Somewhere in my files is a xerox copy of one of these invitations. It's odd to hold a real one. "This will get me into the party. Then you'd like me to introduce myself to Sara Baxter Clarke, and ask her for a copy of her unpublished paper?"

"In a nutshell. I can give you some cash to help, er, convince her if necessary. Frankly, I don't care how you do it. I *want* that paper, Dr. McCullough."

He looks a little agitated now, and there's a shrill undertone to his voice. I suspect Dr. Chambers is planning to take credit for what's in the paper, maybe even hoping for that second Nobel. I think for a minute. Dr. Clarke's will left everything to Jim Kennedy, her assistant and fiancé. Even if Chambers gets the credit, maybe there's a way to reward the people who actually did the work. I make up a large, random number.

"I think $30,000 should do it." I clutch the arm of the chair and rub my thumb nervously over the smooth polished wood.

Dr. Chambers starts to protest, then just waves his hand. "Fine. Fine. Whatever it takes. Funding for this project is not an issue. As I said, we only have enough of the isotope to power one trip into the past and back – yours. If you recover the paper successfully, we'll be able to develop the technology for many, many more excursions. If not—" he lets his sentence trail off.

"Other people *have* tried this?" I ask, warily. It occurs to me I may be the guinea pig, usually an expendable item.

He pauses for a long moment. "No. You'll be the first. Your records indicate you have no family, is that correct?"

I nod. My father died two years ago, and the longest relationship I've ever had only lasted six months. But Chambers doesn't strike me as a liberal. Even if I was still living with Nancy, I doubt if he would count her as family. "It's a big risk. What if I decline?"

"Your post-doc application will be reviewed," he shrugs. "I'm sure you'll be happy at some other university."

So it's all or nothing. I try to weigh all the variables, make a reasoned decision. But I can't. I don't feel like a scientist right now. I feel like a ten-year-old kid, being offered the only thing I've ever wanted – the chance to meet Sara Baxter Clarke.

"I'll do it," I say.

"Excellent." Chambers switches gears, assuming a brisk, businesslike manner. "You'll leave a week from today at precisely 6:32 a.m. You cannot take any-thing – underwear, clothes, shoes, watch – that was manufactured after 1956. My secretary has a list of antique clothing stores in the area, and some fashion magazines of the times." He looks at my jeans with distaste. "Please choose something appropriate for the reception. Can you do anything with your hair?"

My hair is short. Nothing radical, not in Berkeley in the 90s. It's more like early Beatles – what they called a pixie cut when I was a little girl – except I was always too tall and gawky to be a pixie. I run my fingers self-consciously through it and shake my head.

Chambers sighs and continues. "Very well. Now, since we have to allow for the return of Clarke's manuscript, you must take something of equivalent mass – and also of that era. I'll give you the draft copy of my own dissertation. You will also be supplied with a driver's license and university faculty card from the period, along with packets of vintage currency. You'll return with the manuscript at exactly 11:37 Monday morning. There will be no second chance. Do you understand?"

I nod, a little annoyed at his patronizing tone of voice. "If I miss the deadline, I'll be stuck in the past forever. Dr. Clarke is the only other person who could possibly send me home, and she won't be around on Monday morning. Unless—?" I let the question hang in the air.

"Absolutely not. There is one immutable law of tempokinetics, Dr. McCullough. You cannot change the past. I trust you'll remember that?" he says, standing.

Our meeting is over. I leave his office with the biggest news of my life. I wish I had someone to call and share it with. I'd settle for someone to help me shop for clothes.

Friday, February 17, 1995. 6:20 a.m.

The supply closet on the ground floor of LeConte Hall is narrow and dimly lit, filled with boxes of rubber gloves, lab coats, shop towels. Unlike many places on campus, the Physics building hasn't been remodeled in the last 40 years. This has always been a closet, and it isn't likely to be occupied at 6:30 on any Friday morning.

I sit on the concrete floor, my back against a wall, dressed in an appropriate period costume. I think I should feel nervous, but I feel oddly detached. I sip from a cup of lukewarm 7-11 coffee and observe. I don't have any role in this part of the experiment – I'm just the guinea pig. Dr. Chambers's assistants step carefully over my outstretched legs and make the final adjustments to the battery of apparatus that surrounds me.

At exactly 6:28 by my antique Timex, Dr. Chambers himself appears in the doorway. He shows me a thick packet of worn bills and the bulky, rubber-banded typescript of his dissertation, then slips both of them into a battered leather briefcase. He places the case on my lap and extends his hand. But when I reach up to shake it, he frowns and takes the 7-11 cup.

"Good luck, Dr. McCullough," he says formally. Nothing more. What more would he say to a guinea pig? He looks at his watch, then hands the cup to a young man in a black T-shirt, who types in one last line of code, turns off the light, and closes the door.

I sit in the dark and begin to get the willies. No one has ever done this. I don't know if the cool linoleum under my legs is the last thing I will ever feel. Sweat drips down between my breasts as the apparatus begins to hum. There is a moment of intense – sensation. It's not sound, or vibration, or anything I can quantify. It's as if all the fingernails in the world are suddenly raked down all the blackboards, and in the same moment oxygen is transmuted to lead. I am pressed to the floor by a monstrous force, but every hair on my body is erect. Just when I feel I can't stand it any more, the humming stops.

My pulse is racing, and I feel dizzy, a little nauseous. I sit for a minute, half-expecting Dr. Chambers to come in and tell me the experiment has failed, but no one comes. I try to stand – my right leg has fallen asleep – and grope for the light switch near the door.

In the light from the single bulb, I see that the apparatus is gone, but the gray metal shelves are stacked with the same boxes of gloves and shop towels. My leg all pins and needles, I lean against a brown cardboard box stenciled Bayside Laundry Service, San Francisco 3, California.

It takes me a minute before I realize what's odd. Either those are very old towels, or I'm somewhere pre-ZIP code.

I let myself out of the closet, and walk awkwardly down the empty hallway, my spectator pumps echoing on the linoleum. I search for further confirmation. The first room I peer into is a lab – high stools in front of black slab tables with Bunsen burners, gray boxes full of dials and switches. A slide rule at every station.

I've made it.

Friday, February 17, 1956. 7:00 a.m.
The campus is deserted on this drizzly February dawn, as is Telegraph Avenue. The streetlights are still on – white lights, not yellow sodium – and through the mist I can see faint lines of red and green neon on stores down the avenue. I feel like Marco Polo as I navigate through a world that is both alien and familiar. The buildings are the same, but the storefronts and signs look like stage sets or photos from old *Life* magazines.

It takes me more than an hour to walk downtown. I am disoriented by each shop window, each passing car. I feel as if I'm a little drunk, walking too attentively through the landscape, and not connected to it. Maybe it's the colors. Everything looks too real. I grew up with grainy black-and-white TV reruns and 50s technicolor films that have faded over time, and it's disconcerting that this world is not overlaid with that pink-orange tinge.

The warm aromas of coffee and bacon lure me into a hole-in-the-wall cafe. I order the special – eggs, bacon, hash browns and toast. The toast comes dripping with butter and the jelly is in a glass jar, not a little plastic tub. When the bill comes it is 55¢. I leave a generous dime tip then catch the yellow F bus and ride down Shattuck Avenue, staring at the round-fendered black Chevys and occasional pink Studebakers that fill the streets.

The bus is full of morning commuters – men in dark jackets and hats, women in dresses and hats. In my tailored suit I fit right in. I'm surprised that no one looks 50s – retro 50s – the 50s that filtered down to the 90s. No poodle skirts, no DA haircuts. All the men remind me of my pop. A man in a gray felt hat has the *Chronicle*, and I read over his shoulder. Eisenhower is considering a second term. The San Francisco police chief promises a crackdown on vice. *Peanuts* tops the comics page and there's a Rock Hudson movie playing at the Castro Theatre. Nothing new there.

As we cross the Bay Bridge I'm amazed at how small San Francisco looks – the skyline is carved stone, not glass and steel towers. A green Muni streetcar takes me down the middle of Market Street to Powell. I check into the St. Francis, the city's finest hotel. My room costs less than I've paid for a night in a Motel 6.

All my worldly goods fit on the desktop – Chambers's manuscript; a brown leather wallet with a driver's license, a Berkeley faculty card, and twenty-three dollars in small bills; the invitation to the reception tonight; and 30,000 dollars in banded stacks of 50-dollar bills. I pull three bills off the top of one stack and put the rest in the drawer, under the cream-colored hotel stationery. I have to get out of this suit and these shoes.

Woolworth's has a toothbrush and other plastic toiletries, and a tin "Tom Corbett, Space Cadet" alarm clock. I find a pair of pleated pants, an Oxford cloth shirt, and wool sweater at the City of Paris. Macy's Men's Shop yields a pair of "dungarees" and two T-shirts I can sleep in – 69 cents each. A snippy clerk gives me the eye in the Boys department, so I invent a nephew, little Billy, and buy him black basketball sneakers that are just my size.

After a shower and a change of clothes, I try to collect my thoughts, but I'm too keyed up to sit still. In a few hours I'll actually be in the same room as Sara Baxter Clarke. I can't distinguish between fear and excitement, and spend the afternoon wandering aimlessly around the city, gawking like a tourist.

Friday, February 17, 1956. 7:00 p.m.

Back in my spectator pumps and my tailored navy suit, I present myself at the doorway of the reception ballroom and surrender my invitation. The tuxedoed young man looks over my shoulder, as if he's expecting someone behind me. After a moment he clears his throat.

"And you're Mrs.—?" he asks, looking down at his typewritten list.

"Dr. McCullough," I say coolly, and give him an even stare. "Mr. Chambers is out of town. He asked me to take his place."

After a moment's hesitation he nods, and writes my name on a white card, pinning it to my lapel like a corsage.

Ballroom A is a sea of gray suits, crew cuts, bow-ties and heavy black-rimmed glasses. Almost everyone is male, as I expected, and almost everyone is smoking, which surprises me. Over in one corner is a knot of women in bright cocktail dresses, each with a lacquered football helmet of hair. Barbie's cultural foremothers.

I accept a canapé from a passing waiter and ease my way to the corner. Which one is Dr. Clarke? I stand a few feet back, scanning nametags. Mrs. Niels Bohr. Mrs. Richard Feynman. Mrs. Ernest Lawrence. I am impressed by the company I'm in, and dismayed that none of the women has a name of her own. I smile an empty cocktail party smile as I move away from the wives and scan the room. Gray suits with a sprinkling of blue, but all male. Did I arrive too early?

I am looking for a safe corner, one with a large, sheltering potted palm, when I hear a blustery male voice say, "So, Dr. Clarke. Trying the H.G. Wells route, are you? Waste of the taxpayer's money, all that science fiction stuff, don't you think?"

A woman's voice answers. "Not at all. Perhaps I can change your mind at Monday's session." I can't see her yet, but her voice is smooth and rich, with a bit of a lilt or a brogue – one of those vocal clues that says "I'm not an American." I stand rooted to the carpet, so awestruck I'm unable to move.

"Jimmy, will you see if there's more champagne about?" I hear her ask. I see a motion in the sea of gray and astonish myself by flagging a waiter and taking two slender flutes from his tray. I step forward in the direction of her voice. "Here you go," I say, trying to keep my hand from shaking. "I've got an extra."

"How very resourceful of you," she laughs. I am surprised that she is a few inches shorter than me. I'd forgotten she'd be about my age. She takes the glass and offers me her other hand. "Sara Clarke," she says.

"Carol McCullough." I touch her palm. The room seems suddenly bright and the voices around me fade into a murmur. I think for a moment that I'm de-materializing back to 1995, but nothing so dramatic happens. I'm just so stunned that I forget to breathe while I look at her.

Since I was ten years old, no matter where we lived, I have had a picture of Sara Baxter Clarke over my desk. I cut it out of that old physics magazine. It is grainy, black and white, the only photo of her I've ever found. In it, she's who I always wanted to be – competent, serious, every inch a scientist. She wears a white lab coat and a pair of rimless glasses, her hair pulled back from her face. A bald man in an identical lab coat is showing her a piece of equipment. Neither of them is smiling.

I know every inch of that picture by heart. But I didn't know that her hair was a coppery red, or that her eyes were such a deep, clear green. And until this moment, it had never occurred to me that she could laugh.

The slender blond man standing next to her interrupts my reverie. "I'm Jim Kennedy, Sara's assistant."

Jim Kennedy. Her fiancé. I feel like the characters in my favorite novel are all coming to life, one by one.

"You're not a wife, are you?" he asks.

I shake my head. "Post doc. I've only been at Cal a month."

He smiles. "We're neighbors, then. What's your field?"

I take a deep breath. "Tempokinetics. I'm a great admirer of Dr. Clarke's work." The blustery man scowls at me and leaves in search of other prey.

"Really?" Dr. Clarke turns, raising one eyebrow in surprise. "Well then we should have a chat. Are you—?" She stops in mid-sentence and swears almost inaudibly. "Damn. It's Dr. Wilkins and I must be pleasant. He's quite a muckety-muck at the NSF, and I need the funding." She takes a long swallow of champagne, draining the crystal flute. "Jimmy, why don't you get Dr. McCullough another drink and see if you can persuade her to join us for supper."

I start to make a polite protest, but Jimmy takes my elbow and steers me through the crowd to an unoccupied sofa. Half an hour later we are deep in a discussion of quantum field theory when Dr. Clarke appears and says, "Let's make a discreet exit, shall we? I'm famished."

Like conspirators, we slip out a side door and down a flight of service stairs. The Powell Street cable car takes us over Nob Hill into North Beach, the Italian section of town. We walk up Columbus to one of my favorite restaurants – the New Pisa – where I discover that nothing much has changed in 40 years except the prices.

The waiter brings a carafe of red wine and a trio of squat drinking glasses and we eat family style – bowls of pasta with red sauce and steaming loaves of crusty garlic bread. I am speechless as Sara Baxter Clarke talks about her work, blithely answering questions I have wanted to ask my whole life. She is brilliant, fascinating. And beautiful. My food disappears without me noticing a single mouthful.

Over coffee and spumoni she insists, for the third time, that I call her Sara, and asks me about my own studies. I have to catch myself a few times, biting back citations from Stephen Hawking and other works that won't be published for decades. It is such an engrossing, exhilarating conversation, I can't bring myself to shift it to Chambers's agenda. We leave when we notice the restaurant has no other customers.

"How about a nightcap?" she suggests when we reach the sidewalk.

"Not for me," Jimmy begs off. "I've got an 8:30 symposium tomorrow morning. But why don't you two go on ahead. The Paper Doll is just around the corner."

Sara gives him an odd, cold look and shakes her head. "Not funny, James," she says and glances over at me. I shrug noncommittally. It seems they have a private joke I'm not in on.

"Just a thought," he says, then kisses her on the cheek and leaves. Sara and I walk down to Vesuvio's, one of the bars where Kerouac, Ferlinghetti, and Ginsberg spawned the Beat Generation. Make that *will* spawn. I think we're a few months too early.

Sara orders another carafe of raw red wine. I feel shy around her, intimidated, I guess. I've dreamed of meeting her for so long, and I want her to like me. As we begin to talk, we discover how similar, and lonely, our childhoods were. We were raised as only children. We both begged for chemistry sets we never got. We were expected to know how to iron, not know about ions. Midway through her second glass of wine, Sara sighs.

"Oh, bugger it all. Nothing's really changed, you know. It's still just snickers and snubs. I'm tired of fighting for a seat in the old boys' club. Monday's paper represents five years of hard work, and there aren't a handful of people at this entire conference who've had the decency to treat me as anything but a joke." She squeezes her napkin into a tighter and tighter wad, and a tear trickles down her cheek. "How do you stand it, Carol?"

How can I tell her? I've stood it because of you. You're my hero. I've always asked myself what Sara Baxter Clarke would do, and steeled myself to push through. But now she's not a hero. She's real, this woman across the table from me. This Sara's not the invincible, ever-practical scientist I always thought she was. She's as young and as vulnerable as I am.

I want to ease her pain the way that she, as my imaginary mentor, has always eased mine. I reach over and put my hand over hers; she stiffens, but she doesn't pull away. Her hand is soft under mine, and I think of touching her hair, gently brushing the red tendrils off the back of her neck, kissing the salty tears on her cheek.

Maybe I've always had a crush on Sara Baxter Clarke. But I can't be falling in love with her. She's straight. She's 40 years older than I am. And in the back of my mind, the chilling voice of reality reminds me that she'll also be dead in two days. I can't reconcile that with the vibrant woman sitting in this smoky North

Beach bar. I don't want to. I drink two more glasses of wine and hope that will silence the voice long enough for me to enjoy these few moments.

We are still talking, our fingertips brushing on the scarred wooden tabletop, when the bartender announces last call. "Oh, bloody hell," she says. "I've been having such a lovely time I've gone and missed the last ferry. I hope I have enough for the cab fare. My Chevy's over in the car park at Berkeley."

"That's ridiculous," I hear myself say. "I've got a room at the hotel. Come back with me and catch the ferry in the morning." It's the wine talking. I don't know what I'll do if she says yes. I want her to say yes so much.

"No, I couldn't impose. I'll simply—" she protests, and then stops. "Oh, yes, then. Thank you. It's very generous."

So here we are. At 2:00 a.m. the hotel lobby is plush and utterly empty. We ride up in the elevator in a sleepy silence that becomes awkward as soon as we are alone in the room. I nervously gather my new clothes off the only bed and gesture to her to sit down. I pull a T-shirt out of its crinkly cellophane wrapper. "Here," I hand it to her. "It's not elegant, but it'll have to do as a nightgown."

She looks at the T-shirt in her lap, and at the dungarees and black sneakers in my arms, an odd expression on her face. Then she sighs, a deep, achy sounding sigh. It's the oddest reaction to a T-shirt I've ever heard.

"The Paper Doll would have been all right, wouldn't it?" she asks softly.

Puzzled, I stop crinkling the other cellophane wrapper and lean against the dresser. "I guess so. I've never been there." She looks worried, so I keep talking. "But there are a lot of places I haven't been. I'm new in town. Just got here. Don't know anybody yet, haven't really gotten around. What kind of place is it?"

She freezes for a moment, then says, almost in a whisper, "It's a bar for women."

"Oh," I nod. "Well, that's okay." Why would Jimmy suggest a gay bar? It's an odd thing to tell your fiancée. Did he guess about me somehow? Or maybe he just thought we'd be safer there late at night, since—

My musings – and any other rational thoughts – come to a dead stop when Sara Baxter Clarke stands up, cups my face in both her hands and kisses me gently on the lips. She pulls away, just a few inches, and looks at me.

I can't believe this is happening. "Aren't you – isn't Jimmy—?"

"He's my dearest chum, and my partner in the lab. But romantically? No. Protective camouflage. For both of us," she answers, stroking my face.

I don't know what to do. Every dream I've ever had is coming true tonight. But how can I kiss her? How can I begin something I know is doomed? She must see the indecision in my face, because she looks scared, and starts to take a step backwards. And I can't let her go. Not yet. I put my hand on the back of her neck and pull her into a second, longer kiss.

We move to the bed after a few minutes. I feel shy, not wanting to make a wrong move. But she kisses my face, my neck, and pulls me down onto her. We begin slowly, cautiously undressing each other. I fumble at the unfamiliar garter belts and stockings, and she smiles, undoing the rubber clasps for me. Her slender body is pale and freckled, her breasts small with dusty pink nipples.

Her fingers gently stroke my arms, my thighs. When I hesitantly put my mouth on her breast, she moans, deep in her throat, and laces her fingers through my hair. After a minute her hands ease my head down her body. The hair between her legs is ginger, the ends dark and wet. I taste the salty musk of her when I part her lips with my tongue. She moans again, almost a growl. When she comes it is a single, fierce explosion.

We finally fall into an exhausted sleep, spooned around each other, both T-shirts still crumpled on the floor.

Saturday, February 18, 1956. 7:00 a.m.
Light comes through a crack in the curtains. I'm alone in a strange bed. I'm sure last night was a dream, but then I hear the shower come on in the bathroom. Sara emerges a few minutes later, toweling her hair. She smiles and leans over me – warm and wet and smelling of soap.

"I have to go," she whispers, and kisses me.

I want to ask if I'll see her again, want to pull her down next to me and hold her for hours. But I just stroke her hair and say nothing.

She sits on the edge of the bed. "I've got an eleven o'clock lab, and there's another dreadful cocktail thing at Stanford this evening. I'd give it a miss, but Shockley's going to be there, and he's front runner for the next Nobel, so I have to make an appearance. Meet me after?"

"Yes," I say, breathing again. "Where?"

"Why don't you take the train down. I'll pick you up at the Palo Alto station at half-past seven and we can drive to the coast for dinner. Wear those nice black trousers. If it's not too dreary, we'll walk on the beach."

She picks up her wrinkled suit from the floor where it landed last night, and gets dressed. "Half past seven, then?" she says, and kisses my cheek. The door clicks shut and she's gone.

I lie tangled in the sheets, and curl up into the pillow like a contented cat. I am almost asleep again when an image intrudes – a crumpled Chevy on the rocks below Devil's Slide. It's like a fragment of a nightmare, not quite real in the morning light. But which dream is real now?

Until last night, part of what had made Sara Baxter Clarke so compelling was her enigmatic death. Like Amelia Earhart or James Dean, she had been a brilliant star that ended so abruptly she became legendary. Larger than life. But I can still feel where her lips brushed my cheek. Now she's very much life-size, and despite Chambers's warnings, I will do anything to keep her that way.

Saturday, February 18, 1956. 7:20 p.m.
The platform at the Palo Alto train station is cold and windy. I'm glad I've got a sweater, but it makes my suit jacket uncomfortably tight across my shoulders. I've finished the newspaper and am reading the train schedule when Sara comes up behind me.

"Hullo there," she says. She's wearing a nubby beige dress under a dark wool coat and looks quite elegant.

"Hi." I reach to give her a hug, but she steps back.

"Have you gone mad?" she says, scowling. She crosses her arms over her chest. "What on earth were you thinking?"

"Sorry." I'm not sure what I've done. "It's nice to see you," I say hesitantly.

"Yes, well, me too. But you can't just – oh, you know," she says, waving her hand.

I don't, so I shrug. She gives me an annoyed look, then turns and opens the car door. I stand on the pavement for a minute, bewildered, then get in.

Her Chevy feels huge compared to the Toyota I drive at home, and there are no seatbelts. We drive in uncomfortable silence all through Palo Alto and onto the winding, two-lane road that leads to the coast. Our second date isn't going well.

After about ten minutes, I can't stand it any more. "I'm sorry about the hug. I guess it's still a big deal here, huh?"

She turns her head slightly, still keeping her eyes on the road. "Here?" she asks. "What utopia are you from, then?"

I spent the day wandering the city in a kind of haze, alternately giddy in love and worrying about this moment. How can I tell her where – when – I'm from? And how much should I tell her about why? I count to three, and then count again before I answer. "From the future."

"Very funny," she says. I can hear in her voice that she's hurt. She stares straight ahead again.

"Sara, I'm serious. Your work on time travel isn't just theory. I'm a post-doc at Cal. In 1995. The head of the physics department, Dr. Chambers, sent me back here to talk to you. He says he worked with you and Jimmy, back before he won the Nobel Prize."

She doesn't say anything for a minute, then pulls over onto a wide place at the side of the road. She switches off the engine and turns towards me.

"Ray Chambers? The Nobel Prize? Jimmy says he can barely do his own lab work." She shakes her head, then lights a cigarette, flicking the match out the window into the darkness. "Ray set you up for this, didn't he? To get back at Jimmy for last term's grade? Well, it's a terrible joke," she says turning away, "and you are one of the cruelest people I have ever met."

"Sara, it's not a joke. Please believe me." I reach across the seat to take her hand, but she jerks it away.

I take a deep breath, trying deperately to think of something that will convince her. "Look, I know it sounds crazy, but hear me out. In September, *Modern Physics* is going to publish an article about you and your work. When I was ten years old – in 1975 – I read it sitting on the back porch of my father's quarters at Fort Ord. That article inspired me to go into science. I read about you, and I knew when I grew up I wanted to travel through time."

She stubs out her cigarette. "Go on."

So I tell her all about my academic career, and my "assignment" from Chambers. She listens without interrupting me. I can't see her expression in the darkened car.

After I finish, she says nothing, then sighs. "This is rather a lot to digest, you know. But I can't very well believe in my work without giving your story some credence, can I?" She lights another cigarette, then asks the question I've been dreading. "So if you've come all this way to offer me an enormous sum for my paper, does that mean something happened to it – or to me?" I still can't see her face, but her voice is shaking.

I can't do it. I can't tell her. I grope for a convincing lie. "There was a fire. A lot of papers were lost. Yours is the one they want."

"I'm not a faculty member at *your* Cal, am I?"

"No."

She takes a long drag on her cigarette, then asks, so softly I can barely hear her, "Am I—?" She lets her question trail off and is silent for a minute, then sighs again. "No, I won't ask. I think I prefer to bumble about like other mortals. You're a dangerous woman, Carol McCullough. I'm afraid you can tell me too many things I have no right to know." She reaches for the ignition key, then stops. "There is one thing I must know, though. Was last night as carefully planned as everything else?"

"Jesus, no." I reach over and touch her hand. She lets me hold it this time. "No, I had no idea. Other than finding you at the reception, last night had nothing to do with science."

To my great relief, she chuckles. "Well, perhaps chemistry, don't you think?" She glances in the rearview mirror then pulls me across the wide front seat and into her arms. We hold each other in the darkness for a long time, and kiss for even longer. Her lips taste faintly of gin.

We have a leisurely dinner at a restaurant overlooking the beach in Half Moon Bay. Fresh fish and a dry white wine. I have the urge to tell her about the picture, about how important she's been to me. But as I start to speak, I realize she's more important to me now, so I just tell her that. We finish the meal gazing at each other as if we were ordinary lovers.

Outside the restaurant, the sky is cloudy and cold, the breeze tangy with salt and kelp. Sara pulls off her high heels and we walk down a sandy path, holding hands in the darkness. Within minutes we are both freezing. I pull her to me and lean down to kiss her on the deserted beach. "You know what I'd like," I say, over the roar of the surf.

"What?" she murmurs into my neck.

"I'd like to take you dancing."

She shakes her head. "We can't. Not here. Not now. It's against the law, you know. Or perhaps you don't. But it is, I'm afraid. And the police have been on a rampage in the city lately. One bar lost its license just because two men were holding hands. They arrested both as sexual vagrants and for being – oh, what was the phrase – lewd and dissolute persons."

"Sexual vagrants? That's outrageous!"

"Exactly what the newspapers said. An outrage to public decency. Jimmy knew one of the poor chaps. He was in Engineering at Stanford, but after his name and address were published in the paper, he lost his job. Does that still go on where you're from?"

"I don't think so. Maybe in some places. I don't really know. I'm afraid I don't pay any attention to politics. I've never needed to."

Sara sighs. "What a wonderful luxury that must be, not having to be so careful all the time."

"I guess so." I feel a little guilty that it's not something I worry about. But I was four years old when Stonewall happened. By the time I came out, in college, being gay was more of a lifestyle than a perversion. At least in San Francisco.

"It's sure a lot more public," I say after a minute. "Last year there were a quarter of a million people at the Gay Pride parade. Dancing down Market Street and carrying signs about how great it is to be queer."

"You're pulling my leg now. Aren't you?" When I shake my head she smiles. "Well, I'm glad. I'm glad that this witch hunt ends. And in a few months, when I get my equipment up and running, perhaps I shall travel to dance at your parade. But for tonight, why don't we just go to my house? At least I've got a new hi-fi."

So we head back up the coast. One advantage to these old cars, the front seat is as big as a couch; we drive up Highway 1 sitting next to each other, my arm resting on her thigh. The ocean is a flat, black void on our left, until the road begins to climb and the water disappears behind jagged cliffs. On the driver's side the road drops off steeply as we approach Devil's Slide.

I feel like I'm coming to the scary part of a movie I've seen before. I'm afraid I know what happens next. My right hand grips the upholstery and I brace myself for the oncoming car or the loose patch of gravel or whatever it is that will send us skidding off the road and onto the rocks.

But nothing happens. Sara hums as she drives, and I realize that although this is the spot I dread, it means nothing to her. At least not tonight.

As the road levels out again, it is desolate, with few signs of civilization. Just beyond a sign that says "Sharp Park" is a trailer camp with a string of bare light bulbs outlining its perimeter. Across the road is a seedy-looking roadhouse with a neon sign that blinks "Hazel's." The parking lot is jammed with cars. Saturday night in the middle of nowhere.

We drive another hundred yards when Sara suddenly snaps her fingers and does a U-turn.

Please don't go back to the cliffs, I beg silently. "What's up?" I ask out loud.

"Hazel's. Jimmy was telling me about it last week. It's become a rather gay club, and since it's over the county line, out here in the boondocks, he says anything goes. Including dancing. Besides, I thought I spotted his car."

"Are you sure?"

"No, but there aren't that many '39 Packards still on the road. If it isn't, we'll just continue on." She pulls into the parking lot and finds a space at the back, between the trash cans and the ocean.

Hazel's is a noisy, smoky place – a small, single room with a bar along one side – jammed wall-to-wall with people. Hundreds of them, mostly men, but more than a few women. When I look closer, I realize that some of the "men" are actually women with slicked-back hair, ties, and sportcoats.

We manage to get two beers, and find Jimmy on the edge of the dance floor – a minuscule square of linoleum, not more than 10 x 10, where dozens of people are dancing to Bill Haley & the Comets blasting from the jukebox. Jimmy's in a tweed jacket and chinos, his arm around the waist of a young Latino man in a tight white T-shirt and even tighter blue jeans. We elbow our way through to them and Sara gives Jimmy a kiss on the cheek. "Hullo, love," she says.

He's obviously surprised – shocked – to see Sara, but when he sees me behind her, he grins. "I told you so."

"James, you don't know the half of it," Sara says, smiling, and puts her arm around me.

We dance for a few songs in the hot, crowded bar. I take off my jacket, then my sweater, draping them over the railing next to the bottles of beer. After the next song I roll up the sleeves of my button-down shirt. When Jimmy offers to buy another round of beers, I look at my watch and shake my head. It's midnight, and as much as I wanted to dance with Sara, I want to sleep with her even more.

"One last dance, then let's go, okay?" I ask, shouting to be heard over the noise of the crowd and the jukebox. "I'm bushed."

She nods. Johnny Mathis starts to sing, and we slow dance, our arms around each other. My eyes are closed and Sara's head is resting on my shoulder when the first of the cops bursts through the front door.

Sunday, February 19, 1956. 12:05 a.m.

A small army of uniformed men storms into the bar. Everywhere around us people are screaming in panic, and I'm buffeted by the bodies running in all directions. People near the back race for the rear door. A red-faced, heavy-set man in khaki, a gold star on his chest, climbs onto the bar. "This is a raid," he shouts. He has brought reporters with him, and flashbulbs suddenly illuminate the stunned, terrified faces of people who had been sipping their drinks moments before.

Khaki-shirted deputies, nightsticks in hand, block the front door. There are so many uniforms. At least 40 men – highway patrol, sheriff's department, and even some army MPs – begin to form a gauntlet leading to the back door, now the only exit.

Jimmy grabs my shoulders. "Dance with Antonio," he says urgently. "I've just met him, but it's our best chance of getting out of here. I'll take Sara."

I nod and the Latino man's muscular arms are around my waist. He smiles shyly just as someone pulls the plug on the jukebox and Johnny Mathis stops in mid-croon. The room is quiet for a moment, then the cops begin barking orders. We stand against the railing, Jimmy's arm curled protectively around Sara's shoulders, Antonio's around mine. Other people have done the same thing, but there are not enough women, and men who had been dancing now stand apart from each other, looking scared.

The uniforms are lining people up, herding them like sheep toward the back. We join the line and inch forward. The glare of headlights through the half-open back door cuts through the smoky room like the beam from a movie projector. There is an icy draft and I reach back for my sweater, but the railing is too far away, and the crush of people too solid to move any direction but forward. Jimmy sees me shivering and drapes his sportcoat over my shoulders.

We are in line for more than an hour, as the cops at the back door check everyone's ID. Sara leans against Jimmy's chest, squeezing my hand tightly once or twice, when no one's looking. I am scared, shaking, but the uniforms seem to be letting most people go. Every few seconds, a car starts up in the parking lot, and I can hear the crunch of tires on gravel as someone leaves Hazel's for the freedom of the highway.

As we get closer to the door, I can see a line of black vans parked just outside, ringing the exit. They are paneled with wooden benches, filled with the men who are not going home, most of them sitting with their shoulders sagging. One van holds a few women with crew cuts or slicked-back hair, who glare defiantly into the night.

We are ten people back from the door when Jimmy slips a key into my hand and whispers into my ear. "We'll have to take separate cars. Drive Sara's back to the city and we'll meet at the lobby bar in your hotel." "The bar will be closed," I whisper back. "Take my key and meet me in the room. I'll get another at the desk." He nods as I hand it to him.

The cop at the door looks at Sara's elegant dress and coat, barely glances at her outstretched ID, and waves her and Jimmy outside without a word. She pauses at the door and looks back at me, but an MP shakes his head and points to the parking lot. "Now or never, lady," he says, and Sara and Jimmy disappear into the night.

I'm alone. Antonio is a total stranger, but his strong arm is my only support until a man in a suit pulls him away. "Nice try, sweetie," the man says to him. "But I've seen you in here before, dancing with your pansy friends." He turns to the khaki-shirted deputy and says, "He's one of the perverts. Book him." The cop pulls Antonio's arm up between his shoulder blades, then cuffs his hands behind his back. "Time for a little ride, pretty boy," he grins, and drags Antonio out into one of the black vans.

Without thinking, I take a step towards his retreating back. "Not so fast," says another cop, with acne scars across both cheeks. He looks at Jimmy's jacket, and down at my pants and my black basketball shoes with a sneer. Then he puts his hands on my breasts, groping me. "Loose ones. Not all tied down like those other he-shes. I like that." He leers and pinches one of my nipples.

I yell for help, and try to pull away, but he laughs and shoves me up against the stack of beer cases that line the back hallway. He pokes his nightstick between my legs. "So you want to be a man, huh, butchie? Well, just what do you think you've got in there?" He jerks his nightstick up into my crotch so hard tears come to my eyes.

I stare at him, in pain, in disbelief. I am too stunned to move or to say anything. He cuffs my hands and pushes me out the back door and into the van with the other glaring women.

Sunday, February 19, 1956. 10:00 a.m.

I plead guilty to being a sex offender, and pay the $50 fine. Being arrested can't ruin my life. I don't even exist here.

Sara and Jimmy are waiting on a wooden bench outside the holding cell of the San Mateo County jail. "Are you all right, love?" she asks.

I shrug. "I'm exhausted. I didn't sleep. There were ten of us in one cell. The woman next to me – a stone butch? – really tough, Frankie – she had a pompadour – two cops took her down the hall – when she came back the whole side of her face was swollen, and after that she didn't say anything to anyone, but I'm okay, I just—" I start to shake. Sara takes one arm and Jimmy takes the other, and they walk me gently out to the parking lot.

The three of us sit in the front seat of Jimmy's car, and as soon as we are out of sight of the jail, Sara puts her arms around me and holds me, brushing the hair off my forehead. When Jimmy takes the turnoff to the San Mateo bridge, she says, "We checked you out of the hotel this morning. Precious little to check, actually, except for the briefcase. Anyway, I thought you'd be more comfortable at my house. We need to get you some breakfast and a bed." She kisses me on the cheek. "I've told Jimmy everything, by the way."

I nod sleepily, and the next thing I know we're standing on the front steps of a brown shingled cottage and Jimmy's pulling away. I don't think I'm hungry, but Sara makes scrambled eggs and bacon and toast, and I eat every scrap of it. She runs a hot bath, grimacing at the purpling, thumb-shaped bruises on my upper arms, and gently washes my hair and my back. When she tucks me into bed, pulling a blue quilt around me, and curls up beside me, I start to cry. I feel so battered and so fragile, and I can't remember the last time someone took care of me this way.

Sunday, February 19, 1956. 5:00 p.m.

I wake up to the sound of rain and the enticing smell of pot roast baking in the oven. Sara has laid out my jeans and a brown sweater at the end of the bed. I put them on, then pad barefoot into the kitchen. There are cardboard boxes piled in one corner, and Jimmy and Sara are sitting at the yellow formica table with cups of tea, talking intently.

"Oh good, you're awake." She stands and gives me a hug. "There's tea in the pot. If you think you're up to it, Jimmy and I need to tell you a few things."

"I'm a little sore, but I'll be okay. I'm not crazy about the 50s, though." I pour from the heavy ceramic pot. The tea is some sort of Chinese blend, fragrant and smoky. "What's up?"

"First a question. If my paper isn't entirely – complete – could there possibly be any repercussions for you?"

I think for a minute. "I don't think so. If anyone knew exactly what was in it, they wouldn't have sent me."

"Splendid. In that case, I've come to a decision." She pats the battered brown briefcase. "In exchange for the extraordinary wad of cash in here, we shall send back a perfectly reasonable-sounding paper. What only the three of us will know is that I have left a few things out. This, for example." She picks up a pen, scribbles a complex series of numbers and symbols on a piece of paper, and hands it to me.

I study it for a minute. It's very high-level stuff, but I know enough physics to get the gist of it. "If this really works, it's the answer to the energy problem. It's exactly the piece Chambers needs."

"Very, very good," she says, smiling. "It's also the part I will never give him."

I raise one eyebrow.

"I read the first few chapters of his dissertation this afternoon while you were sleeping," she says, tapping the manuscript with her pen. "It's a bit uneven, although parts of it are quite good. Unfortunately, the good parts were written by a graduate student named Gilbert Young."

I raise the other eyebrow. "But that paper's what Chambers wins the Nobel for."

"Son of a bitch." Jimmy slaps his hand down onto the table. "Gil was working for me while he finished the last of his dissertation. He was a bright guy, original research, solid future – but he started having these headaches. The tumor was inoperable, and he died six months ago. Ray said he'd clean out Gil's office for me. I just figured he was trying to get back on my good side."

"We can't change what Ray does with Gil's work. But I won't give him my work to steal in the future." Sara shoves Chambers's manuscript to the other side of the table. "Or now. I've decided not to present my paper in the morning."

I feel very lightheaded. I *know* she doesn't give her paper, but – "Why not?" I ask.

"While I was reading the manuscript this afternoon, I heard that fat sheriff interviewed on the radio. They arrested 90 people at Hazel's last night, Carol, people like us. People who only wanted to dance with each other. But he kept bragging about how they cleaned out a nest of perverts. And I realized – in a blinding moment of clarity – that the university is a branch of the state, and the sheriff is enforcing the state's laws. I'm working for people who believe it's morally right to abuse you – or me – or Jimmy. And I can't do that any more."

"Here, here!" Jimmy says, smiling. "The only problem is, as I explained to her this morning, the administration is likely to take a very dim view of being embarrassed in front of every major physicist in the country. Not to mention they feel Sara's research is university property." He looks at me and takes a sip of tea. "So we decided it might be best if Sara disappeared for a while."

I stare at both of them, my mouth open. I have that same odd feeling of *déjà vu* that I did in the car last night.

"I've cleaned everything that's hers out of our office and the lab," Jimmy says. "It's all in the trunk of my car."

"And those," Sara says, gesturing to the boxes in the corner, "are what I value from my desk and my library here. Other than my Nana's teapot and some clothes, it's all I'll really need for a while. Jimmy's family has a vacation home out in West Marin, so I won't have to worry about rent – or privacy."

I'm still staring. "What about your career?"

Sara puts down her teacup with a bang and begins pacing the floor. "Oh, bugger my career. I'm not giving up my *work*, just the university – and its hypocrisy. If one of my colleagues had a little fling, nothing much would come of it. But as a woman, I'm supposed to be some sort of paragon of unsullied Victorian virtue. Just by being *in* that bar last night, I put my 'career' in jeopardy. They'd crucify me if they knew who – or what – I am. I don't want to live that way any more."

She brings the teapot to the table and sits down, pouring us each another cup. "End of tirade. But that's why I had to ask about your money. It's enough to live on for a good long while, and to buy all the equipment I need. In a few months, with a decent lab, I should be this close," she says, holding her thumb and forefinger together, "to time travel in practice as well as in theory. And that discovery will be mine – ours. Not the university's. Not the government's."

Jimmy nods. "I'll stay down here and finish this term. That way I can keep tabs on things and order equipment without arousing suspicion."

"Won't they come looking for you?" I ask Sara. I feel very surreal. Part of me has always wanted to know *why* this all happened, and part of me feels like I'm just prompting the part I know comes next.

"Not if they think there's no reason to look," Jimmy says. "We'll take my car back to Hazel's and pick up hers. Devil's Slide is only a few miles up the road. It's—"

"It's a rainy night," I finish. "Treacherous stretch of highway. Accidents happen there all the time. They'll find Sara's car in the morning, but no body. Washed out to sea. Everyone will think it's tragic that she died so young," I say softly. My throat is tight and I'm fighting back tears. "At least I always have."

They both stare at me. Sara gets up and stands behind me, wrapping her arms around my shoulders. "So that *is* how it happens?" she asks, hugging me tight. "All along you've assumed I'd be dead in the morning?"

I nod. I don't trust my voice enough to say anything.

To my great surprise, she laughs. "Well, I'm not going to be. One of the first lessons you should have learned as a scientist is never assume," she says, kissing the top of my head. "But what a terrible secret for you to have been carting about. Thank you for not telling me. It would have ruined a perfectly lovely weekend. Now let's all have some supper. We've a lot to do tonight."

Monday, February 20, 1956. 12:05 a.m.

"What on earth are you doing?" Sara asks, coming into the kitchen and talking around the toothbrush in her mouth. "It's our last night – at least for a while. I was rather hoping you'd be waiting in bed when I came out of the bathroom."

"I will. Two more minutes." I'm sitting at the kitchen table, rolling a blank sheet of paper into her typewriter. I haven't let myself think about going back in the morning, about leaving Sara, and I'm delaying our inevitable conversation about it for as long as I can. "While we were driving back from wrecking your car, I had an idea about how to nail Chambers."

She takes the toothbrush out of her mouth. "It's a lovely thought, but you know you can't change anything that happens."

"I can't change the past," I agree. "But I *can* set a bomb with a very long fuse. Like 40 years."

"What? You look like the cat that's eaten the canary." She sits down next to me.

"I've retyped the title page to Chambers's dissertation – with your name on it. First thing in the morning, I'm going to rent a large safe deposit box at the Wells Fargo Bank downtown, and pay the rent in advance. Sometime in 1995, there'll be a miraculous discovery of a complete Sara Baxter Clarke manuscript. The bomb is that, after her tragic death, the esteemed Dr. Chambers appears to have published it under his own name – and won the Nobel Prize for it."

"No, you can't. It's not my work either, it's Gil's and—" she stops in mid-sentence, staring at me. "And he really *is* dead. I don't suppose I dare give a fig about academic credit anymore, should I?"

"I hope not. Besides, Chambers can't prove it's *not* yours. What's he going to say – Carol McCullough went back to the past and set me up? He'll look like a total idiot. Without your formula, all he's got is a time machine that won't work. Remember, you never present your paper. Where I come from it may be okay to be queer, but time travel is still just science fiction."

She laughs. "Well, given a choice, I suppose that's preferable, isn't it?"

I nod and pull the sheet of paper out of the typewriter.

"You're quite a resourceful girl, aren't you?" Sara says, smiling. "I could use an assistant like you." Then her smile fades and she puts her hand over mine. "I don't suppose you'd consider staying on for a few months and helping me set up the lab? I know we've only known each other for two days. But this – I – us – Oh, dammit, what I'm trying to say is I'm going to miss you."

I squeeze her hand in return, and we sit silent for a few minutes. I don't know what to say. Or to do. I don't want to go back to my own time. There's nothing for me in that life. A dissertation that I now know isn't true. An office with a black and white photo of the only person I've ever really loved – who's sitting next to me, holding my hand. I could sit like this forever. But could I stand to live the rest of my life in the closet, hiding who I am and who I love? I'm used to the 90s – I've never done research without a computer, or cooked much without a microwave. I'm afraid if I don't go back tomorrow, I'll be trapped in this reactionary past forever.

"Sara," I ask finally, "are you sure your experiments will work?"

She looks at me, her eyes warm and gentle. "If you're asking if I can promise you an escape back to your own time someday, the answer is no. I can't promise you anything, love. But if you're asking if I believe in my work, then yes. I do. Are you thinking of staying, then?"

I nod. "I want to. I just don't know if I can."

"Because of last night?" she asks softly.

"That's part of it. I was raised in a world that's so different. I don't feel right here. I don't belong."

She kisses my cheek. "I know. But gypsies never belong to the places they travel. They only belong to other gypsies."

My eyes are misty as she takes my hand and leads me to the bedroom.

Monday, February 20, 1956. 11:30 a.m.

I put the battered leather briefcase on the floor of the supply closet in LeConte Hall and close the door behind me. At 11:37 exactly, I hear the humming start, and when it stops, my shoulders sag with relief. What's done is done, and all the dies are cast. In Palo Alto an audience of restless physicists is waiting to hear a paper that will never be read. And in Berkeley, far in the future, an equally restless physicist is waiting for a messenger to finally deliver that paper.

But the messenger isn't coming back. And that may be the least of Chambers's worries.

This morning I taped the key to the safe deposit box – and a little note about the dissertation inside – into the 1945 bound volume of The Astrophysical Journal. My officemate Ted was outraged that no one had checked it out of the physics library since 1955. I'm hoping he'll be even more outraged when he discovers the secret that's hidden inside it.

I walk out of LeConte and across campus to the coffee shop where Sara is waiting for me. I don't like the political climate here, but at least I know that it will change, slowly but surely. Besides, we don't have to stay in the 50s all the time – in a few months, Sara and I plan to do a lot of traveling. Maybe one day some graduate student will want to study the mysterious disappearance of Dr. Carol McCullough. Stranger things have happened.

My only regret is not being able to see Chambers's face when he opens that briefcase and there's no manuscript. Sara and I decided that even sending back an incomplete version of her paper was dangerous. It would give Chambers enough proof that his tempokinetic experiment worked for him to get more funding and try again. So the only thing in the case is an anonymous, undated postcard of the St. Francis Hotel that says:

"Having a wonderful time. Thanks for the ride."

ON THE WATCHTOWER AT PLATAEA

Garry Kilworth

Garry Kilworth is a critically acclaimed British writer with over eighty novels and short-story collections somewhere out there in the ether, mainly fantasy and science fiction, but a few other genres too. He's currently writing a science fiction novel with the working title of *Ring-a-Ring o' Roses*. This story was first published in *Other Edens II* in 1988.

There was the chilling possibility, despite Miriam's assurance that she would dissuade the government from physical confrontation, that I might receive the order to go out and kill my adversary in the temple. They might use the argument that our future existence depended on an answer to be dredged up from the past. I wondered if I could do such a thing: and if so, how? Would I sneak from the watchtower in the night, like an assassin, and murder him in his bed? Or challenge him to single combat, like a true noble warrior is supposed to? The whole idea of such a confrontation made me feel ill and I prayed that if it should come to such a pass, they would send someone else to do the bloody job. I have no stomach for such things.

It was a shock to find that the expedition could go no further back than 429 BC: though for some of us, it was not an unwelcome one. Miriam was perhaps the only one amongst us who was annoyed that we couldn't get to Pericles. He had died earlier, in the part of the year we couldn't reach. So near – but we had hit a barrier, as solid as a rockface on the path of linear time, in the year that the Peloponnesian War was gaining momentum. It was the night that Sparta and its allies were to take positive action against the Athenians by attacking a little walled city-state called Plataea. Plataea, with its present garrison of 400 local hoplites and some eighty seconded Athenians, was virtually the only mainland supporter of Athens in the war amongst the Greeks. It was a tiny city-state, even by ancient world standards – perhaps a mile in circumference – and it was heavily outnumbered by the besieging troops led by the Spartan king, Archidamus. It didn't stand a chance, but by God it put up resistance which rivalled The Alamo for stubbornness, and surpassed it for inventiveness.

Miriam suggested we set up the recording equipment in an old abandoned watchtower on a hill outside the city. From there we could see the main gates, and could record both the Spartan attempts at breaching the walls and the defenders as they battled to keep the invaders at bay. The stonework of the watchtower was unstable, the timber rotting, and it was probably only used to shelter goats. We did not, therefore, expect to be interrupted while we settled in. In any case, while we were "travelling", we appeared as insubstantial beings and were seldom confronted. The tower was ideal. It gave us the height we needed to command a good view, and had aged enough to be a respectable establishment for spectral forms.

There were three of us in the team. Miriam was the expedition's leader; John was responsible for the recording equipment; and I was the official communicator, in contact with base camp, AD 2017. By 429, we were not at our harmonious best, having been away from home for a very long time: long enough for all our habits and individual ways to get on each other's nerves to the point of screaming. I suppose we were all missing home to a certain extent, though why we should want to go back to a world where four-fifths of the population was on the streets, starving, and kept precariously at bay by the private military armies of privileged groups, was never raised. We ourselves, of course, belonged to one of those groups, but we were aware of the instability of the situation and the depressingly obvious fact that we could do nothing to influence it. The *haves* were no longer in a position to help the *have nots,* even given the desire to do such. One of the reasons for coming on the expedition was to escape my guilt – and the constant wars between the groups. It was, as always, a mess.

"What do base say?" asked Miriam.

I could see the watch fires on the nearby city walls through her ghostly form, as she moved restlessly around the walkway of the tower. John was doing something below.

"They believe the vortex must have an outer limit," I said. "It would appear that we've reached it."

This didn't satisfy her, and I didn't expect it to. Miriam did not operate on beliefs. She liked people to *know.*

"But why here? Why now? What's so special about the year 429? It doesn't make any sense."

"You expect it to make sense?"

"I had hoped . . . oh, I don't know. An answer which wasn't still a question I suppose. Doesn't it worry you? That suddenly we come up against a wall, without any apparent reason?"

I shrugged. "Surely natural limitations are a good enough reason. Human endeavour has often come up against such things – the sound barrier, for example. They believed that was impassable at the time, but they got through it in the end. Maybe this is a comparable problem?"

"It's a bitch, I know that much," she replied in a bitter tone. "I really wanted Pericles – and the earlier battles. Marathon. Thermopylae. Damn it, there's so much we'll have to leave. Mycenae and Agamemnon. We could have confirmed all that. If we can't go back any further, Troy will remain covered in mist . . ."

Which was not altogether a bad thing as far as I was concerned. Already too many illusions had been wiped away. Why destroy all myth and legend, simply for the sake of facts? It's a pretty boring world, once the magic has been stripped off.

"Well, perhaps we shouldn't do it all at once," I suggested. "I feel as if I'm drowning as it is . . . let someone else destroy Homer."

She said, "We're not *destroying* anything. We're merely recording . . ."

"The *truth*," I said, unable to keep the sarcasm out of my tone.

She glared at me, a silvery frown marring her handsome features. We had clashed in the same way several times recently and I think she was getting tired of my outbursts.

"You have an attitude problem, Stan – don't make it my problem, too."

"I won't," I said, turning away.

In the distance, I could hear the jingle of brass: the Spartan army tramping through the night, their torches clearly visible. These sounds and sights were the cause of some consternation and excitement amongst the Plataeans on the walls of the city. The enemy had arrived. Little figures ran to and fro, between the watch fires. They had known for a few hours that Archidamus was coming: Theban traitors, spies and double agents had been busy during the day, earning a crust. The warnings had come too late for flight, however, and it was now a case of defying the vastly superior force or surrendering the city. Some of the defenders were relying on the fact that Plataea was sacred ground – it had been consecrated after a successful battle with the Persians earlier in the century – but Archidamus was not a man to take much notice of that. There were ways of appealing to the gods for a suspension of holy rights, if the need was there.

I wondered how the Spartans would react if they knew they were being recorded, visually. They were already pretty good at strutting around in grand macho style, cuffing slaves and flaunting their long hair. We had been told that historical recordings such as this would be studied for possible answers to the problems of our own time. I couldn't help but feel cynical about this idea, though I did not have the whole picture. The future, beyond my own time, had been investigated by another team and the result was a secret known only to that expedition and our illustrious government, but I couldn't help feeling it was a very bleak picture.

Besides Spartans, the invading army consisted of slave auxiliaries, a few mercenaries and volunteer forces from the cities allied with Sparta: Corinth, Megara, Elis, Thebes and many others. These cities looked to their big cousin to lead them against the upstart Athens, a city-state of little significance until the early part of the century, when it had thrashed a hugely superior force of Persians at the Battle of Marathon, and had since become too big for its sandals. If there was one thing the ancient Greeks could not stand, it was someone thinking they were better than everyone else.

Except for Plataea. Athens stood virtually alone in mainland Greece, though its maritime empire encompassed almost all the Aegean islands and the coast of Asia Minor. One of the reasons why the war would last so long was because a stalemate was inevitable. Athens was a strongly walled city, which included its harbour, and could not be penetrated by a land force. Its formidable bronze-toothed fleet of ramming triremes discouraged any idea of a naval blockade. On the other hand, Sparta had no ships to speak of, was an inland unwalled city, but positively encouraged an invasion of their territory since they relished battles and their hoplites were considered almost invincible. Certainly no Spartan would leave a field alive unless victory had been assured. Direct confrontations with such warriors, cool and unafraid of death, were not courted at all keenly, even by brave Athenians.

So, a military might and a naval power, and rarely the twain met. Stalemate. Little Plataea was in fact nothing more than a whipping boy on which Sparta could vent some of its frustration and spleen.

Miriam was looking through night viewers, at the advancing hordes. She said, "This may be the last historical battle we're able to record."

I was glad of that. Expeditions like ours tend to start out fortified by enthusiasms and good nature, only to end in disillusionment and bitter emotions, as any geographical explorer will tell you. Discoveries exact a high price from the finders, who have to pay for them with pieces of their souls.

There was a terrible scream from down below, sending lizards racing up my back. I stared at Miriam. A few moments later, John came up the makeshift ladder, looking disgusted.

"Goatboy," he explained. "Wandered in looking for a place to hide from the troops, I suppose, now that they've closed the city gates. He saw me and ran. That earth floor already stinks to high heaven with goat droppings. They must have been using it for decades."

Miriam said, "Pull up the ladder, John. We may as well settle for the night. Nothing's going to happen until morning."

Below us, the weary Allies began to arrive and put up tents, out of range of any archers who might be on the walls of the city. Trumpets were sounded, informing the Plataeans that a bloody business was about to begin, as if they didn't know that already. They were pretty noisy in unloading their gear, clattering pots and clanking bits of armour; bawling to one another as new groups arrived, in the hearty fashion of the soldier before the killing starts. We required rest, though we did not sleep while we were travelling, any more than we needed to eat or drink.

"Noisy bastards," I grumbled. "I wish they'd shut up." John, saying his prayers as he always did at that time of night, looked up sharply from his kneeling position and frowned. He did not like interruptions during such a time, and I found myself apologizing.

Here we were, making sure these squabbles amongst humankind reached a pitch of historical accuracy nobody needed. What the hell was it all about? And were our recordings doing even that useless job? I doubted it. Going back into history, you tend to get caught in the confusion of one small corner of an issue, just as if you lived in the times. One needs God's eyes to see the whole, and weigh the reasons.

It might be that God dwells beyond some far ripple of the time vortex. If you think of the vortex as an old-fashioned, long-playing record and the groove as linear time, you will have some idea how travellers are able to skip through the ages, as a too light arm of a record deck skates over a disc. It is a mental process, requiring no vehicle. Somewhere beyond those grooves, dwells the Almighty. Who wants to meet God and see *absolute truth* in all its blinding whiteness? Not me. Not me, my friend. *Eyes I dare not meet in dreams,* as the poet Eliot said.

By the next morning the Spartans had surrounded Plataea and were intent on encircling it with a palisade of sharpened stakes, leaning inwards. Archidamus wanted to be sure that no one could escape from the city. He wanted to teach the inhabitants a lesson: that siding with those nasty imperialists and free-thinkers, the Athenians, was a dangerous thing to do.

It was true that Athens had created a confederacy, mostly consisting of island states, which she subsequently milked of funds, using the money to build the Parthenon, generally beautify the city, and increase the number of ships in her fleet. It was true that anyone who requested to leave the confederacy found the equivalent of several British gunboats in their harbour within a few days. But it was equally true that the Spartans, with their two kings (one to stay at home, while the other was at war), really could not give a damn about anyone but themselves. Athens was full of woolly-minded intellectuals who not only indulged in progressive thinking and innovations, but were carefree and undisciplined with it. Sparta had long since fossilized. They had put a stop to progress some time ago. In Sparta it was forbidden to write new songs, poetry or plays, or introduce anything into society with a flavour of change about it, let alone the avant-garde stuff allowed in Athens. Why, the northern city was positively licentious in its attitudes towards art and science. Nothing which would disturb the perfection of the lifestyle Spartans had achieved at an earlier time was permitted in Lacedaemonia. Asceticism, the nobility of war, plain food and state-raised children destined for the army: these were the ideals to be upheld. Give a Spartan a coarse hair shirt, a plate of salty porridge, a lusty 300-year-old song to sing and send him out on to the battlefield, and he'll die thanking you. To the Athenians, who loved good food, new mathematics, eccentric old men asking interminable questions, incomprehensible philosophies, weird inventions, plays making fun of the gods, love, life and the pursuit of happiness – to these people the Spartans were homicidal lunatics.

I suppose it was little wonder that these two Hellenic city-states disliked each other so much.

While the thousands of figures, the keen ones still sweating in their armour, scurried about below us, busy with siege engines, we got on with our regular tasks. John had set up a hologram at the entrance to the tower. It was supposed to represent Apollo and appeared instantly on any human approach, to warn away hoplites who would have otherwise used the tower as a toilet. The hologram uttered its threats in what was probably an appalling accent, but it was the best we could do with the devices at hand. It seemed to do its job, because by noon on the first day gifts had been placed at a respectable distance from the entrance to the watchtower. They could see us, of course, drifting around the top of the tower, but I suppose we were gods, too, witnessing the heroic struggles of mortals. I did my best to assume a Zeus-like posture. We had some "thunder and lightning" for emergencies, but hadn't needed them up to that point.

The heat of the day made us generally testy and irritable, for although many of our bodily functions were suspended, we still had our senses. I found some shade under the parapet and proceeded to contact base. This time they had a little news for us which was still very vague. Something – they were not sure quite what, but told us to watch for the unusual – something was preventing a further spread of the vortex.

Watch for something unusual? Only those bloody deskriders back at base would say something like that, to travellers in an antique world, where the unusual was all around, in almost every facet of daily life. Personally, I hoped they didn't solve the problem. I was weary and homesick and a solution would mean continuing the journey. I didn't say that, of course.

I told Miriam what base had said, and she nodded.

"Thanks. We'll have to wait and see."

Boredom, that's what time travel is mostly about. Like war, it's 5 per cent feverish action, and 95 per cent sitting around with nothing to do. I settled down wearily for a game of chess with John.

"You're the Athenians and I'm the Spartans, so I get to have two kings," he joked.

I thought John uncomplicated and open, and we seemed to get on well together, though he was a good deal younger than me. I was reticent, but he didn't seem to mind that. He had not lost the bubbling enthusiasm of youth, took religion seriously (both of which got on my nerves sometimes, when I was feeling bloody), and had a love for his fellows which was difficult to resist.

Miriam was of a similar disposition to myself. Sometimes to while away the hours, I imagined a romantic connection between us, which was actually as far-fetched as any fairytale romance. Although she is a fine-looking woman, with a strong will and good mind, I was not in the least attracted to her. Interested in her, but not attracted. One of those chemical negatives I suppose. I'm sure the feeling was mutual, if she thought about it at all. She had a husband back home, and two kids, not that she ever talked about them. I expect they were none of our damn business.

"Your move."

John shifted his head, to interfere with my line of vision.

"Oh, yes – sorry. Daydreaming."

"Occupational hazard," he said, with more seriousness than was warranted, but I didn't have time to question his tone. At that moment a bird, a bee-eater I think, flew into the parapet with a *smack*. I picked the beautiful creature up, whereupon it pecked me, struggled from my grasp and took groggily to the air. It seemed to be all right.

John gave me a significant stare. It is one of his theories that the vortex interferes with the orientation of natural creatures (time travellers being unnatural, I expect) and he intended towrite something of the sort when we returned to civilization. He could be right, but if he believed that anyone would care about such things, he was in for a disappointment. It is one of my theories that, back at base camp, they don't even care about the orientation of humans, let alone bee-eaters.

Over the next few weeks we watched the activity below with a little more interest. It became a battle of wits, not swords, the main combatants being the engineering corps of both sides. The Spartan army laboured long and hard to build an earth ramp against the city wall, up which they intended to march and take the city, at the same time catapulting fireballs through the air and making futile attempts at scaling the walls with ladders. Before the ramp was completed the wily Plataeans had raised the height of the wall at that point, cannibalizing their houses for stone blocks. It became a race. The taller grew the ramp, the higher went the wall. In the end, Archidamus put every available man on earth-carrying duty and by this means he managed to gain on the Plataeans, threatening to reach the top of the wall.

Undaunted, the defenders then tunnelled underneath their own wall and through the earth ramp, removing the loose soil until the ramp collapsed. On seeing his beautiful mound fall in on itself, Archidamus stamped around threatening death and destruction. He sacrificed a dozen goats to us, and to another shrine – a small temple about half a mile from our position – hoping we would intervene divinely on his behalf in subduing these irksome Plataeans. He came to us in full armour, wearing the classic Corinthian helmet, with its decorated, elongated cheek-pieces and transverse crest of horsehair, his brass-faced shield and muscled greaves, and a heavy bell cuirass. For a Spartan he was pretty flashy, but then he was a king. It was obvious that he was hot and testy, and I think it took all his reserve to remain polite to the gods who were giving his troops such a hard time. The goats' entrails stank like hell thrown into the copper bowl of flames and we retreated below for a while, leaving a hologram of Athena to receive promises of temples to be erected, and pilgrimages to be undertaken, once victory was within Spartan grasp. On reflection it was not the most tactful thing to have done, since Athena was the goddess protector of Athens, but we didn't think about that at the time. In any case, what was irritating Archidamus was the fact that the enemy would not come out and fight like men. Spartans do not make the best besieging troops in the world. They hate messing around with mud, sticks and stones, when they could be looking their best, charging across a windy plain with their long black hair streaming and their mouths uttering terrible war cries, ready to stick in or be stuck by some sharp instrument. There were lots of jokes about the Spartans, even amongst their own allies. The one about the shrew's brain in a lion's skin was a particular favourite.

After delivering his dubious gifts, Archidamus then went to the small temple, inside the palisade, and repeated the exercise. Miriam became very curious about this rival for our affections and managed to find a spot around the tower wall where she could see the building through her viewers. Finally, she asked John to take some footage, though it was not possible to see directly into the obliquely positioned temple and our line of sight was hampered by the points of some tall stakes on the palisade. We ran this through, afterwards, and managed to catch a glimpse of a figure between the marble columns. He had some kind of tri-legged device with him, the head of which seemed to incorporate revolving flaps of stiff material, that flashed like mirrors when it was operated. More significant than this, however, was the fact that the white-robed figure working this machine seemed to have semi-transparent flesh. Certainly, he was treated with distant, wary reverence by the Hellenes, in the same way that we were ourselves. There was very good reason to suppose that we and this elusive person, and possibly any companions hidden by the temple walls, had a great deal in common.

"Look at those beggars – you've got to hand it to them," said John, with admiration in his voice. He was, of course, talking about the Plataeans. Archidamus's engineers had stopped the Plataeans' little game of removing earth from under the ramp by packing baskets with clay and placing them as foundation blocks for the ramp. These could not be drawn away like loose earth. The defenders met this device by digging a subterranean mine to beyond the ramp and allowing the whole effort to collapse again. By this time, the earth was having to be carried from some considerable distance by the besiegers and they were becoming dispirited and thoroughly disgruntled by the whole affair. Deserters began to drift by our watchtower at night, and one or two minor kings packed their tents and took their citizen-soldiers home. Archidamus executed some malefactors, possibly to create an interesting diversion to the gruelling manual labour, but was unable to stem the increasing tide of dissatisfaction amongst his troops. He had sent for some Scythian archers of his own, but the Plataeans erected animal-hide screens on top of the walls to protect themselves and the bowmen were less than effective. Added to this there was the smell of sickness in the air, which was part of the sordid business of a war in stalemate.

Some time after calling base regarding the possible presence of another group of travellers, we were asked to obtain further information. Miriam had already spent a great deal of time studying the mysterious occupants of the small temple through the viewer, but there were too many obstacles in the way to get anything concrete.

"We'll have to go over there," she said, "and get a closer look."

John and I glanced at one another. Although the watchtower was far from secure against aggressive action, it provided protection for us in that it had become a sacred building to the Greeks and was unlikely to be violated. It ensured that we remained distant, aloof figures which could be avoided simply by giving the crumbling structure a wide berth. Once we started wandering amongst them, like ordinary mortals, we were in danger of becoming too familiar. It was not beyond the realm of possibility that some brave hoplite might decide to challenge the "gods": after all, Odysseus had got away with it. It was a risky business. Of course, we could protect ourselves with our own weapons, but never having had to resort to such drastic action, we were unsure of the consequences.

"What do you suggest?" asked John.

Miriam said, "I'll take the portable and go over there for some close-ups – Stan, you come with me."

Not *too* close, I thought, but nodded in assent. I must admit, the anticipation of some excitement gave me a charge, despite my apprehension.

We set off just as the Hellenic dawn was coming up. Miriam carried the hand recorder, while I self-consciously cradled a weapon in my arms. I knew how to use it, but it was more a question of whether it knew how to use me. I have never had to hurt anyone in my life – physically, that is. We walked between tents and lean-to shacks that had been raised by the invaders, without hindrance, though one or two wide-eyed early risers moved quickly out of our way. When we got to the gate in the palisade of stakes we had a problem. It was closed.

"What do we do?" I said. "We can't walk through the damn thing. And gods don't fiddle with gates, wondering how they open."

Before Miriam could answer, one of the sentries rushed forward and pulled at a leather thong. The gate swung open. He had not, of course, understood the language of the gods, but our intentions were obvious and the mere fact that I had voiced some strange words must have spurred him to action.

We made our way towards the temple. I prayed that the archers on the walls of Plataea would be too overawed by the sight of a pair of semi-transparent beings to fire any arrows.

We stood off about a hundred yards from the temple, where we had a clear view into the interior, and Miriam began recording. Half-hidden in the heavy shadows thrown by the columns we could see a translucent form operating the instrument with the metallic flaps, which was possibly some sort of heliographic recording device, though it looked like something knocked-up in a Swiss toy-maker's workshop for an Anibian prince. The stand was fashioned of polished wood covered in hieroglyphics and there were lead weights on plumblines which balanced wooden arms connected to cogged wheels. Behind the operator, hanging from the pillars, were two elongated scrolls of painted parchment, one with a picture of a dog's body with a monkey's head, the other depicting some sort of wading bird.

As we stood, both he and us, recording each other – a situation that struck me as rather ironical – another wraith-like figure appeared, wearing a long, flowing robe and decorated headcloth. He whispered to his companion, then went back into a side-room. I was sure that the directional mike would capture that whisper, which when amplified would reveal their language. Miriam gestured to me without speaking and we stopped recording, making our way back.

The gate had been left open for us and we passed through without any problem, but on the other side of the palisade it was a different matter. Word had got around that the gods were abroad and a huge crowd had gathered, though there was a wide path through the middle of it leading to the tower. I could see John on the ramparts of the watchtower with a weapon in his hands.

"Okay," said Miriam, "let's go, Stan. Don't look back . . ."

I had no intention of doing anything of the sort. All I wanted to do was reach the tower, safely. As we walked down the avenue a murmuring broke out amongst the troops, which grew in volume to uncoordinated chants. I hadn't any doubt we were being petitioned for various miracles, both collective and individual. Two-thirds of the way along there was a horrible incident. A young man broke from the crowd and threw himself at my feet, attempting to clutch my ankle. Before he could lay a hand on me, he was pinned to the mud by several spears, thrown by his comrades. I wanted to be sick on the spot as I watched him squirming in the dust like some wounded porcupine. We made the tower without any further problems and shortly afterwards the crowd broke up as Spartan officers moved amongst them with whips. The young man's body was removed and as he was carried away I wondered what had made him so desperate as to brave touching a god. Maybe his mother or father was terminally ill? Or a close friend had been killed whom he wished us to raise from the dead? Or perhaps he was just a helot, a slave, who thought we could free him from the oppression of his Spartan masters with a wave of our hands? Poor bastard.

Later, I went to Miriam and asked her about our friends in the temple. We had already mentioned the word *Egyptian* to each other, though all we had as evidence for that were the hieroglyphics and the pictures. A group of future ancient Egyptian revivalists? Just because they wore the costume and carried the artefacts didn't make them residents from the banks of the Nile. Though there didn't seem any logical reason for a masquerade, cults are seldom founded on reason, or by rational thinkers.

"The bird picture was an ibis,' said Miriam, "and the dog-monkey . . . well, the ancient Egyptian god Zehuti was represented by both those symbolic characters."

"Zehuti?" I knew a little of the culture in question, but this was a new one to me.

"Sorry, you probably know him as Thoth – Zehuti is his older name. The Greeks identified him with Hermes, which makes sense. Hermes the messenger – a *traveller*?"

"Anything else?"

"Yes – Thoth was also the patron of science and inventions, the spokesman of the gods and their keeper of the records. Thoth invented all the arts and sciences, including surveying, geometry, astronomy, soothsaying, magic . . . do I need to go on?"

"No. I get the picture. If you wanted a god of time travel, Thoth fits the bill quite nicely. So what do we do now?"

She gave me a grim smile.

"Wait. What else? Once you've transmitted the recording back to base, we wait until they come up with definites."

So we did what we were best, and worst, at: waiting.

One evening the three of us were sitting, more or less in a rough circle, engaged in frivolous tasks. I was actually doing nothing. The stars were out, above us, and I could hear the snuffling of livestock and the clank of pots from down below. The area around Plataea was becoming as unsavoury as the no man's land of World War Two, with cesspits filling the air with an appalling stink and churned mud giving the landscape an ugly, open-wound appearance. We had been discussing our situation. Something was preventing the outer ring of our vortex from going any further, and base believed that what was stopping it was another vortex, coming from the other direction, the distant past. The two whirlpools were touching each other, and neither could proceed before the other retreated. Our friends were indeed early Egyptians. It had taken a while for this idea to sink in, but when I thought deeply about it, it was not at all far-fetched.

On a simple level, time travel involved a psychological state induced by the use of darkness and light, resulting in the fusion of infinites, of space and time. The dark and light became unified into a substance which formed a shape. That shape was common enough in the night sky: a spiral on a flat plane, moving outwards from the centre of the group, some of whom remained behind to form an anchor point for the vortex. The base-camp group. The room in which we had begun the vigil was no longer a room, but something else: a super-physical universe that possibly exists in all minds at some level of perception. There was no technological reason why an earlier civilization could not have made the same mental discovery. On the other hand, people of our rank were still not privy to the source of the discovery, and it could well be that the knowledge had *come* from the past. Egyptian documents perhaps, only recently decoded? I remembered something about mirrors being used to flood the dark interior passages of the pyramids with light from the sun.

A horrible thought occurred to me.

"We're not going to stay here, until they go back?"

Miriam shrugged.

"I don't know. I'm awaiting instructions from base."

"Now look, we're the ones that are here. Not them."

"You know how it is, as well as I do, Stan."

I stared at her.

"I know how it is," I said, bitterly.

Her phantom features produced a faint smile.

I lay awake that night, thinking about the stalemate I had got myself into. Egyptians? If they had had time travel for so long, why hadn't they visited future centuries? But then, of course, they probably had and we had run screaming from them, just as the goatboy had fled from us. They probably had a similar policy to ourselves: no interference, just record and return. So, on their umpteenth journey into the future, they had come to a halt, suddenly, and had no doubt come to the same conclusion as we had: someone was blocking the path.

It wasn't difficult either to see how such a discovery might be lost to future civilizations. Hadn't certain surgical techniques been lost too? Time travel would undoubtedly have been in the hands of an elite: probably a priesthood. Some pharaoh, his brain addled as the result of a long lineage of incestuous relationships, had destroyed the brotherhood in a fit of pique; or the priests had been put to death by invading barbarians, their secret locked in stone vaults.

On the current front, the Plataeans were still one jump ahead of the Spartans. They had abandoned their mining operations and instead had built another crescent-shaped wall inside their own, so that when the ramp was finally completed, the Spartans were faced with a second, higher obstacle. Peltasts tried lobbing spears over the higher wall, only to find the distance was too great. Archidamus had his men fill the gap between the two walls with faggots and set light to it, but a chance storm doused this attempt to burn down the city. We got a few indignant looks from the Spartans after that. As gods, we were responsible for the weather. The war trumpets of the invaders filled the air with bleating notes which we felt sure were a criticism of us and our seeming partiality towards the defenders.

Finally, battering rams were employed, over the gap between the walls, but the Plataeans had a device – a huge beam on chains – which they dropped on to the ram-headed war machines and snapped off the ends.

Archidamus gave up. He ordered yet another wall to be built, outside the palisade of stakes, and left part of his army to guard it. Winter was beginning to set in and the king had had enough of the inglorious mudbath in which he had been wallowing. He went home, to his family in the south.

The majority of the Egyptians also withdrew at this point. One of them remained behind.

We received our orders from base.

"One of us must stay," said Miriam, "until a relief can be sent. If we all go back, the vortex will recede with us and the Egyptians will move forward, gain on us."

"A Mexican stand-off," I said, disgustedly.

"Right. We can't allow them the opportunity to invade the territory we already hold . . ."

"Shit," I said, ignoring a black look from John, "now we've got a cold war on our hands. Even *time* isn't safe from ownership. First it was things, then it was countries . . . now it's time itself. Why don't we build a bloody great wall across this year, like Archidamus, and send an army of guards to defend it?"

Miriam said, "Sarcasm won't help at this stage, Stan."

"No, I don't suppose it will, but it makes me feel good. So what happens now? We draw straws?"

"I suggest we do it democratically." She produced three shards of pottery that she had gathered from the ground below, and distributed one to each of us.

"We each write the name of the person we think most competent to remain behind," she explained, "and then toss them in the middle."

"Most competent – I like the diplomatic language," I muttered. John, I knew, would put down his own name. He was one of those selfless types, who volunteered for everything. His minor household gods were Duty and Honour. He would actually *want* to stay.

I picked up my piece of pot. It was an unglazed shard depicting two wrestlers locked in an eternal, motionless struggle, each seemingly of equal strength and skill, and each determined not to give ground. I turned it over and wrote JOHN in clear letters, before placing it, picture-side up, in the middle of the ring.

Two other pieces clattered against mine. Miriam sorted through them, turning them over.

My name was on two of them.

I turned to John.

"Thanks," I said.

"It had to be somebody. You're the best man for the job."

"Bullshit," I said. I turned to Miriam. "What if I refuse to stay? I'll resign, terminate my contract."

Miriam shook her head. "You won't do that. You'd never get another trip and while you get restless in the field, you get even worse at home. I know your type, Stan. Once you've been back a couple of weeks you'll be yelling to go again."

She was right, damn her. While I got bored in the field, I was twice as bad back home.

"I'm not a type," I said, and got up to go below. Shortly afterwards, Miriam followed me.

"I'm sorry, Stan," She touched my arm. "You see it for what it is – another political attempt at putting up fences by possessive, parochial old farts. Unless I go back and convince them otherwise, they'll be sending death squads down the line to wipe out the Egyptians. You do understand?"

"So it had to be me."

"John's too young to leave here alone. I'll get them to replace you as soon as I can – until then . . ."

She held out her slim hand and I placed my own slowly and gently into her grip. The touch of her skin was like warm silk.

"Goodbye," I said.

She went up the ladder and John came down next.

I said coldly, "What is this? Visiting day?"

"I came to say goodbye," he said, stiffly.

I stared hard at him, hoping I was making it difficult, hoping the bastard was uncomfortable and squirming.

"Why me, John? You had a reason."

He suddenly looked very prim, his spectral features assuming a sharp quality.

"I thought about volunteering myself, but that would have meant you two going back alone – together, that is . . ." He became flustered. "She's a married woman, Stan. She'll go back to her husband and forget you."

I rocked on my heels.

"*What?* What the hell are you talking about?"

"Miriam. I've seen the way you two look at each other."

I stared at him, finding it difficult to believe he could be so stupid.

"You're a fool, John. The worst kind of fool. It's people like you, with twisted minds, that start things like that war out there. Go on – get out of my sight."

He started to climb the ladder, then he looked down and gave me a Parthian shot. "You put *my* name on your shard. Why should I feel guilty about putting yours?"

And he was right, but that didn't stop me from wanting to jerk the ladder from under him and breaking his bloody neck.

They were gone within the hour, leaving me to haunt the Greeks all on my own, a solitary ghost moving restlessly around the parapet of the tower. I saw my Egyptian counterpart once, in the small hours, as a shimmering figure came out into the open to stare at my prison. I thought for a moment he or she was going to wave again, but nothing so interesting happened, and I was left to think about my predicament once more. I knew how slowly things moved back home. They had all the time in the world. I wondered whether Egyptians could learn to play chess. It was a pity Diogenes wasn't yet alive, or I might have been tempted to wander down to Corinth. He would certainly have enjoyed a game, providing I stayed out of his sun. Me and Diogenes, sitting on top of his barrel, playing chess a thousand years before the game was invented – that would have been something. Plato was a newborn babe in arms. Socrates was around, in his early forties, but who would want to play with that cunning man. Once he got the hang of it, you'd never win a game.

Flurries of snow began to drift in, over the mountains. The little Plataeans were in for a hard winter. I knew the result of the siege, of course. Three hundred Plataeans and seconded Athenians would make a break for it in a year's time, killing the sentries left by Archidamus on the outer wall and getting away in the dark. All of them would make it, to Athens, fooling their pursuers into following a false trail, their inventive minds never flagging when it came to survival. Those Plataeans whose hearts failed them when it came to risking the escape, almost two hundred, would be put to death by the irate Spartans. The city itself would be razed. Perhaps the Spartans would learn something from the incident, but I doubted it. There was certainly a lot of patience around in the ancient world.

Patience. I wondered how much patience those people from the land of the pharaohs had, because it occurred to me that the natural movement of time was on their side. Provided we did nothing but maintain the status quo, standing nose to nose on the edges of our own vortices, they would gain, ever so gradually. Hour by hour, day by day, we were moving back to that place I call home.

We might replace our frontier guards, by one or by thousands, but the plain fact of the matter is we will eventually be pushed back to where we belong. Why, they've already gained several months as it is . . . only another twenty-five centuries and I'll be back in my own back yard.

Then again, I might receive that terrible message I have been dreading, which would turn me from being the Athenian I believe I am, into a Spartan. Which would have me laying down my scroll and taking up the spear and shield. A ghost-warrior from the future, running forth to meet a god-soldier from the past. I can only hope that the possible historical havoc such action might cause will govern any decision made back home. I can't help thinking, however, that the wish for sense to prevail must have been in the lips of a million-million such as me, who killed or died in fields, in trenches, in deserts and jungles, on seas and in the air.

The odds are stacked against me.

ALEXIA AND GRAHAM BELL

Rosaleen Love

Rosaleen Love is an Australian writer who has commented on
Australian science and society, in both fiction and nonfiction, for the
past forty years. She has published two collections of short fiction
with The Women's Press in the United Kingdom: *The Total Devotion
Machine* and *Evolution Annie*. Her most recent books are *Reefscape:
Reflections on the Great Barrier Reef*, Sydney and Washington, and
The Traveling Tide, short fiction, with Aqueduct Press, Seattle. She
is the recipient of the Chandler Award for lifetime achievement in
Australian Science Fiction. "Alexia and Graham Bell" was first published in *Aphelion 5* in 1986.

I suppose you know about the telephone by now, and you've heard a version
of its story. Perhaps you think it's an invention we've had for eighty years
or so.

You'll be wrong.

The telephone was invented two months ago by my brother Graham, on a
cold winter's afternoon when he had nothing better to do than fiddle around
with a few tin cans, a thermo-amp, some wires, and a junked teletype I found on
the tip. I heard some strange noises and when he yelled "Alexia" down the hall to
me, I came running, because I thought he was up to his usual dopy experiments,
dropping the cats upside down off the roof to see if they'd land on their paws,
that kind of thing. But it wasn't the cats this time. He'd hitched the teletype up so
it spoke! I saw it myself, the first time he got it working, and it was playing away
like a pianola, but sounding out the words! Words which Graham was speaking
into a tin can on the other side of the room! The telephone! Which you've all
heard about by now, though what you don't know is its secret. That it's only
been around for two months. Truly.

Why should you believe me? When the history books tell the story differently
and antique telephones fetch high prices at the market?

Let me explain. It's one of those things which was never intended to happen.
It was only after the event that all kinds of things fell into place, retrospectively.

I think the responsibility for our present mess must rest firmly with great-grandfather Alexander Graham Bell. Yes, back in 1870 he'd planned to migrate from
England to Canada but he missed the boat! So he stayed at the docks and
caught the next ship out, to Australia. West, east, what's the difference? said

great-grandfather, but he was wrong. Ever since Alexander overslept, the world of invention and discovery has taken an alternative path. Yes, the path of the telegraph and the censors and communal messenging.

Let me explain. It was only after the telephone was invented that it started influencing the past. Graham's explanation goes like this: in our day-to-day activities, we are usually working toward a future goal, I am studying to become a censor in Central Control, or I was then, all that's changed, now, and Graham is saving money so he can invent the ice-aeroplane. Okay, so we're here, in the present, and the way we perceive the future is influencing what we're doing. Equally, our present, now, is at this moment an influence on the past of our former selves and others. Graham says it's obvious to anyone with the intellect of an ant, but I don't know about the ants, they may be smarter than we give them credit for.

I can see that Graham's argument has a certain elementary logic all its own.

"Graham," I had to say, after I'd congratulated him on inventing something that worked for once, even though it was probably going to be good for nothing in the world, then that's my brother Graham, what can I expect? "Graham, what will Mother say when she sees what a mess you've made of her thermo-amp?"

Graham glared at me and made for the cat, but I grabbed it before he could upend it. Surely he knows enough about how the cat uses its tail as an inertial paddle? He doesn't have to go in for the experimental overkill! That's Graham, though, a perfectionist. A perfectionist in the creation of knowledge we could perfectly well do without.

He had all the time to experiment because he was on compo from his job as messenger boy, second class. It's not what Graham thought he was meant for in this life. So he did his best to fall down every flight of stairs between Central Message Control and the jobs he was sent on until finally he broke a few bones and got some time off to recover. Of course what he's done is make himself retrospectively redundant now we've got the telephone, and messenger boys are out of work in a big way. Yes, along the way Graham created our present crisis in unemployment.

This is how it happened. I've been a privileged witness to the scene and I have a responsibility to tell the story properly.

The telephone's great achievement is the contraction of distance. Pick up a phone and dial a number, and it doesn't matter whether the person on the other end is down the street or across the country.

Now mess around with distance, with length, and you're going to be messing around with time. That's what we've just recently come to realize. Though we should have known, I suppose. Einstein told us about it. So, basically, what has happened since Graham got busy is that the last two months have expanded out of all proportion, expanded in time that is. Two months have blown out into eighty years! It's true!

So Graham did something clever, something that worked, for once. The trouble is, it worked only too well.

At first Graham just tinkered about in the workroom. He was excited and chatty about what he was up to, but I'd heard all I wanted to know about cats and aerodynamics and the possibilities of the ice-aeroplane, so I didn't really listen as closely as I should have. "Imagine!" said Graham. "Imagine being able to speak at a distance, without a written record of the conversation! Think what it'd be like! Privacy! No censors snooping into all the details of our lives! We'll be able to talk about something without the entire teletype room knowing what's happening!"

When he said that I was listening, that's for sure, and I tried to argue back. Imagine, a world without censors reading all the messages! I took him to task on that one, I can assure you. "Graham, if someone can pick up your telephone and speak to anyone else without a record being kept, it will lead to the breakdown of law and order as we know it.

"Besides," I added, and Graham grew white about the eyes at this. Ha! I scared him properly! "If the censors get to hear about what you're doing, why, you'll do them out of a job" (and I was right about that!) "and they'll be absolutely livid!"

Graham clutched his throat with a strangled cry. "The censors? After me? No! I'm only a child! My mother loves me! How would they get to know about it?"

"Walls have ears," I said, very smugly.

"Alexia! No! Don't tell on me! I'm your brother! You'd never!"

Ha! I had him worried! But he's right. I'm not a censor-snooper. It's true, I wanted a job as a censor, but I wanted it for the pay packet and the security. I didn't have to believe all the guff they teach us about law and order. "Be careful," I said to Graham, but of course he wasn't. Once he found out what he was able to do, he just had to go ahead and do it. I didn't tell on Graham. I now know I did wrong. After all, Graham succeeded in subverting the social fabric of twentieth-century society.

I was too busy to notice, at the time. I had my work to do. I confided to my friend Greta, though. We worked together at the telegraph office.

"Mind you, if Graham's invention works, we'll soon be out of a job," I said to Greta, between the dots and the dashes.

Greta didn't believe me. "At the telegraph office? At Central Message Control? No, Alexia, that won't happen. No one ever gets sacked from here."

"They can get you for unnatural interference with the messages," I reminded her.

Greta was shocked. "Alexia, that's never happened! No one would do that! It'd be . . . monstrous!"

"What about redundancy? They can get you on that."

I shall always remember Greta's patient reply. "Alexia," she said, "morse code and semaphore and messenger boys have been around longer than your brother Graham and his crazy ideas. How's the cat?"

"On the mend."

"The ice-aeroplane, didn't you say that was another of his latest inventions?"

"Yes, but the telephone is different! I think the telephone is going to work!"

Greta was unconvinced. "We'd be able to talk to each other without everyone in the teletype room knowing the message."

"I know, I know."

"It'll mean the end of twentieth-century society as we know it!"

"No more censors!"

"Shhh!"

"Greta, I just can't get through to Graham. I keep telling him: Graham, the telephone will lead to anarchy."

"It won't ever happen," said Greta, as she lectured me on the moral desirability of the Censored State. "If we were meant to talk to each other down wires then God would have connected us up from birth."

Graham just kept on working. "Today the passageway, tomorrow the world," he announced when I came home one evening.

I found a land-line down the passage and a telephone hook-up in my bedroom. "Graham, you've gone too far this time," I bellowed into the phone when it rang. "Get your inventions out of my room!"

"Alexia, will you step into the next room for a moment?" said Graham on the phone, polite and conscious of the historic moment.

I told him a thing or two. "Greta says you're a social menace, and I agree with her!" This is a true account of the first telephone message. You may know part of the story.

First Graham wired up the passage, then he extended the line to every room in the house. Then he wanted more. He wanted to go down the street and clear across Australia, then out into the world.

And he managed to persuade people! Never mind the censors, they vanished, once the capitalist entrepreneurs took over. Graham had them convinced.

"Gas pipes, water pipes, and telephone pipes!" said Graham, his eyes gleaming and his fingers flying. "One system, one policy, one universal service!"

"One giant monopoly! And money!" replied the capitalist entrepreneur.

"One grand telephonic system linking each farm to its neighbor, each factory to its central office, each nation to the other!" said Graham, still the visionary.

Remember what it said in the paper? "We may confidently expect that Mr. Bell will give us the means of making voice and spoken words audible through the electric wires to an ear hundreds of miles distant." It happened.

I tried to warn Graham. "There may be a few social problems."

Graham didn't pay attention. "Nothing a telephone in every house won't fix," he said.

"There may be a few economic problems," I warned.

"Show me the economic problem that money won't eliminate!" There was no stopping him.

"Contract distance, contract time!"

"Only a little bit! No one will ever notice!"

"Graham, don't do it! You are going into the unknown."

"No need to worry," said Graham, "I know perfectly well what I'm doing."

Of course, he got it wrong and we all paid the price. Poor old Greta was one of the first casualties.

"Alexia, what's wrong? My life . . . it's passing so quickly! It seems only yesterday that we worked in Central Control, and now . . . the telegraph! It's vanished!"

I tried my best to distract her. "Happy birthday, darling! Fifty candles on the cake!"

"Then things changed so quickly. The telephone. . ."

"Time's a funny thing."

Greta blew at the candles. "Everything started to speed up, and things passed me by, so quickly!"

"There, there, you must have been enjoying yourself."

"It's not fair! I haven't had time to enjoy myself!"

Of course, Graham could explain it. "The distinction between past, present, and future is only an illusion," he said.

"It seems real, to me. How can yesterday become tomorrow?"

"If time contracts!"

"That's my problem! What's the solution?"

"I'm working on it," Graham muttered.

"I can't wait," said Greta, "I need it now."

I discovered that time is more than my perception of it. Time depends on the telephone.

"Nonsense!" you will say. "Time has been around for simply ages, but the telephone, why, it's only been around for a couple of years!"

"A couple of years? Did you say a couple of years? Why did you say that? I've got you, there!"

"Did I say a couple of years?" you'll say, puzzled. "Why, of course I meant a hundred years. I don't know why I said a *couple* of years, and with such conviction. It was just a silly mistake."

Aha, but silly mistakes always mean something! You're confused about the issue, admit it. There's something not quite right about the telephone, something that's hovering on the edge of your comprehension but which can't quite make the break out into your conscious mind. You know, more than you can tell.

Greta and I both noticed something happening. I've worked it out since then.

When Graham got the marketing men interested in his invention, and phones started appearing in every home, time started to speed up for most people. You know how it is, you feel that last year was only yesterday, and that the years of your life are flitting by so quickly. There is a perfectly reasonable explanation. It's because last year was only yesterday, for you, though not for me.

The censors joined the unemployed, the messenger boys went off to two world wars, and wherever the telephone spread, time accelerated in its course. It's only in countries where there are no phones that people still get full value for their lives.

I don't know why it was that Graham and I have not shared the experience. We've either been spared, or punished, for our knowledge. We have stayed outside the onward rush of time. Graham's happy. He thinks he must have invented the elixir of youth in that first experiment. Only the elixir isn't a drug made from gold, or precious herbs, or genetically engineered DNA. The elixir is a unique form of radiation which comes from standing too close to a few tin cans, a thermo-amp, old wires, and a teletype junked in a quite specific way, at a time when Jupiter is on the cusp of Uranus and the moon is in the fourth quarter.

I can't turn the clock back. I can't personally dynamite every telephone in Australia. But I see I shall have to hijack Graham and take him off to Antarctica. He'll come with me willingly enough. Where better to design the ice-aeroplane?

There's a new factor entering into the story. Graham's started to mutter about a new device to contract distance, only this time on a cosmic scale. He can do it, too. The problem with space travel, says Graham, is that space is too big. It's one thing to design a spaceship, but then it takes aeons to get anywhere in it. The stars are too far away. So Graham is working on a device to shrink the galaxy.

Instead of us reaching out to the stars, Graham will have the stars reach down to us.

This is the end. The world has suffered enough.

I, Alexia Bell, being of sound mind, must take my brother Graham to Antarctica, and there build him an ice-hangar for his ice-aeroplanes. I shall lock the door and throw the key from a high window. I make this sacrifice, for you.

A NIGHT ON THE BARBARY COAST

Kage Baker

Kage Baker was an American writer who wrote both serious and funny stories and novels, most with a fantastical or science fiction slant. She was a finalist for the Hugo Award and winner of the Theodore Sturgeon Memorial Award and the Nebula Award. "A Night on the Barbary Coast" was the winner of the first of the Emperor Norton awards for San Francisco based speculative fiction in 2003. It was originally published in *The Silver Gryphon* anthology. You can find another Company story, "Noble Mold," elsewhere in this anthology.

I'd been walking for five days, looking for Mendoza. The year was 1850.

Actually, *walking* doesn't really describe traveling through that damned vertical wilderness in which she lived. I'd crawled uphill on hands and knees, which is no fun when you're dressed as a Franciscan friar, with sandals and beads and the whole nine yards of brown burlap robe. I'd slid downhill, which is no fun either, especially when the robe rides up in back. I'd waded across freezing cold creeks and followed thready little trails through ferns, across forest floors in permanent darkness under towering redwoods. I'm talking *gloom*. One day the poets will fall in love with Big Sur, and after them the beats and hippies, but if vampires ever discover the place they'll go nuts over it.

Mendoza isn't a vampire, though she is an immortal being with a lot of problems, most of which she blames on me.

I'm an immortal being with a lot of problems, too. Like father, like daughter.

After most of a week, I finally came out on a patch of level ground about three thousand feet up. I was standing there looking *down* on clouds floating above the Pacific Ocean, and feeling kind of funny in the pit of my stomach as a result – and suddenly saw the Company-issue processing credenza on my left, nicely camouflaged. I'd found Mendoza's camp at last.

There was her bivvy tent, all right, and a table with a camp stove, and five pots with baby trees growing in them. Everything but the trees had a dusty, abandoned look.

Cripes, I thought to myself, how long since she's been here? I looked around uneasily, wondering if I ought to yoo-hoo or something, and that was when I noticed her signal coming from. . . *up?* I craned back my head.

An oak tree rose from the mountain face behind me, huge and branching wide, and high up there among the boughs Mendoza leaned. She gazed out at the sea; but with such a look of ecstatic vacancy in her eyes, I guessed she was seeing something a lot farther away than that earthly horizon.

I cleared my throat.

The vacant look went away fast, and there was something inhuman in the sharp way her head swung around.

"Hi, honey," I said. She looked down and her eyes focused on me. She has black eyes, like mine, only mine are jolly and twinkly and bright. Hers are like flint. Always been that way, even when she was a little girl.

"What the hell are you doing here, Joseph?" she said at last.

"I missed you, too, baby," I said. "Want to come down? We need to talk."

Muttering, she descended through the branches.

"Nice trees," I remarked. "Got any coffee?"

"I can make some," she said. I kept my mouth shut as she poked around in her half-empty rations locker, and I still kept it shut when she hauled out her bone-dry water jug and stared at it in a bewildered kind of way before remembering where the nearest stream was, and I didn't even remark on the fact that she had goddam *moss* in her hair, though what I wanted to yell at the top of my lungs was: *How can you live like this?*

No, I played it smart. Pretty soon we were sitting at either end of a fallen log, sipping our respective mugs of coffee, just like family.

"Mm, good Java," I lied.

"*What* do you want?" she said.

"Okay, kid, I'll tell you," I said. "The Company is sending me up to San Francisco on a job. I need a field botanist, and I had my pick of anybody in the area, so I decided on you."

I braced myself for an explosion, because sometimes Mendoza's a little touchy about surprises. But she was silent for a moment, with that bewildered expression again, and I just knew she was accessing her chronometer because she'd forgotten what year this was.

"San Francisco, huh?" she said. "But I went through Yerba Buena a century ago, Joseph. I did a complete survey of all the endemics. Specimens, DNA codes, the works. Believe me, there wasn't anything to interest Dr. Zeus."

"Well, there might be now," I said. "And that's all you need to know until we get there."

She sighed. "So, it's like that?"

"It's like that. But hey, we'll have a great time! There's a lot more up there now than fog and sand dunes."

"I'll say there is," she said grimly. "I just accessed the historical record for October 1850. There's a cholera epidemic going on. There's chronic arson. The streets are half quicksand. You really take me to some swell places, don't you?"

"How long has it been since you ate dinner in a restaurant?" I coaxed. She started to say something sarcastic in reply, looked down at whatever was floating in the bottom of her coffee, and shuddered.

"See? It'll be a nice change of scenery," I told her, as she tossed the dregs over her shoulder. I tossed out my coffee, too, in a simpatico gesture. "The Road to

Frisco! A fun-filled musical romp! Two wacky cyborgs plus one secret mission equals laughs galore!"

"Oh, shut up," she told me, but rose to strike camp.

It took us longer to get down out of the mountains than I would have liked, because Mendoza insisted on bringing her five potted trees, which were some kind of endangered species, so we had to carry them all the way to the closest Company receiving terminal in Monterey, by which time I was ready to drop the damn things down any convenient cliff. But away they went to some Company botanical garden, and, after requisitioning equipment and a couple of horses, we finally set off for San Francisco.

I guess if we had been any other two people, we'd have chatted about bygone times as we rode along. It's never safe to drag up old memories with Mendoza, though. We didn't talk much, all the way up El Camino Real, through the forests and across the scrubby hills. It wasn't until we'd left San Jose and were picking our way along the shore of the back bay, all black ooze and oyster shells, that Mendoza looked across at me and said: "We're carrying a lot of lab equipment with us. I wonder why?"

I just shrugged.

"Whatever the Company's sending us after, they want it analyzed on the spot," she said thoughtfully. "So possibly they're not sure that it's really what they want. But they need to find out."

"Could be."

"And your only field expert is being kept on a need-to-know basis, which means it's something important," she continued. "And they're sending *you*, even though you're still working undercover in the Church, being Father Rubio or whoever. Aren't you?"

"I am."

"You look even more like Mephistopheles than usual in that robe, did I ever tell you that? Anyway – why would the Company send a friar into a town full of gold miners, gamblers, and prostitutes?" Mendoza speculated. "You'll stick out like a sore thumb. And where does botany fit in?"

"I guess we'll see, huh?"

She glared at me sidelong and grumbled to herself a while, but that was okay. I had her interested in the job, at least. She was losing that thousand-year-stare that worried me so much.

I wasn't worrying about the job at all.

You could smell San Francisco miles before you got there. It wasn't the ordinary mortal aroma of a boom town without adequate sanitation, even one in the grip of cholera. San Francisco smelled like smoke, with a reek that went right up your nose and drilled into your sinuses.

It smelled this way because it had been destroyed by fire four times already, most recently only a month ago, though you wouldn't know it to look at the place. Obscenely expensive real estate where tents and shanties had stood was already filling up with brand-new frame buildings. Hammers pounded day and night along Clay, along Montgomery and Kearney and Washington. All the raw new wood was festooned with red-white-and-blue bunting, and hastily improvised Stars and Stripes flew everywhere. California had only just found out it had been admitted to the Union, and was still celebrating.

The bay was black with ships, but those closest to the shore were never going to sea again – their crews had deserted and they were already enclosed by wharves, filling in on all sides. Windows and doors had been cut in their hulls as they were converted to shops and taverns.

Way back in the sand hills, poor old Mission Dolores – built of adobe blocks by a people whose world hadn't changed in millennia, on a settlement plan first designed by officials of the Roman Empire – looked down on the crazy new world in wonderment. Mendoza and I stared, too, from where we'd reined in our horses near Rincon Hill.

"So this is an American city," said Mendoza.

"Manifest Destiny in action," I agreed, watching her. Mendoza had never liked being around mortals much. How was she going to handle a modern city, after a century and a half of wilderness? But she just set her mouth and urged her horse forward, and I was proud of her.

For all the stink of disaster, the place was *alive*. People were out and running around, doing business. There were hotels and taverns; there were groceries and bakeries and candy stores. Lightermen worked the water between those ships that hadn't yet been absorbed into the city, bringing in prospectors bound for the gold fields or crates of goods for the merchants. I heard six languages spoken before we'd crossed Clay Street. Anything could be bought or sold here, including a meal prepared by a Parisian chef. The air hummed with hunger, and enthusiasm, and a kind of rapacious innocence.

I grinned. America looked like fun.

We found a hotel on the big central wharf, and loaded our baggage into two narrow rooms whose windows looked into the rigging of a landlocked ship. Mendoza stared around at the bare plank walls.

"This is Oregon spruce," she announced. "You can still smell the forest! I'll bet this was alive and growing a month ago."

"Probably," I agreed, rummaging in my trunk. I found what I was looking for and unrolled it to see how it had survived the trip.

"What's that?"

"A subterfuge." I held the drawing up. "A beautiful gift for his Holiness the Pope! The artist's conception, anyway."

"A huge ugly crucifix?" Mendoza looked pained.

"*And* a matching rosary, baby. All to be specially crafted out of gold and – this is the important part – gold-bearing quartz from sunny California, U.S.A., so the Holy Father will know he's got faithful fans out here!"

"That's disgusting. Are you serious?"

"Of course I'm not serious, but we don't want the mortals to know that," I said, rolling up the drawing and sticking it in a carpetbag full of money. "You stay here and set up the lab, okay? I've got to go find some jewelers."

There were a lot of jewelers in San Francisco. Successful guys coming back from the Sacramento sometimes liked to commemorate their luck by having gold nuggets set in watch fobs, or stickpins, or brooches for sweethearts back east. Gold-bearing quartz, cut and polished, was also popular, and much class-ier looking.

Hiram Gainsborg, on the corner of Ohio and Broadway, had some of what I needed; so did Joseph Schwartz at Harrison and Broadway, although J. C. Russ on the corner of Harrison and Sixth had more. But I also paid a visit to Baldwin & Co. on Clay at the Plaza, and to J. H. Bradford on Kearney, and just to play it safe I went over to Dupont and Clay to see the firm of Moffat & Co., Assayers and Bankers.

So I was one pooped little friar, carrying one big heavy carpetbag, by the time I trudged back to our hotel as evening shadows descended. I'd been followed for three blocks by a Sydney ex-convict whose intent was robbery and possible murder; but I managed to ditch him by ducking into a saloon, exiting out the back and across the deck of the landlocked *Niantic,* and cutting through another saloon where I paused just long enough to order an oyster loaf and a pail of steam beer.

I'd lost him for good by the time I thumped on Mendoza's door with the carpetbag.

"Hey, honeybunch, I got dinner!"

She opened the door right away, jittery as hell. "Don't shout, for God's sake!"

"Sorry." I went in and set down the carpetbag gratefully. "I don't think the mortals are sleeping yet. It's early."

"There are three of them on this floor, and seventeen downstairs," she said, wringing her hands. "It's been a while since I've been around so many of them. I'd forgotten how loud their hearts are, Joseph. I can hear them beating."

"Aw, you'll get used to it in no time," I said. I held up the takeout. "Look! Oyster loaf and beer!"

She looked impatient, and then her eyes widened as she caught the scent of the fresh-baked sourdough loaf and the butter and the garlic and the little fried oysters . . .

"Oh, gosh," she said weakly.

So we had another nice companionable moment, sitting at the table where she'd set up the testing equipment, drinking from opposite sides of the beer pail. I lit a lamp and pulled the different paper-wrapped parcels from my carpetbag, one by one.

"What're those?" Mendoza inquired with her mouth full.

"Samples of gold-bearing quartz," I explained. "From six different places. I wrote the name of each place on the package in pencil, see? And your job is to test each sample. You're going to look for a blue-green lichen growing in the crevices with the gold."

She swallowed and shook her head, blank-faced.

"You need a microbiologist for this kind of job, Joseph, surely. Plants that primitive aren't my strong suit."

"The closest microbiologist was in Seattle," I explained. "And Agrippanilla's a pain to work with. Besides, you can handle this! Remember the Black Elysium grape? The mutant saccharomyces or whatever it was? You won yourself a field commendation on that one. This'll be easy!"

Mendoza looked pleased, but did her best to conceal it. "I'll bet your mission budget just wouldn't stretch to shipping qualified personnel down here, eh? That's the Company. Okay; I'll get started right after dinner."

"You can wait until morning," I said.

"Naah." She had a gulp of the beer. "Sleep is for sissies."

So after we ate I retired, and far into the hours of the night I could still see lamplight shining from her room, bright stripes through the plank wall every time I turned over. I knew why she was working so late.

It's not hard to sleep in a house full of mortals, if you tune out the sounds they make. Sometimes, though, just on the edge of sleep, you find yourself listening for one heartbeat that ought to be there, and it isn't. Then you wake up with a start and remember things you don't want to remember.

I opened my eyes and sunlight smacked me in the face, glittering off the bay through my open door. Mendoza was sitting on the edge of my bed, sipping from her canteen. I grunted, grimaced, and sat unsteadily.

"*Coffee,*" I croaked. She looked smug and held up her canteen.

"There's a saloon on the corner. The nice mortal sold me a whole pot of coffee for five dollars. Want some?"

"Sure." I held out my hand. "So . . . you didn't mind going down to the saloon by yourself? There are some nasty mortals in this town, kid."

"The famous Sydney Ducks? Yes, I'm aware of that." She was quietly gleeful about something. "I've lived in the Ventana for years, Joseph, dodging mountain lions! *Individual* nasty mortals don't frighten me anymore. Go ahead, try the coffee."

I sipped it cautiously. It was great. We may have been in America (famous for lousy coffee) now, but San Francisco was already *San Francisco.*

Mendoza cleared her throat and said, "I found your blue-green lichen. It was growing on the sample from Hiram Gainsborg's. The stuff looks like Stilton cheese. What is it, Joseph?"

"Something the Company wants," I said, gulping down half the coffee.

"I'll bet it does," she said, giving me that sidelong look again. "I've been sitting here, watching you drool and snore, amusing myself by accessing scientific journals on bioremediant research. Your lichen's a toxiphage, Joseph. It's perfectly happy feeding on arsenic and antimony compounds found in conjunction with gold. It breaks them down. I suspect that it could make a lot of money for anyone in the business of cleaning up industrial pollution."

"That's a really good guess, Mendoza," I said, handing back the coffee and swinging my legs over the side of the bed. I found my sandals and pulled them on.

"Isn't it?" She watched me grubbing around in my trunk for my shaving kit. "Yes, for God's sake, shave. You look like one of Torquemada's henchmen, with those blue jowls. So Dr. Zeus is doing something altruistic! In its usual corporate-profit way, of course. I don't understand why this has to be classified, but I'm impressed."

"Uh-huh." I swabbed soap on my face.

"You seem to be in an awful hurry."

"Do I?" I scraped whiskers from my cheek.

"I wonder what you're in a hurry to do?" Mendoza said. "Probably hotfoot it back to Hiram Gainsborg's, to see if he has any more of what he sold you."

"Maybe, baby."

"Can I go along?"

"Nope."

"I'm not sitting in my room all day, watching lichen grow in petrie dishes," she said. "Is it okay if I go sightseeing?"

I looked at her in the mirror, disconcerted. "Sweetheart, this is a rough town. Those guys from Australia are devils, and some of the Yankees—"

"I pity the mortal who approaches me with criminal intent," she said, smiling in a chilly kind of way. "I'll just ride out to the Golden Gate. How can I get into trouble? Ghirardelli's won't be there for another two years, right?"

I walked her down to the stable anyway, and saw her safely off before hot-footing it over to Hiram Gainsborg's, as she suspected.

Mr. Gainsborg kept a loaded rifle behind his shop counter. I came in through his door so fast he had it out and trained on me pronto, before he saw it was me.

"Apologies, Father Rubio," he said, lowering the barrel. "Back again, are you? You're in some hurry, sir." He had a white chin beard, wore a waistcoat of red-and-white striped silk, and overall gave me the disconcerting feeling I was talking to Uncle Sam.

"I was pursued by importuning persons of low moral fiber," I said.

"That a fact?" Mr. Gainsborg pursed his lips. "Well, what about that quartz you bought yesterday? Your brother friars think it'll do?"

"Yes, my son, they found it suitable," I said. "In fact, the color and quality are so magnificent, so superior to any other we have seen, that we all agreed only *you* were worthy of this important commission for the Holy Father." I laid the drawing of the crucifix down on his counter. He smiled.

"Well, sir, I'm glad to hear that. I reckon I can bring the job in at a thousand dollars pretty well." He fixed me with a hard clear eye, waiting to see if I'd flinch, but I just hauled my purse out and grinned at him.

"Price is no object to the Holy Mother Church," I said. "Shall we say, half the payment in advance?"

I counted out Chilean gold dollars while he watched, sucking his teeth, and I went on: "In fact, we were thinking of having rosaries made up as a gift for the whole College of Cardinals. Assuming, of course, that you have enough of that *particular* beautiful vein of quartz. Do you know where it was mined?"

"Don't know, sir, and that's a fact," he told me. "Miner brought in a sackful a week ago. He reckoned he could get more for it at a jeweler's because of the funny color. There's more'n enough of it in my back room to make your beads, I bet."

"Splendid," I said. "But do you recall the miner's name, in case we do need to obtain more?"

"Ayeh." Mr. Gainsborg picked up a dollar and inspected it. "Isaiah Stuckey, that was the fellow's name. Didn't say where his claim was, though. They don't tell, as a general rule."

"Understandable. Do you know where I might find the man?"

"No, sir, don't know that. He didn't have a red cent until I paid for the quartz, I can tell you; so I reckon the next place he went was a hotel." Mr. Gainsborg looked disdainful. "Unless he went straight for the El Dorado or a whorehouse, begging your pardon. Depends on how long he'd been in the mountains, don't it?"

I sighed and shook my head. "This is a city of temptation, I am afraid. Can you describe him for me?"

Mr. Gainsborg considered. "Well, sir, he had a beard."

Great. I was looking for a man with a beard in a city full of bearded men. At least I had a name.

So I spent the rest of that day trudging from hotel to boardinghouse to tent, asking if anybody there had seen Isaiah Stuckey. Half the people I asked snickered and said, "No, why?" and waited for a punchline. The other half also replied in the negative, and then asked my advice on matters spiritual. I heard confessions for seventeen prostitutes, five drunks, and a transvestite before the sun sank behind Knob Hill, but I didn't find Isaiah Stuckey.

By twilight, I had worked my way out to the landlocked ships along what would one day be Battery and Sansome Streets, though right now they were just so many rickety piers and catwalks over the harbor mud. I teetered up the gangplank of one place that declared itself the MAGNOLIA HOTEL, by means of a sign painted on a bedsheet hung over the bow. A grumpy-looking guy was swabbing the deck.

"We don't rent to no goddam greasers here," he informed me. "Even if you is a priest."

"Well, now, my son, Christ be my witness I've not come about taking rooms," I said in the thickest Dublin accent I could manage. "Allow me to introduce myself! Father Ignatius Costello. I'm after searching for a poor soul whose family's in sore need of him, and him lost in the gold fields this twelvemonth. Do you rent many rooms to miners, lad?"

"Sure we do," muttered the guy, embarrassed. "What's his name?"

"Isaiah Stuckey, or so his dear old mother said," I replied.

"Him!" The guy looked up, righteously indignant now. He pointed with his mop at a vast expanse of puke on the deck. "That's your Ike Stuckey's work, by God!"

I recoiled. "He's never got the cholera?"

"No, sir, just paralytic drunk. You ought to smell his damn *room*, after he lay in there most of a week! Boss had me fetch him out, plastered or not, on account of he ain't paid no rent in three days. I got him this far and he heaved up all over my clean floor! Then, I wish I may be struck down dead if he don't sober up instant and run down them planks like a racehorse! Boss got a shot off at him, but he kept a-running. Last we saw he was halfway to Kearney Street."

"Oh, dear," I said. "I don't suppose you'd have any idea where he was intending to go, my son?"

"No, I don't," said the guy, plunging his mop in its pail and getting back to work. "But if you run, too, you can maybe catch the son of a—" he wavered, glancing up at my ecclesiastical presence "— gun. He ain't been gone but ten minutes."

I took his advice, and hurried off through the twilight. There actually was a certain funk lingering in the air, a trail of unwashed-Stuckey molecules, that any bloodhound could have picked up without much effort – not that it would have enjoyed the experience – and incidentally any cyborg with augmented senses could follow, too.

So I was slapping along in my sandals, hot on Stuckey's trail, when I ran into Mendoza at the corner.

"Hey, Joseph!" She waved at me cheerily. "You'll never guess what I found!"

"Some plant, right?"

"And how! It's a form of *Lupinus* with—"

"That's fascinating, doll, and I mean that sincerely, but right now I could really use a lift." I jumped and swung up into the saddle behind her, only to find myself sitting on something damp. "What the hell—"

"That's my *Lupinus*. I dug up the whole plant and wrapped the root ball in a piece of my petticoat until I can transplant it into a pot. If you've squashed it, I'll wring your neck," she told me.

"No, it's okay," I said. "Look, could we just canter up the street that way? I'm chasing somebody and I don't want to lose him."

She grumbled, but dug her heels into the horse's sides and we took off, though we didn't go very far very fast because the street went straight uphill.

"It wouldn't have taken us ten minutes to go back and drop my *Lupinus* at the hotel, you know," Mendoza said. "It's a really rare subspecies, possibly a mutant form. It appears to produce photoreactive porphyrins."

"Honey, I haven't got ten minutes," I said, wrootching my butt away from the damn thing. "Wait! Turn left here!" Stuckey's trail angled away down Kearney toward Portsmouth Square, so Mendoza yanked the horse's head around and we leaned into the turn. I peered around Mendoza, trying to spot any bearded guy staggering and wheezing along. Unfortunately, the street was full of staggering bearded guys, all of them converging on Portsmouth Square.

We found out why when we got there.

Portsmouth Square was just a sandy vacant lot, but there were wire baskets full of pitch and redwood chips burning atop poles at its four corners, and bright-lit board and batten buildings lined three sides of it. The fourth side was just shops and one adobe house, like a row of respectable spinsters frowning down on their neighbors, but the rest of the place blazed like happy Gomorrah.

"Holy smoke," said Mendoza, reining up. "I'm not going in there, Joseph."

"It's just mortals having a good time," I said. Painted up on false fronts, garish as any Old West fantasy, were names like The Mazourka, Parker House, The Varsouvienne, La Souciedad, Dennison's Exchange, The Arcade. All of them were torchlit and proudly decked in red, white, and blue, so the general effect was of Hell on the Fourth of July.

"It's brothels and gambling dens," said Mendoza.

"It's theaters, too," I said defensively, pointing at the upstairs windows of the Jenny Lind.

"And saloons. What do you want here?"

"A guy named Isaiah Stuckey," I said, leaning forward. His scent was harder to pick out now, but . . . over *there* . . . "He's the miner who found our quartz.

I need to talk to him. Come on, we're blocking traffic! Let's try that one. The El Dorado."

Mendoza gritted her teeth but rode forward, and as we neared the El Dorado the scent trail grew stronger.

"He's in here," I said, sliding down from the saddle. "Come on!"

"I'll wait outside, thank you."

"You want to wait here by yourself, or you want to enter a nice civilized casino in the company of a priest?" I asked her. She looked around wildly at the happy throng of mortals.

"Damn you anyway," she said, and dismounted. We went into the El Dorado.

Maybe I shouldn't have used the words *nice civilized casino*. It was a big square place with bare board walls, and the floor sloped downhill from the entrance, because it was just propped up on pilings over the ash heaps and was already sagging. Wind whistled between the planks, and there is no night air so cold as in San Francisco. It gusted into the stark booths along one wall, curtained off with thumb tacked muslin, where the whores were working. It was shantytown squalor no Hollywood set designer would dream of depicting.

But the El Dorado had all the other trappings of an Old West saloon, with as much rococo finery as could be nailed up or propped against the plank walls. There were gilt-framed paintings of balloony nude women. There was a grand mirrored bar at one end, cut glass glittering under the oil lamps. Upon the dais a full orchestra played, good and loud, and here again the Stars and Stripes were draped, swagged and resetted in full glory.

At the gambling tables were croupiers and dealers in black suits, every one of them a gaunt Doc Holliday clone presiding over monte, or faro, or diana, or chuck-a-luck, or plain poker. A sideboard featured free food for the high rollers, and a lot of ragged men – momentary millionaires in blue jeans, back from the gold fields for the winter – were helping themselves to pie and cold beef. At the tables, their sacks of gold dust or piles of nuggets sat unattended, as safe as anything else in this town.

I wished I wasn't dressed as a friar. This was the kind of spot in which a cyborg with the ability to count cards could earn himself some money to offset operating expenses. I might have given it a try anyway, but beside me Mendoza was hyperventilating, so I just shook my head and focused on my quarry.

Isaiah Stuckey was in here somewhere. At the buffet table? No . . . At the bar? No . . . Christ, there must have been thirty guys wearing blue jeans and faded red calico shirts in here, and they all stank like bachelors. Was that him? The beefy guy looking around furtively?

"Okay, Mendoza," I said, "if you were a miner who'd just recovered consciousness after a drinking binge, stone broke – where would you go?"

"I'd go bathe myself," said Mendoza, wrinkling her nose. "But a mortal would probably try to get more money. So he'd come in here, I guess. Of course, you can only *win* money in a game of chance if you already have money to bet—"

"*STOP, THIEF!*" roared somebody, and I saw the furtive guy sprinting through the crowd with a sack of gold dust in his fist. The croupiers had risen as one, and from the recesses of their immaculate clothing produced an awesome amount of weaponry. Isaiah Stuckey – boy, could I smell him *now*! – crashed through a back window, pursued closely by bullets and bowie knives.

I said something you don't often hear a priest say and grabbed Mendoza's arm. "Come on! We have to find him before they do!"

We ran outside, where a crowd had gathered around Mendoza's horse.

"Get away from that!" Mendoza yelled. I pushed around her and gaped at what met my eyes. The sorry-looking bush bound behind Mendoza's saddle was . . . glowing in the dark, like a faded neon rose. It was also shaking back and forth, but that was because a couple of mortals were trying to pull it loose.

They were a miner, so drunk he was swaying, and a hooker only slightly less drunk, who was holding the miner up by his belt with one hand and doing her best to yank the mutant *Lupinus* free with the other.

"I *said* leave it alone!" Mendoza shoved me aside to get at the hooker.

"But I'm getting married," explained the hooker, in as much of a voice as whiskey and tobacco had left her. "An' I oughter have me a buncha roses to get married holding on to. 'Cause I ain't never been married before and I oughter have me a buncha roses."

"That is not a bunch of roses, you stupid cow, that's a rare photoreactive porphyrin-producing variant *Lupinus* specimen," Mendoza said, and I backed off at the look in her eyes and so did every sober man there, but the hooker blinked.

"Don't you use that kinda language to me," she screamed, and attempted to claw Mendoza's eyes out. Mendoza ducked and rose with a roundhouse left to the chin that knocked poor Sally Faye, or whoever she was, back on her ass, and her semiconscious fiancé went down with her.

All the menfolk present, with the exception of me, circled eagerly to give the ladies room. I jumped forward and got Mendoza's arm again.

"My very beloved daughters in Christ, is this any way to behave?" I cried, because Mendoza, with murder in her eye, was pulling a gardening trowel out of her saddlebag. Subvocally I transmitted, *Are you nuts? We've got to go after Isaiah Stuckey!* Snarling, Mendoza swung herself back into the saddle. I had to scramble to get up there, too, hitching my robe in a fairly undignified way, which got boffo laughs from the grinning onlookers before we galloped off into the night.

"Go down to Montgomery Street!" I said. "He probably came out there!"

"If one of the bullets didn't get him," said Mendoza, but she urged the horse down Clay and made a fast left onto Montgomery. Halfway along the block we slowed to a canter and I leaned out, trying to pick up the scent trail again.

"Yes!" I punched the air and nearly fell off the horse. Mendoza grabbed my hood, hauling me back up straight behind her.

"Why the hell is it so important you talk to this mortal?" she demanded.

"Head north! His trail goes back toward Washington Street," I said. "Like I said, babe, he sold that quartz to Gainsborg."

"But we already know it tested positive for your lichen," said Mendoza. At the next intersection we paused as I sniffed the air, and then pointed forward.

"He went thataway! Let's go. We want to know where he got the stuff, don't we?"

"Do we?" Mendoza kicked the horse again – I was only grateful the Company hadn't issued her spurs – and we rode on toward Jackson. "Why should we particularly need to know where the quartz was mined, Joseph? I've cultured the lichen successfully. There'll be plenty for the Company labs."

"Of course," I said, concentrating on Isaiah Stuckey's scent. "Keep going, will you? I think he's heading back toward Pacific Street."

"Unless the Company has some other reason for wanting to know where the quartz deposit is," said Mendoza, as we came up on Pacific.

I sat up in the saddle, closing my eyes to concentrate on the scent. There was his earlier track, but . . . yes . . . he was heading uphill again. "Make another left, babe. What were you just saying?"

"What I was *about* to say was, I wonder if the Company wants to be sure nobody else finds this very valuable deposit of quartz?" said Mendoza, as the horse snorted and laid its ears back; it wasn't about to gallop up Pacific. It proceeded at a grudging walk.

"Gee, Mendoza, why would Dr. Zeus worry about something like exclusive patent rights on the most valuable bioremediant substance imaginable?" I said.

She was silent a moment, but I could feel the slow burn building.

"You mean," she said, "that the Company plans to destroy the original source of the lichen?"

"Did I say that, honey?"

"Just so nobody else will discover it before Dr. Zeus puts it on the market, in the twenty-fourth century?"

"Do you see Mr. Stuckey up there anyplace?" I rose in the saddle to study the sheer incline of Pacific Street.

Mendoza said something amazingly profane in sixteenth-century Galician, but at least she didn't push me off the horse. When she had run out of breath, she gulped air and said: "Just *once* in my eternal life I'd like to know I was actually helping to save the world, like we were all promised, instead of making a lot of technocrats up in the future obscenely rich."

"I'd like it too, honest," I said.

"Don't you *honest* me! You're a damned Facilitator, aren't you? You've got no more moral sense than a jackal!"

"I resent that!" I edged back from her sharp shoulder blades, and the glow-in-the-dark mutant *Lupinus* squelched unpleasantly under my behind. "And anyway, what's so great about being a Preserver? You could have been a Facilitator like me, you know that, kid? You had what it took. Instead, you've spent your whole immortal life running around after freaking *bushes*!"

"A Facilitator like you? Better I should have died in that dungeon in Santiago!"

"I saved your *life*, and this is the thanks I get?"

"And as for freaking bushes, Mr. Big Shot Facilitator, it might interest you to know that certain rare porphyrins have serious commercial value in the data storage industry—"

"So, who's making the technocrats rich now, huh?" I demanded. "And have you ever stopped to consider that maybe the damn plants wouldn't *be* so rare if Botanist drones like you weren't digging them up all the time?"

"For your information, that specimen was growing on land that'll be paved over in ten years," Mendoza said coldly. "And if you call me a drone again, you're going to go bouncing all the way down this hill with the print of my boot on your backside."

The horse kept walking, and San Francisco Bay fell ever farther below us. Finally, stupidly, I said:

"Okay, we've covered all the other bases on mutual recrimination. Aren't you going to accuse me of killing the only man you ever loved?"

She jerked as though I'd shot her, and turned around to regard me with blazing eyes.

"You didn't kill him," she said, in a very quiet voice. "You just let him die."

She turned away, and of course then I wanted to put my arms around her and tell her I was sorry. If I did that, though, I'd probably spend the next few months in a regeneration tank, growing back my arms.

So I just looked up at the neighborhood we had entered without noticing, and that was when I really felt my blood run cold.

"Uh – we're in Sydney-Town," I said.

Mendoza looked up. "Oh-oh."

There weren't any flags or bunting here. There weren't any torches. And you would never, *ever* see a place like this in any Hollywood western. Neither John Wayne nor Gabby Hayes ever went anywhere near the likes of Sydney-Town.

It perched on its ledge at the top of Pacific Street and rotted. On the left side was one long row of leaning shacks; on the right side was another. I could glimpse dim lights through windows and doorways, and heard fiddle music scraping away, a half-dozen folk tunes from the British Isles, played in an eerie discord. The smell of the place was unbelievable, breathing out foul through dark doorways where darker figures leaned. Above the various dives, names were chalked that would have been quaint and reassuring anywhere else: The Noggin of Ale. The Tam O'Shanter. The Jolly Waterman. The Bird in Hand.

Some of the dark figures leaned out and bid us "G'deevnin'," and without raising their voices too much let us know about the house specialties. At the Boar's Head, a woman was making love to a pig in the back room; did we want to see? At the Goat and Compass, there was a man who'd eat or drink anything, absolutely *anything,* mate, for a few cents, and he hadn't had a bath in ten years. Did we want to give him a go? At the Magpie, a girl was lying in the back on a mattress, so drunk she'd never wake before morning, no matter what anyone did to her. Were we interested? And other dark figures were moving along in the shadows, watching us.

Portsmouth Square satisfied simple appetites like hunger and thirst, greed, the need to get laid or to shoot at total strangers. Sydney-Town, on the other hand, catered to specialized tastes.

It was nothing I hadn't seen before, but I'd worked in Old Rome at her worst, and Byzantium too. Mendoza, though, shrank back against me as we rode.

She had a white, stunned look I'd seen only a couple of times before. The first was when she was four years old, and the Inquisitors had held her up to the barred window to see what could happen if she didn't confess she was a Jew. More than fear or horror, it was *astonishment* that life was like this.

The other time she'd looked like that was when I let her mortal lover die.

I leaned close and spoke close to her ear. "Baby, I'm going to get down and follow the trail on foot. You ride on, okay? I'll meet you at the hotel."

I slid down from the saddle fast, smacked the horse hard on its rump, and watched as the luminous mutant whatever-it-was bobbed away through the dark, shining feebly. Then I marched forward, looking as dangerous as I could in the damn friar's habit, following Isaiah Stuckey's scent line.

He was sweating heavily, now, easy to track even here. Sooner or later, the mortal was going to have to stop, to set down that sack of gold dust and wipe his face and breathe. He surely wasn't dumb enough to venture into one of these places . . .

His trail took an abrupt turn, straight across the threshold of the very next dive. I sighed, looking up at the sign. This establishment was The Fierce Grizzly. Behind me, the five guys who were lurking paused, too. I shrugged and went in.

Inside the place was small, dark, and smelled like a zoo. I scanned the room. Bingo! There was Isaiah Stuckey, a gin punch in his hand and a smile on his flushed face, just settling down to a friendly crap game with a couple of serial rapists and an axe murderer. I could reach him in five steps. I had taken two when a hand descended on my shoulder.

"Naow, mate, you ain't saving no souls in 'ere," said a big thug. "You clear off, or sit down and watch the exhibition, eh?"

I wondered how hard I'd have to swing to knock him cold, but then a couple of torches flared alight at one end of the room. The stage curtain, nothing more than a dirty blanket swaying and jerking in the torchlight, was flung aside.

I saw a grizzly bear, muzzled and chained. Behind her, a guy I assumed to be her trainer grinned at the audience. The act started.

In twenty thousand years I thought I'd seen everything, but I guess I hadn't.

My jaw dropped, as did the jaws of most of the other patrons who weren't regulars there. They couldn't take their eyes off what was happening on the stage, which made things pretty easy for the pickpockets working the room.

But only for a moment.

Maybe that night the bear decided she'd finally had enough, and summoned some self-esteem. Maybe the chains had reached the last stages of metal fatigue. Anyway, there was a sudden *ping,* like a bell cracking, and the bear got her front paws free.

About twenty guys, including me, tried to get out through the front door at the same moment. When I picked myself out of the gutter, I looked up to see Isaiah Stuckey running like mad again, farther up Pacific Street.

"Hey! Wait!" I shouted; but no Californian slows down when a *grizzly* is loose. Cursing, I rose and scrambled after him, yanking up my robe to clear my legs. I could hear him gasping like a steam engine as I began to close the gap between us. Suddenly, he went down.

I skidded to a halt beside him and fell to my knees. Stuckey was flat on his face, not moving. I turned him over and he flopped like a side of meat, staring sightless up at the clear cold stars. Massive aortic aneurysm. Dead as a doornail.

"No!" I howled, ripping his shirt open and pounding on his chest, though I knew nothing was going to bring him back. "Don't you go and die on me, you mortal son of a bitch! Stupid *jackass—*"

Black shadows had begun to slip from the nearest doorways, eager to begin corpse-robbing; but they halted, taken aback, I guess, by the sight of a priest screaming abuse at the deceased. I glared at them, remembered who I was supposed to be, and made a grudging sign of the Cross over the late Isaiah Stuckey.

There was a clatter of hoofbeats. Mendoza's horse came galloping back downhill.

"Are you okay?" Mendoza leaned from the saddle. "Oh, hell, is that him?"

"The late Isaiah Stuckey," I said bitterly. "He had a heart attack."

"I'm not surprised, with all that running uphill," said Mendoza. "This place really needs those cable cars, doesn't it?"

"You said it, kiddo." I got to my feet. "Let's get out of here."

Mendoza frowned, gazing at the dead man. "Wait a minute. That's Catskill Ike!"

"Cute name," I said, clambering up into the saddle behind her. "You knew the guy?"

"No, I just monitored him in case he started any fires. He's been prospecting on Villa Creek for the last six months."

"Well, so what?"

"So I know where he found your quartz deposit," said Mendoza. "It wasn't mined up the Sacramento at all, Joseph."

"It's in Big *Sur*?" I demanded. She just nodded.

At that moment, the grizzly shoved her way out into the street, and it seemed like a good idea to leave fast.

"Don't take it too badly," said Mendoza a little while later, when we were riding back toward our hotel. "You got what the Company sent you after, didn't you? I'll bet there'll be Security Techs blasting away at Villa Creek before I get home."

"I guess so," I said glumly. She snickered.

"And look at the wonderful quality time we got to spend together! And the Pope will get his fancy crucifix. Or was that part just a scam?"

"No, the Company really is bribing the Pope to do something," I said, "But you don't—"

"— Need to know what, of course. That's okay. I got a great meal out of this trip, at least."

"Hey, are you hungry? We can still take in some of the restaurants, kid," I said.

Mendoza thought about that. The night wind came gusting up from the city below us, where somebody at the Poulet d'Or was mincing onions for a *sauce piperade,* and somebody else was grilling steaks. We heard the pop of a wine cork all the way up where we were on Powell Street . . .

"Sounds like a great idea," she said. She briefly accessed her chronometer. "As long as you can swear we'll be out of here by 1906," she added.

"Trust me," I said happily. "No problem!"

"Trust you?" she exclaimed, and spat. I could tell she didn't mean it, though. We rode on down the hill.

THIS TRAGIC GLASS

Elizabeth Bear

Elizabeth Bear was born on the same day as Frodo and Bilbo Baggins, but in a different year. When coupled with a tendency to read the dictionary for fun as a child, this led her inevitably to penury, intransigence, and the writing of speculative fiction. She is the Hugo, Sturgeon, and Campbell Award–winning author of twenty-five novels and almost a hundred short stories. Her dog lives in Massachusetts; her partner, writer Scott Lynch, lives in Wisconsin. She spends a lot of time on planes.

View but his picture in this tragic glass,
  And then applaud his fortunes as you please.
  Christopher Marlowe, *Tamburlaine the Great*, Part 1. II. 7–8

The light gleamed pewter under gracious, bowering trees; a liver-chestnut gelding stamped one white hoof on the road. His rider stood in his stirrups to see through wreaths of mist, shrugging to settle a slashed black doublet which violated several sumptuary laws. Two breaths steamed as horse and man surveyed the broad lawn of scythe-cut grass that bulwarked the manor house where they had spent the night and much of the day before.

The man ignored the slow coiling of his guts as he settled into the saddle. He reined the gelding about, a lift of the left hand and the light touch of heels. It was eight miles to Deptford Strand and a meeting place near the slaughterhouse. In the name of Queen Elizabeth and her Privy Council, and for the sake of the man who had offered him shelter when no one else under God's dominion would, Christofer Marley must arrive before the sun climbed a handspan above the cluttered horizon.

"That's—" Satyavati squinted at her heads-up display, sweating in the under-air-conditioned beige and grey academia of her computer lab. Her fingers moved with automatic deftness, opening a tin and extracting a cinnamon breath mint from the embrace of its brothers. Absently, she crunched it, and winced at the spicy heat. "—funny."

"Dr. Brahmaputra?" Her research assistant looked up, disconnecting his earplug. "Something wrong with the software?"

She nodded, pushing a fistful of coarse silver hair out of her face as she bent closer to the holographic projection that hung over her desk. The rumble of a semiballistic leaving McCarran Aerospaceport rattled the windows. She rolled her eyes. "One of the undergrads must have goofed the coding on the text. Our gen-derbot just kicked back a truly freaky outcome. Come look at this, Baldassare."

He stood, a boy in his late twenties with an intimidatingly Italian name, already working on an academic's well-upholstered body, and came around her desk to stand over her shoulder. "What am I looking at?"

"Line one fifty-seven," she said, pushing down a fragment of panic that she knew had nothing to do with the situation at hand and everything to do with old damage and ancient history. "See? Coming up as female. Have we a way to see who coded the texts?"

He leaned close, reaching over her to put a hand on her desk. She edged away from the touch. "All the Renaissance stuff was double-checked by Sienna Haverson. She shouldn't have let a mistake like that slip past; she did her dis on Nashe or Fletcher or somebody, and she's just gotten into the Poet Emeritus project, for the love of Mike. And it's not like there are a lot of female Elizabethan playwrights she could have confused—"

"It's not a transposition." Satyavati fished out another cinnamon candy and offered one to Tony Baldassare, who smelled faintly of garlic. He had sense enough to suck on his instead of crunching it; she made a point of tucking hers up between her lip and gum where she'd be less likely to chew on it. "I checked that. This is the only one coming up wrong."

"Well," Baldassare said on a thoughtful breath, "I suppose we can always consider the possibility that Dr. Haverson was drunk that evening—"

Satyavati laughed, brushing Baldassare aside to stand up from her chair, uncomfortable with his closeness. "Or we can try to convince the establishment that the most notorious rakehell in the Elizabethan canon was a girl."

"I dunno," Baldassare answered. "It's a fine line between Marlowe and Jonson for scoundrelhood."

"Bah. You see what I mean. A nice claim. It would do wonders for my tenure hopes and your future employability. And I know you have your eye on Poet Emeritus, too."

"It's a crazy dream." He spread his arms wide and leaned far back, the picture of ecstatic madness.

"Who wouldn't want to work with Professor Keats?" She sighed, twisting her hair into a scrunchie. "Screw it: I'm going to lunch. See if you can figure out what broke."

The air warmed as the sun rose, spilling light like a promise down the road, across the grey moving water of the Thames, between the close-growing trees. Halfway to Deptford, Christofer Marley reined his gelding in to rest it; the sunlight matched his hair to the animal's mane. The man was as beautiful as the horse – groomed until shining, long-necked and long-legged, slender as a girl and fashionably pallid of complexion. Lace cuffs fell across hands as white as the gelding's forehoof.

Their breath no longer steamed, nor did the river.

Kit rubbed a hand across the back of his mouth. He closed his eyes for a moment before glancing back over his shoulder: the manor house – his lover and patron Thomas Walsingham's manor house – was long out of sight. The gelding tossed his head, ready to canter, and Kit let him have the rein he wanted.

All the rein he wants. A privilege Kit himself had rarely been allowed.

Following the liver-colored gelding's whim, they drove hard for Deptford and the house of a cousin of the Queen's beloved secretary of state and closest confidant, Lord Burghley.

The house of Mistress Eleanor Bull.

Satyavati stepped out of the latest incarnation of a vegetarian barbecue joint that changed hands every six months, the heat of a Las Vegas August afternoon pressing her shoulders like angry hands. The University of Nevada campus spread green and artificial across a traffic-humming street; beyond the buildings monsoon clouds rimmed the mountains across the broad, shallow desert valley. A plastic bag tumbled in ecstatic circles near a stucco wall, caught in an eddy, but the wind was against them; there would be no baptism of lightning and rain. She crossed at the new pedestrian bridge, acknowledging Professors Keats and Ling as they wandered past, deep in conversation— "we were going after Plath, but the consensus was she'd just kill herself again" – and almost turned to ask Ling a question when her hip unit beeped.

She dabbed her lips in case of leftover barbecue sauce and flipped the minicomputer open. Clouds covered the sun, but cloying heat radiated from the pavement under her feet. Westward, toward the thunderheads and the mountains, the grey mist of verga – evaporating rain – greased the sky like a thumbsmear across a charcoal sketch by God. "Mr. Baldassare?"

"Dr. Brahmaputra." Worry charged his voice; his image above her holistic communications and computational device showed a thin dark line between the brows. "I have some bad news . . ."

She sighed and closed her eyes, listening to distant thunder echo from the mountains. "Tell me the whole database is corrupt."

"No." He rubbed his forehead with his knuckles; a staccato little image, but she could see the gesture and expression as if he stood before her. "I corrected the Marlowe data."

"And?"

"The genderbot still thinks Kit Marlowe was a girl. I re-entered everything."

"That's—"

"Impossible?" Baldassare grinned. "I know. Come to the lab; we'll lock the door and figure this out. I called Dr. Haverson."

"Dr. Haverson? Sienna Haverson?"

"She was doing Renaissance before she landed in Brit Lit. Can it hurt?"

"What the hell."

Eleanor Bull's house was whitewashed and warm-looking. The scent of its gardens didn't quite cover the slaughterhouse reek, but the house peered through narrow windows and seemed to smile. Kit gave the gelding's reins to a lad from the stable, along with coins to see the beast curried and fed. He scratched under the animal's mane with guilty fingers; his mother would have his hide for not seeing to the chestnut himself. But the Queen's business took precedence, and Kit was – and had been for seven years – a Queen's man.

Bull's establishment was no common tavern, but the house of a respectable widow, where respectable men met to dine in private circumstances and discuss the sort of business not for common ears to hear. Kit squared his shoulders under the expensive suit, clothes bought with an intelligencer's money, and presented himself at the front door of the house. His stomach knotted; he wrapped his inkstained fingers together after he tapped, and waited for the Widow Bull to offer him admittance.

The blond, round-cheeked image of Sienna Haverson beside Satyavati's desk frowned around the thumbnail she was chewing. "It's ridiculous on the face of it. Christopher Marlowe, a woman? It isn't possible to reconcile his biography with – what, crypto-femininity? He was a seminary student, for Christ's sake. People lived in each other's *pockets* during the Renaissance. Slept two or three to a bed, and not in a sexual sense—"

Baldassare was present in the flesh; like Satyavati, he preferred the mental break of actually going home from the office at the end of the day. It also didn't hurt to be close enough to keep a weather eye on university politics.

As she watched, he swung his Chinese-slippered feet onto the desk, his fashionably shabby cryosilk smoking jacket falling open as he leaned back. Satyavati leaned on her elbows, avoiding the interface plate on her desktop and hiding a smile; Baldassare's breadth of gesture amused her.

He said, "Women soldiers managed it during the American Civil War."

"Hundreds of years later—"

"Yes, but there's no reason to think Marlowe had to be a woman. He could have been providing a cover for a woman poet or playwright – Mary Herbert, maybe. Sidney's sister—"

"Or he could have been Shakespeare in disguise," Haverson said with an airy wave of her hand. "It's one anomaly out of a database of two hundred and fifty authors, Satyavati. I don't think it invalidates the work. That's an unprecedented precision of result."

"That's the problem," Satyavati answered, slowly. "If it were a pattern of errors, or if he were coming up as one of the borderline cases – we can get Alice Sheldon to come back just barely as a male author if we use a sufficiently small sample – but it's the entire body of Marlowe's work. And it's *strongly* female. We can't publish until we address this. Somehow."

Baldassare's conservative black braid fell forward over his shoulder. "What do we know about Christopher Marlowe, Dr. Haverson? You've had Early Modern English and Middle English RNA-therapy, haven't you? Does that include history?"

The hologram rolled her eyes. "There's also old-fashioned reading and research," she said, scratching the side of her nose with the gnawed thumbnail. Satyavati grinned at her, and Haverson grinned back, a generational acknowledgment. *Oh, these kids.*

"Christopher Marlowe. Alleged around the time of his death to be an atheist and a sodomite – which are terms with different connotations in the Elizabethan sense than the modern: it borders on an accusation of witchcraft, frankly – author of seven plays, a short lyric poem, and an incomplete long poem that remain to us, as well as a couple of Latin translations and the odd eulogy. And a dedication to Mary Herbert, Countess of Pembroke, which is doubtless where

Baldassare got that idea. The only thing we know about him – really *know* – is that he was the son of a cobbler, a divinity student who attended Corpus Christi under scholarship and seemed to have more money than you would expect and the favor of the Privy Council, and he was arrested several times on capital charges that were then more or less summarily dismissed. All very suggestive that he was an agent – a spy – for Queen Elizabeth. There's a portrait that's supposed to be him—"

Baldassare jerked his head up at the wall; above the bookcases, near the ceiling, a double row of 2-D images were pinned: the poets, playwrights, and authors whose work had been entered into the genderbot. "The redhead."

"The original painting shows him as a dark mousy blond; the reproductions usually make him prettier. If it is him. It's an educated guess, frankly: we don't know who that portrait is of." Haverson grinned, warming to her subject; the academic's delight in a display of useless information. Satyavati knew it well.

Satyavati's field of study was the late 21st century; Renaissance poets hadn't touched her life in more than passing since her undergraduate days. "Did he ever marry? Any kids?" *And why are you wondering that?*

"No, and none that we know of. It's conventionally accepted that he was homosexual, but again, no proof. Men often didn't marry until they were in their late twenties in Elizabethan England, so it's not a deciding factor. He's never been convincingly linked to anyone; for all we know, he might have died a virgin at twenty-nine—" Baldassare snorted heavily, and Haverson angled her head to the side, her steepled hands opening like wings. "There's some other irregularities in his biography: he refused holy orders after completing his degree, and he was baptized some twenty days after his birth rather than the usual three. And the circumstances of his death are very odd indeed. But it doesn't add up to a pattern, I don't think."

Baldassare shook his head in awe. "Dare I ask what you know about Nashe?"

Haverson chuckled. "More than you ever want to find out. I could give you another hour on Marlowe easy: he's a ninety-minute lecture in my Brit Lit class."

The Freshman Intro to British Literature that Haverson taught as wergild for her access to Professor Keats and Ling, and the temporal device. The inside of Satyavati's lip tasted like rubber; she chewed gently. "So you're saying we don't know. And we can prove nothing. There's no period source that can help us?"

"There's some odd stuff in Shakespeare's *As You Like It* that seems to indicate that the protagonist is intended to be a fictionalized reflection of Marlowe, or at least raise questions about his death. We know the two men collaborated on at least two plays, the first part of *Henry VI* and *Edward III*—" Haverson stopped and disentangled her fingers from her wavy yellow hair, where they had become idly entwined. Something wicked danced in her eyes. "And—"

"What?" Satyavati and Baldassare, in unison. Satyavati leaned forward over her desk, closing her hands on the edges.

"The protagonist of *As You Like It* – the one who quotes Marlowe and details the circumstances of his death?"

"Rosalind," Baldassare said. "What about her?"

"Is a young woman quite successfully impersonating a man."

*

Kit ate sparingly, as always. His image, his patronage, his sexuality, his very livelihood were predicated on the contours of his face, the boyish angles of his body, and every year that illusion of youth became harder to maintain. Also, he didn't dare drop his eyes from the face of Robin Poley, his fair-haired controller and – in Kit's educated opinion – one of the most dangerous men in London.

"Thou shalt not be permitted to abandon the Queen's service so easily, sweet Kit," Poley said between bites of fish. Kit nodded, dry-mouthed; he had not expected Poley would arrive with a guard. Two others, Skeres and Frazier, dined heartily and without apparent regard for Kit's lack of appetite.

"'Tis not that I wish any disservice to her Majesty," Kit said. "But I swear on my honor Thomas Walsingham is her loyal servant, good Robin, and she need fear him not. His love for her is as great as any man's, and his family has ever been loyal—"

Poley dismissed Kit's protestations with a gesture. Ingrim Frazier reached the breadth of the linen-laid table with the long blade of his knife and speared a piece of fruit from the board in front of Kit. Kit leaned out of the way.

"You realize of course that textual evidence isn't worth the paper it's printed on. And if you assume Marlowe was a woman, and Shakespeare knew it—"

"You rapidly enter the realm of the crackpots. Indeed."

"We have a serious problem."

"We could just quietly drop him from the data—" He grinned in response to her stare. "No, no. I'm not serious."

"You'd better not be," Satyavati answered. She quelled the rush of fury that Baldassare's innocent teasing pricked out of always-shallow sleep. *What happened a decade ago is not his fault.* "This is my career – my *scholarship* – in question."

A low tap on the office door. Satyavati checked the heads-up display, recognized Haverson, and tapped the key on her desk to disengage the lock. The Rubenesque blonde hesitated in the doorway. "Good afternoon, Satya. Baldassare. Private?"

"Same conversation as before," Satyavati said. "Still trying to figure out how to salvage our research—"

Haverson grinned and entered the room in a sweep of crinkled skirts and tunic. She shut the door behind herself and made very certain it latched. "I have your answer."

Satyavati stood and came around her desk, dragging with her a chair, which she offered to Haverson. Haverson waved it aside, and Satyavati sank into it herself. "It assumes of course that Christopher Marlowe *did* die violently at Eleanor Bull's house in May of 1593 and did not run off to Italy and write the plays of Shakespeare—" Haverson's shrug seemed to indicate that that was a fairly safe assumption.

"The Poet Emeritus project?" Baldassare crowed, swinging his arms wide before clapping his hands. "Dr. Haverson, you're brilliant. And what if Marlowe *did* survive 1593?"

"We'll send back an observer team to make sure he dies. They'll have to exhume the body anyway; we'll need to be able to make that swap for the living Marlowe, assuming the recovery team can get to him before Frazier and company stab him in the eye."

Baldassare shuddered. "I swear that makes my skin crawl—"

"Paradox is an odd thing, isn't it? You start thinking about where the body comes from, and you start wondering if there are other changes happening."

"If there were," Baldassare said, "we'd never know."

Satyavati's dropped jaw closed as she finally forced herself to understand what they were talking about. "No one who died by violence. No one from before 1800. There are rules. Culture shock, language barriers. Professor Ling would never permit it."

Haverson grinned wider, obviously excited. "You know why those rules were developed, don't you?"

"I know it's a History Department and Temporal Studies protocol, and English is only allowed to use the device under their auspices, and competition for its time is extreme—"

"The rule developed after Richard I rose from what should have been his deathbed to run through a pair of History undergrads on the retrieval team. We never did get their bodies back. Or the Lionheart, for that matter—" Baldassare stopped, aware of Haverson's considering stare. "What? I'm gunning for a spot on the Poet Emeritus team. I've been reading up."

"Ah."

"We'd never get the paperwork through to pull Christopher Marlowe, though." He sighed. "Although it would be worth it for the looks on the Marlovians' faces."

"You're awfully certain of yourself, son."

"Dr. Haverson—"

Haverson brushed him off with a turn of her wrist. She kept her light blue eyes on Satyavati. "What if I thought there was a chance that Professor Keats could become interested?"

"Oh," Satyavati said. "*That's* why you came to campus."

Haverson's grin kept growing; as Satyavati watched, it widened another notch. "He doesn't do business by holoconference," she said. "How could Percy Shelley's best friend resist a chance to meet Christopher Marlowe?"

Kit leaned back on his bench, folding his hands in his lap. "Robin, I protest. Walsingham is as loyal to the crown as I."

"Ah." Poley turned it into an accusing drawl: one long syllable, smelling of onions. He straightened, frowning. "And art thou loyal, Master Marley?"

"Thy pardon?" As if a trapdoor had opened under his guts: he clutched the edge of the table to steady himself. "I've proven my loyalty well enough, I think."

"Thou hast grown soft," Poley sneered. Frazier, on Kit's right, stood, and Kit stood with him, toppling the bench in his haste. He found an ale-bottle with his right hand. There was a bed in the close little room in addition to the table, and Kit stepped against it, got his shoulder into the angle the headboard made with the wall.

Ingram Frazier's dagger rose in his hand. Kit looked past him, into Poley's light blue eyes. "Robin," Kit said. "Robin, old friend. What means this?"

Professor Keats looked up as they knocked on his open door: a blatant abrogation of campus security, but Satyavati admitted the cross-breeze felt better than sealed-room climate control. Red curls greying to ginger, his sharp chin softened now by jowls, he leaned back in his chair before a bookshelf stuffed with old leatherbound books and printouts: the detritus of a man who had never abandoned paper. Satyavati's eye picked out the multicolored spines of volumes and volumes of poetry; the successes of the Poet Emeritus project. As a personal and professional friend of the History Department's Bernard Ling, Professor Keats had assumed the chairmanship of Poet Emeritus shortly after the death of its founder, Dr. Eve Rodale.

Who would gainsay the project's greatest success?

The tuberculosis that would have been his death was a preresistant strain, easy prey to modern antibiotics; the lung damage was repairable with implants and grafts. He stood gracefully as Satyavati, Haverson, and Baldassare entered, a vigorous sixty-year-old who might have as many years before him as behind, and laid aside the fountain pen he still preferred. "It's not often lovely ladies come to visit this old poet," he said. "Can I offer you a cup of tea?"

"Soft," Poley said again, and spit among the rushes on the floor. Bits of herbs colored his saliva green; Kit thought of venom and smiled. *If I live, I'll use that—*

The stink of fish and wine was dizzying. Poley kept talking. "Five years ago thou would'st have hanged Tom Walsingham for the gold in thy purse—"

"Only if he proved guilty."

"Guilty as those idiot students thou did'st see hanged at Corpus Christi?"

Kit winced. He wasn't proud of that. The pottery bottle in his hand was rough-surfaced, cool; he shifted his grip. "Master Walsingham is loyal. Frazier, you're in his *service*, man—"

"So fierce in his defense." Poley smiled, toxic and sweet. "Mayhap the rumors of thee dropping thy breeches for Master Walsingham aren't so false, after all—"

"Whoreson—" Kit stepped up, provoked into abandoning the wall. *A mistake*, and as his focus narrowed on Poley, Frazier grabbed his left wrist, twisting. Kit raised the bottle – up, down, smashed it hard across the top of Frazier's head, ducking Frazier's wild swing with the dagger. The weaselly Skeres, so far silent, lunged across the table as Frazier roared and blood covered his face.

Satyavati had turned a student desk around; she sat on it now, her feet on the narrow plastic seat, and scrubbed both hands through her thick silver hair. Professor John Keats stood by the holodisplay that covered one long wall of the classroom, the twelve-by-fourteen card that Baldassare had pulled down off the wall in Satyavati's office pressed against it, clinging by static charge. Pinholes haggled the yellowed corners of the card; at its center was printed a 2-D image of a painfully boyish, painfully fair young man. He was richly dressed, with huge dark eyes, soft features, and a taunting smile framed by a sparse down of beard.

"He would have been eight years older when he died," Keats said.

Haverson chuckled from beside the door. "If that's him."

"If he *is* a him," Baldassare added. Haverson glared, and the grad student shrugged. "It's what we're here to prove, isn't it? Either the software works, or—"

"Or we have to figure out what this weird outlier means."

Keats glanced over his shoulder. "Explain how your program works, Professor?"

Satyavati curled her tongue across her upper teeth and dug in her pocket for the tin of mints. She offered them around the room; only Keats accepted. "It's an idea that's been under development since the late 20th century," she said, cinnamon burning her tongue. "It relies on frequency and patterns of word use – well, it originated in some of the metrics that Elizabethan scholars use to prove authorship of the controversial plays, and also the order in which they were written. We didn't get *Edward III* firmly attributed to Marlowe, with a probable Shakespearean collaboration, until the beginning of the 21st century—"

"And you have a computer program that can identify the biological gender of the writer of a given passage of text."

"It even works on newsfeed reports and textbooks, sir."

"Have you any transgendered authors entered, Satyavati?"

John Keats just called me by my first name. She smiled and scooted forward half an inch on the desk, resting her elbows on her knees. "Several women who wrote as men, for whatever reason. Each of them confirmed female, although some were close to the midline. Two male authors who wrote as women. An assortment of lesbians, homosexuals, and bisexuals. Hemingway—"

Haverson choked on a laugh, covering her mouth with her hand. Satyavati shrugged. "—as a baseline. Anaïs Nin. Ovid, and Edna St. Vincent Millay. Tori Siikanen."

"I've read her," Keats said. "Lovely."

Satyavati shrugged. "The genderbot found her unequivocally male, when her entire body of work was analyzed. Even that written *after* her gender reassignment. We haven't been able to track down any well-known writers of indeterminate sex, unfortunately. I'd like to see how somebody born cryptomale and assigned female, for example, would score—"

"What will your 'bot tell us then?"

"Chromosomal gender, I suppose."

"Interesting. Is gender so very immutable, then?" He raised an eyebrow and smiled, returning his attention to Christopher Marlowe. "That's quite the can of worms—"

"Except for his," Satyavati said, following the line of Keats' gaze to the mocking smile and folded arms of the arrogant boy in the facsimile. "What makes him different?"

"Her," Baldassare said, in a feigned coughing fit. "That moustache is totally gummed on. Look at it."

Keats didn't turn, but he shrugged. "What makes any of us different, my dear?" A long pause, as if he expected an attempt to answer what must have been a rhetorical question. He turned and looked Satyavati in the eye. His gingery eyebrows lifted and fell. "Do you understand the risks and costs of this endeavor?"

Satyavati hunched forward on her chair and shook her head. "It was Sienna's idea—"

"Oh, so quick to cast away credit and blame," the poet said, but his eyes twinkled.

Haverson came to stand beside Satyavati's desk. "Still. Is there any writer or critic who hasn't wondered, a little, what that young man could have done?"

"Were he more prone to temperance?"

Keats was being charming. *But he's still John Keats.*

"Poets are not temperate by nature," he said, and smiled. He folded his hands together in front of his belt buckle. His swing jacket, translucent chromatic velvet, caught the light through the window as he moved.

"In another hundred years we'll change our gender the way we change our clothes." Haverson pressed her warmth against Satyavati's arm, who endured it a moment before she leaned away.

"I confess myself uncomfortable with the concept." Keats' long fingers fretted the cuff of his gorgeous jacket.

Satyavati, watching him, felt a swell of kinship. "I think there is a biological factor to how gender is expressed. I think my genderbot proves that unequivocally: if we can detect birth gender to such a fine degree—"

"And this is important?" Keats' expression was gentle mockery; an emergent trace of archaic Cockney colored his voice, but something in the tilt of his head showed Satyavati that it was a serious question.

"Our entire society is based on gender and sex and procreation. How can it *not* be as vital to understanding the literature as it is to understanding everything else?"

Keats' lips twitched; his pale eyes tightened at the corners. Satyavati shrank back, afraid she'd overstepped, but his voice was still level when he spoke again. "What does it matter where man comes from – or woman either – if the work is true?"

A sore spot. She sucked her lip, searching for the explanation. "One would prefer to think such things no longer mattered." With a sideways glance to Baldassare. He gave her a low thumbs-up. "This isn't my first tenure-track position."

"You left Yale." Just a statement, as if he would not press.

"I filed an allegation of sexual harassment against my department chair. She denied it, and claimed I was attempting to conceal a lack of scholarship—"

"She?"

Satyavati folded her arms tight across her chest, half sick with the admission. "She didn't approve of my research, I think. It contradicted her own theories of gender identity."

"You think she knew attention would make you uncomfortable, and harried you from the department."

"I . . . have never been inclined to be close to people. Forgive me if I am not trusting."

He studied her expression silently. She found herself lifting her chin to meet his regard, in answer to his unspoken challenge. He smiled thoughtfully and said, "I was told a stableman's son would be better to content himself away from poetry, you know. I imagine your Master Marlowe, a cobbler's boy, heard something similar once or twice – and God forbid either one of us had been a girl. It's potent stuff you're meddling in."

Rebellion flared in her belly. She sat up straight on the ridiculous desk, her fingers fluttering as she unfolded her hands and embraced her argument. "If anything, then, my work proves that biology is not destiny. I'd like to force a continuing expansion of the canon, frankly: 'women's books' are still – *still* – excluded. As if war were somehow a more valid exercise than raising a family—" *Shit.* Too much, by his stunned expression. She held his gaze, though, and wouldn't look down.

And then Keats smiled, and she knew she'd won him. "There are dangers involved, beyond the cost."

"I understand."

"Do you?" He wore spectacles, a quaint affectation that Satyavati found charming. But as he glanced at her over the silver wire frames, a chill crept up her neck.

"Professor Keats—"

"John."

"John." And that was worth a deeper chill, for the unexpected intimacy. "Then make me understand."

Keats stared at her, pale eyes soft, frown souring the corners of his mouth. "A young man of the Elizabethan period. A duelist, a spy, a playmaker: a violent man, and one who lives by his wits in a society so xenophobic it's difficult for us to properly imagine. Someone to whom the carriage – the horse-drawn carriage, madam doctor – is a tolerably modern invention, the heliocentric model of the solar system still heresy. Someone to whom your United States is the newborn land of Virginia, a colony founded by his acquaintance Sir Walter Ralegh. Pipe tobacco is a novelty, coffee does not exist, and the dulcet speech of our everyday converse is the yammering of a barbarian dialect that he will find barely comprehensible, at best."

Satyavati opened her mouth to make some answer. Keats held up one angular hand. As if to punctuate his words, the rumble of a rising semiballistic rattled the windows. "A young man, I might add" – as if this settled it—"who must be plucked alive from the midst of a deadly brawl with three armed opponents. A brawl history tells us he instigated with malice, in a drunken rage."

"History is written by the victors," Satyavati said, at the same moment that Baldassare said "Dr. Keats. The man who wrote *Faustus*, sir."

"If a man he is," Keats answered, smiling. "There is that, after all. And there would be international repercussions. UK cultural heritage is pitching a fit over 'the theft of their literary traditions.'"

"Because the world would be a better place without John Keats?" Satyavati grinned, pressing her tongue against her teeth. "Hell, they sold London Bridge to Arizona. I don't see what they have to complain about: if they're so hot to trot, let them build their own time device and steal some of our dead poets."

Keats laughed, a wholehearted guffaw that knocked him back on his heels. He gasped, collected himself, and turned to Haverson, who nodded. "John, how can you possibly resist?"

"I can't," he admitted, and looked back at Haverson.

"How much will it cost?"

Satyavati braced for the answer and winced anyway. Twice the budget for her project, easily.

"I'll write a grant," Baldassare said.

Keats laughed. "Write two. *This* project, I rather imagine there's money for. It will also take a personal favor from Bernard. Which I *will* call in. Although I doubt very much we can schedule a retrieval until next fiscal. Which makes no difference to Marlowe, of course, but does mean, Satyavati, that you will have to push your publication back."

"I'll consider it an opportunity to broaden the database," she said, and Keats and Haverson laughed like true academics at the resignation in her voice.

"And—"

She flinched. "And?"

"Your young man may prove thoroughly uncooperative. Or mentally unstable once the transfer is done."

"Is the transition really so bad?" Baldassare, with the question that had been on the tip of Satyavati's tongue.

"Is there a risk he will reject reality, you mean? Lose his mind, to put it quaintly?"

"Yes."

"I can't say what it will be like for him," he said. "But I, at least, came to you knowing the language and knowing I had been about to die." Keats rubbed his palms together as if clapping nonexistent chalk dust from his palms. "I rather suspect, madam doctors, Mr. Baldassare" – Satyavati blinked as he pronounced Baldassare's name correctly and without hesitation; she hadn't realized Keats even *knew* it— "we must prepare ourselves for failure."

Kit twisted away from the knife again, but Skeres had a grip on his doublet now, and the breath went out of him as two men slammed him against the wall. Cloth shredded; the broken bottle slipped out of Kit's bloodied fingers as Frazier wrenched his arm behind his back.

Poley blasphemed. "*Christ on the cross—*"

Frazier swore too, shoving Kit's torn shirt aside to keep a grip on his flesh. "God's wounds, it's a wench."

A lax moment, and Kit got an elbow into Frazier's ribs and a heel down hard on Poley's instep and his back into the corner one more time, panting like a beaten dog. No route to the window. No route to the door. Kit swallowed bile and terror, tugged the rags of his doublet closed across his slender chest. "Unhand me."

"Where's Marley?" Poley said stupidly as Kit pressed himself against the boards.

"I am Marley, you fool."

"No wench could have written that poetry—"

"I'm no wench," he said, and as Frazier raised his knife, Christofer Marley made himself ready to die as he had lived, kicking and shouting at something much bigger than he.

*

Seventeen months later, Satyavati steepled her fingers before her mouth and blew out across them, warm moist breath sliding between her palms in a contrast to the crisping desert atmosphere. One-way shatterproof bellied out below her; leaning forward, she saw into a retrieval room swarming with technicians and medical crew, bulwarked by masses of silently blinking instrumentation – and the broad space in the middle of the room, walled away from operations with shatterproof ten centimeters thick. Where the retrieval team would reappear.

With or without their quarry.

"Worried?"

She turned her head and looked up at Professor Keats, stylishly rumpled as ever. "Terrified."

"Minstrels in the gallery," he observed. "There's Sienna . . ." Pointing to her blond head, bent over her station on the floor.

The shatterproof walls of the retrieval box were holoed to conceal the mass of technology outside them from whoever might be inside; theoretically, the retrievant should arrive sedated. But it wasn't wise to be too complacent about such things.

The lights over the retrieval floor dimmed by half. Keats leaned forward in his chair. "Here we go."

"Five." A feminine voice over loudspeakers. "Four. Three—"

I hadn't thought he'd look so fragile. Or so young.

Is this then Hell? Curious that death should hurt so much less than living—

"Female," a broad-shouldered doctor said into his throat microphone. He leaned over the sedated form on his examining table, gloved hands deft and quick.

Marlowe lay within an environmentally shielded bubble; the doctor examined her with built-in gloves. She would stay sedated and in isolation until her immunizations were effective and it was certain she hadn't brought forward any dangerous bugs from the 16th century. Satyavati was grateful for the half-height privacy screens hiding the poet's form. *I hadn't thought it would seem like such an invasion.*

"Aged about thirty," the doctor continued. "Overall in fair health although underweight and suffering the malnutrition typical of Elizabethan diet. Probably parasitic infestation of some sort, dental caries, bruising sustained recently – damn, look at that wrist. That must have been one hell of a fight."

"It was," Tony Baldassare said, drying his hands on a towel as he came up on Satyavati's right. His hair was still wet from the showers, slicked back from his classically Roman features. She stepped away, reclaiming her space. "I hope this is the worst retrieval I ever have to go on – although Haverson assures me that I made the grade, and there will be more. Damn, but you sweat in those moonsuits." He frowned over at the white-coated doctor. "When do they start the RNA therapy?"

"Right after the exam. She'll still need exposure to the language to learn it."

Baldassare took a deep breath to sigh. "Poor Kit. I bet she'll do fine here, though: she's a tough little thing."

"She would have had to be," Satyavati said thoughtfully, as much to drown out the more intimate details of the doctor's examination. "What a fearful life—"

Baldassare grinned, and flicked Satyavati with the damp end of his towel. "Well," he said, "she can be herself from now on, can't she? Assuming she acclimates. But anybody who could carry off that sort of a counterfeit for nearly thirty years—"

Satyavati shook her head. "I wonder," she murmured. "What on earth possessed her parents."

Kit woke in strange light: neither sun nor candles. The room smelled harsh: no sweetness of rushes or heaviness of char, but something astringent and pungent, as like the scent of lemons as the counterfeit thud of a pewter coin was like the ring of silver. He would have sat, but soft cloths bound his arms to the strange hard bed, which had shining steel railings along the sides like the bars on a baiting-bear's cage.

His view of the room was blocked by curtains, but the curtains were not attached to the strange, high, narrow bed. They hung from bars near the ceiling. *I am captive,* he thought, and noticed he didn't *hurt*. He found that remarkable; no ache in his jaw where a tooth needed drawing, no burn at his wrist where Frazier's grip had broken the skin.

His clothes were gone, replaced with an open-backed gown. The hysteria he would have expected to accompany this realization didn't; instead, he felt rather drunk. Not unpleasantly so, but enough that the panic that clawed the inside of his breastbone did so with padded claws.

Something chirped softly at the bedside, perhaps a songbird in a cage. He turned his head but could only glimpse the edge of a case in some dull material, the buff color called Isabelline. If his hands were free, he'd run his fingers across the surface to try the texture: neither leather nor lacquer, and looking like nothing he'd ever seen. Even the sheets were strange: no well-pounded linen, but something smooth and cool and dingy white.

"Marry," he murmured to himself. "'Tis passing strange."

"But very clean." A woman's voice, from the foot of the bed. "Good morning, Master Marlowe."

Her accent was strange, the vowels all wrong, the stresses harsh and clipped. A foreign voice. He turned his face and squinted at her; that strange light that was not sunlight but almost as bright glared behind her. It made her hard to see. Still, only a woman. Uncorseted, by her silhouette, and wearing what he realized with surprise were long, loose trousers. *If a wench with a gentle voice is my warden, perhaps there's a chance I shall emerge alive.*

"Aye, very," he agreed as she came alongside the bed. Her hair was silver, loose on her shoulders in soft waves like a maiden's. He blinked. Her skin was mahogany, her eyes angled at the corners like a cat's and shiny as gooseberries. She was stunning and not quite human, and he held his breath before he spoke. "Madam, I beg your patience at my impertinence. But, an it please you to answer – what *are* you?"

She squinted as if his words were as unfamiliar to her as hers to him. "Pray," she said, self-consciously as one speaking a tongue only half-familiar, "say that again, please?"

He tugged his bonds, not sharply. The sensation was dulled, removed. *Drunk or sick*, he thought. *Forsooth, drunk indeed, not to recollect drinking. . .* Robin. Robin and his villains – But Kit shook his head, shook the hair from his eyes, and mastered himself with trembling effort. He said it again, slowly and clearly, one word at a time.

He sighed in relief when she smiled and nodded, apprehending to her satisfaction. In her turn, she spoke precisely, shaping the words consciously with her lips. He could have wept in gratitude at her care. "I'm a woman and a doctor of philosophy," she said. "My name is Satyavati Brahmaputra, and you, Christopher Marlowe, have been rescued from your death by our science."

"Science?"

She frowned as she sought the word. "Natural philosophy."

Her accent, the color of her skin. He suddenly understood. "I've been stolen away to Spain." He was not prepared for the laughter that followed his startled declaration.

"Hardly," she said. "You are in the New World, at a university hospital, a – a surgery? – in a place called Las Vegas, Nevada—"

"Madam, those are Spanish names."

Her lips twitched with amusement. "They are, aren't they? Oh, this is complicated. Here, look." And heedlessly, as if she had nothing to fear from him – *they know, Kit. That's why they left only a wench to guard thee. An Amazon, more like: she's twice my size* – she crouched beside the bed and unknotted the bonds that affixed him to it.

He supposed he could drag down the curtain bars and dash her brains out. But he had no way to know what sort of guards might be at the door; better to bide his time, as she seemed to mean him no injury. And he was tired; even with the cloths untied, lethargy pinned him to the bed.

"They told me not to do this," she whispered, catching his eye with her dark, glistening one. She released a catch and lowered the steel railing. "But in for a penny, in for a pound."

That expression, at least, he understood. He swung his feet to the floor with care, holding the gaping gown closed. The dizziness moved with him, as if it hung a little above and to the left. The floor was unfamiliar too; no rushes and stone, but something hard and resilient, set or cut into tiles. He would have crouched to examine it – and perhaps to let the blood run to his brain – but the woman caught his hand and tugged him past the curtains and toward a window shaded with some ingenious screen. He ran his fingers across the alien surface, gasping when she pulled a cord and the whole thing rose of a piece, hard scales or shingles folding as neatly as a drawn curtain.

And then he looked through the single enormous, utterly transparent pane of glass before him and almost dropped to his knees with vertigo and wonder. His hand clenched on the window ledge; he leaned forward. The drop must have measured hundreds upon hundreds of feet. The horizon was impossibly distant, like the vista from the mast of a sailing ship, the view from the top of a high, lonely down. And before that horizon rose fanciful towers of a dominion vaster than London and Paris made one, stretching twenty or perhaps fifty miles away: however far it took for mountains to grow so very dim with distance.

"God in Hell," he whispered. He'd imagined towers like that, written of them. To see them with his own undreaming eyes – "Sweet Jesu. Madam, what is this?" He spoke too fast, and the brown woman made him repeat himself once more.

"A city," she said quietly. "Las Vegas. A small city, by today's standards. Master Marlowe – or Miss Marlowe, I suppose I should say – you have come some five hundred years into your future, and here, I am afraid, you must stay."

"*Master* Marlowe will do. Mistress Brahma. . ." Marlowe stumbled over Satyavati's name. The warmth and openness Marlowe had shown vanished on a breath. She folded her arms together, so like the Corpus Christi portrait – thinner and wearier, but with the same sardonic smile and the same knowing black eyes – that Satyavati had no doubt that it was the same individual.

"Call me Satya."

"Madam."

Satyavati frowned. "Master Marlowe," she said. "This is a different . . . Things are different now. Look at me, a woman, a blackamoor by your terms. And a doctor of philosophy like your friend Tom Watson, a scholar."

"Poor Tom is dead." And then as if in prophecy, slowly, blinking. "Everyone I know is dead."

Satyavati rushed ahead, afraid that Marlowe would crumple if the revelation on her face ever reached her belly. *A good thing she's sedated, or she'd be in a ball on the floor.* "I'm published, I've written books. I'll be a tenured professor soon." *You will make me that.* But she didn't say it; she simply trusted the young woman, so earnest and wide-eyed behind the brittle defense of her arrogance, would understand. Which of course she didn't, and Satyavati repeated herself twice before she was certain Marlowe understood.

The poet's accent was something like an old broad Scots and something like the dialect of the Appalachian Mountains. *Dammit, it is English.* As long as she kept telling herself it was English, that the foreign stresses and vowels did not mean a foreign language, Satyavati could force herself to understand.

Marlowe bit her lip. She shook her head, and took Satyavati's cue of speaking slowly and precisely, but her eyes gleamed with ferocity. "It bears not on opportunity. I am no woman. Born into a wench's body, aye, mayhap, but as surely a man as Elizabeth is king. My father knew from the moment of my birth. S'death, an it were otherwise, would he have named me and raised me as his son? Have lived a man's life, loved a man's loves. An you think to force me into farthingales and huswifery, know that I would liefer die. I *will* die – for surely now I have naught to fear from Hell – and the man who dares approach me with woman's garb will precede me there."

Satyavati watched Kit – in that ridiculous calico johnny – brace herself, assuming the confidence and fluid gestures of a swordsman, all masculine condescension and bravado. As if she expected a physical assault to follow on her manifesto.

Something to prove. What a life—

The door opened. Satyavati turned to see who entered, and sighed in relief at the gaudy jacket and red hair of Professor Keats, who paused at the edge of the bedcurtain, a transparent bag filled with cloth and books hanging from his hand. "Let me talk to the young man, if you don't mind."

"She's – upset, Professor Keats." But Satyavati stepped away, moving toward Keats and past him, to the door. She paused there.

Keats faced Marlowe. "Are you the poet who wrote *Edward II*?"

A sudden flush, and the eyebrows rose in mockery above the twitch of a grin. "I am that."

"It's a fact that poets are liars," the old man said without turning to Satyavati. "But we *always* speak the truth, and a thing is what you name it. Isn't that so, Marlowe?"

"Aye," she said, her brow furrowed with concentration on the words. "Good sir, I feel that I should know you, but your face—"

"Keats," the professor said. "John Keats. You won't have heard of me, but I'm a poet too."

The door shut behind the woman, and Kit's shoulders eased, but only slightly. "Master Keats—"

"John. Or Jack, if that's more comfortable."

Kit studied the red-haired poet's eyes. Faded blue in the squint of his regard, and Kit nodded, his belly unknotting a little. "Kit, then. I pray you will forgive me my disarray. I have just risen—"

"No matter." Keats reached into his bag. A shrug displayed his own coat, a long loose robe of something that shifted in color, chromatic as a butterfly's wing. "You'll like the modern clothes, I think. I've brought something less revealing."

He laid cloths on the bed: a strange sort of close-collared shirt, trews or breeches in one piece that went to the ankle. Low shoes that looked like leather, but once Kit touched them he was startled by the gummy softness of the soles. He looked up into Keats' eyes. "You prove most kind to a poor lost poet."

"I was rescued from 1821," Keats said dismissively. "I bear some sympathy for your panic."

"Ah." Kit stepped behind the curtain to dress. He flushed hot when the other poet helped him with the closure on the trousers, but once Kit understood this device – the zipper – he found it enchanting. "I shall have much to study on, I wot."

"You will." Keats looked as if he was about to say more. The thin fabric of the shirt showed Kit's small breasts. He hunched forward, uncomfortable; not even sweet Tom Walsingham had seen him so plainly.

"I would have brought you a bandage, if I'd thought," Keats said, and gallantly offered his jacket. Kit took it, face still burning, and shrugged it on.

"What – what year is this, Jack?"

A warm hand on his shoulder; Keats taking a deep breath alerted Kit to brace for the answer. "Anno domini two thousand one hundred and seventeen," he said. The words dropped like stones through the fragile ice of Kit's composure.

Kit swallowed, the implications he had been denying snapping into understanding like unfurled banners. Not the endless changing world, the towers like Babylon or Babel beyond his window. But— "Tom. Christ wept, Tom is dead. All the Toms – Walsingham, Nashe, Kyd. Sir Walter. My sisters. Will. Will and I were at work on a play, *Henry VI*—"

Keats laughed, gently. "Oh, I have something to show you, Kit." His eyes shone with coy delight. "Look here—"

He drew a volume from his bag and pressed it into Kit's hands. It weighed heavy, bound in what must be waxed cloth and stiffened paper. The words on the cover were embossed in gilt in strange-shaped letters. *The Complete Works of William Shakespeare*, Kit read, once he understood how the *esses* seem to work. He gaped, and opened the cover. "His plays . . ." He looked up at Keats, who smiled and opened his hands in a benediction. "This type is so fine and so clear! Marry, how *ever* can it be set by human hands? Tell me true, Jack, have I come to fairyland?" And then, turning pages with trembling fingers and infinite care, his carefulness of speech failing in exclamations. "Nearly forty plays! Oh, the type is so fine – Oh, and his sonnets, they are wonderful sonnets, he's written more than I had seen—"

Keats, laughing, an arm around Kit's shoulders. "He's thought the greatest poet and dramatist in the English language."

Kit looked up in wonder. "T'was I discovered him." Kit held the thick, real book in his hands, the paper so fine and so white he'd compare it to a lady's hand. "Henslowe laughed; Will came from tradesmen and bore no education beyond the grammar school—"

Keats coughed into his hand. "I sometimes think wealth and privilege are a detriment to poetry."

The two men shared a considering gaze and a slow, equally considering smile. "And . . .." Kit looked at the bag, the glossy transparent fabric as foreign as every other thing in the room. There were still two volumes within. The book in his hands smelled of real paper, new paper. With a shock, he realized that the page-ends were trimmed perfectly smooth and edged with gilt. *And how long must that have taken? This poet is a wealthy man, to give such gifts as this.*

"And what of Christopher Marlowe?"

Kit smiled. "Aye."

Keats looked down. "You are remembered, I am afraid, chiefly for your promise and your extravagant opinions, my friend. Very little of your work survived. Seven plays, in corrupted versions. The Ovid. *Hero and Leander*—"

"Forsooth, there was more," Kit said, pressing the heavy book with Will's name on the cover against his chest.

"There will be more," Keats said, and set the bag on the floor. "That is why we saved your life."

Kit swallowed. *What an odd sort of patronage.* He sat on the bed, still cradling the wonderful book. He looked up at Keats, who must have read the emotion in his eyes.

"Enough for one day, I think," the red-haired poet said. "I've given you a history text as well, and" – a disarming smile and a tilt of his head— "a volume of my own poetry. Please knock on the door if you need for anything – you may find the garderobe a little daunting, but it's past that door and the basic functions are obvious – and I will come to see you in the morning."

"I shall amuse myself with gentle William." Kit knew a sort of anxious panic for a moment: it was so necessary that this ginger-haired poet must love him,

Kit – and he also knew a sort of joy when Keats chuckled at the double entendre and clapped him on the shoulder like a friend.

"Do that. Oh!" Keats halted suddenly and reached into the pocket of his trousers. "Let me show you how to use a pen—"

The slow roil of his stomach got the better of Kit for an instant. "I daresay I know well enough how to hold a pen."

Keats shook his head and grinned, pulling a slender black tube from his pocket. "Dear Kit. You don't know how to do anything. But you'll learn soon enough, I imagine."

Satyavati paced, short steps there and back again, until Baldassare reached out without looking up from his workstation and grabbed her by the sleeve. "Dr. Brahmaputra—"

"Mr. Baldassare?"

"Are you going to share with me what the issue is, here?"

One glance at his face told her he knew very well what the issue was. She tugged her sleeve away from him and leaned on the edge of the desk, too far for casual contact. "Marlowe," she said. "She's still crucial to our data—"

"He."

"Whatever."

Baldassare stood; Satyavati tensed, but rather than closer, he moved away. He stood for a moment looking up at the rows of portraits around the top margin of the room – more precisely, at the white space where the picture of Marlowe had been. A moment of consideration, and Satyavati as much as *saw* him choose another tack. "What about Master Marlowe?"

"If I publish—"

"Yes?"

"I tell the world Christopher Marlowe's deepest secret."

"Which Professor Keats has sworn the entire Poet Emeritus project to secrecy about. And if you don't publish?"

She shrugged to hide the knot in her belly. "I'm not going to find a third tenure-track offer. You've got your place with John and Dr. Haverson, at least. All I've got is" – a hopeless gesture to the empty place on the wall— "her."

Baldassare turned to face her. His expressive hands pinwheeled slowly in the air for a moment before he spoke, as if he sifted his thoughts between them. "You keep doing that."

"Doing what?"

"Calling Kit *her*."

"She *is* a her. Hell, Mr. Baldassare, you were the one who was insisting she was a woman, before we brought her back."

"And he insists he's not." Baldassare shrugged. "If he went for gender reassignment, what would you call him?"

Satyavati bit her lip. "Him," she admitted unwillingly. "I guess. I don't know—"

Baldassare spread his hands wide. "Dr. Brahmaputra—"

"Hell. Tony. Call me Satya already. If you're going to put up that much of a fight, you already know that you're moving out of student and into friend."

"Satya, then." A shy smile that startled her. "Why don't you just ask Kit?

He understands how patronage works. He knows he owes you his life. Go tomorrow."

"You think she'd say yes?"

"Maybe." His self-conscious grin turned teasing. "If you remember not to call him *she*."

The strange spellings and punctuation slowed Kit a little, but he realized that they must have been altered for the strange, quickspoken people among whom, apparently, he was meant to make his life. Once he mastered the cadences of the modern speech – the commentaries proving invaluable – his reading proceeded faster despite frequent pauses to reread, to savor.

He read the night through, crosslegged on the bed, bewitched by the brightness of the strange greenish light and the book held open on his lap. The biographical note told him that "Christopher Marlowe's" innovations in the technique of blank verse provided Shakespeare with the foundations of his powerful voice. Kit corrected the spelling of his name in the margin with the pen that John Keats had loaned him. The nib was so sharp it was all but invisible, and Kit amused himself with the precision it leant his looping secretary's hand. He read without passion of Will's death in 1616, smiled that the other poet at last went home to his wife. And did not begin to weep in earnest until halfway through the third act of *As You Like It*, when he curled over the sorcerously wonderful book, careful to let no tear fall upon the pages, and cried silently, shuddering, fist pressed bloody against his teeth, face-down in the rough-textured coverlet.

He did not sleep. When the spasm of grief and rapture passed, he read again, scarcely raising his head to acknowledge the white-garbed servant who brought a tray that was more like dinner than a break-fast. The food cooled and was retrieved uneaten; he finished the Shakespeare and began the history, saving his benefactor's poetry for last.

"I want for nothing," he said when the door opened again, glancing up. Then he pushed the book from his lap and jumped to his feet in haste, exquisitely aware of his reddened eyes and crumpled clothing. The silver-haired woman from yesterday stood framed in the doorway. "Mistress," Kit said, unwilling to assay her name. "Again I must plead your forbearance."

"Not at all," she said. "Mmm – master Marlowe. It is I who must beg a favor of you." Her lips pressed tight; he *saw* her willing him to understand.

"Madam, as I owe you the very breath in my body – Mayhap there is a way I can repay that same?"

She frowned and shut the door behind herself. The latch clicked; his heart raced; she was not young, but he was not certain he understood what *young* meant to these people. And she was lovely. And unmarried, by her hair—

What sort of a maiden would bar herself into a strange man's bedchamber without so much as a chaperone? Has she no care at all for her reputation?

And then he sighed and stepped away, to lean against the windowledge. *One who knows the man in question is not capable as a man. Or* – a stranger thought, one supported by his long night's reading – *or the world has changed more than I could dream.*

"I need your help," she said, and leaned back against the door. "I need to tell the world what you are."

He shivered at the urgency in her tone, her cool reserve, the tight squint of her eyes. *She'll do what she'll do and thou hast no power over her.* "Why speak to me of this at all? Publish your pamphlet, then, and have done—"

She shook her head, lips working on some emotion. "It is not a pamphlet. It's—" She shook her head again. "Master Marlowe, when I say *the world* I mean the world."

Wonder filled him. *If I said no, she would abide it.* "You ask for no less a gift than the life I have made, madam."

She came forward. He watched: bird stalked by a strange silver cat. "People won't judge. You can live as you choose—"

"As you judged me not?"

Oh, a touch. She flinched. He wasn't proud of that, either. "—and not have to lie, to dissemble, to hide. You can even become a man. Truly, in the flesh—"

Wonder. "*Become* one?"

"Yes." Her moving hands fell to her sides. "If it is what you want." Something in her voice, a sort of breathless yearning he didn't dare believe.

"What means this to you? To tell your *world* that what lies between my legs is quaint and not crowing, that is – what benefits it you? Who can have an interest, if your society is so broad of spirit as you import?"

He saw her thinking for a true answer and not a facile one. She came closer. "It is my scholarship." Her voice rose on the last word, clung to it. Kit bit his lip, turning away.

No. His lips shaped the word: his breath wouldn't voice it. Scholarship.

Damn her to hell. *Scholarship.*

She said the word the way Keats said *poetry.*

"Do—" He saw her flinch; his voice died in his throat. He swallowed. "Do what you must, then." He gestured to the beautiful book on his bed, his breath catching in his throat at the mere memory of those glorious words. "It seems gentle William knew well enough what I was, and he forgave me of it better than I could have expected. How can I extend less to a lady who has offered me such kindness, and been so fair in asking leave?"

Satyavati rested her chin on her hand, cupping the other one around a steaming cup of tea. Tony, at her right hand, poked idly at the bones of his tandoori chicken. Further down the table, Sienna Haverson and Bernard Ling were bent in intense conversation, and Keats seemed absorbed in tea and mango ice cream. Marlowe, still clumsy with a fork, proved extremely adept at navigating the intricacies of curry and naan as fingerfood and was still chasing stray tidbits of lamb vindaloo around his plate. She enjoyed watching her – *him*, she corrected herself, annoyed – eat; the weight he'd gained in the past months made him look less like a strong wind might blow him away.

Most of the English Department was still on a quiet manhunt for whomever might have introduced the man to the *limerick.*

She lifted her tea; before she had it to her mouth, Tony caught her elbow, and Marlowe, looking up before she could flinch away, hastily wiped his hand and picked up a butterknife. He tapped his glass as Keats grinned across the table. Marlowe cleared his throat, and Haverson and Ling looked up, reaching for their cups when it became evident that a toast was in the offing.

"To Professor Brahmaputra," Marlowe said, smiling, in his still-strong accent. "Congratulations—"

She set her teacup down, a flush warming her cheeks as glasses clicked and he continued.

"— on her appointment to tenure. In whose honor I have composed a little poem—"

Which was, predictably, sly, imagistic, and *inventively* dirty. Satyavati imagined even her complexion blazed quite red by the time he was done with her. Keats' laughter alone would have been enough to send her under the table, if it hadn't been for Tony's unsettling deathgrip on her right knee. "Kit!"

He paused. "Have I scandalized my lady?"

"Master Marlowe, you have scandalized the very walls. I trust that one won't see print just yet!" Too much time with Marlowe and Keats: she was noticing a tendency in herself to slip into an archaic idiom that owed something to both.

"Not until next year at the earliest," he answered with a grin, but she saw the flash of discomfort that followed.

After dinner, he came up beside her as she was shrugging on her cooling-coat and gallantly assisted.

"Kit," she said softly, bending close so no one else would overhear. He smelled of patchouli and curry. "You are unhappy."

"Madam." A low voice as level as her own. "Not unhappy."

"Then what?"

"Lonely." Marlowe sighed, turning away.

"Several of the Emeritus Poets have married," she said carefully. Keats eyed her over Marlowe's shoulder, but the red-haired poet didn't intervene.

"I imagine it's unlikely at best that I will find anyone willing to marry something neither fish nor fowl—" A shrug.

She swallowed, her throat uncomfortably dry. "There's surgery now, as we discussed—"

"Aye. 'Tis—" She read the word he wouldn't say. *Repulsive.*

Keats had turned away and drawn Tony and Sienna into a quiet conversation with Professor Ling at the other end of the table. Satyavati looked after them longingly for a moment and chewed her lower lip. She laid a hand on Kit's shoulder and drew him toward the rest. "You are what you are," she offered hopelessly, and on some fabulous impulse ducked her head and kissed him on the cheek, startled when her dry lips tingled at the contact. "Someone will have to appreciate that."

The door slides aside. He steps through the opening, following the strange glorious lady with the silver-fairy hair. The dusty scent of curry surrounds him as he walks into the broad spread of a balmy evening roofed with broken clouds.

Christopher Marlowe leans back on his heels and raises his eyes to the sky, the desert scorching his face in a benediction. *Hotter than Hell.* He draws a single deep breath and smiles at the mountains crouched at the edge of the world, tawny behind a veil of summer haze, gold and orange sunset pale behind them. Low trees crouch, hunched under the potent heat. He can see forever across this hot, flat, tempestuous place.

The horizon seems a thousand miles away.

Author's Note: In the years since I wrote this story, it's been brought to my attention that there's a gender-essentialist reading that is so entirely contrary to my intentions that I honestly never realized it existed until someone pointed it out to me. While I'm all for literary ambiguity, a transphobic reading is pretty definitely a flaw in a story that was intended to make the point (among others) that, no matter *what* outside criteria you employ – chromosomal, computational, or otherwise – a person's identity is what they say it is. Sorry about that; I have tried to do better since.

THE GULF OF THE YEARS

Georges-Olivier Châteaureynaud

TRANSLATED BY EDWARD GAUVIN

Georges-Olivier Châteaureynaud is a French novelist and short-story
writer, with over one hundred short stories and nine novels to his
credit. He has been described as one of the most original contemporary French authors. His work has been compared to Kurt Vonnegut,
Franz Kafka, and Julio Cortázar. This story was translated from the
French by Edward Gauvin and published for the first time in English
in the collection *A Life on Paper* in 2011.

In the train, the passengers spoke in hushed voices about the hard times. A
young woman with a yellow star sewn to her breast briefly lifted her gaze
from the dressmaker's pattern she was studying. The boy across from her
pulled the latest issue of *Signal* from a worn satchel and unfolded it right in front
of her face. She lowered her eyes.

Through the window, Manoir watched the few cars, quaint and yet almost
new, on the road beside the tracks. He started at the sight of a military convoy.
He checked his watch, then settled back. It was still early. The bombing wouldn't
start till later that morning. Far away, young men were waking in their bar-
racks . . . or were they on their feet already, assembled in flight suits before
a blackboard with their wing commander? Early rising schoolboys of fire and
death. They were twenty, in fur-lined boots and leather helmets, blue wool and
sheepskin. They drank tea and smoked *gauloises blondes*. Manoir's best wishes
went with them. And yet, in a few hours, one of them would kill his mother.

Manoir got off at S. He walked up the Avenue de la Gare, turned left at the town
hall, and passed the post office, then the elementary school. He hesitated, but not
over which way to go. As a child, he'd pretended he was blind in these streets.
He'd try and make his way to school from home with his eyes closed. Sometimes
he walked right into a lamppost, or someone's legs. He cheated, of course: from
time to time he opened his eyelids just a bit, long enough to see where he was.
But one night he'd managed to make it only cheating three times.

He checked his watch again. In five minutes, a little boy would emerge from
his house a few streets away. On the front steps, his maman would kiss him as
she did every morning. Satchel in hand, he would cross the small yard. With one
last wave, he'd head through the gate and be on his unhurried way to school.

It was seven-fifty. School opened its doors at eight. Would it take him ten
minutes to get there, or just five? If he missed him – God, what if he missed

him? Manoir spotted a boy in a cape, then two more, an older one leading a younger one by the hand, and two more after that ... they were coming out of the woodwork now. Still sleepy, eyes unfocused for the most part, pale and huddled against the cold morning, children were converging on the school. Manoir panicked. They were coming toward him down both sides of the street at once, the bigger ones sometimes hiding the littler ones from view. All he could see of some – hooded, wrapped up in scarves or balaclavas – was their eyes and a bit of nose poking out from the wool. He recalled a yellowish coat, maybe even a beret? Yes, he was sure of the coat. But two out of every three boys were wearing berets.

The crowd of children grew, overflowing the sidewalk for a moment. Manoir almost wept with frustration. None of these children were the one he was looking for! The flood slowed; most of the flock had passed. He'd missed him; he'd let him slip by beneath a brown coat or a black cape. All was lost. His heart broke. The street emptied. He ran into a few breathless latecomers ... and over there, that shape! He dashed forward. An ugly yellow coat. A beret pulled halfway down his forehead. A loose-knit gray scarf. And that odd, moony walk, that dawdling step! He should've known. He slowed his pace, trying to still his beating heart. The boy was only fifteen yards away, now. Their paths were about to cross. The boy looked up at the man. Something – a familial air – had awoken his curiosity. Manoir stopped right in front of him.

"Jean-Jacques?"

The boy took a step back. "How come y'know my name? I don't know yours."

"You're Jean-Jacques Manoir, aren't you? Right? You don't know me, but I know all about you. You're eight years old, in third grade, and your teacher's name is Mr. Crépon. He's got a tiny mustache and is very strict. See – I know all about you!"

At once intrigued by the stranger's omniscience yet worried about being late, Jean-Jacques hopped from foot to foot. "OK, but I'm going to be late. Mr. Crépon's going to make me do lines!"

Mr. Crépon didn't make him do lines as often as he might have. His customarily iron rule softened for the three fatherless boys in his class.

"C'mon, Mr. Crépon's not as bad as all that. If he punished you every time you were late or busy daydreaming instead of working—"

So the stranger knew that, too! The boy gulped. "Wh-who are you?"

"I'm your cousin. Your father's cousin. Don't you think I look like him?"

"Yes, you do," the child replied after looking him over. "But I still don't know you. And my dad's dead."

Manoir nodded. "He died in the war. He was a hero. He got medals: a round one, with a green and yellow ribbon, and another with a green and red ribbon and little swords. Isn't that right?"

"Yes!"

"C'mon, I'll show you something that'll prove I'm his cousin. You know the ring your dad always wore?"

"A ring? I dunno . . ." Jean-Jacques blushed. Through the fabric of his pocket and the handkerchief he'd wrapped it in, the signet ring he'd brought in secret to show his friends seemed to be burning.

The cousin's eyes gleamed with irony. "You must have seen it. A gold ring, with a little *château* on it, like your name – a *manor*."

Jean-Jacques gave in. "Yeah, I've seen it before."

"I've got the same one! Look!" The man took his hand from his pocket, fingers spread, and held it out to the boy. A signet ring, exactly like the one the boy had stolen from his father's desk but moments ago, gleamed in the gray day. "See, there's my proof."

"Why, Jean-Jacques! Jean-Jacques, you're really going to be late today!"

A woman stood before them: a neighbor, the same one who would come fetch the boy after school, after the tragedy. She was speaking to the boy, but looking the man up and down. She did her best to help the young widow: here a pot of broth, there some wool from an old, unraveling sweater. She'd believed the mother and child alone in the world. But who was this man who looked so much like poor Mr. Manoir?

"I'm a friend of the boy's mother," she said. "And you are . . . ?"

"Manoir, " the stranger mumbled. "Jean-Pierre Manoir. *Enchanté.*"

"He's daddy's cousin," Jean-Jacques announced. "I didn't know him, but he knew all about me."

The woman hesitated. If it weren't for the resemblance . . . She didn't dare insist, but she vowed to get to the bottom of this. "I'll drop in on your mother, Jean-Jacques. You should hurry, or Mr. Crépon will yell at you again."

The cousin had other plans. "Jean-Jacques isn't going to school this morning. We're going home together."

"You know Yvonne, of course?"

"Jeanne, you mean? My poor cousin's widow is named Jeanne."

"Jeanne, of course. I'm losing my mind."

"No, we've never met. The hazards of fate . . . But I'm eager to meet her at last. So, if you'll excuse us—"

"Please. Later, perhaps? I'd planned to visit Jeanne this morning anyway." The woman walked off, her fears allayed. Now it was curiosity that gnawed at her. Jean-Pierre Manoir, cousin of the deceased. He looked just like his brother. He'd turned up just like that, with his hands in his pockets, but where from? A cousin fallen from the sky . . . What if he were a Gaullist? A parachutist from the FFL? A terrorist? One didn't quite know what to call them. Shouldn't she stay away from Jeanne's this morning? But then she'd never find out a thing!

Manoir took the boy's hand. Jean-Jacques let him, and this act of trust over-whelmed the man. He quickly wiped his tears away with the back of his free hand. The excited child skipped beside him.

"Are you going to stay for a long time?"

"I don't know. Do you want me to?"

"You'll have to play with me."

"Count on it. Do you have many toys?"

"A whole chest full! And comics, and a train – say, how come you know me if you don't know maman?"

Manoir chuckled, stalling. "Well! You think of everything, don't you! Look, the bakery's open. Do you want some cake?"

"There is no cake."

"Of course there isn't. Some sweets, maybe?"

"It's not real sugar. Maman says they make your tummy hurt."

"I see. But you like them anyway, don't you?"

Jean-Jacques smiled secretively. He didn't really mind them so much, those fake-sugar sweets that made your tummy hurt.

Manoir walked inside the store. The baker watched them with curiosity from behind her empty glass jars. She saw the boy go by every day. Sometimes she sold him sweets made with saccharin. The father had been killed in 1940. The man looked so much like him! His brother, no doubt.

"Good morning, madame. We'd like some sweets."

"Of course. Green? Yellow?"

"A few of each. Let's see . . ." Manoir pulled the few coins he had left from his pocket. "As many as these will buy."

"That'll be a hundred grams."

"Excellent!"

"Do you have ration coupons?"

"Coupons? Oh no, I – I hadn't thought . . ."

The baker scratched her forehead. "A pity. I could give you the cracked ones? Without tickets . . ."

"Of course. Whatever you can spare."

On the doorstep, Manoir handed Jean-Jacques the little bag.

"Thanks."

"Call me Uncle Jean-Pierre, if you'd like."

"Thanks, Uncle Jean-Pierre."

They walked. Jean-Jacques crunched into the broken sweets with relish.

"You know what's good? The raspberry ones."

"And the hard mint ones, and the little eggs with liqueur centers. But—"

"Your father sent me your photo. I don't have it anymore. I lost it in the war."

"Oh. Was I a little baby in the photo?"

"No, not a baby really, or I wouldn't have recognized you. You were five or six."

They were getting close. At the next intersection, on the left, they spotted the house.

"Ow! You're hurting me!"

"I'm sorry." Manoir loosened his grip. Seized with feeling, he'd been crushing the child's hand. His heart was pounding. His mouth was dry. They rounded the corner.

"What's wrong? Are you sick?"

"No, no."

From this angle, the greenish grille, spotted here and there with rust, half masked the millstone and stucco facade. He'd remembered the building being taller, larger, perforated with broad windows like so many eyes wide open on Eden. In reality, it was tiny: the smallest house on the street, nestled in its few acres between two bulging villas that drowned it in shadow.

"C'mon, we're here."

Jean-Jacques dashed off and swung briefly from the handle of the bell. It let out a feeble ring. A minute went by before a window opened upstairs.

"Jean-Jacques? Why aren't you at school? Who is that with you? What's going on?"

"It's daddy's cousin. I met him on the street."

Manoir reeled at the sound of his mother's voice. He couldn't, he wasn't strong enough to see or speak to her. He'd faint, right there on the sidewalk. He had to get away. But his legs refused to obey. With one hand he hung on to the gate and closed his eyes. A thin figure appeared. He was trembling all over, his eyes clouded with tears.

"Monsieur?"

Manoir desperately swallowed his tears and smiled. His mother was as old as she'd ever get: thirty. The bomb would crush a short young woman with even features and skin already dulled by grief and worry. She had but an hour left to live, and stood up straight in her seamstress' blouse over which she'd slipped a man's jacket much too large for her.

"Monsieur?"

She, too, was trembling. This man looked so much like her husband! He'd never mentioned this man, but how could they not be related? He spoke. His very voice, his tone, awoke echoes. He introduced himself. He explained. He was in fact the only relative of the deceased. A few months before his death, he'd written his cousin; he'd even enclosed a photo of his young son with the letter. Manoir caressed Jean-Jacques' hair. The boy let him. Unfortunately, Jean-Pierre Manoir had lost the letter and photo with his belongings near Sedan, in the chaos of the retreat.

Manoir ostentatiously underlined his words with gestures of his ringed hand. Jeanne gave a start.

"Pardon me, but that ring—"

At that moment, Jean-Jacques, who had been watching the two adults silently, chimed in. "Yeah, did you see it, maman? He's got the same ring as Papa. The exact same one!"

Manoir held out his hand. "We ordered them together from a jeweler in P——. Michel drew the chateau on the setting himself on a page of his notebook."

The truthful part of this new lie chased away whatever doubts lingered in the young woman's mind. Her husband had indeed had his ring made in P——, from a sketch by his very own hand. Still, despite everything, it was strange that he'd never brought up this cousin, a dozen years his senior, whom he must have been close to in his youth, it seemed . . . But above all, she was inclined to rejoice in this visit that interrupted the monotony of her day and this revelation of a friendly presence in the desert of her life. She became suddenly aware of her unkempt appearance – this blouse, this shapeless jacket, really! She apologized; she'd been about to sit down to work at her machine. She did a little sewing; her war-widow's pension was quite modest.

They went inside. The impostor's throat tightened as he inhaled the old smells he'd never forgotten and staggering traces of which he sometimes came across by chance on the street. Quince cheese, a canary cage, wax polish, and vegetable soup, and from Jean-Jacques' room, the slightly acrid reek of mouse droppings. The smell of secondhand clothes, for in these penurious times, Jeanne gathered, recut, and repaired more old clothes than she made new ones. The smell of the oilcan for the sewing machine. There it was. The big black Singer with its gilt chasing sat enthroned in the living room, amidst a mess of spools and needles, chalk and scissors. But he remembered a room reserved for special occasions, where you went only if you had to, in a pair of felt slippers . . . that was before, of course! Before the war, and his father's death. The living room had been turned into a workspace, and the slippers peeked out from under a sofa.

Jeanne led them into the kitchen. He sat down in the chair she offered as though his feet had been cut out from under him. The walls, hung with plates, spun around him.

"Jean-Pierre? I can call you Jean-Pierre, can't I? After all, we're related. You look quite tired!"

"Yes. The trip—"

"Did you come a long way?"

"A very long way, yes."

He was overcome with dizziness. He closed his eyes, opened them, tried to smile. She'd turned her back on him and was heating water. Then, standing before the pantry shelves, she pushed aside empty jars and gave each white tin box a shake beside her ear.

"Let's see . . . No more tea, of course. No more real coffee, either. Herbal tea, then, or chicory."

Bit by bit, Manoir's dizziness wore off. The walls slowed their spinning, the plates grew still. There were three, covered with a thin film of grease and dust. The first showed an interior scene: a woman, like Jeanne at that very moment, busying herself in her kitchen. In the second a traveler from the last century, cane in hand, broad hat brim hiding his face, made his way through the woods. The last was a rebus. From where he was sitting he couldn't see the elements very clearly. A note on a musical staff, a pond . . .

"There, it's steeping. It's lime-blossom. Oh, wait, I've got a treat after all."

She pulled a plate from another cupboard. Manoir recognized the dark amber, almost brown sections she used to cut from a block of fruit jelly for his afternoon snack.

"I don't make it as often as I used to. It takes too much sugar. But Jean-Jacques loves it. Where has that boy gone now? Jean-Jacques?"

A clatter of steps echoed in the stairwell. Jean-Jacques appeared.

"What were you up to?"

"I was cleaning my room so I could show Uncle Jean-Pierre."

"But Jean-Pierre isn't your uncle. He's your father's cousin."

"Yes, but he said—"

"No, that's fine," Manoir interrupted. "I'm a bit too old to be a cousin."

"And we'll play, right? Like you said. I cleaned my room just so we could."

"Leave Jean-Pierre alone. Here, have some quince cheese. You, too, Jean-Pierre. Help yourself."

Man and boy started in. The pieces were a bit sticky. Jean-Jacques licked his fingers. Manoir hesitated, then, giving him a complicit glance, did the same.

"*Maman?*"

"Yes, dear?"

"Am I going back to school today?"

"Well . . . not this morning, at least."

"Not this afternoon, either!"

"We'll see. I'll see. Oh, the tea's ready." Jeanne had taken out two bowls. Jean-Jacques didn't much like herbal tea, and he'd just had breakfast. It didn't stop him from digging into the quince paste. For his part, Manoir was dying to have seconds but didn't dare.

"Help yourself, Jean-Pierre! Really!"

"With pleasure. It's delicious." He took a broken piece from the plate.

"Hey, are you coming back?"

They were in Jean-Jacques' room. Jeanne was working below. Jean-Jacques was lying on the linoleum near his toy chest. Manoir set down the little tin airplane he'd been studying.

"Of course, if your mother wants me to."

"She does, I know she does!"

"And why is that?"

"Because you're family. When you've got family, you visit, right?"

"I suppose so. I don't really know. I don't have any – except you two."

"Just like us – all we have is you."

Manoir leaned over the chest, and reached for a box of cubes. "But sometimes you live too far away to visit often."

"Do you live far away? In the free zone?"

"That's right. In the free zone."

"So we won't be able to see each other."

Manoir had opened the box of cubes. He'd already found three faces that represented parts of a single picture. A rodeo scene, no doubt.

"I'm moving."

"Really? Neat! So we'll see each other often, then? We could go boating. Maman won't take me. But you will, right?"

"We'll go everywhere! The circus, and the zoo, and the Ferris wheel at the fair."

"The Ferris wheel! It makes me scared to look around even when we haven't left the ground yet!"

"You won't be scared with me, right?"

"No! Definitely not!"

Suddenly the sirens screamed. Man and boy froze.

"Hear that? It's the bomb warning!"

Manoir checked his watch and nodded. Jeanne's urgent voice reached them from below.

"Jean-Jacques! Jean-Pierre! The sirens!"

"Come."

On the threshold, before closing the door, Manoir took one last look at his childhood room. The red eiderdown on the bed, the white mouse nibbling at the bars of its cage, the plaster coin bank in the shape of a dog on the dresser, the Kipling poem in its gilded pitchpine frame. Good-bye, good-bye forever this time.

They went down. Jeanne was waiting for them at the foot of the stairs. She wasn't alone. The neighbor stood next to her. Curiosity had brought her over, and the sirens surprised her on the front step.

"Hurry up! Didn't you hear the warning!"

"Yes, but it's not for us. I bet they're going to bomb the station."

"We're just next door! Come over, my cellar's deeper underground, and my husband did a good job shoring it up."

"We don't have time," Manoir cut in. "Listen – they've started!"

The engines' roar had grown louder. In a few moments, the squadron would pass right over the town. Muffled explosions broke out.

"It's the AA guns," Jean-Jacques shouted. "Blam! Blam! Vrrr! Vrrr! Blammm!"

"Hurry, downstairs!"

Jeanne grabbed the boy. She opened the cellar door and headed down the steps. Manoir stepped aside to let the neighbor by.

Jeanne lit a small lamp. They were seated on old crates. The ground trembled without stopping. With each detonation, shockwaves shook the walls. In a corner of the cellar, empty bottles clinked.

"They're bombing the station. We have nothing to fear."

"If you say so!" The neighbor was missing her reinforced shelter and her sandbags. Jeanne was quiet. After a momentary brush with fear, Jean-Jacques had regained confidence before "Uncle Jean-Pierre's" demeanor. Manoir smiled. He felt great peace within. Events once gone astray were about to resume their rightful course.

Above, a bomber had been hit. It veered, losing altitude. To lighten the load, the pilot ordered all bombs to be dropped. For a moment, the bombs rocked in the air as though uncertain, then the wind on their fins stabilized them. They were falling straight down now, with a whistling that grew ever higher in pitch. The first ripped the street open two hundred yards from the house. The second crushed a gas truck at the corner of the street. In the cellar, the neighbor, the bearer of bad news, opened her mouth to cry out. Jean-Jacques pressed himself against Jeanne, his face buried in her breast. Manoir rose, threw himself upon them, and held them.

ENOCH SOAMES: A MEMORY OF THE EIGHTEEN-NINETIES

Max Beerbohm

Max Beerbohm's full name was Sir Henry Maximilian Beerbohm, once he accepted the knighthood from King George VI in 1939. An English essayist, parodist, and caricaturist, his first short story was published in 1897 ("The Happy Hypocrite"), and his novel *Zuleika Dobson* was published in 1911, although most of his written works were nonfiction. "Enoch Soames" plays with time travel via a deal with the Devil. It was first published in 1916 in *Century Magazine*.

When a book about the literature of the eighteen-nineties was given by Mr. Holbrook Jackson to the world, I looked eagerly in the index for Soames, Enoch. It was as I feared: he was not there. But everybody else was. Many writers whom I had quite forgotten, or remembered but faintly, lived again for me, they and their work, in Mr. Holbrook Jackson's pages. The book was as thorough as it was brilliantly written. And thus the omission found by me was an all the deadlier record of poor Soames's failure to impress himself on his decade.

I dare say I am the only person who noticed the omission. Soames had failed so piteously as all that! Nor is there a counterpoise in the thought that if he had had some measure of success he might have passed, like those others, out of my mind, to return only at the historian's beck. It is true that had his gifts, such as they were, been acknowledged in his lifetime, he would never have made the bargain I saw him make – that strange bargain whose results have kept him always in the foreground of my memory. But it is from those very results that the full piteousness of him glares out.

Not my compassion, however, impels me to write of him. For his sake, poor fellow, I should be inclined to keep my pen out of the ink. It is ill to deride the dead. And how can I write about Enoch Soames without making him ridiculous? Or, rather, how am I to hush up the horrid fact that he WAS ridiculous? I shall not be able to do that. Yet, sooner or later, write about him I must. You will see in due course that I have no option. And I may as well get the thing done now.

In the summer term of '93 a bolt from the blue flashed down on Oxford. It drove deep; it hurtlingly embedded itself in the soil. Dons and undergraduates stood around, rather pale, discussing nothing but it.

Whence came it, this meteorite? From Paris. Its name? Will Rothenstein. Its aim? To do a series of twenty-four portraits in lithograph. These were to be published from the Bodley Head, London.

The matter was urgent. Already the warden of A, and the master of B, and the Regius Professor of C had meekly "sat." Dignified and doddering old men who had never consented to sit to anyone could not withstand this dynamic little stranger. He did not sue; he invited: he did not invite; he commanded. He was twenty-one years old. He wore spectacles that flashed more than any other pair ever seen. He was a wit. He was brimful of ideas. He knew Whistler. He knew Daudet and the Goncourts. He knew everyone in Paris. He knew them all by heart. He was Paris in Oxford. It was whispered that, so soon as he had polished off his selection of dons, he was going to include a few undergraduates. It was a proud day for me when I – I was included. I liked Rothenstein not less than I feared him; and there arose between us a friendship that has grown ever warmer, and been more and more valued by me, with every passing year.

At the end of term he settled in, or, rather, meteoritically into, London. It was to him I owed my first knowledge of that forever-enchanting little world-in-itself, Chelsea, and my first acquaintance with Walter Sickert and other August elders who dwelt there. It was Rothenstein that took me to see, in Cambridge Street, Pimlico, a young man whose drawings were already famous among the few – Aubrey Beardsley by name. With Rothenstein I paid my first visit to the Bodley Head. By him I was inducted into another haunt of intellect and daring, the domino-room of the Cafe Royal.

There, on that October evening – there, in that exuberant vista of gilding and crimson velvet set amidst all those opposing mirrors and upholding caryatids, with fumes of tobacco ever rising to the painted and pagan ceiling, and with the hum of presumably cynical conversation broken into so sharply now and again by the clatter of dominoes shuffled on marble tables, I drew a deep breath and, "This indeed," said I to myself, "is life!" (Forgive me that theory. Remember the waging of even the South African War was not yet.)

It was the hour before dinner. We drank vermuth. Those who knew Rothenstein were pointing him out to those who knew him only by name. Men were constantly coming in through the swing-doors and wandering slowly up and down in search of vacant tables or of tables occupied by friends. One of these rovers interested me because I was sure he wanted to catch Rothenstein's eye. He had twice passed our table, with a hesitating look; but Rothenstein, in the thick of a disquisition on Puvis de Chavannes, had not seen him. He was a stooping, shambling person, rather tall, very pale, with longish and brownish hair. He had a thin, vague beard, or, rather, he had a chin on which a large number of hairs weakly curled and clustered to cover its retreat. He was an odd-looking person; but in the nineties odd apparitions were more frequent, I think, than they are now. The young writers of that era – and I was sure this man was a writer – strove earnestly to be distinct in aspect. This man had striven unsuccessfully. He wore a soft black hat of clerical kind, but of Bohemian intention, and a gray waterproof cape which, perhaps because it was waterproof, failed to be romantic. I decided that "dim" was the mot juste for him. I had already essayed to write, and was immensely keen on the mot juste, that Holy Grail of the period.

The dim man was now again approaching our table, and this time he made up his mind to pause in front of it.

"You don't remember me," he said in a toneless voice.

Rothenstein brightly focused him.

"Yes, I do," he replied after a moment, with pride rather than effusion – pride in a retentive memory. "Edwin Soames."

"Enoch Soames," said Enoch.

"Enoch Soames," repeated Rothenstein in a tone implying that it was enough to have hit on the surname. "We met in Paris a few times when you were living there. We met at the Cafe Groche."

"And I came to your studio once."

"Oh, yes; I was sorry I was out."

"But you were in. You showed me some of your paintings, you know. I hear you're in Chelsea now."

"Yes."

I almost wondered that Mr. Soames did not, after this monosyllable, pass along. He stood patiently there, rather like a dumb animal, rather like a donkey looking over a gate. A sad figure, his. It occurred to me that "hungry" was perhaps the mot juste for him; but – hungry for what? He looked as if he had little appetite for anything. I was sorry for him; and Rothenstein, though he had not invited him to Chelsea, did ask him to sit down and have something to drink.

Seated, he was more self-assertive. He flung back the wings of his cape with a gesture which, had not those wings been waterproof, might have seemed to hurl defiance at things in general. And he ordered an absinthe. "Je me tiens toujours fidele," he told Rothenstein, "a la sorciere glauque."

"It is bad for you," said Rothenstein, dryly.

"Nothing is bad for one," answered Soames. "Dans ce monde il n'y a ni bien ni mal."

"Nothing good and nothing bad? How do you mean?"

"I explained it all in the preface to 'Negations.'"

"'Negations'?"

"Yes, I gave you a copy of it."

"Oh, yes, of course. But, did you explain, for instance, that there was no such thing as bad or good grammar?"

"N-no," said Soames. "Of course in art there is the good and the evil. But in life – no." He was rolling a cigarette. He had weak, white hands, not well washed, and with finger-tips much stained with nicotine. "In life there are illusions of good and evil, but" – his voice trailed away to a murmur in which the words "vieux jeu" and "rococo" were faintly audible. I think he felt he was not doing himself justice, and feared that Rothenstein was going to point out fallacies. Anyhow, he cleared his throat and said, "Parlons d'autre chose."

It occurs to you that he was a fool? It didn't to me. I was young, and had not the clarity of judgment that Rothenstein already had. Soames was quite five or six years older than either of us. Also – he had written a book. It was wonderful to have written a book.

If Rothenstein had not been there, I should have revered Soames. Even as it was, I respected him. And I was very near indeed to reverence when he said he had another book coming out soon. I asked if I might ask what kind of book it was to be.

"My poems," he answered. Rothenstein asked if this was to be the title of the book. The poet meditated on this suggestion, but said he rather thought of giving the book no title at all. "If a book is good in itself—" he murmured, and waved his cigarette.

Rothenstein objected that absence of title might be bad for the sale of a book.

"If," he urged, "I went into a bookseller's and said simply, 'Have you got?' or, 'Have you a copy of?' how would they know what I wanted?"

"Oh, of course I should have my name on the cover," Soames answered earnestly. "And I rather want," he added, looking hard at Rothenstein, "to have a drawing of myself as frontispiece." Rothenstein admitted that this was a capital idea, and mentioned that he was going into the country and would be there for some time. He then looked at his watch, exclaimed at the hour, paid the waiter, and went away with me to dinner. Soames remained at his post of fidelity to the glaucous witch.

"Why were you so determined not to draw him?" I asked.

"Draw him? Him? How can one draw a man who doesn't exist?"

"He is dim," I admitted. But my mot juste fell flat. Rothenstein repeated that Soames was non-existent.

Still, Soames had written a book. I asked if Rothenstein had read "Negations." He said he had looked into it, "but," he added crisply, "I don't profess to know anything about writing." A reservation very characteristic of the period! Painters would not then allow that anyone outside their own order had a right to any opinion about painting. This law (graven on the tablets brought down by Whistler from the summit of Fuji-yama) imposed certain limitations. If other arts than painting were not utterly unintelligible to all but the men who practiced them, the law tottered – the Monroe Doctrine, as it were, did not hold good. Therefore no painter would offer an opinion of a book without warning you at any rate that his opinion was worthless. No one is a better judge of literature than Rothenstein; but it wouldn't have done to tell him so in those days, and I knew that I must form an unaided judgment of "Negations."

Not to buy a book of which I had met the author face to face would have been for me in those days an impossible act of self-denial. When I returned to Oxford for the Christmas term I had duly secured "Negations." I used to keep it lying carelessly on the table in my room, and whenever a friend took it up and asked what it was about, I would say: "Oh, it's rather a remarkable book. It's by a man whom I know." Just "what it was about" I never was able to say. Head or tail was just what I hadn't made of that slim, green volume. I found in the preface no clue to the labyrinth of contents, and in that labyrinth nothing to explain the preface.

Lean near to life. Lean very near – nearer.
Life is web and therein nor warp nor woof is, but web only.
It is for this I am Catholick in church and in thought, yet do let swift Mood weave there what the shuttle of Mood wills.

These were the opening phrases of the preface, but those which followed were less easy to understand. Then came "Stark: A Conte," about a midinette who, so far as I could gather, murdered, or was about to murder, a mannequin. It was rather like a story by Catulle Mendes in which the translator had either skipped or cut out every alternate sentence. Next, a dialogue between Pan and St. Ursula, lacking, I rather thought, in "snap." Next, some aphorisms (entitled "Aphorismata" [spelled in Greek]). Throughout, in fact, there was a great variety of form, and the forms had evidently been wrought with much care. It was rather the substance that eluded me. Was there, I wondered, any substance at all? It did not occur to me: suppose Enoch Soames was a fool! Up cropped a rival hypothesis: suppose *I* was! I inclined to give Soames the benefit of the doubt. I had read "L'Apres-midi d'un faune" without extracting a glimmer of meaning; yet Mallarmé, of course, was a master. How was I to know that Soames wasn't another? There was a sort of music in his prose, not indeed, arresting, but perhaps, I thought, haunting, and laden, perhaps, with meanings as deep as Mallarmé's own. I awaited his poems with an open mind.

And I looked forward to them with positive impatience after I had had a second meeting with him. This was on an evening in January. Going into the aforesaid domino-room, I had passed a table at which sat a pale man with an open book before him. He had looked from his book to me, and I looked back over my shoulder with a vague sense that I ought to have recognized him. I returned to pay my respects. After exchanging a few words, I said with a glance to the open book, "I see I am interrupting you," and was about to pass on, but, "I prefer," Soames replied in his toneless voice, "to be interrupted," and I obeyed his gesture that I should sit down.

I asked him if he often read here.

"Yes; things of this kind I read here," he answered, indicating the title of his book – "The Poems of Shelley."

"Anything that you really" – and I was going to say "admire?" But I cautiously left my sentence unfinished, and was glad that I had done so, for he said with unwonted emphasis, "Anything second-rate."

I had read little of Shelley, but, "Of course," I murmured, "he's very uneven."

"I should have thought evenness was just what was wrong with him. A deadly evenness. That's why I read him here. The noise of this place breaks the rhythm. He's tolerable here." Soames took up the book and glanced through the pages. He laughed. Soames's laugh was a short, single, and mirthless sound from the throat, unaccompanied by any movement of the face or brightening of the eyes. "What a period!" he uttered, laying the book down. And, "What a country!" he added.

I asked rather nervously if he didn't think Keats had more or less held his own against the drawbacks of time and place. He admitted that there were "passages in Keats," but did not specify them. Of "the older men," as he called them, he seemed to like only Milton. "Milton," he said, "wasn't sentimental." Also, "Milton had a dark insight." And again, "I can always read Milton in the reading-room."

"The reading-room?"

"Of the British Museum. I go there every day."

"You do? I've only been there once. I'm afraid I found it rather a depressing place. It – it seemed to sap one's vitality."

"It does. That's why I go there. The lower one's vitality, the more sensitive one is to great art. I live near the museum. I have rooms in Dyott Street."

"And you go round to the reading-room to read Milton?"

"Usually Milton." He looked at me. "It was Milton," he certificatively added, "who converted me to diabolism."

"Diabolism? Oh, yes? Really?" said I, with that vague discomfort and that intense desire to be polite which one feels when a man speaks of his own religion. "You – worship the Devil?"

Soames shook his head.

"It's not exactly worship," he qualified, sipping his absinthe. "It's more a matter of trusting and encouraging."

"I see, yes. I had rather gathered from the preface to 'Negations' that you were a – a Catholic."

"Je l'étais à cette époque. In fact, I still am. I am a Catholic diabolist."

But this profession he made in an almost cursory tone. I could see that what was upmost in his mind was the fact that I had read "Negations." His pale eyes had for the first time gleamed. I felt as one who is about to be examined viva voce on the very subject in which he is shakiest. I hastily asked him how soon his poems were to be published.

"Next week," he told me.

"And are they to be published without a title?"

"No. I found a title at last. But I sha'n't tell you what it is," as though I had been so impertinent as to inquire. "I am not sure that it wholly satisfies me. But it is the best I can find. It suggests something of the quality of the poems – strange growths, natural and wild, yet exquisite," he added, "and many-hued, and full of poisons."

I asked him what he thought of Baudelaire. He uttered the snort that was his laugh, and, "Baudelaire," he said, "was a bourgeois malgre lui." France had had only one poet – Villon; "and two thirds of Villon were sheer journalism." Verlaine was "an épicier malgre lui." Altogether, rather to my surprise, he rated French literature lower than English. There were "passages" in Villiers de l'Isle-Adam. But, "I," he summed up, "owe nothing to France." He nodded at me. "You'll see," he predicted.

I did not, when the time came, quite see that. I thought the author of "Fungoids" did, unconsciously of course, owe something to the young Parisian decadents or to the young English ones who owed something to THEM. I still think so. The little book, bought by me in Oxford, lies before me as I write. Its pale-gray buckram cover and silver lettering have not worn well. Nor have its contents. Through these, with a melancholy interest, I have again been looking. They are not much. But at the time of their publication I had a vague suspicion that they MIGHT be. I suppose it is my capacity for faith, not poor Soames's work, that is weaker than it once was.

TO A YOUNG WOMAN
THOU ART, WHO HAST NOT BEEN!

Pale tunes irresolute
And traceries of old sounds
Blown from a rotted flute
Mingle with noise of cymbals rouged with rust,
Nor not strange forms and epicene
Lie bleeding in the dust,
Being wounded with wounds.
For this it is
That in thy counterpart
Of age-long mockeries
THOU HAST NOT BEEN NOR ART!

There seemed to me a certain inconsistency as between the first and last lines of this. I tried, with bent brows, to resolve the discord. But I did not take my failure as wholly incompatible with a meaning in Soames's mind. Might it not rather indicate the depth of his meaning? As for the craftsmanship, "rouged with rust" seemed to me a fine stroke, and "nor not" instead of "and" had a curious felicity. I wondered who the "young woman" was and what she had made of it all. I sadly suspect that Soames could not have made more of it than she. Yet even now, if one doesn't try to make any sense at all of the poem, and reads it just for the sound, there is a certain grace of cadence. Soames was an artist, in so far as he was anything, poor fellow!

It seemed to me, when first I read "Fungoids," that, oddly enough, the diabolistic side of him was the best. Diabolism seemed to be a cheerful, even a wholesome influence in his life.

NOCTURNE
Round and round the shutter'd Square
I strolled with the Devil's arm in mine.
No sound but the scrape of his hoofs was there
And the ring of his laughter and mine.
We had drunk black wine.

I scream'd, "I will race you, Master!"
"What matter," he shriek'd, "to-night
Which of us runs the faster?
There is nothing to fear to-night
In the foul moon's light!"

Then I look'd him in the eyes
And I laugh'd full shrill at the lie he told
And the gnawing fear he would fain disguise.
It was true, what I'd time and again been told:
He was old – old.

There was, I felt, quite a swing about that first stanza – a joyous and rollicking note of comradeship. The second was slightly hysterical, perhaps. But I liked the third, it was so bracingly unorthodox, even according to the tenets of Soames's peculiar sect in the faith. Not much "trusting and encouraging" here! Soames triumphantly exposing the Devil as a liar, and laughing "full shrill," cut a quite heartening figure, I thought, then! Now, in the light of what befell, none of his other poems depresses me so much as "Nocturne."

I looked out for what the metropolitan reviewers would have to say. They seemed to fall into two classes: those who had little to say and those who had nothing. The second class was the larger, and the words of the first were cold; insomuch that

"Strikes a note of modernity. . . These tripping numbers." *The Preston Telegraph*

was the only lure offered in advertisements by Soames's publisher. I had hoped that when next I met the poet I could congratulate him on having made a stir, for I fancied he was not so sure of his intrinsic greatness as he seemed. I was but able to say, rather coarsely, when next I did see him, that I hoped "Fungoids" was "selling splendidly." He looked at me across his glass of absinthe and asked if I had bought a copy. His publisher had told him that three had been sold. I laughed, as at a jest.

"You don't suppose I CARE, do you?" he said, with something like a snarl. I disclaimed the notion. He added that he was not a tradesman. I said mildly that I wasn't, either, and murmured that an artist who gave truly new and great things to the world had always to wait long for recognition. He said he cared not a sou for recognition. I agreed that the act of creation was its own reward.

His moroseness might have alienated me if I had regarded myself as a nobody. But ah! Hadn't both John Lane and Aubrey Beardsley suggested that I should write an essay for the great new venture that was afoot—"The Yellow Book"? And hadn't Henry Harland, as editor, accepted my essay? And wasn't it to be in the very first number? At Oxford I was still in statu pupillari. In London I regarded myself as very much indeed a graduate now – one whom no Soames could ruffle. Partly to show off, partly in sheer good-will, I told Soames he ought to contribute to "The Yellow Book." He uttered from the throat a sound of scorn for that publication.

Nevertheless, I did, a day or two later, tentatively ask Harland if he knew anything of the work of a man called Enoch Soames. Harland paused in the midst of his characteristic stride around the room, threw up his hands toward the ceiling, and groaned aloud: he had often met "that absurd creature" in Paris, and this very morning had received some poems in manuscript from him.

"Has he NO talent?" I asked.

"He has an income. He's all right." Harland was the most joyous of men and most generous of critics, and he hated to talk of anything about which he couldn't be enthusiastic. So I dropped the subject of Soames. The news that Soames had an income did take the edge off solicitude. I learned afterward that he was the son of an unsuccessful and deceased bookseller in Preston, but had inherited an annuity of three hundred pounds from a married aunt, and had no surviving relatives of any kind. Materially, then, he was "all right." But there was still a spiritual pathos about him, sharpened for me now by the possibility that even the praises of "The Preston Telegraph" might not have been forthcoming had he not been the son of a Preston man. He had a sort of weak doggedness which I could not but admire. Neither he nor his work received the slightest encouragement; but he persisted in behaving as a personage: always he kept his dingy little flag flying. Wherever congregated the jeunes feroces of the arts, in whatever Soho restaurant they had just discovered, in whatever music-hall they were most frequently, there was Soames in the midst of them, or, rather, on the fringe of them, a dim, but inevitable, figure. He never sought to propitiate his fellow-writers, never bated a jot of his arrogance about his own work or of his contempt for theirs. To the painters he was respectful, even humble; but for the poets and prosaists of "The Yellow Book" and later of "The Savoy" he had never a word but of scorn. He wasn't resented. It didn't occur to anybody that he or his Catholic diabolism mattered. When, in the autumn of '96, he brought out (at his own expense, this time) a third book, his last book, nobody said a word for or against it. I meant, but forgot, to buy it. I never saw it, and am ashamed to say I don't even remember what it was called. But I did, at the time of its publication, say to Rothenstein that I thought poor old Soames was really a rather tragic figure, and that I believed he would literally die for want of recognition. Rothenstein scoffed. He said I was trying to get credit for a kind heart which I didn't possess; and perhaps this was so. But at the private view of the New English Art Club, a few weeks later, I beheld a pastel portrait of "Enoch Soames, Esq." It was very like him, and very like Rothenstein to have done it. Soames was standing near it, in his soft hat and his waterproof cape, all through the afternoon. Anybody who knew him would have recognized the portrait at a glance, but nobody who didn't know him would have recognized the portrait from its bystander: it "existed" so much more than he; it was bound to. Also, it had not that expression of faint happiness which on that day was discernible, yes, in Soames's countenance. Fame had breathed on him. Twice again in the course of the month I went to the New English, and on both occasions Soames himself was on view there. Looking back, I regard the close of that exhibition as having been virtually the close of his career. He had felt the breath of Fame against his cheek – so late, for such a little while; and at its withdrawal he gave in, gave up, gave out. He, who had never looked strong or well, looked ghastly now – a shadow of the shade he had once been. He still frequented the domino-room, but having lost all wish to excite curiosity, he no longer read books there. "You read only at the museum now?" I asked, with attempted cheerfulness. He said he never went there now. "No absinthe there," he muttered. It was the sort of thing that in old days he would have said for effect; but it carried conviction now. Absinthe, erst but a point in the "personality" he had striven so hard to build up, was solace and necessity now. He no longer called it "la sorciere glauque." He had shed away all his French phrases. He had become a plain, unvarnished Preston man.

Failure, if it be a plain, unvarnished, complete failure, and even though it be a squalid failure, has always a certain dignity. I avoided Soames because he made me feel rather vulgar. John Lane had published, by this time, two little books of mine, and they had had a pleasant little success of esteem. I was a – slight, but definite—"personality." Frank Harris had engaged me to kick up my heels in

"The Saturday Review," Alfred Harmsworth was letting me do likewise in "The Daily Mail." I was just what Soames wasn't. And he shamed my gloss. Had I known that he really and firmly believed in the greatness of what he as an artist had achieved, I might not have shunned him. No man who hasn't lost his vanity can be held to have altogether failed. Soames's dignity was an illusion of mine. One day, in the first week of June, 1897, that illusion went. But on the evening of that day Soames went, too.

I had been out most of the morning and, as it was too late to reach home in time for luncheon, I sought the Vingtieme. This little place – Restaurant du Vingtieme Siecle, to give it its full title – had been discovered in '96 by the poets and prosaists, but had now been more or less abandoned in favor of some later find. I don't think it lived long enough to justify its name; but at that time there it still was, in Greek Street, a few doors from Soho Square, and almost opposite to that house where, in the first years of the century, a little girl, and with her a boy named De Quincey, made nightly encampment in darkness and hunger among dust and rats and old legal parchments. The Vingtieme was but a small whitewashed room, leading out into the street at one end and into a kitchen at the other. The proprietor and cook was a Frenchman, known to us as Monsieur Vingtieme; the waiters were his two daughters, Rose and Berthe; and the food, according to faith, was good. The tables were so narrow and were set so close together that there was space for twelve of them, six jutting from each wall.

Only the two nearest to the door, as I went in, were occupied. On one side sat a tall, flashy, rather Mephistophelian man whom I had seen from time to time in the domino-room and elsewhere. On the other side sat Soames. They made a queer contrast in that sunlit room, Soames sitting haggard in that hat and cape, which nowhere at any season had I seen him doff, and this other, this keenly vital man, at sight of whom I more than ever wondered whether he were a diamond merchant, a conjurer, or the head of a private detective agency. I was sure Soames didn't want my company; but I asked, as it would have seemed brutal not to, whether I might join him, and took the chair opposite to his. He was smoking a cigarette, with an untasted salami of something on his plate and a half-empty bottle of Sauterne before him, and he was quite silent. I said that the preparations for the Jubilee made London impossible. (I rather liked them, really.) I professed a wish to go right away till the whole thing was over. In vain did I attune myself to his gloom. He seemed not to hear me or even to see me. I felt that his behavior made me ridiculous in the eyes of the other man. The gangway between the two rows of tables at the Vingtieme was hardly more than two feet wide (Rose and Berthe, in their ministrations, had always to edge past each other, quarreling in whispers as they did so), and any one at the table abreast of yours was virtually at yours. I thought our neighbor was amused at my failure to interest Soames, and so, as I could not explain to him that my insistence was merely charitable, I became silent. Without turning my head, I had him well within my range of vision. I hoped I looked less vulgar than he in contrast with Soames. I was sure he was not an Englishman, but what WAS his nationality? Though his jet-black hair was en brosse, I did not think he was French. To Berthe, who waited on him, he spoke French fluently, but with a hardly native idiom and accent. I gathered that this was his first visit to the Vingtieme; but Berthe was offhand in her manner to him: he had not made a good impression. His eyes were handsome, but, like the Vingtieme's tables, too narrow and set too close together. His nose was predatory, and the points of his mustache, waxed up behind his nostrils, gave a fixity to his smile. Decidedly, he was sinister. And my sense of discomfort in his presence was intensified by the scarlet waistcoat which tightly, and so unseasonably in June, sheathed his ample chest. This waistcoat wasn't wrong merely because of the heat, either. It was somehow all wrong in itself. It wouldn't have done on Christmas morning. It would have struck a jarring note at the first night of "Hernani." I was trying to account for its wrongness when Soames suddenly and strangely broke silence. "A hundred years hence!" he murmured, as in a trance.

"We shall not be here," I briskly, but fatuously, added.

"We shall not be here. No," he droned, "but the museum will still be just where it is. And the reading-room just where it is. And people will be able to go and read there." He inhaled sharply, and a spasm as of actual pain contorted his features.

I wondered what train of thought poor Soames had been following. He did not enlighten me when he said, after a long pause, "You think I haven't minded."

"Minded what, Soames?"

"Neglect. Failure."

"FAILURE?" I said heartily. "Failure?" I repeated vaguely. "Neglect – yes, perhaps; but that's quite another matter. Of course you haven't been – appreciated. But what, then? Any artist who – who gives—" What I wanted to say was, "Any artist who gives truly new and great things to the world has always to wait long for recognition"; but the flattery would not out: in the face of his misery – a misery so genuine and so unmasked – my lips would not say the words.

And then he said them for me. I flushed. "That's what you were going to say, isn't it?" he asked.

"How did you know?"

"It's what you said to me three years ago, when 'Fungoids' was published." I flushed the more. I need not have flushed at all. "It's the only important thing I ever heard you say," he continued. "And I've never forgotten it. It's a true thing. It's a horrible truth. But – d'you remember what I answered? I said, 'I don't care a sou for recognition.' And you believed me. You've gone on believing I'm above that sort of thing. You're shallow. What should YOU know of the feelings of a man like me? You imagine that a great artist's faith in himself and in the verdict of posterity is enough to keep him happy. You've never guessed at the bitterness and loneliness, the" – his voice broke; but presently he resumed, speaking with a force that I had never known in him. "Posterity! What use is it to ME? A dead man doesn't know that people are visiting his grave, visiting his birthplace, putting up tablets to him, unveiling statues of him. A dead man can't read the books that are written about him. A hundred years hence! Think of it! If I could come back to life THEN – just for a few hours – and go to the reading-room and READ! Or, better still, if I could be projected now, at this moment, into that future, into that reading-room, just for this one afternoon!

I'd sell myself body and soul to the Devil for that! Think of the pages and pages in the catalogue: 'Soames, Enoch' endlessly – endless editions, commentaries, prolegomena, biographies" – But here he was interrupted by a sudden loud crack of the chair at the next table. Our neighbor had half risen from his place. He was leaning toward us, apologetically intrusive.

"Excuse – permit me," he said softly. "I have been unable not to hear. Might I take a liberty? In this little restaurant-sans-facon – might I, as the phrase is, cut in?"

I could but signify our acquiescence. Berthe had appeared at the kitchen door, thinking the stranger wanted his bill. He waved her away with his cigar, and in another moment had seated himself beside me, commanding a full view of Soames.

"Though not an Englishman," he explained, "I know my London well, Mr. Soames. Your name and fame – Mr. Beerbohm's, too – very known to me. Your point is, who am *I*?" He glanced quickly over his shoulder, and in a lowered voice said, "I am the Devil."

I couldn't help it; I laughed. I tried not to, I knew there was nothing to laugh at, my rudeness shamed me; but – I laughed with increasing volume. The Devil's quiet dignity, the surprise and disgust of his raised eyebrows, did but the more dissolve me. I rocked to and fro; I lay back aching; I behaved deplorably.

"I am a gentleman, and," he said with intense emphasis, "I thought I was in the company of GENTLEMEN."

"Don't!" I gasped faintly. "Oh, don't!"

"Curious, nicht wahr?" I heard him say to Soames. "There is a type of person to whom the very mention of my name is – oh, so awfully – funny! In your theaters the dullest comedian needs only to say 'The Devil!' and right away they give him 'the loud laugh what speaks the vacant mind.' Is it not so?"

I had now just breath enough to offer my apologies. He accepted them, but coldly, and re-addressed himself to Soames.

"I am a man of business," he said, "and always I would put things through 'right now,' as they say in the States. You are a poet. Les affaires – you detest them. So be it. But with me you will deal, eh? What you have said just now gives me furiously to hope."

Soames had not moved except to light a fresh cigarette. He sat crouched forward, with his elbows squared on the table, and his head just above the level of his hands, staring up at the Devil.

"Go on," he nodded. I had no remnant of laughter in me now.

"It will be the more pleasant, our little deal," the Devil went on, "because you are – I mistake not? – a diabolist."

"A Catholic diabolist," said Soames.

The Devil accepted the reservation genially.

"You wish," he resumed, "to visit now – this afternoon as-ever-is – the reading-room of the British Museum, yes? But of a hundred years hence, yes? Parfaitement. Time – an illusion. Past and future – they are as ever present as the present, or at any rate only what you call 'just round the corner.' I switch you on to any date. I project you – pouf! You wish to be in the reading-room just as it will be on the afternoon of June 3, 1997? You wish to find yourself standing in that room, just past the swing-doors, this very minute, yes? And to stay there till closing-time? Am I right?"

Soames nodded.

The Devil looked at his watch. "Ten past two," he said. "Closing-time in summer same then as now – seven o'clock. That will give you almost five hours. At seven o'clock – pouf! – you find yourself again here, sitting at this table. I am dining tonight dans le monde – dans le higlif. That concludes my present visit to your great city. I come and fetch you here, Mr. Soames, on my way home."

"Home?" I echoed.

"Be it never so humble!" said the Devil, lightly.

"All right," said Soames.

"Soames!" I entreated. But my friend moved not a muscle.

The Devil had made as though to stretch forth his hand across the table, but he paused in his gesture.

"A hundred years hence, as now," he smiled, "no smoking allowed in the reading-room. You would better therefore—"

Soames removed the cigarette from his mouth and dropped it into his glass of Sauterne.

"Soames!" again I cried. "Can't you" – but the Devil had now stretched forth his hand across the table. He brought it slowly down on the tablecloth. Soames's chair was empty. His cigarette floated sodden in his wineglass. There was no other trace of him.

For a few moments the Devil let his hand rest where it lay, gazing at me out of the corners of his eyes, vulgarly triumphant.

A shudder shook me. With an effort I controlled myself and rose from my chair. "Very clever," I said condescendingly. "But – 'The Time Machine' is a delightful book, don't you think? So entirely original!"

"You are pleased to sneer," said the Devil, who had also risen, "but it is one thing to write about an impossible machine; it is a quite other thing to be a supernatural power." All the same, I had scored.

Berthe had come forth at the sound of our rising. I explained to her that Mr. Soames had been called away, and that both he and I would be dining here. It was not until I was out in the open air that I began to feel giddy. I have but the haziest recollection of what I did, where I wandered, in the glaring sunshine of that endless afternoon. I remember the sound of carpenters' hammers all along Piccadilly and the bare chaotic look of the half-erected "stands." Was it in the Green Park or in Kensington Gardens or WHERE was it that I sat on a chair beneath a tree, trying to read an evening paper? There was a phrase in the leading article that went on repeating itself in my fagged mind: "Little is hidden from this August Lady full of the garnered wisdom of sixty years of Sovereignty." I remember wildly conceiving a letter (to reach Windsor by an express messenger told to await answer): "Madam: Well knowing that your Majesty is full of the garnered wisdom of sixty years of Sovereignty, I venture to ask your advice in the following delicate matter. Mr. Enoch Soames, whose poems you may or may not know—" Was there NO way of helping him, saving him? A bargain was a bargain, and I was the last man to aid or abet any one in wriggling out of a reasonable obligation. I wouldn't have lifted a little finger to save Faust. But poor Soames! Doomed to pay without respite an eternal price for nothing but a fruitless search and a bitter disillusioning.

Odd and uncanny it seemed to me that he, Soames, in the flesh, in the water-proof cape, was at this moment living in the last decade of the next century, poring over books not yet written, and seeing and seen by men not yet born. Uncannier and odder still that to-night and evermore he would be in hell. Assuredly, truth was stranger than fiction.

Endless that afternoon was. Almost I wished I had gone with Soames, not, indeed, to stay in the reading-room, but to sally forth for a brisk sight-seeing walk around a new London. I wandered restlessly out of the park I had sat in. Vainly I tried to imagine myself an ardent tourist from the eighteenth century. Intolerable was the strain of the slow-passing and empty minutes. Long before seven o'clock I was back at the Vingtieme.

I sat there just where I had sat for luncheon. Air came in listlessly through the open door behind me. Now and again Rose or Berthe appeared for a moment. I had told them I would not order any dinner till Mr. Soames came. A hurdy-gurdy began to play, abruptly drowning the noise of a quarrel between some Frenchmen farther up the street. Whenever the tune was changed I heard the quarrel still raging. I had bought another evening paper on my way. I unfolded it. My eyes gazed ever away from it to the clock over the kitchen door.

Five minutes now to the hour! I remembered that clocks in restaurants are kept five minutes fast. I concentrated my eyes on the paper. I vowed I would not look away from it again. I held it upright, at its full width, close to my face, so that I had no view of anything but it. Rather a tremulous sheet? Only because of the draft, I told myself.

My arms gradually became stiff; they ached; but I could not drop them – now. I had a suspicion, I had a certainty. Well, what, then? What else had I come for? Yet I held tight that barrier of newspaper. Only the sound of Berthe's brisk footstep from the kitchen enabled me, forced me, to drop it, and to utter:

"What shall we have to eat, Soames?"

"Il est souffrant, ce pauvre Monsieur Soames?" asked Berthe.

"He's only – tired." I asked her to get some wine – Burgundy – and whatever food might be ready. Soames sat crouched forward against the table exactly as when last I had seen him. It was as though he had never moved – he who had moved so unimaginably far. Once or twice in the afternoon it had for an instant occurred to me that perhaps his journey was not to be fruitless, that perhaps we had all been wrong in our estimate of the works of Enoch Soames. That we had been horribly right was horribly clear from the look of him. But, "Don't be discouraged," I falteringly said. "Perhaps it's only that you – didn't leave enough time. Two, three centuries hence, perhaps—"

"Yes," his voice came. "I've thought of that."

"And now – now for the more immediate future! Where are you going to hide? How would it be if you caught the Paris express from Charing Cross? Almost an hour to spare. Don't go on to Paris. Stop at Calais. Live in Calais. He'd never think of looking for you in Calais."

"It's like my luck," he said, "to spend my last hours on earth with an ass." But I was not offended. "And a treacherous ass," he strangely added, tossing across to me a crumpled bit of paper which he had been holding in his hand. I glanced at the writing on it – some sort of gibberish, apparently. I laid it impatiently aside.

"Come, Soames, pull yourself together! This isn't a mere matter of life or death. It's a question of eternal torment, mind you! You don't mean to say you're going to wait limply here till the Devil comes to fetch you."

"I can't do anything else. I've no choice."

"Come! This is 'trusting and encouraging' with a vengeance! This is diabolism run mad!" I filled his glass with wine. "Surely, now that you've SEEN the brute—"

"It's no good abusing him."

"You must admit there's nothing Miltonic about him, Soames."

"I don't say he's not rather different from what I expected."

"He's a vulgarian, he's a swell mobs-man, he's the sort of man who hangs about the corridors of trains going to the Riviera and steals ladies' jewel-cases. Imagine eternal torment presided over by HIM!"

"You don't suppose I look forward to it, do you?"

"Then why not slip quietly out of the way?"

Again and again I filled his glass, and always, mechanically, he emptied it; but the wine kindled no spark of enterprise in him. He did not eat, and I myself ate hardly at all. I did not in my heart believe that any dash for freedom could save him. The chase would be swift, the capture certain. But better anything than this passive, meek, miserable waiting. I told Soames that for the honor of the human race he ought to make some show of resistance. He asked what the human race had ever done for him. "Besides," he said, "can't you understand that I'm in his power? You saw him touch me, didn't you? There's an end of it. I've no will. I'm sealed."

I made a gesture of despair. He went on repeating the word "sealed." I began to realize that the wine had clouded his brain. No wonder! Foodless he had gone into futurity, foodless he still was. I urged him to eat, at any rate, some bread. It was maddening to think that he, who had so much to tell, might tell nothing. "How was it all," I asked, "yonder? Come, tell me your adventures!"

"They'd make first-rate 'copy,' wouldn't they?"

"I'm awfully sorry for you, Soames, and I make all possible allowances; but what earthly right have you to insinuate that I should make 'copy,' as you call it, out of you?"

The poor fellow pressed his hands to his forehead.

"I don't know," he said. "I had some reason, I know. I'll try to remember." He sat plunged in thought.

"That's right. Try to remember everything. Eat a little more bread. What did the reading-room look like?"

"Much as usual," he at length muttered.

"Many people there?"

"Usual sort of number."

"What did they look like?"

Soames tried to visualize them.

"They all," he presently remembered, "looked very like one another."

My mind took a fearsome leap.

"All dressed in sanitary woolen?"

"Yes, I think so. Grayish-yellowish stuff."

"A sort of uniform?" He nodded. "With a number on it perhaps – a number on a large disk of metal strapped round the left arm? D. K. F. 78,910 – that sort of thing?" It was even so. "And all of them, men and women alike, looking very well cared for? Very Utopian, and smelling rather strongly of carbolic, and all of them quite hairless?" I was right every time. Soames was only not sure whether the men and women were hairless or shorn. "I hadn't time to look at them very closely," he explained.

"No, of course not. But—"

"They stared at ME, I can tell you. I attracted a great deal of attention." At last he had done that! "I think I rather scared them. They moved away whenever I came near. They followed me about, at a distance, wherever I went. The men at the round desk in the middle seemed to have a sort of panic whenever I went to make inquiries."

"What did you do when you arrived?"

Well, he had gone straight to the catalogue, of course – to the S volumes – and had stood long before SN-SOF, unable to take this volume out of the shelf because his heart was beating so. At first, he said, he wasn't disappointed; he only thought there was some new arrangement. He went to the middle desk and asked where the catalogue of twentieth-century books was kept. He gathered that there was still only one catalogue. Again he looked up his name, stared at the three little pasted slips he had known so well. Then he went and sat down for a long time.

"And then," he droned, "I looked up the 'Dictionary of National Biography,' and some encyclopedias. I went back to the middle desk and asked what was the best modern book on late nineteenth-century literature. They told me Mr. T. K. Nupton's book was considered the best. I looked it up in the catalogue and filled in a form for it. It was brought to me. My name wasn't in the index, but – yes!" he said with a sudden change of tone, "that's what I'd forgotten. Where's that bit of paper? Give it me back."

I, too, had forgotten that cryptic screed. I found it fallen on the floor, and handed it to him.

He smoothed it out, nodding and smiling at me disagreeably.

"I found myself glancing through Nupton's book," he resumed. "Not very easy reading. Some sort of phonetic spelling. All the modern books I saw were phonetic."

"Then I don't want to hear any more, Soames, please."

"The proper names seemed all to be spelt in the old way. But for that I mightn't have noticed my own name."

"Your own name? Really? Soames, I'm VERY glad."

"And yours."

"No!"

"I thought I should find you waiting here to-night, so I took the trouble to copy out the passage. Read it."

I snatched the paper. Soames's handwriting was characteristically dim. It and the noisome spelling and my excitement made me all the slower to grasp what T. K. Nupton was driving at.

The document lies before me at this moment. Strange that the words I here copy out for you were copied out for me by poor Soames just eighty-two years hence!

From page 234 of "Inglish Littracher 1890-1900" bi T. K. Nupton, publishd bi th Stait, 1992.

Fr egzarmpl, a riter ov th time, naimed Max Beerbohm, hoo woz stil alive in th twentith senchri, rote a stauri in wich e pautraid an immajnari karrakter kauld "Enoch Soames" – a thurd-rait poit hoo beleevz imself a grate jeneus an maix a bargin with th Devvl in auder ter no wot posterriti thinx ov im! It iz a sumwot labud sattire, but not without vallu az showing hou seriusli the yung men ov th aiteen-ninetiz took themselvz. Nou that th littreri profeshn haz bin auganized az a departmnt of publik servis, our riters hav found their levvl an hav lernt ter doo their duti without thort ov th morro. "Th laibrer iz werthi ov hiz hire" an that iz aul. Thank hevvn we hav no Enoch Soameses amung us to-dai!

I found that by murmuring the words aloud (a device which I commend to my reader) I was able to master them little by little. The clearer they became, the greater was my bewilderment, my distress and horror. The whole thing was a nightmare. Afar, the great grisly background of what was in store for the poor dear art of letters; here, at the table, fixing on me a gaze that made me hot all over, the poor fellow whom – whom evidently – but no: whatever down-grade my character might take in coming years, I should never be such a brute as to— Again I examined the screed. "Immajnari." But here Soames was, no more imaginary, alas! than I. And "labud" – what on earth was that? (To this day I have never made out that word.) "It's all very – baffling," I at length stammered.

Soames said nothing, but cruelly did not cease to look at me.

"Are you sure," I temporized, "quite sure you copied the thing out correctly?"

"Quite."

"Well, then, it's this wretched Nupton who must have made – must be going to make – some idiotic mistake. Look here, Soames, you know me better than to suppose that I— After all, the name Max Beerbohm is not at all an uncommon one, and there must be several Enoch Soameses running around, or, rather, Enoch Soames is a name that might occur to any one writing a story. And I don't write stories; I'm an essayist, an observer, a recorder. I admit that it's an extraordinary coincidence. But you must see—"

"I see the whole thing," said Soames, quietly. And he added, with a touch of his old manner, but with more dignity than I had ever known in him, "Parlons d'autre chose."

I accepted that suggestion very promptly. I returned straight to the more immediate future. I spent most of the long evening in renewed appeals to Soames to come away and seek refuge somewhere. I remember saying at last that if indeed I was destined to write about him, the supposed "stauri" had better have at least a happy ending. Soames repeated those last three words in a tone of intense scorn.

"In life and in art," he said, "all that matters is an INEVITABLE ending."

"But," I urged more hopefully than I felt, "an ending that can be avoided ISN'T inevitable."

"You aren't an artist," he rasped. "And you're so hopelessly not an artist that, so far from being able to imagine a thing and make it seem true, you're going to make even a true thing seem as if you'd made it up. You're a miserable bungler. And it's like my luck."

I protested that the miserable bungler was not I, was not going to be I, but T. K. Nupton; and we had a rather heated argument, in the thick of which it suddenly seemed to me that Soames saw he was in the wrong: he had quite physically cowered. But I wondered why – and now I guessed with a cold throb just why – he stared so past me. The bringer of that "inevitable ending" filled the doorway.

I managed to turn in my chair and to say, not without a semblance of lightness, "Aha, come in!" Dread was indeed rather blunted in me by his looking so absurdly like a villain in a melodrama. The sheen of his tilted hat and of his shirt-front, the repeated twists he was giving to his mustache, and most of all the magnificence of his sneer, gave token that he was there only to be foiled.

He was at our table in a stride. "I am sorry," he sneered witheringly, "to break up your pleasant party, but—"

"You don't; you complete it," I assured him. "Mr. Soames and I want to have a little talk with you. Won't you sit? Mr. Soames got nothing, frankly nothing, by his journey this afternoon. We don't wish to say that the whole thing was a swindle, a common swindle. On the contrary, we believe you meant well. But of course the bargain, such as it was, is off."

The Devil gave no verbal answer. He merely looked at Soames and pointed with rigid forefinger to the door. Soames was wretchedly rising from his chair when, with a desperate, quick gesture, I swept together two dinner-knives that were on the table, and laid their blades across each other. The Devil stepped sharp back against the table behind him, averting his face and shuddering.

"You are not superstitious!" he hissed.

"Not at all," I smiled.

"Soames," he said as to an underling, but without turning his face, "put those knives straight!"

With an inhibitive gesture to my friend, "Mr. Soames," I said emphatically to the Devil, "is a Catholic diabolist"; but my poor friend did the Devil's bidding, not mine; and now, with his master's eyes again fixed on him, he arose, he shuffled past me. I tried to speak. It was he that spoke. "Try," was the prayer he threw back at me as the Devil pushed him roughly out through the door— "TRY to make them know that I did exist!"

In another instant I, too, was through that door. I stood staring all ways, up the street, across it, down it. There was moonlight and lamplight, but there was not Soames nor that other.

Dazed, I stood there. Dazed, I turned back at length into the little room, and I suppose I paid Berthe or Rose for my dinner and luncheon and for Soames's; I hope so, for I never went to the Vingtieme again. Ever since that night I have avoided Greek Street altogether. And for years I did not set foot even in Soho Square, because on that same night it was there that I paced and loitered, long and long, with some such dull sense of hope as a man has in not straying far from the place where he has lost something. "Round and round the shutter'd Square" – that line came back to me on my lonely beat, and with it the whole stanza, ringing in my brain and bearing in on me how tragically different from the happy scene imagined by him was the poet's actual experience of that prince in whom of all princes we should put not our trust!

But strange how the mind of an essayist, be it never so stricken, roves and ranges! I remember pausing before a wide door-step and wondering if perchance it was on this very one that the young De Quincey lay ill and faint while poor Ann flew as fast as her feet would carry her to Oxford Street, the "stony-hearted stepmother" of them both, and came back bearing that "glass of port wine and spices" but for which he might, so he thought, actually have died. Was this the very door-step that the old De Quincey used to revisit in homage? I pondered Ann's fate, the cause of her sudden vanishing from the ken of her boy friend; and presently I blamed myself for letting the past override the present. Poor vanished Soames!

And for myself, too, I began to be troubled. What had I better do? Would there be a hue and cry— "Mysterious Disappearance of an Author," and all that? He had last been seen lunching and dining in my company. Hadn't I better get a hansom and drive straight to Scotland Yard? They would think I was a lunatic. After all, I reassured myself, London was a very large place, and one very dim figure might easily drop out of it unobserved, now especially, in the blinding glare of the near Jubilee. Better say nothing at all, I thought.

AND I was right. Soames's disappearance made no stir at all. He was utterly forgotten before any one, so far as I am aware, noticed that he was no longer hanging around. Now and again some poet or prosaist may have said to another, "What has become of that man Soames?" but I never heard any such question asked. As for his landlady in Dyott Street, no doubt he had paid her weekly, and what possessions he may have had in his rooms were enough to save her from fretting. The solicitor through whom he was paid his annuity may be presumed to have made inquiries, but no echo of these resounded. There was something rather ghastly to me in the general unconsciousness that Soames had existed, and more than once I caught myself wondering whether Nupton, that babe unborn, were going to be right in thinking him a figment of my brain.

In that extract from Nupton's repulsive book there is one point which perhaps puzzles you. How is it that the author, though I have here mentioned him by name and have quoted the exact words he is going to write, is not going to grasp the obvious corollary that I have invented nothing? The answer can be only this: Nupton will not have read the later passages of this memoir. Such lack of thoroughness is a serious fault in any one who undertakes to do scholar's work. And I hope these words will meet the eye of some contemporary rival to Nupton and be the undoing of Nupton.

I like to think that some time between 1992 and 1997 somebody will have looked up this memoir, and will have forced on the world his inevitable and startling conclusions. And I have reason for believing that this will be so. You realize that the reading-room into which Soames was projected by the devil was in all respects precisely as it will be on the afternoon of June 3, 1997. You realise, therefore, that on that afternoon, when it comes round, there the selfsame crowd will be, and there Soames will be, punctually, he and they doing precisely what they did before. Recall now Soames's account of the sensation he made. You may say that the mere difference of his costume was enough to make him sensational in that uniformed crowd. You wouldn't say so if you had ever seen him, and I assure you that in no period would Soames be anything but dim. The fact that people are going to stare at him and follow him around and seem afraid of him, can be explained only on the hypothesis that they will somehow have been prepared for his ghostly visitation. They will have been awfully waiting to see whether he really would come. And when he does come the effect will of course be – awful.

An authentic, guaranteed, proved ghost, but only a ghost, alas! Only that. In his first visit Soames was a creature of flesh and blood, whereas the creatures among whom he was projected were but ghosts, I take it – solid, palpable, vocal, but unconscious and automatic ghosts, in a building that was itself an illusion. Next time that building and those creatures will be real. It is of Soames that there will be but the semblance. I wish I could think him destined to revisit the world actually, physically, consciously. I wish he had this one brief escape, this one small treat, to look forward to. I never forget him for long. He is where he is and forever. The more rigid moralists among you may say he has only himself to blame. For my part, I think he has been very hardly used. It is well that vanity should be chastened; and Enoch Soames's vanity was, I admit, above the average, and called for special treatment. But there was no need for vindictiveness. You say he contracted to pay the price he is paying. Yes; but I maintain that he was induced to do so by fraud. Well informed in all things, the Devil must have known that my friend would gain nothing by his visit to futurity. The whole thing was a very shabby trick. The more I think of it, the more detestable the Devil seems to me.

Of him I have caught sight several times, here and there, since that day at the Vingtieme. Only once, however, have I seen him at close quarters. This was a couple of years ago, in Paris. I was walking one afternoon along the rue d'Antin, and I saw him advancing from the opposite direction, overdressed as ever, and swinging an ebony cane and altogether behaving as though the whole pavement belonged to him. At thought of Enoch Soames and the myriads of other sufferers eternally in this brute's dominion, a great cold wrath filled me, and I drew myself up to my full height. But – well, one is so used to nodding and smiling in the street to anybody whom one knows that the action becomes almost independent of oneself; to prevent it requires a very sharp effort and great presence of mind. I was miserably aware, as I passed the Devil, that I nodded and smiled to him. And my shame was the deeper and hotter because he, if you please, stared straight at me with the utmost haughtiness.

To be cut, deliberately cut, by HIM! I was, I still am, furious at having had that happen to me.

TROUSSEAU: FASHION FOR TIME TRAVELERS

Genevieve Valentine

It's a mistake to go. Let's start there.

If you insist, there are some things you're better off knowing.

Jumpsuits. Jumpsuits for Forward motion.

Now you're thinking about some movies you've seen or some ads you've read on the rail about a future where everyone's in skin-tight white. You snickered at how silly it looked, or admired how immaculate, this world where no one is ever carrying coffee and no one sweats and if they have subways instead of personal transport pods then the train cars get wiped down every ten minutes, and nothing ever touches you.

If that's why you're traveling Forward, you should rethink.

Cleanliness is for the people who can afford it. Whatever future you jump to (and the ads are incorrect, there's never just the one), on whatever orbiting body you end up, there is going to be a ruling class, and you are not going to be in it.

The numbers are against you, and the future's a treacherous place even if this isn't your very first jump. Even if you chanced it with a bespoke bioluminescent evening ensemble and lucked out in the right climate to sustain it and enchanted the right social echelon so that they'd take a stranger in to dinner, running with the rich and the beautiful is more than you're ready for.

(If you run with them now, congratulations, and it's no wonder that you're aiming high, but the practicals will undermine you in ways no one has trained you to think of. Depending where you land, the bios that make up your jacket have a labor union, and you're screwed for keeping them out past sunset without paying overtime. Be safe. Stay low.)

You need work boots that don't jog anybody's memory; you need a jumpsuit, unmarked and dark and baggy, with some pockets outside and some pockets inside where no one can reach. The future isn't safe. Have a backup plan strapped to your thigh.

If you think that means a weapon, rethink.

Backward isn't any better, to be honest.

You have to be able to aim before you can plan for the journey, and your first time will be a wash, no matter what they tell you. Nervous people end up on the outskirts of remote Viking camps or out too far in the Dead Sea and have to use their callback in a hurry.

Don't worry. Sensors get sharper every day, and any couture house worth its salt has a satisfaction guarantee. (Give no money to an establishment that won't accommodate.) House of Lewis, the now-vanished icon of the trade, distilled theirs into only six words: "Come back. Look forward. Start again."

Remember that moving through time is a skill; no matter who's holding your hand when that bright machine powers up, there are no chauffeurs for what this is.

When you're headed Backward, wear natural fibers only. Rayon gets you burned as a witch if you're not careful.

A long linen tunic will pass about sixty-five percent of the time. If caught out, claim you were set upon and divested of the rest. It's a prime opportunity to appreciate the immersive experience of being in another place and time as you do labor to earn other garments.

(There are no guarantees that even that cover story will work; the world's a funny thing. You'll be all right in Cleopatra's Egypt, but if you land in feudal Japan and they slice you open for disrespecting the presence of the Emperor, you're on your own.)

Your second-best bet is wool. Wool isn't fancy, but you shouldn't be – sumptuary laws shoot to kill, in some places. Make your sleeves wider than you think you'll need, hems longer than you think is safe. You'll be surprised how cold nights can get in the Andes. You're traveling light; every half-yard of wool you can use is your insurance.

Silk is softer, sometimes finer, but a risk. Make sure your Arabic or Hindi or Chinese dialects are up to snuff, and even then, be prepared to claim the garment is a gift from someone who's dead, and to peel it off to give whoever's asking.

Adornments of any kind should stay out of sight until you have the lay of the land. No exceptions. It doesn't matter when you are or who you're trying to impress. There are no definitive census numbers regarding those Travelers who go missing, killed every year on the roadside, or in alleys, or in dark rooms by someone who knows you're a stranger and will never be missed. No Travel agency is willing to release them.

Think about why that is; leave anything that glitters out of sight.

It's impossible to disappear into your dress.

Everything you wear betrays you – its make, its cost, its cut, its age. Why you have it, or why you don't. Think what a thin gold band on a single finger means;

where you're going, wherever that is, every stitch will give you away.

You might – if you're confident enough to jump, if you aim as you hoped, if you land where you're powerful – be in a place where you can almost disappear. A man in a well-cut dark grey suit can go fifty years from now in either direction, across thousands of miles, and avoid the sort of notice that gets you pointed out to constables.

(It's easy when you're powerful. Anything is. If that's the reason you're traveling local, rethink.)

In eighteenth-century France, a heel less than two inches high is for a man with aspirations past his abilities. An Ethiopian habesha kemis in white signals a guest at a formal occasion. A man in Tokyo in 1872 is a toady or a traitor, whether he wears a kimono or a waistcoat. An unmarried Russian wears her kokoshnik open in the back, and to close it claims a thing you might not mean.

Clothes speak for you; go carefully.

The Persians invented cotton underwear several centuries BC. Maybe start there.

Two hundred years from now, they say, our clothes will be loose and woven through with UVB, cocoons of safety from an ever-warmer sun.

Everyone who goes Forward has said it; whatever future they come from, we're more doomed then.

It's a mistake to go.

Don't wear or carry anything on the cutting edge. You can always explain something a little out of fashion, but rarely can you pass off the new.

If you mention a technology (a fabric, a color, a concept) that doesn't exist, and someone questions you, say, "I saw it on a card." Carry a handful of cigarette cards or postcards or cartes des visites with you in a silver case, and sift through them a moment as if it was just there and you're hoping to find it. Everyone will think you're eccentric, but that's better than the alternative.

If you're somewhen without cards, say, "I heard it from a traveler." If you're in small or far-away places, be prepared to describe someone specific. Make them old; soldiers rarely go after those who sound as if they're about to die on their own.

If all else fails, say, "I saw it in a dream."

People will believe that. They'll expect you to have strange dreams. Anywhere you go will be neck-deep in superstition, but taken one at a time, people aren't fools. Wherever you end up, they know already that you're odd; they can tell you're not theirs.

Black is a color of sophistication, except when it's the color of death. Forward travelers in black might be given responsibilities beyond what they can guess; black is the color of a judge's robes. Black is the color of plague doctors, of people to be taken very seriously.

Red is the color of blood, the color of a hundred feuding houses you'll never be able to keep straight; it's the color of fishing boats you can't steer, the banner of allies who won't reach you in time.

Where purple exists, it's the color of kings. Don't even think about it.

Green is the color of forest outlaws and spring kimono; it's a color of starting over. It's the color of messengers and the Holy Roman Empire. Optimists and armies wear green.

Blue is the color of mystics, the color of weddings, the color of dresses meant to call rain down on the grass. Blue you can make without worry for a throne; blue is safe, as colors go.

White is the color of purity, except when it's the color of mourning. It indicates an absence; it's the color of unfinished things. It's the color of all those sleek, cold spaces we haven't built yet, made for people to stand in and never touch.

Grey is the safest color. It's the color of being undecided; it's the color of never quite belonging, but having no loyalties that might be of concern. It's the color of strangers who have come alone.

Never pick up a watch. Their usefulness is deceptive. Watches are sentimental things, given from people who care about time passing to people who get sensitive about every wasted second. Every watch is a reminder of death. Whoever you steal it from will know it's missing; there will be complications.

Whoever has a watch like that is the sort of person you fall in love with. It's hard not to love a person who can sense what matters.

Whoever has a watch like that will find a way to get it back. Keep time some other way.

There are things, amid the shoes without lefts and rights and the folding of a sari and the way to wrap a fur to outlast the Mongolian cold, that you will have to accept.

Any time someone jumps, a past or a future bursts open. That person comes back from a world that didn't exist before, might never again. The How-To posters you see on the street with their clean lines and destinations stamped in circles like subway stops are Art Deco propaganda, and mean nothing.

Those who jump pull everything apart, if they manage to hold on to it at all. No matter how quiet and careful you try to be, the cut has been made, and when you callback, whatever you've done either ruins us in ways we can't know, or vanishes. If you're going to jump, accept this.

(Don't love anyone, whatever you do. When you leave them behind, it's either to a nightmare or oblivion.

It's a mistake to go.)

There are no lines; there might be circles, or loops, or just holes. Don't think about it. It's important not to think about it. You can get trapped on your way back, if you have doubts while you're traveling.

From there to home is a delicate process; if you doubt it at all, you'll disappear.

Come back. Look forward. Start again.

MAZES AND TRAPS

THE CLOCK THAT WENT BACKWARD

Edward Page Mitchell

Edward Page Mitchell was an American journalist and early science fiction writer. Most of his fiction was published in the 1870s and 1880s in such journals as *Scribner's Monthly* and *The New York Sun*. His best-known story is "The Tachypomp," published in 1874. "The Clock That Went Backward," released in 1881 in *The Sun*, is the first time-travel story ever published, coming out several years before H.G. Wells's *The Time Machine*.

A row of Lombardy poplars stood in front of my great-aunt Gertrude's house, on the bank of the Sheepscot River. In personal appearance my aunt was surprisingly like one of those trees. She had the look of hopeless anemia that distinguishes them from fuller blooded sorts. She was tall, severe in outline, and extremely thin. Her habiliments clung to her. I am sure that had the gods found occasion to impose upon her the fate of Daphne she would have taken her place easily and naturally in the dismal row, as melancholy a poplar as the rest.

Some of my earliest recollections are of this venerable relative. Alive and dead she bore an important part in the events I am about to recount: events which I believe to be without parallel in the experience of mankind.

During our periodical visits of duty to Aunt Gertrude in Maine, my cousin Harry and myself were accustomed to speculate much on her age. Was she sixty, or was she six score? We had no precise information; she might have been either. The old lady was surrounded by old-fashioned things. She seemed to live altogether in the past. In her short half-hours of communicativeness, over her second cup of tea, or on the piazza where the poplars sent slim shadows directly toward the east, she used to tell us stories of her alleged ancestors. I say alleged, because we never fully believed that she had ancestors.

A genealogy is a stupid thing. Here is Aunt Gertrude's, reduced to its simplest forms:

Her great-great-grandmother (1599–1642) was a woman of Holland who married a Puritan refugee, and sailed from Leyden to Plymouth in the ship *Ann* in the year of our Lord 1632. This Pilgrim mother had a daughter, Aunt Gertrude's great-grandmother (1640–1718). She came to the Eastern District of Massachusetts in the early part of the last century, and was carried off by the Indians in the Penobscot wars. Her daughter (1680–1776) lived to see these colonies free and independent, and contributed to the population of the coming republic not less than nineteen stalwart sons and comely daughters. One of the latter (1735–1802) married a Wiscasset skipper engaged in the West India trade, with whom she sailed. She was twice wrecked at sea – once on what is now Seguin Island and once on San Salvador. It was on San Salvador that Aunt Gertrude was born.

We got to be very tired of hearing this family history. Perhaps it was the constant repetition and the merciless persistency with which the above dates were driven into our young ears that made us skeptics. As I have said, we took little stock in Aunt Gertrude's ancestors. They seemed highly improbable. In our private opinion the great-grandmothers and grandmothers and so forth were pure myths, and Aunt Gertrude herself was the principal in all the adventures attributed to them, having lasted from century to century while generations of contemporaries went the way of all flesh.

On the first landing of the square stairway of the mansion loomed a tall Dutch clock. The case was more than eight feet high, of a dark red wood, not mahogany, and it was curiously inlaid with silver. No common piece of furniture was this. About a hundred years ago there flourished in the town of Brunswick a horologist named Cary, an industrious and accomplished work-man. Few well-to-do houses on that part of the coast lacked a Cary timepiece. But Aunt Gertrude's clock had marked the hours and minutes of two full centuries before the Brunswick artisan was born. It was running when William the Taciturn pierced the dikes to relieve Leyden. The name of the maker, Jan Lipperdam, and the date, 1572, were still legible in broad black letters and figures reaching quite across the dial. Cary's masterpieces were plebeian and recent beside this ancient aristocrat. The jolly Dutch moon, made to exhibit the phases over a landscape of windmills and polders, was cunningly painted. A skilled hand had carved the grim ornament at the top, a death's head transfixed by a two-edged sword. Like all timepieces of the sixteenth century, it had no pendulum. A simple Van Wyck escapement governed the descent of the weights to the bottom of the tall case.

But these weights never moved. Year after year, when Harry and I returned to Maine, we found the hands of the old clock pointing to the quarter past three, as they had pointed when we first saw them. The fat moon hung perpetually in the third quarter, as motionless as the death's head above. There was a mystery about the silenced movement and the paralyzed hands. Aunt Gertrude told us that the works had never performed their functions since a bolt of lightning entered the clock; and she showed us a black hole in the side of the case near the top, with a yawning rift that extended downward for several feet. This explanation failed to satisfy us. It did not account for the sharpness of her refusal when we proposed to bring over the watchmaker from the village, or for her singular agitation once when she found Harry on a stepladder, with a borrowed key in his hand, about to test for himself the clock's suspended vitality.

One August night, after we had grown out of boyhood, I was awakened by a noise in the hallway. I shook my cousin. "Somebody's in the house," I whispered.

We crept out of our room and on to the stairs. A dim light came from below. We held breath and noiselessly descended to the second landing. Harry clutched my arm. He pointed down over the banisters, at the same time drawing me back into the shadow.

We saw a strange thing.

Aunt Gertrude stood on a chair in front of the old clock, as spectral in her white nightgown and white nightcap as one of the poplars when covered with snow. It chanced that the floor creaked slightly under our feet. She turned with a sudden movement, peering intently into the darkness, and holding a candle high toward us, so that the light was full upon her pale face. She looked many years older than when I bade her good night. For a few minutes she was motionless, except in the trembling arm that held aloft the candle. Then, evidently reassured, she placed the light upon a shelf and turned again to the clock.

We now saw the old lady take a key from behind the face and proceed to wind up the weights. We could hear her breath, quick and short. She rested a hand on either side of the case and held her face close to the dial, as if subjecting it to anxious scrutiny. In this attitude she remained for a long time. We heard her utter a sigh of relief, and she half turned toward us for a moment. I shall never forget the expression of wild joy that transfigured her features then.

The hands of the clock were moving; they were moving backward.

Aunt Gertrude put both arms around the clock and pressed her withered cheek against it. She kissed it repeatedly. She caressed it in a hundred ways, as if it had been a living and beloved thing. She fondled it and talked to it, using words which we could hear but could not understand. The hands continued to move backward.

Then she started back with a sudden cry. The clock had stopped. We saw her tall body swaying for an instant on the chair. She stretched out her arms in a convulsive gesture of terror and despair, wrenched the minute hand to its old place at a quarter past three, and fell heavily to the floor.

Aunt Gertrude's will left me her bank and gas stocks, real estate, railroad bonds, and city sevens, and gave Harry the clock. We thought at the time that this was a very unequal division, the more surprising because my cousin had always seemed to be the favorite. Half in seriousness we made a thorough examination of the ancient timepiece, sounding its wooden case for secret drawers, and even probing the not complicated works with a knitting needle to ascertain if our whimsical relative had bestowed there some codicil or other document changing the aspect of affairs. We discovered nothing.

There was testamentary provision for our education at the University of Leyden. We left the military school in which we had learned a little of the theory of war, and a good deal of the art of standing with our noses over our heels, and took ship without delay. The clock went with us. Before many months it was established in a corner of a room in the Breede Straat.

The fabric of Jan Lipperdam's ingenuity, thus restored to its native air, continued to tell the hour of quarter past three with its old fidelity. The author of the clock had been under the sod for nearly three hundred years. The combined skill of his successors in the craft at Leyden could make it go neither forward nor backward.

We readily picked up enough Dutch to make ourselves understood by the townspeople, the professors, and such of our eight hundred and odd fellow students as came into intercourse. This language, which looks so hard at first, is only a sort of polarized English. Puzzle over it a little while and it jumps into your comprehension like one of those simple cryptograms made by running together all the words of a sentence and then dividing in the wrong places.

The language acquired and the newness of our surroundings worn off, we settled into tolerably regular pursuits. Harry devoted himself with some assiduity to the study of sociology, with especial reference to the round-faced and not unkind maidens of Leyden. I went in for the higher metaphysics.

Outside of our respective studies, we had a common ground of unfailing interest. To our astonishment, we found that not one in twenty of the faculty or students knew or cared a sliver about the glorious history of the town, or even about the circumstances under which the university itself was founded by the Prince of Orange. In marked contrast with the general indifference was the enthusiasm of Professor Van Stopp, my chosen guide through the cloudiness of speculative philosophy.

This distinguished Hegelian was a tobacco-dried little old man, with a skull-cap over features that reminded me strangely of Aunt Gertrude's. Had he been her own brother the facial resemblance could not have been closer. I told him so once, when we were together in the Stadthuis looking at the portrait of the hero of the siege, the Burgomaster Van der Werf. The professor laughed. "I will show you what is even a more extraordinary coincidence," said he; and, leading the way across the hall to the great picture of the siege, by Wanners, he pointed out the figure of a burgher participating in the defense. It was true. Van Stopp might have been the burgher's son; the burgher might have been Aunt Gertrude's father.

The professor seemed to be fond of us. We often went to his rooms in an old house in the Rapenburg Straat, one of the few houses remaining that ante-date 1574. He would walk with us through the beautiful suburbs of the city, over straight roads lined with poplars that carried us back to the bank of the Sheepscot in our minds. He took us to the top of the ruined Roman tower in the center of the town, and from the same battlements from which anxious eyes three centuries ago had watched the slow approach of Admiral Boisot's fleet over the submerged polders, he pointed out the great dike of the Landscheiding, which was cut that the oceans might bring Boisot's Zealanders to raise the leaguer and feed the starving. He showed us the headquarters of the Spaniard Valdez at Leyderdorp, and told us how heaven sent a violent northwest wind on the night of the first of October, piling up the water deep where it had been shallow and sweeping the fleet on between Zoeterwoude and Zwieten up to the very walls of the fort at Lammen, the last stronghold of the besiegers and the last obstacle in the way of succor to the famishing inhabitants. Then he showed us where, on the very night before the retreat of the besieging army, a huge breach was made in the wall of Leyden, near the Cow Gate, by the Walloons from Lammen.

"Why!" cried Harry, catching fire from the eloquence of the professor's narrative, "that was the decisive moment of the siege."

The professor said nothing. He stood with his arms folded, looking intently into my cousin's eyes.

"For," continued Harry, "had that point not been watched, or had defense failed and the breach been carried by the night assault from Lammen, the town would have been burned and the people massacred under the eyes of Admiral Boisot and the fleet of relief. Who defended the breach?"

Van Stopp replied very slowly, as if weighing every word:

"History records the explosion of the mine under the city wall on the last night of the siege; it does not tell the story of the defense or give the defender's name. Yet no man that ever lived had a more tremendous charge than fate entrusted to this unknown hero. Was it chance that sent him to meet that unexpected danger? Consider some of the consequences had he failed. The fall of Leyden would have destroyed the last hope of the Prince of Orange and of the free states. The tyranny of Philip would have been reestablished. The birth of religious liberty and of self-government by the people would have been postponed, who knows for how many centuries? Who knows that there would or could have been a republic of the United States of America had there been no United Netherlands? Our university, which has given to the world Grotius, Scaliger, Arminius, and Descartes, was founded upon this hero's successful defense of the breach. We owe to him our presence here today. Nay, you owe to him your very existence. Your ancestors were of Leyden; between their lives and the butchers outside the walls he stood that night."

The little professor towered before us, a giant of enthusiasm and patriotism. Harry's eyes glistened and his cheeks reddened.

"Go home, boys," said Van Stopp, "and thank God that while the burghers of Leyden were straining their gaze toward Zoeterwoude and the fleet, there was one pair of vigilant eyes and one stout heart at the town wall just beyond the Cow Gate!"

The rain was splashing against the windows one evening in the autumn of our third year at Leyden, when Professor Van Stopp honored us with a visit in the Breede Straat. Never had I seen the old gentleman in such spirits. He talked incessantly. The gossip of the town, the news of Europe, science, poetry, philosophy, were in turn touched upon and treated with the same high and good humor. I sought to draw him out on Hegel, with whose chapter on the complexity and interdependency of things I was just then struggling.

"You do not grasp the return of the Itself into Itself through its Otherself?" he said smiling. "Well, you will, sometime."

Harry was silent and preoccupied. His taciturnity gradually affected even the professor. The conversation flagged, and we sat a long while without a word. Now and then there was a flash of lightning succeeded by distant thunder.

"Your clock does not go," suddenly remarked the professor. "Does it ever go?"

"Never since we can remember," I replied. "That is, only once, and then it went backward. It was when Aunt Gertrude—"

Here I caught a warning glance from Harry. I laughed and stammered, "The clock is old and useless. It cannot be made to go."

"Only backward?" said the professor, calmly, and not appearing to notice my embarrassment. "Well, and why should not a clock go backward? Why should not Time itself turn and retrace its course?"

He seemed to be waiting for an answer. I had none to give.

"I thought you Hegelian enough," he continued, "to admit that every condition includes its own contradiction. Time is a condition, not an essential. Viewed from the Absolute, the sequence by which future follows present and present follows past is purely arbitrary. Yesterday, today, tomorrow; there is no reason in the nature of things why the order should not be tomorrow, today, yesterday."

A sharper peal of thunder interrupted the professor's speculations.

"The day is made by the planet's revolution on its axis from west to east. I fancy you can conceive conditions under which it might turn from east to west, unwinding, as it were, the revolutions of past ages. Is it so much more difficult to imagine Time unwinding itself; Time on the ebb, instead of on the flow; the past unfolding as the future recedes; the centuries countermarching; the course of events proceeding toward the Beginning and not, as now, toward the End?"

"But," I interposed, "we know that as far as we are concerned the—"

"We know!" exclaimed Van Stopp, with growing scorn. "Your intelligence has no wings. You follow in the trail of Compte and his slimy brood of creepers and crawlers. You speak with amazing assurance of your position in the universe. You seem to think that your wretched little individuality has a firm foothold in the Absolute. Yet you go to bed tonight and dream into existence men, women, children, beasts of the past or of the future. How do you know that at this moment you yourself, with all your conceit of nineteenth-century thought, are anything more than a creature of a dream of the future, dreamed, let us say, by some philosopher of the sixteenth century? How do you know that you are anything more than a creature of a dream of the past, dreamed by some Hegelian of the twenty-sixth century? How do you know, boy, that you will not vanish into the sixteenth century or 2060 the moment the dreamer awakes?"

There was no replying to this, for it was sound metaphysics. Harry yawned. I got up and went to the window. Professor Van Stopp approached the clock.

"Ah, my children," said he, "there is no fixed progress of human events. Past, present, and future are woven together in one inextricable mesh. Who shall say that this old clock is not right to go backward?"

A crash of thunder shook the house. The storm was over our heads.

When the blinding glare had passed away, Professor Van Stopp was standing upon a chair before the tall timepiece. His face looked more than ever like Aunt Gertrude's. He stood as she had stood in that last quarter of an hour when we saw her wind the clock.

The same thought struck Harry and myself.

"Hold!" we cried, as he began to wind the works. "It may be death if you—"

The professor's sallow features shone with the strange enthusiasm that had transformed Aunt Gertrude's.

"True," he said, "it may be death; but it may be the awakening. Past, present, future; all woven together! The shuttle goes to and fro, forward and back—"

He had wound the clock. The hands were whirling around the dial from right to left with inconceivable rapidity. In this whirl we ourselves seemed to be borne along. Eternities seemed to contract into minutes while lifetimes were thrown off at every tick. Van Stopp, both arms outstretched, was reeling in his chair. The house shook again under a tremendous peal of thunder. At the same instant a ball of fire, leaving a wake of sulphurous vapor and filling the room with dazzling light, passed over our heads and smote the clock. Van Stopp was prostrated. The hands ceased to revolve.

The roar of the thunder sounded like heavy cannonading. The lightning's blaze appeared as the steady light of a conflagration. With our hands over our eyes, Harry and I rushed out into the night.

Under a red sky people were hurrying toward the Stadthuis. Flames in the direction of the Roman tower told us that the heart of the town was afire. The faces of those we saw were haggard and emaciated. From every side we caught disjointed phrases of complaint or despair. "Horseflesh at ten schillings the pound," said one, "and bread at sixteen schillings." "Bread indeed!" an old woman retorted: "It's eight weeks gone since I have seen a crumb." "My little grandchild, the lame one, went last night." "Do you know what Gekke Betje, the washerwoman, did? She was starving. Her babe died, and she and her man—"

A louder cannon burst cut short this revelation. We made our way on toward the citadel of the town, passing a few soldiers here and there and many burghers with grim faces under their broad-brimmed felt hats.

"There is bread plenty yonder where the gunpowder is, and full pardon, too. Valdez shot another amnesty over the walls this morning."

An excited crowd immediately surrounded the speaker. "But the fleet!" they cried.

"The fleet is grounded fast on the Greenway polder. Boisot may turn his one eye seaward for a wind till famine and pestilence have carried off every mother's son of ye, and his ark will not be a rope's length nearer. Death by plague, death by starvation, death by fire and musketry – that is what the burgomaster offers us in return for glory for himself and kingdom for Orange."

"He asks us," said a sturdy citizen, "to hold out only twenty-four hours longer, and to pray meanwhile for an ocean wind."

"Ah, yes!" sneered the first speaker. "Pray on. There is bread enough locked in Pieter Adriaanszoon Van der Werf's cellar. I warrant you that is what gives him so wonderful a stomach for resisting the Most Catholic King."

A young girl, with braided yellow hair, pressed through the crowd and con-fronted the malcontent. "Good people," said the maiden, "do not listen to him. He is a traitor with a Spanish heart. I am Pieter's daughter. We have no bread. We ate malt cakes and rapeseed like the rest of you till that was gone. Then we stripped the green leaves from the lime trees and willows in our garden and ate them. We have eaten even the thistles and weeds that grew between the stones by the canal. The coward lies."

Nevertheless, the insinuation had its effect. The throng, now become a mob, surged off in the direction of the burgomaster's house. One ruffian raised his hand to strike the girl out of the way. In a wink the cur was under the feet of his fellows, and Harry, panting and glowing, stood at the maiden's side, shouting defiance in good English at the backs of the rapidly retreating crowd.

With the utmost frankness she put both her arms around Harry's neck and kissed him.

"Thank you," she said. "You are a hearty lad. My name is Gertruyd Van der Wert."

Harry was fumbling in his vocabulary for the proper Dutch phrases, but the girl would not stay for compliments. "They mean mischief to my father"; and she hurried us through several exceedingly narrow streets into a three-cornered market place dominated by a church with two spires. "There he is," she exclaimed, "on the steps of St. Pancras."

There was a tumult in the market place. The conflagration raging beyond the church and the voices of the Spanish and Walloon cannon outside of the walls were less angry than the roar of this multitude of desperate men clamoring for the bread that a single word from their leader's lips would bring them. "Surrender to the King!" they cried, "or we will send your dead body to Lammen as Leyden's token of submission."

One tall man, taller by half a head than any of the burghers confronting him, and so dark of complexion that we wondered how he could be the father of Gertruyd, heard the threat in silence. When the burgomaster spoke, the mob listened in spite of themselves.

"What is it you ask, my friends? That we break our vow and surrender Leyden to the Spaniards? That is to devote ourselves to a fate far more horrible than starvation. I have to keep the oath! Kill me, if you will have it so. I can die only once, whether by your hands, by the enemy's, or by the hand of God. Let us starve, if we must, welcoming starvation because it comes before dishonor. Your menaces do not move me; my life is at your disposal. Here, take my sword, thrust it into my breast, and divide my flesh among you to appease your hunger. So long as I remain alive expect no surrender."

There was silence again while the mob wavered. Then there were mutterings around us. Above these rang out the clear voice of the girl whose hand Harry still held – unnecessarily, it seemed to me.

"Do you not feel the sea wind? It has come at last. To the tower! And the first man there will see by moonlight the full white sails of the prince's ships."

For several hours I scoured the streets of the town, seeking in vain my cousin and his companion; the sudden movement of the crowd toward the Roman tower had separated us. On every side I saw evidences of the terrible chastisement that had brought this stout-hearted people to the verge of despair. A man with hungry eyes chased a lean rat along the bank of the canal. A young mother, with two dead babes in her arms, sat in a doorway to which they bore the bodies of her husband and father, just killed at the walls. In the middle of a deserted street I passed unburied corpses in a pile twice as high as my head. The pestilence had been there – kinder than the Spaniard, because it held out no treacherous promises while it dealt its blows.

Toward morning the wind increased to a gale. There was no sleep in Leyden, no more talk of surrender, no longer any thought or care about defense. These words were on the lips of everybody I met: "Daylight will bring the fleet!"

Did daylight bring the fleet? History says so, but I was not a witness. I know only that before dawn the gale culminated in a violent thunderstorm, and that at the same time a muffled explosion, heavier than the thunder, shook the town. I was in the crowd that watched from the Roman Mound for the first signs of the approaching relief. The concussion shook hope out of every face. "Their mine has reached the wall!" But where? I pressed forward until I found the burgomaster, who was standing among the rest. "Quick!" I whispered. "It is beyond the Cow Gate, and this side of the Tower of Burgundy." He gave me a searching glance, and then strode away, without making any attempt to quiet the general panic. I followed close at his heels.

It was a tight run of nearly half a mile to the rampart in question. When we reached the Cow Gate this is what we saw:

A great gap, where the wall had been, opening to the swampy fields beyond: in the moat, outside and below, a confusion of upturned faces, belonging to men who struggled like demons to achieve the breach, and who now gained a few feet and now were forced back; on the shattered rampart a handful of soldiers and burghers forming a living wall where masonry had failed; perhaps a double handful of women and girls, serving stones to the defenders and boiling water in buckets, besides pitch and oil and unslaked lime, and some of them quoiting tarred and burning hoops over the necks of the Spaniards in the moat; my cousin Harry leading and directing the men; the burgomaster's daughter Gertruyd encouraging and inspiring the women.

But what attracted my attention more than anything else was the frantic activity of a little figure in black, who, with a huge ladle, was showering molten lead on the heads of the assailing party. As he turned to the bonfire and kettle which supplied him with ammunition, his features came into the full light. I gave a cry of surprise: the ladler of molten lead was Professor Van Stopp.

The burgomaster Van der Werf turned at my sudden exclamation. "Who is that?" I said. "The man at the kettle?"

"That," replied Van der Werf, "is the brother of my wife, the clockmaker Jan Lipperdam."

The affair at the breach was over almost before we had had time to grasp the situation. The Spaniards, who had overthrown the wall of brick and stone, found the living wall impregnable. They could not even maintain their position in the moat; they were driven off into the darkness. Now I felt a sharp pain in my left arm. Some stray missile must have hit me while we watched the fight.

"Who has done this thing?" demanded the burgomaster. "Who is it that has kept watch on today while the rest of us were straining fools' eyes toward tomorrow?"

Gertruyd Van der Werf came forward proudly, leading my cousin. "My father," said the girl, "he has saved my life."

"That is much to me," said the burgomaster, "but it is not all. He has saved Leyden and he has saved Holland."

I was becoming dizzy. The faces around me seemed unreal. Why were we here with these people? Why did the thunder and lightning forever continue? Why did the clockmaker, Jan Lipperdam, turn always toward me the face of Professor Van Stopp? "Harry!" I said, "come back to our rooms."

But though he grasped my hand warmly his other hand still held that of the girl, and he did not move. Then nausea overcame me. My head swam, and the breach and its defenders faded from sight.

*

Three days later I sat with one arm bandaged in my accustomed seat in Van Stopp's lecture room. The place beside me was vacant.

"We hear much," said the Hegelian professor, reading from a notebook in his usual dry, hurried tone, "of the influence of the sixteenth century upon the nineteenth. No philosopher, as far as I am aware, has studied the influence of the nineteenth century upon the sixteenth. If cause produces effect, does effect never induce cause? Does the law of heredity, unlike all other laws of this universe of mind and matter, operate in one direction only? Does the descendant owe everything to the ancestor, and the ancestor nothing to the descendant? Does destiny, which may seize upon our existence, and for its own purposes bear us far into the future, never carry us back into the past?"

I went back to my rooms in the Breede Straat, where my only companion was the silent clock.

YESTERDAY WAS MONDAY

Theodore Sturgeon

Theodore Sturgeon was an American writer and critic. He is credited with writing over two hundred stories. He was inducted into the Science Fiction Hall of Fame in 2000 with awards such as the Hugo and the Nebula to his name. His popularity was highest in the 1950s when he had many fans, although many readers today are happy to re-discover his stories. Although he wrote several well-received novels, Sturgeon was best known for his short stories and novellas. This story was first published in *Unknown* in 1941.

HARRY WRIGHT ROLLED over and said something spelled "Bzzzzhha-a-aw!" He chewed a bit on a mouthful of dry air and spat it out, opened one eye to see if it really would open, opened the other and closed the first, closed the second, swung his feet onto the floor, opened them again and stretched. This was a daily occurrence, and the only thing that made it remarkable at all was that he did it on a Wednesday morning, and —

Yesterday was Monday.

Oh, he knew it was Wednesday all right. It was partly that, even though he knew yesterday was Monday, there was a gap between Monday and now; and that must have been Tuesday. When you fall asleep and lie there all night without dreaming, you know, when you wake up, that time has passed. You've done nothing that you can remember; you've had no particular thoughts, no way to gauge time, and yet you know that some hours have passed. So it was with Harry Wright. Tuesday had gone wherever your eight hours went last night.

But he hadn't slept through Tuesday. Oh no. He never slept, as a matter of fact, more than six hours at a stretch, and there was no particular reason for him doing so now. Monday was the day before yesterday; he had turned in and slept his usual stretch, he had awakened, and it was Wednesday.

It *felt* like Wednesday. There was a Wednesdayish feel to the air.

Harry put on his socks and stood up. He wasn't fooled. He knew what day it was. "What happened to yesterday?" he muttered. "Oh – yesterday was Monday." That sufficed until he got his pajamas off. "Monday," he mused, reaching for his underwear, "was quite a while back, seems as though." If he had been the worrying type, he would have started then and there. But he wasn't. He was an easygoing sort, the kind of man that gets himself into a rut and stays there until he is pushed out. That was why he was an automobile mechanic at twenty-three dollars a week; that's why he had been one for eight years now, and would be from now on, if he could only find Tuesday and get back to work.

Guided by his reflexes, as usual, and with no mental effort at all, which was also usual, he finished washing, dressing, and making his bed. His alarm clock, which never alarmed because he was of such regular habits, said, as usual, six twenty-two when he paused on the way out, and gave his room the once-over. And there was a certain something about the place that made even this phlegmatic character stop and think.

It wasn't finished.

The bed was there, and the picture of Joe Louis. There were the two chairs sharing their usual seven legs, the split table, the pipe-organ bedstead, the beige wallpaper with the two swans over and over and over, the tiny corner sink, the tilted bureau. But none of them were finished. Not that there were any holes in anything. What paint there had been in the first place was still there. But there was an odor of old cut lumber, a subtle, insistent air of building, about the room and everything in it. It was indefinable, inescapable, and Harry Wright stood there caught up in it, wondering. He glanced suspiciously around but saw nothing he could really be suspicious of. He shook his head, locked the door and went out into the hall.

On the steps a little fellow, just over three feet tall, was gently stroking the third step from the top with a razor-sharp chisel, shaping up a new scar in the dirty wood. He looked up as Harry approached, and stood up quickly.

"Hi," said Harry, taking in the man's leather coat, his peaked cap, his wizened, bright-eyed little face. "Whatcha doing?"

"Touch-up," piped the little man. "The actor in the third floor front has a nail in his right heel. He came in late Tuesday night and cut the wood here. I have to get it ready for Wednesday."

"This is Wednesday," Harry pointed out.

"Of course. Always has been. Always will be."

Harry let that pass, started on down the stairs. He had achieved his amazing bovinity by making a practice of ignoring things he could not understand. But one thing bothered him— "Did you say that feller in the third floor front was an actor?"

"Yes. They're all actors, you know."

"You're nuts, friend," said Harry bluntly. "That guy works on the docks."

"Oh yes – that's his part. That's what he acts."

"No kiddin'. An' what does he do when he isn't acting?"

"But he— Well, that's all he does do! That's all any of the actors do!"

"Gee— I thought he looked like a reg'lar guy, too," said Harry. "An actor? 'Magine!"

"Excuse me," said the little man, "but I've got to get back to work. We mustn't let anything get by us, you know. They'll be through Tuesday before long, and everything must be ready for them."

Harry thought: this guy's crazy nuts. He smiled uncertainly and went down to the landing below. When he looked back the man was cutting skillfully into the stair, making a neat little nail scratch. Harry shook his head. This was a screwy morning. He'd be glad to get back to the shop. There was a '39 sedan down there with a busted rear spring. Once he got his mind on that he could forget this nonsense. That's all that matters to a man in a rut. Work, eat, sleep, pay day. Why even try to think anything else out?

The street was a riot of activity, but then it always was. But not quite this way. There were automobiles and trucks and buses around, aplenty, but none of them were moving. And none of them were quite complete. This was Harry's own field; if there was anything he didn't know about motor vehicles, it wasn't very important. And through that medium he began to get the general idea of what was going on.

Swarms of little men who might have been twins of the one he had spoken to were crowding around the cars, the sidewalks, the stores and buildings. All were working like mad with every tool imaginable. Some were touching up the finish of the cars with fine wire brushes, laying on networks of microscopic cracks and scratches. Some, with ball peens and mallets, were denting fenders skill-fully, bending bumpers in an artful crash pattern, spider-webbing safety-glass windshields. Others were aging top dressing with high-pressure, needlepoint sandblasters. Still others were pumping dust into upholstery, sandpapering the dashboard finish around light switches, throttles, chokes, to give a finger-worn appearance. Harry stood aside as a half dozen of the workers scampered down the street bearing a fender which they riveted to a 1930 coupe. It was freshly bloodstained.

Once awakened to this highly unusual activity, Harry stopped, slightly open-mouthed, to watch what else was going on. He saw the same process being industriously accomplished with the houses and stores. Dirt was being laid on plate-glass windows over a coat of clear sizing. Woodwork was being cleverly scored and the paint peeled to make it look correctly weather-beaten, and dozens of leather-clad laborers were on their hands and knees, poking dust and dirt into the cracks between the paving blocks. A line of them went down the sidewalk, busily chewing gum and spitting it out; they were followed by another crew who carefully placed the wads according to diagrams they carried, and stamped them flat.

Harry set his teeth and muscled his rocking brain into something like its normal position. "I ain't never seen a day like this or crazy people like this," he said, "but I ain't gonna let it be any of my affair. I got my job to go to." And trying vainly to ignore the hundreds of little, hard-working figures, he went grimly on down the street.

When he got to the garage he found no one there but more swarms of stereo-typed little people climbing over the place, dulling the paint work, cracking the cement flooring, doing their hurried, efficient little tasks of aging. He noticed, only because he was so familiar with the garage, that they were actually *making* the marks that had been there as long as he had known the place. "Hell with it," he gritted, anxious to submerge himself into his own world of wrenches and grease guns. "I got my job; this is none o' my affair."

He looked about him, wondering if he should clean these interlopers out of the garage. Naw – not his affair. He was hired to repair cars, not to police the joint. Long as they kept away from him – and, of course, animal caution told him that he was far, far outnumbered. The absence of the boss and the other mechanics was no surprise to Harry; he always opened the place.

He climbed out of his street clothes and into coveralls, picked up a tool case and walked over to the sedan, which he had left up on the hydraulic rack yester— that is, Monday night. And that is when Harry Wright lost his temper. After all, the car was his job, and he didn't like having anyone else mess with a job he had started. So when he saw his job – his '39 sedan – resting steadily on its wheels over the rack, which was down under the floor, and when he saw that the rear spring was repaired, he began to burn. He dived under the car and ran deft fingers over the rear wheel suspensions. In spite of his anger at this unprecedented occurrence, he had to admit to himself that the job had been done well. "Might have done it myself," he muttered.

A soft clank and a gentle movement caught his attention. With a roar he reached out and grabbed the leg of one of the ubiquitous little men, wriggled out from under the car, caught his culprit by his leather collar, and dangled him at arm's length.

"What are you doing to my job?" Harry bellowed.

The little man tucked his chin into the front of his shirt to give his windpipe a chance, and said, "Why, I was just finishing up that spring job."

"Oh. So you were just finishing up on that spring job," Harry whispered, choked with rage. Then, at the top of his voice, "Who told you to touch that car?"

"Who told me? What do you— Well, it just had to be done, that's all. You'll have to let me go. I must tighten up those two bolts and lay some dust on the whole thing."

"You must *what!* You get within six feet o' that car and I'll twist your head offn your neck with a Stillson!"

"But— It has to be done!"

"You won't do it! Why, I oughta—"

"Please let me go! If I don't leave that car the way it was Tuesday night—"

"When was Tuesday night?"

"The last act, of course. Let me go, or I'll call the district supervisor!"

"Call the devil himself. I'm going to spread you on the sidewalk outside; and heaven help you if I catch you near here again!"

The little man's jaw set, his eyes narrowed, and he whipped his feet upward. They crashed into Wright's jaw; Harry dropped him and staggered back. The little man began squealing, "Supervisor! Supervisor! Emergency!"

Harry growled and started after him; but suddenly, in the air between him and the midget workman, a long white hand appeared. The empty air was swept back, showing an aperture from the garage to blank, blind nothingness. Out of it stepped a tall man in a single loose-fitting garment literally studded with pockets. The opening closed behind the man.

Harry cowered before him. Never in his life had he seen such noble, powerful features, such strength of purpose, such broad shoulders, such a deep chest. The man stood with the backs of his hands on his hips, staring at Harry as if he were something somebody forgot to sweep up.

"That's him," said the little man shrilly. "He is trying to stop me from doing the work!"

"Who are you?" asked the beautiful man, down his nose.

"I'm the m-mechanic on this j-j— Who wants to know?"

"Iridel, supervisor of the district of Futura, wants to know."

"Where in hell did you come from?"

"I did not come from hell. I came from Thursday."

Harry held his head. "What *is* all this?" he wailed. "Why is today Wednesday? Who are all these crazy little guys? What happened to Tuesday?"

Iridel made a slight motion with his finger, and the little man scurried back under the car. Harry was frenzied to hear the wrench busily tightening bolts. He half started to dive under after the little fellow, but Iridel said, "Stop!" and when Iridel said, "Stop!" Harry stopped.

"This," said Iridel calmly, "is an amazing occurrence." He regarded Harry with unemotional curiosity. "An actor on stage before the sets are finished. Extraordinary."

"What stage?" asked Harry. "What are you doing here anyhow, and what's the idea of all these little guys working around here?"

"You ask a great many questions, actor," said Iridel. "I shall answer them, and then I shall have a few to ask you. These little men are stage hands – I am surprised that you didn't realize that. They are setting the stage for Wednesday. Tuesday? That's going on now."

"Arrgh!" Harry snorted. "How can Tuesday be going on when today's Wednesday?"

"Today isn't Wednesday, actor."

"Huh?"

"Today is Tuesday."

Harry scratched his head. "Met a feller on the steps this mornin' – one of these here stage hands of yours. He said this was Wednesday."

"It *is* Wednesday. Today is Tuesday. Tuesday is today. 'Today' is simply the name for the stage set which happens to be in use. 'Yesterday' means the set that has just been used; 'Tomorrow' is the set that will be used after the actors have finished with 'today.' This is Wednesday. Yesterday was Monday; today is Tuesday. See?"

Harry said, "No."

Iridel threw up his long hands. "My, you actors are stupid. Now listen carefully. This is Act Wednesday, Scene 6:22. That means that everything you see around you here is being readied for 6:22 a.m. on Wednesday. Wednesday isn't a time; it's a place. The actors are moving along toward it now. I see you still don't get the idea. Let's see . . . ah. Look at that clock. What does it say?"

Harry Wright looked at the big electric clock on the wall over the compressor. It was corrected hourly and highly accurate, and it said 6:22. Harry looked at it amazed. "Six tw— but my gosh, man, that's what time I left the house. I walked here, an' I been here ten minutes already!"

Iridel shook his head. "You've been here no time at all, because there is no time until the actors make their entrances."

Harry sat down on a grease drum and wrinkled up his brains with the effort he was making. "You mean that this time proposition ain't something that moves along all the time? Sorta— well, like a road. A road don't go no place— You just go places along it. Is that it?"

"That's the general idea. In fact, that's a pretty good example. Suppose we say that it's a road; a highway built of paving blocks. Each block is a day; the actors move along it, and go through day after day. And our job here – mine and the little men – is to . . . well, pave that road. This is the clean-up gang here. They are fixing up the last little details, so that everything will be ready for the actors."

Harry sat still, his mind creaking with the effects of this information. He felt as if he had been hit with a lead pipe, and the shock of it was being drawn out infinitely. This was the craziest-sounding thing he had ever run into. For no reason at all he remembered a talk he had had once with a drunken aviation mechanic who had tried to explain to him how the air flowing over an airplane's wings makes the machine go up in the air. He hadn't understood a word of the man's discourse, which was all about eddies and chords and cambers and foils, dihedrals and the Bernoulli effect. That didn't make any difference; the things flew whether he understood how or not; he knew that because he had seen them. This guy Iridel's lecture was the same sort of thing. If there was nothing in all he said, how come all these little guys were working around here? Why wasn't the clock telling time? Where was Tuesday?

He thought he'd get that straight for good and all. "Just where is Tuesday?" he asked.

"Over there," said Iridel, and pointed. Harry recoiled and fell off the drum; for when the man extended his hand, it *disappeared!*

Harry got up off the floor and said tautly, "Do that agin."

"What? Oh— Point toward Tuesday? Certainly." And he pointed. His hand appeared again when he withdrew it.

Harry said, "My gosh!" and sat down again on the drum, sweating and staring at the supervisor of the district of Futura. "You point, an' your hand – ain't," he breathed. "What direction is that?"

"It is a direction like any other direction," said Iridel. "You know yourself there are four directions – forward, sideward, upward, and" – he pointed again, and again his hand vanished – "*that* way!"

"They never tole me that in school," said Harry. "Course, I was just a kid then, but—"

Iridel laughed. "It is the fourth dimension – it is *duration*. The actors move through length, breadth, and height, anywhere they choose to within the set. But there is another movement – one they can't control – and that is duration."

"How soon will they come . . . eh . . . here?" asked Harry, waving an arm. Iridel dipped into one of his numberless pockets and pulled out a watch. "It is now eight thirty-seven Tuesday morning," he said. "They'll be here as soon as they finish the act, and the scenes in Wednesday that have already been prepared."

Harry thought again for a moment, while Iridel waited patiently, smiling a little. Then he looked up at the supervisor and asked, "Hey – this 'actor' business – what's that all about?"

"Oh – that. Well, it's a play, that's all. Just like any play – put on for the amusement of an audience."

"I went to a play once," said Harry. "Who's the audience?"

Iridel stopped smiling. "Certain— Ones who may be amused," he said. "And now I'm going to ask you some questions. How did you get here?"

"Walked."

"You *walked* from Monday night to Wednesday morning?"

"Naw— From the house to here."

"Ah— But how did you get to Wednesday, six twenty-two?"

"Well I— Damfino. I just woke up an' came to work as usual."

"This is an extraordinary occurrence," said Iridel, shaking his head in puzzlement. "You'll have to see the producer."

"Producer? Who's he?"

"You'll find out. In the meantime, come along with me. I can't leave you here; you're too close to the play. I have to make my rounds anyway."

Iridel walked toward the door. Harry was tempted to stay and find himself some more work to do, but when Iridel glanced back at him and motioned him out, Harry followed. It was suddenly impossible to do anything else.

Just as he caught up with the supervisor, a little worker ran up, whipping off his cap.

"Iridel, sir," he piped, "the weather makers put .006 of one percent too little moisture in the air on this set. There's three sevenths of an ounce too little gasoline in the storage tanks under here."

"How much is in the tanks?"

"Four thousand two hundred and seventy-three gallons, three pints, seven and twenty-one thirty-fourths ounces."

Iridel grunted. "Let it go this time. That was very sloppy work. Someone's going to get transferred to Limbo for this."

"Very good, sir," said the little man. "Long as you know we're not responsible." He put on his cap, spun around three times and rushed off.

"Lucky for the weather makers that the amount of gas in that tank doesn't come into Wednesday's script," said Iridel. "If anything interferes with the continuity of the play, there's the devil to pay. Actors haven't sense enough to cover up, either. They are liable to start whole series of miscues because of a little thing like that. The play might flop and then we'd all be out of work."

"Oh," Harry oh-ed. "Hey, Iridel – what's the idea of that patchy-looking place over there?"

Iridel followed his eyes. Harry was looking at a corner lot. It was tree-lined and overgrown with weeds and small saplings. The vegetation was true to form around the edges of the lot, and around the path that ran diagonally through it; but the spaces in between were a plain surface. Not a leaf nor a blade of grass grew there; it was naked-looking, blank, and absolutely without any color whatever.

"Oh, that," answered Iridel. "There are only two characters in Act Wednesday who will use that path. Therefore it is as grown-over as it should be. The rest of the lot doesn't enter into the play, so we don't have to do anything with it."

"But— Suppose someone wandered off the path on Wednesday," Harry offered.

"He'd be due for a surprise, I guess. But it could hardly happen. Special prompters are always detailed to spots like that, to keep the actors from going astray or missing any cues."

"Who are they – the prompters, I mean?"

"Prompters? G.A.'s – Guardian Angels. That's what the script writers call them."

"I heard o' them,' said Harry.

"Yes, they have their work cut out for them," said the supervisor. "Actors are always forgetting their lines when they shouldn't, or remembering them when the script calls for a lapse. Well, it looks pretty good here. Let's have a look at Friday."

"Friday? You mean to tell me you're working on Friday already?"

"Of course! Why, we work years in advance! How on earth do you think we could get our trees grown otherwise? Here – step in!" Iridel put out his hand, seized empty air, drew it aside to show the kind of absolute nothingness he had first appeared from, and waved Harry on.

"Y-you want me to go in there?" asked Harry diffidently.

"Certainly. Hurry, now!"

Harry looked at the section of void with a rather weak-kneed look, but could not withstand the supervisor's strange compulsion. He stepped through.

And it wasn't so bad. There were no whirling lights, no sensations of falling, no falling unconscious. It was just like stepping into another room – which is what had happened. He found himself in a great round chamber, whose roundness was touched a bit with the indistinct. That is, it had curved walls and a domed roof, but there was something else about it. It seemed to stretch off in that direction toward which Iridel had so astonishingly pointed. The walls were lined with an amazing array of control machinery – switches and ground-glass screens, indicators and dials, knurled knobs, and levers. Moving deftly before them was a crew of men, each looking exactly like Iridel except that their garments had no pockets. Harry stood wide-eyed, hypnotized by the enormous complexity of the controls and the ease with which the men worked among them. Iridel touched his shoulder. "Come with me," he said. "The producer is in now; we'll find out what is to be done with you."

They started across the floor. Harry had not quite time to wonder how long it would take them to cross that enormous room, for when they had taken perhaps a dozen steps they found themselves at the opposite wall. The ordinary laws of space and time simply did not apply in the place.

They stopped at a door of burnished bronze, so very highly polished that they could see through it. It opened and Iridel pushed Harry through. The door swung shut. Harry, panic-stricken lest he be separated from the only thing in this weird world he could begin to get used to, flung himself against the great bronze portal. It bounced him back, head over heels, into the middle of the floor. He rolled over and got up to his hands and knees.

He was in a tiny room, one end of which was filled by a colossal teakwood desk. The man sitting there regarded him with amusement. "Where'd you blow in from?" he asked; and his voice was like the angry bee sound of an approaching hurricane.

"Are you the producer?"

"Well, I'll be darned," said the man, and smiled. It seemed to fill the whole room with light. He was a big man, Harry noticed; but in this deceptive place, there was no way of telling how big. "I'll be most verily darned. An actor. You're a persistent lot, aren't you? Building houses for me that I almost never go into. Getting together and sending requests for better parts. Listening carefully to what I have to say and then ignoring or misinterpreting my advice. Always asking for just one more chance, and when you get it, messing that up too. And now one of you crashes the gate. What's your trouble, anyway?"

There was something about the producer that bothered Harry, but he could not place what it was, unless it was the fact that the man awed him and he didn't know why. "I woke up in Wednesday," he stammered, "and yesterday was Tuesday. I mean Monday. I mean—" He cleared his throat and started over. "I went to sleep Monday night and woke up Wednesday, and I'm looking for Tuesday."

"What do you want me to do about it?"

"Well – couldn't you tell me how to get back there? I got work to do."

"Oh – I get it," said the producer. "You want a favor from me. You know, someday, some one of you fellows is going to come to me wanting to give me something, free and for nothing, and then I am going to drop quietly dead. Don't I have enough trouble running this show without taking up time and space by doing favors for the likes of you?" He drew a couple of breaths and then smiled again. "However – I have always tried to be just, even if it is a tough job sometimes. Go on out and tell Iridel to show you the way back. I think I know what happened to you; when you made your exit from the last act you played in, you somehow managed to walk out behind the wrong curtain when you reached the wings. There's going to be a prompter sent to Limbo for this. Go on now – beat it."

Harry opened his mouth to speak, thought better of it and scuttled out the door, which opened before him. He stood in the huge control chamber, breathing hard. Iridel walked up to him.

"Well?"

"He says for you to get me out of here."

"All right," said Iridel. "This way." He led the way to a curtained doorway much like the one they had used to come in. Beside it were two dials, one marked in days, and the other in hours and minutes.

"Monday night good enough for you?" asked Iridel.

"Swell," said Harry.

Iridel set the dials for 9:30 p.m. on Monday. "So long, actor. Maybe I'll see you again some time."

"So long," said Harry. He turned and stepped through the door.

He was back in the garage, and there was no curtained doorway behind him. He turned to ask Iridel if this would enable him to go to bed again and do Tuesday right from the start, but Iridel was gone.

The garage was a blaze of light. Harry glanced up at the clock – it said fifteen seconds after nine-thirty. That was funny; everyone should be home by now except Slim Jim, the night man, who hung out until four in the morning serving up gas at the pumps outside. A quick glance around sufficed. This might be Monday night, but it was a Monday night he hadn't known.

The place was filled with the little men again!

Harry sat on the fender of a convertible and groaned. "Now what have I got myself into?" he asked himself.

He could see that he was at a different place-in-time from the one in which he had met Iridel. There, they had been working to build, working with a precision and nicety that was a pleasure to watch. But here —

The little men were different, in the first place. They were tired-looking, sick, slow. There were scores of overseers about, and Harry winced with one of the little fellows when one of the men in white lashed out with a long whip. As the Wednesday crews worked, so the Monday gangs slaved. And the work they were doing was different. For here they were breaking down, breaking up, carting away. Before his eyes, Harry saw sections of paving lifted out, pulverized, toted away by the sackload by lines of trudging, browbeaten little men. He saw great beams upended to support the roof, while bricks were pried out of the walls. He heard the gang working on the roof, saw patches of roofing torn away. He saw walls and roof both melt away under that driving, driven onslaught, and before he knew what was happening he was standing alone on a section of the dead white plain he had noticed before on the corner lot.

It was too much for his overburdened mind; he ran out into the night, breaking through lines of laden slaves, through neat and growing piles of rubble, screaming for Iridel. He ran for a long time, and finally dropped down behind a stack of lumber out where the Unitarian church used to be, dropped because he could go no farther. He heard footsteps and tried to make himself smaller. They came on steadily; one of the overseers rounded the corner and stood looking at him. Harry was in deep shadow, but he knew the man in white could see in the dark.

"Come out o' there," grated the man. Harry came out.

"You the guy was yellin' for Iridel?"

Harry nodded.

"What makes you think you'll find Iridel in Limbo?" sneered his captor. "Who are you, anyway?"

Harry had learned by this time. "I'm an actor," he said in a small voice. "I got into Wednesday by mistake, and they sent me back here."

"What for?"

"Huh? Why – I guess it was a mistake, that's all."

The man stepped forward and grabbed Harry by the collar. He was about eight times as powerful as a hydraulic jack. "Don't give me no guff, pal," said the man. "Nobody gets sent to Limbo by mistake, or if he didn't do somethin' up there to make him deserve it. Come clean, now."

"I didn't do nothin'," Harry wailed. "I asked them the way back, and they showed me a door, and I went through it and came here. That's all I know. Stop it, you're choking me!"

The man dropped him suddenly. "Listen, babe, you know who I am? Hey?" Harry shook his head. "Oh – you don't. Well, I'm Gurrah!"

"Yeah?" Harry said, not being able to think of anything else at the moment.

Gurrah puffed out his chest and appeared to be waiting for something more from Harry. When nothing came, he walked up to the mechanic, breathed in his face. "Ain't scared, huh? Tough guy, huh? Never heard of Gurrah, supervisor of Limbo an' the roughest, toughest son of the devil from Incidence to Eternity, huh?"

Now Harry was a peaceable man, but if there was anything he hated, it was to have a stranger breathe his bad breath pugnaciously at him. Before he knew it had happened, Gurrah was sprawled eight feet away, and Harry was standing alone rubbing his left knuckles – quite the more surprised of the two.

Gurrah sat up, feeling his face. "Why, you . . . you hit me!" he roared. He got up and came over to Harry. "You hit me!" he said softly, his voice slightly out of focus in amazement. Harry wished he hadn't – wished he was in bed or in Futura or dead or something. Gurrah reached out with a heavy fist and – patted him on the shoulder. "Hey," he said, suddenly friendly, "you're all right. Heh! Took a poke at me, didn't you? Be damned! First time in a month o' Mondays anyone ever made a pass at me. Last was a feller named Orton. I killed 'im." Harry paled.

Gurrah leaned back against the lumber pile. "Dam'f I didn't enjoy that, feller. Yeah. This is a hell of a job they palmed off on me, but what can you do? Breakin' down – breakin' down. No sooner get through one job, workin' top speed, drivin' the boys till they bleed, than they give you the devil for not bein' halfway through another job. You'd think I'd been in the business long enough to know what it was all about, after more than eight hundred an' twenty million acts, wouldn't you? Heh. Try to tell *them* that. Ship a load of dog houses up to Wednesday, sneakin' it past backstage nice as you please. They turn right around and call me up. What's the matter with you, Gurrah? Them dog houses is no good. We sent you a list o' worn-out items two acts ago. One o' the items was dog houses. Snap out of it or we send someone back there who can read an' put you on a toteline.' That's what I get – act in and act out. An' does it do any good to tell 'em that my aide got the message an' dropped dead before he got it to me? No. Uh-uh. If I say anything about that, they tell me to stop workin' 'em to death. If I do that, they kick because my shipments don't come in fast enough."

He paused for breath. Harry had a hunch that if he kept Gurrah in a good mood it might benefit him. He asked, "What's your job, anyway?"

"Job?" Gurrah howled. "Call this a job? Tearin' down the sets, shippin' what's good to the act after next, junkin' the rest?" He snorted.

Harry asked, "You mean they use the same props over again?"

"That's right. They don't last, though. Six, eight acts, maybe. Then they got to build new ones and weather them and knock 'em around to make 'em look as if they was used."

There was silence for a time. Gurrah, having got his bitterness off his chest for the first time in literally ages, was feeling pacified. Harry didn't know how to feel. He finally broke the ice. "Hey, Gurrah— How'm I goin' to get back into the play?"

"What's it to me? How'd you— Oh, that's right, you walked in from the control room, huh? That it?"

Harry nodded.

"An' how," growled Gurrah, "did you get inta the control room?"

"Iridel brought me."

"Then what?"

"Well, I went to see the producer, and—"

"Th' *producer*! Holy— You mean you walked right in and—" Gurrah mopped his brow. "What'd he say?"

"Why – he said he guessed it wasn't my fault that I woke up in Wednesday. He said to tell Iridel to ship me back."

"An' Iridel threw you back to Monday." And Gurrah threw back his shaggy head and roared.

"What's funny," asked Harry, a little peeved.

"Iridel," said Gurrah. "Do you realize that I've been trying for fifty thousand acts or more to get something on that pretty ol' heel, and he drops you right in my lap. Pal, I can't thank you enough! He was supposed to send you back into the play, and instead o' that you wind up in yesterday! Why, I'll blackmail him till the end of time!" He whirled exultantly, called to a group of bedraggled little men who were staggering under a cornerstone on their way to the junkyard. "Take it easy, boys!" he called. "I got ol' Iridel by the short hair. No more busted backs! No more snotty messages! *Haw haw haw!*"

Harry, a little amazed at all this, put in a timid word, "Hey – Gurrah. What about me?"

Gurrah turned. "You? Oh. *Tel-e-phone!*" At his shout two little workers, a trifle less bedraggled than the rest, trotted up. One hopped up and perched on Gurrah's right shoulder; the other draped himself over the left, with his head forward. Gurrah grabbed the latter by the neck, brought the man's head close and shouted into his ear. "Give me Iridel!" There was a moment's wait, then the little man on his other shoulder spoke in Iridel's voice, into Gurrah's ear, "Well?"

"Hiyah, fancy pants!"

"Fancy— I beg your— Who is this?"

"It's Gurrah, you futuristic parasite. I got a couple things to tell you."

"Gurrah! How *dare* you talk to me like that! I'll have you—"

"You'll have me in your job if I tell all I know. You're a wart on the nose of progress, Iridel."

"What is the meaning of this?"

"The meaning of this is that you had instructions sent to you by the producer an' you muffed them. Had an actor there, didn't you? He saw the boss, didn't he? Told you he was to be sent back, didn't he? Sent him right over to me instead of to the play, didn't you? You're slippin', Iridel. Gettin' old. Well, get off the wire. I'm callin' the boss, right now."

"The boss? Oh – don't do that, old man. Look, let's talk this thing over. Ah – about that shipment of three-legged dogs I was wanting you to round up for me; I guess I can do without them. Any little favor I can do or you—"

"—you'll damn well do, after this. You better, Goldilocks." Gurrah knocked the two small heads together, breaking the connection and probably the heads, and turned grinning to Harry. "You see," he explained, "that Iridel feller is a damn good supervisor, but he's a stickler for detail. He sends people to Limbo for the silliest little mistakes. He never forgives anyone and he never forgets a slip. He's the cause of half the misery back here, with his hurry-up orders. Now things are gonna be different. The boss has wanted to give Iridel a dose of his own medicine for a long time now, but Irrie never gave him a chance."

Harry said patiently, "About me getting back now—"

"My fran'!" Gurrah bellowed. He delved into a pocket and pulled out a watch like Iridel's. "It's eleven forty on Tuesday," he said. "We'll shoot you back there

471

THEODORE STURGEON

now. You'll have to dope out your own reasons for disappearing. Don't spill too much, or a lot of people will suffer for it – you the most. Ready?"

Harry nodded; Gurrah swept out a hand and opened the curtain to nothingness. "You'll find yourself quite a ways from where you started," he said, "because you did a little moving around here. Go ahead."

"Thanks," said Harry.

Gurrah laughed. "Don't thank me, chum. You rate all the thanks! Hey – if, after you kick off, you don't make out so good up there, let them toss you over to me. You'll be treated good; you've my word on it. Beat it; luck!"

Holding his breath, Harry Wright stepped through the doorway.

He had to walk thirty blocks to the garage, and when he got there the boss was waiting for him.

"Where you been, Wright?"

"I – lost my way."

"Don't get wise. What do you think this is – vacation time? Get going on the spring job. Damn it, it won't be finished now till tomorra."

Harry looked him straight in the eye and said, "Listen. It'll be finished tonight. I happen to know." And, still grinning, he went back into the garage and took out his tools.

IS THERE ANYBODY THERE?

Kim Newman

> Kim Newman is an English novelist, critic, and broadcaster. His fiction
> includes *The Night Mayor*, *Bad Dreams*, *Jago*, the Anno Dracula novels
> and stories, *The Quorum*, *The Original Dr. Shade and Other Stories*,
> *Life's Lottery*, *Back in the USSA* (with Eugene Byrne) and *The Man From
> the Diogenes Club* under his own name, and *The Vampire Genevieve*
> and *Orgy of the Blood Parasites* as Jack Yeovil. *Johnny Alucard*, the
> fourth Anno Dracula novel, appeared in 2012; his upcoming novel
> will be *An English Ghost Story*. This story was originally published
> in *The New English Library Book of Internet Stories* (edited by Maxim
> Jakubowski) in 2000.

"**I**s there a presence?" asked Irene.

The parlour was darker and chillier than it had been moments
ago. At the bottoms of the heavy curtains, tassels stirred like the
fronds of a deep-sea plant. Irene Dobson – Madame Irena, to her sitters – was
alert to tiny changes in a room that might preface the arrival of a visitor from
beyond the veil. The fizzing and dimming of still-untrusted electric lamps, so
much less impressive than the shrinking and bluing of gaslight flames she remembered from her earliest seances. A clamminess in the draught, as foglike cold rose
from the carpeted floor. The minute crackle of static electricity, making hair lift
and pores prickle. The tart taste of pennies in her mouth.

"Is there a traveller from afar?" she asked, opening her inner eye.

The planchette twitched. Miss Walter-David's fingers withdrew in a flinch;
she had felt the definite movement. Irene glanced at the no-longer-young woman
in the chair beside hers, shrinking away for the moment. The fear-light in the
sitter's eyes was the beginning of true belief. To Irene, it was like a tug on a
fishing line, the satisfying twinge of the hook going in. This was a familiar stage
on the typical sitter's journey from scepticism to fanaticism. This woman was
wealthy; soon, Irene would taste not copper but silver, eventually gold.

Wordlessly, she encouraged Miss Walter-David to place her fingertips on the
planchette again, to restore balance. Open on the round table before them was
a thin sheet of wood, hinged like an oversized chessboard. Upon the board's
smoothly papered and polished surface was a circle, the letters of the alphabet
picked out in curlicue. Corners were marked for YES – "oui", "ja" – and NO.
The planchette, a pointer on marble castors, was a triangular arrowhead-shape.

Irene and Miss Walter-David lightly touched fingers to the lower points of the planchette, and the tip quivered.

"Is there anybody there?" Miss Walter-David asked.

This sitter was bereft of a fiancé, an officer who had come through the trenches but succumbed to influenza upon return to civilian life. Miss Walter-David was searching for balm to soothe her sense of hideous unfairness, and had come at last to Madame Irena's parlour.

"Is there—"

The planchette moved, sharply. Miss Walter-David hissed in surprise. Irene felt the presence, stronger than usual, and knew it could be tamed. She was no fraud, relying on conjuring tricks, but her understanding of the world beyond the veil was very different than that which she wished her sitters to have. All spirits could be made to do what she wished them to do. If they thought themselves grown beyond hurt, they were sorely in error. The planchette, genuinely independent of the light touches of medium and sitter, stabbed towards a corner of the board, but stopped surprisingly short.

Y

Not YES, but the Y of the circular alphabet. The spirits often used initials to express themselves, but Madame had never encountered one who neglected the convenience of the YES and NO corners. She did not let Miss Walter-David see her surprise.

"Have you a name?"

Y again. Not YES. Was Y the beginning of a name: Youngman, Yokohama, Ysrael?

"What is it?" she was almost impatient.

The planchette began a circular movement, darting at letters, using the lower tips of the planchette as well as the pointer. That also was unusual, and took an instant or two to digest.

M S T R M N D

"Msstrrmnnd," said Miss Walter-David.

Irene understood. "Have you a message for anyone here, Master Mind?"

Y

"For whom?"

U

"For Ursula?" Miss Walter-David's christian name was Ursula.

N U

"U?"

"You," said Miss Walter-David. "You."

This was not a development Irene liked a bit.

*

There were two prospects in his Chat Room. Women, or at least they said they were. Boyd didn't necessarily believe them. Some users thought they were clever.

Boyd was primarily MstrMnd, but had other log-in names, some male, some female, some neutral. For each ISDN line, he had a different code name and e-address, none traceable to his physical address. He lived OnLine, really; this flat in Highgate was just a place to store the meat. There was nothing he couldn't get by playing the web, which responded to his touch like a harpsichord to a master's fingers. There were always backdoors.

His major female ident was Caress, aggressively sexual; he imagined her as a porn site Cleopatra Jones, a black model with dom tendencies. He kept a more puritanical, shockable ident – SchlGrl – as back-up, to cut in when Caress became too outrageous.

These two users weren't tricky, though. They were clear. Virgins, just the way he liked them. He guessed they were showing themselves nakedly to the Room, with no deception.

IRENE D.

URSULA W-D.

Their messages typed out laboriously, appearing on his master monitor a word at a time. He initiated searches, to cough up more on their handles. His system was smart enough to come up with a birth-name, a physical address, financial details and, more often than not, a .jpg image from even the most casually-assumed one-use log-on name. Virgins never realised that their presences always left ripples. Boyd knew how to piggyback any one of a dozen official and unofficial trackers, and routinely pulled up information on anyone with whom he had even the most casual, wary dealings.

IRENE D: Have you a message for anyone here, Master Mind?

Boyd stabbed a key.

Y

IRENE D: For whom?

U

IRENE D: For Ursula?

N U

IRENE D: U?

URSULA W-D: You.

At least one of them got it. IRENE D – why didn't she tag herself ID or I-D? – was just slow. That didn't matter. She was the one Boyd had spotted as a natural. Something about her blank words gave her away. She had confidence and ignorance, while her friend – they were in contact, maybe even in the same physical room – at least understood she knew nothing, that she had stepped into deep space and all the rules were changed. IRENE D – her log-on was probably a variant on the poor girl's real name – thought she was in control. She would unravel very easily, almost no challenge at all.

A MESSAGE FOR U I-D, he typed.

He sat on a reinforced swivel chair with optimum back support and buttock-spread, surveying a semi-circle of keyboards and monitors all hooked up to separate lines and accounts, all feeding into the master-monitor. When using two or more idents, he could swivel or roll from board to board, taking seconds to chameleon-shift. He could be five or six people in any given minute, dazzle a solo into thinking she – and it almost always was a she – was in a buzzing Chat Room with a lively crowd when she was actually alone with him, growing more vulnerable with each stroke and line, more open to his hooks and grapples, her backdoors flapping in the wind.

I KNOW WHO U ARE

Always a classic. Always went to the heart.

He glanced at the leftmost screen. Still searching. No details yet. His system was usually much faster than this. Nothing on either of them, on IRENE or URSULA. They couldn't be smart enough to cover their traces in the web, not if they were really as newbie as they seemed. Even a netshark ace would have been caught by now. And these girls were fighting nowhere near his weight. Must be a glitch. It didn't matter.

I KNOW WHAT U DO

Not DID, but DO. DID is good for specifics, but DO suggests something ongoing, some hidden current in an ordinary life, perhaps unknown even to the user.

U R NOT WHAT U CLAIM 2 B

That was for sure.

*

U R NOT WHAT U CLAIM 2 B

"You are not what you claim to be?" interpreted Miss Walter-David. She had become quickly skilled at picking out the spirit's peculiar, abbreviated language. It was rather irritating, thought Irene. She was in danger of losing this sitter, of becoming the one in need of guidance.

There was something odd about Master Mind. He – it was surely a he – was unlike other spirits, who were mostly vague children. Everything they spelled out was simplistic, yet ambiguous. She had to help them along, to tease out from the morass of waffle whatever it was they wanted to communicate with those left behind, or more often to intuit what it was her sitters wanted or needed most to hear and to shape her reading of the messages to fit. Her fortune was built not on reaching the other world, but in manipulating it so that the right communications came across. No sitter really wanted to hear a loved one had died a meaningless death and drifted in limbo, gradually losing personality like a cloud breaking up. Though, occasionally, she had sitters who wanted to know that those they had hated in life were suffering properly in the beyond and that their miserable post-mortem apologies were not accepted. Such transactions disturbed even her, though they often proved among the most rewarding financially.

Now, Irene sensed a concrete personality. Even through almost-coded, curt phrases, Master Mind was a someone, not a something. For the first time, she was close to being afraid of what she had touched.

Master Mind was ambiguous, but through intent rather than fumble-thinking. She had a powerful impression of him, from his self-chosen title: a man on a throne, head swollen and limbs atrophied, belly bloated like a balloon, framing vast schemes, manipulating lesser beings like chess-pieces. She was warier of him than even of the rare angry spirit she had called into her circle. There were defences against him, though. She had been careful to make sure of that.

"Ugly hell gapes", she remembered from Dr Faustus. Well, not for her.

She thought Master Mind was not a spirit at all.

U R ALLONE

"You are all one," interpreted Miss Walter-David. "Whatever can that mean?"

U R ALONE

That was not a cryptic statement from the beyond. Before discovering her "gift", Irene Dobson had toiled in an insurance office. She knew a type-writing mistake when she saw one.

U R AFRAID

"You are af—"

"Yes, Miss Walter-David, I understand."

"And are you?"

"Not any more. Master Mind, you are a most interesting fellow, yet I cannot but feel you conceal more than you reveal. We are all, at our worst, alone and afraid. That is scarcely a great insight."

It was the secret of her profession, after all.

"Are you not also alone and afraid?"

Nothing.

"Let me put it another way."

She pressed down on the planchette, and manipulated it, spelling out in his own language.

R U NOT ALSO ALONE AND AFRAID

She would have added a question mark, but the ouija board had none. Spirits never asked questions, just supplied answers.

*

IRENE D was sharper than he had first guessed. And he still knew no more about her. No matter.

Boyd rolled over to the next keyboard.

U TELL HIM GRRL BCK OFF CREEP

IRENE D: Another presence? How refreshing. And you might be?

CARESS SISTA.

IRENE D: Another spirit?

Presence? Spirit? Was she taking the piss?

UH HUH SPIRT THAT'S THE STUFF SHOW THAT PIG U CAN STAND UP 4 YRSELF

IRENE D: Another presence, but the same mode of address. I think your name might be Legion.

Boyd knew of another netshark who used Legion as a log-on. IRENE D must have come across him too. Not the virgin she seemed, then. Damn.

His search still couldn't penetrate further than her simple log-on. By now, he should have her mother's maiden name, her menstrual calendar, the full name of the first boy she snogged at school and a list of all the porn sites she had accessed in the last week.

He should close down the Room, seal it up forever and scuttle away. But he was being challenged, which didn't happen often. Usually, he was content to play a while with those he snared, scrambling their heads with what he had found out about them as his net-noose drew tauter around them. Part of the game was to siphon a little from their bank accounts: someone had to pay his phone and access bills, and he was damned if he should cough up by direct debit like some silly little newbie. But mostly it was for the sport.

In the early days, he had been fond of co-opting idents and flooding his playmates' systems with extreme porn or placing orders in their names for expensive but embarrassing goods and services. That now seemed crude. His current craze was doctoring and posting images. If IRENE D was married, it would be interesting to direct her husband to, say, a goat sex site where her face was convincingly overlaid upon an enthusiastic animal-lover's body. And it was so easy to mock up mug shots, complete with guilty looks and serial numbers, to reveal an ineptly-suppressed criminal past (complete with court records and other supporting documentation) that would make an employer think twice about keeping someone on the books. No one ever bothered to double-check by going back to the paper archives before they downsized a job.

Always, he would leave memories to cherish; months later, he would check up on his net-pals – his score so far was five institutionalisations and two suicides – just to see that the experience was still vivid. He was determined to crawl into IRENE D's skull and stay there, replicating like a virus, wiping her hard drive.

URSULA W-D: Do you know Frank? Frank Conynghame-Mars.

Where did that come from? Still, there couldn't be many people floating around with a name like that. Boyd shut off the fruitless backdoor search, and copied the double-barrel into an engine. It came up instantly with a handful of matches. The first was an obituary from 1919, scanned into a newspaper database. A foolish virgin had purchased unlimited access to a great many similar archives, which was now open to Boyd. A local newspaper, the *Ham&High*. He was surprised. It was the World Wide Web after all. This hit was close to home – maybe only streets away – if eighty years back. He looked over the obit, and took a flyer.

DEAD OF FLU

URSULA W-D: Yes. She knows Frank, Madame Irena. A miracle. Have you a message from Frank? For Ursula?

Boyd speed-read the obit. Frank Conynghame-Mars, "decorated in the late conflict", etc. etc. Dead at thirty-eight. Engaged to a Miss Ursula Walter-David, of this parish. Could the woman be still alive? She would have to be well over a hundred.

He launched another search. Ursula Walter-David

Three matches. One the Conynghame-Mars obit he already had up. Second, an article from something called *The Temple*, from 1924 – a publication of the Spiritualist Church. Third, also from the *Ham&High* archive, her own obit, from 1952.

Zoiks, Scooby – a ghost!

This was an elaborate sting. Had to be.

He would string it along, to give him time to think.

U WIL BE 2GETHER AGAIN 1952

The article from *The Temple* was too long and close-printed to read in full while his formidable attention was divided into three or four windows. It had been scanned in badly, and not all of it was legible. The gist was a testimonial for a spiritualist medium called Madame Irena (no last-name given). Among her "sitters", satisfied customers evidently, was Ursula Walter-David.

Weird. Boyd suspected he was being set up. He didn't trust the matches. They must be plants. Though he couldn't see the joins, he knew that with enough work he could run something like this – had indeed done so, feeding prospects their own mocked-up obits with full gruesome details – to get to someone. Was this a vengeance crusade? If so, he couldn't see where it was going.

He tried a search on "Madame Irena" and came up with hundreds of matches, mostly French and porn sites. A BD/SM video titled *The Lash of Madame Irena* accounted for most of the matches. He tried pairing "+Madame Irena" with "+spiritualist" and had a more manageable fifteen matches, including several more articles from *The Temple*.

URSULA W-D: Is Frank at peace?

He had to sub-divide his concentration, again. He wasn't quite ambidextrous, but could pump a keyboard with either hand, working shift keys with his thumbs, and split his mind into segments, eyes rolling independently like a lizard's, to follow several lines.

FRANK IS OVER HIS SNIFFLES

Among the "Madame Irena"/"medium" matches was a *Journal of the Society of Psychical Research* piece from 1926, shout-lined "Fraudulence Alleged". He opened it up, and found from a news-in-brief snippet that a court case was being prepared against one "Irene Dobson", known professionally as "Madame Irena", for various malpractices in connection with her work as a spirit medium. One Catriona Kaye, a "serious researcher", was quoted as being "in no doubt of the woman's genuine psychical abilities but also sure she had employed them in an unethical, indeed dangerous, manner".

Another match was a court record. He opened it: a declaration of the suit against Irene Dobson. Scrolling down, he found it frustratingly incomplete. The document set out what was being tried, but didn't say how the case came out. A lot of old records were like that, incompletely scanned. Usually, he only had current files to open and process. He looked again at the legal rigmarole, and his eye was caught by Irene Dobson's address.

The Laburnums, Feldspar Road, Highgate.

This was 26, Feldspar Road. There were big bushes outside. If he ran a search for laburnum.jpg, he was sure he'd get a visual match.

Irene Dobson lived in this house.

No, she had lived in this house. In the 1920s, before it was converted into flats. When it had a name, not a number.

Now she was dead.

Whoever was running this on Boyd knew where he lived. He was not going to take that.

*

"This new presence," said Miss Walter-David. "It's quite remarkable."

There was no new presence, no "Caress". Irene would have felt a change, and hadn't. This was one presence with several voices. She had heard of such. Invariably malign. She should call an end to the seance, plead fatigue. But Ursula Walter-David would never come back, and the husbandless woman had a private income and nothing to spend it on but the beyond. At the moment, she was satisfied enough to pay heavily for Irene's service. She decided to stay with it, despite the dangers. Rewards were within reach. She was determined, however, to treat this cunning spirit with extreme caution. He was a tiger, posing as a pussycat.

She focused on the centre of the board, and was careful with the planchette, never letting its points stray beyond the ring of letters.

"Caress," said Miss Walter-David, a-tremble, "may I speak with Frank?"

"Caress" was supposed to be a woman, but Irene thought the first voice – "Master Mind" – closer to the true personality.

IN 52

"Why 1952? It seems a terribly long way off."

WHEN U DIE

That did it. Miss Walter-David pulled away as if bitten. Irene considered: it seemed only too likely that the sitter had been given the real year of her death. That was a cruel stroke, typical of the malign spirit.

The presence was a prophet. Irene had heard of a few such spirits – one of the historical reasons for consulting mediums was to discern the future – but never come across one. Could it be that the spirits had true foreknowledge of what was to come? Or did they inhabit a realm outside time and could look in at any point in human history, future as well as past, and pass on what they saw?

Miss Walter-David was still impressed. But less pleased.

The planchette circled, almost entirely of its own accord. Irene could have withdrawn her fingers, but the spirit was probably strong enough to move the pointer without her. It certainly raced ahead of her push. She had to keep the planchette in the circle.

IRENE

Not Irena.

DOBSON

Now she was frightened, but also annoyed. A private part of her person had been exposed. This was an insult and an attack.

"Who's Dobson?" asked Miss Walter-David.

SHE IS

"It is my name," Irene admitted. "That's no secret."

ISNT IT

"Where are you?" she asked.

HERE THERE EVERYWHERE

"No, here and there perhaps. But not everywhere."

This was a strange spirit. He had aspirations to omnipotence, but something about him was overreaching. He called himself "Master Mind", which suggested a streak of self-deluding vanity. Knowledge wasn't wisdom. She had a notion that if she asked him to name this year's Derby winner, he would be able to furnish the correct answer

(an idea with possibilities)

but that he could reveal precious little of what came after death. An insight struck her: this was not a departed spirit, this was a living man.

Living. But where?

No.

When?

"What date is it?" she asked.

*

Good question.

Since this must be a sting, there was no harm in the truth.

JAN 20 01

IRENE D: 1901?

N 2001

URSULA W-D: I thought time had no meaning in the world beyond.

IRENE D: That depends which world beyond our guest might inhabit.

Boyd had run searches on "Irene Dobson" and his own address, independent and cross-matching. Too many matches were coming up. He wished more people had names like "Frank Conynghame-Mars" and fewer like "Irene Dobson". "Boyd Waylo", his birth-name, was a deep secret; his accounts were all in names like "John Barrett" and "Andrew Lee".

Beyond the ring of monitors, his den was dark. This was the largest room in what had once been a Victorian town-house, and was now divided into three flats. Was this where "Madame Irena" had held her seances? His raised ground-floor flat might encompass the old parlour.

He was supposed to believe he was in touch with the past.

One of the "Irene Dobson" matches was a .jpg. He opened the picture file, and looked into a small, determined face. Not his type, but surprising and striking. Her hair was covered by a turban and she wore a Chinese-style jacket, buttoned up to the throat. She looked rather prosperous, and was smoking a black cigarette in a long white holder. The image was from 1927. Was that when she was supposed to be talking to him from?

WHAT DATE 4 U

IRENE D: January 13, 1923. Of course.

Maybe he was supposed to bombard her with questions about the period, to try and catch her out in an anachronism. But he had only general knowledge: Prohibition in America, a General Strike in Britain, talking pictures in 1927, the Lindbergh flight somewhere earlier, the stock market crash a year or two later, *Thoroughly Modern Millie* and P.G. Wodehouse. Not a lot of use. He couldn't even remember who was Prime Minister in January, 1923. He could get answers from the net in moments, though; knowing things was pointless compared with knowing how to find things out. At the moment, that didn't help him.

Whoever these women were – or rather, whoever this IRENE D was, for URSULA W-D plainly didn't count – he was sure that they'd have the answers for any questions he came up with.

What was the point of this?

He could get to IRENE D. Despite everything, he had her. She was in his Room; she was his prey and meat and he would not let her challenge him.

I C U

*

I C U

I see you.

Irene thought that was a lie, but Master Mind could almost certainly hear her. Though, as with real spirits, she wondered if the words came to him as human sounds or in some other manner.

The parlour was almost completely dark, save for a cone of light about the table.

Miss Walter-David was terrified, on the point of fleeing. That was for the best, but there was a service Irene needed of her.

She did not say it out loud, for "Master Mind" would hear.

He said he could see, but she thought she could conceal her hand from him.

It was an awkward move. She put the fingers of her left hand on the shivering planchette, which was racing inside the circle, darting at the letters, trying to break free.

I C U ID

I C U R FRIT

She slipped a pocket-book out of her cardigan, opened it one-handed and pressed it to her thigh with the heel of her hand while extracting the pencil from the spine with her fingernails. It was not an easy thing to manage.

U R FRIT AND FRAUD

This was just raving. She wrote a note, blind. She was trusting Miss Walter-David to read her scrawl. It was strange what mattered.

"This is no longer Caress," she said, trying to keep her voice steady. "Have we another visitor?"

2TRU IM SNAKE

"Im? Ah-ha, "I'm". Snake? Yet another speaker of this peculiar dialect, with unconventional ideas about spelling."

Miss Walter-David was backing away. She was out of her seat, retreating into darkness. Irene offered her the pocket-book, opened to the message. The sitter didn't want to take it. She opened her mouth. Irene shook her head, shushing her. Miss Walter-David took the book, and peered in the dark. Irene was afraid the silly goose would read out loud, but she at least half-understood.

On a dresser nearby was a tea-tray, with four glasses of distilled water and four curls of chain. Bicycle chain, as it happened. Irene had asked Miss Walter-David to bring the tray to the ouija table.

"Snake, do you know things? Things yet to happen?"

2TRU

"A useful accomplishment."

NDD

"Indeed?"

2RIT

There was a clatter. Miss Walter-David had withdrawn. Irene wondered if she would pay for the seance. She might. After all, there had been results. She had learned something, though nothing to make her happy.

"Miss Walter-David will die in 1952?"

Y

Back to Y. She preferred that to 2TRU and 2RIT.

"Of what?"

A pause.

PNEU

"Pneumonia, thank you."

Her arm was getting worn out, dragged around the circle. Her shoulder ached. Doing this one-handed was not easy. She had already set out the glasses at the four points of the compass, and was working on the chains. It was important that the ends be dipped in the glasses to make the connections, but that the two ends in each glass not touch. This was more like physics than spiritualism, but she understood it made sense.

"What else do you know?"

U R FRAUD

"I don't think so. Tell me about the future. Not 2001. The useful future, within the next five or ten years."

STOK MRKT CRSH 29

"That's worth knowing. You can tell me about stocks and shares?"

Y

It was a subject of which she knew nothing, but she could learn. She had an idea that there were easier and less obtrusive fortunes to be made there than in Derby winners. But she would get the names out of him, too.

"Horse races?"

A hesitation.

Y

The presence was less frisky, sliding easily about the circle, not trying to break free.

"This year's Derby?"

*

A simple search (+Epsom +Derby +winner +1923 -Kentucky) had no matches; he took out -Kentucky, and had a few hits, and an explanation. Papyrus, the 1923 winner, was the first horse to run in both the Epsom and Kentucky Derby races, though the nag lost in the States, scuppering a possible chance for a nice long-shot accumulator bet if he really was giving a woman from the past a hot tip on the future. Boyd fed that all to IRENE D, still playing along, still not seeing the point. She received slowly, as if her system were taking one letter at a time.

Click. It wasn't a monitor. It was a ouija board.

That was what he was supposed to think.

IRENE D: I'm going to give you another name. I should like you to tell me what you know of this man.

OK

IRENE D: Anthony Tallgarth. Also, Basil and Florence Tallgarth.

He ran multiple searches and got a cluster of matches, mostly from the 20s – though there were birth and death announcements from the 1860s through to 1968 – and, again, mostly from the *Ham&High*. He picked one dated February 2, 1923, and opened the article.

TYCOON FINDS LOST SON.

IRENE D: Where is Anthony? Now.

According to the article, Anthony was enlisted in the Royal Navy as an Able Seaman, under the name of T.A. Meredith, stationed at Portsmouth and due to ship out aboard the HMS *Duckett*. He had parted from his wealthy parents after a scandal and a quarrel – since the brat had gone into the Navy, Boyd bet he was gay – but been discovered through the efforts of a "noted local spiritualist and seeress". A reconciliation was effected.

He'd had enough of this game. He wasn't going to play any more.

He rolled back in his chair, and hit an invisible wall.

IRENE D: I should tell you, Master Mind, that you are bound. With iron and holy water. I shall extend your circle, if you co-operate.

He tried reaching out, through the wall, and his hand was bathed with pain.

IRENE D: I do not know how you feel, if you can feel, but I will wager that you do not care for that.

It was as if she was watching him. Him!

IRENE D: Now, be a good little ghostie and tell me what I wish to know.

With his right hand lodged in his left armpit as the pain went away, he made keystrokes with his left hand, transferring the information she needed. It took a long time, a letter at a time.

IRENE D: There must be a way of replacing this board with a type-writer. That would be more comfortable for you, would it not?

FO, he typed.

A lash at his back, as the wall constricted. She had understood that. Was that a very 1923 womanly quality?

IRENE D: Manners, manners. If you are good to me, I shall let you have the freedom of this room, maybe this floor. I can procure longer chains.

He was a shark in a play-pool, furious and humiliated and in pain. And he knew it would last.

*

Mr and Mrs Tallgarth had been most generous. She could afford to give Master Mind the run of the parlour, and took care to refresh his water-bindings each day. This was not a task she would ever entrust to the new maid. The key to the parlour was about Irene's person at all times.

People would pay to be in contact with the dead, but they would pay more for other services, information of more use in the here and now. And she had a good line on all manner of things. She had been testing Master Mind, and found him a useful source about a wide variety of subjects, from the minutiae of any common person's life to the great matters which were to come in the rest of the century.

Actually, knowing which horse would win any year's Derby was a comparatively minor advantage. Papyrus was bound to be the favourite, and the race too famous for any fortune to be made. She had her genie working on long-shot winners of lesser races, and was sparing in her use of the trick. Bookmakers were the sort of sharp people she understood only too well, and would soon tumble to any streak of unnatural luck. From now on, for a great many reasons, she intended to be as unobtrusive as possible.

This morning, she had been making a will. She had no interest in the disposal of her assets after death, when she herself ventured beyond the veil, for she intended to make the most of them while alive. The entirety of her estate was left to her firm of solicitors on the unusual condition that, when she passed, no record or announcement of her death be made, even on her gravestone. It was not beyond possibility that she mightn't make it to 2001, though she knew she would be gone from this house by then. From now on, she would be careful about official mentions of her name; to be nameless, she understood, was to be invisible to Master Mind, and she needed her life to be shielded from him as his was from her.

The man had intended her harm, but he was her genie now, in her bottle.

She sat at the table, and put her hands on the planchette, feeling the familiar press of resistance against her.

"Is there anybody there?"

YYYYYYYYYYYYYYYYYYYYYY

"Temper temper, Master Mind. Today, I should like to know more about stocks and shares . . ."

*

Food was brought to him from the on-line grocery, handed over at the front door. He was a shut-in forever now. He couldn't remember the last time he had stepped outside his flat; it had been days before IRENE D, maybe weeks. It wasn't like he had ever needed to post a letter or go to a bank.

Boyd had found the chains. They were still here, fixed into the skirting boards, running under the doorway, rusted at the ends, where the water traps had been. It didn't matter that the water had run out years ago. He was still bound.

Searches told him little more of Irene Dobson. At least he knew someone would have her in court in four years time – a surprise he would let her have – but he had no hopes that she would be impeded. He had found traces of her well into the 1960s, lastly a piece from 1968 that didn't use her name but did mention her guiding spirit, "Master Mind", to whom she owed so much over the course of her long and successful career as a medium, seeress and psychic sleuth.

From 1923 to 1968. Forty-five years. Realtime. Their link was constant, and he moved forward as she did, a day for a day.

Irene Dobson's spirit guide had stayed with her at least that long.

Not forever. Forty-five years.

He had tried false information, hoping to ruin her – if she was cast out of her house (though she was still in it in 1927, he remembered) he would be free – but she always saw through it and could punish him.

He had tried going silent, shutting everything down. But he always had to boot up again, to be OnLine. It was more than a compulsion. It was a need. In theory, he could stop paying electricity and phone bills – rather, stop other people paying his – and be cut off eventually, but in theory he could stop himself breathing and suffocate. It just wasn't in him. His meat had rarely left the house anyway, and as a reward for telling her about the extra-marital private habits of a husband whose avaricious wife was one of her sitters, she had extended his bindings to the hallway and – thank heavens – the toilet.

She had his full attention.

IRENE D: Is there anybody there?

Y DAMNIT Y

FISH NIGHT

Joe Lansdale

Joe Lansdale is an American writer who has published over thirty
novels and numerous short stories. He has received the Edgar Award,
nine Bram Stokers, the Grinzane Cavour Prize for literature, and
many others. His novella *Bubba Ho-Tep* was filmed by Don Coscarelli,
starring Bruce Campbell and Ossie Davis, and has become a cult
classic. He lives and works in Nacogdoches, Texas. This story was
first published in the Arbor House Books anthology *Specter!* in 1982.

It was a bleached-bone afternoon with a cloudless sky and a monstrous sun.
The air trembled like a mass of gelatinous ectoplasm. No wind blew.

Through the swelter came a worn, black Plymouth, coughing and belch-
ing white smoke from beneath its hood. It wheezed twice, backfired loudly, died
by the side of the road.

The driver got out and went around to the hood. He was a man in the hard
winter years of life, with dead brown hair and a heavy belly riding his hips. His
shirt was open to the navel, the sleeves rolled up past his elbows. The hair on his
chest and arms was gray.

A younger man climbed out on the passenger side, went around front too.
Yellow sweat-explosions stained the pits of his white shirt. An unfastened,
striped tie was draped over his neck like a pet snake that had died in its sleep.

"Well?" the younger man said.

The old man said nothing. He opened the hood. A calliope note of steam blew
out from the radiator in a white puff, rose to the sky, turned clear.

"Damn," the old man said, and he kicked the bumper of the Plymouth as if he
were kicking a foe in the teeth. He got little satisfaction out of the action, just a
nasty scuff on his brown wingtip and a jar to his ankle that hurt like hell.

"Well?" the young man repeated.

"Well what? What do you think? Dead as the can-opener trade this week.
Deader. The radiator's chicken-pocked with holes."

"Maybe someone will come by and give us a hand."

"Sure."

"A ride anyway."

"Keep thinking that, college boy."

"Someone is bound to come along," the young man said.

They seated themselves on the hot ground with their backs to the car. That way
it provided some shade – but not much. They sipped on a jug of lukewarm water
from the Plymouth and spoke little until the sun fell down. By then they had both
mellowed a bit. The heat had vacated the sands and the desert chill had settled in.

Where the warmth had made the pair snappy, the cold drew them together.

The old man buttoned his shirt and rolled down his sleeves while the young man rummaged a sweater out of the backseat. He put the sweater on, sat back down. "I'm sorry about this," he said suddenly.

"Wasn't your fault. Wasn't anyone's fault. I just get to yelling sometime, taking out the can-opener trade on everything but the can-openers and myself. The days of the door-to-door salesman are gone, son."

"And I thought I was going to have an easy summer job," the young man said.

The old man laughed. "Bet you did. They talk a good line, don't they?"

"I'll say!"

"Make it sound like found money, but there ain't no found money, boy. Ain't nothing simple in this world. The company is the only one ever makes any money. We just get tireder and older with more holes in our shoes. If I had any sense I'd have quit years ago. All you got to make is this summer—"

"Maybe not that long."

"Well, this is all I know. Just town after town, motel after motel, house after house, looking at people through screen wire while they shake their heads No. Even the cockroaches at the sleazy motels begin to look like little fellows you've seen before, like maybe they're door-to-door peddlers that have to rent rooms too."

The young man chuckled. "You might have something there."

They sat quietly for a moment, welded in silence. Night had full grip on the desert now. A mammoth gold moon and billions of stars cast a whitish glow from eons away.

The wind picked up. The sand shifted, found new places to lie down. The undulations of it, slow and easy, were reminiscent of the midnight sea. The young man, who had crossed the Atlantic by ship once, said as much.

"The sea?" the old man replied. "Yes, yes, exactly like that. I was thinking the same. That's part of the reason it bothers me. Part of why I was stirred up this afternoon. Wasn't just the heat doing it. There are memories of mine out here," he nodded at the desert, "and they're visiting me again."

The young man made a face. "I don't understand."

"You wouldn't. You shouldn't. You'd think I'm crazy."

"I already think you're crazy. So tell me."

The old man smiled. "All right, but don't you laugh."

"I won't."

A moment of silence moved in between them. Finally the old man said, "It's fish night, boy. Tonight's the full moon and this is the right part of the desert if memory serves me, and the feel is right – I mean, doesn't the night feel like it's made up of some fabric, that it's different from other nights, that it's like being inside a big dark bag, the sides sprinkled with glitter, a spotlight at the top, at the open mouth, to serve as a moon?"

"You lost me."

The old man sighed. "But it feels different. Right? You can feel it too, can't you?"

"I suppose. Sort of thought it was just the desert air. I've never camped out in the desert before, and I guess it is different."

"Different, all right. You see, this is the road I got stranded on twenty years back. I didn't know it at first, least not consciously. But down deep in my gut I must have known all along I was taking this road, tempting fate, offering it, as the football people say, an instant replay."

"I still don't understand about fish night. What do you mean, you were here before?"

"Not this exact spot, somewhere along in here. This was even less of a road back then than it is now. The Navajos were about the only ones who traveled it. My car conked out like this one today, and I started walking instead of waiting. As I walked the fish came out. Swimming along in the starlight pretty as you please. Lots of them. All the colors of the rainbow. Small ones, big ones, thick ones, thin ones. Swam right up to me . . . *right through me!* Fish just as far as you could see. High up and low down to the ground.

"Hold on boy. Don't start looking at me like that. Listen: You're a college boy, you know what was here before we were, before we crawled out of the sea and changed enough to call ourselves men. Weren't we once just slimy things, brothers to the things that swim?"

"I guess, but—"

"Millions and millions of years ago this desert was a sea bottom. Maybe even the birthplace of man. Who knows? I read that in some science books. And I got to thinking this: If the ghosts of people who have lived can haunt houses, why can't the ghosts of creatures long dead haunt where they once lived, float about in a ghostly sea?"

"Fish with a soul?"

"Don't go small-mind on me, boy. Look here: Some of the Indians I've talked to up North tell me about a thing they call the manitou. That's a spirit. They believe everything has one. Rocks, trees, you name it. Even if the rock wears to dust or the tree gets cut to lumber, the manitou of it is still around."

"Then why can't you see these fish all the time?"

"Why can't we see ghosts all the time? Why do some of us never see them? Time's not right, that's why. It's a precious situation, and I figure it's like some fancy time lock – like the banks use. The lock clicks open at the bank; and there's the money. Here it ticks open and we get the fish of a world long gone."

"Well, it's something to think about," the young man managed.

The old man grinned at him. "I don't blame you for thinking what you're thinking. But this happened to me twenty years ago and I've never forgotten it. I saw those fish for a good hour before they disappeared. A Navajo came along in an old pickup right after and I bummed a ride into town with him. I told him what I'd seen. He just looked at me and grunted. But I could tell he knew what I was talking about. He'd seen it too, and probably not for the first time.

"I've heard that Navajos don't eat fish for some reason or another, and I bet it's the fish in the desert that keep them from it. Maybe they hold them sacred. And why not? It was like being in the presence of the Creator; like crawling around in the liquids with no cares in the world."

"I don't know. That sounds sort of . . ."

"Fishy?" The old man laughed. "It does, it does. So this Navajo drove me to town. Next day I got my car fixed and went on. I've never taken that cutoff again – until today, and I think that was more than accident. My subconscious was driving me. That night scared me, boy, and I don't mind admitting it. But it was wonderful too, and I've never been able to get it out of my mind."

The young man didn't know what to say.

The old man looked at him and smiled. "I don't blame you," he said. "Not even a little bit. Maybe I am crazy."

They sat awhile longer with the desert night, and the old man took his false teeth out and poured some of the warm water on them to clean them of coffee and cigarette residue.

"I hope we don't need that water," the young man said.

"You're right. Stupid of me! We'll sleep awhile, start walking before daylight. It's not far to the next town. Ten miles at best." He put his teeth back in. "We'll be just fine."

The young man nodded.

No fish came. They did not discuss it. They crawled inside the car, the young man in the front seat, the old man in the back. They used their spare clothes to bundle under, to pad out the cold fingers of the night.

Near midnight the old man came awake suddenly and lay with his hands behind his head and looked up and out the window opposite him, studied the crisp desert sky.

And a fish swam by.

Long and lean and speckled with all the colors of the world, flicking its tail as if in good-bye. Then it was gone.

The old man sat up. Outside, all about, were the fish – all sizes, colors, and shapes.

"Hey, boy, wake up!"

The younger man moaned.

"Wake up!"

The young man, who had been resting face down on his arms, rolled over. "What's the matter? Time to go?"

"The fish."

"Not again."

"Look!"

The young man sat up. His mouth fell open. His eyes bloated. Around and around the car, faster and faster in whirls of dark color, swam all manner of fish.

"Well, I'll be . . . *How?*"

"I told you, I told you."

The old man reached for the door handle, but before he could pull it a fish swam lazily through the back window glass, swirled about the car, once, twice, passed through the old man's chest, whipped up and went out through the roof.

The old man cackled, jerked open the door. He bounced around beside the road. Leaped up to swat his hands through the spectral fish. "Like soap bubbles," he said. "No. Like smoke!"

The young man, his mouth still agape, opened his door and got out. Even high up he could see the fish. Strange fish, like nothing he'd ever seen pictures of or imagined. They flitted and skirted about like flashes of light.

As he looked up, he saw, nearing the moon, a big dark cloud. The only cloud in the sky. That cloud tied him to reality suddenly, and he thanked the heavens for it. Normal things still happened. The whole world had not gone insane.

After a moment the old man quit hopping among the fish and came out to lean on the car and hold his hand to his fluttering chest.

"Feel it, boy? Feel the presence of the sea? Doesn't it feel like the beating of your own mother's heart while you float inside the womb?"

And the younger man had to admit that he felt it, that inner rolling rhythm that is the tide of life and the pulsating heart of the sea.

"How?" the young man said. "Why?"

"The time lock, boy. The locks clicked open and the fish are free. Fish from a time before man was man. Before civilization started weighing us down. I know it's true. The truth's been in me all the time. It's in us all."

"It's like time travel," the young man said. "From the past to the future, they've come all that way."

"Yes, yes, that's it . . . Why, if they can come to our world, why can't we go to theirs? Release that spirit inside of us, tune into their time?"

"Now wait a minute . . ."

"My God, that's it! They're pure, boy, pure. Clean and free of civilization's trappings. That must be it! They're pure and we're not. We're weighted down with technology. These clothes. That car."

The old man started removing his clothes.

"Hey!" the young man said. "You'll freeze."

"If you're pure, if you're completely pure," the old man mumbled, "that's it . . . yeah, that's the key."

"You've gone crazy."

"I won't look at the car," the old man yelled, running across the sand, trailing the last of his clothes behind him. He bounced about the desert like a jack-rabbit. "God, God, nothing is happening, nothing," he moaned. "This isn't my world. I'm of that world. I want to float free in the belly of the sea, away from can-openers and cars and—"

The young man called the old man's name. The old man did not seem to hear.

"I want to leave here!" the old man yelled. Suddenly he was springing about again. "The teeth!" he yelled. "It's the teeth. Dentist, science, foo!" He punched a hand into his mouth, plucked the teeth free, tossed them over his shoulder.

Even as the teeth fell the old man rose. He began to stroke. To swim up and up and up, moving like a pale pink seal among the fish.

In the light of the moon the young man could see the pooched jaws of the old man, holding the last of the future's air. Up went the old man, up, up, up, swimming strong in the long-lost waters of a time gone by.

The young man began to strip off his own clothes. Maybe he could nab him, pull him down, put the clothes on him. Something . . . God, something . . . but, what if *he* couldn't come back? And there were the fillings in his teeth, the metal rod in his back from a motorcycle accident. No, unlike the old man, this was his world and he was tied to it. There was nothing he could do.

A great shadow weaved in front of the moon, made a wriggling slat of darkness that caused the young man to let go of his shirt buttons and look up.

A black rocket of a shape moved through the invisible sea: a shark, the grand-daddy of all sharks, the seed for all of man's fears of the deep.

And it caught the old man in its mouth, began swimming upward toward the golden light of the moon. The old man dangled from the creature's mouth like a ragged rat from a house cat's jaws. Blood blossomed out of him, coiled darkly in the invisible sea.

The young man trembled. "Oh God," he said once.

Then along came that thick dark cloud, rolling across the face of the moon. Momentary darkness.

And when the cloud passed there was light once again, and an empty sky.

No fish.

No shark.

And no old man.

Just the night, the moon and the stars.

THE LOST PILGRIM

Gene Wolfe

Gene Wolfe has been called the best living American writer regardless of genre. Some of his awards include the World Fantasy Award for Lifetime Achievement, the Nebula Award, the Locus Award, the Rhysling Award (for poetry), and the British Science Fiction Association Award as well as eight nominations for the Hugo Award. "The Lost Pilgrim" was first published in the anthology *The First Heroes* (edited by Harry Turtledove) in 2004.

Before leaving my own period, I resolved to keep a diary; and indeed I told several others I would, and promised to let them see it upon my return. Yesterday I arrived, captured no Pukz, and compiled no text. No more inauspicious beginning could be imagined.

I will not touch my emergency rations. I am hungry, and there is nothing to eat; but how absurd it would be to begin in such a fashion! No. Absolutely not. Let me finish this, and I will go off in search of breakfast.

To begin. I find myself upon a beach, very beautiful and very empty, but rather too hot and much too shadeless to be pleasant. "Very empty," I said, but how can I convey just how empty it really is? (Pukz 1-3)

As you see, there is sun and there is water, the former remarkably hot and bright, the latter remarkably blue and clean. There is no shade, and no one who –

A sail! Some kind of sailboat is headed straight for this beach. It seems too small, but this could be it. (Puk 4)

*

I cannot possibly describe everything that happened today. There was far, far too much. I can only give a rough outline. But first I should say that I am no longer sure why I am here, if I ever was. On the beach last night, just after I arrived, I felt no doubts. Either I knew why I had come, or I did not think about it. There was that time when they were going to send me out to join the whateveritwas expedition – the little man with the glasses. But I do not think this is that; this is something else.

Not the man getting nailed up, either.

It will come to me. I am sure it will. In such a process of regression there cannot help but be metal confusion. Do I mean metal? The women's armor was gold or brass. Something like that. They marched out onto the beach, a long line of them, all in the gold armor. I did not know they were women.

I hid behind rocks and took Pukz. (See Pukz 5-9) The reflected glare made it difficult, but I got some good shots just the same.

They banged their spears on their shields and made a terrible noise, but when the boat came close enough for us to see the men on it (Pukz 10 and 11) they marched back up onto the hill behind me and stood on the crest. It was then that I realized they were women; I made a search for "women in armor" and found more than a thousand references, but all those I examined were to Joan of Arc or similar figures. This was not one woman but several hundreds.

I do not believe there should be women in armor, anyway. Or men in armor, like those who got off the boat. Swords, perhaps. Swords might be all right. And the name of the boat should be two words, I think.

The men who got off this boat are young and tough-looking. There is a book of prayers in my pack, and I am quite certain it was to be a talisman. "O God, save me by thy name and defend my cause by thy might." But I cannot imagine these men being impressed by any prayers.

Some of these men were in armor and some were not. One who had no armor and no weapons left the rest and started up the slope. He has an intelligent face, and though his staff seemed sinister, I decided to risk everything. To tell the truth I thought he had seen me and was coming to ask what I wanted. I was wrong, but he would surely have seen me as soon as he took a few more steps. At any rate, I switched on my translator and stood up. He was surprised, I believe, at my black clothes and the buckles on my shoes; but he is a very smooth man, always exceedingly polite. His name is Ekkiawn. Or something like that. (Puk 12) Ekkiawn is as near as I can get to the pronunciation.

I asked where he and the others were going, and when he told me, suggested that I might go with them, mentioning that I could talk to the Native Americans. He said it was impossible, that they had sworn to accept no further volunteers, that he could speak the language of Kolkkis himself, and that the upper classes of Kolkkis all spoke English.

I, of course, then asked him to say something in English and switched off my translator. I could not understand a word of it.

At this point he began to walk again, marking each stride with his beautiful staff, a staff of polished hardwood on which a carved snake writhes. I followed him, switched my translator back on, and complimented him on his staff.

He smiled and stroked the snake. "My father permits me to use it," he said. "The serpent on his own is real, of course. Our tongues are like our emblems, I'm afraid. He can persuade anyone of anything. Compared to him, my own tongue is mere wood."

I said, "I assume you will seek to persuade those women that you come in peace. When you do, will they teach you to plant corn?"

He stopped and stared at me. "Are they women? Don't toy with me."

I said I had observed them closely, and I was quite sure they were.

"How interesting! Come with me."

As we approached the women, several of them began striking their shields with their spears, as before. (Puk 13) Ekkiawn raised his staff. "My dear young ladies, cease! Enchanting maidens, desist! You suppose us pirates. You could not be more mistaken. We are the aristocracy of the Minyans. Nowhere will you find young men so handsome, so muscular, so wealthy, so well bred, or so well connected. I myself am a son of Hodios. We sail upon a most holy errand, for we would return the sacred ramskin to Mount Laphystios."

The women had fallen silent, looking at one another and particularly at an unusually tall and comely woman who stood in the center of their line.

"Let there be peace between us," Ekkiawn continued. "We seek only fresh water and a few days' rest, for we have had hard rowing. We will pay for any supplies we receive from you, and generously. You will have no singing arrows nor blood-drinking spears from us. Do you fear sighs? Languishing looks? Gifts of flowers and jewelry? Say so if you do, and we will depart in peace."

A woman with gray hair straggling from under her helmet tugged at the sleeve of the tall woman. (Puk 14) Nodding, the tall woman stepped forward. "Stranger, I am Hupsipule, Queen of Lahmnos. If indeed you come in peace—"

"We do," Ekkiawn assured her.

"You will not object to my conferring with my advisors."

"Certainly not."

While the queen huddled with four other women, Ekkiawn whispered, "Go to the ship like a good fellow, and find Eeasawn, our captain. Tell him these are women and describe the queen. Name her."

Thinking that this might well be the boat I was supposed to board after all and that this offered as good a chance to ingratiate myself with its commander as I was ever likely to get, I hurried away. I found Eeasawn without much trouble, assured him that the armed figures on the hilltop were in fact women in armor ("both Ekkiawn and I saw that quite clearly") and told him that the tallest, good-looking, black-haired, and proud, was Queen Hupsipule.

He thanked me. "And you are . . .?"

"A humble pilgrim seeking the sacred ramskin, where I hope to lay my heartfelt praise at the feet of God."

"Well spoken, but I cannot let you sail with us, Pilgrim. This ship is already as full of men as an egg is of meat. But should—"

Several members of the crew were pointing and shouting. The women on the hilltop were removing their armor and so revealing their gender, most being dressed in simple frocks without sleeves, collars, or buttons. (Puk 15) There was a general rush from the ship.

Let me pause here to comment upon the men's clothing, of which there is remarkably little, many being completely naked. Some wear armor, a helmet and a breastplate, or a helmet alone. A few more wear loose short-sleeved shirts that cover them to mid-thigh. The most remarkable is certainly the captain, who goes naked except for a single sandal. (Pukz 16 and 17)

For a moment or two, I stood watching the men from the ship talking to the women. After conversations too brief to have consisted of much more than introductions, each man left with three or more women, though our captain departed with the queen alone (Puk 18), and Ekkiawn with five. I had started to turn away when the largest and strongest hand I have ever felt closed upon my shoulder.

"Look 'round here, Pilgrim. Do you really want to go to Kolkkis with us?"

The speaker was a man of immense size, bull-necked and pig-eyed (Puk 19); I felt certain that it would be dangerous to reply in the negative.

"Good! I promised to guard the ship, you see, the first time it needed guarding."

"I am not going to steal anything," I assured him.

"I didn't think so. But if you change your mind, I'm going to hunt you down and break your neck. Now, then, I heard you and Eeasawn. You watch for me, hear? While I go into whatever town those splittailed soldiers came out of and get us some company. Two enough for you?"

Not knowing what else to do, I nodded.

"Me?" He shrugged shoulders that would have been more than creditable on a bull gorilla. "I knocked up fifty girls in one night once. Not that I couldn't have done it just about any other night, too, only that was the only time I've had a crack at fifty. So a couple for you and as many as I can round up for me. And if your two have anything left when you're done up, send 'em over. Here." He handed me a spear. "You're our guard 'til I get back."

I am waiting his return; I have removed some clothing because of the heat and in the hope of ingratiating myself with any women who may return with him. Hahraklahs is his name.

*

Hours have passed since I recorded the account you just read. No one has come, neither to molest our boat nor for any other reason. I have been staring at the stars and examining my spear. It has a smooth hardwood shaft and a leaf-shaped blade of copper or brass. I would not have thought such a blade could be sharpened, but it is actually very sharp.

It is also wrong. I keep thinking of spears with flared mouths like trumpets. And yet I must admit that my spear is a sensible weapon, while the spears with trumpet mouths would be senseless as well as useless.

These are the most beautiful stars in the world. I am beginning to doubt that I have come at the right period, and to tell the truth I cannot remember what the right period was. It does not matter, since no one can possibly use the same system. But this period in which I find myself has the most beautiful stars, bar none. And the closest.

There are voices in the distance. I am prepared to fight, if I must.

*

We are at sea. I have been rowing; my hands are raw and blistered. We are too many to row all at once, so we take turns. Mine lasted most of the morning. I pray for a wind.

I should have brought prophylactics. It is possible I have contracted some disease, though I doubt it. The women (Apama and Klays, Pukz 20-25, infrared) were interesting, both very eager to believe that I was the son of some king or other and very determined to become pregnant. Apama has killed her husband for an insult, stabbing him in his sleep.

Long after we had finished and washed ourselves in this strange tideless sea, Hahraklahs was still engaged with his fifteen or twenty. (They came and went in a fashion that made it almost impossible to judge the exact number.) When the last had gone, we sat and talked. He has had a hard life in many ways, for he is a sort of slave to one Eurustheus who refuses to speak to him or even look at him. He has been a stableman and so forth. He says he strangled the lion whose skin he wears, and he is certainly very strong. I can hardly lift his brass-bound club, which he flourishes like a stick.

If it were not for him, I would not be on this boat. He has taken a liking to me because I did not want to stay at Lahmnos. He had to kidnap about half the crew to get us out to sea again, and two could not be found. Kaeneus (Puk 26) says the crew wanted to depose Captain Eeasawn and make Hahraklahs captain, but he remained loyal to Eeasawn and would not agree. Kaeneus also confided that he himself underwent a sex-change operation some years ago. Ekkiawn warned me that Kaeneus is the most dangerous fighter on the boat; I suppose he was afraid I would ridicule him. He is a chief, Ekkiawn says, of the Lapiths; this seems to be a Native American tribe.

I am certainly on the wrong vessel. There are two points I am positive of. The first is the name of the captain. It was Jones. Captain Jones. This cannot be Eeasawn, whose name does not even begin with J. The second is that there was to be someone named Brewster on board, and that I was to help this Brewster (or perhaps Bradford) talk with the Lapiths. There is no one named Bradford among my present companions – I have introduced myself to all of them and learned their names. No Brewsters. Thus this boat cannot be the one I was to board.

On the positive side, I am on a friendly footing now with the Lapith chief. That seems sure to be of value when I find the correct ship and reach Atlantis.

I have discussed this with Argos. Argos (Puk 27) is the digitized personality of the boat. (I wonder if the women who lay with him realized that?) He points out – wisely, I would say – that the way to locate a vessel is to visit a variety of ports, making inquiries at each. In order to do that, one should be on another vessel, one making a long voyage with many ports of call. That is my situation, which might be far worse.

We have sighted two other boats, both smaller than our own.

Our helmsman, said to be an infallible weather prophet, has announced that we will have a stiff west wind by early afternoon. Our course is northeast for Samothrakah, which I take to be another island. We are forty-nine men and one woman.

She is Atalantah of Kaludon (Pukz 28-30), tall, slender, muscular, and quite beautiful. Ekkiawn introduced me to her, warning me that she would certainly kill me if I tried to force her. I assured her, and him, that I would never do such a thing. In all honesty I cannot say I have talked with her, but I listened to her for some while. Hunting is the only thing she cares about. She has hunted every large animal in her part of the world and joined Eeasawn's expedition in hope of hunting grups, a fierce bird never seen west of our destination. They can be baited to a blind to feed upon the bodies of horses or cattle, she says. From that I take them to be some type of vulture. Her knowledge of lions, stags, wild swine, and the dogs employed to hunt all three is simply immense.

*

At sea again, course southeast and the wind dead astern. Now that I have leisure to bring this account up to date, I sit looking out at the choppy waves pursuing us and wonder whether you will believe even a fraction of what I have to relate.

In Samothrakah we were to be initiated into the Cult of Persefonay, a powerful goddess. I joined in the preparations eagerly, not only because it would furnish insight into the religious beliefs of these amoral but very superstitious men, but also because I hoped – as I still do – that the favor of the goddess would bring me to the rock whose name I have forgotten, the rock that is my proper destination.

We fasted for three days, drinking water mixed with wine but eating no solid food. On the evening of the third day we stripped and daubed each other with a thin white mixture which I suspect was little more than chalk dispersed in water. That done, we shared a ritual supper of boiled beans and raw onions. (Pukz 31 and 32)

Our procession reached the cave of Persefassa, as she is also called, about midnight. We extinguished our torches in an underground pool and received new ones, smaller torches that burned with a clear, almost white flame and gave off a sweet scent. Singing, we marched another mile underground.

My companions appeared undaunted. I was frightened, and kept my teeth from chattering only by an effort of will. After a time I was able to exchange places with Erginos and so walk behind Hahraklahs, that tower of strength. If that stratagem had not succeeded, I think I might have turned and run.

The throne room of the goddess (Pukz 33-35) is a vast underground chamber of spectacular natural columns where icy water drips secretly and, as it were, stealthily. The effect is of gentle, unending rain, of mourning protracted until the sun burns out. The priestesses passed among us, telling each of us in turn, "All things fail. All decays, and passes away."

Ghosts filled the cavern. Our torches rendered them invisible, but I could see them in the darkest places, always at the edge of my field of vision. Their whispers were like a hundred winds in a forest, and whenever one came near me I felt a cold that struck to the bone.

Deep-voiced horns, melodious and tragic, announced the goddess. She was preceded by the Kabeiri, stately women and men somewhat taller than Hahraklahs who appeared to have no feet. Their forms were solid to the knees, where they became translucent and quickly faded to nothing. They made an aisle for Persefonay, a lovely young woman far taller than they.

She was robed in crimson, and black gems bound her fair hair. (Pukz 36 and 37) Her features are quite beautiful; her expression I can only call resigned. (She may revisit the upper world only as long as the pomegranate is in bloom – so we were taught during our fast. For the rest of the year she remains her husband's prisoner underground.) She took her seat upon a rock that accommodated itself to her as she sat, and indicated by a gesture that we were to approach her.

We did, and her Kabeiri closed about us as if we were children shepherded by older children, approaching a teacher. That and Puk 38 will give you the picture; but I was acutely conscious, as I think we all were, that she and her servants were beings of an order remote from biological evolution. You will be familiar with such beings in our own period, I feel sure. I do not recall them, true. I do recall that knowledge accumulates. The people of the period in which I find myself could not have sent someone, as I have been sent, to join in the famous voyage whose name I have forgotten.

Captain Eeasawn stepped forward to speak to Persefonay. (Pukz 39 and 40) He explained that we were bound for Aea, urged upon our mission by the Pythoness and accompanied by sons of Poseidon and other gods. Much of what he said contradicted what I had been told earlier, and there was much that I failed to understand.

When he had finished, Persefonay introduced the Kabeiri, the earliest gods of Samothrakah. One or more, she said, would accompany us on our voyage, would see that our boat was never wrecked, and would rescue us if it were. Eeasawn thanked her in an elaborate speech, and we bowed.

At once every torch burned out, leaving us in utter darkness. (Pukz 39a and 40a infrared) Instructed by the priestesses, we joined hands, I with Hahraklahs and Atalantah, and so were led out of the cave. There our old torches were restored to us and rekindled. (Puk 41) Carrying them and singing, we returned to our ship, serenaded by wolves.

*

We have passed Ilion! Everyone agrees that was the most dangerous part of our voyage. Its inhabitants control the strait and permit no ships other than their own to enter or leave. We remained well out of sight of the city until night.

Night came, and a west wind with it. We put up the mast and hoisted our sail, and Periklumenos dove from the prow and took the form of a dolphin (Puk 42 infrared) to guide us though the strait. As we drew near Ilion, we rowed, too, rowing for all we were worth for what seemed half the night. A patrol boat spotted us and moved to intercept us, but Phaleros shot its helmsman. It sheered off – and we passed! That shot was five hundred meters if it was one, and was made by a man standing unsupported on a bench aboard a heeling, pitching boat urged forward by a bellying sail and forty rowers pulling for all they were worth. The arrow's flight was as straight as any string. I could not see where the helmsman was hit, but Atalantah says the throat. Knowing that she prides herself on her shooting, I asked whether she could have made that shot. She shrugged and said, "Once, perhaps, with a quiver-full of arrows."

We are docked now at a place called Bear Island. We fear no bears here, nor much of anything else. The king is the son of an old friend of Hahraklahs's. He has invited us to his wedding, and all is wine and garlands, music, dancing, and gaiety. (Pukz 43-48) Eeasawn asked for volunteers to guard the boat. I volunteered, and Atalantah offered to stay with me. Everyone agreed that Eeasawn and Hahraklahs would have to be present the whole time, so they were excused; the rest drew lots to relieve us. Polydeukahs the Clone and Kaeneus lost and were then subjected to much good-natured raillery. They promise to relieve us as soon as the moon comes up.

Meanwhile I have been leaning on my spear and talking with Atalantah. Leaning on my spear, I said, but that was only at first. Some kind people came down from the town (Puk 49) to talk with us, and left us a skin of wine. After that we sat side by side on one of the benches and passed the tart wine back and forth. I do not think that I will ever taste dry red wine again without being reminded of this evening.

Atalantah has had a wretched life. One sees a tall, athletic, good-looking young woman. One is told that she is royal, the daughter of a king. One assumes quite naturally that hers has been a life of ease and privilege. It has been nothing of the sort. She was exposed as an infant – left in the forest to die. She was found by hunters, one of whom had a captive bear with a cub. He washed her in the bear's urine, after which the bear permitted her to nurse. No one can marry her who cannot best her in a foot-race, and no one can. As if that were not enough, she is compelled to kill the suitors she outruns. And she has, murdering half a dozen fine young men and mourning them afterward.

I tried to explain to her that she could still have male friends, men other than suitors who like her and enjoy her company. I pointed out that I could never make a suitable mate for a beautiful young woman of royal blood but that I would be proud to call myself her friend. I would make no demands, and assist her in any way I could. We kissed and became intimate.

*

Have I gone mad? Persefonay smiled at me as we left. I shall never forget that. I cannot. Now this!

*

No, I am not mad. I have been wracking my brain, sifting my memory for a future that does not yet exist. There is a double helix of gold. It gives us the power to make monsters, and if it exists in that age it must exist in this. Look! (Pukz 50-58) I have paced off their height, and find it to be four and a half meters or a little more.

Six arms! All of them have six arms. (Pukz 54-57 show this very clearly.) They came at us like great white spiders, then rose to throw stones, and would have brained us with their clubs.

God above have mercy on us! I have been reading my little book by firelight. It says that a wise warrior is mightier than a strong warrior. Doubtless that is true, but I know that I am neither. We killed three. I killed one myself. Good Heavens!

*

Let me go at this logically, although every power in this mad universe must know that I feel anything but logical.

I have reread what I recorded here before the giants came. The moon rose, and not long after – say, three quarters of an hour – our relief arrived. They were somewhat drunk, but so were we.

Kastawr came with his clone Polydeukahs, not wanting to enjoy himself without him. Kaeneus came as promised. Thus we had five fighters when the giants came down off the mountain. Atalantah's bow served us best, I think, but they rushed her. Kaeneus killed one as it ran. That was simply amazing. He crouched under his shield and sprang up as the giant dashed past, severing an artery in the giant's leg with his sword. The giant took a few more steps and fell. Polydeukahs and Kastawr attacked another as it grappled Atalantah. I actually heard a rib break under the blows of Polydeukahs's fists. They pounded the giant's side like hammers.

People who heard our war cries, the roars of the giants, and Atalantah's screams came pouring down from the town with torches, spears, and swords; but they were too late. We had killed four, and the rest were running from us. None of the townspeople I talked to had been aware of such creatures on their island. They regarded the bodies with superstitious awe. Furthermore, they now regard us with superstitious awe – our boat and our whole crew, and particularly Atalantah, Kastawr, Polydeukahs, Kaeneus, and me. (Puk 59)

About midnight Atalantah and I went up to the palace to see if there was any food left. As soon as we were alone, she embraced me. "Oh, Pilgrim! Can you . . .Could anyone ever love such a coward?"

"I don't ask for your love, Atalantah, only that you like me. I know very well that everyone on our boat is braver than I am, but—"

"Me! Me! You were – you were a wild bull. I was terrified. It was crushing me. I had dropped my bow, and I couldn't get to my knife. It was about to bite my head off, and you were coming! Augah! Oh, Pilgrim! I saw fear in the monster's eyes, before your spear! It was the finest thing that has ever happened to me, but when the giant dropped me I was trembling like a doe with an arrow in her heart."

I tried to explain that it had been nothing, that Kastawr and his clone had already engaged the giant, and that her own struggles were occupying its attention. I said, "I could never have done it if it hadn't had its hands full."

"It had its hands full?" She stared, and burst into laughter. In another minute I was laughing too, the two of us laughing so hard we had to hold onto each other. It was a wonderful moment, but her laughter soon turned to tears, and for the better part of an hour I had to comfort a sobbing girl, a princess small, lonely, and motherless, who stayed alive as best she could in a forest hut with three rough men.

Before I go on to speak of the extraordinary events at the palace, I must say one thing more. My companions shouted their war cries as they battled the giants; and I, when I rushed at the one who held Atalantah, yelled, "Mayflower! Mayflower!" I know that was not what I should have said. I know I should have said mayday, but I do not know what "mayday" means, or why I should have said it. I cannot offer even a hint as to why I found myself shouting mayflower instead. Yet I feel that the great question has been answered. It was what I am doing here. The answer, surely, is that I was sent in order that Atalantah might be spared.

The whole palace was in an uproar. (Pukz 60-62) On the day before his wedding festivities began, King Kuzikos had killed a huge lion on the slopes of Mount Dindumon. It had been skinned and its skin displayed on the stoa, no one in his country having seen one of such size before.

After Kaeneus, Polydeukahs, and Kastawr left the banquet, this lion (we were told) was restored to life, someone filling the empty skin with new lion, so to speak. (Clearly that is impossible; another lion, black-maned like the first and of similar size, was presumably substituted for the skin.) What mattered was that the new or restored lion was loose in the palace. It had killed two persons before we arrived and had mauled three others.

Amphiareaws was in a trance. King Kuzikos had freed his hounds, piebald dogs the size of Great Danes that were nearly as dangerous as any lion. (Pukz 63 and 64) Eeasawn and most of our crew were hunting the lion with the king. Hahraklahs had gone off alone in search of it but had left word with Ekkiawn that I was to join him. Atalantah and I hurried away, knowing no more than that he had intended to search the east wing of the palace and the gardens. We found a body, apparently that of some worthy of the town but had no way of knowing whether it was one of those whose deaths had already been reported or a fresh kill. It had been partly devoured, perhaps by the dogs.

We found Hahraklahs in the garden, looking very much like a lion on its hind legs himself with his lion skin and huge club. He greeted us cordially and seemed not at all sorry that Atalantah had come with me.

"Now let me tell you," he said, "the best way to kill a lion – the best way for me, anyhow. If I can get behind that lion and get my hands on its neck, we can go back to our wine. If I tried to club it, you see, it would hear the club coming down and jerk away. They've got sharp ears, and they're very fast. I'd still hit it – they're not as fast as all that – but not where I wanted, and as soon as I hit it, I'd have it in my lap. Let me get a grip on its neck, though, and we've won."

Atalantah said, "I agree. How can we help?"

"It will be simple, but it won't be easy. When we find it, I'll front it. I'm big enough and mean enough that it won't go straight for me. It'll try to scare me into running, or dodge around and look for an opening. What I need is for somebody to distract it, just for a wink. When I killed this one I'm wearing, Hylas did it for me, throwing stones. But he's not here."

I said I could do that if I could find the stones, and Atalantah remarked that an arrow or two would make any animal turn around to look. We had begun to tell Hahraklahs about the giants when Kalais swooped low and called, "It's coming! Path to your left! Quick!"

I turned my head in time to see its final bound, and it was like seeing a saddle horse clear a broad ditch. Three sparrows could not have scattered faster than we. The lion must have leaped again, coming down on Hahraklahs and knocking him flat. I turned just in time to see him throw it off. It spun through the air, landed on its feet, and charged him with a roar I will never forget.

I ran at it, I suppose with the thought of spearing it, if I had any plan at all. One of Atalantah's arrows whistled past and buried itself in the lion's mane. Hahraklahs was still down, and I tried to pull the lion off him. His club, breaking the lion's skull, sounded like a lab explosion.

And it was over. Blood ran from Hahraklahs's immense arms and trickled from his fingers, and more ran down his face and soaked his beard. The lion lay dead between us, bigger than any horse I have ever seen. Kalais landed on its side as he might have landed on a table, his great white wings fanning the hot night air.

Atalantah embraced me, and we kissed and kissed again. I think that we were both overjoyed that we were still alive. I know that I had already begun to shake. It had happened much too fast for me to be afraid while it was happening, but when it was over, I was terrified. My heart pounded and my knees shook. My mouth was dry. But oh how sweet it was to hold Atalantah and kiss her at that moment, and have her kiss me!

By the time we separated, Hahraklahs and Kalais were gone. I took a few Pukz of the dead lion. (Pukz 65-67) After that, we returned to the wedding banquet and found a lot of guests still there, with Eeasawn and most of our crew. As we came in, Hahraklahs called out, "Did you ever see a man that would take a lion by the tail? Here he is! Look at him!"

That was a moment!

＊

We held a meeting today, just our crew. Eeasawn called it, of course. He talked briefly about Amphiareaws of Argolis, his high reputation as a seer, famous prophecies of his that have been fulfilled, and so on. I had already heard most of it from Kaeneus, and I believe most of our crew is thoroughly familiar with Amphiareaws's abilities.

Amphiareaws himself stepped forward. He is surprisingly young, and quite handsome, but I find it hard to meet his eyes; there is poetry in them, if you will, and sometimes there is madness. There may be something else as well, a quality rarer than either, to which I can put no name. I say there may be, although I cannot be sure.

He spoke very quietly. "We had portents last night. When we were told the lion had been resurrected, I tried to find out what god had done it, and why. At that time, I knew nothing about the six-armed giants. I'll come to them presently.

"Hrea is one of the oldest gods, and one of the most important. She's the mother of Father Zeus. She's also the daughter of Earth, something we forget when we shouldn't. Lions are her sacred animals. She doesn't like it when they are driven away. She likes it even less when they are killed. She's old, as I said, and has a great deal of patience, as old women generally do. Still, patience doesn't last forever. One of us killed one of her favorite lions some time ago."

Everyone looked at Hahraklahs when Amphiareaws said this; I confess I did as well.

"That lion was nursed by Hrea's daughter Hahra at her request, and it was set in the heavens by Hahra when it died – again at her mother's request. The man who killed it changed his name to 'Hahra's Glory' to avert her wrath, as most of us know. She spared him, and her mother Hrea let the matter go, at least for the present."

Amphiareaws fell silent, studying us. His eyes lingered on Hahraklahs, as was to be expected, but lingered on me even longer. (Puk 68) I am not ashamed to say they made me acutely uncomfortable.

"King Kuzikos offended Hrea anew, hunting down and killing another of her finest animals. We arrived, and she determined to avenge herself. She called upon the giants of Hopladamus, the ancient allies who had protected her and her children from her husband." By a gesture, Amphiareaws indicated the six-armed giants we had killed.

"Their plan was to destroy the *Argo*, and with most of us gone, they anticipated little difficulty. I have no wish to offend any of you. But had only Kaeneus and Polydeukahs been present, or only Atalantah and Pilgrim, I believe they would have succeeded without much difficulty. Other gods favored us, however. Polydeukahs and Kastawr are sons of Zeus. Kaeneus is of course favored by the Sea God, as are ships generally. Who can doubt that Augah favors Atalantah? Time is Pilgrim's foe – something I saw plainly as I began to speak. But if Time detests him, other gods, including Father Zeus, may well favor him.

"Whether that is so or otherwise, our vessel was saved by the skill in arms of those five, and by their courage, too. We must not think, however, that we have won. We must make what peace we can with Hrea, and so must King Kuzikos. If we fail, we must expect disaster after disaster. Persefonay favors our cause. This we know. Father Zeus favors it as well. But Persefonay could not oppose Hrea even if she dared, and though Father Zeus may oppose his mother in some things, there will surely be a limit to his friendship.

"Let us sacrifice and offer prayers and praise to Hrea. Let us urge the king to do likewise. If our sacrifices are fitting and our praise and prayers sincere, she may excuse our offenses."

We have sacrificed cattle and sheep in conjunction with the king. Pukz 69-74 show the entire ceremony.

I have been hoping to speak privately with Amphiareaws about Time's enmity. I know that I will not be born for many years. I know also that I have traveled the wrong way through those many years to join our crew. Was that in violation of Time's ordinances? If so, it would explain his displeasure; but if not, I must look elsewhere.

Is it lawful to forget? For I know that I have forgotten. My understanding of the matter is that knowledge carried from the future into the past is clearly out of place, and so exists only precariously and transitorily. (I cannot remember who taught me this.) My offense may lie in the things I remember, and not in the far greater number of things I have forgotten.

I remember that I was a student or a scholar.

I remember that I was to join the crew of a boat (was it this one?) upon a great voyage.

I remember that I was to talk with the Lapiths.

I remember that there is some device among my implants that takes Pukz, another implant that enables me to keep this record, and a third implant that will let me rush ahead to my own period once we have brought the ramskin back to Mount Laphysios.

Perhaps I should endeavor to forget those things. Perhaps Time would forgive me if I did.

I hope so.

*

We will put to sea again tomorrow morning. The past two days have been spent making ready. (Pukz 75-81) The voyage to Kolkkis should take a week or ten days. The capital, Aea, is some distance from the coast on a navigable river. Nauplios says the river will add another two days to our trip, and they will be days of hard rowing. We do not care. Call the whole time two weeks. Say we spend two more in Aea persuading the king to let us return the ramskin. The ghost of Phreexos is eager to be home, Amphiareaws says. It will board us freely. In a month we may be homeward bound, our mission a success. We are overjoyed, all of us.

Atalantah says she will ask the king's permission to hunt in his territory. If he grants it, she will go out at once. I have promised to help her.

This king is Aeeahtahs, a stern ruler and a great warrior in his youth. His queen is dead, but he has a daughter, the beautiful and learned Mahdaya. Atalantah and I agree that in a kingdom without queen or prince, this princess is certain to wield great influence, the more so in that she is reported to be a woman of ability. Atalantah will appeal to her. She will certainly be interested in the particulars of our voyage, as reported by the only woman on board. Atalantah will take every opportunity to point out that her hunt will bring credit to women everywhere, and particularly to the women of Kolkkis, of whom Mahdaya is the natural leader. Should her hunt fail, however, there will be little discredit if any – everyone acknowledges that the grups is a terribly difficult quarry. I will testify to Atalantah's prowess as a huntress. Hahraklahs offers his testimony as well; before our expedition set out they went boar hunting together.

We are loaded – heavily loaded, in fact – with food, water, and wine. It will be hard rowing, but no one is complaining so early, and we may hope for a wind once we clear the harbor. There is talk of a rowing contest between Eeasawn and Hahraklahs.

*

Is it possible to be too tired to sleep? I doubt it, but I cannot sleep yet. My hands burn like fire. I splashed a little wine on them when no one was looking. They could hurt no worse, and it may prevent infection. Every muscle in my body aches.

I am splashing wine in me, as well – wine mixed with water. Half and half, which is very strong.

If I had to move to write this, it would not be written.

We put out in fair weather, but the storm came very fast. We took down the sail and unshipped the mast. It was as dark as the inside of a tomb, and the boat rolled and shipped water, and rolled again. We rowed and we bailed. Hour after hour after hour. I bailed until someone grabbed my shoulder and sat me down on the rowing bench. It was so good to sit!

I never want to touch the loom of an oar again. Never!

More wine. If I drink it so fast, will I get sick? It might be a relief, but I could not stand, much less wade out to spew. More wine.

No one knows where we are. We were cast ashore by the storm. On sand, for which we thank every god on the mountain. If it had been rocks, we would have died. The storm howled like a wolf deprived of its prey as we hauled the boat higher up. Hahraklahs broke two ropes. I know that I, and a hundred more like me, could not have broken one. (Pukz 82 and 83, infrared) Men on either side of me – I do not know who. It does not matter. Nothing does. I have to sleep.

*

The battle is over. We were exhausted before they came, and we are exhausted now; but we were not exhausted when we fought. (Pukz 84, infrared, and 85-88) I should write here of how miraculously these heroes revived, but the fact is that I myself revived in just the same way. I was sound asleep and too fatigued to move when Lugkeos began shouting that we were being attacked. I sat up, blearily angry at being awakened and in the gray dawnlight saw the ragged line of men with spears and shields charging us from the hills above the beach.

All in an instant, I was wide awake and fighting mad. I had no armor, no shield, nothing but my spear, but early in the battle I stepped on somebody's sword. I have no idea how I knew what it was, but I did, and I snatched it up and fought with my spear in my right hand and the sword in my left. My technique, if I can be said to have had one, was to attack furiously anyone who was fighting Atalantah. It was easy since she frequently took on two or three at a time. During the fighting I was much too busy to think about it, but now I wonder what those men thought when they were confronted with a breastplate having actual breasts, and glimpsed the face of a beautiful woman under her helmet.

Most have not lived to tell anyone.

What else?

Well, Eeasawn and Askalafos son of Arahs were our leaders, and good ones, too, holding everybody together and going to help wherever the fighting was hottest. Which meant that I saw very little of them; Kaeneus fought on Atalantah's left, and his swordsmanship was simply amazing. Confronted by a man with armor and a shield, he would feint so quickly that the gesture could scarcely be seen. The shield would come down, perhaps only by five centimeters. Instantly Kaeneus's point would be in his opponent's throat, and the fight would be over. He was not so much fighting men as butchering them, one after another after another.

Hahraklahs fought on my right. Spears thrust at us were caught in his left hand and snapped like so many twigs. His club smashed every shield in reach, and broke the arm that held it. We four advanced, walking upon corpses.

*

Oh, Zeus! Father, how could you! I have been looking at my Pukz of the battle (84-88). King Kuzikos led our attackers. I recognized him at once, and he appears in 86 and 87. Why should he welcome us as friends, then attack us when we were returned to his kingdom by the storm? The world is mad!

I will not tell Eeasawn or Hahraklahs. We have agreed not to loot the bodies until the rain stops. If the king is among the dead, someone is sure to recognize him. If he is not, let us be on our way. A protracted quarrel with these people is the last thing we require.

I hope he is still alive. I hope that very much indeed.

*

The king's funeral games began today. Foot races, spear-throwing, all sorts of contests. I know I cannot win, but Atalantah says I must enter several to preserve my honor, so I have. Many will enter and all but one will lose, so losing will be no disgrace.

Eeasawn is buying a chariot and a team so that he can enter the chariot race. He will sacrifice both if he wins.

Hahraklahs will throw the stone. Atalantah has entered the foot races. She has had no chance to run for weeks, and worries over it. I tried to keep up with her, but it was hopeless. She runs like the wind. Today she ran in armor to build up her legs. (Puk 89)

Kastawr has acquired a fine black stallion. Its owner declared it could not be ridden by any man alive. Kastawr bet that he could ride it, laying his place on our boat against the horse. When its owner accepted the bet, Kastawr whistled, and the horse broke its tether to come to him. We were all amazed. He whispered in its ear, and it extended its forelegs so that he could mount more easily. He rode away bareback, jumped some walls, and rode back laughing. (Pukz 90-92)

"This horse was never wild," he told its previous owner. "You merely wanted to say that you nearly had a place on the *Argo*."

The owner shook his head. "I couldn't ride him, and neither could anyone else. You've won. I concede that. But can I try him just once more, now that you've ridden him?"

Polydeukahs got angry. "You'll gallop away, and my brother will never see you again. I won't permit it."

"Well, I will," Kastawr declared. "I trust him – and I think I know a way of fetching him back."

So the previous owner mounted; the black stallion threw him at once, breaking his neck. Kastawr will enter the stallion in the horse race. He is helping Eeasawn train his chariot horses as well.

The games began with choral singing. We entered as a group, our entire crew. I was our only tenor, but I did the best I could, and our director singled me out for special praise. Atalantah gave us a mezzosoprano, and Hahraklahs supplied a thundering bass. The judges chose another group, but we were the popular favorites. These people realize, or at any rate most of them seem to, that it was King Kuzikos's error (he mistook us for pirates) that caused his death, a death we regret as much as they do.

As music opened the games today, so music will close them. Orfius of Thrakah, who directed our chorus, will play and sing for us. All of us believe he will win.

*

The one-stade race was run today. Atalantah won, the only woman who dared run against men. She is celebrated everywhere. I finished last. But wait —
My performance was by no means contemptible. There were three who were no more than a step or two ahead of me. That is the first thing. I paced myself poorly, I know, running too fast at first and waiting until too late to put on a final burst of speed. The others made a final effort, too, and I had not counted on that. I will know better tomorrow.

Second, I had not known the customs of these people. One is that every contestant wins a prize of some kind – armor, clothing, jewelry, or whatever. The other is that the runner who comes in last gets the best prize, provided he accepts his defeat with good humor. I got a very fine dagger of the hard, yellowish metal all armor and weapons are made of here. There is a scabbard of the same metal, and both display extraordinary workmanship. (Pukz 93-95)

Would I rather have won? Certainly. But I got the best prize as well as the jokes, and I can honestly say that I did not mind the jokes. I laughed and made jokes of my own about myself. Some of them were pretty feeble, but everybody laughed with me.

I wanted another lesson from Kaeneus, and while searching for him I came upon Idmon, looking very despondent. He tells me that when the funeral games are over, a member of our crew will be chosen by lot to be interred with King Kuzikos. Idmon knows, he says, that the fatal lot will fall upon him. He is a son of Apollawn and because he is, a seer like Amphiareaws; long before our voyage began, he learned that he would go and that he would not return alive. (Apollawn is another of their gods.) I promised Idmon that if he was in fact buried alive I would do my utmost to rescue him. He thanked me but seemed as despondent as ever when I left him. (Puk 96)

*

The two-stade race was run this morning, and there was wrestling this afternoon. Both were enormously exciting. The spectators were beside themselves, and who can blame them?

In the two-stade race, Atalantah remained at the starting line until the rest of us had rounded the first turn. When she began to run, the rest of us might as well have been walking.

No, we were running. Our legs pumped, we gasped for breath, and we streamed with sweat. Atalantah was riding a turbocycle. She ran effortlessly, her legs and arms mere blurs of motion. She finished first and was already accepting her prize when the second-place finisher crossed the line.

Kastawr wrestled. Wrestlers cannot strike, kick, gouge or bite, but everything else seems to be permitted. To win, one must throw one's opponent to the ground while remaining on one's feet. When both fall together, as often happens, they separate, rise, and engage again. Kastawr threw each opponent he faced, never needing more than a minute or two. (Pukz 97-100) No one threw him, nor did he fall with his opponent in any match. He won, and won as easily, I thought, as Atalantah had won the two-stade race.

I asked Hahraklahs why he had not entered. He said he used to enter these things, but he generally killed or crippled someone. He told me how he had wrestled a giant who grew stronger each time he was thrown. Eventually Hahraklahs was forced to kill him, holding him over his head and strangling him. If I had not seen the six-armed giants here, I would not have believed the story, but why not? Giants clearly exist. I have seen and fought them myself. Why is there this wish to deny them? Idmon believes he will die, and that nothing can save him. I would deny giants, and the very gods, if I were not surrounded by so many of their sons.

Atalantah says she is of purely human descent. Why did her father order her exposed to die? Surely it must have been because he knew he was not her father save in name. I asked about Augah, to whom Atalantah is so often compared. Her father was Zeus, her mother a Teetan. May not Father Zeus (as he is rightly called) have fathered another, similar, daughter by a human being? A half sister?

When I congratulated Kastawr on his win, he challenged me to a friendly fencing match, saying he wanted to see how much swordcraft I had picked up from Kaeneus. I explained that Kaeneus and I have spent most of our time on the spear.

Kastawr and I fenced with sticks and pledged ourselves not to strike the face. He won, but praised my speed and resource. Afterward he gave me a lesson and taught me a new trick, though like Kaeneus he repeated again and again that tricks are of no value to a warrior who has not mastered his art, and of small value even to him.

He made me fence left-handed, urging that my right arm might someday be wounded and useless; it has given me an idea. Stone-throwing this morning; we will have boxing this afternoon. The stadium is a hollow surrounded by hills, as my Pukz (101-103) show. There are rings of stone seats all around the oval track on which we raced, nine tiers of them in most places. Stone-throwing, boxing, and the like take place in the grassy area surrounded by the track.

Hahraklahs was the only member of our crew to enter the stone-throwing, and it is the only event he has entered. I thought that they would measure the throws, but they do not. Two throw together, and the one who makes the shorter throw is eliminated. When all the pairs have thrown, new pairs are chosen by lot, as before. As luck would have it, Hahraklahs was in the final pair of the first pairings. He went to the farther end of the stadium and warned the spectators that his stone might fall among them, urging them to leave a clear space for it. They would not take him seriously, so he picked up one of the stones and warned them again, tossing it into the air and catching it with one hand as he spoke. They cleared a space as he had asked, though I could tell that he thought it too small. (Puk 104)

He went back to the line at the other end of the field, picking up the second stone on his way. In his huge hands they seemed scarcely larger than cheeses. When he threw, his stone sailed high into the air and fell among the spectators like a thunderbolt, smashing two limestone slabs in the ninth row. It had landed in the cleared space, but several people were cut by flying shards even so.

*

After seeing the boxing, I wonder whether I should have entered the spear-dueling after all. The boxers' hands are bound with leather strips. They strike mostly at the face. A bout is decided when one contestant is knocked down; but I saw men fighting still when they were half blinded by their own blood. (Pukz 105-110) Polydeukahs won easily.

Since I am to take part in the spear-dueling, I had better describe the rules. I have not yet seen a contest, but Kaeneus has explained everything. A shield and a helmet are allowed, but no other armor. Neither the spears nor anything else (stones for example) may be thrown. First blood ends the contest, and in that way it is more humane than boxing. A contestant who kills his opponent is banished at once – he must leave the city, never to return. In general a contestant tries to fend off his opponent's spear with his shield, while trying to pink his opponent with his own spear. Wounds are almost always to the arms and legs, and are seldom deep or crippling. It is considered unsportsmanlike to strike at the feet, although it is not, strictly speaking, against the rules.

Reading over some of my earlier entries, I find I referred to a "turbocycle." Did I actually know what a turbocycle was when I wrote that? Whether I did or not, it is gone now. A cycle of turbulence? Kalais might ride turbulent winds, I suppose. No doubt he does. His father is the north wind. Or as I should say, his father is the god who governs it.

*

I am alone. Kleon was with me until a moment ago. He knelt before me and raised his head, and I cut his throat as he wished. He passed swiftly and with little pain. His spurting arteries drenched me in blood, but then I was already drenched with blood.

I cannot remember the name of the implant that will move me forward in time, but I hesitate to use it. (They are still shoveling dirt upon this tomb. The scrape of their shovels and the sounds of the dirt falling from them are faint, but I can hear them now that the others are dead.) Swiftly, then, before they finish and my rescuers arrive.

Eeasawn won the chariot race. (Pukz 111-114) I reached the semifinals in spear-dueling, fighting with the sword I picked up during the battle in my left hand. (Pukz 115-118)

Twice I severed a spear shaft, as Kastawr taught me. (Pukz 119 and 120) I was as surprised as my opponents. One must fight without effort, Kaeneus said, and Kaeneus was right. Forget the fear of death and the love of life. (I wish I could now.) Forget the desire to win and any hatred of the enemy. His eyes will tell you nothing if he has any skill at all. Watch his point, and not your own.

I was one of the final four contestants. (Pukz 121) Atalantah and I could not have been happier if I had won. (Pukz 122 and 123)

*

I have waited. I cannot say how long. Atalantah will surely come, I thought. Hahraklahs will surely come. I have eaten some of the funeral meats, and drunk some of the wine that was to cheer the king in Persefonay's shadowy realm. I hope he will forgive me.

We drew pebbles from a helmet. (Pukz 124 and 125) Mine was the black pebble (Pukz 126), the only one. No one would look at me after that.

The others (Pukz 127 and 128) were chosen by lot, too, I believe. From the king's family. From the queen's. From the city. From the palace servants. That was Kleon. He had been wine steward. Thank you, Kleon, for your good wine. They walled us in, alive.

"Hahraklahs will come for me," I told them. "Atalantah will come for me. If the tomb is guarded—"

They said it would be.

"It will not matter. They will come. Wait. You will see that I am right."

They would not wait. I had hidden the dagger I won and had brought it into the tomb with me. I showed it to them, and they asked me to kill them.

Which I did, in the end. I argued. I pleaded. But soon I consented, because they were going to take it from me. I cut their throats for them, one by one.

And now I have waited for Atalantah.

Now I have waited for Hahraklahs.

Neither has come. I slept, and sat brooding in the dark, slept, and sat brooding. And slept again, and sat brooding again. I have reread my diary, and reviewed my Pukz, seeing in some things that I had missed before. They have not come. I wonder if they tried?

*

How long? Is it possible to overshoot my own period? Surely not, since I could not go back to it. But I will be careful just the same. A hundred years – a mere century. Here I go!

*

Nothing. I have felt about for the bodies in the dark. They are bones and nothing more. The tomb remains sealed, so Atalantah never came. Nobody did. Five hundred years this time. Is that too daring? I am determined to try it.

*

Greece. Not that this place is called Greece, I do not think it is, but Eeasawn and the rest came from Greece. I know that. Even now the Greeks have laid siege to Ilion, the city we feared so much. Agamemnawn and Akkilleus are their leaders.

*

Rome rules the world, a rule of iron backed by weapons of iron. I wish I had some of their iron tools right now. The beehive of masonry that imprisons me must surely have decayed somewhat by this time, and I still have my emergency rations. I am going to try to pry loose some stones and dig my way out.

*

The *Mayflower* has set sail, but I am not aboard her. I was to make peace. I can remember it now – can remember it again. We imagined a cooperative society in which Englishmen and Indians might meet as friends, sharing knowledge and food. It will never happen now, unless they have sent someone else.

The tomb remains sealed. That is the chief thing and the terrible thing, for me. No antiquarian has unearthed it. King Kuzikos sleeps undisturbed. So does Kleon. Again . . .

*

This is the end. The Chronomiser has no more time to spend. This is my own period, and the tomb remains sealed; no archeologist has found it, no tomb robber. I cannot get out, and so must die. Someday someone will discover this. I hope they will be able to read it.

Good-bye. I wish that I had sailed with the Pilgrims and spoken with the Native Americans – the mission we planned for more than a year. Yet the end might have been much the same. Time is my enemy. Cronus. He would slay the gods if he could, they said, and in time he did.

Revere my bones. This hand clasped the hand of Hercules.

These bony lips kissed the daughter of a god. Do not pity me.

The bronze blade is still sharp. Still keen, after four thousand years. If I act quickly I can cut both my right wrist and my left. (Pukz 129 and 130, infrared)

PALINDROMIC

Peter Crowther

Peter Crowther is a British journalist, short-story writer, novelist, editor, publisher, and anthologist. The founder of PS Publishing, he is also the recipient of the World Fantasy Award, the HWA Bram Stoker Award, and the British Fantasy Award. His work has been widely translated, and his short stories have been adapted for television on both sides of the Atlantic and collected in several collections. "Palindromic" was first published in the anthology *First Contact*, edited by Martin H. Greenberg and Larry Segriff, in 1997.

> *What seest thou else*
> *In the dark backward and abysm of time?*
> William Shakespeare, *The Tempest*

It was on the third day after the aliens arrived that we made the fateful discovery which placed the future of the entire planet in our hands. That discovery was that they hadn't arrived yet.

There were three of us went over to the vacant lot alongside Sycamore . . . that's me, Derby – like the hat – McLeod, plus my good friend and local genius Jimmy-James Bannister and Ed Brewster, Forest Plains' very own bad boy . . . except there was nothing bad about Ed. Not really.

We went up into that giant tumbleweed cloud thing that served as some kind of interstellar flivver – it had been at the aliens' invitation, or so we thought: our subsequent discovery called that particular fact into some considerable dispute – purely to get a look at whatever this one alien was doing. Jimmy reckoned – and he was right, as it turned out – he was keeping tabs on what was going on and recording everything in some kind of 'book'.

Not that he – if the alien *was* a 'he': we never did find out – was writing the way you or I would write, because he wasn't. We didn't even know if he was writing at all until later that night, when Jimmy-James had taken a long look in that foam-book of theirs.

Not that this book was like any other book you ever saw. It wasn't. Just like the ship that brought them to Forest Plains wasn't like any other ship you ever saw, not in *Earth vs The Flying Saucers* or even on *Twilight Zone* – both of which were what you might call 'current' back then. And the aliens themselves weren't like any kind of alien you ever saw in the dime comicbooks or even dreamed about . . . not even maybe after eating warmed-over two-day-old pizza last thing at night on top of a gutful of Michelob and three or four plates of Ma

Chetton's cheese surprises, the small pieces of toasted cheese flapjack that Ma used to serve up when we were holding the monthly Forest Plains Pool Knockout Competition.

It was during one of those special nights, with the moon hanging over the desert like a crazy Jack o'Lantern and the heat making your shirt stick to your back and underarms, that the whole thing actually got itself started. That was the night that creatures from outer space arrived in Forest Plains. Then again, it wasn't.

But I'm getting way ahead of myself here . . .

So maybe that's the best place to start the story, that night.

It was a Monday, the last one in November, at about 9 o'clock. The year was 1964.

Ma Chetton was sweeping the few remaining cheese surprises from her last visit to the kitchen down onto a plate of freshly-made cookies, their steam rising up into the smokey atmosphere of her husband Bill's Pool Emporium over on Sycamore, when the place shook like jello and the strains of The Trashmen's *Surfin' Bird*, which had been playing on Bill's pride-and-joy Wurlitzer, faded into a wave of what sounded like static. Only thing was we'd never heard of a jukebox suffering from static before. Then the lights went out and the machine just ground itself to a stop.

Jerry Bucher was about to take a shot – six-ball off of two cushions into the far corner as I recall . . . all the other pockets being covered by Ed Brewster's stripes: funny how you remember details like that – and he stood up ramrod tall like someone had just dropped a firecracker or something crawly down the back of his shorts.

"What the hell was that?" Jerry asked nobody in particular, switching the half-chewed matchstalk from one side of his mouth to the other while he glanced around to put the blame on somebody for almost fouling up his shot. Ed was never what you might call a calm player and he was an even worse loser.

Ed Brewster was crouched over, his shoulders hunched up, watching the dust drifting down from the rafters and settling on the pool table, his girlfriend Estelle's arms clamped around his waist.

Ma was standing frozen behind the counter, empty plate in her hand, staring at the lights shining through the windows. "Felt like some kind of earthquake," she ventured.

Bill Chetton's head was visible through the hatch into the kitchen, his mouth hanging open and eyes as wide as dinner plates. "Everyone okay?"

I leaned my pool cue against the table and walked across to the windows. By rights, it should have been dark outside but it was bright as a night-time ballgame, like someone was shining car headlights straight at the windows, and when I took a look along the street I saw sand and stuff blowing across towards us from the vacant lot opposite.

"Some kind of power failure is what it is," Estelle announced, her voice sounding even higher and squeakier than usual and not at all reassuring.

Leaning against the table in front of the window, my face pressed up against the glass, I saw that the cause of that power failure was not something simple and straightforward like power lines being down between Forest Plains and Bellingham, some 35 miles away. It was something far more complicated.

Settling down onto the empty lot across the street was something that resembled a cross between a gigantic metal canister and an equally gigantic vegetable, its sides billowing in and out.

"Is it a helicopter?" Old Fred Wishingham asked from alongside me, his voice soft and nervous. Fred had ambled over from the booth he occupied every night of the year and was standing on the other side of the table staring out into the night. "Can't be a plane," he said, "so it must be some kind of helicopter." There sounded like a good deal of wishful thinking in that last statement.

But wishful thinking or not, the thing descending on the spare ground across the street didn't look like any helicopter I'd ever seen – not that I'd seen many, mind you – and I told Fred as much.

"It's some kind of goddam hot air balloon," Ed Brewster said, crouching down so's he could get a better look at the top of the thing – it was tall, there was no denying that.

"Looks more like some kind of furry cloud," Abel Bodeen muttered to himself. I figured he was speaking so softly because he didn't feel like making that observation widely known because it sounded a mite foolish. And it did, right enough. The truth of the matter was that the thing *did* look like a furry cloud . . . or maybe a giant lettuce or the head of a cauliflower, with lights flashing on and off deep inside it.

Pretty soon we were all gathered around the window watching, nobody saying anything else as the thing settled down on the ground.

Within a minute or two, the poolroom lights came back on and the shaking stopped. "You going out to see what it is?" Fred asked. Nobody responded. "I guess *some*body should go out there to see what it is," he said.

Right on cue, the screen door squeaked behind us and we saw the familiar figure of Jimmy-James Bannister step out onto the sidewalk. He glanced back at the window at us all and gave a shrug. Then he started across the street.

"Hope that damn fool knows what he's doing." Ed Brewster was a past master at putting everyone's thoughts into words.

The truth of the matter was Jimmy-James knew a whole lot of things that none of the rest of us had any idea at all about. And anything he didn't know about he just kept on at until he did. Jimmy-James – born James Ronald Garrison Bannister (he'd made his first name into a double to go partways to satisfying his father and partways to keep the mickey-taking down to an acceptable minimum) – was the resident big brain of Forest Plains. Still only 22 years old – same age as me, at the time – he was finishing up his Master's course over at Princeton, studying languages and applied math.

Jimmy-James could do long division problems in his head and cuss in fourteen languages which, along with the fact that he could drink anyone else in town – including Ed – under the table, made him a pretty popular member of any group gathering . . . particularly one where any amount of liquor or even just beer was to be consumed. He was home for Thanksgiving, taking the week off, and there's a lot of folks owes him a debt of gratitude for that fact.

Anyway, there went Jimmy-James, large as life and twice as bold – though some might say 'stupid' – walking across the street, his hands thrust deep into his trouser pockets and his head held high, proud and fearless. There were a couple of muted gasps from somewhere behind me and then the sound of shuffling as folks tried to get closer to the window to get a good look. After all, we'd all seen from the *War Of The Worlds* movie what happened to people who got a little too close to these objects . . . and we'd all pretty much decided that the thing across the street was about as likely to have come from anyplace on Earth as it was to have flown up to us from Vince and Molly Waldon's general store down the street. Nobody actually came right out and said it was from another planet but we all knew that it was. But why it was here was another matter, though we weren't in any great rush to find out the answer to that question. None of us except Jimmy-James Bannister, that is.

"Go call the Sherrif," Ma Chetton whispered.

I could hear Bill Chetton pressing the receiver and saying *Hello? Hello?* like his life depended on it. It didn't come as any surprise when Bill announced to the hushed room that the line seemed like it was dead. Then the jukebox kicked in again with a loud and raucous *A papapapapapa . . .* the needle somehow having returned to the start of the Trashmen's hit record.

The street outside seemed like it was holding its breath in much the same way as the folks looking out of the window were holding their breath . . . both it and us waiting to see what was going to happen.

What happened was both awesome and kind of an anticlimax.

Just as Jimmy-James reached the sidewalk across the street, the sides of the giant vegetable balloon canister from another world dropped down and became a kind of shiny skirt reaching all the way to the ground. No sooner had that happened than a whole group of smaller vegetable things – smaller but still twice the size of Jimmy-James . . . and, at almost six-four, JJ is not a small man – came sliding down the platform onto terra firma . . . and into the heart of Forest Plains.

We could hear their caterwauling from where we were, even over the drone of The Trashmen telling anyone who would listen that *the Bird was the Word* . . . and, as we watched, we saw the vegetable-shapes come to a halt on the sidewalk right in front of Jimmy-James where they kind of spun around and then gathered around him in a tight circle. Then all but one of them moved back a few feet and then the last one moved back, too.

At this point, Jimmy-James turned around and waved to us. "Come on out," he yelled.

"You think it's safe?" Ed Brewster asked.

I shrugged. "Doesn't seem to be they mean any harm," Ma Chetton said softly, the wonder in her voice as plain as the streaks of grey coloring the hair around her ears and temples.

"They come all the way from wherever it is they come from, seems to me that if they'd had a mind to do us any harm they'd have done it by now," said Old Fred Wishingham. "That said, mind you," he added, "I'm not about to go charging out there until we see what it is they *have* come for."

"Maybe they haven't come for nothing at all," Estelle suggested.

Somebody murmured that such an unlikely scenario could be the case but they weren't having none of it. That was the way folks were in Forest Plains in those days – the way folks were all over this country, in fact. Nobody (with the possible exception of Ed Brewster, and even he only did it for fun) wanted to make anyone look or feel a damned fool and hurt their feelings if they could get away without doing so. With Estelle it could be difficult. Estelle had turned making herself look a damned fool into something approaching an artform.

"You mean, like they're exploring . . . something like that?" Abel Bodeen said to help her out a mite.

"Yeah," Estelle agreed dreamily, "exploring."

"Well, I'm going out," Ma said. And without so much as a second glance or a pause to allow someone to talk her out of it, she rested the empty plate on the counter-top and strode over to the door. A minute or so later she was walking across the street. It seemed like the things had sensed she was going to come out because they'd moved across the street like to greet her, swivelling around at the last minute – just as Ma came to a stop – and ringing her just the way they had done with Jimmy-James.

They seemed harmless enough but I felt like we should have the law in on the situation. "Phone still out, Bill?" I shouted. Bill Chetton lifted the receiver and tried again. He nodded and returned it to the cradle.

"Okay Ed," I said, "let's me and you scoot out the back and run over to the Sherriff's office."

Ed said okay, after thinking about that for a second or two, and then the two of us slipped behind the counter and into Bill's and Ma's kitchen, then out of the back door and into the yard, past the trashcans towards the fence . . . and then I heard someone calling.

"What was that?" I whispered across to Ed.

Ed had stopped dead in his tracks on the other side of the fence. He was staring ahead of him. When I got to the fence I looked in the directioon Ed was looking and there they were. Three of them. Right in front of us, wailing. I'll never forget that sound . . . like the wind in the desert, lost and aimless.

The door we'd just come out of opened up again behind us and Fred Wishingham's voice shouted, "Hold it right where you . . ." and then trailed off when Fred saw the things. "I was just going to tell you that some of those things had just turned around and headed over to where you'd be appearing . . . and, well, you already saw that." Fred had lowered his voice like he'd just been caught shooting craps in Church.

Ed nodded and I told Fred to get back inside.

As I heard the lock click on the door, I whispered to Ed. "You think maybe they can read our minds?"

Ed shrugged.

The things were about 10, maybe 12 feet high and seemed to float above the ground on a circular frilled platform. I say 'floated' because they didn't leave any marks as they moved along, not even in the soft dirt of the alleyway that ran behind Bill's and Ma's store.

The platform was about a foot deep and, above that, the thing's body kind of tapered up like a glass stem until it reached another frilly overhang – like a mushroom's head – at the top. Halfway between the two platforms a collar of tendrils or thin wings – like the gossamer veils of a jellyfish – stuck out from the stem a foot or so and then drooped down limply about three feet. These seemed to twitch and twirl of their own accord, no matter whether a wind was blowing or not, and it didn't take me too long to figure out these were what passed for arms and hands on the things' own world.

I looked up at the first creature's top section, trying to see if there were any kind of air-holes or eyes but there was nothing, although the texture of the skin-covering was kind of opaque or translucent . . . see-through, for want of a better phrase, and I could see things moving around in there, shifting and re-forming. Where the noise they made came out, I couldn't tell. And we never did find out.

We watched as the creatures moved closer. Suddenly, the one at the front turned around real fast and the hand-arm things fluttered outwards, like a sheet settling on a bed, and, just for a moment, they touched my shoulder. There was something akin to affection there. At the time, I thought I was maybe imagining it . . . maybe reading the creature's thought-waves or something, but I was later to discover that there was, if not an outright affection, then at least a feeling of familiarity on the creature's part.

This confrontation lasted only a few seconds, a minute at the most, and then the creatures moved back away from us in the direction of the Sherriff's office, the wing things outstretched towards us as they went.

"What did you make of that?" Ed Brewster said, his voice a little croaky and hoarse.

"I have absolutely no idea at all," I said.

I kept watching because one of the creatures intrigued me more than the others. This one carried what seemed to be some kind of foam box, thick with piled-up layers of what looked like cotton candy. All the time we'd been 'meeting' with the leader – we supposed the thing that had touched me *was* the leader – this other creature was removing small pieces of foam which it seemed to absorb into its tendrils. It was still doing it as the three of them moved down the alleyway. Just as they reached the back of the Sherriff's office, the leader put down its wings, turned around and, leaving the other two behind, moved up onto the sidewalk and out of sight.

I turned at the sound of hurried footsteps behind me and saw Jimmy-James running along the alleyway, his face beaming a wide smile. Ma Chetton was following him, her head still turned in the direction of the street to see if any of the creatures were following *her*.

"What about *that*!" JJ said. Then, "What *about* that!"

I nodded and when I turned to look at Ed, he was nodding too. There didn't seem much else to do.

"Did they say anything?" Jimmy-James asked. "Did they say where they've come from?"

"Nope," I said. "Not a word. Just that mournful wailing. Gives me the creeps . . . sounds like a coyote."

"Or a baby teething," Ma said breathlessly.

"Same here," said JJ. "I tried them with everything I know . . . English, French, German, Spanish, Russian . . . quite a few more. And I tried out a couple of hybrids, too."

"Like standing in the United Nations," Ma Chetton muttered testily, her breath rasping. "Or hanging atop the Tower of Babel come Doomsday."

"What the hell are hybrids?" Ed Brewster asked.

"Mixtures of two or three languages," JJ explained. "In the old days, that was the way most folks communicated . . . I mean before any one single language or dialect had gained enough of a footing to be commonplace. And I tried them with all kinds of signs and stuff but they didn't seem to know what I was doing. I thought maybe they would have known all about our language by listening to our radio waves out there in outer space. But it was no-go. I can't figure out how they communicate with each other at all," he said. "Unless it's that wailing noise or maybe through that thing that one of them's carrying around."

"You mean the box-thing? The thing that looks like a pile of cotton candy?"

JJ nodded. "He's messing with that thing all the time, changing it even as I'm trying to talk to them."

"Yeah," I agreed, "but did you notice he's taking things *out* instead of adding to what's already in there."

"I'd noticed that," JJ said. "I was wondering if that stuff is absorbed into him and enables him to communicate to the others. Like a translator."

I shrugged. It was all too much for me.

Ed glanced around to make sure none of those creatures had sneaked up on him and said, "We figure they can read our minds."

"Really?" said JJ. "How's that?"

"Well," Ed said, matter-of-factly, "they knew we were coming out here into the alleyway."

JJ frowned and glanced at me before returning his full attention to Ed.

Ed gave a characteristic shrug. "Why else would they come on down here from the street if they didn't know we were coming out?"

While JJ mulled that over, I said, "What do you figure they want, JJ?"

The back door to the poolroom opened and Abel Bodeen peered out. "Is there any of those things out there?"

"Nope, they've gone down to see the Sherriff," I said.

Abel pulled a face and gave a wry smile. "That should please Benjamin no end," he said with a chuckle.

The fact was that the creatures *did* please Sherriff Ben Travers, as it turned out. Or they didn't *dis*please him anyway. The truth of the matter was that the aliens didn't do anything to upset or irritate anyone. In fact, they didn't do anything at all.

"Why the hell did they come, Derby?" Abel Bodeen asked me a couple of days after they'd . . . after we'd first seen them.

"Beats me," I said.

We were sitting out on the old straight-backed chairs Molly Waldon had left out in front of her and Vince's General Store, watching the creatures wander around the town, just as they had been doing all the time. But I was watching a little more intently than I had done at first. The folks around town had become used to the aliens after two full days and nobody seemed to care much *what* they were there for. So it's probably fair to say that people hadn't picked up that the attitude of the creatures was changing. It wasn't changing by much, but it *was* changing.

"You've noticed, haven't you?"

I shielded my eyes from the glare of the late afternoon November sunshine and looked across at Jimmy-James. "Noticed what?"

He looked across at two of the creatures gliding along the other side of the street. "They're slowing down."

I followed his gaze and, sure enough, the creatures did seem to be slower than they had been at first. But it was more than that. They seemed to be more cautious. I mentioned this to JJ and Abel, and to Ed and Estelle who were leaning on what remained of an old hitching rail at the edge of the sidewalk.

Ed snorted. "That don't make no sense at all," he said. "Why would they be cautious now, when they've been here two goddam days."

"Ed, watch your mouth," Estelle whined in her high-pitched voice.

"He's right," agreed Jimmy-James.

"Who?" Ed asked. "Me or him?"

"Both of you." JJ got to his feet and strode across to the post behind Ed and leaned. "They *are* getting slower and they do seem to be more . . . more careful," he said, choosing his words. "And, no, it doesn't make any sense for them to be more careful the longer they're here."

"Nothing for them to be nervous about, that's for sure," Abel said. "They've got us wrapped up neat as a Christmas gift."

The aliens had effectively cut off the town. There were no phone lines and the roads were . . . well, they were impassible. It was Doc Maynard had seen it first, trying to get his old Ford Fairlane out to check on Sally Iaccoca's father, over towards Bellingham. Frank Iaccoca had taken a bad fall – cracked a couple of ribs, Doc said – and Doc had him trussed up like Boris Karloff in the old *Mummy* movie.

The car had cut out three miles out of Forest Plains and there was nothing Doc could do to get it going again. So he'd come back into town for help, without even taking a look under the hood, and Abel, Johnny Deveraux and me had gone out there to give him some help. Johnny, who works at Phil Masham's garage, had taken some tools and a spare battery in case it was something simple he could fix out on the road. Doc Maynard was not renowned for looking after his automobile.

When we got out there, Johnny tried the ignition and it was dead. But when he made to move around to the front of the car to open the hood he suddenly started floundering and dropped the battery. That's when we found the barrier.

A 'force field' is what Jimmy-James called it.

Everything looked completely normal up ahead in front of Doc Maynard's Fairlane but there was no way for us to get to it. It felt like cloth but not porous. JJ said it was an invisible synthetic membrane – whatever *that* was – and he reckoned the creatures had set it up around the town to protect their spaceship. Sure enough, the same barrier travelled all the way around town . . . or so we figured. We tried different points on farm tracks and woodland paths and each one came to a complete halt.

Like it or not, we were caught like fish in a bowl. But that didn't seem to matter . . . at least not until JJ took a look in the creatures' 'book'.

"There he goes, if it is a 'he'," said Jimmy-James, pointing to the creature with the box of cotton candy. The funny thing was that the box now looked to have a lot less of the stuff in it than it had done at first. The first time we'd seen it, the thing had looked to be almost full.

"The other thing," said JJ in a soft voice that made you think he was realising what he was about to say at exactly the same time as he said it, "is they seem not to be touching people with those . . . those veil-things."

"Yeah," I agreed. "I guess that was what I meant about them being more cautious. Part of it, anyway."

Ed snorted. "Maybe it's a case of the more they see of us the less they like."

Estelle rubbed Ed Brewster's oiled hair and puckered up her mouth. "I'm sure they like what they see of you, honey," she trilled without changing the shape of her mouth. "Anyone would." It sounded as though Estelle was talking to a newborn babe sitting in a stroller. Ed must've thought so, too, because he told her to can it while he readjusted his quiff.

"We need to get a look in that box-thing," JJ said.

"How we going to do that?" I asked. "And what good is it going to do us anyway? Just looks like a load of gunk to me."

JJ stepped away from the rail and out onto the street. "That's just it," he shouted over his shoulder as he strode across to the creature with the box. "None of us has seen what's in there, not up close."

We watched the confrontation.

Jimmy-James stopped right in front of the creature and it turned around. Almost immediately, the little veil-arms wafted out as though blown by a breeze and settled on JJ's shoulders, the wailing sound rising a pitch or two in the process. Then it started to back away, its arms still blowing free.

JJ shouted over to me to come on along. Ed Brewster stood up and moved alongside me. "I'm coming, too," he said.

"Now you be careful what you're doing, Ed, honey," Estelle warbled.

"I will, Estelle, I will," Ed said, with maybe just a hint of a sigh. And the two of us walked onto the street to join JJ. Which was how we got into the creatures' spaceship.

The alien with the book kept on backing away from the three of us and we just kept on walking after it. Eventually, we reached the ship where we discovered two more of the creatures standing by the ramp.

The creatures then backed on up into the ship. We kept on following.

A few minutes later the three of us were standing amidst a whole array of what looked to be lumps of foam, all of various size, piled up on or stuck against other lumps. Some of the lumps were circular – cylindrical, JJ said – and others looked like tears of modelling clay thumbed into place by a gigantic hand without design or reason.

Up inside the ship, the things' wing-arms were fluttering faster and more frequently than ever . . . and the alien that we reckoned to be recording the whole visit was mightily busy, removing small pieces of foam with the tendrils and absorbing them. When I glanced inside the box, I saw there was hardly anything in it.

Over to one side of the crowded room a wide lamp-thing stood by itself. Standing beneath the lamp, two aliens were seemingly absorbed in another of the boxes, their wings-arms fluttering like a leaf caught in a draft. This particular box was completely full, a collection of multi-colored shapes and lumps and pieces, all pressed into each other or standing alone.

"We need to get a look at that," JJ whispered to Ed and me.

"Leave it to me," Ed Brewster said. He walked across to the box and lifted it with both hands. "Okay if I borrow this for a while, ol' buddy?" he said, waving the box in front of the two creatures.

The things didn't seem to do anything as Ed stepped back and moved back alongside us, although their arms were fluttering faster than ever. Then, suddenly, the little arm-wings dropped limp and the two creatures turned around. As they did this, the creature standing in front of the other two in the center of the room waved its arms and then it, too, spun around.

"Let's get out of here," Jimmy-James said. "I'm starting to get a bad feeling about this."

As we ran down the platform leading back onto Sycamore Street I asked Jimmy-James what he'd meant by that last remark. But he just shook his head.

"It's too fantastic to even think about," was all he'd say. "Just let me take a look at the box and then maybe I'll be able to get an idea."

We high-tailed it back to Jack and Edna Bannister's house down on Beech Avenue and, while me and Ed drank cup after cup of JJ's mom's strong coffee, JJ himself pored over the contents of the alien box. It was almost three in the morning when a wild-eyed Jimmy-James rushed into the Bannisters' lounge and slammed the box onto the table. Ed was asleep, curled up like a baby on the sofa, and I was reading the TV Guide.

"I have to look at the other box," he said. "Now!"

Ed smacked his lips together loudly and shuffled around on the sofa.

I looked up from a feature on *Gilligan's Island* and was immediately surprised to see how much Jimmy-James resembled that hapless shipwreck survivor. "What's up?"

JJ shook his head and ran his hands through his hair. I noticed straight away that they were shaking. "A lot, maybe . . . maybe nothing. I don't know."

"You want to—"

"I've been through all of the usual coding techniques," JJ said, ticking off on his outstretched fingers. "I've applied the Patagonian Principle of repeated shapes, colour motifs, spacing . . . I've run the Spectromic Law of shading relationships and the old Inca constructional communication dynamics . . ."

I held up a hand and waved for him to stop. "Whoa, boy . . . what the hell are you talking about?"

JJ crouched down in front of me and looked up into my eyes. "It makes sense," he said. "I've made it work . . . made the patterns fit."

"You *understand* it?" I glanced across at the box of jumbled shapes. "*That*?"

JJ nodded emphatically. "Yes!" he said. Then, "No! Oh, God, I don't know. That's why I need to check. And I need to do it tonight. Tomorrow may be too late."

"I still don't know what you're—"

The resident genius of Forest Plains placed a hand on my knee. "No time," he said. "No time to talk. It has to be *now*."

I studied his face for a few seconds, saw the look in his eyes: there was an urgent need there, sure . . . but there was something else, too. It was fear. Jimmy-James Bannister looked as scared as any man could be. "Okay, let's go do it."

He stood up and looked at Ed. "What about him?"

"He'll be fine. We expecting any trouble in there?"

"I don't think so."

"Okay. Let's go."

And we went.

The ship was silent and dark. JJ borrowed his old man's flashlight and the two of us crept up that platform and into the depths of the creatures' rocketship. The place was deserted, which was just as well. It didn't take too long before JJ found the second box – the one the creature had been using all the time – and he scooped it into his arms and rushed back out of the ship.

We were back in the house almost as soon as we had left. The whole thing had taken less than ten minutes.

I watched as JJ sat in front of the new box – now containing but a few lumps and dollops of that clay-stuff – wringing his hands and muttering to himself. I couldn't stand it any more and I grabbed a hold of JJ and shook him until I could hear his teeth clattering. "What the hell *is* it, JJ . . . why don't you tell me for God's sake."

He seemed to come to his senses then and he quietened down. Then he said, softly, "It's the aliens."

"What about them?" I said.

"Theyre . . ." He seemed to be trying hard to find the right words. "They're palindromic."

"They're *what*?"

"They run backwards . . . their time is different to ours."

"Their time is *different* to ours? Like *how* different?"

"It moves in a different direction . . . backwards instead of forwards – except to them it *is* forwards. But to us it's—" JJ waved his arms around like he was about to take off. "Well, it's bass-ackwards is what it is."

"What the hell is all the goddam noise about?" Ed said, turning over on the sofa. He reached for his pack of Luckies and shook one into the corner of his mouth, lit it with a match.

I didn't know what to say and looked across at Jimmy-James. "Maybe you'd better tell him – *us*!"

JJ sat down at the table next to the two boxes, one full and one almost empty. He smiled and said, calmly, "It's this way.

"I've broken the basics of their language. It wasn't really too difficult once I'd eliminated the obvious no-go areas." He pointed to the almost empty box. "This is the 'book' they're using now . . . the one that's recording everything that happens *here* . . . here on Earth."

"Looks like a mound of clay to me," Ed said, blowing smoke across the table and shuffling one edge of the box away from him.

"That's because you're you," JJ said impatiently, "because you're from Earth. To them, it's the equivalent of a diary . . . a ship's log, if you like."

Ed settled back on the sofa. "Okay. What's it say?"

"It starts at the very moment they opened the doors. It says they found a group of creatures standing outside watching them disembark . . . get out. These creatures, their record says, held instruments . . . they thought at first the things might be gifts."

I frowned. "When was that? I never held no instrument."

JJ leaned forward. "That's just it. You didn't. It didn't happen. At least it didn't happen yet." He lifted the box onto his knee and pointed at the shapes inside. "See, it's all arranged in a linear fashion, with each piece linking to others, building across the box in waves and doubling back to the other side. It's like layers of pasta furled over on itself. But see the way that it's arranged . . . you can pull pieces out of place and the gap stays. It's an intricate constructional form of basic communication. I say 'basic' because I've only been able to pick up the very basic fundamentals. There's much much more to it . . . but I don't have the time to work it out. Not now, anyway."

Ed tapped his cigarette ash onto the carpet and rubbed it in with his free hand. "*Why* don't you have the time? What's the panic?"

"The panic is that the record goes on to say how surprised they all were to find creatures—"

"Not half as surprised as we were to see them!" I said.

JJ carried on without comment. "It goes on to say how they came out and stood in front of us and nobody – none of *us* – moved or did anything. We just stood there. Then we all moved away and went to some structures. They walked around and looked at the outside of these structures and then went back into their ship. They were concerned that they had somehow created the situation by their ship's power."

"Huh?"

JJ waved for Ed to keep quite and continued.

"Listen. Then it says that, after some early investigations – they say that much more research has to be carried out – after these early investigations, we came on board the ship and borrowed their log."

"Yeah, well, we've got the log," I said. "For what good it's doing us."

"But none of that other stuff happened," JJ said. "This stuff in here . . ." He pointed at the individual pieces of clay . . . lifted one end of the carefully interwoven sheet of linked pieces and tiny constructions. "This only amounts to less than one single day. The creatures have been here almost three days now. There's no mention of all the other things that have happened. And bear this in mind . . . the stuff in here is what's *left*, as far as we're concerned."

I figured someone had to ask so it might as well be me. "How do you mean 'what's left'?"

"I mean, we've been watching the creature remove stuff from this box all the time he's been here, right?" I nodded and saw Ed Brewster do the same. "*And*," JJ continued, emphasising the word, "what we have here, *now* – and which represents what's left in the box after he's been removing the clay stuff for almost three days – is a record of when they first *arrived*. The creature has been removing the stuff from the *top* – I've watched him . . . so have you, Derby; you, too, Ed – and leaving the stuff at the bottom completely intact. And that stuff records them *arriving*."

Ed and I sat silently, watching Jimmy-James. I didn't have the first idea of what to say and I was sure Ed didn't either. JJ must have sensed it because he started speaking again without giving us much of a chance to comment.

"Derby, the creatures . . . have you noticed how they seem always to be turned away from you when you go up to speak to them?"

We'd already figured that the clear part of the mushroom tops more or less worked as the things' faces. And it was true, now that Jimmy-James mentioned it, that the things always had that part of themselves turned away whenever you went up to them.

"That's because at the moment you start trying to communicate with them, they've actually just finished trying to do the same with you."

"That sounds like horseshit," Ed said. "Not even Perry Mason could convict somebody on that evidence."

"And have you noticed how they keep facing you when they move away? That's because, in their time-frame, they're *approaching* you."

Some of it was beginning to make some kind of sense to me and JJ noticed that.

"And we've all commented on how their attitude to us is changing," he said. "You said they seemed to be getting slower . . . more cautious."

"That I did," I remembered.

"Well, they're getting more cautious because where they are now is they've just *arrived*. Where they were when we first saw them was in their third or fourth day around us. They were *used* to us then . . . they're not now."

"Okay, okay, I hear what you say, JJ," I said. "Maybe the creatures' time does move in reverse, if that's what you're saying. I don't understand it, but then I don't understand a lot of things. The thing that puzzles me is why you're getting so hot under the collar about this. Everything's going to go okay: we saw them 'arrive' – which you say is when they left – and nothing happened in the meantime. All we have to worry about is our future which is their past . . . and they've come through that okay haven't—"

I saw JJ's face screw up like he'd just sucked on a lemon. He reached over and pulled the full box across to the edge of the table, held up another of those interlaced jigsaw puzzles of multi-colored clay pieces. "This is the previous diary," he said, "the one before the one they started after they had arrived.

"You remember I said there was an entry in the current ship's log about the creatures being concerned that they had somehow created the situation they found when they arrived?" We both nodded. "Well, that situation is explained in a little more detail in the previous record." At this point, Jimmy-James sat back on his chair and seemed to draw in his breath.

"Okay: the log says that they were following the course taken by an earlier ship – one that had disappeared a long time ago – when they experienced some kind of terrible space storm the like of which had never previously been recorded. For a time, it was touch and go that they would survive, though survive they did. But when the storm subsided, they were nowhere that they recognised. After a few of their time periods – which, based on the limited information in the new book, I would put at quarter days . . . give or take an hour – there was a sudden blinding flash of light and a huge explosion. When they checked their instruments, they discovered that the ship was about to impact upon a planet which had apparently appeared out of nothingness."

Ed looked confused. "So this explosion went off *before* they hit the planet?"

JJ nodded.

"I don't get it," Ed said.

I said to let Jimmy-James finish.

"There hadn't been any planet there at all until then," JJ said. "Then, there it was. And that planet was Earth.

"They narrowly averted the collision," JJ went on, "and settled onto the planet's surface. After checking atmospheric conditions they prepared to go outside. The log finished with them wondering what they'll find there."

While JJ had been talking I'd been holding my breath without even realising it. I let it out with a huge sigh. "Are you sure?"

The owner of the best mind in town shook his head sadly.

"But you *think* you're right."

"I think I'm right, yes."

"And they found us, right?"

"Right, Ed," JJ said. "They found us." He waited.

I thought over everything I had heard and knew there was something there that should bother me . . . but I couldn't for the life of me figure out what it was. Then it hit me. "The blinding flash," I said. "If before that blinding flash there was nothing and after it there was the Earth . . . then, if the creatures' time *does* move backwards, and their version of their arrival is – or *will* be – our version of their departure, that means the aliens will destroy the planet when they leave."

JJ was nodding. "That's the way I figure it, too," he said.

I looked across at Ed and he looked across at me. "What are we going to do?" I asked JJ.

JJ shrugged. "We have to stop them leaving . . . in terms of our *own* time progression."

"But, in their terms, that would be to stop them *arriving* . . . and they're already here."

"Yes, that's true. In just the same way, if we do something to stop them – and I see only one course of action there – then, again in our time, they never actually 'arrive' . . . though, of course, they've arrived already as far as we're concerned. What we do, is prevent their departure in our terms."

Ed Brewster shook his head and pushed himself off the sofa onto the floor. "Jesus Christ, I'm getting a goddam headache here," he said. "Their arrival is our departure . . . their departure is our arrival . . . but if they don't do this, how could they do that . . . and as for *palindoodad* . . ." He stood up and rubbed his hands through his hair. "This all sounds like something off *Howdy Doody*. What does it all mean? How can we play about with time like that? How can *any*body play about with time like that?"

"I think it may have been the space storm," JJ said. "I think, maybe, their time normally progresses in exactly the same way as our own . . . although Albert Einstein said we shouldn't allow ourselves to be railroaded about time being a one-way linear progre—"

"Jesus, Jimmy-James!" Ed shouted, and JJ winced . . . glancing upwards towards his parents' bedroom while we all waited for sounds of people moving around to see what all the noise was about. "Jesus," Ed continued in a hoarse whisper, "I can't keep up with all of this stuff. Just keep it simple."

"Okay," JJ said. "I figure one of two things: either the aliens always move backwards in time or they don't.

"If we go for the first option, then we have to ask how they found their way into our universe."

"The space storm?" I suggested.

"I think so," said JJ. "If we go for the second option – that they *don't* normally travel backwards in time – then we have to ask what might have caused the change." He looked across at me again and gave a small smile.

I nodded. "The space storm."

"Kee-rect! So either way, the storm did the deed. But whatever the cause, the fact remains that they're here and we have to prevent whatever it was that caused the explosion."

We sat for a minute or so considering that. I didn't like the sound of what I'd heard but I liked the sound of the silence that followed even less. I looked at Ed. He didn't seem too happy either. "So how do we do that, JJ?" I said.

JJ shrugged. "We have to kill them . . . kill them *all*," he said. He pulled across the almost empty box that we all reckoned was the alien's current ship's log and lifted up the few lace-like constructions of interwoven clay pieces. "And we have to do it *tonight*."

I don't remember the actual rounding up of people that night. And I don't recall listening to JJ telling his story again and again. But tell it he did, and the people got rounded up. There was me, Sherriff Ben, Ed, Abel, Jerry and Jimmy-James Bannister himself. We walked silently out to the spaceship and weren't at all surprised to see faint wisps of steam coming out from the sides or that the platform was up for the first time since . . . well, the first time since three days ago. As the platform lowered itself slowly to the dusty ground of the vacant lot across from Bill's and Ma's poolroom, I heard JJ call out my name.

"Derby . . ."

I turned around and he held up his rifle, then nodded to the others standing there on Sycamore Street, all of them carrying the same kind of thing. "Instruments," he said.

By then it was too late. The bets were placed.

As soon as they appeared we started firing. We moved forward as one mass, vigilantes, firing and clearing, firing and clearing. The creatures never knew what hit them. They just folded up and fell to the ground, some inside the ship and others onto Sycamore Street. When they were down, Sherriff Ben went up to each one and put a couple of bullets into its head from his handgun.

We continued into the ship and finished the job.

There were sixteen of them. We combed the ship from top to bottom like men in a fever, a destructive killing frenzy, pulling out pieces of foam and throwing them out into the street . . . in much the same way as you might rip out the wires in the back of a radio to stop it from playing danceband music. God, but we were scared.

When the sun came up, we put the aliens back on the ship and doused the whole thing in gasoline. Then we put a match to it. It burned quietly, as we might have expected of any vehicle operated by such gentle creatures. It burned for two whole days and nights. When it had finished, we loaded the remains onto Vince Waldon's flatbed truck and took them out to Darien Lake. The barrier – or 'force field', as JJ called it – had gone. Things were more or less back to normal. For a time.

It turned out that JJ found more of those ship's logs that night, when the rest of us were tearing and destroying. Turned out that he sneaked them off the ship and kept them safe until he could get back for them. I didn't find that out right away.

He came round to my house about a week later.

"Derby, we have to talk," he said.

"What about?"

"The aliens."

"Oh, for cris'sakes, I—" I was going to tell him that I couldn't stand to talk about those creatures any more, couldn't stand to think about what we'd done to them. But his face looked so in need of conversation that I stopped short. "What about the aliens?" I said.

That was when Jimmy-James told me he'd taken the old diaries from inside the ship.

Walking along Sycamore, he said, "Have you ever thought about what we did?"

I groaned.

"No, not about us shooting the aliens . . . about how we changed their past?" Someone had left a soda bottle lying on the sidewalk and JJ kicked it gently into the gutter. The clatter it made somehow set off a dog barking and I tried to place the sound but couldn't. It did sound right, though, that mixture of a lonely dog barking and the night and talking about the aliens . . . like it all belonged together. "I mean," JJ went on, "we changed our future – which is okay: anyone can do that – but we actually changed things that, as far as they were concerned, had already happened. Did you think about that?"

"Nope." We walked in silence for a minute or so, then I said, "Did you?"

"A little – at first. Then, when I'd read the diaries, I thought about it a lot." He stopped and turned to me. "You know the big diary, the full box? The one that ended with details of the explosion?"

I didn't say anything but I knew what he was talking about.

"I went into more of the details about the missing ship . . . the one that had disappeared? The last message they received from this other ship was at these same co-ordinates."

"So?"

He shrugged. "The message said they'd been moving along when they suddenly noticed a planet that was not there before."

"Do I want to hear this?"

"I think the Earth is destined for destruction. The aliens were fulfilling some kind of cosmic plan."

"JJ, you're starting to lose me."

"Yeah, I'm starting to lose *me*," he said with a short laugh. But there was no humor there. "This other ship – the first one, the one that the diary talks about – I've calculated that it's about forty years in their past. Or in our future."

I grabbed a hold of his arm and spun him around. "You mean there's more of those things coming?"

JJ nodded. "In about forty years, give or take. And they're going to be going through this section of the universe and BOOM! . . ." He clapped his hands loudly. "'Hey, Captain,'" JJ said in an accent that sounded vaguely foreign, "'there's a planet over there!' And there's no kewpie doll for guessing the name of that planet."

"So, if they're moving backwards, too . . . then that means they'll destroy us." The dog barked again somewhere over to our right.

"Yep. But if the aliens we just killed were going to do the job, how could the others have done it, too?"

"Another planet?"

JJ shook his head. "The co-ordinates seemed quite specific . . . as far as I could make out. That's another problem right there."

"What's that?"

"The diaries are gone. They liquefied . . . turned into mulch."

"All of it?"

"Every bit. But it *was* Earth they were talking about. I'd bet my life on it . . . hell, I'd even bet yours."

That was when I fully realised just how much of a friend Jimmy-James Bannister truly was. He placed a greater value on my life than on his own.

"Which means, of course," JJ said, "that we were destined to stop the aliens the way we did."

"We were *meant* to do it?"

"Looks that way to me." He glanced at me and must have seen me relax a little. "That make you feel better?"

"A little."

"Me too."

"What is it? What is it that's causing the destruction?"

"Hey, if I knew *that* . . . Way I figure it, they're maybe warping across space somehow – kind of like matter transference. The magazines have been talking about that kind of thing for years: they call them black funnels or something.

"But maybe they're also warping across time progressions, too . . . without even realising they're doing it. Then, as soon as they appear into our dimension or plane, one that operates on a different time progression . . . it's like a chemical reaction and . . ."

I clapped my hands. "I know," I said. "BOOM!"

"Right."

"So what do we do?"

"Right now? Nothing. Right now, the balance has been restored. But the paradox will be repeated . . . around 2003, 2004." He smiled at me. "Give or take."

We went on walking and talking but that's about all I can remember of that night.

The next day, or maybe the one after, we told Ed Brewster. And we made ourselves a pact.

We couldn't bring ourselves to tell anyone about what had happened. Who would believe us? Where was the proof? A few boxes of slime? Forget it. And if we showed them the blackened stuff at the bottom of Darien Lake . . . well, it was just a heap of blackened stuff at the bottom of a lake.

But there was another reason we didn't want to tell anyone outside of Forest Plains about what we'd done. Just like nobody else in town wanted to tell anyone. We were ashamed.

So we made a pact. We'd keep our eyes peeled – keep watching the skies, as the newspaperman said in *The Thing* movie . . .

And when something happens, we'll know what to do.

What really gets to me – still, after all this time – is not just that there's a bunch of aliens somewhere out there, maybe heading on a disaster course with Earth . . . but that, back on their own planet or dimension there's another bunch of creatures listening to their messages . . . a bunch we killed on the streets of Forest Plains almost 40 years ago.

AUGUSTA PRIMA

Karin Tidbeck

Karin Tidbeck is a Swedish writer who has published short stories and poetry in Swedish since 2002, and in English since 2010. Her 2010 book debut, the short-story collection *Vem är Arvid Pekon?*, awarded her the coveted one-year working grant from the Swedish Authors' Fund. Her English-language collection *Jagannath* (2012) won the Crawford Award and was short-listed for the Tiptree Award. Her English publication history includes *Weird Tales*, *Shimmer* magazine, *Tor.com*, *Lightspeed*, *Strange Horizons*, *Unstuck Annual*, and the anthology *Odd?*. Her first novel, *Amatka*, was released by Sweden's largest publisher in 2012. "Augusta Prima" was her first published story in English, appearing in *Weird Tales* in 2011.

Augusta stood in the middle of the lawn with the croquet club in a two-handed grasp. She had been offered to open the game. Mnemosyne's prized croquet balls were carved from bone, with inlaid enamel and gold. The ball at Augusta's feet stared up at her with eyes of bright blue porcelain. An invitation to a croquet game in Mnemosyne's court was a wonderful thing. It was something to brag about. Those who went to Mnemosyne's games saw and were seen by the right people. Of course, they also risked utter humiliation and ridicule.

Augusta was sweating profusely. It trickled down between her breasts, eventually forming damp spots on the front of her shirt. She could feel a similar dampness spreading in the seat of her too-tight knee pants. More moisture ran down her temples, making tracks in the thick layers of powder. Her artful corkscrew curls were already wilting.

The other guests spread out across the lawn, waiting for her move. Everyone who meant something was here. Our Lady Mnemosyne sat under a lace umbrella on her usual podium. Her chamberlain Walpurgis lounged in the grass in his white surtout, watching Augusta with heavy-lidded eyes. At his side, the twin lovers Vergilia and Hermine shared a divan, embracing as usual. Today one of them was dressed in a crinoline adorned with leaves; the other wore a dress made of gray feathers. Their page, a changeling boy in garish makeup, stood behind them holding a tray of drinks.

Further away, Augusta's sister Azalea had grown tired of waiting. She had stripped naked next to a shrubbery, methodically plucking leaves off its branches. Everyone except Azalea were watching Augusta. The only sound was that of tearing leaves.

Augusta took a deep breath, raised her club and swung it with a grunt. The ball flew in a high arc, landing with a crunch in the face of the twins' page who dropped his tray and doubled over. The garden burst into cheers and applause. Mnemosyne smiled and nodded from her podium. Augusta had passed the test.

The game thus opened, the other guests threw themselves into play. In a series of magnificent hits, Walpurgis knocked out two pages who were carried off with crushed eyebrows, broken teeth and bleeding noses. The twins were in unusually bad shape, mostly hitting balls instead of pages. Augusta played very carefully, mostly focusing on not getting hit. There were a few breaks for cake, games and flogging a servant. Finally Hermine and Vergilia, one hand each on the club, hit Augusta's ball and sent it into the woods beyond the gardens. The hit was considered so stylish that Augusta was sent out of the game. She wandered in among the trees to find her ball.

Under one of the dog-rose bushes lay a human corpse: a man in a grey woolen suit. They sometimes wandered into the woods by mistake. This one had come unusually far. It was difficult to tell what had killed him. He had begun to putrefy; the swollen belly had burst his waistcoat open. A gold chain trailed from one of the pockets. Augusta bent forward, gingerly grasped the chain and pulled it. A shiny locket emerged on the end of the chain, engraved with flowers. Augusta swung the locket up in the air and let it land in her palm. The touch sent a little chill along her arm, and for a moment she felt faint. She wrapped the locket in a handkerchief, put it in a pocket, and returned to the croquet green to announce that there was a new and interesting corpse.

Augusta returned to her rooms, a little medal pinned to her chest as thanks for her find. No one had noticed her taking the metal thing for herself. She shooed out her page and sat down on the bed to examine the thing further.

It seemed to be made of gold, engraved on both sides with flowery strands. It was heavy and cold in her palm. The vertigo gradually subsided, but the chills remained like an icy stream going from her hand to her neck. The chain attached to the locket by a little knob on the side. Another, almost invisible button sat across from it. She pressed it, and the locket sprung open to reveal a white disc painted with small lines. Three thin rods were attached to the centre. One of them moved around the disc in twitching movements, making a ticking noise like a mouse's heart.

It was a machine. Augusta had seen things like it a few times, among the belongings of houses or humans who had been claimed by the gardens. They had always been broken, though. Mechanical things usually fell apart as soon as they came into the gardens' domain. It was a mystery how this thing could still be in one piece and working.

The chills had become an almost pleasant sensation. Augusta watched the rod chasing around the disc until she fell asleep.

She woke up in the same position as she'd fallen asleep in, on her side with the little machine in her hand. It was still now. Augusta frowned and called on her page. There were a handful of pages in the family, most of them nameless changelings raised in servitude. For various reasons there were only two of them that could carry a conversation, should one be so inclined. Augusta's page wasn't one of them.

"Fetch Azalea's page," she told him when he arrived.

Augusta watched the machine until there was a scratch at her door and Azalea's page stepped inside. He was a half-grown boy, with dark hair in oiled locks and eyes rimmed with kohl; a beautiful specimen that Azalea had insisted on taking into service despite his being too old to train properly. The boy stood in the middle of the room, having the audacity to stare directly at Augusta. She slapped him with the back of her hand. He shrunk back, turning his gaze to the floor. He walked over to the bed and started to remove his clothes.

"No, not now," Augusta said.

The boy froze halfway out of his surtout. Augusta tossed him the little locket.

"You will tell me what this is," she said.

"You don't know?" he said.

Augusta slapped him again.

"You will tell me what this is," she repeated.

He sniffled.

"It's a watch."

"And what does a watch do?"

"It measures time."

He pointed at the different parts of the watch, explaining their functions. The rods were called hands, and chased around the clockface in step with time. The clockface indicated where in time one was located. It made Augusta shudder violently. Time was an abhorrent thing, a human thing. It didn't belong here. It was that power which made flesh rot and dreams wither. The gardens were supposed to lie beyond the grasp of time, in constant twilight; the sun just under the horizon, the moon shining full over the trees. Augusta told the boy as much:

"Time doesn't pass here. Not like that, not for us."

The boy twisted the little bud on the side of the locket, and the longest hand started to move again.

"But look," he said. "The hands are moving now. Time is passing now."

"But does it know how time flows? Does it measure time, or does it just move forward and call that time?"

The changeling stared at her. "Time is time," he said.

Augusta cut his tongue out before she let him go. Azalea would be furious, but it was necessary.

She laid down on her bed again, but couldn't seem to fall asleep. How could the hands on the watch keep moving here? The sun didn't go up or down. Didn't that mean time stood still here? It was common knowledge. Whenever one woke up, it was the same day as the day before.

She sat down at her writing desk, jotting down a few things on paper. It made her head calm down a little. Then she opened a flask of poppy wine and drank herself back to sleep.

*

When Augusta woke up, her page was scratching at the door with a set of clothes in his arms and an invitation card between his teeth. It was an invitation to croquet. With a vague feeling that there was something she ought to remember, Augusta let the page dress and powder her.

She returned with a bump in the back of her head and a terrific headache. It had been a fantastic game. There had been gorging, Walpurgis had demonstrated a new dance, and the twins had – sensationally – struck each other senseless. Augusta had been behind everyone else in the game, eventually having her ball sent into the woods again, needing to go fetch it just like that time she'd found something under the dog-rose bush . . . under the dog-rose bush. She looked at her writing desk, where a little silk bundle sat on a piece of paper. She moved the bundle out of the way and read:

> *A minute is sixty seconds.*
> *An hour is sixty minutes.*
> *A day is twelve hours.*
> *A day and a night is twenty-four hours.*

Augusta opened the bundle and looked at the little locket. Some images appeared in her mind: her first croquet game. The corpse in the grey suit. The watch. The page who told her about time. A thirst to *know* how it worked. *What is time?* she wrote under the first note. *Is it here?*

Augusta took the watch and left her room. She wandered down to the orangery, which was lit from inside. Tendrils of steam rose from the roof. Inside, three enormous mounds lay on couches. The Aunts were as always immersed in their holy task to fatten. Three girls hovered around them, tiny in comparison. The girls were servants and successors, keeping the Aunts fed until they eventually perished, and then taking their places to begin the process anew. Augusta opened the watch, peeking at the clockface. The longest hand moved slowly, almost imperceptibly.

She walked from the orangery to the outskirts of the apple orchard, and from there to Porla's fen; then to the dog-rose shrubs in the woods outside Mnemosyne's court. Everywhere, the hands on the clockface moved; sometimes forward, sometimes backward. Sometimes they lifted from the clockface, hitting the glass protecting it, as if trying to escape.

Augusta woke up in Azalea's arms, under a canopy in Our Lady's arbour. The orgy they were visiting was still going on; there were low cries and the sound of breaking glass. Augusta couldn't remember what they had been doing, but she felt sore and bloated and her sister was snoring very loudly. She was still wearing her shirt. Something rustled in her left breast pocket; she dug it out. It was a note. A little map, seemingly drawn in her own hand. Below the map was written a single sentence: *The places float just like time.* She had been wandering around, drawing maps and measuring distances. At some point, Mnemosyne's garden had first been on the right-hand side from Augusta's rooms. The next time she had found herself walking straight ahead to get there. The places floated. Augusta turned the note over. On the other side were the words: *Why is there time here? Why does it flow differently in different places? And if the places float, what is the nature of the woods?*

She returned to her rooms in a state of hangover. Papers were strewn everywhere, it seemed: on and under the bed, on the dresser, in droves on the writing-desk. Some of the notes were covered in dust. She couldn't remember writing some of them. But every word was in her own handwriting.

There was a stranger in Mnemosyne's court, towering over the other guests. She was dressed in simple robes, hooded and veiled, golden yellow eyes showing through a thin slit. They shone down on Walpurgis, who made a feeble attempt to offer her a croquet club. Everyone else gave the stranger a wide berth.

"It is a djinneya. She is visiting Mnemosyne to trade information," the twins mumbled to Augusta.

"We wonder what information that is," Vergilia added.

"Those creatures know everything," Hermine said.

The djinneya sat by Mnemosyne's side during the whole game, seemingly deep in conversation with her hostess. Neither the twin's spectacular knock-out of Walpurgis nor Azalea's attempt to throttle one of the pages caught her attention. Having been knocked out with a ball over her left knee, Augusta retreated to a couch where she wrote an invitation.

Augusta woke up by her writing-desk by a knock at her door. A cloaked shape entered without asking permission. The djinneya seemed even taller indoors.

"Come in," said Augusta.

The djinneya nodded, unfastening the veil. Her skin was the colour of fresh bruises. She grinned with a wide mouth, showing deep blue gums and long teeth filed into points.

"I thank you for your invitation, Augusta Prima." She bent down over Augusta's bed, fluffing the pillows, and sat down. A scent of sweat and spice spread in the room. "You wanted to converse."

Augusta straightened, looking at the papers and notes on her desk. She remembered what it was she wanted to ask.

"You and your sort, you travel everywhere. Even beyond the woods. You know things."

The djinneya flashed her toothy smile. "That we do."

"I would like to know the nature of time," Augusta said. "I want to know why time can't be measured properly here, and why everything moves around."

The djinneya laughed. "Your kind doesn't want to know about those things. You can't bear it."

"But I do. I want to know."

The djinneya raised her thin eyebrows. "Normally, you are tedious creatures," she said. "You only want trivial things. Is that person dead yet? Does this person still love that person? What did they wear at yesterday's party? I know things that could destroy worlds, and all you wish to know is if Karhu from Jumala is still unmarried." She scratched her chin. "I believe this is the first time one of your sort has asked me a good question. It's an expensive one, but I shall give you the answer. If you really are sure."

"I have to know," said Augusta. "What is the nature of the world?"

The djinneya smiled with both rows of teeth. "Which one?"

Augusta woke up by the writing desk. The hangover throbbed behind her temples. She had fallen asleep with her head on an enormous stack of papers. She peered at it, leafing through the ones at the top. *There are eight worlds,* the first one said. *They lie side by side, in degrees of perfection. This world is the most perfect one.* Below these lines, written in a different ink, was: *There is one single world, divided into three levels which are partitioned off from each other by greased membranes.* Then in red ink: *There are two worlds and they overlap. The first is the land of Day, which belongs to the humans. The second is the land of Twilight, which belongs to the free folk, and of which the woods is a little backwater part. Both lands must obey Time, but the Twilight is ruled by the Heart, whereas the Day is ruled by Thought.* At the bottom of the page, large block letters proclaimed: *ALL OF THIS IS TRUE.*

It dawned on Augusta that she remembered very clearly. The endless parties, in detail. The finding of the corpse, the short periods of clarity, the notes. The djinneya bending down to whisper in her ear.

A sharp yellow light stung Augusta's eyes. She was sitting at her writing desk in a very small room with wooden walls. A narrow bed with tattered sheets filled the rest of the space. The writing desk stood beneath a window. On the other side of the glass, the woods bathed in light.

There was a door next to the bed. Augusta opened it, finding herself in a narrow hallway with another door at the end. A full-length mirror hung on the opposite wall. It showed a woman dressed in what had once been a blue surtout and knee pants. The fabrics were heavily stained with dirt and greenish mold and in some places worn through. Concentric rings of sweat radiated from the armpits. The shirt front was stiff with red and brown stains. Augusta touched her face. White powder lay in cracked layers along her nose and cheeks. Deep lines ran between her nose and mouth; more lines spread from the corners of her eyes. A golden chain hung from her breast pocket. She pulled on it, swinging the locket into her hand. It was ticking in a steady rhythm.

Augusta opened the other door and stepped out onto a landing. An unbearably bright light flooded over her. She backed into the hallway again, slamming the door.

"I told you. Your kind can't bear that question."

The djinneya stood behind her in the hallway, shoulders and head hunched under the low ceiling.

"What did you do?" Augusta said.

"What did *I* do? No. What did *you* do, Augusta Prima?" She patted Augusta's shoulder. "It started even before you invited me, Augusta Prima. You tried to measure time in a land that doesn't *want* time. You tried to map a floating country."

The djinneya smiled. "The woods spit you out, Augusta. Now you're in the land that measures time and draws maps."

Augusta gripped the hand on her shoulder. "I want to go home. You have to take me home again."

"So soon? Well. All you have to do is forget what you have learned." The djinneya squeezed past Augusta and stepped out onto the porch, where she stretched to her full height with a sigh.

"Goodbye, Augusta," she said over her shoulder. "And do try to hurry if you want to make it back. You're not getting any younger."

LIFE TRAP

Barrington J. Bayley

Barrington J. Bayley was born in Birmingham, England, and educated in Newport, Shropshire. He worked a number of jobs before joining the Royal Air Force in 1955. In the 1960s, Bayley became friends with Michael Moorcock, who described himself as "the dumb one in the partnership," and joined science fiction's New Wave movement. His short stories appeared regularly in Moorcock's *New Worlds* magazine and then later in various *New Worlds* paperback anthologies. His first book, *The Star Virus*, was followed by more than a dozen other novels; his downbeat, gloomy approach to novel writing has been cited as influential on the likes of M. John Harrison, Bruce Sterling, and Iain M. Banks. His story "Life Trap" was first published in the collection *The Seed of Evil* in 1979.

Although we of the Temple of Mysteries have devoted our energies to the pursuit of life's secrets, it has never been guaranteed that what we may learn will be in any way pleasant, or conducive to our peace of mind. What becomes known cannot be made unknown, until death intervenes, and all seekers after hidden knowledge run the risk of finding that ignorance was after all the happier state.

The experiment was conducted at midnight, this being the hour when the subject, by his own account, customarily knows greatest clarity of mind. This subject was in fact my good friend Marcus, Aspirant of the Third Grade of the Arcanum – the highest rank our hierarchy affords, entitling him, when the occasion arises, to wear the mantle of High Priest. The mixture had been prepared earlier in the day, and was a combination of ether, poppy, a certain mushroom, and other consciousness-altering drugs, all substances which, when taken singly or in various simpler compounds, produced effects already well known to us from our years of investigative labour. Never before, however, had we designed a concoction for so ambitious or so hazardous a purpose: to take the mind, while still fully conscious, beyond the point of death, and after an interval to return it to the living world.

Vainly I had begged Marcus to be less precipitous; to test the compound beforehand, possibly using partial samples on a candidate acolyte. But Marcus, adamant that nothing less than the full dose would be effective, consented only to test it on a dog belonging to our drug expert, Lucius the apothecary. When forced to inhale the fumes the animal became rigid and appeared to be dead for the space of about an hour. After this it quickly recovered, but for a further hour it showed some nervousness, barking and cringing when anyone came near. Eventually this, too, wore off, and Marcus announced that the symptoms were as would be expected.

On the appointed night Marcus and I were alone in the Temple, the others having left at Marcus's own request. In the changing room I helped him into a robe of crisp clean linen on which the emblem of the Temple was sewn. Then, for a period, we sat together, while the water-clock dripped away the moments. We said little, for all aspects of the enterprise had already been thoroughly discussed.

The pan of the clock began to tremble. "Soon we may know the truth," Marcus said with a smile.

"Or I shall lose a friend," I replied.

Just then the balance tipped and the water-clock chimed the hour of midnight. We both rose.

I accompanied Marcus to the inner sanctum. As we went down the short corridor, flanked by two pillars, which leads to the door of the adytum, the possibility that I might be seeing him alive for the last time suddenly weighed heavily on me, but I tried to show no emotion. I opened the heavy oak door, whose edges are trimmed with lambswool so as to shut out extraneous noises, and we entered.

I looked around to ensure that everything was in place and the surroundings harmonious. For us, the inner sanctum serves the same function in our activities as the preliminary ritual of donning ceremonial garb: to help calm the mind and divert it from trivial thought. Hence everything is arranged to invoke the feeling of departure from the mundane. The room is oval in shape and painted in restful hues. On the walls are mandalas and one or two specially selected paintings. Earlier I had placed a vase of peonies on the small table of polished walnut.

The nostrum had already been left in a crucible over the brazier. While Marcus reclined himself on the couch I moved the brazier closer, so he would gain the direct benefit of the vapours, and lit the oil-soaked charcoal with a taper. Quickly the brazier began to blaze and the nostrum to bubble.

With no further glance at Marcus, I left.

The Temple of Mysteries subscribes to none of the traditional doctrines, since all of these are in varying degrees erroneous or at best blur the distinction between what is truly known and what is merely deduced or speculated upon. Our approach, once we have formulated an area of ignorance, is to try to gain the truth first-hand.

On the subject of what follows death, there are many preferred answers. The most pragmatic, of course, is that death is simply extinction. But most schools of thought claim some kind of survival, either in a different condition – in a spiritual realm or else by way of rebirth into another body – or actually in the same condition. The latter version, the bleakest of theories of this kind, represents time as a circle and says that following death we are born again into the same life as before, to repeat everything that has happened. Then again there is the doctrine that death means the end of individual consciousness, but that the mind is absorbed into a universal consciousness.

While sitting by myself in the changing room I reviewed these ideas as a means of taking my mind off Marcus. Close to an hour had passed, for the pan of the water-clock was again almost full, when I heard a hoarse shout from the inner sanctum, followed by the thud of falling furniture.

In seconds I had gained the corridor. As I did so the oak door flew open and Marcus staggered forth, his face grey. I rushed to assist him; he all but collapsed against me. His eyes, I noticed, were stricken and not glazed, as though he had seen something that horrified him.

Through the door, I saw that both the couch and the walnut table had been overturned. The brazier still glowed; but only a black stain on the crucible recorded the presence of the nostrum, whose fragrance yet drifted on the air.

I helped Marcus to the changing room and sat him down. He begged for wine. Though apprehensive of what its effect might be on top of so many drugs, I took a flask from the cupboard, uncorked it and poured him a goblet. He gulped it greedily, at which a little colour came to his cheeks.

"I shall be all right," he said in answer to my solicitations. "Just give me a minute or so to recover."

I stood by while he slumped in the chair, breathing heavily. At length I could forbear no longer. What, I enquired, had been the outcome of the experiment? Had it been successful? He groaned, and in sombre tones told me that it had; indeed (his voice fell to a mutter) the whole secret of death had been revealed to him. "Do not ask me to reveal this secret," he said. "Better not to know."

Astonished, I reminded him of the rule of our order forbidding any member to withhold from his brothers anything he has learned as a result of his work in the Temple, and again I eagerly pressed him to relate his new knowledge. He nodded resignedly and asked for more wine. Then, uttering a deep sigh, he related what is essentially the following.

Death (he said) is reversal. Reversal of consciousness, and reversal of time.

What do I mean by this? I will take consciousness first, for that is the first thing to be reversed. As we are now, our consciousness is within our bodies. I perceive you through my eyes, and within my brain I derive, through my senses, a picture of the outside world. Of myself I have no direct perception. I know myself only indirectly, through my relations with others, or through beholding myself in a mirror.

After death all this changes. Consciousness remains; but it is consciousness external to one's body. It becomes an objective consciousness, similar to experiences of ecstasy we have had accounts of, where one sees oneself from outside. One watches while one's body is laid out. One is present when it is placed on a bier and, accompanied by one's friends and relatives, carried to the grave.

Then one seems to be present in the grave, watching the cast-off body decay for several months. From this there is no escape, for one's consciousness is always where one's body is. This, you might think, is a harrowing experience. But wait.

The reason why one becomes conscious of one's dead body is that consciousness has momentum and, for a spell, coasts forward through time. But after a while the second reversal takes place. *Time reverses.*

(Emptying his goblet, Marcus reached for the flask, ignoring my anxious glance in that direction.) Time reverses. Do you understand me? Time runs backwards. Death truly is the end of life, but only in the sense that a road ends in a particular place. After that one turns round and retraces one's steps. One finds oneself watching as one's corpse slowly mends, is taken up from the ground, is carried home, and comes to life. So one's life resumes, from death to birth. Reversed time. Reversed consciousness.

Eventually birth must come again. The shock of this is like the shock of death, and indeed it is, for this reversed life, the same as death. And again one's consciousness coasts past it, but made internal now, living as a shrinking foetus until time again reverses itself and the foetus expands again, and one is born, a new babe, seeing the world through the senses as before.

This, then, Clinias, is the manner of our lives. The soul oscillates eternally between the poles of birth and death, though we know it not, and not one whit of what has happened can be changed. Therein, in our ignorance, lies our happiness for the present. But wait. You will not be happy. Wait until you stand outside yourself and must see yourself . . .

Marcus's voice trailed off. "So the doctrine of an eternally repeating life comes closest to the truth," I ventured.

"Yes. We have lived this life many, many times before."

"But why so gloomy, Marcus? It is immortality after a fashion."

Marcus looked up at me with a startled look on his face. "Have you not understood, Clinias? Do you not see? This is the worst of all possibilities! Each of us is doomed to see himself as he appears to the external world, and in that stance to live again through every detail of his existence! Every unworthy act, every self-deception, every last piece of shame we hide even from ourselves – all is presented to our gaze, and for a lifetime! How can one endure it? There is no one who lives with such dignity that this could be bearable!"

Slowly the horror of Marcus's revelation began to dawn on me. Unsteadily he rose to his feet and placed his hand on my shoulder. For long moments the silence of the Temple seemed to descend on us, while I pondered on what I had heard and stood there with my friend.

"That nothing can be changed is the worst aspect of it," Marcus said wearily. "How one longs and aches to be able to change what one sees!"

"We are in a trap," I observed.

He nodded. "Normally the traumas of birth and death wipe memory clean. For our temerity the gods have allowed me to glimpse the truth, and to remember it. That is our reward, and our punishment. But I can speak no more tonight. Let us go home. We have done enough."

Suddenly Marcus was violently sick. I cleaned him up, conducted him to his house, and saw to it that he was put to bed, leaving only after he had fallen soundly asleep.

Although the secret of death has been imparted to the full membership of the Temple, not all have understood its import. Several members, driven by curiosity, have repeated Marcus's experiment, with results that more or less confirm his findings, but to most it is interesting merely; they do not grasp its terror. To live a life which, because lacking external awareness of itself, is contemptible and mean, and then to be given that awareness which alone could have improved it – and be condemned at the same time to do no more than watch the wretched and loathsome spectacle! The gods do indeed chuckle when they look down on the human condition.

A change of outlook has been forced on we senior members of the Arcanum who do understand the meaning of Marcus's discovery. Suicide, which once seemed an honourable escape from undignified circumstance, is now realised to be no escape at all. And yet from this trap of life there should be, if the world is just, some escape.

Marcus has sickened, but fears to die. We all of us fear to die, knowing what awaits us. Men, who take refuge in never seeing themselves as they really are, invariably will shun such a vision.

Our work now is in how to end the eternal oscillation, whether to gain oblivion or a new life does not matter. But how may it be done? On that we have not a single idea. The gods may know. The gods, whom we have spurned as confusers and defilers of the minds of men, perhaps in the end we must turn to the gods.

LOST CONTINENT

Greg Egan

Greg Egan is an Australian science fiction writer and a computer programmer. Currently he is the author of ten novels and many short stories, some published in multiple short-story collections. He has been active in immigration detention reform and this story illustrates the hardships and inhumane treatment of this policy as a time traveler seeks refuge from war in his own time by traveling to the future. This story was first published in *The Starry Rift*, edited by Jonathan Strahan in 2008.

1.

Ali's uncle took hold of his right arm and offered it to the stranger, who gripped it firmly by the wrist.

"From this moment on, you must obey this man," his uncle instructed him. "Obey him as you would obey your father. Your life depends on it."

"Yes, uncle." Ali kept his eyes respectfully lowered.

"Come with me, boy," said the stranger, heading for the door.

"Yes, haji," Ali mumbled, following meekly. He could hear his mother still sobbing quietly in the next room, and he had to fight to hold back his own tears. He had said good-bye to his mother and his uncle, but he'd had no chance for any parting words with his cousins. It was halfway between midnight and dawn, and if anyone else in the household was awake they were huddled beneath their blankets, straining to hear what was going on but not daring to show their faces.

The stranger strode out into the cold night, hand still around Ali's wrist like an iron shackle. He led Ali to the Land Cruiser that sat in the icy mud outside his uncle's house, its frosted surfaces glinting in the starlight, an apparition from a nightmare. Just the smell of it made Ali rigid with fear; it was the smell that had presaged his father's death, his brother's disappearance. Experience had taught him that such a machine could only bring tragedy, but his uncle had entrusted him to its driver. He forced himself to approach without resisting.

The stranger finally released his grip on Ali and opened a door at the rear of the vehicle. "Get in and cover yourself with the blanket. Don't move, and don't make a sound, whatever happens. Don't ask me any questions, and don't ask me to stop. Do you need to take a piss?"

"No, haji," Ali replied, his face burning with shame. Did the man think he was a child?

"All right, get in there."

As Ali complied, the man spoke in a grimly humorous tone. "You think you show me respect by calling me 'haji'? Every old man in your village is 'haji'! I haven't just been to Mecca. I've been there in the time of the Prophet, peace be upon him." Ali covered his face with the ragged blanket, which was imbued with the concentrated stench of the machine. He pictured the stranger standing in the darkness for a moment, musing arrogantly about his unnatural pilgrimage. The man wore enough gold to buy Ali's father's farm ten times over. Now his uncle had sold that farm, and his mother's jewelry – the hard-won wealth of generations – and handed all the money to this boastful man, who claimed he could spirit Ali away to a place and a time where he'd be safe.

The Land Cruiser's engine shuddered into life. Ali felt the vehicle moving backward at high speed, an alarming sensation. Then it stopped and moved forward, squealing as it changed direction; he could picture the tracks in the mud.

It was his first time ever in one of these machines. A few of his friends had taken rides with the Scholars, sitting in the back in the kind with the uncovered tray. They'd fired rifles into the air and shouted wildly before tumbling out, covered with dust, alive with excitement for the next ten days. Those friends had all been Sunni, of course. For Shi'a, rides with the Scholars had a different kind of ending.

Khurosan had been ravaged by war for as long as Ali could remember. For decades, tyrants of unimaginable cruelty from far in the future had given their weapons to factions throughout the country, who'd used them in their squabbles over land and power. Sometimes the warlords had sent recruiting parties into the valley to take young men to use as soldiers, but in the early days the villagers had banded together to hide their sons, or to bribe the recruiters to move on. Sunni or Shi'a, it made no difference; neighbor had worked with neighbor to outsmart the bandits who called themselves soldiers, and keep the village intact.

Then four years ago, the Scholars had come, and everything had changed.

Whether the Scholars were from the past or the future was unclear, but they certainly had weapons and vehicles from the future. They had ridden triumphantly across Khurosan in their Land Cruisers, killing some warlords, bribing others, conquering the bloody patchwork of squalid fiefdoms one by one. Many people had cheered them on, because they had promised to bring unity and piety to the land. The warlords and their rabble armies had kidnapped and raped women and boys at will; the Scholars had hung the rapists from the gates of the cities. The warlords had set up checkpoints on every road, to extort money from travelers; the Scholars had opened the roads again for trade and pilgrimage in safety.

The Scholars' conquest of the land remained incomplete, though, and a savage battle was still being waged in the north. When the Scholars had come to Ali's village looking for soldiers themselves, they'd brought a new strategy to the recruitment drive: they would only take Shi'a for the front line, to face the bullets of the unsubdued warlords. Shi'a, the Scholars declared, were not true Muslims, and this was the only way they could redeem themselves: laying down their lives for their more pious and deserving Sunni countrymen.

This deceit, this flattery and cruelty, had cleaved the village in two. Many friends remained loyal across the divide, but the old trust, the old unity was gone. Two months before, one of Ali's neighbors had betrayed his older brother's hiding place to the Scholars. They had come to the farm in the early hours of the morning, a dozen of them in two Land Cruisers, and dragged Hassan away. Ali had watched helplessly from his own hiding place, forbidden by his father to try to intervene. And what could their rifles have done against the Scholars' weapons, which sprayed bullets too fast and numerous to count?

The next morning, Ali's father had gone to the Scholars' post in the village, to try to pay a bribe to get Hassan back. Ali had waited, watching the farm from the hillside above. When a single Land Cruiser had returned, his heart had swelled with hope. Even when the Scholars had thrown a limp figure from the vehicle, he'd thought it might be Hassan, unconscious from a beating but still alive, ready to be nursed back to health.

It was not Hassan. It was his father. They had slit his throat and left a coin in his mouth.

Ali had buried his father and walked half a day to the next village, where his mother had been staying with his uncle. His uncle had arranged the sale of the farm to a wealthy neighbor, then sought out a *mosarfar-e-waqt* to take Ali to safety.

Ali had protested, but it had all been decided, and his wishes had counted for nothing. His mother would live under the protection of her brother, while Ali built a life for himself in the future. Perhaps Hassan would escape from the Scholars, God willing, but that was out of their hands. What mattered, his mother insisted, was getting her youngest son out of the Scholars' reach.

In the back of the Land Cruiser, Ali's mind was in turmoil. He didn't want to flee this way, but he had no doubt that his life would be in danger if he remained. He wanted his brother back and his father avenged, he wanted to see the Scholars destroyed, but their only remaining enemies with any real power were murderous criminals who hated his own people as much as the Scholars themselves did. There was no righteous army to join, with clean hands and pure hearts.

The Land Cruiser slowed then came to a halt, the engine still idling. The *mosarfar-e-waqt* called out a greeting, then began exchanging friendly words with someone, presumably a Scholar guarding the road.

Ali's blood turned to ice; what if this stranger simply handed him over? How much loyalty could mere money buy? His uncle had made inquiries of people with connections up and down the valley, and had satisfied himself about the man's reputation, but however much the *mosarfar-e-waqt* valued his good name and the profits it brought, there'd always be some other kind of deal to be made, some profit to be found in betrayal.

Both men laughed, then bid each other farewell. The Land Cruiser accelerated.

For what seemed like hours, Ali lay still and listened to the purring of the engine, trying to judge how far they'd come. He had never been out of the valley in his life, and he had only the sketchiest notion of what lay beyond. As dawn approached, his curiosity overwhelmed him, and he moved quietly to shift the blanket just enough to let him catch a glimpse through the rear window. There was a mountain peak visible to the left, topped with snow, crisp in the predawn light. He wasn't sure if this was a mountain he knew, viewed from an unfamiliar angle, or one he'd never seen before.

Not long afterward they stopped to pray. They made their ablutions in a small, icy stream. They prayed side by side, Sunni and Shi'a, and Ali's fear and suspicion retreated a little. However arrogant this man was, at least he didn't share the Scholars' contempt for Ali's people.

After praying, they ate in silence. The *mosarfar-e-waqt* had brought bread, dried fruit and salted meat. As Ali looked around, it was clear that they'd long ago left any kind of man-made track behind. They were following a mountain pass, on higher ground than the valley but still far below the snow line.

They traveled through the mountains for three days, finally emerging onto a wind-blasted, dusty plain. Ali had grown stiff from lying curled up for so long, and the second time they stopped on the plain he made the most of the chance to stretch his legs, wandering away from the Land Cruiser for a minute or two.

When he returned, the *mosarfar-e-waqt* said, "What are you looking for?"

"Nothing, haji."

"Are you looking for a landmark, so you can find this place again?"

Ali was baffled. "No, haji."

The man stepped closer, then struck him across the face, hard enough to make him stagger. "If you tell anyone about the way you came, you'll hear some more bad news about your family. Do you understand me?"

"Yes, haji."

The man strode back to the Land Cruiser. Ali followed him, shaking. He'd had no intention of betraying any detail of their route, any secret of the trade, to anyone, but now his uncle had been named as hostage against any indiscretion, real or imagined.

Late in the afternoon, Ali heard a sudden change in the sound of the wind, a high-pitched keening that made his teeth ache. Unable to stop himself, he lifted his head from beneath the blanket.

Ahead of them was a small dust storm, dancing across the ground. It was moving away from them, weaving back and forth as it retreated, like a living thing trying to escape them. The Land Cruiser was gaining on it. The heart of the storm was dark, thick with sand, knotted with wind. Ali's chest tightened. This was it: the *pol-e-waqt*, the bridge between times. Everyone in his village had heard of such things, but nobody could agree what they were: the work of men, the work of djinn, the work of God. Whatever their origin, some men had learned their secrets. No *mosarfar-e-waqt* had ever truly tamed them, but nobody else could find these bridges or navigate their strange depths.

They drew closer. The dust rained onto the windows of the Land Cruiser, as fine as any sand Ali had seen, yet as loud as the hailstones that fell sometimes on the roof of his house. Ali forgot all about his instructions; as they vanished into the darkness, he threw off the blanket and started praying aloud.

The *mosarfar-e-waqt* ignored him, muttering to himself and consulting the strange, luminous maps and writing that changed and flowed in front of him through some magic of machinery. The Land Cruiser plowed ahead, buffeted by dust and wind but palpably advancing. Within a few minutes, it was clear to Ali that they'd traveled much further than the storm's full width as revealed from the outside. They had left his time and his country behind, and were deep inside the bridge.

The lights of the Land Cruiser revealed nothing but a hand's-breadth of flying dust ahead of them. Ali peered surreptitiously at the glowing map in the front, but it was a maze of branching and reconnecting paths that made no sense to him. The *mosarfar-e-waqt* kept running a fingertip over one path, then cursing and shifting to another, as if he'd discovered some obstacle or danger ahead. Ali's uncle had reassured him that at least they wouldn't run into the Scholars in this place, as they had come to Khurosan through another, more distant bridge. The entrance to that one was watched over night and day by a convoy of vehicles that chased it endlessly across the desert, like the bodyguards of some staggering, drunken king.

A hint of sunlight appeared in the distance, then grew slowly brighter. After a few minutes, though, the *mosarfar-e-waqt* cursed and steered away from it. Ali was dismayed. This man had been unable to tell his uncle where or when Ali would end up, merely promising him safety from the Scholars. Some people in the village – the kind with a friend of a friend who'd fled into the future – spoke of a whole vast continent where peace and prosperity reigned from shore to shore. The rulers had no weapons or armies of their own, but were chosen by the people for the wisdom, justice and mercy they displayed. It sounded like paradise on Earth, but Ali would believe in such a place when he saw it with his own eyes.

Another false dawn, then another. The body of the Land Cruiser began to moan and shudder. The *mosarfar-e-waqt* cut the engine, but the vehicle kept moving, driven by the wind, or the ground itself. Or maybe both, but not in the same direction: Ali felt the wheels slipping over the treacherous river of sand. Suddenly there was a sharp pain deep inside his ears, then a sound like the scream of a giant bird, and the door beside him was gone. He snatched at the back of the seat in front of him, but his hands closed over nothing but the flimsy blanket as the wind dragged him out into the darkness.

Ali bellowed until his lungs were empty. But the painful landing he was braced for never came: the blanket had snagged on something in the vehicle, and the force of the wind was holding him above the sand. He tried to pull himself back toward the Land Cruiser, hand over hand, but then he felt a tear run through the blanket. Once more he steeled himself for a fall, but then the tearing stopped with a narrow ribbon of cloth still holding him.

Ali prayed. "Merciful God, if you take me now please bring Hassan back safely to his home." For a year or two his uncle could care for his mother, but he was old, and he had too many mouths to feed. With no children of her own, her life would be unbearable.

A hand stretched out to him through the blinding dust. Ali reached out and took it, grateful now for the man's iron grip. When the mosarfar-e-waqt had dragged him back into the Land Cruiser, Ali crouched at the stranger's feet, his teeth chattering. "Thank you, haji. I am your servant, haji." The *mosarfar-e-waqt* climbed back into the front without a word.

Time passed, but Ali's thoughts were frozen. Some part of him had been prepared to die, but the rest of him was still catching up.

Sunlight appeared from nowhere: the full blaze of noon, not some distant promise. "This will suffice," the *mosarfar-e-waqt* announced wearily.

Ali shielded his eyes from the glare, then when he uncovered them the world was spinning. Blue sky and sand, changing places.

The bruising thud he'd been expecting long before finally came, the ground slapping him hard from cheek to ankle. He lay still, trying to judge how badly he was hurt. The patch of sand in front of his face was red. Not from blood: the sand itself was red as ocher.

There was a sound like a rapid exhalation, then he felt heat on his skin. He raised himself up on his elbows. The Land Cruiser was ten paces away, upside down, and on fire. Ali staggered to his feet and approached it, searching for the man who'd saved his life. Behind the wrecked vehicle, a storm like the one that the mouth of the bridge had made in his own land was weaving drunkenly back and forth, dancing like some demented hooligan pleased with the havoc it had wreaked.

He caught a glimpse of an arm behind the flames. He rushed toward the man, but the heat drove him back.

"Please God," he moaned, "give me courage."

As he tried again to breach the flames, the storm lurched forward to greet him. Ali stood his ground, but the Land Cruiser spun around on its roof, swiping his shoulder and knocking him down. He climbed to his feet and tried to circle around to the missing door, but as he did the wind rose up, fanning the flames.

The wall of heat was impenetrable now, and the storm was playing with the Land Cruiser like a child with a broken top. Ali backed away, glancing around at the impossible red landscape, wondering if there might be anyone in earshot with the power to undo this calamity. He shouted for help, his eyes still glued to the burning wreck in the hope that a miracle might yet deliver the unconscious driver from the flames.

The storm moved forward again, coming straight for the Land Cruiser. Ali turned and retreated; when he looked over his shoulder the vehicle was gone and the darkness was still advancing.

He ran, stumbling on the uneven ground. When his legs finally failed him and he collapsed onto the sand, the bridge was nowhere in sight. He was alone in a red desert. The air was still now, and very hot.

After a while he rose to his feet, searching for a patch of shade where he could rest and wait for the cool of the evening. Apart from the red sand there were pebbles and some larger, cracked rocks, but there was no relief from the flatness: not so much as a boulder he could take shelter beside. In one direction there were some low, parched bushes, their trunks no thicker than his fingers, their branches no higher than his knees. He might as well have tried to hide from the sun beneath his own thin beard. He scanned the horizon, but it offered no welcoming destination.

There was no water for washing, but Ali cleaned himself as best he could and prayed. Then he sat cross-legged on the ground, covered his face with his shawl, and lapsed into a sickly sleep.

He woke in the evening and started to walk. Some of the constellations were familiar, but they crossed the sky far closer to the horizon than they should have. Others were completely new to him. There was no moon, and though the terrain was flat he soon found that he lost his footing if he tried to move too quickly in the dark.

When morning came, it brought no perceptible change in his surroundings. Red sand and a few skeletal plants were all that this land seemed to hold.

He slept through most of the day again, stirring only to pray. Increasingly, his sleep was broken by a throbbing pain behind his eyes. The night had been chilly, but he'd never experienced such heat before. He was unsure how much longer he could survive without water. He began to wonder if it would have been better if he'd been taken by the wind inside the bridge, or perished in the burning Land Cruiser.

After sunset, he staggered to his feet and continued his hopeful but unguided trek. He had a fever now, and his aching joints begged him for more rest, but if he resigned himself to sleep he doubted he'd wake again.

When his feet touched the road, he thought he'd lost his mind. Who would take the trouble to build such a path through a desolate place like this? He stopped and crouched down to examine it. It was gritty with a sparse layer of wind-blown sand; beneath that was a black substance that felt less hard than stone, but resilient, almost springy.

A road like this must lead to a great city. He followed it.

An hour or two before dawn, bright headlights appeared in the distance. Ali fought down his instinctive fear; in the future such vehicles should be commonplace, not the preserve of bandits and murderers. He stood by the roadside awaiting its arrival.

The Land Cruiser was like none he'd seen before, white with blue markings. There was writing on it, in the same European script as he'd seen on many machine parts and weapons that had made their way into the bazaars, but no words he recognized, let alone understood. One passenger was riding beside the driver; he climbed out, approached Ali, and greeted him in an incomprehensible tongue.

Ali shrugged apologetically. "*Salaam aleikom,*" he ventured. "*Bebakhshid agha, mosarfar hastam. Ba tawarz' az shoma moharfazat khahesh mikonam.*"

The man addressed Ali briefly in his own tongue again, though it was clear now that he did not expect to be understood any more than Ali did. He called out to his companion, gestured to Ali to stay put, then went back to the Land Cruiser. His companion handed him two small machines; Ali tensed, but they didn't look like any weapons he'd seen.

The man approached Ali again. He held one machine up to the side of his face, then lowered it again and offered it to Ali. Ali took it, and repeated the mimed action.

A woman's voice spoke in his ear. Ali understood what was happening; he'd seen the Scholars use similar machines to talk with each other over great distances. Unfortunately, the language was still incomprehensible. He was about to reply, when the woman spoke again in what sounded like a third language. Then a fourth, then a fifth. Ali waited patiently, until finally the woman greeted him in stilted Persian.

When Ali replied, she said, "Please wait." After a few minutes, a new voice spoke. "Peace be upon you."

"And upon you."

"Where are you from?" To Ali, this man's accent sounded exotic, but he spoke Persian with confidence.

"Khurosan."

"At what time?"

"Four years after the coming of the Scholars."

"I see." The Persian-speaker switched briefly to a different language; the man on the road, who'd wandered halfway back to his vehicle and was still listening via the second machine, gave a curt reply. Ali was amazed at these people's hospitality: in the middle of the night, in a matter of minutes, they had found someone who could speak his language.

"How did you come to be on this road?"

"I walked across the desert."

"Which way? From where? How far did you come?"

"I'm sorry, I don't remember."

The translator replied bluntly, "Please try."

Ali was confused. What did it matter? One man, at least, could see how weary he was. Why were they asking him these questions before he'd had a chance to rest?

"Forgive me, sir. I can't tell you anything, I'm sick from my journey."

There was an exchange in the native language, followed by an awkward silence. Finally the translator said, "This man will take you to a place where you can stay for a while. Tomorrow we'll hear your whole story."

"Thank you, sir. You have done a great thing for me. God will reward you."

The man on the road walked up to Ali. Ali held out his arms to embrace him in gratitude. The man produced a metal shackle and snapped it around Ali's wrists.

2.

The camp was enclosed by two high fences, topped with glistening ribbons of razor-sharp metal. The space between them was filled with coils of the same material. Outside the fences there was nothing but desert as far as the eye could see. Inside there were guards, and at night everything was bathed in a constant harsh light. Ali had no doubt that he'd come to a prison, though his hosts kept insisting that this was not the case.

His first night had passed in a daze. He'd been given food and water, examined by a doctor, then shown to a small metal hut that he was to share with three other men. Two of the men, Alex and Tran, knew just enough Persian to greet Ali briefly, but the third, Shahin, was an Iranian, and they could understand each other well enough. The hut's four beds were arranged in pairs, one above the other; Ali's habit was to sleep on a mat on the floor, but he didn't want to offend anyone by declining to follow the local customs. The guards had removed his shackles then put a bracelet on his left wrist – made from something like paper, but extraordinarily strong – bearing the number "3739". The last numeral was more or less the same shape as a Persian nine; he recognized the others from machine parts, but he didn't know their values.

Every two hours, throughout the night, a guard opened the door of the hut and shone a light on each of their faces in turn. The first time it happened Ali thought the guard had come to rouse them from their sleep and take them somewhere, but Shahin explained that these "head counts" happened all night, every night.

The next morning, officials from the camp had taken Ali out in a vehicle and asked him to show them the exact place where he'd arrived through the bridge. He'd done his best, but all of the desert looked the same to him. By midday, he was tempted to designate a spot at random just to satisfy his hosts, but he didn't want to lie to them. They'd returned to the camp in a sullen mood. Ali couldn't understand why it was so important to them.

Reza, the Persian translator who'd first spoken with Ali through the machine, explained that he was to remain in the camp until government officials had satisfied themselves that he really was fleeing danger, and hadn't merely come to the future seeking an easy life for himself. Ali understood that his hosts didn't want to be cheated, but it dismayed him that they felt the need to imprison him while they made up their minds. Surely there was a family in a nearby town who would have let him stay with them for a day or two, just as his father would have welcomed any travelers passing through their village.

The section of the camp where he'd been placed was fenced off from the rest, and contained about a hundred people. They were all travelers like himself, and they came from every nation Ali had heard of, and more. Most were young men, but there were also women, children, entire families. In his village, Ali would have run to greet the children, lifted them up and kissed them to make them smile, but here they looked so sad and dispirited that he was afraid the approach of even the friendliest stranger might frighten them.

Shahin was a few years older than Ali, but he had spent his whole life as a student. He had traveled just two decades through time, escaping a revolution in his country. He explained that the part of the camp they were in was called "Stage One"; they were being kept apart from the others so they wouldn't learn too much about the way their cases would be judged. "They're afraid we'll embellish the details if we discover what kind of questions they ask, or what kind of story succeeds."

"How long have you been here?" Ali asked.

"Nine months. I'm still waiting for my interview."

"Nine months!"

Shahin smiled wearily. "Some people have been in Stage One for a year. But don't worry, you won't have to wait that long. When I arrived here, the Center Manager had an interesting policy: nobody would have their cases examined until they asked him for the correct application form. Of course, nobody knew that they were required to do that, and he had no intention of telling them. Three months ago, he was transferred to another camp. When I asked the woman who replaced him what I needed to do to have my claims heard, she told me straight away: ask for Form 866."

Ali couldn't quite follow all this. Shahin explained further.

Ali said, "What good will it do me, to get this piece of paper? I can't read their language, and I can barely write my own."

"That's no problem. They'll let you talk to an educated man or woman, an expert in these matters. That person will fill out the form for you, in English. You only need to explain your problem, and sign your name at the bottom of the paper."

"English?" Ali had heard about the English; before he was born they'd tried to invade both Hindustan and Khurosan, without success. "How did that language come here?" He was sure that he was not in England.

"They conquered this country two centuries ago. They crossed the world in wooden ships to take it for their king."

"Oh." Ali felt dizzy; his mind still hadn't fully accepted the journey he'd made. "What about Khurosan?" he joked. "Have they conquered that as well?"

Shahin shook his head. "No."

"What is it like now? Is there peace there?" Once this strange business with the English was done, perhaps he could travel to his homeland. However much it had changed with time, he was sure he could make a good life there.

Shahin said, "There is no nation called Khurosan in this world. Part of that area belongs to Hindustan, part to Iran, part to Russia."

Ali stared at him, uncomprehending. "How can that be?" However much his people fought among themselves, they would never have let invaders take their land.

"I don't know the full history," Shahin said, "but you need to understand something. This is not your future. The things that happened in the places you know are not a part of the history of this world. There is no pol-e-waqt that connects past and future in the same world. Once you cross the bridge, everything changes, including the past."

With Shahin beside him, Ali approached one of the government officials, a man named James, and addressed him in the English he'd learned by heart. "Please Mr James, can I have Form 866?"

James rolled his eyes and said, "OK, OK! We were going to get around to you sooner or later." He turned to Shahin and said, "I wish you'd stop scaring the new guys with stories about being stuck in Stage One forever. You know things have changed since Colonel Kurtz went north."

Shahin translated all of this for Ali. "Colonel Kurtz" was Shahin's nickname for the previous Center Manager, but everyone, even the guards, had adopted it. Shahin called Tran "The Rake", and Alex was "Denisovich of the Desert".

Three weeks later, Ali was called to a special room, where he sat with Reza. A lawyer in a distant city, a woman called Ms Evans, spoke with them in English through a machine that Reza called a "speakerphone". With Reza translating, she asked Ali about everything: his village, his family, his problems with the Scholars. He'd been asked about some of this the night he'd arrived, but he'd been very tired then, and hadn't had a chance to put things clearly.

Three days after the meeting, he was called to see James. Ms Evans had written everything in English on the special form, and sent it to them. Reza read through the form, translating everything for Ali to be sure that it was correct. Then Ali wrote his name on the bottom of the form. James told him, "Before we make a decision, someone will come from the city to interview you. That might take a while, so you'll have to be patient."

Ali said, in English, "No problem."

He felt he could wait for a year, if he had to. The first four weeks had gone quickly, with so much that was new to take in. He had barely had space left in his crowded mind to be homesick, and he tried not to worry about Hassan and his mother. Many things about the camp disturbed him, but his luck had been good: the infamous "Colonel Kurtz" had left, so he'd probably be out in three or four months. The cities of this nation, Shahin assured him, were mostly on the distant coast, an infinitely milder place than the desert around the camp. Ali might be able to get a laboring job while studying English at night, or he might find work on a farm. He hadn't quite started his new life yet, but he was safe, and everything looked hopeful.

By the end of his third month Ali was growing restless. Most days he played cards with Shahin, Tran, and a Hindustani man named Rakesh, while Alex lay on his bunk reading books in Russian. Rakesh had a cassette player and a vast collection of tapes. The songs were mostly in Hindi, a language that contained just enough Persian words to give Ali some sense of what the lyrics were about: usually love, or sorrow, or both.

The metal huts were kept tolerably cool by machines, but there was no shade outside. At night the men played soccer, and Ali sometimes joined in, but after falling badly on the concrete, twice, he decided it wasn't the game for him. Shahin told him that it was a game for grass; from his home in Tehran, he'd watched dozens of nations compete at it. Ali felt a surge of excitement at the thought of all the wonders of this world, still tantalizingly out of reach: in Stage One, TV, radio, newspapers, and telephones were all forbidden. Even Rakesh's tapes had been checked by the guards, played from start to finish to be sure that they didn't contain secret lessons in passing the interview. Ali couldn't wait to reach Stage Two, to catch his first glimpse of what life might be like in a world where anyone could watch history unfolding, and speak at their leisure with anyone else.

English was the closest thing to a common language for all the people in the camp. Shahin did his best to get Ali started, and once he could converse in broken English some of the friendlier guards let him practice with them, often to their great amusement. "Not every car is called a Land Cruiser," Gary explained. "I think you must come from Toyota-stan."

Shahin was called to his interview. Ali prayed for him, then sat on the floor of the hut with Tran and tried to lose himself in the mercurial world of the cards. What he liked most about these friendly games was that good and bad luck rarely lasted long, and even when they did it barely mattered. Every curse and every blessing was light as a feather.

Shahin returned four hours later, looking exhausted but satisfied. "I've told them my whole story," he said. "It's in their hands now." The official who'd interviewed him had given him no hint as to what the decision would be, but Shahin seemed relieved just to have had a chance to tell someone who mattered everything he'd suffered, everything that had forced him from his home.

That night Shahin was told that he was moving to Stage Two in half an hour. He embraced Ali. "See you in freedom, brother."

"God willing."

After Shahin was gone, Ali lay on his bunk for four days, refusing to eat, getting up only to wash and pray. His friend's departure was just the trigger; the raw grief of his last days in the valley came flooding back, deepened by the unimaginable gulf that now separated him from his family. Had Hassan escaped from the Scholars? Or was he fighting on the front line of their endless war, risking death every hour of every day? With the only *mosarfar-e-waqt* Ali knew now dead, how would he ever get news from his family, or send them his assistance?

Tran whispered gruff consolations in his melodic English. "Don't worry kid. Everything OK. Wait and see."

Worse than the waiting was the sense of waste: all the hours trickling away, with no way to harness them for anything useful. Ali tried to improve his English, but there were some concepts he could get no purchase on without someone who understood his own language to help him. Reza rarely left the government offices for the compound, and when he did he was too busy for Ali's questions.

Ali tried to make a garden, planting an assortment of seeds that he'd saved from the fruit that came with some of the meals. Most of Stage One was covered in concrete, but he found a small patch of bare ground behind his hut that was sheltered from the fiercest sunlight. He carried water from the drinking tap on the other side of the soccer ground and sprinkled it over the soil four times a day. Nothing happened, though. The seeds lay dormant, the land would not accept them.

Three weeks after Shahin's departure, Alex had his interview, and left. A week later, Tran followed. Ali started sleeping through the heat of the day, waking just in time to join the queue for the evening meal, then playing cards with Rakesh and his friends until dawn.

By the end of his sixth month, Ali felt a taint of bitterness creeping in beneath the numbness and boredom. He wasn't a thief or a murderer, he'd committed no crime. Why couldn't these people set him free to work, to fend for himself instead of taking their charity, to prepare himself for his new life?

One night, tired of the endless card game, Ali wandered out from Rakesh's hut earlier than usual. One of the guards, a woman named Cheryl, was standing outside her office, smoking. Ali murmured a greeting to her as he passed; she was not one of the friendly ones, but he tried to be polite to everyone.

"Why don't you just go home?" she said.

Ali paused, unsure whether to dignify this with a response. He'd long ago learned that most of the guards' faces became stony if he tried to explain why he'd left his village; somewhere, somehow it had been drummed into them that nothing their prisoners said could be believed.

"Nobody invited you here," she said bluntly. "You want to live in a civilized country? Go home and build one for yourself. You've got a war back there? *My ancestors* fought wars, they died for their freedom. What do you expect – five hundred years of progress to be handed to you on a plate? Nobody owes you a comfortable life. Go home and earn it."

Ali wanted to tell her that his life would have been fine if the meddlers from the future hadn't chosen Khurosan as their fulcrum for moving history, but his English wasn't up to the task.

He said, "I'm here. From me, big tragedy for your nation? I'm honest man and hard worker. I not betray your hospitality."

Cheryl snickered. Ali wasn't sure if she was sneering at his English or his sentiments, but he persisted. "Your leaders did agreement with other nations. Anyone asking protection gets fair hearing." Shahin had impressed that point on Ali. It was the law, and in this society the law was everything. "That is my right."

Cheryl coughed on her cigarette. "Dream on, Ahmad."

"My name is Ali."

"Whatever." She reached out and caught him by the wrist, then held up his hand to examine his ID bracelet. "Dream on, 3739."

James called Ali to his office and handed him a letter. Reza translated it for him. After eight months of waiting, in six days' time he would finally have his interview.

Ali waited nervously for Ms Evans to call him to help him prepare, as she'd promised she would when they'd last spoken, all those months before. On the morning of the appointed day, he was summoned again to James's office, and taken with Reza to the room with the speakerphone, the "interview room". A different lawyer, a man called Mr Cole, explained to Ali that Ms Evans had left her job and he had taken over Ali's case. He told Ali that everything would be fine, and he'd be listening carefully to Ali's interview and making sure that everything went well.

When Cole had hung up, Reza snorted derisively. "You know how these clowns are chosen? They put in tenders, and it goes to the lowest bidder." Ali didn't entirely understand, but this didn't sound encouraging. Reza caught the expression on Ali's face, and added, "Don't worry, you'll be fine. Fleeing from the Scholars is flavor of the month."

Three hours later, Ali was back in the interview room.

The official who'd come from the city introduced himself as John Fernandez. Reza wasn't with them; Fernandez had brought a different interpreter with him, a man named Parviz. Mr Cole joined them on the speakerphone. Fernandez switched on a cassette recorder, and asked Ali to swear on the Quran to give truthful answers to all his questions.

Fernandez asked him for his name, his date of birth, and the place and time he'd fled. Ali didn't know his birthday or his exact age; he thought he was about eighteen years old, but it was not the custom in his village to record such things. He did know that at the time he'd left his uncle's house, twelve hundred and sixty-five years had passed since the Prophet's flight to Medina.

"Tell me about your problem," Fernandez said. "Tell me why you've come here."

Shahin had told Ali that the history of this world was different from his own, so Ali explained carefully about Khurosan's long war, about the meddlers and the warlords they'd created, about the coming of the Scholars. How the Shi'a were taken by force to fight in the most dangerous positions. How Hassan was taken. How his father had been killed. Fernandez listened patiently, sometimes writing on the sheets of paper in front of him as Ali spoke, interrupting him only to encourage him to fill in the gaps in the story, to make everything clear.

When he had finally recounted everything, Ali felt an overwhelming sense of relief. This man had not poured scorn on his words the way the guards had;

instead, he had allowed Ali to speak openly about all the injustice his family and his people had suffered.

Fernandez had some more questions.

"Tell me about your village, and your uncle's village. How long would it take to travel between them on foot?"

"Half a day, sir."

"Half a day. That's what you said in your statement. But in your entry interview, you said a day." Ali was confused. Parviz explained that his "statement" was the written record of his conversation with Ms Evans, which she had sent to the government; his "entry interview" was when he'd first arrived in the camp and been questioned for ten or fifteen minutes.

"I only meant it was a short trip, sir, you didn't have to stay somewhere halfway overnight. You could complete it in one day."

"Hmm. OK. Now, when the smuggler took you from your uncle's village, which direction was he driving?"

"Along the valley, sir."

"North, south, east, west?"

"I'm not sure." Ali knew these words, but they were not part of the language of everyday life. He knew the direction for prayer, and he knew the direction to follow to each neighboring village.

"You know that the sun rises in the east, don't you?"

"Yes."

"So if you faced in the direction in which you were being driven, would the sun have risen on your left, on your right, behind you, where?"

"It was night time."

"Yes, but you must have faced the same direction in the valley in the morning, a thousand times. So where would the sun have risen?"

Ali closed his eyes and pictured it. "On my right."

Fernandez sighed. "OK. Finally. So you were driving north. Now tell me about the land. The smuggler drove you along the valley. And then what? What kind of landscape did you see, between your valley and the bridge?"

Ali froze. What would the government do with this information? Send someone back through their own bridge, to find and destroy the one he'd used? The *mosarfar-e-waqt* had warned him not to tell anyone the way to the bridge. That man was dead, but it was unlikely that he'd worked alone; everyone had a brother, a son, a cousin to help them. If the family of the *mosarfar-e-waqt* could trace such a misfortune to Ali, the dead man's threat against his uncle would be carried through.

Ali said, "I was under a blanket, I didn't see anything."

"You were under a blanket? For how many days?"

"Three."

"Three days. What about eating, drinking, going to the toilet?"

"He blindfolded me," Ali lied.

"Really? You never mentioned that before." Fernandez shuffled through his papers. "It's not in your statement."

"I didn't think it was important, sir." Ali's stomach tightened. What was happening? He was sure he'd won this man's trust. And he'd earned it: he'd told him the truth about everything, until now. What difference did it make to his problem with the Scholars, which mountains and streams he'd glimpsed on the way to the bridge? He had sworn to tell the truth, but he knew it would be a far greater sin to risk his uncle's life.

Fernandez had still more questions, about life in the village. Some were easy, but some were strange, and he kept asking for numbers, numbers, numbers: how much did it weigh, how much did it cost, how long did it take? What time did the bazaar open? Ali had no idea, he'd been busy with farm work in the mornings, he'd never gone there so early that it might have been closed. How many people came to Friday prayers in the Shi'a mosque? None, since the Scholars had arrived. Before that? Ali couldn't remember. More than a hundred? Ali hesitated. "I think so." He'd never counted them, why would he have?

When the interview finished, Ali's mind was still three questions behind, worrying that his answers might not have been clear enough. Fernandez was rewinding the tapes, shaking his hand formally, leaving the room.

Mr Cole said, "I think that went well. Do you have any questions you want to ask me?"

Ali said, "No, sir." Parviz had already departed.

"All right. Good luck." The speakerphone clicked off. Ali sat at the table, waiting for the guard to come and take him back to the compound.

3.

Entering Stage Two, Ali felt as if he had walked into the heart of a bustling town. Everything was noise, shouting, music. He'd sometimes heard snatches of this cacophony wafting across the fenced-off "sterile area" that separated the parts of the camp, but now he was in the thick of it. The rows of huts, and the crowds moving between them, seemed to stretch on forever. There must have been a thousand people here, all of them unwilling travelers fleeing the cruelties of their own histories.

He'd moved his small bag of belongings into the hut allocated to him, but none of his new roommates were there to greet him. He wandered through the compound, dizzy from the onslaught of new sights and sounds. He felt as if he'd just had a heavy cloth unwound from around his head, and his unveiled senses were still struggling to adjust. If he was reeling from this, how would he feel when he stepped onto the streets of a real city, in freedom?

The evening meal was over, the sun had set, and the heat outside had become tolerable. Almost everyone seemed to be out walking, or congregating around the entrances of their friends' huts, taped music blaring through the open doorways. At the end of one row of huts, Ali came to a larger building, where thirty or forty people were seated. He entered the room, and saw a small box with a window on it, through which he could see an oddly-colored, distorted, constantly changing view. A woman was dancing and singing in Hindi.

"TV," Ali marveled. This was what Shahin had spoken about; now the whole world was open to his gaze.

An African man beside him shook his head. "It's a video. The TV's on in the other common room."

Ali lingered, watching the mesmerizing images. The woman was very beautiful, and though she was immodestly dressed by the standards of his village, she seemed dignified and entirely at ease. The Scholars would probably have stoned her to death, but Ali would have been happy to be a beggar in Mumbai if the streets there were filled with sights like this.

As he left the room, the sky was already darkening. The camp's floodlights had come on, destroying any hope of a glimpse of the stars. He asked someone, "Where is the TV, please?" and followed their directions.

As he walked into the second room, he noticed something different in the mood at once; the people here were tense, straining with attention. When Ali turned to the TV, it showed an eerily familiar sight: an expanse of desert, not unlike that outside the camp. Helicopters, four or five, flew over the landscape. In the distance, a tight funnel of swirling dust, dancing across the ground.

Ali stood riveted. The landscape on the screen was brightly lit, which meant that what he was watching had already happened: earlier in the day, someone had located the mouth of the bridge. He peered at the small images of the helicopters. He'd only ever seen a broken one on the ground, the toy of one warlord brought down by a rival, but he recognized the guns protruding from the sides. Whoever had found the bridge, it was now in the hands of soldiers.

As he watched, a Land Cruiser came charging out of the storm. Then another, and another. This was not like his own arrival; the convoy was caked with dust, but more or less intact. Then the helicopters descended, guns chattering. For a few long seconds Ali thought he was about to witness a slaughter, but the soldiers were firing consistently a meter or so ahead of the Land Cruisers. They were trying to corral the vehicles back into the bridge.

The convoy broke up, the individual drivers trying to steer their way past the blockade. Curtains of bullets descended around them, driving them back toward the meandering storm. Ali couldn't see the people inside, but he could imagine their terror and confusion. This was the future? This was their sanctuary? Whatever tyranny they were fleeing, to have braved the labyrinth of the pol-e-waqt only to be greeted with a barrage of gunfire was a fate so cruel that they must have doubted their senses, their sanity, their God.

The helicopters wheeled around the mouth of the bridge like hunting dogs, indefatigable, relentless in their purpose. Ali found the grim dance unbearable, but he couldn't turn away. One of the Land Cruisers came to a halt; it wasn't safely clear of the storm, but this must have seemed wiser than dodging bullets. Doors opened and people tumbled out. Weirdly, the picture went awry at exactly that moment, clumps of flickering color replacing the travelers' faces.

Soldiers approached, guns at the ready, gesturing and threatening, forcing the people back into the car. A truck appeared, painted in dappled green and brown. A chain was tied between the vehicles. Someone emerged from the Land Cruiser; the face was obscured again, but Ali could see it was a woman. Her words could not be heard, but Ali could see her speaking with her hands, begging, chastising, pleading for mercy. The soldiers forced her back inside.

The truck started its engines. Sand sprayed from its wheels. Two soldiers climbed into the back, their weapons trained on the Land Cruiser. Then they towed their cargo back into the storm.

Ali watched numbly as the other two Land Cruisers were rounded up. The second stalled, and the soldiers descended on it. The driver of the third gave up, and steered his own course into the mouth of the bridge.

The soldiers' truck emerged from the storm, alone. The helicopters spiraled away, circling the funnel at a more prudent distance. Ali looked at the faces of the other people in the room; everyone was pale, some were weeping.

The picture changed. Two men were standing, indoors somewhere. One was old, white-haired, wizened. In front of him a younger man was talking, replying to unseen questioners. Both were smiling proudly.

Ali could only make sense of a few of their words, but gradually he pieced some things together. These men were from the government, and they were explaining the events of the day. They had sent the soldiers to "protect" the bridge, to ensure that no more criminals and barbarians emerged to threaten the peaceful life of the nation. They had been patient with these intruders for far too long. From this day on, nobody would pass.

Behind the men there was a huge banner. It bore a picture of the face of the younger man, and the words KEEPING THE PAST IN THE PAST.

"What about the law?" someone was asking. An agreement had been signed: any traveler who reached this country and asked for protection had a right to a fair hearing.

"A bill has been drafted, and will be introduced in the House tomorrow. Once passed, it will take force from nine o'clock this morning. The land within twenty kilometers of the bridge will, for the purposes of the Act, no longer be part of this nation. People entering the exclusion zone will have no basis in law to claim our protection."

Confused, Ali muttered, "Chi goft?" A young man sitting nearby turned to face him. "Salaam, chetori? Fahim hastam."

Fahim's accent was unmistakably Khurosani. Ali smiled. "Ali hastam. Shoma chetori?"

Fahim explained what the man on the TV had said. Anyone emerging from the mouth of the bridge, now, might as well be on the other side of the world. The government here would accept no obligation to assist them. "If it's not their land anymore," he mused, "maybe they'll give it to us. We can found a country of our own, a tribe of nomads in a caravan following the bridge across the desert."

Ali said nervously, "My interview was today. They said something about nine o'clock—"

Fahim shook his head dismissively. "You made your claim months ago, right? So you're still covered by the old law."

Ali tried to believe him. "You're still waiting for your decision?"

"Hardly. I got refused three years ago."

"Three years? They didn't send you back?"

"I'm fighting it in the courts. I can't go back, I'd be dead in a week." There were dark circles under Fahim's eyes. If he'd been refused three years before, he'd probably spent close to four years in this prison.

Fahim, it turned out, was one of Ali's roommates. He took him to meet the other twelve Khurosanis in Stage Two, and the whole group sat together in one of the huts, talking until dawn. Ali was overjoyed to be among people who knew his language, his time, his customs. It didn't matter that most were from provinces far from his own, that a year ago he would have thought of them as exotic strangers.

When he examined their faces too closely, though, it was hard to remain joyful. They had all fled the Scholars, like him. They were all in fear for their lives. And they had all been locked up for a very long time: two years, three years, four years, five.

In the weeks that followed, Ali gave himself no time to brood on his fate. Stage Two had English classes, and though Fahim and the others had long outgrown them, Ali joined in. He finally learned the names for the European letters and numbers that he'd seen on weapons and machinery all his life, and the teacher encouraged him to give up translating individual words from Persian, and reshape whole sentences, whole thoughts, into the alien tongue.

Every evening, Ali joined Fahim in the common room to watch the news on TV. There was no doubt that the place they had come to was peaceful and prosperous; when war was mentioned, it was always in some distant land. The rulers here did not govern by force, they were chosen by the people, and even now this competition was in progress. The men who had sent the soldiers to block the bridge were asking the people to choose them again.

When the guard woke Ali at eight in the morning, he didn't complain, though he'd had only three hours' sleep. He showered quickly, then went to the compound's south gate. It no longer seemed strange to him to move from place to place this way: to wait for guards to come and unlock a succession of doors and escort him through the fenced-off maze that separated the compound from the government offices.

James and Reza were waiting in the office. Ali greeted them, his mouth dry. James said, "Reza will read the decision for you. It's about ten pages, so be patient. Then if you have any questions, let me know."

Reza read from the papers without meeting Ali's eyes. Fernandez, the man who'd interviewed Ali, had written that there were discrepancies between things Ali had said at different times, and gaps in his knowledge of the place and time he claimed to have come from. What's more, an expert in the era of the Scholars had listened to the tape of Ali talking, and declared that his speech was not of that time. "Perhaps this man's great-grandfather fled Khurosan in the time of the Scholars, and some sketchy information has been passed down the generations. The applicant himself, however, employs a number of words that were not in use until decades later."

Ali waited for the litany of condemnation to come to an end, but it seemed to go on forever. "I have tried to give the applicant the benefit of the doubt," Fernandez had written, "but the overwhelming weight of evidence supports the conclusion that he has lied about his origins, his background, and all of his claims."

Ali sat with his head in his hands.

James said, "Do you understand what this means? You have seven days to lodge an appeal. If you don't lodge an appeal, you will have to return to your country."

Reza added, "You should call your lawyer. Have you got money for a phone card?"

Ali nodded. He'd taken a job cleaning the mess, he had thirty points in his account already.

Every time Ali called, his lawyer was busy. Fahim helped Ali fill out the appeal form, and they handed it to James two hours before the deadline. "Lucky Colonel Kurtz is gone," Fahim told Ali. "Or that form would have sat in the fax tray for at least a week."

Wild rumors swept the camp: the government was about to change, and everyone would be set free. Ali had seen the government's rivals giving their blessing to the use of soldiers to block the bridge; he doubted that they'd show the prisoners in the desert much mercy if they won.

When the day of the election came, the government was returned, more powerful than ever.

That night, as they were preparing to sleep, Fahim saw Ali staring at the long white scars that criss-crossed his upper arms and chest. "I use a razor blade," Fahim admitted. "It makes me feel better. The one power I've got left: to choose my own pain."

"I'll never do that," Ali swore.

Fahim gave a hollow laugh. "It's cheaper than cigarettes."

Ali closed his eyes and tried to picture freedom, but all he saw was blackness. The past was gone, the future was gone, and the world had shrunk to this prison.

4.

"Ali, wake up, come see!"

Daniel was shaking him. Ali swatted his hands away angrily. The African was one of his closest friends, and there'd been a time when he could still drag Ali along to English classes or the gym, but since the appeal tribunal had rejected him, Ali had no taste for anything. "Let me sleep."

"There are people. Outside the fence."

"Escaped?"

"No, no. From the city!"

Ali clambered off the bunk. He splashed water on his face, then followed his friend.

Dozens of prisoners had gathered at the south-west corner of the fence, blocking the view, but Ali could hear people on the outside, shouting and banging drums. Daniel tried to clear a path, but it was impossible. "Get on my shoulders." He ducked down and motioned to Ali.

Ali laughed. "It's not that important."

Daniel raised a hand angrily, as if to slap him. "Get up, you have to see." He was serious. Ali obeyed.

From his vantage, he could see that the mass of prisoners pressed against the inner fence was mirrored by another crowd struggling to reach the outer one. Police, some on horses, were trying to stop them. Ali peered into the scrum, amazed. Dozens of young people, men and women, were pushing against the cordon of policemen, and every now and then someone was slipping through and running forward. Some distance away across the desert stood a brightly colored bus. The word "freedom" was painted across it, in English, Persian, Arabic, and probably ten or twelve languages that Ali couldn't read. The people were chanting, "Set them free! Set them free!" One young woman reached the fence and clung to it, shouting defiantly. Four policemen descended on her and tore her away.

A cloud of dust was moving along the desert road. More police cars were coming, reinforcements. A knife twisted in Ali's heart. This gesture of friendship astonished him, but it would lead nowhere. In five or ten minutes, the protesters would all be rounded up and carried away.

A young man outside the fence met Ali's gaze. "Hey! My name's Ben."

"I'm Ali."

Ben looked around frantically. "What's your number?"

"What?"

"We'll write to you. Give us your number. They have to deliver the letters if we include the ID number."

"Behind you!" Ali shouted, but the warning was too late. One policeman had him in a headlock, and another was helping wrestle him to the ground.

Ali felt Daniel stagger. The crowd on his own side was trying to fend off a wave of guards with batons and shields.

Ali dropped to his feet. "They want our ID numbers," he told Daniel. Daniel looked around at the melee. "Got anything to write on?"

Ali checked his back pocket. The small notebook and pen it was his habit to carry were still there. He rested the notebook on Daniel's back, and wrote "Ali 3739 Daniel 5420." Who else? He quickly added Fahim and a few others.

He scrabbled on the ground for a stone, then wrapped the paper around it. Daniel lifted him up again.

The police were battling with the protesters, grabbing them by the hair, dragging them across the dirt. Ali couldn't see anyone who didn't have more pressing things to worry about than receiving his message. He lowered his arm, despondent.

Then he spotted someone standing by the bus. He couldn't tell if it was a man or a woman. He, or she, raised a hand in greeting. Ali waved back, then let the stone fly. It fell short, but the distant figure ran forward and retrieved it from the sand.

Daniel collapsed beneath him, and the guards moved in with batons and tear gas. Ali covered his eyes with his forearm, weeping, alive again with hope.

THE MOUSE RAN DOWN

Adrian Tchaikovsky

Adrian Tchaikovsky is a British fantasy author with eight novels out
currently in his Shadows of the Apt series from Tor UK, and about a
dozen short stories in various anthologies. "The Mouse Ran Down"
was first published in *Carnage: After the End 2* in 2012.

Will Kempe was just starting his comic turn when Ellie pushed her way
through the crowd to prod me in the shoulder.

"It's time," she hissed. "We've got to go."

I missed Kempe's standard opener, the joke about lawyers, and the whooping
roar of the groundlings around us obliterated Ellie's next words.

"Give me five minutes, come on," I slipped into the next lull. "I never get to
hear this. I'm all packed."

Ellie prodded me again. "Move, John." She was got up as an apprentice, a
young lad with the first growth of moustache feathering his lip and out on the
prowl in his master's cast-off doublet. A man's clothes made it easier to move
about London in the Year of Our Lord 1598. Small wonder Shakespeare had
cross-dressing on the brain.

"They've got the Complete Works back at Permian One." Ellie's finger jabbed
even harder. "Besides, you could have gone to see it yesterday."

"It's Will Kempe. He does a different skit each night. No-one wrote it down."
But I was letting myself be dragged off, as Ellie drove a path through the crowd,
leading with her elbows.

I never did get to hear that routine of Kempe's. You could keep the rest of the
play, the stuff Shakespeare wrote, but Kempe was a comedian's comedian, and
I was always having to move just as he got into his flow, hearing the joke but
never the punchline.

But we were running out of time, approaching the jagged end of history. Ellie
was right: we had to get out.

There was a warehouse near the river that was the subject of a furious
inheritance lawsuit. It was piled high with crates and boxes, imperishable goods
brought in from the Indies and tied up in the courts until one of seven warring
brothers would finally prevail over the others in around 1603. That was our
home, for the nine months of the years 1597-8 that history had snapped off
and preserved. We always arrived in the bitter cold of December, laden with our
meagre possessions, hurrying through the snow-scattered streets to our makeshift saunctuary. We left in a September that was just being leached of the heat
of summer, just as Will Kempe was making them laugh at the Curtain.

Four times. I had crept into this London four times with Ellie and Marcus, with a handful of families at our heels, living in the untenanted spaces of history by borrowing and theft and subterfuge, and then moving on.

We got back to the warehouse double time, by all the secret ways of that close-pressed, cluttered London, roofs and alleyways and connecting cellars. We were dressed as locals, but we were not supposed to be there, surplus to temporal requirements. It was best to avoid being noticed.

And there were always the hunters. We'd lost four fragments in the past year – my personal year, that was cut loose from all calendars – and nobody knew where would be next. We refugees were running short of safe havens. We were always on the move. It was no life, not for me, and certainly not for the children, the infirm. So few of us had made it out from the fall of history. We did our best to look after everyone.

Marcus had a look like sour milk when we turned up. "Do you know how late you are?"

"Plenty of time," I told him, but it wasn't true. Everything around us was starting to look grainy, shot through with streaks and fuzzy spots: noise in the signal, signs that a fragment was coming to its end. Out there, Old London Town was unravelling, breaking apart against the rocks of end time. Nobody would notice except us. The inhabitants, Will Kempe, all the theatregoers, they would disintegrate into nothing and never know it. If we didn't get out we'd join them, only we'd not be made anew when the fragment began its nine month round again. We'd just be gone.

Patrick Scarrow and his family were ready to move, and Beth Nguyen and her kids, and the Wietzels, and the Morrow girls. We had twenty-one souls in our care, eternal refugees from when they'd destroyed the Now. The kids were complaining, mostly in whispers. It didn't matter how many times, the life was still too disjointed to be good for them. Worse than just having to move school every year or so: each time they packed their bags they might be headed for the halls of Prester John or Dark Age Siberia or some time before mammals had even evolved.

Speaking of which. "Where're we headed? You've taken a reading?"

Marcus gave me another look. "Just as well someone did. One month of Babylon. We're overlapping with another troupe but it's the only safe shard I could plot to. After that it's a year in the Palaeolothic."

"Make the most of Babylon then," Ellie said dryly.

I passed amongst the others, making sure all the kids were keeping close to their folks, and that everyone had shouldered their backs and bags. Everyone had dressed for the occasion: robes and skirts, bare chests for the men, jewellery for the women. Babylon was a soft touch, but if there were other refugees already eking out a living there, we'd be in each others' way and on each others' toes every day. A populated fragment has its advantages – plenty of food to steal, plenty of comforts and conveniences if you're sly about how you take advantage of them. Living space is tough to find, though – there just aren't many places in any city of any time that will stay overlooked for the duration. The invisible spaces of Babylon in 1700BC would already be staked out and claimed by whoever was taking refuge there.

That this sort of doubling up was becoming more common as fragments were lost to us must have been in all our minds, but nobody said it. Nobody wanted to admit we were losing.

Not even losing the war. A war suggests we could fight back. We had been on the run since the end of time, desperately trying to put back the clock, and our enemies had hunted us through the eras and the ages, taking away our hiding places one by one. One day they would find this old London we were abandoning, and then Will Kempe would be no more, and his humorous monologue would be forever lost to human recollection.

"All right, let's move!" Marcus called, opening the doors from one ruined dog-end of time to the next, keeping us one step ahead of the enemy. Everyone began to file through, and I cast a backwards glance at the warehouse even as the sight was riven with cracks and discoloured stains. I would be back, I hoped: back for another of 1597's endless supply of Decembers, and many more after that.

There had indeed been a war. Did we win? The question has no meaning. It was a cold war. Nobody was actually fighting, because that would have been boorish and uneconomic. Instead, competing commercial and ideological interests – one of them ours – were spinning the wheels frantically behind the scenes to find a way to beat the others without ever having to fight.

You heard about all sorts, from those who remembered those lost, last years. There were gene bombs and attack memes. There were viral ideas gone feral, adverse mental programming on a vast scale. You didn't know what to believe, they said, and even when you did, you didn't trust your own faith because someone might have slipped it into your drink. It was a strange war. It killed ideas but left people standing. Every day our society was written and rewritten.

Small wonder that they had started looking at taking the war into time. Surely the ultimate piece of passive aggression was to pre-empt the bad guys before they even knew what they were going to do.

It didn't work out.

We hit the cooling night of Babylon after the rains had come and gone, creeping out from the cracks of the world into the shadows of the temples. The air was still, scented with fragrant smoke, with distant decay. Around us the darkened city was quiet, but there would surely be locals abroad who would not want to see this ragged band of refugees struggling through their streets. Getting to the safe house would be risky. If we had arrived at the beginning of the fragment, when everything had reset to its earliest surviving moment, then we could know exactly where all the inhabitants would be, and follow a pre-determined path that would get us under cover, unseen, before dawn. This fragment was months into its cycle, though, and the mere presence of other refugees would have exercised a cumulative effect on the routines of the city, despite their best efforts to stay below the radar. We would have to rely on stealth and misdirection.

Marcus and Ellie and I would take turns to lead away anyone who looked like they would take issue with a group of foreigners skulking through their streets, and still we expected to be seen by a fair assortment of beggars, prostitutes and drunken artisans. We could only hope we wouldn't cause any problems for the incumbents. We would be waiting just a month before we skipped off for the Eocene, whilst they were fixing to stay here for the duration and would have to ride out any ripples that we had made.

We made it in the end, just as dawn was clawing at the eastern sky. There were almost no locals about that night, and those we saw were only glimpsed distantly and were as keen to avoid us as we were to dodge them. At the time I thought that we'd been lucky.

The safe house here was a tomb, or at least a tomb in waiting. The intended resident would be alive and well throughout the fragment's term, still clinging grimly to life when time called a fractured halt to this slice of Babylon. In the meantime his forward planning and the vanity of his wanting a grand monument to his posterity gave us a roof over our heads.

"Who's here, anyway?" I asked Marcus as we hurried and skulked in turn through the moon-shrouded streets.

"Maria, Leon, Sun, maybe another thirty all told," he told me. "Going to be real crowded. We won't be making any friends. Everyone on their best behaviour."

"It's not like it's our fault—" I objected, but he cut me off.

"Doesn't matter. Going to be standing room only for a month, and that's not their fault, either. If Comoy could only step up the work—"

It was my turn to butt in. "Doctor Comoy is doing all he can to fix this."

We were practically in sight of the tomb and Marcus gave out a long sigh, and only through that did he show just how tired he was. "John, it's been almost forty years we've lived like this. I was a kid, when it all went to crap. You weren't born. Comoy's had all the time in the world to put the fucking egg back together again."

"He's not given up hope."

"That's what he says. Come on."

Marcus and I had our charges, Scarrow and Nguyen and the rest, and we got them huddled down in a small street within sight of the tomb, while Ellie went to make contact with the incumbents. By that time everyone was exhausted, the children dead on their feet, backs bowed under their loaded lives, all they had of where we'd all come from, mementos of a past and future that no longer existed.

"We can't keep doing this," Marcus said. I made an urgent expression towards the others, who were all within earshot, but he shrugged. "I don't care," he went on. "It's too hard. We can't just keep running."

"We can if we want to live." The old party line. "It won't be forever."

His laughter was forced out of him like bile from a wound. "Forever? The end of time won't be forever? Oh, you fucking naïf."

Then Ellie was on her way back – too soon and too fast. Marcus and I exchanged glances. We were already on our feet by the time she reached us.

"They're gone," she told us.

"Is this the right fragment—?" I started and:

"The locals—?" from Marcus, but she was shaking her head to both of us.

"They were here. They're gone. Not the locals."

"No," I heard myself say, but Ellie was already continuing.

"There are burn-marks all over, spent shell casings. Someone put up a fight. This fragment is compromised."

"No," I said again, and I was aware of a gathering murmur of despair and fear from everyone around us, but Marcus hissed for quiet.

Somewhere across the city the enemy was abroad. Small wonder we'd seen so few locals. There would be a genocide underway even as we crouched there. This small, jagged fragment of space and time was being cleansed and sterilized. We had lost Babylon. One more piece of history was no longer safe for human habitation.

"We need to move," Ellie said.

"We need somewhere to move to," Marcus pointed out sourly.

"Give me a chance. There must be somewhere we can reach from here. John, you too. I'll take upstream, you take down."

We did the math, over an hour, calculating our way out of fallen Babylon. At any moment the enemy could have found us, and we would all have died. I had glimpsed the enemy once before, during an escape that was far too tight and diminished the surviving population of human history by another twenty souls. They were sufficiently advanced that there was no resisting them. Hiding was all we had.

They were things left over from the war that had stopped the wheels of history, ended the world and robbed us not only of all we had but of all that was to come. The only thing we knew was that they were hunting us down, we refugees from the war, one rough-edged piece of time after another. Vermin. That's what we were to them: vermin to be exterminated.

I searched and searched. I found a dozen mapped fragments within reach, not one of them to anywhere with dry land, and some without even a breathable atmosphere. So much of our own past is denied to us, a planet hostile to the meek who would one day inherit it.

"One," I said at last. Marcus checked my results: the middle of a Carboniferous ice age, a frozen forest where a spark would set off a firestorm.

"No," he said, and Ellie chimed, "I've found another." She was always faster than me.

"Then why didn't you—?"

"I was hoping you'd do better," she said sadly. "We can get to Warsaw."

"No," I breathed, aware of all the eyes on us: the desperate, the lost, the eternally displaced. "There must be something else."

I was seriously going to argue for the ice, for the giant bugs, for the dizzying high oxygen atmosphere of the Carboniferous. He was right, though. The difference between that time – near inimitable to human life – and the Warsaw ghetto was slight, but we might have a chance. There would be a way out, if only we could find it.

They broke time, in that war. Because we can never go back there, we'll never know who was responsible: whether it was everyone incrementally twisting at the fabric of time, or whether the continuum just fractured the moment the first time engine went online. Or perhaps, as Marcus says, it was just the concept of mutually-assured destruction taken to its logically illogical extreme. A pre-emptive strike against time itself to stop it falling into the hands of the enemy. Perhaps they meant to do it.

The cracks coursed through history like a mouse running down a clock. Some small number of us – and by 'us' I mean the seven billion human beings who were alive to see those final days of sanity – were snatched out of time before it broke, preserved by brilliant men like Doctor Comoy. We are, theoretically, the lucky ones. At least we still exist.

Doc Comoy and his team are still mapping the expanding debris cloud that is time itself. When we find a fragment we can reach, we catalogue it, plot it, inventory it. The science is not academic. We are looking for sanctuary, temporary shelters from the storm. For the first few decades it was us against the end of the world, blazing our trails through the monsters of prehistory and the depredations of our own ancestors to find places that would be safe to hide in, even for a little while. Then we discovered that one other thing had survived the annihilation: the enemy, whoever and whatever they were. As we scurried from fragment to fragment, eking out our miserable existence in the spaces between, they were hunting us. Even this tenuous life was more than they were prepared to allow us.

Warsaw 1943, and it is an insult to that city's name that only this shard of it remains: its darkest hour, the last three months of the ghetto. Jewish and Polish resistance fighters, desperate and poorly armed, clashing with Nazi troops and collaborator police; a thousand plans of getting out, so few of which came to anything; an implacable enemy; the doom of utter annihilation hanging in the air. The only advantage to that terrible place was that we fit right in. No point in trying to hide, because every hidden part of that city was already crammed with the fearful.

"We can't stay here long." We'd got everyone into a shelter, the cellar of a collapsed house. There were a dozen families already there, pushed together, on top of one another. Starved, dirty faces stared at us, seeing our bizarre clothes, our mix of ethnicities, the fact that we were all far too well fed. They would all be dead, I knew. They were already dead. The Nazis would storm the ghetto as this fragment of time began to fail. Every one of these people had been preserved by that malevolent cripple, history, solely to suffer, to hope and fear, dread and die, over and over again.

"We need a proper sanctuary," Ellie said. "There's nothing I can see where we'd be safe hiding up. Someone has to make it to Comoy and get him to find us somewhere. We don't have enough data here."

"Can we even get someone to Comoy?" Marcus asked her.

"I have a path," she confirmed. It was nineteen fragments long, skipping from time-piece to time-piece, in and out of history like a rat in the skirting, scant minutes to cross between the shards. We could never have got the children through it, probably not most of the adults. But then staying in Warsaw for any length of time was no better.

Time would be of the essence.

"I'll do it." And it was my creeping shame that courage did not motivate me. I could not face the end in Warsaw another time. I had seen it too often. The broken fragments of history have sharp edges.

Marcus nodded bluntly, and I looked over Ellie's obstacle course. It was mostly out of recorded time, a worm-trail through monster-haunted spaces that man had no place travelling in.

My finger tracked to a projected five late Devonian minutes and I raised my eyebrow.

"Hold your breath," said Ellie, and kissed me lightly on the cheek.

I walked the tops of glaciers when they ruled the world, huddling and hurrying in my too-thin clothes. I lurched from them into a desert that spanned the horizons, that could have been anywhere, save that in this time it was near everywhere. The sun tried to kill me; elsewhere it was pelycosaurs at my heels with their razor teeth. For one minute I walked the streets of Pompeii where the ash had yet to fall. The eruption would never come to this fragment, and yet its work had already been done. The locals were gone, removed entirely, not a living thing remaining. The enemy had been there. We had lost another crumb of our past.

I held my breath and ran through the uncertain Devonian, crushing liverworts beneath my feet, a pelting figure from a lost future dashing through the ferns and towering hands of fungus.

Ellie had plotted my escape well. She always did have the best head for it. Me? The only things I was really good at were running and hiding.

We had retained a lot of the Permian, snapped-off pieces of it scattered like stones across the broken substrate of time. Some of those fragments were years long, even centuries. They were harsh, dry times, the age before the dinosaurs, populated by starving monsters; each shard a memento of a time when all life on earth was sliding inexorably towards an extinction that would claim very nearly everything that lived. The world would know only one greater disaster, and that was ours. It was fitting that Doctor Comoy had made his home there, cycling between a dozen bestial, inhospitable fragments and taking his laboratory with him. Nobody else was permitted to set up in residence along the course of his peregrinations in case they got in his way. He was not a man fond of company, or of the human race much. He was its only hope, though, so it had no choice but to be fond of him.

Permian One was his migratory home, where he and his staff and guards were trying to start the clocks again. It was the hope of every lost, scattered, desperate soul who crept in and out of the fragments and scurried from era to era. *Doc Comoy will fix it.*

I believed. I thought I believed. I had lived all my life to that mantra. We will remake the world again, glue the fragments back into a whole. Somehow the misanthropic genius would save us all, give the universe CPR, turn back time.

I hadn't been to Permian One in six years of personal time. My faith had sat at the back of my mind, comforting in its presence, never needing to be unsheathed. When I had talked with Marcus, the doubter, I had taken Comoy's side, always. Of course he would succeed in fixing it all. What other alternative was there, that was worth the consideration?

I found his prefab compound exactly as before, that set of metal boxes that they took down and put up each time he moved his base to another piece of doomed Permian time. I went in, seeing the faces I remembered, his subordinate scientists, his guards, all their grim and drawn expressions, harried and weary just like before. Just like before, all of it. I think that was when it broke. My faith had sat back there for so long it had corroded into nothing, and when I tried to test it, it just broke.

Doctor Comoy himself was in his high chair, a cherry-picker affair that lifted him up and down the bank of screens that displayed the secrets of the universe, or at least those few pieces of it that we could still access. He was an old man now, older than last time, skin like sun-cracked leather, liver-spotted, pouchy about the eyes, sunken in about his cheeks. Old, he looked old but, other than that, I might as well have just left a moment before. Here was the saviour of the human race, the engineer of time.

I had the utter conviction, then, that nothing was being done, no progress was being made. Doc Comoy, after jury-rigging together the calculations that allowed the dozens of refugee bands to limp from timepiece to timepiece, had achieved nothing. In all of my life he had just been marking time.

I did not voice it. I could not have brought forward the maths to prove it. I could not shake the belief, though. I had a new faith, and it was pure nihilism.

I got out the problem, my band stranded in Warsaw's darkness. I needed an exit, and I needed it yesterday. We had to get them out.

This small service he could provide, this prolonging of the end. His great computers and his greater mind gave me the path they must follow, and my own to get back to them. Even as I looked at the sequences, though, I was doubting them. Was this why even our precarious hold on time was breaking down? Was this why the enemy was winning?

Was Doctor Comoy fallible in everything? Were we just now seeing the inevitable disintegration of a system that he had not thought through?

I left Permian One. I had two hundred and fifty million years to cover and no time at all to do it in. I wove my way in and out of history, dodging cavemen and dinosaurs, revolutionaries and the Golden Horde. In my mind was the distant candle flame that was Warsaw, so soon to be snuffed out. I was always a runner, and I ran. Nobody could have made better use of time than I. I did not stop for man or beast or cataclysm.

And I was late. I was too late. Was I slow or were the calculations wrong? Perhaps it never had been possible, just as the long-term survival of all that we knew was only a dream. I arrived in Warsaw, but it was a different Warsaw. The fragment had ended and begun again, all the pieces, Jews and Poles and Nazis, reset on the board. And no Ellie, no Marcus, no Scarrows or Nguyen or the rest of them. I was too late.

They might have got out. Knowing the end was coming – of the ghetto and of time, one and then the other in a great wave of pain and fear and utter oblivion – perhaps they calculated an exit. Ellie was always good at the figures, after all. There were fragments they could have made – or Doc Comoy's calculations said there were. Unless it was a lie.

Or perhaps the enemy had come and wiped them away, shot them and removed them from the ruptured track of history. Or the Nazis had stormed the ghetto as they always did, and Ellie and the others had been just more corpses amongst so many, so very many.

Or the end had come, the real end, where time's frayed edge caught up with them, and when the fragment began again they were gone, erased from time and space, made as if they never were.

In the ghetto, I knelt down and wept, screamed out my frustrations to the sky and shrugged off the attempts of those doomed and desperate people to comfort me.

I was alone, and Doc Comoy's escape route was consigned to history. I sat there in the ruins and the ashes, amongst that other fugitive people, and did my own maths – not elegant Ellie maths, but my hamfisted imitation. I had to get out.

Even with nothing to get out for, a part of me wanted to live. Life has its own momentum. Ask the people in the Warsaw ghetto: no matter how bad it is, everyone wants to live.

It took me two years of my life, and I walked from one end of time to the other, but I made it back to Permian One. I hid in the Rome of the Medicis and cowered back from the wise, cold eyes of Neanderthals. I did what I did best: I ran, from the Mughals and the Zulus and the Iceni and Tyrannosaurus rex.

When at last I found the jump into the Permian fragment that the doctor was using, I saw it was true. Nothing had changed at all. He was older – they were all older, the clocks of their bodies marching on in ignorance of what had happened to wider time – but that was all. Oh, they were all busy, and there was the great impression of *things being done*, but I knew I was right. It was all a show, even if Doctor Comoy himself believed in it.

"They're gone," I told him, and from his expression he either did not know who I meant, or did not care.

That was when the enemy arrived.

I had never seen them properly before. I did not do so then, quite. They were humanoid, armoured, but what they were armoured in was proof against mere light as well as more violent measures. They shifted and warped and flickered and yet, at the same time, they were the most definite, concrete things in that complex. They were death, after all. There's nothing more real than death.

Like death, they were patient hunters. They had been stalking me for a long time, following me from fragment to fragment, effortless in their transitions, whilst I scratched and strained at the mathematics. They had tried to hide from me, but I was too much of an experienced fugitive. I had known they were there.

I led them to Permian One. I led them to Doctor Comoy. It wasn't as if I was doing anything else with my time. None of us were. That was the problem.

I had not known whether they were people at all, before that. They were the enemy, from before time broke, but I had thought they were no more than machines following the last orders of history. Until one spoke, I chose to believe that they were simple annihilators, the things that come at the end of the day, to close the shutters and put out the sun.

"Doctor Robert Comoy," one of them said – impossible to tell which one, but it was a woman's human voice, strong and stern. "You and your accomplices will be taken into custody for trial and disposal. Any attempt at escape will be met with force."

The old man on his ridiculous high chair goggled down at them. "What are you doing?" his frail voice demanded. "Can't you see I'm trying to put the world back together?"

"We are already restoring time," the woman returned flatly. "The only thing standing between us and a unified timestream is the interference caused by the presence of you and your people. We cannot repair time with your vermin running riot amongst the pieces. You will either come with us and be rehabilitated, or you will be removed."

Removed. She said it as though it had a capital letter: excised from time. Even then I could not have said whether it was true. Were they able to put the egg back together again? Were we the problem, rather than the solution?

Perhaps there was no solution.

Doctor Comoy was spitting, trying to force out words that were too big for the gape of his mouth, but then someone started shooting. Someone always starts shooting. Give a man a gun and he will want to use it. Perhaps that mentality is what caused this mess in the first place.

The enemy opened fire in return, beams of energy scorching and scouring whatever they touched. I wanted no part of it. Ellie and Marcus and the rest were gone, and I was on nobody's side but my own.

I had my calculations already made. While they were fighting, while the enemy were triumphing over Doc Comoy and his wretched little Permian dream, I fled.

It had taken me long hours of patient calculation, but once I knew the enemy were content to follow me, I realized that I had time, for the first time in a long time, to get it right. There was a fragment of the Eocene, that dawn age after the extinction of all the old dinosaurs, that was three years long, and I stepped from the burning confusion of Comoy's compound into a bright new day.

The enemy would hunt me. If what they said was true then I would gum up their works just by daring to exist. The Eocene was a big place, though, and running and hiding are what I'm good at, after all. As long as the enemy leave me fragments, I will find a hole to shelter in. I've the whole of my life ahead of me.

And when I'm old, when I've seen it all, that pitiful miscellany that is all that is left, perhaps I'll go back to that cluttered London, if the enemy have left it. I'll stand amongst the groundlings at the Curtain and listen to Will Kempe's final routine, his farewell speech to all of creation. I'll laugh out the end of the fragment into painless extinction, and let them save the universe.

But not yet. Not when I'm still using it. I've got a long way left to run.

THE GREAT CLOCK

Langdon Jones

Langdon Jones is an English short-story writer, editor, and musician whose stories appeared in *New Worlds*. He was part of the New Wave of literary science fiction in the 1960s, along with Michael Moorcock, J.G. Ballard, M. John Harrison, and several others. "The Great Clock" was first published in *New Worlds* #160 in 1966 and later appeared in his short-story collection *The Eye of the Lens*.

1

The light of the sky could be seen dimly through the small slits in the ceiling of the Great Chamber.

The Great Clock worked.

The Pendulum swung slowly in its giant arc and with every tick the whole Clock shuddered. The Great Wheel rose above the rest of the Clock mechanism in a great and static arc and the Fast Wheel whirled, humming, its sound rising above the noises made by the workings of the Clock. The other wheels turned at their various speeds, some smoothly, while some advanced one notch with every tick of the Clock. Pins engaged, wedges dropped, springs uncoiled. On the floor was thrown a shadow of wheels which formed an abstract pattern.

And the man sleeping naked on the pallet at the Posterior Wall stirred a little.

2

He was awakened by the whistle of the clock within the Clock.

It was fixed on one wall of the Great Chamber. It was made of wood and the sound of its ticking was lost in the constant sounds of the Great Clock. It was powered by a weight on a long chain, the other end of the chain having a metal loop through which projected the end of a lever coming through the wall. At this moment the lever, powered in some way by the Great Clock, was lowering itself smoothly, pulling down the free end of chain and winding up the clock. Below the clock, projecting upward from the floor was a four-foot metal flue pipe. The whistle was coming from this, a deafening note that was calling him to his duties. He covered his ears against the raucous sound. Eventually the note began to drop in volume and pitch, for a second broke down the octave to its fundamental, and then became quiet except for the hiss of escaping air. Behind the wooden wall could be heard intensive creaking as the giant bellows exhausted themselves.

The Clock ticked.

It was a thunderous sound, and it shook his body there on the pallet. It was a sound composed of a mosaic of sounds, some too high, others too low to be heard. But the high sounds irritated the eardrums and the low ones stirred the bowels. The sounds that could be heard were a million. Metallic and wooden, high and low, muffled and clear, they all combined in a shattering rumble that made thought impossible. The tick was composed primarily of four separate groups of sound that peaked at intervals of about half a second. At the end of each tick, a creak from somewhere high in the building ran up the scale to silence.

When the echoes had died away he could hear the other sounds of the Clock. The whole Chamber was alive with noise. There were creakings all around; cogs met with metallic clashes; wooden parts knocked hollowly. From high in the Chamber on the opposite side to his pallet the Fast Wheel hummed loudly.

He opened his eyes. Light was filtering in dimly through the two tiny slits in the ceiling of the Great Chamber. He could see the black outlines of the Great Wheel where it vaulted overhead, partly obscured by a supporting column. He groaned, then sat up on the pallet, looking across toward the clock on the wall. The clock was made entirely of wood, and only one hand pointed toward the irregular marks scored around the edge of the dial. The marks indicated the times at which he had to perform his duties; they extended three-quarters round the face. When the hand reached any of the marks, the bellows, now filling slowly behind the wall, would drop a short distance and the metal flue pipe would give a short call. The hand was about five degrees from the first mark, and this gave him a short while to eat his breakfast. He wondered dully if there was a little man inside the wall-clock, just getting up, ready for his day's work maintaining the mechanism.

The Clock ticked.

When the floor had stopped vibrating, he got up and walked across the Great Chamber. Dust rose in acrid clouds about him, making him sneeze. He urinated in the corner, lifting his nose against the sharp smells that arose from the inter-section of the walls that he always used for this purpose. Then he turned and walked back past the pile of bones in the other corner, skulls like large pieces of yellow putty, twigs of ribs, half buried by dust, and made his way to the door on the far side of the Chamber, moving among the bronzed supports of the Clock mechanism as he did so. He arrived at the low arched door and turned the iron handle, pushing open the wooden slab with effort.

The Clock ticked.

Now he was in the Small Chamber. The room was about nine feet long by seven wide, and was lined by wooden planks. The whole of the left-hand side of the Small Chamber was covered by a mass of wheels, thousands upon thousands, interlocking in frightening complexity. He had never tried to work out their arrangement and purpose; he just knew that they were an integral part of the workings of the Great Clock. The wheels were plain-rimmed—not cogged—and were of silver metal. They varied in size from about four feet down to one inch, and were all turning at varied rates. They whirred and clicked softly as they worked. The sounds of the Clock were muffled here in the Small Chamber, with the door closed, and only the tick was still just as disturbing, as disruptive to logical thought.

The Clock ticked.

He watched the chains from the wheels disappearing through the myriad holes in the wooden walls at either end of the Chamber. Some of the wheels were partly obscured, with just a tiny segment of their arc appearing through the space between the ceiling and the left-hand wall. Once, he had wondered whether he saw all the wheels or whether in fact there were more, many more, stretching away upward and downward.

The rest of the room was taken up mainly by the only compromise to his welfare, apart from the pallet in the Great Chamber. There was a wooden table and a small wooden chair. On the table were three objects, all of metal, a plate, a spoon, and a heavy goblet. At the far end of the Chamber by the cupboard set into the wall were two silver faucets. Above the faucets were two wheels of iron, to which worn wooden handles were attached.

The Clock ticked.

He walked across the Chamber and picked the plate off the table. He placed it on the floor below the nearer of the faucets. He stood up and began to turn the wheeled handle. A white mash poured out of the wide mouth of the faucet and slopped onto the plate. After he had turned the handle about ten complete revolutions there was a click, the handle spun free and no more mash came from the mouth. He picked up the plate and carried it back to the table, burying the spoon upright in the mash. Then he repeated the performance with the goblet and the other faucet, and filled the vessel with cold water.

The Clock ticked.

He settled down listlessly and began to spoon the mash into his mouth. It was completely tasteless, but he accepted it as he accepted everything else. The Clock ticked five times before he had finished his meal. He left half the mash and inverted the plate over the primitive drain in the floor. Rotting food from previous meals still remained, and at one time the stench would have appalled him.

A short, sharp blast from the pipe informed him that it was time for his duties to start. There was a lot of work in front of him. A vague memory came into his mind of when he used to eat all the mash and still have a little time to relax quietly before starting his work. Now he toyed with his food and needed less.

The Clock ticked and dispersed the thought.

He walked with heavy steps over to the cupboard and opened the door. Inside were his tools. To the left was a rack of hammers for testing the wheels. They ranged in size from a tiny hammer all of metal, the head of which was about the size of the first joint of his little finger, to a giant sledgehammer with a large iron head and a thick wooden shaft, which was used for testing the Great Wheel. The trolley was just as he had left it the previous night. Everything was just as he had left it. The trolley was made of black cracked wood with iron wheels. On it was a giant drum with an opened top. A great faucet extended down from the top of the cupboard above the drum, and now the container was filled with yellow sweetly-smelling grease. Every night it was the same.

The Clock ticked.

On a shelf on the right was a can, below yet another, small, faucet, and the can was now filled by the dark translucent beauty of thin oil. He lifted the hammers from the rack and slowly placed them on the trolley beside the drum. He lifted down the oil can and placed that on the rack designed for the purpose.

He grasped the pulling rail and began to heave the trolley backward out of the cupboard. His body strained with the effort. Surely, at one time it had all been easier . . .

The Clock ticked.

The trolley was finally right out of the cupboard, and he walked round it, so that he would be able to push it from the back. Before he started pushing, he suddenly realized that he had forgotten to move the table out of the way. He sighed deeply and walked back to the table, folding up the legs and resting it on its side against the wall.

"Getting old . . ." he muttered, " . . . getting old . . ." Those were the first words he had spoken in a long time, and his voice sounded thin and weak. He pushed the trolley through the Small Chamber, past the whirring wheels. His last duty of the day would be to oil those wheels. He realized that he had forgotten to open the door, opened it, and pushed the trolley into the Great Chamber. He stopped the trolley at the point where he always stopped it.

The Clock ticked.

He went up to the nearest of the wheels. It was a large wheel, about five feet in diameter. Most of the wheel could be seen clearly, unobscured by other mechanism, and the black metal was pitted, as if by age. He selected the correct hammer, a large one, weighing several pounds, and swung it into contact with the edge of the wheel. The wheel shivered, and rang like a gong. Satisfied, he placed the hammer back on the trolley, and pushed it on a little further. On he went, wheel after wheel. Some of the wheels boomed hollowly, others tinkled like tiny bells. Never had they done otherwise.

When he came to the first supporting column, he selected the second largest hammer. The column was of a diameter of about a foot, and it was made of a golden metal, either copper or brass. Later these columns would have to be cleaned.

The Clock ticked exactly at the moment he swung the hammer. But after the sounds had died away, the column still reverberated with a shrill brightness. Now he had come to the Fast Wheel. There was a wooden ladder set against its supports, and he picked up the oil can and began to mount the ladder.

The Fast Wheel was different from most of the others. It was difficult to observe, owing to its rate of travel, but the lack of fuzziness at the edges indicated that it possessed no cogs. It appeared to be a double wheel, having two rims, its spokes tapering inward to the single hub. It was driven by a taut chain which was an insubstantial blur that stretched to a hole in the Anterior Wall, opposite his pallet. The ladder vibrated with the wheel's motion, and air fanned his face strongly as he climbed upward. The wheel ran in oil, and a reservoir arched above it with two ducts that fell past its eighteen-inch radius to the hub. The hum of the wheel was almost intolerable at this closeness.

The Clock ticked and for a couple of seconds drowned the hum of the Fast Wheel.

He poured half the contents of the oil can into the reservoir, then quickly descended the ladder. Now there was just the Great Wheel and then four smaller cogs over the other side of the mechanism. He picked the largest hammer from the trolley and dragged it across the floor. The Great Wheel was only exposed at one point, and then only about a foot of its surface. This was about the nearest it was possible for him to get to the Anterior Wall. The Great Wheel was about a foot thick and was constructed of matt black metal; a foot from where it disappeared into the space between the floor and the Anterior Wall the other mechanism of the Clock terminated. He dragged the hammer into a convenient position and tensed the muscles of his arms and stomach.

The Clock ticked.

He swung in an imaginary back stroke, the hammer not moving, then, reaching as far back as he could and starting to swing forward, transformed the stroke into actuality by dragging the hammer along the floor toward the wheel. The head lifted just before the hammer came into contact with the black metal. It hit, and his stomach was churned by the deep vibration of the Great Wheel. Along with the almost subsonic fundamental, an upper partial screamed briefly. The sounds almost made him vomit, but he checked this and instead coughed the dust from his throat. During the time when his duties had always seemed to be much easier and quicker, and there had been time to spare, he had watched the twenty-foot Great Wheel very carefully for long periods, and had never seen it move a fraction of an inch.

The Clock ticked as he walked away.

He went to his trolley and plunged his hands into the drum, withdrawing two gobs of grease. He went up to the Great Wheel again and slapped the grease into the reservoir at its side. There would be more points to grease later in the day.

Now there were just the other four cogs to test, and then it would be time to check the Meter.

The flue pipe blew piercingly.

Shock raced through his body, and the grunt he made was lost in the sounds of the Clock. *Had he been so slow?* He never remembered having a job unfinished when the time came to begin the next. He looked unbelievingly at the clock on the wall; the hand stood unquestionably at the second of the scored marks.

For a moment he was lost; his knees trembled and his body shook. What should he do? Should he finish his job or hurry to check the Meter? Normally he liked checking the Meter; there was rarely any need to make an adjustment, the pointer always resting at the zero position. This meant that he would have at least fifteen minutes to himself. But now he was in an agony of uselessness, for the first time being faced with a decision. A thought began to bubble up through his shock, and forced itself into consciousness for a fraction of a second.

Why?

The Clock ticked, dissolving the thought in a torrent of sound.

He decided to check the Meter. He could always come back and sound the remaining four wheels; it would mean losing a little of the precious spare time, but that didn't matter.

He wiped his greasy hands on his thighs and walked across to the Posterior Wall and the little panel behind which lay the Meter. He pulled aside the wooden panel with effort, and then groaned in dismay. The pointer stood at minus two.

He was plunged into panic; an adjustment would have to be made. When would he have time to sound the remaining four wheels? He would have to hurry. He pulled aside the adjacent panel with trembling hands. He stepped inside the lift and began to turn the large wheeled handle. The Great Chamber was lost to view as the lift began to travel down the shaft. Little light filtered down from the Chamber, but he was able to see the joints in the wood of the shaft. Going down, he was fighting the counterweight and the work was much more difficult. He wished that he was coming up, the adjustment having been made.

After what seemed like hours, the dim light of the Pendulum Well traveled up the open front of the lift and he stopped.

The Clock ticked, very slightly muffled at this depth.

He clambered out of the lift and then finally stood upright in the Pendulum Well. The Well was vast. It stretched up and up, many times his own height, and the top was marked by a light rectangle where the mouth of the Well met the lighter Great Chamber at the very front of the Clock. Cogs jutted blackly above, and the tall cylinder of the Pendulum Rod inclined itself gracefully and slowly toward one side of the Well. Once he had wondered on the unusual nature of the Escapement Mechanism. The Escapement itself appeared to be almost independent of the Pendulum, its action only being triggered by the Pendulum's motion. The Pendulum swung freely for almost its whole arc, and the Escapement Lever only inclined at the extremes of its swing. At the top the Escapement Lever quivered, preparing for its giant pivoting movement, and its sound came to him like a clanking of great chains. The Pendulum had a wide arc, about forty-five degrees, and at the moment it was reaching the peak of its swing. The Pendulum was so vast that at this point of its swing it scarcely seemed to be moving. It was only when the Bob was whistling past his head at the bottom of its swing that he could really appreciate how fast it was moving.

At the top of the Clock the Escapement quivered again. The Pendulum had slowed now and seemed to be poised impossibly, hanging without movement, a vast distance from him. There was a rumble and, with a screech of metal, the Escapement Lever roused itself and began to pivot its great weight. With a shattering crash, it fell heavily into its new position.

And the Clock ticked.

Now the Pendulum was moving back again, increasing speed second by second.

The walls of the Pendulum Well were, like the Small Chamber, lined by planks of wood, although black. The sounds of the clock came to him here with a wooden consistency as they were reflected and diffused by the Well. On the near side of the Well, iron rungs were set into the wall, which would enable him to reach the giant bulk of the Weight. He glanced up, looking at the dark shadow that loomed overhead. He stepped forward into the path of the rapidly approaching Pendulum Bob, which would pass about a foot above his head. At the far end of the Well was another ladder which led up to a platform far above, which would enable him to meet the Bob as it rose up to the top of its swing, and from which he would step on to the Bob to carry out the adjustment.

From its highest point, above the Escapement Mechanism, to a point about one sixth of the way down the Well, the Pendulum Rod consisted of a cylinder of shining golden metal, probably brass, with a diameter of about four feet. From there to the Bob, a distance of at least fifty feet, it was made up of a frame of several smaller tubes of various colored metals, probably some kind of temperature compensation. The Bob itself was a ten-foot lens of gray metal, tapering at the edges to knife-blade-thinness. As the Pendulum rushed through the air, eddies formed on alternate sides like the ripples running along a flag, setting the Pendulum, as it rode the turbulence, into vibration.

And the Pendulum sang.

A deep, clear ringing vibration filled the Well, like an organ note, but with a chiming quality. He felt the vibration through the soles of his feet as he stood there on the wooden floor. He kept his mouth slightly slack, for if his teeth touched together they would buzz unpleasantly with a higher version of the same note.

The Bob was now rushing down upon him, and with a sudden gust of air, it was past him and away, climbing rapidly toward the peak of its swing.

With a shock he realized that there was no time to stand here watching. There were still four wheels left unsounded. He turned and began to climb the nearer ladder. There was a catwalk leading round the Well past the Weight, and he always came this way to check on the Weight as he passed. After a long time of climbing the iron rungs he eventually arrived at the catwalk. The Weight was a vast bulk to his rear; he was fortunate that he had come down at this time, for often the Weight was further toward the floor, or too high, which necessitated painful maneuvering on the rungs.

He turned and looked at the Weight. It was a block of black metal, about two feet deep and four feet high, and it stretched the length of the Well. It was supported by thin wire, which branched out from a single strand far up the Well and culminated in hundreds of strands spread out in an angular delta. At the top of the Weight was a complex of cogs, the largest of which was about six inches across, the smallest about half an inch, and some of them were revolving quite rapidly. The fine wire passed up and down in the complex of wheels, circling some of them. These grooved wheels turned as the wire moved round them, and the vast Weight was lowering itself, so slowly that its motion could scarcely be seen.

The Clock ticked.

He glanced at the Pendulum, now at the fullest extent of its swing at the far end of the Well. He would be able to get to the platform in one-and-a-half strokes, by which time the Bob would be in the correct position for him to mount it. He began to move along the catwalk, his bare feet pattering on the wooden planks. There was no safety rail and he kept close to the wall, as he was now about twenty feet from the floor. As the Pendulum overtook him on its way back, the Bob dropped to far below his level, and then began to climb past him.

The Clock ticked before he reached the corner of the Well.

Past the corner he went, and he walked across the width of the Well, a distance of only about thirty feet. The platform projected out from the wall, and he stood out on it, waiting for the Bob to arrive. There was a long, thin chain hanging beside him, that stretched up into the mechanism of the Escapement. He guessed that his weight was computed by the strain on the platform, and pulling the iron ring at the end of the chain caused some kind of weight compensation to be applied to the Pendulum, so that his weight on the Pendulum for one whole swing had no effect on the accuracy of the Clock. The Bob was now at the bottom of its return swing and was rising, apparently slowly, toward him. Mounting the Pendulum was a difficult feat, one that had caused him trouble in the early days.

The early days? He dismissed the distracting thought: he must concentrate on mounting the Pendulum. The difficulty was in the apparent motion of the Bob. When one stood in the center of the Well at the bottom, at the higher points of its swing the Pendulum scarcely seemed to be moving, while at its center its true speed could be appreciated. Here, at the high point of its swing, the opposite illusion occurred, but was made more complex by the fact that the Pendulum *did* actually slow at this point of its arc.

The apparent speed of the Bob was increasing rapidly as it approached him. His muscles tensed as its bulk loomed up toward him. He slipped his hand into the iron ring, and pulled the chain downward. Then, as the Bob was almost on him it suddenly appeared to slow. Now he could see the corresponding platform that jutted out from the Bob. He watched the platform and nothing else. The edges of the two platforms came smoothly together. There was a pause. He stepped swiftly across on to the other surface. There was a brass rail on the inside of the platform with a strap looped from it. With fumbling fingers he hurriedly buckled the strap about his waist and pulled it tight, just as the Pendulum began to move downward.

And the Clock ticked, shaking the Pendulum.

He looked over his shoulder and watched the other platform and the catwalk moving rapidly upward and away from him. The acceleration became greater, and he felt his stomach lift within him as he traveled yet faster. The air rushed past his face, and he tried to draw his attention from the distressing physical sensations. The bulk of his body, tiny though it was in relation to the Bob, disturbed the flow of the air, breaking the current into smaller eddies. As the new vibration tried to impose itself on the old, the Pendulum groaned with tearing dissonance. Then, abruptly, the note broke up to its second partial, and the sound was now bright, ringing and intense. As the Bob began to level out, his stomach felt a little more normal, and he squatted down to make the adjustment. The platform on which he was squatting was slung at the lowest part of the Bob, and hung down below. At the very lowest point of the Bob was fitted the Adjustment Weight, for making the incredibly small adjustments to the frequency of the Pendulum's swing. A piece of thin metal rod was fixed from the Bob, hanging downward. This rod was scored across at regular intervals, about a quarter of an inch apart, and attached about halfway down was a small weight, of about an ounce, with a sprung clip that attached to one of the grooves in the rod. The Meter had read minus two; this meant that the weight had to be slid two spaces upward. Obviously the Clock was running slow by an infinitesimal amount, and this adjustment would correct its running. As he put out his hand the Pendulum began to rise on its upward swing, and his arm felt heavy and approached the weight much lower than it should have done.

He paused as the nausea gripped him again. After a few seconds the feeling began to diminish as the Pendulum reached its high point. He knew better than to attempt to adjust the weight at this moment.

The Clock ticked, vibrating the Pendulum, and almost throwing him on to his back. He gripped the brass rail and waited for the wrenching of his stomach as he fell in the sweeping arc. The Pendulum began to move downward. The adjustment would have to be made this time; he knew that he would be incapable of standing more than one complete swing of the Pendulum. Air rushed past him as he dropped with the Bob and he gritted his teeth against the sickness that rose inside. At least the new high note of the Pendulum did not buzz in his head as would have done the fundamental. As the Pendulum leveled out, he reached out and grasped the weight. He pushed upward, and the weight moved up slowly with a double click. He tested it with a light pull, and then sighed with relief and began to stand, fighting the downward push caused by the upward motion of the Bob.

At the top of the swing he stepped on to the platform before the tick of the Clock commenced its vibration. His legs were shaking as he began to climb down the iron rungs.

As he walked across the floor of the Well his mind was feverishly calculating. Would he still have time to sound the wheels before his next task? He clambered down the narrow tunnel into the lift. His next task was the Winding, and he tried not to think of this. It was a task that took about an hour of his time every day, and left him a weak, trembling old man. Even so, he still sometimes wondered how it was that such a comparatively small amount of energy could sustain the vast mechanism all about him. From his fuddled memory he vaguely recalled that on similar occasions, the whistle had blown shortly after he had arrived in the Great Chamber.

As the lift arrived at the top of its shaft, the Clock ticked, the sound of it jangling afterwards in his ears, contrasting with the sounds of the Pendulum Well. Here, the noises were all about him again; the grinding of the cogs, the humming of the Fast Wheel; the oil smells and the sharp tang of metal were in his nostrils again. His trolley was there, as he had left it. He began to walk across the floor, dust rising in clouds about him as he moved. He reached the trolley and grasped his hammer, ready for sounding the next wheel, and he used a small hammer that could comfortably be held in one hand. He swung the hammer and struck the wheel.

The whistle screamed, drowning all other sounds. He groaned out loud. The whistle stopped, and he stood there, hammer in hand, wanting to strike the wheel again. Why could not the whistle have blown one second later? At least he would have been able to hear this wheel. He almost swung at the wheel again, but he could not; it was time for the Winding. He felt tears springing to his eyes at the unfairness of it all. He was old, and tired . . . He walked across to the Posterior Wall and slid open the panel that led to the Winding Room.

The Clock ticked.

This was only a small room and it was lined with planks like the others. It was completely featureless save for the Winding Handle which was set into the far wall and projected out into the room. He stepped inside and grasped the Handle. He put his weight on to it and it gradually moved downward, a ratchet clicking rapidly somewhere behind the wall. When the Handle was at its lowest extent, he slightly released the pressure and it rose up under his hands to its original position. He pressed down again. He would wind until the whistle blew again, a period he estimated to be about an hour, but a very long hour indeed. After the Winding he would be allowed a short time from his labor for lunch. Perhaps he could sound the remaining wheels in his lunch time?

The Clock ticked.

This would mean that he would miss his mash. He didn't mind about that too much; what really worried him was that he would miss his valuable rest period. The handle rose under his hands to its highest position. He was worried about the afternoon; how could he work if he missed his rest? He was weak enough now. He pressed down the handle. Sweat was beginning to run down his forehead; he felt terrible. Surely, at one time he had not felt so weak and tired. At one time?

At what time? For a second he was distracted from his task.

He slipped.

His foot went from under him and he fell forward, toward the handle. His hands slid from it and it swung up, catching him under the chin and throwing him backward on to the floor.

Lights flashed under his eyelids and his head buzzed, cutting out all other sound. When he came to he found that he was standing in the Great Chamber, swaying slightly.

Where was he?

For the first time his routine had been upset. The blow had jogged his mind from its well-worn paths. He realized that all the events of this day had conspired to open his senses to this apocalypse.

He looked about himself in amazement.

All was as it had been; the Fast Wheel hummed to itself and the cogs moved round at their various speeds.

But now the Clock mechanism looked alien and frightening to him as he regarded it with eyes unclouded by time.

How had he got here?

The stench of his own excrement arose from the corner of the Great Chamber, mixed with the acrid tang of the metal that surrounded him.

His head moved from side to side as he tried to see everything at once.

The Clock ticked, unexpectedly, causing him to clap his hands to his ears.

He had been so frightened; what had forced him to carry out these awful duties that had wasted so much of his life? He walked across to the far end of the Great Chamber and looked at the bones in the corner. He could see about four complete skeletons among the crumbling fragments of many others. They were all supported on a billowing pile of dust that came from innumerable others. Were these the bones of the others, who, before him, had tended the Clock? Did they, one day, suddenly know that their time was up, and did they, obeying a dim and contrived instinct, slowly, painfully drag themselves over to the pile and quietly lie upon it? And then did the next person come here and immediately settle into his ritual of duties, ignoring the twitching bundle in the corner, and later the odor of its corruption?

He walked back to his pallet and sat on it, burying his face in his hands. When *he* came to the Clock, was there a body in the corner? Did he sit in the Small Chamber eating his mash whilst the air was full of the taint of death?

What was his life before he came here?

Who was he?

He could not remember. Nor could he remember how long he had been here.

He felt round the back of his head; his hair was hanging down almost to his shoulders. He estimated from this that he had been inside the Clock for a whole year of his life. He remembered something else. His age. He was twenty-five years old.

Twenty-five?

Then why was he so weak and tired?

Something wrong made a shudder crawl its way down his back. His hands had been registering something for some time, and now he consciously accepted their message. His hands told him that the skin hung loose and wrinkled round his face. His hands told him that his features were covered by wrinkled and flaccid parchment.

He sat up on the pallet in fear. He suddenly pulled out a little clump of hair, bringing tears to his eyes. But the tears did not obscure his vision completely, and he could see that the hair was snowy white. He looked up in agony.

"I'm old!"

The Clock ticked.

"I'm old . . ."

He looked down at his body. It was the body of an old, old man.

He slowly stood and then staggered to one of the supporting columns. He embraced the column, resting his cheek against the golden surface. His hand stroked the smooth metal of the column's surface, almost as if he were caressing a woman. He giggled.

"Look at me," he muttered to the Clock. "Look what you've done to me!"

The Fast Wheel hummed; the cogs turned.

"You've taken my life! I was young when I came here a year ago! Young! What have you done?"

His voice had become high and quavering and was swallowed in the sounds of the Clock.

"Oh God!" he said, and slumped against the column. He stayed there a long time, thinking. He was going to have his revenge. The Clock would run down, with no one to wind it. It would die, without him.

The Clock ticked, and he pushed his shoulders from the column, standing erect. He began to walk round the Great Chamber, putting out his hand here, stroking a wheel there. He blew kisses to the Fast Wheel and ran his flat hand gently over the surface of the Great Wheel. Wheedling, coquettish, he minced extravagantly through the Great Chamber, quietly talking to the Clock.

"Why?" he said. "Why? I've given you my life; what have you given in return? You have taken eighty years from me—what have you done with them? Are they stored vilely away in a cupboard? If I searched long enough, could I find them, stacked on a shelf? Could I put out my hands and slip them on, like clothes? Eh? Why did you steal them?"

His muttering suddenly became ominous in tone.

"I'll fix you; I won't even give you the pleasure of running quietly down, as you would have done with me. Oh no, my friend, you shall die violently; I'll show you no quarter.'

He moved across to the trolley. He painfully lifted off the largest of the hammers and dragged it to the floor. A wheel of moderate size, about four feet across, was quite near to him. With all his strength he swung the hammer in a low arc and relaxed only as it smashed into the wheel. The giant hammer broke off one of the cogs completely, and bent part of the wheel at an impossible angle. He dropped the hammer, and, filled with emotion, crammed his fists against his opened mouth.

The Clock ticked.

He found that he was weeping; why, he didn't understand.

The cog turned slowly, the damaged section moving nearer to its inevitable interaction with another wheel. He screwed up his eyes, and felt the warm tears running freely down his face.

"I've killed you," he said. He stood, thin, bleached and naked, paralysed and sobbing. Something would happen soon.

The damaged section interacted.

The wrecked cog spun suddenly and rapidly before its teeth engaged again. A shower of sparks flew out, burning his flesh. He started, both at the pain and at the sheer noise of that dreadful contact. At the threshold of his hearing, far below the other sounds of the Clock, he could hear the buckling of metal, the scraping of part on part. The other wheel buckled and spun in its turn. A spring burst from somewhere behind the wheel and scattered metal splinters all over the Chamber. Strange smells were in the air; the death-smells of the Clock.

A trail of damage was running across the mechanism of the Clock like an earthquake fissure running across land. It could not be seen, and outwardly practically everything was normal, but his ears could hear the changes in what had been familiar sounds. The grinding and destruction spreading like a canker could be heard clearly enough.

The Clock ticked, and even the tick sounded slightly weaker.

Louder and louder came the sounds of invisible destruction. He stood, still weeping, shaking as if with fever. The changed sounds of the Clock plunged him into a new and unfamiliar world.

A different sound made him look up. Above him the Fast Wheel was running eccentrically. It was wavering from side to side in its supports, oil spurting from its reservoirs. As it spun, it whined, jarringly.

Abruptly it broke free of its supports and, still whining, it dropped to the floor. It screamed as it hit the floor and was covered by the roaring flame of its friction. And then it was gone, only the hint of a bright streak in the air indicating its trajectory. It smashed into the far wall scattering dust from the bones as the wooden wall dissolved into splintering wreckage.

An uluation came from the Small Chamber. Inside, the mass of wheels screamed as they were tortured by the new disorder spreading through their myriad ranks. The Clock shook in its ague, shivering itself to death. Suddenly through the open door of the Small Chamber came the wheels, thousands of them. The Great Chamber was full of smooth silver wheels, some broken and flying through the air, others rolling lazily.

The Clock ticked, gratingly, and then screamed again. The Escapement Mechanism jammed rigid, but the Pendulum wanted to continue its swing. It did, bending its great four-foot-diameter column in a grotesque shape.

Dust was everywhere, flying metal whistled about his ears. As the sound became unbelievable the destruction became complete.

His last sight was of light streaming brightly in as the whole Clock collapsed in a mass of falling wood and metal cogs.

3

And it was everybody else's last sight, too. They may, for a brief period, have seen their world freezing itself in grotesque lack of activity. They may have seen water, solidifying in its fall to complete immobility; they may have seen birds flying through air that was like treacle, finally coming to rest above the ground; they may even have seen their own faces beginning to register terror, but never completing the expression . . .

But after that, there was no time to see anything.

TRAVELLER'S REST

David I. Masson

David I. Masson was a British science fiction writer and librarian. *The Caltraps of Time* is his only short-story collection, containing all of his fiction, all of the stories he published in *New Worlds*, and three additional stories. "Traveller's Rest" was originally published in 1965 in *New Worlds* magazine.

It was an apocalyptic sector. Out of the red-black curtain of the forward sight-barrier, which at this distance from the Frontier shut down a mere twenty metres north, came every sort of meteoric horror: fission and fusion explosions, chemical detonations, a super-hail of projectiles of all sizes and basic velocities, sprays of nerve-paralysants and thalamic dopes. The impact devices burst on the barren rock of the slopes or the concrete of the forward stations, some of which were disintegrated or eviscerated every other minute. The surviving installations kept up an equally intense and nearly vertical fire of rockets and shells. Here and there a protectivized figure could be seen sprinting up, down or along the slopes on its mechanical walker like a frantic ant from an anthill attacked by flamethrowers. Some of the visible oncoming trajectories could be seen snaking overhead into the indigo gloom of the rear sight-curtain, perhaps fifty metres south, which met the steep-falling rock surface forty-odd metres below the observer's eye. The whole scene was as if bathed in a gigantic straight rainbow. East and west, as far as the eye could see, perhaps some forty miles in this clear mountain air despite the debris of explosion (but cut off to west by a spur from the range) the visibility-corridor witnessed a continual onslaught and counter-onslaught of devices. The visible pandemonium was shut in by the sight-barriers' titanic canyon walls of black, reaching the slim pale strip of horizon-spanning light at some immense height. The audibility-corridor was vastly wider than that of sight; the many-pitched din, even through left ear in helm, was considerable.

"Computer-sent, must be," said H's transceiver into his right ear. No sigil preceded this statement, but H knew the tones of B, his next-up, who in any case could be seen a metre away saying it, in the large concrete bubble whence they watched, using a plaspex window and an infrared northviewer with a range of some hundreds of metres forward. His next-up had been in the bunker for three minutes, apparently overchecking, probably for an appreciation to two-up who might be in station VV now.

"Else how can they get minutely impacts here, you mean?" said H.

"Well, of course it could be long range low-frequency – we don't really know how Time works over There."

"But if the conceleration runs asymptotically to the Frontier, as it should if Their Time works in mirror-image, would anything ever have got over?"

"Doesn't have to, far's I can see – maybe it steepens a lot, then just falls back at the same angle the other Side," said B's voice; "anyway, I didn't come to talk science: I've news for you, if we hold out the next few seconds here, you're Relieved."

H felt a black inner sight-barrier beginning to engulf him, and a roaring in his ears swallowed up the noise of the bombardment. He bent double as his knees began to buckle, and regained full consciousness. He could see his replacement now, an uncertain-looking figure in prot-suit (like everybody else up here) at the far side of the bunker.

"XN 3, what orders then?" he said crisply, his pulse accelerating.

"XN 2: pick em-kit now, repeat now, rocket 3333 to VV, present tag" – holding out a luminous orange label printed with a few coarse black characters – "and proceed as ordered thence."

H stuck up his right thumb from his fist held at elbow length, in salute. It was no situation for facial gestures or unnecessary speech. "XN 3, yes, em-kit, 3333 rocket, tag" (he had taken it in his left glove) "and W orders; parting!"

He missed B's nod as he skimmed on soles to the exit, grabbed a small bundle hanging (one of fifteen) from the fourth hook along, slid down the greasy slide underground ten metres to a fuel-cell-lit cavern, pressed a luminous button in the wall, watched a lit symbol passing a series of marks, jumped into the low car as it ground round the corner, and curled up foetuswise. His weight having set off the door mechanism, the car shut, slipped down and (its clamps setting on H's body) roared off down the chute.

Twenty-five seconds after his parting word H uncurled at the forward receiver cell of station VV nearly half a mile downslope. He crawled out as the rocket ground off again, walked ten steps onward in this larger version of his northward habitat, saluted thumb-up and presented his tag to two-up (recognized from helm-tint and helm-sign), saying simultaneously, "XN 3 rep, Relieved."

"XN 1 to XN 3: take this" (holding out a similar orange tag plucked from his pocket) "and take mag-lev train down, in – seventy seconds. By the way, ever seen a prehis?"

"No, sir."

"Spot through here, then; look like pteros but more primitive."

The infrared telescopic viewer looking north-west passed through the forward sight-barrier which due north was about forty metres away here. Well upslope yet still well clear of the dark infrared-radiation barrier could be seen, soundlessly screaming and yammering, two scaly animals about the size of large dogs, but with two legs and heavy wings, flopping around a hump or boulder on the rock. They might have been hit on their way along, and could hardly have had any business on that barren spot, H thought.

"Thanks; odd," he said. Eleven seconds of the seventy had gone. He pulled out a squirter-cup from the wall and took a drink from the machine through his helm. Seventeen seconds gone, fifty-three to go.

"XN 1 to XN 3: how are things up there?"

Naturally a report was called for: XN 2 might never return, and communication up-time and down-time was nearly impossible at these latitudes over more than a few metres.

"XN 3. Things have been hotting up all day; I'm afraid a burst through may be attempted in the next hour or so – only my guess, of course. But I've never seen anything like it all this time up here. I suppose you'll have noticed it in VV too?"

"XN 1, thanks for report," was all the answer he got. But he could hear for himself that the blitz was much more intense than any he had known at this level either.

Only twenty-seven seconds remained. He saluted and strode off across the bunker with his em-kit and the new tag. He showed the tag to the guard, who stamped it and pointed wordlessly down a corridor. H ran down this, arriving many metres down the far end at a little gallery. An underslung rail-guided vehicle with slide-doors opening into cubicles glided quietly alongside. A gallery-guard waved as H and two others waiting opened doors whose indicators were unlit, the doors slid to, and H found himself gently clamped in on a back-tilted seat as the mag-lev train accelerated downhill. After ten seconds it stopped at the next checkhalt; a panel in the cubicle ceiling lit up to state DIVERSION, LEFT, presumably because the direct route had been destroyed. The train now appeared to accelerate but more gently, swung away to left (as H could feel) and stopped at two more checkhalts before swinging back right and finally decelerating, coming to rest and opening some 480 seconds after its start, by Had's personal chronograph, instead of the 200 he had expected.

At this point daylight could again be seen. From the top bunker where XN 2 had discharged him, Had had now gone some ten miles south and nearly 3000 metres down, not counting detours. The forward sight-barrier here was hidden by a shoulder of mountain covered in giant lichen, but the southern barrier was evident as a violet-black fog-wall a quarter of a mile off. Lichens and some sort of grass-like vegetation covered much of the neighbouring landscape, a series of hollows and ravines. Noise of war was still audible, mingled with that of a storm, but nearby crashes were not frequent and comparatively little damage could be seen. The sky overhead was turbulent. Some very odd-looking animals, perhaps between a lizard and a stoat in general appearance, were swarming up and down a tree-fern near by. Six men in all got out of the mag-lev train, besides Had. Two and three marched off in two groups down track eastward. One (not one of those who had got in at VV) stayed with Had.

"I'm going down to the Great Valley; haven't seen it for twenty days; everything'll be changed. Are you sent far?" said the other man's voice in Had's right ear through the transceiver.

"I— I— I'm Relieved," tried Had uncertainly.

"Well, I'm . . . disintegrated!" was all the other man could manage. Then after a minute, "Where will you go?"

"Set up a business way south, I think. Heat is what suits me, heat and vegetation. I have a few techniques I could put to good use in management of one sort or another. I'm sorry – I never meant to plume it over you with this – but you did ask me."

"That's all right. You certainly must have Luck, though. I never met a man who was Relieved. Make good use of it, won't you. It helps to make the Game worthwhile up here – I mean, to have met a man who is joining all those others we're supposed to be protecting – it makes them real to us in a way."

"Very fine of you to take it that way," said Had.

"No, I mean it. Otherwise we'd wonder if there was any people to hold the Front for."

"Well, if there weren't, how'd the techniques have developed for holding on up here?" put Had.

"Some of the Teccols I remember in the Great Valley might have developed enough techniques for that."

"Yes, but think of all the pure science you need to work up the techniques from; I doubt if that could have been studied inside the Valley Teccols."

"Possibly not – that's a bit beyond me," said the other's voice a trifle huffily, and they stood on in silence till the next cable-car came up and round at the foot of the station. Had let the man get in it – he felt he owed him that – and a minute later (five seconds only, up in his first bunker, he suddenly thought ironically and parenthetically) the next car appeared. He swung himself in just as a very queer-looking purple bird with a long bare neck alighted on the stoat-lizards' tree-fern. The cable-car sped down above the ravines and hollows, the violet southern curtain backing still more swiftly away from it. As the time-gradient became less steep his brain began to function better and a sense of well-being and meaningfulness grew in him. The car's speed slackened.

Had was glad he still wore his prot-suit when a couple of chemical explosions burst close to the cable line, presumably by chance, only fifty metres below him. He was even more glad of it when flying material from a third broke the cable itself well downslope and the emergency cable stopped him at the next pylon. He slid down the pylon's lift and spoke with his transceiver close to the telephone at the foot. He was told to make west two miles to the next cable-car line. His interlocutor, he supposed, must be speaking from an exchange more or less on the same latitude as that of his pylon, since communication even here was still almost impossible north–south except at ranges of some metres. Even so, there was a squeaky sound about the other voice and its speech came out clipped and rapid. He supposed his own voice would sound gruff and drawled to the other.

Using his walker, he picked his way across ravines and gullies, steering by compass and watching the sight-barriers and the Doppler tint-equator ahead for yawing. All very well for that man to talk about Teccols, he thought, but he must realize that no civilization could have evolved from anywhere as far north as the Great Valley: it's far too young to have even evolved Men by itself – at least at this end; I'm not sure how far south the eastern end goes.

The journey was not without its hazards: there were several nearby explosions, and what looked like a suspicious artificial miasma, easily overlooked, lay in two hollows which he decided to go round. Moreover, an enraged giant bear-sloth came at him in a mauve shrub-thicket and had to be eliminated with his quickgun. But to one who had just come down from that mountain hell all this seemed like a pleasant stroll.

Finally he came upon the line of pylons and pressed the telephone button at the foot of the nearest, after checking that its latitude-number was nearly right. The same voice, a little less outlandish and rapid, told him a car would arrive in three quarters of a minute and would be arranged to stop at his pylon; if it did not, he was to press the emergency button nearby. Despite his walker, nearly an hour had gone by since he set out for it. Perhaps ninety minutes had passed since he first left the top bunker – well over a minute and a half of their time there.

The car came and stopped, he scrambled up and in, and this time the journey passed without incident, except for occasional sudden squalls, and the passage of flocks of nervous crows, until the car arrived at its terminus, a squat tower on the heathy slopes. The car below was coming up, and a man in it called through his transceiver as they crept past each other, "First of a bunch!" Sure enough the terminus interior was filled with some twenty men all equipped – almost enough to have warranted sending them up by polyheli, thought Hadol, rather than wait for cars at long intervals. They looked excited and not at all cast down, but Hadol refrained from giving away his future. He passed on to the ratchet-car way and found himself one of a group of men more curious about the landscape than about their fellows. A deep reddish curtain of indeterminate thickness absorbed the shoulders of the heights about a quarter-mile northward, and the bluish fog terminated the view over the valley at nearly half a mile southward, but between the two the latitudinal zone was tolerably clear and devoid of obvious signs of war. Forests of pine and lower down of oak and ash covered the slopes, until finally these disappeared in the steepening edge of the Great Valley, whose mead-ows could however be glimpsed past the bluff. Swirling cloud-shadows played over the ground, skirts and tassels of rain and hail swept across it, and there was the occasional flash and rumble of a storm. Deer could be seen briefly here and there, and dense clouds of gnats danced above the trees.

A journey of some fifty minutes took them down, past two empty stations, through two looped tunnels and among waterfalls and under cliffs where squir-rels leapt across from dangling root to root, through steadily warmer and warmer air to the pastures and cornfields of the Great Valley, where a narrow village of concrete huts and wooden cabins, Emmel, nestled on a knoll above the winding river, and a great road ran straight to the east, parallel to a railway. The river was not large here – a shallow, stony but attractive stream – and the Great Valley (all of whose breadth could now be seen) was at this western point no more than a third of a mile across. The southward slopes terminating the North-Western Plateau, now themselves visible, were rich in shrubland.

The utter contrast with what was going on above and, in top bunker time, per-haps four minutes ago, made Hadolar nearly drunk with enjoyment. However, he presented his luminous tag and had it (and his permanent checktab) checked for radiation, countersigned and stamped by the guard commander at the military terminal. The detachable piece at the end of the tag was given back to him to be slipped into the identity disc, which was, as always, let into a slot in one of his ribs; the other portion was filed away. He got out of his prot-suit and walker, gave up his gun, ammunition and em-kit, was given two wallets of one thousand credit tokens each and a temporary civsuit. An orderly achieved the identity-disc operation. The whole ceremony from his arrival took 250 seconds flat – two seconds up in the top bunker. He walked out like an heir to the earth.

The air was full of scents of hay, berries, flowers, manure. He took intoxicated gulps of it. At the freshouse he ordered, paid for, and drank four decis of light ale, then ordered a sandwich and an apple, paid and ate. The next train east, he was told, would be in a quarter of an hour. He had been in the place perhaps half an hour. No time to spend watching the stream, but he walked to the railhead, asked for a ticket to Veruam by the Sea some 400 miles east and, as the detailed station map showed him, about thirty miles south, paid, and selected a compartment when the train arrived from its shed.

A farm girl and a sleepy-looking male civilian, probably an army contractor, got in one after the other close behind Hadolar, and the compartment contained just these three when the train left. He looked at the farm girl with interest – she was blonde and placid – as the first female he had seen for a hundred days. Fashions had not changed radically in thirty-odd years, he saw, at least among Emmel farm girls. After a while he averted his gaze and considered the landscape. The valley was edged by bluffs of yellowish stone now to north and now to south. Even here their difference in hue was perceptible – the valley had broadened slightly; or perhaps he was being fanciful and the difference was due solely to normal light-effects. The river meandered gracefully from side to side and from cliff to cliff, with occasional islands, small and crowned with hazel. Here and there a fisher could be seen by the bank, or wading in the stream. Farmhouses passed at intervals. North above the valley rose the great slopes, apparently devoid of signs of human life except for funicular stations and the occasional heliport, until they vanished into the vast crimson-bronze curtain of nothingness which grew insensibly out of a half cloud-covered green sky near the zenith. Swirls of whirlwind among the clouds told of the effects of the time-gradient on weather, and odd lightning-streaks, unnoticed further north amid the war, appeared to pirouette among them. To the south the plateau was still hidden by the height of the bluffs, but the beginnings of the dark blue haze grew out of the sky above the valley skyline. The train stopped at a station and the girl, Hadolar saw with a pang, got out. Two soldiers got in in light dress and swapped minor reminiscences: they were on short-term leave to the next stop, a small town, Granev, and eyed Hadolar's temporary suit but said nothing.

Granev was mostly built of steel and glass: not an exciting place, a one-block twenty-storey five-mile strip on either side of the road, with overpass-canopy. (How lucky, thought Hadolar, that speech and travel could go so far down this Great Valley without interlatitude problems: virtually the whole 450 miles.) Industry and some of the Teccols now appeared. The valley had broadened until, from the line, its southern cliffs began to drown in the blue haze half a mile off. Soon the northern slopes loomed a smoky ruddy brown before they too were swallowed up. The river, swollen by tributaries, was a few hundred metres across now and deep whenever the line crossed it. So far they had only gone fifty-odd miles. The air was warmer again and the vegetation more lush. Almost all the passengers were civilians now, and some noted Hadolar's temporary suit ironically. He would buy himself a wardrobe at Veruam at the first opportunity, he decided. But at the moment he wished to put as many miles as possible between himself and that bunker in the shortest personal time.

Some hours later the train arrived at Veruam by the North-Eastern Sea. Thirty miles long, forty storeys high, and 500 metres broad north–south, it was an imposing city. Nothing but plain was to be seen in the outskirts, for the reddish fog still obliterated everything about four miles to the north, and the bluish one smothered the view southward some seven. A well-fed Hadolaris visited one of the city's Rehabilitation Advisers, for civilian techniques and material resources had advanced enormously since his last acquaintance with them, and idioms and speech-sounds had changed bewilderingly, while the whole code of social behaviour was terrifyingly different. Armed with some manuals, a pocket recorder, and some standard speech-form and folkway tapes, he rapidly purchased thin clothing, stormwear, writing implements, further recording tools, lug-bags and other personal gear. After a night at a good guestery, Hadolaris sought interviews with the employing offices of seven subtropical development agencies, was tested and, armed with seven letters of introduction, boarded the night liner mag-lev train for the south past the shore of the North-Eastern Sea and to Oluluetang some 360 miles south. One of the tailors who had fitted him up had revealed that on quiet nights very low-pitched rumblings were to be heard from, presumably, the mountains northward. Hadolaris wanted to get as far from that north as he conveniently could.

He awoke among palms and savannah-reeds. There was no sign of either sight-barrier down here. The city was dispersed into compact blocks of multistorey buildings, blocks separated by belts of rich woodland and drive-like roadways and monorails. Unlike the towns of the Great Valley, it was not arranged on an east–west strip, though its north–south axis was still relatively short. HadolArisóndamo found himself a small guestery, studied a plan of the city and its factory areas, bought a guide to the district and settled down to several days of exploration and inquiry before visiting the seven agencies themselves. His evenings were spent in adult classes, his nights absorbing the speech-form recordings unconsciously in sleep. In the end after nineteen days (about four hours at Veruam's latitude, four minutes at that of Emmel, less than two seconds at the higher bunker, he reflected) he obtained employment as a minor sales manager of vegetable products in one of the organizations.

Communication north and south, he found, was possible verbally for quite a number of miles, provided one knew the rules. In consequence the zoning here was far from severe and travel and social facilities covered a very wide area. One rarely saw the military here. Hadolarisóndamo bought an automob and, as he rose in the organization's hierarchy, a second one for pleasure. He found himself well liked and soon had a circle of friends and a number of hobbies. After a number of love-affairs he married a girl whose father was higher up in the organization, and, some five years after his arrival in the city, became the father of a boy.

"Arisón!" called his wife from the boat. Their son, aged five, was puttering at the warm surface of the lake with his fists over the gunwale. Hadolarisóndamo was painting on the little island, quick lines and sweeps across the easelled canvas, a pattern of light and shade bursting out of the swamp trees over a little bay. "Arisón! I can't get this thing to start. Could you swim over and try?"

"Five minutes more, Mihányo. Must get this down."

Sighing, Karamihányolasve continued, but without much hope, to fish from the bows with her horizontal yo-yo gadget. Too quiet round here for a bite. A parakeet flashed in the branches to right. Derestó, the boy, stopped hitting the water, pulled over the tube-window, let it into the lake and got Mihányo to slide on its lightswitch. Then he peered this way and that under the surface, giving little exclamations as tiny fish of various shapes and hues shot across. Presently Arisón called over, folded up his easel, pulled off his trousers, propped paints and canvas on top of everything, and swam over. There were no crocs in this lake, hippo were far off, filariasis and bilharzia had been eliminated here. Twenty minutes' rather tense tinkering got things going, and the silent fuel-cell driven screw was ready to pilot them over to the painting island and thence across the lake to where a little stream's current pushed out into the expanse. They caught four. Presently back under the westering sun to the jetty, tie up and home in the automob.

By the time Derestó was eight and ready to be formally named Lafonderestónami, he had a sister of three and a baby brother of one. He was a keen swimmer and boatman, and was developing into a minor organizer, both at home and in school. Arisón was now third in the firm, but kept his balance. Holidays were spent either in the deep tropics (where one could gain on the time-exchange) or among the promontories on the southern shores of the North-Eastern Sea (where one had to lose), or, increasingly, in the agricultural stream-scored western uplands, where a wide vista of the world could in many areas be seen and the cloudscapes had full play. Even there the sight-barriers were a mere fogginess near the north and south horizons, backed by a darkness in the sky.

Now and then, during a bad night, Arisón thought about the past. He generally concluded that, even if a breakthrough had been imminent in, say, half an hour from his departure, this could hardly affect the lives of himself and his wife, or even of their children, down here in the south, in view of the time-contraction southwards. Also, he reflected, since nothing ever struck further south than a point north of Emmel's latitude, the ballistic attacks must be mounted close to the Frontier; or if they were not, then the Enemy must lack all knowledge of either southern time-gradients or southern geography, so that the launching of missiles from well north of the Frontier to pass well south of it would not be worthwhile. And even the fastest heli which could be piloted against time conceleration would, he supposed, never get through.

Always adaptable, Arisón had never suffered long from the disabilities incident on having returned after a time at the Front. Mag-lev train travel and other communications had tended to unify the speech and the ethos, though naturally the upper reaches of the Great Valley and the military zone in the mountains of the north were linguistically and sociologically somewhat isolated. In the western uplands, too, pockets of older linguistic forms and old-fashioned attitudes still remained, as the family found on its holidays. By and large, however, the whole land spoke the tongue of the "contemporary" subtropical lowlands, inevitably modified of course by the onomatosyntomy or "shortmouth" of latitude. A "contemporary" ethical and social code had also spread. The southern present may be said to have colonized the northern past, even geological past, somewhat as the birds and other travelling animals had done, but with the greater resources of human wits, flexibility, traditions and techniques.

Ordinary people bothered little about the war. Time conceleration was on their side. Their spare mental energies were spent in a vast selection of plays and ploys, making, representing, creating, relishing, criticizing, theorizing, discussing, arranging, organizing, co-operating, but not so often out of their own zone. Arisón found himself the member of a dozen interweaving circles, and Mihányo was even more involved. Not that they were never alone: the easy tempo of work and life with double "weeks" of five days' work, two days free, seven days' work and six days free, the whole staggered across the population and in the organizations, left much leisure time which could be spent on themselves. Arisón took up texture-sculpting, then returned after two years to painting, but with magneto-brush instead of spraypen; purified by his texture-sculpting period, he achieved a powerful area control and won something of a name for himself. Mihányo, on the other hand, became a musician. Derestó, it was evident, was going to be a handler of men and societies, besides having, at thirteen, entered the athletic age. His sister of eight was a great talker and arguer. The boy of six was, they hoped, going to be a writer, at least in his spare time: he had a keen eye for things, and a keen interest in telling about them. Arisón was content to remain, when he had reached it, second in the firm: a chiefship would have told on him too much. He occasionally lent his voice to the administration of local affairs, but took no major part.

Mihányo and Arisón were watching a firework festival on the North-Eastern Sea from their launch off one of the southern promontories. Up here, a fine velvety backdrop for the display was made by the inky black of the northern sight-barrier, which cut off the stars in a gigantic arc. Fortunately the weather was fine. The silhouettes of the firework boats could just be discerned. In a world which knew no moon the pleasures of a "white night" were often only to be got by such displays. The girl and Derestó were swimming round and round the launch. Even the small boy had been brought out, and was rather blearily staring northward. Eventually the triple green star went up and the exhibition was over; at the firework boats a midnight had been reached. Derestó and Venoyyè were called in, located by a flare, and ultimately prevailed on to climb in, shivering slightly, and dry off in the hot-air blaster, dancing about like two imps. Arisón turned the launch for the shore and Silarre was found to be asleep. So was Venoyyè when they touched the jetty. Their parents had each to carry one in and up to the beach house.

Next morning they packed and set out in the automob for home. Their twenty days' holiday had cost 160 days of Oluluetang time. Heavy rain was falling when they reached the city. Mihányo, when the children were settled in, had a long talk on the opsiphone with her friend across the breadth of Oluluetang: she (the friend) had been with her husband badger-watching in the western uplands. Finally Arisón chipped in and, after general conversation, exchanged some views with the husband on developments in local politics.

"Pity one grows old so fast down here," lamented Mihányo that evening; "if only life could go on forever!"

"For ever is a big word. Besides, being down here makes no difference to the feeling – you don't feel it any slower up on the Sea, do you now?"

"I suppose not. But if only . . ."

To switch her mood, Arisón began to talk about Derestó and his future. Soon they were planning their children's lives for them in the way parents cannot resist doing. With his salary and investments in the firm they would set up the boy for a great administrator, and still have enough to give the others every opportunity.

Next morning it was still in something of a glow that Arisón bade farewell to his wife and went off to take up his work in the offices. He had an extremely busy day and was coming out of the gates in the waning light to his automob in its stall, when he found standing round it three of the military. He looked inquiringly at them as he approached with his personal pulse-key in hand.

"You are VSQ 389 MLD 194 RV 27 XN 3, known as HadolArisóndamo, resident at" (naming the address) "and sub-president today in this firm." The cold tones of the leader were a statement, not a question.

"Yes," whispered Arisón as soon as he could speak.

"I have a warrant for your immediate re-employment with our Forces in the place at which you first received your order for Release. You must come with us forthwith." The leader produced a luminous orange tag with black markings.

"But my wife and family!"

"They are being informed. We have no time."

"My firm?"

"Your chief is being informed. Come now."

"I— I— I must set my affairs in order."

"Impossible. No time. Urgent situation. Your family and firm must do all that between them. Our orders override everything."

"Wh— wh— what is your authority? Can I see it please?"

"This tag should suffice. It corresponds to the tag-end which I hope you still have in your identity disc – we will check all that en route. Come on now."

"But I must see your authority. How do I know, for instance, that you are not trying to rob me, or something?"

"If you know the code you'll realize that these symbols can only fit one situation. But I'll stretch a point: you may look at this warrant, but don't touch it."

The other two closed in. Arisón saw that they had their quickguns trained on him. The leader pulled out a broad screed. Arisón, as well as the dancing characters would let him, resolved them in the light of the leader's torch into an order to collect him, Arisón, by today at such and such a time, local Time, if possible immediately on his leaving his place of work (specified); and below, that one man be detailed to call Mihányo by opsiphone simultaneously, and another to call the president of the organization. The Remployee and escort to join the military mag-lev train to Veruam (which was leaving within about fifteen minutes). The Remployee to be taken as expeditiously as possible to the bunker (W) and thence to the higher bunker (from which he had come some twenty years before, but only about ten minutes in the Time of that bunker, it flashed through Arisón's brain – apart from six or seven minutes corresponding to his journey south).

"How do they know if I'm fit enough for this job after all these years?"

"They've kept checks on you, no doubt."

Arisón thought of tripping one and slugging two and doing a bolt, but the quickguns of the two were certainly trained upon him. Besides, what would that gain him? A few hours' start, with unnecessary pain, disgrace and ruin on

Mihányo, his children and himself, for he was sure to be caught.

"The automob," he said ridiculously.

"A small matter. Your firm will deal with that."

"How can I settle my children's future?"

"Come on, no use arguing. You are coming now, alive or dead, fit or unfit."

Speechless, Arisón let himself be marched off to a light military vehicle.

In five minutes he was in the mag-lev train, an armoured affair with strong windows. In ten more minutes, with the train moving off, he was stripped of his civilian clothes and possessions (to be returned later to his wife, he learnt), had his identity disc extracted and checked and its Relief tag-end removed, and a medical checkup was begun on him. Apparently this was satisfactory to the military authorities. He was given military clothing.

He spent a sleepless night in the train trying to work out what he had done with this, what would be made of that, who Mihányo could call upon in need, who would be likely to help her, how she would manage with the children, what (as nearly as he could work it out) they would get from a pension which he was led to understand would be forthcoming from his firm, how far they could carry on with their expected future.

A grey pre-dawn saw the train's arrival at Veruam. Foodless (he had been unable to eat any of the rations) and without sleep, he gazed vacantly at the marshalling yards. The body of men travelling on the train (apparently only a few were Remployees) was got into closed trucks and the long convoy set out for Emmel.

At this moment Hadolaris' brain began to re-register the conceleration situation. About half a minute must have passed since his departure from Oluluetang, he supposed, in the Time of his top bunker. The journey to Emmel might take up another two minutes. The route from Emmel to that bunker might take a further two and a half minutes there, as far as one could work out the calculus. Add the twenty-years' (and southward journey's) sixteen to seventeen minutes, and he would find himself in that bunker not more than some twenty-two minutes after he had left it. (Mihan, Deres and the other two would all be nearly ten years older and the children would have begun to forget him.) The blitz was unprecedentedly intense when he had left, and he could recall (indeed it had figured in several nightmares since) his prophecy to XN 1 that a breakthrough might be expected within the hour. If he survived the blitz, he was unlikely to survive a breakthrough; and a breakthrough of what? No one had ever seen the Enemy, this Enemy that for Time immemorial had been striving to get across the Frontier. If it got right over, the twilight of the race was at hand. No horror, it was believed at the Front, could equal the horror of that moment. After a hundred miles or so he slept, from pure exhaustion, sitting up in a cramped position, wedged against the next man. Stops and starts and swerves woke him at intervals. The convoy was driving at maximum speeds.

At Emmel he stumbled out to find a storm lashing down. The river was in spate. The column was marched to the depot. Hadolar was separated out and taken into the terminal building where he was given inoculations, issued with walker, quickgun, em-kit, prot-suit and other impedimenta, and in a quarter of an hour (perhaps seven or eight seconds up at the top bunker) found himself entering a polyheli with thirty other men. This had barely topped the first rise and into sunlight when explosions and flarings were visible on all sides. The machine forged on, the sight-curtains gradually closing up behind and retreating grudgingly before it. The old Northern vertigo and somnambulism re-engulfed Had. To think of Kar and their offspring now was to tap the agony of a ghost who shared his brain and body. After twenty-five minutes they landed close to the foot of a mag-lev train line. The top-bunker lapse of twenty-two minutes was going, Had saw, to be something less. He was the third to be bundled into the mag-lev train compartments, and 190 seconds saw him emerging at the top and heading for bunker VV. XN 1 greeted his salute merely with a curt command to proceed by rocket to the top bunker. A few moments more and he was facing XN 2.

"Ah, here you are. Your Relief was killed so we sent back for you. You'd only left a few seconds." A ragged hole in the bunker wall testified to the incident. The relief's cadaver, stripped, was being carted off to the disposal machine.

"XN 2. Things are livelier than ever. They certainly are hot stuff. Every new offensive from here is pitched back at us in the same style within minutes, I notice. That new cannon had only just started up when back came the same shells – I never knew They had them. Tit for tat."

Into H's brain, seemingly clarified by hunger and exhaustion and much emotion, flashed an unspeakable suspicion, one that he could never prove or disprove, having too little knowledge and experience, too little overall view. No one had ever seen the Enemy. No one knew how or when the War had begun. Information and communication were paralysingly difficult up here. No one knew what really happened to Time as one came close to the Frontier, or beyond it. Could it be that the conceleration there became infinite and that there was nothing beyond the Frontier? Could all the supposed missiles of the Enemy be their own, somehow returning? Perhaps the war had started with a peasant explorer lightheartedly flinging a stone northwards, which returned and struck him? Perhaps there was, then, no Enemy?

"XN 3. Couldn't that gun's own shells be reflected back from the Frontier, then?"

"XN 2. Impossible. Now you are to try to reach that forward missile post by the surface – our tunnel is destroyed – at 15° 40' east – you can just see the hump near the edge of the I/R viewer's limit – with this message; and tell him verbally to treble output."

The ragged hole was too small. H left by the forward port. He ran, on his walker, into a ribbon of landscape which became a thicket of fire, a porcupine of fire, a Nessus-shirt to the Earth, as in a dream. Into an unbelievable supercrescendo of sound, light, heat, pressure and impacts he ran, on and on up the now almost invisible slope . . .

DELHI

Vandana Singh

Vandana Singh teaches physics at a state university near Boston and writes in her non-existent spare time. She was born and raised in the city of Dilli (aka Delhi, India), where medieval ruins lie strewn among modern-day edifices. Her work has been published in numerous magazines and anthologies and has frequently been reprinted in year's-best publications. She is a winner of the Carl Brandon Parallax Award. Her most recent publication is a story for *Lightspeed* magazine. "Delhi" was first published in *So Long Been Dreaming: Postcolonial Science Fiction and Fantasy*, edited by Nalo Hopkinson and Uppinder Mehan, in 2004.

Tonight he is intensely aware of the city: its ancient stones, the flat-roofed brick houses, threads of clotheslines, wet, bright colors waving like pennants, neem-tree lined roads choked with traffic. There's a bus going over the bridge under which he has chosen to sleep. The night smells of jasmine, and stale urine, and the dust of the cricket field on the other side of the road. A man is lighting a bidi near him: face lean, half in shadow, and he thinks he sees himself. He goes over to the man, who looks like another layabout. "My name is Aseem," he says. The man, reeking of tobacco, glares at him, coughs and spits, "kya chahiye?" Aseem steps back in a hurry. No, that man is not Aseem's older self; anyway, Aseem can't imagine he would take up smoking bidis at any point in his life. He leaves the dubious shelter of the bridge, the quiet lane that runs under it, and makes his way through the litter and anemic streetlamps to the neon-bright highway. The new city is less confusing, he thinks; the colors are more solid, the lights dazzling, so he can't see the apparitions as clearly. But once he saw a milkman going past him on Shahjahan road, complete with humped white cow and tinkling bell. Under the stately, ancient trees that partly shaded the streetlamps, the milkman stopped to speak to his cow and faded into the dimness of twilight.

When he was younger he thought the apparitions he saw were ghosts of the dead, but now he knows that is not true. Now he has a theory that his visions are tricks of time, tangles produced when one part of the time-stream rubs up against another and the two cross for a moment. He has decided (after years of struggle) that he is not insane after all; his brain is wired differently from others, enabling him to discern these temporal coincidences. He knows he is not the only one with this ability, because some of the people he sees also see him, and shrink back in terror. The thought that he is a ghost to people long dead or still to come in this world both amuses and terrifies him.

He's seen more apparitions in the older parts of the city than anywhere else, and he's not sure why. There is plenty of history in Delhi, no doubt about that – the city's past goes back into myth, when the Pandava brothers of the epic Mahabharata first founded their fabled capital, Indraprastha, some three thousand years ago. In medieval times alone there were seven cities of Delhi, he remembers, from a well-thumbed history textbook – and the eighth city was established by the British during the days of the Raj. The city of the present day, the ninth, is the largest. Only for Aseem are the old cities of Delhi still alive, glimpsed like mysterious islands from a passing ship, but real, nevertheless. He wishes he could discuss his temporal visions with someone who would take him seriously and help him understand the nature and limits of his peculiar malady, but ironically, the only sympathetic person he's met who shares his condition happened to live in 1100 A.D. or thereabouts, the time of Prithviraj Chauhan, the last great Hindu ruler of Delhi.

He was walking past the faded white colonnades of some building in Connaught Place when he saw her: an old woman in a long skirt and shawl, making her way sedately across the car park, her body rising above the road and falling below its surface in parallel with some invisible topography. She came face to face with Aseem – and saw him. They both stopped. Clinging to her like gray ribbons were glimpses of her environs – he saw mist, the darkness of trees behind her. Suddenly, in the middle of summer, he could smell fresh rain. She put a wondering arm out toward him but didn't touch him. She said: "What age are you from?" in an unfamiliar dialect of Hindi. He did not know how to answer the question, or how to contain within him that sharp shock of joy. She, too, had looked across the barriers of time and glimpsed other people, other ages. She named Prithviraj Chauhan as her king. Aseem told her he lived some 900 years after Chauhan. They exchanged stories of other visions – she had seen armies, spears flashing, and pale men with yellow beards, and a woman in a metal carriage, crying. He was able to interpret some of this for her before she began to fade away. He started toward her as though to step into her world, and ran right into a pillar. As he picked himself off the ground he heard derisive laughter. Under the arches a shoeshine boy and a man chewing betel leaf were staring at him, enjoying the show.

Once he met the mad emperor, Mohammad Shah. He was walking through Red Fort one late afternoon, avoiding clumps of tourists and their clicking cameras. He was feeling particularly restless; there was a smoky tang in the air, because some gardener in the grounds was burning dry leaves. As the sun set, the red sandstone fort walls glowed, then darkened. Night came, blanketing the tall ramparts, the lawns through which he strolled, the shimmering beauty of the Pearl Mosque, the languorous curves of the now distant Yamuna that had once flowed under this marble terrace. He saw a man standing, leaning over the railing, dressed in a red silk sherwani, jewels at his throat, a gem studded in his turban. He smelled of wine and rose attar, and he was singing a song about a night of separation from the Beloved, slurring the words together.

Bairan bhayii raat sakhiya . . .

Mammad Shah piya sada Rangila . . .

Mohammad Shah Rangila, early 1700's, Aseem recalled. The Emperor who loved music, poetry and wine more than anything, who ignored warnings that the Persian king was marching to Delhi with a vast army . . . "Listen, king," Aseem whispered urgently, wondering if he could change the course of history, "You must prepare for battle. Else Nadir Shah will overrun the city. Thousands will be butchered by his army . . ."

The king lifted wine-darkened eyes. "Begone, wraith!"

Sometimes he stops at the India Gate lawns in the heart of modern Delhi and buys ice-cream from a vendor, and eats it sitting by one of the fountains that Lutyens built. Watching the play of light on the shimmering water, he thinks about the British invaders, who brought one of the richest and oldest civilizations on earth to abject poverty in only two hundred years. They built these great edifices, gracious buildings and fountains, but even they had to leave it all behind. Kings came and went, the goras came and went, but the city lives on. Sometimes he sees apparitions of the goras, the palefaces, walking by him or riding on horses. Each time he yells out to them: "Your people are doomed. You will leave here. Your Empire will crumble." Once in a while they glance at him, startled, before they fade away.

In his more fanciful moments he wonders if he hasn't, in some way, caused history to happen the way it does. Planted a seed of doubt in a British officer's mind about the permanency of the Empire. Despite his best intentions, convinced Mohammad Shah that the impending invasion is not a real danger but a ploy wrought against him by evil spirits. But he knows that apart from the Emperor, nobody he has communicated with is of any real importance in the course of history, and that he is simply deluding himself about his own significance.

Still, he makes compulsive notes of his more interesting encounters. He carries with him at all times a thick, somewhat shabby notebook, one half of which is devoted to recording these temporal adventures. But because the apparitions he sees are so clear, he is sometimes not certain whether the face he glimpses in the crowd, or the man passing him by on a cold night, wrapped in shawls, belong to this time or some other. Only some incongruity – spatial or temporal – distinguishes the apparitions from the rest.

Sometimes he sees landscapes, too, but rarely – a skyline dotted with palaces and temple spires, a forest in the middle of a busy thoroughfare – and, strangest of all, once, an array of tall, jeweled towers reaching into the clouds. Each such vision seems to be charged with a peculiar energy, like a scene lit up by lightning. And although the apparitions are apparently random and don't often repeat, there are certain places where he sees (he thinks) the same people again and again. For instance, while traveling on the Metro he almost always sees people in the subway tunnels, floating through the train and the passengers on the platforms, dressed in tatters, their faces pale and unhealthy as though they have never beheld the sun. The first time he saw them, he shuddered. "The Metro is quite new," he thought to himself, "and the first underground train system in Delhi. So what I saw must be in the future . . ."

One day, he tells himself, he will write a history of the future.

*

The street is Nai Sarak, a name he has always thought absurd. New Road, it means, but this road has not been new in a very long time. He could cross the street in two jumps if it wasn't so crowded with people, shoulder to shoulder. The houses are like that too, hunched together with windows like dull eyes, and narrow, dusty stairways and even narrower alleys in between. The ground floors are taken up by tiny, musty shops containing piles of books that smell fresh and pungent, a wake-up smell like coffee. It is a hot day, and there is no shade. The girl he is following is just another Delhi University student looking for a bargain, trying not to get jostled or groped in the crowd, much less have her purse stolen. There are small, barefoot boys running around with wire-carriers of lemon-water in chipped glasses, and fat old men in their undershirts behind the counters, bargaining fiercely with pale, defenseless college students over the hum of electric fans, rubbing clammy hands across their hairy bellies, while they slurp their ice drinks, signaling to some waif when the transaction is complete, so that the desired volume can be deposited into the feverish hands of the student. Some of the shopkeepers like to add a little lecture on the lines of "Now, my son, study hard, make your parents proud . . ." Aseem hasn't been here in a long time (since his own college days in fact); he is not prepared for any of this, the brightness of the day, the white dome of the mosque rising up behind him, the old stone walls of the old city engirdling him, enclosing him in people and sweat and dust. He's dazzled by the white kurtas of the men, the neat beards and the prayer caps, this is of course the Muslim part of the city, Old Delhi, but not as romantic as his grandmother used to make it sound. He has a rare flash of memory into a past where he was a small boy listening to the old woman' tales. His grandmother was one of the Hindus who never went back to old Delhi, not after the madness of Partition in 1947, the Hindu-Muslim riots that killed thousands, but he still remembers how she spoke of the places of her girlhood: parathe-walon-ki-gali, the lane of the paratha-makers, where all the shops sell freshly-cooked flatbreads of every possible kind, stuffed with spiced potatoes or minced lamb, or fenugreek leaves, or crushed cauliflower and fiery red chillies; and Dariba Kalan, where after hundreds of years they still sell the best and purest silver in the world, delicate chains and anklets and bracelets. Among the crowds that throng these places he has seen the apparitions of courtesans and young men, and the blood and thunder of invasions, and the bodies of princes hanged by British soldiers. To him the old city, surrounded by high, crumbling, stone walls, is like the heart of a crone who dreams perpetually of her youth.

The girl who's caught his attention walks on. Aseem hasn't been able to get a proper look at her – all he's noticed are the dark eyes, and the death in them. After all these years in the city he's learned to recognize a certain preoccupation in the eyes of some of his fellow citizens: the desire for the final anonymity that death brings.

Sometimes, as in this case, he knows it before they do.

The girl goes into a shop. The proprietor, a young man built like a wrestler, is dressed only in cotton shorts. The massage-man is working his back, kneading and sculpting the slick, gold muscles. The young man says: "Advanced Biochemistry? Watkins? One copy, only one copy left." He shouts into the dark, cavernous interior, and the requisite small boy comes up, bearing the volume as though it were a rare book. The girl's face shows too much relief; she's doomed even before the bargaining begins. She parts with her money with a resigned air, steps out into the noisy brightness, and is caught up with the crowd in the street like a piece of wood tossed in a river. She pushes and elbows her way through it, fending off anonymous hands that reach toward her breasts or back. He loses sight of her for a moment, but there she is, walking past the mosque to the bus stop on the main road. At the bus stop she catches Aseem's glance and gives him the pre-emptive cold look. Now there's a bus coming, filled with people, young men hanging out of the doorways as though on the prow of a sailboat. He sees her struggling through the crowd toward the bus, and at the last minute she's right in its path. The bus is not stopping but (in the tantalizing manner of Delhi buses) barely slowing, as though to play catch with the crowd. It is an immense green and yellow metal monstrosity, bearing down on her, as she stands rooted, clutching her bag of books. This is Aseem's moment. He lunges at the girl, pushing her out of the way, grabbing her before she can fall to the ground. There is a roaring in his ears, the shriek of brakes, and the conductor yelling. Her books are scattered on the ground. He helps pick them up. She's trembling with shock. In her eyes he sees himself for a moment: a drifter, his face unshaven, his hair unkempt. He tells her: don't do it, don't ever do it. Life is never so bereft of hope. You have a purpose you must fulfill. He's repeating it like a mantra, and she's looking bewildered, as though she doesn't understand that she was trying to kill herself. He can see that he puzzles her: his grammatical Hindi and his fair English labels him middle class and educated, like herself, but his appearance says otherwise. Although he knows she's not the woman he is seeking, he pulls out the computer printout just to be sure. No, she's not the one. Cheeks too thin, chin not sharp enough. He pushes one of the business cards into her hand and walks away. From a distance he sees that she's looking at the card in her hand and frowning. Will she throw it away? At the last minute she shoves it into her bag with the books. He remembers all too clearly the first time someone gave him one of the cards. "Worried About Your Future? Consult Pandit Vidyanath. Computerized and Air-Conditioned Office. Discover Your True Purpose in Life." There is a logo of a beehive and an address in South Delhi.

Later he will write up this encounter in the second half of his notebook. In three years he has filled this part almost to capacity. He's stopped young men from flinging themselves off the bridges that span the Yamuna. He's prevented women from jumping off tall buildings, from dousing themselves with kerosene, from murderous encounters with city traffic. All this by way of seeking her, whose story will be the last in his book.

But the very first story in this part of his notebook is his own . . .

Three years ago. He is standing on a bridge over the Yamuna. There is a heavy, odorous fog in the air, the kind that mars winter mornings in Delhi. He is shivering because of the chill, and because he is tired, tired of the apparitions that have always plagued him, tired of the endless rounds of medications and appointments with doctors and psychologists. He has just written a letter to his fiancée, severing their already fragile relationship. Two months ago he stopped attending his college classes. His mother and father have been dead a year and two years respectively, and there will be no one to mourn him, except for relatives in other towns who know him only by reputation as a person with problems. Last night he tried, as a last resort, to leave Delhi, hoping that perhaps the visions would stop. He got as far as the railway station. He stood in the line before the ticket counter, jostled by young men carrying hold-alls and aggressive matrons in bright saris. "Name?" said the man behind the window, but Aseem couldn't remember it. Around him, in the cavernous interior of the station, shouting, red-clad porters rushed past, balancing tiers of suitcases on their turbaned heads, and vast waves of passengers swarmed the stairs that led up across the platforms. People were nudging him, telling him to hurry up, but all he could think of were the still trains between the platforms, steaming in the cold air, hissing softly like warm snakes, waiting to take him away. The thought of leaving filled him with a sudden terror. He turned and walked out of the station. Outside, in the cold, glittering night, he breathed deep, fierce breaths of relief, as though he had walked away from his own death.

So here he is, the morning after his attempted escape, standing on the bridge, shivering in the fog. He notices a crack in the concrete railing, which he traces with his finger to the seedling of a pipal tree, growing on the outside of the rail. He remembers his mother pulling pipal seedlings out of walls and the paved courtyard of their house, over his protests. He remembers how hard it was for him to see, in each fragile sapling, the giant full-grown tree. Leaning over the bridge he finds himself wondering which will fall first – the pipal tree or the bridge. Just then he hears a bicycle on the road behind him, one that needs oiling, evidently, and before he knows it some rude fellow with a straggly beard has come out of the fog, pulled him off the railing and on to the road. "Don't be a fool, don't do it," says the stranger, breathing hard. His bicycle is lying on the roadside, one wheel still spinning. "Here, take this," the man says, pushing a small card into Aseem's unresisting hand. "Go see them. If they can't give you a reason to live, your own mother wouldn't be able to."

The address on the card proves to be in a small marketplace near Sarojini Nagar. Around a dusty square of withered grass, where ubiquitous pariah dogs sleep fitfully in the pale sun, there is a row of shops. The place he seeks is a corner shop next to a vast jamun tree. Under the tree, three humped white cows are chewing cud, watching him with bovine indifference. Aseem makes his way through a jangle of bicycles, motor-rickshaws and people, and finds himself before a closed door, with a small sign saying, only, "Pandit Vidyanath, Consultations." He goes in.

The Pandit is not in, but his assistant, a thin, earnest-faced young man, waves Aseem to a chair. The assistant is sitting behind a desk with a PC, a printer, and a plaque bearing his name: Om Prakash, BSc. Physics (Failed), Delhi University. There is a window with the promised air-conditioner (apparently defunct) occupying its lower half. On the other side of the window is a beehive in the process of completion. Aseem feels he has come to the wrong place, and regrets already the whim that brought him here, but the beehive fascinates him, how it is still and in motion all at once, and the way the bees seem to be in concert with one another, as though performing a complicated dance. Two of the bees are crawling on the computer and there is one on the assistant's arm. Om Prakash seems completely unperturbed; he assures Aseem that the bees are harmless, and tries to interest him in an array of bottles of honey on the shelf behind him. Apparently the bees belong to Pandit Vidyanath, a man of many facets, who keeps very busy because he also works for the city. (Aseem has a suspicion that perhaps the great man is no more than a petty clerk in a municipal office). Honey is ten rupees a bottle. Aseem shakes his head, and Om Prakash gets down to business with a noisy clearing of his throat, asking questions and entering the answers into the computer. By now Aseem is feeling like a fool.

"How does your computer know the future?" Aseem asks.

Om Prakash has a lanky, giraffe-like grace, although he is not tall. He makes a deprecating gesture with his long, thin hands that travels all the way up to his mobile shoulders.

"A computer is like a beehive. Many bits and parts, none is by itself intelligent. Combine together, and you have something that can think. This computer is not an ordinary one. Built by Pandit Vidyanath himself."

Om Prakash grins as the printer begins to whir.

"All persons who come here seek meaning. Each person has their own dharma, their own unique purpose. We don't tell future, because future is beyond us, Sahib. We tell them why they need to live."

He hands a printout to Aseem. When he first sees it, the page makes no sense. It consists of x's arranged in an apparently random pattern over the page. He holds it at a distance and sees – indistinctly – the face of a woman.

"Who is she?"

"It is for you to interpret what this picture means," says Om Prakash. "You must live because you need to meet this woman, perhaps to save her or be saved. It may mean that you could be at the right place and time to save her from some terrible fate. She could be your sister or daughter, or a wife, or a stranger."

There are dark smudges for eyes, and the hint of a high cheekbone, and the swirl of hair across the cheek, half-obscuring the mouth. The face is broad and heart-shaped, narrowing to a small chin.

"But this is not very clear. It could be almost anyone. How will I know. . ."

"You will know when you meet her," Om Prakash says with finality. "There is no charge. Thank you sir, and here are cards for you to give other unfortunate souls."

Aseem takes the pack of business cards and leaves. He distrusts the whole business, especially the bit about no charge. No charge? In a city like Delhi?

But despite his doubts he finds himself intrigued. He had expected the usual platitudes about life and death, the fatalistic pronouncements peculiar to charlatan fortune tellers, but this fellow, Vidyanath, obviously is an original. That Aseem must live simply so he might be there for someone at the right moment: what an amusing, humbling idea! As the days pass it grows on him, and he comes to believe it, if for nothing else than to have something in which to believe. He scans the faces of the people in the crowds, on the dusty sidewalks, the overladen buses, the Metro, and he looks for her. He lives so that he will cross her path some day. Over three years he has convinced himself that she is real, that she waits for him. He's made something of a life for himself, working at a photocopy shop in Lajpat Nagar, where he can sleep on winter nights, or making deliveries for shopkeepers in Defence Colony, who pay enough to keep him in food and clothing. Over three years he has handed out hundreds of the little business cards, and visited the address in South Delhi dozens of times. He's become used to the bees, the defunct air-conditioner, and even to Om Prakash. Although there is too much distance between them to allow friendship (a distance of temperament, really), Aseem has told Om Prakash about the apparitions he sees. Om Prakash receives these confidences with his rather foolish grin and much waggling of the head in wonder, and says he will tell Pandit Vidyanath. Only, each time Aseem visits there is no sign of Pandit Vidyanath, so now Aseem suspects that there is no such person, that Om Prakash himself is the unlikely mind behind the whole business.

But sometimes he is scared of finding the woman. He imagines himself saving her from death or a fate worse than death, realizing at last his purpose. But after that what awaits him? The oily embrace of the Yamuna?

Or will she save him in turn?

One of the things he likes about the city is how it breaks all rules. Delhi is a place of contradictions – it transcends thesis and anti-thesis. Here he has seen both the hovels of the poor and the opulent monstrosities of the rich. At major intersections, where the rich wait impatiently in their air-conditioned cars for the light to change, he's seen bone-thin waifs running from car to car, peddling glossy magazines like Vogue and Cosmopolitan. Amid the glitzy new high-rises are troupes of wandering cows, and pariah dogs; rhesus monkeys mate with abandon in the trees around Parliament House.

He hasn't slept well – last night the police raided the Aurobindo Marg sidewalk where he was sleeping. Some foreign VIP was expected in the morning so the riffraff on the roadsides were driven off by stick-wielding policemen. This has happened many times before, but today Aseem is smarting with rage and humiliation: he has a bruise on his back where a policeman's stick hit him, and it burns in the relentless heat. Death lurks behind the walled eyes of the populace – but for once he is sick of his proximity to death. So he goes to the only place where he can leave behind the city without actually leaving its borders – another anomaly in a city of surprises. Amid the endless sprawl of brick houses and crowded roads, within Delhi's borders, there lies an entire forest: the Delhi Ridge, a green lung. The coolness of the forest beckons to him.

Only a little way from the main road, the forest is still, except for the subdued chirping of birds. He is in a warm, green womb. Under the acacia trees he finds an old ruin, one of the many nameless remains of Delhi's medieval era. After checking for snakes or scorpions, he curls up under a crumbling wall and dozes off.

Some time later, when the sun is lower in the sky and the heat not as intense, he hears a tapping sound, soft and regular, like slow rain on a tin roof. He sees a woman – a young girl – on the paved path in front of him, holding a cane before her. She's blind, obviously, and lost. This is no place for a woman alone. He clears his throat and she starts.

"Is someone there?"

She's wearing a long blue shirt over a salwaar of the same color, and there is a shawl around her shoulders. The thin material of her dupatta drapes her head, half-covering her face, blurring her features. He looks at her and sees the face in the printout. Or thinks he does.

"You are lost," he says, his voice trembling with excitement. He's fumbling in his pockets for the printout. Surely he must still be asleep and dreaming. Hasn't he dreamed about her many, many times already? "Where do you wish to go?"

She clutches her stick. Her shoulders slump.

"Naya Diwas lane, good sir. I am traveling from Jaipur. I came to meet my sister, who lives here, but I lost my papers. They say you must have papers. Or they'll send me to Neechi Dilli with all the poor and the criminals. I don't want to go there! My sister has money. Please, sir, tell me how to find Naya Diwas."

He's never heard of Naya Diwas lane, or Neechi Dilli. New Day Lane? Lower Delhi? What strange names. He wipes the sweat off his forehead.

"There aren't any such places. Somebody has misled you. Go back to the main road, turn right, there is a marketplace there. I will come with you. Nobody will harm you. We can make enquiries there."

She thanks him, her voice catching with relief. She tells him she's heard many stories about the fabled city, and its tall, gem-studded minars that reach the sky, and the perfect gardens. And the ships, the silver udan-khatolas, that fly across worlds. She's very excited to be here at last in the Immaculate City.

His eyes widen. He gets up abruptly but she's already fading away into the trees. The computer printout is in his hand, but before he can get another look at her, she's gone.

What has he told her? Where is she going, in what future age, buoyed by the hope he has given her, which (he fears now) may be false?

He stumbles around the ruin, disturbing ground squirrels and a sleepy flock of jungle babblers, but he knows there is no hope of finding her again except by chance. Temporal coincidences have their own unfathomable rules. He's looked ahead to this moment so many times, imagined both joy and despair as a result of it, but never this apprehension, this uncertainty. He looks at the computer printout again. Is it mere coincidence that the apparition he saw looked like the image? What if Pandit Vidyanath's computer generated something quite random, and that his quest, his life for the past few years has been completely pointless? That Om Prakash or Vidyanath (if he exists) are enjoying an intricate joke at his expense? That he has allowed himself to be duped by his own hopes and fears?

But beyond all this, he's worried about this girl. There's only one thing to do – go to Om Prakash and get the truth out of him. After all, if Vidyanath's computer generated her image, and if Vidyanath isn't a complete fraud, he would know something about her, about that time. It is a forlorn hope, but it's all he has.

He takes the Metro on his way back. The train snakes its way under the city through the still-new tunnels, past brightly lit stations where crowds surge in and out and small boys peddle chai and soft drinks. At one of these stops he sees the apparitions of people, their faces clammy and pale, clad in rags; he smells the stench of unwashed bodies too long out of the sun. They are coming out of the cement floor of the platform, as though from the bowels of the earth. He's seen them many times before; he knows they are from some future he'd rather not think about. But now it occurs to him with the suddenness of a blow that they are from the blind girl's future. Lower Delhi – Neechi Dilli – that is what this must be: a city of the poor, the outcast, the criminal, in the still-to-be-carved tunnels underneath the Delhi that he knows. He thinks of the Metro, fallen into disuse in that distant future, its tunnels abandoned to the dispossessed, and the city above a delight of gardens and gracious buildings, and tall spires reaching through the clouds. He has seen that once, he remembers. The Immaculate City, the blind girl called it.

By the time he gets to Vidyanath's shop, it is late afternoon, and the little square is filling with long shadows. At the bus stop where he disembarks there is a young woman sitting, reading something. She looks vaguely familiar; she glances quickly at him but he notices her only peripherally.

He bursts into the room. Om Prakash is reading a magazine, which he sets down in surprise. A bee crawls out of his ear and flies up in a wide circle to the hive on the window. Aseem hardly notices.

"Where's that fellow, Vidyanath?"

Om Prakash looks mildly alarmed.

"My employer is not here, sir."

"Look, Om Prakash, something has happened, something serious. I met the girl of the printout. But she's from the future. I need to go back and find her. You must get Vidyanath for me. If his computer made the image of the girl, he must know how I can reach her."

Om Prakash shakes his head sadly.

"Panditji speaks only through the computer." He looks at the beehive, then at Aseem. "Panditji cannot control the future, you know that. He can only tell you your purpose. Why you are important."

"But I made a mistake! I didn't realize she was from another time. I told her something and she disappeared before I could do anything. She could be in danger! It is a terrible future, Om Prakash. There is a city below the city where the poor live. And above the ground there is clean air and tall minars and udan khatolas that fly between worlds. No dirt or beggars or poor people. Like when the foreign VIPs come to town and the policemen chase people like me out of the main roads. But Neechi Dilli is like a prison, I'm sure of it. They can't see the sun."

Om Prakash waves his long hands.

"What can I say, Sahib?"

Aseem goes around the table and takes Om Prakash by the shoulders.

"Tell me, Om Prakash, am I nothing but a strand in a web? Do I have a choice in what I do, or am I simply repeating lines written by someone else?"

"You can choose to break my bones, sir, and nobody can stop you. You can choose to jump into the Yamuna. Whatever you do affects the world in some small way. Sometimes the effect remains small, sometimes it grows and grows like a pipal tree. Causality as we call it is only a first-order effect. Second-order causal loops jump from time to time, as in your visions, sir. The future, Panditji says, is neither determined nor undetermined."

Aseem releases the fellow. His head hurts and he is very tired, and Om Prakash makes no more sense than usual. He feels emptied of hope. As he leaves he turns to ask Om Prakash one more question.

"Tell me, Om Prakash, this Pandit Vidyanath, if he exists – what is his agenda? What is he trying to accomplish? Who is he working for?"

"Pandit Vidyanath works for the city, as you know. Otherwise he works only for himself."

He goes out into the warm evening. He walks toward the bus stop. Over the chatter of people and the car horns on the street and the barking of pariah dogs, he can hear the distant buzzing of bees.

At the bus stop the half-familiar young woman is still sitting, studying a computer printout in the inadequate light of the streetlamp. She looks at him quickly, as though she wants to talk, but thinks better of it. He sits on the cement bench in a daze. Three years of anticipation, all for nothing. He should write down the last story and throw away his notebook.

Mechanically, he takes the notebook out and begins to write.

She clears her throat. Evidently she is not used to speaking to strange men. Her clothes and manner tell him she's from a respectable middle-class family. And then he remembers the girl he pushed away from a bus near Nai Sarak.

She's holding the page out to him.

"Can you make any sense of that?"

The printout is even more indistinct than his. He turns the paper around, frowns at it and hands it back to her.

"Sorry, I don't see anything."

She says: "You could interpret the image as a crystal of unusual structure, or a city skyline with tall towers. Who knows? Considering that I'm studying biochemistry and my father really wants me to be an architect with his firm, it isn't surprising that I see those things in it. Amusing, really."

She laughs. He makes what he hopes is a polite noise.

"I don't know. I think the charming and foolish Om Prakash is a bit of a fraud. And you were wrong about me, by the way. I wasn't trying to. . . to kill myself that day."

She's sounding defensive now. He knows he was not mistaken about what he saw in her eyes. If it wasn't then, it would have been some other time – and she knows this.

"Still, I came here on an impulse," she says in a rush, "and I've been staring at this thing and thinking about my life. I've already made a few decisions about my future."

A bus comes lurching to a stop. She looks at it, and then at him, hesitates. He knows she wants to talk, but he keeps scratching away in his notebook. At the last moment before the bus pulls away she swings her bag over her shoulder, waves at him and climbs aboard. The look he had first noticed in her eyes has gone, for the moment. Today she's a different person.

He finishes writing in his notebook, and with a sense of inevitability that feels strangely right, he catches a bus that will take him across one of the bridges that span the Yamuna.

At the bridge he leans against the concrete wall looking into the dark water. This is one of his familiar haunts; how many people has he saved on this bridge? The pipal tree sapling is still growing in a crack in the cement – the municipality keeps uprooting it but it is buried too deep to die completely. Behind him there are cars and lights and the sound of horns, the jangle of bicycle bells. He sets his notebook down on top of the wall, wishing he had given it to someone, like that girl at the bus stop. He can't make himself throw it away. A peculiar lassitude, a detachment, has taken hold of him and he can think and act only in slow motion.

He's preparing to climb on to the wall of the bridge, his hands clammy and slipping on the concrete, when he hears somebody behind him say "wait!" He turns. It is like looking into a distorting mirror. The man is hollow-cheeked, with a few days' stubble on his chin, and the untidy thatch of hair has thinned and is streaked with silver. He's holding a bunch of cards in his hand. A welt mars one cheek, and the left sleeve is torn and stained with something rust-colored. The eyes are leopard's eyes, burning with a dreadful urgency. "Aseem," says the stranger who is not a stranger, panting as though he has been running, his voice breaking a little. "Don't . . ." He is already starting to fade. Aseem reaches out a hand and meets nothing but air. A million questions rise in his head but before he can speak the image is gone.

Aseem's first impulse is a defiant one. What if he were to jump into the river now – what would that do to the future, to causality? It would be his way of bowing out of the game that the city's been playing with him, of saying: I've had enough of your tricks. But the impulse dies. He thinks, instead, about Om Prakash's second-order causal loops, of sunset over the Red Fort, and the twisting alleyways of the old city, and death sleeping under the eyelids of the citizenry. He sits down slowly on the dusty sidewalk. He covers his face with his hands; his shoulders shake.

After a long while he stands up. The road before him can take him anywhere, to the faded colonnades and bright bustle of Connaught Place, to the hush of public parks, with their abandoned cricket balls and silent swings, to old government housing settlements where, amid sleeping bungalows, ancient trees hold court before somnolent congresses of cows. The dusty by-lanes and broad avenues and crumbling monuments of Delhi lie before him, the noisy, lurid marketplaces, the high-tech glass towers, the glitzy enclaves with their citadels of the rich, the boot-boys and beggars at street corners. . . He has just to take a step and the city will swallow him up, receive him the way a river receives the dead. He is a corpuscle in its veins, blessed or cursed to live and die within it, seeing his purpose now and then, but never fully.

Staring unseeingly into the bright clamor of the highway, he has a wild idea that, he realizes, has been bubbling under the surface of his consciousness for a while. He recalls a picture he saw once in a book when he was a boy: a satellite image of Asia at night. On the dark bulge of the globe there were knots of light; like luminous fungi, he had thought at the time, stretching tentacles into the dark. He wonders whether complexity and vastness are sufficient conditions for a slow awakening, a coming-to-consciousness. He thinks about Om Prakash, his foolish grin and waggling head, and his strange intimacy with the bees. Will Om Prakash tell him who Pandit Vidyanath really is, and what it means to "work for the city?" He thinks not. What he must do, he sees at last, is what he has been doing all along: looking out for his own kind, the poor and the desperate, and those who walk with death in their eyes. The city's needs are alien, unfathomable. It is an entity in its own right, expanding every day, swallowing the surrounding countryside, crossing the Yamuna which was once its boundary, spawning satellite children, infant towns that it will ultimately devour. Now it is burrowing into the earth, and even later it will reach long fingers towards the stars.

What he needs most at this time is someone he can talk to about all this, someone who will take his crazy ideas seriously. There was the girl at the bus stop, the one he had rescued in Nai Sarak. Om Prakash will have her address. She wanted to talk; perhaps she will listen as well. He remembers the printout she had shown him and wonders if her future has something to do with the Delhi-to-come, the city that intrigues and terrifies him: the Delhi of udan-kha-tolas, the "ships that fly between worlds", of starved and forgotten people in the catacombs underneath. He wishes he could have asked his future self more questions. He is afraid because it is likely (but not certain, it is never that simple) that some kind of violence awaits him, not just the violence of privation, but a struggle that looms indistinctly ahead, that will cut his cheek and injure his arm, and do untold things to his soul. But for now there is nothing he can do, caught as he is in his own time-stream. He picks up his notebook. It feels strangely heavy in his hands. Rubbing sticky tears out of his eyes, he staggers slowly into the night.

COME-FROM-AWAYS

Tony Pi

Tony Pi is a Canadian writer with a Ph.D. in linguistics. While pursuing his graduate studies, he had the chance to observe and spend time with two purported amnesiacs. Those incidents inspired this story. His work can be found in *Clarkesworld* magazine, *InterGalactic Medicine Show*, *On Spec Magazine*, and *The Improbable Adventures of Sherlock Holmes*, among others. "Come-From-Aways" was originally published in *On Spec, the Canadian Magazine of the Fantastic* in 2009.

Madoc was a striking man in his thirties, his eyes bluer than the sea. I could well imagine him as an ancient prince.

I sat next to his hospital bed and smiled. "*Siw mae*, Madoc."

He paused, the way I would whenever I heard a phrase in Newfoundland English to make sure I hadn't misheard. Then he sat up and spoke excitedly, but I couldn't understand what he was saying. Contrary to what people believe, linguists don't all speak twenty languages or pick up a new language instantly. Where we excel was figuring out linguistic patterns.

Doctor Liu smirked. "Did you call him *pork dumpling*?"

I understood the confusion. *Siw mae* sounded like *siu mai* in Cantonese, which meant *pork dumpling*. "It means *how are you* in modern Southern Welsh. Madoc would have been from Snowdon, Northern Wales, so I should have said *sut mae*."

Two weeks ago, on December twenty-sixth, a strange ship had drifted into the Harbour of St. John's. Found aboard the replica of the Viking longship were four dead men and one survivor. Will Monteith from the Royal Newfoundland Constabulary contacted me to help him pinpoint the man's origin through his language. Analyzing the tapes of the man's speech, I came to the strange conclusion that the man who called himself Madoc had been speaking two archaic languages: Middle English and Middle Welsh.

To be certain, I asked Will to arrange a face-to-face interview. Sometimes linguistic evidence was visual. For example, the *v* sound in Modern Welsh was produced like in Modern English, with the upper teeth against the lower lip, but the *v* in Middle Welsh was produced with both lips, like in Spanish.

I turned on the tape recorder and pointed to myself. "Kate." I indicated Detective Monteith and Doctor Liu. "Will. Philip. *Meddic*." Doctor, in Middle Welsh. The double *dd* sounded like the first sound in the English word, *they*.

He repeated the names and grinned.

Madoc was a puzzle indeed. The theory that made most sense was that he and the other men were trying to recreate the Madoc voyage. Prince Madoc of Gwynedd was a Welsh legend, believed to have sailed west from Wales in 1170. He returned seven years later to tell of a new land of untouched bounty across the sea. Intending to settle the new land, he set out with a fleet of ten ships of settlers, and disappeared from history.

This man could be a Middle Ages scholar with damage to Wernicke's area. Wernicke's aphasics had no problems with articulation, but their utterances made little sense. For the most severe cases, sounds were randomly chosen, spliced together to sound real, but contained few actual words. 'Madoc' might be suffering from a similar *jargonaphasia*. However, the MRI and PET scans showed no such damage to his brain's left hemisphere.

But how authentic was Madoc's command of Middle Welsh? I had two tests in mind.

I gave Madoc two poems I had found, one by Gwalchmai ap Meilyr, another by Dafydd ap Gwilym, both printed in a font called Neue Hammer Unziale. The font seemed closest to Insular Majescule, the script a twelfth-century prince might have been familiar with. "*Darlle.*" I prompted him to read.

Madoc read the first poem easily, but tripped over some of the words in the second.

Will raised an eyebrow. "Shouldn't he be able to read both poems?" he asked, his detective's instincts coming to the fore.

"I made it difficult on purpose," I explained. "The first poem was by a court poet who lived around the same time as Madoc. The second poem, however, was poetry written in the fourteenth century, and is usually designated as early Modern Welsh. I expected him to have more difficulty with that one. It's like Chaucer trying to read Shakespeare, or Shakespeare reading Tennessee Williams; different time, different language."

"You're trying to trip him up! Police work and linguistics are a lot alike," Will said. "Patterns and mistakes."

"I've never quite heard it put that way, but you're right." Will and I shared a smile.

Second test was a production task. I took out a colour pictorial of England, and opened it to a photograph with nine men in a pub.

"*Gwyr. Pet?*" Men. How many?

"*Naw.*" Nine.

I shook my head. "*Naw wyr.*" Nine men. I prompted him to use compounds, as I wanted to test a phenomenon called lenition or mutation. In Welsh, if a word came after a number, the first sound sometimes changed or was dropped, as in the case of *gwyr* to *wyr*. Mutations appeared elsewhere as well, but seeing as I was only dabbling in Celtic, I kept it simple for myself.

Madoc caught on fast; we went through the book counting people and things. When we came to a picture of a boat, Madoc pointed to it, then himself. "*Gwyr. Pet?*" How many survived from his ship?

I cast a sidewise glance at Will.

"*Un,*" I answered. One.

A shocked expression overtook Madoc's face.

"That's enough for today," I said. I gave him a bottle of ink, a sketchbook, and a seagull feather I had cut into a quill pen, and mimed writing motions. I wanted to analyze his writing.

Madoc took my hand and drew it close for a kiss.

Will smiled. "He might not be able to say it, Kate, but I think you're after making a friend for life."

A week of interviews later, at Detective Will Monteith's request, I presented my findings to the other experts at the R.N.C. Headquarters downtown: Doctor Birley from the Provincial Coroner's Office; Rebecca Shannon, a lawyer working *pro bono* for Madoc; and Professor Connon from the Department of Anthropology at Memorial University.

I had reservations about coming. My linguistic analysis had led me to a strange and inescapable conclusion: there was no doubting Madoc's native fluency in Middle Welsh. Even if a hoaxer had learned Middle Welsh, he might pronounce words wrong, or not know the words for common things. Madoc never tripped over syntax or vocabulary, except when it involved a modern object. Could he be the genuine Madoc, lost at sea over eight hundred years ago, found at last in St. John's?

Was it a mad fancy? Perhaps. The academic in me scoffed at the idea. But the romantic in me wanted to believe. Here in Newfoundland, it seemed like anything was possible. I didn't know how to describe it, but there was something magical and mystical about this place. I wouldn't be surprised to find a leprechaun at my house, for instance. Time had stopped this winter, snow falling every day like the weather was stuck and couldn't move ahead to anything different. I felt like I was living in a snow-globe, and the same guy kept turning it upside-down and shaking it. In his world it was only five minutes of playing; but inside the snow-globe, an entire month passed.

But could I convince the others?

"He's a native speaker of Middle Welsh, with some training in Middle English," I said. "He did quite well on the reading passages, and the way he pronounced his vowels and consonants were consistent with my expectations. The written evidence further supports it."

"Preposterous!" Connon said. "A good scholar could learn a second language well enough to fool you. It's a hoax by someone in the Society of Creative Anachronism, I wager."

"We spoke to the Seneschal at Memorial University and contacted everyone on their Shire Roll, but no one from their group is missing, and no one heard about any re-enactment of the Madoc voyage," Will said.

"I hear he's learning English," Connon continued. "How do we know that it wasn't his plan, fake the Madoc story long enough to ease back into English?"

"You can't stop someone from learning a new language. He's a human being, not an artifact from some dig!" I said.

"'Ang on, 'Arry," said old Doctor Birley. He had that Newfoundlander tendency to drop his *h*'s and add them back on words that shouldn't have them. "It might be plausible that h'one man didn't 'ave vaccination scars or dental work.

I meself was vaccinated in '72, but I don't 'ave a scar. But h'all *four* bodies, plus Madoc? The h'odds of that are right slim. Unless they were h'all raised in the backwoods, of course. But a person who 'as the wherewithal to pull off an 'oax like this wouldn't be so isolated from society. Or do you think someone planned this for forty years?"

"I'll admit the boat is the work of a meticulous forger." Connon passed out some photographs of the ship and items found aboard. "The design's consistent with what we know about twelfth-century ships. A Viking longship with a high prow, carved with a lion's head. That's an interesting point. You might have expected the red dragon typically associated with Wales, but the Lions of Gwynedd were in use in the Gwynedd arms, up until the time of the Tudors."

I set aside a picture of a twisted iron nail and studied the weather-worn red lion's head that Professor Connon described.

"I was expecting a coracle," Philip Liu interjected. "I was reading Severin's *The Brendan Voyage* about the seaworthiness of oxhide boats, and whether they were used to reach North America."

Connon shook his head. "That was sixth-century Ireland. By the twelfth century, the Welsh made alliances with Norse raiders, and there were Norse settlements in Wales. Legend has it that the *Gwennan Gorn*, Madoc's ship, was made from oak, but held together with stag's horn instead of iron. The seafaring myths of those times warned of magnetic islands, which would have spelled doom to ships built with iron nails. The ship's authentic in that respect. Nice touch, that. However, I have concrete proof that it's all an elaborate hoax." He showed us a photograph of a pipe. "One of the artifacts recovered from the ship. Note the five-petal white rose on top of the five-petal red, stamped on its heel."

Philip recognized it. "A Tudor rose."

"Right! Henry the Seventh created it to symbolize the union of the red rose of Lancaster and the white rose of York. But the Tudors didn't begin their reign until 1485. If Madoc's from the twelfth century, where did this anachronism come from?" Connon asked.

"Maybe he stopped off to have a smoke," Rebecca joked.

Everyone laughed, but an intriguing idea came to mind. "Why not?" I said. "We're thinking a single trip. Maybe it's not his first and only trip through time?"

Connon snorted. "We're *scientists*! The very idea of time-travel . . ."

"It's not impossible," Philip said. "Einstein's theory of relativity allows for time-travel in the forward direction. Time dilation will keep a man from aging as fast, if he's too close to a serious gravity well. Who knows? I'm starting to wonder if he isn't the genuine article!"

Connon shook his head. "You're on your own. I won't jeopardize my reputation with a cockamamie time-travel theory. I'm denouncing him as a fraud, Detective Monteith. Good day." He grabbed his photos and stormed out.

Connon's departure left us all in a state of unease. Will sighed. "He's right. If we announce that Madoc is a time-traveler, they'll call us crackpots."

Rebecca, Will and I went for muffins and coffee at Tim Horton's after the meeting. The line took forever. The girls at the counter made one thing at a time, but by George they made it right. People didn't hurry here.

"Linguistics is the best evidence we have, Kate. Without you, Madoc will look like a fraud," Rebecca said.

I picked at my partridgeberry muffin. "I know. His future's in my hands. Where does he stand, legally?"

"If he's a fraud, he could be charged with public mischief," Rebecca answered. "Maybe breaking immigration laws, if we can establish that he isn't Canadian. If he's a real time-traveler, well, I don't think there are laws that are applicable. But as a Newfoundlander, my instinct's to welcome him to the Island, not lock him up."

"The press will eat us alive," Will said.

"I know a way to appease the press. A screech-in," Rebecca suggested.

"What's that?" I asked.

"You don't know what a screech-in is?" Will asked. He laughed. "We'll have to initiate you too, Kate!"

"It's a grand old Newfoundland tradition," Rebecca explained. "It's a ceremony to initiate a CFA to honorary citizenship. CFA stands for 'Come-From-Aways', or people who aren't from Newfoundland. Like mainlanders and time-travelers."

"What do you do at a 'screech-in'?"

"We drink 'screech' – that's Newfoundland rum. Kiss a cod, dip your toe into the Atlantic. Good fun for all," said Rebecca. "Then you become a proud member of the Royal Order of Screechers, and get a certificate to prove it."

"Kiss a fish?"

"Don't knock it till you try it," said Rebecca, with a wink.

"What you said, about Madoc's multiple trips in time?" Will said. "Maybe this isn't the first time he's been to Newfoundland. Maybe he stopped in Avalon."

"Avalon?"

"You might know it as Ferryland, a historical site about an hour-and-a-half away, halfway to Trepassey," explained Rebecca. "It's a tourist stop, but I go out there to collect rocks, sometimes. The beach is amazing. Lord Baltimore set up the Colony of Avalon there in 1620, before he moved to the States because of the cold."

"Maybe he'll recognize the area? Will, can we bring him to Ferryland?"

"If my superiors say it's fine, we can go tomorrow. But I think Professor Connon should come along," Will said.

I didn't like the idea, but we did need a historian. I nodded. "Tomorrow."

On our way to Ferryland, Harry Connon went on and on about Sir George Calvert, Lord Baltimore. I sat with Madoc in the back of the car. Will had taken him to a barber and dressed him with modern clothes, so he wouldn't look out of place. Madoc watched in wonder as we passed cars and trucks on the highway. I had half-expected him to react with fear and horror at the strange technology, but he seemed fascinated instead. He truly had the soul of an explorer!

Madoc was skimming through time like a skipping stone, and I wanted to know how he was doing it, and why. I had cobbled together some simple questions in Middle Welsh.

Did he know where he was? *Yes.*

Did he know what year it was? *No.*

Did things change when he sailed? *Yes.*

How many times did things change? *Eleven.*

Eleven! Assuming he first set sail around 1179, and that each trip shunted him forward the same number of years, that would average seventy-five years per journey. His sixth stop would have been 1629, around the time of the Colony of Avalon.

What was he looking for? *The end of the whale-road. To learn. To see if it takes me back home to my people, my brother*, he said.

I recalled that in the legend, his brother Rhiryd went with Madoc to settle the new land.

How did he travel through time? *Storm comes every eighty-three days. Help me, Kate.*

I checked my datebook. Madoc arrived on Boxing Day. Eighty-three days from that would place the next storm on March eighteenth.

Poor Madoc! I thought my first winter in Newfoundland was long, and I'd only lived a couple months of it. He arrived from each journey in winter, only to leave at winter's end for a future winter. That was at least two years of fog and snow.

"Will, is there any significance to March eighteenth in Newfoundland?" I asked.

"The day after Paddy's Day? Yeah. Sheila's Brush. That's a big snowstorm that always happens on or around St. Patrick's Day. Not quite the same as Paddy's Broom, another storm that also comes around then. Sheila is Patrick's wife, see. She's always mad at him, chasing after him with her brush and painting everything with ice. Why?"

"Because that's the day the time portal opens again, to seventy-five years in the future," I said.

The dig was closed on weekends, but Connon had research privileges here, facilitating our visit. To my surprise, the anthropologist was getting along with Madoc. As we traipsed through the snow at Ferryland, he spoke to Madoc in English, taking for granted that he would understand. Madoc was animated, pointing to places, speaking to me in Middle Welsh, but I caught only a few words. Clearly he had been here before. Frustrated, Connon put a pencil in Madoc's hand, and made him draw in his sketchbook.

Madoc led Connon through the dig, sketching out a map of Avalon as he remembered it. "His sketches seem consistent with the buildings we know to be in the Colony at the time. These buildings he drew are the bakery and brewhouse, which don't exist today. They tore them down in 1637 to build Kirke House," Connon explained. "You've done your homework, Madoc."

Will and I left them to their explorations for a quiet stroll along the shore. Like Rebecca said, the rocky beach had some beautiful stones. I knelt and picked up a smooth green stone. I showed Will the lovely lines in the rock.

"That's what we call a 'salt water rock'," said Will. "Rounded and smoothed by the sea."

A tall, elderly gentleman down the beach waved at us. "You two look like a charming couple," said the man, smiling.

Will furrowed his brow.

Embarrassed, I corrected him. "Thank you, but we're not together."

"Take it from a man who's seen much in his lifetime. You two belong together." The old man tipped his hat and continued along the shore.

"Did you know him?" I asked.

Will shook his head. "He reminds me of my father, is all."

"What will happen to Madoc?"

Will sighed. "He has no money, no citizenship. Kind folk like you'd find anywhere in Newfoundland will help him out, but he'll be a burden unless he learns some English. Maybe he could sell his story; I don't know. But he'll end up in limbo, without Canadian citizenship."

"I have an idea about that, but I need to discuss it with Rebecca first," I hinted. As Madoc's *pro bono* lawyer, she would know whether the legal loophole I saw would actually work. "But in the end, wouldn't it be simpler to let him go back on his ship? Imagine finding out what the world would be like in seventy-five, a hundred-and-fifty, three hundred years from now. See how future generations live!"

"He'll be adrift and alone."

"No one needs to be." I took a risk and took Will's hand. He didn't pull away.

"Have dinner with me tonight, Kate?" he asked sheepishly.

"I'd like that."

"Come in, Kate, and shut the door." Professor Claudia Seif had recently been appointed the Chair of Linguistics at Memorial.

I knew why she wanted to see me.

"I had a call from Harry Connon," she said. "When I recommended you to the detective, I was expecting diligent, responsible analysis. Instead, you've made yourself a laughingstock of the field. It reflects badly on the department."

"I stand by my judgment, Claudia. It's not the orthodox answer or the safe answer, but it's what I believe. I won't lie."

"Watch what you say to the press, Kate. Think about your future."

I sighed. "What future? I've been paying my dues for the last five years, moving from city to city, and I've yet to make any short lists for tenure-track positions."

"Kate, you're a good linguist." Her voice was softer now. "The breaks will come. Drop this 'Madoc' madness."

There would be no convincing her. "Thanks for the talk, Claudia. You've given me much to think about," I said, and left.

O'Reilly's Irish Pub was packed for the screech-in/press conference, and the journalists were chattering excitedly among themselves. Claudia stared daggers at me from the back row.

Will introduced himself, then began, "On December twenty-sixth, a Viking longship was discovered in the Harbour of St. John's. Five men were found aboard, but only one was alive. Autopsies by the Coroner's Office indicate that the men died of hypothermia. The survivor was in quarantine for fourteen days as required by the Quarantine Act, but showed no signs of disease. However, when the man regained consciousness, we discovered that he didn't speak English, French or any other modern language.

"Several experts examined the body of evidence about our mystery man. The ship and his language point to the man's identity as Prince Madoc of Gwynedd, a twelfth century Welsh legend." The journalists whispered and chuckled when they heard this. "Whether this is a hoax or a case of time-travel, remains in dispute among our experts. At this point, I'll yield the floor to them: but please save your questions until they all have had a chance to speak."

We each took a turn presenting the evidence. Connon expounded on the hoax hypothesis, while the doctor and the coroner expressed ambivalence. When it was my turn, I glanced at Claudia. What if she was right? Was I throwing away my career by standing behind what I believed?

I looked at Madoc, wondering what would become of him. He smiled.

I was as alone as he was. My feeling of being disconnected wasn't because of the fog and the rain. If I really looked, that sense of not belonging stretched back for years. We were two of a kind: I too wanted to see the future and start afresh. I knew then that I couldn't hedge like the others did. I *had* to be Madoc's voice in this matter, even if it meant my career. I took a deep breath, and spoke.

"Based on the linguistic evidence, I must conclude Madoc is truly a man out of time." I went on to discuss why it was nearly impossible to fake pronunciation and grammar as consistently as a native speaker. "Given his native fluency in Middle Welsh, I must conclude that he is, indeed, from the twelfth century."

Claudia stood, shook her head in disappointment, and left.

All eyes were on me. I felt like The Fool on a tarot card, about to step off a cliff.

Rebecca saved me from the press. "I'm representing Madoc *pro bono*, ensuring that his rights aren't being violated. Currently, we're unable to ascertain his nationality. But suppose that he really is Madoc. He would have been among the first Europeans to settle in Newfoundland. There's no disputing that he's Welsh; all the evidence pointed to that. But is he *Canadian*? Ah.

"The legend tells that Madoc set out with settlers to a newly found land across the sea. We know he was at the Colony of Avalon. Even Professor Connon admits that Madoc knew things about Avalon only an expert would know. And later this spring, archaeologists will begin excavations at a previously unknown site, to see if Madoc was right about a hitherto undiscovered building that existed in Calvert's time. If he lived in Avalon, then by the Newfoundland Act that admitted Newfoundland to Confederation in 1948, that would also make him a citizen of Canada."

"But he wasn't alive at Confederation, was he?" a reporter shouted.

"Well, he certainly wasn't dead." Laughter. "He truly is one of the first immigrants to Newfoundland. I say we, a people known for our hospitality, take him in with open arms. To that effect, we're throwing a 'screech-in' here at

O'Reilly's, and you're all invited!"

The question period was chaotic. I thought I handled most of the questions well, but the ones that asked if this was all a joke were frustrating. Will finally announced it was time for the screech-in. As a native-born Newfoundlander had to perform the ceremony, Will would do the honours. They dragged us to the center and crowned us with yellow, plastic sou'wester hats. Then, we were given a full shot of screech rum.

"Hold your screech up high and repeat after me. *Long may your big jib draw!*" shouted Will.

"*Long may your big jib draw!*" I yelled, even though I had no idea what that meant. I only knew I needed a stiff drink. I squealed when the rum hit my taste buds and gut.

"That's why they call it *screech*!" someone shouted. The crowd laughed.

They prompted Madoc to repeat the same. "*Long mei ywr bug si'ib dra*'?"

"Close enough! Bring out the cod!"

I woke in my bed with a hangover and an upset stomach, not remembering how I got home. Rum and fried baloney definitely didn't belong together.

I found Will asleep on my couch. He must have driven me home.

Not wanting to wake Will, I went into the bedroom and called Rebecca. "I think we need to help Madoc back on his journey. And I'm seriously thinking about joining him."

"You mean, going to the future?" Rebecca asked. "Kate, think it through! What would you do there? End up like him, a living museum?"

"I'll find something," I said. "Imagine, a chance to put theories of language change to the test!"

"What about your classes?"

"I doubt I still have a job." I twisted the phone cord. "I'd like to leave instructions to take care of unfinished business."

"Kate, give it more thought! People *died* on that last voyage."

"I thought of that. We can stock up on supplies, prepare ourselves better."

Rebecca sighed. "You're serious about this? What about a crew? And a ship?"

"I'll think of something."

After the call, I gently woke Will. "Good morning, sleepyhead. Thanks for looking after me."

"My pleasure," he said, rubbing his eyes. "Can I make you breakfast?"

I smiled to hide my troubled thoughts. "Know how to make peach pancakes?"

I told Will about my plan as we ate. "We need to give him back his ship, Will, by St. Patrick's Day."

"What? We can't."

"It's his property. His destiny. His journey doesn't end here, I know it."

"The brass will never allow it!"

"One day, that's all I ask. Call it a re-enactment of the Madoc voyage, a heritage moment, something. If it doesn't work, you can repossess the boat, and us."

"Us? What are you saying?"

"I'm going with Madoc."

Silence hung between us.

"I'd like you to stay, Kate," Will said at last, taking my hands.

I squeezed his hands. "Come with us."

"'Now' is enough for me, Kate. Is it for you?"

"A chance like this comes once in a lifetime. I think there was a reason I met Madoc, here and now. He's the adventure I've been looking for."

"Not stability?"

"That, too," I admitted. "Perhaps I can't have both, not yet. Maybe there isn't a bright future seventy-five years from now. But to give up a chance to experience something extraordinary? I don't think I can."

"Isn't that what love can be?"

I looked into his eyes. He was the sweetest man I had met in a long time. I didn't want to break his heart. "Help us."

Will sighed. "You're a stubborn one, Kate Tannhauser. Very well, the future is yours. But for now, the present is ours."

He leaned over the table and kissed me. It was a long, unhurried kiss, just as I imagined.

The media frenzy that followed in the weeks after was not unexpected. Our time-travel theory was portrayed as ridiculous by most, praised by few, and always controversial. I had a spate of invitations for television, newspaper and radio interviews, and I agreed to the reputable ones, but ignored the sensational ones. The consensus was, *this could only happen in Newfoundland.*

Rebecca and her husband opened their guest room to Madoc, after he was discharged from the hospital. I met with him to discuss joining him on his journey. "*We will return you to your ship, to your storm,*" I said in his language. "*I am coming with you.*"

There was a look of surprise and joy on Madoc's face. "*I am honoured, Lady Kate. But we need more men.*"

"*I will find them,*" I said.

Madoc nodded. "*Bring no iron. Mistake. Danger.*"

As far as I could tell, the phenomenon that allowed him to travel through time was based on powerful magnetic fields. Passing through such a gateway with ferrous metals over a certain size either disrupted the field, or made the transition dangerous. He had discovered it on his first journey, finding that objects made of iron aboard their ship burned with *canwyll yr ysbryd,* 'spirit candles' or what we called St. Elmo's Fire, followed by a sudden snowstorm. Although they tossed all their iron off the ship, he still lost two men to the waves. On his last journey, someone must have accidentally brought iron onto the *Gwennan Gorn, a theory supported by that twisted iron nail found aboard the ship.*

We still needed a crew.

I met with the Society of Creative Anachronism Seneschal of the Shire of *An n-Eilean-ne,* which was Scots Gaelic for 'an island of our own', and gave him the details of my plan. "Imagine, a chance to see the future, a one-way trip. I know it's a lot to ask, leaving this time behind. But I need people who are willing to take a risk, and soon."

"It's an unusual request, but let me send out a notice. You never know, with us lot. We mostly look to the past, but some of us also look to the future. After all, what could be more appealing than becoming anachronisms ourselves?" He smiled. "But it seems to me, you could do a great deal of good for people who have lost hope."

"What do you mean?"

"There are some diseases modern medicine can't cure, but what about future medicine? Some people don't have seventy-five years, but they hang on to hope."

He was right. There might be new cures in the future. Then again, there might not be. All I could promise them was a gamble.

Slowly, the calls and emails came. People had heard about the opportunity through the SCA. I told them it might be a dangerous, one-way trip, but the journey would be the adventure of a lifetime. I never heard back from the majority again; but to my surprise, some were serious about joining the crew.

Though he disapproved of my plans, Will helped weed the jokesters and the dangerous from the list of volunteers. "It's not cheap to fly to Newfoundland. Only the serious ones will come," Will said. We whittled the list to twelve, ten men and two women. Four had sailing experience, and one was a Welshman who offered to expedite translations with Madoc.

The crew arrived a week before St. Patrick's Day. They were a diverse crowd: fisherman, physicist, historian, ex-marine, writer, student, trucker, doctor, and more. They all had their own reasons to come with us.

We prepared provisions, avoiding ferromagnetic materials altogether. The SCA rallied and made period clothing appropriate to Madoc's time. We chose the four lions of Gwynedd for our symbol, stitched onto white and green cloth.

Madoc and I continued teaching each other our languages. "*It's not too late, Lady Kate. You can stay with good Will. I promise to see them safely into the future.*"

I shook my head. "*It's what I want.*"

Alas, St. Patrick's Day came all too soon. Tomorrow, we would set sail.

I spent that night with Will, cradled in his arms.

I asked him one last time. "Come with me."

He held me tighter. "I need certainty." He reached for his coat by the bed, and took out a small black box from his pocket. My heart pounded. A ring?

No. Inside the box was a golden necklace, its pendant adorned with the salt water rock I had so admired at Avalon. He put it around my neck and fastened it. "It's not iron, so it's safe. Something to remember me by. I love you, Kate."

I couldn't hold back the tears anymore. "And I you. Remember me, Will."

The next morning, the harbourfront was packed with students, strangers and friends who came to see us off. Most of them expected the whole thing to be a publicity stunt. I saw Rebecca, Philip, and Harry Connon, but there was no sign of Will. Was it too hard for him to see me off?

It had been Will who convinced the Coast Guard to return the *Gwennan Gorn* to us temporarily. High-prowed, she creaked as we set foot aboard her. The sound was strangely reassuring. This ship had survived many journeys and the test of countless years. She would serve us well.

What would the world be like, seventy-five years from now? Would Newfoundland be exactly the same as now, as though no time had passed? I didn't know. All I knew was that the Will I loved would not be there, waiting for me.

I distracted myself from that thought, focusing on our preparations. We loaded food and other supplies onto the ship, within the roofed enclosure built into the center. We checked and double-checked the manifest, and we swept the ship and crew with a metal detector, looking for forgotten iron. The last crew might have been lost because of a nail. I didn't want to make the same mistake.

When we were fit to launch, I stood at the head of the boat with a hand on Madoc's shoulder. "Fellow travelers!" I shouted. "I trust you've said your goodbyes. We might go into the storm and go no further than today. We might meet with disaster. Worst of all, we sail into uncertainty. But throughout history, haven't there always been men and women with adventurous souls, who have left behind loved ones to find new horizons? In the future, men will build ships to the stars. They will choose to do as we do today, to leave behind everything we love to explore the unknown."

I paused and met the eyes of my shipmates. "It's a frightening prospect, I know. But I know if I never took this chance, I will regret it for the rest of my life. I hope you all feel the same. Let's *make* history!"

My crew cheered.

The snow began to fall, and the wind picked up. Sheila's Brush was on its way.

Upon Madoc's signal, the crew began to row. The *Gwennan Gorn* glided through the harbour waters past the ice floes. I looked for Will and spied him pushing through the cheering crowd, an old man following behind. It was the gentleman Will and I had met on the beach at Avalon.

Will waved from the docks, wearing civilian clothes. "Kate! Wait!" He leapt onto the ice floes, the pans, between the docks and the ship.

"Stop rowing!" I cried.

Will leapt from pan to pan, ignoring the danger. He clambered into the boat, took off his watch, and dropped it in the water. "My last piece of iron."

I embraced him. "What made you change your mind?" I asked.

"Madoc convinced me," Will said.

I looked at Madoc. Had he learned enough English from me to talk to Will? Or had he been a fraud, all this time?

Will saw my confusion. "No, not him. The man we met at Avalon? Madoc Monteith. Our son."

It took a while for it to sink in. "How?"

He showed me the golden pendant he wore beneath his clothes. The stone was identical to the one he gave me, striations and all, but old and worn. My hand flew to my neck. Mine was still there!

"They did find another way back. Remember I told you about Paddy's Broom, the other storm that comes around the same time as Sheila's Brush? Our son came back through that gate, and gave me this as proof. It's the certainty I need. Let's face the future together, come-what-may."

I understood.

Madoc hollered. Ahead, a rainbow halo appeared in the whiteness of snow and fog. The gate!

There was no turning back. Into the storm and into the future.

"Come-what-may," I said, and kissed Will.

TERMINÓS

Dean Francis Alfar

Dean Francis Alfar is a Filipino playwright, novelist, and writer of speculative fiction. His plays have been performed in venues across the country, while his articles and fiction have been published both in his native Philippines and abroad in *Strange Horizons*, *Rabid Transit*, *The Year's Best Fantasy and Horror*, and the Exotic Gothic series. His latest short-story collection is *How to Traverse Terra Incognita* (2012). "Terminós" was first published in *Rabid Transit: Menagerie*, edited by Christopher Barzak, Alan DeNiro, and Kristin Livdahl, in 2005.

Mr. Henares thinks about time

From the moment he opened his eyes in the morning to the instant before he fell asleep alone at night, Mr. Henares thought only about time.

He reflected about how time slowed down when he was engaged in an unpleasant activity, such as dyeing his thinning grey hair over the broken antique basin installed by his son-in-law Alvaro in his blue-tiled bathroom; and how time went faster during the rare instances when he felt happy, such as when his brace of grandchildren came for the cold weather holidays, their hypnotic music invariably loud and invigorating.

Mr. Henares recalled days when time did not move at all: waking up one morning convinced that it was the exact same day as the day before, watching the red display of his tableside clock blinking fruitlessly. The experience of the twin miércoles was to be repeated thrice more, adding jueves, viernes and sábado to his list of repeating days. He endured the repeated conversations and graceless routines, read the same stories in the newspapers and watched the same interviews on television.

Once, when he was a much younger man, Mr. Henares went back in time. The incident caught him completely unaware – he realized he was walking backwards and thinking thoughts in reverse. This unfortunate event flustered him so much that when it was suddenly over, he broke down in tears and resolved never to travel back in time if he could help it.

One morning Mr. Henares thought about the future, methodically spooning sweetsop into his mouth and spitting out the seeds into a cup. He sat at the breakfast alcove of his house that adjoined his little shop and squinted at the sun outside the windows.

"The future is always happening," he said to the empty kitchen. "If it is always happening, then it is, in fact, the present; and any instances of the future having occurred are, in fact, the past."

Mr. Henares stood up, wiped sweetsop juice from his chin, washed his hands, crossed the connecting corridor and went about opening his shop for the day.

Mr. Henares makes some sales

His first visitors were a trio of young men, all sporting nose rings and dressed in last year's affectation of jeans and tulle.

"Vueño arao, Mr. Henares," the thinnest one said, removing his Pepsi-blue hat as he entered the shop.

"Good morning," Mr. Henares replied. "What can I do for you gentlemen?"

"We would like to sell," the stoutest one replied, wiping beads of perspiration from his forehead with a swipe of a ruffled sleeve. "We've been waiting for you to open."

"Ah," the old merchant said, "And what do you have for me?"

"We have time to kill," the tallest one told him, offering his hands, palms up. He looked at Mr. Henares with half-lidded eyes.

Mr. Henares shook his head. "You understand, of course, that rates have really gone down. With the new teatros and entretenimientos, people are finding things to occupy themselves with."

"Certainly, Mr. Henares," the stoutest one replied. "We will take what you will offer. You are the fairest merchant in all of Ciudad Manila."

Mr. Henares brought out his tools, brass and glass and wood, and extracted the precise amount of time each young man wanted to sell. They waited patiently as he labeled each vial, heads tilted to the mellow bossa nova tracks that emanated from a pair of speakers from behind the counter. When he had finished putting everything away, he gave them their payment, wrapped in blue encaje.

The three young men opened the package then and there, much to the discomfort of Mr. Henares. The tallest one took out the Planet Hollywood shot glass and read aloud what was written around the logo, as his two companions unabashedly held hands and closed their eyes.

Silence is foolish if we are wise, but wise if we are foolish

By early evening, Mr. Henares had completed four more transactions.

A young mother, fresh from the provinces, who sold all her memories of childhood: Mr. Henares's payment was etched on a Flores bandalore, the inscription set deep in the yo-yo's polished wooden rim.

A drop hollows out a stone

A pair of lovers, who entered his store and left it hand-in-hand, traded in five separate occasions of romance: when they first knew they were in love, when they first kissed, when they first made love, when they first reconciled, and when they decided to stay together for as long as they could, despite all inconvenience, difficulty or portent. Mr. Henares gave them, in exchange, words written on yellowed Badtz Maru stationery, sweat and ink staining the image of the little black Japanese penguin.

Night follows day

A bored widow was next, bartering away two years of future solitude. "I'm certain someone will want that," she said wryly, "I certainly don't." Mr. Henares gave her a polished citrine carved into the form of a tiny fluted flower with even smaller engraved words.

We do not care of what we have, but we cry when it is lost

The widow sniffed, "True, true," and asked if she could purchase some romance. Mr. Henares offered her the vials he obtained from the lovers earlier. She took two and stepped out into the humidity.

The fourth customer was a proud-looking soldier, the buttons on his dress uniform shiny and golden. "My maternal grandaunt told me that I would lose my right arm in war across the sea. If it must be so, then I'd like to sell the time of actual loss and recovery."

Mr. Henares studied the man's resigned face and offered him, in exchange for his future pain, words woven in sawali.

An empty barrel makes the greatest sound

Mr. Henares prepares for bed

As he closed the shop, he reflected on how time's ebb and flow meant different things to different people. He once had a customer, a dark-skinned young man from Cabarroquis, who protested against his good fortune in the game of love.

"Everyone I meet wants me," the dark-eyed man sighed in Mr. Henares's bed. "Everyone wants to devour me. I never have time for myself. I am certain that even you will soon speak to me of love."

Mr. Henares had not really been listening to him then, but was instead enraptured by the young man's skin, marveling at the game of hide-and-seek the candlelight and shadows played upon it. It was only much later when he remembered the words the man spoke.

As he prepared his frugal dinner of salted fish and boiled aubergine, Mr. Henares thought about how some people believed in time as a panacea for all hurt, all pain, all woes.

A pair of sisters, veiled and somber, once asked him if he had thirty years of uninterrupted time for sale. He sadly told them he did not, that no one had ever sold him a block of personal time greater than a handful of years. But inwardly, he cringed at the notion that there were people who believed in a blessed future, guaranteed happiness by imbibing his vials or selling their sorrow, whether past or yet-to-come.

He felt too old to believe in what he sold.

Before going to bed in the house that adjoined his shop, Mr. Henares checked on his trading stock, arranging various items containing words, phrases and maxims. Behind a shelf, almost hidden from his eyesight, he found a faded adarna plume etched with

Vision is the art of seeing things invisible

and a handkerchief embroidered with

What we see depends on what we look for

That night, as he stripped his clothes and slipped into bed, Mr. Henares thought about how time, whether bought or sold or unsold, robbed everyone of everything in the end. He chuckled at himself, surprised by his cynical perspective, scratched at a sore spot on his spotted arms, and went to sleep, thinking about time.

Miguel Lopez Vicente's drought

Three days later, on the eve of his thirty-second natal day, the storyteller Miguel Lopez Vicente came to terms with the fact that he had nothing more to write. His body of work, unmatched in terms of scope and volume, was testament to his genius, read, devoured and performed in various venues all over Hinirang. In years past, he tilled the soil of his homeland and harvested the loves and hopes of its people, transmuting their mundane lives into great dramas of passion. He listened to the tales of sailors, merchants and ambassadors to foreign lands and improved upon what he heard, spinning marvels from the barest descriptions and epics from whispered rumors. But with each year that passed, his ideas dwindled and diminished, leaving a profound void in the center of his heart. He found himself staring at virgin pages, his quill sapped by the ennui of waiting.

"There is nothing left," he said to his reflection in the mirror. "I don't want to grow old."

He recalled the first time he knew he would be a writer, how the sight of farmers during rice-planting season triggered a sudden rapture in him. But the matter of age and the ravages of time had been weighing heavily on his head for the past few months. When he passed the halfway mark of a healthy man's lifespan the year prior, he did it in a wine-induced stupor, drinking in an effort to obliterate the fact that he had written only one wondrous play the previous year.

This year, he thought about doing something else, to ward off the thoughts of another year ending, a fruitless year of utter desolation – perhaps by losing himself in the arms of some unknown young man, but decided against it. A young man's embrace would repeat a story he already knew (no doubt the boy's arms would be strong; his skin perfect and tight; his eyes round; his life exactly the same as every other young man that Miguel had known), a futile exercise. And so Miguel simply resolved to determine his own story's ending.

Miguel Lopez Vicente selects an ending

The afternoon of the next day, Miguel walked to the Encanto lu Caminata to the shop of Mr. Henares. The shop was empty of people when he arrived, but filled to the rafters with all manner of jars, pots and woven baskets; vials, censers and tsino incense stick holders; beads, feathers, and boxes and bowls of various sizes, shapes and colors. A peculiar scent permeated the room, swirling slowly around a large storm lantern on the counter – the mingled smells of an eclipse, stolen kisses, and newly-opened luggage fresh from an airplane's belly.

Miguel was about to touch the lantern when he decided instead to ring the tiny porcelain bell whose intricate details seemed to never end.

"Vueño arao, what can I do for you?" Mr. Henares said, appearing from an adjoining room.

"Good morning, Mr. Henares," Miguel Lopez Vicente replied. "I have come to trade away all my days."

"All your days? Are you certain?" The old merchant looked him straight in the eye and for a moment Miguel felt himself dissolve into sad and heavy motes that just barely kept the shape of a man.

"Yes," Miguel nodded. "Believe me, this decision was not at all spontaneous."

"I cannot buy them all," Mr. Henares said. "This is not that kind of place."

"Do you know who I am?" Miguel asked him.

"It makes no difference, sir," Mr. Henares replied. "But, yes. I do."

"This way, at least, let someone benefit," Miguel told him with an unflinching gaze.

"I see," said Mr. Henares. He leaned forward until the space between him and Miguel was no wider than a fist. "But I have nothing in stock to give you for what you want to give me. It is quite early in the month. The value of your—"

"Sir," Miguel interrupted him, taking a step back. "Just give me the first thing you see and we'll call it an exchange fair and well-made."

"Very well," the old man said, before vanishing into the other room. He returned a moment later with his tools, brass and glass and wood, and took precisely the amount of time Miguel Lopez Vicente wanted to exchange. Afterwards, he handed Miguel a silver thimble, discolored and slightly dented.

"This was found in a ship sleeping at the bottom of the sea, off the island of Siqui'jor. The vessel sank fleeing pirates – it is a story old but true." Mr. Henares said in a soft tone. "Sometimes, one cannot run away."

"I am aware of that story," Miguel sighed as he looked closely at the thimble for the inscription.

"Of course. Of course, you are," Mr. Henares nodded, scratching at a sore on his left arm. He left Miguel alone to read.

Around the rim of the thimble, almost worn away, were the words

There is a reason why past is past.

That night at his home, Miguel Lopez Vicente dismissed his maidservant early, mixed water with his last supper's vino, a simple claret from the vineyards of Sevilla in Ispancio, undressed himself, taking care to empty his bowels beforehand to maintain a semblance of dignity for the benefit of those who would find him, and stretched out on his lonely bed built for two.

His final thoughts, as he slipped into a dreamless sleep, were how he wished he were a man half his age again, at the height of his powers. That bittersweet conceit kept him occupied as cold seawater rushed to submerge his bed.

And so his story ended.

-terminó-

"Cumpleaños felices," the dark-skinned Katao boy from Cabarroquis whispered, his eyes soft and liquid brown. "I am your birthday present."

Miguel Lopez Vicente fought his almost overwhelming excitement and sought his voice. "You— you are?"

"Yes," the boy smiled, trailing a slender finger down his bare chest, stopping short at a point past his hairless navel. "Your uncle engaged me for tonight. For you."

"Oh," Miguel managed, "I see."

"Do you like what you see?"

Whatever words Miguel had suddenly dried on his tongue as he watched the boy disrobe.

"There is no need to feel anxious."

"No, no, I am— not anxious."

"You only turn sixteen once. It should be special. It will be special." The boy had crossed the distance between them in the span of a thunderous heartbeat and Miguel shuddered when he felt the intense heat the boy seemed to radiate. He did not know if it was the result of his imagination or barely controlled desire but he feared that he would burn.

"You cannot possibly be older than me," Miguel said, casting his gaze to the side, suddenly conscious of the boy's nearness.

"I am fifteen. Or thirteen. Unless you prefer me to be older," the boy spoke as he began unbuttoning Miguel's shirt. "I can be eighteen. Or twenty. Just let me know."

"I—" Miguel began, but as the boy's fingers found his skin he lost all words, the language abandoning him to the trails of heat left by the boy's explorations. When their tongues met, he was certain he would be consumed by fire, losing himself in the intense moment of unadulterated sunlight that reduced everything that he was into a throbbing cinder, wanting only the explosive release that was as inevitable as life and death.

"Never leave me," he told the boy.

"Everyone loves me," the boy answered. "You must live only for the moment."

"Then I'll never be old."

Later, after his birthday gift had left, he lay trembling in a bed built for one, his body weak with the demarcation of new frontiers, while his soul, not quite anywhere, exulted in the epiphany that he was his own boundary and that it was as wide or as narrow as he wanted.

What Miguel Lopez Vicente did not know, what he could not know, was that his heart was ill-suited for single nights' passion. It was fragile and tender and rare, wanting only true love, and collapsed upon itself, heavy with imagined loss in the small hours before dawn, feeling lost, betrayed and old before its time.

And so his story ended.

-terminó-

When Miguel Lopez Vicente turned eight, his father brought him to see the End of the World.

The spectacle, held only once every generation and lasting for fourteen nights, was staged on a massive series of sculpted sets within the Baluarte of the Plaza Miranda. Ciudad Manila spared no expense – the costumed cast numbered in the hundreds and great machines, made invisible by cloth and convention, spewed fire, blew wind and rained artificial hailstones the size of macopas but with the consistency of cotton. The Beast of the Apocalypse (a magnificent contraption maneuvered by three alternating shifts of eighteen people) towered over the amazed audience, clawing its way out of a bottomless pit; its words and imprecations resounded with the voice of the Most Excellent Primo Orador herself.

Much of the performance went over Miguel Lopez Vicente's head; instead he was terrified by the sights and sounds of the Apocalypse, much to his father's regret.

"Did you not enjoy the show?" Antonio Manuel Vicente asked him afterwards, visibly irritated at his son's obvious pallor.

"Yes, Papa," Miguel lied with little difficulty.

"It is important that you know about things like this," Antonio continued, not hearing him. "The world ends in horror if the will of the Three Sisters is not followed."

"Yes, Papa."

"That is why you must pray every day, every night, before you eat, before you sleep. Pray for their mercy."

"Yes, Papa."

"When you grow older, you'll understand that we are all servants of the Three."

"Yes, Papa," Miguel replied, but in his heart he had decided never to grow old.

When they returned home, Miguel rushed to his room and trembled in a corner, his thoughts ablaze with images of endings and destruction. He cried for over an hour, caught off-guard by the tears his fear provoked, feeling helpless, alone and destined to die in the Apocalypse that could occur tomorrow or the day after that.

The young boy turned his back on the faith of his father that day, with the fierce determination of the very young, and resolved that he would rather die than live to see the End of the World.

Before he went to sleep, he deliberately did not say his bedtime prayers and turned the statue of the Three Sisters away from his bed. He did not want them watching him.

The Apocalypse arrived that night, triggered by the loss of one little boy's faith. In their fury, radiant devas came to Miguel's room on shimmering wings, shattering the walls of the house. "So this is the one who brought about the End of Things," the fiercest among them said, pointing to the sleeping boy with a sword that burned with a flame unseen since the Beginning of All Things. With a soundless cry she struck down the remnants of the house then flew with her legion into the sky that wept stars.

And so his story ended.

-terminó-

Miguel Lopez Vicente's mother, dead just a week, came to him on the eve of his fourth birthday, saying something her son could not quite hear.

He sat up, straining to listen to her words, having no fear of the woman who had shown him only love.

"Miguel."

"Mama?"

"I am lonely here. Will you come with me?"

"Yes, Mama."

When his mother kissed him on the forehead, Miguel felt suddenly cold and embraced her, his heavy heart, lately engorged by sorrow, shrinking to the size of a child's perfect love.

"You are the only one I have ever loved, my Miguel," she told him as they stepped into the shadows.

"Yes, Mama."

"You will always be my little boy."

"Yes, Mama."

"Do not forget to take your smile with you."

Miguel set his face into a smile of unconditional trust and walked forward.

And so his story ended.

-terminó-

Antonio Manuel Vicente, the rising dramatist, stood at the balcony of his tower residence and contemplated his life, like pages in a chapbook he felt he had only partially authored.

A soft wind, heavy with the suggestion of salt, blew in from the nearby harbor, carrying muted voices that sang, argued, lied or whispered promises. He pulled his dressing robe closer to his body, thinking about the sad and strange paths his life had taken, the people he had loved and left behind, and how the simplicity of a change of perspective – the height of a balcony – could provoke thoughts of drastic action.

In his arms he carried his sleeping son, Miguel; a two-year-old result of a dalliance with a woman he could honestly not remember. He had found the boy sitting alone, silent and stone-faced, on the stairs of his residence, with a brief letter that held even briefer introductions. That was a week ago.

Antonio had his entire life before him and felt that the unwelcome weight in his arms was an unfair burden. When he felt his son stir in his arms, he summoned up all the paternal inclinations in his heart and came up with an absolute emptiness.

He looked at the son he had never wanted, never even dreamed of, and without a single other thought, hurled him off the balcony. He felt no remorse, prepared to act the distraught parent when tomorrow brought news of the horrible accident to his ears, already composing the lines of dialogue that he, grief-stricken, would speak.

Miguel Lopez Vicente watched the ground rush up to welcome him with the same stoicism he had when he was abandoned by his mother.

And so his story ended.

-terminó-

Mr. Henares looks at his inventory

In the storeroom of his shop along the Encanto lu Caminata, Mr. Henares looked at the eighty four vials he had distilled from the future days of his largest customer of the year.

He gently swirled the closest one between thumb and forefinger and watched the marvelous stories of Miguel Lopez Vicente unfold in a glimmer of effervescent, liquid tales brimming with potential. He paused and thought about the nature of stories, the vagaries of time and the single, long road of desire and shook his head, resigned to the fact that for as long as people were people, his business would continue.

Mr. Henares replaced the vial of Miguel Lopez Vicente among the eighty-three others, put off for the next day the task of determining their relative prices (perhaps he would bundle two or three – one of his regulars, a famous astronomer when he was young, wanted some more time for stargazing), and went about closing the shop.

"We all burn sunlight," he muttered to no one in particular, scratching an arm with a motion that could almost be mistaken as a caress.

-terminó-

THE WEED OF TIME

Norman Spinrad

Norman Spinrad is an American writer who has published more than twenty novels and sixty or so short stories, feature film scripts, television scripts, songs, and much assorted other stuff. He has won the Hugo Award and the Nebula Award for his fiction. "The Weed of Time" was originally published in *Vertex: The Magazine of Science Fiction* in August of 1973.

I, me, the spark of mind that is my consciousness, dwells in a locus that is neither place nor time. The objective duration of my life-span is one hundred and ten years, but from my own locus of consciousness, I am immortal – my awareness of my own awareness can never cease to be. I am an infant am a child am a youth am an old, old man dying on clean white sheets. I am all these have always been all these mes will always be all mes in the place where my mind dwells in an eternal moment divorced from time.

A century and a tenth is my eternity. My life is like a biography in a book; immutable, invariant, fixed in length, in duration. On April 3, 2040, I am born. On December 2, 2150, I die. The events in between take place in a single instant. Say that I range up and down them at will, experiencing each of them again and again and again eternally. Even this is not really true; I experience all in my century and a tenth simultaneously, once forever . . . How can I tell my story? How can you understand? The language we have in common is based on concepts of time which we do not share.

For me, time as you think of it does not exist. I do not move from moment to moment sequentially like a blind man groping his way down a tunnel. I am at all points in the tunnel simultaneously, and my eyes are open wide. Time is to me, in a sense, what space is to you, a field over which I move in more directions than one. How can I tell you? How can I make you understand? We are, all of us, men born of women, but in a way you have less in common with me than you do with an ape or an amoeba. Yet I *must* tell you, somehow. It is too late for me, will be too late, has been too late. I am trapped in this eternal hell and I can never escape, not even into death. My life is immutable, invariant, for I have eaten of Temp, the Weed of Time. But you must not! You must listen! You must understand! Shun the Weed of Time! I must try to tell you in my own way. It is pointless to try to start at the beginning. There is no beginning. There is no end. Only significant time-loci. Let me describe these loci. Perhaps I can make you understand . . .

September 8, 2050. I am ten years old. I am in office of Dr. Phipps, who is the director of the mental hospital in which I have been for the past eight years.

June 12, 2053, they will finally understand that I am not insane. It is all they will understand, but it will be enough for them to release me. But on September 8, 2050, I am in a mental hospital.

September 8, 2050 is the day the first expedition returns from Tau Ceti. The arrival is to be televised, and why I am in Dr. Phipps's office watching television with the director. The Tau Ceti expedition is the reason I am in the hospital. I have been babbling about it for the previous ten years. I have been demanding that the ship be quarantined, that the plant samples it will bring back be destroyed, not allowed to grow in the soil of Earth. For most of my life this has been regarded as an obvious symptom of schizophrenia – after all, before July 12, 2048, the ship has not left for Tau Ceti, and until today it has not returned.

But on September 8, 2050, they wonder. This is the day I have been babbling about since I emerged from my mother's womb and now it is happening. So now I am alone with Dr. Phipps as the image of the ship on the television set lands on the image of a wide concrete apron . . .

"Make them understand!" I shout, knowing that it is futile. "Stop them, Dr. Phipps, stop them!"

Dr. Phipps stares at me uneasily. His small blue eyes show a mixture of pity, confusion, and fright. He is all too familiar with my case. Sharing his desktop with the portable television set is a heavy oaktag folder filled with my case history, filled with hundreds of therapy session records. In each of these records, this day is mentioned: September 8, 2050. I have repeated the same story over and over and over again. The ship will leave for Tau Ceti on July 12, 2048. It will return on September 8, 2050. The expedition will report that Tau Ceti has twelve planets . . . The fifth alone is Earth-like and bears plant and animal life . . . The expedition will bring back samples and seeds of a small Cetan plant with broad green leaves and small purple flowers . . . The plant will be named *tempis ceti* . . . It will become known as Temp . . . Before the properties of the plant are fully understood, seeds will somehow become scattered and Temp will flourish in the soil of Earth . . . Somewhere, somehow, people will begin to eat the leaves of the Temp plant. They will become changed. They will babble of the future, and they will be considered mad – until the future events of which they speak begin to come to pass . . .

Then the plant will be outlawed as a dangerous narcotic. Eating Temp will become a crime . . . But, as with all forbidden fruit, Temp will continue to be eaten . . . And finally, Temp addicts will become the most sought-after criminals in the world. The governments of the Earth will attempt to milk the secrets of the future from their tortured minds . . .

All this is in my case history, with which Dr. Phipps is familiar. For eight years, this has been considered only a remarkably consistent psychotic delusion.

But now it is September 8, 2050. As I have predicted, the ship has returned from Tau Ceti. Dr. Phipps stares at me woodenly as the gangplank is erected and the crew begins to debark. I can see his jaw tense as the reporters gather around the captain, a tall, lean man carrying a small sack.

The captain shakes his head in confusion as the reporters besiege him. "Let me make a short statement first," he says crisply. "Save wear and tear on all of us." The captain's thin, hard, pale face fills the television screen. "The expedition is a success," he says. "The Tau Ceti system was found to have twelve planets, the fifth is Earth-like and bears plant and simple animal life. Very peculiar animal life . . ."

"What do you mean, peculiar?" a reporter shouts. The captain frowns and shrugs his wide shoulders. "Well, for one thing, they all seem to be herbivores and they seem to live off one species of plant which dominates the planetary flora. No predators. And it's not hard to see why. I don't quite know how to explain this, but all the critters seem to know what the other animals will do before they do it. And what we were going to do, too. We had one hell of a time taking specimens. We think it has something to do with the plant. Does something strange to their time sense."

"What makes you say that?" a reporter asks.

"Well, we fed some of the stuff to our lab animals. Same thing seemed to happen. It became virtually impossible to lay a hand on 'em. They seemed to be living a moment in the future, or something. That's why Dr. Lominov has called the plant *tempis ceti*."

"What's this tempis look like?" a reporter says.

"Well, it's sort of . . ." the captain begins. "Wait a minute," he says, "I've got a sample right here."

He reaches into the small sack and pulls something out. The camera zooms in on the captain's hand.

He is holding a small plant. The plant has broad leaves and small purple blossoms.

Dr. Phipps's hands begin to tremble uncontrollably. He stares at me. He stares and stares and stares . . . •

May 12, 2062. I am in a small room. Think of it as a hospital room. Think of it as a laboratory, think of it as a cell: it is all three. I have been here for three months.

I am seated on a comfortable lounge-chair. Across a table from me sits a man from an unnamed government intelligence bureau. On the table is a tape recorder. It is running. The man seated opposite is frowning in exasperation.

"The subject is December, 2081," he says. "You will tell me all you know of the events of December, 2081."

I stare at him silently, sullenly. I am tired of all the men from intelligence sections, economic councils, scientific bureaus, with their endless, futile demands.

"Look," the man snaps, "we know better than to appeal to your nonexistent sense of patriotism. We are all too well aware that you don't give a damn about what the knowledge you have can mean to your country. But just remember this: you're a convicted criminal. Your sentence is indeterminate. Cooperate, and you'll be released in two years. Clam up, and we'll hold you here till you rot or until you get it through your head that the only way for you to get out is to talk. The subject is the month of December in the year 2081. Now, *give*!"

I sigh. I know that it is no use trying to tell any of them that knowledge of the future is useless, that the future cannot be changed because it was not changed because it will not be changed. They will not accept the fact that choice is an illusion caused by the fact that future time-loci are hidden from those who advance sequentially along the time-stream one moment after the other in blissful ignorance. They refuse to understand that moments of future time are no different from moments of past or present time; fixed, immutable, invariant. They live in the illusion of sequential time.

So I begin to speak of the month of December in the year 2081. I know they will not be satisfied until I have told them all I know of the years between this time-locus and December 2, 2150. I know they will not be satisfied because they are not satisfied, have not been satisfied, will not be satisfied . . .

So I tell them of that terrible December nine years in their future . . .

December 2, 2150. I am old, old, a hundred and ten years old. My age-ruined body lies on the clean, white sheets of a hospital bed, lungs, heart, blood vessels, organs, all failing. Only my mind is forever untouched, the mind of an infant-child-youth-man-ancient. I am, in a sense, dying. Beyond this day, December 2, 2150, my body no longer exists as a living organism. Time to me forward of this date is as blank to me as time beyond April 3, 2040 is in the other temporal direction.

In a sense, I am dying. But in another sense, I am immortal. The spark of my consciousness will not go out. My mind will not come to an end, for it has neither end nor beginning. I exist in one moment that lasts forever and spans one hundred and ten years.

Think of my life as a chapter in a book, the book of eternity, a book with no first page and no last. The chapter that is my life-span is one hundred and ten pages long. It has a starting point and an ending point, but the chapter exists as long as the book exists, the infinite book of eternity.

Or, think of my life as a ruler one hundred and ten inches long. The ruler "begins" at one and "ends" at one hundred and ten, but "begins" and "ends" refer to length, not duration.

I am dying. I experience dying always, but I never experience death. Death is the absence of experience. It can never come for me.

December 2, 2150 is but a significant time-locus for me, a dark wall, an end-point beyond which I cannot see. The other wall has the time-locus April 3, 2040.

April 3, 2040. Nothingness abruptly ends, non-nothingness abruptly begins. I am born.

What is it like for me to be born? How can I tell you? How can I make you understand? My life, my whole life-span of one hundred and ten years comes into being once, in an instant. At the "moment" of my birth I am at the moment of my death and all moments in between. I emerge from my mother's womb and I see my life as one sees a painting, a painting of some complicated landscape; all at once, whole, a complete gestalt. I see my strange, strange infancy, the incomprehension as I emerge from the womb speaking perfect English, marred only by my undeveloped vocal apparatus, as I emerge from my mother's womb demanding that the ship from Tau Ceti in the time-locus September 8, 2050 be quarantined, knowing that my demand will be futile because it was futile, will be futile, is futile, knowing that at the moment of my birth I am have been will be all that I ever was/am/will be and that I cannot change a moment of it.

I emerge from my mother's womb and I am dying in clean white sheets and I am in the office of Dr. Phipps watching the ship land and I am in the government cell for two years babbling of the future and I am in a clearing in some woods where a plant with broad green and small purple flowers grows and I am picking the plant and eating it as I know I will do have done am doing . . .

I emerge from my mother's womb and I see the gestalt-painting of my life-span, a pattern of immutable events painted on the stationary and eternal canvas of time . . .

But I do not merely *see* the "painting", I *am* the "painting" and I am the painter and I am also outside the painting viewing the whole and I am none of these.

And I see the immutable time-locus that determines all the rest – March 4, 2060. Change that and the painting dissolves and I live in time like any other man, moment after blessed moment, freed from this all-knowing hell. But change itself is illusion.

March 4, 2060 in a wood not too far from where I was born. But knowledge of the horror that day brings, has brought, will bring can change nothing. I will do as I am doing will do did because I did it will do it am doing it . . .

April 3, 2040, and I emerge from my mother's womb, an infant-child-youth-man-ancient, in a government cell in a mental hospital dying in clean white sheets . . .

March 4, 2060. I am twenty. I am in a clearing in the woods. Before me grows a small plant with broad green leaves and purple blossoms – Temp, the Weed of Time, which has haunted, haunts, will haunt my never-ending life. I know what I am doing will do have done because I will do have done am doing it.

How can I explain? How can I make you understand that this moment is una-voidable, invariant, that though I have known, do know, will know its dreadful consequences, I can do nothing to alter it?

The language is inadequate. What I have told you is an unavoidable half-truth. All actions I perform in my one hundred and ten year life-span occur simultaneously. But even that statement only hints around the truth, for "simul-taneously" means "at the same time" and "time" as you understand the word has no relevance to my life. But let me approximate.

Let me say that all actions I have ever performed, will perform, do perform, occur simultaneously. Thus no knowledge inherent in any particular time-locus can affect any action performed at any other locus in time. Let me construct another useful lie, Let me say that for me action and perception are totally inde-pendent of each other. At the moment of my birth, I did everything I would ever do in my life, instantly, blindly, in one total gestalt. Only in the next "moment" do I perceive the results of all those myriad actions, the horror that March 4, 2060 will make has made is making of my life.

Or . . . they say that at the moment of death, one's entire life flashes instan-taneously before one's eyes. At the moment of my birth, my whole life flashed before me, not merely before my eyes, but in reality. I cannot change any of it because change is something that exists only as a function of the relationship between different moments in time and for me life is one eternal moment that is one hundred and ten years long . . .

So this awful moment is invariant, inescapable.

March 4, 2060. I reach down, pluck the Temp plant. I pull off a broad green leaf, put it in my mouth. It tastes bittersweet, woody, unpleasant. I chew it, bolt it down.

The Temp travels to my stomach, is digested, passes into my bloodstream, reaches my brain. There changes occur which better men than I are powerless, will be powerless to understand, at least up till December 2, 2150 beyond which is blankness. My body remains in the objective time-stream, to age, grow old, decay, die. But my mind is abstracted out of time to experience all moments as one.

It is like a *déjà vu*. Because this happened on March 4, 2060, I have already experienced it in the twenty years since my birth. Yet this is the beginning point for my Temp-consciousness in the objective time-stream. But objective time-stream has no relevance to what happens . . .

The language, the very thought patterns are inadequate. Another useful lie: in the objective time-stream I was a normal human being until this dire March 4, experiencing each moment of the previous twenty years sequentially, in order, moment, after moment, after moment . . .

Now on March 4, 2060, my consciousness expands in two directions in the time-stream to fill my entire lifespan: forward to December 2, 2150 and my death, backward to April 3, 2040 and my birth. As this time-locus of March 4 "changes" my future, so too it "changes" my past, expanding my Temp-consciousness to both extremes of my life-span.

But once the past is changed, the previous past has never existed and I emerge from my mother's infant-child-youth-man-ancient in a government cell a mental hospital dying in clean white sheets . . . And—

I, me, the spark of mind that is my consciousness, dwells in a locus that is neither place nor time. The objective duration of my life-span is one hundred and ten years, but from my own locus of consciousness, I am immortal, my awareness of my own awareness can never cease to be. I am an infant am a child am a youth am an old, old man dying on clean white sheets. I am all these mes, have always been all these mes will always be all these mes in the place where my mind dwells in an eternal moment divorced from time . . .

THE WAITABITS

Eric Frank Russell

Eric Frank Russell was a British writer best known for his science fiction novels and short stories. Most of his work was first published in the United States in magazines such as *Astounding Stories*, *Weird Tales*, *Strange Stories*, and *Tales of Wonder*. "The Waitabits" gives a different perspective on time and was first published in *Astounding Science Fiction* in 1955.

He strode toward the Assignment Office with quiet confidence born of long service, much experience and high rank. Once upon a time a peremptory call to this department had made him slightly edgy exactly as it unnerved the fresh-faced juniors today. But that had been long, long ago. He was grey-haired now, with wrinkles around the corners of his eyes, silver oak-leaves on his epaulettes. He had heard enough, seen enough and learned enough to have lost the capacity for surprise.

Markham was going to hand him a tough one. That was Markham's job: to rake through a mess of laconic, garbled, distorted or eccentric reports, pick out the obvious problems and dump them squarely in the laps of whoever happened to be hanging around and was considered suitable to solve them. One thing could be said in favour of this technique: its victims often were bothered, bedevilled or busted but at least they were never bored. The problems were not commonplace, the solutions sometimes fantastic.

The door detected his body-heat as he approached, swung open with silent efficiency. He went through, took a chair, gazed phlegmatically at the heavy man behind the desk.

"Ah, Commodore Leigh," said Markham pleasantly. He shuffled some papers, got them in order, surveyed the top one. "I am informed that the Thunderer's overhaul is complete, the crew has been recalled and everything is ready for flight."

"That is correct."

"Well now, I have a task for you." Markham put on the sinister smile that invariably accompanied such an announcement. After years of reading what had followed in due course, he had conceived the notion that all tasks were funny except when they involved a massacre. "You are ready and eager for another trip, I trust?"

"I am always ready," said Commodore Leigh. He had outgrown the eagerness two decades back.

"I have here the latest consignment of scout reports," Markham went on. He made a disparaging gesture. "You know what they're like. Condensed to the minimum and in some instances slightly mad. Happy the day when we receive a report detailed with scientific thoroughness."

"You'll get that only from a trained mind," Leigh commented. "Scouts are not scientists. They are oddities who like roaming the loneliest reaches of space with no company but their own. Pilot-trained hoboes willing to wander at large, take brief looks and tell what they've seen. Such men are useful and necessary. Their shortcomings can be made up by those who follow them."

"Precisely," agreed Markham with suspicious promptness. "So this is where we want you to do some following."

"What is it this time?"

"We have Boydell's latest report beamed through several relay stations. He is way out in the wilds." Markham tapped the paper irritably. "This particular scout is known as Gabby Boydell because he is anything but that. He uses words as if they cost him fifty dollars apiece."

"Meaning he hasn't said enough?" asked Leigh smiling.

"Enough? He's told us next to nothing!" He let go an emphatic snort.

"Eighteen planets scattered all over the shop and not a dozen words about each. He discovers a grand total of eighteen planets in several previously unexplored systems and the result doesn't occupy half a page."

"Going at that speed, he'd not have time for much more," Leigh ventured. "You can't write a book about a world without taking up residence for a while."

"That may be. But these crackpot scouts could do better and it's time they were told as much." He pointed an accusative finger. "Look at this item. The eleventh planet he visited. He has named it Pulok for some reason that is probably crazy. His report employs exactly four words: 'Take it and welcome.' What do you make of that?"

Leigh thought it over carefully. "It is inhabitable by humankind. There is no native opposition, nothing to prevent us grabbing it. But in his opinion it isn't worth possessing."

"Why, man, why?"

"I don't know, not having been there."

"Boydell knows the reason." Markham fumed a bit and went on, "And he ought to state it in precise, understandable terms. He shouldn't leave a mystery hanging in mid-air like a bad smell from nowhere."

"He will explain it when he returns to his sector headquarters, surely?"

"That may be months hence, perhaps years, especially if he manages to pick up fuel and replacement tubes from distant outposts. Those scouts keep to no schedule. They get there when they arrive, return when they come back. Galactic gypsies, that's how they like to think of themselves."

"They've chosen freedom," Leigh offered.

Ignoring that remark, Markham continued, "Anyway, the problem of Pulok is a relatively minor one to be handled by somebody else. I'll give it to one of the juniors; it will do something for his education. The more complicated and possibly dangerous tangles are for older ones such as yourself."

"Tell me the worst."

"Planet fourteen on Boydell's list. He has given it the name of Eterna and don't ask me why. The code formula he's registered against it reads O/1.1/D.7. That means we can live on it without special equipment, it's an Earth-type planet of one-tenth greater mass and is inhabited by an intelligent life form of different but theoretically equal mental power. He calls this life form the Waitabits. Apparently he tags everything and everybody with the first name that pops into his mind."

"What information does he offer concerning them?"

"Hah!" said Markham, pulling a face. "One word. Just one word." He paused, then voiced it. "Unconquerable."

"Eh?"

"Unconquerable," repeated Markham. "A word that should not exist in scout-language." At that point he became riled, jerked open a drawer, extracted a notebook and consulted it. "Up to last survey, four hundred and twenty-one planets had been discovered, charted, recorded. One hundred and thirty-seven found suitable for human life and large or small groups of settlers placed thereon. Sixty-two alien life forms mastered during the process." He shoved the book back. "And out there in the dark a wandering tramp picks a word like unconquerable."

"I can think of only one reason that makes sense," suggested Leigh.

"What is that?"

"Perhaps they really are unconquerable."

Markham refused to credit his ears. "If that is a joke, commodore, it's in bad taste. Some might think it seditious."

"Well, can you think up another and better reason?"

"I don't have to. I'm sending you there to find out. The Grand Council asked specifically that you be given this task. They feel that if any yet unknown aliens have enough to put the wind up one of our own scouts then we must learn more about them. And the sooner the better."

"There's nothing to show that they actually frightened Boydell. If they had done so he'd have said more, much more. A genuine first-class menace is the one thing that would make him talk his head off."

"That's purely hypothetical," said Markham. "We don't want guesses. We want facts."

"All right."

"Consider a few other facts," Markham added. "So far no other life form has been able to resist us. I don't see how any can. Any creatures with an atom of sense soon see which side their bread is buttered, if they eat bread and like butter. If we step in and provide the brains while they furnish the labour, with mutual benefit to both parties, the aliens are soon doing too well for themselves to complain. If a bunch of Sirian Wimpots slave all day in our mines, then fly in their own helicopters back to homes such as their forefathers never owned, what have they got to cry about?"

"I fail to see the purpose of the lecture," said Leigh, dryly.

"I'm emphasizing that by force, ruthlessness, argument, persuasion, precept and example, appeal to commonsense or any other tactic appropriate to the circumstances we can master and exploit any life-form in the cosmos. That's the theory we've been using for a thousand years – and it works. We've proved that it works. We have made it work. The first time we let go of it and admit defeat we're finished. We go down and disappear along with all the other vanished hordes." He swept his papers to one side. "A scout has admitted defeat. He must be a lunatic. But lunatics can create alarm. The Grand Council is alarmed."

"So I am required to seek soothing syrup?"

"Yes. See Parrish in the charting department. He'll give you the coordinates of this Eterna dump." Standing up, he offered a plump hand.

"A smooth trip and a safe landing, commodore."

"Thanks."

The Thunderer hung in a balanced orbit while its officers examined the new world floating below. This was Eterna, second planet of a sun very much like Sol. Altogether there were four planets in this particular family but only the second harboured life in any detectable form.

Eterna was a pretty sight, a great blue-green ball shining in the blaze of full day. Its land masses were larger than Earth's, its oceans smaller. No vast mountain ranges were visible, no snow-caps either, yet lakes and rivers were numerous. Watersheds lay in heavily forested hills that crinkled much of the surface and left few flat areas. Cloud-banks lay over the land like scatterings of cotton-wool, small in area, widely dispersed, but thick, heavy and great in number.

Through powerful glasses towns and villages could be seen, most of them placed in clearings around which armies of trees marched down to the rivers. There were also narrow, winding roads and thin, spidery bridges. Between the larger towns ran vague lines that might be railroad tracks but lacked sufficient detail at such a distance to reveal their true purpose.

Pascoe, the sociologist, put down his binoculars and said, "Assuming that the night side is very similar, I estimate their total strength at no more than one hundred millions. I base that on other planetary surveys. When you've counted the number of peas per bottle in a large and varied collection of them you develop the ability to make reasonably accurate guesses. One hundred millions at most."

"That's low for a planet of this size and fertility, isn't it?" asked Commodore Leigh.

"Not necessarily. There were no more of us in the far past. Look at us now."

"The implication is that these Waitabits are comparatively a young species?"

"Could be. On the other hand they may be old and senile and dying out fast. Or perhaps they're slow breeders and their natural increase isn't much."

"I don't go for the dying out theory," put in Walterson, the geophysicist. "If once they were far bigger than they are today, the planet should still show signs of it. A huge inheritance leaves its mark for centuries. Remember that city-site we found on Hercules? Even the natives didn't know of it, the markings being visible only from a considerable altitude."

They used their glasses again, sought for faint lines of orderliness in wide tracts of forest. There were none to be seen.

"Short in history or slow to breed," declared Pascoe. "That's my opinion for what it's worth."

Frowning down at the blue-green ball, Leigh said heavily. "By our space-experienced standards a world of one hundred millions is weak. It's certainly not sufficiently formidable to turn a hair on a minor bureaucrat, much less worry the Council itself." He turned, lifted a questioning eyebrow as a signals-runner came up to him. "Well?"

"Relay from Sector Nine, sir."

Unfolding the message, he found it duly decoded, read it aloud.

19.12. ex Terra. *Defence H.Q. to C.O. battleship* Thunderer. *Light cruiser* Flame, *Lieut. Mallory commanding, assigned your area for Pulok check. Twentieth heavy cruiser squadron readied Arlington port, Sector Nine. This authorizes you to call upon and assume command of sail forces in emergency only. Rathbone. Com. Op. Dep. D.H.Q. Terra.*

He filed the message, shrugged and said, "Seems they're taking few chances."

"Yes," agreed Pascoe, a trifle sardonically. "So they've assembled reinforcements near enough to be summoned but too far away to do us any good. The *Flame* could not get here in less than seven weeks. The ships at Arlington couldn't make it in under nineteen or twenty weeks even at super-drive. By then we could be cooked, eaten, burped and forgotten."

"I don't see what all this jumpiness is about," complained Walterson.

"That scout Boydell went in and came out without losing his edible parts, didn't he? Where one can go a million can follow."

Pascoe regarded him with pity. "A solitary invader rarely frightens anyone. That's where scouts have an advantage. Consider Remy 11. Fellow name of James finds it, lands, makes friends, becomes a blood brother, finally takes off amid a huzzah of fond farewells. Next, down comes three shiploads of men, uniforms and guns. That's too much for the locals to stomach. In Remitan psychology the number represents critical mass. Result: the Remy war which, if you remember your history, was long, costly and bitter."

"I remember history well enough to recall that in those primitive days they used blockheaded space-troopers and had no specially trained contact-men," Walterson retorted.

"Nevertheless, what has happened before can happen again."

"That's my problem right now," Leigh interjected. "Will the sight of a battleship a mile in length cause them to start something that can't be finished without considerable slaughter? Had I better risk the crew of a lifeboat in an effort to smooth the introduction? I wish Boydell had been a little more informative." He chewed his bottom lip with vexation, picked up the intercom phone, flipped the signals-room switch. "Any word from Boydell yet?"

"No, commodore," responded a voice. "Sector Nine doesn't think there will be any, either. They've just been through saying he doesn't answer their calls. They believe he's now out of range. Last trace they got of him showed him to be running beyond effective communication limits."

"All right." He dumped the phone, gazed through the port. "Several hours we've waited. Nothing has come up to take a look at us. We can detect no signs of excitement down there. Therefore it's a safe bet that they have no ships, perhaps not even rudimentary aircraft. Neither do they keep organized watch on the sky. They're not advanced in our sense of the term."

"But they may be in some other sense," Pascoe observed.

"That is what I implied." Leigh made an impatient gesture. "We've hung within telescopic view long enough. If they are capable of formidable reaction, we should be grimly aware of it by now. I don't feel inclined to test the Waitabits at the expense of a few men in an unarmed lifeboat. We'll take the *Thunderer* itself down and hope they're sane enough not to go nuts."

Hastening forward to the main control-cabin he issued the necessary orders.

The landing place was atop a treeless bluff nine miles south of a large town. It was as good a site as any that could have been chosen. The settling of great tonnage over a mile-long area damaged nobody's property or crops, the ground was solid enough not to furrow under the ship's weight, the slight elevation gave a strategic advantage to the *Thunderer's* guns.

Despite its nearness the town was out of sight, being hidden by intervening hills. A narrow road ran through the valley but nothing moved thereon. Between the road and the base of the bluff lay double railroad tracks of about twenty-inch gauge with flat-topped rails of silvery metal.

The rails had no spikes or ties and appeared to be held firmly in position by being sunk into long, unbroken ridges of concrete or some similar rock-like substance.

The *Thunderer* reposed, a long, black, ominous shape with all locks closed and gun-turrets open, while Leigh stared speculatively at the railroad and waited for the usual call from the metering lab. It came within short time. The phone rang, he answered it, heard Shallom speaking: "The air is breathable, commodore."

"We knew that in advance. A scout sniffed it without dropping dead."

"Yes, commodore," agreed Shallom, patiently. "But you asked for an analysis."

"Of course. Because we don't know how long Boydell was here. Perhaps a day, perhaps a week. Whatever it was, it wasn't enough. He might have curled up his toes after a month or two. In his brief visit he'd have avoided any long-term accumulative effect. What we want to know is whether this atmosphere is safe for keeps."

"Quite safe, commodore. It's rather rich in ozone and argon but otherwise much like Earth's."

"Good. We'll open up and let the men stretch their legs."

"There's something else of interest," Shallom went on. "Preliminary observation time occupied seven hours and twenty-two minutes. Over that period the longitudinal shift of a selected equatorial point amounted to approximately three-tenths of a degree. That means this planet's period of axial rotation is roughly equivalent to an Earth-year. Its days and nights are each about six months long."

"Thanks, Shallom." He cut off without surprise, switched the intercom, gave orders to Bentley in the main engine room to operate the power locks. Then he switched again to Lieutenant Harding, officer commanding ground forces, gave permission for one-quarter of his men to be let out for exercise providing they bore arms and did not stray beyond direct cover of the ship's guns.

That done, he swivelled his pneumatic chair to face the port, put his feet up with heels resting on a wall-ridge and quietly contemplated the alien landscape. Walterson and Pascoe mooched around the room in the restless manner of men waiting for a possibly burning fuse to reach a hypothetical gunpowder barrel.

Shallom phoned again, recited gravitational and magnetic field readings, went off. A few minutes later he came through once more with details of atmospheric humidity, barometric variations and radioactivity.

Apparently he cared nothing for what might be brewing beyond the hills so long as it failed to register on his meters and screens. To his mind no real danger could exist without advertising itself through a needle-wagging or a fluorescent blip.

Outside, two hundred men scrambled noisily down the edge of the bluff, reached soft greensward that was not grass but something resembling short, heavily matted clover. There they kicked a ball around, wrestled, leap-frogged or were content to lie full-length on the turf, look at the sky, enjoy the sun. A small group strolled half a mile to the silent railroad, inspected it, trod precariously along its rails with extended arms jerking and swaying in imitation of tightrope walkers.

Four of Shallom's staff went down, two of them carrying buckets and spades like kids making for the seashore. A third bore a bug-trap. The fourth had a scintilloscope. The first pair dug clover and dirt, hauled it up to the ship for analysis and bacteria-count. Bug-trap dumped his box, went to sleep beside it. Scintilloscope marched in a careful zigzag around the base of the bluff.

After two hours Harding's whistle recalled the outside lotus-eaters who responded with reluctance. They slouched back into the gigantic bottle that already had contained them so long. Another two hundred went out, played all the same tricks including the tightrope act on the rails.

By the time that gang had enjoyed its ration of liberty the mess bells announced a main meal ready. The crew ate, after which Number One Watch took to its berths and the deepest sleep within memory. A third freedom party cavorted on the turf. The indefatigable Shallom passed along the news that nine varieties of flea-sized bugs were awaiting introduction to Garside, the entomologist, whenever that worthy gentleman deigned to crawl out of bed.

By the time the fourth and last section of the crew returned from its two-hour spree, Pascoe had had enough. He was baggy-eyed from lack of slumber, disappointed with having curiosity left unsatisfied.

"More than seven hours waiting in the sky," he complained to Leigh, "and another eight down here. That's over fifteen hours all told. Where has it got us?"

"It has given the men a badly-needed break," Leigh reproved. "The first rule of captaincy is to consider the men before considering an exterior problem. There is no real solution to any predicament unless there is also the means to apply it. The men are the means and more so than is the ship or any part of it. Men can build ships but ships cannot manufacture men."

"All right. They've had their outing. They are refreshed and their morale is boosted, all in accordance with the best psychological advice. What next?"

"If nothing turns up it will enable them to catch up on their sleep. The first watch is snoring its collective head off right now. The other two watches are entitled to their turn."

"But that means sitting idle for another eighteen hours," Pascoe protested.

"Not necessarily. The Waitabits may arrive at any time, in unguessable numbers, with unknown intentions and with unknown means of enforcing them. If so, everyone will have a rude awakening and you may get enough action to last you a lifetime," Leigh jerked a thumb toward the door. "Meanwhile, take to bed while the going is good. If trouble starts, it's likely to be days before you get another chance. Exhausted men are crippled men in a situation such as this."

"What about you?"

"I intend to slump into sweet dreams myself as soon as Harding is ready to take over."

Pascoe snorted with impatience, glanced at Walterson, gained no support from that quarter. Walterson was dozing on his feet at mere mention of bed. Pascoe snorted again, more loudly this time, departed with the other following.

They returned within ten hours, found Leigh freshly shaved and spruced. A look through the port revealed the same landscape as before.

Some two dozen of the crew were fooling around outside, beneath a Sun that had not visibly changed position in the sky. The road still wound through the valley and over the hills without a soul upon it. The railroad track still reposed with all the impassive silence of a long abandoned spur.

Pascoe said, thoughtfully, "This is a good example of how one can deduce something from nothing."

"Meaning what?" inquired Leigh, showing interest. "The town is nine miles away. We could walk there in about two hours. They've had several times that long in which to sound the alarm, summon the troops, launch an assault." He gestured toward the peaceful scene. "Where are they?"

"You tell us," Walterson prompted.

"Any life form capable of constructing roads and rails obviously must have eyes and brains. Therefore it is pretty certain that they've seen us either hanging above or coming down. I don't believe that they remain unaware of our existence." He studied his listeners, went on, "They haven't shown up because they're deliberately keeping away from us. That means they're afraid of us. And that in turn means they consider themselves far weaker, either as result of what they've see of us so far or maybe as result of what they learned from contact with Boydell."

"I don't agree with that last bit," opined Leigh.

"Why not?"

"If they saw us either up above or coming down, what did they actually see? A ship and nothing more. They observed nothing to indicate that we are of Boydell's own kind though it would be reasonable to assume it. Factually, we're still a bunch of unknowns to them."

"That doesn't make hay of my reasoning."

"It spoils it on two counts," Leigh insisted. "Firstly, not having weighed and measured us, how can they tell that they're weaker? Secondly, Boydell himself called them unconquerable. That suggests strength. And strength of a redoubtable order."

"Look," said Pascoe, "it doesn't really matter whether they're stronger or weaker in their own estimation. In the long run they can't buck the power of the human race. The cogent point right now is that of whether they are friendly or antagonistic."

"Well?"

"If friendly, they'd have been around dickering with us hours ago. There's no sign of them, not a spit or a button. Ergo, they don't like us. They've crawled into a hole because they lack the muscle to do something effective. They've ducked under cover hoping we'll go away and play some place else."

"An alternative theory," put in Walterson, "is that they're tough and formidable just as Boydell implied. They have kept their distance because they're wise enough to fight on ground of their own choosing and not on ours. If they refuse to come here, we've got to go there or accept stalemate. So they are making ready for us to walk into their parlour, after which" – he wiped a forefinger across his throat – "*skzzt!*"

"Bunk!" said Pascoe.

"We'll soon learn where we stand one way or the other," Leigh informed. "I've ordered Williams to get the helicopter out. The Waitabits can't avoid seeing that thing whooshing around. We'll learn plenty if they don't shoot it down."

"And if they do shoot it down?" inquired Pascoe.

"That question will be answered if and when it arises," Leigh assured. "You know as well as I do the law that hostility must not be accepted until demonstrated."

He went to the port, gazed across the scene to the tree-swathed hills beyond. After a while he reached for his binoculars, focused them upon the mid-distance.

"Holy smoke!" he said.

Pascoe ran to his side. "What's the matter?"

"Something's coming at last. And it's a train, no less." He handed over the glasses. "Take a look for yourself."

A dozen crewmen were on the track industriously filing from a rail sufficient metallic powder to be analysed in the lab. They straightened up as the line conducted sounds of the newcomer's approach. Shading their eyes, they stood like men paralysed while they gaped toward the east.

A couple of miles away the streamlined express came tearing around the base of a hill at nothing less than one and a half miles per hour. The men remained staring incredulously for ten minutes during which time the phenomenon covered a full quarter mile.

The *Thunderer*'s siren wailed a warning, the sample-takers recovered their wits and without undue exertion made more speed up the forty-degree bluff than the possible menace was doing on the flat. The last of them had sufficient presence of mind to bring with him an ounce of dust that Shallom later defined as titanium alloy.

Monstrous and imposing, the *Thunderer* sat waiting for first official contact. Every port held at least three expectant faces watching the track and the train. Every mind took it for granted that the oncoming machine would halt at the base of the bluff and things weird in shape emerge therefrom in readiness to parley. Nobody thought for a moment that it might pass on.

It did pass on.

The train consisted of four linked metal coaches and no locomotive, the source of power not being evident. The tiny cars, less than the height of a man, rolled by holding a score of crimson-faced, owl-eyed creatures some of whom were looking absently at the floor, some at each other, out the sides, anywhere but directly at the great invader atop the bluff.

From the time the train was first observed until realization dawned that it was not going to stop occupied precisely one hour and twenty-four minutes. That was its speed record from the eastward hill to the bluff.

Lowering his binoculars, Commodore Leigh said in baffled tones to Pascoe,

"Did you get a clear, sharp view of them?"

"Yes. Red-faced with beak noses and blinkless eyes. One had his hand resting on a window ledge and I noticed it was five-fingered like ours but with digits more slender."

"Far less than walking pace," commented Leigh. "That's what it's doing. I can amble faster even with corns on both feet." He had another puzzled look outside. The train had gained forty yards in the interval. "I wonder whether the power Boydell attributed to them is based on some obscure form of cunning."

"How do you mean?"

"If they cannot cope with us while we hold the ship in force, they've got to entice us out of it."

"Well, we aren't out of it, are we?" Pascoe countered. "Nobody has developed a mad desire to catch that train. And, if anybody did, he'd overtake it so fast he'd get wherever it's going before he had time to pull up. I don't see how they can bait us into being foolhardy merely by crawling around."

"The tactic would be according to their own logic, not ours," Leigh pointed out. "Perhaps on this world to crawl is to invite attack. A wild-dog pack reacts that way: the animal that limps gets torn to pieces." He thought it over, continued, "I'm suspicious of this episode. I don't like the ostentatious way in which they all kept their eyes fixed on something else as they went past. It isn't natural."

"Hah!" said Pascoe, prepared to argue.

Leigh waved him down. "I know it's a childish blunder to judge any species by the standards of our own, but I still say it isn't natural to have eyes and not use them."

"On Terra," chipped in Walterson, seriously, "some folk have arms, legs, eyes and even brains that they don't use. That's because they have the misfortune to be incurably afflicted, as you know." He went on, encouraged by the other's silence. "What if this track is a connecting link between the town and a sanatorium or hospital? Maybe its sole purpose is to carry sick people."

"We'll soon find out." Leigh resorted to the intercom. "Williams, is the 'copter ready yet?"

"Assembled and now being fuelled, commodore. It can take off in ten minutes' time."

"Who is duty pilot?"

"Ogilvy."

"Tell him to fly ahead of that train and report what's at the other end of the tracks. He's to do that before taking a look at the town." He turned to the others, added, "Shallom should have a panorama of the whole area taken on the way down, but it won't provide the details Ogilvy can get us."

Pascoe, again standing at the port, asked, "How much slower is slower?"

"Eh?"

"When a thing is already creeping as though next year will do, how can you tell that it has decided to apply the brakes?" He elucidated further, "It may be my imagination but I fancy that train has reduced velocity by a few yards per hour. I hope none of its passengers suffered injury by being slung from one end to the other."

Leigh had a look. The train had now gone something less than half a mile from his observation point. The tedious speed and slight foreshortening made it impossible to decide whether or not Pascoe was correct. He had to keep watch a full fifteen minutes before he too agreed that the train was slowing down.

During that time the helicopter took off with a superfast *whoosh-whoosh* from whirling vanes. Soaring over the track, it fled ahead of the train, shrank into the hills until its plastic-egg cabin resembled a dewdrop dangling from a spinning sycamore seed.

Contacting the signals room, Leigh said, "Put Ogilvy's reports through the speaker here." He returned to the port, continued watching the train.

All the crew not asleep or on duty were similarly watching.

"Village six miles along line," blared the speaker. "A second four miles farther on. A third five miles beyond that. Eight thousand feet. Climbing."

Five minutes later, "Six-coach train on tracks, headed eastward. Appears stalled from this height, but may be moving."

"Coming the other way and at a similar crawl," remarked Pascoe, glancing at Walterson. "Bang goes your sick people theory if that one also holds a bunch of zombies."

"Altitude twelve thousand," announced the loudspeaker. "Terminal city visible beyond hills. Distance from base twenty-seven miles. Will investigate unless recalled."

Leigh made no move to summon him back. There followed a long silence. By now the train was still less than a mile away and had cut progress down to about one yard per minute. Finally it stopped, remained motionless for a quarter of an hour, began to back so gradually that it had inched twenty yards before watchers became certain that it had reversed direction. Leigh levelled powerful glasses upon it. Definitely it was returning to the base of the bluff.

"Funny thing here," bawled Ogilvy from the wall. "Streets full of people all struck stiff. It was the same in those villages now that I come to think of it. I went over them too fast for the fact to register."

"That's crazy," said Pascoe. "How can he tell from that height?"

"I'm hovering right over the main stem, a tree-lined avenue with crowded sidewalks," Ogilvy continued. "If anyone is moving, I can't detect it. Request permission to examine from five hundred."

Using the auxiliary mike linked through the signals room, Leigh asked, "Is there any evidence of opposition such as aircraft, gun emplacements or rocket pits?"

"No, commodore, not that I can see."

"Then you can go down but don't drop too fast. Sheer out immediately if fired upon."

Silence during which Leigh had another look outside. The train was continuing to come back at velocity definable as chronic. He estimated that it would take most of an hour to reach the nearest point.

"Now at five hundred," the loudspeaker declared. "Great Jupiter, I've never seen anything like it. They're moving all right. But they're so sluggish I have to look twice to make sure they really are alive and in action." A pause, then, "Believe it or not, there's a sort of street-car system in operation. A baby eighteen months old could toddle after one of those vehicles and catch it."

"Come back," Leigh ordered sharply. "Come back and report on the nearby town."

"As you wish, commodore." Ogilvy sounded as if he were obeying with reluctance.

"Where's the point of withdrawing him from there?" asked Pascoe, irritated by this abrupt cutting-off of data. "He's in no great danger. What will he learn from one place that he cannot get from another?"

"He can confirm or deny the thing that is all-important, namely, that conditions are the same elsewhere and are not restricted to one locale. When he's had a look at the town I'll send him a thousand miles away for a third and final check." His grey eyes were thoughtful as he went on, "In olden times a Martian visitor could have made a major blunder if he'd judged Earth by one of its last remaining leper colonies. Today we'd make precisely the same mistake if this happens to be a quarantined area full of native paralytics."

"Don't say it," put in Walterson, displaying some nervousness. "If we've sat down in a reservation for the diseased, we'd better get out mighty fast. I don't want to be smitten by any alien plague to which I've no natural resistance. I had a narrow enough escape when I missed that Hermes expedition six years ago. Remember it? Within three days of landing the entire complement was dead, their bodies growing bundles of stinking strings later defined as a fungus."

"We'll see what Ogilvy says," Leigh decided. "If he reports what we consider more normal conditions elsewhere, we'll move there. If they prove the same, we'll stay."

"Stay," echoed Pascoe, his features expressing disgust. "Something tells me you picked the right word – stay." He gestured toward the port beyond which the train was a long time coming. "If what we've seen and what we've heard has any meaning at all, it means we're in a prize fix."

"Such as what?" prompted Walterson.

"We can stay a million years or go back home. For once in our triumphant history we're well and truly thwarted. We'll gain nothing whatever from this world for a good and undefeatable reason, namely, life's too short."

"I'm jumping to no hasty conclusions," said Leigh. "We'll wait for Ogilvy."

In a short time the loudspeaker informed with incredulity: "This town is full of creepers, too. And trolleys making the same speed, if you can call it speed. Want me to go down and tell you more?"

"No," said Leigh into the mike. "Make a full-range sweep eastward. Loop out as far as you can go with safety. Watch especially for any radical variation in phenomena and, if you find it, report at once." He racked the microphone, turned to the others. "All we can do now is wait a bit."

"You said it!" observed Pascoe pointedly. "I'll lay odds of a thousand to one that Boydell did no more than sit futilely around picking his teeth until he got tired of it."

Walterson let go a sudden laugh that startled them.

"What's the matter with you?" demanded Pascoe, staring at him.

"One develops the strangest ideas sometimes," said Walterson apologetically. "It just occurred to me that if horses were snails they'd never be compelled to wear harness. There's a moral somewhere but I can't be bothered to dig it out."

"City forty-two miles eastward from base," called Ogilvy. "Same as before. Two speeds: dead slow and slower than dead."

Pascoe glanced through the port. "That train is doing less than bug-rate. I reckon it intends to stop when it gets here." He thought a bit, finished, "If so, we know one thing in advance: they aren't frightened of us."

Making up his mind, Leigh phoned through to Shallom. "We're going outside. Make a record of Ogilvy's remarks while we're gone. Sound a brief yelp on the alarm-siren if he reports rapid movement any place." Then he switched to Nolan, Hoffnagle and Romero, the three communications experts. "Bring your Keen charts along in readiness for contact."

"It's conventional," reminded Pascoe, "for the ship's commander to remain in control of his vessel until contact has been made and the aliens found friendly or, at least, not hostile."

"This is where convention gets dumped overboard for once," Leigh snapped. "I'm going to pick on the load in that train. It's high time we made some progress. Please yourselves whether or not you come along."

"Fourteen villages so far," chipped in Ogilvy from far away over the hills. "Everyone in them hustling around at the pace that kills – with boredom. Am heading for city visible on horizon."

The communicators arrived bearing sheaves of coloured charts. They were unarmed, being the only personnel forbidden to wear guns. The theory behind this edict was that obvious helplessness established confidence. In most circumstances the notion proved correct and communicators survived. Once in a while it flopped and the victims gained no more than decent burial.

"What about us?" inquired Walterson, eyeing the newcomers. "Do we take weapons or don't we?"

"We'll chance it without any," Leigh decided. "A life form sufficiently intelligent to trundle around in trains should be plenty smart enough to guess what will happen if they try to take us. They'll be right under the ship's guns while we're parleying."

"I've no faith in their ability to see reason as we understand it," Pascoe put in. "For all their civilized veneer they may be the most treacherous characters this side of Sirius." Then he grinned and added, "But I've faith in my legs. By the way these aliens get into action I'd be a small cloud of dust in the sunset before one of them could take aim."

Leigh smiled, led them through the main lock. Every port was filled with watching faces as they made their way down to the track.

Gun-teams stood ready in their turrets, grimly aware that they could not beat off an attempted snatch except at risk of killing friends along with foes. But if necessary they could thwart it by wrecking the rails behind and ahead of the train, isolating it in readiness for further treatment. For the time being their role was the static one of intimidation. Despite this world's apparent lack of danger there was a certain amount of apprehension among the older hands in the ship. A pacific atmosphere had fooled humans before and they were wary of it.

The six reached the railroad a couple of hundred yards in advance of the train, walked toward it. They could see the driver sat behind a glass-like panel in front. His big yellow eyes were staring straight ahead, his crimson face was without expression. Both his hands rested on knobbed levers and the sight of half-a-dozen other-worlders on the lines did not make him so much as twitch a finger.

Leigh was first to reach the cab door and stretch out a hand to grasp incurable difficulty number one. He took hold of the handle, swung the door open, put a pleasant smile upon his face and uttered a cordial "Hello!"

The driver did not answer. Instead, his eyeballs began to edge round sidewise while the train continued to pelt along at such a rate that it started pulling away from Leigh's hand. Perforce, Leigh had to take a step to keep level. The eyes reached their corners by which time Leigh was compelled to take another step. Then the driver's head started turning. Leigh took a step. More turn. Another step. Behind Leigh his five companions strove to stay with them. It wasn't easy. In fact it was tough going. They could not stand still and let the train creep away. They could not walk without getting ahead of it. The result was a ludicrous march based on a hop-pause rhythm with the hops short and the pauses long.

By the time the driver's head was halfway round, the long fingers of his right hand had started uncurling from the knob it was holding. At the same overstretched instant the knob commenced to rise on its lever. He was doing something, no doubt of that. He was bursting into action to meet a sudden emergency.

Still gripping the door, Leigh edged along with it. The others went hop-pause in unison. Pascoe wore the pained reverence of one attending the tedious funeral of a rich uncle who has just cut him out of his will.

Imagination told Leigh what ribald remarks were being tossed around among the audience in the ship.

He solved the problem of reclaiming official dignity by the simple process of stepping into the cab. That wasn't much better, though. He had avoided the limping procession but now had the choice of standing half-bent or kneeling on the floor.

Now the driver's head was right round, his eyes looking straight at the visitor. The knob had projected to its limit. Something that made hissing noises under the floor went silent and the train's progress was only that of its forward momentum against the brakes. A creep measurable in inches or fractions of an inch.

"Hello!" repeated Leigh, feeling that he had never voiced a sillier word.

The driver's mouth opened to a pink oval, revealed long, narrow teeth but no tongue. He shaped the mouth and by the time he'd got it to his satisfaction the listener could have smoked half a cigarette. Leigh perked his ears for the expected greeting. Nothing came out, not a sound, a note, a decibel. He waited a while, hoping that the first word might emerge before next Thursday. The mouth made a couple of slight changes in form while pink palps at the back of it writhed like nearly-dead worms. And that was all.

Walterson ceased ultra-slow mooching on the tangled clover and called, "It has stopped, commodore."

Stepping backward from the cab, Leigh shoved hands deep into pockets and gazed defeatedly at the driver whose formerly blank face was now acquiring an expression of surprised interest. He could watch the features registering with all the lackadaisical air of a chameleon changing colour, and at about the same rate.

"This is a hell of a note," complained Pascoe, nudging Leigh. He pointed at the row of door handles projecting from the four cars. Most of them had tilted out of the horizontal and were moving a degree at a time toward the vertical. "They're falling over themselves to get out."

"Open up for them," Leigh suggested.

Hoffnagle, who happened to be standing right by an exit, obligingly twisted a handle and lugged the door. Out it swung complete with a clinging passenger who hadn't been able to let go. Dropping his contact charts, Hoffnagle dexterously caught the victim, planted him on his feet. It took forty-eight seconds by Romero's watch for this one to register facial reaction, which was that of bafflement.

After this, doors had to be opened with all the caution of a tax collector coping with a mysterious parcel that ticks. Pascoe, impatient as usual, hastened the dismounting process by lifting aliens from open doorways and standing them on the greensward. The quickest-witted one among the lot required a mere twenty-eight seconds to start mulling the problem of how he had passed from one point to another without crossing intervening space. He would solve that problem – given time.

With the train empty there were twenty-three Waitabits hanging around. None exceeded four feet in height or sixty pounds Eterna-weight.

All were well-clothed in manner that gave no clue to sex. Presumably all were adults, there being no tiny specimens among them. Not one bore anything remotely resembling a weapon.

Looking them over Leigh readily conceded that no matter how sluggish they might be they were not dopey. Their outlandishly coloured features held intelligence of a fairly high order. That was already self-evident from the tools they made and used, such as this train, but it showed in their faces, too.

The Grand Council, he decided, had good cause for alarm in a way not yet thought of by its members. If the bunch standing before him were truly representative of their planet, then they were completely innocuous.

They embodied no danger whatsoever to Terran interests anywhere in the cosmos. Yet, at the same time, they implied a major menace of which he hated to think.

With their easily comprehensible charts laid out on the ground the three communicators prepared to explain their origin, presence and purposes by an effective sign-and-gesture technique basic for all first contacts. The fidgety Pascoe speeded up the job by arranging Waitabits in a circle around the charts, picking them up like so many lethargic dolls and placing them in position.

Leigh and Walterson went to have a look at the train. If any of its owners objected to this inspection, they didn't have enough minutes in which to do something about it.

The roofs of all four cars were of pale yellow, transparent plastic extending down the sides to a line flush with the door-tops. Beneath the plastic lay countless numbers of carefully-arranged silicon wafers. Inside the cars, beneath plates forming the centre aisles, were arrays of tiny cylinders rather like nickel-alloy cells. The motors could not be seen, they were hidden beneath small driving-cabs of which there was one to each car.

"Sun power," said Leigh. "The prime motive force is derived from those solar batteries built into the roofs." He paced out the length of a car, made an estimate. "Four feet by twenty apiece. Including the side-strips, that's six-forty square feet of pickup area."

"Nothing marvellous about it," ventured Walterson, unimpressed. "They use better ones in the tropical zones of Earth and have similar gadgets on Dramonia and Werth."

"I know. But here the night-time lasts six months. What sort of storage batteries will last that long without draining? How do they manage to get around on the night-side? Or does all transport cease while they snore in bed?"

"Pascoe could make a better guess at their boudoir habits. For what it's worth, I'd say they sleep, six months being to them no more than a night is to us. Anyway, why should we speculate about the matter? We'll be exploring the night-side sooner or later, won't we?"

"Yes, sure. But I'd like to know whether this contraption is more advanced in any single respect than anything we've got."

"To discover that much we'd have to pull it to pieces," Walterson objected. "Putting Shallom and his boys on a wrecking job would be a lousy way of maintaining friendship. These Waitabits wouldn't like it even though they can't stop us."

"I'm not that ham-handed," Leigh reproved. "Apart from the fact that destruction of property belonging to non-hostile aliens could gain me a court-martial, why should I invite trouble if we can get the information from them in exchange for other data? Did you ever hear of a genuinely intelligent Me form that refused to swap knowledge?"

"No," said Walterson. "And neither did I ever hear of one that took ten years to pay for what it got in ten minutes." He grinned with malicious satisfaction, added, "We're finding out what Boydell discovered, namely, that you've got to give in order to receive – and in order to receive you've got to wait a bit."

"Something inside of me insists that you're dead right." Leigh shrugged and went on, "Anyway, that's the Council's worry. Right now we can do no more until the contact men make their report. Let's get back to the ship."

They mounted the bluff. Seeing them go, Pascoe hastened after them, leaving the trio of communicators to play with Keen charts and make snakes of their arms.

"How's it going?" Leigh inquired as they went through the lock.

"Not so good," said Pascoe. "You ought to try it yourself. It would make you whirly."

"What's the trouble?"

"How can you synchronize two values when one of them is unknown? How can you make rhythm to a prolonged and completely silent beat? Every time Hoffnagle uses the orbit-sign he is merely demonstrating that the quickness of the hand deceives the eye so far as the audience is concerned. So he slows, does it again and it still fools them. He slows more." Pascoe sniffed with disgust. "It's going to take those three luckless characters all of today and maybe most of a week to find, practise and perfect the quickest gestures that register effectively. They aren't teaching anybody anything – they're learning themselves. It's time-and-motion study with a vengeance."

"It has to be done," Leigh remarked quietly. "Even if it takes a lifetime."

"Whose lifetime?" asked Pascoe, pointedly.

Leigh winced, sought a satisfactory retort, failed to find one.

At the corner of the passageway Garside met them. He was a small, excitable man whose eyes looked huge behind thick spectacles. The great love of his life was bugs, any size, shape, colour or origin so long as they were bugs.

"Ah, commodore," he exclaimed, bubbling with enthusiasm, "a most remarkable discovery, most remarkable! Nine species of insect life, none really extraordinary in structure, but all afflicted with an amazing lassitude. If this phenomenon is common to all native insects, it would appear that local metabolism is—"

"Write it down for the record," advised Leigh, patting him on the shoulder. He hastened to the signals room. "Anything special from Ogilvy?"

"No, commodore. All his messages have been repeats of his first ones. He is now most of the way back and due to arrive here in about an hour."

"Send him to me immediately he returns."

"As you order, sir."

Ogilvy appeared in the promised time. He was a lanky, lean-faced individual given to irritating grins. Entering the room he held hands behind his back, hung his head and spoke with mock shame.

"Commodore, I have a confession to make."

"So I see from the act you're putting on. What is it?"

"I landed, without permission, right in the main square of the biggest city I could find."

Leigh raised his eyebrows. "And what happened?"

"They gathered around and stared at me."

"Is that all?"

"Well, sir, it took them twenty minutes to see me and assemble, by which time the ones farther away were still coming. I couldn't wait any longer to discover what they'd do next. I estimated that if they fetched some rope and tied down my landing gear they'd have the job finished about a year next Christmas."

"Humph! Were things the same everywhere else?"

"Yes, sir. I passed over more than two hundred towns and villages, reached extreme range of twelve-fifty miles. Conditions remained consistent." He gave his grin, continued, "I noticed a couple of items that might interest you."

"What were those?"

"The Waitabits converse with their mouths but make no detectable noises. The 'copter has a supersonic converter known as Bat-ears which is used for blind flying. I tuned its receiver across its full range when in the middle of that crowd but didn't pick up a squeak. So they're not talking high above us. I don't see how they can be subsonic either. It must be something else."

"I've had a one-sided conversation with them myself," Leigh informed. "It may be that we're overlooking the obvious while seeking the obscure."

Ogilvy blinked and asked, "How d'you mean, sir?"

"They're not necessarily employing some unique faculty such as we cannot imagine. It is quite possible that they communicate visually. They gaze into each other's gullets and read the waggling palps. Something like you semaphoring with your tonsils." He dismissed the subject with a wave of his hand. "And what's your other item?"

"No birds," replied Ogilvy. "You'd think that where insects exist there would also be birds or at least things somewhat birdlike. The only airborne creature I saw was a kind of membrane-winged lizard that flaps just enough to launch itself, then glides to wherever it's going. On Earth it couldn't catch a weary gnat."

"Did you make a record of it?"

"No, sir. The last magazine was in the camera and I didn't want to waste strip. I didn't know if anything more important might turn up later."

"All right."

Leigh watched the other depart, picked up the phone, said to Shallom, "If those 'copter reels prove sharp enough for long-range beaming, you'd better run off an extra copy for the signals room. Have them boost it to Sector Nine for relay to Earth."

As he put down the phone Romero entered looking desperate.

"Commodore, could you get the instrument mechs to concoct a phenakistoscope with a revolution-counter attached?"

"We can make anything, positively anything," chimed in Pascoe from near the port. "Given enough centuries in which to do it."

Ignoring the interruption, Leigh asked, "What do you want it for?"

"Hoffnagle and Nolan think we could use it to measure the precise optical register of those sluggards outside. If we can find out at what minimum speed they see pictures merge into motion it would be a great help."

"Wouldn't the ship's movie projector serve the same purpose?"

"It isn't sufficiently variable," Romero objected. "Besides, we can't operate it independently of our own power supply. A phenakistoscope can be carried around and cranked by hand."

"This becomes more fascinating every moment," Pascoe interjected. "It can be cranked. Add a few more details and I'll start to get a hazy idea of what the darned thing is."

Taking no notice of that either, Leigh got through to Shallom again, put the matter to him.

"Holy Moses!" ejaculated Shallom. "The things we get asked for! Who thought up that one?" A pause, followed by, "It will take two days."

"Two days," Leigh repeated to Romero.

The other looked aghast.

"What's eating you?" asked Pascoe. "Two days to get started measuring visual retention is mighty fast in this world. You're on Eterna now. Adapt, boy, adapt!"

Leigh eyed Pascoe carefully and said, "Becoming rather pernickety this last hour or two, aren't you?"

"Not yet. I have several dregs of patience left. When the last of them has trickled away you can lock me in the brig because I'll be nuts."

"Don't worry. We're about to have some action."

"Haha!" said Pascoe disrespectfully.

"We'll drag out the patrol wagon, go to town and have a look around in the middle of them."

"About time, too," Pascoe endorsed.

The armoured, eight-seater car rumbled down the ramp on heavy caterpillars, squatted in the clover. Only a short, flared nozzle in its bonnet and another in its tail revealed the presence of button-controlled snort-guns. The boxed lens on its roof belonged to an automatic camera.

The metal whip atop the box was a radio antenna.

They could have used the helicopter which was capable of carrying four men with equipment but, once landed, that machine would be of little good for touring the streets.

Leigh shared the front seat with Lieutenant Harding and the duty driver. Behind him were two of Harding's troop and Pascoe. At back sat the radio operator and the snort gunner.

Walterson, Garside and all the other specialists remained with the ship.

Rolling forward, they passed the circle of Waitabits who were now sitting cross-legged on the turf and staring at a Keen chart which Nolan was exhibiting with an air of complete frustration. Nearby, Hoffnagle was masticating his nails while trying to decide how much of the lesson was being absorbed and how much missed. Not one of this bunch showed the slightest surprise when the car charged down the steep bluff and clattered by them.

With jerks and heaves the car crossed the lines behind the stalled train, gained the road. Here the surface proved excellent, the running smooth.

The artery would have done justice to a Terran racing-track. Before they had gone five miles they encountered an alien using it for exactly that.

This one half-sat, half-reclined in a long, narrow, low-slung single-seater that had "hot-rod" written all over it. He came along like a maniac, face strained, eyes popping, hands clinging firmly to the wheel. According to the photoelectric telltale on the patrol wagon's instrument board he roared past them at fifty-two and a quarter miles per hour. Since the speedometer on the same board recorded precisely fifty, it meant that the other was going all out at a harrowing two and a quarter.

Twisting his head to gaze through the rear window, Pascoe said, "As a sociologist I'll tell you something authoritatively; some of this crowd are downright reckless. If that lunatic is headed for the city now about thirty miles away he'll make it in as little as twelve hours." Then he frowned, became serious as he added, "Seeing that their reactions are in keeping with their motions, one being as tedious as the other, it wouldn't surprise me if they have traffic problems comparable with those of any other world."

Nobody got a chance to comment on that. The entire eight bowed in unison as the brakes went on. They were entering the suburbs with pedestrians, cars and trolleys littering the streets. After that it was strictly bottom-gear work; the driver had to learn a completely new technique and it wasn't easy.

Crimson-faced people in the same sexless attire ambled across the roads in a manner suggesting that for two pins they'd lie down and go to sleep. Some moved faster than others but the most nimble ones among the lot were an obstacle for an inordinate while. Not one halted and gaped at the invading vehicle as it trundled by, but most of them stopped and took on a baffled expression by the time they'd been left a mile behind.

To Leigh and his companions there was a strong temptation to correlate slowness with stupidity. They resisted it. Evidence to the contrary was strong enough not to be denied.

The streets were level, straight and well-made, complete with sidewalks, gulleys and drains. No buildings rose higher than sixty feet but all were solidly built and far from primitive. Cars were not numerous by Terran standards but had the appearance of engineering jobs of no mean order.

The street-trolleys were small, sun-powered, languidly efficient and bore two dozen passengers apiece.

For a few minutes they halted near a building in course of construction, maintained attention upon a worker laying a brick, estimated that the job required twenty minutes. Three bricks per hour.

Doing some fast figuring, Leigh said, "Taking their days and nights as six months apiece and assuming they put in the equivalent of an eight-hour day, that fellow is laying something over a thousand bricks per hour." He pursed his lips, gave a brief whistle. "I know of no life form capable of building half as fast. Even on Earth it takes a robot to equal it."

The others considered that aspect of the matter in silence. The patrol wagon moved on, reached a square in which was a civic car-park containing some forty machines. The sight was irresistible. Driving straight in past two uniformed attendants they lined their vehicle neatly at the end of a row. The attendants' eyeballs started edging around.

Leigh spoke to the driver, radio man and gunner. "You three stay here. If anyone interferes, pick him up, put him down a hundred yards away and leave him to try all over again. If they show signs of getting organized to blow you sky-high, just move the wagon to the other end of the park. When they catch you up, move back here."

"Where are you going?" inquired Harding.

"Over there." He pointed toward an official-looking building. "To save time I'd like you, your men and Pascoe to try the other places. Take one apiece, go inside, see if you can learn anything worth picking up." He glanced at his watch. "Be back promptly at three. No dallying. The laggard will be left to take a nine-mile walk."

Starting off, he found an attendant twenty yards away and moving toward him with owl-eyes wide. Going boldly up to him, he took the book of tickets from an unresisting hand, tore one off, pressed the book back into crimson fingers, added a silver button by way of payment and passed on. He derived amused satisfaction from that honest gesture. By the time he'd crossed the square and entered the building the recipient had got around to examining the button.

At three they returned to find chaos in the square and no sign of the patrol wagon in the park. A series of brief wails on its siren drew them to a side street where it was waiting by the kerb.

"Slow as they may be, they can get places given long enough," said the driver. "They started creeping around us in such numbers that we looked like being hemmed in for keeps. We wouldn't have been able to get out without running over fifty of them. I beat it while there was still a gap to drive through." He pointed through the windshield. "Now they're making for here. The tortoise chasing the hare."

One of Harding's men, a grizzled veteran of several space-campaigns, remarked, "It's easier to cope when you're up against guppies that are hostile and fighting mad. You just shoot your way out." He grunted a few times. "Here, if you sit around too long you've got to let yourself be trapped or else run over them in cold blood. That's not my idea of how to do things." Another grunt. "Hell of a planet. The fellow who found it ought to be made to live here."

"Find anything in your building?" Leigh asked him.

"Yes, a dozen cops."

"What?"

"Cops," repeated the other. "It was a police station. I could tell because they all had the same uniforms, all carried duralumin bludgeons. And there were faces on the wall with queer printing beneath. I can't recognize one face from another. They are all alike to me. But something told me those features hadn't been stuck to the wall to commemorate saintliness."

"Did they show any antagonism toward you?"

"They didn't get the chance," he said with open contempt. "I just kept shifting around looking at things and that had them foxed."

"My building was a honey," informed Pascoe. "A telephone exchange."

Leigh twisted around to stare at him. "So they are supersonic speakers after all?"

"No. They use scanners and three-inch visi-screens. If I've looked down one squirming gizzard, I've looked down twenty. What's more, a speaker sometimes removes his palps from the screen and substitutes a sort of slow-motion display of deaf-and-dumb talk with his fingers. I have a vague idea that some of those digital acrobatics represent vitriolic cussing."

The driver put in nervously, "If we squat here much longer the road will be blocked both ends."

"Then let's get out while there's time."

"Back to the ship, sir?"

"Not yet. Wander around and see if you can find an industrial area."

The car rolled forward, went cautiously past a bunch of oncoming pedestrians, avoided the crowded square by trundling down another side street.

Lying back in comfort, Pascoe held his hands together over his stomach and inquired interestedly, "I suppose none of you happened to find himself in a fire station?" Nobody had.

"That's what I'd give a thousand credits to see," he said. "A couple of pumps and a hook-and-ladder squad bursting out to deal with a conflagration a mile away. The speed of combustion is no less on this world than on our own. It's a wonder to me the town hasn't burned down a dozen times."

"Perhaps it has," offered Harding. "Perhaps they're used to it. You can get accustomed to anything in the long run."

"In the long run," agreed Pascoe. "Here it's long enough to vanish into the mists of time. And it's anything but a run."

He glanced at Leigh. "What did you walk into?"

"A public library."

"That's the place to dig up information. How much did you get?"

"One item only," Leigh admitted with reluctance. "Their printed language is ideographic and employs at least three thousand characters."

"There's a big help," said Pascoe, casting an appealing glance heavenward. "Any competent linguist or trained communicator should be able to learn it from them. Put Hoffnagle on the job. He's the youngest among us and all he needs is a couple of thousand years."

The radio burped, winked its red eye, and the operator switched it on. Shallom's voice came through.

"Commodore, an important-looking specimen has just arrived in what he probably thinks of as a racing car. It may be that he's a bigwig appointed to make contact with us. That's only our guess but we're trying to get confirmation of it. I thought you'd like to know."

"How's progress with him?"

"No better than with the others. Possibly he's the smartest boy in college. Nevertheless, Nolan estimates it will take most of a month to convince him that Mary had a little lamb."

"Well, keep trying. We'll be returning shortly." The receiver cut off and Leigh added to the others, "That sounds like the road-hog we passed on the way here." He nudged the driver, pointed leftward. "That looks like a sizeable factory. Stop outside while I inspect it."

He entered unopposed, came out after a few minutes, told them, "It's a combined flour-mill, processing and packaging plant. They're grinding up a mountain of nut-kernels, probably from surrounding forests. They've a pair of big engines down in the basement that beat me. Never seen anything like them. I think I'll get Bentley to come and look them over. He's the expert on power supplies."

"Big place for a mill, isn't it?" ventured Harding.

"They're converting the flour into about twenty forms. I took a lick at some of it."

"What did it taste like?"

"Bill-sticker's paste." He nudged the driver again. "There's another joint." Then to Harding, "You come with me."

Five minutes later they returned and said, "Boots, shoes and slippers. And they're making them fast."

"Fast?" echoed Pascoe, twitching his eyebrows.

"Faster than they can follow the process themselves. The whole layout is fully automatic and self-arresting if anything goes wrong. Not quite as good as we've got on Earth but not so far behind, either." Leigh sat with pursed lips, musing as he gazed through the windshield. "I'm going back to the ship. You fellows can come for further exploration if you wish."

None of them registered enthusiasm.

There was a signal waiting on the desk, decoded and typed.

C.O. Flame *to* C.O. Thunderer. *Atmosphere Pulok analysed good in fact healthy. So instruments insist. Noses say has abominable stench beyond bearing. Should be named Puke. Proceeding Arlington Port 88.137 unless summoned by you. Mallory.*

Reading it over Leigh's shoulder, Pascoe commented, "That Boydell character has a flair for picking ugly ones right out of the sky. Why doesn't someone choke him to death?"

"Four hundred twenty-one recorded in there," reminded Leigh, tapping his big chart book. "And about two-thirds of them come under the heading of ugly ones."

"It would save a lot of grief if the scouts ignored those and reported only the dumps worth having."

"Grief is the price of progress, you know that." Leigh hurriedly left his desk, went to the port as something whirred outside. He picked up the phone. "Where's the 'copter going?"

"Taking Garside and Walterson some place," replied a voice. "The former wants more bugs and the latter wants rock-samples."

"All right. Has that film been finished yet?"

"Yes, commodore. It has come out good and clear. Want me to set it up in the projection room?"

"You might as well. I'll be there right away. Have somebody get to work on the magazine in the patrol wagon. About half of it has been exposed."

"As you order, sir."

Summoning the rest of the specialist staff, of whom there were more than sixty, he accompanied them to the projection room, studied the record of Ogilvy's survey. When it had finished the audience sat in glum silence. Nobody had anything to say. No comment was adequate.

"A nice mess," griped Pascoe after they had returned to the main cabin.

"In the last one thousand years the human race has become wholly technological. Even the lowest ranking space-marine is considerably a technician, especially by standards of olden times."

"I know." Leigh frowned futilely at the wall.

"We are the brains," Pascoe went on, determining to rub salt into the wounds. "And because we're the brains we naturally dislike providing the muscle as well. We're a cut above the mere hewing of wood and drawing of water."

"You're telling me nothing."

Down to telling it anyway, Pascoe continued, "So we've planted settlers on umpteen planets. And what sort of settlers are they? Bosses, overseers, boys who inform, advise, point and tell while the less advanced do the doing."

Leigh offered no remark.

"Suppose Walterson and the others find this lousy world rich in the things we need," he persisted. "How are we going to get at the stuff short of excavating it ourselves? The Waitabits form a big and probably willing labour force but what's the use of them if the most rudimentary job gets completed ten, twenty or fifty years hence? Who's going to settle here and become a beast of burden as the only way of getting things done in jig time?"

"Ogilvy went over a big dam and what looked like a hydroelectric plant," observed Leigh, thoughtfully. "On Earth the entire project might have cost two years at most. How long it required here is anyone's guess. Two hundred years perhaps. Or four hundred. Or more." He tapped fidgety fingers on his desk. "It worries me."

"We're not worried. We're frustrated. It's not the same thing."

"I tell you I'm worried. This planet is like a lighted fuse long ignored but now noticed. I don't know where it leads or how big a bang is waiting at the other end."

"That's frustration," insisted Pascoe, completely missing the point because he hadn't thought of it yet. "We're thwarted and don't like it. We're the irresistible force at long last meeting the immovable object. The bang is within our own minds. No *real* explosion big enough to shake us can ever come from this world's life forms. They're too slow to catch cold."

"I'm not bothered about them in that respect. They worry me by their very existence."

"There always have been sluggards, even on our own world."

"Precisely!" endorsed Leigh with emphasis. "And that is what's raising my hackles right now."

The loudspeaker interrupted with a polite cough and said, "Ogilvy here, sir. We've picked up granite chippings, quartz samples and other stuff. At the moment I'm at sixteen thousand feet and can see the ship in the distance. I don't like the looks of things."

"What's the matter?"

"The town is emptying itself. So are nearby villages. They've taken to the road in huge numbers and started heading your way. The vanguard should reach you in about three hours." A brief silence, then, "There's nothing to indicate hostile intentions, no sign of an organized advance. Just a rabble motivated by plain curiosity as far as I can tell. But if you get that mob gaping around the ship you won't be able to move without incinerating thousands of them."

Leigh thought it over. The ship was a mile long. Its lifting blasts caromed half a mile each side and its tail blast was equally long. He needed about two square miles of clear ground from which to take off without injury to others.

There were eleven hundred men aboard the *Thunderer*. Six hundred were needed to attend the boost. That left five hundred to stay grounded and keep the mob at bay around the perimeter of two square miles. And they'd have to be transferred by 'copter, a few at a time, to the new landing place. Could it be done? It could – but it was hopelessly inefficient.

"We'll move a hundred miles before they get here," he informed Ogilvy. "That should hold them for a couple of days."

"Want me to come in, sir?"

"Please yourself."

"The passengers aren't satisfied and want to add to their collections. So I'll stay out. If you drop out of sight I'll home on your beacon."

"Very well." Leigh turned to the intercom. "Sound the siren and bring in those yaps outside. Check crew all present and correct. Prepare to lift."

"Rule Seven," said Pascoe, smirking. "Any action causing unnecessary suffering to non-hostile life will be deemed a major offence under the Contact Code." He made a derisive gesture. "So they amble toward us like a great army of sloths and we have to tuck in our tails and run."

"Any better solution?" Leigh asked, irritably.

"No. Not one. That's the devil of it."

The siren yowled. Soon afterward the *Thunderer* began a faint but steady shuddering as combustion chambers and ventur is warmed up.

Hoffnagle rushed into the cabin. He had a roll of crumpled Keen charts in one fist and a wild look in his eyes.

"What's the idea?" he shouted, flourishing the charts and forgetting to say "sir". "Two successive watches we've spent on this, given up our off-duty time into the bargain and have just got one of them to make the orbit-sign. Then you recall us." He waited, fuming.

"We're moving."

"Moving?" He looked as if he'd never heard of such a thing. "Where?"

"A hundred miles off."

Hoffnagle stared incredulously, swallowed hard, opened his mouth, closed it, opened it once more. "But that means we'll have to start over again with some other bunch."

"I'm afraid so," agreed Leigh. "The ones you've been trying to talk to could come with us but it would take far too long to make them understand what's wanted. There's nothing for it but to make a new start."

"No!" bawled Hoffnagle, becoming frenzied. "Oh, no! Anything but that!"

Behind him, Romero barged in and said, "Anything but what?" He was breathing heavily and near the end of his tether.

Trying to tell him the evil news, Hoffnagle found himself lost for words, managed no more than a few feeble gestures. "A Communicator is unable to communicate with another communicator," observed Pascoe, showing academic interest.

"They're shifting the ship," Hoffnagle got out with considerable effort. He made it sound dastardly.

Releasing a violent, "*What*?" Romero went two shades redder than the Waitabits. In fact, for a moment he looked like one as he stood there pop-eyed and half-paralysed.

"Get out," snapped Leigh. "Get out before Nolan comes in and makes it three to two. Go some place where you can cool down. Remember, you're not the only ones caught in this fix."

"No, maybe we aren't," said Hoffnagle, bitterly. "But we're the only ones carrying the entire onus of— "

"Everybody's carrying onuses of one sort or another," Leigh retorted. "And everybody's well and truly bollixed by them. Beat it before I lose my own temper and summon an escort for you."

They departed with unconcealed bad grace. Leigh sat at his desk, chewed his bottom lip while he tended to official papers. Twenty minutes went by. Finally, he glanced at the wall chronometer, switched the intercom, spoke to Bentley. "What's holding us up?"

"No signal from control room, sir."

He re-switched to control room. "What are we waiting for?"

"That bunch from the train is still lounging within burning distance, commodore. Either nobody's told them to go back or, if they have been told, they haven't got around to it yet."

Leigh seldom swore but he did it this time, one potent word uttered with vigour. He switched a third time, got Harding.

"Lieutenant, rush out two platoons of your men. They are to return all those alien passengers to their train. Pick them up, carry them there, tuck them into it and return as quickly as possible."

He resumed with his papers while Pascoe sat in a corner nibbling his fingers and grinning to himself. After half an hour Leigh voiced the word again and resorted to the intercom.

"What is it now?"

"Still no signal, commodore," said Bentley in tones of complete resignation.

Onto the control room. "I gave the order to lift immediately there's clearance. Why haven't we done so?"

"One alien is still within the danger area, sir."

Next to Harding. "Didn't I tell you to get those aliens onto their train?"

"Yes, sir, you did. All passengers were restored to their seats fifteen minutes ago."

"Nonsense, man! They've left one of them hanging around and he's holding up the entire vessel."

"That one is not from the train, sir," said Harding, patiently. "He arrived in a car. You gave no order concerning him."

Leigh used both hands to scrabble the desk, then roared, "Get him out of it. Plant him in his contraption and shove it down the road. At once."

Then he lay back in his chair and muttered to himself.

"How'd you like to resign and buy a farm?" Pascoe asked.

The new landing-point was along the crest of the only bald hill for miles around. Charred stumps provided evidence of a bygone forest fire which had started on the top, spread down the sides until halted, probably by heavy rain.

Thickly wooded hills rolled away in every direction. No railroad tracks ran nearby but there was a road in the valley and a winding river beyond it. Two villages were visible within four miles' distance and a medium-sized town lay eleven miles to the north.

Experience of local conditions enabled a considerable speed-up in investigation. Earnshaw, the relief pilot, took out the 'copter with Walterson and four other experts crowded inside. The patrol wagon set off to town bearing a load of specialists including Pascoe. Three botanists and an arboriculturalist took to the woods accompanied by a dozen of Harding's men who were to bear their spoils.

Hoffnagle, Romero and Nolan traipsed cross-country to the nearest village, spread their explanatory charts in the small square and prayed for a rural genius able to grasp the meaning of a basic gesture in less than a week. A bunch of ship's engineers set forth to examine lines strung on lattice masts across hills to the west and south.

A piscatorial expert, said to have been conditioned from birth by the cognomen of Fish, sat for hours on the river bank dangling his lines without knowing what bait to use, what he might catch, or whether it could be caught in less than a lifetime.

Leigh stayed by the ship during this brief orgy of data-gathering. He had a gloomy foreboding concerning the shape of things to come. Time proved him right. Within thirty hours Earnshaw had handed over to Ogilvy twice and was flying for the third time. He was at fifteen thousand above the *Thunderer* when he called.

"Commodore, I hate to tell you this, but they're coming again. They seem to have caught on quicker. Maybe they were warned over that visi-screen system they've got."

"How long do you give them?"

"The villagers will take about two hours. The mob from the town want five or six. I can see the patrol wagon heading back in front of them."

"You'd better bring in whoever you're carrying and go fetch those three communicators right away," said Leigh. "Then pick up anyone else on the loose."

"All right, sir."

The siren moaned eerily across the valleys. Over in the village Hoffnagle suddenly ceased his slow-motion gesturing and launched into an impassioned tirade that astonished the Waitabits two days later. Down in the woods the arboriculturalist fell off a tree and flattened a Marine who also became vocal.

It was like the ripple effect of a stone cast into a pond. Somebody pressed an alarm-stud and a resulting wave of adjectives spread halfway to the horizon.

They moved yet again, this time to within short range of the terminator.

At least it served to shift the sun which had hung stubbornly in mid-sky and changed position by no more than one degree per Earth-day.

The third watch took to bed, dog-tired and made more than ready for slumber by a semblance of twilight. Data-hunters went out feeling that paradoxically time was proving all too short on a planet with far too much of it. Ogilvy whirred away for a first look at the night-side, discovered half a world buried in deep sleep with nothing stirring, not a soul, not a vehicle.

This situation lasted twenty-one hours at the end of which all natives for miles around had set out for the circus. Once more the sight stimulated enrichment of Earth-language. The *Thunderer* went up, came down four hundred miles within the night-side.

That tactic, decided Leigh, represented a right smart piece of figuring.

Aroused aliens on the day-side would now require about twelve days to reach them. And they'd make it only if some insomniac had spotted and phoned the ship's present location. Such betrayal was likely enough because the *Thunderer*'s long rows of ports poured a brilliant blaze into the darkness and caused a great glow in the sky.

It wasn't long before he gained assurance that there was little danger of a give-away. Nolan entered the cabin and stood with fingers twitching as if he yearned to strangle someone very, very slowly, much as a Waitabit would do it. His attitude was accentuated by possession of unfortunate features. Of all the personnel aboard the *Thunderer*, nobody better resembled the popular notion of a murderer.

"You will appreciate, commodore," he began, speaking with great restraint, "the extreme difficulty of knocking sense into or getting sense out of creatures that think in hours rather than split-seconds."

"I know it's tough going," Leigh sympathized. He eyed the other carefully. "What's on your mind?"

"What is on my mind," informed Nolan in rising tones, "is the fact that there's one thing to be said in favour of previous subjects." He worked the fingers around. "At least they were awake."

"That is why we had to move," Leigh pointed out. "They're no nuisance to us while dead abed."

"Then," Nolan burst forth, "how do you expect us to make contact with them?"

"I don't. I've given it up. If you wish to continue trying, that's your affair. But you're under no compulsion to do so." Crossing the room, he said more gently, "I've sent a long signal to Earth giving full details of what we're against. The next move is up to them. Their reply should come in a few days' time. Meanwhile, we'll sit tight, dig out whatever information we can, leave what we can't."

Nolan said morbidly, "Hoff and I went to a hamlet far down the road. Not only is everyone asleep but they can't be wakened. They can be handled like dolls without stirring in their dreams. The medics came and had a look at them after we'd told them about this wholesale catalepsy."

"What did they say?"

"They're of the opinion that the Waitabits are active only under stimulus of sunlight. When the sun goes down they go down with it." He scowled at his predicament, suggested hopefully, "But if you could run us a power line out there and lend us a couple of sunray lamps, we could rouse a few of them and get to work."

"It isn't worth it," said Leigh.

"Why not?"

"Chances are that we'll be ordered home before you can show any real progress."

"Look, sir," pleaded Nolan, making a final effort. "Everyone else is raking in results. Measurements, meterings and so forth. They've got bugs, nuts, fruits, plants, barks, timber-sections, rocks, pebbles, soil-samples, photographs, everything but shrunken heads. The communicators are the only ones asked to accept defeat and that's because we've not had a fair chance."

"All right," Leigh said, taking up the challenge. "You fellows are best placed to make an accurate estimate. So tell me: how long would a fair chance be?"

That had him tangled. He shuffled around, glowered at the wall, examined his fingers.

"Five years?" prompted Leigh.

No answer.

"Ten maybe?"

No reply.

"Perhaps twenty?"

Nolan growled, "You win," and walked out. His face still hankered to create a corpse.

You win, thought Leigh. Like heck he did. The winners were the Waitabits. They had a formidable weapon in the simple, incontrovertible fact that life can be too short.

Four days later Sector Nine relayed the message from Earth.

37.14 *ex Terra. Defence H.Q. to C.O. battleship* Thunderer. *Return route*

D9 calling Sector Four H.Q. Leave ambassador if suitable candidate available. Position in perpetuity. Rathbone. Com. Op. Dep.

D.H.Q. Terra.

He called a conference in the long room amidships. Considerable time was spent coordinating data ranging from Walterson's findings on radioactive life to Mr. Fish's remarks about creeping shrimps. In the end three conclusions stood out clearly.

Eterna was very old as compared with Earth. Its people were equally old as compared with humankind, estimates of life-duration ranging from eight hundred to twelve hundred for the average Waitabit. Despite their chronic sluggishness the Waitabits were intelligent, progressive and had advanced to about the same stage as humankind had reached a century before the first jump into space.

There was considerable argument about whether the Waitabits would ever be capable of a short rocket-flight even with the aid of automatic, fast-functioning controls. Majority opinion was against it but all agreed that in any event none would live to see it.

Then Leigh announced, "An Earth Ambassador is to be left here if anyone wants the job." He looked them over, seeking signs of interest.

"There's little point in planting anybody on this planet," someone objected.

"Like most alien people, the Waitabits have not developed along paths identical with our own," Leigh explained. "We're way ahead of them, know thousands of things that they don't, including many they'll never learn. By the same token they've picked up a few secrets we've missed. For instance, they've types of engines and batteries we'd like to know more about. They may have further items not apparent in this first superficial look-over. And there's no telling what they've got worked out theoretically. If there's one lesson we've learned in the cosmos it's that of never despising an alien culture. A species too big to learn soon goes small."

"So?"

"So somebody's got to take on the formidable task of systematically milking them of everything worth a hoot. That's why we are where we are: the knowledge of creation is all around and we get it and apply it."

"It's been one time and again on other worlds," agreed the objector. "But this is Eterna, a zombie-inhabited sphere where the clock ticks about once an hour. Any Earthman marooned in this place wouldn't have enough time if he lived to be a hundred."

"You're right," Leigh told him. "Therefore this ambassadorial post will be strictly an hereditary one. Whoever takes it will have to import a bride, marry, raise kids, hand the grief to them upon his deathbed. It may last through six generations or more. There is no other way." He let them stew that a while before he asked, "Any takers?"

Silence.

"You'll be lonely except for company provided by occasional ships but contact will be maintained and the power and strength of Terra will be behind you. Speak up!"

Nobody responded.

Leigh consulted his watch. "I'll give you two hours to think it over. After that, we blow. Any candidate will find me in the cabin."

At zero-hour the *Thunderer* flamed free, leaving no representative of the world. Some day there would be one, no doubt of that. Some day a willing hermit would take up residence for keeps. Among the men of Terra an oddity or a martyr could always be found.

But the time wasn't yet. On Eterna the time never was quite yet.

The pale pink planet that held Sector Four H.Q. had grown to a large disc before Pascoe saw fit to remark on Leigh's meditative attitude.

"Seven weeks along the return run and you're still broody. Anyone would think you hated to leave that place. What's the matter with you?"

"I told you before. They make me feel apprehensive."

"That's illogical," Pascoe declared. "Admittedly we cannot handle the slowest crawlers in existence. But what of it? All we need do is drop them and forget them."

"We can drop them, as you say. Forgetting them is something else. They have a special meaning that I don't like."

"Be more explicit," Pascoe suggested.

"All right, I will. Earth has had dozens of major wars in the far past. Some were caused by greed, ambition, fear, envy, desire to save face or downright stupidity. But there were some caused by sheer altruism."

"Huh?"

"Some," Leigh went doggedly on, "were brought about by the unhappy fact that the road to hell is paved with good intentions. Big, fast-moving nations tried to lug small, slower-moving ones up to their own superior pace. Sometimes the slow-movers couldn't make it, resented being forced to try, started shooting to defend their right to mooch. See what I mean?"

"I see the lesson but not the point of it," said Pascoe. "The Waitabits couldn't kill a lame dog. Besides, nobody is chivvying them."

"I'm not considering that aspect at all."

"Which one then?"

"Earth had a problem never properly recognized. If it had been recognized, it wouldn't have caused wars."

"What problem?"

"That of pace-rate," said Leigh. "Previously it has never loomed large enough for us to see it as it really is. The difference between fast and slow was always sufficiently small to escape us." He pointed through the port at the reef of stars lying like sparkling dust against the dark. "And now we know that out there is the same thing enormously magnified. We know that included among the numberless and everlasting problems of the cosmos is that of pace-rate boosted to formidable proportions."

Pascoe thought it over. "I'll give you that. I couldn't argue it because it has become self-evident. Sooner or later we'll encounter it again and again. It's bound to happen somewhere else eventually."

"Hence my heebies," said Leigh.

"You scare yourself to your heart's content," Pascoe advised. "I'm not worrying. It's no hair off my chest. Why should I care if some loony scout discovers life forms even slower than the Waitabits? They mean nothing whatever in my young life."

"Does he have to find them slower?" Leigh inquired.

Pascoe stared at him. "What are you getting at?"

"There's a pace-rate problem, as you've agreed. Turn it upside-down and take another look at it. What's going to happen if we come up against a life form twenty times faster than ourselves? A life form that views us much as we viewed the Waitabits?"

Giving it a couple of minutes, Pascoe wiped his forehead and said, unconvincingly, "Impossible!"

"Is it? Why?"

"Because we'd have met them long before now. They'd have got to us first."

"What, if they've a hundred times farther to come? Or if they're a young species one-tenth our age but already nearly level with us?"

"Look here," said Pascoe, taking on the same expression as the other had worn for weeks, "there are troubles enough without you going out of your way to invent more."

Nevertheless, when the ship landed he was still mulling every possible aspect of the matter and liking it less every minute.

A Sector Four official entered the cabin bearing a wad of documents.

"Lieutenant Vaughan, at your service, commodore," he enthused. "I trust you have had a pleasant and profitable run."

"It could have been worse," Leigh responded.

Radiating good will, Vaughan went on, "We've had a signal from Markham at Assignment Office on Terra. He wants you to check equipment, refuel and go take a look at Binty."

"What name?" interjected Pascoe.

"Binty."

"Heaven preserve us! Binty!" He sat down hard, stared at the wall.

"Binty!" He played with his fingers, voiced it a third time. For some reason best known to himself he was hypnotized by Binty. Then in tones of deep suspicion he asked, "Who reported it?"

"Really, I don't know. But it ought to say here." Vaughan obligingly sought through his papers. "Yes, it does say. Fellow named Archibald Boydell."

"I knew it," yelped Pascoe. "I resign. I resign forthwith."

"You've resigned forthwith at least twenty times in the last eight years," Leigh reminded.

"I mean it this time."

"You've said that, too." Leigh sighed.

Pascoe waved his hands around. "Now try to calm yourself and look at this sensibly. What space-outfit which is sane and wearing brown boots would take off for a dump with a name like Binty?"

"We would," said Leigh. He waited for blood pressure to lower, then finished, "Wouldn't we?"

Slumping into his seat Pascoe glowered at him for five minutes before he said,

"I suppose so. God help me, I must be weak." A little glassy-eyed, he shifted attention to Vaughan. "Name it again in case I didn't hear right."

"Binty," said Vaughan, unctuously apologetic. "He has coded it 0/0.9/E5 which indicates the presence of an intelligent but backward life form."

"Does he make any remark about the place?"

"One word," informed Vaughan, consulting the papers again. "Ugh!"

Pascoe shuddered.

MUSIC FOR TIME TRAVELERS

Jason Heller

To listen to music is to travel through time.

When we listen to music, we're being asked to exist – for the length of a performance or recording – not only elsewhere, but else*when*. That travel through time doesn't have to be profound. It can be barely perceptible. Often songwriters wish to shift us just a few moments of either side of today, more of a puddle-jump than a voyage. "Yesterday, all my troubles seemed so far away," sings Paul McCartney in "Yesterday" by The Beatles. "Will you still love me tomorrow?" wonder The Shirelles in their girl-group anthem of the same name. These songs aren't mere functions of memory or premonition. Both of them – and thousands more like them – jar us from the here-and-now. Tethered only loosely to the present, we become uprooted in time.

Space, too, becomes a variable. That's only natural, considering the interrelation of space and time, not to mention the way music seeks to transport us. There's a third axis, though: sound. Far more than language alone, the confluence of lyrics and music is able to strike a resonant cluster of notes, a chord of timelessness. Or time*ful*ness.

H.G. Wells's *The Time Machine* was published in 1895, the same year the seven-inch record was introduced to music consumers and phonograph parlors. Each in their own way, these innovative watersheds augured a new way of seeing time in the twentieth century: as a substance that could be defined, contained, and even manipulated – a notion that was soon manifested in everything from Einstein's Special Theory of Relativity to the forty-hour workweek. By midcentury, the seven-inch single had become the staple of commercial music recordings. Its technical limitation was a temporal one, too: The further a seven-inch record exceeded four minutes per side, the more compressed its single, spiral groove became – and the more distorted it sounded. It's hard to picture a more vivid analogy for time travel.

Upon its advent in 1948, the twelve-inch long-playing record (or LP) began overtaking its seven-inch counterpart. In a conspicuously consumerist, postwar world, more meant better, music included. Rising parallel to this was the notion of leisure time, which in turn allowed society to indulge, more than ever before, its imagination – nostalgia for the past, a mixture of hope and fear about the future. The former became the fodder of literary fantasy; the latter fueled science fiction. J.R.R. Tolkien's The Lord of the Rings was published in 1954 and '55, half a decade after George Orwell's *1984*.

Throughout the rest of the century, those two works would inspire dozens of popular songs, from Led Zeppelin's "Ramble On" to David Bowie's "1984." Neither The Lord of the Rings nor *1984* is about time travel per se, but they helped codify the polyglot genre of speculative fiction, one that gazed imaginatively both backward and forward. This paradox – along with the breakneck acceleration of atomic and space-travel technologies throughout the Cold War – presented mankind with a previously unthinkable dilemma: Did they live in the past, the present, or the future?

Sun Ra didn't answer any questions, but he posed some astounding ones. In the 1950s, the LP format – and its elongation of songtime – allowed recording artists to expand the spectrum of their vision. Through this new aural telescope, Sun Ra ogled at the cosmos. Born Herman Poole Blount in Birmingham, Alabama, the pianist and bandleader claimed that, early in his career, he had traveled astrally to Saturn; his obsession with Ancient Egypt reflected an equal affinity for time travel. Drawing anachronistically from both the far future and the remote past, Blount crafted an elaborate, pharaoh-from-the-stars stage persona – complete with dazzling costumes – that made him appear as a wanderer through space-time, stranded here and now only long enough to make music.

And make music he did. Launching the movement of Afrofuturism, he used big-band bebop and abstract, chilling modulations of sound to turn his rotating LPs into virtual flying saucers. His 1960 song "Music from the World Tomorrow" – recorded with his Myth Science Arkestra – is just one of the many dense, discordant compositions that Sun Ra used to free his music, and his listeners, from the chains of spacetime.

Throughout the rest of the '60s, popular music became a vehicle for increasingly ambitious sounds and ideas. But it wasn't until the psychedelic movement blossomed in the last half of the decade that Sun Ra's music-as-time-travel concept began to take root. One of the most otherworldly practitioners of psychedelic rock, the Texan bard Roky Erickson, led his band The 13th Floor Elevators through a subdued yet trippy track titled "She Lives (in a Time of Her Own)". Released in 1967 as the psychedelic zeitgeist reached its cusp, the song hints at the way psychotropic substances can alter the way one's consciousness flows through the chronological continuum. Erikson fixates on an ethereal young woman who seems to traverse time according to her own velocity and rhythm.

Psychedelia crossed over with folk as the '60s oozed into the '70s, softening the sharper edges of such transcendental sounds. Accordingly, folk artists picked up on time travel. In 1969, the duo of Zager and Evans had a fluke hit with the eerie single "In the Year 2525," which skips like a stone across a still pond, revealing various dystopian scenarios between 2525 and the mind-numbingly distant 9595. It's nowhere near as far-off as the year 802,701, which is where the Time Traveler of Wells's *The Time Machine* finds himself. But the song is clearly inspired by Wells, pessimism and all. Less famously but more potently, English folkie Mick Softley released a song called "Time Machine" in 1970. "Who were you in 2000 B.C.?" Softley asks before demanding, "Who will you be in 5000 A.D.?" By grafting the more traditional sounds of folk music to the science-fictional possibilities of time travel, these artists became the first to traffic openly in temporal paradox and anachronism – elements that would surface more frequently as music pushed further into the future.

Progressive rock, as its name implies, sought to probe tomorrow with a restlessness that bordered on vengeance. Hard rock rose to satisfy the demands of the masses – Grand Funk Railroad's 1969 song "Time Machine" is an ode to sex with groupies, nothing deeper – but progressive rock took that heaviness to a cerebral extreme. Rejecting the short, crude, simple formula of the conventional pop-rock song, the genre of "prog" – as it became both affectionately and derogatorily known – infused jazz and classical structures into rock. Not only did this allow prog musicians to distend and distort the skin of popular music to a previously unimaginable degree, it encouraged the tackling of headier subject matter such as time travel. With twenty-minute-plus songs that routinely took up entire sides of LPs, prog bands dabbled routinely in science fiction and fantasy. Despite the stereotype, though, prog's conceptual palette was much broader, and time travel didn't factor significantly into it – at least not literally. Rather than *singing* about journeys to the future, prog artists tended to act like they were already there.

Curiously, time travel as a lyrical theme is most prominent in the early '70s in the overlap of prog and hard rock. Uriah Heep and Hawkwind were two British bands who could only marginally be considered prog; in fact, they had more in common with the emerging sound of heavy metal. Yet in 1972, each band immortalized itself in the annals of time-travel music: Uriah Heep with "Traveller in Time" and Hawkwind with "Silver Machine." (Three years later, Hawkwind would release an album titled *Warrior on the Edge of Time*, based on the books of science-fiction/fantasy author Michael Moorcock and his time-bending Eternal Champion.) More startlingly, the German jazz-rock outfit Dzyan – associated with the movement known as Krautrock, which would birth the futuristic group Kraftwerk – released an instrumental record in 1973 titled *Time Machine*. Free of vocals or lyrics, it instead uses intricate, radically shifting tempos and time signatures as metaphors for time travel.

Some of the strains of progressivism reached the mainstream in the '70s – and many of those bands are now considered staples of classic rock. Many such acts managed to smuggle an incredible amount of weirdness onto the airwaves, though. Time travel included. Although the lyrics of Steely Dan's 1974 hit "Pretzel Logic" are as arch and abstruse as most of their work, songwriter Donald Fagen revealed years later that the song was, in its own cryptic way, about time travel. In 1975, two of classic rock's biggest bands, Led Zeppelin and Queen, touched on the time-travel theme: Zeppelin's "Kashmir" contains the mysticism-laden lines, "I am a traveler of both time and space," while Queen's "'39" – sung by guitarist and future Ph.D. in astrophysics Brian May – relates the tale of space explorers who, much to their alarm, return to Earth a century after they depart due to Einstein's Special Theory of Relativity. Also in 1975, a scrappy, lurid stage production called *The Rocky Horror Picture Show* made it to the big screen. With it came its indelibly glammed-up theme song, "Time Warp." Although neither the film nor the song deal explicitly with time travel, their grab-bag pastiche of eras and aesthetics took the free-for-all anachronism of the decade and spun it into a catchy, danceable, cult-worthy anthem.

Things got grimmer in the '80s. The imminent approach of the year 1984 was an almost oppressive reminder that Orwell's dystopic predictions half a century earlier had been specious in some ways, prescient in others. The future had arrived, and it was both more boring and more chilling than predicted. Brian Eno, former keyboardist of the temporally unhinged band Roxy Music, got a jump on the '80s with 1977 album *Before and After Science*. As if its title was enough of an indication that Eno viewed time from multiple angles at once, many of the album's songs brush on time travel – including "Here He Comes,"in which Eno sings of "the boy who tried to vanish to the future or the past."

Eno – along with his most notable collaborator in the '70s, David Bowie – was an architect of '80s new wave. One of his many disciples was the band The Human League. Driven by synthesizers, robotic vocals, and the cryogenically frozen remnants of prog, The Human League wrote "Almost Medieval" – a 1979 song obsessed with century-hopping and jumbled timelines – before morphing into a romantic, soft-pop band as the '80s progressed. New wave was an amalgam of the punk, glam, and art-rock movements of the '70s, so it only makes sense that the '80s bands most conversant with time travel were comprised of actual '70s holdovers. In 1980, former Hawkwind frontman Nik Turner led his punk-fueled freakout ensemble Inner City Unit through a frenzied song titled "Watching the Grass Grow", which opens with the shrieked lines, "We are the survivors / The eternal survivors / Androgynous energies / Traveling through time!" A year later, the iconic Krautrock group Kraftwerk reached the zenith of its android-encased electronica. Their 1981 song "Computer World" mentions "time, travel, communication, entertainment" as four of the vectors of existence that will be precisely regulated in its cybernetic vision of the future. The fact that "time" and "travel" are mentioned in the same breath seems like no coincidence.

Another band that came of age in the '70s was Electric Light Orchestra. Led by mastermind Jeff Lynne, ELO became one of the '80s most accomplished proponents of time-travel music. In fact, the band's 1981 album *Time* is the first major concept album devoted entirely to time travel. The basic premise: A man from the 1980s is catapulted to the year 2095, where he's confronted by the dichotomy between technological advancement and ages-old heartache. "Though you ride on the wheels of tomorrow," Lynne sings poignantly on the *Time* song "21st Century Man", "You still wander the fields of your sorrow."

After 1984 came and passed, the future seemed not so terrifying. That milestone had passed without major incident; it was time to start looking fondly backward – or at least recalibrating our sensibilities so that we realized, once and for all, that we were now living in the world of tomorrow. Cue *Back to the*

Future. The 1985 film not only gave the musty old time machine a spiffy chrome finish, it produced one of the most recognizable time-travel songs of all time: the equally shiny "Back in Time" by Huey Lewis and the News, who, oxymoronically, played an entirely retroactive kind of old-school, meat-and-potatoes pop rock.

Catchy, cozy, and utterly unchallenging on a musical level, "Back in Time" ushered in a decade of music – the mid-'80s to the mid-'90s – that was relatively quiet in regard to time travel. The exception was heavy metal. Unafraid to keep the dread of the future and the wonder of the past alive, metal masterpieces like Fates Warning's 1985 song "Traveler in Time", Iron Maiden's 1986 album *Somewhere in Time*, and Blue Öyster Cult's 1988 album *Imaginos* reimagined time travel in harder, darker ways. In particular, *Somewhere in Time* has stood the test of time. Lean, menacing, and yet subliminally progressive, the album's loose concept covers everything from memory to history to destiny – all aspects of the mercurial commodity of time.

Perhaps because they were starting to feel the march of time themselves, many rock veterans worked time travel into their music from the late '80s through the late '90s. While alternative rockers like Nirvana to Beck became fixated on irony and emotional expressionism rather than high concept, prog legend Rick Wakeman and metal stalwarts Black Sabbath kept time travel on life support – the former with his 1988 album *Time Machine*, the latter with their 1992 song "Time Machine". (That formula would repeat itself in 1999, when prog legend Alan Parsons released his album *The Time Machine* and metal stalwarts Saxon unleashed their song "Are We Travellers in Time.") Still, it was clear by the mid-'90s that that time-travel music had hit a slump.

Then came Dr. Octagon. One of many alter egos assumed by the rapper Kool Keith, Dr. Octagon is both the creator and the main character of his 1996 album *Dr. Octagonecologyst*. Not only is it one of the most vital and enduring hip-hop albums of the '90s, it almost singlehandedly revived the concept of time travel in popular music. In a scrambled conglomeration of genres and storylines, the album follows the twisted trajectory of its time-traveling, extraterrestrial doctor. Fans of *Doctor Who* might notice some basic similarities, but The Doctor is only one of many time-warping, science-fiction archetypes Dr. Octagon weaves into his dizzying mosaic of beats, rhymes, and spacetime.

Inspired by that madcap genius, hip-hop crew Arsonists weighed in with their clock-spinning 1999 song "Rhyme Time Travel." As if to offset those teeming expressions of lyrical acumen, the long-standing experimental project Coil recorded their 1998 album *Time Machines*. According to Coil's leader, the late John Balance, the vocal-free, minimalist, electronic tones that make up the album might sound hypnotic, but they're actually intended to induce a mental state that would facilitate time travel. With the help of choice hallucinogens, of course.

As with 1984, the year 2000 defused much of the mystique surrounding a chronological milestone. If 1984 marked the end of yesterday, 2000 truly marked the start of tomorrow. Following the comical-in-hindsight panic that occurred during the buildup to Y2K, though, the twenty-first century wasn't as terrifying as everyone thought it might be. (The fact that the year 2000 was technically part of the twentieth century didn't seem to bother anyone.) Then the terror attacks of September 11, 2001, cast a new kind of shadow across the future. Music grew either grim or escapist – but few musicians were thinking of time travel as thematic vessel for those impulses.

Leave it to the cheerful, acid-damaged indie rockers The Flaming Lips to breathe new life into time-travel music. With the post-9/11 clouds beginning to part slightly, there was a sliver of sunlight for The Lips' 2006 song "Time Travel . . . Yes!!" to flourish. Released in no less than three different versions that year, the song features guest singer Steve Burns, former host of the children's show *Blue's Clues*. Accordingly, the song is breezily innocent in its celebration of skipping through time.

The rise of geek rock in the new millennium was certainly inspired in part by the science-fiction whimsy of The Flaming Lips. But it was Barenaked Ladies that formed a cornerstone of that foundation. The Canadian pop band's 1998 song "It's All Been Done" is one of the more imaginative examples of time-travel music: the witty tale of two lovers who cross each other's paths throughout time, only to wind up disenchanted. Geek rock's rap-centric cousin, nerdcore, also came into prominence in the '00s. And the subgenre's prime mover, MC Lars, naturally dabbled in time travel; the title of his 2006 song "If I Had a Time Machine, That Would Be Fresh" pretty much says it all.

But the most unique, involved, and innovative of all twenty-first-century musical time travelers is the avant-R&B artist Janelle Monáe. The backstory of her 2007 album *Metropolis: Suite I (The Chase)* is so elaborate, it might as well be the product of its own time-travel paradox. Actually, it sort of is: Like Dr. Octagon, Monáe obliterates the fourth wall in her interweaving of artist and character – to the point where she's stated that the protagonist of her songs, the twenty-eighth-century android Cindi Mayweather, has traveled back in time to inspire Monae herself. She also draws sounds and/or inspiration from generations of Afrofuturists, from Sun Ra to Parliament Funkadelic to Grace Jones. To a far lesser degree, rapper T-Pain does the same with his 2007 song "Time Machine" – but what it lacks in complexity it makes up for in hooks, sweetness, and old-school nostalgia. And when rapper Dead Prez delivers Egyptological verses about hieroglyphics and the Eye of Horus in his 2012 song "Time Travel", it completes the Afrofuturist circuit Sun Ra established over fifty years earlier.

And the circle keeps on spinning. Indie-pop collective The Apples in Stereo released its geeky, infectious concept album *Travellers in Space and Time* in 2010 – and it's a direct descendent of ELO's *Time* from thirty years prior. A profusion of pop artists of all levels of notoriety have kept the time-travel flame alive in the twenty-first century. Mega-successful pop singer Robyn released the single "Time Machine" in 2007, complete with frigid, futuristic beats. On a more modest scale, Never Shout Never and Blouse – both of whom released songs titled "Time Travel" in 2011 – have explored different sides of tomorrow-pop.

Metal bands are still in on the time-travel act as well, with brutal groups like Agoraphobic Nosebleed and High on Fire slicing through the time stream with 2009's *Agorapocalypse* and 2012's *De Vermis Mysteriis*, respectively. And then there's Mastodon's masterful, metallic epic *Crack the Skye*. The 2009 album posits the traversal of spacetime via astral projection, much as Sun Ra did; the result is a voyage through a wormhole, back to czarist Russia, and into the soul of Rasputin.

Like Sun Ra, Dzyan, and Coil before them, some current groups have found instrumental music to be the most efficient method of conveyance through time. The one-woman electronic project Motion Sickness of Time Travel – comprising Rachel Evans on tone generators, oscillators, and other supposedly archaic analog noisemakers – composes symphonic paeans to the temporal slipstream. Meanwhile the maestro known as Mickey Moonlight crafts uncategorizable albums such as 2011's *The Time Axis Manipulation Corporation,* a kaleidoscopic blend of space-age kitsch lounge music and adrift-in-spacetime electronica. Even seasoned electronic artists like Thomas Dolby (of "She Blinded Me with Science" fame) have hitched their wagon to time travel – in Dolby's case, literally. His 2012 Time Machine Tour was conducted in a chrome-plated trailer of his own design, a self-defined "time capsule" cobbled together from bits of technology from the past, the present, and presumably the future.

As the twenty-first century loses its new-car smell, musicians intrigued by time travel must find new ways to interpret the musty old notions of H.G. Wells – and the recording limitations of the past. Where the evolution of recording formats, from the seven-inch phonograph to the compact disc, once gave artists more conceptual spacetime to play with, the ascendancy of digital recording and streaming means the cloud is the limit. Neither music creators nor listeners are beholden to outmoded interpretations of the future.

The future, actually, doesn't even have to be futuristic at all. The literary genre of steampunk has catalyzed a movement of music that acts as its unofficial soundtrack – a genre, not coincidentally, that counts Thomas Dolby as one of its godfathers. Thriving in the same anachronistic soup as the literature that spawned it, steampunk music draws from a variety of historical eras, past and future, both real and imaginary. Alternate history clashes with retro-futurism; Victorian and/or Edwardian values jostle with cybernetics and post-humanism. In most of twentieth-century time-travel lore, paradox is a thing to be avoided or explained away as logically as possible. With steampunk, chronological quirk is embraced, not buried. So when a prominent steampunk group like Abney Park constructs an overarching meta-narrative about the band's tenure on a time-traveling dirigible, it all plays into the immersive listening experience of being both audience and scientific observer. And when steampunk troubadours Vernian Process fuse together a panoply of centuries-spanning styles – from ragtime to progressive rock to trip-hop – the polyglot sound represents the fractured linearity and immediate accessibility of music in the digital age. Vernian Process' 2013 album is titled *The Consequences of Time Travel* – and for the first time in the history of recorded music, it feels as though the possibilities of time-travel music are finally, fully being embraced with a sense of adventure.

We are living, these old-fashioned, newfangled steampunks might say, in a post-chronological world. But this isn't a new idea. As the brainy punk-pop band the Buzzcocks sang in their 1978 time-paradox anthem "Nostalgia," "Sometimes there's a song in my brain / And I feel that my heart knows the refrain / I guess it's just the music that brings on nostalgia / For an age yet to come."

Or, in other words: To travel through music is to listen to time.

A Time Travel Playlist

13th Floor Elevators, "She Lives (in a Time of Her Own)"
Abney Park, *The End of Days*
Agoraphobic Nosebleed, *Agorapocalypse*
The Apples in Stereo, *Travellers in Space and Time*
Arsonists, "Rhyme Time Travel"
Ayrean, *Universal Migrator Parts 1 and 2*
Barenaked Ladies, "It's All Been Done"
Black Sabbath, "Time Machine"
Blouse, "Time Travel"
Blue Öyster Cult, *Imaginos*
Brian Eno, *Before and After Science*
Buzzcocks, "Nostalgia"
Coil, *Time Machines*
Dead Prez, "Time Travel"
Dr. Octagon, *Dr. Octagonecologyst*
Dzyan, *Time Machine*
Electric Light Orchestra, *Time*
Fates Warning, "Traveler in Time"
The Flaming Lips, "Time Travel . . . Yes!!"
Grand Funk Railroad, "Time Machine"
Hawkwind, "Silver Machine"
High on Fire, *De Vermis Mysteriis*
Huey Lewis and the News, "Back in Time"
The Human League, "Almost Medieval"
Inner City Unit, "Watching the Grass Grow"
Iron Maiden, *Somewhere in Time*
Isis, "In Fiction"
Jonelle Monáe, *Metropolis: Suite I (The Chase)*
Klaxons, "Gravity's Rainbow"
Kraftwerk, "Computer World"
Led Zeppelin "Kashmir"
Mastodon, *Crack the Skye*
MC Lars, "If I Had a Time Machine, That Would Be Fresh"
Mick Softley, "Time Machine"
Mickey Moonlight, *The Time Axis Manipulation Corporation*
Motion Sickness of Time Travel, *Eclipse Studies*
Muse, "Knights of Cydonia"
Nena, "Irgendwie, Irgendwo, Irgendwann"
Never Shout Never, "Time Travel"
Queen, "'39"
Rick Wakeman, *Time Machine*
Robyn, "Time Machine"
The Rocky Horror Picture Show Cast, "Time Warp"
Rush, "Cygnus X-1 Book I: The Voyage" and
"Cygnus X-1 Book II: Hemispheres"

Steely Dan, "Pretzel Logic"
Sun Ra and His Myth Science Arkestra, "Music from the World Tomorrow"
T-Pain, "Time Machine"
Uriah Heep, "Traveller in Time"
Vernian Process, *The Consequences of Time Travel*
"Weird Al" Yankovic, "Everything You Know is Wrong"
Wings, "Backward Traveler"
Zager and Evans, "In the Year 2525"

COMMUNIQUÉS

WHAT IF

Isaac Asimov

Isaac Asimov was one of the most prolific and beloved science fiction writers of the twentieth century. In addition to his popular fiction, he wrote quite a lot of nonfiction. Some say he published over 500 books altogether. He had a knack for taking complex scientific ideas and presenting them so that the layman could understand these concepts. This story was first published in *Fantastic Story Magazine* in the summer of 1952.

Norman and Livvy were late, naturally, since catching a train is always a matter of last-minute delays, so they had to take the only available seat in the coach. It was the one toward the front, the one with nothing before it but the seat that faced the wrong way, with its back hard against the front partition. While Norman heaved the suitcase onto the rack, Livvy found herself chafing a little.

If a couple took the wrong-way seat before them, they would be staring self-consciously into each other's faces all the hours it would take to reach New York; or else, which was scarcely better, they would have to erect synthetic barriers of newspaper. Still, there was no use in taking a chance on there being another unoccupied double seat elsewhere in the train.

Norman didn't seem to mind, and that was a little disappointing to Livvy. Usually they held their moods in common. That, Norman claimed, was why he remained sure that he had married the right girl.

He would say, "We fit each other, Livvy, and that's the key fact. When you're doing a jigsaw puzzle and one piece fits another, that's it. There are no other possibilities, and of course there are no other girls."

And she would laugh and say, "If you hadn't been on the streetcar that day, you would probably never have met me. What would you have done then?"

"Stayed a bachelor. Naturally. Besides, I would have met you through Georgette another day."

"It wouldn't have been the same."

"Sure it would."

"No, it wouldn't. Besides, Georgette would never have introduced me. She was interested in you herself, and she's the type who knows better than to create a possible rival."

"What nonsense."

Livvy asked her favorite question: "Norman, what if you had been one minute later at the streetcar corner and had taken the next car? What do you suppose would have happened?"

"And what if fish had wings and all of them flew to the top of the mountains? What would we have to eat on Fridays then?"

But they had caught the streetcar, and fish didn't have wings, so that now they had been married for five years and ate fish on Fridays. And because they had been married five years, they were going to celebrate by spending a week in New York.

Then she remembered the present problem. "I wish we could have found some other seat."

Norman said, "Sure. So do I. But no one has taken it yet, so we'll have relative privacy as far as Providence, anyway."

Livvy was unconsoled, and felt herself justified when a plump little man walked down the central aisle of the coach. Now, where had he come from? The train was halfway between Boston and Providence, and if he had had a seat, why hadn't he kept it? She took out her vanity and considered her reflection. She had a theory that if she ignored the little man, he would pass by. So she concentrated on her light-brown hair which, in the rush of catching the train, had become disarranged just a little; at her blue eyes, and at her little mouth with the plump lips which Norman said looked like a permanent kiss. Not bad, she thought.

Then she looked up, and the little man was in the seat opposite. He caught her eye and frowned widely. A series of lines curled about the edges of his smile. He lifted his hat hastily and put it down beside him on top of the little black box he had been carrying. A circle of white hair instantly sprang up stiffly about the large bald spot that made the center of his skull a desert.

She could not help smiling back a little, but then she caught sight of the black box again and the smile faded. She yanked at Norman's elbow.

Norman looked up from his newspaper. He had startlingly dark eyebrows that almost met above the bridge of his nose, giving him a formidable first appearance. But they and the dark eyes beneath bent upon her now with only the usual look of pleased and somewhat amused affection.

He said, "What's up?" He did not look at the plump little man opposite.

Livvy did her best to indicate what she saw by a little unobtrusive gesture of her hand and head. But the little man was watching and she felt a fool, since Norman simply stared at her blankly.

Finally she pulled him closer and whispered, "Don't you see what's printed on his box?"

She looked again as she said it, and there was no mistake. It was not very prominent, but the light caught it slantingly and it was a slightly more glistening area on a black background. In flowing script it said, "What If."

The little man was smiling again. He nodded his head rapidly and pointed to the words and then to himself several times over.

Norman put his paper aside. "I'll show you." He leaned over and said, "Mr. If?"

The little man looked at him eagerly.

"Do you have the time, Mr. If?"

The little man took out a large watch from his vest pocket and displayed the dial.

"Thank you, Mr. If," said Norman. And again in a whisper, "See, Livvy."

He would have returned to his paper, but the little man was opening his box and raising a finger periodically as he did so, to enforce their attention. It was just a slab of frosted glass that he removed – about six by nine inches in length and width and perhaps an inch thick. It had beveled edges, rounded corners, and was completely featureless. Then he took out a little wire stand on which the glass slab fitted comfortably. He rested the combination on his knees and looked proudly at them.

Livvy said, with sudden excitement, "Heavens, Norman, it's a picture of some sort."

Norman bent close. Then he looked at the little man. "What's this? A new kind of television?"

The little man shook his head, and Livvy said, "No, Norman, it's us."

"What?"

"Don't you see? That's the streetcar we met on. There you are in the back seat wearing that old fedora I threw away three years ago. And that's Georgette and myself getting on. The fat lady's in the way. Now! Can't you see us?"

He muttered, "It's some sort of illusion."

"But you see it too, don't you? That's why he calls this, 'What If.' It will *show* us what if. What if the streetcar hadn't swerved . . ."

She was sure of it. She was very excited and very sure of it. As she looked at the picture in the glass slab, the late afternoon sunshine grew dimmer and the inchoate chatter of the passengers around and behind them began fading.

How she remembered that day. Norman knew Georgette and had been so embarrassed that he was forced into gallantry and then into conversation. An introduction from Georgette was not even necessary. By the time they got off the streetcar, he knew where she worked.

She could still remember Georgette glowering at her, sulkily forcing a smile when they themselves separated. Georgette said, "Norman seems to like you."

Livvy replied, "Oh, don't be silly! He was just being polite. But he is nice-looking isn't he?"

It was only six months after that that they married.

And now here was that same streetcar again, with Norman and herself and Georgette. As she thought that, the smooth train noises, the rapid clack-clack of wheels, vanished completely. Instead, she was in the swaying confines of the streetcar. She had just boarded it with Georgette at the previous stop.

Livvy shifted weight with the swaying of the streetcar, as did forty others, sitting and standing, all to the same monotonous and rather ridiculous rhythm. She said, "Somebody's motioning at you, Georgette. Do you know him?"

"At me?" Georgette directed a deliberately casual glance over her shoulder. Her artificially long eyelashes flickered. She said, "I know him a little. What do you suppose he wants?"

"Let's find out," said Livvy. She felt pleased and a little wicked.

Georgette had a well-known habit of hoarding her male acquaintances, and it was rather fun to annoy her this way. And besides, this one seemed quite . . . interesting.

She snaked past the lines of standees, and Georgette followed without enthusiasm. It was just as Livvy arrived opposite the young man's seat that the streetcar lurched heavily as it rounded a curve. Livvy snatched desperately in the direction of the straps. Her fingertips caught and she held on. It was a long moment before she could breathe. For some reason, it had seemed that there were no straps close to be reached. Somehow, she felt that by all the laws of nature she should have fallen.

The young man did not look at her. He was smiling at Georgette and rising from his seat. He had astonishing eyebrows that gave him a rather competent and self-confident appearance. Livvy decided that she definitely liked him. Georgette was saying, "Oh no, don't bother. We're getting off in about two stops."

They did. Livvy said, "I thought we were going to Sachs."

"We are. There's just something I remember having to attend to here. It won't take but a minute."

"Next stop, Providence!" the loudspeakers were blaring. The train was slowing and the world of the past had shrunk itself into the glass slab once more. The little man was still smiling at them.

Livvy turned to Norman. She felt a little frightened. "Were you through all that, too?"

He said, "What happened to the time? We can't be reaching Providence yet?" He looked at his watch. "I guess we are." Then, to Livvy, "You didn't fall that time."

"Then you did see it?" She frowned. "Now, that's like Georgette. I'm sure there was no reason to get off the streetcar except to prevent my meeting you. How long had you known Georgette then, Norman?"

"Not very long. Just enough to be able to recognize her at sight and to feel that I ought to offer her my seat."

Livvy curled her lip.

Norman grinned, "You can't be jealous of a might-have-been, kid. Besides, what difference would it have made? I'd have been sufficiently interested in you to work out a way of meeting you."

"You didn't even look at me."

"I hardly had the chance."

"Then how would you have met me?"

"Some way. I don't know how. But you'll admit this is a rather foolish argument we're having."

They were leaving Providence. Livvy felt a trouble in her mind. The little man had been following their whispered conversation, with only the loss of his smile to show that he understood. She said to him, "Can you show us more?"

Norman interrupted, "Wait now, Livvy. What are you to try to do?"

She said, "I want to see our wedding day. What it would have been if I hadn't caught the strap."

Norman was visibly annoyed. "Now, that's not fair. We might not have been married on the same day, you know."

But she said, "Can you show it to me, Mr. If?" and the little man nodded.

The slab of glass was coming alive again, glowing a little. Then the light collected and condensed into figures. A tiny sound of organ music was in Livvy's ears without there actually being sound.

Norman said with relief, "Well, there I am. That's our wedding. Are you satisfied?"

The train sounds were disappearing again, and the last thing Livvy heard was her own voice saying, "Yes, there you are. But where am I?"

*

Livvy was well back in the pews. For a while she had not expected to attend at all. In the past months she had drifted further and further away from Georgette, without quite knowing why. She had heard of her engagement only through a mutual friend, and, of course, it was to Norman. She remembered very clearly that day, six months before, when she had first seen him on the streetcar. It was the time Georgette had so quickly snatched her out of sight. She had met him since on several occasions, but each time Georgette was with him, standing between.

Well, she had no cause for resentment; the man was certainly none of hers. Georgette, she thought, looked more beautiful than she really was. And he was very handsome indeed.

She felt sad and rather empty, as though something had gone wrong – something that she could not quite outline in her mind. Georgette had moved up the aisle without seeming to see her, but earlier she had caught his eyes and smiled at him. Livvy thought he had smiled in return.

She heard the words distantly as they drifted back to her, "I now pronounce you—"

The noise of the train was back. A woman swayed down the aisle, herding a little boy back to their seats. There were intermittent bursts of girlish laughter from a set of four teenage girls halfway down the coach. A conductor hurried past on some mysterious errand.

Livvy was frozenly aware of it all.

She sat there, staring straight ahead, while the trees outside blended into a fuzzy, furious green and the telephone poles galloped past.

She said, "It was she you married."

He stared at her for a moment and then one side of his mouth quirked a little. He said lightly, "I didn't really, Olivia. You're still my wife, you know. Just think about it for a few minutes."

She turned to him. "Yes, you married me – because I fell in your lap. If I hadn't, you would have married Georgette. If she hadn't wanted you, you would have married someone else. You would have married anybody. So much for your jigsaw-puzzle pieces."

Norman said very slowly, "Well-I'll-be-darned!" He put both hands to his head and smoothed down the straight hair over his ears where it had a tendency to tuft up. For the moment it gave him the appearance of trying to hold his head together. He said, "Now, look here, Livvy, you're making a silly fuss over a stupid magician's trick. You can't blame me for something I haven't done."

"You would have done it."

"How do you know?"

"You've seen it."

"I've seen a ridiculous piece of – hypnotism, I suppose." His voice suddenly raised itself into anger. He turned to the little man opposite. "Off with you, Mr. If, or whatever your name is. Get out of here. We don't want you. Get out before I throw your little trick out the window and you after it."

Livvy yanked at his elbow. "Stop it. Stop it! You're in a crowded train."

The little man shrank back into the corner of the seat as far as he could go and held his little black box behind him. Norman looked at him, then at Livvy, then at the elderly lady across the way who was regarding him with patent disapproval.

He turned pink and bit back a pungent remark. They rode in frozen silence to and through New London.

Fifteen minutes past New London, Norman said, "Livvy!"

She said nothing. She was looking out the window but saw nothing in the glass.

He said again, "Livvy! Livvy! Answer me!"

She said dully, "What do you want?"

He said, "Look, this is all nonsense. I don't know how the fellow does it, but even granting it's legitimate, you're not being fair. Why stop where you did? Suppose I had married Georgette, do you suppose you would have stayed single? For all I know, you were already married at the time of my supposed wedding. Maybe that's why I married Georgette."

"I wasn't married."

"How do you know?"

"I would have been able to tell. I knew what my own thoughts were."

"Then you would have been married within the next year."

Livvy grew angrier. The fact that a sane remnant within her clamored at the unreason of her anger did not soothe her. It irritated her further, instead. She said, "And if I did, it would be no business of yours, certainly."

"Of course it wouldn't. But it would make the point that in the world of reality we can't be held responsible for the 'what ifs'. "

Livvy's nostrils flared. She said nothing.

Norman said, "Look! You remember the big New Year's celebration at Winnie's place year before last?"

"I certainly do. You spilled a keg of alcohol all over me."

"That's beside the point, and besides, it was only a cocktail shaker's worth. What I'm trying to say is that Winnie is just about your best friend and had been long before you married me."

"What of it?"

"Georgette was a good friend of hers too, wasn't she?"

"Yes."

"All right, then. You and Georgette would have gone to the party regardless of which one of you I had married. I would have had nothing to do with it. Let him show us the party as it would have been if I had married Georgette, and I'll bet you'd be there with either your fiancée or your husband."

Livvy hesitated. She felt honestly afraid of that.

He said, "Are you afraid to take the chance?"

And that, of course, decided her. She turned on him furiously, "No, I'm not! And I hope I am married. There's no reason I should pine for you. What's more, I'd like to see what happens when you spill the shaker all over Georgette. She'll fill both your ears for you, and in public, too. I know her. Maybe you'll see a certain difference in the jigsaw pieces then." She faced forward and crossed her arms angrily and firmly across her chest.

Norman looked across at the little man, but there was no need to say anything.

The glass slab was on his lap already. The sun slanted in from the west, and the white foam of hair that topped his head was edged with pink.

Norman said tensely, "Ready?"

Livvy nodded and let the noise of the train slide away again.

*

Livvy stood, a little flushed with recent cold, in the doorway. She had just removed her coat, with its sprinkling of snow, and her bare arms were still rebelling at the touch of open air.

She answered the shouts that greeted her with "Happy New Year's" of her own, raising her voice to make herself heard over the squealing of the radio. Georgette's shrill tones were almost the first thing she heard upon entering, and now she steered herself toward her. She hadn't seen Georgette, or Norman, in weeks.

Georgette lifted an eyebrow, a mannerism she had lately cultivated, and said, "Isn't anyone with you, Olivia?" Her eyes swept the immediate surroundings and then returned to Livvy.

Livvy said indifferently, "I think Dick will be around later. There was something or other he had to do first." She felt as indifferent as she sounded.

Georgette smiled tightly. "Well, Norman's here. That ought to keep you from being lonely, dear. At least, it's turned out that way before."

As she said so, Norman sauntered in from the kitchen. He had a cocktail shaker in his hand, and the rattling of ice cubes castanetted his words. "Line up, you rioting revelers, and get a mixture that will really revel your riots – Why, Livvy!"

He walked toward her, grinning his welcome, "Where've you been keeping yourself? I haven't seen you in twenty years, seems like. What's the matter? Doesn't Dick want anyone else to see you?"

"Fill my glass, Norman," Georgette said sharply.

"Right away," he said, not looking at her. "Do you want one too, Livvy? I'll get you a glass." He turned, and everything happened at once.

Livvy cried, "Watch out!" She saw it coming, even had a vague feeling that all this had happened before, but it played itself out inexorably. His heel caught the edge of the carpet; he lurched, tried to right himself, and lost the cocktail shaker. It seemed to jump out of his hands, and a pint of ice-cold liquor drenched Livvy from shoulder to hem.

She stood there, gasping. The noises muted about her, and for a few intolerable moments she made futile brushing gestures at her gown, while Norman kept repeating "Damnation!" in rising tones.

Georgette said coolly, "It's too bad, Livvy. Just one of those things. I imagine the dress can't be very expensive."

Livvy turned and ran. She was in the bedroom, which was at least empty and relatively quiet. By the light of the fringe-shaded lamp on the dresser, she poked among the coats on the bed, looking for her own.

Norman had come in behind her. "Look, Livvy, don't pay any attention to what she said. I'm devilishly sorry. I'll pay—"

"That's all right. It wasn't your fault." She blinked rapidly and didn't look at him. "I'll just go home and change."

"Are you coming back?"

"I don't know. I don't think so."

"Look, Livvy . . ." His warm fingers were on her shoulders—

Livvy felt a queer tearing sensation deep inside her, as though she were ripping away, clinging cobwebs and—

*

—and the train noises were back.

Something did go wrong with the time when she was in there – in the slab. It was deep twilight now. The train lights were on. But it didn't matter. She seemed to be recovering from the wrench inside her.

Norman was rubbing his eyes with thumb and forefinger. "What happened?"

Livvy said, "It just ended. Suddenly."

Norman looked uneasily, "You know, we'll be putting into New Haven soon." He looked at his watch and shook his head.

Livvy said wonderingly, "You spilled it on me."

"Well, so I did in real life."

"But in real life I was your wife. You ought to have spilled it on Georgette this time. Isn't that queer?" But she was thinking of Norman pursuing her; his hands on her shoulders . . .

She looked up at him and said with warm satisfaction, "I wasn't married."

"No, you weren't. But was that Dick Reinhardt you were going around with?"

"Yes."

"You weren't planning to marry him, were you, Livvy?"

"Jealous, Norman?"

Norman looked confused. "Of that? Of a slab of glass? Of course not."

"I don't think I would have married him."

Norman said, "You know, I wish it hadn't ended when it did. There was something that was about to happen, I think." He stopped, then added slowly, "It was as though I would rather have done it to anybody else in the room."

"Even to Georgette."

"I wasn't giving two thoughts about Georgette. You don't believe me, I suppose."

"Maybe I do." She looked up at him. "I've been silly, Norman. Let's – let's live our real life. Let's not play with all the things that just might have been."

But he caught her hands. "No, Livvy. One last time. Let's see what we would have been doing right now, Livvy! This very minute! If I had married Georgette."

Livvy was a little frightened. "Let's not, Norman." She was thinking of his eyes, smiling hungrily at her as he held the shaker, while Georgette stood beside her, and regarded. She didn't want to know what happened afterward. She just wanted this life now, this good life.

New Haven came and went.

Norman said again, "I want to try, Livvy."

She said, "If you want to, Norman." She decided fiercely that it wouldn't matter. Nothing would matter. Her hands reached out and encircled his arm. She held it tightly, and while she held it she thought: "Nothing in make-believe can take him from me."

Norman said to the little man, "Set 'em up again."

In the yellow light the process seemed to be slower. Gently the frosted slab cleared, like clouds being torn apart and dispersed by an unfelt wind.

Norman was saying, "There's something wrong. That's just the two of us, exactly as we are now."

He was right. Two little figures were sitting in a train on the seats which were the farthest toward the front. The field was enlarging now – they were merging into it. Norman's voice was distant and fading.

"It's the same train," he was saying. "The window in back is cracked just as—"

*

Livvy was blindingly happy. She said, "I wish we were in New York."

He said, "It will be less than an hour, darling." Then he said, "I'm going to kiss you." He made a movement, as though he were about to begin.

"Not here! Oh, Norman, people are looking."

Norman drew back. He said, "We should have taken a taxi."

"From Boston to New York?"

"Sure. The privacy would have been worth it."

She laughed. "You're funny when you try to act ardent."

"It isn't an act." His voice was suddenly a little somber. "It's not just an hour, you know. I feel as though I've been waiting five years."

"I do, too."

"Why couldn't I have met you first. It was such a waste."

"Poor Georgette," Livvy sighed.

Norman moved impatiently. "Don't be sorry for her, Livvy. We never really made a go of it. She was glad to get rid of me."

"I know that. That's why I say 'Poor Georgette'. I'm just sorry for her for not being able to appreciate what she had."

"Well, see to it that you do," he said. "See to it that you're immensely appreciative, infinitely appreciative – or more than that, see that you're at least half as appreciative as I am of what I've got."

"Or else you'll divorce me, too?"

"Over my dead body," said Norman.

Livvy said, "It's all so strange. I keep thinking, What if you hadn't spilt the cocktails on me that time at the party? You wouldn't have followed me out; you wouldn't have told me; I wouldn't have known. It would have been so different . . . everything."

"Nonsense. It would have been just the same. It would have all happened another time."

"I wonder," said Livvy softly.

*

Train noises merged into train noises. City lights flickered outside, and the atmosphere of New York was about them. The coach was astir with travelers dividing the baggage among themselves.

Livvy was an island in the turmoil until Norman shook her.

She looked at him and said, "The jigsaw pieces fit after all."

He said, "Yes."

She put a hand on his. "But it wasn't good, just the same. I was very wrong. I thought that because we had each other, we should have all the possible each others. But all of the possibilities are none of our business. The real is enough. Do you know what I mean?"

He nodded.

She said, "There are millions of other what ifs. I don't want to know what happened in any of them. I'll never say, 'What if', again."

Norman said, "Relax, dear. Here's your coat." And he reached for the suitcases.

Livvy said with sudden sharpness, "Where's Mr. If?"

Norman turned slowly to the empty seat that faced them. Together they scanned the rest of the coach.

"Maybe," Norman said, "he went into the next coach."

"But why? Besides, he wouldn't leave his hat." And she bent to pick it up.

Norman said, "What hat?"

And Livvy stopped her fingers hovering over nothingness. She said, "It was here – I almost touched it." She straightened and said, "Oh, Norman, what if—"

Norman put a finger on her mouth. "Darling . . ."

She said, "I'm sorry. Here, let me help you with the suitcases."

The train dived into the tunnel beneath Park Avenue, and the noise of the wheels rose to a roar.

AS TIME GOES BY

Tanith Lee

Tanith Lee is a highly respected English writer of science fiction, horror, and fantasy, with over seventy novels and hundreds of short stories to her credit. She has been a regular contributor over many years to *Weird Tales* magazine. She has won the World Fantasy Award, the British Fantasy Award, and the Nebula Award multiple times. This story was first published in *Chrysalis 10* in 1983.

We had half a crew in here two twenties ago, swore they passed the *Napoleon,* coming up into the Parameter. But you know what spacers are, particularly when they're in a Static Zone. Two-thousand-plus time streams colliding in space, and a white ironex wheel, fragile as a leaf, spinning round at the center of it all. You're bound to get time-ghosts, and superstitions of all sorts.

The wheel here at Tempi was the first way station ever created, in the first Parameter they ever hit when they finally figured how Time operates out in deep space. You'll know most, if not all of it, of course. How every star system functions in a different time sphere, everything out of kilter with everything else, and that the universe is composed of a million strands of time, of which only two thousand have as yet been definitely charted and made navigable. And you know too that Tempi, and her sister Zones – what they jokingly call the *white holes* in space – are the safe houses where time is, forever and always, itself at a stop. And that, though wheelers reckon in twenty-hour units, and though, like anywhere else, we have a jargon of past, present and future – yestertwenty, today, tomorrow – temporal stasis actually obtains all around a wheel. *We* move all right, but over the face of a frozen clock, over the face of a clock without any hands at all. Which means that whatever ship blows in, out of whichever of those two-thousand-odd time continuums, can realign here, or in another of the white holes, docked against a white ironex wheel, having come back, as it were, to square one. It's here they wipe the slate clean before flying out again into chaos. A tract of firm ground in the boiling seas. In scientific terms: a Parameter, one constant sphere in a differential Infinity. In common parlance, just another way of keeping sane.

But sanity, like time, is relative. As I say, Tempi has its share of "ghosts"; like the Lyran wildflowers that are sometimes supposed to manifest on the Sixth Level. Not that I ever saw those. I did see the *Napoleon,* once.

It was back in the twenties when they still had that bar here on the Third Level–Rouelle Etoile, Star Alley. Maybe you've heard of it. It owed quite a lot to early-twentieth-century celluloid, you know those old movies, like thin acidulous slices of lemon. The Rouelle had that square-shouldered furniture, and the glass chunk ashtrays. The walls had rose and black satin poured down them. And some of the women would get out of their coveralls, and come into the Rouelle with satin poured down them too, and those long, dark scarlet nails and those long earrings like chandeliers. There was also a chandelier in the roof. You should have seen it. Like ice on fire. And under the chandelier there was a real piano, and a real pianist, a Sirtian, blue as coal, with the face of a prince, and hands like sea waves. The sounds that came out of the piano were the shape and color of the blades of light snowing off the chandelier. You should have seen that chandelier.

But I was telling you about the time I saw the *Napoleon.*

I was up on the Fourth Walk, one level over the Rouelle Etoile, where you can watch the ship explode in out of nothing, leaving the Warp Lanes at zero 50. Space was blind-clear as a pool of ink, without stars obviously, since you never see stars inside a Parameter. Incoming traffic was listed as over for that twenty. When I saw this great bottlenose dolphin surging up out of nowhere, I started to run for the Alert panel. Then something made me look back when I was two thirds along the gantry. And the ship just wasn't there anymore.

I'm not given to hallucinations, and besides, I have a pretty good Recall. I remember sitting down on the gantry, and putting that ship together again on the blackboard of my mind, and taking a hard long look at her. And I realized, inside a second, she couldn't be any crate left on the listings. The numerals and date-codings, you see, were Cycles out – about nineteen years or more, by Confederation reckoning. With the time-tangle out here, every code gets changed once every Cycle. Naturally, there's the occasional tin can comes careening out of Warp, with its dating markers legally a few points overdue. But they're little ships, freelance dippers nobody makes much fuss over. This was a big ship, a cool, pale giant. She had the old-fashioned diesel-pod at her stern too, burning like a ruby. But there was something else. My Recall was showing me enough to know her markings weren't just out of date, they were *wrong*. And she had a device. Anyone who's ever heard of the Trade War knows about the pirate ships, and the blazons they used to carry. Quite a few people know what the device of the *Napoleon* was: an eagle over a sunburst. And that's precisely what this ship had on her bow.

I didn't report anything. Just hinted around, you know the kind of thing. Then I began to get comparison sightings, and there were quite a lot. To my knowledge, nobody's ever come face to face with Day Curtis himself. Except, there is one story.

Curtis had a reputation all his own, something of a legend going for him, even before *Napoleon* disappeared with almost all hands. The Trade War had broken the Confederation in three neat pieces, and there were plenty of captains running through the guns on all three sides, taking cargo to wherever it was meant, or not meant, to go, for a suitable fee, and not averse to accumulating extra merchandise if they came across it in the Warp Lanes. Curtis was unique in that he'd hire out to any side at any time, and simultaneously commit acts of piracy against the very side he was running for. The reason he still got paid was he could make *Napoleon* play games with the time streams and the Warp that are technically impossible, even today. If you could outbid everyone else and buy him, he'd get whatever it was that had to be got to wherever it was it had to go. No matter what was in the way: Sonic barriers, radiation strips, a flotilla of fully armed attack vessels. More than once he split a fleet in two, led one half away through the Warps, now visible and now not, eventually bringing them back by the hand straight into the cannon of the second half who were still waiting for him. He would slip between like a coin through a slot, while they, reacting to pre-primed targets, inadvertently blasted hell out of each other. But you'll have heard the stories about Curtis and his ship, everyone has.

Tempi Parameter was a truce zone then, because it had to be. There were only two wheels spinning in those days, and everybody needed them, whichever part of the Confederation owned you. There was every kind of craft passing in and out: patrol runners, battle cruisers, destroyers, merchantmen, smugglers and privateers. And the crews knew better than not to keep quiet when they met each other in the corridors, the diners and the bars. With ships diving in and out of time like fish through water, and only a couple of safe places to go between, you bowed to the rule and you left your gun at the entry port. Some of the most notorious desperadoes that ever took to space came through here, time and time again, on their way to and from mayhem. But even in that kind of company, Day Curtis stood out.

A slight dark man, with the somber pallor most spacers get, a type of moon-tan, and those thick-fringed Roman-Byzantine eyes you find in frescoes on Earth. You may have seen news-video of him. There was some, the Cycle *Napoleon* towed that shelled liner, the *Aurigos,* through her enemy lines into harbor on Lyra – for the bounty, of course. Or the occasion the entire three segments of the split Confederation each put a price on his head, and most of his brother pirates went out to get him and never got him. He was even finer-made than he looks in those old videos, but the expression was the same. He never joked, he never even smiled. It wasn't any act, anything he'd lost or become. Whatever it is that smooths the edges of human isolation, that was the item he'd come into life without. His crew treated him like a stone king. They knew he could run the show, and with something extra, a sort of cold genius, and they trusted him to do it. But they hated him in about the same measure as they respected him, which was plenty. He had a tongue like a razor blade. You got cut once, and that was enough. Since he was handsome, women liked him all right, until they learned they couldn't get anywhere with him. The ones that kept trying were usually sorry. All that being the case, the story, this last story I ever heard about Day Curtis, is probably apocryphal. The man who told it to me didn't claim it wasn't.

I heard that last story two years after I saw the *Napoleon* from the Fourth Walk. I heard it on the twenty that they closed up the Rouelle Etoile. It was the ninth Cycle, and the day after the tempest smashed those fifteen ships to tinder between Sirtis and the Dagon Strip. I can remember it very well, even without Recall. The bar despoiled, naked and hollow, seeming to echo, the way a dying venue does, with all the voices, the music, the colors that have ever existed in it. A team of men were portioning up that huge glissade of a chandelier, lifting it on to dollies, and carrying it away. The piano was long gone, but there were the dim sheer notes of a girl quietly sobbing to herself, somewhere nearby. I never knew the reason; someone on one of those ships, maybe, had belonged to her . . . The man and I were finishing the last flask of Noira brandy, at the counter in the midst of the suspiring desolation. And we grew warm and sad, and he told me the story.

And outside the oval ports, innocent and terrible, the field of space and time-lessness hung on the rim of the vignette, a starless winter night.

The Rouelle Etoile was almost deserted, that twenty. There was some big action out at zero 98, and the ships had lifted off like vultures, to join in or to scavenge. The tall marble clock against the wall said nineteen fifteen, but the blue pianist was still rolling the tide of his hands up and down the keys. About four or five customers were sitting around chewing trouble, or playing Shot over on the indigo baize. And in one of the corner booths was Day Curtis. *Napoleon* was in dock, had come in two twenties before with a hole in her flank, and the crew were going all out to patch her over well enough to take her out into 98 and see what was left worth mopping up. But it didn't look as if the repairs were going to make it in time, and at eighteen hundred Curtis had walked into the Rouelle with a look like dead lightning in the backs of his eyes. Curtis seldom showed when he was angry, but he could drink like dry sand, and that's what he was doing, steadily and coldly draining the soul out of the bar, when the woman came in.

She looked late twenties, with hair black as the blackest thing you ever saw, which might be space, or an afterimage of some sun, cropped short across the crown, but growing out into one long free-slung black comma across her neck and shoulders. She had the spacer's tawny paleness otherwise, and one of the poured dresses that went with the Rouelle, almost the same color as she was. She was off one of the ships that had stayed in dock, an artisan's shuttle that had no quarrel with anyone in particular, but she walked in as if she'd come on a dare, ready to fight, or to run. She went straight to the bar counter and ordered one of the specialty cocktails, which she drank straight down, not looking at anyone or anything. Then she ordered another, and holding it poised in the long stems of her fingers, she turned and confronted the room. She moved like a dancer, and she had the unique magic which comes with a beauty that surpasses its name, a glamour that doesn't fit in any niche or under any label. Four or five of the men in the bar were staring at her, but her gaze passed on over them with a raking indifference. She was obviously searching for something and, the impression was, hoping not to find it. Then her eyes reached the corner booth, and Curtis.

It's possible he may have noticed her when she came in, or he may not. But implacable scrutiny, even in a truce zone, is frequently the prologue to trouble. After a second or so, he lifted his head slowly, and looked back at her. Her face didn't change, but the glass dropped through her fingers and smashed on the polished floor.

For about a quarter of a minute she kept still, but there was a sort of electric-ity playing all around her, the invisible kind a wire exudes when there's a storm working up in the stratosphere. Then, she kicked the broken glass lightly out of her way, and she walked very fast and direct, over to Curtis' table. He'd kept on watching her, they all had, even the Sirtian pianist, though his hands never missed the up and down flow of the piano keys. The woman had the appearance of being capable of anything, up to and including the slinging of a fine-honed stiletto right across the bar into Curtis' throat. Only a blind man would have ignored her. Maybe not even a blind man.

When she reached the table, the slim hand that had let go the glass flared out like a cobra and slashed Curtis across the face.

"Well," she said, "you win the bet. What am I supposed to pay you?"

He'd had these one-sided scenes with women before, and supposedly assumed this was only another, one more girl he had forgotten. He said to her, matter-of-factly, "I'm sure you can find your own way out of here."

"Yes," she said, "I remember now. You warned me. Last time."

"I probably warned you you were a fool, too. Either get out of the bar, or I will."

"Fifteen years is a long time," she said. Her eyes were like scorched freckled topaz, and there were white flowers enameled on her crimson nails. "I presume I've changed. Even if you haven't. Oh, but I don't expect you to recollect me. How could you? I just wanted to see, to understand—"

Curtis got up. He was moving by her when she caught at his arms. Her face was stark with the genuine terror the anger had been all along, and she said flatly, "Suddenly I've worked it out. I do understand. I've been afraid for years, and now I know why. You're dead, Curtis. Or you will be. Tomorrow – soon—"

She'd started to retreat from him even while she said it, in a dazed, bewildered glide, but of course now he reached out and caught her back. A threat was a threat, and even a woman off an artisan's vessel could be in Confederation pay.

"All right," he said, holding her pinned. I'm interested. Tell me more about my death."

"I'm sorry," she said. "Please let go."

"I let go when I hear what you have to say. Perhaps."

"I don't, after all, have anything to say."

"What a shame. Let me prompt you. You're dead, Curtis. Or you will be."

"We all could be," she said with an attempt at somber lightness. 'There's a war going on out there."

"There's a war going on in here," he said. "You just started it."

"You're hurting me."

"Not yet."

She went on looking at him and he went on holding her. The room was full of piano currents and utter listening silence.

"I'll tell you," she said. "Let me sit down, and I'll tell you."

He nodded, and she slid into the booth, but he kept a grip on her wrist. They sat facing each other, almost holding hands, almost like lovers, ignoring the rest of the room, and he said to her gently, "In case you forget this is a truce zone, you'd better bear it in mind I can break your wrist in two seconds flat."

She smiled dismally.

"I believe you would."

"What's more important, I believe it."

She looked at the tabletop between them.

'This is going to be difficult."

"Only for you."

She said bitterly, "You know, you're almost funny."

"The word 'funeral'," he said, "also begins with the word 'fun'. Think about it."

"All right." Her eyelids tensed like two pale golden wings pasted across her eyes. Then her face smoothed out, relaxed, lost every trace of character. She might have been a doll, and her voice might have been a tape. 'When I was sixteen, around half my lifetime ago, I was here in Tempi. I was traveling in my grandfather's ship, the *Hawk*, before the war really hotted up. We'd come from Sirtis and we were heading for Syracuse. The ship was just a little cargo runner, completely legitimate and authorized up to the hilt. He wasn't expecting any trouble – the cargo was safe and dull – and he'd brought me along to get me out of military school for a few months. I was so glad to be away, glad to be playing female and adult, and not just guns. He brought me in here, and gave me my first sunburst in a tall narrow glass. About seventeen hundred all the Alert panels started going off. An unscheduled lifeboat had blown into the Parameter. The markings were scalded off, and when they got the casings open, there was only one man in it. There was quite a squall then, because the name of the vessel he claimed to have come from wasn't down on any of the listings. Besides, he was talking about a tempest out on zero 98, a time gale that cost him his ship, and there was no gale registering anywhere. Even so, he kept insisting there must be other survivors to be pulled in, but no one came, and when they used the sonar to scan, they picked up nothing, just as they weren't picking up the gale. They questioned the man from the lifeboat until about nineteen hundred, and then they let him come into the Rouelle Etoile, with an official escort. He went over to the bar counter, and then he turned and looked right round the room. There was quite a crowd. My granddaddy was playing Shot over on the baize, and I was sitting exactly where you are now, in my grown-up frock, with one of the young helmsmen off the *Hawk*. The man who'd come in out of space looked at everyone until he got to me. Then he walked across. He dragged me to my feet and held me by my shoulders, and he swore at me. Jove, my helmsman, landed out at him, and the stranger thunked poor Jove across the head. Granddaddy came running with the official escort, and there was something of a fight. When somebody finally laid the stranger out with one of those chunk ashtrays from the bar, I took stock of my feelings. I was scared, horrified, and very flattered. It was all crazy. But I looked at the crazy stranger on the floor, with blood running through his hair, and he was the most beautiful man I'd ever seen, and, for whatever reason, I was the one he'd singled out. Quite logically, though I didn't know it at the time, I fell in love with him. And it was you, Day Curtis." She raised her eyes again, and gazed at him again. "You. Exactly as you are now. And I was sixteen."

There was a pause. Curtis appeared bored, and simultaneously very dangerous. When she didn't continue, he said, "If I let you go on, I imagine you'll eventually reveal why you're giving me this time cliché myth."

"The nature of time," she said, as coldly as he. "What do we really know about it? Two thousand streams, and us playing about in them like salmon."

"The kind of time paradox you're doling out is the sort of junk a Parameter is there to invalidate. Assuming it could even happen. You should change your brand of dream pills."

"All right, mister," she said. "Do I go on, or do I get out?"

He sat and studied her. He said, "You can tell it to the end."

"Thank you," she said icily.

"It'll be interesting, seeing you hit the rotten wood and fall right through it."

"Damn you," she said.

"It takes more than you to do that."

She stared at the tabletop again. She said, "They put you – it *was* you, Curtis – in the Medical Center on the Second Level. Guess what I did?" She glanced at him, and away. "I was sixteen, and I was in love. I went to your room. You were sitting staring out of the port at that blind-black Parameter sky, and your eyes looked just as black . . . though they're not black at all, are they? Never mind. You said, 'What the hell do you want?' Wasn't that a tender greeting? I didn't know what to do, whether to fight you or surrender, or go away, or stay. I stayed. I stayed, Curtis. And gradually you started to tell me. About the time storm, about the number of the Cycle – fifteen years on from where it really was. You told me how I'd be when I was thirty-one, and how I'd walk into the Rouelle in the last hours of this twenty, and I'd see you, and drop my glass on the floor . . . I had to come in here tonight, to act it out. I didn't think you'd be here. No. I did think you would. But if you were, it had to be some joke. You'd be in your forties. You'd laugh at me. But you're not in your forties, and, my God, you're not laughing. You're just the way you told me, warned me, you'd be, that night I was sixteen and you told me not to come to Tempi ever again. But I had to. You can see that. Anyway, my ship came through Tempi, I didn't have any choice this time. I could hardly have avoided it."

She stopped, and detached one of the long white cigarettes from the dispenser. She drew on it and the ignition crystal broke, and the end glowed a pale, dull rose. The smoke made a design round her words as she said, "Tomorrow you take your ship out and you meet the storm. Your ship dies out there in the Warp Lanes. So do you. It's just some part of you that's left wandering there, lost, unaligned. And somehow, I draw you back, to the wrong Cycle, the wrong time, back to that night I was sixteen and I sat here in the Rouelle Etoile. I said, some part of you. Much more than that. You. It had to be because—" She faltered remotely, as if reading from a board abruptly obscured. Then: "I made you come back out of nowhere, and you hated me for it. It was the first intense emotion you'd ever felt for any human being. I think you wanted to kill me more than anything. And I think I'd have let you kill me. My own first really intense emotion, too."

"So," he said, "you got laid to the sound of discordant violins."

She smiled tightly. "You should know. Unfortunately, you can't. It's my past, your future."

"There are two alternatives," he said. "Either you're insane, or someone paid you to spook me about the next flight I take. Which is it?"

"No one paid me."

"Which means you were paid. I hope you kept the money. You may need it for medical expenses."

"Even if you kill me tonight, which you don't, I'd still be waiting for you, in my yesterday. Tomorrow you'll come out of space, and I'll be there." She finished the cigarette, and let it die in the glass ashtray. "I don't think," she said, "you had any right to come back out of death and time and space and haunt me, and ruin my life. I don't think you have any right to be here, in my future, and ruin it again. I shouldn't have tried to find you. But how could I resist?"

Curtis was no longer touching her, just his eyes, fixed on her, long lids blinking now and then, that was all. The rest of the room hadn't been able to hear their conversation once it was trapped inside the booth, a low, coldly impassioned murmur of two voices, but mostly her voice, saying what she claimed to be the truth to him, as if it were a poem, the monologue from some play. So the room cast a look at them now and then, but nothing else. The two Shot players had even finished up and left the bar. And the pianist kept the dark blue tides coming and going on the piano keys, and the chandelier snowed its lights.

"I don't want you to die," she said finally.

"I can make you deliriously happy then," he said, "because I don't intend to."

"I wish," she said, "I could show you the proof of what happened. If I could prove it to you – if I could convince you – But I was sixteen, and the proof got lost, snatched and swept away, like everything else." She met his eyes again, for a long, long time, and then she said, "I don't think you have a soul anyway. Not this Cycle. I gave you a soul. It grew inside you, like the hate you felt for me, unless it wasn't hate at all. And in the end, it looked back at me out of your eyes. But your eyes tonight are like the flat disks of sunglasses."

He said, "If it meant so much, why didn't I stay with you?"

It was the first, and the only admission, that he accepted what she said – not as factual or possible, certainly neither of those – but as a fiction worthy of analysis. But he said it with an edge to his voice that could have skinned an apple.

She said softly, "You couldn't or wouldn't, or weren't allowed to. Or maybe, if you were some extraordinary kind of ghost, the power to survive in time is limited. Like light-cells. Or an echo. Except—" She put her hands together as if examining some element caught between them. "Next twenty you were gone. They searched. The theory was you'd stolen one of the wheel's own lifeboats. I suppose one might have been missing. My grandfather said none was. But that was the theory. The wreck you'd come in on had disintegrated under the tests they'd been subjecting it to. They'd been careful, and that surprised them, but it can happen. As I say, you'd vanished without trace. Almost. Almost." She waited, long enough for seven or eight bars of piano melody to fill the gap between them. At last she said, "You're not going to ask me what, if anything, you left behind. Are you?"

The piano shivered like silver leaves, and he was no longer watching her. Two tears, like silken streamers, unraveled from her eyes. They didn't spoil either her looks or her makeup, and presently they dried and might never have been.

The glow dawned through the Rouelle's marble clock that showed one twenty was folding over into another.

The woman got up. She walked to the bar counter and bought a triple Noira brandy, and took it to the piano, setting the black-gold glass where the Sirtian could reach it. He bowed to her, like the prince he was, and she leaned forward and said something in his ear. He let the waves roll on over the keys while he thought, searching back through the storerooms of his brain to look out what she'd asked for, then, not breaking the rhythm, he tipped the tides of the music over into it. It was one of those old songs the Rouelle Etoile was so adept at conjuring. One of the songs from the celluloid era of twentieth-century Earth. In those same years, in Sirtis, they'd been raising temples of cloudy fire, like blue winter suns. But on the screens of Earth, the black-and-white flickering women, in their high-shouldered dresses that clung to them like snakes, the thin, bruised-eyed men, burning smokily out like the cigarettes in their mouths, had danced and fought and wise-cracked and loved. And all the while the wild pure stars had been waiting, and the Nature of Time, and, two hundred years away another era, of looking back, full circle, amazed, into recognizable eyes and hearts and minds. Everything changes; people, never. No, they never do.

The woman leaned by the piano, listening to the Sirtian play the song, her head averted from the booth. When the song ended, she turned, and Curtis was gone.

About five hours later, her own ship pulled off from the wheel. Nothing happened to the ship, she got wherever she was going, and so did the woman who had sat in the bar with Curtis. Afterwards, no one knew her name. The artisan ship's listing had ten female crew aboard, three female passengers. She could have been any one of those. She became a beautiful strange event, a story that got told around. Because nobody in the bar heard much of the conversation between her and Curtis, guesswork calcified round it, staled it, defused it, and, at length, changed it into just another anecdote, which probably isn't true.

What happened with Day Curtis himself, of course, is known pretty precisely.

At one-oh-seven of the new twenty, he walked along the gantry to the bay where *Napoleon* lay in her repair webbing like a vast wounded whale. Despite earlier predictions, her crew had got her patched, welded, and in fair shape. Certainly she looked sound enough to take the trip out to 98. Sonic reports were still coming in on that one, and a couple of liners were reportedly adrift, split wide open, and treasure-trove swirling out of them as if from a cornucopia. Some of the little lazy ships were even sneaking out now into Warp; the lions and the jackals would be feeding together.

Curtis' crew were eager to be part of the show, and they hadn't anticipated he would be any different in his reaction. Then Curtis knocked the walkway from under them by canceling the drive order and grounding the ship.

He didn't give any reason, but that wasn't uncommon. Generally the reason for anything he did would have been self-explanatory. Not now, of course.

If you credit the story of the black-haired woman, obviously you can figure out what the reason may have been. Curtis didn't credit her, but he did credit she was working on him, and for a larger stake than a fifteen-year-old love affair. Whoever was really behind the scene in the Rouelle had made particular deductions based on Curtis' presumed psychological patterns. Warned off going back into Warp that twenty, Curtis would, contradictorily, throw himself and his ship into immediate action. Or so somebody might have supposed. And if that was what they had predicted and wanted him to do, there must be some excellent reason also for their desires. Perhaps some very special welcome had been rigged for him, out in the Warp. Or the ship herself might have received some extra-special attention . . . If the girl in the Rouelle had been meant to push him into some type of contrary and precipitate heroism, she had failed. Though not believing her warning, he could act as if he did. Intended to race *Napoleon* away into space, he could stay put, and watch for what new developments occurred. And for which individuals or which organization was revealed by them.

Curtis gave his grounding order, and walked back along the gantry.

He had a crew who respected him totally, and, in most cases, hated him in equal measure. Up until then, their wants and their ambitions had run concurrently with his own. Now they'd been slaving on the tall white hip of *Napoleon*, in a blaze of sweat, steam and laserburn, and he strolled over from the bar and tolled their hopes of loot and blood, the reward they always needed to have from him in lucre or kind, because he never offered it any other way.

Half an hour after Curtis walked off the gantry, *Napoleon*'s Second Officer, a man named Doyeneau, led a ten-minute mutiny. By two-thirty, *Napoleon* was free of the Parameter and scorching out toward zero 98.

At two thirty-five, a message was sent back to Curtis at Tempi. He'd made the one immortal mistake of his career, and the message showed it. They were angry enough, that crew of his, to steal his ship, but much too afraid of him to sue for pardon. They would never be back. He must have known he'd lost everything, and when the second message came in, the automatic tracker on sonic, it was only the second most terrible error that twenty.

An hour out into the Warp, a little storm came up. It was so small it could have passed like the blow of a child's fist striking the hull. But Doyeneau, already in a kind of panic, panicked himself into an avoidance maneuver Curtis had contrived maybe a hundred times. Doyeneau dove the ship at the eye of the storm, to break the barriers and get through, but there was no eye in this storm, only a center of spurling matter. And when, caught up in that, Doyeneau gave his order to jump the stream, one continuum to another, *Napoleon*'s patched casing blew, and took out most of the side of the ship.

There is no sound in space, we all know that. No sound, no air, no stopping place. A long fall that never ends, the bottomless pit. Picture a great white fish, cloven in one curving side, shriveling away and away down those empty rivers, her diesel-pod fluttering like a scarlet ember, dying.

At least, that's how it goes. No one was ever entirely sure, since no one ever got back from *Napoleon*. They pieced a few fragments together from sounds picked up, a whole Cycle after, on the delay playback of the sonar here at Tempi. Her death is surmise. Like a lot of things.

Curtis lit off somewhere, at some time. The scenario and the characterization grow vague from the moment that his ship vanished, as if he had lost his soul. The last salient fact is that, one seven-mooned night on Syracuse, in an alley near the space-dock, someone, who is supposed to have resembled Curtis closely, negotiated a deal to rim an unspecified cargo out beyond Andromeda, in a merchantman whose name has not survived. This may or may not have been Curtis, but the far stars are pretty far away. Legends burn out there, good and bad, and reputations dwindle. And there was never anything to stop him altering his name, beyond a touch of legal wrangling. Whatever caused it, you lose him, like an echo, somewhere out among the rumors and the cold green suns.

As for the story about the woman in the Rouelle Etoile, as I said before, it's probably apocryphal. If it weren't, that sort of time paradox is too absurd to handle. It would be crazy enough for a man to get free of an exploding ship, take off in a lifeboat, and then home in on a timeless zone – in the wrong time. And to arrive Cycles out of synchronization, because a girl had drawn him there simply by forewarning him that she would – for that, actually, is what her warning entails . . . Yes, all that's crazy enough. But then to add this other crazier time paradox on top of it: He ducked. The one thing the time cliché can't take, that was what he did. He avoided it. He wasn't *on* the *Napoleon* when she perished. So how could he home in, a magnetized time-ghost, to this whirling ironex wheel, outside of which, in the cool pool of the Parameter, time stands irreparably static?

Clever of you to spot I'm heading somewhere. There is a sort of epilogue. Take it as you find it.

Remember, I said the story was told me on the twenty that they closed the Rouelle Etoile for keeps, the twenty after the tempest. The girl was softly crying her little lost piano notes in the background, the dead chandelier had been trundled away, and the brandy flask was almost dry. Remember too, I said no one here had ever come face to face with the ghost of Day Curtis, on the wheel at Tempi – except there is one story. It's mine. I came face to face with that ghost, and all through that somber twenty, I sat in the Rouelle with him, drinking brandy. Listening to what he had to say. It truly was Curtis, at least to look at, the elegant build, the moon-tan skin, the dark hair, the Roman eyes. But he was about thirty-five years of age, and Curtis wasn't his name. And he wasn't a ghost.

You may have wondered how I knew, or how he knew to tell me, what their conversation was, the woman and Curtis, in the booth, which had been so low the rest of the room couldn't hear it. But maybe she told someone. Found them and told them. Remember what she said to Curtis? About proof, and how it had been snatched away? Or perhaps my Curtis-who-wasn't made it up. Perhaps he'd seen the old videos and a freak likeness to another man, and it took his fancy to pretend, and that's all he was doing. Playing pirates. Sons of pirates.

But if you accept the story, only for a moment, she was sixteen, and very likely quite innocent. She could have had a child, although how, in anyone's book, can a time-ghost convey biological life?

The place where the Rouelle used to be is a storage bay now. But sometimes, when you're alone up there with black nothing crowding against the ports, you can hear the Sirtian's piano still playing, far away. It's the stutter of the sonar link-pipes in the walls, it has to be. There's no time in a white hole, and no true past, and no true future, no matter what the future brings. As for lovers, they come and go, welcome or not. And as for time, outside the Confederation's thirty-eight Parameters, and the thirty-six spinning ironex wheels, it's there. It goes by.

AT DORADO

Geoffrey A. Landis

Geoffrey A. Landis is an American scientist and writer, working for
NASA on planetary exploration, interstellar propulsion, solar power,
and photo-voltaics. He has published over eighty short stories translated into over twenty languages and several novels. He has won the
Nebula, Hugo, and Sturgeon awards for his fiction. "At Dorado" was
first published in *Asimov's Science Fiction Magazine* in 2002.

A man Cheena barely knew came running to the door of the bar. For a
brief second she thought that he might be a customer, but then Cheena
saw he was wearing a leather harness and jockstrap and almost nothing
else. One of the bar-boys from a dance house along the main spiral-path to the
downside.

In the middle of third shift, there was little business in the bar. Had there
been a ship in port, of course, the bar would be packed with rowdy sailors, and
she would have been working her ass off trying to keep them all lubricated and
spending their port-pay. But between dockings, the second-shift maintenance
workers had already finished their after-work drinks and left, and the place was
mostly empty.

It was unusual that a worker from one of the downside establishments would
drop into a bar so far upspinward, and Cheena knew instantly that something
was wrong. She flicked the music off – nobody was listening anyway – and
he spoke.

"Hoya," he said. "A wreck, a wreck. They fish out debris now." The door
hissed shut, and he was gone.

Cheena pushed into the crowd that was already gathered at the maintenance dock.
The gravity was so low at the maintenance docks that they were floating more
than standing, and the crowd slowly roiled into the air and back down. Cheena
saw the bar-boy who had brought the news, and a gaggle of other barmaids and
bar-boys, a few maintenance workers, some Cauchy readers, navigators, and a
handful of waiting-for-work sailors. "Stand back, stand back," a lone security
dockworker said. "Nothing to see yet." But nobody moved back. "Which ship
was it?" somebody shouted, and two or three others echoed: "What ship? What
ship?" That was what everybody wanted to know.

"Don't know yet," the security guy said. "Stand back now, stand back."

"*Hesperia*," said a voice behind. Cheena turned, and the crowd did as well.
It was a tug pilot, still wearing his fluorescent yellow flight suit, although his
helmet was off. "The wreck was *Hesperia*."

There was a moment of silence, and then a soft sigh went through the crowd, followed by a rising babble of voices, some of them relieved, some of them curious, some dazed by the news. *Hesperia*, Cheena thought. The word was like a silken ribbon suddenly tied around her heart.

"They're bringing debris in now," said the tug pilot.

Some of the girls Cheena knew had many sailors as husbands. It was no great risk; any given ship only came to port once or twice a year, and each sailor could believe the carefully-crafted fiction that Zee or Dayl or whoever it was was alone, was waiting patient and hopeful for him and only him. If the unlikely happens, and two ships with two different sailor-husbands come in to port at the same time – well, with luck and connivance and hastily-fabricated excuses, the two husbands will never meet.

Cheena, however, believed in being faithful, and for her there was only one man: Daryn, a navigator. She might earn a few florins by drinking beer with another sailor, and leading him on, if a ship was in port, and Dari was not on it. What of it? That was, after all, what the barmaids were paid for; drinks could just as easily be served by automata. But her heart could belong to only one man, and would only be satisfied if that one man loved only her. And Daryn had loved her. Or so he had once proclaimed, before they had fought.

Daryn.

Daryn Bey was short and dark, stocky enough that one might take him for a dockworker instead of a navigator. His skin was the rich black of a deep-space sailor, a color enhanced with biochemical dye to counter ultraviolet irradiation. Against the skin, luminescent white tattoos filigreed across every visible centimeter of his body. When he had finally wooed her and won her and taken her to where they could examine each other in private, she found the rest of him had been tattooed as well, most deliciously tattooed. He was a living artwork, and she could study each tiny centimeter of him for hours.

And Daryn sailed with *Hesperia*.

The wormholes were the port's very reason for existing, the center of Cheena's universe. In view of their importance it was odd, perhaps, that Cheena almost never went to look at them. In her bleak, destructive mood, she closed the bar and headed upspiral. Patryos, owner of the Subtle Tiger, would be angry at her, because in the hours after news of a wreck, when nobody had yet heard real information and everybody had heard rumors, people would naturally come to the bar; business would be good. Let him come and serve drinks himself, she thought; she needed some solitude. The thought of putting on a show of cheerfulness and passing around gossip along with liquor made her feel slightly sick.

Still, sailors – even navigators – sometimes changed ships. Daryn might not have been on *Hesperia*. It might not be certain that the ship had been *Hesperia*; it could be debris from an ancient wreck, just now washing through the strange time tides of the wormhole. Or it could even be wreckage from far in the future, perhaps some other ship to be named *Hesperia*, one not yet even built. The rigid laws of relativity mean that a wormhole pierces not space alone, but also time.

Half of the job of a navigator, Daryn had explained to her once – and the most important half at that – came in making sure that the ship sailed to the right when as well as to the right where. Sailing a Cauchy loop would rip the ship apart; it was the navigator's calculation to make sure the ship never entered its own past, unless it was safely light years away. The ship could skim, but never cross, its own Cauchy horizon.

Cheena made her way upspiral, until at last she came to the main viewing lounge. It featured a huge circular window, five meters across, a window that looked out on the emptiness, and on the wormhole. She entered, and then instantly pulled back: the usually-empty lounge was throbbing with spectators. Of course it would be, she thought; they are watching a disaster.

She couldn't stay there, but as she stood indecisive, there drifted into her mind like a piece of floating debris the thought that once Daryn had taken her to another viewing area, not exactly a lounge, but a maintenance hangar with a viewport. It was out of the public areas, of course, but Cheena had been at the station since she had been born, and knew that if she always moved briskly, as if she belonged, and arrived at a door just after an authorized person had opened it, nobody would question her. And after a few minutes she found her maintenance hangar empty.

There was no gravity here, and she floated in front of it, trying to blank away her thoughts.

The port station orbited slowly around the wormhole named *Dorado*, largest of the three wormholes in the nexus. They floated in interstellar space, far from any star, but light was redundant here: there was nothing there to see.

The Dorado wormhole, a thousand kilometers across, could only be seen after the eyes had adapted to the star field, and realized that the stars seen through the wormhole were different from the stars drifting slowly in the background. After her eyes adapted, she could see a dozen tiny sparkles of light orbiting the wormhole, automated beacons to guide starships to correct transit trajectories through the hole. And now she could see ships, tiny one-man maintenance dories, no larger than a coffin with metal arms, drifting purposefully through space, collecting debris.

Cheena deliberately made her mind blank. She didn't want to think about debris, and what that might mean. She stared at the wormhole, telling herself that it was a hole in space ten thousand light years long, that through the wormhole she was seeing stars nearly on the other side of the galaxy, impossibly distant and yet just a tiny skip away.

Cheena had never been to any of them. She had been born on the station, and would die on the station. Sailors lived for the star passage, loved the disruption of space as they fell through the topological incongruence of the wormholes. To Cheena, the thought filled her with dread. She had never wanted to be any-where else.

She had explained this to Daryn once. He loved her, couldn't he stay home, with her, make a home on the port? He had laughed, a gentle laugh, a good-hearted laugh that she loved to hear, but still a laugh.

"No, my beautiful one. The stars get into your blood, don't you know? If I stay in port too long, the stars call to me, and if I do not find a ship then, I will go mad." He kissed her gently. "But you know that I will always come back to you."

She nodded, contented but not contented, for she had always known that this was all she could hope for.

Hesperia, she thought. He sailed out on *Hesperia*. She knew that she would never again hear that ship's name spoken, for there was a superstition among the sailors, and the port crew, never to say the name of a wrecked ship aloud. From now on it would be "the ship," or "that ship, you know the one," and everybody would know.

She floated, staring without seeing, for what must have been hours. The tiny dories were returning now, the robotic arms of each cluttered with debris, and tangled in with the debris, they were bringing in the first of the dead.

The port crew had their legends. Some of them might even have been true. Once, according to a story, a ship of ancient design had come unexpectedly to Pskov station. Pskov was a station circling Viadei wormhole, two jumps away from the port. Cheena had never been there, had never left the port, but the rumors circulated through all of the network. Even before the ship had docked, the portkeepers located the records: the ship was *Tsander*. *Tsander* had entered Viadei three hundred and seventy years ago, during a massive solar flare, one of the largest flares ever recorded, and was lost.

Tsander tumbled out of the wormhole mouth with all sensors blind from flare damage, and the tug crew of Pskov station had found it, caught it, stabilized it, and towed it to the docks.

At liberty in the port, the crew of the *Tsander* spoke in strange accents that were barely understandable. It was a miracle that the ship had emerged at all; all its navigation systems – of an unreliable design long since obsolete – were burned out. *Tsander*'s crew had marveled at the size and sophistication of the entertainments of Pskov port, had been incredulous to hear of the extent of the wormhole network. They offered as payment archaic coins of an ancient nation that was now nearly forgotten, coins that had worth only for their value as curiosities.

After a week of repairing their ship, the crew took their ship *Tsander* back into the wormhole Viadei, vowing that they would return to their own time with a story that would earn drinks for them forever.

No one at the station told them that the ancient logs held comprehensive records of every wormhole passage, and the logs, meticulously kept despite revolutions and disasters and famine, had no record of *Tsander* ever re-emerging in the past.

Perhaps they had known. They were sailors, the crew of *Tsander*: for all that they wore quaint costumes and spoke in archaic accents, they were sailors.

Back at the maintenance dock, Cheena watched, waiting and dreading. She should never have let him go, should have held him tight, instead of pushing him away. The crowd was larger than it had been before, and Cheena was pushed up against a man wearing only a feather cloak over a fur loincloth. "Sorry," she said, and as she said it, she realized that it was the bar-boy from the downspin dance hall, the one who had first come to the Subtle Tiger and told her that there had been a wreck. On an impulse, she touched his arm. "Name's Cheena," she told him.

He looked back at her, perhaps startled that she had spoken. "Tayo," he said. "You're the mid-shift girl from Subtle Tiger. I seen you around." He was breathing shallowly and his eyes trembled, perhaps blinking back tears.

"You had somebody on that ship, the one we talked about?" she asked.

"I dunno." He trembled. "I—I hope not. A navigator."

Suddenly, irrationally, Cheena was certain that his sailor was Daryn too, that Daryn had had two lovers in the port. But then he continued, "He shipped out on *Singapore*," and she knew it wasn't Daryn after all.

A spray of relief washed over Cheena, although she knew it had been silly for her to have thought Daryn had two lovers in port. When would he have had time?

"—but you know how sailors are. He said he'd be back to me on the next ship this direction, and, and if *Hes* – if that ship was coming inbound . . ."

She put her arm around Tayo. "He's okay. He wouldn't be on that ship, I'm sure of it."

Tayo chewed his lip, but he seemed more cheerful. "Are you sure?"

Cheena nodded sagely, although she knew no such thing. "Positive."

When a ship comes to disaster at a wormhole, the wreckage sprays through both time and space. Cheena didn't even know when *Hesperia* had wrecked, possibly years or even centuries in the future. She held on to that thought.

And another ship came in, not through the Dorado wormhole, but via Camino Estrella, the smallest of the three wormholes, one that led toward an old, rich cluster of worlds in the Orion arm. It would stay at the port for three days, letting its crew relax, and then depart through Dorado for the other side of the galaxy.

And there was nothing for it but to prepare for the arrival of the sailors. With a ship coming into port, Patryos could not spare her, and there was no place at the port for a person without a job. But when her shift ended, she drifted over to the maintenance port, wordlessly waiting for them to post names of the bodies.

Nothing.

Tayo, the boy from the downside bar, dropped in at the beginning of her next shift and updated her with the latest gossip from the maintenance investigation. They had finished gathering the pieces, he told her, and had gathered enough to date the wreck. It was very nearly contemporal, he told her, and her heart suddenly chilled.

"Past or future?" she said.

"Two hundred hours pastward of standard," he told her. "They said."

Eight days. She did a quick calculation in her head. Right now, through the Dorado wormhole mouth, the port stood fifty-two days pastward of Viadei mouth, and Viadei was forty days in the future of Standard. So – if the mouths had not drifted further apart, and if *Hesperia* had taken the straightforward loop, and not some strange path through – the wreckage came from six days into their future.

Everybody at the port would be doing the same calculations, she knew. "How about your sailor?" Cheena asked, but from the radiance of Tayo's face, she already knew the answer.

"He went out via Dorado."

And so he was almost certainly safe, she thought, unless he took a very long passage pastward. Dorado opened fifty-two days futureward. Not quite impossible, if he took a long-enough loop, but unlikely enough that Tayo could consider his lover safe. Cheena has no such consolation; she knew that Dari had crewed the doomed ship.

Tayo looked up. "Thought you might want to know the latest," he said. "Sorry, but I gotta get to the hall. Sailors will be arriving in maybe an hour, and the boss wants me on the floor."

She nodded. "Give 'em hell," she said.

Tayo looked at her. "You going to be okay?"

"Sure." She smiled. "I'm fine."

Cheena went back to cleaning the bar, went back to hating herself. She had kicked Daryn out, called him a two-timing bastard, and worse; told him that he didn't love her. Daryn had protested, tried to soothe her, but the one thing he didn't say was that what she had heard was wrong.

It was another sailor who told her, a sailor she didn't know, who had remarked that he wished he was as lucky with women as Daryn. "Who?" she had asked, although in her heart she knew. "Daryn Bey," the sailor had said. "Lucky bastard has a wife in every port."

"Excuse me," she had told him, "I'll be back in a moment." She had put on a modest dress and gone upspin, gone into a bar near officers' quarters that she knew he would never frequent. "I'm looking for Daryn Bey," she told a man at the bar. "I've got a message sent from his wife in Pskov port. Anybody know him?"

"A message from Karina?" one of the officers at the bar asked. "She only saw him two days ago, why would she have a message?"

"That Daryn," one of the officers said, shaking his head. "I wonder how he keeps them all straight?"

She had been in no mind to listen. She went back and threw his clothes out of her apartment, scattered his books and papers and simulation disks down the corridor with a savage glee. Then she bolted the door and refused to listen to his pounding or shouted apologies. Later, she heard, he had shipped out on the *Hesperia*, and she had felt glad that he was gone.

She was still cleaning the bar when the owner Patryos came in. "You going to be okay?" he asked.

It was the same thing Tayo had asked. Cheena nodded, without saying anything.

"I heard that the names are being listed," Patryos said, "up in maintenance."

She turned her head a little toward him, enough to show she was listening.

"You want to go up? I expect the first hour after the sailors start coming in will still be pretty calm." He shrugged. "I can spare you for a little, if you want to go up."

She didn't look up, just shook her head.

"Go!" he told her, and she looked up at him in surprise. "Anybody can see you haven't been worth anything, and you won't be worth anything until you know for certain. One way or the other."

He lowered his voice, and said, more calmly, "One way or the other, it's better to know. Take it from me. Go."

Cheena nodded, dropped her rag on the bar, and left.

She knew where to go in the maintenance quarter, although she had never had any reason to go there. Everybody knew. Behind the door was a desk, and behind the desk a door. Sitting at the desk was a single maintenance man. She came up to him, and said quietly, "Daryn Bey."

His eyes flickered. "Relationship?"

"I'm his downspin wife." It was a marriage that was only recognized within the boundaries of the port, but a fully legal one. The maintenance man looked away for a moment, and then said, "I'm sorry." He paused for a moment, and then asked, "would you like to see him?"

She nodded, and the maintenance man gestured toward the door behind him.

The room was cold. Death is cold, she thought. She was alone, and wondered what to do. A second maintenance man appeared through another door, and gestured to her to follow. This close to spin axis, gravity was light, and he moved in an eerie, slow-motion bounce. She almost floated behind him, her feet nearly useless. She wasn't used to low gravity.

He stopped at a pilot's chair. No, Daryn wasn't a pilot, she thought, this is the wrong man, and then she saw him.

The maintenance man withdrew, and she stared into Daryn's face.

Vacuum hematoma had been hard on him, and he looked like he had been beaten by a band of thugs. His eyes were closed. The tattoos still glowed, faintly, and that was the worst thing of all, that his tattoos still were alive, and Daryn wasn't.

She reached out and put her fingertips against his cheek with a feather's touch, stroking along his jawline with a single finger. Suddenly, irrationally, she was angry at him. She wanted to tell him how inconsiderate he was, how selfish and idiotic and, and, and – but he was not listening. He was never going to listen.

The anger helped her to keep from crying.

By the time she returned to the Subtle Tiger, knots of sailors were walking upspin and downspin the corridors, talking and sometimes singing, dropping into a bar for a moment to see if it felt like a place to spend the rest of the shift, and then moving on, or staying for a drink. She passed a ferret crew going upspin toward the docks. The ferrets, slender and lithe as snakes with legs, squirmed in their cages, nearly insane with excitement over the prospect of being set free on the just-docked ship to hunt for stowaway rats.

She took over the bar from Patryos, serving drinks in a daze, unable to think of any quick responses to the double entendres and light-hearted suggestions offered by the sailors. Most of them knew that she had a sailor husband, though, and didn't press her very hard, and of course they wouldn't know that he had been in the wreck.

In fact, none of them would even know about the wreck yet; unless they had transferred across through an uptime wormhole, it was still in their future, and the port workers would be careful not to say anything that would cause a catastrophe. An incipient contradiction due to a loop in history would close the wormhole. A little information can leak from the future into the past, but history must be consistent. If enough information leaks downtime to threaten an inconsistency, the offending wormhole connection can snap.

The port circled the wormhole cluster, light-years from any star. If their passage to the rest of civilization by the wormhole connection failed, it would be a thousand years of slower-than-light travel to reach the fringes of civilization. So the port crew did not need to be reminded to avoid incipient contradiction; it was as natural to them as manufacturing oxygen.

Slowly the banter and the routine of serving elevated Cheena's mood. One of the sailors asked to buy her a drink, and she accepted it and drank philosophically. It was hard to stay gloomy when liquor and florins were flowing so freely. She had kicked him out, after all; he was nothing to her. She could replace him any night from any of a dozen eager suitors – maybe even this one, if he was as nice as he seemed.

And the bar was suddenly especially hectic, with a dozen sailors asking for drinks at once, and half of them asking for more than that, and two more singing a rather clever duet she hadn't heard before, a song about a navigator who kept a pet mouse in the front of his pants, with the heavyset sailor singing the mouse's part in a squeaky falsetto. She was busy smiling and serving and taking orders, so it wasn't surprising at all that she didn't see him come in. He was quiet, after all, and took a seat at the bar and waited for her to come to him.

Daryn.

She was so surprised that she started to drop the beer she was holding, and caught it with a jerk, spilling a great splash of it across the bar and half across two sailors. The one she'd caught full-on jumped up, staring down at his splattered uniform. The one sitting with him started to laugh. "Now you've had your baptism in beer, and the night is still young, say now," he said. After a moment the one who had been splashed started to laugh as well. "A good sign, then, wouldn't you say?"

"Sorry, there," she said, bringing them both fresh drinks, waving her hand when they started to pay. "The last one was on you, so this one's on the house," she told them, and they both laughed. All the time she carefully avoided looking toward Daryn.

Daryn.

He sat at the end of the bar, drinking the beer that the other barmaid had brought him, not gesturing for her to come over, but smugly aware that, sooner or later, she would. He said something that made the other barmaid giggle, and she wondered what it might have been. She served a few of the other sailors, and then, knowing that sooner or later she would, she went to talk to him.

"Alive, alive," she said. It was barely more than a whisper.

"Myself, in the flesh," Daryn said. He smiled his huge, goonish smile. "Surprised to see me, yes?"

"How can you be here?" she said. "I thought you were on – on that ship."

"*Hesperia*? Yeah. But we docked alongside *Lictor* at Tarrytown port, and *Lictor* was short a navigator, and *Hesperia* could spare me for a bit, and I knew that *Lictor* was heading to stop here, and I'd have a chance to see you, and—" he spread his hands. "I can't stay."

"You can't stay," she repeated.

"No, I have to sail with *Lictor*, so I can catch up with *Hesperia* at Dulcinea." He looked up at her. She was still standing stupidly there over him. "But I had to see you."

"You had to see me," she repeated slowly, as if trying to understand.

"I had to tell you," he said. "You have to know that you're the only one."

You are such a sweet liar, she thought, how can I trust you? But his smile brought back a thousand memories of time they had spent together, and it was like a sweet ache in her throat. "The only one," she repeated, still completely unable to think of any words of her own to say.

"You aren't still angry, are you?" he said. "Please, tell me you're not still angry. You know that you've always been the only one."

Morning came to the second-shift, and she propped her head up on one elbow to look across the bed at him. The glow of his tattoos cast a mottled pattern of soft light against the walls and ceiling.

Daryn awoke, rolled over, and looked at her. He smiled, a radiant smile, with his eyes still smoky with sleep, and leaned forward to kiss her. "There will be no other," he said. "This time I promise."

She kissed him, her eyes closed, knowing it would be the last kiss they would ever have.

"I know," she said.

3 RMS, GOOD VIEW

Karen Haber

Karen Haber is an American writer who has published nine novels,
including *Star Trek Voyager: Bless the Beasts*. She is also the coauthor
of *The Science of the X-Men* and an art critic and historian. Her short
fiction has been published in *Asimov's Science Fiction Magazine*, *The
Magazine of Fantasy & Science Fiction* and many others. This story was
first published in *Asimov's Science Fiction Magazine* in 1990.

"Apartment for rent," said the net ad. "3 rms, gd view. Potrero Hill
area, $1200 a month, utilities pd."

It sounded like a dream. Every San Francisco apartment I had
seen in the last six months had waiting lists for their waiting lists.

"Southern exp. Pets OK."

Better and better.

Then I found the catch. The apartment was available, all right. In 1968.

Don't misunderstand me. I'm not one of those with a temporal bias. And God
knows, I've always wanted to live in San Francisco.

I first came north in '07 on a family expedition to the Retro-Pan-Pacific
Exposition. The fair was fun, but what I loved even better was San Francisco:
the sunswept hillsides, the streets lined with bright flower boxes, the digital-
ized ding-a-ling of the streetcar bells floating in the cool air, the fog creeping
in at dusk. Heaven, especially after thirteen summers spent baking in the San
Fernando Valley. I vowed to come back.

It took me seventeen years and a divorce, but I did it. Right after I graduated
from Boalt and passed the bar.

Unfortunately, housing was tight – in fact, strangulated. The city had instituted
severe building restrictions back in '03 and got what it asked for: all residential
construction not only stopped but vanished, gone eastward to the greener pastures of Contra Costa County.

I got on the waiting list of every real estate agent in the Bay Area, but the best
digs I would find was a studio apartment – more like a large walk-in closet with
plumbing – in a renovated duplex in Yuba City. Add on a three-hour commute to
my job in San Francisco's financial district, and we're not exactly talking about
positive quality of life.

So when I saw the net ad, I jumped. And stopped in midair. As I said, I have no
temporal biases. But I'm not one of those sentimental history nuts just dying to
travel back to the Crucifixion, either. I like real time just fine, thank you. Always
have. It's a peculiar trait, considering my family.

My grandmother lives in 1962, and has for the last ten years. She said it was the last time that America believed in itself as a country. And it's safe. She likes the peace and quiet of the pre-computer era. "Loosen up, Chrissy," she said to me before she left. "You should be more flexible. There's nothing wrong with living in the past."

My brother lives in 1997 where he's pierced his nose, lip, eyebrows, and had his scalp tattooed in concentric circles of red and black. Every now and then I get a note from him through e-mail: "Come visit. We'll hit the clubs. Don't you ever take a vacation? I thought girls wanted to have fun."

As for Mom, well, she likes 1984. But then, she always did have an odd sense of humor.

Pardon me if I like realtime best. I've always had my feet planted firmly in the present. Practical, sturdy Christine. In the lofty hierarchy of Mount Olympus, I'd be placed just to the left of Zeus in the marble frieze, in the Athena position. Yes, I even have the gray eyes and brown hair to go with the no-nonsense attitude. I'm tall and muscular, as befits your basic warrior goddess/business attorney type. My stature is useful, too – who wants a lawyer who doesn't look intimidating?

And I've never wanted to go backward. We all remember the first reports of time-travel glitches. Shari, one of my prelaw classmates at Berkeley, wanted to spend her Christmas break in the village where her French great-great-great-grandmother lived. But a power surge from Sacramento sent her to the fourteenth century instead. Talk about your bad neighborhoods. If she hadn't gotten her shots before she left – complaining all the way – she'd probably have come back sporting buboes the size and color of rotten nectarines.

After Shari's brush with the Black Death, I told myself I was immune to the allure of era-hopping. I ignored the net ads for Grand Tours: the Crucifixion and sack of Rome package, $1,598. Dark Ages through the Enlightenment, two weeks for $2,100, all meals and tips included. (These packages are especially popular with the Japanese, who have become time-travel junkies. And why not? They can go away and come back without losing any realtime at work.)

Even when the Koreans made portable transport units for home or office, I shrugged and stuck by realtime. But when I saw the listing in the paper, I looked around the stucco walls of my apartment/cell and threw all my sturdy, practical notions to the wind. An apartment on Potrero Hill? In a nanosecond, Pallas Athena transmuted into impulsive Mercury.

My hands trembled with excitement and impatience as I sent my credit history to Jerry Raskin, the real estate agent listed on the ad. Almost immediately I received an appointment to view the apartment. This Raskin sure didn't waste any time.

We met at his office in the Tenderloin. He was a short man, barely reaching my shoulder, with thinning dark hair and a doughy nose that looked like a half-baked biscuit. A matte black Mitsubishi temp transport unit sat behind his desk. I stared at it uneasily.

"Want to look over the premises?" he asked. He gestured toward the unit.

"Uh, yes. Of course." I took a deep breath and stepped over the threshold of the transport.

There was a sudden fragmentation of color, of sound. I was in a high white space, falling. I was stepping into an apartment on Potrero Hill, shaking my head in wonder.

Even before the shimmering transport effect had diminished, Jerry had launched into his sales pitch. "It's a gem," he said proudly. "I hardly ever get this kind of listing." He flicked an invisible piece of lint from the shoulder of his green silk suit. "Once every five years."

It was perfect. Big sunny rooms paneled in pine, full of light, ready for plants. Hardwood floors. There was even a little balcony off the bedroom where I could watch the fog drift in over Twin Peaks in the summer afternoons.

All wound up and oblivious to my rapture, Raskin rattled on. "You can install a transport unit in the closet for your morning and evening commute to realtime. It's a steal. What's your rail commute cost from Yuba City?"

I didn't need much convincing. "I'll take it."

"Two year lease," he said. "Sign here." Then he brandished an additional piece of paper. "This too."

"What is it?" I was Pallas Athena again, staring down suspiciously onto the sweaty center of his bald spot. "If this is a pet restriction clause, I'm going to protest. Your ad didn't say anything about it. I've got a cat." I didn't bother to mention that I kept MacHeath at work – there was more room for him there than at home. But wherever – and whenever – I went, he went.

"Sure, sure," Raskin said. "You can keep your kitty as long as you pay a deposit. This is just your standard noninterference contract."

"Noninterference contract?"

He looked at me like I was stupid. It rarely happens. When it does, I don't like it.

"You know," he said, and recited in a sing-song voice: "Don't change the past or the past will change you. The time laws. You lawyers understand this kind of thing. You, and you alone, are responsible for any dislocation of past events, persons or things, et cetera, et cetera. Read the small print and sign."

A sudden chill teased my upper vertebrae. Noninterference? Well, why would I interfere with the past? The morning sunlight streamed in through the big window in the front room. High clouds scudded over the hillside. I shook off the shivers and signed.

A week later, I took up residence, hanging my tiny collection of photos, putting down rugs, and glorying in my privacy. MacHeath didn't care much for the transport effect but he approved of his new improved situation. After sniffing every corner of the place, he made an appointment with the sun and spent the rest of the day following it from window to window.

Life's pendulum swung me between work and home, uptime and downtime, in an easy arc. Thanks to the transport I could leave the house at any time of day and return a moment later. This made for a great deal of quality time, spent snuggled up with MacHeath on the red corduroy sofa, and on my own in the heart of a smaller, cozier city. I wandered gratefully along the waterfront, bought sourdough bread and lingered over coffee in North Beach jazz clubs. Everywhere was color and life and music: garish psychedelic posters printed in what I think were called Day-Glo inks, announcing musical groups with odd names like the

Jackson's Airplane. Shaggy-haired, brightly dressed, childishly friendly people piled in casual groups on the street, in buses, and in the old houses lining Haight Street and Ashbury. I fell in love with the past – at least with San Francisco's past.

Uptime, at work, they asked me how I could stand to watch history go by without comment.

"Don't you ever want to warn somebody?" said Bill Hawthorne, the senior partner. "Don't you ever want to call up Martin Luther King or Robert Kennedy and say, 'Stay away from hotel balconies,' or 'Don't go in the kitchen'?"

"Shame on you, Bill," I said. "You know that's against the law."

In fact, I watched, agog, as the alarming parade of assassinations and demonstrations took place. History on the hoof. I began to see why people got hooked on the past. It's a much realer form of video.

And during the year I lived in 1968, Martin Luther King was assassinated in Memphis, and Robert Kennedy in Los Angeles. And somebody moved into the downstairs apartment.

It had remained empty for so long that I'd begun to think of it as part of my domain. Oh, I knew that some uptime renter would probably appear one morning, strangely dressed, keeping to him or herself. I'd seen one or two folks in the neighborhood whom I suspected of being residential refugees from uptime like me, but I had avoided them, and they, me. We all played the game with discretion.

I was out of town, uptime, when the people downstairs moved in. The first sign I had of their presence was the primal beat of rock music reverberating through my lovingly stained floorboards, occasionally punctuated by the high manic whine of amplified electric guitars. Boom-boom-bah. Boom-boom-bah. For five hours I considered various legal strategies showing just cause for murder. Sorry, Your Honor, but it was self-defense. Their music made me psychotic and if I hadn't stopped it, the entire neighborhood would have been at risk and all of history would have been changed so I had to do it, don't you see?

About three in the morning, somebody turned off the music.

The next day, as I was blearily putting out my garbage, I met my neighbor. He was sitting in the backyard, smoking a sweet-smelling cigarette. The pungent smoke curled up above his head in lazy circles. Long wavy blond hair fell to the middle of his back. He was wearing jeans and a brown suede vest but aside from that his interest in clothing seemed minimal. His toenails were black with grime.

"Name's Duffy," he said. He jerked his head at a hefty woman in a long muslin skirt and peasant blouse who stood in the doorway, smiling spacily at me. "That's Parvati." Parvati's strawberry-blond hair was gathered into two fat braids that fell past her knees. She was wearing metal-rimmed eyeglasses whose lenses flashed prismatic reflections on the grass. I stared, fascinated. I'd forgotten that in this era people used external devices to correct their vision.

The head jerked again, this time toward an urchin with a dirty face, stringy blond hair, and big blue eyes. "Our kid, Rainbow."

Rainbow wiped her nose against the back of her hand and stared at me. All three of them stared at me, at my burr haircut, severe business suit, dark shoes, glossy briefcase. I realized that, to my new hippie neighbors, I must have looked like some kind of strange male impersonator.

"Hi," I said. "Nice to meet you." I began to climb the stairs to my apartment.

"Far out," Duffy said. He was staring at my briefcase. "You some kind of secretary or actress or something?"

"Something." I was through my door and had closed it behind me before he could ask anything else.

Weekends I took long walks through Golden Gate Park. It was green, beautiful, and filled with people who were probably Duffy's relatives.

"Peace," they said, and I nodded.

"Love."

I smiled.

"Could you lay a little bread on me, please?"

I shook my head and walked away, confused – did I look like a baker?

For trips to the grocery store I bought a lime-green Volkswagen Beetle – the classic – with a dented purple fender, third-hand, and after some abrupt bucking rides down the block, mastered the quaint antique stick shift and clutch.

As for clothing, well, I found used jeans in the neighborhood Army-Navy store and a loose-fitting top of muslin tie-dyed pink and red. The shirt itched a bit when I wore it and turned my underwear gray-pink in the washer, but it was good camouflage. With a red bandana wrapped around my head to cover my short hair, I almost managed to look inconspicuous.

I quickly learned my neighbors' schedule: they stayed up all night vibrating my apartment with their music and slept all day.

Apparently Rainbow didn't go to school. Once, I glanced out my window to see her staring up hungrily at my place. I tried not to see her. I really tried.

One night, late, as the guitars whined and I was about to switch on my noise dampers, there was a knock at the door.

"Who is it?"

"Duffy."

I opened the door a crack. "What's up?"

Lids at half-mast, he peered at me and smiled muzzily. "Thought you might want to come to a party." He smiled muzzily.

"No thanks. I need my sleep."

"C'mon, don't be such a hard lady," he said. "Parvati's gone to see her folks. Just you 'n me."

I almost laughed. Men rarely looked at me the way he was looking at me now. While I might have welcomed it from one or two of the attorneys I knew in realtime, I was not interested in this dirty, lazy, antediluvian jerk.

"That's too small a party for me. No thanks."

"Hey, Parvati won't mind. Whatever goes down is cool with her."

"Congratulations. Hope she knows a good lawyer when things start to warm up." I shut the door.

The apartment was blissfully quiet after that – in fact, I didn't hear Duffy's music for at least a week. Didn't see him or Rainbow, or any of their friends except for once, when I was putting out the garbage, Rainbow appeared at the front window, pressed her little hands against the pane, and stared out at me. I smiled. She didn't smile back. When she turned to walk away, I saw that her hands had left dirty smudges on the glass.

I spent a week in realtime on an important case, and when I got back, discovered that I had new neighbors.

Duffy and his family were gone. In their place were two skinny guys in their twenties with long dark hair, beards, and the same interest in the same kind of loud guitar music. They barely acknowledged my presence, which was fine.

One night, late, after my noise dampers had cycled and shut down, I heard a child crying. It was the high, keening, hopeless sound of one who doesn't expect to be comforted. The kind of sound no child should ever have to make, any time or place.

I got out of bed, listened, heard it again, opened the front door. Then I couldn't hear it any more. The night was silent save for the creaking floorboards under my feet. Was I imagining things?

MacHeath yawned elaborately as I got back into bed and made a sleepy inquisitive sound.

"It's nothing," I said. "Bad dream."

The next night I heard it again – the sound of a child crying hopelessly, long after everybody else in the world was asleep.

Two days later, I saw her.

Rainbow was standing in the backyard, weaving back and forth.

Her eyes were half-closed as though she were stoned.

I took a step toward her. "Honey, are you all right?"

She opened her eyes. The pupils were massive, almost engulfing the blue irises.

"Rainbow, where's your mommy?"

"Mommy?" She looked at me, her face crumpled into tears, and she ran into the house.

I didn't hear the crying again after that.

But I did meet one of Rainbow's babysitters. He was waiting outside one morning as I brought out the garbage.

"Hey, sister."

I ignored him, thinking about torts, about deed restrictions. About Rainbow.

Suddenly there was a hand on my shoulder. "Hey. You deaf?" Another hand attached itself to my ass.

I leaned toward him. He came closer. I grabbed his arm and, ducking, pulled hard. He landed headfirst, sprawled among the garbage cans. For a moment, I thought that I'd killed him. Then he groaned and rolled over onto his side. He lay there, stunned, peering up at me.

"Hands off," I said, enunciating carefully. "I don't know you. I don't want to." I kicked the can beside his head to emphasize the point. He winced and nodded.

After that, he left me alone. But I came home one night to find that the door to my apartment had been vandalized: somebody had tried to force the lock. Good thing I'd brought a security sealer from uptime and installed it. Whoever had attempted the deed had contented themselves with carving the word "bitch" into the wood just above the doorknob.

Don't you forget it.

I left the graffito exactly where it was.

The crying at night resumed. I began to wonder if I should call somebody. But who? Where were Duffy and Parvati? Were they really even her parents? And what kind of child welfare agencies were available in the 1960s in San Francisco? Could Rainbow hope for anything better than what she had right now? Besides, the time laws were explicit: No interference.

I didn't know what to do, so I waited. She who hesitates, loses.

I transported home one night at eleven o'clock into a dark smoke-filled apartment. Fire. Where? I couldn't find the source. I felt the floor – hot, too hot. No time to waste. I called the fire department, grabbed MacHeath, and was halfway out the door before I remembered the transport unit. Cursing, I disconnected it, threw it into my briefcase, and ran down the stairs, arms full of squirming orange cat.

By the time I got to the pavement, the lower apartment was completely engulfed, the flames roaring. As the upper story caught I watched the flames dance up the curtains and part my front window. Imagined them licking and consuming my rugs, quilts, clothing. My life. I could hear the deafening screams of sirens as fire trucks raced down the street.

Lights came on in houses up and down the block and sleepy faces peered through windows, through open doors. Tears – from smoke or fear, I don't know which – ran down my face to soak MacHeath's fur. He struggled furiously, trying to get away from the strange sounds, the people, the dark. Finally I stowed him in my Beetle.

Firemen kicked in the door downstairs and played water from a rubber hose into the inferno. It might have all been interestingly antique if it hadn't been happening to me.

Those firemen did good work. Within an hour the flames had subsided. The charred timbers sent plumes of smoke high into the air, but the fire was dead.

Shivering, I watched as the bodies were carried out: blackened beyond recognition, more like burned logs than people. Nine corpses, nine flaking, reeking corpses. And one more, smaller than the rest. The last to be brought out. Rainbow.

"Found her by the back window." The fireman's face was blackened, his voice hoarse. "I think she was trying to open it and get out. But the damned thing was painted shut." Gently he set her down. "Jesus, I've got two at home around her age. Damned shame."

"Yeah." I didn't trust myself to say more. Quickly as I could, I turned around and got out of there. I spent the night at a neighbor's house. The next morning, I waited until my Good Samaritan had left for work at the shipyards, then I plugged in the transport, set it for autoretrieve, and took MacHeath back to realtime, right into Jerry Raskin's office.

"You son of a bitch!" I grabbed him by the lapel of his cheap silver coat. "You knew that place was going to burn down when you rented it to me."

"What?" He stared at my soot-stained face and there was real fear in his eyes.

"I had no idea. Chrissy, you've got to believe me."

I shook him until his teeth chattered. "You are required by law to do a time sweep in order to alert tenants to potential dangers."

"I did. I did. The records came up clean. The former owner must have lied to the insurance company."

"Reckless endangerment," I said. "How does that sound, for starters? How would you like to be charged with a felony?"

Raskin's eyes were huge with terror now. I put him down and he backed away from me until the desk separated us. "Now let's just calm down," he said. "You look okay to me. You got out all right, didn't you? I'll refund your deposit. I swear, I didn't know."

I decided not to waste my energy. Raskin wasn't worth it. Back I went to Yuba City. Found a studio apartment that almost had room for me and MacHeath. Tried to forget.

By day it was easy. San Francisco put on her best show for me: The Golden Gate Bridge glistened in the sunlight. The bay was dotted by solar-powered sailboats. The cable cars' recorded bells rang. The scent of coffee and chocolate wafted up from the power-blowers installed at Ghiradelli Square. My work was blessedly absorbing.

But at night my dreams were filled with little girls with dirty faces and large blue eyes, terrified little girls with their hands and faces pressed against a wall of unyielding glass as flames raced up behind them.

"Help," they cried. "Help me, Mommy!"

"Help me, Daddy!"

"Help me, Christine!"

On my way to work one morning, I glanced through the window as we pulled into Powell Station. Another train had come in on the parallel track, and in it a small girl with big blue eyes stared at me with great seriousness. Her hands were pressed against the window. I looked down at my net paper. When I looked up again, she was gone. But two small handprints smudged the glass where she had been.

That night I went back.

I went back to 1968 and stood outside the house and watched as the fire gained strength. Watched, paralyzed, as choking smoke billowed upward. Saw a woman – me – peer out the upstairs window with fierce, frightened eyes as she held an orange cat in her arms. Was that severe face really mine? I didn't have time to wonder.

I saw a flash at the downstairs window. A small face, eyes huge. Rainbow, struggling with the latch. The smoke filled the room behind her. She beat against the window, coughing.

I moved, then. Picked up a rock.

The fire engines howled in the distance.

I saw myself coming down the stairs and darted to the side, out of sight, quickly, quickly, until I knew that I was putting MacHeath in the car with my back to the house.

Awkwardly, then, I changed history. Smashed the window. Reached through jagged glass that scratched my hands and arms, grabbed the child, and pulled her through. The flames chased her right up to the edge of the sill, but they couldn't have her. No. Not this time.

Rainbow clung to me, sobbing, and I rocked her gently.

"It's okay, honey," I whispered. My hands smeared blood and soot on her face. I didn't care. She was alive.

When she had calmed enough to fall into an exhausted sleep, I handed her to a neighbor and crept away. I didn't want anybody to notice that there were two of me there.

Back in realtime, I took a long shower, bandaged my wounds, and had two glasses of smooth old scotch, vintage 1991.

The next morning, I called in a favor from Jimmy Wu, keeper of the SFPD database.

"Her name's Rainbow."

Good old Jimmy searched for her, beginning in late 1968. He looked and looked for Rainbow. He never found a trace of her.

"Shit, Chrissy," he said. "They were all called Rainbow that year. "Or Morning Star or Peacelove. I need a real name, like Tammy or Katie or Sarah, and a social security number. A last name would be really nice."

So the trail fizzled out in the backyard of a smoldering house on Potrero Hill, fifty-six years ago. And nothing anomalous ever happened that I could detect – not one ripple of difference in the timeline. MacHeath didn't turn green, I didn't grow wings. San Francisco glittered as always in the chilly summer sunlight. I guess some people are just throwaway people. They don't make any difference at all, in any time.

Did she survive to adulthood? Or did she overdose in some gas station bathroom near Reseda when she was twelve? Did I break every time law on the books merely to postpone her fate? I don't know – but I do know one thing. I sleep better now.

The rhythms of routine distracted me. My cuts healed. My memories receded to a comfortable distance.

About three days ago, I got a call from a real estate agent in the Castro.

"Christine? I got your name from Jerry Raskin."

"I'm not interested in downtime apartments."

She laughed a breathy laugh. "Oh, I only deal in realtime estate. And I've got two places I want to show you. The first is a beauty: a three-bedroom apartment in the Potrero Hill area. Upstairs and down. Used to be a two-family unit. You've got to see it to believe it."

Everything inside me stilled to a whisper. I could see the window again, that window with its small dirty fingerprints.

"Hello? Hello?"

Somehow I found my voice. "I've seen it."

"But that's impossible. This apartment just came on the market."

"Believe me, I've seen it. In fact, you might say that I've spent way too much time on it already." And then I hung up.

TWENTY-ONE, COUNTING UP

Harry Turtledove

Harry Turtledove is an American writer and editor best known for his work in science fiction, alternate histories, and historical fiction. With well over twenty novels and hundreds of short stories, his work has been nominated for just about every award in the industry. He has won the Hugo, the Sidewise, and the Prometheus awards. "Twenty-one, Counting Up" was first published in *Analog Science Fiction and Fact* in 1999. It is a companion piece to his other story in this anthology, "Forty, Counting Down," which features the same main character, Justin Kloster.

Justin Kloster looked from his blue book to his watch and back again. He muttered under his breath. Around him, a hundred more people in the American history class were looking at their watches, too. Fifteen minutes left. After that, another breadth requirement behind him. His junior year behind him, too. Three down, one to go.

At precisely four o'clock, the professor said, "Time! Bring your blue books up to the front of the lecture hall."

Like everybody else, Justin squeezed out another couple of sentences before doing as he was told. He wrung his hand to show writer's cramp, then stuck the pen in the pocket of his jeans and headed for the door.

"How do you think you did?" somebody asked him.

"I'm pretty sure I got a B, anyhow," he answered. "That's all I really need. It's not like it's my major or anything." The prof could hear him, but he didn't much care. This wasn't a course for history majors, not that Cal State Northridge had many of those. It was a school for training computer people like him, business types, and teachers. After a moment, he thought to ask, "How about you?"

"Probably about the same," the other fellow said. "Well, have a good summer."

"Yeah, you, too." Justin opened the door and stepped from air conditioning and pale fluorescent light into the brassy sun and heat of the San Fernando Valley. He blinked a couple of times as his eyes adapted. Sweat started pouring off him. He hurried across campus to the parking lot where his Toyota waited. He was very blond and very fair, and sunburned if you looked at him sideways. He was also a little – only a little – on the round side, which made him sweat even more.

When he unlocked the car, he fanned the door back and forth a couple of times to get rid of the furnacelike air inside. He cranked the AC as soon as he started the motor. After he'd gone a couple of blocks, it started doing some good. He'd just got comfortable when he pulled into the gated driveway of his apartment building.

The Acapulco was like a million others in Los Angeles, with a below-ground parking lot and two stories of apartments built above it around a courtyard that held a swimming pool, a rec room, and a couple of flower beds whose plants kept dying.

The key that opened the security gate also opened the door between the lot and the lobby. Justin checked his snailmail and found, as he'd hoped, a check from his father and another from his mother. His lip curled as he scooped the envelopes from his little mailbox. His folks had gone through a messy divorce his senior year in high school. These days, his father was living with a redheaded woman only a couple of years older than he was – and his mother was living with a dark-haired woman only a couple of years older than he was. They both sent money to help keep him in his apartment . . . and so they wouldn't have to have anything more to do with him. That suited him fine. He didn't want to have anything to do with them these days, either.

He used the security key again to get from the lobby to the courtyard behind it, then walked back to his apartment, which wasn't far from the rec room. That had worried him when he first rented the place, but hardly anybody played table tennis or shot pool or lifted weights, so noise wasn't a problem.

His apartment was no neater than it had to be. His history text and lecture notes covered the kitchen table. He chuckled as he shoved them aside. "No more pencils, no more books, no more teachers' dirty looks," he chanted – and how long had people escaping from school been singing that song? He grabbed a Coke from the refrigerator and started to sit down in front of the space he'd cleared. Then he shook his head and carried the soda back into the bedroom instead.

He really lived there. His iMac sat on a desk in a corner by the closet. Justin grinned when he booted it up. It didn't look like all the boring beige boxes other companies made. As soon as the desktop came up, he logged onto Earthlink to check his e-mail and see what was going on in some of the newsgroups he read.

None of the e-mail was urgent, or even very interesting. The newsgroups . . . "How about that?" he said a couple of minutes later. Dave and Tabitha, who'd both been posting in the Trash Can Sinatras newsgroup for as long as he'd been reading it, announced they were getting married. Justin sent congratulations. He hoped they'd get on better than his own folks had. His girlfriend's parents were still together, and still seemed to like each other pretty well.

Thinking of Megan made him want to talk to her. He logged off Earthlink – having only one line in the apartment was a pain – and went over to the phone on the nightstand. He dialed and listened to it ring, once, twice . . . "Hello?" she said.

"What's the story, morning glory?" Justin said – Megan was wild for Oasis. He liked British pop, too, though he preferred Pulp, as someone of his parents' generation might have liked the Stones more than the Beatles.

"Oh. Hiya, Justin." He heard the smile in her voice once she recognized his. He smiled, too. With exams over for another semester, with his girlfriend glad to hear from him, the world looked like a pretty good place. Megan asked, "How'd your final go?"

"Whatever," he answered. "I don't think it's an A, but I'm pretty sure it's a B, and that's good enough. Want to go out tonight and party?"

"I can't," Megan told him. "I've got my English lit final tomorrow, remember?"

"Oh, yeah. That's right." Justin hadn't remembered till she reminded him. "I bet you're glad to get through with most of that lower-division stuff." She was a year behind him.

"This wasn't so bad." Megan spoke as if telling a dark, shameful secret: "I kind of like Shakespeare."

"Whatever," Justin said again. All he remembered from his literature course was that he'd been damn lucky to escape with a B-minus. "I'll take you to Sierra's. We can get margaritas. How's that?"

"The bomb," Megan said solemnly. "What time?"

"How about six-thirty? I start at CompUSA tomorrow, and I'll get off a little past five."

"Okay, see you then," Megan said. "I've got to get back to *Macbeth*. 'Bye." She hung up.

Justin put *This Is Hardcore*, his favorite Pulp album, in the CD player and pulled dinner out of the freezer at random. When he saw what he had, he put it back and got another one: if he was going to Sierra's tomorrow night, he didn't want Mexican food tonight, too. Plain old fried chicken would do the job well enough. He nuked it, washed it down with another Coke, then threw the tray and the can in the trash and the silverware into the dishwasher. When he started running out of forks, he'd get everything clean at once.

He went back into the bedroom, surfed the Net without much aim for a while, and then went over to bungie.com and got into a multiplayer game of *Myth II*. His side took gas; one of the guys didn't want to follow their captain's orders, even though his own ideas were a long way from brilliant. Justin logged off in disgust. He fired up his *Carmageddon* CD-ROM and happily ran down little old ladies in walkers till he noticed in some surprise that it was after eleven. "Work tomorrow," he sighed, and shut down and went to bed.

Freshly showered, freshly shaved, a gold stud in his left ear, he drove over to Megan's parents' house to pick her up. Her mother let him in. "How are you, Justin?" she said. "How do you like your new job?"

"I'm fine, Mrs. Tricoupis," he answered. "The job's – okay, I guess." One day had been plenty to convince him his supervisor was a doofus. The guy didn't know much about computers, and, because he was pushing thirty, he thought he could lord it over Justin and the other younger people at the store.

Megan's mom caught Justin's tone. Laughing, she said, "Welcome to the real world." She turned and called toward the back of the house: "Sweetie! Justin's here!"

"I'm *coming*," Megan said. She hurried into the living room. She was a slim, almost skinny brunette with more energy than she sometimes knew what to do with. "Hiya," she told Justin. The way she looked at him, she might have invented him.

"Hi." Justin felt the same way about her. He wanted to grab her right then and there. If her mother hadn't been standing three feet away, he would have done it.

Mrs. Tricoupis laughed again, on a different note. It didn't occur to Justin that she could see through Megan and him. She said, "Go on, kids. Have fun. Drive carefully, Justin."

"Whatever," Justin said, which made Megan's mom roll her eyes up to the heavens. But he'd been in only one wreck since getting his license, and that one hadn't quite been his fault, so he couldn't see why she was ragging on him.

He didn't grab Megan when they got into the car, either. At the first red light, though, they leaned toward each other and into a long, wet kiss that lasted till the light turned green and even longer – till, in fact, the old fart in the SUV behind them leaned on his horn and made them both jump.

Sierra's had stood at the corner of Vanowen and Canoga for more than forty years, which made it a Valley institution. They both ordered margaritas as they were seated, Megan's strawberry, Justin's plain. The waiter nodded to her but told Justin, "I'm sorry, *señor*, but I'll need some ID."

"Okay." Justin displayed his driver's license, which showed he'd been born in April 1978, and so had been legal for a couple of months.

"*Gracias, señor*," the waiter said. "I'll get you both your drinks." Justin and Megan didn't start quietly giggling till he was gone. Megan was only twenty, but people always carded Justin.

The margaritas were good. After a couple of sips of hers, Megan said, "You didn't even ask me how I did on my final."

"Duh!" Justin hit himself in the forehead with the heel of his hand. "How *did* you do?"

"Great," she said happily. "I think I might even have gotten an A."

"That rocks." Justin made silent clapping motions. Megan took a seated bow. He went on, "How do you feel like celebrating?"

"Well, we probably ought to save club-hopping for the weekend, since you've got to go to work in the morning." Megan stuck out her tongue at him. "See? *I* think about what's going on with *you*." Justin started to get chuffed, but didn't let it show. A couple of seconds later, he was glad he didn't, because Megan went on, "So why don't we just go back to your place after dinner?"

"Okay," he said, and hoped he didn't sound slaveringly eager. Maybe he did; Megan started laughing at him. But it wasn't mean laughter, and she didn't change what she'd said. He raised his margarita to his lips. At twenty-one, it's easy to think you've got the world by the tail.

He hardly noticed what he ordered. When the waiter brought it, he ate it. It was good; the food at Sierra's always was. Afterwards, he had to remember to stay somewhere close to the speed limit as he drove up Canoga toward the Acapulco. Getting a ticket would interrupt everything else he had in mind.

When he opened the door to let Megan into his apartment, she said, "You're so lucky to have a place of your own."

"I guess so," Justin answered. He thought she was pretty lucky to have parents who cared enough about her to want her to stay at home while she went through college. As far as he was concerned, the checks his father and mother sent counted for a lot less than some real affection would have. He'd tried explaining that, but he'd seen it made no sense to her.

She bent down and went pawing through his CDs and put on *I've Seen Everything*, the Trash Can Sinatras' second album. As "Easy Road" started coming out of the stereo, she sighed. "They were *such* a good band. I wish they'd made more than three records before they broke up."

"Yeah," Justin said. However much he liked the Sinatras, though, he didn't pay that much attention to the music. Instead, he watched her straighten and get to her feet. He stepped forward to slip an arm around her waist.

She turned and smiled at him from a range of about six inches, as if she'd forgotten he was there and was glad to be reminded. "Hiya," she said brightly, and put her arms around him. Who kissed whom first was a matter of opinion. They went back into the bedroom together.

They'd been lovers for only a couple of months. Justin was still learning what Megan liked. He didn't quite get her where she was going before he rather suddenly arrived himself. "Sorry," he said as his heartrate slowed toward normal. "Wait a few minutes and we'll try it again." It was only a few minutes, too. At his age, he could – and did – take that for granted. After the second time, he asked, "Better?"

"Yeah," Megan answered in a breathy voice that meant it was quite a bit better. Or maybe that breathy voice meant something else altogether, for she was still using it as she went on, "Get up, will you? You're squashing me."

"Oh." Justin slid his weight – *too much weight*, he thought, not for the first time – off her. "I didn't mean to."

"A gentleman," she said darkly, "takes his weight on his elbows." But she laughed as she said it, so she couldn't have been really mad.

Justin scratched his stomach, which gave him an excuse to feel how too much of it there was. He wasn't really tubby. He'd never been really tubby. But he would never have six-pack abs, either. Twelve-pack or maybe a whole case, yeah. Six-pack? Real live muscles? Fuhgeddaboutit. Unlike some other girls he'd known, Megan had never given him a hard time about it.

"Shall we go down to the Probe Friday night?" he said. "They don't have me working Saturday, so we can close the place and see what kind of after-hours stuff we can dig up."

"All *right*," Megan said. She slid off the bed and went into the bathroom. When she came back, she started dressing. Justin had half hoped for a third round, but it wasn't urgent. He put his clothes on again, too.

The drive back to Megan's house passed in happy silence. Justin kept glancing over at her every so often. *I'm a pretty lucky fellow*, he thought, *finding a girl I can* . . . Then he clicked his tongue between his teeth. He didn't even want to think the word love. After he'd watched his parents' messy breakup, that word scared the hell out of him. But it kept coming back whether he wanted it to or not. He told himself that was a good sign, and came close to believing it.

The Probe lay a couple of blocks off Melrose, the heart of the L.A. scene. Justin snagged a parking space in front of a house not far away. Megan gave him a hand. "I thought we'd have to hike for, like, miles," she said.

"Well, we've got the shoes for it," Justin said, which made her grin. They both wore knockoffs of Army boots, big and black and massive, with soles that looked as if they'd been cut from tractor tire treads. Justin made sure he put the Club on the steering wheel before he got out of the car. Things in this neighborhood had a way of walking with Jesus if you weren't careful.

He and Megan had no trouble snagging a table when they got inside the Probe. "Guard it with your life," he told her, and went over to the bar to buy a beer. He got carded again, and had to haul out his license. He brought the brew back to Megan, who couldn't pass the ID test, then got another one for himself.

They both eyed the deejay's booth, which was as yet uninhabited. "Who's it supposed to be tonight?" Megan asked. Before Justin could answer, she went on, "I hope it's Helen. She plays the best mix of anybody, and she's not afraid to spin things you don't hear every day."

"I dunno," Justin said. "I like Douglas better, I think. He won't scramble tempos the way Helen does sometimes. You can really dance when he's playing things."

Megan snorted. "Give me a break. I have to drag you out there half the time."

"Proves my point," Justin said. "I need all the help I can get."

"Well, maybe," Megan said: no small concession. She and Justin analyzed and second-guessed deejays the way football fans played Monday-morning quarterback. Their arguments got just as abstruse and sometimes just as heated, too. Megan didn't drop it cold here: she said, "As long as it's not Michael."

Justin crossed his forefingers, as if warding off a vampire. "Anybody but Michael," he agreed. "I don't know how they can keep using him. His list is so lame – my *father* would like most of it." He could find no stronger condemnation.

A couple of minutes later, a skinny redheaded guy with a buzz cut even shorter than Justin's, little tiny sunglasses, and a silver lip ring that glittered under the blazing spots sauntered across the stage to the booth. "It's Douglas," Megan said. She didn't sound too disappointed; she liked him next best after Helen.

"Yeah!" Justin let out a whoop and clapped till his hands hurt. A lot of people in the club were doing the same; Douglas had a considerable following. But there were also scattered boos, and even one raucous shout of, "We want Michael!" Justin and Megan looked at each other and both mouthed the same word: *losers*.

Douglas didn't waste time with chatter. That was another reason Justin liked him – he didn't come to the Probe for foreplay. As soon as the music started blaring out, an enormous grin spread over his face. He didn't even grumble when Megan sprang up, grabbed him, and hauled him out onto the floor. He gave it his best shot. With the bass thudding through him like the start of an earthquake, how could he do anything else?

Tomorrow, he knew, his ears would ring and buzz. His hearing wouldn't be quite right for a couple of days. But he'd worry about that later, if he worried at all. He was having a good time, and nothing else mattered.

Somewhere a little past midnight, a guy with a pierced tongue drifted through the crowd passing out fliers xeroxed on poisonously pink paper. RAVE! was the headline in screamer type – and in a fancy font that was barely legible; Justin, who'd just taken a desktop-publishing course, would never have chosen it. Below, it gave an address a few blocks from the Probe and a smudgy map.

"Wanna go?" Justin asked when the thundering music stopped for a moment.

Megan tossed her head to flip back her hair, then wiped her sweaty forehead with the sleeve of her tunic. "Sure!" she said.

After the Probe closed at two, people streamed out to their cars. The not quite legal after-hours action – at which Justin saw a lot of the same faces – was in an empty warehouse. He'd never been to this one before, but he'd been to others like it. Dancing till whenever was even more fun than dancing till two, and there was always the chance the cops would show up and run everybody out.

There were other ways to have fun at raves, too. A pretty blonde girl carried an enormous purse full of plastic vials half full of orange fluid. "Liquid Happiness?" she asked when she came up to Justin and Megan.

They looked at each other. Justin pulled out ten bucks. The girl gave him two vials. She went on her way. He handed Megan a vial. They both pulled out the stoppers and drank. They both made faces, too. The stuff tasted foul. The drugs you got at raves usually did. Justin and Megan started dancing again, waiting for the Liquid Happiness to kick in.

As far as Justin was concerned, it might as well have been Liquid Wooziness. He felt as if his head were only loosely attached to the rest of him. It was fun. It would have been even more fun if he'd been more alert to what was going on.

Things broke up about a quarter to five. Justin's head and the rest of him seemed a little more connected. He didn't have too much trouble driving back to the Valley. "Take you home or go back to my place?" he asked Megan as he got off the Ventura Freeway and onto surface streets.

"Yours," Megan said at once. "We're so late now, another half hour, forty-five minutes won't matter at all."

He reached out and set his hand on her thigh. "I like the way you think."

His boss knew even less about Macs than he did about other computers. Since said boss was convinced he knew everything about everything, persuading him of that took all the tact Justin had, and maybe a little more besides. He got home from CompUSA feeling as if he'd gone through a car wash with his doors open.

As usual, he sorted through his snailmail walking from the lobby to his apartment. As usual, the first thing he did when he got to the apartment was toss most of it in the trash. And, as usual, the first worthwhile thing he did was turn on his computer and check e-mail. That was more likely to be interesting than what he got from the post office.

At first, though, he didn't think it would be, not today. All he had were a couple of pieces of obvious spam and something from somebody he'd never heard of who used AOL. His lip curled. As far as he was concerned, AOL was for people who couldn't ride a bicycle without training wheels.

But, with nothing more interesting showing on the monitor, he opened the message. He didn't know what he'd been expecting. Whatever it was, it wasn't what he got. *Who but you*, the e-mail read, *would know that the first time you jacked off, you were looking at Miss March 1993, a little before your fifteenth birthday? Gorgeous blonde, wasn't she? The only way I know is that I am you, more or less. Let me hear from you.*

The signature line read, *Justin Kloster, age 40.*

Justin Kloster, age twenty-one, stared at that: stared and stared and stared. He remembered Miss March 1993 very, very well. He remembered sneaking her into the bathroom at his parents' house, back in the days before they'd decided to find themselves and lose him. He remembered not quite being sure what would happen as he fumbled with himself, and how much better reality had been than anything he'd imagined.

What he didn't remember was ever telling anybody about it. It wasn't the sort of thing you advertised, that was for damn sure. Could he have mentioned it when he was shooting the bull with his buds, maybe after they'd all had a few beers, or more than a few? He shook his head. No way.

He looked at the signature line again. *Justin Kloster, age 40*? "Bullshit," he muttered. He wasn't forty, thank God. Forty was the other side of the moon, the side old men lived on. Not really old, ancient, but old like his father. Old enough. The only thing that made the idea getting to forty even halfway appealing was that he might do it with Megan. After all, she'd only be thirty-nine then.

What to do about the message? He was tempted to delete it, forget it. But he couldn't, not quite. He chose the REPLY function and typed, *What kind of stupid joke is this? Whatever it is, it's not funny*. He thought about adding *Justin Kloster, age 21* to it, but he didn't want to acknowledge it even enough to parody. He sent the bald e-mail just the way it was.

He walked out to the kitchen and threw a Hungry Man dinner in the micro-wave. As soon as it started, he opened the refrigerator and dithered between Coke and a beer. He seldom drank alcohol when he was by himself. Today, he made an exception. He popped open a can of Coors Light and took a long pull. The beer slid down his throat, cold and welcome.

As if drawn by a magnet, he went back to the computer. He had no way of knowing when the smartass on AOL who signed himself with his own name would send more e-mail soon, or even if he'd send any more at all. But the fellow might – and Justin spent a lot of time online just about every evening anyhow.

Sure as hell, new e-mail from that same address came in before the microwave buzzed to tell him his dinner was done. He took another big swig of beer, then opened the mail.

No joke, it read. *Who else but you would know you lost your first baby tooth in a pear at school when you were in the first grade? Who else would know your dad fed you Rollos when he took you to work with him that day when you were eight or nine? Who else would know you spent most of the time while you were losing your cherry staring at the mole on the side of Lindsey Fletcher's neck? Me, that's who: you at 40. Justin Kloster.*

"Jesus!" Justin said hoarsely. His hands were shaking so much, the beer slopped and splashed inside the can. He had to put the can down on the desk, or he would have spilled beer on his pants.

Out in the kitchen, the microwave did let him know his dinner was ready. He heard it, but he hardly noticed. He couldn't take his eyes off the iMac's monitor. Nobody knew that stuff about him. *Nobody*. He would have bet money neither his mother nor his father could have told how he lost his first tooth, or when. He would have bet more money his dad couldn't have remembered those Rollos to save himself from a firing squad.

As for Lindsey Fletcher . . . "No way," he told the words, the impossible words, on the screen. Telling them that didn't make them go away. Lindsey was a cute little blonde he'd known in high school. They'd never even broken up, not in the sense of a fight or anything, but she'd moved out to Simi Valley with her folks the summer his parents' marriage struck a mine, and they'd stopped dating. A damn cute little blonde – but she did have that mole.

Justin went to the kitchen, opened up his dinner, and carried it and a couple of dish towels and (almost as an afterthought) a knife and fork back into the bedroom. He put the towels in his lap so the dinner tray wouldn't burn his legs and started to eat. He hardly noticed what he was shoveling into his face. *What do I say?* he kept wondering. *What the hell do I say?*

That depended on what he believed. He didn't know what the hell to believe. "Time travel?" he said, and then shook his head. "Bullshit." But if it was bullshit, how did the guy sending him e-mail know so goddamn much? The truth, no doubt, was out there, but how could anybody go about getting his hands on it?

The line made him decide how to answer. *I don't watch* X-Files *much,* he typed, *but maybe I ought to. How could you know all that about me? I never told anybody about Lindsey Fletcher's neck.*

Whoever the other guy was, he answered in a hurry. Justin imagined him leaning toward his computer, waiting for AOL's stupid electronic voice to tell him, "You've got mail!" and then writing like a bastard. *How do I know?* he said. *I've told you twice now – I know because I am you, you in 2018. It's not* X-Files *stuff – it's good programming. Believe me, I'm back here for a good reason.*

"Believe you?" Justin yelped, as if the fellow sending him e-mail were there in the bedroom with him. "How am I supposed to believe you when you keep telling me shit like this?" His fingers said the same thing, only a little more politely. *But that's impossible,* he wrote, and sent the message.

Okay. The reply came back almost instantly. *But if it is impossible, how do I know all this stuff about you?*

That was a good question, what his grandfather called the sixty-four dollar question. Justin would have been a lot happier had he had a sixty-four dollar answer for it. Since he didn't, being flip would have to do. *I don't know,* he wrote. *How do you know all this stuff about me?*

Because it's stuff about me, too, said the fellow on the other end of the computer hookup. *You don't seem to be taking that seriously yet.*

Justin snorted. "Yeah, right," he said. "Like I'm supposed to take any of this crap seriously. Like anybody would." He snapped his fingers and laughed out loud. "I'll fix you, you son of a bitch. Hassle me, will you?" His fingers flew over the keyboard. *If you're supposed to be me, then you'll look like me, right?*

He laughed again. That'd shut Mr. Mindgames up, by God. Except it didn't. Again, the reply came back very fast. *Right,* wrote the stranger who claimed to be his older self. *Meet me in front of the B. Dalton's in the Northridge mall tomorrow night at 6:30 and I'll buy you dinner. You'll see for yourself.*

"Huh," Justin said. He hadn't expected to have his bluff called. He hadn't thought it was a bluff. He typed three defiant words – *See you there* – sent them off, and shut down his iMac. It was still early, but he'd had enough electronic weirdness for one night.

Like Topanga Plaza, the Northridge mall was one of Justin's favorite places. He'd spent a lot of time at both of them, shopping and killing things at the arcade (though Topanga, for some reason, didn't have one) and hanging out with his buds and just being by himself. He'd been especially glad of places to be by himself when his parents' marriage went south. Northridge had just reopened then, after staying shut for a year and a half after the big quake in '94. If they'd let him, he would have visited it while it was in ruins. Even that would have beat the warfare going on at his house.

He parked in the open lot on the south side of the mall, near the Sears. Everyone swore up and down that the new parking structures they'd built since the earthquake wouldn't come crashing down the way the old ones had. Maybe it was even true. Justin didn't care to find out by experiment.

His apartment was air-conditioned. His Toyota was air-conditioned. He worked up a good sweat walking a hundred feet from the car to the entrance under the Sears façade that was also new since the quake. Summer was here early this year, and felt ready to stay for a long time. *Global warming*, he thought. He opened the door. The mall, thank God, was also air-conditioned. He sighed with pleasure at escaping the Valley heat again.

He walked through the Sears toward the entryway into the rest of the mall. None of the men's clothing he passed looked interesting. Some of it was for businessmen – not particularly successful businessmen, or they wouldn't shop at Sears. The rest of the clothes were casual, but just as unexciting.

An escalator took Justin up to the second level. The B. Dalton's was on the right-hand side as he went north, not too far past the food court in the middle of the mall. He paused a couple of times to eye pretty girls sauntering past – yeah, he was seeing Megan all the time and happy about that, but it didn't mean he was blind. One of the girls smiled at him. He wasn't foolish enough to let himself get distracted. Not quite.

Past the food court, on toward the bookstore. A guy was leaning against the brushed-aluminum rail – a blond, slightly chunky guy in a black T-shirt, baggy jeans, and Army boots. He'd been looking the other way. Now he swung his head back toward Justin – and he had Justin's face.

Justin stopped in his tracks. He felt woozy, almost ready to pass out, as if he'd stood up too suddenly from a chair. He had to grab the rail himself, to keep from falling down. He didn't know what he'd expected. That the other guy's e-mail might be simple truth had never crossed his mind.

He wanted to get the hell out of there. His older self also looked a little green around the gills. And why not? He was meeting himself for the first time, too. Justin made himself keep going.

When he got up to himself-at-forty, his older self stuck out a hand and said, "Hi. Thanks for coming." His voice didn't sound the way Justin's did in his own ears, but it did sound the way he sounded when he got captured on videotape.

Both Justins looked down at the hands that matched so well. "Maybe I'm not crazy," Justin said slowly. "Maybe you're not crazy, either. You look just like me." He studied his older self. Despite the buzz cut that matched his own, despite the Cow Pi T-shirt, he thought himself-at-forty did look older. But he didn't look a lot older. He didn't look anywhere close to the age he was claiming.

"Funny how that works," his older self said with a tight smile.

He was sharper, more abrupt, than Justin. He acted like a goddamn adult, in other words. And, acting like an adult, as if he knew everything there was to know just because he had some years under his belt, he automatically ticked Justin off. Justin put his hands on his hips and said, "Prove you're from the future." Maybe this guy was a twin separated at birth. Maybe he was no relation, but a double anyhow. Maybe . . . Justin didn't know what.

His older self reached into the pocket of his jeans and pulled out a little blue plastic coin purse, the kind only a grownup would use. Squeezing it open, he took out a quarter. "Here – this is for you." He gave it to Justin.

It lay in Justin's hand eagle side up. Justin turned it over. It still looked like any other quarter . . . till he saw the date. He thought his eyes would bug out of his head. "It's from 2012," he whispered. "Jesus. You weren't kidding." Four little numbers stamped onto a coin, and the reality of what he'd just walked into hit him over the head like a club.

"I told you I wasn't." His older self sounded like an adult talking down to a kid. That helped convince him, too. Himself-at-forty continued, "Come on. What's the name of that Korean barbecue place over on Reseda?"

"The Pine Tree?" Justin said. He liked the restaurant. He'd taken Megan there once, and she'd liked it, too.

"Yeah." Himself-at-forty sounded as if he'd needed reminding. Did that mean he didn't go there in 2018? Before the question could do anything more than cross Justin's mind, his older self went on, "Let's go over there. I'll buy you dinner, like I said in e-mail, and we can talk about things."

Justin was hungry – he usually ate dinner earlier – but that wasn't tops on his list. He came out with what was: "Like what you're doing here."

His older self nodded. "Yeah. Like what I'm doing here."

As often as not, Justin and whomever he was with turned out to be the only Caucasians in the Pine Tree. He and Megan had been. He and his older self were, too. The waitresses were all Korean; none of them spoke a whole lot of English.

Himself-at-forty ordered marinated beef and pork they could cook themselves at the gas grill set into the tabletop. He ordered a couple of tall OB beers, too. Justin nodded at that. God knew he could use a beer right now.

As their waitress wrote down the order, she kept looking from his older self to Justin and back again. "Twins," she said at last.

"Yeah," himself-at-forty said. Justin wondered if he was lying or telling the truth. *Damned if I know*, he thought as the waitress headed back to the kitchen. He wanted to giggle. This whole business was too bizarre for words.

Instead of giggling, he pointed at his older self. "Tell me one thing," he said in deep and portentous tones.

"What?" Himself-at-forty looked alarmed. Heaven only knew what he thought would come out of Justin's mouth.

Justin leered at him. "That the Rolling Stones aren't still touring by the time you're – I'm – forty."

"Well, no." Now his older self looked irked, as if he couldn't believe Justin would come out with anything as off-the-wall as that. *Don't have much fun at forty, do you?* Justin thought.

Here came the waitress with the beer. She hadn't asked either of the Justins for his driver's license. *A good thing, too.* Justin wondered what kind of license his older self had, or if himself-at-forty had one at all. But he had more important things to worry about. After the waitress went off to deal with a party of Koreans at another table, Justin said, "Okay, I believe you. I didn't think I would, but I do. You know too much – and you couldn't have pulled that quarter out of your ear from nowhere." He took a big sip of his OB.

"That's right," himself-at-forty said. Again, he sounded as if he knew everything there was to know. That rubbed Justin the wrong way. But, goddamn it, his older self did know more than Justin. *How much more?* Justin didn't know. *Too much more.* He was sure of that.

He drank his glass empty, and filled it from the big bottle the waitress had set in front of him. Pretty soon, that second glass was empty, too. Justin killed the bottle pouring it for a third time. He waved to the waitress for another beer. Why not? His older self was buying. Himself-at-forty hadn't even refilled his glass once yet. *Terrific*, Justin thought. *I turn into a wet blanket.*

Not only did the waitress bring his new beer, but also dinner: plates of strange vegetables (many of them potently flavored with garlic and chilies) for Justin and his older self to share, and the marinated beef and pork. She started the gas fire under the grill and used a pair of tongs to put some meat on to cook for them. As the thinly sliced strips started sizzling, Justin pointed at them and said, "Oh my God! They killed Kenny!"

"Huh?" His older self clearly didn't remember *South Park*. *Wet blanket*, Justin thought again. Then a light came in his older self's eyes. "Oh." Himself-at-forty laughed – a little.

Justin said, "If you'd have said that to me, I'd have laughed a lot harder." He decided to cut his older self some slack: "But the show's not big for you any more, is it? No, it wouldn't be. 2018. Jesus." He made a good start on the new OB.

His older self grabbed the tongs and took some meat. So did Justin. They both ate with chopsticks. Justin wasn't real smooth with them, but he looked down his nose at people who came to Asian restaurants and reached for the knife and fork. They could do that at home. Himself-at-forty handled the chopsticks almost as well as the Koreans a couple of tables over. *More practice*, Justin thought.

After they'd made a fair dent in dinner, Justin said, "Well, *will* you tell me what this is all about?"

His older self answered the question with another question: "What's the most important thing in your life right now?"

Justin grinned. "You mean, besides trying to figure out why I'd travel back in time to see me?" Himself-at-forty nodded, his face blank like a poker player's. Justin went on, "What else could it be but Megan?"

"Okay, we're on the same page," himself-at-forty said. "That's why I'm here, to set things right with Megan."

"Things with Megan don't need setting right." Justin could feel the beer he'd drunk. It made him sound even surer than he would have otherwise. "Things with Megan are great. I mean, I'm taking my time and all, but they're great. And they'll stay great, too. How many kids do we have now?" That was the beer talking, too. Without it, he'd never have spoken so freely.

"None." Himself-at-forty touched the corner of his jaw, where a muscle was twitching.

"None?" That didn't sound good. The way his older self said the word didn't sound good, either. Justin noticed something he should have seen sooner: "You're not wearing a wedding ring." His older self nodded. He asked, "Does that mean we don't get married?"

"We get married, all right," his older self answered grimly. "And then we get divorced."

Ice ran through Justin. "That can't happen," he blurted.

He knew too goddamn much about divorce, more than he'd ever wanted to. He knew about the shouts and the screams and the slammed doors. He knew about the silences that were even deadlier. He knew about the lies his parents had told each other. He knew about the lies they'd told him about each other, and the lies they'd told him about themselves. He had a pretty fair notion of the lies they'd told themselves about themselves.

One of the biggest lies each of them had told him was, *Of course I'll still care for you just as much afterwards as I did before.* Megan wasn't the only one who envied him his apartment – a lot of people his age did. What the apartment meant to him was that his folks would sooner give him money to look out for himself than bother looking out for him. He envied Megan her parents who cared.

And now his older self was saying he and Megan would go through that? He sure was. His voice hard as stone, he squashed Justin's protest: "It can. It did. It will." That muscle at the corner of his jaw started jumping again.

"But – how?" Justin asked, sounding even in his own ears like a little boy asking how his puppy could have died. He tried to rally. "We aren't like Mom and Dad – we don't fight all the time, and we don't look for something on the side wherever we can find it." He took a long pull at his beer, trying to wash the taste of his parents out of his mouth. And he hadn't smiled back at that girl in the mall. He really hadn't.

With weary patience, his older self answered, "You can fight about sex, you can fight about money, you can fight about in-laws. We ended up doing all three, and so . . ." Himself-at-forty leaned his chopsticks on the edge of his plate and spread his hands. "We broke up – will break up – if we don't change things. That's why I figured out how to come back: to change things, I mean."

Justin poured the last of the second OB into his glass and gulped it down. After a bit, he said, "You must have wanted to do that a lot."

"You might say so." His older self drank some more beer, too. He still sounded scratchy as he went on, "Yeah, you just might say so. Since we fell apart, I've never come close to finding anybody who makes me feel the way Megan did. If it's not her, it's nobody. That's how it looks from here, anyhow. I want to make things right for the two of us."

"Things *were* going to be right." But Justin couldn't make himself sound as if he believed it. Divorce? He shuddered. From everything he'd seen, anything was better than that. In a small voice, he asked, "What will you do?"

"I'm going to take over your life for the next couple of months." His older self sounded absolutely sure, as if he'd thought it all through and this was the only possible answer. Was that how doctors sounded, recommending major surgery? Justin didn't get a chance to wonder for long; himself-at-forty plowed ahead, relentless as a landslide: "I'm going to be you. I'm going to take Megan out. I'm going to make sure things are solid – and then the superstring I've ridden to get me here will break down. You'll live happily ever after. I'll brief you to make sure you don't screw up what I've built. And when I get back to 2018, *I will have lived* happily ever after. How does that sound?"

"I don't know." Now Justin regretted pouring down two tall beers one right after the other. He needed to think clearly, and he couldn't quite. "You'll be taking Megan out?"

"That's right." Himself-at-forty nodded.

"You'll be . . . taking Megan back to the apartment?"

"Yeah," his older self said. "But she'll think it's you, remember, and pretty soon it'll be you, and it'll keep right on being you till you turn into me, if you know what I mean."

"I know what you mean. Still . . ." Justin grimaced. "I don't know. I don't like it." When you imagined your girlfriend being unfaithful to you, you pictured her making love with somebody else. Justin tried to imagine Megan being unfaithful to him by picturing her making love with somebody who looked just like him. It made his mental eyes cross.

His older self folded his arms across his chest and sat there in the booth. "You have a better idea?" he asked. He must have known damn well that Justin had no ideas at all.

"It's not fair," Justin protested. "You *know* all this shit, and I've gotta guess."

With a cold shrug, himself-at-forty said, "If you think I did this to come back and tell you lies, go ahead. That's fine. You'll see what happens. And we'll both be sorry."

"I don't know. I just don't know." Justin shook his head. He felt trapped, caught in a spider's web. "Everything sounds like it hangs together, but you could be bullshitting, too, just as easy."

"Yeah, right." Amazing how much scorn his older self could pack into two words.

Justin got to his feet, so fast it made him lightheaded for a couple of seconds – or maybe that was the beer, too. "I won't say yes and I won't say no, not now I won't. I've got your e-mail address. I'll use it." Out he went, planting his feet with exaggerated care at every stride.

Night had fallen while he and himself-at-forty were eating. He drove back to his apartment building as carefully as he'd walked. Picking up a 502 for driving under the influence was the last thing he wanted. One thought pounded in his head the whole way back. *What do I do? What the hell do I do?*

He'd just come out of the bathroom – the revenge of those two tall OBs – when the telephone rang. He wondered if it was his older self, calling to give him another dose of lecture. If it was, he intended to tell himself-at-forty where he could stick that lecture. "Hello?" he said suspiciously.

But it wasn't his older self. "Hiya," Megan said.

"Oh!" Justin shifted gears in a hurry. "Hi!"

"I just called up to say I think you're the bomb," she told him, and hung up before he could answer.

He stared at the telephone handset, then slowly set it back in its cradle. "God damn you," he whispered, cursing not Megan but his older self. "Oh, God damn you." He had a girl like this, and himself-at-forty was saying he'd lose her? *I can't do that*, he thought. *Whatever it takes, I can't do that.*

Even if it means bowing out of your own life for a while? Even if it means letting him stick his nose in? But his older self sticking his nose in didn't worry Justin. His older self sticking something else in . . .

I don't have to make up my mind right away. I'm not going to make up my mind right away. This is too important. And if my older self can't figure that out, tough shit, that's all.

Justin checked his e-mail even before he brushed his teeth the next morning. Himself-at-forty hadn't started nagging, anyhow. There was e-mail from Megan, though. Everything else could wait, but he opened that. It said, *The bomb.* ;-)

He grinned and shook his head. But the grin slipped a moment later. *I can't let her get away from me. Knowing she might* . . . He ground his teeth. He didn't just know she might. He knew she would. He'd never thought of being blind to the future as a blessing, but knowing some of it sure felt like a curse.

At work, his boss chewed him out for not paying attention to anything going on around him. He couldn't even blame the guy; he *wasn't* paying attention to anything going on around him. Too many important things spun through his mind.

He gulped lunch at the Burger King four doors down from the CompUSA, then went to the pay phones around the side of the building. He fed in a quarter – *not* the one from 2012; he was saving that – and a dime and called Megan. "Hello?" she said.

"Hi. I think you're the bomb, too." It wasn't *I love you* – it wasn't even close to *I love you* – but it was the best he could do.

Megan giggled, as if she'd been waiting by the telephone for him to call. "I bet you say that whenever you phone a girl who isn't wearing any clothes," she answered – and hung up on him again.

He spluttered, which did him no good. He reached into his pants pocket for more change to call her back and find out why she wasn't wearing any clothes – or if she really wasn't wearing any clothes. But that didn't matter. He had the image of her naked stuck in his head – which had to be just what she'd had in mind.

As he walked back, he realized he'd made up his mind. *I can't lose her. No matter what, I can't lose her.* If that meant letting his older self fix things up – whatever there was that needed fixing – then it did, and that was all there was to it.

Despite deciding, he took another day and a half to write the e-mail that admitted he'd decided. *All write, dammit*, he typed. *I still don't know about this, but I don't think I have any choice. If me and Megan are going to break up, that* can't *happen. You better make sure it doesn't.*

After he'd sent the e-mail, he looked at it again. It wasn't exactly gracious. He shrugged. He didn't feel exactly gracious, either.

An answer came back almost at once. Himself-at-forty must have been hanging around the computer waiting for him to say something. *You won't be sorry*, the e-mail told him.

Whatever, Justin wrote. His hands balled into fists. He made them unclench. *How do you want to make the switch?*

Meet me in front of the B. Dalton's again, himself-at-forty replied. *Park by the Sears. I will, too. Bring whatever you want in your car. You can move it to the one I'm driving. I'll do the same here. See you in two hours?*

Justin sighed. *Whatever*, he said again. Packing didn't take anything like two hours. He thought about bringing the iMac along, but ended up leaving it behind and taking his PowerBook instead. It was old, but it would do for games and for the Net. He scribbled a note and set it by the iMac's keyboard: *In case you don't remember, here's Megan's phone number and e-mail. Don't screw it up, that's all I've got to tell you.*

Once he'd stuffed everything he thought he needed into a pair of suitcases, he put them in the trunk of his Toyota and headed for the mall. He'd gone only a couple of blocks when he snapped his fingers and swung down to the Home Depot on Roscoe first.

Even with the stop, he still took his place in front of the bookstore before his older self got there. This time, seeing himself-at-forty made him grim, not boggled. "Let's get this over with," he said.

"Come on. It's not a root canal," his older self said. Justin shrugged. He'd never had one. Himself-at-forty went on, "Let's go do it. We'll need to swap keys, you know."

"Yeah," Justin said. "I had spares made. How about you?"

"Me, too." His older self grinned a lopsided grin. "We think alike. Amazing, huh?"

"Amazing. Right." Justin abruptly turned away and started walking toward Sears and the lot beyond it. "This better work."

"It will." Himself-at-forty sounded disgustingly confident.

The two Toyotas sat only a couple of rows apart. They were almost as much alike as Justin and his older self. Justin moved his things into the other car, while himself-at-forty put stuff in his. They traded keys. "You know where I live," Justin said. "What's my new address?"

"Oh." His older self gave it to him. He knew where it was – not as good a neighborhood as the one the Acapulco was in. Himself-at-forty went on, "The car's insured, and you'll find plenty of money in the underwear drawer." His older self patted him on the shoulder, the only time they'd touched other than shaking hands. "It'll be fine. Honest. You're on vacation for a couple of months, that's all."

"On vacation from my *life*," Justin exclaimed. He glared at his older self. "Don't fuck up, that's all."

"It's my life, too, remember." Himself-at-forty got into the car Justin had driven to the mall. Justin went to his older self"s Toyota. Still half wondering if this were some elaborate scam, he tried the key. The car started right up. Justin drove off to see where the hell he'd have to wait this out.

Sure enough, the Yachtsman and the apartment buildings on the block with it were older and tireder-looking than the Acapulco and its surroundings. It wasn't a neighborhood where guys sold crack from parked cars, but it might be heading that way in a few years. The one bright spot Justin saw was the Denny's on the corner. If he got sick of frozen dinners and his own bad cooking, he could always eat there.

He found his parking space under the apartment building. When he went out to the lobby, a mailbox had KLOSTER Dymo-taped onto it. He checked. His older self hadn't got any mail. Justin went inside and found his apartment. The door key and dead-bolt key both worked. "Well, what have we got?" he wondered.

When he discovered what he had, his first impulse was to walk right out again. The TV just plugged into the wall: no cable, not even a VCR hooked up. The stereo had to have come out of an antique store. It played cassettes and vinyl, but not CDs. He could play CDs on the PowerBook, but even so . . .

He opened the underwear drawer, more than half expecting BVDs and nothing else. But under the briefs lay . . . "Christ!" he exclaimed. How much was there? He picked up wad after wad of cash, threw them all down on the bed, and started counting. By the time he was through, he'd had almost as much fun as he'd ever had in his life.

Close to seventy grand, he thought dazedly. *Jesus*. All at once, he stopped doubting his older self's story. Nobody – but nobody – would spend, or let him spend, that kind of money on a scam. The bills weren't even crisp and new, as they might have been if they were counterfeits. They'd all been circulating a good long while, and couldn't be anything but genuine.

"Okay," he said, fighting the impulse to count them again. "I'm on vacation. Let the good times roll." He *did* recount a couple of thousand dollars' worth, just for the hell of it.

He'd never been in a spot where he could spend all the money he wanted, do whatever he felt like doing. If he wanted to go out and get a VCR, he could – and he intended to. He could charge right down to Circuit City or Best Buy or Fry's and . . .

"Uh-oh," he muttered. If he went to any of those places, there was some chance he'd run into Megan. His older self didn't want him running into Megan for a while, and his older self had left him all this money to play around with so he wouldn't. He shrugged. He could go over to Burbank or out to Simi Valley or wherever and get a VCR. Then he could charge right down to Blockbuster and rent enough tapes to keep him from getting too . . .

Uh-oh. He didn't say it this time, but he thought it. Megan was liable to show up at either of the local Blockbusters; she liked watching movies on video as much as everybody else did.

"Okay," Justin said, as if somebody were arguing with him. "I'll find some video place out in the boonies, too."

That made him happier. He had time to kill – nothing but time to kill – and movies were a great way to kill it. But he couldn't watch movies and play computer games all the damn time. *I can go down to . . .* But that thought stopped before it was even half formed. He couldn't go to the mall, not to Northridge, not to Topanga Plaza, not even to the half-dead Promenade farther down Topanga or to tacky Fallbrook. Megan visited all of them.

"Shit," he said in a low voice. And he really couldn't go to any of his favorite restaurants, because where would himself-at-forty be taking Megan? To one of them or another, sure as hell. What would she think if she were with his older self and then saw him come in by himself in different clothes? Nothing good, that was for damn sure.

Great, Justin thought. *I can do whatever I want, as long as I don't do it in any of the places I usually go to. Or I can just sit here in this miserable apartment and jack off.* He suspected he'd end up doing a lot of that. Thinking about Megan immediately made him want to do more than think about Megan: he was, after all, twenty-one.

Down, boy, he told himself. Himself didn't want to listen. While he was holed up here by his lonesome, himself-at-forty would be taking Megan out, taking Megan home, taking Megan to bed. No, he didn't like that worth a rat's ass. He tried again to imagine Megan being unfaithful to him with somebody with his own face. He came a lot closer to succeeding this time.

He paced out to the kitchen. Even looking at the bed turned him on and pissed him off, regardless of whether it had cash strewn all over it. When he opened the refrigerator, he found a couple of six-packs of microbrews along with fresh vegetables and other things he was unlikely to eat. He tried to unscrew the cap from one of the beers, only to discover it didn't unscrew. That meant he had to rummage in the drawer till he came up with an opener. Once he got the cap off, he threw it at the wastebasket – and missed. He had to bend down and drop it in – and even then he almost missed again.

Sighing, Justin sipped the hard-won Anchor Porter . . . and made a horrible face. "People pay a buck a bottle for *this*?" he said. "Jesus! Gimme Coors Light any day."

When he opened the freezer, he found steaks and chops and chicken in there. He supposed he could do up the steaks in a pan on the stove, but chicken was out of his culinary league. Fortunately, there were also several frozen dinners. He didn't know what he would have done if his older self had turned into a total foodie.

Like hell I don't know, he thought, and grinned. *I'd just eat out all the time. With that Denny's right at the end of the block, I might anyway.*

After watching network TV that night, he realized he would have to get a VCR ASAP if he wanted to stay anywhere close to sane. He ate bacon and eggs and hash browns at the Denny's the next morning, then drove over to an electronics place he knew on Ventura Boulevard in Encino – only twenty minutes' drive from the Yachtsman, but not a place where he was at all likely to run into Megan. He bought the VCR, put the box in his trunk, and headed to a Blockbuster a few doors away to get some tapes.

His address came up on their computer system. "You do know we have locations closer to your home, sir?" the clerk said.

"Yeah." Justin nodded. "This is near where I work."

He'd never been a great liar. He was, at the moment, wearing a Dilbert T-shirt and a pair of baggy shorts. The clerk raised an eyebrow. But Justin's credit checked out okay, so that was all she did.

Having lugged the VCR into his apartment, he discovered, not for the first time, that being a computer-science major didn't make the damn thing easy to set up. He fumed and mumbled and cussed and finally got the gadget acting the way it was supposed to. With *Deep Impact* on the TV and a Coke in his hand, life looked better.

He put his feet on the coffee table and belched enormously. Nothing to do but kick back and watch movies for a couple of months? *Okay, I can handle it*, he thought. Then he snapped his fingers. "Potato chips!" he said out loud. "Doritos. Whatever."

That day went fine. The next day went all right. By the middle of the afternoon on the third day, he was sick of movies and computer games and hoped he'd never see another nacho-cheese Dorito as long as he lived. He went into the bedroom and picked up the phone. He'd dialed four digits of Megan's number before he remembered he wasn't supposed to call her.

"God damn it," he muttered. "This is so lame. What am I going to do, stay cooped up here till I get all dusty?"

His older self wanted him to do exactly that. His older self had left him plenty of money so he would do exactly that. But what good was the money if he had trouble finding places to blow it? After staring at the walls – and the TV screen, and his laptop's monitor – for two days straight, his affection for his older self, which had never been high, sank like the Dow on an especially scary day. He'd never understood people saying money couldn't buy happiness. Now maybe he did.

He wanted to talk with his girlfriend. Hell, he wanted to lay his girlfriend. Himself-at-forty was telling him he couldn't do either. Himself-at-forty, the son of a bitch, was probably doing both. Justin was no better at handling frustration than anyone else his age. The hornier he got, the worse he got, too.

If he couldn't talk to Megan, he damn well could talk to his older self. He dialed the number at his apartment, which felt funny. He never called there. Why would he? If he wasn't home, who would answer? A burglar?

But somebody was home to answer now. And, after three rings, somebody did. "Hello?" Himself-at-forty sounded as if he were talking from deep underwater.

"Hi," Justin said cheerfully; he had all he could do not to say *hiya*, the way Megan did. "How are things?"

"Things are fine," his older self answered after a longish pause. He still sounded like hell; if he hadn't been ridden hard and put away wet, Justin had never heard anybody who had. Another pause. Then himself-at-forty tried again: "Or they were till you called. I was asleep."

"*Now*?" Justin exclaimed in disbelief. He looked at his watch: half past two. He didn't think he'd been asleep at half past two since he was three years old and quit taking naps. "I called now 'cause I figured you wouldn't be."

"Never mind." His older self yawned, but seemed a little less fuzzy when he went on, "Yeah, things are okay. We went to the Probe last night, and—"

"*Did* you?" Justin broke in. He didn't like the way that sounded: him stuck here in this miserable place, himself-at-forty having a good time at his favorite club. No, he didn't like that at all. "What else did you do?"

"That after-hours place," his older self answered. "Some guy came through with fliers, so I knew how to get there."

Yeah, you'd have forgotten, wouldn't you, you sorry bastard? Aloud, Justin said, "Lucky you. And what *else* did you do?" He could imagine Megan in his older self's arms, all right. Now he could. He'd had plenty of time to try. Practice made perfect, dammit. He could hate what he imagined, too.

"About what you'd expect," himself-at-forty said. Christ, he sounded arrogant. "I'm you, remember. What would you have done?" Justin sighed. He knew what he would have done, by God. But no. He'd stayed here by his lonesome – by his very lonesome – so his older self could do it instead. He sucked in a long, angry breath preparatory to telling himself-at-forty where to head in. Before he could, his older self went on, "And when I took her home, I told her I loved her."

"Jesus!" Justin yelped, forgetting whatever else he might have said. "What did you go and do that for?"

"It's true, isn't it?" his older self asked.

"That doesn't mean you've got to *say* it, for Christ's sake," Justin answered. He shook his head in disbelief, though his older self wasn't there to see it. His parents must have said they loved each other once upon a time, too, and how had that turned out? "What am I supposed to do when you go away?"

"Marry her, doofus," himself-at-forty said, as if it were just that simple. "Live happily ever after, so I get to live happily ever after, too. Why the hell do you think I came back here?"

"For your good time, man, not mine," Justin snarled. "I'm sure not having a good time, I'll tell you." He belched again. No surprise – how many Cokes had he poured down since he got to this place? Too many. With the carbonation, he tasted stale nacho cheese.

His older self took a deep breath, too, and said, "Look, chill for a while, okay? I'm doing fine."

That only made Justin angrier. "Sure you are. You're doing fucking great. What about me?"

"You're fine. Chill. You're on vacation," himself-at-forty answered. If he didn't know everything, he didn't know he didn't know everything. "Go ahead. Relax. Spend my money. That's what it's there for."

When his older self mentioned the money, Justin forgot how chuffed he was, at least for a little while. "Where'd you get so much?" he asked. "What did you do, rob a bank?"

"It's worth a lot more now than it will be then," his older self told him. "Inflation. Have some fun. Just be discreet, okay?"

Which brought Justin back to square one. His older self kept trying to blow him off, and he didn't want to put up with it. "You mean, get out of your hair."

"In a word, yes." Himself-at-forty sounded as if he was having trouble putting up with Justin, too.

"While you're in Megan's hair." No, Justin had no trouble at all seeing pictures in his mind, pictures nastier than any he could have pulled off the Net. He sighed, trying to make them go away. "I don't know, dude."

"It's for you," himself-at-forty said. "It's for her and you."

That, goddammit, was the trump card. If Justin-now was fated to break up with Megan, he didn't see that he had any choice other than letting his older self set things right. He hated the idea. Every minute he spent in this miserable apartment made him hate it more. But he couldn't find any way around it. Get married and get divorced? That was worse. "Yeah," he said, and hung up.

Every minute he spent in that miserable apartment . . . from then on, he spent as little time as he could there. That worked better than staring at the TV and the PowerBook's monitor and, most of all, the four walls. When he was out and doing things, he didn't think about himself-at-forty and Megan . . . so much.

Getting out would have worked better still if he'd been able to go to the places he really liked, the local malls and the movie theaters and coffeehouses and restaurants where he'd gone with Megan. But he didn't dare. He couldn't imagine what he'd do if he saw her and his older self together. And what would himself-at-forty do? And Megan? Those were all terrific questions, and he didn't want to find out the answers to any of them.

So he went to places where he could be sure he wouldn't run into Megan or anybody else he knew. He killed an afternoon at the Glendale Galleria. He killed a whole day at the enormous Del Amo mall down in Torrance, which was supposed to be the biggest shopping center this side of the Mall of America. By the time he'd trekked from one end of it to the other, he believed all the hype. He hadn't come close to hitting all the stores that looked interesting.

He grabbed some pizza down there, and stayed for a movie after the shops closed. That turned out to be a mistake. Sitting in a theater by himself was the loneliest thing he'd ever done, much worse than watching a movie on the VCR without any company. All the other people there seemed to have somebody else to have a good time with, and he didn't.

And he was sure Megan would have loved this flick. She'd have gone all slobbery over the male star, and he could have had a good time teasing her about it. And she would have told him he only went to movies for the special effects – and they were pretty damn special. And then they would have gone back to his place and screwed themselves silly.

He went back to the place that wasn't his: a long haul up the San Diego Freeway, which had plenty of traffic even after eleven at night. When he got there, he masturbated twice in quick succession. It wasn't the same – it wasn't close to the same – but it let him fall asleep.

The next morning, he drove out Topanga Canyon Boulevard to the ocean and spent the day at Zuma Beach. That would have been better with Megan along, too, but it wasn't so bad by itself, either: nothing to do but lie there and watch girls and keep himself well greased with sunscreen. It let him get through another day without being too unhappy.

But, in spite of all the sunscreen, he came home with a burn. He was so fair, he could sunburn in the moonlight. Hot and uncomfortable, he couldn't fall asleep. Finally, he quit trying. He put on some shorts and a T-shirt and went out front to watch TV. That experiment didn't last long: nothing there but crap of the purest ray serene. After about twenty minutes, he turned it off in disgust.

"Now what?" he muttered. He still wasn't sleepy. He walked back into the bedroom and got his car keys. He was an L.A. kid, all right: when in doubt, climb behind the wheel.

Driving around with a Pulp cassette in the stereo and the volume cranked made Justin feel better for a while. But he wasn't just driving around. His hands and feet figured that out a little before his head did. The conscious part of his mind was surprised to discover they'd sent him down his own street toward his own apartment building.

If he parked between the Acapulco and the building next to it, he could look between them and see his bedroom window, a foreshortened rectangle of light. The curtain was drawn, so light was all he could see, light and, briefly, a moving shadow. Was that his older self? Megan? Were they both there? If they were, what were they doing? *Like I don't know*, Justin thought.

"I've got spare keys," he told himself in conversational tones. "I could walk in there and . . ."

Instead, he started up the car and drove away, fast. What would he do if he did walk in on himself-at-forty and Megan? He didn't want to find out.

The sunburn bothered him enough the next day that staying in the apartment and being a lump suited him fine. The day after, though, he felt better, which meant he also started feeling stir-crazy. He went out and drove some more: west on the 118 into Ventura County. Simi Valley and Moorpark were bedroom communities for the Valley, the way the Valley had been a bedroom community for downtown L.A. when his parents were his age.

I could be going to Paris or Prague or Tokyo, he thought as he put the pedal to the metal to get on the freeway, *and I'm going to Simi Valley?* But, in fact, he couldn't go to Paris or Prague or Tokyo, not without a passport, which he didn't have. And he didn't really want to. He just wanted to go on living the way he had been living. He'd spent his whole life in the Valley, and was in some ways as much a small-town kid as somebody from Kokomo or Oshkosh.

Justin didn't think of himself like that, of course. As far as he was concerned, he stood at the top of the cool food chain. And so, when he'd pulled off the freeway and driven the couple of blocks to what his Thomas Brothers guide showed as the biggest shopping center in Simi Valley, he made gagging noises. "It's not even a mall!" he exclaimed. And it wasn't, not by his standards: no single, enormous, air-conditioned building in which to roam free. If he wanted to go from store to store, he had to expose his tender hide to the sun for two, sometimes three, minutes at a time.

He almost turned around and drove back to his apartment. In the end, with a martyred sigh, he parked the car and headed toward a little mom-and-pop software store. It turned out to be all PC stuff. He had Virtual PC, so he could run Windows programs on his Macs, but he left in a hurry anyway. They'd go okay on the iMac, which was a pretty fast machine, but they'd be glacial on the old PowerBook he had with him.

The Wherehouse a couple of doors down was just as depressing. Grunge, metal, rap, bands his parents had listened to – yeah, they had plenty of that stuff.

British pop? He found one, count it, one Oasis CD, filed under THE REST OF O. Past that? Nada.

"Boy, this is fun," he said as he stomped out in moderately high dudgeon. He spotted a Borders halfway across the shopping center and headed toward it. Even as he did, he wondered why he bothered. The way his luck was running, it would stock a fine assortment of computer magazines from 1988.

Behind him, somebody called, "Justin!" He kept walking. Half the guys in his generation – all the ones who weren't Jasons – were Justins. But the call came again, louder, more insistent: "Hey, Justin!"

Maybe it is me, he thought, and turned around. A startled smile spread over his face. "Lindsey!" he said. Sure as hell, Lindsey Fletcher came running up to him, rubber-soled sandals scuffing on the sidewalk. He opened his arms. They gave each other a big hug.

"I can't believe it," Lindsey said. "What are you doing up here? You never come up here. I've never seen you up here, anyway." She spoke as if one proved the other.

She'd always liked to talk, Justin remembered. He remembered the mole on the side of her neck, too. It was still there, a couple of inches above the top of her T-shirt. "How are you?" he said. "How've you been?"

"I'm fine." She looked him up and down. "God, you haven't changed a bit."

"Yeah, well," Justin said, a little uncomfortably. He knew how little he would change, too, which she didn't.

"What are you doing up here?" Lindsey asked again.

"Whatever," Justin answered. "A little shopping. Hanging out. You know."

"Here? It's a lot better in the Valley." She looked astonished and sounded wistful.

"Yeah, well," he said again: he'd already discovered that. "Something new."

"Slumming," Lindsey told him. "But as long as you're here, that donut place over there isn't too bad." She pointed. "I mean, if you want to get something and, you know, talk for a little while."

"Sure," Justin said. Like a lot of the little donut shops in Southern California, this one was run by Cambodians: a middle-aged couple who spoke with accents and a teenage boy who talked just like Justin and Lindsey. Lindsey tried to buy; Justin wouldn't let her, not with his older self's money burning a hole in his wallet. They got jelly donuts and big fizzy Cokes, sat down at one of the half dozen or so little tables in the shop, and proceeded to get powdered sugar all over their faces.

"What have you been up to?" Lindsey asked, dabbing at herself with a paper napkin.

"Finished my junior year at CSUN," Justin answered, pronouncing it *C-sun* the way anybody who went there would.

"What's your major?"

"Computer science. It's pretty interesting, and it'll pay off, too – I've got a summer job at the Northridge CompUSA." *Which my older self is welcome to.* Half a beat slower than he should have, Justin asked, "How about you?"

"I've been going to Moorpark Community College kind of on and off," Lindsey said. "I've got a part-time job, too – pet grooming."

"Ah, cool," Justin said. "You always did love animals. I remember."

She nodded. "Maybe I'll end up doing that full-time. If I can save some money, maybe I'll try and get into breeding one of these days." She sipped at her Coke, then asked, "Do I want to know about your parents?"

"No!" Justin exclaimed. "God no! Let's see . . . I think you'd already moved here when my mom came out of the closet."

"Oh, Lord." Lindsey's eyes got big. "That must have been fun."

"Yeah, right," Justin said. "Somebody shoot me quick if I ever set out to discover myself." He turned his mother's favorite phrase into a curse.

Lindsey didn't ask about his father. The bad news there had been obvious while she still lived in the Valley. After some hesitation, she did ask, "What about you? Are you . . . seeing anybody?"

Justin had just taken a big bite of jelly donut, so he didn't have to answer right away. When he did, he did his best to make it sound casual: "Uh-huh."

"Oh." Lindsey looked disappointed, which was flattering. And Justin couldn't have sounded too casual, because she asked, "Are you serious?"

"Well, it kinda looks that way," he admitted. And then, not so much out of politeness as because he didn't want to think about how he *wasn't* seeing Megan right this minute and his older self *was*, he said, "What about you?"

Lindsey shook her head. A strand of her short blonde hair – she'd worn it longer in high school – fell down onto her nose. She brushed it away with her hand. "Not right now. Not so it matters, anyhow, I mean. I've gone with a few guys since I got up here, but nobody I'd want to settle down with. You're lucky."

She sounded wistful again. She also sounded as if she really meant it. She'd never begrudged happiness to anybody else. Justin would have had trouble saying the same thing – he was mad as hell thinking about himself-at-forty having a good time with Megan. And how lucky was he if his older self had to come back from 2018 to try to straighten things out? But Lindsey didn't – couldn't – know about that, of course.

He finished the donut in a couple of big bites. "I better get going. I have to be at work before too long." He could almost feel his nose getting longer, but the lie gave him an excuse to get away.

"Okay." Lindsey stood up, too. "It was great to see you. I'm glad you're doing so well." She sounded as if she really meant that, too. Nope, not a mean bone in her body. She gave him another hug, this one a little more constrained than the one when they first ran into each other. "Listen, if you ever want to just talk or anything, I'm in the book." She made a face. "I sorta wish I wasn't, but I am. I get more damn telemarketers than you can shake a stick at."

"Always at dinnertime, too," Justin said, and she nodded. "They ought to do something about 'em." He didn't know who *they* were or what they could do, but that didn't stop him from complaining. He headed for the door. "So long."

"So long, Justin." Lindsey followed, but more slowly, making it plain she wasn't going to come with him once they got outside. He headed for his car. Lindsey walked in the direction of the Wherehouse he'd already found wanting. He looked back toward her once. She was looking toward him. They both smiled and waved. Justin pulled out his keys, unlocked the Toyota, and slid inside. Lindsey went into the Wherehouse. Justin drove back to the Valley. For some reason he couldn't quite fathom, he didn't feel so bad once he got there.

He kept feeling halfway decent, or even a little better than halfway decent, for a while afterwards. The driving need to call up either his older self or Megan and find out how things were going went away. What that amounted to, of course, was finding out whether anybody in the whole wide world cared if he was alive – and a good-sized fear the answer was no. Lindsey Fletcher cared. Justin didn't think of it in those terms – on a conscious level, he hardly thought of it at all – but that was what it added up to.

And so, over about the next ten days, he found things to do and places to go that let him kill time without seeming to be doing nothing but killing time. He drove over to the Sherman Oaks Galleria, which had gone from the coolest place in the world to semi-ghost town in one fell swoop after the '94 quake. He beat the parking hassles at the new Getty Museum looming over the San Diego Freeway by taking a cab there – *spending my older self's money*, he thought, feeling half virtuous and half *so there*! He found a pretty good Japanese restaurant, Omino's, on Devonshire near Canoga. It'd be a good place to take Megan once himself-at-forty got the hell back to 2018 where he belonged.

"Superstrings," Justin muttered in the apartment that wasn't his. He'd fought his way through his physics classes; he couldn't say much more than that. He wished he knew more. His older self did, dammit. That was definitely something to think about when he planned his schedule for his senior year.

Before so very long, though, he started muttering other, more incendiary, things. His decent mood didn't last, not least because he didn't fully understand what had caused it in the first place. The apartment in the Yachtsman started feeling like a prison cell again. Going out stopped being fun. Minutes crawled past on hands and knees.

Justin thought about calling his older self to complain: he thought about it for a good second and a half, as a matter of fact. Then he laughed a bitter laugh that lasted a lot longer. He knew just what his older self would say. *Live with it*. He could tell himself that and save the price of a phone call. It wasn't quite *fuck off and die*, but close enough for government work.

Besides, he didn't really want to talk to himself-at-forty. He wanted to talk to Megan. His older self had given him all sorts of reasons why that wasn't a good idea. Justin had only one reason why it was: he was going out of his tree because he couldn't. Eventually, that swamped everything his older self had said.

He felt as if he'd just pulled off a jailbreak when he dialed her number. Her father answered the phone. "Hi, Mr. Tricoupis," he said happily. "Can I talk to Megan, please?"

Instead of saying *Sure* or *Hang on a second* or anything like that, Megan's father answered, "Well, I don't know, Justin. I'll see if she wants to talk to you."

I'll see if she wants to talk to you? Justin thought. *What the hell's going on here?* But he couldn't even ask, because a clunking noise meant Mr. Tricoupis had put the phone down. He could only wait.

After what seemed like forever but couldn't have been more than half a minute, Megan said, "Hello?" He needed no more than the one word to hear that she didn't sound happy.

But he felt something close to delirious joy at hearing her voice. "Hi!" he burbled. "How you doing?"

Another pause. Then, very carefully, Megan said, "Justin, didn't I tell you last night not to call here for a while? Didn't I say that?"

He knew what that meant. It meant his older self wasn't as goddamn smart as he thought he was. By the look of things, it also meant he'd have to bail himself-at-forty out instead of the other way round. He wondered if he could. He and Megan hadn't had any great big fights, which meant he had no sure feel for how to fix one.

Silly seemed a good idea. "Duh," he said, the standard idiot-noise of the late '90s, and then, "My big mouth." That wasn't just an apology; it was also the title of an Oasis song Megan liked.

"Your big mouth is right," she said, but a little of the hard edge left her voice – either that or wishful thinking was running away with Justin. She wasn't going to let him down easy, though; she went on, "Do you have any idea how far over the line you were? Any idea at all?"

"Definitely maybe," he answered: an Oasis album title that had the added virtue of keeping him off the hook.

He wasn't sure Megan had noticed the first title he used, but she definitely noticed the second; he heard her snort. "You're funny now," she said, as if fighting to stay mad. "You weren't funny last night after the movie, believe me you weren't."

Which movie? Justin wondered. He could hardly ask; he was supposed to know. He couldn't even waste any more time cursing his older self, not when he was trying to jolly Megan back into a good mood. "Charmless man, that's me," he said. It wasn't just him – it was also a track on a recent Blur CD.

"Justin . . ." But Megan was fighting back laughter now. "What am I supposed to do about you?"

"Roll with it, my legendary girlfriend," Justin said: one Oasis song, one from Pulp. "I'm just a killer for your love. Advert." Two from Blur. He didn't know how long he could keep it up, but he was having fun while it lasted.

With that, Megan gave up the fight and giggled. "Okay," she said. "Okay. I didn't think you could do anything to make me forget last night, but you did. How did you manage?"

"Only tongue will tell," he answered gravely. "Worked a miracle." That set Megan off again. She recognized Trash Can Sinatra's titles, sure enough, and there probably weren't three other people in the San Fernando Valley who would have.

"I'll see you soon, Justin," she said, and hung up.

But she wouldn't be seeing him, dammit. She'd be seeing his older self. Justin started to call his old apartment to tell himself-at-forty what he thought of him, but held off. He didn't see what good it would do. He wasn't quite ready to throw his older self out of his place on his ear, and nothing short of that would make a nickel's worth of difference. *I'll wait*, he thought. *For a little while.*

He didn't have to wait long. Twenty minutes later, the phone rang. He hurried into the bedroom from the kitchen, hoping it was Megan. He'd just picked up the phone when he remembered she didn't have the number here. By then, he was already saying, "Hello?"

"Oh, good. You're home." His older self sounded half disappointed Justin hadn't walked in front of a truck.

"Oh, it's you," Justin answered, still wishing it were Megan. Throwing himself-at-forty out on his ear suddenly looked more attractive. He went on, "No, *you're* home. I'm stuck here." He looked around the little bedroom, feeling like a trapped animal again.

His older self had gone into dictator mode: "Didn't I tell you to lay low till I was done here? God damn it, you'd better listen to me. I just had to pretend I knew what Megan was talking about when she said I'd been on the phone with her."

"She's my girl, too," Justin said. "She was my girl first, you know. I've got a *right* to talk with her." As talking with Lindsey Fletcher out in the wilds of Simi Valley had, it reminded him he was alive.

But himself-at-forty didn't want to hear any of that. Maybe he wasn't a dictator; maybe he was just a grownup talking down to a kid. Whatever he was, he sure sounded like somebody convinced he knew it all: "Not if you want her to keep being your girl, you don't. You're the one who's going to screw it up, remember?"

"That's what you keep telling me." Justin was getting sick of hearing it, too. "But you know what? I'm not so sure I believe you any more. When I called her, Megan sounded like she was really torqued at me – at you, I mean. So it doesn't sound like you've got all the answers."

"*Nobody* has *all* the answers." His older self sounded as if he believed that. Justin didn't; like *The X-Files*, he was convinced the truth was out there, provided he could find it. And then, throwing gasoline on the fire, his older self added, "If you think you've got more of them than I do, you're full of shit."

That did it. Justin wanted to turn his head real fast to see if he had smoke coming out of his ears. "You want to be careful how you talk to me," he ground out, biting off each word. "Half the time, I still think your whole setup is bogus. If I decide to, I can wreck it. You know damn well I can."

If that didn't scare the crap out of himself-at-forty, Justin didn't know what would. But if it did, his older self didn't show it, damn him. Instead, he kicked back with both feet, like a mule: "Yeah, go ahead. Screw up your life for good. Keep going like this and you will."

And that scared the crap out of Justin. Himself-at-forty had to know it would. It was the only weapon he had, but it was a nuke. Justin tried not to let on that he knew it, saying, "You sound pretty screwed up now. What have I got to lose?"

Maybe, for once, he got through to himself-at-forty, because his older self, also for once, stopped trying to browbeat him and started trying to explain: "I had something good, and I let it slip through my fingers. You wreck what I'm doing now, you'll go through life without knowing what a good thing was." And then he trotted out the ICBMs again. "You want that? Just keep sticking your nose in where it doesn't belong. You want to end up with Megan or not?"

There it was. Justin did want that. He wanted it more than anything else in the world, and he couldn't let on that he didn't. If himself-at-forty was bluffing, he'd just got away with it. "All right," Justin said, though it was anything but all right, and he didn't think he sounded as if it were. "I'll back off – for now."

He got the last word by hanging up. Then he masturbated again. It made him feel good, but it didn't come close to making him feel better.

He rented *Titanic* and watched it several times over the next few days, which certainly went a long way toward keeping him out of circulation. He wasn't watching it for the romance. Christ, no. Jack died. He wanted his life with Megan to go on and on, even if he couldn't stand Celine Dion.

What he watched obsessively was the way the enormous liner took on water and sank after it hit the iceberg. Here in this apartment that wasn't his, as far out of the loop as he could be, he felt he was taking on water, too.

Running into Lindsey Fletcher, sitting down with her and eating messy jelly donuts and talking, had let him believe for quite a while that he wasn't alone in the world. He cared about Megan a lot more, but talking with her on the phone didn't satisfy his people jones nearly as long. For one thing, talking on the phone was like looking at a picture of a great dinner – pretty, yeah, but not the real thing.

And, for another, he'd had the row with himself-at-forty just afterwards. He might have stayed happier longer if he hadn't. The main reason – the only reason – he'd gone along with his older self and this whole craziness was that he couldn't stand the idea of losing Megan, of having to go through a divorce. If his older self could smooth things out now, make sure that never happened, great.

But if his older self was fighting with Megan, was making her angry at him . . . Where the hell did that leave Justin? He'd already saved the day once, which made him want to gallop back into the scene like a knight in shining armor coming to rescue the fair maiden. Would he rescue her, though? Or would he gallop in and screw things up, the way his older self said?

He didn't hop into his car – which was actually his older self's car – and drive over and throw himself-at-forty out of his rightful apartment. But he couldn't stand staying here and doing nothing, either, not for very long he couldn't.

After a bit more sitting on his hands, he hit on a compromise – or, to look at it another way, he found an excuse for doing what he wanted to do anyhow. *I'll call Megan,* Justin thought. *I did some good the last time. Maybe I can do some more now. And then I'll brief my older self on what we talked about, so he doesn't get caught short.*

Man is the rationalizing animal.

Justin felt good, felt alive, felt part of things again, as he dialed the phone. It rang a couple of times, then somebody picked it up. "Hello?" Hearing Megan's voice made him smile big and wide. It also made him horny as hell.

"Hiya!" He gave her back her own favorite greeting.

Silence, about fifteen seconds' worth, on the other end of the line. Then Megan said, "Justin, this is way over, I mean *way* over, the top. Didn't I tell you not two hours ago that I didn't want to see you any more, I didn't want to talk to you any more, I didn't want to have anything to do with you any more? Didn't I?"

"But—" Justin heard the words, but he had a hard time making them mean anything.

Megan didn't give him much of a chance, either. She went on, "Didn't I tell you that if I ever changed my mind, *I'd* call *you*? Didn't I? I don't want to be on the phone with you any more, Justin, I mean I really don't." She sounded furious, bigtime furious.

"Wait a minute," Justin said frantically. "What—?"

He was trying to say, *What are you talking about*? But he never got the chance. Megan filled in the blank for him: "What about the sex? I already told you, I don't care how good it was. I don't care that it got better the last couple weeks, either. I don't want you treating me like I was twelve years old, and I *do* care about that. Now get out of my life, goddammit. Goodbye!" The phone crashed down.

Slowly, like a man in shock – which he was – Justin hung up, too. *I don't care that it got better the last couple weeks, either*? One day, when he had time to think about it, that would be a separate torment of its own. Right now, it was just part of the general disaster.

"What do I do?" he asked, as if the bedroom could tell him. What he wanted to do was call Megan back and explain, really explain, but that wasn't gonna fly. If he got in even two words before she hung up on him, it'd be a miracle.

"E-mail!" he exclaimed, and ran for his PowerBook. He wrote the message. He sent it. Less than a minute later, it came back, with PERMANENT FATAL ERROR at the top and an explanatory paragraph underneath saying that she was refusing all mail from his address. "Jesus!" he cried in real anguish. "I've been bozo-filtered!" That added insult to injury, and none of this, not one single thing, was his fault.

He knew whose fault it was, though. Anguish didn't last. Rage replaced it.

The phone rang four times before his older self answered. "Hello?" He sounded groggy.

Justin didn't much care how he sounded. "You son of a bitch," he snarled. "You goddamn stupid, stinking, know-it-all son of a bitch."

"I'm sorry," himself-at-forty said. Of all the useless words in the world right now, those were the big two. "I tried to—"

"I just tried calling Megan," Justin said, interrupting his older self the way Megan had interrupted him. "She said she didn't want to talk to me. She said she never wanted to talk to me again. She said she'd told me she never wanted to talk to me again, so what was I doing on the phone right after she told me that? Then she hung up on me." He didn't say anything about the refused e-mail. Somehow, that hurt even worse, too much to talk about.

"I'm sorry," his older self said again. "I—"

"Sorry?" Justin yelled. If he hadn't had a buzz cut, he might have pulled his hair. "You think you're sorry now? You don't know what sorry is, but you will. I'm gonna beat the living shit out of you, dude. You think you can get away with that, you're full of—" He hung up on himself-at-forty even harder than Megan had hung up on him.

He hadn't been in a fight since middle school, and he'd lost that one. It didn't matter. He stormed out of the apartment, slamming the door behind him. He ran down to his car – no, to his older self's car – and headed to his old apartment, his proper apartment, as fast as he could go.

That meant somewhere between ten and fifteen minutes. He was still incandescent when he got there. He turned the key in the lock to the security gate and drove into the Acapulco's parking lot. His own car, the one himself-at-forty had been driving, was still in its space.

"You thought I was kidding, did you, you bastard?" Justin's lips skinned back from his teeth in a savage smile. "I'll show you who was kidding, asshole."

Finding a parking space out on the street took another minute (a well-trained Southern Californian, he never thought to use one of the empty ones in the parking garage; those weren't his). Then he stormed up the steps into the lobby, opened the security door, and charged toward his apartment.

Click! One key in the dead bolt. *Click!* The other in the lock. The door opened. Justin slammed it shut behind him. "All right, you fucker, now you're gonna get it," he growled.

No one answered. Justin strode into the bedroom. It was as empty of life – except his own – as the front room and kitchen had been. He checked the bathroom. He checked the closets. He checked under the bed. He didn't take long to decide he was the only one in the place.

But his older self hadn't taken his car. "He can't have gone far," Justin muttered: again, the Southern California assumption that nobody without wheels could do much. Justin scratched his head. Was himself-at-forty running for his life? Hopping a cab? Waiting for a bus? None of those made much sense.

But the chair in the bedroom was pulled a long way out from the desk. You couldn't use the iMac with the chair out there. You could sure as hell use a laptop, though. What would a laptop from 2018 be able to do? Justin didn't know, but the mere thought was plenty to make him salivate.

His older self had said coming back from then to now was a matter of good programming. If he had a machine like that, if he had the program on the hard drive, could he go back the way he'd come?

"How should I know?" Justin asked nobody in particular. But the apartment felt very, very empty. Maybe his older self had fled where he couldn't hope to follow for nineteen years.

Or could he? He knew some things he wouldn't have if his older self hadn't come back and . . . *And screwed up my life*, Justin thought. He knew going back in time involved superstrings and programming. The combination wouldn't have crossed his mind in a million years – no, in something close to nineteen years – if himself-at-forty hadn't returned to 1999 to meddle.

And he knew the thing could be done in the first place. Knowing that was half the battle, maybe more than half. He'd never let himself get discouraged. No matter how bleak things looked, he wouldn't give up and decide he was chasing something impossible.

And . . . A slow smile stole over his face. He had a nest egg now that he hadn't had before, thanks to the cash his older self had left behind. He hadn't blown very much of it. If he made some investments and they worked out, he could be sitting pretty by the time he got to the frontiers of middle age.

"Inflation," he said, reminding himself. "Gotta watch out for inflation."

Himself-at-forty had said his stash of cash wouldn't be worth nearly so much in 2018 as it was now. Whatever he put the money into, he'd have to make sure rising prices didn't erode it into chump change.

What he had to do right now was get his hands on the cash, which was still sitting back at the other apartment. Then he'd have to figure out how to put it into his bank account without getting busted as a drug runner or money launderer. You could put only so much cash in at a time, or else the bank had to report you to the Feds. He knew that. But what was the upper limit? He had no idea. *I'll find out on the Net*, he thought, and put it out of his mind for the time being.

As he drove over to the other apartment, something else struck him: *I can get rid of this car. That'll bring in some more money to help set me up.*

All that assumed his older self wasn't hanging around in 1999. Justin didn't *know* himself-at-forty wasn't, not for a fact. If his older self *did* remain here in the twentieth century, Justin still intended to punch his lights out the first chance he got.

He was loading twenties and fifties and hundreds into shopping bags, feeling a lot like a gangster, when he thought, *I can move out of this apartment, too, and get back whatever security deposits my older self paid – part of them, anyway.* In spite of the handfuls of greenbacks he was taking out of the drawer, every dollar felt important.

He wondered what his quarter from 2012 would be worth, and whether it would be worth anything at all. But then he shook his head. "I'll keep it," he declared, as if someone had told him not to. "It'll remind me what I'm shooting for."

More than a little nervously, he took the cash down to the car. He managed it without getting mugged. He didn't think he'd ever driven so carefully in his life as on the trip back to the Acapulco. He'd never watched the rear-view mirror so much, either. *Don't want to get rear-ended now. Oh, Jesus, no.*

As he parked in front of the apartment building, a nasty thought hit him. *What'll I do if he just walked away for a few minutes and now he's back in my place?* Punching his older self's lights out still seemed like a good plan.

But the apartment was empty. With a sigh of relief, Justin stashed the bags of cash in the little closet in the hallway that led from the living room back to the bedroom. Then he put a couple of pans by the door. He'd have to get the lock changed, but in the meantime at least he'd have some warning if his older self was still around and tried to come in.

"Have to get the rest of my stuff out of that other place, too," he said. But, for the time being, that could wait.

He quickly went through the apartment, looking for whatever his older self had left behind. Finding a laptop from 2018 – if himself-at-forty had had one with him – would have been the grand prize. He didn't. But he did find a statement from a bank he wouldn't have patronized if a stagecoach had run over him. When he saw how much it was for, his eyes bugged out of his head: about as much as he had in those bags in the closet.

And it's mine, too, he thought dazedly. *If he's gone, it's mine. I can prove I'm*

Justin Kloster just as well as he could. I know my mother's maiden name just as well as he did.

For a moment, thinking of only one thing at a time, he actually felt grateful toward his older self. A twenty-one-year-old guy with six figures' worth of money in the bank and with a plan to get ahead . . . What couldn't he do?

I can't have Megan. His joy blew out. Cash was great, but without his girl? Whatever his older self had done there, he'd screwed it up bigtime. And he'd said he'd never found anybody else who came close to her.

Maybe I can get her back, Justin thought. *Maybe in a couple weeks, or when school starts again and I see her. Or something.*

He shoved the thought aside. He couldn't do anything about it now.

Himself-at-forty had seen to that. Justin started getting angry all over again.

And he didn't get any happier when he looked at what was in the refrigerator. It was all stuff he'd have to cook if he wanted to eat it: even worse stuff than had been in his older self's other place when he first got there. What were you supposed to do with ginger root or hoisin sauce? He didn't know, and he wasn't interested in learning. But then he started to laugh. He could afford to eat out, by God.

Eat out he did. Yang Chow was odds-on the best Chinese place in this end of the Valley. He devoured kung-pao chicken and chili shrimp, with a Tsingtao beer to put out the fire from the peppers. No sign of his older self when he got back.

Justin called the other place. The phone rang and rang. After it had gone on ringing for more than a minute, he hung up again, nodding. His older self wasn't there, either. The more he wasn't there, the more convinced Justin was that he'd gone back to 2018.

"He should have stayed there, the son of a bitch," Justin said. "Maybe Megan and me would have made it. Shit – even if we didn't, I'd still have the good memories he did. What have I got now? Not one damn thing."

Before he went to bed, he changed the sheets and bedspread. He didn't even want to think about what had happened on the ones he threw in the clothes basket.

He slept late the next morning, which annoyed him. He had a lot of stuff he wanted to do that day: formally leave the other apartment, close his older self's banking account and move the money to his own, sell that other Toyota and put the proceeds from the deal in the bank, too. He was just heading out the door when the phone rang.

"Jesus!" he said, and hurried back to the bedroom. Maybe it was his older self. That would screw things up. Or maybe it was Megan. That would do anything but. "Hello?"

It wasn't himself-at-forty. It wasn't Megan, either, dammit. It was his boss at CompUSA, and he sounded pissed to the max. "Where the hell are you, Kloster?" he shouted. "That graphic-design outfit is coming in this morning to order their new Macs, and they don't want to deal with anybody but you." He said something under his breath about "Macintosh primadonnas," then went back to bellowing: "What are you doing there when you're supposed to be here?"

Justin had forgotten all about his CompUSA job. Evidently, his older self had been holding it down pretty well. With all the money he had, he was tempted to tell his boss to stuff it, but he didn't. That would look bad on a résumé. He gave the best excuse he could think of: "I must have forgotten to set my alarm last night. I'll be right there."

His boss promptly tempted him to regret his choice, roaring, "If they show up before you do, you're toast!" and hanging up hard.

He did get there first, and had enough time to review things before the graphic designers trooped in. Before they trooped out again, they'd bought about fifty grand worth of computers and peripherals, and his boss was acting amazingly human. Said boss even took him to lunch at a Mexican place not nearly so good as Sierra's – though he wouldn't have wanted to go there now – and didn't say boo when he ordered a margarita to go with his enchilada and rice and refried beans.

After lunch, he was upgrading system software on one of the iMac demos when he heard footsteps behind him. He turned around to see who it was; the Macintosh ministore inside the CompUSA didn't get nearly the foot traffic he thought it deserved. "Lindsey!" he exclaimed. "What are you doing here?"

"Well, you told me where you worked." She looked nervous. "I just thought I'd come over and say hi. Hi!" She fluttered her fingers at him in an arch little wave, then quickly went on. "I don't want to make trouble or anything. I know you said you were seeing somebody." By the way she stood on the balls of her feet, she was poised to flee if Justin barked at her.

But that, right this second, was the last thing he wanted to do. "I was, yeah," he answered, and watched her eyes widen at the past tense, "but we just broke up. Somebody came between us, I guess you'd say."

"Oh, my God!" Lindsey exclaimed, and then frowned anxiously. "I hope you don't mean me. She wasn't, like, jealous 'cause you went up to Simi Valley and ran into me or anything? That'd be awful."

"No, no, no," Justin assured her. "Had nothing to do with you. It was another guy. An older guy." The first and last parts of that were true, anyway. The middle? He wasn't so sure.

"That's terrible!" Lindsey said. "You must be all torn up inside." She reached out and put a sympathetic hand on his arm.

"I was bummed," he admitted – about as much as a male his age was likely to say. "It's really nice, that you came all the way from Simi to see me." They both laughed, even though Justin hadn't quite made the joke on purpose. Lindsey smiled at him. He wasn't always fast on the uptake, but something got through. He set his hand on hers. "Who knows?" he said. "Maybe it won't work out too bad after all."

LOOB

Bob Leman

Bob Leman was an American science fiction and horror short-story writer, most often associated with *The Magazine of Fantasy & Science Fiction*. Leman's first story appeared when he was forty-five. His most famous story, "Window" (1980), was nominated for the Nebula Award and adapted for an episode of *Night Visions*, directed by and starring Bill Pullman. Another of Leman's stories, "How Dobbstown Was Saved," was to have been published in the Harlan Ellison anthology *The Last Dangerous Visions* but eventually appeared in the collection *Feesters in the Lake and Other Stories* (2002). This story, "Loob," was first published in *The Magazine of Fantasy & Science Fiction* in 1979.

I t may be that none of this happened.

That is badly put. Let me say it another way: none of this *will have happened* at the instant – which I believe must come eventually – the instant that Loob permits my great-grandfather to pass unscathed through the drawing room door.

I believe that one day Loob will permit it. I think he must. Because if he does not, my existence is an impossibility. And I do exist. *Cogito, ergo sum.* Besides which, I have an actual physical presence: yesterday I cut myself when I shaved (there is a decided tremor in my hands), I have a blister on my right foot, these seedy clothes cover a breathing body.

Officially, though, and perhaps in law, I do not exist. Neither the county nor the state has any record of my birth (nor my father's; my grandmother's birth, however, is duly recorded). Lawrenceville and Princeton have no record of my attendance and graduation. Even the United States Army, that indefatigable maker and keeper of records has no paper that acknowledges my three years of servitude. And it is a melancholy fact that no one in the world seems to know or remember me; not friends from prep school days, not college classmates or fellow officers, not a soul in the old home town. My precise and detailed recollection of my twenty-five years of life is always and everywhere belied by records both public and private, and by every reality of the world around me.

Yet I am real, I am a living, breathing, thinking human being, as solid and sentient as any of the degenerates who surround me here. As I skulk about this decrepit travesty of my native town, I reflect endlessly upon my impossible existence, upon the resemblances and differences between this world and my own, upon an explanation for the situation in which I find myself. And I have found the explanation, and in finding it I find some hope. I can only wait, and watch Loob.

It is true that certain parts of my explanation are, perhaps, in a way, to a certain degree (if you like) conjectural; nonetheless, it hangs together, it hangs together. Up to a certain August day in 1905 this world and my own were identical; my explanation rests, therefore, on simple, unarguable fact. On that day there was a divergence, a forking, and Loob was the cause. It took me some time to figure that out.

To identify Loob as the villain, that is. I was much quicker at the rest of it, at accounting for the existence of this town. It is located where the town of my birth is located, it bears the same name, it has the same history up to a point. It is composed of the same streets and buildings that make up the older part of my own town, horribly run-down here, all in a state of slovenly desuetude, with buildings vacant and boarded up, trash in the deserted streets, insolent weeds growing in and around the ruins of structures that have burned or fallen down. It is a depressed and depressing place, forming a most bleak and demoralizing contrast with the self-confident bustle and gloss of the town I knew.

My own situation is also considerably different. There I am the heir apparent, the young master, indulged in expensive toys – a Ferrari, a string of polo ponies – by a doting grandmother. Here I work as a swamper in a saloon; the Top Hat Bar and Grill, to be exact. It is the only work available to a nameless unperson. (They call me Tom Perkins. I don't know where they got that. Back when I still talked, I used to ask them to use my real name, but the request always generated so much laughter that I gave it up.) At that, I am one of the very few people here who work; most of the town is on welfare, as I might be myself if I could establish the fact that I exist. Ironically, they have volunteered to put me on the welfare rolls under the name of Tom Perkins, an offer which I declined. That also caused a good deal of laughter.

Day after day, as I cleaned the spittoons (three-pound coffee cans, actually) and mopped the foul floor, my mind was occupied by a sustained effort to discover, through the application of the most rigorous logic, a theory to account for my presence in a world where my presence is impossible. (This was after my parole from the state hospital, after I had achieved a measure of resignation to my plight.) The initial stages of my analysis were simple enough: I postulated that any occurrence, anywhere, anytime, is a cause that has a consequent effect. A major occurrence has a major effect and changes history. Now, from the beginning, history has been an infinity of forks in a road, with the road not taken disappearing forever after it is passed, so that a backward look shows only a single thoroughfare stretching to the rear. But suppose that somehow, from our present position on this thoroughfare, a barricade could be hurled backward, back to one of those forks in the road, compelling events to travel on the alternative route. As time went by, and fork after fork came and went, a retrospective survey of the route taken would not show that the main road was missed long ago. It would not show that we now travel on a detour, a sad, sick, degenerate, abominable detour. But the main road is still there, is still there. I think logic dictates that we must believe it is still there.

The exercise of pure reason had brought me to that point, but there my search for the truth began to appear to be almost hopeless. Reduced to essentials, it had become a search for the villain. Someone had erected the barricade that shunted history into the detour and exiled me from the main road to this wretched byway, and whoever he was, he had to be found and compelled to undo his villainy. But the world is a big place, containing a very considerable number of people, and I had not the least vague clue to his identity. A mad scientist? A military secret project? A lama spinning a prayer wheel in Tibet?

My problem was further complicated by the fact that I am not permitted to leave town. The people at the state hospital have decreed that I must be brought in once a month to be questioned and tested, presumably for reassurance that I can safely continue to be farmed out to the Top Hat Bar and Grill. I gather that before my incarceration I sometimes did violent things. (When I compare my mashed-in face with the way I used to look, I can believe it.) Okie Perkins, Prop. of the Top Hat Bar and Grill, drives me to these monthly vettings, where I steadfastly maintain silence despite the often ingenious subterfuges the headshrinkers use to get me to talk. I have promised myself that I shall speak no word until I am back where I belong. Obviously this vow was a further impediment to my investigation.

But I had some good luck, which served me as well as cold reason and sedulous research could have done. I found Loob. At some point in my despairing prowlings through the town, I became aware of him, and I came gradually to realize that I had found the culprit. It was no blazing revelation, or anything of that sort; but as soon as I began to suspect him I undertook to weigh his qualifications as a suspect against the indisputable facts, and, little by little, it became perfectly plain that it was indeed Loob who had done this unspeakable thing. I matched the history of the town – one history until 1905, and then two, both of which I had pondered obsessively – with what I knew about Loob, and at last the whole grim story was laid out for me.

I said that finding him was good luck, but it was bad luck as well, because my plan to compel an undoing of the evil has come to nothing; quite clearly there is no way to compel Loob to do anything at all. There is not even any way to talk to him – which I would be eager to do if he could understand. But he cannot talk, and so certain portions of the story must remain forever conjecture. But they fit the facts, the whole thing coheres.

So now I watch him and wait for the day when he will undo what he did. Because there is nothing to do but watch and wait. And (I cannot help it) hope. I stalk him through the town, willing him to go to the house, to sit in the window. That is where he must be to change things back. When he is in the house, I usually lurk somewhere outside, not because I can affect what may happen, but simply out of an unexplainable feeling that I should be there. And then, too, looking at the house can sometimes evoke my real life so strongly that for a moment I forget where I am.

The house, my grandmother's house in the real world. A mansion with many chimneys, enduringly built of the pale-gray local sandstone, still displaying a basic elegance of line and proportion. Its walls remain as stout as the day they were built, and the slates of the roof still turn the rain; but there is no glass in any window, nor a door in any doorway, and the winds sweep through, blowing dust and trash in squalid patterns across the floor. There are no rooms on the first story; the interior walls were torn out years ago and replaced by a number of steel poles to bear the weight of the upper floors. In the cavernous space thus created, a foredoomed machine shop had existed precariously for a few years before it sank into bankruptcy and abandoned its worn-out lathes and drills to the scavengers and vandals. This is where Loob likes to be.

He likes to sit on a box in one of the oriel windows. From there he looks down to the river, across the junk piles and weeds that were once a smooth lawn sloping to the edge of the woods, across the rusty railroad tracks and decaying sheds that stand where great trees grew in the days when the house was in history's mainstream. He sits there for a large part of almost every day, watching an inconstant landscape: seeing sometimes a squirm of rats among frozen weeds, sometimes a small giggling girl frolicking with a patient dog on a summer lawn, sometimes other things. Loob feels no curiosity about these alterations of the view. Most things in life are incomprehensible to him, and all phenomena are equally unexpected and equally unsurprising. But the little girl engages somewhat more of his attention than do the rats; the pretty lady at the piano is marginally more interesting than a ruined milling machine. Loob is happier (if that is the word for the viscid stirring within him) when he is watching the past.

During all the eighteen years of his life the past has been his milieu as often as the present. He does not distinguish between them. Some things can be touched and some cannot; that is one of the things he knows, and it is his sole perception of the difference between past and present. His questing hand will pass through the piano but be arrested by the milling machine; neither occurrence surprises him. If the piano were suddenly to become palpable and the milling machine insubstantial, he would not remember that it had ever been otherwise.

He answers to "Loob," short for "Loober," which is as close as he can come to pronouncing Luther. His name is another of the things he knows. Boys used to use that fact to bait him.

"Hey, Loob. What's your name, Loob?"

"Loo – ber." Thick, slow, forced out after a struggle.

Laughter. "Make him do it again."

"What's your name, Loob?"

"Loo – ber."

And laughter again. But now he has grown to several inches over six feet and weighs three hundred pounds. They no longer tease him. He has never been known to harm anyone, but his size and appearance have emancipated him from the role of butt. When he walks in the streets now, they say, "Hi, Loob," or even, "Hello, Luther." All of the people here know each other. A stranger may say, "My God, what's that?" and someone will tell him, "Oh, that's Luther Rankin. One of our village idiots. Perfectly harmless."

The speaker will be mistaken; Loob is anything but perfectly harmless. He can do – has done – abominable things, as no one knows better than I. But he has not done them with malice; he has not intended harm. He has never in his life intended anything at all and indeed is incapable of having intentions. The abominations happened simply because Loob is what he is; they came about as suddenly, and with as little premeditation, as the collapse of a river bank in a flood. But it is because of Loob that the house is what it is. That the town is what it is.

For three quarters of a century the town has been dying. At the turn of the century it passed almost overnight from its lusty prime into senescence, but ever since it has clung with a kind of weak tenacity to a spark of life, and now, shrunken and listless, it squats and decays on its mountainside, still housing in decrepit grimy dwellings a few hundred dispirited clients of the welfare system. Trains still make runs along the track that winds down the valley beside the river, but it has been many years since the train has stopped here, and the town's name on the depot has almost weathered away. A new interstate highway carries most of the traffic that formerly used the river road, and the town's last filling station stands boarded up at the corner where Main Street meets the road. There are only two stores left, and one saloon. The school has been abandoned, and all but one of the churches. It is a town without hope and without pride, a place with no reason for existing except to provide shelter of a sort for people who are themselves without hope or pride.

Once long ago it was a prosperous confident town, whose citizens believed it might one day rival Pittsburgh. It was not a wholly impossible vision. The Dappling Iron Works, which had grown prodigiously during the Civil War, leagued itself with the railroads when the war ended, and if Henry Dappling had been another kind of man, he might have pushed himself into the company of Carnegie and Frick and made his town a city like theirs. But he was not driven by ambition, and his factory and his town in the first years of the new century were exactly as he wanted them to be: healthy, bustling, productive – and of manageable size. He was comfortable in his role as First Citizen and Squire, and he approved of a community that was not too large for every citizen to know him and know his position. He liked the town as it was, and he liked his own position within it.

He took a keen pleasure in his daily trip to the plant, the ceremony and style of it. Every morning at eight, his polished buggy passed between the gateposts of the estate and proceeded briskly into town along Dappling Road, Dappling portly and erect in the seat, snugly buttoned into well-tailored sober broadcloth, in firm control of a team of matched chestnuts. There were no doffed hats or tugged forelocks as he passed, but those who shouted good morning to him called him Mr. Dappling.

Dappling Road curved around a hill and sloped downward to meet Main Street; Dappling's house was in fact quite near the town, but hidden from it by the cheek of the hill. At Main Street he turned left, down into the town, past houses that became progressively larger as he approached the square. The block nearest the square had mansions on both sides of the street, large dark buildings of brick or stone, heavily ginger-breaded, standing at the backs of deep lawns. These were the homes of Dappling's superintendents and the banker and the most prosperous of the merchants. The retail commerce of the town took place around the square, and most of the merchants contrived to be at their doors to greet Dappling as the buggy passed smartly by. He returned to each a sober inclination of the head, a nod calculated precisely to indicate relative social positions. On the lower side of the square was another block of fine houses, and then the row houses of the mill workers down to the wrought-iron gates of the Dappling Iron Works.

In the cobbled courtyard, McVay would be waiting to take the horses, a lean grim mountaineer with a crooked leg. The leg had been crippled in a mill accident, and because McVay had a family, a job as hostler and janitor had been found for him. If he had been killed, his widow would have received a small sum every payday until the oldest boy was old enough to work in the mill. When a mill hand grew too old or too infirm to work, the son or son-in-law who took him in found his pay envelope somewhat augmented each week for so long as the old man lived. No one starved in Dappling's town. No one had any luxuries, either, except for the people in the big houses on Main Street. And Dappling.

The townspeople were content with that arrangement. They were proud, illiterate people who made a point of asking for no more than they felt they had earned, and they were in fact more prosperous and lived more comfortably (if perhaps with a little less freedom) than their cousins who lived in mountain cabins. They were all people indigenous to the mountains, some still owning steep remnants of the land granted to ancestors in recognition of service as soldiers in the Revolution. There were no foreigners in Dappling's mill. He had observed with fastidious disgust the consequences of Pittsburgh's resort to immigrant labor: the swarms of evil-smelling clownish peasants, gabbling in strange tongues and devouring loathsome foods, creating squalid enclaves that reproduced with hideous fidelity the degenerate East European or Mediterranean villages that had spawned them. Dappling would have none of it. Who would be squire where the tenants were the likes of these?

No, he would forego becoming a great man, if becoming a great man entailed such things. In his lifetime, at least, things would not change here. This neat prospering town where dwelt contented respectful citizens; this bustling prof-itable mill where free Americans labored; these wooded hills surrounding his elegant great house: these were what he prized; these he would keep. These and his family.

His days were so ordered that there was time for each of them: he would be in his office (he still called it a counting house, a small room darkly furnished in mahogany and green plush) until noon precisely, sitting deliberate and magiste-rial behind the broad desk, guiding the affairs of his mill with a concentration of attention indistinguishable from love. That part of his life that belonged to the mill was the mill's absolutely. But with the first sound of the noon whistle he was at the door, and before the sound of the whistle had died the chestnuts were in motion, retracing the morning's journey. With the closing of the door, Dappling shut business out of his mind until tomorrow; the rest of the day belonged to the estate and the family.

He always felt a lift in his spirits as the buggy approached the gates of the manor, an emotion identical with the one he felt as he neared the mill in the morning. Twice each day on six days of the week he enjoyed this feeling of pleasurable anticipation. He relished each morning's work, the solid satisfaction of bringing order to confused situations, the pride in his honest profit from his honest product. He relished equally the afternoons: a farmer's lunch, a change into boots and breeches, and then into the outdoors – sometimes afoot and sometimes riding – to verify that all went well with his acres.

There were about twenty thousand of them, forest mostly, lofty virgin stands of oak and walnut steeply rising above valleys where swift cold streams ran. Where the land was reasonably flat, there were wheat and cornfields, and on steeper clearings grew lush pasturage for the fat cattle and blooded horses that won ribbons for Dappling at the fair. He liked to take his big gray gelding on a tour of the fields on a summer afternoon, using not the farm roads but his private bridle paths, cantering through the silent forest on a crooked course that took him from the stable down to the fat fields of the bottomland, thence upward as far as the high mountain meadow, and from there back again to his house in the last hour before sunset. He would emerge from the trees at the top of the home meadow, whose long slope ran from the edge of the woods down to Dappling Road. There he always pulled up to absorb the view for a few minutes: in the foreground the dairy herd making its way in a peaceable file towards the barn for the evening milking; then the road; and then, beyond treetops, his house, solid, permanent, and shapely, on its broad expanse of lawn. The best part of the day was still to come. If the gelding was not overheated, Dappling would give him his head and, with deliberate theatricality, thunder up to the stable at a dead run. More often than not, Emily would be there waiting for him.

His Emily, his sunshine; the radiance that lighted his life, the small grand-daughter whom he loved with an intensity of devotion that sometimes – as he was well aware – made him appear faintly ridiculous. He doted; and was aware that his doting was a cause of laughter, and did not care, this staid industrialist who prized his dignity above most things. He saw in this merry child a recrea-tion of her grandmother, the adored wife who had died young and whose loss inflicted a wound that had remained as raw as the day it was new through all the years until Emily's birth.

He had remained fond enough of his son Sam and never been so unhinged by grief as to blame the boy because his birth had killed his mother; nonetheless, he had been more a dutiful than a loving father. But if he did not cheer at Sam's triumphs, neither did he chide him for his failures, and they did not quarrel. They did not embrace, either, and Sam no more filled the empty part of Dappling's life than did the mill and the estate. All three were good things, important to him and sources of satisfaction, but it was not until the baby's birth that they fell snugly into place as parts of a life that seemed now to be whole and unflawed. He was able at last to love Sam as a son and to become fond of Sam's wife Olivia, the aristocrat Sam had fetched home to the mountains from a decaying Main Line mansion.

Sam, for his part, not only loved his father, he admired him above all men. He accounted himself very lucky, did plain decent Sam, with the great Henry Dappling his father and the beautiful Olivia his wife. Sam knew his limitations, knew that his father and his wife had quicker, keener minds than his own. At Harvard, where his father had been graduated *cum laude* after an indolent and sociable four years, Sam had had to toil mightily for his Gentleman's Cs, and he was never able to comprehend at all the formidable books that his wife inces-santly read. But what he learned he remembered, and Dappling was a patient teacher. Sam had come to be of value in the mill and on the farm, and when the proper time came round (in ten years, Dappling thought, or fifteen), he would be fit to command both. His ways were not his father's ways, but Dappling had gradually come to realize that Sam's pleasant, almost diffident orders were carried out with as much alacrity as his own, and undoubtedly more cheerfully. The men respected and to some degree feared Dappling, but they were fond of Sam. They were beginning to respect him, as well; and a few, who had failed him in one way or another, had learned that there were times when he, too, was to be feared.

They dined early, so that Emily could eat with the family. Each evening as they entered the dining room, Mrs. McVay would pop Emily in through the other door, starched and ruffled, fragrant from her bath, her small face serious with the effort of making a ladylike entrance, her eyes on Dappling. It was a game. If Dappling's expression did not change, she was able to make her way to her chair with suitable gravity; but if he winked, or permitted the corner of his mouth to twitch with an incipient grin, she broke into giggles and ran to him to be picked up and deposited in her chair. She was in fact a beautiful child, with a regularity of feature and a shapeliness of the underlying bone that indicated an inevitable growth into a beautiful woman. She glowed with health; the round cheeks bloomed, the blue eyes sparkled. Merriment bubbled always just beneath the surface of her mood of the moment, so that even when she was irritated or sullen, the bad behavior somehow gave the impression of being no more than a pose. It was not to be doubted that all of her life people would be charmed by her and forgive her almost any offense. She was a delightful small person and seemed so not only to her besotted grandfather but to the whole populace of Dappling's demesne. In the row houses the grannies were already worrying about a suitable husband being found for her, and eminent fiddlers from the mountain cabins often turned up at the door with tenders of music to be played for the Missy. These were not sycophantish people; they felt a very genuine affection for her. Everyone did.

They ate the food of the region, roast beef or fried pork or game, with corn-bread and boiled greens. But the plain food was served on delicate china and eaten with monogrammed silver; the napery was heavy linen, snowy white. Olivia's code of manners had not been relaxed by removal to the west. The Dapplings were gentlefolk, after all, and if they had tended to live coarsely during the years when the house was without a chatelaine, it was only her duty, now that she was mistress, to set things back on the correct path. Dappling was amiable about it, and the adoring Sam, as anxious to please as a puppy, pretended great enthusiasm for her amendments to their style of living. They drew the line at formal dinner wear, but were agreeable to changing from outdoor clothes for dinner, and Olivia settled for that.

The men ate hugely, minding their table manners to set an example for Emily and to please Olivia. The conversation would no doubt have surprised a chance visitor: Dappling's education had been excellent, and he was that rarity among industrialists, a man who loved books. Olivia, too, was a reader. She had had no more than the education considered appropriate for females of her class and time – genteel reading, manners, a little music – but she had very early displayed, to the utter astonishment of the improvident sportsmen and flighty belles who comprised her family, a formidable intellect, an attribute that the clan found as exotic as the ability to charm snakes, and about as desirable in a lady. Her father had leaped at the chance to marry her off to rich Sam Dappling, who was, although perhaps not out of the very top drawer, a lad much to the old man's liking, a good shot, bold at a jump, well-tailored, and in no way bookish. Indeed, he felt a certain sympathy for Sam, anticipating that the boy might have a difficult time with his blue-stocking daughter. But it had turned out that Dappling's library had afforded her all she could ask in the way of books, and she had found her father-in-law's conversation to be modestly learned and sometimes even witty. It more than compensated for the occasional whiff of the frontier she discerned in the atmosphere around her.

Sometimes there were guests. Men came from New York and Pittsburgh to talk about iron and steel, or from the capitol to talk politics. At dinner and afterwards until bedtime they talked their business or politics, with Sam utterly absorbed in the conversation and Dappling joining in with a certain detached amusement, while Olivia sat rigid with boredom, mechanically making the proper responses. But there were other visitors, people from Olivia's former world who came for extended visits to rest and restore their failing energies in the mountain air. When there were houseguests in residence, dinners were leisurely affairs, deliberately protracted by Olivia; it was the time of the best conversation, and meals were the chief – almost the only – entertainment there in the country. There might be cards in the late evening, or Olivia would play Chopin or Schubert with passable skill. Sometimes they gathered around the piano and sang; often they sat on the lawn late into the night, the talk incessant under the stridulation of night insects until it was time for bed.

Sam was always glad of bedtime; indeed, he found himself looking forward to it almost from the time he rose in the morning. One of his amusements, when conversation about paintings or cotillions had bored him to the point of numbness, was to picture Olivia as she would be later in their bedroom; he liked to imagine the expressions on the faces around the table if they suddenly found themselves conversing not with the cool hostess who was explicating Darwin, but with the Olivia that only he had ever seen, who came into being after the bedroom door had closed. Both Sam and Olivia had been at first enormously surprised and then intensely grateful for the depth of her sexuality; but both were quite certain that it was somehow discreditable, and they were in agreement that it should be utterly secret. Their public manner towards each other was almost formal; they lived in the innocent belief that their passion was wholly concealed.

Dappling was much amused by their affectation of coolness, but it was a benign and complacent amusement. They were a happy couple, and their happiness was a cornerstone of Emily's world. Whatever made Emily happy met with Dappling's unqualified approval. It was his intent that her life was to be without sorrow, that her merriment was to continue all of her days. It was to this end that he directed the affairs of his mill, his estate, and his people, so that Emily could never know want, would always have responsible protectors, would always have her path smooth and the way open, no matter what happened to him, no matter what happened to Sam and Olivia. Large sums of money were so placed that she was forever assured of opulence, whatever the vagaries of the economy; banks in Pittsburgh and lawyers in New York were committed by pledge and self-interest to protect her as a jewel; young matrons in the best circles of Eastern Seaboard cities were already anticipating the day when they would sponsor her; and throughout Goster County hard men and their tough women, bound to Dappling by a fealty that was near-feudal, had come to understand that the welfare of this child was to be protected in any and all circumstances, by whatever means were necessary.

Dappling had done what he could, and he did not doubt that it was enough. In any case, he saw his safeguards only as an excess of caution. There was no reason why he should not live until Emily herself was a grandmother, and he proposed to guard her tenderly through all those years. But such speculation about the far future was confined to moments of active planning; in his heart, in his day-to-day thought, she was forever five years old, forever a golden child laughing among flowers in a long golden afternoon. And that would be the reality, in a way.

Or, at any rate, *a* reality; one of the realities perceived by Loob, peering uncomprehendingly down the chasm of the years from his seat in the oriel window. He watched her often at play, skipping blithely with bare feet over sun-warmed grass, as he sat hunched motionless on his box, strange and gross, scoured by a gritty cold wind that he did not seem to feel, staring with lusterless eyes at the pantomime he watched almost every day without ever remembering that he had seen it before. There had never been pattern or sequence to his perception of the past, and scenes came and went apparently at random, but the child on the lawn was there for him almost every day. He looked through the window and saw her at play, and behind him in the room, if he turned his head to look, the pretty lady was playing the piano while a slim man with a mustache turned the pages of music for her, and through the door another man was entering the room.

It always ended then; abruptly Loob was looking at the desolate present or a different time in the past. No one could have said whether it mattered to him. No expression crossed the broad pallid face, the dull eyes neither brightened nor dimmed. But somewhere in the cloudy corridors of his brain something found that particular scene appealing, and it was endlessly repeated for Loob, child and dog in the sunlight, man and woman at the piano, the other man entering. And some sort of censor existed there, as well, cutting off his view each time at the same point; even Loob could not have borne to see again the scene played to its end.

Or perhaps he could have, and the shift in time had quite another explanation. There was no way of knowing what he felt, or indeed if he had feelings at all. What went on inside his head differed utterly – differed in kind – from the thinking processes of other people. He was not stupid or insane; those words apply to a mind's efficiency in the handling of reality and rational thought, and what happened inside Loob's skull bore no relation to those things. There was a power there that normal brains do not have, and Loob could see things long invisible to everyone else, but he did not – could not – think.

He had been born with a brain that was skewed and misshapen; the conduits that carry the impulses called thought were twisted and awry, in no way resembling the complex, symmetrical network which the genetic blueprint prescribes.

They coiled upon themselves in tight nodes, forked where they should have continued singly, came to dead ends where they should have made a juncture, joined fortuitously where no connection should have been made. The energies that passed along them traveled unprecedented routes, and the result was not thought but something new and unique.

In a different age Loob would have been exposed and abandoned to die, and in a different place he would have been locked into an institution and forgotten. Here in this mountain town he was kept alive and, for what it was worth to him, permitted almost total freedom. The people clung to their immemorial folkways, and it had never been their way to send defective people to institutions. When seventeen-year-old Carolee Rankin came home to bear her bastard and depart again, this time to disappear forever, her mother, as a matter of course, kept the child to raise as one of the moil of children swarming through the ruinous house the welfare people supplied her. Loob shared his grandmother's breast with his uncle, who was a year older than Loob. By his third birthday he was an inch taller than the uncle. It was by then evident, even to the grandmother, who herself lived at a certain remove from reality, that something was amiss inside Loob's head. He walked into furniture and followed with his eyes the movements of invisible people and became frightened at the sight of things that were not there. It could not be doubted that he was in some way cracked.

The grandmother did not regard the fact as a major tragedy; most of the families she knew produced at least one natural in each generation. Loob received neither more nor less than his share of her fitful offerings of affection, and perhaps less than his share of the cuffings. He continued to grow with unnatural speed, almost visibly acquiring inches of height and layers of fat, feeding greedily on enormous quantities of the starchy foods provided by bureaucratic charity. When he was seven the grandmother died.

The day after her death, her mother, the matriarch of the clan, appeared in the town. She began a long wrangle with the young woman from the welfare department, who proposed to put into foster homes all of the children except Loob, who was to go to an asylum. The old woman was wise in all the ways and regulations of the welfare department, and she was unshakably determined that her kin would not be raised by strangers. In the end she prevailed; the government would continue to rent the house, regular checks would continue to issue, and the children, including Loob, would be kept together. But her scheming had gone beyond that: she was able, as a part of the same settlement, to make provision for another of her feckless brood. Her youngest son, a cowboy-togged frequenter of honky-tonks, who had reached his early thirties, without ever having had a job, was given a stipend by the government to move with his wife into the house and make a home for the children. He had no children of his own; his wife, a skinny alcoholic named Dolores, did not like them.

As time passed she came to like them less and less, her new charges in particular. The littlest of them cried or screamed a good deal of the time, and those of school age were frequently the cause of visitations by the welfare lady, who tended to be quite fierce after hearing school teachers' shocked reports about the clothing and grooming of the children. Dolores was infuriated by these intrusions upon her effort to live as she liked. She had experienced the fulfillment of an old daydream: enough money to keep the refrigerator well-filled with beer, and a rent-free dim room where the days could be passed in a mindless fog of alcohol and rock music. She did not ask for more than this, but having tasted it, she would not settle for less. When reality insisted upon invading her misty paradise, she was at first irritated and then filled with sullen rage. These children, she came to see, were her enemies. She would treat them as they deserved to be treated.

And so they grew, an undernourished gaggle of delinquents, vicious and unpredictable, pale of eyes and hair, each with the chinless face and crooked pointed teeth of the family. One by one, as they reached their middle teens, they left the house, to find dens elsewhere in the town or to run away and vanish utterly. Dolores was left at last with only Loob.

And even he had stumbled into habits that kept him out of her reach most of the time. In his early years it had been otherwise; he had not been able to learn, like the others, to make himself inconspicuous or to hide, nor was he able to read the signs that foretold explosions of her wrath. He had thus been almost always conveniently available to her, a ready victim, a swollen speechless lump too lethargic to evade blows and incapable of argument. In summer he would squat in the dusty backyard, and in winter in a corner of the kitchen, staring at whatever it was that he saw. When he was eleven or twelve he began to follow along behind the uncle who was near his own age, and he remained a faithful shadow until the uncle ran away a year or two later. That was the period when the boys used Loob as a butt.

By the time of the uncle's disappearance Loob seemed to have come to a vague awareness that things were somehow better when he was away from Dolores, that he felt no blows and did not hear the shrill vituperative voice. It came to be his habit to go to the house only to sleep and to eat when he could not find food elsewhere. He became a wanderer through the town and its purlieus, an enormous shambling creature with arms that were disproportionately short and a tongue too large for his mouth who made mysterious detours as he walked and clutched a shapeless bundle of rags that had once been a stuffed toy dog. At some point his wanderings brought him to the window of the old Dappling house. Thereafter he was usually to be found at that place.

Dolores knew where he was, and she had no objection. She had never con- sciously made a connection between Loob's absence from the house and a rise in her spirits, but her subconscious mind had for many years observed and recorded the fact that acts of cruelty to Loob were likely to have distressing consequences. The appalling depressions of spirit that sometimes engulfed her, dropping her into a black hell of melancholy and terror, were blamed on her boozing, and she ascribed to the same cause the endless succession of accidents that made bandages or splints a standard part of her costume. That Loob was the cause of her afflictions was not an idea that would have occurred to her.

It did not occur to Loob, either, of course. Loob did not have ideas, any more than he had memories. He lived from moment to moment, and each new moment of his life found him in something very close to a whole new world. The few things he had learned had been absorbed so gradually, over so long a time, that they had merged with, and become indistinguishable from, instinct; no reasoning from cause to effect had ever been the motive of an action of his.

He was in fact totally unaware of what he was doing when he made use of his power. It was his, wholly by chance, an effect of the same clots in the circuitry of his brain that deprived him of an effective memory and the faculty of reason, and he used it instinctively and without forethought. Afterwards he would have no memory of what he had done, nor any awareness of consequences. There was the matter of the Goster County dogs, for example.

A lean starving dog of enormous size, driven to mindless ferocity by hunger and the pain of a festering paw, one day sprang at Loob's throat. Loob reached with cobra swiftness, his instincts serving him, far better than reason would have. The dog seemed to crumple in midair; a savage predator had leaped, and a cowed and broken creature hit the ground. It fled in howling terror to its nest under a stump and remained there until it died of starvation and fear a week later.

If Loob had failed to react, no harm would have been done him; the dog's attack had actually taken place on a day a century and a half in the past, and Loob had struck at a wraith, an apparition that had no substance in Loob's time. It is probable that it was not attacking Loob at all, but some beast or person actually there; but it may have sensed somehow Loob's uncomprehending observation and blindly attacked the unseen. Either way, they were in different times, Loob and the dog, and neither of them had any physical reality for the other. But Loob's dreadful bolt was not affected by time. Time had no meaning for Loob or his power. And the dog was smitten.

The dog was a wild animal, an amalgam of large breeds, the possessor of a rich strain of wolf blood. He killed sheep and bred bitches on most of the farms in the county and ventured sometimes into the town itself when the wind brought the scent of a bitch in heat. By the time he was brought low by a farmer's bullet, he had sired feral litters throughout the area, all of which fruitfully interbred. His blood was passed on and enriched by the inbreeding, and his descendants came to be almost a distinct breed, huge rangy dogs with blunt muzzles and smooth black pelts, who stood baleful guard over the farms of the county and patrolled the streets of the town with a forbidding, proprietary air.

They disappeared when Loob struck the attacker; or, rather, did not disappear: they had never existed. The old progenitor had died of terror in a hole before he could breed their ancestors, and other dogs lived – had always lived – here. Reality had been amended in a small way: a race of dogs did not exist; the bloodlines of the local sheep were imperceptibly different; the phrase, "As mean as a Goster County dog" did not have currency in that end of the state. Most of the people had memories of their pasts that were somewhat different from what they had been; a great many snapshots showed other dogs or no dogs at all. Not much else. Loob's mindless interference with the past had harmed no one, all things considered, and the world was in fact in no worse condition than it would otherwise have been.

But of course that was not the only occasion on which he altered the past, and that other tampering had consequences that scarcely bear thinking about, that were indeed so incomparably dreadful that one has difficulty in restraining himself from committing atrocities upon Loob's person. But that would be self-defeating, that would be something worse than suicide. Loob is not to be interfered with; he must be left to do as he is moved to do.

Loob once had a dog of his own. When he was twelve or thirteen years old, an emaciated stray mongrel had one summer evening peered through a hole in the fence and watched him as he sat in a corner of the yard hunched over his tin basin of pork and potatoes. The dog had sat staring with hopeless longing at the pieces that fell into the dust as Loob crammed the food into his mouth until, unable to restrain itself any longer, it made a frantic and despairing foray into the yard, snatched a loathly ort from under Loob's feet, and scrambled in terror back through the hole. Loob took no notice whatever. The dog, observing this, made a second raid, again without retribution. By the time the basin was empty, the ground was clear of food, and the dog was sitting beside Loob waiting for the next scrap to fall.

Thereafter they took their meals together, and after a time the dog began to follow Loob wherever he went and to lie down touching Loob when Loob was at rest. Loob appeared not to be aware of the dog at all until the evening when the dog for the first time attempted to follow him into the house and was hastily ejected by Dolores. Loob began an enormous bellowing, a noise so offensive and sustained that one of the older children admitted the animal as soon as Dolores had returned to her room. After that time they were not separated by day or night until a coal truck ran over the dog on Main Street one morning, not only killing it instantly but flattening it to something unrecognizable as a dog.

Loob saw the incident; at any rate his eyes were turned toward it at the moment it happened. But he gave no sign that he recognized what had taken place, and he continued his lurching progress up the street without pausing. That night he did not eat, however, a thing that had not happened before in his lifetime. During all of the next day and the day after that, he took no food. The other children, astonished and frightened, told Dolores, who two days later told the welfare lady. Loob's skin was by then beginning to hang in pale folds, and he staggered even more than usual as he wandered through the town.

"I don't know," the welfare lady said. "Maybe this time he'll have to go to Murdock." Murdock is a state mental hospital. I know it well.

"It was the dog gettin' kilt done it," one of the children said. Maybe if he had another dog—"

"Another dog," the welfare lady said. "Aid to Dependent Dogs." She spoke to Dolores: "Do you have any idea – No. Of course you don't. I'll talk to the doctor. I'm afraid it will have to be Murdock." But she came back later in the day with a toy dog, a stylized stuffed Airdale covered in plush. "Let's try it, anyhow," she said. "You never know."

Loob stared at the toy as emptily as he stared at the rest of the world. After a while the welfare lady said, "Well, I'm not surprised. It was worth trying, though." She turned to go. Loob reached out and took the toy. His face did not change, but he raised the dog and squeezed it to his chest with both hands, and that evening he devoured his usual enormous meal. For the next five years of his life he was never seen without the toy in his hand.

He did not play with it or show it any sign of affection, or indeed seem to be aware that he held it, but even in his sleep his grip did not wholly relax. In time the plastic stuffing hardened and crumbled and sifted out through rips in the seams of the plush, so that at last Loob carried only a filthy rag; but to all appearances the rag had the same value to him that the new toy had had. It may have been that the sticky wad of cloth provided the only continuity in his life, the only thing of permanence in his inconstant world. Or perhaps he was after all capable of some murky analogue of emotion and felt something akin to affection for the ruined toy. It is even possible that he had never perceived it as a representation of a dog, but simply as an object tendered in kindness, and hence not to be relinquished. Whatever the reason, it was unique in the world, a thing that appeared to matter to Loob.

Dolores took it from him one day, took it and burned it and so created her own beginnings and condemned a town. She took Loob's rag out of simple malice, out of a heartfelt desire to cause him pain; but she never knew whether or not the confiscation had really hurt him, any more than in the past she had been able to tell if he had heard her voice when she railed at him or felt the blows when she struck him. This time, though, she had achieved her purpose.

It was a bad morning for her, a morning when the thrum and jangle of her nerves had begun before she awoke, so that she came to consciousness depressed and apprehensive, with a yellow taste in her mouth and an incipient tremor in her limbs. She was well aware of the cause, which was a lack of alcohol in her system; and she remembered clearly and with despair that before going to sleep she had drunk the last drop in the house, having debated leaving a pick-me-up in the vodka bottle and deciding against it. She had had this experience before, and she knew precisely the course it would take. It was absolutely necessary that she have a bottle within the next hour, or the shaking and nausea would utterly incapacitate her.

The car would not start. She sat behind the wheel and cursed, a stringy woman with bad teeth and lank hair, musty and disheveled and becoming frantic. Without pause in her swearing she left the car and, sweating, returned to the house to use the telephone. The taxicab company told her the town's only taxi would not be available until the afternoon.

She stood clutching the telephone, frozen by panic. She did not see how she could walk the mile to the liquor store, but no matter how desperately she tried, she could think of no alternative. She was quite unable to cope with the problem. Until her brain had received its wonted portion of alcohol, it scarcely functioned at all, and getting the alcohol to make thinking possible was itself her problem. Frustration squeezed her in a clawed vice and became anger, a red extremity of rage that she thought might burst her head with its intensity.

Through the door to the kitchen she caught sight of Loob, sitting dumbly in his corner staring at nothing. "You bastard!" she shouted. "You goddam crazy dummy, you old goddam crazy dummy! Sit and hold your goddam crazy rag all day, you goddam crazy dummy! Why can't you *do* something?"

Loob did not move, did not blink. She rushed into the kitchen and struck him on the cheek with her fist. He gave no sign of feeling it. "Goddam you!" she shouted. "Goddam, oh, goddam!" Loob sat and stared emptily. "You bastard," she said, panting now. "Oh, you big dummy bastard." Her eye fell upon the rag. "Oh, you big dummy bastard with your rag."

She snatched suddenly, and the rag was in her hand. Without hesitation she pulled a lid off the stove and dropped the rag inside, where coals still glowed.

"There, you crazy dummy!" she said. "There's your crazy rag." There was a crackle of flame inside the stove.

Still Loob made no sign. She gave a wordless shriek, a yelp of pure, helpless rage, and struck him again, to no effect whatever. She stood trembling for a moment and then ran from the room and from the house and stood sobbing beside the road. A car came, and she held up her hand. The car stopped and picked her up.

In the kitchen Loob sat without movement for some time. Then his hand opened, lay so for a moment, and clenched again. He repeated the movement two or three times. He rose ponderously, lurched out through the kitchen door, and made his way through the litter of the back yard to a gap in the fence, and thence through a vacant lot to Dappling Road. He proceeded erratically down the road, as he had a thousand times before, and turned in at the derelict slag lane that led down to the old house. When he reached the house he climbed the discolored stone steps, entered, and took his seat in the window. His hand was slowly clenching and unclenching.

Something new had happened – was happening – to him: he was, improbably, in the grip of an emotion. Somewhere in the ruinous labyrinth of his mind there was adumbrated a feeling of loss, something nameless that was forever gone. There was no way for him to weigh the matter, to reflect upon the strangeness of this phenomenon; he could only react instinctively: *Danger. Strike.* He struck.

It was toward the end of a long August afternoon in 1905, and Sam Dappling was opening a door, entering the room where Olivia was playing Chopin. A house-guest, a cousin from Philadelphia, stood beside the piano and turned the pages of the music, and two other visitors, another cousin and his wife, listened from seats on a divan. As he crossed the threshold, placid, genial Sam Dappling went mad; the black discharge of Loob's strange ordnance smashed into his brain, instantly exploding a million subtle connections, and in the moment of passing through the doorway Sam Dappling ceased to exist. In his stead was something monstrous, a thing bulging with insensate ferocity, that ran suddenly into the room and tore from the wall the Civil War saber that hung under a portrait of old General Dappling. It whirled with the saber in its hand and without the slightest pause accelerated into frenzied motion, filling the room with a demented fury of destruction and dismemberment; and when the butchery at last was done, it again did not pause, but rushed dripping out of that place of blood and stink and twitching scraps into the outdoors, onto the lawn where a child and a dog played in the sunshine.

It left unspeakable things scattered there on the grass and plunged, howling, into the barn, where it found only a mare and her foal, upon whom it fell in undiminished frenzy. When there was no more movement in the stall, it paused for a fraction of a moment. In the loft pigeons were fluttering; it heard the sound and went swarming up the ladder, in no way slowed by the saber. The pigeons were out of reach, swooping just under the roof, far above. At the end of the loft was another ladder, leading up to the great opening under the ridge pole through which the hay was hauled into the mow. It scuttled up with the agility of a great feral monkey. A startled pigeon flapped in confusion and then flew hastily through the opening, and the thing that had been Sam Dappling leaped for it, wildly cutting with its sword. The pigeon rose gracefully and curved back to alight on the roof. The thing sailed outward and dropped, still slicing and hacking at the air through which it fell. It struck the hard-packed earth and bounced slightly and was still. In the house the screaming had just begun.

For Henry Dappling it never stopped. He lived for the seven years that remained of his life with a never-ending scream in his ears. It was not the screaming from the house that he heard; it was the demented noise that came from Mrs. McVay, who was standing on the lawn with her face to the sky as he rode the gray out of the woods that evening. He had emerged from the sun-shot cool gloom and silence of the forest into the full evening sunlight and pulled up as usual. He heard it then, a mindless howl of terror and loss and unutterable grief, ripping through the bright clear air with ugly insistence, smirching the evening. He put the gray into a dead run, down the meadow and the drive and over the lawn to where she stood screaming and screaming. He saw what she held in her hands.

That was the real end of Henry Dappling's life. His remaining seven years were something worse than death. He would have made a quick end of it almost immediately, except that he did not see how he could die without knowing *why*. Even a vindictive maniac God must have had a reason for so gross an affront to decency, so loathsome and abominable a cruelty as permitting him to see the bulging small blue eyes and yellow curls of what was frozen in Mrs. McVay's clawed hands. The question became almost the sole tenant of his mind, a consuming obsession that was never absent for a second of his years as a mad hermit in his mansion. He did not find his answer, of course, and he died at last with the screaming still in his ears, alone in the great house where mildew and dry rot were crumbling the interior and weeds and branches besieged the walls. Long before his death the house had come to look desolate and abandoned, and it was known as a haunted house while its master still lived within its walls.

He had attended the funeral; indeed, he had taken charge from the very first, from the moment he had pried Mrs. McVay's hands away from their awful burden. He had shouted at her in so loud and peremptory a voice that her hysteria was punctured, and she took hold of herself and obeyed his instructions to gather together the men whom he named and to have the sheriff sent for. He himself told the men what to do, evincing no emotion at the sight of the shambles in the house or the pitiful thing that had been his son lying broken on the ramp of the barn. He went about for the three days, with an expressionless face, speaking, when speech was needful, in a precise cold voice, glassy-hard and without apparent grief or rage. He was watched warily: at any moment full realization might strike him, and he could be expected to do something strange – to become violent and murderous or perhaps lose his mind entirely and gibber and drool.

In fact he did none of those things. After the funeral he took the superintendent of the mill aside. "Pay off everybody," he said. "Yourself, too. Lock it up."

"What?" said the superintendent. "Pay—? Lock—? What?"

"Do it," Dappling said. The superintendent did. The town stopped. The big houses lost their people first, as the men who had run the mill betook themselves to Pittsburgh and Gary. Then some of the row houses emptied; venturesome or ambitious men severed their roots and went to Wheeling or Youngstown, while others, in whom the old highland blood ran strong, satisfied a perennial urge and returned to the cabins. A majority stayed. They stayed and watched the town decay around them, a passive indolent community bereft of leadership and energy, doomed now to a long sleep and then extinction.

It stirred to life, briefly, during the First World War; money and importunities from Washington effected a partial resolution of the chaos into which Dappling's estate had fallen and the mill was put into operation for a year, although the already archaic equipment was hopelessly inefficient. After the Armistice the ponderous machinery of the law again clanked into operation; the gates were re-locked, the new railroad sidings left to rust. The tedious succession of suit and countersuit, stay and deferral, lien and attachment and injunction was resumed and dragged its dusty way through courtrooms and sheriff's offices and lawyers' chambers. If Dappling had died with his family, there would have been no problem; his affairs would have been carried on without even a pause by an existing establishment. But he lived on for seven years, and there was no way to appoint an executor or administrator for a living man. They might have had him certified incompetent, but no one dared. And so no taxes were paid or rents collected; no one voted shares of stock or gave proxies for them; no one guarded or was responsible for property and accounts. Sheriff's deputies nailed notices to doors; servers of process came and went; various bank accounts stagnated or were looted. Numbers of small suppliers went bankrupt; certain bankers and lawyers prospered greatly.

And all the while the town shrank and rotted and waited for the better times that had to come, and Henry Dappling, grown hairy and filthy and emaciated, crept through the dark haunted rooms of his mansion and endlessly asked his unanswerable question. One day in the seventh summer, McVay, who each week left a supply of food for the hermit at the kitchen door, found the previous week's provisions still on the step. He called the sheriff, who came with a fat deputy, broke into the shuttered house, and found Dappling's body. The screaming had stopped at last.

Lawful administration of the estate began at once, but it was too late. Except for the federal cutting of the Gordian Knot for wartime purposes, there had never been a hope of bringing enough order out of the chaos to make the mill a going enterprise again. Vultures and then beetles picked the carcass clean and left the town to its own devices.

It could devise nothing but stagnation. When the Great Depression came, the event would have passed unnoticed by the people had it not been for the fact that money began to arrive from the government. They were at first too proud to accept it, and then they accepted it and were ashamed, and in due course they were not ashamed but came to think of it as rightfully theirs. The relief checks became the way of life of the town, an assurance of a livelihood for even the most indolent and feckless. When times at last improved, there was a leaching away of the brighter and abler young, who went to seek a future elsewhere; and by the time "relief" became "welfare," no one there worked at all except for a few torpid merchants, whose customers paid with government checks. The town would not die, but it lived – or half-lived – as a parasite.

The citizens know no other life. Loob was born to it, and so was his mother, and his grandmother came to it before her adolescence. These are people who do not know want, but have never known prosperity. They do not know ambition or thrift; neither do they know toil or hunger. Their possessions are cheap and gaudy and soiled, their diet deficient in nourishment and abundant in sugar, their music a commercial debasement of the folk music of their fathers. They drink fiercely and are given to casual incest and sometimes slice each other with knives. Their only dreams are of winning prizes on television giveaway shows. These are the descendants of the stern mountaineers who were Henry Dappling's people. Down the years each generation has been more misshapen than its predecessor. Loob is their ultimate fruit.

And so a circle is completed. Because Loob is what he is, he shattered the mind of Sam Dappling and so damned the town. Because the town was damned, Loob is what he is.

There is no point of entry into this circle: Loob created the events that created Loob. And since that cannot be, it is necessary to consider the possibility that these things did not happen at all. It may be that someday, as Loob sits in the window, his censor may not operate, he may see the scene through to its end; and now, with the loss of his toy no longer a fresh wound, and indeed probably no longer even a scar, he may let Sam come through the door and enter the room unchanged. If that should come about, then none of this happened; if Sam comes unscathed across the threshold, the past has once more been changed. Or left unchanged. The entry into the room of a sane Sam Dappling will mean that the horrors of that evening never occurred, that through the years ahead events will take place with Sam and Emily and Olivia alive, with Henry Dappling a fulfilled and happy man. It will mean that at the moment Loob fails to loose his bolt, he will never have existed.

One would perhaps then find in the bay of the window not a pale gross cretin crouched on a box, but an old lady in a Sheraton chair, who contemplates with eyes that are still merry and blue the long slope of lawn outside the window. The old piano is still in the room, its top covered with photographs, among them those of her great-grandchildren. Her great-grandfather's portrait as a general hangs on the wall and under it his saber, unblooded since Bull Run. The woodwork of the room glows with the deep luster of fervent polishings, the metal is bright, the glass sparkles. It is an old room and a happy one, sunny and filled with good things well cared for, an appropriate setting for this patrician lady.

She is waiting for someone, perhaps her grandson, almost certainly her grandson. He will no doubt arrive in the Ferrari, sending up a spray of white gravel when he brakes in front of the house. A manservant will hurry down to get his luggage, but he is already halfway up the steps, a trim athletic young man in flannels and tweed jacket. He has been in the East for a month of polo, but now he is home again, home where he is heir to the town and the big house. The townspeople had smiled and waved as the Ferrari growled up steep Main Street past the busy mill and the gleaming row houses, around the square with its sleek shops and smug shopkeepers, and up to where Dappling Road curled around the hill to the monumental gates of the estate.

Grandmother has laid on champagne for the occasion, chilled in a monogrammed silver bucket. She raises her glass in a toast to the happy homecoming, and the happy homecomer responds. We make a pretty picture there in that elegant room, beaming at each other: she slim, erect, and proud, wearing her years with grace; I the golden youth, handsome, cultured, immensely rich, at play for a while before settling down to my responsibilities. This is who I am. I am not the man they call Tom Perkins, the crazy sweeper of a sleazy bar in a decayed simulacrum of my town. This – *this* is the real world, this world with the champagne and the Ferrari, not the shoddy horror where the Perkins creature lives, where I am standing now.

And the real world is so very close. If once, only once, Loob permits Sam to enter the room, Loob never existed, and the town's history followed the main, the real thoroughfare, and I am safely where I belong, and none of this vile scenario ever took place. I think I will not be aware of the transition – indeed, there will not be a transition: all this simply will not have been, and there will nowhere be the faintest memory or even dream of this grim place. I will be sipping my champagne in my grandmother's drawing room, and all will be as it always was.

That is what I believe as I stand here among the cold weeds watching Loob in the window, as I wait for the instant that I am real again. And that is going to happen. I have no doubt that it will happen, none at all. None at all. Because I have positive proof that Loob can undo his interference with the past.

The proof is this: they are here, the Goster County dogs. They are here, gravely patrolling the streets of the town and the country round about, alert, watchful, and intimidating, as much a part of the landscape as the ridge above the town. *And they have always been here.* That is the point, that is the proof. Never since about the time of the Mexican War has the town been without these dogs. Think about that. It is quite obvious that a day came when there was a repetition of the circumstances surrounding the destruction of the old ancestor dog, with Loob in the same location when that same segment of the past unreeled itself. This time, though, Loob's vacant stare was directed elsewhere when the dog attacked. There was thus no instinctive reaction to the attacks; the dog lived on to beget his progeny. There is no fact in the universe more certain than the existence of these dogs. One of them is watching me now.

If Loob can do that, he can put right his other, greater, his infinitely tragic interference. And when he does, he and the wretched Tom Perkins will never have been. The world will be back on its true path, the path where there is love and comfort and safety.

It will.

THE HOUSE THAT MADE THE SIXTEEN LOOPS OF TIME

Tamsyn Muir

Tamsyn Muir is a New Zealand writer based in Auckland, where she divides her time between writing, her dogs, and teaching high school English. A graduate of the Clarion Writers' Workshop 2010, her work has previously appeared in *Fantasy Magazine*, *Weird Tales*, and *Nightmare Magazine*. Her stories have also been selected for *The Year's Best Science Fiction & Fantasy 2013* and *Best Horror of the Year*. This story first appeared in *Fantasy Magazine* in 2011.

14 Arden Lane suffered from bad plumbing and magical build-up. There Dr. Rosamund Tilly had raised two children, bred sixteen chinchillas and written her thesis, and because her name was on the deed had become the medium of all the house's whims and wishes. She liked it, most of the time, but her best friend in all the world liked it less: "Your house is a spoiled brat," said Danny Tsai, "and I feel inane saying that."

The house was an old, old two-storey lump, very square and not graceful, made of red brick that had to peep through thick trellises of ivy creeper and a roof that liked shedding tiles. Dr. Tilly knew it was horribly untidy and ran risk of being burnt down by vigilantes from the Neighbourhood Association – only that it was at the end of the road, and hidden by a thick yew hedge. Even then the hedge was never even at the top, and it was her neighbours' hobby to send letters seeing if they could get her to cut it down.

But Rosamund loved 14 Arden Lane; it had been willed to her by her grandmother, who died conveniently when she was twenty and had needed a house. She had admired it for its slippery wooden floors, its wide stairs and weird chimney, the poky bathrooms and the wheezing refrigerator in the kitchen. She had carefully and thoroughly checked for ants' nests and termites, following guides. Satisfied, she recklessly painted the walls in unlikely colours like lipstick red, and moved all her coats into the closets that would shelter her coats and later the coats of her daughters. When the house turned out to be magical Rosamund Tilly just accepted this as fact.

Magic built up like a breath waiting to be exhaled. On a bad day, she could touch a coffee mug and have it erupt in delicate little spikes of ceramic, a fretwork of stalactites extending outward as she pulled her hand back. Tap water might avoid her fingers when she turned on the tap. And that was just the house when it was in a *good* mood, because when it was upset or in a fit of bad behaviour it could make her life a misery. A spoiled brat, like Daniel said.

Once Dr. Tilly had grown welts under her arms that burst and released dozens of tiny, transparent crabs, which made Danny nauseated and her daughters shriek. She had finally swept the crabs into a dustpan and let them go outside, where they crept into the bushes. Rosamund had been more disturbed than afraid, and good at choking down things that made her disturbed: her daughters Snowdrop and Sparrow were disturbed, afraid and disquieted, but in rebellion from being named Snowdrop and Sparrow they were creatures of logic who'd always despaired of the house and dreamt of air-conditioned flats. At that point she hadn't really blamed them.

Daniel, though, had bore up well. He'd only once really lost his temper, when her kitchen parsley bit his fingers: "Why can't you have a normal house instead of— this stupid, temperamental Disney *shack*," he'd snapped. "And the water pressure is terrible." For five weeks neither of his cellphones got reception there and Danny banged all the doors.

But with Daniel, any annoyance he demonstrated was usually awkwardness, and under the staid curtness of his day-to-day chartered stockbroker face he liked chinchillas as well as laptops. They were two people who understood each other completely: she understood his irritability, his privacy, his inability to be serious with her when he was serious all day with everyone else. He understood just about everything with her, including a lot of things she wished he didn't. They were as devoted to each other as two people could be, and every lunchtime when he was at his office desk and she was marking university papers they would ring up to ask what the other was eating. Accepting her magical house was a small issue.

Anyway, anything 14 Arden Lane did never lasted; when the house felt it had made its point, it stopped. Usually. One of the chinchillas had been purple forever.

Now that she was forty-two Rosamund Tilly could tell when the build-ups were reaching explosion point. The ivy trellises around the house would be taut and trembling, the pretty crazy-paved path curling inward trying to claw the long grass verge. Even the dust would smell like firework smoke as she dragged a cloth haphazardly over her collections of glass cats. Years ago a build-up had made her accidentally wipe off her youngest daughter's eyebrows, and Snowdrop had gone around with her fringe brushed down and full of bitter complaints. Her tweenage feelings had been further hurt by her mother finding it hilarious, but the point was underscored: Rosamund Tilly really couldn't control what happened or when.

Thursday week the house made her hiccup a butterfly, and at that point she knew there was going to be a problem. 14 Arden Lane was of late empty and lonely now that it had lost the children and most of the chinchillas, and the house would sullenly take it out on her in sometimes vicious ways. Just a month ago great snakelike twists of wormy mud slithered out of the kitchen sink, coiling over her dishes and bending her forks, and that had made Dr. Tilly remember the crabs.

That night Danny came over from the office after a long day of chartered stockbrokering and surfed pictures of cats on his laptop as she fidgeted. "A watched pot never boils," he said.

"Don't give the house ideas with 'boil', you animal."

"Remember how aggressive it got when you put down new carpet, with the chimney and the goats?" He was clicking through pictures of disapproving rabbits, sitting next to her on the sofa. "I'm waiting for the day when you form a new plane of existence and your evil self replaces you, and I'll be able to tell her by the moustache."

"You are so flip," said Rosamund. "Why do you have to be so *flip*."

"I'm just here to look after you, Rose," he said, and that was pretty adorable so she put her feet into his lap and prodded his computer with her socks. Daniel Tsai had longsufferingly helped her raise two children, sixteen chinchillas and read her thesis, but he'd been obliged to: in primary school they had exchanged teal and fuschia friendship bracelets, a lifelong commitment if ever there was one. "Well? Go on and tell the house to hurry up, as the suspense is killing me."

Rosamund Tilly folded herself into a lotus pose instead, which always gently bemused him and disgusted her two daughters. Being able to fold oneself into a lotus was a payoff from having done yoga when it wasn't popular and being a hippie when it wasn't fun any more, when she'd prided herself on having the widest bellbottoms in all Hartford and fifty-six recipes involving carob. When she had moved into 14 Arden Lane she'd had carrot-coloured hair so long she could sit on it and towered three inches over Danny, who wasn't short, so she supposed the house had liked her out of pure shock.

Her ears popped, like they did on a descending airplane. "I think something's coming," she said.

Danny was looking at cats again. "So's Christmas."

Not a lot happened, at first. There was a little tingly smell like ozone, and a sense that she'd just breathed in a lungful of water and had to spit it out. Needle-sharp shivers started at her ankles and worked their way up. She closed her eyes very tightly, and when she opened them again there was Danny, waiting, eyes crinkling a little quizzically.

"Well?" he said. "Did worlds collide?"

"Not for me," she said, and the sensation flared briefly again: more like the shadow of a feeling than the first sharp injection of it. Her vision blurred a little, but she wasn't sure as they hadn't turned on all the lights in the sitting-room. The house liked it when they thought conscientiously about the environment. Dr. Tilly worried that something dreadful was about to happen.

"Well?" Danny said. "Did worlds collide?"

"You already said that, you broken record," she said. A third little stab. The room shifted again, and her fingers fretted at her eyes.

"Well?" he said. "Did worlds collide?"

The little flurries of sensation were making her palms prickle with sweat. Danny wasn't reacting. He had barely moved an inch – hadn't even moved – same expression, the same tonal quality, the same lift to the I in *collide* and slight Yorkshire slur to the *s*. When looked at, the room wasn't doing anything particularly interesting: the wallpaper wasn't turning into sugar and the arm-chairs weren't growing feet.

"I'm admitting defeat," she said.

"Well?" Danny said. "Did worlds collide?"

For long moments Rosamund just breathed. She pinched the bridge of her nose to make that nearly-a-headache sensation go away, suddenly horribly certain that she had turned her best friend into a space mannequin and that at forty-two she would never be able to get another half as good, but the man opposite reached out and took her hand to keep her steady. Rosamund was stupidly relieved at that. "Ease up," he said. "What's happened?"

Now they were both looking around. She was having no apparent effect. The rug was not bleeding, the air tasted of nothing but air, and they both had their fingerprints. Once when she was younger and pregnant she'd made soap bubbles every time she blinked, which had distracted her from being younger and pregnant and thinking listlessly about marrying the father. Danny got worried and jogged her elbow: "Earth to Rosamund Tilly. How many fingers am I holding up?"

"You're not holding up any fingers, you egg."

The room blurred again. Right before her Danny-on-the-sofa unzipped and re-zipped back to where he'd been sitting, so fast that it was like he hadn't moved at all. Lamplight caught all the worn patches on his suit. His expression was vague and somehow familiar—

"Well?" Danny said. "Did worlds collide?"

Even then she didn't get frightened, she told herself. Three cheers for Dr. Tilly.

*

Time for a test. She was a doctor, after all, and though she was a doctor of Medieval Literature she still retained a duty to Science. She launched herself off the sofa like a shell firing and went to the clock, took down the time, wrote it on the back of a grocery bill – 8:14 – and put it on the coffee table. Dr. Tilly stood beside it like a guard, scrunching up her hands in her daffodil-coloured skirt and feeling ridiculous as the clock marched on to 8:15. Nothing happened.

Danny was leaning over to read. "8:14?"

Oh, well, what the hell. Dr. Tilly tensed up before she said, "Testing?"

*

Another big blur, another jerk of dislocation as she found herself back on the sofa, totally discombobulated. Once more Danny wore that pensive, waiting expression and she couldn't even look at it as his mouth started to round out the words, as her grocery list sat next to the clock pristine and un-written-on. The clock read: 8:14.

"Well?" said Danny. "Did worlds collide?"

Time travel! The house had never mixed up *time* before. Dr. Tilly thought that she must have done something really rotten to have it drop something like this in her lap. She would have been excited if she hadn't been so horrified: the house was probably destroying the space-time continuum right now and forming a thousand glittering paradoxes all because she hadn't really cleaned the kitchen. Once she'd forgotten to weed the window boxes and the house had dissolved her feet right up to the ankle.

She knew three scientific things: 1. she was caught in a time loop, set off by 2. speaking, and 3. all of this was incredibly unscientific. So Dr. Tilly got her grocery bill again and scribbled on the back, worried that perhaps this too would send her careening back to the start:

CAUSED TIME LOOP, D

—but nothing happened. Whew.

Danny Number Six looked at her, then looked at the grocery list, then looked at her, and had the reaction that she'd guessed he had; he was completely delighted. He took his ballpoint pen out of his pocket and clicked it on and off, a sure sign of ecstasy in a stockbroker. "Are you sure?" She nodded again. "Good God. Why no verbal?"

Her writing was getting increasingly cramped. SPEAKING = SWITCH. SOUND???

"All right. Don't worry, I'm a licensed professional," he said, leaning forward and putting the laptop away. "A time loop means you've already gone back. How many iterations of the loop so far, Rose?" She raised her fingers. "Six? This is insane."

Dr. Tilly wrote again: got to break it though, this is ridiculous!!

"This is beyond ridiculous. Did you forget to defrost the fridge again?"

Will experiment. You forget what happens each time I reset the loop. Judiciously she added a sad face, :(

"Let's not go into the physics and assume you're creating endless worlds in 14 Arden Lane with each new loop, it will give the chinchillas and I a logistics headache," he said, leaning back and drumming his fingers on his knee. "Go ahead. What's the worst that can happen? Goodbye from the future, you know – I as Future Daniel Tsai will cease to be."

that is horrible do not put it that way!!

"I'm sorry," he said. "Do what you have to do, Rosamund."

"I will, I promise," she said, and—

*

"Well?" said Danny Seven. "Did worlds collide?"

*

Dr. Tilly went around and touched all the walls and the photographs, hoping the house would respond. New try. "Did worlds collide?" asked Danny Eight. On the next loop she went and made sure all of the chinchillas were coping in their hutch as Danny Nine craned his head, nonplussed, and that didn't do anything either. Next. Danny Ten followed her as she left the house but going out into the street did nothing more than make her eyes squint in the chill lemon-rind glare of the lamps, and at 8:18 in that iteration her eldest daughter Sparrow sent her a text message she didn't read. The neighbours peered at her through their curtains. "Did worlds collide?" asked Danny Eleven. In the throes of despair and rattling around the house like an old car, Dr. Tilly dusted her glass cats. Nothing happened, though at one point her cellphone tweeted in her pocket.

Sitting there on the sofa with what felt like an ice-cream headache, Dr. Tilly permitted herself an expletive: "Jesus H. Christ," she said.

"Well?" said Danny Twelve. "Did worlds collide?"

She said a ruder word.

Dr. Tilly put her head in her hands, which caught Danny Thirteen's attention immediately as he reached over to touch her shoulder. "What happened?" he said, and for a moment she was tempted to explain everything again; to rely on his thoughtfulness and candor, but instead she sighed and went to get her notebook. Perhaps waiting was another experiment too, and she didn't have to worry him in the process.

I'm mute. The house is not happy with me.

"Is that all?" The relief in her best friend's voice was palpable. "Well, that's nothing. We could play Charades."

NO

"We could enjoy the quiet." Rosamund made a very rude motion like a gunshot salute, and seeing her so uncharacteristically hangdog he relented: "Well, come here and we'll watch TV until the house forgives you, but we just missed the news."

They both pretended to watch the Food Network on mute. 14 Arden Lane was silent except for the low burble of the dishwasher and the muffled sound of chinchillas in the next room. She put her head on the shoulder of his dusty coat and allowed herself five seconds of frustrated self-pity, and enjoyed those five seconds immensely. When she and Daniel were alone she pretended that he never flinched slightly or was given pause by anything, and she just smelled the old familiar smell of his shampoo and overheated laptop. At 8:18 her cellphone buzzed in her pocket, which she ignored.

She and Danny had once both sworn that they would be presidents, astronauts and rock stars, and now in their forties they shared mid-life crises in the same way they'd used to share chocolates. She knew she could be careless and cavalier and hard to deal with, and had won the lottery with Daniel. As best friends went he was reliably fantastic. She liked the way his dark hair was cut short, with sprigs of early grey at the temples, liked his hair in general: it was a pretty shallow thing to like about a person, but she liked so much about Danny that she was amazed by every new thing she found charming. There were lines at his eyes and mouth that made his rare smile a little lopsided and piratical, no asset for a chartered stockbroker. When she touched his hair he hesitated.

"It's bizarre not to have you talking," he said. "I have to admit, I don't actually like it."

Rosamund wrote afresh in her notebook:

Sometimes I think you're angry at me.

"Don't even try to have a conversation like this," he said, avoiding the issue like a champ, "it annoys me watching you painstakingly write that out."

There was a terrible loneliness in her as she touched his neck, folded down a piece of his collar. It wasn't 14 Arden Lane that was lonely, she suddenly thought, it was *her*; she was an armoured creature, self-sufficient, but for the terrible fact of needing her best friend all the time excepting when she wanted to finish a book. Her fingers curled at his neck and she was aware of everything, aware of the outside night-time and how her clothes felt on her skin, of how his face was a mask and how he wouldn't look at her. Her fingers brushed his cheek and his jaw and the side of his mouth, sifted through his hair. Rosamund Tilly was an empty glass.

"Don't," said Danny.

At university they'd draped all over each other and never cared. They'd both had their gay periods then, reverting straight the next semester when Rosamund admitted she couldn't do all the clogged-up sinks and he admitted he couldn't deal with the late nights, and life proceeded from there. Daniel had one and a half divorces and Dr. Tilly had littered Hartford with a committed lack of commitment. She'd also littered Hartford with Snowdrop and Sparrow Tilly, who were the delights of her life, or at least would be when one or the other stopped texting her, and now that they were grown up being without Daniel was a terrible chore. Rosamund had never been lonely for anyone except Daniel Tsai, and when she pressed closer she could feel the beat of his heart slithering arrhythmically against her arm.

"Don't," he said again. Her mouth was very close to his mouth. Danny's dark eyes were fathomless and closed. "We can't handle change, Rosamund. I love you too much and know you too well. Think about this."

The room closed down claustrophobically on her. She wanted to say: *do you know how long I've thought about this?* Or: *I want you more than anyone I ever thought I wanted.* And: *I'm so sorry.* Instead she accidentally said, "I—"

*

"Well?" Danny Fourteen said. "Did worlds collide?"

*

Dr. Tilly quit wasting time. She shot to her feet, made a beeline for her notebook, laptop jabbing into her thigh and irritated at the faint smell of chinchillas as she wrote. He said, "What," as she flipped over pages, pretty patient as she gestured him away from trying to look – all he did was eventually get up and get himself a glass of water, as though this were a perfectly normal evening.

"Just nod your head for *all's well* and shake it for *things not well*," said Daniel, "maybe flailing a little for something in the middle, God knows, I didn't learn how to deal with this in school."

Now used to gestures, she jabbed a finger at him until he sat back down on the squashy sofa and looked up at her expectantly. Dr. Tilly did not expect to feel so shaky. She tasted nervousness in her saliva as she flipped up the notebook—

Don't stop me, Daniel.

"Oh, yes, that calms me down," said Danny. "*That* makes me feel perfectly at ease."

Flip. *We need to talk.*

"Okay. Any reason you're using flashcards?"

Flip. *& what I'm saying here is all true and nothing to do with any house magic.*

Danny still looked pretty buttoned-up and patient, but his voice had that overly reasonable cast people took on if they thought you were a bit loopy. "Okay. Go on."

what did you have for lunch today??

"Rose, you already asked, and it was a peanut butter protein bar."

Mr. Daniel Tsai, are you in love with me?

He didn't even take it in. He read it, looked at her face, saw the question there as well, and smiled as gently as a chartered stockbroker could when faced with a woman for whom the date was over – self-effacing, running one hand through that grey-sprigged hair as though trying to consider how best to put things. "So that's what you're worried about," he said carefully. "Rosamund, you know I care about you, don't you? You and the girls are the most important people in my life who don't share my genetic code."

This was not going well. She had made some mistake. When Danny decided the best defense was a good offense, he went in with irritated guns blazing. "I know we joke around a lot," he was saying. "Is it the flirting? We can stop if it makes you uncomfortable. To be honest, I do love you. But I haven't been *in* love with you since I was eighteen."

It was incredible. She hadn't thought you could physically feel your heart breaking, a sort of sucking sensation near the aorta as it imploded into itself. Dr. Tilly hadn't thought her heart would break at all. "Don't worry," he added, "nothing's going to change, Rose. Nothing."

"Let me try this again," she said.

*

"Well?" Danny Fifteen said. "Did worlds collide?"

*

It was a little funny, even, how his reactions didn't change, how she noticed the quirk of his eyebrows once he got to halfway through her litany. Her handwriting had perhaps been a little messier this time. There was only one change now, a question of semantics—

"Rose, you already asked," said Danny, "and it was a peanut butter protein bar."

Mr. Daniel Tsai: I am in love with you.

Dr. Tilly held that one for the longest time, gripped between her knees. Once she'd gotten to forty she thought she'd been an emotional bulwark, but now she felt as though all her insides were scooped out and replaced with packing peanuts. She felt thick and heavy. Danny re-read the sign six times, eyes darting to her face before going back and reading it again, and she thought she imagined him swallowing.

"Well," he said, with admirable calmness, "what do I do with that information, Dr. Rosamund Tilly?"

She scribbled inanely: *I'm not sure? Romantic embraces??*

"So you immediately assume I'm in love with you, in a fit of o'erweening hubris," snapped her best friend, but even as she gaped and horrible dread filled her he made the queerest half-smile expression. The smell of sofa and dusty chinchillas no longer irritated Dr. Tilly. "Don't mind me," he said, and Danny leaned over to kiss her. He kissed her kindly until she didn't want to be kissed kindly any more, at which point he smeared her chapstick from her top lip to her bottom lip. "Please just talk," he said, and she was too busy trying to memorize the way that his mouth felt and how the cradle of his hips were against her own. "I love you. Say it again."

"I've never loved anyone else," said Dr. Tilly.

*

"Well?" Danny Sixteen said. "Did worlds collide?"

*

This time all she did was unfold herself: got up wearily off the sofa and could not look him in the eye, had that quizzical expression of his burned repulsively into her brain forevermore. Dr. Tilly stood up and paced around the room, hating every hair on her head and every brick in 14 Arden Lane's walls, and at one point kicked the chimney grate until it hurt her big toe. Danny just watched.

The cellphone buzzed for the umpteenth time in the pocket of her skirt, and now she yanked it out savagely to read:

8:18 PM
Sent from: Sparrow
Dont forget to fix the fridge mum!

Dr. Tilly imagined that the house was a little sorry as she got the hairdryer and proceeded to defrost everything up to and including the freezer, cartons of milk and meat sitting on the countertop as Danny watched and provided towels. If there had been a Queen's Award for feeling exhausted, she would have won it. Feeling tired made one feel sadder and when one was sad one felt tireder, and she got down on her knees and scrubbed out the remnants of old carrots as she half-daydreamed about being kissed.

"There," she said, "are you happy now, you wretched house?" Nothing happened. Her brain burst into tears.

Danny looked at her expression and said, "All right. Plan B," and did what he did every time she had a pressure headache, which was to turn off the lights so that only a thin filter from the kitchen made its way into the sitting-room. He spread the sofa blanket out on their laps and put his arm around her, and they listened to the far-off roar of cars in the street and the tiny squeaks of chinchillas dust-bathing. Dr. Tilly thought she understood why he was angry: there they were, two people who knew each other so well that just by an expression he could tell what she needed, and all they did was stand and stare at opposite sides of the crevasse.

"A time loop?" he said, when she finally told him. "You've got to be kidding me. A *time loop*? You met my doppelgangers?" The expression on her face must have been like a coffee stain that couldn't be wiped clean, so he relented: "Well, I suppose worlds really did collide."

The house tried to get back into her good books by making tiny mandarin-coloured lights appear like fireflies, and she nearly forgave it when Danny reached out and let one alight on his finger. When he passed it to her it was sweet and warm like tumbledryer lint. So was his hand.

"Yes," said Dr. Tilly, "they did, now that I think about it."

*

When everyone else in the faculty asked about her tired face the next day, she said "House troubles," and everyone nodded as though that made any sort of sense. The neighbours had stuffed two notes about the hedge in 14 Arden Lane's letterbox and the house had retaliated by covering them in snails; the water pressure in her morning shower had been shocking; the house had made jasmine bloom from the ivy trellises, but Rosamund Tilly informed it that this was a poor show and botanically incorrect. It was Danny who had to call her at lunchtime as she sat down to mark some coursework, and she hadn't any lunch.

"Tuna salad and three crackers," said Daniel. "You?"

She looked in her desk drawer. "Five Peppermint Tic-Tacs."

"Rose, that's disgusting," he said, and she could hear him drumming a pen on his desk. Danny didn't mince words: "Look, you can't go on like this, and I don't mean your lunch. God only knows what your house will do the next time."

"It's lonely," she said, though her heart wasn't really into defending it. "The girls are too far away. I was thinking of getting another chinchilla."

"I was thinking more along the lines of a roommate," he said a bit crisply, "and before you say anything else – I was thinking of me. For one, I'm at your house so often I think I'm legally your common-law friendship-bracelet wife. What do you say?"

Her eyelids undrooped. Her headache cleared. Dr. Tilly's Tic-Tacs melted on her tongue, sharp and clean and sweet. "I think that might do the trick," she said.

It did. The plumbing was still terrible, but in Rosamund's opinion 14 Arden Lane was good as gold.

AGAINST THE LAFAYETTE ESCADRILLE

Gene Wolfe

Gene Wolfe is an award-winning American science fiction and fantasy writer. His best-known and most highly regarded work is the multi-volume novel The Book of the New Sun. He has written over thirty novels and many short stories. He was inducted into the Science Fiction Hall of Fame in 2007. "Against the Lafayette Escadrille" was first published in the anthology *Again, Dangerous Visions* (edited Harlan Ellison) in 1972.

I have built a perfect replica of a Fokker triplane, except for the flammable dope. It is five meters, seventy-seven centimeters long and has a wing span of seven meters, nineteen centimeters, just like the original. The engine is an authentic copy of an Oberursel UR II. I have a lathe and a milling machine and I made most of the parts for the engine myself, but some had to be farmed out to a company in Cleveland, and most of the electrical parts were done in Louisville, Kentucky.

In the beginning I had hoped to get an original engine, and I wrote my first letters to Germany with that in mind, but it just wasn't possible; there are only a very few left, and as nearly as I could find out none in private hands. The Oberursel Werke is no longer in existence. I was able to secure plans though, through the cooperation of some German hobbyists. I redrew them myself, translating the German when they had to be sent to Cleveland. A man from the newspaper came to take pictures when the Fokker was nearly ready to fly and I estimated then that I had put more than three thousand hours into building it. I did all the airframe and the fabric work myself, and carved the propeller.

Throughout the project I have tried to keep everything as realistic as possible, and I even have two 7.92 mm Maxim "Spandau" machine-guns mounted just ahead of the cockpit. They are not loaded of course, but they are coupled to the engine with the Fokker Zentralsteuerung interrupter gear.

The question of dope came up because of a man in Oregon I used to correspond with who flies a Nieuport Scout. The authentic dope, as you're probably aware, was extremely flammable. He wanted to know if I'd used it, and when I told him I had not he became critical.

As I said then. I love the Fokker too much to want to see it burn authentically, and if Antony Fokker and Reinhold Platz had had fireproof dope they would have used it. This didn't satisfy the Oregon man and he finally became so abusive

I stopped replying to his letters. I still believe what I did was correct, and if I had it to do over my decision would be the same.

I have had a trailer specially built to move the Fokker, and I traded my car in on a truck to tow it and carry parts and extra gear, but mostly I leave it at a small field near here where I have rented hangar space, and move it as little as possible on the roads. When I do because of the wide load I have to drive very slowly and only use certain roads. People always stop to look when we pass, and sometimes I can hear them on their front porches calling to others inside to come and see. I think the three wings of the Fokker interest them particularly, and once in a rare while a veteran of the war will see it – almost always a man who smokes a pipe and has a cane. If I can hear what they say it is often pretty foolish, but a light comes into their eyes that I enjoy.

Mostly the Fokker is just in its hangar out at the field and you wouldn't know me from anyone else as I drive out to fly. There is a black cross painted on the door of my truck, but it wouldn't mean anything to you. I suppose it wouldn't have meant anything even if you had seen me on my way out the day I saw the balloon.

It was one of the earliest days of spring, with a very fresh, really indescribable feeling in the air. Three days before I had gone up for the first time that year, coming after work and flying in weather that was a little too bad with not quite enough light left; winter flying, really. Now it was Saturday and everything was changed. I remember how my scarf streamed out while I was just standing on the field talking to the mechanic.

The wind was good, coming right down the length of the field to me, getting under the Fokker's wings and lifting it like a kite before we had gone a hundred feet. I did a slow turn then, getting a good look at the field with all the new, green grass starting to show, and adjusting my goggles.

Have you ever looked from an open cockpit to see the wing struts trembling and the ground swinging far below? There is nothing like it. I pulled back on the stick and gave it more throttle and rose and rose until I was looking down on the backs of all the birds and I could not be certain which of the tiny roofs I saw was the house where I live or the factory where I work. Then I forgot looking down, and looked up and out, always remembering to look over my shoulder especially, and to watch the sun where the S.E. 5a's of the Royal Flying Corps love to hang like dragonflies, invisible against the glare.

Then I looked away and I saw it, almost on the horizon, an orange dot. I did not, of course, know then what it was; but I waved to the other members of the Jagstaffel I command and turned toward it, the Fokker thrilling to the challenge. It was moving with the wind, which meant almost directly away from me, but that only gave the Fokker a tailwind, and we came at it – rising all the time.

It was not really orange-red as I had first thought. Rather it was a thousand colors and shades, with reds and yellows and white predominating. I climbed toward it steeply with the stick drawn far back, almost at a stall. Because of that I failed, at first, to see the basket hanging from it. Then I leveled out and circled it at a distance. That was when I realized it was a balloon. After a moment I saw, too, that it was of very old-fashioned design with a wicker basket for the passengers and that someone was in it. At the moment the profusion of colors interested me more, and I went slowly spiraling in until I could see them better, the Easter egg blues and the blacks as well as the reds and whites and yellows.

It wasn't until I looked at the girl that I understood. She was the passenger, a very beautiful girl, and she wore crinolines and had her hair in long chestnut curls that hung down over her bare shoulders. She waved to me, and then I understood. The ladies of Richmond had sewn it for the Confederate army, making it from their silk dresses. I remembered reading about it. The girl in the basket blew me a kiss and I waved to her, trying to convey with my wave that none of the men of my command would ever be allowed to harm her; that we had at first thought that her craft might be a French or Italian observation balloon, but that for the future she need fear no gun in the service of the Kaiser's Flugzeugmeisterei.

I circled her for some time then, she turning slowly in the basket to follow the motion of my plane, and we talked as well as we could with gestures and smiles. At last when my fuel was running low I signaled her that I must leave. She took, from a container hidden by the rim of the basket, a badly shaped, corked brown bottle. I circled even closer, in a tight bank, until I could see the yellow, crumbling label. It was one of the very early soft drinks, an original bottle. While I watched she drew the cork, drank some, and held it out symbolically to me.

Then I had to go. I made it back to the field, but I landed dead stick with my last drop of fuel exhausted when I was half a kilometer away. Naturally I had the Fokker refueled at once and went up again, but I could not find her balloon.

I have never been able to find it again, although I go up almost every day when the weather makes it possible. There is nothing but an empty sky and a few jets. Sometimes, to tell the truth, I have wondered if things would not have been different if, in finishing the Fokker, I had used the original, flammable dope. She was so authentic. Sometimes toward evening I think I see her in the distance, above the clouds, and I follow as fast as I can across the silent vault with the Fokker trembling around me and the throttle all the way out; but it is only the sun.

SWING TIME

Carrie Vaughn

Carrie Vaughn is an American writer who has written several novels in her *New York Times* bestselling series about a werewolf named Kitty. She also wrote the young-adult novels *Voices of Dragons* and *Steel* (which was named to the ALA's 2012 Amelia Bloomer list of the best books for young readers with strong feminist content), and the novels *Discord's Apple* and *After the Golden Age*. She is a contributor to the Wild Cards series of shared-world superhero books edited by George R.R. Martin, and her short stories have appeared in numerous magazines and anthologies. An Air Force brat, she survived her nomadic childhood and managed to put down roots in Boulder, Colorado. This story originally appeared in the June 2007 issue of *Jim Baen's Universe*.

He emerged suddenly from behind a potted shrub. Taking Madeline's hand, he shouldered her bewildered former partner out of the way and turned her toward the hall where couples gathered for the next figure.

"Ned, fancy meeting you here." Madeline deftly shifted so that her voluminous skirts were not trod upon.

"Fancy? You're pleased to see me then?" he said, smiling his insufferably ironic smile.

"Amused is more accurate. You always amuse me."

"How long has it been? Two, three hundred years? That volta in Florence, wasn't it?"

"Si, signor. But only two weeks subjective."

"Ah yes." He leaned close, to converse without being overheard. "I've been meaning to ask you: have you noticed anything strange on your last few expeditions?"

"Strange?"

"Any doorways you expected to be there not opening. Anyone following you and the like?"

"Just you, Ned."

He chuckled flatly.

The orchestra's strings played the opening strains of a Mozart piece. She curtseyed – low enough to allure, but not so low as to unnecessarily expose décolletage. Give a hint, not the secret. Lower the gaze for a demure moment only. Smile, tempt. Ned bowed, a gesture as practiced as hers. Clothed in white silk stockings and velvet breeches, one leg straightened as the other leg stepped back. He made a precise turn of his hand and never broke eye contact.

They raised their arms – their hands never quite touched – and began to dance. Elegant steps made graceful turns, a leisurely pace allowed her to study him. He wore dark green velvet trimmed with white and gold, sea spray of lace at the cuffs and collar. He wore a young man's short wig powdered to perfection.

"I know why you're here," he said, when they stepped close enough for conversation. "You're after Lady Petulant's diamond brooch."

"That would be telling."

"I'll bet you I take it first."

"I'll make that bet."

"And whoever wins—"

Opening her fan with a jerk of her wrist, she looked over her shoulder. "Gets the diamond brooch."

The figure of the dance wheeled her away and gave her to another partner, an old man whose wig was slipping over one ear. She curtseyed, kept one eye on Lady Petulant, holding court over a tray of bonbons and a rat-like lap dog, and the other on Ned.

With a few measures of dancing, a charge of power crept into Madeline's bones, enough energy to take her anywhere: London 1590. New York 1950. There was power in dancing.

The song drew to a close. Madeline begged off the next, fanning herself and complaining of the heat. Drifting off in a rustle of satin, she moved to the empty chair near Lady Petulant.

"Is this seat taken?"

"Not at all," the lady said. The diamond, large as a walnut, glittered against the peach-colored satin of her bodice.

"Lovely evening, isn't it?"

"Quite."

For the next fifteen minutes, Madeline engaged in harmless conversation, insinuating herself into Lady Petulant's good graces. The lady was a widow, rich but no longer young. White powder caked the wrinkles of her face. Her fortune was entailed, bestowed upon her heirs and not a second husband, so no suitors paid her court. She was starved for attention.

So when Madeline stopped to chat with her, she was cheerful. When Ned appeared and gave greeting, she was ecstatic.

"I do believe I've found the ideal treat for your little dear," he said, kneeling before her and offering a bite-sized pastry to the dog.

"Why, how thoughtful! Isn't he a thoughtful gentleman, Frufru darling? Say thank you." She lifted the creature's paw and shook it at Ned. "You are too kind!"

Madeline glared at Ned, who winked back.

A servant passed with a silver tray of sweets. When he bowed to offer her one, she took the whole tray. "Marzipan, Lady Petulant?" she said, presenting the tray.

"No thank you, dear. Sticks to my teeth dreadfully."

"Sherry, Lady Petulant?" Ned put forward a crystal glass which he'd got from God knew where.

"Thank you, that would be lovely." Lady Petulant took the glass and sipped.

"I'm very sorry, Miss Madeline, but I don't seem to have an extra glass to offer you."

"That's quite all right, sir. I've always found sherry to be rather too sweet. Unpalatable, really."

"Is that so?"

"Hm." She fanned.

And so it went, until the orchestra roused them with another chord. Lady Petulant gestured a gloved hand toward the open floor.

"You young people should dance. You make such a fine couple."

"Pardon me?" Ned said.

Madeline fanned faster. "I couldn't, really."

"Nonsense. You two obviously know each other quite well. It would please me to watch you dance."

Madeline's gaze met Ned's. She stared in silence, her wit failing her. She didn't need another dance this evening, and she most certainly did not want to dance with him again.

Giving a little smile that supplanted the stricken look in his eyes, he stood and offered his hand. "I'm game. My lady?"

He'd thought of a plan, obviously. And if he drew her away from Lady Petulant – she would not give up that ground.

The tray of marzipan sat at the very edge of the table between their chairs. As she prepared to stand, she lifted her hand from the arm of her chair, gave her fan a downward flick – and the tray flipped. Miniature daisies and roses shaped in marzipan flew around them. Madeline shrieked, Lady Petulant gasped, the dog barked. Ned took a step back.

A ruckus of servants descended on them. As Madeline turned to avoid them, the dog jumped from Lady Petulant's lap – for a brief moment, its neck seemed to grow to a foot long – and bit Madeline's wrist. A spot of red welled through her white glove.

"Ow!" This shriek was genuine.

"Frufru!" Lady Petulant collected the creature and hugged it to her breast. "How very naughty of you, Frufru darling. My dear, are you all right?"

She rubbed her wrist. The blood stain didn't grow any larger. It was just a scratch. It didn't even hurt. "I— I—" Then again, if she played this right. . .

"I – oh my, I do believe I feel faint." She put her hand to her neck and willed her face to blush. "Oh!"

She fell on Lady Petulant. With any luck, she crushed Frufru beneath her petticoats. Servants convulsed in a single panicked unit, onlookers gasped, even Ned was there, murmuring and patting her cheek with a cool hand.

Lady Petulant wailed that the poor girl was about to die on top of her. Pressed up against the good lady, Madeline took the opportunity to reach for the brooch. She could slip it off and no one would notice—

The brooch was already gone.

She did not have to feign a stunned limpness when a pair of gallant gentlemen lifted her and carried her to a chaise near a window. Ned was nowhere to be seen. Vials of smelling salts were thrust at her, lavender water sprinkled at her. Someone was wrapping her wrist – still gloved – in a bandage, and someone who looked like a doctor – good God, was the man wielding a razor? – approached.

She shoved away her devoted caretakers and tore off the bandage. "Please, give me air! I've recovered my senses. No, really, I have. If-you-please, sir!"

As if nothing had happened, she stood, straightened her bodice over her corset, smoothed her skirts, and opened her fan with a snap.

"I thank you for your attention, but I am quite recovered. Goodbye."

She marched off in search of Ned.

He was waiting for her toward the back of the hall, a fox's sly grin on his face. Before she came too close, he turned his cupped hand, showing her a walnut-sized diamond that flashed against the green velvet of his coat.

Turning, he stepped sideways behind the same potted fern where he had ambushed her.

He disappeared utterly.

"Damn him!" Her skirts rustled when she stamped her foot.

Ignoring concerned onlookers and Lady Petulant's cries after her welfare, she cut across the hall to the glass doors opening to the courtyard behind the hall, and across the courtyard to a hideously baroque statue of Cupid trailing roses off its limbs. She stopped and took a breath, trying to regain her composure. No good brooding now. It was over and done. There would be other times and places to get back at him. Stepping through required calm.

A handful of doorways collected here in this hidden corner of the garden. One led to an alley in Prague 1600; tilting her head one way, she could just make out a dirty cobbled street and the bricks of a Renaissance façade. Another led to a space under a pier in Key West 1931. Yet another led home.

She danced for this moment; this moment existed because she danced.

Behind the statue Madeline turned her head, narrowed her eyes a certain practiced way, and the world shifted. Just a bit. She put out her hand to touch the crack that formed a line in the air. Confirming its existence, she stepped sideways and through the doorway, back to her room.

Her room: sealed in the back of a warehouse, it had no windows or doors. In it, she stored the plunder taken from a thousand years of history – what plunder she could carry, at least: Austrian crystal, Chinese porcelain, Aztec gold, and a walk-in closet filled with costumes spanning millennia.

She dropped her fan, pulled the pins out of her wig, unfastened her dress and unhooked her corset. Now that she could breathe, she paced and fumed at Ned properly.

She really ought to go someplace with a beach next time. Hawaii 1980, perhaps. Definitely someplace without corsets. Someplace like—

The band played Glenn Miller from a gymnasium stage with a USO banner draped overhead. There must have been a couple hundred G.I.s drinking punch, crowding along the walls, or dancing with a couple hundred local girls wearing bright dresses and big grins. Madeline only had to wait a moment before a G.I. in dress greens swept her up and spun her into the mob.

Of all periods of history, of all forms of dance, this was her favorite. Such exuberance, such abandon in a generation that saw the world change before its eyes. No ultra-precise curtseys and bows here.

Her soldier lifted her, she kicked her feet to the air and he brought her down, swung her to one side, to the other, and set her on the floor at last to Lindy hop and catch her breath. Her red skirt caught around her knees, and sweat matted her hair to her forehead.

Her partner was a good-looking kid, probably nineteen or twenty, clean-faced and bright-eyed. Stuck in time, stuck with his fate – a ditch in France, most likely. Like a lamb to slaughter. It was like dancing a minuet in Paris in 1789, staring at a young nobleman's neck and thinking, you poor chump.

She could try to warn him, but it wouldn't change anything.

The kid swung her out, released her and she spun. The world went by in a haze and miraculously she didn't collide with anyone.

When a hand grabbed hers, she stopped and found herself pulled into an embrace. Arm in arm, body to body, with Ned. Wearing green again. Arrogant as ever, he'd put captain bars on his uniform. He held her close, his hand pressed against the small of her back, and two-stepped her in place, hemmed in by the crowd. She couldn't break away.

"Dance with me, honey. I ship out tomorrow and may be dead next week."

"Not likely, Ned. Are you following me?"

"Now how would I manage that? I don't even know when you live. So, what are you here for, the war bonds cash box?"

"Maybe I just like the music."

As they fell into a rhythm, she relaxed in his grip. A dance was a dance after all, and if nothing else he was a good dancer.

"I didn't thank you for helping me with Lady Petulant. Great distraction. We should be a team. We both have to dance to do what we do – it's a perfect match."

"I work alone."

"You might think about it."

"No. I tried working with someone once. His catalyst for stepping through was fighting. He liked to loot battlefields. All our times dancing ended in brawls."

"What happened to him?"

"Somme 1916. He stayed a bit too long at that one."

"Ah. I met a woman once whose catalyst was biting the heads off rats."

"You're joking! How on earth did she figure that out?"

"One shudders to think."

The song ended, a slow one began, and a hundred couples locked together.

"So, how did you find me?" she asked.

"I know where you like to go."

She frowned and looked aside, across his shoulder to a young couple clinging desperately to one another as they swayed in place.

"Tell me Ned, what were you before you learned to step through? Were you always a thief?"

"Yes. A highwayman and a rogue from the start. You?"

"I was a good girl."

"So what changed?

"The cops can't catch me when I step through."

"That doesn't answer my question. If you were a good girl, why do you use stepping through to rob widows, and not to do good? Don't tell me you've never tried changing anything. Find a door to the Ford Theater and take John Wilkes Booth's gun."

"It never works. You know that."

"But history doesn't notice when an old woman's diamond disappears. So – what do you use the money you steal for? Do you give it to the war effort? The Red Cross? The Catholic Church? Do you have a poor family stashed away somewhere that you play fairy godmother to?"

She tried to pull away, but the beat of the music and the steps of the dance carried her on.

The song changed to something relentless and manic. She tried to break out of his grasp, to spin and hop like everyone else was doing, but he tightened his grip and kept her cheek to cheek.

"You don't do any of those things," she said.

"How do you know?"

He was right, of course. She only had his word for it when he said he was a rogue.

"What are you trying to say?"

He brought his lips close to her ear and purred. "You were never a good girl, Madeline."

She slapped him, a nice crack across the cheek. He seemed genuinely stunned – he stopped cold in the middle of the dance and touched his face. A few bystanders laughed. Madeline turned, shoving her way off the dance floor, dodging feet and elbows.

She went all the way to the front doors before looking back. Ned wasn't following her. She couldn't see him at all, through the mob.

In the women's room she found her doorway to Madrid 1880 where she'd stashed a gown and danced flamenco, then to a taverna in Havana 1902, and from there to her room. He wouldn't possibly be able to follow that path.

Unbelievable, how out of a few thousand years of history available to them and countless millions of locations around the world, they kept running into each other.

Ned wore black. He had to, really, because they were at the dawn of the age of the tuxedo, and all the men wore black suits: black pressed trousers, jackets with tails, waistcoats, white cravats. Madeline rather liked the trend, because the women, in a hundred shades of rippling silk and shining jewels, glittered against the monotone backdrop.

Gowns here didn't require the elaborate architecture they had during the previous three centuries. She wore a corset, but her skirt was not so wide as to prevent walking through doorways. The fabric, pleated and gathered in back, draped around her in slimming lines. She glided tall and elegant, as a Greek statue.

He hadn't seen her yet. For once, she had the advantage. She watched behind the shelter of a neoclassical pillar. He moved like he'd been born to this dance. Perhaps he had. Every step made with confidence, he and his partner might have been the same unit as they turned, stepped, turned, not looking where they were going yet never missing a step. It always amazed her, how a hundred couples could circle a crowded ballroom like this and never collide.

He was smiling, his gaze locked on his partner's the whole time. For a moment, Madeline wished she were dancing with him. Passing time had cooled her temper.

She'd already got what she came for, a few bits of original Tiffany jewelry. After a dance or two, she could open a door and leave. In a room this large, she could dance a turn and Ned would never have to know she'd been here.

But she waited until his steps brought him close to her. She moved into view, caught his gaze and smiled. He stumbled on the parquet.

He managed to recover without falling and without losing too much of his natural grace. "Madeline! I didn't see you."

"I know."

He abandoned his partner – turned his back on her and went straight to Madeline. The woman glared after him with a mortally offended expression that Ned didn't seem to notice.

"Been a while, eh?"

"Only a month, subjective."

"So – what brings you here?"

"That's my secret. I've learned my lesson about telling you anything. You?"

He looked around, surveying the ballroom, the orchestra on the stage, the swirl of couples dancing a pattern like an eddy in a stream. Each couple was independent, but all of them together moved as one entity, as if choreographed.

"Strauss," he said at last. "Will you dance with me, Miss Madeline?"

He offered his hand, and she placed hers in it. They joined the pattern.

"Have you forgiven me for that comment from last time?"

"No," Madeline said with a smile. "I'm waiting for the chance to return the favor."

Step two three turn two three —

"Do you believe in fate?" Ned said.

"Fate? I suppose I have to, considering some of the things I've seen. Why do you ask?"

"It's a wonderful thing, really. You see, we never should have met. I should have died before you were born – or vice versa, since I still don't know when you're from. But here we are."

"That's fate? I thought you were following me."

"Ah yes."

Madeline tilted her head back. Crystal chandeliers sparkled overhead, turning, turning. Ned didn't take his eyes off her.

"Have you thought of why I might follow you?" he said.

"To reap the benefits of my hard work. I do the research and case the site, and you arrive to take the prize. It's all very neat and I'd like you to stop."

"I can't do that, Madeline."

"Why not? Isn't there enough history for you to find your own hunting grounds without taking mine?"

"Because that isn't the reason I'm following you. At least not anymore." He paused. He wasn't smiling, he wasn't joking. "I think I'm in love with you."

Her feet kept doing what they were supposed to do. The music kept them moving, which was good because her mind froze. "No," she murmured.

"Will you give me a chance? A chance to show you?"

It was a trick. A new way to make a fool of her, and it was cruel. But she had never seen him so serious. His brow took on furrows.

She stopped dancing, and he had to stop with her, but he wouldn't let go. There, stalled in the middle of the ballroom floor, the dance turned to chaos around them.

"No. I can't love you back, Ned. We're too much alike."

For a long moment, a gentle strain of music, he studied her. His expression turned drawn and sad.

"Be careful, Madeline. Watch your back." He kissed her hand, a gentle press of lips against her curled fingers, then let it go and walked off the dance floor, shouldering around couples as they passed.

He left her alone, lost, in the middle of the floor. She touched her hand where he had kissed it.

"Ned!" she called, the sound barely audible over the orchestra. "Ned!"

He didn't turn around.

The song ended.

She left the floor, hitched up her skirt and ran everywhere, looking behind every door and every potted fern. But he was gone.

If Ned followed her, it stood to reason others could as well.

Her room had been trashed. The mirror over the vanity was shattered, chairs smashed, a dresser toppled. Powdered cosmetics dusted the wreckage. The wardrobe was thrown open, gowns and fabric torn and strewn like streamers over the furniture.

She didn't have windows or doors precisely to keep this sort of thing from happening. There was only one way into the room – through a sideways door, and only if one knew just the right way to look through it. So how—

Someone grabbed her in a bear hug. Another figure appeared from behind her and pointed a bizarre vice-grip and hairbrush-looking tool at her in the unmistakable stance of holding a weapon. A third moved into view.

She squirmed in the grasp of the first, but he was at least a foot taller than she and he quickly worked to secure bindings around her arms and hands that left her immobile. All wore black militaristic suits with goggles and metallic breathing masks hiding their features.

The third spoke, a male voice echoing mechanically through the mask. "Under Temporal Transit Authority Code forty-four A dash nine, I hereby take you into custody and charge you—

"The what?" Madeline said with a gasp. Her captor wrenched her shoulders back. Any struggle she made now was merely out of principle. "Temporal Transit Authority? I've never heard of such a thing!"

"You've never stepped through to the twenty-second century, then."

"No." Traveling to one's own future was tough – there was no record to study, no way to know what to expect. She'd had enough trouble with her past, she never expected the future to come back to haunt her.

"I hereby take you into custody and charge you with unregulated transportation along the recognized timeline, grand theft along the recognized timeline, historic fraud—"

"You can't be serious—"

He held up a device, something like an electric razor with a glowing wand at one end and flashing lights at the other. He pressed a button and drew a line in the air. The line glowed, hanging in midair. He pressed another button, the line widened into a plane, a doorway through which a dim scene showed: pale tiled walls and steel tables.

He opened a door, he stepped through, and all he needed to do was push a button.

In that stunned moment, the two flunkies picked her up and carried her through.

They entered a hospital room and unloaded her onto a gurney. More figures appeared, doctors hiding behind medical scrubs, cloth masks, and clinical gazes. With practiced ease they strapped her face-down, wrists and legs bound with padded restraints. When she tried to struggle, a half-dozen hands pressed her into the thin mattress. Her ice-blue skirt was hitched up around her knees, wrinkling horribly.

"Don't I get a lawyer? A phone call? Something?" She didn't even know where or when she was. Who would she call?

A doctor spoke to the thug in charge. "Her catalyst?"

"Dancing."

"I know just the thing. Nurse, prep a local anesthetic."

Madeline tensed against her bindings. "What are you doing? What are you doing to me?"

"Don't worry, we can reverse the procedure. If you're found innocent at the trial."

She lost track of how many people were in the room. A couple of the thugs, a couple of people in white who must have been nurses or orderlies. A couple who looked like doctors. Someone unbuttoned her shoes. Her silk stockings ripped.

Needle-pricks stabbed each foot, then pins of sleep traveled up her legs. She screamed. It was the only thing she could do. A hand pushed her face into the mattress. Her legs went numb up to her knees. She managed to turn her face, and through the awkward, foreshortened perspective she saw them make incisions above her heels, reach a thin scalpel into the wounds, and cut the Achilles' tendons. There was no pain, but she felt the tissues snap inside her calves.

She screamed until her lungs hurt, until she passed out.

She awoke in a whitewashed cell, lying on a cot that was the room's only furnishing. There was a door without a handle. She was no longer tied up, but both her ankles were neatly bandaged, and she couldn't move her legs.

Gingerly sitting up, she unfastened the bodice of her gown, then released the first few hooks of her corset. She took a deep breath, arching her back. Her ribs and breasts were bruised from sleeping in the thing. Not to mention the manhandling she'd received.

She didn't want to think about her legs.

Curling up on her side, she hugged her knees and cried.

She fell asleep, arms curled around her head. The light, a pale fluorescent filtering through a ceiling tile, stayed on. Her growling stomach told her that time passed. Once, the door opened and an orderly brought in a tray of food, leaving it on the floor by the bed. She didn't eat. Another time, a female orderly brought in a contraption, a toilet seat and bedpan on wheels, and offered to help her use it. She screamed, batted and clawed at the woman until she left.

She pulled apart her elegant, piled coif – tangled now – and threw hairpins across the room.

When the door opened again, she had a few pins left to hurl at whomever entered. But it wasn't an orderly, a doctor, or a thug.

It was Ned, still in his tails and cravat.

He closed the door to the thinnest crack and waited a moment, listening. Madeline clamped her hand over her mouth to keep from crying out to him.

Apparently satisfied, Ned came to the bed, knelt on the floor, and gathered her in an embrace.

"You look dreadful," he said gently, holding her tightly.

She sobbed on his shoulder. "They cut my tendons, Ned. They cut my legs."

"They're bastards, Madeline," he muttered, between meaningless noises of comfort.

Clutching the fabric of his jacket, she pushed him away suddenly. "Did they get you too? What did they do to you?" She looked him over, touched his face – nothing seemed wrong. "How did you get here?"

He gave her a lopsided smile. "I used to be one of the bastards."

She edged away, pushing herself as far to the wall as she could. Ned, with his uncanny ability to follow her where and whenever she went. He didn't move, didn't try to stop her or grapple with her. She half expected him to.

"Used to be," she said. "Not still?"

"No. It began as a research project, to study what people like me – like us – can do, and what that meant about the nature of space and time. But there were other interests at work. They developed artificial methods of finding doorways and stepping through. They don't need us anymore and hate competition. The Temporal Transit Authority was set up to establish a monopoly over the whole business."

"And you – just left? Or did you lead them to me?"

"Please, Madeline. I'm searching for a bit of redemption here. I followed you. I couldn't stop following you. I knew they were looking for you. I found your place right after they did. I wish – I should have told you. Warned you a little better than I did."

"Why didn't you?" she said, her voice thin and desperate.

"I didn't think you'd believe me. You've never trusted me. I'm sorry."

No, she thought, remembering that last waltz, the music and his sad face and the way he disappeared. *I'm sorry.*

"You were following me all along. We didn't meet by chance."

"Oh no. It was chance. Fate. I didn't know about you, wasn't looking for you. But when I met you, I knew the Authority would find you sooner or later. I didn't want them to find you."

"But they did."

"Once again I apologize for that. Now, we're getting out of here."

He started to pick her up, moving one arm to her legs and the other to her shoulders. She leaned away, pressing herself against the wall in an effort to put more distance between them.

"Please trust me," he said.

Why should she believe anything he said? She didn't know anything about him. Except that he was a marvelous dancer. And she needed to dance.

She put her arms around his neck and let him lift her.

"Come on, then." He picked her up, cradling her in his arms. She clung to him. "Get the door, would you?"

She pulled the door open. He looked out. The corridor was empty. Softly, he made his way down the hall.

Then Ned froze. Voices echoed ahead of them, moving closer. Without a word, he turned and walked the other direction. If he had been able to run, he would have rounded the next corner before the owners of the voices saw him. But he held her, and he couldn't do more than walk carefully.

Footsteps sounded behind him. She looked over his shoulder and saw a doctor flanked by a couple of orderlies enter the corridor.

"Hey! Stop there!" The doctor pointed and started running.

"All these bloody doors lock on the outside," Ned muttered. "Here, open that one."

She stared. The door had no handle, no visible hinges or latches. Ned hissed a breath of frustration and bumped a red light panel on the wall with his elbow. The door popped in with a little gasp of hydraulics.

He pushed through into what turned out to be a supply closet, about ten foot square, filled with shelves and boxes, and barely enough room to turn around. He set her on the floor and began pushing plastic tubs at the door. He soon had enough of a blockade to stop their pursuers from shoving through right away. He kept piling, though, while the people outside pounded on the door and shouted.

Madeline cowered on the floor, her legs stuck out awkwardly. "You can't dance for both of us, and I'm too big for you to carry me through."

"Yes."

"You shouldn't have come. Now you're caught too."

"But I'm with you," he said, turning to her with the brightest, most sincere smile she had ever seen. "It makes all the difference." He went back to throwing boxes on the stack.

She caught her breath and wondered what she'd have to do to see that smile again.

"Help me stand." She hooked her fingers on a shelving post as far above her as she could reach and pulled. Grunting, she shifted her weight to try and get her feet under her.

"Madeline, good god what are you doing?"

"Standing. Help me."

He went to her and pulled her arm over his shoulders, reaching his own arm around her waist. Slowly, he raised her. She straightened her legs, and her feet stayed where she put them.

There. She was standing. She clenched her jaw. Her calves were exploding with pain.

"Do you think there's a door in here?" she said, her voice tight.

"There're doors everywhere. But you can't—"

"We have to."

"But—"

"I can. Help me."

He sighed, adjusting his grip so he supported her more firmly. "Right. What should we dance?"

She took a breath, cleared her mind so she could think of a song. She couldn't even tap her toe to keep a beat. She began humming. The song sounded out of tune and hopeless in her ears.

"Ravel. 'Pavane for a Dead Princess'," Ned said. "Come on, dear, you're not done yet. One and two and—"

She held her breath and moved her right leg. It did move, the foot dragging, and she leaned heavily on Ned because she didn't dare put any weight on it. Then the left foot. She whimpered a little. Ned was right behind her, stepping with her.

The pavane had the simplest steps she could think of. At its most basic, it was little more than walking very slowly – perfect for a crippled dancer. It was also one of the most graceful, stately, elegant dances ever invented. Not this time. She couldn't trust her legs. She dragged them forward and hoped they went where they needed to be. Ned wasn't so much dancing with her as lurching, ensuring she stayed upright.

There was a kind of power, even in this: bodies moving in desperation.

She tried to keep humming, but her voice jerked, pain-filled, at every step. They hummed together, his voice steadying her as his body did.

Then came a turn. She attempted it – a dance was a dance, after all. Put the left foot a little to the side, step out—

Her leg collapsed. She cried out, cutting the sound off mid-breath. Ned caught her around the waist and leaned her against the shelving. This gave her something to sit on, a little support.

Without missing a beat, he took her hand and stepped a half-circle around her. He held her hand lightly, elevated somewhat, and tucked his other hand behind his back. Perfect form.

"This just doesn't feel right if I'm not wearing a ruff," he said, donning a pompous, aristocratic accent.

Hiccupping around stifled tears, she giggled. "But I like being able to see your neck. It's a handsome neck."

"Right, onto the age of disco then."

The banging on the door was loud, insistent, like they'd started using a battering ram, and provided something of a beat. The barricade began to tumble.

"And so we finish." He bowed deeply.

She started to dip into a curtsey – just the tiniest of curtsies – but Ned caught her and lifted her.

"I think we're ready."

She narrowed her eyes and looked a little bit sideways.

Space and time made patterns, the architecture of the universe, and the lines crossed everywhere, cutting through the very air. Sometimes, someone had a talent that let them see the lines and use them.

"There," Ned said. "That one. A couple of disheveled Edwardians won't look so out of place there. Do you see it?"

"Yes," she said, relieved. A glowing line cut before them, and if they stepped a little bit sideways—

She put out her hand and opened the door so they could step through together.

Lady Petulant's diamond paid for reconstructive surgery at the best unregistered clinic in Tokyo 2028. Madeline walked out the door and into the alley, where Ned was waiting for her. Laughing, she jumped at him and swung him around in a couple of steps of a haphazard polka.

"Glad to see you're feeling better," he said. And there was that smile again.

"Polycarbon filament tissue replacement. I have the strongest tendons in the world now."

They walked out to the street – searching the crowd of pedestrians, always looking over their shoulders.

"Where would you like to go?" he said.

"I don't know. It's not so easy to pick, now that we're fugitives. Those guys could be anywhere."

"But we have lots of places to hide. We just have to keep moving."

They walked for a time along a chaotic street, nothing like a ballroom, the noises nothing like music. The Transit Authority people knew they had to dance; if they were really going to hide, it would be in places like this, where dancing was next to impossible.

But they couldn't do that, could they?

Finally, Ned said, "We could go watch Rome burn. And fiddle."

"Hm. I'd like to find a door to the Glen Island Casino. 1939."

"Glenn Miller played there, didn't he?"

"Yes."

"We could find one, I think."

"If we have to keep moving anyway, we'll hit on it eventually."

He took her hand, pulled her close and pressed his other hand against the small of her back. Ignoring the tuneless crowd, he danced with her.

"Lead on, my dear."

THE MASK OF THE REX

Richard Bowes

Richard Bowes has won two World Fantasy awards, an International Horror Guild Award, and a Million Writers Award. He has published six novels, four short-story collections and seventy stories. His most recent novel *Dust Devil on a Quiet Street* just appeared from Lethe Press, which also republished his Lambda Award–winning 1999 novel *Minions of the Moon*. His most recent collections are *The Queen, the Cambion, and Seven Others* from Aqueduct Press and *If Angels Fight* from Fairwood Press, both in 2013. This story was first published in *The Magazine of Fantasy & Science Fiction* in 2002.

1.

The last days of summer have always been a sweet season on the Maine coast. There's still warmth in the sun, the crickets' song is mellow and the vacationers are mostly gone. Nowhere is that time more golden than on Mount Airey Island.

Late one afternoon in September of 1954, Julia Garde Macauley drove north through the white shingled coastal towns. In the wake of a terrible loss, she felt abandoned by the gods and had made this journey to confront them.

Then, as she crossed Wenlock Sound Bridge which connects the island with the world, she had a vision. In a fast montage, a man, his face familiar yet changed, stood on crutches in a cottage doorway, plunged into an excited crowd of kids, spoke defiantly on the stairs of a plane.

The images flickered like a TV with a bad picture and Julia thought she saw her husband. When it was over, she realized who it had been. And understood even better the questions she had come to ask.

The village of Penoquot Landing on Mount Airey was all carefully preserved clapboard and widow's walks. Now, after the season, few yachts were still in evidence. Fishing boats and lobster trawlers had full use of the wharves.

Baxter's Grande Hotel on Front Street was in hibernation until next summer. In Baxter's parlors and pavilions over the decades, the legends of this resort and Julia's own family had been woven.

Driving through the gathering dusk, she could almost hear drawling voices discussing her recent loss in same way they did everything having to do with Mount Airey and the rest of the world.

"Great public commotion about that fly-boy she married."

"The day their wedding was announced, marked the end of High Society."

"In a single engine plane in bad weather. As if he never got over the war."

"Or knew he didn't belong where he was."

Robert Macauley, thirty-four years old, had been the junior senator from New York for a little more than a year and a half.

Beyond the village, Julia turned onto the road her grandfather and Rockefeller had planned and had built. "Olympia Drive, where spectacular views of the mighty Atlantic and piney mainland compete for our attention with the palaces of the great," rhapsodized a writer of the prior century. "Like a necklace of diamonds bestowed upon this island."

The mansions were largely shut until next year. Some hadn't been opened at all that summer. The Sears estate had just been sold to the Carmelites as a home for retired nuns. Where the road swept between the mountain and the sea, Julia turned onto a long driveway and stopped at the locked gates. Atop a rise stood Joyous Garde, all Doric columns and marble terraces. Built at the dawn of America's century, its hundred rooms overlooked the ocean, "One of the crown jewels of Olympia Drive."

Joyous Garde had been closed and was, in any case, not planned for convenience or comfort. Julia was expected. She beeped and waited.

Welcoming lights were on in Old Cottage just inside the gates. Itself a substantial affair, the Cottage was on a human scale. Henry and Martha Eder were the permanent caretakers of the estate and lived here year round. Henry emerged with a ring of keys and nodded to Julia.

Just then, she caught flickering images, of this driveway and what looked at first like a hostile, milling mob.

A familiar voice intoned. "Beyond these wrought iron gates and granite pillars, the most famous private entryway in the United States, and possibly the world, the Macauley family and friends gather in moments of trial and tragedy."

Julia recognized the speaker as Walter Cronkite and realized that what she saw was the press waiting for a story.

Then the gates clanged open. The grainy vision was gone. As Julia rolled through, she glanced up at Mt. Airey. It rose behind Joyous Garde covered with dark pines and bright foliage.

Martha Eder came out to greet her and Julia found herself lulled by the old woman's Down East voice. Julia had brought very little luggage. When it was stowed inside, she stood on the front porch of Old Cottage and felt she had come home. The place was wooden-shingled and hung with vines and honeysuckle. Her great-grandfather, George Lowell Stoneham, had built it seventy-five years before. It remained as a guest house and gate house and as an example of a fleeting New England simplicity.

2.

George Lowell Stoneham was always referred to as one of the discoverers of Mt. Airey. The Island, of course, had been found many times. By seals and gulls and migratory birds, by native hunters, by Hudson and Champlain and Scotch-Irish fishermen. But not until after the Civil War was it found by just the right people: wealthy and respectable Bostonians.

Gentlemen, such as the painter Brooks Carr looking for proper subjects, or the Harvard naturalist George Lowell Stoneham trying to loose memories of Antietem, came up the coast by steamer, stayed in the little hotels built for salesmen and schooner captains. They roamed north until they hit Mt. Airey.

At first, a few took rooms above Baxter's General Provisions And Boarding House in Penoquot Landing. They painted, explored, captured bugs in specimen bottles. They told their friends, the nicely wealthy of Boston, about it. Brooks Carr rented a house in the village one summer and brought his young family.

To Professor Stoneham went the honor of being the first of these founders to build on the island. In 1875, he bought (after hard bargaining) a chunk of land on the seaward side of Mt. Airey and constructed a cabin in a grove of giant white pine that overlooked Mirror Lake.

In the following decades, others also built: plain cabins and studios at first, then cottages. In those days, men and boys swam naked and out of sight at Bachelor's Point on the north end of the island. The women, in sweeping summer hats and dresses that reached to the ground, stopped for tea and scones at Baxter's which now offered a shady patio in fine weather. There, they gossiped about the Saltonstall boy who had married the Pierce girl then moved to France, and about George Stoneham's daughter Helen and a certain New York financier.

This filet of land in this cream of a season did not long escape the notice of the truly wealthy. From New York they came and Philadelphia. They acquired large chunks of property. The structures they caused to rise were still called studios and cottages. But they were mansions on substantial estates. By the 1890's those who could have been anywhere in world chose to come in August to Mount Airy.

Trails and bridle paths were blazed through the forests and up the slopes of the mountain. In 1892 John D. Rockefeller and Simon Garde constructed a paved road, Olympia Drive, around the twenty-five mile perimeter of the island.

Hiking parties into the hills, to the quiet glens at the heart of the island, always seemed to find themselves at Mirror Lake with its utterly smooth surface and unfathomable depths.

The only work of man visible from the shore, and that just barely, was Stoneham Cabin atop a sheer granite cliff.

Julia Garde Macauley didn't know what caused her great-grandfather to build on that exact spot. But she knew it wasn't whim or happenstance. The old tintypes showed a tall man with a beard like a wizard's and eyes that had gazed on Pickett's Charge.

Maybe the decision was like the one Professor Stoneham himself described in his magisterial WASPS OF THE EASTERN UNITED STATES. "In the magic silence of a summer's afternoon, the mud wasp builds her nest. Instinct, honed through the eons guides her choice."

Perhaps, though, it was something more. A glimpse. A sign. Julia knew for certain that once drawn to the grove, George Stoneham had discovered that it contained one of the twelve portals to an ancient shrine. And that the priest, or the Rex as the priest was called, was an old soldier, Lucius, a Roman centurion who worshipped Lord Apollo. Lucius had been captured and enslaved during Crassus' invasion of Parthia in the century before Christ. He escaped with the help of his god who then led him to one of the portals of the shrine. The reigning priest at that time was a devoted follower of Dionysus. Lucius found and killed the man, put on the silver mask and became Rex in his place.

Shortly after he built the cabin, George Lowell Stoneham built a cottage for his family at the foot of the mountain. But he spent much time up in the grove. After the death of his wife, he even stayed there, snowbound, for several winters researching, he said, insect hibernation.

In warmer seasons, ladies in the comfortable new parlors at Baxter's Hotel, alluded to the professor's loneliness.

Conversation over brandy in the clubrooms of the recently built Bachelor's Point Aquaphiliacs Society, dwelt on the 'fog of war' that sometimes befell a hero.

There was some truth in all that. But what only Stoneham's daughter Helen knew was that beyond the locked door of the snowbound cabin, two old soldiers talked their days away in Latin. They sat on marble benches overlooking a cypress grove above a still lake in second century Italy. Lucius would look out into the summer haze, and come to attention each time a figure appeared, wondering, the professor knew, if this was the agent of his death.

Then on a morning one May, George Lowell Stoneham was discovered sitting in his cabin with a look of peace on his face. A shrapnel splinter, planted in a young soldier's arm during the Wilderness campaign thirty-five years before, had worked its way loose and found his heart. Professor Stoneham's daughter and only child, Helen, inherited the Mt. Airey property. Talk at the Thursday Cotillions in the splendid summer ballroom of Baxter's Grande Hotel had long spun around the daughter, "With old Stoneham's eyes and Simon Garde's millions."

For Helen was the first of the Boston girls to marry New York money. And such money and such a New York man! Garde's hands were on all the late nineteenth century levers: steel, railroads, shipping. His origins were obscure. Not quite, a few hinted, Anglo-Saxon. The euphemism used around the Aquaphiliacs' Society was, "Eastern".

In the great age of buying and building on Mt. Airey, none built better or on a grander scale than Mr. and Mrs. Garde. The old Stoneham property expanded, stretched down to the sea. The new "cottage", Joyous Garde, was sweeping, almost Mediterranean, with its Doric columns and marble terraces, its hundred windows that flamed in the rising sun.

With all this, Helen did not neglect Stoneham Cabin up on the mountain. Over the years, it became quite a rambling affair. The slope on which it was built, the pine grove in which it sat, made its size and shape hard to calculate. In the earliest years of the century, after the birth of her son, George, it was remarked that Helen Stoneham Garde came up long before the season and stayed well afterwards. And that she was interested in things Chinese. Not the collections of vases and fans that so many clipper-captain ancestors had brought home, but earthenware jugs, wooden sandals, bows and arrows. And she studied the language. Not high Mandarin, apparently, but some guttural peasant dialect.

Relations with her husband were also a subject for discussion. They were rarely seen together. In 1906, the demented millionaire Harry Thaw shot the philandering architect Stanford White on the rooftop of Madison Square Garden in New York. And the men taking part in the Bachelor's Point Grand Regatta that year joked about how Simon Garde had been sitting two tables away. "As easily it might have been some other irate cuckold with a gun and Sanford White might be building our new yacht club right now."

At the 1912 Charity Ball for the Penoquot Landing Fisherfolk Relief Fund in Baxter's Grande Pavilion, the Gardes made a joint entrance. This was an event rare enough to upstage former President Teddy Roosevelt about to campaign as a Bull Moose.

Simon Garde, famously, mysteriously, died when the French liner *Marseilles* was sunk by a U-boat in 1916. Speculation flourished as to where he was bound and the nature of his mission. When his affairs, financial and otherwise, were untangled, his widow was said to be one of the wealthiest women in the nation.

Helen Stoneham Garde, a true child of New England, never took her attention far from the money. Horses were her other interest besides chinoise. She bred them and raced them. And they won. Much of her time was spent on the Mt. Airey estates. Stories of her reclusivity abounded. The truth, her granddaughter Julia knew, would have stunned even the most avid of the gossips. For around the turn of the century, Lucius had been replaced. A single arrow in the eye had left the old Rex sprawling on the stone threshold of the shrine. His helmet, his sword and the matched pair of Colt naval revolvers which had been a gift from George Stoneham, lay scattered like toys.

A new Rex, or more accurately a Regina, picked the silver mask out of the dust and put it on. This was Ki Mien from north China, a servant of the goddess of forests and woods and a huntress of huge ability. From a few allusions her grandmother dropped, Julia deduced that Helen Garde and the priestess had, over the next two decades, forged a union. Unknown to any mortal on the Island or in the world, they formed what was called in those days a Boston marriage.

In the years that Helen was occupied with Ki Mien, motorcars came to Mt. Airey. Their staunchest supporter was George "Flash" Garde, Simon and Helen's son and only child. "A damned fine looking piece of American beef," as a visiting Englishman remarked. Whether boy or man, Flash Garde could never drive fast enough. His custom-built Locomobile, all brass and polish and exhaust, was one of the hazards of Olympia Drive. "Racing to the next highball and low lady," it was said at Bachelor's Point. "Such a disappointment to his mother," they sighed at Baxter's. In fact, his mother seemed unbothered. Perhaps this was because she had, quite early on, arranged his marriage to Cissy Custis, the brightest of the famous Custis sisters. The birth of her granddaughter Julia guaranteed the only succession that really mattered to her.

3.

In 1954, on the evening of the last day of summer, Julia had supper in Old Cottage kitchen with the Eders. Mrs. Eder made the same comforting chicken pie she remembered. The nursery up at Joyous Garde was vast. On its walls were murals of the cat playing the fiddle and the cow jumping the moon. It contained a puppet theater and a play house big enough to walk around in if you were small enough. But some of Julia's strongest memories of Mt. Airey centered on Old Cottage. The most vivid of all, began one high summer day in the early 1920's. Her grandmother, as she sometimes did, had taken Julia out of the care of her English nurse and her French governess.

When it was just the two of them, Helen Stoneham Garde raised her right hand and asked, "Do you swear on the head of Ruggles the One Eared Rabbit, not to tell anybody what we will see today?"

Time with her grandmother was always a great adventure. Julia held up the stuffed animal worn featureless with love and promised. Then they went for a walk. Julia was in a pinafore and sandals and held Ruggles by his remaining ear. The woman of incalculable wealth wore sensible shoes and a plain skirt and carried a picnic basket. Their walk was a long one for somebody with short legs. But finches sang, fledglings chirped on oak branches. Invisible through the leaves, a woodpecker drilled a maple trunk. Red squirrels and jays spread news of their passage.

Up the side of Mt. Airey, Helen led her grandchild, to the silent white pine grove that overlooked deep, still waters. The Cabin itself was all odd angles, gray shingles and stone under a red roof. It was Julia's first visit to the place.

Years later, when she was able to calculate such things, she realized that the dimensions of Stoneham Cabin did not quite pan out. But only a very persistent visitor would note that something was missing, that one room always remained unexplored.

That first time, on a sunny porch, visible from no angle outside the Cabin, Helen Garde set down the basket, unpacked wine and sandwiches along with milk and a pudding for Julia. Then she stood behind her granddaughter and put her hands on the child's shoulders.

"Julia, I should like you to meet Alcier, whom we call the Rex."

The man in the doorway was big and square-built with dark skin and curly, black hair. His voice was low, and, like Mademoiselle Martine, he spoke French, though his was different. He wore sandals and a white shirt and trousers. The priest bowed and said, "I am happy to meet the tiny lady."

He was not frightening at all. On the contrary, morning doves fed out of his hand and he admired Ruggles very much. When they had finished lunch, the Rex asked her grandmother if he could show Julia what lay inside.

The two of them passed through a curtain which the child could feel but couldn't see. She found herself in a round room with doors open in all directions. It was more than a small child could encompass. That first time, she was aware only of a cave opening onto a snowy winter morning and an avenue of trees with the moon above them.

Then Alcier faced her across a fire which flickered in the center of the room even on this warm day. He put on a silver mask that covered his face, with openings for his eyes, nostrils and mouth, and said, "Just as your grandmother welcomed me to her house, so, as servant of the gods, I welcome you to the Shrine of the Twelve Portals."

But even as gods spoke through him, Julia could see that Alcier smiled and that his eyes were kind. So she wasn't a bit afraid. When it was time to say good-by, the Rex stood on the porch and bowed slightly. A red tailed hawk came down and sat on his wrist. Because of Alcier's manners, Julia was never frightened of the Rex. Even later when she had seen him wiping his machete clean.

As a small child, Julia didn't know why her grandmother made her promise not to tell anyone about the hawk and the invisible curtain and the nice black man who lived up in the cabin. But she didn't.

Children who tell adults everything are trying to make them as wise as they. Just as children who ask questions, already know why the sky is blue and where the lost kitten has gone.

What they need is the confirmation that the odd and frightening magic which has turned adults into giants has not completely addled their brains. That Julia didn't need such reassurance she attributed to her grandmother and to Alcier. On her next visit, she learned to call the place with the flame, the Still Room. She found out that it was a shrine, a place of the gods, and that Alcier was a priest, though much different than the ones in the Episcopal church. On the second visit she noticed Alcier's slight limp.

Her grandmother never went inside with them. On Julia's next few visits over several summers, she and Alcier sat on stools in the Still Room and looked out through the twelve doors. The Rex patrolled each of these entrances every day. He had a wife and, over the years, several children whom Julia met. Though she never was told exactly where they lived. Soon, she had learned the name of what lay beyond each portal: jungle, cypress grove, dark forest, tundra, desert, rock-bound island, marsh, river valley, mountain, cave, plains, sandy shore.

At first she was accompanied up the mountain by her grandmother. Then, in the summer she turned twelve, Julia was allowed to go by herself. By that time, she and Alcier had gone through each of the doors and explored what lay beyond. The hour of the day, the climate, even Julia came to realize, the continent varied beyond each portal. All but one, in those years, had a shrine of some kind. This might be a grove or a cave, or a rocky cavern, with a fire burning and, somewhere nearby, a body of water still as a mirror. The plains, even then, had become a wasteland of slag heaps and railroad sidings. Julia did not remember ever having seen it otherwise.

If she loved Alcier, and she did, it was not because he spared her the truth in his quiet voice and French from the Green Antilles. Early on he showed her the fascinating scar on his left leg and explained that he was an escaped slave, "Like each Rex past and to be." He told her how he had been brought over the wide waters when he was younger than she, how he had grown up on a plantation in the Sugar Islands. How he had been a house servant, how he had run away and been brought back in chains with his leg torn open.

Julia already knew how one Rex succeeded another. But on that first summer she visited the cabin alone, she and Alcier had a picnic on the wide, empty beach on the Indochina Sea and she finally asked how it had happened.

Before he answered, Alcier drew the silver mask out of the satchel he always carried. Julia noticed that he hardly had to guide it. The mask moved by itself to his face. Then he spoke.

"Where I lived, we had a public name for the bringer of wisdom And a private name known only by those to whom She spoke. When I was very young, She sent me dreams. But after I was taken beyond the sea, it was as if I was lost and She couldn't find me.

"Then, after I had escaped and been recaptured and brought back to my owner, She appeared again and told me what to do. When I awoke, I followed Her command.

"With the chains that bound my hands, I broke the neck of one who came to feed me. With that one's knife, I killed him who bore the keys. With the machete he dropped, I made the others flee. My left leg carried me well. My right was weak. I did not run as I once had.

"In the forest, hunters chased me. But the goddess drew me into a mist and they passed by. Beside a stream, a hare came down to drink. I killed her and drank her blood. That morning, hunters went to my left and to my right. I slipped past them as before.

"Then it was past mid-day. I stood in shadows on the edge of a glade. And all was silent and still. No leaf moved. In the sky directly above me, the sun and a hawk stood still. And I knew gods were at work here. I heard no sounds of hunters. For I was at the heart of the forest.

"I saw the lodge made of wood and stone and I knew it was mine for the taking. If I killed the King of this place. I said a prayer to the goddess and let her guide me.

"Not a leaf moved, not a bird sang. Then I saw the silver mask and knew the Rex was looking for me. My heart thumped. I commanded it to be still. The head turned one way then another. But slowly. The Rex was complacent, maybe, expecting to find and kill me easily. Or old and tired.

"My goddess protected me. Made me invisible. Balanced on my good leg and my bad, I stood still as the Rex crossed the glade. I studied the wrinkled throat that hung below the mask. And knew I would have one chance. Just out of range of my knife, the priest hesitated for an instant. And I lunged. One great stride. I stumbled on my bad leg. But my arm carried true. The knife went into the throat. And I found it was a woman and that I was king in her place.

"The shrine has existed as long as the gods. Along one of the paths some day, will come the one who succeeds me," he told her. "When the gods wish, that one will do away with me."

The Rex could speak of his own death the same way he might about a change of the seasons. But some time after that, on a visit to the Still Room, Julia noticed derricks and steel tanks on the rocky island. When she asked Alcier about the destruction of another shrine, he seemed to wince, shook his head and said nothing.

4.

At night in Old Cottage years later, Julia looked out the windows into the dark. And saw Mount Airey by daylight. The cabin and the grove were gone. The bare ground they had stood on was cracked and eroded. She told Mrs. Eder that she was going to visit Stoneham Cabin next morning. Falling asleep, Julia remembered the resort as it had been. As a child, she had learned to swim at Bachelor's Point and heard the story of Mount Airey being spun. Men tamed and in trunks, women liberated in one piece suits, swam together now and talked of the useful Mr. Coolidge and, later, the traitorous Franklin Delano Roosevelt.

When she was fifteen, her father died in an accident. Nothing but the kindest condolences were offered. But Julia, outside an open door, heard someone say, "Ironic, Flash Garde's being cut down by a speeding taxi."

"In front of the Stork Club, though, accompanied by a young lady described as a 'hostess'. He would have wanted it that way." She heard them all laugh.

By then, cocktail hour had replaced afternoon tea at Baxter's. In tennis whites, men sat with their legs crossed, women with their feet planted firmly on the ground. Scandal was no longer whispered. Julia knew that her mother's remarriage less than two months after her father's death would have been fully discussed. As would the decision of this mother she hardly ever saw to stay in Europe.

Julia's grandmother attended her son's funeral and shed not a tear. Her attitude was called stoic by some. Unfeeling by others. No one at Baxter's or Bachelor's Point had the slightest idea that the greatest love of Helen Garde's life had, over their twenty years together, given her hints of these events yet to come.

After her father's death and her mother's remarriage, Julia visited the Rex. From behind the silver mask, Alcier spoke. "The gods find you well. You will wed happily with their blessings," he said. "The divine ones will shield your children."

Much as she adored Alcier, Julia thought of this as fortune-teller stuff. She began, in the way of the young, to consider the Rex and the Shrine of the Twelve Portals as being among the toys of childhood.

That Fall, she went to Radcliffe as her grandmother wished. There, the thousand and one things of a wealthy young woman's life drove thoughts of the gods to the back of her mind. They didn't even re-emerge on a sunny day on Brattle Street in her senior year.

Julia and her friend Grace Shipton were headed for tennis lessons. At the curb, a young man helped a co-ed from Vassar into the seat of an MG Midget. He looked up and smiled what would become a well-known smile. And looked again, surprised. It was the first time he had laid eyes on the woman he would marry.

Before this moment, Julia had experienced a girl's tender thoughts and serious flirtations. Then her eyes met those of the young man in the camel-hair jacket. She didn't notice the boy who watched them, so she didn't see his mischievous smile or feel the arrow. But in a moment of radiance her heart was riven.

When Julia asked Grace who the young man was, something in her voice made the Shipton heiress look at her, "That's Robert Macauley," came the answer. "The son of that lace curtain thug who's governor of New York."

Julia Garde and young Robert Macauley were locked in each other's hearts. All that afternoon she could think of nothing else. Then came the telegram that read, "Sorry to intrude. But I can't live without you."

"Until this happened, I never believed in this," she told him the next afternoon when they were alone and wrapped in each others' arms.

Robert proposed a few days later. "The neighbors will burn shamrocks on your front lawn," he said when Julia accepted.

She laughed, but knew that might be true. And didn't care. Polite society studied Helen Stoneham Garde's face for the anger and outrage she must feel. The heiress to her fortune had met and proposed to marry an Irishman, A CATHOLIC, A DEMOCRAT! But when Julia approached her grandmother in the study at Joyous Garde and broke the news, Helen betrayed nothing. Her eyes were as blue as the wide Atlantic that lay beyond the French doors. And as unknowable.

"You will make a fine-looking couple," she said. "And you will be very happy."

"You knew."

"Indirectly. You will come to understand. The wedding should be small and private. Making it more public would serve no immediate purpose."

"Best political instincts I've encountered in a Republican," the governor of the Empire State remarked on hearing this. "Be seen at mass," he told his son. "Raise the children in the Church. With the Garde money behind you, there'll be no need to muck about with concrete contracts."

"There will be a war and he will be a fighter pilot," Helen told Julia after she had met Robert. Before her granddaughter could ask how she knew, she said impatiently, "All but the fools know a war is coming. And young men who drive sports cars always become pilots."

It was as she said. Robert was in Naval Flight Training at Pensacola a month after Pearl Harbor. The couple's song was, "They can't take that away from me".

Their son, Timothy, was not three and their daughter Helen was just born when Robert Macauley sailed from San Francisco on the aircraft carrier *Constellation*. Julia saw him off, then found herself part of the great, shifting mass of soldiers and sailors home on leave, women returning after saying good-by to husbands, sons, boyfriends.

On a crowded train, with sailors sleeping in the luggage racks, she and a Filipino nurse cried about their men in the South Pacific. She talked with a woman, barely forty, who had four sons in the army.

Julia felt lost and empty. She reread the *Metamorphoses* and the *Odyssey* and thought a lot about Alcier and the Still Room. It had been two years since she had visited Mount Airey. She felt herself drawn there all that winter. Early in Spring, she left her children in the care of nurses and her grandmother and went by train from New York to Boston and from Boston to Bangor. She arrived in the morning and Mr. Eder met her at the station. They drove past houses with victory gardens and V's in the windows if family members were in the service. A sentry post had been established on the mainland end of Wenlock Sound Bridge. The Army Signal Corps had taken over Bachelor's Point for the duration of the war.

The bar at Baxter's was an officers' club. On Olympia Drive, some of the great houses had been taken for the duration. Staff cars, jeeps, canvas-topped trucks stood in the circular drives.

It was just after the thaw. Joyous Garde stood empty. Patches of snow survived on shady corners of the terraces. The statues looked as if they still regretted their lack of clothes. Julia found a pair of rubber boots that fit and set off immediately for Stoneham Cabin. In summer, Mt. Airey was nature in harness, all bicycle paths and hiking parties. In Mud Time, dry beds ran with icy water, flights of birds decorated a gray sky, lake-sized puddles had appeared, the slopes lay leafless and open.

Julia saw the stranger as she approached the cabin. But this was her land and she did not hesitate. Sallow faced, clean-shaven with the shadow of a beard, he was expecting her. When she stepped onto the porch, he came to attention. She knew that sometime in the recent past he had murdered Alcier.

"Corporal John Smalley, Her Britannic Majesty's London Fusiliers," he said. "Anxious to serve you, my lady." In the Still Room, when they entered, Julia looked around, saw wreckage in the desert shrine, smashed tanks on the sand.

Dead animals lay around the oasis and she guessed the water was poisoned. The murderer put on the silver mask and spoke. His voice rang. Julia felt a chill.

"It's by the will of the gods that I'm here today. By way of a nasty scrap in the hills. Caught dead to rights and every one of us to die. Officers down. No great moment. But the sergeant major was gone. A spent round richoted off my Worsley helmet and I was on me back looking up.

"I lay still but I could hear screams and thought it was up and done with and I would dance on hot coals for as long as it took. For cheating and philandering and the cove I stabbed in Cheapside. And I prayed as I'd never done.

"Then He appeared. Old Jehovah as I thought, all fiery eyes and smoke behind his head. Then He spoke and it seems it was Mars himself. I noticed he wore a helmet and carried a flaming sword. He told me I was under His protection and nothing would happen to me.

"Good as His word. No one saw when, I rose up and took my Enfield. He led the way all through the night, talking in my ear. About the shrine and the priest that lives here.

"A runaway slave it always is who kills the old priest and takes over. And I choked at that. Not the killing, but Britains never will be slaves and all.

"Lord Mars told me enlistment in Her Majesty's Army came close enough. New thinking, new blood was what was needed. Led me to a hill shrine before dawn. Left me to my own devices.

"The shrine's that one through that portal behind your ladyship. A grove with the trees all cut short by the wind and a circle of stone and a deep pool. When I was past the circle and beside the pool, the wind's sound was cut off and it was dead still.

"A path led down to the pool and on it was a couple of stones and a twig resting on them. And I knew not to disturb that. So I went to ground. Oiled my Enfield. Waited. Took a day or two. But I was patient. Ate my iron rations and drank water from the pool.

"When he came, it was at dusk and he knew something was up. A formidable old bugger he was. But . . ."

He trailed off. Removed the mask. "You knew him. Since you were a little girl, I hear."

Julia's eyes burned. "He had a wife and children."

"I've kept them safe. He'd put a sum aside for them from shrine offerings and I saw they had that. Got my own bit of bother and strife tucked away. We know in this job we aren't the first. And won't be the last. Living on a loan of time so to speak."

He pointed to the ruined shrines. "The gods have gotten wise that things will not always go their way." The corporal told her about defense works and traps he was building. Like a tenant telling the landlady about improvements he is making, thought Julia. She knew that was the way it would be between them and that she would always miss her noble Alcier.

Just before she left, Smalley asked, "I wonder if I could see your son, m'lady. Sometime when it's convenient." Julia said nothing. She visited her grandmother, eighty and erect, living in Taos in a spare and beautiful house. Her companion was a woman from the Pueblo, small, silent and observant.

"Timothy is the whole point of our involvement," said the old woman. She sat at a table covered with breeding charts and photos of colts. "You and I are the precursors."

"He's just a child."

"As were you when you were taken to the shrine. Think of how you loved Alcier. He would have wanted you to do this. And you shall have your rewards. Just as I have."

"And they are?"

"At this point in your life, you would despise them if I told you. In time, they will seem more than sufficient."

Julia knew that she would do as the Rex had asked. But that summer Robert was stationed in Hawaii. So she went out to be with him instead of going to Mount Airey. The next August, she gave birth to Cecilia, her second daughter. The year after that, Robert was in a naval hospital in California, injured in a crash landing on a carrier flight deck. His shoulder was smashed but healed nicely. A three inch gash ran from his left ear to his jaw. It threw his smile slightly off-kilter.

He seemed distant, even in bed. Tempered like a knife. And daring. As if he too sensed death and destiny and the will of the gods. When the war was over Robert had a Navy Cross, a trademark smile and a scar worth, as he put it, "Fifty-thousand votes while they still remember." Over his own father's objections, the young Macauley ran for Congress from the West Side of Manhattan. The incumbent, one of the old man's allies, was enmeshed in a corruption scandal.

Robert won the primary and the election. His lovely wife and three young children were features of his campaign. Julia paid a couple of fast visits to the cabin. On one of them the corporal told her, "I know it's a kid will be my undoing. But it will be a little girl." On another he said, "The gods would take it as a great favor, if you let me speak to your son." Thus it was that one lovely morning the following summer. Julia left her two little daughters in the huge nursery at Joyous Garde and brought Timothy to Stoneham Cabin. As if it was part of a ritual, she had Mrs. Eder pack lunch.

Julia stuck a carton of the Luckies she knew the Corporal favored into the basket and started up the hill. Her son, age seven and startlingly like the father he rarely saw, darted around, firing a toy gun at imaginary enemies.

The corporal, tanned and wiry, sat on the back porch, smoking and cleaning his rifle. Tim stared at him wide eyed.

"Are you a commando?" he asked after the introductions were made and he'd learned that their guest was English

"Them's Navy," Smalley said. "And I'm a soldier of the Queen. Or King as it is." Julia stared down at Mirror Lake. Except when Smalley spoke, she could imagine that Alcier was still there. Something even more intense than this must have happened to her grandmother after the death of Ki Mien.

"Have you killed anybody?"

"Killing's never a nice thing, lad. Sometimes a necessity. But never nice," Smalley said. "Now what do you say that we ask your mother if I can show you around?"

Later, on their way back to the cottage, Timothy was awestruck. "He showed me traps he had set! In a jungle! He told me I was going to be a great leader!"

As her grandmother had with her, Julia demanded his silence. Timothy agreed and kept his word. In fact, he rarely mentioned the cabin and the shrine. Julia wondered if Smalley had warned him not to. Then and later, she was struck by how easily her son accepted being the chosen of the gods.

Fashion had passed Mt. Airey by. That summer, the aging bucks at Bachelor's Point drawled on about how Dewey was about to thrash Truman. And how the Rockefellers had donated their estate to the National Parks Service.

"What else now that the Irish have gotten onto the island."

"And not even through the back door." That summer, Helen Stoneham Garde stayed in New Mexico. But Joyous Garde jumped. "Prominent Democrats from the four corners of the nation come to be bedazzled," as Congressman Macauley murmured to his wife. Labor leaders smoked cigars in the oak and leather splendor of Simon Garde's study. Glowing young Prairie Populists, drank with entrenched Carolina Dixiecrats. The talk swirled around money and influence, around next year's national elections and Joe Kennedy's boy down in Massachusetts.

Above them, young Macauley with his lovely wife stood on the curve of the pink and marble stairs. Julia had grown interested in this game. It reminded her of her grandmother's breeding charts and race horses.

The following summer, Helen Stoneham Garde returned to her estate. Afternoons at Baxter's were drowsy now and dowager-ridden.

"Carried in a litter like royalty."

"Up the mountain to the cabin."

"Returned there to die it seems."

"Her daughter and son-in-law will have everything."

Shudders ran around the room. On an afternoon of warm August sun and a gentle sea breeze, Julia sat opposite her grandmother on the back porch of Stoneham Cabin. "Only the rich can keep fragments of the past alive," Helen told her. "To the uneducated eye, great wealth can be mistaken for magic."

Below them, a party had picnicked next to Mirror Lake a bit earlier. Hikers had passed though. But at the moment, the shore was deserted, the surface undisturbed. The Rex was not in evidence. Helen's eye remained penetrating, her speech clear. "A peaceful death," she said. "Is one of the gifts of the gods."

Julia wished she had thought to ask her grandmother more questions about how their lives had been altered by the shrine.

She realized that her own introduction to it at so young an age had occurred because Helen could not stand dealing with the man who had murdered the one closest to her.

The two sat in a long silence. Then the old woman said, "My dearest child, I thought these might be of interest," and indicated a leather folder on the table.

Julia opened it and found several photos. She stared, amazed at the tree-lined Cambridge Street and the young couple agape at their first glimpse of each other. She couldn't take in all the details at once: the deliveryman hopping from his cart, the elderly gent out for a stroll, the boy who walked slightly behind what must have been his parents. Small, perhaps foreign in his sandals, he alone saw the tall, dark-haired young man, the tall blond young woman, stare at each other in wonder.

"You knew before . . ." Julia said looking up. She didn't dare breathe. Her grandmother still smiled slightly. Her eyes were wide. Beside her stood a figure in a silver mask. Tall and graceful. Not Corporal Smalley. Not at all. He wore only a winged helmet and sandals. Hermes, Lord Mercury, touched Helen with the silver caduceus staff he carried.

Julia caught her breath. Her grandmother slumped slightly. Helen Stoneham Garde's eyes were blank. Her life was over. The figure was gone.

5.

"First day of Autumn," Martha Eder said when Julia came down the Old Cottage stairs the morning after her return. A picnic basket had been packed. Julia had not brought cigarettes for Smalley, had reason to think they weren't necessary. The air was crisp but the sun was warm enough that all Julia needed was a light jacket. As she set out, Henry Eder, interrupted his repair of a window frame. "I can go with you, see if anything needs doing." When she declined, he nodded and went back to his work.

Grief was a private matter to Mainers. Besides, even after three quarters of a century, Julia's family were still "summer folk" and thus unfathomable. The walk up Mount Airey was magnificent. Julia had rarely seen it this late in the year. Red and gold leaves framed green pine. Activity in the trees and undergrowth was almost frantic. A fox, intent on the hunt, crossed her path. After her grandmother's death, she had returned to the cabin only on the occasions when she brought Tim. In the last few years, she hadn't been back at all.

She remembered a day when she and Robert sat in the study of their Georgetown mansion and Timothy knocked on the door. Just shy of twelve, he wore his Saint Anthony's Priory uniform of blazer and short pants. In 1951, the American upper class kept its boys in shorts for as long as possible. A subtle means of segregating them from the masses.

Representative Robert Macauley (D-NY) was maneuvering for a Senate nomination in what promised to be a tough year for Democrats. He looked up from the speech he was reviewing. Julia, busy with a guest list, watched them both. Timothy said, "What I would like for my birthday this year is a crewcut. Lots of the kids have them. And I want long pants when I'm not in this stupid monkey suit. And this summer I want to be allowed to go up to the cabin on Mount Airey by myself."

Julia caught the amusement and look of calculation in her husband's eyes. Did his kid in short pants gain him more votes from women who thought it was adorable than he lost from men who thought it was snooty?

"In matters like this, we defer to the upper chamber," he said with a quick, lopsided smile and nodded to Julia.

She felt all the pangs of a mother whose child is growing up. But she negotiated briskly. The first demand was a throwaway as she and her son both knew.

"No crewcut. None of the boys at your school have them. The brothers don't approve." The brothers made her Protestant skin crawl. But they were most useful at times like this.

"Long pants outside school? Please!" he asked. "Billy Chervot and his brothers all get to wear blue jeans!" Next year would be Timothy's last with the brothers. Then he'd be at Grafton and out in the world.

"Perhaps. For informal occasions."

"Jeans!"

"We shall see." He would be wearing them, she knew, obviously beloved, worn ones. On a drizzly morning in Maine. His hair would be short. He'd have spent that summer in a crewcut.

Julia had studied every detail of a certain photo. She estimated Tim's age at around fifteen. The shot showed him as he approached Stoneham Cabin. He wore his father's old naval flight jacket, still too big for him, though he had already gotten tall.

"Mount Airey?" the eleven-year-old Tim had asked. She heard herself saying. "Yes. That should be fine. Check in with Mrs. Eder when you're going. And tell her when you come back. Be sure to let me know if anything up there needs to be done." Her son left the room smiling. "What's the big deal about that damned cabin?" her husband asked.

Julia shrugged. "THE WASPS OF THE EASTERN UNITED STATES," she said and they both laughed. The title of her grandfather's tome was a joke between them. It referred to things no outsider could ever understand or would want to. Julia returned to her list. She had memorized every detail of the photo of their son. He had tears in his eyes. The sight made her afraid for them all.

Her husband held out a page of notes. "Take a look. I'm extending an olive branch to Mrs. Roosevelt. Her husband and my dad disagreed." He grinned. Franklin Roosevelt, patrician reformer and Timothy Macauley, machine politician, had famously loathed each other.

Julia stared at her husband's handwriting. Whatever the words said would work. The third photo in the leather folder her grandmother had given her showed FDR's widow on a platform with Robert. Julia recognized a victory night.

She could trace a kind of tale with the photos. She met her husband. He triumphed. Their son went for comfort to the Rex. A story was told. Or, as in the *Iliad*, part of one.

That day in the study in Georgetown, she looked at Robert Macauley, in the reading glasses he never wore publicly, and felt overwhelming tenderness. Julia could call up every detail of the photo of their meeting.

Only the boy in the background looked directly at the couple who stared into each other's eyes. He smiled. His hand was raised. Something gold caught the sun. A ring? A tiny bow?

Had Robert and she been hit with Eros' arrow? All she knew was that the love she felt was very real.

How clever they were, the gods, to give mortals just enough of a glimpse of their workings to fascinate. But never to let them know everything.

That summer, her son went up Mount Airey alone. It bothered Julia as one more sign he was passing out of her control. "The gods won't want to lose this one m'lady," Smalley had told her.

Over the next few years, Timothy entered puberty, went away to school, had secrets. His distance increased. When the family spent time at Joyous Garde, Tim would go to the Cabin often and report to her in privacy. Mundane matters like "Smalley says the back eaves need to be reshingled." Or vast, disturbing ones like, "That jungle portal is impassable now. Smalley says soon ours will be the only one left."

Then came a lovely day in late August 1954. Sun streamed through the windows of Joyous Garde, sailboats bounced on the water. In the ballroom, staff moved furniture. A distant phone rang. A reception was to be held that evening. Senator Macauley would be flying in from Buffalo that afternoon. Julia's secretary, her face frozen and wide-eyed held out a telephone and couldn't speak. Against all advice, trusting in the good fortune which had carried him so far, her husband had taken off in the face of a sudden Great Lakes storm. Thunder, lightning and hail had swept the region. Radio contact with Robert Macauley's one-engine plane had been lost.

The crash site wasn't found until late that night. The death wasn't confirmed until the next morning. When Julia looked for him, Timothy was gone. The day was cloudy with a chill drizzle. She stood on the porch of Old Cottage a bit later when he returned. His eyes red. Dressed as he was in the photo.

As they fell into each others' arms, Julia caught a glimpse that was gone in an instant. Her son, as in the photo she had studied so often, approached Stoneham Cabin. This time, she saw his grief turn to surprise and a look of stunned betrayal. Timothy didn't notice. The two hugged and sobbed in private sorrow before they turned toward Joyous Garde and the round of public mourning.

As they did, he said, "You go up there from now on. I never want to go back."

FINALE

Julia approached the grove and Cabin on that first morning of Fall. She was aware that it lay within her power to destroy this place. Julia had left a sealed letter to be shown to Timothy if she failed to return. Though she knew that was most unlikely to happen.

A young woman, casual in slacks and a blouse, stood on the porch. In one hand she held the silver mask. "I'm Linda Martin," she said. "Here by the will of the gods."

Julia recognized Linda as contemporary and smart. "An escaped slave?" she asked.

"In a modern sense, perhaps." The other woman shrugged and smiled. "A slave of circumstances."

"I've had what seem to be visions." Julia said as she stepped onto the porch. "About my son and about this property."

"Those are my daughter's doing, I'm afraid. Sally is nine," Linda was apologetic yet proud. "I've asked her not to. They aren't prophecy. More like possibility."

"They felt like a promise. And a threat."

"Please forgive her. She has a major crush on your son. Knows everything he has done. Or might ever do. He was very disappointed last month when he was in pain and wanted to talk to the corporal. And found us."

"Please forgive Tim. One's first Rex makes a lasting impression." Julia was surprised at how much she sounded like her grandmother.

The living room of Stoneham Cabin still smelled of pine. The scent reminded Julia of Alcier and her first visit. As before, a door opened where no door had been. She and Linda passed through an invisible veil and the light from the twelve portals mingled and blended in the Still Room.

"Sally, this is Julia Garde Macauley. Timothy's mother." The child who sat beyond the flame was beautiful. She wore a blue tunic adorned with a silver boy riding a dolphin. She bowed slightly. "Hello Mrs. Macauley. Please explain to Timothy that the corporal knew what happened was Fate and not me."

Julia remembered Smalley saying, "It's a child will be my undoing." She smiled and nodded. Linda held out the mask which found its way to Sally's face.

"This is something I dreamed about your son."

What Julia saw was outdoors and in winter. It was men mostly. White mostly. Solemn. Formally dressed. A funeral? No. A man in judicial robes held a book. He was older, but Julia recognized an ally of her husband's, a young congressman from Oregon. This was the future.

"A future," said the voice from behind the mask. Julia froze. The child was uncanny. Another man, seen from behind, had his hand raised as he took the oath of office. An inauguration. Even with his back turned, she knew her son.

"And I've seen this. Like a nightmare." Flames rose. The Cabin and the grove burned.

"I don't want that. This is our home." She was a child and afraid.

Later, Linda and Julia sat across a table on the rear porch and sipped wine. The foliage below made Mirror Lake appear to be ringed with fire.

"It seems that the gods stood aside and let my husband die. Now they want Tim."

"Even the gods can't escape Destiny," Linda said. "They struggle to change it by degrees."

She looked deep into her glass. "I have Sally half the year. At the cusps of the four seasons. The rest of the time she is with the Great Mother. Once her abilities were understood, that was as good an arrangement as I could manage. Each time she's changed a little more."

Another mother who must share her child, Julia thought. We have much to talk about. How well the Immortals know how to bind us to their plans. She would always resent that. But she was too deeply involved not to comply. Foreknowledge was an addiction.

A voice sang, clear as mountain air. At first Julia thought the words were in English and that the song came from indoors.

Then she realized the language was ancient Greek and that she heard it inside her head. The song was about Persephone, carried off to the Underworld, about Ganymede abducted by Zeus. The voice had an impossible purity. Hypnotic, heartbreaking, it sang about Time flowing like a stream and children taken by the gods.

MESSAGE IN A BOTTLE

Nalo Hopkinson

Nalo Hopkinson is a Jamaican science fiction writer formerly from Canada now living in the United States. Her first novel, *Brown Girl in the Ring*, received substantial critical acclaim and was short-listed for the Philip K. Dick Award. In addition to her novels and short fiction, she has also edited various anthologies, including *Skin Folk* and *So Long Been Dreaming*. This story was first published in *Futureways* (New York's Whitney Museum and Arsenal Pulp Press) in 2004.

"**W**hatcha doing, Kamla?" I peer down at the chubby-fingered kid who has dug her brown toes into the sand of the beach. I try to look relaxed, indulgent. She's only a child, about four years old, though that outsize head she's got looks strangely adult. It bobs around on her neck as her muscles fight for control. The adoption centre had told Babette and Sunil that their new daughter checked out perfectly healthy otherwise.

Kamla squints back up at me. She gravely considers my question, then holds her hand out, palm up, and opens it like an origami puzzle box. "I'm finding shells," she says. The shell she proffers has a tiny hermit crab sticking out of it. Its delicate body has been crushed like a ball of paper in her tight fist. The crab is most unequivocally dead.

I've managed to live a good many decades as an adult without having children in my life. I don't hate them, though I know that every childless person is supposed to say that so as not to be pecked to death by the righteous breeders of the flock. But I truly don't hate children. I just don't understand them. They seem like another species. I'll help a lost child find a parent, or give a boost to a little body struggling to get a drink from a water fountain – same as I'd do for a puppy or a kitten – but I've never had the urge to be a father. My home is also my studio, and it's a warren of tangled cables, jury-rigged networked computers, and piles of books about as stable as playing-card houses. Plus bins full of old newspaper clippings, bones of dead animals, rusted metal I picked up on the street, whatever. I don't throw anything away if it looks the least bit interesting. You never know when it might come in handy as part of an installation piece. The chaos has a certain nest-like comfort to it.

Gently, I take the dead hermit crab in its shell from Kamla's hand. She doesn't seem disturbed by my claiming her toy. "It's wrong," she tells me in her lisping child's voice. "Want to find more."

She begins to look around again, searching the sand. This is the other reason children creep me out. They don't yet grok that delicate, all-important boundary between the animate and inanimate. It's all one to them. Takes them a while to figure out that travelling from the land of the living to the land of the dead is a one-way trip.

I drop the deceased crab from a shaking hand. "No, Kamla," I say. "It's time to go in for lunch now."

I reach for her little brown fist. She pulls it away from me and curls it tightly towards her chest. She frowns up at me with that enfranchised hauteur that is the province of kings and four-year-olds. She shakes her head. "No, don't want lunch yet. Have to look for shells."

They say that play is the work of children. Kamla starts scurrying across the sand, intent on her task. But I'm responsible to Kamla's mother, not to Kamla. I promised to watch the child for an hour while Babette prepared lunch. Babs and Sunil have looked tired, desperate and drawn for a while now. Since they adopted Kamla.

There's still about twenty minutes left in my tenure as Kamla's sitter. I'm counting every minute. I run after her. She's already a good hundred yards away, stuffing shells down the front of her bright green bathing suit as quickly as she can. When I catch up with her, she won't come.

Fifteen minutes left with her. Finally, I have to pick her up. Fish-slippery in my arms, she struggles, her black hair whipping across her face as she shakes her head, "No! No!"

I haul her bodily back to the cottage, to Babette. By then, Kamla is loudly shrieking her distress, and the neighbours are watching from their quaint summer cottages. I dump Kamla into her mother's arms. Babette's expression as she takes the child blends frustration with concern. She cradles the back of Kamla's head. Kamla is prone to painful whiplash injuries.

Lunch consists of store-bought cornmeal muffins served with hot dogs cut into fingerjoint-sized pieces, and bright orange carrot sticks. The muffins have a sticky-fake sweetness. Rage forgotten, Kamla devours her meal with a contented, tuneless singing. She has slopped grape juice down the front of her bathing suit. She looks at me over the top of her cup. It's a calm, ancient gaze, and it unnerves me utterly.

Babette has slushed her grape juice and mine with vodka and lots of ice. "Remember Purple Cows?" she asks. "How sick we got on them at Frosh Week in first year?"

"What's Frosh Week?" asks Kamla.

"It's the first week of university, love. University is big people's school."

"Yes, I do know what a university is," pipes the child. Sometimes Kamla speaks in oddly complete sentences. "But what in the world is a frosh?"

"It's short for freshman," I tell her. "Those are people going to university for the first time."

"Oh." She returns to trying to stab her hot dog chunks with a sharp spear of carrot. Over the top of her head, I smile vaguely at Babette. I sip at the awful drink, gulp down my carrot sticks and sausages. As soon as my plate is empty, I make my excuses. Babette's eyes look sad as she waves me goodbye from the kitchen table. Sunil is only able to come up to their summer cottage on weekends. When he does so, Babs tells me that he sleeps most of the weekend away, too exhausted from his job to talk much to her, or to play with Kamla on the beach.

On my way out the door, I stop to look back. Kamla is sitting in Babette's lap. There's a purple Kamla-sized handprint on Babette's stained yellow T-shirt. Kamla is slurping down more grape juice, and doesn't look up as I leave.

When I reached the age where my friends were starting to spawn like frogs in springtime – or whenever the hell frogs spawn – my unwillingness to do the same became more of a problem. Out on a date once with Sula, a lissom giraffe of a woman with a tongue just as supple, I mentioned that I didn't intend to have kids. She frowned. Had I ever seen her do that before?

"Really?" she said. "Don't you care about passing on your legacy?"

"You mean my surname?"

She laughed uncomfortably. "You know what I mean."

"I really don't. I'm not a king and I'm never going to be rich. I'm not going to leave behind much wealth for someone to inherit. It's not like I'm building an empire."

She made a face as though someone had dropped a mouse in her butter churn. "What are you going to do with your life, then?"

"Well," I chuckled, trying to make a joke of it, "I guess I'm going to go home and put a gun to my head, since I'm clearly no use to myself or anyone else."

Now she looked like she was smelling something rotten. "Oh, don't be morbid," she snapped.

"Huh? It's morbid to not want kids?"

"No, it's morbid to think your life has so little value that you might as well kill yourself."

"Oh, come on, Sula!"

I'd raised my voice above the low-level chatter in the restaurant. The couple at the table closest to us glanced our way. I sighed and continued: "My life has tons of value. I just happen to think it consists of more than my genetic material. Don't you?"

"I guess." But she pulled her hand away from mine. She fidgeted with her napkin in her lap. For the rest of dinner, she seemed distracted. She didn't meet my eye often, though we chatted pleasantly enough. I told her about this bunch of Sioux activists, how they'd been protesting against a university whose archaeology department had dug up one of their ancestral burial sites. I'm Rosebud Sioux on my mum's side. When the director of the department refused to reconsider, these guys had gone one night to the graveyard where his great-grandmother was buried. They'd dug up her remains, laid out all the bones, labelled them with little tags. They did jail time, but the university returned their ancestors' remains to the band council.

Sula's only response to the story was, "Don't you think the living are more important?" That night's sex was great. Sula rode me hard and put me away wet. But she wouldn't stay the night. I curled into the damp spot when she'd left, warming it with my heat. We saw each other two or three times after that, but the zing had gone out of it.

Babette and Sunil began talking about moving away from St. John's. Kamla was about to move up a grade in school. Her parents hoped she'd make new friends in a new school. Well, any friends, really. Kids tended to tease Kamla, call her names.

Babette found a job before Sunil did. She was offered a post teaching digital design at the Emily Carr Institute in Vancouver. Construction was booming there, so Sunil found work pretty easily afterwards. When she heard they were moving, Kamla threw many kinds of fits. She didn't want to leave the ocean. Sunil pointed out that there would be ocean in Vancouver. But Kamla stamped her foot. "I want *this* ocean right here. Don't you understand?" Sunil and Babette had made their decision, though, and Kamla was just a kid. The whole family packed up kit and caboodle in a move that Babette later told me was the most tiring thing she'd ever done.

On the phone, Babette tells me, "A week after we got here, we took Kamla down to Wreck Beach. The seals come in real close to shore, you know? You can see them peeking at you as they hide in the waves. We thought Kamla would love it."

"Did she?" I ask, only half-listening. I'm thinking about my imminent date with Cecilia, who I've been seeing for a few months now. She is lush and brown. It takes both of my hands to hold one of her breasts, and when we spoon at night, her belly fits warm in my palm like a bowl of hot soup on a cold day.

"You know what Kamla did?" Babette asks, bringing me back from my jism-damp haze. I hear the inhale and "tsp" sound of someone smoking a cigarette. Babette has started smoking again during the move. "She poked around in the sand for a few minutes, then she told us we were stupid and bad and she wasn't going to talk to us any more. Sulked the rest of the day, and wouldn't eat her dinner that night. She's still sulking now, months later."

That's another thing about kids; their single-mindedness. They latch onto an idea like a bulldog at a rabbit hole, and before you know it, you're arranging your whole life around their likes and dislikes. They're supposed to be your insurance for the future; you know, to carry your name on, and shit? My mother's been after me to breed, but I'm making my own legacy, thank you very much. A body of art I can point to and document. I'm finally supporting myself sort of decently through a combination of exhibition fees, teaching and speaking gigs. I want to ask Cecilia to move in with me, but every time I come close to doing so, I hear Sula's words in my head: *No children? Well, what are you going to do with yourself, then?* I don't know whether Cecilia wants kids, and I'm afraid to ask.

"Greg?" says Babette's voice through the telephone. "You still there?"

"Yeah. Sorry. Mind wandering."

"I'm worried about Kamla."

"Because she's upset about the move? I'm sure she'll come around. She's making friends in school, isn't she?"

"Not really. The other day, the class bully called her Baby Bobber. For the way her head moves."

I suppress a snort of laughter. It's not funny. Poor kid. "What did you do?"

"We had the school contact his parents. But it's not just that she doesn't have many friends. She's making our lives hell with this obsession for Bradley's Cove. And she's not growing."

"You mean she's, like, emotionally immature?" *Or intellectually?* I think.

"No, physically. We figure she's about eight, but she's not much bigger than a five-year-old."

"Have you taken her to the doctor?"

"Yeah. They're running some tests."

Cecilia can jerry-rig a computer network together in a matter of minutes. We geekspeak at each other all the time. When we're out in public, people fall silent in linguistic bafflement around us.

"They say Kamla's fine," Babette tells me, "and we should just put more protein in her diet."

Cecilia and I are going to go shopping for a new motherboard for her, then we we're going to take blankets and pillows to the abandoned train out in the old rail yards and hump like bunnies till we both come screaming. Maybe she'll wear those white stockings under her clothes. The sight of the gap of naked brown thigh between the tops of the stockings and her underwear always makes me hard.

Babette says, "There's this protein drink for kids. Makes her pee bright yellow."

The other thing about becoming a parent? It becomes perfectly normal to discuss your child's excreta with anyone who'll sit still for five minutes. When we were in art school together, Babette used to talk about gigabytes, Cronenberg and post-humanism.

I can hear someone else ringing through on the line. It's probably Cecilia. I mutter a quick reassurance at Babette and get her off the phone.

Kamla never does get over her obsession with the beach, and with shells. By the time she is nine, she's accumulated a library's worth of reference books with names like *Molluscs of the Eastern Seaboard*, and *Seashells: Nature's Wonder*. She continues to grow slowly. At ten years old, people mistake her for six. Sunil and Babette send her for test after test.

"She's got a full set of adult teeth," Babette tells me as we sit in a coffee shop on Churchill Square. "And all the bones in her skull are fused."

"That sounds dangerous," I say.

"No, it happens to all of us once we've stopped growing. Her head's fully grown, even if the rest of her isn't. I guess that's something. You gonna eat those fries?"

Babette's come home to visit relatives. She's quit smoking, and she's six months pregnant. If she'd waited two more months, the airline wouldn't have let her travel until the baby was born. "Those symptoms of Kamla's," says Babette, "they're all part of the DGS."

The papers have dubbed it "Delayed Growth Syndrome". Its official name is Diaz Syndrome, after the doctor who first identified it. There are thousands of kids with Kamla's condition. It's a brand new disorder. Researchers have no clue what's causing it, or if the bodies of the kids with it will ever achieve full adulthood. Their brains, however, are way ahead of their bodies. All the kids who've tested positive for DGS are scarily smart.

"Kamla seems to be healthy," Babette tells me. "Physically, anyway. It's her emotional state I'm worried about."

I say, "I'm gonna have some dessert. You want anything?"

"Yeah, something crunchy with meringue and caramel. I want it to be so sweet that the roof of my mouth tries to crawl away from it."

Cecilia's doing tech support for somebody's office today. Weekend rates. My mum's keeping an eye on our son Russ, who's two and a half. Yesterday we caught him scooping up ants into his mouth from an anthill he'd found in the backyard. He was giggling at the way they tickled his tongue, chomping down on them as they scurried about. His mouth was full of anthill mud. He didn't even notice that he was being bitten until Cecilia and I asked him. That's when he started crying in pain, and he was inconsolable for half an hour. I call him our creepy little alien child. We kinda had him by accident, me and Cece. She didn't want kids any more than I did, but when we found out she was pregnant, we both got . . . curious, I guess. Curious to see what this particular life adventure would be; how our small brown child might change a world that desperately needs some change. We sort of dared each other to go through with it, and now here we are. Baby's not about changing anyone's world but ours just yet, though. We've both learned the real meaning of sleep deprivation. That morning when he was so constipated that trying to shit made him scream in pain, I called Babette in panic. Turns out poo and pee are really damned important, especially when you're responsible for the life of a small, helpless being that can barely do anything else. Russ gurgles with helpless laughter when I blow raspberries on his tummy. And there's a spot on his neck, just under his ear, that smells sweet, even when the rest of him is stinky. He's a perfect specimen; all his bits are in proportion. I ask Babette what new thing is bothering her about her kid, if not the delayed growth.

"She gets along fine with me and Sunil, you know? I feel like I can talk to her about anything. But she gets very frustrated with kids her age. She wants to play all these elaborate games, and some of them don't understand. Then she gets angry. She came stomping home from a friend's place the other day and went straight to her room. When I looked in on her, she was sitting looking in her mirror. There were tears running down her cheeks. 'I bloody hate being a kid,' she said to me. 'The other kids are stupid, and my hand-eye coordination sucks'."

"She said that her hand-eye coordination sucked? That sounds almost too . . ."

"Yeah, I know. Too grown up for a ten-year-old. She probably had to grow up quickly, being an adoptee."

"You ever find out where she came from before you took her?"

Babette shakes her head. She's eaten all of her pavlova and half of my carrot cake.

It just so happens that I have a show opening at Eastern Edge while Babette and Sunil are in town. "The Excavations", I call it. It was Russ's anthill escapade that gave me the idea. I've trucked in about half a ton of dirt left over from a local archaeological dig. I wish I could have gotten it directly from Mexico, but I couldn't afford the permit for doing that. I seeded the soil with the kinds of present-day historical artifacts that the researchers tossed aside in their zeal to get to the iconic past of the native peoples of the region: a rubber boot that had once belonged to a Mayan Zapatista from Chiapas; a large plastic jug that used to hold bleach, and that had been refitted as a bucket for a small child to tote water in; a scrap of hand-woven blanket with brown stains on it. People who enter the exhibition get basic excavation tools. When they pull something free of the soil, it triggers a story about the artifact on the monitors above. Sunil is coming to the opening. Babette has decided to stay at her relatives' place and nap. Six months along in her pregnancy, she's sleepy a lot.

I'm holding court in the gallery, Cecilia striding around the catwalk above me, doing a last check of all the connections, when Sunil walks in. He's brought Kamla. She doesn't alarm me any more. She's just a kid. As I watch her grow up, I get some idea of what Russ's growing years will be like. In a way, she's his advance guard.

Kamla scurries in ahead of her dad, right up to me, her head wobbling as though her neck is a column of gelatin. She sticks out her hand. "Hey, Greg," she says. "Long time." Behind her, Sunil gives me a bashful smile.

I reach down to shake the hand of what appears to be a six-year-old.

"Uh, hey," I say. Okay, I lied a little bit. I still don't really know how to talk to kids.

"This looks cool," she tells me, gazing around. "What do we do?" She squats down and starts sifting soil through her fingers.

"Kamla, you mustn't touch the art," says Sunil.

I say, "Actually, it's okay. That's exactly what I want people to do."

Kamla flashes me a grateful glance. I give her a small spade and take her through the exhibition. She digs up artifact after artifact, watches the stories about them on the video displays, asks me questions. I get so caught up talking to her about my project that I forget how young she is. She seems really interested. Most of the other people are here because they're friends of mine, or because it's cool to be able to say that you went to an art opening last weekend. The gallery owner has to drag me away to be interviewed by the guy from *Art(ext)/e*. I grin at Kamla and leave her digging happily in the dirt.

While I'm talking to the interviewer, Kamla comes running up to me, Sunil behind her, yelling, "Kamla! Don't interrupt!"

She ignores him, throws her mushroom-shaped body full tilt into my arms, and gives me a whole body hug. "It was you!" she says. "It was you!" She's clutching something in one dirt-encrusted fist. The guy from *Art(ext)/e* kinda freezes up at the sight of Kamla. But he catches himself, pastes the smile back on, motions his camerawoman to take a picture.

"I'm so sorry," Sunil says. "When she gets an idea in her head . . ."

"Yeah, I know. What'd you find, chick?" I ask Kamla. She opens her palm to show me. It's a shell. I shake my head. "Honestly? I barely remember putting that in there. Some of the artifacts are 'blanks' that trigger no stories. The dig where I got it from used to be underwater a few centuries ago."

"It's perfect!" says Kamla, squeezing me hard.

Perfect like she isn't. Damn.

"I've been looking everywhere for this!" she tells me.

"What, is it rare or something?" I ask her.

She rears back in my arms so that she can look at me properly. "You have no idea," she says. "I'm going to keep this so safe. It'll never get out of my sight again."

"Kamla!" scolds Sunil. "That is part of Greg's exhibition. It's staying right here with him."

The dismay on Kamla's face would make a stone weep. It's obvious that it hadn't even occurred to her that I mightn't let her have the shell. Her eyes start to well up.

"Don't cry," I tell her. "It's just an old shell. Of course you can take it."

"You shouldn't indulge her," Sunil says. "You'll spoil her."

I hitch Kamla up on my hip, on that bone adults have that seems tailor-made for cotching a child's butt on. "Let's call it her reward for asking some really smart questions about the exhibition."

Sunil sighs. Kamla's practically glowing, she's so happy. My heart warms to her smile.

When the phone rings at my home many hours later, it takes me awhile to orient myself. It's 3:05 a.m. by the clock by our bedside. "Hello?" I mumble into the phone. I should have known better than to have that fifth whiskey at the opening. My mouth feels and tastes like the plains of the Serengeti, complete with lion spoor.

"Greg?" The person is whispering. "Is this Greg?"

It's a second or so before I recognise the voice. "Kamla? What's wrong? Is your mum okay?"

"They're fine. Everyone's asleep."

"Like you should be. Why the fuck are you calling me at this hour?" I ask, forgetting that I'm talking to a child. Something about Kamla's delivery makes it easy to forget.

"I've been on the Net. Listen, can you come get me? The story's about to break. It's all over Twitter and YouTube already. It'll be on the morning news here in a few hours. Goddamned Miles. We told them he was always running his mouth off."

"What? Told who? Kamla, what's going on?"

Cecilia is awake beside me. She's turned on the bedside lamp. *Who?* She mouths. I make my lips mime a soundless *Kamla*.

"It's a long story," Kamla says. "Please, can you just come get me? You need to know about this. And I need another adult to talk to, someone who isn't my caretaker."

Whatever's going on, she really sounds upset. "Okay, I'll be there soon."

Kamla gives me the address, and I hang up. I tell Cecilia what's going on.

"You should just let Babs and Sunil know that she's disturbed about something," she says. "Maybe it's another symptom of that DGS."

"I'll talk to them after Kamla tells me what's going on," I say. "I promised her to hear her out first."

"You sure that's wise? She's a child, Greg. Probably she just had a nightmare."

Feeding our child has made Cecilia's breasts sit lower on her ribcage. Her hips stretch out the nylon of her nightgown. Through the translucent fabric I can see the shadow of pubic hair and the valley that the curves of her thighs make. Her eyes are full of sleep, and her hair is a tousled mess, and she's so beautiful I could tumble her right now. But there's this frightened kid waiting to talk to me. I kiss

Cecilia goodbye and promise to call her as soon as I've learned more.

Kamla's waiting for me outside the house when I pull up in my car. The night air is a little chilly, and she's a lonely, shivering silhouette against the front door. She makes to come in the passenger side of the car, but I motion her around to my side. "We're going to leave a note for your parents first," I tell her. I have one already prepared. "And we're just going sit right here in the car and talk."

"We can leave a note," she replies, "but we have to be away from here long enough so you can hear the whole story. I can't have Sunil and Babette charging to the rescue right now."

I've never heard her call her parents by their first names; Babs and Sunil aren't into that kind of thing. Her face in her weirdly adult head looks calm, decisive. I find myself acquiescing. So I slip the note under the front door. It tells Babette and Sunil that Kamla's with me, that everything's all right. I leave them my cell phone number, though I'm pretty sure that Babette already has it.

Kamla gets into the car. She quietly closes the door. We drive. I keep glancing over at her, but for a few minutes, she doesn't say anything. I'm just about to ask her what was so urgent that she needed to pull a stunt like this when she says, "Your installation had a certain antique brio to it, Greg. Really charming. My orig – I mean, I have a colleague whose particular interest is in the nascent identity politics as expressed by artists of the twentieth and twenty-first centuries, and how that expression was the progenitor of current speciesism."

"Have you been reading your mum's theory books?"

"No," she replies. There was so much bitterness in that one word. "I'm just a freak. Your kid's almost three, right?"

"Yeah."

"In a blink of an eye, barely a decade from now, his body will be entering puberty. He'll start getting erections, having sexual thoughts."

"I don't want to think about all that right now," I say. "I'm still too freaked that he's begun making poo-poo jokes. Kamla, is this the thing you wanted to tell me? Cause I'm not getting it."

"A decade from now, I'll have the body of a seven-year-old."

"You can't know that. There aren't any DGS kids who've reached their twenties yet."

"I know. I'm the oldest of them, by a few weeks."

Another thing she can't know.

"But we're all well past the age where normal children have achieved adolescence."

Goggling at her, I almost drive through a red light. I slam on the brakes. The car jolts to a halt. "What? What kind of shit is that? You're ten years old. A precocious ten, yes, but only ten."

"Go in there." She points into the parking lot of a nearby grocery store. "It won't be open for another three hours."

I pull into the lot and park, leave the engine running so we can have some heat in the car. "If the cops come by and see us," I say, "I could be in a lot of shit. They'll think I'm some degenerate Indian perv with a thing for little girls."

Shit. I shouldn't be talking to a ten-year-old this way. Kamla always makes me forget. It's that big head, those big words.

"DGS people do get abused," she tells me. "Just like real children do."

"You *are* a real child!"

She glares at me, then looks sad. She says, "Sunil and Babette are going to have to move soon. It's so hard for me to keep up this pretence. I've managed to smartmouth so much at school and in our neighbourhood that it's become uncomfortable to live there anymore."

My eyes have become accustomed enough to the dark that I can see the silent tears running down her cheeks. I want to hold her to me, to comfort her, but I'm afraid of how that will look if the cops show up. Besides, I'm getting the skin-crawly feeling that comes when you realise that someone with whom you've been making pleasant conversation is as mad as a hatter. "I'm taking you back home," I whisper. I start turning the key in the ignition.

"Please!" She puts a hand on my wrist. "Greg, please hear me out. I'll make it quick. I just don't know how to convince you."

I take my hand off the key. "Just tell me," I said. "Whatever it is, your parents love you. You can work it out."

She leans back against the passenger side door and curls her knees up to her chest, a little ball of misery. "Okay. Let me get it all out before you say anything else, all right?"

"All right."

"They grew us from cells from our originals; ten of us per original. They used a viral injection technique to put extra-long tails on one of the strands of our DNA. You need more telomeres to slow down aging."

The scientific jargon exiting smoothly from the mouth of a child could have been comic. But I had goose bumps. She didn't appear to be repeating something she'd memorised.

"Each batch of ten yielded on average four viable blastocytes. They implanted those in womb donors. Two-thirds of them took. Most of those went to full term and were delivered. Had to be C-sections, of course. Our huge skulls presented too much of a risk for our birth mothers. We were usually four years old before we were strong enough to lift our own heads, and that was with a lot of physiotherapy. They treated us really well; best education, kept us fully informed from the start of what they wanted from us."

"Which was?" I whisper, terrified to hear the answer.

"Wait. You said you would." She continues her story. "Any of us could back out if we wanted to. Ours is a society that you would probably find strange, but we do have moral codes. Any of us who didn't want to make the journey could opt to undergo surgical procedures to correct some of the physical changes. Bones and muscles would lengthen, and they would reach puberty normally and thereafter age like regular people. They'll never achieve full adult height, and there'll always be something a little bit odd about their features, but it probably won't be so bad.

"But a few of us were excited by the idea, the crazy, wonderful idea, and we decided to go through with it. They waited until we were age thirteen for us to confirm our choice. In many cultures, that used to be the age when you were allowed to begin making adult decisions."

"You're ten, Kamla."

"I'm twenty-three, though my body won't start producing adult sex hormones for another fifty years. I won't attain my full growth till I'm in my early hundreds. I can expect—"

"You're delusional," I whisper.

"I'm from your future," she says. God. The child's been watching too many B-movies. She continues, "They wanted to send us here and back as full adults, but do you have any idea what the freight costs would have been? The insurance? Arts grants are hard to get in my world, too. The gallery had to scale the budget way back."

"Gallery?"

"National gallery. Hush. Let me talk. They sent small people instead. Clones of the originals, with their personalities superimposed onto our own. They sent back children who weren't children."

I start the car. I'm taking her back home right now. She needs help; therapy, or something. The sky's beginning to brighten. She doesn't try to stop me this time.

Glumly, she goes on. "The weird thing is, even though this body isn't interested in adult sex, I *remember* what it was like, remember enjoying it. It's those implanted memories from my original."

I'm edging past the speed limit in my hurry to get her back to her parents. I make myself slow down a little.

"Those of us living in extremely conservative or extremely poor places are having a difficult time. We stay in touch with them by email and cell phone, and we have our own closed Facebook group, but not all of us have access to computer technology. We've never been able to figure out what happened to Kemi. Some of us were never adopted, had to make our own way as street kids. Never old enough to be granted adult freedoms. So many lost. This fucking project better have been worth it."

I decide to keep her talking. "What project, Kamla?"

"It's so *hard* to pretend you don't have an adult brain! Do you know what it's like turning in schoolwork that's at a grade-five level, when we all have PhDs in our heads? We figured that one of us would crack, but we hoped it'd be later, when we'd reached what your world would consider the age of majority."

We're cruising past a newspaper box. I look through its plastic window to see the headline: **"I'm From the Future," Says Bobble-Headed Boy.** Ah. One of our more erudite news organs.

Oh, Christ. They all have this delusion. All the DGS kids. For a crazy half-second, I find myself wondering whether Sunil and Babette can return Kamla to the adoption centre. And I'm guiltily grateful that Russ, as far as we can tell, is normal.

"Human beings, we're becoming increasingly post-human," Kamla says. She's staring at the headline, too. "Things change so quickly. Total technological upheaval of society every five to eight years. Difficult to keep up, to connect amongst the generations. By the time your Russ is a teenager, you probably won't understand his world at all."

She's hit on the thing that really scares me about kids. This brave new world that Cecelia and I are trying to make for our son? For the generations to follow us? We won't know how to live in it.

Kamla says, "Art helps us know how to do change. That's made it very valuable to us."

"Thank heaven for that," I say, humouring her. "Maybe I'd like your world."

She sits up in her seat, buckles herself in. Shit. I should have made her do that the minute she got in the car. I have one of those heart-in-the-mouth moments that I have often, now that I'm a parent. "In my world," she says, "what you do would be obsolete." She sniggers a little. "Video monitors! I'd never seen a real one, only minibeams disguised to mimic ancient tech. Us DGSers have all become anthropologists here in the past, as well as curators."

"Wait; you're a what?"

"I'm a curator, Greg. I'm trying to tell you; our national gallery is having a giant retrospective; tens of thousands of works of art from all over the world, and all over the world's history. They sent us back to retrieve some of the pieces that had been destroyed. Expensive enough to send living biomaterial back; their grant wasn't enough to pay for returning us to our time. So we're going to *grow* our way there. Those of us that survive."

There are more cars out on the road, more brakes squealing, more horns honking. "I'm not going to miss mass transit when I finally get home," she says. "Your world stinks."

"Yeah, it does." We're nearly to her parents' place. From my side, I lock her door. Of course she notices. She just glances at the sound. She looks like she's being taken to her death.

"I didn't know it until yesterday," she tells me, "but it was you I came for. That installation."

And now the too-clever bloody child has me where I live. Though I know it's all air pie and Kamla is as nutty as a fruitcake, my heart's performing a tympanum of joy. "My installation's going to be in the retrospective?" I ask. Even as the words come out of my mouth, I'm embarrassed at how eager I sound, at how this little girl, as children will, has dug her way into my psyche and found the thing which will make me respond to her.

She gasps and puts her hand to her mouth. "Oh, Greg! I'm so sorry; not you, the shell!"

My heart suicides, the brief, hallucinatory hope dashed. "The shell?"

"Yes. In the culture where I live, speciesism has become a defining concept through which we understand what it means to be human animals. Not every culture or subculture ascribes to it, but the art world of my culture certainly does." She's got her teacher voice on again. She does sound like a bloody curator. "Human beings aren't the only ones who make art," she says.

All right. Familiar territory. "Okay, perhaps. Bower birds make pretty nests to attract a mate. Cetaceans sing to each other. But we're the only ones who make art *mean*; who make it comment on our everyday reality."

From the corner of my eye, I see her shake her oversized head. "No. We don't always know what they're saying, we can't always know the reality on which they're commenting. Who knows what a sea cucumber thinks of the conditions of its particular stretch of ocean floor?"

A sea cucumber? We've just turned onto her parents' street. She'll be out of my hands soon. Poor Babette.

"Every shell is different," she says.

My perverse brain instantly puts it to the tune of "Every Sperm Is Sacred".

She continues, "Every shell is a life journal, made out of the very substance of its creator, and left as a record of what it thought, even if we can't understand exactly what it thought. Sometimes interpretation is a trap. Sometimes we need to simply observe."

"And you've come all this way to take that . . . shell back?" I can see it sticking out of the chest pocket of her fleece shirt.

"It's difficult to explain to you, because you don't have the background, and I don't have the time to teach you. I specialise in shell formations. I mean, that's Vanda's specialty. She's the curator whose memories I'm carrying. Of its kind, the mollusc that made this shell is a genius. The unique conformation of the whorls of its shell expresses a set of concepts that haven't been explored before by the other artists of its species. After this one, all the others will draw on and riff off its expression of its world. They're the derivatives, but this is the original. In our world, it was lost."

Barmy. Loony. "So how did you know that it even existed, then? Did the snail or slug that lived inside it take pictures or something?" I've descended into cruelty. I'm still smarting that Kamla hasn't picked me, my work. My legacy doesn't get to go to the future.

She gives me a wry smile, as though she understands.

I pull up outside the house, start leaning on the horn. Over the noise, she shouts, "The creature didn't take a picture. You did."

Fuck, fuck, fuck. With my precious video camera. I'd videotaped every artifact with which I'd seeded the soil that went onto the gallery floor. I didn't tell her that.

She nods. "Not all the tape survived, so we didn't know who had recorded it, or where the shell had come from. But we had an idea where the recording had come from."

Lights are coming on in the house. Kamla looks over there and sighs. "I haven't entirely convinced you, have I?"

"No," I say regretfully. But damn it, a part of me still hopes that it's all true.

"They're probably going to institutionalise me. All of us."

The front door opens. Sunil is running out to the car, a gravid Babette following more slowly.

"You have to help me, Greg. Please? We're going to outlive all our captors. We will get out. But in the meantime . . ."

She pulls the shell out of her pocket, offers it to me on her tiny palm. "Please keep it safe for me?"

She opens the car door. "It's your ticket to the future," she says, and gets out of the car to greet her parents.

I lied. I fucking hate kids.

THE TIME TELEPHONE

Adam Roberts

Adam Roberts is a University of London professor and writer of science fiction, the most recently published of his fourteen novels being *Jack Glass* (Gollancz 2012) and *Twenty Trillion Leagues Under the Sea* (Gollancz 2013). He lives a little way west of London, England, with his wife, two children, and no cats. "The Time Telephone" was first published in *Infinity Plus* in 2002.

1.

A mother phones her daughter. The call costs her nearly €18,000. The number she dials is several hundred digits long, but it has been calculated carefully and stored as a series of tones, so the dialling process takes only seconds. The ring tone at the far end makes its distant musical drumroll once, twice, three times, and with a clucking noise the receiver is lifted.

'Hello?'

The mother takes a quick breath. 'Marianne?'

'Speaking. Who's this, please?'

'This is your mother, Marianne.'

'Ma? I thought you were in Morocco. You calling from Morocco?'

'No, dear, I'm here, I'm in London.'

'Here?'

'This is a call from the past, my darling,' says the mother, her heart stabbing at her ribs. 'As I speak now, as I speak to you now, I'm actually pregnant with you. You're inside my tummy *here*, and I'm speaking to you *there*.'

For a moment there is only the polluted silence of a phone line; that slightly hissing, leaf-rustle emptiness of a line where the person at the other end is quiet. Then the daughter says, 'Wow, ma. Really?'

'Yes my dear.'

'It's that time telephone thing? Yeah? I read about that, or, or I watched a thing about it, on TV. You're really calling me from the past?'

'Yes my dear. I have a question I want to ask you.'

'Wow, ma. Like, wow. I watched this programme about it on TV, it was a whole big thing, like, decades ago. And now it's actually happening to me! And I'm only on a, like, regular phone.'

'It uses the ordinary phone system, you know.'

'It's incredible, though. Isn't it?'

'I want to ask you this thing, my darling, and I want you to answer truthfully. I know that you are sixteen *there*, aren't you. Aren't you?'

'Sweet sixteen.'

'Well, from where I'm calling you're not born yet. So I want to ask you.' She takes a breath. 'Are you *glad* you were born? Are you pleased to have come into the world?' The drizzly silence of the phone line. 'I mean the question absolutely seriously, my darling, absolutely. I mean the question, in the way that a child will say . . .' But she finds it hard to find the words. 'The way a child will say *I hate you, I wish I'd never been born*. That's an unbearable thing for a parent to hear, my darling. Do you see?'

'You're weirding me out, ma. This whole conversation is weirding me out. This whole concept is weirding me out.'

'But I have to ask it of you, because now you're sixteen, you can tell me. Are you glad you were born?'

'Sure.'

'Are you sure? Really sure?'

'Ok, sure I'm sure, I'm really sure.'

Which is what the mother hoped to hear. She even sighs. And the remainder of the question is conversational scree, just talk about the weather and the chit-chat. So I go to Morocco? Well, yeah, ma. Hey, Scannell just won the board championship. You should make a bet. You could be rich. I don't think it works that way, my darling. You look after yourself. Hey, you too. That sort of thing. You know the sort of thing, the sort of chit-chat a mother and daughter will make on the phone.

2.

The world cable telephone network is some 7,672,450,000 miles long in total, when the different international, national and local lines are added up. And they are all interconnected. They would hardly function as a telephone network if they weren't. We are talking about *cable*, copper or some other electron-conducting material; optical fibre is no good for us, because photons travel only at the speed of light no matter how you slice and dice them. Neutroelectrons – a self-contradictory-sounding name, but better than the alternative mooted by the Italians of 'anti-electrons', for surely an anti-electron is a proton? – anyway – these ghostly particles travel so fast as effectively to travel instantaneously, but they can only do it in a material that conducts their shadowy anti-selves, their phase-inverted electrons. By plotting out a pathway along the telephone network, a neutroelectron can be passed instantly across the seven billion miles of cabling. The phone line becomes a gateway into the past; when they arrive they arrive from the past, if you see what I mean. This is because it would take light about eleven hours to travel the pathway mapped diligently through the phone lines. Which means that the far end of the cable is eleven hours away, so that the instantaneous transmission of the phased particle actually passes eleven hours back in time. For it to happen any other way would violate laws of cause-and-effect. I'm sure you're following me.

Technicians carefully map out a route around the millions of miles of telephone cabling, turning innumerable sharp corners, fleeting back and forth underneath the oceans, rushing along smile-sagging lines propped up every fifty yards by another pole, curling and spinning around the electronic spaghetti of the bigger cities. A path through all this is mapped, and particles are fired along it.

In a year, light travels approximately 5,865,696,000,000 miles.

Looping the signal 900-or-so times around this loop, the neutroelectron effectively opens a phone line a year into the past. The problem is that the repeated passage through the same cable degrades the integrity of the signal. The scientists experimenting with this new phenomenon were able to obtain fax signals, and internet connection, over the time distance of eleven hours. Extending it to just under a day, looping the signal twice, the internet connection becomes choppy, unreliable, and painfully slow: too slow, in fact, to be cost-effective, when the large expense of running the time telephone system is taken into account. The fax signal works better, but only a small amount of visual information is carried by fax tweetings. Any more than a day and the bandwith is too small and too fragile to allow internet access. But even looping it two thousand times allowed a signal of reasonable, if crackly, integrity. More than this and the noise and static swallowed meaningful information exchange.

The initial researchers established an integral network of connections to the past: in effect they set up standing-wave each-way passageways for the neutroelectron connection. The theory owes something to wormhole physics, but it is much more limited on account of its need for a physical infrastructure. They phoned scientists from the past; sometimes phoning themselves, sometimes others. They explained the situation, giving them the know-how necessary to set up neutroelectron generators themselves, and plumbing them back into the phone line. And once the network was established, and people in the past had been contacted, it became evident that people in the past could reuse the connections to speak to people in their future, many years, to such phone terminals as had been utilised by the original scientists.

Soon crosstalk filled the time-phone lines. The future-people move through time at an hour an hour, dragging their envelope of past-talk with them at an hour an hour. But the past-time scientists could act as way-stations, taking the signal and relaying it further back, or further forward. In this way the envelope was extended to more than sixteen years. But no further. The generation of scientists at this blockage time, back in 2004, refused, for some reason, to be beguiled by these whispery voices on the phone, that declared themselves future humans; refused to spend the money on the ridiculous expense of setting up neutroelectronic generators, refused to believe the physics of it. Without their assistance the reach of the time telephones stopped dead. People before a certain date had no knowledge of the technology at all; for them, it had not happened yet.

In the future, researchers tried and failed, tried again and failed, to raise the money to build an enormous cable, billions upon billions of miles long. They wanted a space probe sent to an asteroid, to mine and refine and spool out huge stretches of cable through space, cable that earth people could hook up to the phone line and use to call back further in time. To call back in time *before* the 2004 blockage. But the expense was too much, and the project had not brought about any useful improvement in the quality of life. A person could place a bet in 2010, and call up an internet page from the following day to guide him; with the result that, under such circumstances, betting shrank to long-term wagers only. People could find out tomorrow's news today, but almost always tomorrow's news is merely an extrapolation of today's news.

As the network grew, people called their friends and family in the past, warned loved ones of imminent death and told them which stock to buy, but the past is fixed in curious, physics-consistent ways. *You* are not fixed, as you read this sentence, I'm not suggesting that! But, then again, as you read this sentence you are at the now, between the past and the future. That is where you always are. I, writing it, am in the past. That's just the truth. And even if you could call me up, so that my telephone here on my desktop, this blueblack-plastic Buddha-shaped machine here would ring and you could talk to me, it would make no difference, almost certainly no difference, in almost every case. You can't really reach me, not easily, hardly at all. I'm sorry to tell you this, but it is the truth, it's better you know the truth. Information *does* flow backwards, but sluggishly, treacly. It rushes much more forcefully the other way. So although people warned loved ones of imminent death and told them which stock to buy, the loved ones still died, and nobody found themselves suddenly rich because their earlier selves had invested more wisely. None of that happened. It might still happen, of course. There is nothing in the theory that suggests it could *never* happen.

And so 2019 turned into 2020, and 2020 into 2021, and people could talk to one another from any time from 2004 to 2038, but nobody built the superlong cabling that would have enabled the technicians to get clear neutroelectron signals that reached further back in time than 2004, to get internet access from the past and into the future. There seemed little point.

3.

A phone rings.

The phone is shaped something like a tapered loaf, cast from blood-brown plastic, with a broad steel ring like a buckle on the front that is rimmed with little circular holes. The receiver, bone-shaped, shivers in its cradle in time to the rings. The bell is a mechanical bell, located inside the hollow body of the thing, so that, ringing, it vibrates the whole device a little bit. The receiver is connected to the body of the phone with a brown flex, a flex which had come from the manufacturer curled as precisely as DNA, but which now is gnarled and knotted, unwound in places, scrunched up in others.

The phone sits by the wall on a shelf in a small kitchen area. You might, perhaps, describe the area as a kitchenette. Against the west wall there is a unit containing a small sink, and next to it a dwarf-fridge on a shelf, with a kettle on top of it, and next to that a two-ring hob. On the south wall at tummy-height is a shelf upon which storage jars of coffee and of tea and of sugar, and three mugs, stand next to the phone. A door in the east wall, the north wall decorated with a poster for the film *Gladiator*. Somebody has pasted a photocopy of the face of an individual called Vernon St Lucia over the face of the star of the film, the humour of this gesture deriving from the ironic contrast between the muscular good looks of the film star and the weedy, querulous nature of St Lucia, who has authority over the three laboratory technicians who work here.

Only one of these technicians is in the building. It is shortly after seven o'clock in the evening, and everybody else has gone home for the night. The single technician remaining is called Roger. He comes through to the kitchenette.

The penetrating chirrup of the phone-bell stops.

'Extension three-five-one-one?'

A rainy, white-noise sound, overlaid with a rhythmic distant thudding, and behind it, as if very far away, a tinny vocalisation, or singsong, or whistling. But no words.

'Hello?' says Roger. 'Hello?'

The hissing swells and subsides like surf, the crackles pop more frequently. The *oo-aa-oo*ing in the background might be words. . . . *couldn't get through earlier . . .*

'Hello? The connection,' Roger says, 'is not good.'

Crunching and flushing noises, and then sudden clarity: '. . . imperative that we get a message through . . .' but then, with a swinging, horn-like miaow the line dissipates into static.

'Hello? This is a very bad line.'

Nothing but noise.

Roger replaces the receiver in its cradle. He meanders back to his desk, and switches on a light. He cannot decide whether to go home or not. There is nothing for him at home this evening. His girlfriend, a woman called Stella, is having a girl's night out with four friends. These friends' names are Susan, Susan, Miranda and Belle. He doesn't fancy going back to an empty flat. But the prospect of staying at the lab and working on into the evening is not appealing either. His brain feels muffled, fuzzy. He can't concentrate on his job-in-hand.

He mooches back into kitchen and turns the kettle on. He inspects one of the mugs standing beside the telephone, and, fussily, runs a finger inside the rim. Behind him, the kettle's spout turns into a miniature chimney. Steam pillows out.

Roger changes his mind. He drinks, he tells himself, too much coffee anyway. Six or seven mugs, most days, and strong stuff too.

He walks back to his bench and turns the anglepoise off.

The phone goes again.

As he shuffles back to the kitchen to answer it, he finds himself thinking how annoying the sound of a phone ringing is. How insistent. A mechanical baby's cry that it is almost impossible to ignore. He resents it.

'tension three-five-one-un?'

This time the voice is clearer, although the static is still thorny and distracting. 'Please don't hang up! It's vital you listen to . . . information we have to give you.' The sentence is broken in half by a crack, like a plank breaking.

'I'm sorry,' says Roger, annoyed rather than intrigued. 'Who were you trying to reach?'

'The institute . . .' A whoosh and a clatter drown the rest of the sentence.

'I'll tell you what you've done,' says Roger, prissily. 'You've dialled the one twice by mistake. You want extension three five one seven, but your finger has accidentally pushed the one twice and it's put you through here. There's nobody here, except me and I'm about to go home. Three five one seven will get you the night secretary.'

'No! No!' The panic in the person's voice is evident enough to break through the hisses and spatters of interference. '*Please* don't hang up. We're calling as far back as we can, and the boundary withdraws all the time, one second per second. In a very little time it will be *too late*. Do you understand?'

'No,' says Roger, crossly, 'I don't.'

'I can't stress *too greatly*, your future is at stake. All our futures. The people much further along the line from us have only just encountered the disaster, and they have called us, and we have called you. This may sound *strange* to you. The chance to change things . . . it must happen *there*, in your time. It's got to be *you*.'

'I have no idea what you are on about,' says Roger. 'Is this a prank? Is this Seb?' This, he thinks, is exactly the sort of practical joke that Seb would try.

'Please, no, just *listen*. You don't have to believe me, it doesn't matter if you believe me, the thing you have to do is so simple, so simple it won't take you a moment. All you have to do . . .'

But Roger has put the phone down again. He stands looking at the kettle for a moment, his mind floating free. He thinks of Seb, a man he has never really liked. By a chain of association too oblique to be represented here with any ease, he thinks of a holiday in France, and then of another friend, and then of Stella, and finally of Susan, one of Stella's friends. He and Susan had kissed the previous week, but both had pulled away, startled, before things had proceeded any further. It had been at a party at another friend's house, at the bottom of their garden away from everybody, in the darkness. Two cigarette smokers underneath the stars, the noise and chatter and muffled music of the party sounding very far away. Kissing, and then pulling away. The path not taken. But then again, who knows? It wouldn't be a good idea to tell Stella. He feels sure Susan thinks this too. Best not mention it at all, and certainly not tell Stella.

He puts on his coat, and is about to lock up the lab when the phone rings again.

RED LETTER DAY

Kristine Kathryn Rusch

Kristine Kathryn Rusch is an American writer of award-winning mystery, romance, science fiction, and fantasy. She has written many novels under various names. Her novels have made the bestseller lists worldwide and have been published in fourteen countries and thirteen different languages. Her awards range from the Ellery Queen Readers Choice Award to the John W. Campbell Award. She is the only person in the history of the science fiction field to have won a Hugo Award both for editing and for fiction. "Red Letter Day" was originally published in *Analog Science Fiction and Fact* in 2010.

Graduation rehearsal – middle of the afternoon on the final Monday of the final week of school. The graduating seniors at Barack Obama High School gather in the gymnasium, get the wrapped packages with their robes (ordered long ago), their mortarboards, and their blue and white tassels. The tassels attract the most attention – everyone wants to know which side of the mortarboard to wear it on, and which side to move it to.

The future hovers, less than a week away, filled with possibilities.

Possibilities about to be limited, because it's also Red Letter Day.

I stand on the platform, near the steps, not too far from the exit. I'm wearing my best business casual skirt today and a blouse that I no longer care about. I learned to wear something I didn't like years ago; too many kids will cry on me by the end of the day, covering the blouse with slobber and makeup and aftershave.

My heart pounds. I'm a slender woman, although I'm told I'm formidable. Coaches need to be formidable. And while I still coach the basketball teams, I no longer teach gym classes because the folks in charge decided I'd be a better counselor than gym teacher. They made that decision on my first Red Letter Day at BOHS, more than twenty years ago.

I'm the only adult in this school who truly understands how horrible Red Letter Day can be. I think it's cruel that Red Letter Day happens at all, but I think the cruelty gets compounded by the fact that it's held in school.

Red Letter Day should be a holiday, so that kids are at home with their parents when the letters arrive.

Or don't arrive, as the case may be.

And the problem is that we can't even properly prepare for Red Letter Day. We can't read the letters ahead of time: privacy laws prevent it.

So do the strict time travel rules. One contact – only one – through an emissary, who arrives shortly before rehearsal, stashes the envelopes in the practice binders, and then disappears again. The emissary carries actual letters from the future. The letters themselves are the old-fashioned paper kind, the kind people wrote 150 years ago, but write rarely now. Only the real letters, handwritten, on special paper get through. Real letters, so that the signatures can be verified, the paper guaranteed, the envelopes certified.

Apparently, even in the future, no one wants to make a mistake.

The binders have names written across them so the letter doesn't go to the wrong person. And the letters are supposed to be deliberately vague.

I don't deal with the kids who get letters. Others are here for that, some professional bullshitters – at least in my opinion. For a small fee, they'll examine the writing, the signature, and try to clear up the letter's deliberate vagueness, make a guess at the socio-economic status of the writer, the writer's health, or mood.

I think that part of Red Letter Day makes it all a scam. But the schools go along with it, because the counselors (read: me) are busy with the kids who get no letter at all.

And we can't predict whose letter won't arrive. We don't know until the kid stops mid-stride, opens the binder, and looks up with complete and utter shock.

Either there's a red envelope inside or there's nothing.

And we don't even have time to check which binder is which.

I had my Red Letter Day thirty-two years ago, in the chapel of Sister Mary of Mercy High School in Shaker Heights, Ohio. Sister Mary of Mercy was a small co-ed Catholic High School, closed now, but very influential in its day. The best private school in Ohio according to some polls – controversial only because of its conservative politics and its willingness to indoctrinate its students.

I never noticed the indoctrination. I played basketball so well that I already had three full-ride scholarship offers from UCLA, UNLV, and Ohio State (home of the Buckeyes!). A pro scout promised I'd be a fifth round draft choice if only I went pro straight out of high school, but I wanted an education.

"You can get an education later," he told me. "Any good school will let you in after you've made your money and had your fame."

But I was brainy. I had studied athletes who went to the Bigs straight out of high school. Often they got injured, lost their contracts and their money, and never played again. Usually they had to take some crap job to pay for their college education – if, indeed, they went to college at all, which most of them never did.

Those who survived lost most of their earnings to managers, agents, and other hangers-on. I knew what I didn't know. I knew I was an ignorant kid with some great ball-handling ability. I knew that I was trusting and naïve and undereducated. And I knew that life extended well beyond thirty-five, when even the most gifted female athletes lost some of their edge.

I thought a lot about my future. I wondered about life past thirty-five. My future self, I knew, would write me a letter fifteen years after thirty-five. My future self, I believed, would tell me which path to follow, what decision to make.

I thought it all boiled down to college or the pros.

I had no idea there would be – there could be – anything else.

You see, anyone who wants to – anyone who feels so inclined – can write one single letter to their former self. The letter gets delivered just before high school graduation, when most teenagers are (theoretically) adults, but still under the protection of a school.

The recommendations on writing are that the letter should be inspiring. Or it should warn that former self away from a single person, a single event, or a single choice.

Just one.

The statistics say that most folks don't warn. They like their lives as lived. The folks motivated to write the letters wouldn't change much, if anything.

It's only those who've made a tragic mistake – one drunken night that led to a catastrophic accident, one bad decision that cost a best friend a life, one horrible sexual encounter that led to a lifetime of heartache – who write the explicit letter.

And the explicit letter leads to alternate universes. Lives veer off in all kinds of different paths. The adult who sends the letter hopes their former self will take their advice. If the former self does take the advice, then the kid receives the letter from an adult they will never be. The kid, if smart, will become a different adult, the adult who somehow avoided that drunken night. That new adult will write a different letter to their former self, warning about another possibility or committing bland, vague prose about a glorious future.

There're all kinds of scientific studies about this, all manner of debate about the consequences. All types of mandates, all sorts of rules.

And all of them lead back to that moment, that heartstopping moment that I experienced in the chapel of Sister Mary of Mercy High School, all those years ago.

We weren't practicing graduation like the kids at Barack Obama High School. I don't recall when we practiced graduation, although I'm sure we had a practice later in the week.

At Sister Mary of Mercy High School, we spent our Red Letter Day in prayer. All the students started their school days with Mass. But on Red Letter Day, the graduating seniors had to stay for a special service, marked by requests for God's forgiveness and exhortations about the unnaturalness of what the law required Sister Mary of Mercy to do.

Sister Mary of Mercy High School loathed Red Letter Day. In fact, Sister Mary of Mercy High School, as an offshoot of the Catholic Church, opposed time travel altogether. Back in the dark ages (in other words, decades before I was born), the Catholic Church declared time travel an abomination, antithetical to God's will.

You know the arguments: If God had wanted us to travel through time, the devout claim, he would have given us the ability to do so. If God had wanted us to travel through time, the scientists say, he would have given us the ability to understand time travel – and oh! Look! He's done that.

Even now, the arguments devolve from there.

But time travel has become a fact of life for the rich and the powerful and the well-connected. The creation of alternate universes scares them less than the rest of us, I guess. Or maybe the rich really don't care – they being different from you and I, as renowned (but little read) 20th century American author F. Scott Fitzgerald so famously said.

The rest of us – the nondifferent ones – realized nearly a century ago that time travel for all was a dicey proposition, but this being America, we couldn't deny people the *opportunity* of time travel.

Eventually time travel for everyone became a rallying cry. The liberals wanted government to fund it, and the conservatives felt only those who could afford it would be allowed to have it.

Then something bad happened – something not quite expunged from the history books, but something not taught in schools either (or at least the schools I went to), and the federal government came up with a compromise.

Everyone would get one free opportunity for time travel – not that they could actually go back and see the crucifixion or the Battle of Gettysburg – but that they could travel back in their own lives.

The possibility for massive change was so great, however, that the time travel had to be strictly controlled. All the regulations in the world wouldn't stop someone who stood in Freedom Hall in July of 1776 from telling the Founding Fathers what they had wrought.

So the compromise got narrower and narrower (with the subtext being that the masses couldn't be trusted with something as powerful as the ability to travel through time), and it finally became Red Letter Day, with all its rules and regulations. You'd have the ability to touch your own life without ever really leaving it. You'd reach back into your own past and reassure yourself, or put something right.

Which still seemed unnatural to the Catholics, the Southern Baptists, the Libertarians, and the Stuck in Time League (always my favorite, because they never did seem to understand the irony of their own name). For years after the law passed, places like Sister Mary of Mercy High School tried not to comply with it. They protested. They sued. They got sued.

Eventually, when the dust settled, they still had to comply.

But they didn't have to like it.

So they tortured all of us, the poor hopeful graduating seniors, awaiting our future, awaiting our letters, awaiting our fate.

I remember the prayers. I remember kneeling for what seemed like hours. I remember the humidity of that late spring day, and the growing heat, because the chapel (a historical building) wasn't allowed to have anything as unnatural as air conditioning.

Martha Sue Groening passed out, followed by Warren Iverson, the star quarterback. I spent much of that morning with my forehead braced against the pew in front of me, my stomach in knots.

My whole life, I had waited for this moment.

And then, finally, it came. We went alphabetically, which stuck me in the middle, like usual. I hated being in the middle. I was tall, geeky, uncoordinated, except on the basketball court, and not very developed – important in high school. And I wasn't formidable yet.

That came later.

Nope. Just a tall awkward girl, walking behind boys shorter than I was. Trying to be inconspicuous.

I got to the aisle, watching as my friends stepped in front of the altar, below the stairs where we knelt when we went up for the sacrament of communion.

Father Broussard handed out the binders. He was tall but not as tall as me. He was tending to fat, with most of it around his middle. He held the binders by the corner, as if the binders themselves were cursed, and he said a blessing over each and every one of us as we reached out for our futures.

We weren't supposed to say anything, but a few of the boys muttered, "Sweet!" and some of the girls clutched their binders to their chests as if they'd received a love letter.

I got mine – cool and plastic against my fingers – and held it tightly. I didn't open it, not near the stairs, because I knew the kids who hadn't gotten theirs yet would watch me.

So I walked all the way to the doors, stepped into the hallway, and leaned against the wall.

Then I opened my binder.

And saw nothing.

My breath caught.

I peered back into the chapel. The rest of the kids were still in line, getting their binders. No red envelopes had landed on the carpet. No binders were tossed aside.

Nothing. I stopped three of the kids, asking them if they saw me drop anything or if they'd gotten mine.

Then Sister Mary Catherine caught my arm, and dragged me away from the steps. Her fingers pinched into the nerve above my elbow, sending a shooting pain down to my hand.

"You're not to interrupt the others," she said.

"But I must have dropped my letter."

She peered at me, then let go of my arm. A look of satisfaction crossed her fat face, then she patted my cheek.

The pat was surprisingly tender.

"Then you are blessed," she said.

I didn't feel blessed. I was about to tell her that, when she motioned Father Broussard over.

"She received no letter," Sister Mary Catherine said.

"God has smiled on you, my child," he said warmly. He hadn't noticed me before, but this time, he put his hand on my shoulder. "You must come with me to discuss your future."

I let him lead me to his office. The other nuns – the ones without a class that hour – gathered with him. They talked to me about how God wanted me to make my own choices, how He had blessed me by giving me back my future, how He saw me as without sin.

I was shaking. I had looked forward to this day all my life – at least the life I could remember – and then this. Nothing. No future. No answers.

Nothing.

I wanted to cry, but not in front of Father Broussard. He had already segued into a discussion of the meaning of the blessing. I could serve the church. Anyone who failed to get a letter got free admission into a variety of colleges and universities, all Catholic, some well known. If I wanted to become a nun, he was certain the church could accommodate me.

"I want to play basketball, Father," I said.

He nodded. "You can do that at any of these schools."

"Professional basketball," I said.

And he looked at me as if I were the spawn of Satan.

"But, my child," he said with a less reasonable tone than before, "you have received a sign from God. He thinks you Blessed. He wants you in his service."

"I don't think so," I said, my voice thick with unshed tears. "I think you made a mistake."

Then I flounced out of his office, and off school grounds.

My mother made me go back for the last four days of class. She made me graduate. She said I would regret it if I didn't.

I remember that much.

But the rest of the summer was a blur. I mourned my known future, worried I would make the wrong choices, and actually considered the Catholic colleges. My mother rousted me enough to get me to choose before the draft. And I did.

The University of Nevada in Las Vegas, as far from the Catholic Church as I could get.

I took my full ride, and destroyed my knee in my very first game. God's punishment, Father Broussard said when I came home for Thanksgiving.

And God forgive me, I actually believed him.

But I didn't transfer – and I didn't become Job, either. I didn't fight with God or curse God. I abandoned Him because, as I saw it, He had abandoned me.

Thirty-two years later, I watch the faces. Some flush. Some look terrified. Some burst into tears.

But some just look blank, as if they've received a great shock.

Those students are mine.

I make them stand beside me, even before I ask them what they got in their binder. I haven't made a mistake yet, not even last year, when I didn't pull anyone aside.

Last year, everyone got a letter. That happens every five years or so. All the students get Red Letters, and I don't have to deal with anything.

This year, I have three. Not the most ever. The most ever was thirty, and within five years it became clear why. A stupid little war in a stupid little country no one had ever heard of. Twenty-nine of my students died within the decade. Twenty-nine.

The thirtieth was like me, someone who has not a clue why her future self failed to write her a letter.

I think about that, as I always do on Red Letter Day.

I'm the kind of person who *would* write a letter. I have always been that person. I believe in communication, even vague communication. I know how important it is to open that binder and see that bright red envelope.

I would never abandon my past self.

I've already composed drafts of my letter. In two weeks – on my fiftieth birthday – some government employee will show up at my house to set up an appointment to watch me write the letter.

I won't be able to touch the paper, the red envelope or the special pen until I agree to be watched. When I finish, the employee will fold the letter, tuck it in the envelope and earmark it for Sister Mary of Mercy High School in Shaker Heights, Ohio, thirty-two years ago.

I have plans. I know what I'll say.

But I still wonder why I didn't say it to my previous self. What went wrong? What prevented me? Am I in an alternate universe already and I just don't know it?

Of course, I'll never be able to find out.

But I set that thought aside. The fact that I did not receive a letter means nothing. It doesn't mean that I'm blessed by God any more than it means I'll fail to live to fifty.

It is a trick, a legal sleight of hand, so that people like me can't travel to the historical bright spots or even visit the highlights of their own past life.

I continue to watch faces, all the way to the bitter end. But I get no more than three. Two boys and a girl.

Carla Nelson. A tall, thin, white-haired blonde who ran cross-country and stayed away from basketball, no matter how much I begged her to join the team. We needed height and we needed athletic ability.

She has both, but she told me, she isn't a team player. She wanted to run and run alone. She hated relying on anyone else.

Not that I blame her.

But from the devastation on her angular face, I can see that she relied on her future self. She believed she wouldn't let herself down.

Not ever.

Over the years, I've watched other counselors use platitudes. *I'm sure it's nothing. Perhaps your future self felt that you're on the right track. I'm sure you'll be fine.*

I was bitter the first time I watched the high school kids go through this ritual. I never said a word, which was probably a smart decision on my part, because I silently twisted my colleagues' platitudes into something negative, something awful, inside my own head.

It's something. We all know it's something. Your future self hates you or maybe – probably – you're dead.

I have thought all those things over the years, depending on my life. Through a checkered college career, an education degree, a marriage, two children, a divorce, one brand new grandchild. I have believed all kinds of different things.

At thirty-five, when my hopeful young self thought I'd be retiring from pro ball, I stopped being a gym teacher and became a full-time counselor. A full-time counselor and occasional coach.

I told myself I didn't mind.

I even wondered what would I write if I had the chance to play in the Bigs? *Stay the course?* That seems to be the most common letter in those red envelopes. It might be longer than that, but it always boils down to those three words.

Stay the course.

Only I hated the course. I wonder: would I have blown my knee out in the Bigs? Would I have made the Bigs? Would I have received the kind of expensive nanosurgery that would have kept my career alive? Or would I have washed out worse than I ever had?

Dreams are tricky things.

Tricky and delicate and easily destroyed.

And now I faced three shattered dreamers, standing beside me on the edge of the podium.

"To my office," I say to the three of them.

They're so shell-shocked that they comply.

I try to remember what I know about the boys. Esteban Rellier and J.J. Feniman. J.J. stands for . . . Jason Jacob. I remembered only because the names were so very old-fashioned, and J.J. was the epitome of modern cool.

If you had to choose which students would succeed based on personality and charm, not on Red Letters and opportunity, you would choose J.J.

You would choose Esteban with a caveat. He would have to apply himself.

If you had to pick anyone in class who wouldn't write a letter to herself, you would pick Carla. Too much of a loner. Too prickly. Too difficult. I shouldn't have been surprised that she's coming with me.

But I am.

Because it's never the ones you suspect who fail to get a letter.

It's always the ones you believe in, the ones you have hopes for.

And somehow – now – it's my job to keep those hopes alive.

I am prepared for this moment. I'm not a fan of interactive technology – feeds scrolling across the eye, scans on the palm of the hand – but I use it on Red Letter Day more than any other time during the year.

As we walk down the wide hallway to the administrative offices, I learn everything the school knows about all three students which, honestly, isn't much.

Psych evaluations – including modified IQ tests – from grade school on. Addresses. Parental income and employment. Extracurriculars. Grades. Troubles (if any reported). Detentions. Citations. Awards.

I already know a lot about J.J. already. Homecoming king, quarterback, would've been class president if he hadn't turned the role down. So handsome he even has his own stalker, a girl named Lizbet Cholene, whom I've had to discipline twice before sending to a special psych unit for evaluation.

I have to check on Esteban. He's above average, but only in the subjects that interest him. His IQ tested high on both the old exam and the new. He has unrealized potential, and has never really been challenged, partly because he doesn't seem to be the academic type.

It's Carla who is still the enigma. IQ higher than either boy's. Grades lower. No detentions, citations, or academic awards. Only the postings in cross-country – continual wins, all state three years in a row, potential offers from colleges, if she brought her grades up, which she never did. Nothing on the parents. Address in a middle-class neighborhood, smack in the center of town.

I cannot figure her out in a three-minute walk, even though I try.

I usher them into my office. It's large and comfortable. Big desk, upholstered chairs, real plants, and a view of the track – which probably isn't the best thing right now, at least for Carla.

I have a speech that I give. I try not to make it sound canned.

"Your binders were empty, weren't they?" I say.

To my surprise, Carla's lower lip quivers. I thought she'd tough it out, but the tears are close to the surface. Esteban's nose turns red and he bows his head. Carla's distress makes it hard for him to control his.

J.J. leans against the wall, arms folded. His handsome face is a mask. I realize then how often I'd seen that look on his face. Not quite blank – a little pleasant – but detached, far away. He braces one foot on the wall, which is going to leave a mark, but I don't call him on that. I just let him lean.

"On my Red Letter Day," I say, "I didn't get a letter either."

They look at me in surprise. Adults aren't supposed to discuss their letters with kids. Or their lack of letters. Even if I had been able to discuss it, I wouldn't have.

I've learned over the years that this moment is the crucial one, the moment when they realize that you will survive the lack of a letter.

"Do you know why?" Carla asks, her voice raspy.

I shake my head. "Believe me, I've wondered. I've made up every scenario in my head – maybe I died before it was time to write the letter—"

"But you're older than that now, right?" J.J. asks, with something of an angry edge. "You wrote the letter this time, right?"

"I'm eligible to write the letter in two weeks," I say. "I plan to do it."

His cheeks redden, and for the first time, I see how vulnerable he is beneath the surface. He's as devastated – maybe more devastated – than Carla and Esteban. Like me, J.J. believed he would get the letter he deserved – something that told him about his wonderful, successful, very rich life.

"So you could still die before you write it," he said, and this time, I'm certain he meant the comment to hurt.

It did. But I don't let that emotion show on my face. "I could," I say. "But I've lived for thirty-two years without a letter. Thirty-two years without a clue about what my future holds. Like people used to live before time travel. Before Red Letter Day."

I have their attention now.

"I think we're the lucky ones," I say, and because I've established that I'm part of their group, I don't sound patronizing. I've given this speech for nearly two decades, and previous students have told me that this part of the speech is the most important part.

Carla's gaze meets mine, sad, frightened and hopeful. Esteban keeps his head down. J.J.'s eyes have narrowed. I can feel his anger now, as if it's my fault that he didn't get a letter.

"Lucky?" he asks in the same tone that he used when he reminded me I could still die.

"Lucky," I say. "We're not locked into a future."

Esteban looks up now, a frown creasing his forehead.

"Out in the gym," I say, "some of the counselors are dealing with students who're getting two different kinds of tough letters. The first tough one is the one that warns you not to do something on such and so date or you'll screw up your life forever."

"People actually get those?" Esteban asks, breathlessly.

"Every year," I say.

"What's the other tough letter?" Carla's voice trembles. She speaks so softly I had to strain to hear her.

"The one that says *You can do better than I did*, but won't – can't really – explain exactly what went wrong. We're limited to one event, and if what went wrong was a cascading series of bad choices, we can't explain that. We just have to hope that our past selves – you guys, in other words – will make the right choices, with a warning."

J.J.'s frowning too. "What do you mean?"

"Imagine," I say, "instead of getting no letter, you get a letter that tells you that none of your dreams come true. The letter tells you simply that you'll have to accept what's coming because there's no changing it."

"I wouldn't believe it," he says.

And I agree: he wouldn't believe it. Not at first. But those wormy little bits of doubt would burrow in and affect every single thing he does from this moment on.

"Really?" I say. "Are you the kind of person who would lie to yourself in an attempt to destroy who you are now? Trying to destroy every bit of hope that you possess?"

His flush grows deeper. Of course he isn't. He lies to himself – we all do – but he lies to himself about how great he is, how few flaws he has. When Lizbet started following him around, I brought him into my office and asked him not to pay attention to her.

It leads her on, I say.

I don't think it does, he says. *She knows I'm not interested.*

He knew he wasn't interested. Poor Lizbet had no idea at all.

I can see her outside now, hovering in the hallway, waiting for him, wanting to know what his letter said. She's holding her red envelope in one hand, the other lost in the pocket of her baggy skirt. She looks prettier than usual, as if she's dressed up for this day, maybe for the inevitable party.

Every year, some idiot plans a Red Letter Day party even though the school – the culture – recommends against it. Every year, the kids who get good letters go. And the other kids beg off, or go for a short time, and lie about what they received.

Lizbet probably wants to know if he's going to go.

I wonder what he'll say to her.

"Maybe you wouldn't send a letter if the truth hurt too much," Esteban says.

And so it begins, the doubts, the fears.

"Or," I say, "if your successes are beyond your wild imaginings. Why let yourself expect that? Everything you do might freeze you, might lead you to wonder if you're going to screw that up."

They're all looking at me again.

"Believe me," I say. "I've thought of every single possibility, and they're all wrong."

The door to my office opens and I curse silently. I want them to concentrate on what I just said, not on someone barging in on us.

I turn.

Lizbet has come in. She looks like she's on edge, but then she's always on edge around J.J.

"I want to talk to you, J.J." Her voice shakes.

"Not now," he says. "In a minute."

"*Now*," she says. I've never heard this tone from her. Strong and scary at the same time.

"Lizbet," J.J. says, and it's clear he's tired, he's overwhelmed, he's had enough of this day, this event, this girl, this school – he's not built to cope with something he considers a failure. "I'm busy."

"You're not going to marry me," she says.

"Of course not," he snaps – and that's when I know it. Why all four of us don't get letters, why I didn't get a letter, even though I'm two weeks shy from my fiftieth birthday and fully intend to send something to my poor past self.

Lizbet holds her envelope in one hand, and a small plastic automatic in the other. An illegal gun, one that no one should be able to get – not a student, not an adult. No one.

"Get down!" I shout as I launch myself toward Lizbet.

She's already firing, but not at me. At J.J. who hasn't gotten down.

But Esteban deliberately drops and Carla – Carla's half a step behind me, launching herself as well.

Together we tackle Lizbet, and I pry the pistol from her hands. Carla and I hold her as people come running from all directions, some adults, some kids holding letters.

Everyone gathers. We have no handcuffs, but someone finds rope. Someone else has contacted emergency services, using the emergency link that we all have, that we all should have used, that I should have used, that I probably had used in another life, in another universe, one in which I didn't write a letter. I probably contacted emergency services and said something placating to Lizbet, and she probably shot all four of us, instead of poor J.J.

J.J., who is motionless on the floor, his blood slowly pooling around him. The football coach is trying to stop the bleeding and someone I don't recognize is helping and there's nothing I can do, not at the moment, they're doing it all while we wait for emergency services.

The security guard ties up Lizbet and sets the gun on the desk and we all stare at it, and Annie Sanderson, the English teacher, says to the guard, "You're supposed to check everyone, today of all days. That's why we hired you."

And the principal admonishes her, tiredly, and she shuts up. Because we know that sometimes Red Letter Day causes this, that's why it's held in school, to stop family annihilations and shootings of best friends and employers. Schools, we're told, can control weaponry and violence, even though they can't, and someone, somewhere, will use this as a reason to repeal Red Letter Day, but all those people who got good letters or letters warning them about their horrible drunken mistake will prevent any change, and everyone – the pundits, the politicians, the parents – will say that's good.

Except J.J.'s parents, who have no idea their son had no future. When did he lose it? The day he met Lizbet? The day he didn't listen to me about how crazy she was? A few moments ago, when he didn't dive for the floor?

I will never know.

But I do something I would never normally do. I grab Lizbet's envelope, and I open it.

The handwriting is spidery, shaky.

Give it up. J.J. doesn't love you. He'll never love you. Just walk away and pretend that he doesn't exist. Live a better life than I have. Throw the gun away.

Throw the gun away.

She did this before, just like I thought.

And I wonder: was the letter different this time? And if it was, how different? *Throw the gun away.* Is that line new or old? Has she ignored this sentence before?

My brain hurts. My head hurts.

My heart hurts.

I was angry at J.J. just a few moments ago, and now he's dead.

He's dead and I'm not.

Carla isn't either.

Neither is Esteban.

I touch them both and motion them close. Carla seems calmer, but Esteban is blank – shock, I think. A spray of blood covers the left side of his face and shirt.

I show them the letter, even though I'm not supposed to.

"Maybe this is why we never got our letters," I say. "Maybe today is different than it was before. We survived, after all."

I don't know if they understand. I'm not sure I care if they understand.

I'm not even sure if I understand.

I sit in my office and watch the emergency services people flow in, declare J.J. dead, take Lizbet away, set the rest of us aside for interrogation. I hand someone – one of the police officers – Lizbet's red envelope, but I don't tell him we looked.

I have a hunch he knows we did.

The events wash past me, and I think that maybe this is my last Red Letter Day at Barack Obama High School, even if I survive the next two weeks and turn fifty.

And I find myself wondering, as I sit on my desk waiting to make my statement, whether I'll write my own red letter after all.

What can I say that I'll listen to? Words are so very easy to misunderstand. Or misread.

I suspect Lizbet only read the first few lines. Her brain shut off long before she got to *Walk away* and *Throw away the gun.*

Maybe she didn't write that the first time. Or maybe she's been writing it, hopelessly, to herself in a continual loop, lifetime after lifetime after lifetime.

I don't know.

I'll never know.

None of us will know.

That's what makes Red Letter Day such a joke. Is it the letter that keeps us on the straight and narrow? Or the lack of a letter that gives us our edge?

Do I write a letter, warning myself to make sure Lizbet gets help when I meet her? Or do I tell myself to go to the draft no matter what? Will that prevent this afternoon?

I don't know.

I'll never know.

Maybe Father Broussard was right; maybe God designed us to be ignorant of the future. Maybe He wants us to move forward in time, unaware of what's ahead, so that we follow our instincts, make our first, best – and only – choice.

Maybe.

Or maybe the letters mean nothing at all. Maybe all this focus on a single day and a single note from a future self is as meaningless as this year's celebration of the Fourth of July. Just a day like any other, only we add a ceremony and call it important.

I don't know.

I'll never know.

Not if I live two more weeks or two more years.

Either way, J.J. will still be dead and Lizbet will be alive, and my future – whatever it is – will be the mystery it always was.

The mystery it should be.

The mystery it will always be.

DOMINE

Rjurik Davidson

Rjurik Davidson has written short stories, essays, reviews, and screenplays, and has been short-listed for and won a number of awards. Davidson's collection *The Library of Forgotten Books* was published in 2010 by PS Publishing. His novel *Unwrapped Sky* will be published in early 2014. His script *The Uncertainty Principle* (cowritten with Ben Chessell) is currently in development with Lailaps films and Neon Park films. "Domine" was first published in *Aurealis* in 2007.

I'm off the monorail and through streets littered with cigarette packets and strips of last month's posters, peeled from the yellow and grey chipped walls. The air smells of rubbish and urine. A breeze would only blow the odour away for a moment; I'm in the City.

Genie and I moved into the place temporarily, with the hope of shifting farther out a few months later, where there might be a park for Max to play in, neighbours to help out, a house with a separate dining room and kitchen. Genie remained after I moved out, so every now and then I'm back in the old neighbourhood, with light rain misting through the little inner-city streets, trying not to look past the pavement in front of me in case I see one of the real things that happen here.

A shuttle slashes the sky overhead, taking someone rich to meet other rich people somewhere else. They don't bother with travelling by land – easier to skip over the city like a stone over water. The deep red of the shuttle's burners gives the illusion of warmth.

"Hey Mister, hey!"

One of the boys; there are a million around here.

"Hey Mister, *bliss, bliss*?"

I shake my head and keep my eyes on the stained pavement. No need to encourage them.

"Hey Mister, you come back."

I'm there, at the old five-storey yellow apartment building. Bars on every window, so people don't get in and others don't throw themselves out. It's a fair balance.

The city is still all stairs and four, five, six-storey buildings. Everything new or important happens out in the Towers, little islands of commerce in the suburbs, where things are clean and fresh and everyone's teeth are white and gleaming and the girls in all the shops remind you of your hopes when you were young.

I'm into the stairwell and up. Three sets of stairs, four doors along the walkway. I knock.

I hear scrabbling from behind the door and wait for a while, noticing that my hands seem wrinkled. I am only thirty-eight but I'm getting old.

"Don't you ever call?" I can see one side of Genie's face through the partly opened door, her lank, colourless hair falling across her forehead. She has that look of exhaustion as usual, as if the world has worn her out and everything now is an effort.

"Hi Genie."

"Look, it's not a good time."

"I brought something for Max."

The door opens and I'm inside. The place is tiny: one bedroom, a one-room lounge and kitchen, a bathroom and toilet.

"He doesn't even know who you are." Genie starts picking up odd bits and pieces of junk from the lounge room floor: some socks, a fluffy toy bird, opened envelopes with their contents still inside. She always starts cleaning when I arrive. Max is playing by a water-filled bucket in the corner. The smell of something rotten floats from the bin in the kitchen.

"Hey, Maxy," I say, and my one-year-old son looks up at me, his face round with splotchy, rosy cheeks, and his mouth open. A line of dribble runs from his mouth to his chest.

I walk over to him and squat next to him. "Hey Maxy." Should I reach out to him? I'm not sure. It's hard with children: they're strange things. He looks at me and I'm scared he'll start crying. At the moment he's just frowning.

"So what did you bring him?"

I have no present so I change the subject. "Dany's coming back you know." I say. "Really soon. August thirtieth."

"I know the date, Marek, but I don't care. It's too late for me to care," Genie says. "You should concentrate on your own stuff. Think about Max for once."

"But what am I going to do?" I reach forward and touch Max on the arm. But he senses my tension and tries to pull away, still frowning at me as if I'm an impostor.

A key rattles in the door and a big brawny man, his body too big for his legs, wanders in. He wears baggy khaki work-shorts and a blue singlet over a too-tanned body.

"I told you this was a bad time," Genie says to me. "Oh well, this is Rick. Rick, this is Marek."

"Oh, hi," Rick says and walks over to Genie, gives her a kiss, walks over to Max, ruffles his thin blonde hair.

I'm out of the door and on the landing, but Genie follows me. "I love him," she says, "and he treats me well. Better than you ever did."

"Yeah," I say, still walking, my teeth clenched like a vice.

"What did you come back for?" Her voice is suddenly shrill. "Did you come back to fuck me?"

Another shuttle burns overhead, and I wonder where it's going. The Towers no doubt.

"Come back and visit Max, though," she says suddenly, hopefully, "He needs his father. You of all people should know that."

*

Later that evening I'm in the small unit I can afford, out in the vast expanse of houses and apartments that encircle the Towers. The suburbs are like a sea surrounding a chain of islands, running all the way to the City. It's a nothing space, each section interchangeable with another. The view from a shuttle would be of one infinitely repeating series of buildings and roads. It's how I like it. You can get lost here; you can feel hidden and safe. It allows me to write my music in peace, away from all the demands of the world: partners and children and work. Still, I don't compose much. All my creativity gets drained by the soundscapes I'm forced to design for the Towers. All my originality is sucked away into those.

Tonight, for some reason, I'm agitated, disturbed even. It's August twenty-eighth.

The phone buzzes. I press the button and my older sister Leila appears on the screen. Though she doesn't really like me, we keep in touch. Even now her hair is sculpted, like a blonde helmet. Not a hair out of place.

"I can't sleep," she says.

"Yeah."

"I don't want to see Dany."

"Right."

"I don't want anything to do with him." Leila clenches her jaw (we both inherited that from mum) and crosses her arms emphatically.

"Do you think that Mum was happy in her last years?"

"Christ, Marek, you've always been introspective. That's your problem."

"I think she was. I think finally, after everything, she found some happiness."

Leila brushes her hair back with her hand, but it bounces back to its perfect shape. "So if you talk to him, tell him I don't want to see him."

"Someone's got to be there when he comes back."

"Well it's not going to be me. And Marek, what good is it going to do if you show up? Huh?"

"She wanted to hold on, didn't she? Just another year, just one more year. But she couldn't."

Someone is crying behind Leila. Must be her kid, whose name I can't, for the life of me, remember. Leila turns from the phone to look over her shoulder, then back. "Look Marek, I gotta go."

"It's been all over the news," I say, but she's gone.

August thirtieth arrives and I'm in McArthur Tower: the procession has finished, the speeches are over; there have been medals and descriptions and hologram footage and everything else. I saw him on stage with the others, in their uniforms, but I could barely make it out from up the back. Now I'm sitting at the exit to the conference centre and people in suits are milling about being official and I wonder if I should go in and look around for him, but no, I stay put. Secretly I don't want to see him. I think of leaving, eyeing the lifts far away down the corridor, but something makes me stay. It must have been a hell of a thing, after all, out there in space. The government made a fuss of Dany and the rest of the crew, that's for sure.

A soundscape full of triumphant brass and rolling drums plays in the background.

I notice the captain walk out, officials surrounding him, talking in hushed, respectful tones.

To my right, windows open out to the evening. The vast bulk of another Tower stands opposite, its own windows appearing tiny in the gigantic structure. I struggle to see if I can make out figures, but all I can see is flickering, and that's probably just my eyes playing up.

I look away and suddenly Dany's there, with another of the crew, and they're coming past me. It hits me like a physical blow: he looks in his early twenties. His light hair is short and jagged, his eyes slightly too close together, spoiling his otherwise beautiful looks. It hits me again: he looks just like I once did.

"See you soon then, Dan," the other one says.

He nods and grins like a little boy, runs his hands through his hair and then says, "Yep."

He walks towards the lift as the other one turns back.

"Hey," I say weakly, and then stronger, embarrassed by the strain in my voice, "Dany."

He turns and looks at me and my breath is suddenly taken away. He cocks his head and frowns for a minute. Then says, "Yeah?"

"It's me," I say, and am struck by the banality of it, "Marek."

He grins uncomfortably, cocks his head to the other side and raises his hands as if to say: well, imagine that.

I stand up from my chair, take a few steps and say again, "It's me, Marek."

"Where's your mother?"

"She died."

A look of confusion crosses his face and then passes. "Well, come on then," he says.

I follow him. Neither of us speak as we make our way to the elevator and then wind through one of the prospects: a wide boulevard with ground cars and unicycles zipping along in a chaotic frenzy, the stall holders at the side of the road, with their designer tattoos, calling to us as we pass. Another elevator, spiralling through the Tower in odd directions, takes us up to the Hotel Sector in the fifteen hundreds where Dany has been given a room.

He has an amazing sense of direction amid the massive structure of the Tower, with its thousands of winding corridors. He finds his penthouse calmly and easily. When he arrives he says to me, the first words in some time, "I'm going to get ready. I have to see some of this."

He retreats to the bathroom while I sit and wait.

The view from the giant windows is magnificent. Two Towers, one at an oblique angle, and then the lights of the suburbs, flickering like a thousand shining insects. The clarity of it strikes me.

"We don't wear makeup much anymore," I say.

"Oh . . . What do you wear?"

"I don't really know. I mean, I'm not really up with it. But there's a fashion channel."

Dany comes out, fully shaven. He looks even younger, though the dark makeup around the eyes makes him look like a thirty-year throwback. "Should I take it off?" He looks suddenly anxious.

"No, don't worry. Some people still wear it."

"I've got this card." He says, "They gave me this card. It'll get me clothes, all sorts of things."

"Leila called me a couple of days ago."

He walks across the room, presses a button and the fridge door slides up.

"Drink?" he asks, ignoring me.

"She's doing well. All settled down: husband, kids, you know."

Dany takes a big swig of something, throws back his head, and lets out a roar. Turns around, passes me a glass. "C'mon boy, this'll put a glint back in your eye." He grins his distinctive grin.

I sip the drink and try to stifle a cough. My throat is on fire, my eyes blurred. I hear a laugh off in the distance. "God," I say.

Nightville, up in the eighteen and nineteen hundreds, is a complex of Middle-Eastern and African restaurants, hanging gardens filled with the scent of stone-fruit and dotted with indoor lakes, labyrinthine clubs climbing up through the Tower like ant-colonies so that after a few hours you don't know what level you're on. Nightville is a carefully planned planlessness, designed to give the sense of spontaneity, of a vast and sprawling confusion, imitating the red-light districts in the old cities. But nothing in the Towers is unplanned. So there's always the element of irreality to it, a sense of the manufactured. Shambling through a club one might, lo and behold, stumble upon an Armenian restaurant run by the club's owners, aimed at the very same patrons, in an expression of monopoly apparent only to those not doped up on rapture or blurred by alcohol. Nightville is one big franchise.

We're in *Arabian Nights*, one of the popular clubs in the sector, a ramshackle series of levels where patrons surround hookahs in dark tent-like chambers, where everything is in the deep colours and intricate patterns of the Middle East, where belly dancers and pipe-players, tootling in exotic quarter-tones, make their way through the passageways, where camel-trains ridden by adventurers head for the mini-desert on the western side of the club.

Dany, dressed ridiculously in his space-suit and dark makeup (all blue shadow and grey undertones), is entertaining a small crowd in a side room. I've been edged out of the circle and have to crane my neck over a couple of skip-girls.

"Of course," he says, "you're unconscious during close-to-light-speed. A deep dark sleep filled with magnificent dreams. And then, suddenly, consciousness hits you like a blow, and you're throwing up all over yourself, and you're wondering who you are and what you're doing there. And me, *I'm* thinking I could have bought this feeling for a hundred bucks at *Arabian Nights*."

He pauses for the laughter and then continues in slightly more hushed tones.

"But then you look out and you see Centauri and everything is in a strange new light, filled with blues and greens that you've never seen before, as if you've been reborn into a world just slightly different from this one, and you know nothing will ever be the same again."

Around him there is hushed silence, only the bass from dance music in the main rooms, audible behind his voice.

One of the skip-girls puts her hand on his thigh.

"Hey," he says to me, "Come here." He pulls me toward him and wraps an arm around my shoulder. "I want you to meet Marek. You have to look after him."

Someone passes me a fluorescent blue drink, *Ottoman Ice*, and I down it in one hit.

He continues to tell his stories but his arm is around my neck and I keep thinking to myself: isn't this what you came for, isn't time with Dany what you wanted?

The *Ottoman Ice* has rapture in it, and before long everything has that tinge of silver, those floating motes of light dancing around the room like emblems of joy. I have another and the waves of heat begin to course up and down my body.

"Are you his brother? You look just like him," one of the skip-girls asks me. They're not that quick, skip-girls.

"What's your name?" I say.

"Sandy."

All the skip-girls have names like that: Sandy, Cherry, Peta, Ruby. Her lips are full and red and suddenly her little cherubic face sets off some reaction in my stomach. Skip-girls, I think, are gorgeous.

The *Ottoman Ice* no longer burns in my throat. Now it's just a soft warmth, as if my throat is adjusting itself to the heat emanating from my body. Through a window on my left the mini-desert stretches out and in the distance I can see a little oasis.

"Can you see that?" I say, but there's no one beside me. Everyone is at a table about ten feet away. When did we arrive at the observation deck? I wonder. I join them at the table. Dany is still entertaining: he's charismatic, just as I imagined.

"And there, on the asteroid," he says, "was what looked like a complex machine or engine, too structured to be natural, I swear. But how much fuel did we have? Who knew? Let's go down, I said. I mean, here we were, how many light years from home, and there, within arm's reach is evidence of alien civilisation. Let's go, I said. Take it now, seize our chance. No, said the captain. Yes, said I. No, he said. When else will we get this chance? I said. We can't risk it, said the captain. So that was that." He grins his childlike grin.

Breaths of amazement. I look out over the desert again, not believing a word of it and suddenly we're in the Turkish steam baths and soaking everything up and my body is on fire. All I can do is lie there, head back as the steam invades my body and I feel like I'm somehow dissolving and becoming the water and the water is me and I'm suddenly aware of Dany above me leaning down and he says, "Look, I'm sorry, okay? I'm sorry." He touches my shoulder and then walks off quickly and Sandy is looking at me from the sofa as I look over to the Towers from Dany's penthouse while Christy and Dany are in the bedroom next door.

"You skip-girls," I say. "You're so full of life." I notice her lips again, and this time the freckles on her little round cheeks. She must be in her early twenties, like most skip-girls employed to advertise the Tower, to give it a sense of glamour and sex. She looks out over the city and yawns.

"Do you and Christy work tandem?"

She ignores me and walks to the window. She looks across at the opposite

Tower. "It's amazing, isn't it? That over there, there's a whole 'nother city, and that people don't ever have to leave if they don't want to. A whole world."

I walk up behind her, and there are little muscles outlined just so on her back, perfect, as if sculpted from marble.

"I've been to all of them," I say, "every Tower."

"Wow."

From the bedroom, I can hear a high-pitched whining, and then I think I hear Christy say, "Oh, yes, that."

"Each one has my own little mark," I say. "Soundscape Design. I'm part of the Soundscape Design Team."

"Really?" Her eyes flicker with interest for a moment.

"Well, you know, part of the team."

I'm looking down at her and have an urge to lean forward and touch her hair, metallic green and artificial, a typical mark of a skip-girl.

"I'll be back in a minute," she says, and she walks swiftly across to the bedroom and is gone. I wait for five minutes and then let myself out.

The next day I spend at home, occasionally staring at my computers and synths, turning them on, pretending I'm going to compose. But it's too hard and my head feels like it's been squeezed like a lemon. Oh no, I think, I'm getting old. Once I would have been fine on a day like today, but now my body has perfected the art of sabotage. I wander around distracted, moving from thing to thing, unable to settle. The synths sit in the corner of the room accusingly.

In the afternoon the phone rings and I shuffle towards it, press the button.

"So, what's he like?" I can see Leila leaning forward, so she can see my expression more clearly on the screen.

"I don't know."

"Oh, come on, what's he like?"

"He's a great storyteller, I guess. I mean, he had a fan-club all around. You know, charismatic, I guess, kept everyone mesmerised." I think of Sandy the skip-girl and her full lips, her cherubic face, her metallic hair. Some feeling washes over me that I'd prefer not to acknowledge.

"Is he immature? I bet he's immature."

"I don't know."

"Christ, Marek, listen to you. It's always the same with you. You're still under his spell."

"I guess he's young."

"He must be. He left when he was young."

"It's like looking at me, only fifteen years ago . . . really, like looking back in time. I am, you know, older than him."

"Yeah: the bastard." Leila spits the words with satisfaction.

"He's okay."

"You were too young when he left. I was what, eight? You, though, you were too young. That's your problem. That's why you can't see."

"He used to play with us though, remember? He used to build things with us, little ships that flew through the air, orbited that old planet we had hanging in our room. Remember that?"

Leila grimaces a moment. "He hit mum. Remember that? He hit mum."

"She loved him. She waited for him all her life."

"You're both as bad as each other. Both of you. Look where it got her, Marek."

"*You're* the one calling to find out."

"Fine. Listen, gotta go. Why don't you come over for dinner?"

But I'm off the phone and I put Mozart on with the volume up. I close my eyes and lean back in the chair as the chorus comes in: *Requiem aeternam dona eis, Domine, et lux perpetua luceat eis.*

I meet Dany again the following week up in the Towers. His makeup is gone, he is in the latest fashion – as far as I can tell – all straight sharp lines and black, of course. It's always black.

"Have you seen this holographic porn?" he asks. "It's amazing, really, I mean, God."

I lean from one foot to the other, wondering what to say.

"God," he says, "some of those girls. Some of those positions." He shakes his head.

To change the subject I say, "Remember we used to play with little ships that flew around a toy planet?"

He cocks his head. "Do you still have those?"

I nod.

"Christ, I loved those little things," he says.

"You can come to my place and see them if you want."

"No, can't. I've got to get ready."

"What for?"

"We're going back."

"Back?"

"The machine. We're supposed to examine the alien machine."

"But there is no machine," I say, calling his bluff.

He shakes his head for a second, then adds, "No, you're right. There isn't." He walks into the bedroom and I am left shifting my balance from foot to foot. Then he's back again: "Here, I have something for you: I brought it back for her, but now I want you to have it. It's from Centauri." He leans over and passes me a piece of strange, black swirling rock, attached to a chain, alien and beautiful.

"She died of cancer, you know. Even now cancer takes people." I hold the rock in my hand, and now I want to cry again, but in a different way. I want to reach out to him.

"Wanna go to a strip show?"

"Uh, I don't know."

"I know! I know just the place: baths! That's one thing you miss in space: real water to float in. Come on."

So I follow him to the elevator, and we rise, past the eighteen hundreds, nineteen hundreds, and then at twenty-two hundred we're off the elevator and into the cavernous deck of the shuttle-port. Shuttles taxi around like strange beetles threatening to burst into flight at any moment. Others line a far wall at an angle.

"What are we doing?"

"We're going to Holsen's Tower, north."

"By shuttle?"

"Yep."

There is a line of taxis along the walkway and Dany presses a button, there's a quick sound as the pressurised door opens – shhht – and we hop in.

The shuttle is a lot smaller on the inside than I imagined, only one long seat facing forward, a series of panels across the back of the seat in front. A glass window so we can see the driver, who has great rolls of fat at the back of his head and neck. The taxi shuttles across the tarmac, turns left, and I can see the runway, which opens out into the clear blue of the sky. We sit for a moment and another shuttle emerges slightly in front of us, lines itself up with the runway, stops for a minute and then suddenly its burners are a deep red, the air behind it shimmers, and it is gone.

Our taxi starts to shudder and I take a gasp of breath: surely we're not going to be able to fly. We'll get to the end of the runway and plummet to our deaths. This taxi, I realise, will crash. This is the one, the one out of a million that will break down in mid-flight, lose power, send us to our deaths. The unbelievable shuddering as we power along the runway confirms this, and I close my eyes. Suddenly the shuddering stops and I open them again, afraid of what I might see, and sure enough, beneath us the great metropolis lies like a model of itself. I gasp. Good God, there's nothing holding us up.

"You can let go of my hand now." Dany laughs.

"This is the first time I've flown."

"It's all right. It'll be all right." He gives my hand a squeeze and I feel calmer.

"Look," he says. "Look at the city off there in the distance. Isn't it beautiful? Like a ruined civilisation."

The little city does look like an ancient ruin. As if it has been through a storm that left some of the weaker buildings as rubble, or just a few walls surrounding a mess, while others it stripped of their outer layer, leaving their mottled under-coats visible.

"I have a son down there."

"Really? What's his name?"

"Max."

"You didn't want to give him a Czech name? Keep your mother's tradition?"

"No. We're not Czechs anymore. Would you like to meet him?"

He sits for a while in silence, and then says, "You know, I think I would."

Before long we're north of the city and then into another Tower and the flight is over. Down in the eleven hundreds is Japantown and I find myself lying in a steaming bath, a sparse garden surrounding me and a pot of green tea just out of arm's reach so I have to lift myself out of the bath to pour it. The roof is camouflaged and gives the impression of being sky. Thankfully there is no view of the city whatsoever. There are no sounds at all. Just silence – the Japanese really know how to do it.

"The silence is funny," I say. "The Towers are almost all soundscaped."

"Really."

"Yep. That's what I do. Soundscaping."

"I see."

"Yeah, wanted to be a musician, but you know. Soundscaping's a good job. Keeps me afloat."

"So you compromised."

"No. I just, you know, you have to be realistic."

"Christ, Marek."

"What's so fucking bad about that?"

"That sort of realism isn't for me."

I pull myself out of the bath to pour more tea and wonder, annoyed: why didn't I pull the pot closer last time?

We sit in silence for quite a while and I don't know, perhaps it's the silence, or the beauty of the garden, or the heat of the bath, but suddenly I begin to cry.

"Hey buddy, what's wrong?"

I don't say anything for a while, and then manage to get out between the sobs: "I've made some terrible mistakes, in my life, Dad. I've made some bad mistakes."

Leila lives at the crest of a hill, and her husband, George, is a fitness fanatic with a shaven head. George invested in the Towers, or his parents did, and now they live in a mansion overlooking the aqua sea. They have two boats and three cars and a swimming pool in a basement underneath their house. "The sea," George always says, "is for looking at, not swimming in." At those times I want to break his teeth, but I always nod and smile and say, "Hey, who would swim in the sea nowadays? I mean, with all that pollution." George works out and has huge muscles. He and Leila have one child, about three years old, whose name I can't remember. George and Leila have everything.

The dinner is tiny and served on gigantic white plates: a piece of unidentified meat with two red slivers of what I take to be capsicum on one side.

"A work of art," I say.

"Don't be rude," says Leila.

"He's not," says George, "He said it was a work of art."

"A pure work of art," I say to annoy Leila.

The kid starts crying at the end of the table.

"Here sweetie," says Leila, and she reaches over to give him a drink. He keeps crying.

"Listen to 'im," says George.

"I am," I say.

"All day," says George.

"Oh, shut up," says Leila.

"What's his name?" I say.

But Leila continues at George, "Like you'd know. I'm the one here all bloody day."

"What's his name?"

Leila turns to me. "Families," she says, "take a lot of energy. You'll know—"

But I cut her off, "That's because you had him when you were too old."

She looks as if she's been slapped and I turn to my meal with satisfaction.

A moment later she says to me, "So did you. You had Max too old."

Now it's my turn to look shocked. No matter how hard I try, I know I look crestfallen. I look back to Leila and she meets my eye. The side of her mouth twitches and suddenly we're both laughing at ourselves.

"You really should meet up with Dany, you know," I say.

"I can't. I just can't."

I reach over and place my hand over hers. "You should face him. You know. Say what should be said."

"Is that what you're going to do?"

"Yes. I think so. Yes."

Before Mum died she looked an impossible colour, a kind of composite grey-orange. She was swollen, but in her inimitable way acted as if it was all some kind of joke.

"Look at me," she said, "I'm a fish from the deep sea," and she opened and closed her mouth and we all laughed.

I want to tell Dany something about Mum now, as we head to the city, but some part of me holds back. I know, somehow, that he's not equipped to cope with it. He is, after all, in his early twenties. He's young, I tell myself.

A minute later and we're off the monorail together and Dany turns to me and says, "Jesus, look at this place. What have they done to the city?" I keep my eyes focused on the refuse: empty packages, indeterminate plastic things, toilet paper, but Dany, of course, doesn't know about the street-sellers and suddenly there are three kids around us.

"*Bliss, bliss?*"

"It's not really *bliss* though, is it?" Dany says.

"It is, swear brother, purest I eva had meself. Look mister, look at me eyes."

"You can get your eyes wide like that with all sorts of poisons," says Dany, enjoying the debate.

When we arrive at the building I turn to the kid and say, "Okay, you can fuck off now."

"Aw mister, it's good stuff," one of the little kids says but they leave us alone as we scale the stairs. Three sets of stairs, four doors along the walkway. I knock. Again there is shuffling behind the door and then it opens quicker than I expected. Genie stands there, disappointment written on her face.

"Oh, it's you, hi." She says, then notices Dany and quietly adds, as if he's not there, "My God, Marek, he looks just like you when we met. My god, he's so beautiful."

"Can we come in?"

She opens the door.

"Where's Rick?"

"That bastard."

Dany sweeps Max up from the corner and says, "Hello grubby-chubby." Max grins, revealing a little tooth and letting out another big dribble to join the one connecting his chin and chest.

"I'm moving out of this place soon," says Genie, sweeping back her limp mousy hair, only to have it fall back across her forehead, another symbol of the world's resistance to her desires.

"I'm amazed you stayed so long," I say, looking over to Dany and Max, who are playing with a toy that hovers in the air but avoids being caught when you reach out to it. Both have child-like expressions on their faces.

Genie looks over and says again, quietly, "amazing."

"I'm thinking of going back and being a musician," I say.

"Oh yeah."

"No, really."

Genie looks away from Dany and Max to me. "God, Marek. It would have been alright if you had really wanted to play music, but you always sat in that grey zone your whole life. You didn't really try music, you always held onto it so you wouldn't try anything else."

"The openings were never there; you have to be lucky."

"You were never ready, never good enough. You never wanted to work at it."

"Jesus, Genie, you don't understand how hard it is."

She reaches over and takes my hand, and just looks at me.

After a moment I say, "I'll try to come more often."

"You won't though, you know you won't."

There's nothing else for me to say, standing there looking back and forth at the one real love of my life and the thin blond hair of my son, as he sits comfortably on Dany's lap. Her hand feels soft in mine.

On Dany's last day, before he shoots off to Centauri, I arrive at his penthouse and Christy the skip-girl is wandering about, topless, with a skirt that sits high enough to show her knickers underneath. "Where's that top?" she asks no one in particular.

Dany is still in the shower and I can hear the running water above the soft sound of the ocean soundscape, carefully designed for relaxation but actually infuriating. Relaxation soundscapes make me want to smash something.

"Here it is." Christy pulls the top out from under a couch, puts it straight on and then holds her stomach, looking down at it with curiosity.

Oh no, I think, not again.

Christy looks over at me, smiles, grabs her bag and heads for the door.

"Hey Christy?"

She turns.

"You . . ." My voice trails off with my confidence.

"Yeah?"

"Oh, it's okay."

She waits for a second to see if I have anything else to add, decides I don't and then lets herself out.

A few moments later Dany comes in, drying his hair with a towel. "Turn that fucking sea-sound off would you?" he says. "It's annoying."

I smile, head to the panel and turn all the soundscapes off.

He throws the towel on the floor, sits down, and raises his eyebrows as if to say, well, there you go.

So I hit him with it: "So, you're going to leave, just like that?"

A look of confusion crosses his face and he says, "Don't."

He gets up, walks across to the windows and looks over to the opposite Tower. "This place is so strange," he adds.

I look at him, and he looks small and young and out of place. I know now, that it is time to let him go. I know who he is: He's Dany; he's my father.

"I came to say goodbye," I say.

"Okay," he says and continues to look out over to the mammoth structure, with its thousands of floors containing whole social ecosystems. Whole worlds even. And beyond that the suburbs: filled with people who fell short of their aims and now settle in the grey zone of their life, their quiet desperation muffled. And even further, beyond that, the tiny speck of the ruined city, the dead heart of things, where lights once flashed and people once gathered before everything slipped off track so subtly, so we didn't notice and found ourselves in a world new and strange and hard to bear. That's how I leave him, staring over the geographies of our lives, a man who should have looked older than me, but could have been my own son. He is gone the next day, back out to the stars where he belongs and a few days after that, as I sit in my chair at home, Mozart's requiem surrounding me and filling me. *Lord grant them eternal rest*, the chorus sings, *and let the perpetual light shine upon them*. I know it's time to call Leila. She is, after all, my sister.

When Genie opens the door she says, "Oh, it's you."

I shrug, as if to say, "well there you go."

"Come in. Come in."

The place is still a mess but I don't mind. Max is in a high chair and waves his arms around. I stand awkwardly across from Genie as she starts picking clothes up from the ground. She always starts cleaning when I arrive.

"He's gone," I say.

"I know."

I look over at Max, who has now stopped waving his arms and is examining me curiously. I walk over to him, pick him up and sit him on my hip. He stares impassively and I'm afraid he'll cry.

"Hi Max," I say quietly, and then turn to Genie, hoping that if I act naturally, he'll feel comfortable. "Leila . . . she really should have talked to Dany."

"Yeah, why didn't she? I thought he was nice. And so pretty." Her eyes sparkle mischievously.

"You'll never guess what's happened."

"What?"

"One of the skip-girls that Dany was seeing – I think she's pregnant."

"No!"

"I don't know. Maybe I'm wrong. I nearly asked her but . . . it was awkward."

Genie shakes her head: "He'll never change, will he?"

"He's okay," I say, "He doesn't really hurt . . ." I stop myself.

Max starts to cry and holds his arms out to Genie, who laughs. She takes him from me. Safe once more Max turns and frowns at me. I'm getting used to the frown.

"Don't worry," says Genie, "he's like that with everyone."

"Hey," I say, "do you want to hear my new composition?"

"Sure," she says.

"I got the idea from Mozart. It's sort of a requiem."

I walk over to the old computer in the corner of the room – my old computer. I start it up, touching its old keys lovingly.

Shortly afterwards the piece is playing, filling the room with the sound of deep voices and high strings. No complex beats but a few electronic noises fading in and out – I wanted to keep the classic feel. Genie and I sit on the couch together, Max on Genie's lap, listening as the music fills the room around us. I close my eyes and listen as the voices come in, singing back at the past.

IN THE TUBE

E.F. Benson

E.F. Benson was an English writer best known for his ghost stories and gothic tales. Writers like China Miéville have expressed great admiration for Benson, who was not just prolific but also a clever and sometimes profound writer. He was greatly influenced by J.W. Dunne's theories about time. Dunne put forth a theory that time possessed a geography that could be explored. "In the Tube" was Benson's exploration of this idea, first published in 1923 in *Hutchinson's Magazine*.

"It's a convention," said Anthony Carling cheerfully, "and not a very convincing one. Time, indeed! There's no such thing as Time really; it has no actual existence. Time is nothing more than an infinitesimal point in eternity, just as space is an infinitesimal point in infinity. At the most, Time is a sort of tunnel through which we are accustomed to believe that we are travelling.

"There's a roar in our ears and a darkness in our eyes which makes it seem real to us. But before we came into the tunnel we existed for ever in an infinite sunlight, and after we have got through it we shall exist in an infinite sunlight again. So why should we bother ourselves about the confusion and noise and darkness which only encompass us for a moment?"

For a firm-rooted believer in such immeasurable ideas as these, which he punctuated with brisk application of the poker to the brave sparkle and glow of the fire, Anthony has a very pleasant appreciation of the measurable and the finite, and nobody with whom I have acquaintance has so keen a zest for life and its enjoyments as he. He had given us this evening an admirable dinner, had passed round a port beyond praise, and had illuminated the jolly hours with the light of his infectious optimism. Now the small company had melted away, and I was left with him over the fire in his study. Outside the tartoo of wind-driven sleet was audible on the window-panes, over-scoring now and again the flap of the flames on the open hearth, and the thought of the chilly blasts and the snow-covered pavement in Brompton Square, across which, to skidding taxicabs, the last of his other guests had scurried, made my position, resident here till to-morrow morning, the more delicately delightful. Above all there was this stimulating and suggestive companion, who, whether he talked of the great abstractions which were so intensely real and practical to him, or of the very remarkable experiences which he had encountered among these conventions of time and space, was equally fascinating to the listener.

"I adore life," he said. "I find it the most entrancing plaything. It's a delightful game, and, as you know very well, the only conceivable way to play a game is to treat it extremely seriously. If you say to yourself, 'It's only a game,' you cease to take the slightest interest in it. You have to know that it's only a game, and behave as if it was the one object of existence. I should like it to go on for many years yet. But all the time one has to be living on the true plane as well, which is eternity and infinity. If you come to think of it, the one thing which the human mind cannot grasp is the finite, not the infinite, the temporary, not the eternal."

"That sounds rather paradoxical," said I.

"Only because you've made a habit of thinking about things that seem bounded and limited.

Look it in the face for a minute. Try to imagine finite Time and Space, and you find you can't.

Go back a million years, and multiply that million of years by another million, and you find that you can't conceive of a beginning. What happened before that beginning? Another beginning and another beginning? And before that? Look at it like that, and you find that the only solution comprehensible to you is the existence of an eternity, something that never began and will never end. It's the same about space. Project yourself to the farthest star, and what comes beyond that?

Emptiness? Go on through the emptiness, and you can't imagine it being finite and having an end. It must needs go on for ever: that's the only thing you can understand. There's no such thing as before or after, or beginning or end, and what a comfort that is! I should fidget myself to death if there wasn't the huge soft cushion of eternity to lean one's head against. Some people say – I believe I've heard you say it yourself – that the idea of eternity is so tiring; you feel that you want to stop. But that's because you are thinking of eternity in terms of Time, and mumbling in your brain, 'And after that, and after that?' Don't you grasp the idea that in eternity there isn't any 'after,' any more than there is any 'before'? It's all one. Eternity isn't a quantity: it's a quality."

Sometimes, when Anthony talks in this manner, I seem to get a glimpse of that which to his mind is so transparently clear and solidly real, at other times (not having a brain that readily envisages abstractions) I feel as though he was pushing me over a precipice, and my intellectual faculties grasp wildly at anything tangible or comprehensible. This was the case now, and I hastily interrupted.

"But there is a 'before' and 'after'," I said. "A few hours ago you gave us an admirable dinner, and after that – yes, after – we played bridge. And now you are going to explain things a little more clearly to me, and after that I shall go to bed—"

He laughed.

"You shall do exactly as you like," he said, "and you shan't be a slave to Time either tonight or tomorrow morning. We won't even mention an hour for breakfast, but you shall have it in eternity whenever you awake. And as I see it is not midnight yet, we'll slip the bonds of Time, and talk quite infinitely. I will stop the clock, if that will assist you in getting rid of your illusion, and then I'll tell you a story, which to my mind, shows how unreal so-called realities are; or, at any rate, how fallacious are our senses as judges of what is real and what is not."

"Something occult, something spookish?" I asked, pricking up my ears, for Anthony has the strangest clairvoyances and visions of things unseen by the normal eye.

"I suppose you might call some of it occult," he said, "though there's a certain amount of rather grim reality mixed up in it."

"Go on; excellent mixture," said I.

He threw a fresh log on the fire.

"It's a longish story," he said. "You may stop me as soon as you've had enough. But there will come a point for which I claim your consideration. You, who cling to your 'before' and 'after', has it ever occurred to you how difficult it is to say when an incident takes place? Say that a man commits some crime of violence, can we not, with a good deal of truth, say that he really commits that crime when he definitely plans and determines upon it, dwelling on it with gusto? The actual commission of it, I think we can reasonably argue, is the mere material sequel of his resolve: he is guilty of it when he makes that determination. When, therefore, in the term of 'before' and 'after', does the crime truly take place? There is also in my story a further point for your consideration. For it seems certain that the spirit of a man, after the death of his body, is obliged to re-enact such a crime, with a view, I suppose we may guess, to his remorse and his eventual redemption. Those who have second sight have seen such re-enactments. Perhaps he may have done his deed blindly in this life; but then his spirit re-commits it with its spiritual eyes open, and able to comprehend its enormity. So, shall we view the man's original determination and the material commission of his crime only as preludes to the real commission of it, when with eyes unsealed he does it and repents of it? . . . That all sounds very obscure when I speak in the abstract, but I think you will see what I mean, if you follow my tale. Comfortable? Got everything you want? Here goes, then."

He leaned back in his chair, concentrating his mind, and then spoke:

"The story that I am about to tell you," he said, "had its beginning a month ago, when you were away in Switzerland. It reached its conclusion, so I imagine, last night. I do not, at any rate, expect to experience any more of it. Well, a month ago I was returning late on a very wet night from dining out. There was not a taxi to be had, and I hurried through the pouring rain to the tube-station at Piccadilly Circus, and thought myself very lucky to catch the last train in this direction. The carriage into which I stepped was quite empty except for one other passenger, who sat next the door immediately opposite to me. I had never, to my knowledge, seen him before, but I found my attention vividly fixed on him, as if he somehow concerned me. He was a man of middle age, in dress-clothes, and his face wore an expression of intense thought, as if in his mind he was pondering some very significant matter, and his hand which was resting on his knee clenched and unclenched itself. Suddenly he looked up and stared me in the face, and I saw there suspicion and fear, as if I had surprised him in some secret deed.

At that moment we stopped at Dover Street, and the conductor threw open the doors, announced the station and added, 'Change here for Hyde Park Corner and Gloucester Road.' That was all right for me since it meant that the train would stop at Brompton Road, which was my destination. It was all right apparently, too, for my companion, for he certainly did not get out, and after a moment's stop, during which no one else got in, we went on. I saw him, I must insist, after the doors were closed and the train had started. But when I looked again, as we rattled on, I saw that there was no one there. I was quite alone in the carriage.

Now you may think that I had had one of those swift momentary dreams which flash in and out of the mind in the space of a second, but I did not believe it was so myself, for I felt that I had experienced some sort of premonition or clairvoyant vision. A man, the semblance of whom, astral body or whatever you may choose to call it, I had just seen, would sometime sit in that seat opposite to me, pondering and planning."

"But why?" I asked. "Why should it have been the astral body of a living man which you thought you had seen? Why not the ghost of a dead one?"

"Because of my own sensations. The sight of the spirit of someone dead, which has occurred to me two or three times in my life, has always been accompanied by a physical shrinking and fear, and by the sensation of cold and of loneliness. I believed, at any rate, that I had seen a phantom of the living, and that impression was confirmed, I might say proved, the next day. For I met the man himself. And the next night, as you shall hear, I met the phantom again. We will take them in order.

I was lunching, then, the next day with my neighbour Mrs. Stanley: there was a small party, and when I arrived we waited but for the final guest. He entered while I was talking to some friend, and presently at my elbow I heard Mrs. Stanley's voice – 'Let me introduce you to Sir Henry Payle,' she said.

I turned and saw my vis-à-vis of the night before. It was quite unmistakably he, and as we shook hands he looked at me I thought with vague and puzzled recognition.

'Haven't we met before, Mr. Carling?' he said. 'I seem to recollect—' For the moment I forgot the strange manner of his disappearance from the carriage, and thought that it had been the man himself whom I had seen last night.

'Surely, and not so long ago,' I said. 'For we sat opposite each other in the last tube-train from Piccadilly Circus yesterday night.' He still looked at me, frowning, puzzled, and shook his head.

'That can hardly be,' he said. 'I only came up from the country this morning.' Now this interested me profoundly, for the astral body, we are told, abides in some half-conscious region of the mind or spirit, and has recollections of what has happened to it, which it can convey only very vaguely and dimly to the conscious mind. All lunch-time I could see his eyes again and again directed to me with the same puzzled and perplexed air, and as I was taking my departure he came up to me.

'I shall recollect some day,' he said, 'where we met before, and I hope we may meet again. Was it not—?' and he stopped. 'No: it has gone from me,' he added."

The log that Anthony had thrown on the fire was burning bravely now, and its high-flickering flame lit up his face.

"Now, I don't know whether you believe in coincidences as chance things," he said, "but if you do, get rid of the notion. Or if you can't at once, call it a coincidence that that very night I again caught the last train on the tube going westwards. This time, so far from my being a solitary passenger, there was a considerable crowd waiting at Dover Street, where I entered, and just as the noise of the approaching train began to reverberate in the tunnel I caught sight of Sir Henry Payle standing near the opening from which the train would presently emerge, apart from the rest of the crowd. And I thought to myself how odd it was that I should have seen the phantom of him at this very hour last night and the man himself now, and I began walking towards him with the idea of saying, 'Anyhow, it is in the tube that we meet to-night.' . . . And then a terrible and awful thing happened. Just as the train emerged from the tunnel he jumped down on to the line in front of it, and the train swept along over him up the platform.

For a moment I was stricken with horror at the sight, and I remember covering my eyes against the dreadful tragedy. But then I perceived that, though it had taken place in full sight of those who were waiting, no one seemed to have seen it except myself. The driver, looking out from his window, had not applied his brakes, there was no jolt from the advancing train, no scream, no cry, and the rest of the passengers began boarding the train with perfect nonchalance.

I must have staggered, for I felt sick and faint with what I had seen, and some kindly soul put his arm round me and supported me into the train. He was a doctor, he told me, and asked if I was in pain, or what ailed me. I told him what I thought I had seen, and he assured me that no such accident had taken place.

It was clear then to my own mind that I had seen the second act, so to speak, in this psychical drama, and I pondered next morning over the problem as to what I should do. Already I had glanced at the morning paper, which, as I knew would be the case, contained no mention whatever of what I had seen. The thing had certainly not happened, but I knew in myself that it would happen. The flimsy veil of Time had been withdrawn from my eyes, and I had seen into what you would call the future. In terms of Time of course it was the future, but from my point of view the thing was just as much in the past as it was in the future. It existed, and waited only for its material fulfilment. The more I thought about it, the more I saw that I could do nothing."

I interrupted his narrative.

"You did nothing?" I exclaimed. "Surely you might have taken some step in order to try to avert the tragedy."

He shook his head.

"What step precisely?" he said. "Was I to go to Sir Henry and tell him that once more I had seen him in the tube in the act of committing suicide? Look at it like this. Either what I had seen was pure illusion, pure imagination, in which case it had no existence or significance at all, or it was actual and real, and essentially it had happened. Or take it, though not very logically, somewhere between the two. Say that the idea of suicide, for some cause of which I knew nothing, had occurred to him or would occur. Should I not, if that was the case, be doing a very dangerous thing, by making such a suggestion to him? Might not the fact of my telling him what I had seen put the idea into his mind, or, if it was already there, confirm it and strengthen it? 'It's a ticklish matter to play with souls,' as Browning says."

"But it seems so inhuman not to interfere in any way," said I, "not to make any attempt."

"What interference?" asked he. "What attempt?"

The human instinct in me still seemed to cry aloud at the thought of doing nothing to avert such a tragedy, but it seemed to be beating itself against something austere and inexorable. And cudgel my brain as I would, I could not combat the sense of what he had said. I had no answer for him, and he went on.

"You must recollect, too," he said, "that I believed then and believe now that the thing had happened. The cause of it, whatever that was, had begun to work, and the effect, in this material sphere, was inevitable. That is what I alluded to when, at the beginning of my story, I asked you to consider how difficult it was to say when an action took place. You still hold that this particular action, this suicide of Sir Henry, had not yet taken place, because he had not yet thrown himself under the advancing train. To me that seems a materialistic view. I hold that in all but the endorsement of it, so to speak, it had taken place. I fancy that Sir Henry, for instance, now free from the material dusks, knows that himself."

Exactly as he spoke there swept through the warm lit room a current of ice-cold air, ruffling my hair as it passed me, and making the wood flames on the hearth to dwindle and flare. I looked round to see if the door at my back had opened, but nothing stirred there, and over the closed window the curtains were fully drawn. As it reached Anthony, he sat up quickly in his chair and directed his glance this way and that about the room.

"Did you feel that?" he asked.

"Yes: a sudden draught," I said. "Ice-cold."

"Anything else?" he asked. "Any other sensation?"

I paused before I answered, for at the moment there occurred to me Anthony's differentiation of the effects produced on the beholder by a phantasm of the living and the apparition of the dead. It was the latter which accurately described my sensations now, a certain physical shrinking, a fear, a feeling of desolation. But yet I had seen nothing. "I felt rather creepy," I said.

As I spoke I drew my chair rather closer to the fire, and sent a swift and, I confess, a somewhat apprehensive scrutiny round the walls of the brightly lit room. I noticed at the same time that Anthony was peering across to the chimney-piece, on which, just below a sconce holding two electric lights, stood the clock which at the beginning of our talk he had offered to stop. The hands I noticed pointed to twenty-five minutes to one.

"But you saw nothing?" he asked.

"Nothing whatever," I said. "Why should I? What was there to see? Or did you—"

"I don't think so," he said.

Somehow this answer got on my nerves, for the queer feeling which had accompanied that cold current of air had not left me. If anything it had become more acute.

"But surely you know whether you saw anything or not?" I said.

"One can't always be certain," said he. "I say that I don't think I saw anything. But I'm not sure, either, whether the story I am telling you was quite concluded last night. I think there may be a further incident. If you prefer it, I will leave the rest of it, as far as I know it, unfinished till tomorrow morning, and you can go off to bed now."

His complete calmness and tranquillity reassured me.

"But why should I do that?" I asked.

Again he looked round on the bright walls.

"Well, I think something entered the room just now," he said, "and it may develop. If you don't like the notion, you had better go. Of course there's nothing to be alarmed at; whatever it is, it can't hurt us. But it is close on the hour when on two successive nights I saw what I have already told you, and an apparition usually occurs at the same time. Why that is so, I cannot say, but certainly it looks as if a spirit that is earth-bound is still subject to certain conventions, the conventions of time for instance. I think that personally I shall see something before long, but most likely you won't. You're not such a sufferer as I from these – these delusions—"

I was frightened and knew it, but I was also intensely interested, and some perverse pride wriggled within me at his last words. Why, so I asked myself, shouldn't I see whatever was to be seen? . . .

"I don't want to go in the least," I said. "I want to hear the rest of your story."

"Where was I, then? Ah, yes: you were wondering why I didn't do something after I saw the train move up to the platform, and I said that there was nothing to be done. If you think it over, I fancy you will agree with me . . . A couple of days passed, and on the third morning I saw in the paper that there had come fulfilment to my vision. Sir Henry Payle, who had been waiting on the platform of Dover Street Station for the last train to South Kensington, had thrown himself in front of it as it came into the station. The train had been pulled up in a couple of yards, but a wheel had passed over his chest, crushing it in and instantly killing him.

An inquest was held, and there emerged at it one of those dark stories which, on occasions like these, sometimes fall like a midnight shadow across a life that the world perhaps had thought prosperous. He had long been on bad terms with his wife, from whom he had lived apart, and it appeared that not long before this he had fallen desperately in love with another woman. The night before his suicide he had appeared very late at his wife's house, and had a long and angry scene with her in which he entreated her to divorce him, threatening otherwise to make her life a hell to her. She refused, and in an ungovernable fit of passion he attempted to strangle her. There was a struggle and the noise of it caused her manservant to come up, who succeeded in overmastering him. Lady Payle threatened to proceed against him for assault with the intention to murder her. With this hanging over his head, the next night, as I have already told you, he committed suicide."

He glanced at the clock again, and I saw that the hands now pointed to ten minutes to one.

The fire was beginning to burn low and the room surely was growing strangely cold.

"That's not quite all," said Anthony, again looking round. "Are you sure you wouldn't prefer to hear it tomorrow?"

The mixture of shame and pride and curiosity again prevailed.

"No: tell me the rest of it at once," I said.

Before speaking, he peered suddenly at some point behind my chair, shading his eyes. I followed his glance, and knew what he meant by saying that sometimes one could not be sure whether one saw something or not. But was that an outlined shadow that intervened between me and the wall? It was difficult to focus; I did not know whether it was near the wall or near my chair. It seemed to clear away, anyhow, as I looked more closely at it.

"You see nothing?" asked Anthony.

"No: I don't think so," said I. "And you?"

"I think I do," he said, and his eyes followed something which was invisible to mine. They came to rest between him and the chimney-piece. Looking steadily there, he spoke again.

"All this happened some weeks ago," he said, "when you were out in Switzerland, and since then, up till last night, I saw nothing further. But all the time I was expecting something further. I felt that, as far as I was concerned, it was not all over yet, and last night, with the intention of assisting any communication to come through to me from – from beyond, I went into the Dover Street tube-station at a few minutes before one o'clock, the hour at which both the assault and the suicide had taken place. The platform when I arrived on it was absolutely empty, or appeared to be so, but presently, just as I began to hear the roar of the approaching train, I saw there was the figure of a man standing some twenty yards from me, looking into the tunnel. He had not come down with me in the lift, and the moment before he had not been there. He began moving towards me, and then I saw who it was, and I felt a stir of wind icy-cold coming towards me as he approached. It was not the draught that heralds the approach of a train, for it came from the opposite direction. He came close up to me, and I saw there was recognition in his eyes. He raised his face towards me and I saw his lips move, but, perhaps in the increasing noise from the tunnel, I heard nothing come from them. He put out his hand, as if entreating me to do something, and with a cowardice for which I cannot forgive myself, I shrank from him, for I knew, by the sign that I have told you, that this was one from the dead, and my flesh quaked before him, drowning for the moment all pity and all desire to help him, if that was possible.

Certainly he had something which he wanted of me, but I recoiled from him. And by now the train was emerging from the tunnel, and next moment, with a dreadful gesture of despair, he threw himself in front of it."

As he finished speaking he got up quickly from his chair, still looking fixedly in front of him.

I saw his pupils dilate, and his mouth worked.

"It is coming," he said. "I am to be given a chance of atoning for my cowardice. There is nothing to be afraid of: I must remember that myself."

As he spoke there came from the panelling above the chimney-piece one loud shattering crack, and the cold wind again circled about my head. I found myself shrinking back in my chair with my hands held in front of me as instinctively I screened myself against something which I knew was there but which I could not see. Every sense told me that there was a presence in the room other than mine and Anthony's, and the horror of it was that I could not see it. Any vision, however terrible, would, I felt, be more tolerable than this clear certain knowledge that close to me was this invisible thing. And yet what horror might not be disclosed of the face of the dead and the crushed chest . . . But all I could see, as I shuddered in this cold wind, was the familiar walls of the room, and Anthony standing in front of me stiff and firm, making, as I knew, a call on his courage. His eyes were focused on something quite close to him, and some semblance of a smile quivered on his mouth. And then he spoke again.

"Yes, I know you," he said. "And you want something of me. Tell me, then, what it is."

There was absolute silence, but what was silence to my ears could not have been so to his, for once or twice he nodded, and once he said, "Yes: I see. I will do it." And with the knowledge that, even as there was someone here whom I could not see, so there was speech going on which I could not hear, this terror of the dead and of the unknown rose in me with the sense of powerlessness to move that accompanies nightmare. I could not stir, I could not speak. I could only strain my ears for the inaudible and my eyes for the unseen, while the cold wind from the very valley of the shadow of death streamed over me. It was not that the presence of death itself was terrible; it was that from its tranquillity and serene keeping there had been driven some unquiet soul unable to rest in peace for whatever ultimate awakening rouses the countless generations of those who have passed away, driven, no less, from whatever activities are theirs, back into the material world from which it should have been delivered. Never, until the gulf between the living and the dead was thus bridged, had it seemed so immense and so unnatural. It is possible that the dead may have communication with the living, and it was not that exactly that so terrified me, for such communication, as we know it, comes voluntarily from them. But here was something icy-cold and crime-laden, that was chased back from the peace that would not pacify it.

And then, most horrible of all, there came a change in these unseen conditions. Anthony was silent now, and from looking straight and fixedly in front of him, he began to glance sideways to where I sat and back again, and with that I felt that the unseen presence had turned its attention from him to me. And now, too, gradually and by awful degrees I began to see . . .

There came an outline of shadow across the chimney-piece and the panels above it. It took shape: it fashioned itself into the outline of a man. Within the shape of the shadow details began to form themselves, and I saw wavering in the air, like something concealed by haze, the semblance of a face, stricken and tragic, and burdened with such a weight of woe as no human face had ever worn. Next, the shoulders outlined themselves, and a stain livid and red spread out below them, and suddenly the vision leaped into clearness. There he stood, the chest crushed in and drowned in the red stain, from which broken ribs, like the bones of a wrecked ship, protruded. The mournful, terrible eyes were fixed on me, and it was from them, so I knew, that the bitter wind proceeded . . .

Then, quick as the switching off of a lamp, the spectre vanished, and the bitter wind was still, and opposite to me stood Anthony, in a quiet, bright-lit room. There was no sense of an unseen presence any more; he and I were then alone, with an interrupted conversation still dangling between us in the warm air. I came round to that, as one comes round after an anaesthetic. It all swam into sight again, unreal at first, and gradually assuming the texture of actuality.

"You were talking to somebody, not to me," I said. "Who was it? What was it?"

He passed the back of his hand over his forehead, which glistened in the light.

"A soul in hell," he said.

Now it is hard ever to recall mere physical sensations, when they have passed. If you have been cold and are warmed, it is difficult to remember what cold was like: if you have been hot and have got cool, it is difficult to realise what the oppression of heat really meant. Just so, with the passing of that presence, I found myself unable to recapture the sense of the terror with which, a few moments ago only, it had invaded and inspired me.

"A soul in hell?" I said. "What are you talking about?"

He moved about the room for a minute or so, and then came and sat on the arm of my chair.

"I don't know what you saw," he said, "or what you felt, but there has never in all my life happened to me anything more real than what these last few minutes have brought. I have talked to a soul in the hell of remorse, which is the only possible hell. He knew, from what happened last night, that he could perhaps establish communication through me with the world he had quitted, and he sought me and found me. I am charged with a mission to a woman I have never seen, a message from the contrite . . . You can guess who it is . . ."

He got up with a sudden briskness.

"Let's verify it anyhow," he said. "He gave me the street and the number. Ah, there's the telephone book! Would it be a coincidence merely if I found that at No. 20 in Chasemore Street, South Kensington, there lived a Lady Payle?"

He turned over the leaves of the bulky volume.

"Yes, that's right," he said.

BAD TIMING

Molly Brown

Molly Brown has been an armed guard and a stand-up comedienne, in addition to her writing exploits. "Bad Timing" was Brown's first published story. It won the BSFA (British Science Fiction Association) Award for best short story of 1991, and was in feature film development for several years with Hollywood's Bel Air Entertainment. It was first published in *Interzone*.

"Time travel is an inexact science. And its study is fraught with paradoxes." Samuel Colson, b. 2301 d. 2197.

Alan rushed through the archway without even glancing at the inscription across the top. It was Monday morning and he was late again. He often thought about the idea that time was a point in space, and he didn't like it. That meant that at this particular point in space it was always Monday morning and he was always late for a job he hated. And it always had been. And it always would be. Unless somebody tampered with it, which was strictly forbidden.

"Oh my Holy Matrix," Joe Twofingers exclaimed as Alan raced past him to register his palmprint before losing an extra thirty minutes pay. "You wouldn't believe what I found in the fiction section!"

Alan slapped down his hand. The recorder's metallic voice responded with, "Employee number 057, Archives Department, Alan Strong. Thirty minutes and seven point two seconds late. One hour's credit deducted."

Alan shrugged and turned back towards Joe. "Since I'm not getting paid, I guess I'll put my feet up and have a cup of liquid caffeine. So tell me what you found."

"Well, I was tidying up the files – fiction section is a mess as you know – and I came across this magazine. And I thought, 'what's *this* doing here?' It's something from the twentieth century called *Woman's Secrets*, and it's all knitting patterns, recipes, and gooey little romance stories: 'He grabbed her roughly, bruising her soft pale skin, and pulled her to his rock hard chest' and so on. I figured it was in there by mistake and nearly threw it out. But then I saw this story called 'The Love That Conquered Time' and I realised that must be what they're keeping it for. So I had a look at it, and it was . . ." He made a face and stuck a finger down his throat. "But I really think you ought to read it."

"Why?"

"Because you're in it."

"You're a funny guy, Joe. You almost had me going for a minute."

"I'm serious! Have a look at the drebbing thing. It's by some woman called

Cecily Walker, it's in that funny old vernacular they used to use, and it's positively dire. But the guy in the story is definitely you."

Alan didn't believe him for a minute. Joe was a joker, and always had been. Alan would never forget the time Joe laced his drink with a combination aphrodisiac-hallucinogen at a party and he'd made a total fool of himself with the section leader's overcoat. He closed his eyes and shuddered as Joe handed him the magazine.

Like all the early relics made of paper, the magazine had been dipped in preservative and the individual pages coated with a clear protective covering which gave them a horrible chemical smell and a tendency to stick together. After a little difficulty, Alan found the page he wanted. He rolled his eyes at the painted illustration of a couple locked in a passionate but chaste embrace, and dutifully began to read.

It was all about a beautiful but lonely and unfulfilled woman who still lives in the house where she was born. One day there is a knock at the door, and she opens it to a mysterious stranger: tall, handsome, and extremely charismatic.

Alan chuckled to himself.

A few paragraphs later, over a candle-lit dinner, the man tells the woman that he comes from the future, where time travel has become a reality, and he works at the Colson Time Studies Institute in the Department of Archives.

Alan stopped laughing.

The man tells her that only certain people are allowed to time travel, and they are not allowed to interfere in any way, only observe. He confesses that he is not a qualified traveller – he broke into the lab one night and stole a machine. The woman asks him why and he tells her, "You're the only reason, Claudia. I did it for you. I read a story that you wrote and I knew it was about me and that it was about you. I searched in the Archives and I found your picture and then I knew that I loved you and that I had always loved you and that I always would."

"But I never wrote a story, Alan."

"You will, Claudia. You will."

The Alan in the story goes on to describe the Project, and the Archives, in detail. The woman asks him how people live in the twenty-fourth century, and he tells her about the gadgets in his apartment.

The hairs at the back of Alan's neck rose at the mention of his Neuro-Pleasatron. He'd never told anybody that he'd bought one, not even Joe.

After that, there's a lot of grabbing and pulling to his rock hard chest, melting sighs and kisses, and finally a wedding and a "happily ever after" existing at one point in space where it always has and always will.

Alan turned the magazine over and looked at the date on the cover. March 14, 1973.

He wiped the sweat off his forehead and shook himself. He looked up and saw that Joe was standing over him.

"You wouldn't really do that, would you," Joe said. "Because you know I'd have to stop you."

Cecily Walker stood in front of her bedroom mirror and turned from right to left. She rolled the waistband over one more time, making sure both sides were even. Great; the skirt looked like a real mini. Now all she had to do was get out of the house without her mother seeing her.

She was in the record shop wondering if she really should spend her whole allowance on the new Monkees album, but she really liked Peter Tork, he was so cute, when Tommy Johnson walked in with Roger Hanley. "Hey, Cess-pit! Whaddya do, lose the bottom half of your dress?"

The boys at her school were just so creepy. She left the shop and turned down the main road, heading toward her friend Candy's house. She never noticed the tall blonde man that stood across the street, or heard him call her name.

When Joe went on his lunch break, Alan turned to the wall above his desk and said, "File required: Authors, fiction, twentieth century, initial 'W'."

"Checking," the wall said. "File located."

"Biography required: Walker, Cecily."

"Checking. Biography located. Display? Yes or no."

"Yes."

A section of wall the size of a small television screen lit up at eye-level, directly in front of Alan. He leaned forward and read: Walker, Cecily. b. Danville, Illinois, U.S.A. 1948 d. 2037. Published works: "The Love That Conquered Time", March, 1973. Accuracy rating: fair.

"Any other published works?"

"Checking. None found."

Alan looked down at the magazine in his lap.

"I don't understand," Claudia said, looking pleadingly into his deep blue eyes. Eyes the colour of the sea on a cloudless morning, and eyes that contained an ocean's depth of feeling for her, and her alone. "How is it possible to travel through time?"

"I'll try to make this simple," he told her, pulling her close. She took a deep breath, inhaling his manly aroma, and rested her head on his shoulder with a sigh. "Imagine that the universe is like a string. And every point on that string is a moment in space and time. But instead of stretching out in a straight line, it's all coiled and tangled and it overlaps in layers. Then all you have to do is move from point to point."

Alan wrinkled his forehead in consternation. "File?"

"Yes. Waiting."

"Information required: further data on Walker, Cecily. Education, family background."

"Checking. Found. Display? Yes or . . ."

"Yes!"

Walker, Cecily. Education: Graduate Lincoln High, Danville, 1967. Family background: Father Walker, Matthew. Mechanic, automobile. d. 1969. Mother no data.

Alan shook his head. Minimal education, no scientific background. How could she know so much? "Information required: photographic likeness of subject. If available, display."

He blinked and there she was, smiling at him across his desk. She was oddly dressed, in a multi-coloured tee-shirt that ended above her waist and dark blue trousers that were cut so low they exposed her navel and seemed to balloon out below her knees into giant flaps of loose-hanging material. But she had long dark hair that fell across her shoulders and down to her waist, crimson lips and the most incredible eyes he had ever seen – huge and green. She was beautiful. He looked at the caption: Walker, Cecily. Author: Fiction related to time travel theory. Photographic likeness circa 1970.

"File," he said, "Further data required: personal details, i.e. marriage. Display."

Walker, Cecily m. Strong, Alan.

"Date?"

No data.

"Biographical details of husband, Strong, Alan?"

None found.

"Redisplay photographic likeness. Enlarge." He stared at the wall for several minutes. "Print," he said.

Only half a block to go, the woman thought, struggling with two bags of groceries. The sun was high in the sky and the smell of Mrs. Henderson's roses, three doors down, filled the air with a lovely perfume. But she wasn't in the mood to appreciate it. All the sun made her feel was hot, and all the smell of flowers made her feel was ill. It had been a difficult pregnancy, but thank goodness it was nearly over now.

She wondered who the man was, standing on her front porch. He might be the new mechanic at her husband's garage, judging by his orange cover-alls. Nice-looking, she thought, wishing that she didn't look like there was a bowling ball underneath her dress.

"Excuse me," the man said, reaching out to help her with her bags. "I'm looking for Cecily Walker."

"My name's Walker," the woman told him. "But I don't know any Cecily."

"Cecily," she repeated when the man had gone. What a pretty name.

Alan decided to work late that night. Joe left at the usual time and told him he'd see him tomorrow.

"Yeah, tomorrow," Alan said.

He waited until Joe was gone, and then he took the printed photo of Cecily Walker out of his desk drawer and sat for a long time, staring at it. What did he know about this woman? Only that she'd written one published story, badly, and that she was the most gorgeous creature he had ever seen. Of course, what he was feeling was ridiculous. She'd been dead more than three hundred years.

But there were ways of getting around that.

Alan couldn't believe what he was actually considering. It was lunacy. He'd be caught, and he'd lose his job. But then he realised that he could never have read about it if he hadn't already done it and got away with it. He decided to have another look at the story.

It wasn't there. Under Fiction: Paper Relics: 20th Century, sub-section Magazines, American, there was shelf after shelf full of *Amazing Stories,*

Astounding, Analog, Weird Tales and *Isaac Asimov's Science Fiction Magazine,* but not one single copy of *Woman's Secrets.*

Well, he thought, if the magazine isn't there, I guess I never made it after all. Maybe it's better that way. Then he thought, but if I never made it, how can I be looking for the story? I shouldn't even know about it. And then he had another thought.

"File," he said. "Information required: magazines on loan."

"Display?"

"No, just tell me."

"*Woman's Secrets*, date 1973. *Astounding*, date . . ."

"Skip the rest. Who's got *Woman's Secrets*?"

"Checking. Signed out to Project Control through Joe Twofingers."

Project Control was on to him! If he didn't act quickly, it would be too late.

It was amazingly easy to get into the lab. He just walked in. The machines were all lined up against one wall, and there was no one around to stop him. He walked up to the nearest machine and sat down on it. The earliest model developed by Samuel Colson had looked like an English telephone box (he'd been a big *Doctor Who* fan), but it was hardly inconspicuous and extremely heavy, so refinements were made until the latest models were lightweight, collapsible, and made to look exactly like (and double up as) a folding bicycle. The control board was hidden from general view, inside a wicker basket.

None of the instruments were labelled. Alan tentatively pushed one button. Nothing happened. He pushed another. Still nothing.

He jumped off and looked for an instruction book. There had to be one somewhere. He was ransacking a desk when the door opened.

"I thought I'd find you here, Alan."

"Joe! I . . . uh . . . was just . . ."

"I know what you're doing, and I can't let you go through with it. It's against every rule of the Institute and you know it. If you interfere with the past, who knows what harm you might do?"

"But Joe, you know me. I wouldn't do any harm. I won't do anything to affect history, I swear it. I just want to see her, that's all. Besides, it's already happened, or you couldn't have read that magazine. And that's another thing! You're the one who showed it to me! I never would have known about her if it hadn't been for you. So if I'm going now, it's down to you."

"Alan, I'm sorry, but my job is on the line here, too, you know. So don't give me any trouble and come along quietly."

Joe moved towards him, holding a pair of handcuffs. Attempted theft of Institute property was a felony punishable by five years' imprisonment without pay. Alan picked up the nearest bike and brought it down over the top of Joe's head. The machine lay in pieces and Joe lay unconscious. Alan bent down and felt his pulse. He would be okay. "Sorry, Joe. I had to do it. File!"

"Yes."

"Information required: instruction manual for usage of . . ." he checked the number on the handlebars, "Colson Model 44B Time Traveller."

"Checking. Found. Display?"

"No. Just print. And fast."

The printer was only on page five when Alan heard running footsteps. Five pages would have to do.

Dear Cher, My name is Cecily Walker and all my friends tell me I look just like you. Well, a little bit. Anyway, the reason that I'm writing to you is this: I'm starting my senior year in high school, and I've never had a steady boyfriend. I've gone out with a couple of boys, but they only want one thing, and I guess you know what that is. I keep thinking there's gotta be somebody out there who's the right one for me, but I just haven't met him. Was it love at first sight for you and Sonny?

Alan sat on a London park bench with his printout and tried to figure out what he'd done wrong. Under Location: Setting, it just said "See page 29." Great, he thought. And he had no idea what year it was. Every time he tried to ask someone, they'd give him a funny look and walk away in a hurry. He folded up the bike and took a walk. It wasn't long before he found a news-stand and saw the date: July 19, 1998. At least he had the right century.

Back in the park, he sat astride the machine with the printout in one hand, frowning and wondering what might happen if he twisted a particular dial from right to left.

"Can't get your bike to start, mate?" someone shouted from nearby. "Just click your heels three times and think of home."

"Thanks, I'll try that," Alan shouted back. Then he vanished.

"I am a pirate from yonder ship," the man with the eye patch told her, "and well used to treasure. But I tell thee, lass, I've never seen the like of you."

Cecily groaned and ripped the page in half. She bit her lip and started again.

"I have travelled many galaxies, Madeleine," the alien bleeped. "But you are a life-form beyond compare."

"No, don't. Please don't," Madeleine pleaded as the alien reached out to pull her towards its rock hard chest.

Her mother appeared in the doorway. "Whatcha doin' hon?"

She dropped the pen and flipped the writing pad face down. "My homework."

The next thing Alan knew he was in the middle of a cornfield. He hitched a lift with a truck driver who asked a lot of questions, ranging from "You work in a gas station, do you?" to "What are you, foreign or something?" and "What do you call that thing?" On being told "that thing" was a folding bicycle, the man muttered something about whatever would they think of next, and now his kid would be wanting one.

There were several Walker's listed in the Danville phone book. When he finally found the right house, Cecily was in the middle of her third birthday party.

He pedalled around a corner, checked his printout, and set the controls on "Fast Forward". He folded the machine and hid it behind a bush before walking back to the house. It was big and painted green, just like in the story. There was an apple tree in the garden, just like in the story. The porch swing moved ever so slightly, rocked by an early summer breeze. He could hear crickets chirping and birds singing. Everything was just the way it had been in the story, so he walked up the path, nervously clearing his throat and pushing back a stray lock of hair, just the way Cecily Walker had described him in *Woman's Secrets*, before finally taking a deep breath and knocking on the door. There was movement inside the house. The clack of high-heeled shoes across a wooden floor, the rustle of a cotton dress.

"Yes?"

Alan stared at her, open-mouthed. "You've cut your hair," he told her.

"What?"

"Your hair. It used to hang down to your waist, now it's up to your shoulders."

"Do I know you?"

"You will," he told her. He'd said that in the story.

She was supposed to take one look at him and realise with a fluttering heart that this was the man she'd dreamed of all her life. Instead, she looked at his orange jumpsuit and slapped her hand to her forehead in enlightenment. "You're from the garage! Of course, Mack said he'd be sending the new guy." She looked past him into the street. "So where's your tow truck?"

"My what?" There was nothing in "The Love That Conquered Time" about a tow truck. The woman stared at him, looking confused. Alan stared back, equally confused. He started to wonder if he'd made a mistake. But then he saw those eyes, bigger and greener than he'd ever thought possible. "Matrix," he said out loud.

"What?"

"I'm sorry. It's just that meeting you is so bullasic."

"Mister, I don't understand one word you're saying." Cecily knew she should tell the man to go away. He was obviously deranged; she should call the police. But something held her back, a flicker of recognition, the dim stirrings of a memory. Where had she seen this man before?

"I'm sorry," Alan said again. "My American isn't very good. I come from English-speaking Europe, you see."

"English-speaking Europe?" Cecily repeated. "You mean England?"

"Not exactly. Can I come inside? I'll explain everything."

She let him come in after warning him that her neighbours would come running in with shotguns if they heard her scream, and that she had a black belt in Kung Fu. Alan nodded and followed her inside, wondering where Kung Fu was, and why she'd left her belt there.

He was ushered into the living room and told to have a seat. He sat down on the red velveteen-upholstered sofa and stared in awe at such historical artefacts as a black and white television with rabbit-ear antennae, floral-printed wall-paper, a phone you had to dial, and shelf after shelf of unpreserved books. She picked up a wooden chair and carried it to the far side of the room before sitting down. "Okay," she said. "Talk."

Alan felt it would have been better to talk over a candle-lit dinner in a restaurant, like they did in the story, but he went ahead and told her everything, quoting parts of the story verbatim, such as the passage where she described him as the perfect lover she'd been longing for all her life.

When he was finished, she managed a frozen smile. "So you've come all the way from the future just to visit little ole me. Isn't that nice."

Oh Matrix, Alan thought. She's humouring me. She's convinced I'm insane and probably dangerous as well. "I know this must sound crazy to you," he said.

"Not at all," she told him, gripping the arms of her chair. He could see the blood draining out of her fingers.

"Please don't be afraid. I'd never harm you." He sighed and put a hand to his forehead. "It was all so different in the story."

"But I never wrote any story. Well, I started one once, but I never got beyond the second page."

"But you will. You see, it doesn't get published until 1973."

"You do know this is 1979, don't you?"

"WHAT?"

"Looks like your timing's off," she said. She watched him sink his head into his hands with an exaggerated groan. She rested her chin on one hand and regarded him silently. He didn't seem so frightening now. Crazy, yes, but not frightening. She might even find him quite attractive, if only things were different. He looked up at her and smiled. It was a crooked, little boy's smile that made his eyes sparkle. For a moment, she almost let herself imagine waking up to that smile . . . She pulled herself up in her chair, her back rigid.

"Look," he said. "So I'm a few years behind schedule. The main thing is I found you. And so what if the story comes out a bit later, it's nothing we can't handle. It's only a minor problem. A little case of bad timing."

"Excuse me," Cecily said. "But I think that in this case, timing is everything. If any of this made the least bit of sense, which it doesn't, you would've turned up before now. You said yourself the story was published in 1973 – if it was based on fact, you'd need to arrive here much earlier."

"I did get here earlier, but I was too early."

Cecily's eyes widened involuntarily. "What do you mean?"

"I mean I was here before. I met you. I spoke to you."

"When?"

"You wouldn't remember. You were three years old, and your parents threw a party for you out in the garden. Of course I realised my mistake instantly, but I bluffed it out by telling your mother that I'd just dropped by to apologise because my kid was sick and couldn't come – it was a pretty safe bet that someone wouldn't have shown – and she said, 'Oh you must be little Sammy's father' and asked me in. I was going to leave immediately, but your father handed me a beer and started talking about something called baseball. Of course I didn't have a present for you . . ."

"But you gave me a rose and told my mother to press it into a book so that I'd have it forever."

"You remember."

"Wait there. Don't move." She leapt from her chair and ran upstairs. There was a lot of noise from above – paper rattling, doors opening and closing, things being thrown about. She returned clutching several books to her chest, her face flushed and streaked with dust. She flopped down on the floor and spread them out in front of her. When Alan got up to join her, she told him to stay where he was or she'd scream. He sat back down.

She opened the first book, and then Alan saw that they weren't books at all; they were photo albums. He watched in silence as she flipped through the pages and then tossed it aside. She tossed three of them away before she found what she was looking for. She stared open-mouthed at the brittle yellow page and then she looked up at Alan. "I don't understand this," she said, turning her eyes back to the album and a faded black and white photograph stuck to the paper with thick, flaking paste. Someone had written in ink across the top: Cecily's 3rd birthday, August 2nd, 1951. There was her father, who'd been dead for ten years, young and smiling, holding out a bottle to another young man, tall and blonde and dressed like a gas station attendant. "I don't understand this at all." She pushed the album across the floor towards Alan. "You haven't changed one bit. You're even wearing the same clothes."

"Did you keep the rose?"

She walked over to a wooden cabinet and pulled out a slim hardback with the title, "*My First Reader*". She opened it and showed him the dried, flattened flower. "You're telling me the truth, aren't you?" she said. "This is all true. You risked everything to find me because we were meant to be together, and nothing, not even time itself, could keep us apart."

Alan nodded. There was a speech just like that in "The Love That Conquered Time".

"Bastard," she said.

Alan jumped. He didn't remember that part. "Pardon me?"

"Bastard," she said again. "You bastard!"

"I . . . I don't understand."

She got up and started to pace the room. "So you're the one, huh? You're 'Mister Right', Mister Happily Ever After, caring, compassionate and great in bed. And you decide to turn up now. Well, isn't that just great."

"Is something the matter?" Alan asked her.

"Is something the matter?" she repeated. "He asks me if something's the matter! I'll tell you what's the matter. I got married four weeks ago, you son of a bitch!"

"You're married?"

"That's what I said, isn't it?"

"But you can't be married. We were supposed to find perfect happiness together at a particular point in space that has always existed and always will. This ruins everything."

"All those years . . . all those years. I went through hell in high school, you know. I was the only girl in my class who didn't have a date for the prom. So where were you then, huh? While I was sitting alone at home, crying my goddamn eyes out? How about all those Saturday nights I spent washing my hair? And even worse, those nights I worked at Hastings' Bar serving drinks to salesmen pretending they don't have wives. Why couldn't you have been around then, when I needed you?"

"Well, I've only got the first five pages of the manual . . ." He walked over to her and put his hands on her shoulders. She didn't move away. He gently pulled her closer to him. She didn't resist. "Look," he said, "I'm sorry. I'm a real zarkhead. I've made a mess of everything. You're happily married, you never wrote the story . . . I'll just go back where I came from, and none of this will have ever happened."

"Who said I was happy?"

"But you just got married."

She pushed him away. "I got married because I'm thirty years old and figured I'd never have another chance. People do that, you know. They reach a certain age and they figure it's now or never . . . Damn you! If only you'd come when you were supposed to!"

"You're thirty? Matrix, in half an hour you've gone from a toddler to someone older than me." He saw the expression on her face, and mumbled an apology.

"Look," she said. "You're gonna have to go. My husband'll be back any minute."

"I know I have to leave. But the trouble is, that drebbing story was true! I took one look at your photo, and I knew that I loved you and I always had. Always. That's the way time works, you see. And even if this whole thing vanishes as the result of some paradox, I swear to you I won't forget. Somewhere there's a point in space that belongs to us. I know it." He turned to go. "Good-bye Cecily."

"Alan, wait! That point in space – I want to go there. Isn't there anything we can do? I mean, you've got a time machine, after all."

What an idiot, he thought. The solution's been staring me in the face and I've been too blind to see it. "The machine!" He ran down the front porch steps and turned around to see her standing in the doorway. "I'll see you later," he told her. He knew it was a ridiculous thing to say the minute he'd said it. What he meant was, "I'll see you earlier."

Five men sat together inside a tent made of animal hide. The land of their fathers was under threat, and they met in council to discuss the problem. The one called Swiftly Running Stream advocated war, but Foot Of The Crow was more cautious. "The paleface is too great in number, and his weapons give him an unfair advantage." Flying Bird suggested that they smoke before speaking further.

Black Elk took the pipe into his mouth. He closed his eyes for a moment and declared that the Great Spirit would give them a sign if they were meant to go to war. As soon as he said the word, "war", a paleface materialised among them. They all saw him. The white man's body was covered in a strange bright garment such as they had never seen, and he rode a fleshless horse with silver bones. The vision vanished as suddenly as it had appeared, leaving them with this message to ponder: *Oops*.

There was no one home, so he waited on the porch. It was a beautiful day, with a gentle breeze that carried the scent of roses: certainly better than that smoke-filled teepee.

A woman appeared in the distance. He wondered if that was her. But then he saw that it couldn't be, the woman's walk was strange and her body was misshapen. She's pregnant, he realised. It was a common thing in the days of overpopulation, but he couldn't remember the last time he'd seen a pregnant woman back home – it must have been years. She looked at him questioningly as she waddled up the steps balancing two paper bags. Alan thought the woman looked familiar; he knew that face. He reached out to help her.

"Excuse me," he said. "I'm looking for Cecily Walker."

"My name's Walker," the woman told him. "But I don't know any Cecily."

Matrix, what a moron, Alan thought, wanting to kick himself. Of course he knew the woman; it was Cecily's mother, and if she was pregnant, it had to be 1948. "My mistake," he told her. "It's been a long day."

The smell of roses had vanished, along with the leaves on the trees. There was snow on the ground and a strong northeasterly wind. Alan set the thermostat on his jumpsuit accordingly and jumped off the bike.

"So it's you again," Cecily said ironically. "Another case of perfect timing." She was twenty pounds heavier and there were lines around her mouth and her eyes. She wore a heavy wool cardigan sweater over an oversized tee-shirt, jeans, and a pair of fuzzy slippers. She looked him up and down. "You don't age at all, do you?"

"Please can I come in? It's freezing."

"Yeah, yeah. Come in. You like a cup of coffee?"

"You mean liquid caffeine? That'd be great."

He followed her into the living room and his mouth dropped open. The red sofa was gone, replaced by something that looked like a giant banana. The television was four times bigger and had lost the rabbit-ears. The floral wallpaper had been replaced by plain white walls not very different from those of his apartment. "Sit," she told him. She left the room for a moment and returned with two mugs, one of which she slammed down in front of him, causing a miniature brown tidal wave to splash across his legs.

"Cecily, are you upset about something?"

"That's a good one! He comes back after fifteen years and asks me if I'm upset."

"Fifteen years!" Alan sputtered.

"That's right. It's 1994, you bozo."

"Oh darling, and you've been waiting all this time . . ."

"Like hell I have," she interrupted. "When I met you, back in 1979, I realised that I couldn't stay in that sham of a marriage for another minute. So I must have set some kind of a record for quickie marriage and divorce, by Danville standards, anyway. So I was a thirty-year-old divorcee whose marriage had fallen apart in less than two months, and I was back to washing my hair alone on Saturday nights. And people talked. Lord, how they talked. But I didn't care, because I'd finally met my soul-mate and everything was going to be all right. He told me he'd fix it. He'd be back. So I waited. I waited for a year. Then I waited two years. Then I waited three. After ten, I got tired of waiting. And if you think I'm going through another divorce, you're crazy."

"You mean you're married again?"

"What else was I supposed to do? A man wants you when you're forty, you jump at it. As far as I knew, you were gone forever."

"I've never been away, Cecily. I've been here all along, but never at the right time. It's that drebbing machine; I can't figure out the controls."

"Maybe Arnie can have a look at it when he gets in, he's pretty good at that sort of thing – what am I saying?"

"Tell me, did you ever write the story?"

"What's to write about? Anyway, what difference does it make? *Woman's Secrets* went bankrupt years ago."

"Matrix! If you never wrote the story, then I shouldn't even know about you. So how can I be here? Dammit, it's a paradox. And I wasn't supposed to cause any of those. Plus, I think I may have started an Indian war. Have you noticed any change in local history?"

"Huh?"

"Never mind. Look, I have an idea. When exactly did you get divorced?"

"I don't know, late '79. October, November, something like that."

"All right, that's what I'll aim for. November, 1979. Be waiting for me."

"How?"

"Good point. Okay, just take my word for it, you and me are going to be sitting in this room right here, right now, with one big difference: we'll have been married for fifteen years, okay?"

"But what about Arnie?"

"Arnie won't know the difference. You'll never have married him in the first place." He kissed her on the cheek. "I'll be back in a minute. Well, in 1979. You know what I mean." He headed for the door.

"Hold on," she said. "You're like the guy who goes out for a pack of cigarettes and doesn't come back for thirty years."

"What guy?"

"Never mind. I wanna make sure you don't turn up anywhere else. Bring the machine in here."

"Is that it?" she said one minute later.

"That's it."

"But it looks like a goddamn bicycle."

"Where do you want me to put it?"

She led him upstairs. "Here," she said. Alan unfolded the bike next to the bed. "I don't want you getting away from me next time," she told him.

"I don't have to get away from you now."

"You do. I'm married and I'm at least fifteen years older than you."

"Your age doesn't matter to me," Alan told her. "When I first fell in love with you, you'd been dead three hundred years."

"You really know how to flatter a girl, don't you? Anyway, don't aim for '79. I don't understand paradoxes, but I know I don't like them. If we're ever gonna get this thing straightened out, you must arrive before 1973, when the story is meant to be published. Try for '71 or '72. Now that I think about it, those were a strange couple of years for me. Nothing seemed real to me then. Nothing seemed worth bothering about, nothing mattered; I always felt like I was waiting for something. Day after day I waited, though I never knew what for."

She stepped back and watched him slowly turn a dial until he vanished. Then she remembered something.

How could she ever have forgotten such a thing? She was eleven and she was combing her hair in front of her bedroom mirror. She screamed. When both her parents burst into the room and demanded to know what was wrong, she told them she'd seen a man on a bicycle. They nearly sent her to a child psychiatrist.

Damn that Alan, she thought. He's screwed up again.

The same room, different decor, different time of day. Alan blinked several times; his eyes had difficulty adjusting to the darkness. He could barely make out the shape on the bed, but he could see all he needed to. The shape was alone, and it was adult size. He leaned close to her ear. "Cecily," he whispered. "It's me." He touched her shoulder and shook her slightly. He felt for a pulse.

He switched on the bedside lamp. He gazed down at a withered face framed by silver hair, and sighed. "Sorry, love," he said. He covered her head with a sheet, and sighed again.

He sat down on the bike and unfolded the printout. He'd get it right eventually.

IF EVER I SHOULD LEAVE YOU

Pamela Sargent

Pamela Sargent is an American writer who has won the Nebula and Locus awards, been a finalist for the Hugo Award, Theodore Sturgeon Award, and Sidewise Award, and was honored in 2012 with the Pilgrim Award, given for lifetime achievement in science fiction and fantasy scholarship by the Science Fiction Research Association. She has written many novels including *Cloned Lives*, *Eye of the Comet*, *Homesmind*, *Alien Child*, and *The Shore of Women*. Her short fiction has appeared in *The Magazine of Fantasy & Science Fiction*, *Asimov's Science Fiction Magazine*, *New Worlds*, *Rod Serling's The Twilight Zone Magazine*, *Universe*, and *Nature*, among others. "If Ever I Should Leave You" was first published in a much different form in *Worlds of If*, February 1974, and in this preferred text in *Afterlives*, edited by Pamela Sargent and Ian Watson, Vintage, 1986.

When Yuri walked away from the Time Station for the last time, his face was pale marble, his body only bones barely held together by skin and the weak muscles he had left. I hurried to him and grasped his arm, oblivious to the people who passed us in the street. He resisted my touch at first, embarrassed in front of the others; then he gave in and leaned against me as we began to walk home.

I knew that he was too weak to go to the Time Station again. His body, resting against mine, seemed almost weightless. I guided him through the park toward our home. Halfway there, he tugged at my arm and we rested against one of the crystalline trees surrounding the small lake in the center of the park.

Yuri had aged rapidly in the last six months, transformed from a young man into an aged creature hardly able to walk by himself. I had expected it. One cannot hold off old age indefinitely, even now. But I could not accept it. I knew that his death could be no more than days away.

You can't leave me now, not after all this time, I wanted to scream. Instead, I helped him sit on the ground next to the tree, then sat at his side.

His blue eyes, once clear and bright, now watery with age and surrounded by tiny lines, watched me. He reached inside his shirt and fumbled for something. I had always teased Yuri about his shirts: sooner or later he would tear them along the shoulder seams while flexing the muscles of his broad back and sturdy arms. Now the shirt, like his skin, hung on his bones in wrinkles and folds. At last he pulled out a piece of paper and pressed it into my hand with trembling fingers.

"Take care of this," he whispered to me. "Copy it down in several places so you won't lose it. All the coordinates are there, all the places and times I went to these past months. When you're lonely, when you need me, go to the Time Station and I'll be waiting on the other side." He was trying to comfort me. Because of his concern, he had gone to the Time Station every day for the past six months and had traveled to various points in the past. I could travel to any of those points and be with him at those times. It suddenly struck me as a mad idea, an insane and desperate thing.

"What happens to me?" I asked, clutching the paper. "What am I like when I see you? You've already seen me at all those times. What do I do, what happens to me?"

"I can't tell you, you know that. You have to decide for yourself. Anything I say might affect what you do."

I looked away from him and toward the lake. Two golden swans glided by, the water barely rippling in their wake. Their shapes blurred and I realized I was crying silently. Yuri's blue-veined hand rested on my shoulder.

"Don't cry. Please. You make it harder for me."

At last the tears stopped. I reached over and stroked his hair, once thick and blond, now thin and white. Only a year before we had come to this same tree, our bodies shiny with lake water after a moonlight swim, and made love in the darkness. We were as young as everyone else, confident that we would live forever, forgetting that our bodies could not be rejuvenated indefinitely.

"I'm not really leaving you," Yuri said. His arms held me firmly and for a moment I thought his strength had returned. "I'll be at the other side of the Time Station, any time you need me. Think of it that way."

"All right," I said, trying to smile. "All right." I nestled against him, my head on his chest, listening to his once-strong heart as it thumped against my ear.

Yuri died that night, only a few hours after we returned home.

The relationships among our friends had been an elaborate web, always changing, couples breaking up and recombining in a new pattern. We were all eternally young and time seemed to stretch ahead of us with no end. Throughout all of this, Yuri and I stayed together, the strands of our love becoming stronger instead of more tenuous. I was a shy, frightened girl when I met Yuri and was attracted in part by his boldness; he had appeared at my door one day, introduced himself and told me a friend of his had made him promise he would meet me. I could not have looked very appealing with my slouched, bony body, the thick black hair that would not stay out of my face, my long legs marked with bruises by my clumsiness. But Yuri had loved me almost on sight and I discovered, in time, that his boldness was the protective covering of a serious and intense young man.

Our lives became intertwined so tightly that, after a while, they were one life. It was inconceivable that anything could separate us, even though our relationship may have lacked the excitement of others' lives. With almost three centuries to live at the full height of our physical and mental powers, and the freedom to live several different kinds of lives, changing our professions and pursuits every twenty or thirty years, we know how rarely anyone chooses to stay with the same person throughout. Yet Yuri and I had, even through our changes, fallen in love with each other over and over again. We were lucky, I thought.

We were fools, I told myself when Yuri was gone. I had half a life after his death. I was a ghost myself, wandering from friend to friend seeking consolation, then isolating myself in my house for days, unwilling to see anyone.

But Yuri had not really left me. I had only to walk down to the Time Station, give them the coordinates he had given me, and I would be with him again, at least for a little while. Yet during those first days alone I could not bring myself to go there. He's gone, I told myself angrily; you must learn to live without him. And then I would whisper, Why? You have no life alone, you are an empty shell. Go to him.

I began to wander past the Time Station, testing my resolve. I would walk almost to the door, within sight of the technicians, then retreat, racing home, my hands shaking. Yuri.

I would make the time and trouble he took useless. He had wanted to be with me when I needed him, but he had also wanted to see my future self, what I would become after his death. The Time Station could not penetrate the future, that unformed mass of possibilities. I would be denying Yuri the chance to see it through my eyes, and the chance to see what became of me.

At last I walked to the Time Station and through its glassy door into the empty hall. Time Portals surrounded me on all sides, silvery cubicles into which people would step, then disappear. A technician approached me, silently offering assistance. I motioned her away and went over to one of the unoccupied cubicles. I fumbled for the piece of paper in my pocket, then pulled it out and stared at the first set of coordinates. I stepped inside the cubicle, reciting the coordinates aloud – time, place, duration of my stay.

Suddenly I felt as though my body were being thrown through space, that my limbs were being torn from my torso. The walls around me had vanished. The feeling lasted only an instant. I was now standing next to a small, clear pool of water shadowed by palm trees.

I turned from the pool. In front of me stretched a desolate waste, a rocky desert bleached almost white by the sun. I retreated farther into the shade of the oasis, and knelt by the pool.

"Yuri," I whispered as I dipped my hand into the coolness of the water. A pebble suddenly danced across the silvery surface before me, and the ripples it made mingled with those my hand had created.

I looked around. Yuri stood only a few feet away. He had barely begun to age. His face was still young, his skin drawn tightly across high cheekbones, and his hair was only lightly speckled with silver.

"Yuri," I whispered again, and then I was running to him.

After we swam, we sat next to each other by the small pool with our feet in the water. I was intoxicated, my mind whirling from one thing to another with nothing needing to be said. Yuri smiled at me and skipped pebbles across the pool. Some of my thoughts seemed to skip with them, while another part of me whispered, He's alive, he's here with me, and he'll be with me at a hundred other places in a hundred other times.

Yuri started to whistle a simple tune, one that I had heard for as long as I knew him. I pursed my lips and tried to whistle along but failed, as I always had.

"You'll never learn to whistle now," he said. "You've had two and a half centuries to learn and you still haven't figured it out."

"I will," I replied. "I've done everything else I ever wanted to do and I can't believe that a simple thing like whistling is going to defeat me."

"You'll never learn."

"I will."

"You won't."

I raised my feet, then lowered them forcefully, splashing us both. Yuri let out a yell, and I scrambled to my feet, stumbled and tried to run. He grabbed me by the arm.

"You still won't learn how," he said again, laughing.

I looked into his eyes, level with my own.

I pursed my lips again, and Yuri disappeared. My time was up and I was being thrown and torn at again. I was in the cubicle once more. I left the Time Station and walked home alone.

I became a spendthrift, visiting the Time Station several times a week, seeing Yuri as often as I wanted. We met on the steps of a deserted Mayan pyramid and argued about the mathematical theories of his friend Alney, while jungle birds shrieked around us. I packed a few of his favorite foods and wines and found him in Hawaii, still awaiting the arrival of its first inhabitants. We sat together on a high rocky cliff in Africa, while far below us apelike creatures with primitive weapons hunted for food.

I became busy again, and began work with a group who was designing dwelling places inside the huge trees that surrounded the city. The biologists who had created the trees hundreds of years before had left the trunks hollow. I would hurry to the Time Station with my sketches of various designs, anxious to ask Yuri for advice or suggestions.

Yet during this time I had to watch Yuri grow old again. Each time I saw him he was a little older, a little weaker. I began to realize that I was watching him die all over again, and our visits took on a tone of panic and desperation. He grew more cautious in his choice of times and sites, and I was soon meeting him on deserted island beaches or inside empty summer homes in the twentieth century. Our talks with each other grew more muted, as I was afraid of arguing too vigorously with him and thus wasting the little time we had left. Yuri noticed this and understood what it meant.

"Maybe I was wrong," he said to me after I showed him the final plans for the tree dwellings. I had been overly animated, trying to be cheerful, ignoring the signs of age that reminded me of his death. I couldn't fool him. "I wanted to make it easier for you to live without me, but I might have made things worse. If I hadn't planned these visits, maybe you would have recovered by now, maybe—"

"Don't," I whispered. We were sitting near a sunny stretch of beach in southern France, hiding ourselves behind a large rock from the family picnicking below us. "Don't worry about me, please."

"You've got to face it. I can't make too many more of these journeys. I'm growing weaker."

I tried to say something but my vocal cords were locked, frozen inside my throat. The voices of the family on the beach were piercing. I wondered, idly, how many of them would die in their coming world war.

Yuri held my hand, opened his lips to say something else, then vanished. I clutched at the empty air in desperation. "No!" I screamed. "Not yet! Come back!"

I found myself, once again, at the Time Station.

I had been a spendthrift. Now I became a miser, going to the Time Station only two or three times a month, trying not to waste the few remaining visits I had with Yuri. I was no longer working on the tree dwellings. We had finished our designs and now those who enjoyed working with their hands had begun construction.

A paralysis seized me. I spent days alone in my house, unable even to clothe myself, wandering from room to room. I would sleep fitfully, then rise and, after sitting for a few hours alone, would sleep again.

Once, I forced myself to walk to the Slumber House and asked them to put me to sleep for a month. I felt the same after awakening, but at least I had been able to pass that lonely month in unconsciousness. I went to the Time Station, visited Yuri, and went back to the Slumber House to ask for another month of oblivion. When I awoke the second time, two men were standing over me, shaking their heads. They told me I would have to see a Counselor before they would put me to sleep again.

I had been a Counselor once myself, and I knew all their tricks. Instead, I went home and waited out the time between my visits to the Time Station.

This could not go on indefinitely. The list of remaining coordinates grew shorter until there was only one set left, and I knew I would see Yuri for the last time.

We met by a large wooden summer home that overlooked a small lake. It was autumn there and Yuri began to shiver in the cool air. I managed to open the back door of the house and we went inside, careful not to disturb anything.

Yuri lay on one of the couches, his head on my lap. Outside, the thick wooded area that surrounded the house was bright with colors, orange, red, yellow. A half-grown fawn with white spots on its back peered in the window at the other end of the room, then disappeared among the trees.

"Do you regret anything?" Yuri suddenly asked. I stroked his white hair and managed a smile.

"No, nothing."

"You're sure."

"Yes," I said, trying to keep my voice from quavering.

"I have one regret, that I didn't meet you sooner. But I wouldn't have met you at all, except for that promise I made."

"I know," I said. We had talked about our meeting at least a thousand times. The conversation had become a ritual, yet I wanted to go over it again. "You were so blatant, Yuri, coming to my door like that, out of nowhere. I thought you were a little crazy."

He smiled up at me and repeated what he had said then. "Hello, I'm Yuri Malenkov. I know this is a little strange, but I promised a friend of mine I met today I'd see you. Do you mind if I come in for a little while?"

"And I was so surprised I let you in."

"And I never left."

"I know, and you're still around." Tears stung my eyes.

"You were the only person aside from that friend that I could talk to honestly right away."

By then tears were running down my cheeks. "You never told me anything about your friend," I said abruptly, breaking the ritual.

"An acquaintance, really. I never saw that person again after that."

"Oh, Yuri, what will I do now? You can't leave me. I can't let you die again."

"Don't," he murmured. "You don't have much longer. Can't you see what's happening to you?"

"No."

"Get up and look in the mirror over the fireplace."

I rose, wandered over to the mirror, and looked. The signs were unmistakable. My once jet-black hair was lightly sprinkled with silver and tiny lines were etched into the skin around my eyes.

"I'm dying," I said. "My body isn't rejuvenating itself anymore." I felt a sudden rush of panic; then the fear vanished as quickly as it came, replaced by calm. I hurried back to Yuri's side.

"It won't be long," he said. "Try to do something meaningful with those last months. We'll be together again soon, just keep thinking of that."

"All right, Yuri," I whispered. Then I kissed him for the last time.

I did not fear death and do not fear it now. I became calmer, consoled by the fact that I would not be alone much longer.

How ironic it would be if my many recent uses of the Time Station had caused my sudden aging, if Yuri's gift to me had condemned me instead. Yet I knew this was not so. We all imagine that we'll have our full three centuries; most of us do, after all. But not everyone, and not I. The irony is part of life itself. It was the work not of any Time Station, but of the final timekeeper, Death, who had decided to come for me a few decades early.

What was I to do with the time left to me? I had trained as a Counselor many years ago and had worked as one before choosing a new profession. I decided to use my old experience in helping those who, like me, had to face death.

The dying began to come to me, unable to accept their fate. They were used to their youthfulness and their full lives, feeling invulnerable to anything except an accident. The suddenness with which old age had descended on them drove some to hysteria, and they would concoct wild schemes to bring about the return of their youth. One man, a biologist, spoke to me and then decided to spend his last months involved in the elusive search for immortality. Another man, who had recently fallen in love with a young girl, cried on my shoulder and I didn't know whether to weep for him or for the young woman he was leaving behind. A woman came to me, only seventy and already aging, deprived of what should have been her normal life span.

I began to forget about myself in talking with these people. Occasionally I would walk through the city and visit old friends. My mind was aging too, and on these walks I found myself lost in memories of the past, clearer to me than more recent events. As I passed the Time Station, I would contemplate a visit to my past and then shake my head, knowing that was impossible.

I might have gone on that way if I had not passed the Time Station one warm evening while sorting through my thoughts. As I walked by, I saw Onel Lialla, dressed as a technician, looking almost exactly the same as when I had known him.

An idea occurred to me. Within seconds it had formed itself in my mind and become an obsession. I can do it, I thought. Onel will help me.

Onel had been a mathematician. He had left the city some time before and I had heard nothing about him. I hurried over to his side.

"Onel," I said, and waited. His large black eyes watched me uncertainly and anxiety crossed his classically handsome face. Then he recognized me.

He clasped my arms. He said nothing at first, perhaps embarrassed by the overt signs of my approaching death. "Your eyes haven't changed," he said finally.

We walked toward the park, talking of old times. I was surprised at how little he had changed. He was still courtly, still fancied himself the young knight in shining armor. His dark eyes still paid me homage, in spite of my being an old gray-haired woman. Blinded perhaps by his innate romanticism, Onel saw only what he wished to see.

Years before, while barely more than a boy, Onel had fallen in love with me. It had not taken me long to realize that Onel, being a romantic, did not really wish to obtain the object of his affections and had unconsciously settled on me because I was so deeply involved with Yuri. He would follow me almost everywhere, pouring out his heart. I tried to be kind, not wanting to make him bitter, and spent as much time as I could in conversation with him about his feelings. Onel had finally left the city, and I let him go, knowing he would forget and realizing that this, too, was part of his romantic game.

Onel remembered all this. We sat in the park under one of the crystalline willows and he paid court again. "I never forgot your kindness," he said to me. "I swore I would repay it someday. If there's anything I can do for you now, I will." He sighed dramatically at this point.

"There is," I replied.

"What is it?"

The opportunity had fallen into my lap with no effort. "I want you," I went on, "to come to the Time Station with me and send me back to this park two hundred and forty years in the past. I want to see the scenes of my youth one last time."

Onel seemed stunned. "You know I can't," he said. "The Portal can't send you to any time you've already lived through. We'd have people bumping into themselves, or going back to give their earlier selves advice. It's impossible."

"The Portal can be overridden for emergencies," I said. "You can override it, you know how. Send me through."

"I can't."

"Onel, I don't want to change anything. I don't even want to talk to anybody."

"If you changed the past—"

"I won't. It would already have happened then, wouldn't it? Besides, why should I? I had a happy life, Onel. I'll go back to a day when I wasn't in the park. It would just give me a little pleasure before I die to see things as they were. Is that asking too much?"

"I can't," he said. "Don't ask this of me."

In the end he gave in, as I knew he would. We went to the Station. Onel, his hands shaking, adjusted a Portal for me and sent me through.

Onel had given me four hours. I appeared in the park behind a large refreshment tent. Inside the tent, people sat at small round tables enjoying delicacies and occasionally rising to sample the pink wine that flowed from a fountain in the center. As a girl I had worked as a cook in that tent, removing raw foodstuffs from the transformer in the back and spending hours in the small kitchen making desserts, which were my specialty. I had almost forgotten the tents, which had been replaced later on by more elaborate structures.

I walked past the red tent toward the lake. It too was as I remembered it, surrounded by oaks and a few weeping willows. Biologists had not yet developed the silvery vines and glittering crystal trees that would be planted later. A peacock strutted past me as I headed for a nearby bench. I wanted only to sit for a while near the lake, then perhaps visit one of the tents before I had to return to my own time.

I watched my feet as I walked, being careful not to stumble. Most of those in the park ignored me rather pointedly, perhaps annoyed by an old woman who reminded them of their eventual fate. I had been the same, I thought, avoiding those who would so obviously be dead soon, uncomfortable around those who were dying when I had everything ahead of me.

Suddenly a blurred face was in front of me and I collided with a muscular young body. Unable to retain my balance, I fell.

A hand was held out to me and I grasped it as I struggled to my feet. "I'm terribly sorry," said a voice, a voice I had come to know so well, and I looked up at the face with its wide cheekbones and clear blue eyes.

"Yuri," I said.

He was startled. "Yuri Malenkov," I said, trying to recover.

"Do I know you?" he asked.

"I attended one of your lectures," I said quickly, "on holographic art."

He seemed to relax a bit. "I've only given one," he said. "Last week. I'm surprised you remember my name."

"Do you think," I said, anxious now to hang on to him for at least a few minutes, "you could help me over to that bench?"

"Certainly."

I hobbled over to it, clinging to his arm. By the time we sat down, he was already expanding on points he had covered in the lecture. He was apparently unconcerned about my obvious aging and seemed happy to talk to me.

A thought struck me forcefully. I suddenly realized that Yuri had not yet met my past self. I had never attended that first lecture, having met him just before he was to do his second. Desperately, I tried to recall the date I had given Onel, what day it was in the past.

I had not counted on this. I was jumpy, worried that I would change something, that by meeting Yuri in the park like this I might somehow prevent his meeting me. I shuddered. I knew little of the circumstances that had brought him to my door. I could somehow be interfering with them.

Yuri finished what he had to say and waited for my reaction. "You certainly have some interesting insights," I said. "I'm looking forward to your next lecture." I smiled and nodded, hoping that he would now leave and go about his business.

Instead he looked at me thoughtfully. "I don't know if I'll give any more lectures."

My stomach turned over. I knew he had given ten more. "Why not?" I asked as calmly as I could.

He shrugged. "A lot of reasons."

"Maybe," I said in desperation, "you should talk about it with somebody, it might help." Hurriedly I dredged up all the techniques I had learned as a Counselor, carefully questioning him, until at last he opened up and flooded me with his sorrows and worries.

He became the Yuri I remembered, an intense person who concealed his emotions under a cold, business-like exterior. He had grown tired of the city's superficiality, uncomfortable with those who grew annoyed at his seriousness and penetration. He was unsuited to the gaiety and playfulness that surrounded him, wanting to pursue whatever he did with single-minded devotion.

He looked embarrassed after telling me all this and began once more to withdraw behind his shield. "I have some tentative plans," he said calmly, regaining control. "I may be leaving here in a couple of days with one of the scientific expeditions for Mars. I prefer the company of serious people and have been offered a place on the ship."

My hands trembled. Neither of us had gone with an expedition until five years after our meeting. "I'm sorry for bothering you with my problems," he went on. "I don't usually do that to strangers, or anyone else for that matter. I'd better be on my way."

"You're not bothering me."

"Anyway, I have a lot of things to do. I appreciate the time you took to listen to me."

He stood up and prepared to walk away. No, I thought, you can't, I can't lose you like this. But then I realized something and was shocked that I hadn't thought of it before. I knew what I had to do.

"Wait!" I said. "Wait a minute. Do you think you could humor an old lady, maybe take some advice? It'll only be an hour or so of your time."

"It depends," he said stiffly.

"Before you go on that expedition, do you think you could visit a person I think might enjoy talking to you?"

He smiled. "I suppose," he said. "But I don't see what difference it makes."

"She's a lot like you. I think you'd find her sympathetic." And I told him where I lived and gave him my name. "But don't tell her an old woman sent you, she'll think I'm meddling. Just tell her it was a friend."

"I promise." He turned to leave. "Thank you, friend." I watched him as he ambled down the pebbled path that would lead him to my home.

PALIMPSEST

Charles Stross

Charles Stross is an English science fiction, fantasy, and horror writer. His first piece of fiction, "The Boys", was published in *Interzone* in 1987 and he's been writing steadily ever since, with several novels and many short stories to his name. His fiction has won the Hugo Award, the Locus Award, and the Prometheus Award. This novella, "Palimpsest," won the Hugo Award in 2010 and was first published in his collection *Wireless* in 2009.

FRESH MEAT

This will never happen:

You will flex your fingers as you stare at the back of the youth you are going to kill, father to the man who will never now become your grandfather; and as you trail him home through the snowy night, you'll pray for your soul, alone in the darkness.

Memories are going to come to you unbidden even though you'll try to focus on the task in hand. His life – that part of it which you arrived kicking and squalling in time to share with him before the end – will pass in front of your eyes. You will remember Gramps in his sixties, his hands a bunch of raisin-wrinkled grape joints as he holds your preteen wrists and shows you how to cast the fly across the water. And you'll remember the shrunken husk of his seventies, standing speechless and numb by Gran's graveside in his too-big suit, lying at last alone in the hospice bed, breath coming shallow and fast as he sleeps alone with the cancer. These won't be good memories. But you know the rest of the story too, having heard it endlessly from your parents: young love and military service in a war as distant as faded sepia photographs from another generation's front, a good job in the factory and a wife he will quietly adore who will in due course give him three children, from one of whose loins you in turn are drawn. Gramps will have a good, long life and live to see five grandchildren and a myriad of wonders, and this boy-man on the edge of adulthood who you are compelled to follow as he walks to the recruiting office holds the seeds of the man you will remember . . . But it's him or you.

Gramps would have had a good life. You must hold on to that. It will make what's coming easier.

You will track the youth who will never be your grandfather through the snow-spattered shrubbery and long grass along the side of the railroad tracks, and the wool-and-vegetable-fiber cloth that you wear – your costume will be entirely authentic – chafes your skin. By that point you won't have bathed for a week, or shaved using hot water: you are a young thug, a vagrant, and a wholly bad sort. That is what the witnesses will see, the mad-eyed young killer in the sweat-stained suit with the knife and his victim, so vulnerable with his throat laid open almost to the bone. He'll sprawl as if he is merely sleeping. And there will be outrage and alarm as the cops and concerned citizens turn out to hunt the monster that took young Gerry from his family's arms, and him just barely a man: but they won't find you, because you'll push the button on the pebble-sized box and Stasis Control will open up a timegate and welcome you into their proud and lonely ranks.

When you wake up in your dorm two hundred years-objective from now, bathed in stinking fear-sweat, with the sheet sucking onto your skin like a death-chilled caul, there will be nobody to comfort you and nobody to hold you. The kindness of your mother's hands and the strength of your father's wrists will be phantoms of memory, ghosts that echo round your bones, wandering homeless through the mausoleum of your memories.

They'll have no one to remember their lives but you; and all because you will believe the recruiters when they tell you that to join the organization you must kill your own grandfather, and that if you do not join the organization, you will die.

(It's an antinepotism measure, they'll tell you, nodding, not unkindly. And a test of your ruthlessness and determination. And besides, we all did it when it was our turn.)

Welcome to the Stasis, Agent Pierce! You're rootless now, an orphan of the time stream, sprung from nowhere on a mission to eternity. And you're going to have a remarkable career.

Yellowstone

"You've got to remember, humanity always goes extinct," said Wei, staring disinterestedly at the line of women and children shuffling toward the slave station down by the river. "Always. A thousand years, a hundred thousand, a quarter million – doesn't matter. Sooner or later, humans go extinct." He was speaking Urem, the language the Stasis used among themselves.

"I thought that was why we were here? To try and prevent it?" Pierce asked, using the honorific form appropriate for a student questioning his tutor, although Wei was, in truth, merely a twelfth-year trainee himself: the required formality was merely one more reminder of the long road ahead of him.

"No." Wei raised his spear and thumped its base on the dry, hard-packed mud of the observation mound. "We're going to relocate a few seed groups, several tens of thousands. But the rest are still going to die." He glanced away from the slaves: Pierce followed his gaze.

Along the horizon, the bright red sky darkened to the color of coagulated blood on a slaughterhouse floor. The volcano, two thousand kilometers farther around the curve of the planet, had been pumping ash and steam into the stratosphere for weeks. Every noon, in the badlands where once the Mississippi delta had writhed, the sky wept brackish tears.

"You're from before the first extinction epoch, aren't you? The pattern wasn't established back then. That must be why you were sent on this field trip. You need to understand that this always happens. Why we do this. You need to know it in your guts. Why we take the savages and leave the civilized to die."

Like Wei, and the other Stasis agents who had silently liquidated the camp guards and stolen their identities three nights before, Pierce was disguised as a Benzin warrior. He wore the war paint and beaten-aluminum armbands, bore the combat scars. He carried a spear tipped with a shard of synthetic diamond, mined from a deep seam of prehistoric automobile windshields. He even wore a Benzin face: the epicanthic folds and dark skin conferred by the phenotypic patches had given him food for thought, an unfamiliar departure from his white-bread origins. Gramps (he shied from the memory) would have died rather than wear this face.

Pierce was not yet even a twelve-year trainee: he'd been in the service for barely four years-subjective. But he was ready to be sent out under supervision, and this particular operation called for warm bodies rather than retrocausal subtlety.

Fifty years ago, the Benzin had swept around the eastern coastline of what was still North America, erupting from their heartland in the central isthmus to extend their tribute empire into the scattered tribal grounds of post-Neolithic nomads known to Stasis Control only by their code names: the Alabamae, the Floridae, and the Americae. The Benzin were intent on conquering the New World, unaware that it had been done at least seventeen times already since the start of the current Reseeding. They did not understand the significance of the redness in the western sky or the shaking of the ground, ascribing it to the anger of their tribal gods. They had no idea that these signs heralded the end of the current interglacial age, or that their extinction would be a side effect of the coming Yellowstone eruption – one of a series that occurred at six-hundred-thousand-year intervals during the early stages of the Lower First Anthropogenic epoch.

The Benzin didn't take a long view of things, for although their priest-kings had a system of writing, most of them lived in the hazily defined ahistorical myth-world of the preliterate. Their time was running out all the same. Yellowstone was waking, and even the Stasis preferred to work around such brutal geological phenomena, rather than through them.

"Yes, but why take them?" Pierce nodded toward the silently trudging Alabamae women and children, their shoulders stooped beneath the burden of their terror. They'd been walking before the spear points of their captors for days; they were exhausted. The loud ones had already died, along with the lame. The raiders who had slain their men and stolen them away to a life of slavery sat proudly astride their camels, their enemies' scalps dangling from their kotekas like bizarre pubic wigs. "The Benzin may be savages, but these people are losers – they came off worse."

Wei shook his head minutely. "The adults are all female, and mostly pregnant at that. These are the healthy ones, the ones who survived the march. They're gatherers, used to living off the land, and they're all in one convenient spot."

Pierce clenched his teeth, realizing his mistake. "You're going to use them for Reseeding? Because there are fewer bodies, and they're more primitive, more able to survive in a wilderness . . . ?"

"Yes. For a successful Reseeding we need at least twenty thousand bodies from as many diverse groups as possible, and even then we risk a genetic bottleneck. And they need to be able to survive in the total absence of civilization. If we dumped you in the middle of a Reseeding, you would probably not last a month. No criticism intended; neither would I. Those warriors" – Wei raised his spear again, as if saluting the raiders – "require slaves and womenfolk and a hierarchy to function. The tip of your spear was fashioned by a slave in the royal armories, not by a warrior. Your moccasins and the cloth of your pants were made by Benzin slaves. They are halfway to reinventing civilization: given another five thousand years-subjunctive, their distant descendants might build steam engines and establish ubiquitous recording frameworks, bequeathing their memories to the absolute future. But for a Reseeding they're as useless as we are."

"But they don't have half a deci—"

"Be still. They're moving."

The last of the slaves had been herded between the barbed hedges of the entrance passageway, and the gate guards lifted the heavy barrier back into position. Now the raiders kicked their mounts into motion, beating and poking them around the side of the spiny bamboo fence in a circuit of the guard posts. Wei and Pierce stood impassively as the camel riders spurred down on them. At the last moment, their leader pulled sideways, and his mount snorted and pawed at the ground angrily as he leaned toward Wei.

"Hai!" he shouted, in the tonal trade tongue of the northern Benzin. "I don't remember you!"

"I am Hawk! Who in the seventh hell are you?"

Wei glared at the rider, but the intruder just laughed raucously and spat over the side of his saddle: it landed on the mud, sufficiently far from Wei to make it unclear whether it was a direct challenge.

Pierce tightened his grip on his spear, moving his index finger closer to the trigger discreetly printed on it. High above them, a vulturelike bird circled the zone of confrontation with unnatural precision, its fire-control systems locked on.

"I am Teuch," said the rider, after a pause. "I captured these women! In the name of our Father I took them, and in the name of our Father I got them with children to work in the paddies! What have you done for our Father today?"

"I stand here," Wei said, lifting the butt of his spear. "I guard our Father's flock while assholes like you are out having fun."

"Hai!" The rider's face split in a broad, dust-stained grin. "I see you, too!" He raised his right fist and for an instant Pierce had an icy vision of his guts unraveling around a barbarian's spear; but the camel lifted its head and brayed as Teuch nudged it in a surprisingly delicate sidestep away from Wei, away from the hedge of thorns, away from the slave station. And away from the site of the timegate through which the evacuation team would drive the camp inmates in two days' time. The prisoners would be deposited at the start of the next Reseeding. But none of the Benzin would live to see that day, a hundred thousand years-objective or more in the future.

Perhaps their camels would leave their footprints in the choking, hot rain of ash that would roll across the continent with tomorrow's sunset. Perhaps some of those footprints would fossilize, so that the descendants of the Alabamae slaves would uncover them and marvel at their antiquity in the age to come. But immortality, Pierce thought, was a poor substitute for not dying.

Paying Attention in Class

It was a bright and chilly day on the roof of the world. Pierce, his bare head shaved like the rest of the green-robed trainees, sat on a low stool in a courtyard beneath the open sky, waiting for the tutorial to begin. Riding high above the ancient stone causeway and the spiral minarets of the Library Annex, the moon bared her knife-slashed cheeks at Pierce, as if to remind him of how far he'd come.

"Good afternoon, Honorable Students."

The training camp nestled in a valley among the lower peaks of the Mediterranean Alps. Looming over the verdant lowlands of the Sahara basin, in this epoch they rose higher than the stumps of the time-weathered Himalayas.

"Good afternoon, Honorable Scholar Yarrow," chanted the dozen students of the sixth-year class.

Urem, like Japanese before it, paid considerable attention to the relative status of speaker and audience. Many of the cultures the Stasis interacted with were sensitive to matters of gender, caste, and other signifiers of rank, so the designers of Urem had added declensions to reflect these matters. New recruits were expected to practice the formalities diligently, for a mastery of Urem was important to their future – and none of them were native speakers.

"I speak to you today of the structure of human history and the ways in which we may interact with it."

Yarrow, the Honorable Scholar, was of indeterminate age: robed in black, her hair a stubble-short golden halo, she could have been anywhere from thirty to three hundred. Given the epigenetic overhaul the Stasis provided for their own, the latter was likelier – but not three thousand. Attrition in the line of duty took its toll over the centuries. Yarrow's gaze, when it fell on Pierce, was clear, her eyes the same blue as the distant horizon. This was the first time she had lectured Pierce's class – not surprising, for the college had many tutors, and the path to graduation was long enough to tax the most disciplined. She was, he understood, an expert on what was termed the Big Picture. He hadn't looked her up in the local Library Annex ahead of time. (In his experience it was generally better to approach these lessons with an open mind. And in any case, students had only patchy access to the records of their seniors.)

"As a species, we are highly unstable, prone to Malthusian crises and self-destructive wars. This apparent weakness is also our strength – when reduced to a rump of a few thousand illiterate hunter-gatherers, we can spread out and tame a planet in mere centuries, and build high civilizations in a handful of millennia.

"Let me give you some numbers. Over the two and a half million epochs accessible to us – each of which lasts for a million years – we shall have reseeded starter populations nearly twenty-one million times, with an average extinction period of sixty-nine thousand years. Each Reseeding event produces an average of eleven-point-six planet-spanning empires, thirty-two continental empires, nine hundred and sixty-odd languages spoken by more than one million people, and a total population of one-point-seven trillion individuals. Summed over the entire life span of this planet – which has been vastly extended by the cosmological engineering program you see above you every night – there are nearly twenty billion billion of us. We are not merely legion – we rival in our numbers the stars of the observable universe in the current epoch.

"Our species is legion. And throughout the vast span of our history, ever since the beginning of the first panopticon empire during our first flowering, we have committed to permanent storage a record of everything that has touched us – everything but those events that have definitively unhappened."

Pierce focused on Yarrow's lips. They quirked slightly as she spoke, as if the flavor of her words was bitter – or as if she was suppressing an unbidden humor, intent on maintaining her gravitas before the class. Her mouth was wide and sensual, and her lips curiously pale, as if they were waiting to be warmed by another's touch. Despite his training, Pierce was as easily distracted as any other twentysomething male, and try as he might, he found it difficult to focus on her words: he came from an age of hypertext and canned presentations and found that these archaic, linear tutorials challenged his concentration. The outward austerity of her delivery inflamed his imagination, blossoming in a sensuous daydream in which the wry taste of her lips blended with the measured cadences of her speech to burn like fire in his mind.

"Uncontrolled civilization is a terminal consumptive state, as the victims of the first extinction discovered the hard way. We have left their history intact and untouched, that we might remember our origins and study them as a warning; some of you in this cohort have been recruited from that era. In other epochs we work to prevent wild efflorescences of resource-depleting overindustrialization, to suppress competing abhuman intelligences, and to prevent the pointless resource drain of attempts to colonize other star systems. By shepherding this planet's resources and manipulating its star and neighboring planets to maximize its inhabitable duration, we can achieve Stasis – a system that supports human life for a thousand times the life of the unmodified sun, and that remembers the time line of every human life that ever happened."

Yarrow's facts and figures slid past Pierce's attention like warm syrup. He paid little heed to them, focusing instead on her intonation, the little twitches of the muscles in her cheeks as she framed each word, the rise and fall of her chest as she breathed in and out. She was impossibly magnetic: a puritan sex icon, ascetic and unaware, attractive but untouchable. It was foolish in the extreme, he knew, but for some combination of tiny interlocking reasons he found her unaccountably exciting.

"All of this would be impossible without our continued ownership of the timegate. You already know the essentials. What you may not be aware of is that it is a unique, easily depleted resource. The timegate allows us to open wormholes connecting two openings in four-dimensional space-time. But the exclusion principle prevents two such openings from overlapping in time. Tear-up and tear-down is on the order of seven milliseconds, a seemingly tiny increment when you compare it to the trillion-year span that falls within our custody. But when you slice a period of interest into fourteen-millisecond chunks, you run out of time fast. Each such span can only ever be touched by us once, connected to one other place and time of our choosing.

"Stasis Control thus has access to a theoretical maximum of 5.6 times 10^{21}

slots across the totality of our history – but our legion of humanity comes perilously close, with a total of 2 times 10 19 people. Many of the total available slots are reserved for data, relaying the totality of recorded human history to the Library – fully ninety-six percent of humanity lives in eras where ubiquitous surveillance or personal life-logging technologies have made the recording of absolute history possible, and we obviously need to archive their lifelines. Only the ur-historical prelude to Stasis, and periods of complete civilizational collapse and Reseeding, are not being monitored in exhaustive detail.

"To make matters worse: in practice there are far fewer slots available for actual traffic, because we are not, as a species, well equipped for reacting in spans of less than a second. The seven-millisecond latency of a timegate is shorter by an order of magnitude than the usual duration of a gate used for transport.

"We dare not use gates for iterated computational processes, or to open permanent synchronous links between epochs, and while we could in theory use it to enable a single faster-than-light starship, that would be horribly wasteful. So we are limited to blink-and-it's-gone wormholes connecting time slices of interest. And we must conclude that the slots we allocate to temporal traffic are a scarce resource because—"

Yarrow paused and glanced across her audience. Pierce shifted slightly on his stool, a growing tension in his crotch giving his distraction a focus. Her gaze lingered on him a moment too long, as if she sensed his inattention: the slight hint of amusement, imperceptible microexpressions barely glimpsed at the corners of her mouth, sent a panicky shiver up his spine. She's going to ask questions, he realized, as she opened her lips. "What applications of the timegate are ruled out by the slot latency period, class? Does anyone know? Student Pierce? What do you know?" She looked at him directly, expectantly. The half smile nibbled at her cheeks, but her eyes were cool.

"I, um, I don't—" Pierce flailed for words, dragged back to the embarrassing present from his sensual daydream. "The latency period?"

"You don't what?" Honorable Scholar Yarrow raised one perfect eyebrow in feigned disbelief at his fluster. "But of course, Student Pierce. You don't. That has always been your besetting weakness: you're easily distracted. Too curious for your own good." Her smile finally broke, icy amusement crinkling around her eyes. "See me in my office after the tutorial," she said, then turned her attention back to the rest of the class, leaving him to stew in fearful anticipation. "I do hope you have been paying more attention—"

The rest of Yarrow's lecture slid past Pierce in a delirium of embarrassment as she spoke of deep time, of salami-sliced vistas of continental drift and re-formation, of megayears devoted to starlifting and the frozen, lifeless gigayears during which the Earth had been dislodged from its celestial track, to drift far from the sun while certain necessary restructuring was carried out. She knows me, he realized sickly, watching the pale lips curl around words that meant nothing and everything. She's met me before. These things happened in the Stasis; the formal etiquette was deliberate padding to break the soul-shaking impact of such collisions with the consequences of your own future. She must think I'm an idiot—

The lecture ended in a flurry of bowing and dismissals. Confused, Pierce found himself standing before the Scholar on the roof of the world, beneath the watching moon. She was very beautiful, and he was utterly mortified. "Honorable Scholar, I don't know how to explain, I—"

"Silence." Yarrow touched one index finger to his lips. His nostrils flared at the scent of her, floral and strange. "I told you to see me in my office. Are you coming?"

Pierce gaped at her. "But Honorable Scholar, I—"

"—Forgot that, as your tutor, I am authorized to review your Library record." She smiled secretively. "But I didn't need to: You – your future self – told me why you were distracted, many years-subjective ago. There is a long history between us." Her humor dispersed like mist before a hot wind. "Will you come with me now? And not make an unhappening of our life together?"

"But I—" For the first time he noticed she was using the honorific form of "you," in its most intimate and personal case. "What do you mean, our life?"

She began to walk toward the steps leading down to the Northern Courtyard. "Our life?" He called after her, dawning anger at the way he'd been manipulated lending his voice an edge. "What do you mean, our life?"

She glanced back at him, her expression peculiar – almost wistful. "You'll never know if you don't get over your pride, will you?" Then she looked back at the two hundred stone steps that lay before her, inanimate and treacherous, and began to descend the mountainside. Her gait was as steady and dignified as any matron turning her back on young love and false memories.

He watched her recede for almost a minute before his injured dignity gave way, and he ran after her, stumbling recklessly from step to stone, desperate to discover his future.

HACKING HISTORY

Pleasure Empires

They will welcome you as a prince among princes, and they will worship you as a god among gods. They will wipe the sweat from your brow and the dust of the road from your feet, and they will offer to you their sons and daughters and the wine of their vineyards. Their world exists only to please the angels of the celestial court, and we have granted you this leave to dwell among our worshippers, with all the rights and honors of a god made flesh.

They will bring wine unto you, and the fruit of the dream poppy. They will clothe you in silk and gold, and lie naked beneath your feet, and abase themselves before your every whim. They are the people of the Pleasure Empires, established from time to time by the decree of the lords of Stasis to serve their loyal servants, and it is their honor and their duty to obey you and demonstrate their love for you in any way that you desire, for all their days and lifetimes upon the Earth. And you will dwell among them in a palace of alabaster, surrounded by gardens of delight, and you shall want for nothing.

Your days of pleasure will number one thousand and one; your lovers will number a thousand or one as you please; your pleasures will be without number; and the number of tomorrow's parties shall be beyond measure. You need not leave until the pleasures of flesh and mind pale, and the novelty of infinite luxury becomes a weight on your soul. Then and only then, you will yearn for the duty which lends meaning to life; energized, you will return to service with serenity and enthusiasm. And your colleagues will turn aside from their tasks and wonder at your eagerness: for though you may have spent a century in the Pleasure Empires, your absence from your duty will have lasted barely a heartbeat. You are a loyal servant of the Stasis: and you may return to paradise whenever it pleases you, because we want you to be happy in your work.

Palimpsest Ambush

Almost a hundred kiloyears had passed since the Yellowstone eruption that wiped out the Benzin and the hunter-gatherer tribes of the Gulf Coast. The new Reseeding was twelve thousand years old; civilization had taken root again, spreading around the planet with the efflorescent enthusiasm of a parasitic vine. It was currently going through an expansionist-mercantilist phase, scattered city-states and tribute empires gradually coalescing and moving toward a tentative enlightenment. Eventually they'd rediscover electronics and, with the institution of a ubiquitous surveillance program, finally reconquer the heights of true civilization. Nobody looking at the flourishing cities and the white-sailed trade ships could imagine that the people who built them were destined for anything but glory.

Pierce stumbled along a twisty cobbled lane off the Chandler's Street in Carnegra, doing his faux-drunken best to look like part of the scenery. Sailors fresh ashore from Ipsolian League boats weren't a rarity here, and it'd certainly explain his lack of fluency in Imagra, the local creole. It was another training assignment, but with six more years-subjective of training and a Stasis phone implant, Pierce now had some degree of independence. He was trusted to work away from the watchful eyes of his supervisor, on assignments deemed safe for a probationer-agent.

"Proceed to the Red Duck on Margrave Way at the third hour of Korsday. Take your detox first, and stay on the small beer. You're there as a level-one observer and level-zero exit decoy to cover our other agent's departure. There's going to be a fight, and you need to be ready to look after yourself; but remember, you're meant to be a drunken sailor, so you need to look the part until things kick off. Once your target is out of the picture, you're free to leave. If it turns hot, escalate it to me, and I'll untangle things retroactively."

It was all straightforward stuff, although normally Pierce wouldn't be assigned to a job in Carnegra, or indeed to any job in this epoch. Training to blend in seamlessly with an alien culture was difficult enough that Stasis agents usually worked in their home era, or as close to it as possible, where their local knowledge was most useful. As it was, two months of full-time study had given him just enough background to masquerade as a foreign sailor – in an archipelagean society that was still three centuries away from reinventing the telegraph. It's a personalized test, he'd realized with a jittery shudder of alertness, as if he'd just downed a mug of maté. Someone up the line in Operational Analysis would be watching his performance, judging his flexibility. He determined to give it his all.

It took him two months of hard training, in language and cultural studies and local field procedures – all for less than six hours on the ground in Carnegra.

And the reason he was certain it was a test: Supervisor Hark had changed the subject when he'd asked who he was there to cover for.

Margrave Way was a cobblestoned alley, stepped every few meters to allow for the slope of the hillside, lined on either side with the single-story bamboo shopfronts of fishmongers and chandlers. Pierce threaded his wobbly way around servants out shopping for the daily catch, water carriers, fruit and vegetable sellers, and beggars; dodged a rice merchant's train of dwarf dromedaries loaded with sacks; and avoided a pair of black-robed scholars from one of the seminaries that straggled around the flanks of the hill like the thinning hair on the pate of an elderly priest. Banners rippled in the weak onshore breeze; paper skull-lanterns with mirror-polished eyes to repel evil spirits bounced gaudily beneath the eaves as he entered the inn.

The Red Duck was painted the color of its namesake. Pierce hunched beneath the low awning and probed the gloom carefully, finally emerging into the yard out back with his eyes watering. At this hour the yard was half-empty, for the tavern made much of its trade in food. The scent of honeysuckle hung heavy over the decking; the hibiscus bushes at the sides of the yard were riotously red. Pierce staked out a bench near the rear wall with a clear view of the entrance and the latrines, then unobtrusively audited the other patrons, careful to avoid eye contact. Even half-empty, the yard held the publican's young sons (shuffling hither and yon to fill cups for the customers), four presumably genuine drunken sailors, three liveried servants from the seminaries, a couple of gaudily clad women whose burlesque approach to the sailors was blatantly professional, and three cloak-shrouded pilgrims from the highlands of what had once been Cascadia – presumably come to visit the shrines and holy baths of the southern lands. At least, to a first approximation.

One of the lads was at Pierce's elbow, asking something about service and food. "Give beer," Pierce managed haltingly. "Good beer light two coin value." The tap-boy vanished, returned with a stoneware mug full of warm suds that smelled faintly of bananas. "Good, good." Pierce fumbled with his change, pawing over it as if unsure. He passed two clipped and blackened coins to the kid – both threaded with passive RF transceivers, beacons to tell his contact that they were not alone.

As Pierce raised his mug to his lips in unfeigned happy anticipation, his phone buzzed. It was a disturbing sensation, utterly unnatural, and it had taken him much practice to learn not to jump when it happened. He scanned the beer garden, concealing his mouth with his mug as he did so. A murder of crows – seminary students flocking to the watering hole – was raucously establishing its pecking order in the vestibule, one of the sailors had fallen forward across the table while his fellow tried to rouse him, and a working girl in a red wrap was walking toward the back wall, humming tunelessly. Bingo, he thought, with a smug flicker of satisfaction.

Pierce twitched a stomach muscle, goosing his phone. The other Stasis agent would feel a shiver and buzz like an angry yellow jacket – and indeed, as he watched, the woman in red glanced round abruptly. Pierce twitched again as her gaze flickered over him: this time involuntarily, in the grip of something akin to déjà vu. Can't be, he realized an instant later. She wouldn't be on a field op like this!

The woman in red turned and sidestepped toward his bench, subvocalizing. "You're my cover, yes? Let's get out of here right now, it's going bad."

Pierce began to stand. "Yarrow?" he asked. The sailor who was trying to rouse his friend started tugging at his shoulder.

"Yes? Look, what's your exit plan?" She sounded edgy.

"But—" He froze, his stomach twisting. She doesn't know me, he realized. "Sorry. Can you get over the wall if I create a diversion?" he sent, his heart hammering. He hadn't seen her in three years-subjective – she'd blown through his life like a runaway train, then vanished as abruptly as she'd arrived, leaving behind a scrawled note to say she'd been called uptime by Control, and a final quick charcoal sketch.

"I think so, but there are two—" The sailor stood up and shouted incoherently at her just as Pierce's phone buzzed again. "Who's that?" she asked.

"Hard contact in five seconds!" The other agent, whoever he was, sounded urgent. "Stay back."

The sailor shouted again, and this time Pierce understood it: "Murderer!" He climbed over the table and drew a long, curved knife, moving forward.

"Get behind me." Pierce stepped between Yarrow and the sailor, his thoughts a chaotic mess of This is stupid and What did she do? and Who else? as he paged Supervisor Hark. "Peace," he said in faltering Carnegran, "am friend? Want drink?"

Behind the angry sailor the priest-students were standing up, black robes flapping as they spread out, calling to one another. Yarrow retreated behind him: his phone vibrated again, then, improbably, a fourth time. There were too many agents. "What's happening?" asked Hark.

"I think it's a palimpsest," Pierce managed to send. Like an inked parchment scrubbed clean and reused, a section of history that had been multiply overwritten. He held his hands up, addressed the sailor, "You want. Thing. Money?"

The third agent, who'd warned of contact: "Drop. Now!"

Pierce began to fall as something, someone – Yarrow? – grabbed his shoulder and pushed sideways.

One of the students let his robe slide open. It slid down from his shoulders, gaping to reveal an iridescent fluidity that followed the rough contours of a human body, flexing and rippling like molten glass. Its upper margin flowed and swelled around its wearer's neck and chin, bulging upward to engulf his head as he stepped out of the black scholar's robe.

The sailor held his knife high, point down as he advanced on Pierce. Pierce's focus narrowed as he brought his fall under control, preparing to roll and trigger the telescopic baton in his sleeve—

A gunshot, shockingly loud, split the afternoon air. The sailor's head disappeared in a crimson haze, splattering across Pierce's face. The corpse lurched and collapsed like a dropped sack. Somebody – Yarrow? – cried out behind him, as Pierce pushed back with his left arm, trying to blink the red fog from his vision.

The student's robe was taking on a life of its own, contracting and standing up like a malign shadow behind its master as the human-shaped blob of walking water turned and raised one hand toward the roof. A chorus of screams rose behind it as one of the other seminarians, who had unwisely reached for the robe, collapsed convulsing.

"Stay down!" It was the third agent. "Play dead."

"My knee's—"

Pierce managed a sidelong look that took in Yarrow's expression of fear with a shudder of self-recognition. "I'll decoy," he sent. Then, a curious clarity of purpose in his mind, he rolled sideways and scrambled toward the interior of the tavern.

Several things happened in the next three seconds:

First, a brilliant turquoise circle two meters in diameter flickered open, hovering directly in front of the rear wall of the beer garden. A double handful of enormous purple hornets burst from its surface. Most arrowed toward the students, who had entangled themselves in a panicky crush at the exit: two turned and darted straight up toward the balcony level.

Next, a spark, bright as lightning, leapt between the watery humanoid's upraised hand and the ceiling.

Finally, something punched Pierce in the chest with such breath-taking violence that he found, to his shock and surprise, that his hands and feet didn't seem to want to work anymore.

"Agent down," someone signalled, and it seemed to him that this was something he ought to make sense of, but sense was ebbing fast in a buzz of angry hornets as the pinkness faded to gray. And then everything was quiet for a long time.

Internal Affairs

"Do you know anyone who wants you dead, scholar-agent?" The investigator from Internal Affairs leaned over Pierce, his hands clasped together in a manner that reminded Pierce of a hungry mantis. His ears (Pierce couldn't help but notice) were prominent and pink, little radar dishes adorning the sides of a thin face. It had to be an ironic comment if not an outright insult, his adoption of the likeness of Franz Kafka. Or perhaps the man from Internal Affairs simply didn't want to be recognized.

Pierce chuckled weakly. The results were predictable: when the coughing fit subsided, and his vision began to clear again, he shook his head.

"A pity." Kafka rocked backward slightly, his shoulders hunched. "It would make things easier."

Pierce risked a question. "Does the Library have anything?"

Kafka sniffed. "Of course not. Whoever set the trap knew enough to scrub the palimpsest clean before they embarked on their killing spree."

So it was a palimpsest. Pierce felt vaguely cheated. "They assassinated themselves first? To remove the evidence from the time sequence?"

"You died three times, scholar-agent, not counting your present state." He gestured at the dressing covering the cardiac assist leech clamped to the side of Pierce's chest. It pulsed rhythmically, taking the load while the new heart grew to full size between his ribs. "Agent Yarrow died twice and Agent-Major Alizaid's report states that he was forced to invoke Control Majeure to contain the palimpsest's expansion. Someone" – Kafka leaned toward Pierce again, peering intently at his face with disturbingly dark eyes – "went to great lengths to kill you repeatedly."

"Uh." Pierce stared at the ceiling of his hospital room, where plaster cherubs clutching overflowing cornucopiae cavorted with lecherous satyrs. "I suppose you want to know why?"

"No. Having read your Branch Library file, there are any number of whys: what I want to know is why now." Kafka smiled, his mouth widening until his alarmingly unhinged head seemed ready to topple from the plinth of his jaw. "You're still in training, a green shoot. An interesting time to pick on you, don't you think?"

Fear made Pierce tense up. "If you've read my Library record, you must know I'm loyal . . ."

"Peace." Kafka made a placating gesture. "I know nothing of the kind; the Library can't tell me what's inside your head. But you're not under suspicion of trying to assassinate yourself. What I do know is that so far your career has been notably mundane. The Library branches are as prone to overwrites as any other palimpsest; but we may be able to make deductions about your attacker by looking for inconsistencies between your memories and the version of your history documented locally."

Pierce lay back, drained. *I'm not under suspicion.* "What is to become of me?" he asked.

Kafka's smile vanished. "Nothing, for now: you may convalesce at your leisure, and sooner or later you will learn whatever it is that was so important to our enemies that they tried to erase you. When you do so, I would be grateful if you would call me." He rose to leave. "You will see me again, eventually. Meanwhile, you should bear in mind that you have come to the attention of important persons. Consider yourself lucky – and try to make the best of it."

Three days after Kafka's departure – summoned back, no doubt, to the vasty abyss of deep time in which Internal Affairs held their counsel – Pierce had another visitor.

"I came to thank you," she said haltingly. "You didn't need to do that. To decoy, I mean. I'm very grateful."

It had the sound of a prepared speech, but Pierce didn't mind. She was young and eye-wrenchingly desirable, even in the severe uniform of an Agent Initiate. "You would have died again," he pointed out. "I was your backup. It's bad form to let your primary die. And I owed you."

"You owed me? But we haven't met! There's nothing about you in my Library file." Her pupils dilated.

"It was an older you," he said mildly. While the Stasis held a file on everyone, agents were only permitted to see – and annotate – those of their own details that lay in their past. After a pause, he admitted, "I was hoping we might meet again sometime."

"But I—" She hesitated, then stared at him, narrowing her eyes. "I'm not in the market. I have a partner."

"Funny, she didn't tell me that." He closed his eyes for a few seconds. "She said we had a history, though. And to tell her when I first met her that her first pet – a cat named Chloe – died when a wild dog took her." Pierce opened his eyes to stare at the baroque ceiling again. "I'm sorry I asked, Ya – esteemed colleague. Please forgive me; I didn't think you were for sale. My heart is simply in the wrong place."

After a second he heard a shocked, incongruous giggle.

"I gather armor-piercing rounds usually have that effect," he added.

When she was able to speak again she shook her head. "I am sincere, Scholar-Agent – Pierce? – Pierced? Oh dear!" She managed to hold her dignity intact, this time, despite a gleam of amusement. "I'm sorry if I – I don't mean to doubt you. But you must know, if you know me, I have never met you, yes?"

"That thought has indeed occurred to me." The leech pulsed warmly against his chest, squirting blood through the aortic shunt. "As you can see, right now I am not only heartless but harmless, insofar as I won't even be able to get out of bed unaided for another ten days; you need not fear that I'm going to pursue you. I merely thought to introduce myself and let you know – as she did to me – that we could have a history, if you're so inclined, someday. But not right now. Obviously."

"But obviously not—" She stood up. "This wasn't what I was expecting."

"Me neither." He smiled bitterly. "It never is, is it?"

She paused in the doorway. "I'm not saying no, never, scholar-agent. But not now, obviously. Some other time . . . We'll worry about that if we meet again, perhaps. History can wait a little longer. Oh, and thank you for saving my life some of the times! One out of three is good going, especially for a student."

ELITE

A Brief Alternate History of the Solar System: Part One
What has already happened:

SLIDE 1.

Our solar system, as an embryo. A vast disk of gas and infalling dust surrounds and obscures a newborn star, little more than a thickening knot of rapidly spinning matter that is rapidly sucking more mass down into its ever-steepening gravity well. The sun is glowing red-hot already with the heat liberated by its gravitational collapse, until . . .

SLIDE 2.

Ignition! The pressure and temperature at the core of the embryo star has risen so high that hydrogen nuclei floating in a degenerate soup of electrons are bumping close to one another. A complex reaction ensues, rapidly liberating gamma radiation and neutrinos, and the core begins to heat up. First deuterium, then the ordinary hydrogen nuclei begin to fuse. A flare of nuclear fire lashes through the inner layers of the star. It will take a million years for the gamma-ray pulse to work its way out through the choking, blanketing layers of degenerate hydrogen, but the neutrino pulse heralds the birth cry of a new star.

SLIDE 3.

A million years pass as the sun brightens, and the rotating cloud of gas and dust begins to partition. Out beyond the dew line, where ice particles can grow, a roiling knot of dirty ice is forming, and like the sun before it, it greedily sucks down dirt and gas and grows. As it plows through the cloud, it sprays dust outward. Meanwhile, at the balancing point between the star and the embryonic Jovian gravity well, other knots of dust are forming . . .

SLIDE 4.

A billion years have passed since the sun ignited, and the stellar nursery of gas and dust has been swept clean by a fleet of new-formed planets. There has been some bickering – in the late heavy bombardment triggered by the outward migration of Neptune, entire planetary surfaces were re-formed – but now the system has settled into long-term stability. The desert planet Mars is going through the first of its warm, wet interludes; Venus still has traces of water in its hot (but not yet red-hot) atmosphere. Earth is a chilly nitrogen-and-methane-shrouded enigma inhabited only by primitive purple bacteria, its vast oceans churned by hundred-meter tides dragged up every seven-hour day by a young moon that completes each orbit in little more than twenty-four hours.

SLIDE 5.

Another three billion years have passed. The solar system has completed almost sixteen orbits of the galactic core, and is now unimaginably distant from the stellar nursery which birthed it. Mars has dried, although occasional volcanic eruptions periodically blanket it in cloud. Venus is even hotter. But something strange is happening to Earth. Luna has drifted farther from its primary, the tides quieting; meanwhile, the atmosphere has acquired a strange bluish tinge, evident sign of contamination by a toxic haze of oxygen. The great landmass Rodina, which dominated the southern ocean beneath a cap of ice, has broken up and the shallow seas of the Panthalassic and Panafrican Oceans are hosting an astonishing proliferation of multicellular life.

SLIDE 6.

Six hundred and fifty million years later, the outlines of Earth's new continents glow by night like a neon diadem against the darkness, shouting consciousness at the sky in a blare of radio-wavelength emissions as loud as a star.

There have been five major epochs dominated by different families of land-based vertebrates in the time between slides 5 and 6. All the Earth's coal and oil deposits were laid down in this time, different animal families developed flight at least four times, and the partial pressure of oxygen in the atmosphere rose from around 4 percent to well over 16 percent. At the very end, a strangely bipedal, tailless omnivore appeared on the plains of Africa – its brain turbocharged on a potent mixture of oxygen and readily available sugars – and erupted into sentience in a geological eyeblink.

Here's what isn't going to happen:

SLIDE 7.

The continents of Earth, no longer lit by the afterglow of intelligence, will drift into strange new configurations. Two hundred and fifty million years after the sixth great extinction, the scattered continents will reconverge on a single equatorial supercontinent, Pangea Ultima, leaving only the conjoined landmass that was Antarctica and Australia adrift in the southern ocean. As the sun brightens, so shall the verdant plains of the Earth; oceanic algal blooms raise the atmospheric oxygen concentration close to 25 percent, and lightning-triggered wildfires rage across the continental interior. It will be an epoch characterized by rapid plant growth, but few animal life-forms can survive on land – in the heady air of aged Earth, even waterlogged flesh will burn. And the sun is still brightening . . .

SLIDE 8.

Seven hundred and fifty million years later. The brightening sun will glare down upon cloud-wreathed ancient continents, weathered and corroded to bedrock. Even the plant life has abandoned the land, for the equatorial daytime temperature is perilously close to the boiling point of water. What life there is retreats to the deep ocean waters, away from the searing ultraviolet light that splits apart the water molecules of the upper atmosphere. But there's no escape: the oceans themselves are slowly acidifying and evaporating as the hydrogen liberated in the ionosphere is blasted into space by the solar wind. A runaway greenhouse effect is well under way, and in another billion years Earth will resemble parched, hell-hot Venus.

SLIDE 9.

Four-point-two billion years after the brief cosmic eyeblink of Earthly intelligence, the game is up. The dead Earth orbits alone, its moon a separate planet wandering in increasingly unstable ellipses around the sun. Glowing dull red beneath an atmosphere of carbon dioxide baked from its rocks, there will be no sign that this world ever harbored life. The sun it circles, a sullen-faced ruddy ogre, is nearing the end of its hydrogen reserves. Soon it will expand, engulfing the inner planets.

But events on a larger scale are going to spare the Earth this fate. For billions of years, the galaxy in which this star orbits has been converging with another large starswarm, the M-31 Andromeda galaxy. Now the spiraling clouds of stars are interpenetrating and falling through each other, and the sun is in for a bumpy ride as galaxies collide.

A binary system of red dwarfs is closing with the solar system at almost five hundred kilometers per second. They are going to pass within half a billion kilometers of the sun, a hairbreadth miss in cosmic terms: in the process they will wreak havoc on the tidy layout of the solar system. Jupiter, dragged a few million kilometers sunward, will enter an unstable elliptical orbit, and over the course of a few thousand years it will destabilize all the other planets. Luna departs first, catapulted out of the plane of the ecliptic; Earth, most massive of all, will spend almost five million years wobbling between the former orbits of Venus and Saturn before it finally caroms past Jupiter and drifts off into the eternal night, the tattered remnants of its atmosphere condensing and freezing in a shroud of dry ice.

Slow Recovery

Pierce was to remain on official convalescent leave for an entire year-subjective. His heart had been torn to shreds by a penetrator round; repairing the peripheral damage, growing a new organ in situ, and restoring him to physical condition was a nontrivial matter. Luckily for him, the fatal shooting had happened in the middle of a multiple-overwrite ambush that was finally shut down by Control Majeure using weapons of gross anachronism, and they'd whisked his bleeding wreckage out through a timegate before he'd finished drumming his heels.

Nevertheless, organ regeneration – not to mention psychological recovery from a violent fatal injury – took time. So, rather than shipping him straight to the infirmary in the alpine monastery in Training Zone 25, he was sent to recover in the Rebirth Wing of the Chrysanthemum Clinic, on the Avenue of the Immortals of Medicine, in the city of Leng, on the northeastern seaboard of the continent of Nova Zealantis, more than four billion years after the time into which he had been born.

The current Reseeding was Enlightened; not only were they aware of the existence of the Stasis, but they were a part of the greater transtemporal macroculture: speakers of Urem, obedient to the Stasis, even granted dispensation to petition for use of the timegate in extraordinary circumstances. In return, the Hegemony was altogether conscientious in observing their duties to the guardians of history, according Pierce honors that, in other ages, might have been accorded to a diplomat or minor scion of royalty. Unfortunately, this entailed rather more formality than Pierce was used to. The decor, for one thing: they'd clearly studied his epoch, but modeling his hospital suite on Louis XV's bedroom at Versailles suggested they had strange ideas about his status.

"If it pleases you, my lord, would you like to describe how you entered the celestial service?" The journalist, who his bowing and shuffling concierge explained had been sent by the city archive to document his life, was young, pretty, and shiny-eyed. She'd obviously studied his public records and the customs of his home civilization, and decided to go for the throat. Local fashion echoed the Minoan empire of antiquity, and her attire, though scholarly, was disconcerting: a flash of well-turned ankle, nipples rouged and ringed – Pierce realized he was staring and turned his face away, chagrined.

"Please?" she repeated, her plump lower lip quivering. Her cameras flittered below the ceiling like lazy bluebottles, iridescent in the afternoon sunlight, logging her life for posterity.

"I suppose so . . ." Pierce trailed off, staring through the open window at the lower slopes of the hillside on which the clinic nestled. "But there's no secret, really, none at all. You don't approach them – they approach you. A tap on the shoulder at the right time, an offer of a job, at first I didn't think it was anything unusual."

"Was there anything leading up to that? My lord? What was your life like before the service?"

Pierce frowned slightly as he forced his sullen memory to work. There were gaps. "I'm not sure; I think I was in a car crash, or maybe a war . . ."

His cardiac leech pulsed against his chest like a contented cat. Sunlight warmed the side of his face as he watched her sidelong, from the corner of his eye. How far will she go for a story? he wondered idly. Play your cards right and . . . well, maybe. His temporarily heartless condition had rendered amorous speculations – or anything else calculated to raise the blood pressure – purely academic for the time being.

"My lord?" He pretended to miss the moue of annoyance that flitted across her face, but the very deliberate indrawn breath that followed it was so transparent that he nearly gave the game away by laughing.

"I'm not your lord," he said gently. "I'm just a scholar-agent, halfway through my twenty years of training. What I know about the Guardians of Time" – that was what the Hegemonites called the Stasis, those in power who had polite words for them – "and can tell you is mere trivia. I'm sure your Archive already has it all."

This was a formally declared Science Epoch, in which a whole series of consecutive Reseedings were dedicated to collating the mountain-sized chunks of data returned by the Von Neumann probes that had been launched during the last Science Epoch, a billion years earlier. They and their descendants had quietly fanned out throughout the local group of galaxies, traveling at barely a hundredth of the speed of light, visiting and mapping every star system and extrasolar planet within ten million light-years. There was a lot of material to collate; The Zealantian Hegemony's army of elite astrocartographers, millions strong, would labor for tens of thousands of years to assemble just their one corner of the big picture. And their obsession with knowledge didn't stop at the edge of the solar system.

("A civilization of obsessive-compulsive stamp collectors," Wei had called them when he briefly visited his ex-student. "You've got to watch these Science Cults; sooner or later they'll turn all the carbon in the deep biosphere into memory diamond, then where will we be?")

"The Archive doesn't know everything, my lord. It's not like the Library of Time." There was a strangely reverent note in her voice, as if the Library was somehow different. "We don't have permission to read the forbidden diaries, my lord. We have to accept whatever crusts of wisdom our honored guests choose to let fall from their trenchers."

"I'm not your lord. You can call me Pierce, if you like."

"Yes, my, ah. Pierce? My lord."

"What should I call you?" he asked after a pause.

"Me? I am nobody, lord Pierce! I am a humble journal-keeper—"

"Rubbish." He looked directly at her, taking in everything: her flounced scholar-lady's dress, the jeweled rings through her ears and nipples, her painstakingly knotted chignon. This was a high-energy civilization, but a very staid, conservative one with strict sumptuary laws: were she a commoner, she would risk a flogging for indecency, or worse, dressing above her station. "Who are you really? And why are you so interested in me?"

"Oh! If you must know, I am doctor-postulant Xiri, daughter of doctor-professor archivist His Excellency Dean Imad of the College of History, and Her Ladyship doctor-professor emeritus Leila of the faculty of hot super-Jovian moons" – she smiled coyly – "and I have been charged, by my duty and my honor as a scholar, to study you in absolute detail by my tutors. They have assigned you to me as the topic of my first dissertation. On the hero-guardians of time."

"Your first dissertation—" Her parents were a professor and a dean; she might as well have said sheikh or baron. "Do I have any choice in the matter?"

"You can refuse, of course." She shivered and tugged her filmy shawl back into position. "But I can't."

"Why? What happens if you refuse?"

She shivered. "I would forfeit my doctorate. The shame! My parents" – for a moment the bright-eyed optimism cracked – "would blame themselves. It would cast doubt on my commitment."

Was failure to make tenure track justification for an honor killing? Pierce shook his head, staring at her. "I'm just a trainee!" He reached for the bed's control, stabbing the button to raise his back. The interview was out of control, heading for deep waters, and lying down gave him an unaccountable fear of drowning. "I'm the nobody around here!"

"How do you know that, my lord? For all you know, you might be destined for glory." She tugged at her shawl again and smiled, an ingenue trying to look mysterious.

"But I don't have any—" He switched off the bed lift once he was level with her, looked her in the eyes, and changed the subject in midsentence. "Have your people ever met me before?"

The hardest part of arguing with her, he found, was avoiding staring at her chest. She was really very pretty, but her pedigree suggested he'd be wise to abandon that line of thought; she'd be about as safe to seduce as a rattlesnake.

"No." Her smile widened. "A handsome man of mystery and a time hero to boot: yes, they told us why you were here." Her gaze briefly covered his chest.

For the first time in many months, Pierce resorted to his native language. "Oh, hell." He glanced at the window, then back at Xiri. "Everybody wants to study me," he confessed. "I don't know why, I really don't . . ." He crossed his arms, looked at her. "Study away. I am at your disposal." At least it promised to be a less harrowing experience than Kafka's cross-examination.

"Oh! Thank you, my lord!" She placed a proprietorial hand on the side of his bed. "I will do my utmost to make it an enjoyable experience."

"Really?" There was something about her tone of voice that took him aback, as if he'd answered a question that he didn't remember being asked. The idea of being studied struck Pierce as marginally more enjoyable than banging his head on the wall, but on the upside, Xiri was high-quality eye candy. On the downside – Don't go there, he reminded himself. "Where would you like to begin?"

"Right here, I think," she said, sliding her hand under the covers.

"Hey! I! Huh." Pierce found, to his mild alarm, that her busy hand was getting results. "Um. I don't want to sound ungrateful, but we really shouldn't – why are you – aren't you going to shut off your cameras—"

"I have read about your culture." She sat down on the bed beside him with a rustle of silk. "In some ways, it sounded very familiar. Did they not record everything that happened to them? Did they not talk about people marrying their work? Well, that is just how we do that here."

"But that's just a metaphor!" He tried to push her hand away, but his heart wasn't in it.

"Hush." She responded by making him shudder. "You're the subject of my dissertation! I'm going to find out all about you. It's to be my life's work! I'm so happy! Just relax, my lord, and everything will be wonderful. Don't worry, I have studied the customs of your time, and they are not so very alien. We can talk about the wedding tomorrow, after you've met my father."

Empty Mansions

Resistance was futile: nearly twenty years-subjective passed Pierce by with the eyeblink impact of another bullet, half of them shared with his new wife. Xiri, true to her word, wrapped her life around his twisted time line: at first as an adoring wife, and then, to his bemused and growing pride, mother to three small children and doctor-professor in her own right. Her dissertation was his life: merely glancing lightly off the skin of time was, it seemed, a passport to wealth and status in the Hegemony, and he found life as the consort of a beautiful noblewoman no less congenial than he might have expected.

Xiri did not complain at Pierce's eyeblink excursions from their family home (provided by the grace of her father the dean), which usually lasted only for seconds of subjective time. Nor did she complain about the inward-looking silences and moody introspection that followed, and were of altogether greater duration. On the contrary: they invariably provided additional data for her life's work, once she delicately untangled the story from his memories of unhistory. Sometimes he would age an entire year in an hour's working absence, but the medical privileges of the Stasis extended also to the Enlightened; there would be plenty of time to catch up, over the decades and centuries.

Pierce, for his part, found it oddly easier to deal with the second half of his training with a stable family life to fall back on. The Stasis were spread surprisingly thin across their multitrillion-year empire. The defining characteristic of his job seemed to be that he was only called for in turbulent, interesting times. Between peak oil and Spanish flu, from Carthage to the Cold War, his three-thousand-year beat sometimes seemed no more than a vale of tears – and a thin, poor, nightmare of a world at that, far from the mannered, drowsy contentment of the ten-thousand-year-long Hegemony. Most of his fellow students seemed to prefer the hedonistic abandon proffered by the Pleasure Empires, but Pierce held his own counsel and congratulated himself on his discovery of a more profound source of satisfaction.

On his first return to training after his convalescence, Pierce was surprised to be summoned to Superintendent-of-Scholars Manson's chambers.

"You have formed attachments while convalescing." Manson fixed him with a watery stare. "That is inadvisable, as you will no doubt learn for yourself. However, Operations have noted that there is no permanent Resident in place within a millennium either side of your, ah, domestic anchor-point. It is a tranquil society, but not that tranquil; you are therefore instructed and permitted to maintain your attachment and develop your ability to work there. Purely as a secondary specialty, you understand."

Pierce had almost fallen over with shock. Once he regained his self-control, he asked, "To whom shall I report, master?"

"To your wife, student. Tell her to write up everything. We read all such dissertations, in the end."

Manson looked away, dismissing him. Pierce nudged his phone, weak-kneed, not trusting his ability to make a dignified exit; after a brief routing delay, the timegate responded to his heartfelt wish, and the ground opened up and swallowed him.

One day very late in his training, with perhaps half a year-subjective remaining until his graduation as a full-fledged agent of the Stasis, Pierce returned home from a week sampling the plague-pits of fourteenth-century Constantinople. He found Xiri in an unusually excited state, the household all abuzz around her. "It's fantastic!" she exclaimed, hurrying to meet him across the atrium of their summer residence. "Did you know about it? Tell me you knew about it! This was why you came to our time, wasn't it?"

Pierce, greeting her with a fond smile, lifted young Magnus (who had been attempting to scale his back, with much snarling, presumably to slay the giant) and handed him to his nursemaid. "What's happened?" he asked mildly, trying to give no sign of the frisson he'd momentarily felt (for their youngest son could have no idea of how his father had just spent a week taking tissue samples, carving chunks of mortal flesh from the bubo-stricken bodies of boys of an age to be his playmates in another era). "What's got everyone so excited?"

"It's the probes! They've found something outrageous in Messier 33, six thousand light-years along the third arm!"

Pierce – who could not imagine finding anything outrageous in a galaxy over a million light-years away, even if mapping it was the holy raison d'être of this Civilization – decided to humor his wife. "Indeed. And tell me, what precisely is there that brings forth such outrage? As opposed to mere excitement, or curiosity, or perplexity?"

"Look!" Xiri gestured at the wall, which obligingly displayed a dizzying black void sprinkled with stars. "Let's see. Wall, show me the anomaly I was discussing with the honorable doctor-professor Zun about two hours ago. Set magnification level plus forty, pan left and up five – there! You see it!"

Pierce stared for a while. "Looks like just another rock to me," he said. Racking his brains for the correct form: "an honorable sub-Earth, airless, of the third degree, predominantly siliceous. Yes?"

"Oh!" Xiri, nobly raised, did nothing so undignified as to stamp her foot; nevertheless, Magnus's nursemaid swept up her four-year-old charge and beat a hasty retreat. (Xiri, when excited, could be as dangerously prone to eruption as a Wolf-Rayet star.) "Is that all you can see? Wall, magnification plus ten, repeat step, step, step. There. Look at that, my lord, look!"

The airless moon no longer filled the center of the wall; now it stretched across it from side to side, so close that there was barely any visible curvature to its horizon. Pierce squinted. Craters, rills, drab, irregular features and a scattering of straight-edged rectangular crystals. Crystals? He chewed on the thought, found it curiously lacking as an explanation for the agitation. Gradually, he began to feel a quiet echo of his wife's excitement. "What are they?"

"They're buildings! Or they were, sixty-six million years ago, when the probes were passing through. And we didn't put them there . . ."

THE LIBRARY AT THE END OF TIME

A Brief Alternate History of the Solar System: Part Two

. . . And then the Stasis happened:

SLIDE 7.

After two hundred and fifty million years, the continents of Earth, strobe-lit by the mayfly flicker of empires, will have converged on a single equatorial super-continent, Pangea Ultima. These will not be good times for humanity; the vast interior deserts are arid and the coastlines subject to vast hurricanes sweeping in from the world-ocean. As the sun brightens, so shall the verdant plains of the Earth; but the Stasis have long-laid plans to deflect the inevitable.

Deep in the asteroid belt, their swarming robot cockroaches have dismantled Ceres, used its mass to build a myriad of solar-sail-powered flyers. Now a river of steerable rocks with the mass of a dwarf planet loops down through the inner system, converting solar energy into momentum and transferring it to the Earth through millions of repeated flybys.

Already, Earth has migrated outward from the sun. Other adjustments are under way, subtle and far-reaching: the entire solar system is slowly changing shape, creaking and groaning, drifting toward a new and more useful configuration. Soon – in cosmological terms – it will be unrecognizable.

SLIDE 8.

A billion years later, the Earth lies frozen and fallow, its atmosphere packed down to snow and nitrogen vapor in the chilly wilderness beyond Neptune. This was never part of the natural destiny of the homeworld, but it is only a temporary state – for in another ten million years, the endlessly cycling momentum shuttles will crank Earth closer to the sun. Fifty million years after that, the Reseedings will recommence, from the prokaryotes and algae on up; but in this era, the Stasis want the Earth safely mothballed while their technicians from the Engineering Republics work their magic.

For thirty million years the Stasis will devote their timegate to lifting mass from the heart of a burning star, channeling vast streams of blazing plasma into massive, gravitationally bound bunkers, reserves against a chilly future. The sun will gutter and fade to red, raging and flaring in angry outbursts as its internal convection systems collapse. As it shrinks and dims, they will inflict the final murderous insult, and inject an embryonic black hole into the stellar core. Eating mass faster than it can reradiate it through Hawking radiation, the hole will grow, gutting the stellar core.

By the time the Earth drops back toward the frost line of the solar system, the technicians will have roused the zombie necrosun from its grave. Its accretion disk – fed with mass steadily siphoned from the brown dwarfs orbiting on the edges of the system – will cast a strange, harsh glare across Earth's melting ice caps.

Replacing the fusion core of the sun with a mass-crushing singularity is one of the most important tasks facing the Stasis; annihilation is orders of magnitude more efficient than fusion, not to say more controllable, and the mass they have so carefully husbanded is sufficient to keep the closely orbiting Earth lit and warm not for billions, but for trillions of years to come.

But another, more difficult task remains . . .

SLIDE 9.

Four and a quarter billion years after the awakening of consciousness, and the Milky Way and Andromeda galaxies will collide. The view from Earth's crowded continents is magnificent, like a chaos of burning diamond dust strewn across the emptiness void. Shock waves thunder through the gas clouds, creating new stellar nurseries, igniting millions of massive, short-lived new stars; for a brief ten-million-year period, the nighttime sky will be lit by a monthly supernova fireworks display. The huge black holes at the heart of each galaxy have shed their robes of dust and gas and blaze naked in ghastly majesty as they streak past each other, ripping clusters of stars asunder and seeding more, in a starburst of cosmic fireworks that will be visible nearly halfway across the universe.

But Earth is safe. Earth is serene. Earth is no longer in the firing line.

The Long Burn is by far the largest program of the Stasis. Science Empires will rise and flourish, decay and gutter into extinction, to provide the numerical feedstock for the Navigators. The delicate task of ejecting a star system from its galaxy without setting the planets and moons adrift in their orbits is monstrously difficult. Planets are not bound to their stars by physical cords, and gravity is weak; innumerable adjustments to the orbits of all the significant planets will be required if they are to be carried along. The mass flow of Ceres alone will not suffice. Rocky Mercury has already been dismantled to provide the control mechanisms that keep the necrostar's accretion disk burning steadily; it's Venus's turn to supply the swarming light-sail-driven mass tugs. A brown dwarf ten times the size of Jupiter will fuel the rocket, an entire stellar embryo pumped down to the blazing maw in the course of a million years.

Galactic escape velocity is high, and escape velocity from the local group is even higher. The Long Burn will last ten thousand centuries. Each year that passes, the necrostar will be moving a meter per second faster. And when it comes to an end, the drastically redesigned solar system will be racing away from the local group of galaxies at almost a thousandth the speed of light – straight toward the Bootes Void.

SLIDE 10.

Over the next billion years, Starship Earth and its dead star will rendezvous with the other components of their lifeboat fleet; an even hundred brown dwarf stars, ten to fifty times as massive as Jupiter and every last one dislodged and sent tumbling from its home galaxy by the robot probes of the Engineering Empires.

Their mass will be gratefully received. For Earth is going on a voyage of discovery, where no star has gone before, into the heart of darkness.

Continent of Lies

Nothing in his earlier life had prepared Pierce for what came next. It beggared belief: a series of synthetic aperture radar scans transmitted by a probe millions of years ago in another galaxy had triggered a diplomatic crisis, threatening world war and civilizational autocide.

The Hegemony, despite being a Science Empire, was not the only nation in this age. (True world governments were rare, cumbersome dinosaurs notorious for their absolute top-down corruption and catastrophic-failure modes: the Stasis tended to discourage them.) The Hegemony shared their world with the Autonomous Directorate of Zan, a harshly abstemious land of puritanical library scientists (located on a continent which had once been attached to North America and Africa); sundry secular monarchies, republics, tyrannies, autarchies, and communes (who thought their superpower neighbors mildly insane for wasting so much of their wealth on academic institutions, rather than the usual aimless and undirected pursuit of human happiness); and the Kingdom of Blattaria (whose inhabitants obeyed the prehistoric prophet Haldane with fanatical zeal, studying the arthropoda in ecstatic devotional raptures).

The Hegemony was geographically the largest of the great powers, unified by a set of common filing and monitoring protocols; but it was not a monolithic entity. The authorities of the western principality of Stongu (special area of study: the rocky moons of Hot Jupiters in M-33) had reacted to the discovery of Civilization on the moon of a water giant with a spectacular display of sour grapes, accusing the northeastern Zealantians of fabricating data in a desperate attempt to justify a hit-and-run raid on the Hegemony's federal tax base. Quite what the academics of Leng were supposed to do with these funds was never specified, nor was it necessary to say any more in order to get the blood boiling in the seminaries and colleges. Fabricating data had a deadly ring to it in any Science Empire, much like the words crusade and jihad in the millennium prior to Pierce's birth. Once the accusation had been raised, it could not be ignored – and this presented the Hegemony with a major internal problem.

"Honored soldier of the Guardians of Time, our gratitude would be unbounded were you to choose to intercede for us," said the speaker for the delegation from the Dean's Lodge that called on his household barely two days after the discovery. "We would not normally dream of petitioning your eminence, but the geopolitical implications are alarming."

And indeed, they were; for the Hegemony supplied information to the Autonomous Directorate, in return for the boundless supplies of energy harvested by the solar collectors that blanketed the Directorate's inland deserts. Allegations of fabricating data could damage the value of the Hegemony's currency; indeed, the aggressive and intolerant Zanfolk might consider it grounds for war (and an excuse for yet another of their tiresome attempts to obtain the vineyards and breadbasket islands of the Outer Nesh archipelago).

"I will do what I can." Pierce bowed deeply to the delegates, who numbered no less than a round dozen deans and even a vice-chancellor or two: he studiously avoided making eye contact with his father-in-law, who stood at the back. "If you are absolutely sure of the merits of your case, I can consult the Library, then testify publicly, insofar as I am authorized to do so. Would that be acceptable?"

The vice-chancellor of the Old College of Leng – an institution with a history of over six thousand years at this point – bowed in return, his face stiff with gratitude. "We are certain of our case, and consequently willing to abide by the word of the Library of the Guardians of Time. Please permit me to express my gratitude once more—"

After half an hour of formalities, the delegation finally departed. Xiri reemerged from her seclusion to direct the servants and robots in setting the receiving room of their mansion aright; the boys also emerged, showing no sign of understanding what had just happened. "Xiri, I need to go to the Final Library," Pierce told her, taking her hands in his and watching for signs of understanding.

"Why, that's wonderful, is it not? My lord? Pierce?" She stared into his eyes. "Why are you worried?"

Pierce swallowed bitter saliva. "The Library is not a place, Xiri, it's a time. It contains the sum total of all recorded human knowledge, after the end of humanity. I'm near to graduation, I'm allowed to go there to use it, but it's not, it's not safe. Sometimes people who go to the Library disappear and don't come back. And sometimes they come back changed. It's not just a passive archive."

Xiri nodded, but looked skeptical. "But what kind of danger can it pose, given the question you're going to put to it? You're just asking for confirmation that we've been honoring our sources. That's not like asking for the place and time of your own death, is it?"

"I hope you're right, but I don't know for sure." Pierce paused. "That's the problem." He raised her hands to his lips and kissed the backs of her fingers. If it must be done, best do it fast. "I'll go and find out. I'll be back soon . . ."

He stepped back a pace and activated his phone. "Agent-trainee Pierce, requesting a Library slot."

There was a brief pause while the relays stored his message, awaited a transmission slot, then fired them through the timegate to Control. Then he felt the telltale buzzing in the vicinity of his left kidney that warned of an incoming wormhole. It opened around him, spinning out and engulfing him in scant milliseconds, almost too fast to see: then he was no longer standing in the hall of his own mansion but on a dark plain of artificial limestone, facing a doorway set into the edge of a vast geodesic dome made from some translucent material: the Final Library.

A Brief Alternate History of the Solar System: Part Three

SLIDE 11.

One hundred billion years will pass.

Earth orbits a mere twenty million kilometers from its necrosun in this epoch, and the fires of the accretion disk are banked. Continents jostle and shudder, rising and falling, as the lights strobe around their edges (and occasionally in low equatorial orbit, whenever the Stasis permits a high-energy civilization to arise).

By the end of the first billion years of the voyage, the night skies are dark and starless. The naked eye can still – barely, if it knows where to look – see the Chaos galaxy formed by the collision of M-31 and the Milky Way; but it is a graveyard, its rocky planets mostly supernova-sterilized iceballs ripped from their parent stars by one close encounter too many. Unicellular life (once common in the Milky Way, at least) has taken a knock; multicellular life (much rarer) has received a mortal body blow. Only the Stasis's lifeboat remains.

Luna still floats in Terrestrial orbit – it is a useful tool to stir Earth's liquid core. Prone to a rocky sclerosis, the Earth's heart is a major problem for the Stasis. They can't let it harden, lest the subduction cycle and the deep carbon cycle on which the biosphere depends grind to a halt. But there are ways to stir it up again. They can afford to wait half a billion years for the Earth to cool, then reseed the reborn planet with archaea and algae. After the first fraught experiment in reterraforming, the Stasis find it sufficient to reboot the mantle and outer core once every ten billion years or so.

The universe changes around them, slowly but surely.

At the end of a hundred billion years, uranium no longer exists in useful quantities in the Earth's crust. Even uranium 238 decays eventually, and twenty one half-lives is more than enough to render it an exotic memory, like the bright and early dawn of the universe. Other isotopes will follow suit, leaving only the most stable behind.

(The Stasis have sufficient for their needs, and might even manufacture more – were it necessary – using the necrostar's ergosphere as a forge. But the Stasis don't particularly want their clients to possess the raw materials for nuclear weapons. Better by far to leave those tools by the wayside.)

The sky is dark. The epoch of star formation has drawn to a close in the galaxies the Earth has left. No bright new stellar nurseries glitter in the void. All the bright, fast-burning suns have exploded and faded. All the smaller main-sequence stars have bloated into dyspeptic ruddy giants, then exhausted their fuel and collapsed. Nothing bright remains save a scattering of dim red and white dwarf stars.

Smaller bodies – planets, moons, and comets – are slowly abandoning their galaxies, shed from stars as their orbits become chaotic, then ejecting at high speed from the galaxy itself in the wake of near encounters with neighboring stars. Like gas molecules in the upper atmosphere of a planet warmed by a star, the lightest leave first. But the process is inexorable. The average number of planets per star is falling slowly.

(About those gas molecules: the Stasis have, after some deliberation, taken remedial action. Water vapor is split by ultraviolet light in the upper atmosphere, and the Earth can ill afford to lose its hydrogen. A soletta now orbits between Earth and the necrosun, filtering out the short-wavelength radiation, and when they periodically remelt the planet to churn the magma, they are at pains to season their new-made hell with a thousand cometary hydrogen carriers. But eventually more extreme measures will be necessary.)

The sky is quiet and deathly cold. The universe is expanding, and the wavelength of the cosmic microwave background radiation has stretched. The temperature of space itself is now only thousandths of a degree above absolute zero. The ripples in the background are no longer detectable, and the distant quasars have reddened into invisibility. Galactic clusters that were once at the far edge of detection are now beyond the cosmic event horizon, and though Earth has only traveled two hundred million light-years from the Local Group, the gulf behind it is nearly a billion light-years wide. This is no longer a suitable epoch for Science Empires, for the dynamic universe they were called upon to study is slipping out of sight.

SLIDE 12.

A trillion years will pass.

The universe beyond the necrosun's reach is black. Far behind it, the final stars of the Local Group have burned out. White dwarfs have cooled to the temperature of liquid water; red dwarfs have guttered into chilly darkness. Occasionally stellar remnants collide, then the void is illuminated by flashes of lightning, titanic blasts of radiation as the supernovae and gamma-ray bursters flare.

But the explosions are becoming rare. Now it isn't just planets that are migrating away from the chilly corpses of the galaxies. Stellar remnants are ejected into the void as the galaxies themselves fall apart with age.

Space is empty and cold, barely above absolute zero. The necrostar's course has passed through what was once the Bootes Void, but there is no end to the emptiness in sight: there are voids in all directions now. The Stasis and their clients have abandoned the practice of astronomy. They maintain a simple radar watch in the direction of travel, sending out a gigawatt ping every year against the tiny risk of a rogue asteroid, but they haven't encountered an extrasolar body larger than a grain of sand for billions of years.

As for the necrosun's planetary attendants . . .

One day they will burn Jupiter to keep themselves warm. And Saturn, and icy Neptune, water bunker for the oceans of Earth. These days have not yet come, for they are still working through the titans, through Rhea and Oceanus, Crius and Hyperion – the brown dwarfs built with Sol's stolen mass, and the other dwarfs stolen from the Milky Way during the Long Burn. Each brown dwarf burns for many times the age of the universe at the birth of humanity; black holes are nothing if not efficient. But one day they will be used up, the last titan reduced to a dwarfish cinder; and it will be time to start eating the planets.

Not long thereafter, it will be time for the final Reseeding.

Spin Control

Pierce stood uncertainly before the door in the dome. It glowed blue-green with an inner light, and when he looked around, his shadow stretched into the night behind him.

"Don't wait outside for too long," someone said waspishly. "The air isn't safe."

The air? Pierce wondered as he entered the doorway. The glassy slabs of an airlock slid aside and closed behind him, thrice in rapid succession. He found himself in a spacious vivarium, illuminated by a myriad of daylight-bright lamps shining from the vertices of the dome wall's triangular segments. There were plants everywhere, green and damp-smelling cycads and ferns and crawling, climbing vines. Insect life hidden in the undergrowth creaked and rattled loudly.

Then he noticed the Librarian, who stood in the clearing before the doors, as unnaturally still as a plastinated corpse.

"I haven't been here before," Pierce admitted as he approached the robed figure. "I've used outlying branches, but never the central Library itself."

"I know." The Librarian pushed back the hood of his robe to reveal a plump, bald head, jowly behind its neat goatee, and gimlet eyes that seemed to drill straight through him.

Pierce stopped, uncertain. "Do I know you?"

"Almost certainly not. Call me Torque. Or Librarian." Torque pointed to a path through the vegetation. "Come, walk with me. I'll show you to your reading room, and you can get started. You might want to bookmark this location in case you need to return."

Pierce nodded. "Is there anybody else here?"

"Not at present." Torque sniffed. "You and I are the only living human beings on the planet right now, although there may be more than one of you present. You have the exclusive use of the Library's resources this decade, within reason."

"Within reason?"

"Sometimes our supervisors – yours or mine – take an interest. They are not required to notify me of their presence." There was a fork in the path, around a large outcropping of some sort of rock crystal, like quartz; Torque turned left. "Ah, here we are. This is your reading room, Student-Agent Pierce."

A white-walled roofless cubicle sat in the middle of a clearing, through which ran a small brook, its banks overgrown with moss and ferns. The walls were only shoulder high, a formality and a signifier of privacy; they surrounded a plain wooden desk and a chair. "This is everything?" Pierce asked, startled.

"Not entirely. Look up." Torque gestured at the dome above them. "In here we maintain a human-compatible biosphere to reprocess your air and waste. We provide light, and heat, although the latter is less important than it will be in a few million years hereabouts. We've turned down the sun to conserve mass, but it's still radiating brightly in the infrared; the real problems will start when we work through the last bunker reserve in about eighteen million years. The dome should keep the Library accessible to readers for about thirty million years after that, well into Fimbulwinter."

Fimbulwinter: the winter at the end of the world, after the last fuel for the necrosun's accretion disk had been consumed, leaving Earth adrift in orbit around a cold black hole, billions of light-years from anything else. Pierce shivered slightly at the thought of it. "What's the problem with the outside air?"

"We were losing hydrogen too fast, and without hydrogen, there's no water, and without water, we can't maintain a biosphere, and without a biosphere the planet rapidly becomes less habitable – no free oxygen, for one thing. So about thirty billion years ago we deuterated the biosphere as a conservation measure. Of course, that necessitated major adjustments to the enzyme systems of all the life-forms from bacteria on up, and you – and I – are not equipped to run on heavy water; the stuff 's toxic to us." Torque pointed at the stream. "You can drink from that, if you like, or order refreshments by phone. But don't drink outside the dome. Don't breathe too much, if you can help it."

Pierce looked around. "So this is basically just a reading room, like a Branch Library. Where's the real Library? Where are the archives?"

"You're standing on them." Torque's expression was one of restrained impatience: Weren't you paying attention in class the day they covered this? "The plateau this reading room is built on – in fact, the entire upper crust – is riddled with storage cells of memory diamond, beneath a thin crust of sedimentary rock laid down to protect it. We switched the continental-drift cycle off for good about five billion years ago, after the last core cooling cycle. That's when we began accumulating the Library deposits.

"Oh." Pierce looked around. "Well, I suppose I'd better get started. Do you mind?"

"Not at all." Torque turned his back on Pierce and walked away. "I'll be around if you call me," he sent.

Pierce sat down in front of the empty desk and laid his hands palm down on the blotter. A continent of memory diamond? The mere idea of that much data beggared the imagination. "It'll be in here somewhere," he muttered, and smiled.

Unhistory

One of the first things that any agent of the Stasis learns is patience. It's not as if they are short of time; their long lives extend beyond the easy reach of memory, and should they avoid death through violence or accident or suicide, they can pursue projects that would exceed the life expectancy of ordinary mortals. And that is how they live in the absence of the principal aspect of their employment, the ability to request access to the timegate.

Pierce thought at first that the vice-chancellor's request would be trivial, a matter of taking a few hours or days to dig down into the stacks and review the historical record. He'd return triumphant, a few minutes upstream of his departure, and present his findings before the council. Xiri would be appropriately adoring, and would doubtless write a series of sonnets about his Library visit (for poetics were in fashion as the densest rational format for sociological-academic case studies in Leng): and his adoptive home time would be spared the rigor and pity of a needless doctrinal war. That was his plan.

It came unglued roughly a week after his arrival, at the point when he stopped flailing around in increasing panic and went for a long walk around the paths of the biome, brooding darkly, trying to quantify the task.

Memory diamond is an astonishingly dense and durable data substrate. It's a lattice of carbon nuclei, like any other diamond save that it is synthetic, and the position of atoms in the lattice represents data. By convention, an atom of carbon 12 represents a zero, and an atom of carbon 13 represents a one; and twelve-point-five grams of memory diamond – one molar weight, a little under half an old-style ounce – stores 6×10^{23} bits of data – or 10^{23} bytes, with compression.

The continent the reading room is situated on is fifteen kilometers thick and covers an area of just under forty million square kilometers, comparable to North and South America combined in the epoch of Pierce's birth. Half of it is memory diamond. There's well over 10^{18} tons of the stuff, roughly 10^{23} molar weights. One molar weight of memory diamond is sufficient to hold all the data ever created and stored by the human species prior to Pierce's birth, in what was known at the time as the twenty-first century.

The civilizations over which the Stasis held sway for a trillion years stored a lot more data. And when they collapsed, the Stasis looted their Alexandrian archives, binged on stolen data and vomited it back up at the far end of time.

Pierce's problem was this: more than 90 percent of the Library consisted of lies.

He'd started out, naturally enough, with two pieces of information: the way-point in his phone that identified the exact location of the porch of his home in

Leng, and the designation of the planetary system in M-33 that had aroused such controversy. It was true, as Xiri had said, that the Hegemony was reveling in the feed from the robot exploration fleet that had swept through the Triangulum galaxy tens of millions of years ago. And he knew – he was certain! – that Xiri, and the Hegemony, and the city of Leng with its Mediterranean airs and absurdly scholastic customs existed. He had held her as his wife and lover for nearly two decades-subjective, dwelt there and followed their ways as an honored noble guest for more than ten of those years: he could smell the hot, damp summer evening breeze in his nostrils, the scent of the climbing blue rose vines on the trellis behind his house —

The first time he gave the Library his home address and the identities to search for, it took him to a set of war grave records in the Autonomous Directorate, two years before his first interview with Xiri. He was unamused to note the names of his father- and mother-in-law inscribed in the list of terrorist wreckers and resisters who had been liquidated by the Truth Police in the wake of the liberation of Leng by Directorate forces.

He tried again: this time he was relieved to home in on his return from the field trip to Constantinople – seen through the omnipresent eyes of Xiri's own cams – but was perplexed by her lack of excitement. He backtracked, his search widening out until he discovered to his surprise that according to the Library, the Hegemony was not, in fact, investigating the Triangulum galaxy at all, but focusing on Maffei 1, seven million light-years farther out.

That night he ordered up two bottles of a passable Syrah and drank himself into a solitary stupor for the first time in some years. It was a childish and short-sighted act, but the repeated failures were eating away at his patience. The day after, wiser but somewhat irritable, he tried again, entering his home coordinates into the desk and asking for a view of his hall.

There was no hall, and indeed no Leng, and no Hegemony either; but the angry spear-wielding raccoons had discovered woad.

Pierce stood up, shaking with frustration, and walked out of the reader's cubicle. He stood for a while on the damp green edge of the brook, staring at the play of light across the running water. It wasn't enough. He shed his scholar's robe heedlessly, turned to face the dirt trail that had led him to this dead end, and began to run. Arriving at the entrance airlock, he didn't stop: his legs pounded on, taking him out of the dome and then around it in a long loop, feet thumping on the bony limestone pavement, each plate like the scale of a monstrous fossilized lizard beneath his feet. He kept the glowing dome to his left as he circled it, once, then twice. By the end of the run he was flagging, his chest beginning to burn, the hot, heavy lassitude building in his legs as the sweat dripped down his face.

He slowed to a walk as the airlock came into view again. When he was ready to speak, he activated his phone. "Torque. Your fucking Library is lying to me. Why is that?"

"Ah, you've just noticed." Torque sounded amused. "Come inside and we'll discuss it."

I don't want to discuss it; I want it to work, Pierce fumed to himself as he trudged back to the airlock. Overhead, three planets twinkled redly across the blind vault of the nighttime sky.

Torque was waiting for him in the clearing, holding a bottle and a pair of shot glasses. "You're going to need this," he said, a twinkle in his eyes. "Everybody does, the first time around."

"Feh." Pierce shuffled stiffly past him, intending to return to the reading cubicle. "What use is a Library full of lies?"

"They're not lies." Torque's response was uncharacteristically mild. "They're unhistory."

"Un—" Pierce stopped dead in his tracks. "There was no unhistory in the Branch Libraries I used," he said tonelessly.

"There wouldn't be. Have you given thought to what happens every time you step through a timegate?"

"Not unduly. What does that have to do with—"

"Everything." Torque allowed a note of irritation to creep into his voice. "You need to pay more attention to theory, agent. Not all problems can be solved with a knife."

"Huh. So the Library is contaminated with unhistory, because . . . ?"

"Students. When you use a timegate, you enter a wormhole, and when you exit from it – well, from the reference frame of your point of emergence, a singularity briefly appears and emits a large gobbet of information. You. The information isn't consistent with the time leading up to its sudden appearance – causality may be violated, for one thing, and for another, the information, the traveler, may remember or contain data that wasn't there before. You're just a bundle of data spewed out by a wormhole; you don't have to be consistent with the universe around you. That's how you remember your upbringing and your recruitment, even though nobody else does. Except for the Library."

They came to a clearing and instead of taking the track to the reading room, Torque took a different path.

"Let's suppose you visit a temporal sector – call it A-one – and while you're there, you do something that changes its historical pattern. You're now in sector A-two. A-one no longer exists, it's been overwritten. If there's a Branch Library in A-one, it's now in A-two, and it, too, has changed, because it is consistent with its own history. But the real Library – tell me, how does information enter the Library?"

Pierce floundered. "I thought that was an archival specialty? Every five seconds throughout eternity a listener slot opens for a millisecond, and anything of interest is sent forward to Control."

"Not exactly." Torque stopped on the edge of another clearing in the domed jungle. "The communication slots send data backward in time, not forward. There's an epoch almost a billion years long, sitting in the Archaean and Proterozoic eras, where we run the Library relays. The point is – back in the Cryptozoic-relay era, there are no palimpsests. There's no human history to contaminate, nothing there but a bunch of store-and-forward relays. So reports from sector A-one are relayed back to the Cryptozoic, as are reports from sector A-two. And when they're transmitted uptime to the Final Library for compilation, we have two conflicting reports from sector A."

Pierce boggled. "Are you telling me that we don't destroy time lines when we change things? That everything coexists? That's heretical!"

"I'm not preaching heresy." Torque turned to face him. "The sector is indeed overwritten with new history: the other events are unhistory now, stuff that never happened. Plausible lies. Raw data that pops out of a wormhole mediated by a naked singularity, if you ask the theorists: causally unconnected with reality. But all the lies end up in the Library. Not only does the Library document all of recorded human history – and there is a lot of it, for ubiquitous surveillance technology is both cheap and easy to develop, it's how we define civilization after all – it documents all the possible routes through history that end in the creation of the Final Library. That's why we have the Final Library as well as all the transient, palimpsest-affected Branch Libraries."

It was hard to conceive of. "All right. So the Library is full of internally contradictory time lines. Why can't I find what I'm looking for?"

"Well. If you're using your waypoints correctly, the usual reason why you get a random selection of incorrect views is that someone has rewritten that sector. It's a palimpsest. Not only is the information you came here to seek buried in a near-infinite stack of unhistories, it's unlikely you'll ever be able to return to it – unless you can find the point where that sector's history was altered and undo the alteration."

REPEATEDLY KILLING THE BUDDHA

Graduation Ceremony

You will awaken early on that day, and you will dress in the formal parade robes of a probationary agent of the Stasis for the last time ever. You have worn these robes many times over the past twenty years, and you are no longer the frightened teenager whose hands held the knife of the aspirant and whose ears accepted their ruthless first order. Had you declined the call, were you still in the era of your birth, you would already be approaching early middle age, the great plague of senescence digging its claws deep beneath your skin; and as it is, even though the medical treatments of the Stasis have given you the appearance of a twenty-five-year-old, your eyes are windows onto the soul of an ancient.

Your mind will be honed as sharp and purposeful as a razor blade, for you will have spent six months preparing for this morning; six months of lonesome despair following Torque's explanation of your predicament, spent in training on the roof of the world, obsessively focused on your final studies. You have completed your internship and your probationary assignments, worked alone and unsupervised in perilous times: now you will present yourself to the examiners to undergo their final and most severe examination, in hope of being accepted at last as an agent of Stasis. As a full agent, you will no longer be limited in your access to the Library: nor will your license to summon timegates be restricted. You will be a trustee, a key-holder in the jailhouse of history, able to rummage through lives on a whim, free to search for what you have lost (or have had taken from you: as yet you are unsure whether it was malice or negligence that destroyed your private life).

You will dress in a saffron robe bound with the black belt of your current rank, and place on your head the beret of an agent-aspirant. Elsewhere in the complex, a dozen other probationers are similarly preparing themselves. You will hang on your belt the dagger that you honed to lethal sharpness the night before, obsessively polishing the symbol of your calling. Before the sun reaches the day's zenith, it will have taken a life: it is your duty to ensure that the victim dies swiftly, painlessly.

Out on the time-weathered flagstones, beneath the deep blue dome of a sky bisected by a glittering torque of orbital-momentum-transfer bodies, you will stand in a row before your teachers and tyrants. Not for the first time, you will find yourself asking if it was all worth it. They will stare down at you and your classmates, ready to pronounce judgment – ready perhaps to admit you to their number as a peer, or to anathematize and cauterize, to unmake and consign into unhistory those who are unworthy. They outnumber your fellow trainees three to one, for they take the training of new eumortals very seriously indeed. They are the eternal guardians of historicity, the arbiters of what really happened. And for no reason you can clearly comprehend, they offered you, you in particular out of a field of a billion contenders, an opportunity.

And there will be speeches. And more speeches. And then Superintendent-of-Scholars Manson will utter a sermon, along exactly the lines one would expect on such an occasion. "This momentous and solemn occasion marks the end of your formal training, but not the end of your studies and your search for excellence. You entered this academy as orphans and strangers, and you shall leave it as agents of the Stasis, sworn to serve our great cause – the total history of the human species." He's going to go on in like vein for nearly an hour, you realize: one homily after another, orthodox ideology personified. Theory before praxis.

"We accept you as you are, human aspirants with human weaknesses and human strengths. We are all human; that is our weakness and strength, for we are the agency of human destiny, charged with the holy duty of preserving our species from the triple threat of extinction, transcendental obsolescence, and a cosmos fated to unwind in darkness – notwithstanding your weaknesses, you brother Chee Yun with your obsessive exploration of the extremes of pain, you sister Gretz with your enthusiasm for the fruit of the dream poppy, you brother Pierce with your palimpsest family hobby – we understand all your little vices, and we accept you as you are, despite your weaknesses, despite knowing that only through service to the Stasis will you achieve all that you are destined for—"

You will not bridle angrily when Superintendent-of-Scholars Manson tramples on the grave of your family's unhistory, even though the scars are still raw and weeping, because you know that this is how the ritual unfolds. You will have reviewed the recording delivered in the internal post some days before, heard the breathy rasp of your own voice wavering on the razor edge of horror as he explains the graduation ritual to you-in-the-present. Your fingers will whiten on the sweat-stained leather hilt of your dagger as you await the signal. Though outwardly you remain at peace, inside you will be in turmoil, wondering if you can go through with it. Slaying your grandfather, cutting yourself free from the fabric of history, was one thing; this is something else.

"Stasis demands eternal vigilance, brothers and sisters. It is easier to shape by destruction than to force creation on the boughs of historicity, but we must stand vigilant and ready, if necessary, to intervene even against ourselves should our hands stray from the straightest of strokes. Every time we step from a timegate, we are born anew as information entering the universe from a singularity: we must not allow our hands to be stilled by fear of personal continuity—"

You will realize then that Manson is on track, that he really is going to give the order your older self described with shaking voice, and you tense in readiness as you call up a channel to Control, requesting the gate through which you must graduate.

"Weakness is forgivable in one's personal life, but not in the great work. We humans are weak, and sooner or later many of us stray, led into confusion and solipsism by our human grief and hubris. But it is our glory and our privilege that we can change ourselves. We do not have to accept a false version of our selves which have fallen into the errors of wrong thought or despair! Shortly you will be called on to undertake the first of your autosurveillance duties, monitoring your own future self for signs of deviation. Keep a clear head, remember your principles, and be firm in your determination to destroy your own errors: that is all it takes to serve the Stasis well. We are our own best police force, for we can keep track of our own other selves far better than any eternal invigilator." Manson will clap his hands. And then, without further ado, he will add: "You have all been told what it is that you must do in order to graduate. Do it. Prove to me that you have what it takes to be a stalwart pillar of the Stasis. Do it now."

You will draw your dagger as your phone sends out the request for a timegate two seconds back in time and a meter behind you. Control acknowledges your request, and you begin to step toward the opening hole in front of you, but as you do so you will sense wrongness, and as you draw breath you will begin to turn, raising your knife to block with a scream forming in the back of your mind: No! Not me! But you will be too late. The stranger with your face stepping out of the singularity behind you will tighten his grip on your shoulders, and as you twist your neck to look around, he will use your momentum to aid the edge of the knife you so keenly sharpened. It will whisper through your carotid artery and your trachea, bringing your life to a gurgling, airless fadeout.

The graduation ceremony always concludes this way, with the newly created agents slaughtering their Buddha nature on the stony road beneath the aging stars. It is a pity that you won't be alive to see it in person; it is one of the most profoundly revealing rituals of the time travelers, cutting right to the heart of their existence. But you needn't worry about your imminent death – the other you, born bloody from the singularity that opened behind your back, will regret it as fervently as you ever could.

The Trial

The day after he murdered himself in cold blood, agent Pierce received an urgent summons to attend a meeting in the late nineteenth century.

It was, he thought shakily, par for the course: pick an agent, any agent, as long as their home territory was within a millennium or so of the dateline. From Canada in the twenty-first to Germany in the nineteenth, what's the difference? If you were an inspector from the umpty-millionth, it might not look like a lot, he supposed: they were all exuberant egotists, these faceless teeming ur-people who had lived and died before the technologies of total history rudely dispelled the chaos and uncertainty of the pre-Stasis world. And Pierce was a very junior agent. Best to see what the inspector wanted.

Kaiserine Germany was not one of Pierce's areas of interest, so he took a subjective month to study for the meeting in advance – basic conversational German, European current events, and a sufficient grounding in late-Victorian London to support his cover as a more than usually adventuresome entrepreneur looking for new products to import – before he stepped out of a timegate in the back of a stall in a public toilet in Spittelmarkt.

Berlin before the century of bombs was no picturesque ginger-bread confection: outside the slaughterhouse miasma of the market, the suburbs were dismal narrow-fronted apartment blocks as far as the eye could see, soot-stained by a million brown-coal stoves, the principal olfactory note one of horse shit rather than gasoline fumes (although Rudolf Diesel was even now at work on his engines in a more genteel neighborhood). Pierce departed the public toilet with some alacrity – the elderly attendant seemed to take his emergence as a personal insult – and hastily hailed a cab to the designated meeting place, a hotel in Charlottenberg.

The hotel lobby was close and humid in the summer heat; bluebottles droned around the dark wooden paneling as Pierce looked around for his contact. His phone tugged at his attention as he looked at the inner courtyard, where a cluster of cast-iron chairs and circular tables hinted at the availability of waiter service. Sure enough, a familiar face nodded affably at him.

Pierce approached the table with all the enthusiasm of a condemned man approaching the gallows. "You wanted to see me," he said. There were two goblets of something foamy and green on the table, and two chairs. "Who else?"

"The other drink's for you. Berliner Weiss with Waldmeistersirup. You'll like it. Guaranteed." Kafka gestured at the empty chair. "Sit down."

"How do you know—" Silly question. Pierce sat down. "You know this isn't my time?"

"Yes." Kafka picked up a tall, curved glass full of dark brown beer and took a mouthful. "Doesn't matter." He peered at Pierce. "You're a new graduate. Damn, I don't like this job." He took another mouthful of beer.

"What's happened now?" Pierce asked.

"I don't know. That's why I want you here."

"Is this to do with the time someone tried to assassinate me?"

"No." Kafka shook his head. "It's worse, I'm afraid. One of your tutors may have gone off the reservation. Observation indicated. I'm putting you on the case. You may need – you may need to terminate this one."

"A tutor." Despite himself, Pierce was intrigued. Kafka, the man from Internal Affairs (but his role was unclear, for was it not the case that the Stasis police their own past and future selves?) wanted him to investigate a senior agent and tutor? Ordering him to bug his future self would be understandable, but this —

"Yes." Kafka put his glass down with a curl of his lower lip that bespoke distaste. "We have reason to believe she may be working for the Opposition."

"Opposition." Pierce raised an eyebrow. "There is no opposition—"

"Come, now: don't be naive. Every ideology in every recorded history has an opposition. Why should we be any different?"

"But we're—" Pierce paused, the phrase bigger than history withering on the tip of his tongue. "Excuse me?"

"Work it through." Kafka was atwitch with barely concealed impatience. "You can't possibly not have thought about setting yourself up as a pervert god, can you? Everybody thinks about it, this we know; seed the universe with life, create your own Science Empires, establish a rival interstellar civilization in the deep Cryptozoic, and use it to invade or secede Earth before the Stasis notices – that sort of thing. It's not as if thinking about it is a crime: the problems start when an agent far gone in solipsism starts thinking they can do it for real. Or worse, when the Opposition raise their snouts."

"But I—" Pierce stopped, collected his thoughts, and continued. "I thought that never happened? That the self-policing thing was a, an adequate safeguard?"

"Lad." Kafka shook his head. "You clearly mean well. And self-policing does indeed work adequately most of the time. But don't let the security theater at your graduation deceive you: there are failure modes. We set you a large number of surveillance assignments to muddy the water – palimpsests all, of course, we overwrite them once they deliver their reports so that future-you retains no memory of them – but you can't watch yourself all the time. And there are administrative errors. You're not only the best monitor of your own behavior, but the best-placed individual to know how best to corrupt you. We are human and imperfect, which is why we need an external Internal Affairs department. Someone has to coordinate things, especially when the Opposition are involved."

"The Opposition?" Pierce picked up his glass and drank deeply, studying Kafka. "Who are they?" Who do you want me to rat out? he wondered. Myself? Surely Kafka couldn't have overlooked his history with Xiri, now buried beneath the dusty pages of a myriad of rewrites?

"You'll know them when you meet them." Kafka emitted a little mirthless chuckle and stood up. "Come upstairs to my office, and I'll show you why I requested you for this assignment."

Kafka's office occupied the entire top floor of the building and was reached by means of a creaking mesh-fronted elevator that rose laboriously through the well of a wide staircase. It was warm, but not obnoxiously so, as Pierce followed Kafka out of the elevator cage. "The door is reactive," Kafka warned, placing a protective hand on the knob. Hidden glands were waiting beneath a patina of simulated brass, ready to envenomate the palm of an unwary intruder. "Door: accept agent Pierce. General defenses: accept Agent Pierce with standard agent privilege set. You may follow me now."

Kafka opened the door wide. Beyond it, ranks of angled wooden writing desks spanned the room from wall to wall. A dark-suited iteration of Kafka perched atop a high stool behind each one of them, pens moving incessantly across their ledgers. A primitive visitor (one not slain on the spot by the door handle, or the floor, or the wallpaper) might have gaped at the ever-changing handwriting and spidery diagrams that flickered on the pages, mutating from moment to moment as the history books redrew themselves, and speculated about digital paper. Pierce, no longer a primitive, felt the hair under his collar rise as he polled his phone, pulling up the number of rewrites going on in the room. "You're really working Control hard," he said in the direction of Kafka's receding back.

"This is the main coordination node for prehistoric Germany." Kafka tucked his hands behind his back as he walked, stoop-shouldered, between desks. "We're close enough to the start of Stasis history to make meddling tricky – we have to keep track of continuity, we can't simply edit at will." Meddling with prehistory, before the establishment of the ubiquitous monitoring and recording technologies that ultimately fed the Library at the end of time, ought to be risk-free: if a Neolithic barbarian froze to death on a glacier, unrecorded, the implications for deep history were trivial. But the rules were fluid, and interference was risky: if a time traveler were to shoot the Kaiser, for example, or otherwise derail the ur-history line leading up to the Stasis, it could turn the entire future into a palimpsest. "The individual I am investigating is showing an unhealthy interest in the phase boundary between Stasis and prehistory."

One of the deskbound Kafkas looked up, his eyebrows furrowing with irritation. "Could you take this somewhere else?" he asked.

"I'm sorry," Pierce's Kafka replied with abrupt humility. "Agent Pierce, this way."

As Kafka led Pierce into an office furnished like an actuary's hermitage, Pierce asked, "Aren't you at risk of anachronism yourselves? Multitasking like that, so close to the real Kafka's datum?"

Kafka smiled sepulchrally as he sat down behind the heavy oak desk. "I take precautions. And the fewer individuals who know what's in those ledgers, the better." He gestured at a small, hard seat in front of it. "Be seated, Agent Pierce. Now, in your own words. Tell me about your relationship with Agent-Scholar Yarrow. Everything , if you please." He reached into his desk drawer and withdrew a smart pad. "I have a transcript of your written correspondence here. We'll go through it line by line next . . ."

Funeral in Berlin

The interrogation lasted three days. Kafka didn't even bother to erase it from Pierce's time line retroactively: clearly he was making a point about the unwisdom of crossing Internal Affairs.

Afterward, Pierce left the hotel and wandered the streets of Berlin in a neurasthenic daze.

Does Kafka trust me? Or not? On balance, probably not: the methodical, calm grilling he'd received, the interrogation about the precise meaning of Yarrow's love letters (faded memories from decades ago, to Pierce's mind), had been humiliating, an emotional strip search. Knowing that Kafka understood his dalliance with Yarrow as a youthful indiscretion, knowing that Kafka clearly knew of (and tolerated) his increasingly desperate search for the point at which his history with Xiri had been overwritten, only made it worse. We can erase everything that gives meaning to your life if we feel like it. Feeling powerless was a new and shocking experience for Pierce, who had known the freedom of the ages: a return to his pre-Stasis life, half-starved and skulking frightened in the shadows of interesting times.

And then there was the incipient paranoia that any encounter with Internal Affairs engendered. Am I being watched right now? he wondered as he walked. A ghost-me surveillance officer working for Internal Affairs, or something else?

Kafka would be mad not to assign him a watcher, he decided. If Yarrow was under investigation, then he himself must be under suspicion. Guilt by association was the first rule of counterespionage, after all.

A soul-blighting sense of depression settled into his bones. He'd had an inkling of it for months, ever since his increasingly frantic search in the Library, but Kafka's quietly pedantic examination had somehow catalyzed a growing certainty that he would never see Xiri, or Magnus and Liann, ever again – that if he could ever find them, shadows cast from his mind by the merciless inspection-lamp glare of Internal Affairs would banish them farther into unhistory.

Therefore, he wandered.

Civilization lay like a heavy blanket upon the land, rucked up in gray-faced five-story apartment blocks and pompous stone-faced business establishments, their pillars and porticoes and cornicework swollen with self-importance like so many amorous street pigeons. The city sweated in the summer heat, the stench and flies of horse manure in the streets contributing a sour pungency to the sharp stink of stove smoke.

Other people shared the Strasse with him; here a peddler selling apples from a handcart, there a couple taking the air together. Pierce walked slowly along the sidewalk of a broad street, sweating in his suit and taking what shelter he could from the merciless summer sun beneath the awnings of shops, letting his phone's navigation aid guide his footsteps even as he wondered despondently if he would ever find his way home. He could wander through the shadowy world of historicity forever, never finding his feet – for though the Stasis and their carefully cultivated tools of ubiquitous monitoring had nailed down the sequence of events that comprised history, history was a tangled weave, many threads superimposed and redyed and snipped out of the final pattern . . .

The scent was his first clue that he was not alone, floral and sweet and tickling the edge of his nostrils with a half-remembered sense of illicit excitement that made his heart hammer. The shifting sands of memory gave way: *I know that smell —*

His phone vibrated. "Show no awareness," someone whispered inside his skull in Urem. "They are watching you." The voice was his own.

The strolling couple taking the air arm in arm were ahead of him. It was her scent, the familiar bouquet, but – "Where are you?" he sent. "Show yourself."

The phone buzzed again like an angry wasp trapped inside his ribs. "Not with watchers. Go to this location and wait," said the traitor voice, as a spatial tag nudged the corner of his mind. "We'll pick you up." The rendezvous was a couple of kilometers away, in a public park notorious by night: a French-letter drop for a dead-letter drop.

He tried not to stare. *It might be her,* he thought, trying to shake thirty-year-old jigsaw memories into something that matched a glimpse of a receding back in late-nineteenth-century dress and broad-brimmed hat. He turned a corner in his head even as they turned aside into a residential street: "Internal Affairs just interrogated me about Yarrow."

"You told us already. Go now. Leave the rest to us."

Pierce's phone fell silent. He glanced sideways out of the corners of his eyes, but the strolling couple were no longer visible. He sniffed, flaring his nostrils in search of an echo of that familiar scent, but it, too, was gone. Doubtless they'd never been here at all; they were Stasis, after all. Weren't they?

Guided by his phone's internal nudging, Pierce ambled slowly toward the park, shoulders relaxed and hands clasped behind his back as if enjoying a quiet afternoon stroll. But his heart was pounding and there was an unquiet sensation in the pit of his stomach, as if he harbored a live grenade in his belly. You told us already. Go now. Leave the rest to us. His own traitor voice implying lethally spiraling cynicism. They are watching you. The words of a self-crowned pervert god, hubris trying to dam the flow of history; or the mysterious Opposition that Kafka had warned him of? It was imponderable, intolerable. I could be walking into a trap, Pierce considered the idea, and immediately began to activate a library of macros in his phone that he'd written for such eventualities. As Superintendent-of-Scholars Manson had ceaselessly reminded him, a healthy paranoia was key to avoiding further encounters with cardiac leeches and less pleasant medical interventions.

Pierce crossed the street and walked beside a canal for a couple of blocks, then across a bridge and toward the tree-lined gates of a park. Possibilities hummed in the dappled shadows of the grass like a myriad of butterfly wings broken underfoot, whispering on the edge of actuality like distant thunder. This part of history, a century and more before the emergence of the first universal-surveillance society, before the beginning of the history to which the Stasis laid claim, was mutable in small but significant ways. Nobody could say for sure who might pass down any given street in any specified minute, and deem it disruptive: the lack of determinism lent a certain flexibility to his options.

Triggering one of his macros as he stepped through the gate to the park, between one step and the next Pierce walked through a storeroom in the basement of a Stasis station that had been dust and ruins a billion years before the ice sheets retreated from the North German plains. It had lain disused for a century or so when he entered it, and nobody else would use it for at least a decade thereafter – he'd set monitors, patient trip wires to secure his safe time. He tarried there for almost three hours, picking items from a well-stocked shelf and sending out messages to order them from a factory on a continent that didn't yet exist, eating a cold meal from a long-storage ration pack, and trying to regain his emotional balance in time for the meeting that lay ahead.

An observer close on his tail would have seen a flicker; when he completed the stride his suit was heavier, the fabric stiffer to the touch, and his shoulders slightly stooped beneath the weight concealed within. There were other changes, some of them internal. Perhaps the observers would see, but: Leave the rest to us. He slipped his hands into his pockets, blinked until the itching subsided and the heads-up display settled into place across the landscape, scanning and amplifying. He had summoned watchers, circling overland: invisible and silent, nerves connected to his center. Fuck Kafka's little game, he thought furiously. Fuck them all. Three hours in his unrecorded storeroom in the Cryptozoic had given him time for his depression to ferment into anger. I want answers!

It was a hot day, and the park was far from empty. There were young women, governesses or maids, pushing the prams of their bourgeois employers; clerks or office workers skipping work and some juvenile ne'er-do-wells playing truant from the gymnasium; here a street sweeper and there a dodgy character with a barrel organ and behind him a couple of vagrants sharing a bottle of schnapps. At the center of a well-manicured lawn, an ornate stone pedestal supported a clock with four brass faces. Pierce, letting his phone drive his feet, casually glanced around while his threat detector scanned through the chaff. Nobody – His phone buzzed again.

"What was the tavern where you fell for me called?" An achingly familiar voice whispered in his ear.

"Something to do with wildfowl, in Carnegra, the Red Goose or Red Duck or something like that—"

"Hard contact in three seconds," his own voice interrupted from nowhere. "Button up and hit the ground on my word. Now."

Pierce dived toward the grassy strip beside the path as flaring crimson threat markers appeared all around him. As he fell, his suit bloated and darkened: rubbery cones expanded like a frightened hedgehog's quills as his collar expanded and rotated, hooding him. In the space of a second the park's population doubled, angular metallic figures flickering into being all around. Time flickered and strobed as timegates snapped open and shut, expelling sinister cargo. Pierce twitched ghost muscles convulsively, triggering camouflage routines as the incoming drones locked onto each other and spat missiles and laser fire.

"What's going on?"

"Palimpsest ambush! Hard . . ."

The signal stuttered into silence, hammered flat by jammers and raw, random interference. Pierce began to roll, rising to sit as his suit's countermeasures flared. This is crazy, he thought, shocked by the violence of the attack. They can't hope to conceal—

The sky turned violet-white, the color of lightning: the grass around him began to smoke.

The temperature rose rapidly. His suit was just beginning to char from the prompt radiation pulse as the ground opened under him, toppling him backward into darkness.

REDUX

Army of You

When you see the ground swallow Pierce you will breathe a sigh of relief – you'll finally have the luxury of knowing that one of your iterations has made it out of death ground. But the situation will be too deadly to give you respite. If Internal Affairs are willing to start with combat drones and orbital X-ray lasers, then escalate from there, where will they stop? How badly do they want you?

Very badly, it seems.

There's going to be hell to pay when it's time for the cleanup; ur-history doesn't have room for a nuclear blitzkrieg on the capital of the Second Reich. The calcinated, rapidly skeletonizing remains of the governesses and the organ grinders contort and burst in the searing wind from the Hiroshima miscarriage, and the four faces of the clock glow cherry red and slump to the ground as a dozen more of you flicker into view, anonymous in their heat-flash-silvered battle armor. The echo-armies of your combat drones fan out all around, furiously dumping heat through transient timegates into the cryogenic depths of the far future as they exchange fire with the enemy's soldiers. "Extraction complete. Prepare to move out," says your phone; the iteration tag of that version of you is astronomical, in the millions. This isn't just a palimpsest ambush: it's an entire talmud of rewrites and commentaries and attempted paradoxes piled up in a threatening tsunami of unhistory and dumped on your heads.

You'll grab your future self's metadata and jump toward a timegate to a dispersal zone drifting high in orbit above ruddy Jupiter's north pole, nearly a billion years in the future: the rocket motors at your suit's shoulders and ankles kick hard, and as you loft, you'll catch a flashing glimpse of the Mach wave from the first heat strike surging outward, lifting and crumpling schools and hospitals and churches and apartments and houses and shops in the iron name of Internal Affairs.

They won't find this dispersal zone. They won't uncover the truth about Control, either, or about the Opposition – you'll be sure of that for as long as you continue to live and breathe.

You will look down, between your feet, at the swirling orange-and-cream chaos of Jupiter's upper atmosphere. Your armor will ping and tick quietly as it cools, and you will wait while the star trackers get a fix on your position, your mind empty of everything but a quiet satisfaction, the reward for a job well-done: the extraction of your cardinal iterant from the grasp of Internal Affairs. Somewhere else in time – millions of years ago – the rewrite war is still going on, the virtual legions of you playing a desperate shell game with Kafka: but you've won. All that's left to do is to deftly insert the zombie ringer into ur-history on his way into Kafka's court, primed to tell Internal Affairs exactly what you want them to know, then to orchestrate a drawdown and withdrawal from the ruins of Berlin before Kafka overwrites the battle zone and restores the proper flow of history.

Your suit will beep quietly for attention. "Scan complete," it announces. "Acceleration commencing." The thrusters will push briefly, reorienting you, sliding Jupiter out of sight behind your back. And then the rockets will kick in again, pushing you toward the yard, and the fleet of thirty-kilometer-long starships a-building, and Yarrow.

He Got Your Girl

I'm alive, thought Pierce, then did a double take. I'm alive? Everything was black, and he couldn't tell which way was up. There was a metallic taste in his mouth, and he ached everywhere.

"Where am I?" he asked.

"You'll have to wait while we cut you out of that," said a stranger. Their voice sounded oddly muffled, and he realized with surprise that it wasn't coming from inside him. "You took an EMP that fried your suit. You only just made it out in time – you took several sieverts. We've got a bed waiting for you."

Something pushed at his side, and he felt a strange tipping motion. "Am I in free fall?" he asked.

"Of course. Try not to move."

I'm not on Earth, he realized. It was strange; he'd effectively visited hundreds of planets with ever-shifting continents and biospheres, but he'd never been off Earth before. They were all aspects of Gaia, causally entangled slices through the set of all possible Earths that the Stasis called their own.

Someone tugged on his left foot, and he felt a chill of cold air against his skin. His toes twitched. "That's very good, keep doing that. Tell me if anything hurts." The voice was still muffled by the remains of his hood, but he could place it now. Kari, a quiet woman, one of the trainees from the class above him. He tensed, panic rising in a choking wave. "Hey – Yarrow! He's stressing out—"

"Hold still, Pierce." Yarrow's voice in his ears, also fuzzy. "Your phone's offline, it took a hit too. Kari's with us. It's going to be all right."

You don't have any right to tell me that, he thought indignantly, but the sound of her voice had the desired effect. So Kari's one of them too. Was there no end to the internal rot within the Stasis? In all honesty, considering his own concupiscence – possibly not. He tried to slow his breathing, but it was slowly getting stuffy and hot inside the wreckage of his survival suit.

More parts detached themselves from his skin. He was beginning to itch furiously, and the lack of gravity seemed to be making him nauseous. Finally, the front of his hood cracked open and floated away. He blinked teary eyes against the glare, trying to make sense of what his eyes were telling him.

"Kari—"

The spherical drone floating before his face wore her face on its smartskin. A flock of gunmetal lampreys swam busily behind it, worrying at pieces of the dead and mildly radioactive suit. Some distance beyond, a wall of dull blue triangles curved around him, dish-like, holes piercing it in several places.

"Try not to speak," said Kari's drone. "You've taken a borderline-fatal dose, and we're going to have to get you to a sick bay right away."

His throat ached. "Is Yarrow there?"

Another spherical drone floated into view from somewhere behind him. It wore Xiri's face. "My love? I'll visit you as soon as you've cleared decontamination. The enemy are always trying to sneak bugs in: they wouldn't let me through to see you now. Be strong, my lord." She smiled, but the worry-wrinkles at the corners of her eyes betrayed her. "I'm very proud of you."

He tried to reply, but his stomach had other ideas and attempted to rebel. "Feel. Sick . . ."

Someone kissed the back of his neck with lips of silver, and the world faded out.

Pierce regained consciousness with an abrupt sense of rupture, as if no time at all had passed: someone had switched his sense of awareness off and on again, just as his parents might once have power-cycled a balky appliance.

"Love? Pierce?"

He opened his eyes and stared at her for a few seconds, then cleared his throat. It felt oddly normal: the aches had all evaporated. "We've got to stop meeting like this." The bed began to rise behind his back. "Xiri?"

Her clothing was outrageous to Hegemonic forms (not to say anachronistic or unrevealing), but she was definitely his Xiri; as she leaned forward and hugged him fiercely he felt something bend inside him, a dam of despair crumbling before a tidal wave of relief. "How did they find you?" he asked her shoulder, secure in her embrace. "Why did they reinstate—"

"Hush. Pierce. You were so ill—"

He hugged her back. "I was?"

"They kept me from you for half a moon! And the burns, when they cut that suit away from you. What did you do?"

Pierce pondered the question. "I changed my mind about . . . something I'd agreed to do . . ."

They lay together on the bed until curiosity got the better of him. "Where are we? When are we?" Where did you get that jumpsuit?

Xiri sighed, then snuggled closer to him. "It's a long story," she said quietly. "I'm still not sure it's true."

"It must be, now," he pointed out reasonably, "but perhaps it wasn't, for a while. But where are we?"

She eased back a little. "We're in orbit around Jupiter. But not for much longer."

"But I—" He stopped. "Really?"

"They disconnected your phone, or I could show you. The colony fleets, the shipyards."

He blinked at her, astonished. "How?"

"We all have phone implants, here." Her eyes sparkled with amusement. "This isn't the Stasis you know."

"I'd guessed." He swallowed. "How long has it been for you?"

"Since" – her breath caught, a little ragged – "two years. A little longer."

He gently trapped her right hand in his, ran his thumb across the smooth, plump skin on the back of her wrist. She let him. "Almost the same." He swallowed once more. "I thought I'd never see you again. Anyone would think they'd planned this."

"Oh, but they did." She gave a nervous little laugh. "He said they didn't want us to, to desynchronize. Get too far apart." Her fingers closed around his thumb, constricting and warm.

"Who is 'he'?" asked Pierce, although he thought he knew.

"He used to be you, once. That's what he told me." Her grip tightened suddenly. "He's not you, love, it's not the same. At all."

"I must see him."

Pierce tried to sit up: Xiri clung to him, dragging him down. "No! Not yet," she hissed.

Pierce stopped struggling before he hurt her. His arms and his stomach muscles felt curiously strong, almost as if they'd never been damaged. "Why not?"

"Scholar Yarrow asked me to, to intercede. She said you'd want to confront him." She tensed when she spoke Yarrow's name. "She was right. About lots of things."

"What's her position here?"

"She's with him." Xiri hesitated. "It took much getting used to. I made a fool of myself once, early on."

He raised a hand to stroke her hair. "I can understand that." Pierce pondered his lack of reaction. "It's been years since I knew her, you know. And if he's who – what – I think he is, he was never married to you. Was he?"

"No." She lay against him in silence for a while. "What are you going to do?" she asked in a small voice.

Pierce smiled at the ceiling. (It was low, and bare of decoration: another sign, if he needed one, that he was not back in the Hegemony.) For the time being, the shock and joy of finding her again had left him giddy with relief. "Where are the children?" he asked, forcing himself: one last test.

"I left Liann with a nurse. Magnus is away, in the ship's scholasticos." Concern slowly percolated across her expression. "They've grown a lot: do you think—"

He breathed out slowly, relieved. "There will be time to get to know them again, yes." She reached over his chest and hugged him tight. He stroked her hair, content for the moment but sadly aware that everything was about to change. "But tell me one thing. What is it that you're so desperate to keep from me?"

Nation of Me

"Good to see you, Pierce," said the man on the throne. He smiled pleasantly but distantly. "I gather you've been keeping well."

Pierce had already come to understand that the truly ancient were not like ordinary humans. "Do you remember being me?" he asked, staring.

The man on the throne raised an eyebrow. "Wouldn't you like to know?" He gestured at the bridge connecting his command dais to the far side of the room. "You may approach." Combat drones and uniformed retainers withdrew respectfully, giving Pierce a wide berth.

He tried not to look down as he walked across the bridge, with only partial success. The storms of Jupiter swirled madly beneath his feet. It had made him nauseous the first time he'd seen them, through a dumb-glass window aboard the low-gee shuttle that had brought him hence – evidently his captors wanted to leave him in no doubt that he was a long way from home. Occulting the view of the planet was the blue-tinged quicksilver disk of the largest timegate he'd ever seen, holding open in defiance of protocol with preposterous, scandalous persistence.

"Why am I here?" Pierce demanded.

A snort. "Why do you think?"

"You're me." Pierce shrugged. "Me with a whole lot more experience and age, and an attitude problem." They'd dressed him in the formal parade robes of a Stasis agent rather than the black jumpsuits that seemed to be de rigueur around this place. It was a petty move, to enforce his alienation: and besides, it had no pockets. To fight back, he focused on the absurd. Black jumpsuits and shiny boots, on a spaceship? Someone around here clearly harbored thespian fantasies. "And now you've got me."

His older self stiffened. "We need to talk alone." His eyes scanned the throne room. "You lot: dismissed."

Pierce glanced round just in time to see the last of the human audience flicker into unhistory. He looked back toward the throne. "I was hoping we could keep this civilized," he said mildly. "You've got all the leverage you need. I'm in your power." There: it was out in the open. Not that there'd been any doubt about it, even from the beginning. This ruthless ancient with his well-known mirror-face and feigned bonhomie had made Pierce's position crystal clear with his choice of greeters. All that was left was for Pierce to politely bare his throat and hope for a favorable outcome.

"I didn't rescue you from those scum in order to throw you away again" – his older self seemed almost irritated – "though what you see in her . . ." He shook his head. "You're safe here."

Pierce rolled his eyes. "Oh, really. And I suppose if I decline to go along with whatever little proposition you're about to put to me, you'll just let me walk away, is that it? Rather than, oh, rewind the audience and try again with a clean-sheet me?" He met the even gaze of the man in the throne and suddenly felt finger high.

"No," said the man on the throne, after a momentary pause. "That won't be necessary. I'm not going to ask you to do anything you wouldn't ask me to let you do."

"Oh." Pierce considered this for a moment. "You're with the Opposition, though. Aren't you? And you know I'm not." Honesty made him add, "Yet."

"I told you he'd say that," said Yarrow, behind him. Pierce's head whipped round. She nodded at him, but kept her smile for the man on the throne. "He's young and naive. Go easy on him."

The man on the throne nodded. "He's not that naive, my lady." He frowned. "Pierce, you slit the throat of your own double, separated from you by seconds. You joined the Stasis, after all. But do you really imagine it gets easier with age, when you've had time to meditate on what you've done? There's a reason why armies send the flower of their youth to do the killing and dying, not the aged and cynical. We have a name for those who find murder gets easier with experience: 'monsters.' "

He raised a hand. "Chairs all around." A pair of seats appeared on the dais, facing him: ghosts of carved diamond, fit for the lords of creation. "I think you should be the one to tell him the news," he suggested to Yarrow. "I'm not sure he'd believe me. He hasn't had time to recover from the trauma yet."

"All right." Yarrow slid gratefully into her own chair, then glanced at Pierce. "You'd better sit down."

"Why?" Pierce lowered himself into his seat expectantly.

"Because" – she nodded at Pierce's elder self, who returned the nod with a drily amused smile – "he's not just a member of the Opposition: he's our leader. That's why Internal Affairs have been all over you like ants. And that's why we had to extract you and bring you here."

"Rubbish." Pierce crossed his arms. "That's not why you had to grab me. You've already got him: I assume I'm a palimpsest or leftover from an assassination attempt. So what do you want with me? In the here and now, I mean?"

Yarrow looked flustered. "Pierce—"

His older self placed a restraining hand on her knee as he leaned forward. "Allow me?" He looked Pierce in the eyes. "The Opposition is not – you probably already worked this out – external to the Stasis; we come from within. The Stasis is broken, Pierce, it's drifting rudderless toward the end of time. We've got a, an alternative plan for survival. Internal Affairs is tasked with maintaining internal standards; they're opposed to structural change at all costs. They overwrote your wife's epoch because they discovered possible evidence of our success."

The evidence of abandoned cities on an alien moon, the fleet of gigantic slower-than-light colony starships – was this all just internal politics within the Stasis hierarchy?

"Whatever would they want to do that for?" he asked. "They're not interested in deep space." Except insofar as there were threats to the survival of humanity that had to be dealt with.

Yarrow shook her head. "We disagree. They're very interested in deep space – specifically, in keeping us out of it." She inhaled deeply. "Did you notice, when you were consulting the Library, any sign of histories that touched on extraterrestrial settlement? Even though we have reterraformed the Earth thousands of times over, strip-mined the sun, rearranged gas giants, built black holes, and ripped an entire star system from its native galactic cluster?" Pierce shook his head, uncertain. "We've built and destroyed thousands of biospheres, sculpted continents, we outnumber the stars in the cosmos – but we've never spread to other solar systems! Doesn't that strike you as a little odd?"

"But we coevolved with our planet, we're not adapted to life elsewhere—" Pierce stopped. We can do terraforming, and timegates, he realized. Even if we can only have one wormhole end open at any given time. We rebuilt the sun. We've mapped every planet within ten million light-years. "Are we?" he asked, plaintively.

"There's a Science Empire running down on Earth right now," said the man on the throne. "They've been studying that question for twelve thousand years. We brought them the probe fleet reports. They say it can be done, and they've been building and launching a colony ship a year for the past six centuries." He frowned. "We've had that big gate in place ever since the dawn of civilization, to block Internal Affairs from detecting and overwriting our operation here. Officially we're in the middle of a fallow epoch, and the system should be uninhabited and uninhabitable: we moved in ahead of the first scheduled Reseeding. But they never give up. Sooner or later they'll notice us and start looking for the other side of our barricade, the static drop we funneled you through."

"What happens when they find it?" asked Pierce.

"Six hundred inhabited worlds die, and that's just for starters," Yarrow said quietly. "Call it unhistory if you like euphemisms – but did your graduation kill feel unreal to you? Unlike your" – her nose wrinkled in the ghost of a sniff – "wife and children, the inhabitants of the colony worlds won't be retrievable through the Library."

"And those six hundred planets are just the seed corn," his older self chimed in. "The start of something vast."

"But why?" he asked. "Why would they . . . ?" He stopped.

"The Stasis isn't about historicity," said Yarrow. "That might be the organization's raison d'être, but the raw truth of the matter is that the Stasis is about power. Like any organization, it lives and grows for itself, not for the task with which it is charged. The governing committee – it's very sad. But it's been like this as long as there's been a Stasis."

"We rescued you because we specifically want you – my first iteration, or as near to it as we've been able to get, give or take the assassination ambush in

Carnegra," said the man on the throne. "We need your help to cut us free from the dead hand of history."

"But what—" Pierce lowered his hands to touch his belly. "My phone," he said slowly. "It's damaged, but you could have repaired it. It's not there anymore, is it?"

Yarrow nodded slowly. "Can you tell me why?" she asked.

RESEEDING

A Brief Alternate History of the Universe

SLIDE 1.

Our solar system under the Stasis, first epoch.

Continents slide and drift, scurrying and scraping across the surface of the mantle. Lights flicker around the coastlines, strobing on and off in kiloyear cycles as civilizations rise and fall. In space, the swarm of orbital-momentum-transfer robots built from the bones of Ceres begin to cycle in and out, slowly pumping energy downwell to the Earth to drag it farther from the slowly brightening sun.

SLIDE 2.

Snapshot: something unusual is happening.

We zoom in on a ten-thousand-year slice, an eyeblink flicker of geological time. For millions of years beforehand, the Earth was quiet, its continents fallen dark in the wake of a huge burping hiccup of magma that flooded from the junction of the Cocos and Nazca continental plates. But now the lights are back, jewels sprinkled across the nighttime hemispheres of unfamiliar continents. Unusually, they aren't confined to the surface – three diamond necklaces ring the planet in glory, girdling the equator in geosynchronous orbit. And floating beyond them, at the L1 Lagrange point betwixt Earth and Luna, sits the anomalous glowing maw of an unusually large timegate.

The natives appear to be restless . . .

SLIDE 3.

A slow slide of viewpoint out to Jupiter orbit shows that the anomaly is spreading. Already some of the smaller Jovian moons are missing; Thebe and Amalthea have vanished, and something appears to be eating Himalea. A metallic cloud of smaller objects swarms in orbit around Europa, pinpricks of light speckling their surface.

Meanwhile, the shoals of momentum-transfer bodies are thinning, their simple design replaced by numerous perversions of form and purpose. Still powered by light sails, the new vehicles carry exotic machines for harvesting energy from the solar wind and storing it as antimatter. Shuttles move among them like ants amidst an aphid farm, harvesting and storing their largesse as they swing out to Jupiter before dropping back in toward Mercury.

Some of the hundreds of metal moons that orbit Europa are glowing at infra-red wavelengths, their temperature suspiciously close to three hundred degrees Kelvin. Against the planetary measure of the solar system they are tiny – little bigger than the moons of Mars. But they're among the largest engineered structures ever built by the dreaming apes; vaster than cities and more massive than pyramids. And soon they will start to move.

SLIDE 4.

Three thousand years pass.

Earth lies dark and unpopulated once more, for humanity – as always – has gone extinct. Of the great works in Jupiter orbit few traces remain. The great ships have gone, the shipyards have long since been deorbited into the swirling chaos of the gas giant's atmosphere, and the malformed, warped transfer bodies have been cannibalized and restored to their original purpose.

Five small moons have disappeared, and slowly healing gouges show the sites of huge mining works on Io and Europa, but by the time the Stasis reseed Earth (two-thirds of a million years hence) even the slow resurfacing of Europa's icy caul will have obscured the signs of industry. It may be thousands of years after that before anybody notices.

SLIDE 5.

Twenty million years pass, and the galaxy slowly lights up with a glare of coherent light, waste energy from the communications traffic between the inhabited worlds.

The first generation colonies have long since guttered into senescence and extinction; so have the third and fourth generations. Of the first generation, barely one in five prospered – but that was sufficient. Those that live spawn prolifically. Planets are common, rocky terrestrial bodies far from rare, and even some of the more exotic types (water giants, tide-locked rocky giants in orbit around red dwarfs, and others) are amenable to human purpose. Where no planets are available, life is harder, prone to sudden extinction events: nobody survives the collapse of civilization aboard a space colony. But the tools and technologies of terraforming are well-known, and best practice, of a kind, develops. Many of the dwellers have adapted to their new habitats so well that they're barely recognizable as primates anymore, or even mammals.

SLIDE 6.

Three billion years pass.

Two huge, glittering clouds of sentience fall through each other, a magnificently coordinated flypast of fleets of worlds meshing across the endless void. Shock waves thunder through the gas clouds, and millions of massive, short-lived new stars ignite and detonate like firecrackers. The starburst is indeed enormous. But for the most part, the inhabited worlds are safe: swarms of momentum-transfer robots, their numbers uncountable, work for millions of years ahead of and behind the event to direct the closest encounters. Emergent flocking rules and careful plans laid far in advance have steered colonies clear of the high-risk territories, marshaling brown dwarfs as dampers and buffers to redirect the tearaway suns – and both galaxies are talking to each other, for the expanding sphere of sentience now encompasses the entire Local Group.

Earth is no longer inhabited in this epoch; but the precious timegate remains, an oracular hub embedded in a cluster of exotic artificial worlds, conducting and orchestrating the dance of worlds.

There are now a hundred million civilizations within the expanding bubble of intelligence, each with an average population of billions. They are already within an order of magnitude of the Stasis's ultimate population, and they are barely a thousandth of its age. The universe, it appears, has started to wake up.

SLIDE 7.
The crystal ball is clouded . . .

The Kindest Lies
They walked along a twisting path between walls of shrubs and creepers, and a few short trees, growing from mounds of damp-smelling soil. The path appeared to be of old sandstone, shot through with seams of a milky rock like calcite: appearances were deceptive.

"You played me like a flute," said Pierce. He held his hands behind his back, as was his wont, keeping an arm's reach aside from her.

"I did not!" Her denial was more in hurt than in anger. "I didn't know about this until he, you, recruited me." Her boot scuffed a rock leaning like a rotten tooth from the side of a herbaceous border: tiny insects scuttled from her toes, unnoticed. "I was still in training. Like you, when you were tapped for, for other things."

They walked in silence for a minute, uphill and around a winding corner, then down a flight of steps cut into the side of a low hill.

"If this is all simply an internal adjustment, why doesn't Internal Affairs shut everything down?" he asked. "They must know who is involved . . ."

"They don't." She shook her head. "When you call in a request for a time-gate, your phone doesn't say, 'By the way, this iteration of Pierce is a member of the Opposition.' All of us were compliant – once. If they catch us, they can backtrack along our history and undo the circumstances that led to our descent into dissidence; and sometimes we can catch and isolate them, put them in an environment where doubt flourishes. If they started unmaking every agent suspected of harboring disloyal thoughts, it would trigger a witch hunt that would tear Stasis apart: we're not the kind who'd go quietly. Hence their insistence on control, alienation from family and other fixed reference points, complicity in shared atrocity. They aim to stifle disloyal thoughts before the first germination."

"Huh." They came to a fork in the path. A stone bench, stained gray and gently eroded by lichen, sat to one side. "Were you behind the assassination attempt, then?"

"No." She perched tentatively at one side of the bench. "That was definitely Internal Affairs. They were after him, not you."

"Him—"

"The iteration of you that never stayed in the Hegemony, never met Xiri, eventually drifted into different thoughts and met Yarrow again under favorable circumstances—"

Pierce slowly turned around as she was speaking, but in every direction he looked there was no horizon, just a neatly landscaped wall of mazes curving gently toward the zenith. "It seems to me that they're out of control."

"Yes." She became intent, focused, showing him her lecturer's face. "All organizations that are founded for a purpose rapidly fill with people who see their role as an end in itself. Internal Affairs are a secondary growth. If they ever succeed, there won't be anything left of the Stasis but Internal Affairs, everyone spying on themselves for eternity and a day, trying to preserve a single outcome without allowing anyone to ask why . . ."

Not everything added up. Still thinking, Pierce sat down gingerly at the other side of the bench. Not looking at her, he said: "I met Imad and Leila, Xiri's parents. How could they have survived? Everyone kills their own grandparents, it's the only way to get into the Stasis."

"How did you survive your graduation?" She turned and looked at him, her eyes glistening with unshed tears. "You can be very slow at times, Pierce."

"What—"

"You don't have to abide by what they made you do, my love. Corrupt practices, the use of complicity in shared atrocities to bind new recruits to a cause: it was a late addition to the training protocol, added at the request of Internal Affairs. It may even be what sparked the first muttering of Opposition. We've got the luxury of unmaking our mistakes – even to go back, unmake the mistake, and not enter the Stasis, despite having graduated. Agents do that, sometimes, when they're too profoundly burned-out to continue: they go underground, they run and cut themselves off. That's why there was no agent covering the Hegemony period you landed in. They'd erased their history with the Stasis, going into deep cover."

"You say 'they.' Are you by any chance trying to disown their action?" he asked gently.

"No!" Now she sounded irritated. "I regret nothing. She regrets nothing. Withholding the truth from you for all those years – well, what would you have done if you'd known that your adoring Xiri, the mother of your children, was a deep-cover agent of the Opposition? What would you have done? " She reached across and seized his elbow, staring at him, searching for some truth he couldn't articulate.

"I . . . don't . . . know." His shoulders slumped.

"All those years, you were under observation by other instances of yourself, sworn in service to Internal Affairs, reporting to Kafka," she pointed out. "Honesty wasn't an option. Not unless you can guarantee that all of those ghost-instances would be complicit in keeping the secret, from the moment you were recruited by the Stasis."

"That's why, back in college—" The moment of enlightenment was shocking. Yarrow's mouth, seen for the first time, wide and sensual, the pale lips, his reaction. He looked across the bench, saw the brightness in her eyes as she nodded. "I'd never betray her."

"It happened more than once, according to the Final Library. They can make you betray anyone if they get their claws into you early enough. The only way to prevent it is to make a palimpsest of your whole recruitment into the Stasis – to replace your conscript youth with a disloyal impostor from the outset, or to decline the invitation altogether, and go underground."

"But, I. Him. I'm not him, exactly."

She let go of his elbow. "Not unless you want to be, my love."

"Am I your love? Or is he?"

"That depends which version of you you want to be."

"You're telling me that essentially I can only be free of Internal Affairs if I undo what they made me do."

"There's a protocol," she said, looking away. "We can reactivate your phone. You don't have to reenlist in the Stasis if you don't want to. There are berths waiting for all of us on the colony ships . . ."

"But that's just exchanging one sort of reified destiny for another, isn't it? Expansion in space, instead of time. Why is that any better than, say, freeing the machines, turning over all the available temporal bandwidth to timelike computing to see if the wild-eyed prophets of artificial intelligence and ghosts uploaded in the machines were onto something after all?"

She looked at him oddly. "Do you have any idea how weird you can be at times?"

He snorted. "Don't worry, I'm not serious about that. I know my limits. If I don't do this thing we're discussing, him upstairs will be annoyed. Because Kafka will have all those naively loyal young potential me's to send on spy missions, won't he?" Pierce took a deep breath. "I don't see that there's any alternative, really. And that's what rankles. I had hoped that the Opposition would be willing to give me a little more freedom of action than Kafka, that's all." He felt the ghostly touch of a bunch of raisin-wrinkled grape joints holding his preteen wrists, showing him how to cast a line. He owed it to Grandpa, he felt: to leave his own children a universe with elbow room unconstrained by the thumbcuffs of absolute history. "Will you still be here when I get back?"

She regarded him gravely. "Will you still want to see me afterward?"

"Of course."

"See you later, then." She smiled as she stood up, then departed.

He stared at the spot where she'd been sitting for what seemed like a long, long time. But when he tried to remember her face all he could see was the two of them, Xiri and Yarrow, superimposed.

Saying Good-bye to Now

Twenty years in Stasis. Numerous deaths, many of them self-inflicted, ordered with the callous detachment of self-appointed gods. They feed into the unquiet conscience of a man who knows he could have been better, can still be better – if only he can untangle the Gordian knot of his destiny after it's been tied up and handed to him by people he's coming to despise.

That's you in a nutshell, Pierce.

You're at a bleak crossroads, surrounded by lovers and allies and oh, so isolated in your moment of destiny. Who are you going to be, really? Who do you want to be?

All the myriad ways will lie before you, all the roads not taken at your back: who do you want to be?

You have met your elder self, the man-machine at the center of an intrigue that might never exist if Kafka gets his way. And you'll have mapped out the scope of the rift with Xiri, itself rooted in her despair at Stasis. You can examine your life with merciless, refreshing clarity, and find it wanting if you wish. You can even unmake your mistakes: let Grandpa flower, prune back your frightened teenage nightmare of murder. You can step off the murderous infinite roundabout whenever you please, resign the game or rejoin and play to win – but the question you've only recently begun to ask is, who writes the rules?

Who do you want to be?

The snow falls silently around you as you stand in darkness, knee-deep in the frosted weeds lining the ditch by the railroad tracks. Alone in the night, a young man walks between islands of light. A headhunter stalks him unseen, another young man with a heart full of fears and ears stuffed with lies. There's a knife in his sleeve and a pebble-sized machine in his pocket, and you know what he means to do, and what will come of it. And you know what you need to do.

And now it's your turn to start making history . . .

ACKNOWLEDGEMENTS

We would like to thank the following people for their talent and assistance: our UK editor, Nic Cheetham, at Head of Zeus and our U.S. editor, Liz Gorinsky, at Tor as well as our agents, Sally Harding and Ron Eckel, and all the good folks at the Cooke Agency for making this adventure come to pass. Thanks also to Dan Read, a good friend and bookseller extraordinaire, for finding and sharing obscure books with us and to Paula Guran, for her much appreciated friendship. Many thanks to the remarkable Michael Moorcock for his continued support and for also pointing us in more than one right direction, to the tireless Theresa Goulding who is always there to lend a hand and a smile, to Richard Scott for helping us track down a couple of stories; to Fritz Foy for help finding our way through the permissions maze; to Edward Gauvin for his expertise and translation talents; and to those editors who helped us along the way, including John Joseph Adams, Jetse de Vries, Gavin Grant, Alisa Krasnostein, Samuel Montgomery-Blinn, Bill Schafer, and Jonathan Strahan. We'd also like to thank Tyler Owen and the good people over at the Fermentation Lounge. Sustenance for both the brain and body! And last but not least, we owe a huge debt of gratitude to our editorial assistants, Dominik Parisien and Tessa Kum, for embarking on this adventure with us and keeping us sane. We couldn't have done it without you.

About the Editors & Nonfiction Contributors

For twenty-five years, Hugo Award winner **Ann VanderMeer** and World Fantasy Award winner **Jeff VanderMeer** have been traveling into the past to bring back incredible stories for generations of readers. Their recent *The Weird: A Compendium of Strange & Dark Stories* (Atlantic Books, UK) covered 100 years of weird fiction in a single massive 750,000-word, 1,200-page volume. The VanderMeers have also edited such iconic compilations as *Steampunk* and *The New Weird*, both considered definitive for those subgenres. Other recent books include *The Thackery T. Lambshead Cabinet of Curiosities* and *The Kosher Guide to Imaginary Animals*. This "literary power couple" (*Boing Boing*) has been profiled on national NPR, the Weather Channel, Wired.com, and the *New York Times*'s book blog. Together or separately, they have been keynote speakers around the world, including at MIT, the Library of Congress, and Utopiales. They also have been brought in to conduct creativity workshops for the likes of Blizzard Entertainment (World of Warcraft) and help run Wofford College's Shared Worlds, a unique SF/Fantasy teen writing camp. Ann served as editor in chief of *Weird Tales* for five years and currently serves as a consulting editor for Tor.com. She also recently edited *Steampunk III: Steampunk Revolution*. Jeff's recent *Wonderbook: An Illustrated Guide to Creating Imaginative Fiction* is the world's first image-driven writing book. His forthcoming Southern Reach trilogy was optioned by Paramount Pictures through Scott Rudin Productions and will be published by Farrar, Straus and Giroux (U.S.), HarperCollins Canada, and Fourth Estate (UK). The VanderMeers live in Tallahassee, Florida, with four cats and twenty thousand books.

Jason Heller is the author of the alternate history novel *Taft 2012* (Quirk Books) and a Hugo-nominated editor for his work at *Clarkesworld* magazine. He's also a contributing writer and former editor for *The Onion*'s *A.V. Club*. In addition, his fiction and nonfiction have appeared in *Apex Magazine*, *Sybil's Garage*, *Weird Tales*, *Alternative Press*, *Tor.com*, and others. He lives in Denver, where he plays in punk bands and subjects his writing students to merciless doses of Bob Dylan.

Rian Johnson is an award-winning writer and director whose films include *Brick*, *The Brothers Bloom*, and the time-travel movie *Looper*. He lives in Los Angeles.

Tessa Kum's work has appeared in *Halo: Evolutions*, *Baggage*, *Daikaiju*, *ASIM*, and other places. A Clarion South 2005 graduate, she was an editorial assistant at *Weird Tales* while under the command of Ann VanderMeer and is now a freelance editor. She lives in Melbourne.

Stan Love is a planetary scientist, NASA astronaut, and lifelong science fiction fan. He holds a bachelor's degree in physics from Harvey Mudd College, where they use rhinoceroses to teach relativity, and a master's and doctorate in astronomy from the University of Washington. He gives frequent public presentations on space science and exploration based on his professional background and his experience as a Space Shuttle crewmember. Dr. Love admires the interplay between speculative fiction, which can imagine better futures, and science and technology, which can make them real.

Dominik Parisien is a Franco-Ontarian living in Montreal, Quebec. He holds an MA in English literature from the University of Ottawa. His poetry has appeared or is forthcoming in *Goblin Fruit*, *Stone Telling*, *Mythic Delirium*, *Ideomancer*, *Shock Totem*, *Strange Horizons*, and *Tesseracts Seventeen*, amongst others. Dominik provides editorial support to Cheeky Frawg Books and is a former editorial assistant for *Weird Tales*.

Genevieve Valentine's first novel, *Mechanique*, won the 2012 Crawford Award and was nominated for the Nebula. Her second, *The Girls at the Kingfisher Club*, is forthcoming from Atria in 2014. Her short fiction has been nominated for the World Fantasy Award and the Shirley Jackson Award; her stories have appeared in *Clarkesworld*, *Strange Horizons*, *Journal of Mythic Arts*, and others, and anthologies *Federations*, *The Living Dead 2*, *After*, *Teeth*, and more. Her nonfiction has appeared at NPR.org, *Strange Horizons*, io9.com, *Weird Tales*, and *Tor.com*, and she's a coauthor of pop-culture book *Geek Wisdom* (Quirk).

Charles Yu received the National Book Foundation's 5 Under 35 Award for his short-story collection, *Third Class Superhero*. His first novel, *How to Live Safely in a Science Fictional Universe*, was a *New York Times* Notable Book and named by *Time* magazine as one of the Best Books of 2010. His latest book is *Sorry Please Thank You*, which was named one of the best books of the year by the *San Francisco Chronicle*. He lives in Santa Monica.

EXTENDED COPYRIGHT

Kathryn Rusch. Originally published in *Analog Science Fiction and Fact* (Sep 2010).

Eric Frank Russell: 'The Waitabits'. Originally published in *Astounding Science Fiction*, July 1955.

Pamela Sargent: 'If Ever I Should Leave You', copyright © 1974, 1986 by Pamela Sargent. Originally published in a much different form in *Worlds of If*, February 1974, and in this preferred text in *Afterlives*, edited by Pamela Sargent and Ian Watson, Vintage, 1986.

Eric Schaller: 'How the Future Got Better', copyright © 2010 by Eric Schaller. Originally published in *Sybil's Garage* #7.

Robert Silverberg: 'Needle in a Timestack', copyright © 1983 by Robert Silverberg. Originally published in *Playboy* (June 1983).

Vandana Singh: 'Delhi', copyright © 2004 by Vandana Singh. Originally published in *So Long Been Dreaming* (ed. Nalo Hopkinson).

Cordwainer Smith: 'Himself in Anachron', copyright © 1993 by the estate of Paul Linebarger. Originally published in *The Rediscovery of Man: The Complete Short Fiction of Cordwainer Smith* (NESFA Press). Reprinted by permission of the author's estate and Spectrum Literary Agency.

Norman Spinrad: 'The Weed of Time', copyright © 1973 by Norman Spinrad. Originally published in *Vertex: The Magazine of Science Fiction* (Aug 1973).

Charles Stross: 'Palimpsest', copyright © 2009 by Charles Stross. Originally published in *Wireless* (Ace, Orbit). Reprinted by permission of the author and Little, Brown Book Group.

Theodore Sturgeon: 'Yesterday Was Monday', copyright © 1941 by the estate of Theodore Sturgeon. Originally published in *Unknown* (June 1941). Reprinted by permission of the author's estate and the Chris Lotts Literary Agency.

Michael Swanwick: 'Triceratops Summer', copyright © 2005 by Michael Swanwick. Originally published in *Amazon Shorts* (Sep 2005).

Adrian Tchaikovsky: 'The Mouse Ran Down', copyright © 2012 by Adrian Tchaikovsky. Originally published in *Carnage: After the End 2* (2012).

Karin Tidbeck: 'Augusta Prima', copyright © 2011 by Karin Tidbeck. Originally published in *Weird Tales* (Spring 2011).

Harry Turtledove: 'Forty, Counting Down', copyright © 1999 by Harry Turtledove. Originally published in *Asimov's Science Fiction Magazine* (Dec 1999).

Harry Turtledove: 'Twenty-One, Counting Up', copyright © 1999 by Harry Turtledove. Originally published in *Analog Science Fiction and Fact* (Dec 1999).

Steve Utley: 'Where or When', copyright © 1991 by the estate of Steve Utley. Originally published in *Asimov's Science Fiction Magazine* (Jan 1991). Reprinted by permission of the author's estate.

Carrie Vaughn: 'Swing Time', copyright © 2007 by Carrie Vaughn, LLC. Originally published in *Jim Baen's Universe* (June 2007).

H.G. Wells: Excerpt from 'The Time Machine'. Originally published by William Heinemann in 1895. Reprinted by permission of United Agents on behalf of: The Literary Executors of the Estate of H.G. Wells.

Connie Willis: 'Fire Watch', copyright © 1982 by Connie Willis. Originally published in *Isaac Asimov's Science Fiction Magazine* (Feb 1982). Reprinted by permission of the author and Chris Lotts Literary Agency.

Gene Wolfe: 'Against the Lafayette Escadrille', copyright © 1972 by Gene Wolfe. Originally published in *Again, Dangerous Visions* (ed. Harlan Ellison). Reprinted by permission of the author and the Virginia Kidd Literary Agency.

Gene Wolfe: 'The Lost Pilgrim', copyright © 2004 by Gene Wolfe. Originally published in *The First Heroes* (ed. Harry Turtledove). Reprinted by permission of the author and the Virginia Kidd Literary Agency.